Journey of the Daggers

[the Complete 2012 Trilogy]

A Novel by

Peter Galarneau Jr.

Journey of the Daggers is a work of fiction. All names, characters, places and incidents either are the culmination of the author's imagination or are used fictitiously. Any resemblance to actual events, places or people, living or dead, is purely coincidental.

ISBN: 978-0-9825129-7-5

Text set in Times New Roman

This book is printed on acid-free paper.

Printed in the United States of America

Published by:

PTW
P.T. WILLIAM PUBLISHING CO.

P.T. William Publishing Company
P.O. Box 611
Buckhannon, WV 26201

www.PTWilliam.com

Illustration Credits:

Cover Art by Peter Galarneau Jr.
Based upon original artwork "Phoenix" by Eric Newport, licensed under the Creative Commons Attribution 3.0 United States License.

Web Address: www.kethinov.com/art.php

Interior Artwork: *The Dagger and Book* and *The Parchment Map*, by Roger Fallin.
Original art created for *Journey of the Daggers*.

Fallin Graphics
805 Terra Bella
Irvine, CA 92602

Web Address: www.FallinGraphics.com

Interior Artwork by Peter Galarneau Jr.
The Cubit
Original cover art created for *The Cubit*, 2008

The Djed
Original cover art created for *The Djed*, 2009

Glyphs from the Page of Symbols
Original art created for *Journey of the Daggers*

Web Address: www.PeterGalarneau.com

Also by Peter Galarneau Jr.

Short Stories
The Worms Within Us (1994)

The Edge of Hell (1994)

Blood Barters (1996)

Muldoon's Nursery (1997)

Novels
The Cubit: The 2012 Trilogy I (2008)

The Djed: The 2012 Trilogy II (2009)

O-Time: PUSH* (2010)

Dedicated to:

Nelda, Forrest and Bobbi
For providing support for it all

The Drunken Sausage
For providing a place from it all

Peter Galarneau Sr.
Author of the son

Arah Edgel Galarneau Cox Maloney
Who finally found Paradise

FOREWARD

It was near midnight on December 31, 1999. I'll never forget it. Beyond thinking about Prince and how he wanted to "Party Like It's 1999," I could not assure myself that all of the lights would not go out, that all of the computers would not shut down, that Mankind would not, in the next five minutes, find itself without the electronic means to support itself. The Computers would finally win. And my poor ass, along with thousands of others, standing dazed on, or near, the Roberto Clemente Bridge in Pittsburgh, would become nothing more than statistics. In all of my well-reasoned, left-brained conglomerations of experiences, I still imagined, on that starry night, that life was going to change in some dramatic way that made all of the idiotic soothsayers…intelligent.

Didn't we all?

If the clock turning "00" would have been the end of the world, then all of us—me, my wife, my brother-in-law, everyone I cared about (which suddenly included a couple of thousand people standing on a bridge)—would have met a collective, untimely death, one that had been invented by man, accelerated by man and promulgated by the information channels that man had crafted.

And that got me thinking…about End Times, about all the End Times that had already ended. You know, like the ones said to be predicted by Revelation. Names such as Joseph Smith, William

Miller, The Watchtower Society, Herbert W. Armstrong, Jim Jones, Pat Robertson, Osho, David Koresh, Marshall Applewhite (the list really is very long) surfaced. Of course, so many of these "prophets" took with them too many innocent lives. These "prophets" were the antitheses of what prophets were really meant to be. For every Good there is Evil. For every real prophet there is a false prophet and in many cases, it's hard to tell them apart.

Taking the idea one step further, I started wondering why good people turn bad, why that wonderful mother who leads PTA meetings and takes SUV loads of kids to soccer practices ends up throwing her own children into a lake. What gets into people? What makes them turn? What nests inside us waiting to be released and what is the "thing" that induces such darkness to surface? Something ancient? Certainly, something not created by man. Something like… the Cubit, an antithesis in its own right.

I have always believed that the very best way to scare someone is to base a selected fear on truths rooted to reality. I started thinking about Revelation, rereading it for the umpteenth time, and how rote the idea was since, if you follow the scholarly theologians' way of thinking, Revelation is nothing more than a sign of its own time. But that's not how most of us think about the final book of the Bible. We think like fundamentalists. It's more exciting this way. We get to ask ourselves a whole slew of What If questions that can never, really, truly have answers, not unless you ally those answers to first-century Rome, and what fun is that?

Unfortunately (for me anyway), there are as many interpretations of Revelation as there are those who believe in it. And that can be quite daunting to wrap one's head around. So, in my search for an End Time that we could all believe in and that provided for me and my readers lots of possible twists and turns in plot, I chose an End Time rooted in reality—one that is just around the corner and was created by no one who has been alive for about a thousand years.

The ancient Mayans had their Gods but their calendar was not based on belief and therefore their End Date is not up for interpretation. The ancient Mayans used the Earth and the Sun and the planets and the stars as ultimate predictors and who can argue with such celestial magnates? Unlike the Bible that never really dates anything, for me, the Mayan calendar dated everything, beginning 26,000 years ago. How could such a primitive culture know of the precession of the Earth? How could such a primitive culture know that at the culmination of a 26,000 year cycle, the Earth and Sun would align on the Galactic Center? While Europe debated the flatness of Earth and how our planet was the center of the universe, the Mayans were documenting facts that would have proven these European thinkers wrong. And that primitive culture nailed down a date that would have, today, scientists and faith-mongers alike promoting ideas that *will* happen on December 21, 2012. What if this will be the end of the world…or, at least, the end of the world as we've lived it?

It's a human necessity to think about What If? The world that we know can't work correctly without a big, heaping helping of the unknown. What if everything had shut down on December 31, 1999? We will never know because, of course, Y2K was only as important as a calendar day clicking forward. The year 2000 came, nobody died on that beautifully yellow (they call it gold in Pittsburgh) bridge, and we all drank something to commemorate our continued, ignorant control of this planet.

Earth…

Time…

Humanity…

No wonder there continues to be a quagmire of confusion that ultimately culminates in masses of people wandering aimlessly on yellow bridges in big American cities waiting for The End.

Computer "geeks" told me I was going to be changed (and perhaps die) one second after December 31, 1999. I didn't believe them, only after I found that, since nobody threw me over the yellow bridge, I remained standing and everyone else looked depressed.

It was the first day of the new millennium: a day I had always looked forward to, more in regret of getting older than of the scant significance of the date (still, I did collect bottles of water and cans of green beans). But it was also a time for looking forward to the next End Date scenario. That is when The 2012 Trilogy was born.

You see, I AM only human and I will always drive myself crazy thinking about how people die (particularly me). How much better is it to die not alone, but with everyone else on the planet? That is why, I think, we hold onto these extinction scenarios. We live as social creatures and we should, therefore, die as social creatures. As one. Together.

So what does The 2012 Trilogy have to do with all of this opportunistic End Days' forecasting, the unending sagas presented by the rich exclamations of past fears, present ideals, and future ramifications emboldened by electromagnetic mind feeds?

It has nothing to do with them at all! It has to do with you and me and perceptions. Because, like all dates, December 21, 2012, will come and pass. Either humanity will continue to live by such Gregorian time capsules afterward, or some other planet will witness the bright light of a distant primitive culture as it quits.

But…sorry…there I go again.

Prophesying.

Book One
The Cubit

The Cubit

PART I

THE CUBIT: PART I

ENDANGERED

SUMMER 2007

Lenny's mother had warned him about the dangers of hitchhiking.

"I said, LET ME OUT OF THIS CAR!"

The driver's fist struck Lenny's left eye. The driver growled, "And I said, shut 'yer goddamn mouth!"

The station wagon fishtailed around the sharp corner at Pickett's Crossing and accelerated, sending a box, the size of a small coffin, to the back of the cargo bay and into the rear hatch. Behind them in close pursuit fishtailed two Kansas State Police cruisers. The lead cruiser lost its slide, hit the gravel shoulder and scraped the guardrail with a metal-to-metal screech that easily overpowered its siren.

The old man began mumbling again, talking to the steering wheel, slamming his large fists against its hard plastic. He looked in the rearview mirror and then abruptly at Lenny.

"See! I told you they were chasing me. Christ, they're gonna kill us both."

The old man whimpered. His eyes drooped; wrinkles rippled from the horrified brown marbles in sagging circular waves. He'd not slept in a long time—at least, that's the story he'd given Lenny when he'd picked him up that afternoon.

Lenny had been waiting for an hour at a 76 station near I-70 when the dusty 1984 Oldsmobile Custom station wagon had pulled in.

"Where you headed?" the old man had asked while topping off his tank.

"Pickett's Crossing, Kansas."

"Kansas!" The old man had scratched his gray stubby chin. "Yeah," he'd said. "Kansas. They'll never think of that."

"Excuse me?" Standing on the other side of the pump, Lenny had not heard the old man's mumble.

"Oh, nothing. Forgive an old man and his blabbering. I've not slept in several days."

He'd replaced the pump, had plucked a twenty from a thick wad of bills and had shoved it at the station attendant who'd walked from the garage to stare precariously when the old man had pulled in. "Come on, son. We got miles to cross."

Just a lonely soul out for a relaxing weekend drive, Lenny had thought—a simple farmer who'd suddenly decided that Pickett's Crossing, Kansas, would make a wonderful destination even if it was five hundred miles out of his way.

And the wad of money? His life's savings? Or, more realistically, blood money picked from a dead convenience store clerk, bank teller, or gas station attendant.

Lenny should have known. He should have listened to his mother.

It wasn't until they'd crossed the Missouri line into Kansas that Lenny had become concerned. The old man had become increasingly jittery, keeping his eyes more on the falling sun than on the road. He'd stopped talking about his lovely wife who'd died a few years back, about his grand kids (one of which had died recently), and about the beautiful state of Missouri and all the good years he'd lived there. Then, when the sun had disappeared and night had grown dense, the old man had clammed up altogether. He'd stared at length in his rearview mirror, often weaving across the four-lane interstate and onto the grass median or rocky shoulder like a blindfolded drunk driver.

That's when Lenny had noticed the box. Turning out of curiosity to see what attracted so much of the old man's attention, Lenny had seen it in the cargo area shoved tightly against the back side of the rear seat.

A wooden box the size of a small coffin.

Lenny had remembered their earlier conversation—the recent tragic death of the old man's three-year-old grandson—and Lenny had wondered. The box seemed to be just about the right size for...

"Shit!" the old man grumbled as one of the police cruisers rammed the tail of the station wagon. The old man hit the brakes, the cruiser collided with the tail bumper, glass from the rear hatch imploded, and the coffin rushed backward then forward, crashing into the back side of the rear seat as splinters of window stabbed Lenny's head and neck. The crumpled front end of the police cruiser sped up alongside the station wagon and veered into the rear door behind the old man. The squelch of the police cruiser's PA startled Lenny.

"Pull the fuck over, Professor Cower! You ain't got no escape this time! We'll make sure of that!"

Lenny saw two uniformed outlines in the front seat of the cruiser. The passenger raised his revolver and fired. Lenny flinched as the bullet webbed the front windshield, having missed his nose by the smallest inch.

"I'm gonna blow your goddamn head off," the officer warned, "if you don't stop this shit right now!"

The second cruiser came up from behind and smacked the tail of the station wagon as the lead cruiser continued to press the car from the left. Suddenly, the professor jerked the steering wheel hard to the right. Lenny saw the rushing guardrail as it snaked by his door at sixty miles an hour. He lowered his head and clutched the seat, readying himself for impact.

But none came.

The professor had found a side road, had abruptly turned onto it. Lenny raised his head in time to see the fiery inferno as the police cruisers collided, flipped, split the guardrail, and disappeared in a tumbling blaze down a steep embankment on the far side of the road.

The professor sat rigid. His foot seemed glued to the accelerator pedal. Stalks of corn a month from harvest sped by on either side of the station wagon, slapped the headlights and windshield as if trying to prevent passage. "Okay, kid. Where to now?" he grumbled.

The voice seemed far away. Lenny's mind was too busy sorting out the terror of being kidnapped and shot at. Hell, the cop's bullet had almost taken his head off. He stared at the windshield, his left eye swelling, and imagined his brains scattered across the dashboard, blood pasted in sticky masses to the webbed glass. Absently, he groped his face with his fingertips, assuring himself that his head was still there.

Kid, someone was saying. God, how he hated that name. His stepfather had always called him that. The wife-beating alcoholic had once threatened to blow Lenny's brains out, had placed a .44 magnum handgun right to his temple and had pulled back the hammer. "Okay, *Kid*," he'd slurred. "Tell me who the fuck your mama's been whoring around with."

Of course, his mother had never "whored" around with anyone. The accusation was his stepfather's Jim Beam delusion and Lenny had told him so. That's when his stepfather had pulled the trigger on an empty weapon. Click! And Lenny had seen his brains and blood scattered throughout his bedroom in much the same colorful way as he now saw them stuck to the windshield. The fear of death in 3-D Technicolor. It had made him sick then as it did now.

"Goddammit, kid! You're from around here. How do I get back to the main road?" The professor pulled a gun from under the seat and pointed it at him. "I said, how do we get the fu…?"

Lenny puked in a thin stream onto the dashboard, then turned and continued spraying across the gun and the professor's lap.

"Shit!" the professor yelled and stomped the brake pedal. The station wagon jumped off the dirt road into the corn field, sliced through green stalks, and settled in a cloud of heavy dust. The professor quickly opened his door and rolled out. "Shit, shit, shit," he growled as he scoured his lap with dirt and crumpled stalks.

Lenny had the opportunity to run but his stomach was in control of the situation. He hiccupped a tiny amount of bile and rolled out of the car. The crisp smell of broken corn stalks deodorized the acidic stench of vomit. He took a deep breath, removed his shirt and wiped his mouth and chin, then spit the remaining taste.

The professor crossed in front of the station wagon's headlights and Lenny turned to run. "Wait!" the professor demanded. Lenny stood still, believing the gun was pointed at his spine. "Please. I need your help."

"You might as well shoot," Lenny said, "I'm not aiding and abetting any criminal."

"Ease up. I don't have the gun. And even if I did, I wouldn't shoot you." Lenny heard the shuffle of the professor's feet, felt him at his back. "Turn around, for God's sake."

Lenny thrashed out as he turned, throwing a kick to the groin and a backhand to the face. But the professor was quick—too quick for someone who looked to be nearly sixty years-old. He kicked Lenny's leg out from under him while grabbing his wrist in the same motion, then tossed Lenny aside as if batting away an annoying insect.

"Listen!" The professor knelt. "I haven't enough time for this. You're just going to have to trust me." The professor stared into the broken cornfield. His eyes were wild, intense. His nose flared, sucking in deep breaths. His hands played nervously with broken corn stalks. "They won't stop until they retrieve the Cubit," he whispered to the summer breeze, his voice quivering, acknowledging some fact that apparently scared the living hell out of him.

"The Cubit?" Lenny said.

The professor grabbed Lenny's upper arm and pulled as he rose. "Sorry about all of this. I shouldn't have involved you. It's just that...I needed some help. I'm getting tired. They won't let me sleep. The last time I had a solid meal was in Philly and that was two days ago."

"I thought you said you were from Missouri," Lenny said, backing a step from the professor's wrinkled stare.

"I lied."

"And your wife—your grand kids?"

"Dead as I've said. Murdered in their sleep the night I took off."

Murdered, Lenny thought. Now that made more sense than any of the lies the professor had told so far. Of course they'd been murdered—by the good professor no doubt. The police chase, the gun under his seat, his crazy mood swings and occasional unleashed anger, each a check mark in the "yes" column for Lenny's description of a psychotic killer on the run.

"Hey kid—listen to me." The professor grabbed Lenny's shoulders and Lenny flinched. "I'm not going to hurt you. You got that?" Lenny's tears dropped and the professor shoved him away. His eyebrows drew tight with anger. The folds around his eyes deepened. "You think I killed them, don't you. DON'T YOU!" Lenny nodded. "It wasn't me, dammit." He slammed a fist against his thigh. "It wasn't me."

Suddenly, the professor stiffened. He looked around like a bloodhound on the scent. The station wagon had traveled twenty yards from the dirt road into the cornfield. The engine had died but the lights were still on. The rear hatch had opened and lying in the trampled stalks halfway between the station wagon and the road was the box. It lay askew on a tiny ridge of plowed earth and glowed red from the taillights.

Lenny stared at it, thought that a three-year-old could easily fit inside, that maybe a wife—if chopped finely enough—could have been stuffed inside as well.

The box shifted on the mound of earth as if something alive was inside. And then a knock—knuckles on wood. Something inside the box wanted out. The rapping of knuckles turned into the thrashing of fists as the trapped beat feverishly from within the box.

"Let—them—out," came a voice, seemingly from within the box. The pronunciation was slow, disoriented, sounding like a cassette tape running at half speed. "Let—them—out—now."

Standing on the dirt road, a shadow highlighted in pink, was one of the state troopers.

"Can't—you see—they—want out—pro—fes—sor…" the trooper said while raising his revolver.

"Tough shit," the professor responded, standing near the opened passenger door, eyeing the gun that lay in a puddle of puke on the front seat.

The trooper fired and the professor jerked backward. Lenny dropped to his knees as the professor dove through the shattered rear passenger door window, flipped into the car, and grabbed the gun. The trooper ran into the plowed lane created by the station wagon as the professor brought his gun out and steadied it on the roof of the car.

Bang!

The trooper lifted off the ground and fell flat on his back ten feet from the box.

Lenny crouched at the professor's heels wondering what to do. Everything was moving too fast. There was too much information and too little time to sort it out. Murders, gunfights, psycho killers—Come on! He was just hitchhiking home to see his mother for Christ's sake. *Let them out*, the trooper had said. Let who out? Of what? Shouldn't his demand have been, *Halt, you crazy murderous scumbag or I'll blow your damned head off.* Didn't anyone watch T.V. around here?

Stop thinking, Lenny, and act.

Save your ass.

Get the gun from the professor.

Lenny dove at the back of the professor's legs, yanked them up and away and the professor went down. He grabbed the gun and pointed it at the professor's head. "Enough of this shit! You hear me?" The gun shook in his hands. His voice trembled. His body quivered. This was much different than in the movies. Real guns, real blood—*really* a matter of life or death. "You...You stay there or I'll blow your—" *Go ahead. Say it. Or I'll blow your goddamn head off. Clint Eastwood would say it. Hell, he'd do it; he loved blowing holes in things*. But Lenny couldn't say it, couldn't do it; he just wanted to go home and get this nightmare over with.

Fortunately for Lenny's cowardice, the professor was in no shape to go anywhere. The trooper had shot him in the right breast and his stomach was gashed open from the shards of window glass that he'd dove through to get the gun. His mouth worked as if he were chewing gum and Lenny moved closer, pointing the gun haphazardly at the bullet hole in the professor's chest.

"Watch out," the professor gasped and slid an arm through the crumpled corn stalks with his index finger pointed in the direction of the felled trooper. Lenny jerked, thinking the professor was stretching for some hidden weapon.

"You killed him, man," Lenny said now steadying the gun with both hands. "There's nothing to watch out for except you." That's what Clint

Eastwood would say, he thought.

"No. Not dead. Never dead. Watch out." Blood trickled from the corner of the professor's mouth and red bubbles escaped as he coughed up more.

In the distance, a gun fired and Lenny felt the buzz of a giant insect nip his left ear. He turned. The trooper advanced with his revolver raised. Lenny dropped as the trooper fired another round.

"Hey!" Lenny yelled. "I'm innocent! I'm one of the good guys!"

"Don't let him get the Cubit," the professor moaned. "Trust me." He closed his eyes and exhaled.

"The Cubit? What?"

The trooper had acquired the box and was now carrying it back toward the road. "Hey, professor. He's got the Cubit. Professor?" His hands shook. He wasn't Clint Eastwood. In fact, his actions resembled those of Clint Eastwood's victims. Men too big for their britches. Men too scared to draw and shoot straight. Men who were kids.

What are ya gonna do, kid? Draw or whistle Dixie?

The state trooper turned and fired again. The bullet missed his head by fractions of an inch; he heard it buzzing, like a fly stuck in his ear. Was he actually going to shoot a cop?

You gotta start livin' or you gotta start dyin'—

"Yes, Clint. I know," Lenny yelled out then squinted and fired two rounds. The trooper flinched and returned fire as Lenny dropped face first near the rear bumper of the station wagon. Something stung his shoulder; glass shattered in the distance. His right arm went numb and, lying face down in the cornfield, he transferred the gun to his left hand.

This was it. He was going to die. He should have known better than to ignore his mother. He should not have hitchhiked. Hitchhiking was the same as stealing, she'd say, and stealing was against God's Commandments. He could see her crooked finger slashing the sign of the cross in a cumulative gesture of accusation and forgiveness.

The crunch of snapping corn stalks assaulted his ears and a scorched black shoe appeared in front of his nose. The trooper's pant leg was burned away and in the red taillight luminance, a bare, bubbled calf and shin offered Lenny the nauseating odor of burned flesh. A shoe heel prodded Lenny's spine. A toe poked his ribs. Lenny gasped.

The trooper's breath became deep and excited, sounding like a mad scientist who'd just seen the first jerky signs of life from his monster masterpiece.

And then—

Click!

It was his stepfather again, pointing and firing an empty .44 at his head. Again, the visions of brains and blood in his bedroom—across the dashboard. His stomach churned.

Not this time, coward, Clint had the nerve to remind him. *You keep that puke to yourself.*

Click! Click! Click!

Lenny quickly rolled and lifted his gun with a wavering left hand, leveled it at—

But, it couldn't be alive—the trooper—this thing. It stood naked. Bone poked through brittle black skin across the length of its body. Its genitals, dangling directly in Lenny's line of sight, resembled an unattended weenie roast at a Boy Scout camp. The pin from the trooper's badge punctured its left breast and dangled from abused, blackened tissue. The badge had a bullet hole through its center. The flesh around the things lips, nose and eyes was totally burned away leaving a grin full of teeth, a white stare, and a broken jaw. It struggled to breathe, sucking air through dime-sized holes just above the charred gum line as it gawked with two lidless eyeballs down the barrel of Lenny's gun.

But this was a human being, wasn't it? Lenny thought. What if the guy was just burned real bad—maybe the fire had gotten to his brain and had burned some part of his logical center. He could be just whacked out, disabled, not knowing what the hell he was doing. Yeah—that had to be it. Lenny couldn't shoot someone who wasn't responsible for their own actions. Besides, it was against God's Commandments to murder.

Shoot the Mother Fucker! Clint demanded.

The thing that had been a Kansas state trooper kicked the gun from Lenny's hand. Its black shoe tore loose and followed the gun into the cornstalks. Lenny's body wanted to roll away as the thing leapt at him but his mind was too busy listening to advice from his mother and Clint. Bony fingers wrapped around his throat, tightened their grip. A gritty trail of brittle flesh broke from the things flexing hand and fell underneath his shirt. Its bulging eyeballs, gnashing teeth, and whistled gasps floated within a black mask above Lenny's face.

Lenny beat and shoved with his left arm as his throat was strangled but this only broke away more burnt pieces of the thing's body. Soot came out of its nose and fell into Lenny's gasping mouth. The trooper's white teeth hovered over his lips as if it wanted a kiss and this took Lenny over the edge. His mind shut down. His vision dulled.

Before blacking out, Lenny saw the white glimmer of what he thought was the holy light.

Heaven was dark red and it kind of smelled like Kansas. Lenny opened his eyes, believing himself dead. The pain had eased in his shoulder but his right arm remained mostly functionless. He rose with the intent of propping himself with his left elbow but hit his head on the rear bumper of the station wagon. It was still night. He was still in the cornfield. He wasn't dead, this wasn't heaven and worse: all of it—the professor, the gun fight, the burnt thing—had not been a dream.

Lenny kicked himself from under the car and wearily stood. First, he examined his shoulder, bending toward the red glow of the station wagon's taillights for assistance. The bullet had passed cleanly through the meat near his collarbone. What little blood he'd lost was drying in a splotchy half-moon above his breast. Then, he gave the station wagon a troubled stare. Somehow, the box that the professor had called a Cubit had jumped back into the cargo area, had closed the rear hatch and had turned off the engine. Finally, he noticed that the professor and trooper were gone.

Lenny slipped around to the front of the station wagon while looking back across his injured shoulder. Corn rustled in the dim red taillights. An arm rose from the cover of the stalks, revealing a wrist and five fingers that were tightly wrapped around a knife. Down went the wrist, stabbing what hid in the cornstalks, then back up to reveal wrist, fist and knife. Something screeched, sounding, to Lenny, like the villain Scorpio when Eastwood shot him in *Dirty Harry*.

Then…silence. The professor stood.

Lenny looked for the gun and found it sitting atop the Cubit in the back of the station wagon. He ran for it as the professor yelled, "No!"

As Lenny fingered the steel of the pistol's barrel a small blue spark grabbed his left pinky. There was a gentle tug that lasted for the slightest moment, an electrical tingle not unlike the static touch of hand on metal. The blue spark changed to red so quickly that Lenny was not sure the vision had occurred at all. And then the gun was in his hand. He turned it toward the approaching professor though his eyes remained where the blue-red spark no longer existed. He leveled the gun.

"The Cubit," the professor said. "You touched it."

"No. You're wrong. Stand back or I'll…"

Lenny then noticed the knife in the professor's hand. Its blade was quite long and it appeared to glow in the station wagon's taillights.

"Put it down," the professor demanded with a bit of exasperation and a lot of fatigue. "The gun's empty."

Lenny fired. Fired again. Click. Click.

The professor snatched the empty gun and flung it into the back of the station wagon. "Let's get out of here," he said, then added something before he fainted and collapsed that Lenny thought was quite strange. "You've got to protect me. Help...please."

The drive would take less than fifteen minutes. Lenny sat on thin remnants of the vomit he had swiped from the car seat before climbing in. His right shoulder ached and he could lift it only enough to manage the steering wheel. The professor's injury looked more serious. A large red spot soaked his plaid shirt on the same side as Lenny's injury but his was a few inches lower, more centered around the upper breast than the collarbone. In the dashboard's dim light, Lenny saw a drop of blood trickle from the professor's mouth. The injured man no longer gazed apprehensively into the rearview or side view mirrors which meant that he was either satisfied they were no longer being chased or that he was much too tired to care.

Lenny turned onto a dirt road that led to the Bender's farm. A newspaper protruded from his mother's mailbox and Lenny stopped to fetch it. As he exited the car, he suddenly felt that he'd made a grave mistake. He suddenly realized that he had now placed his mother in great danger, not from the professor so much as from those that were hunting him. He suddenly realized his own selfishness, how getting home and climbing into bed with a warm, home-cooked meal in his tummy was all that had been on his mind. As he snatched the large Sunday edition of the *Topeka Capital Journal* from rusted steel, he gazed hopelessly in all directions, into the middle-of-the-night solitude. The smell of corn rustled his nostril hairs as a thin wave of wind rolled across the darkness. He imagined a legion of burnt, ashen state troopers converging on his mother's house. He imagined Clint Eastwood leading the charge. Clint was no longer big, tough and good-looking. He was now bubbly, torched, and grotesque. He could not see them now but he felt that they were on their way. Somewhere beyond the corn. Somewhere, stalking.

When Lenny climbed back into the station wagon the professor was looking at him with a silent stare that acknowledged understanding. Now you know, the stare said.

Two miles down the front road, between a hundred acres of unplanted farmland (barren due to the neglect of his stepfather) sat the Bender barn and farmhouse. Two years ago, before his father's death, the Benders had made a pretty good living on cotton and corn. Today, Lenny's mother survived as a self-employed seamstress for the Pickett's Crossing community. Her new husband, Albert, had sold nearly all of the farm animals, including several dozen head of cattle, horses, and a pair of prize-winning Labrador Retrievers that had brought substantial added income to the Bender household, not to mention notoriety. Cash from this 'liquidation' had gone to feed Albert's alcohol and gambling addictions. It would not be long before the land itself would be traded for booze, cards and craps. It all depended on how lucky Albert remained at the Vegas tables. It all depended on whether cheating would one day get the best of him. How Lenny prayed that his stepfather's card-counting would one day summon some large man named Vito to a hotel suite on the outskirts of Las Vegas with a gun in hand and bullets marked for cheatin' Albert Stine. Perhaps Lenny would return home for good, help his mother get the farm back on its feet, help his mother get her life back together. Right now it was impossible. Lenny was afraid of Albert. Lenny had very little courage. Lenny could not protect a fly from a spider with a can of Raid in hand. The puke at his feet was a reminder of his cowardice, a summation of his life really, a putrid digestion of lost chances, lack of responsibility and selfishness. A tear emerged and dropped to the red stain encircling his right collarbone. Crying was not a manly thing to do either.

He figured it was somewhere close to two in the morning since the Sunday paper was already in the mailbox. Paper delivery was very efficient in Pickett's Crossing. The paper's circulation depended on early delivery to early-rising farm folk.

He doubted his mother would be awake, doubted even more that she'd appreciate being intruded upon on the Lord's day of rest, and was certain that a stranger at her doorstep would not sit well. She trusted few people outside of the Crossing's community. Her extreme reclusion had started after his father's tragic death and had only become worse since Albert's continuing yard sale of all that she and her husband had built together.

As she'd promised Lenny in a letter he'd received a week ago, Albert would be in Vegas. It would be "safe" for him to come home and see his mother. He could help her clean up the barn and do a few field chores. He could share a little love that had become so elusive between them.

Albert's car was not in the yard. His mother's F150 was. As he turned to park beside the truck, the headlights revealed the Ford's rusty shade of white paint. When he switched off the station wagon the professor sighed, closed his eyes and propped his head against the car door window. A circular pattern of breath-fog emerged against the window at the point where lips touched glass. And then he said something that made Lenny think he was dreaming again.

"You need to kill yourself," he said with shallow breaths. "When it comes out, and it will, you need to kill..." His eyes fluttered as if he were about to pass out. "...to kill you."

Lenny's gaze shifted to the wooden box then back toward the professor.

"The Cubit," the professor said. "Yes. And it won't be long."

Lenny remembered the tiny blue-red spark of electricity no stronger than that of a static charge. He remembered his arm tingling. He remembered that the moment had lasted much longer than the split second it took for the tingle to subside. He rubbed his left hand and now studied it, turned it in the palm of his right hand which still did not work well with the bullet hole through his collarbone. When he looked up again, the knife was in the professor's hand. Lenny flinched.

"Take it," he said. "It's the only way."

Lenny immediately reached forward but paused just inches from the blade. It glistened as if containing a light source of its own. To take it would involve him further. He would become a murderer of children and wives. He would get his own little box and...

The professor shoved the haft of the knife into Lenny's motionless hand. And as Lenny began to study the weapon which looked more like a dagger with a long thin blade, three things happened simultaneously. The professor passed out, the porch light came on, and his mother emerged with shotgun in hand. She chambered a shot and pointed it at the trespassing car.

Lenny didn't want to emerge from the station wagon with a weapon at two o'clock in the morning while his mother pointed a loaded shotgun at his head, so he quickly tossed the dagger in the glove box.

"Mom," he yelled as he opened the car door. "It's me...Lenny."

Janine Bender would not lower the shotgun until she was absolutely sure that the man in the car was really her son. Albert's latest acquaintances made her untrusting of all strange cars, especially those that appeared on her doorstep in the middle of the night.

She moved across the porch to her right, avoided a pair of wicker chairs that she'd refinished last week, and poked the barrel of the shotgun across the hood of her pickup to the two men sitting in the front seat of an old station wagon.

The porch light reflection bouncing off the car's windshield made it difficult to see. The passenger appeared motionless, head to window.

Something stained his shirt but she couldn't tell what it was. The driver was her son; she could see him clearly as he stood from the car. His thin brown hair cropped above the ears outlined the small face of a boy who'd moved another six months toward manhood since she'd last seen him. His shirt was also stained in about the same location as the passenger's. She looked past him, following the gray outline of the front road beyond the barn, until she was satisfied that nothing else was out there.

"Mom," Lenny repeated. "Please. Don't shoot."

It was then that Janine realized she had the shotgun pointed at her son's head and immediately lowered it. "What in Moses' name are you doin' out here in the middle of the night, Lenny?" Janine gazed at the man beside Lenny as her son emerged from the station wagon. "And who's that? You know me and strangers."

"He's hurt real bad." Lenny walked around his mother's truck and ascended the five wooden steps to the porch. "He gave me a lift but then we had a little..."

"And you?" She grabbed his shoulder, lightly. Lenny flinched. "Are *you* hurt real bad?" She pulled him closer to her with one arm while setting the gun on the wicker table with the other.

"Oww," he yelped and pulled away like a little boy whose mother had just touched his little boo-boo.

"Gun shot," Janine said, surprised. "Who in Moses' name has been shooting you?" She turned him to look at the hole in his shirt where the bullet had exited.

"Long story," Lenny said, exasperated. "The professor—he's worse off. Probably needs a doctor."

Janine held her son gently by the sides of his head, looked into his brown eyes for answers that she was certain would not be revealed until much later, if at all. "Doctor!" she said. "You know me and doctors." She didn't wait for an answer; she could see that Lenny was concerned. She didn't like strangers and she didn't like doctors but she couldn't turn away an injured man, especially on the Holy day. She'd have to repent for months. "Come on. Let's get him inside."

His mother was much grayer than when he'd last seen her. She looked as old as the professor though Lenny was certain she was at least ten years younger. Her eyes were grayer as well having shifted from azure shortly after his father's death. It had been a strange transformation: blue eyes to gray. He'd never heard of a person's eyes changing color in the middle of adulthood. It had started with little gray flecks here and there. Now the pupils' were completely gray. They walked together to the passenger's side door of the station wagon.

"He doesn't look well," his mother said. "Lost a lot of blood."

Lenny opened the door slowly and the professor's body slid sideways. He was awake but terribly weak. Lenny helped him into a sitting position.

"We're going to move you inside," Lenny said. The professor responded but Lenny could not understand. He slurred as if drunk. "We're gonna need your help. Okay?"

Lenny reached under the professor's left thigh and arm and scooted him toward the edge of the seat. The professor helped, but not much. When Lenny looked around for his mother he saw her standing motionless and staring into the cargo bay of the station wagon.

"Mom. A little help. Please?"

She remained motionless.

"Mom—"

Lenny was about to loose his balance. His thin frame could not withstand the professor's weight much longer.

"Ka-yaa-buut," the professor moaned. "No Tuuchh."

It took Lenny less than a second to realize what the professor was saying since, simultaneous with this understanding, Lenny watched as his mother leaned into the glass-shattered rear window, her right arm stretched toward the Cubit.

It was the feeling associated with knowing something no one else knew. It was the feeling that she'd seen it somewhere before but was uncertain if it had been something real or something that had been a part of a dream. It felt like desire and fear and helplessness wrapped together into one extremely unwanted emotion. She could not control herself. She had to touch it. Every fiber of her Christian being screamed for resistance, and this caused her arm and hand to shake as she reached into the station wagon.

"No! Mom! No!"

Its smooth wooden surface was a foot away. She hesitated.

"Don't touch it!"

A little red star was buried in the wood at its top edge, centered, as if serving the function of a hasp but it had no latch. It winked at her, or so she thought. She smiled. Giggled. She hadn't giggled in years. The pads of her fingers wanted to gently caress it…its electricity…and in one quick motion, she was suddenly jerked forcefully backwards.

"Mom!" Lenny screamed.

She glared at the box, at Lenny, at the man who now lay on the gravel driveway after Lenny had let him fall. The man attempted to roll onto a knee, pushing himself upward with his good arm, before falling back onto the gravel.

"Come on, Mom," Lenny said, exhausted. "Let's get the professor inside."

The man whom her son had called the professor had only enough strength to allow the limited combined efforts of herself and Lenny to guide him into the house and onto the couch. His blood quickly marred the green and white fabric and Janine thought, briefly, how terribly difficult it was going to be to remove those stains. The professor eased onto his back without aid from either of them, blinked a few quick times while studying the ceiling, then closed his eyes. A few driveway pebbles were stuck in his short, matted gray and white beard and Janine brushed them away.

"Go to the bathroom and get me a couple of washcloths," she said to Lenny. "And bring me a small pan of cool water."

Lenny exited the living room and disappeared into a hallway that led to the bathroom as Janine unbuttoned the professor's shirt and peeled it from sticky skin. She rolled the right half of the shirt to fully uncover the bullet wound. Blood still oozed from it, creating a darker pattern in the center that resembled a red star.

And she was suddenly back outside, dazed and confused, wanting to caress the smooth wood surface of the box in the station wagon. The red glistening star. The desire. The fear. Uncontrollable.

"Here ya go." Lenny's voice broke the spell. "Is it bad?"

She grabbed both washcloths from her son's hand, dipped one into the plastic mixing bowl that Lenny had filled with water, then folded it lengthwise and draped it across the professor's forehead. She wetted the second washcloth and began mopping up the sticky mess of blood from the skin surrounding the wound. She rinsed the washcloth several times until the bowl of water turned crimson.

"He'll live for now but I'm afraid the bullet is still inside him," she said over her shoulder, not looking at Lenny. "I'm afraid he's going to need a hospital. Don't know what the bullet's done to him inside but he needs to have it removed."

The professor suddenly snapped his eyes open and started to rise but was gently forced down by Janine's hand.

"No," he demanded without shouting. "No doctors. No hospitals. No policemen. They'll find me if you do. They'll find the Cubit. You can't let that happen." He grasped Janine's hand and searched her gray eyes. "*You* can't let that happen."

She immediately connected the word 'Cubit' with the wooden box outside. Again, there was that feeling of knowing something but not remembering just how you knew it.

"You'll die without help," Janine demanded and reached forward to flip the wet washcloth on the professor's forehead.

"The dagger," he moaned. "Use the dagger." Then he closed his eyes and became silent. His breathing came in short spurts. A tiny runner of blood emerged from the right corner of his mouth. Janine guessed that he had little life left.

"What about this dagger?" she asked Lenny. "You know what he's talking about?"

"Yeah. It's out in the car. But I don't understand how it's gonna help matters." Janine rose from the professor's side and turned to her son. "I mean, he used it to kill a cop."

She could have asked him to explain in more detail and probably would later. Right now she believed that the man on the couch would soon die. She didn't know what the dagger was nor how it could possibly help the situation but the professor's last words had been: *Use the dagger.*

"Please get it for me," she said and reached forward to pull the collar of Lenny's T-shirt away from his neck. "Once we take care of him, I'll dress you up."

Lenny's first thoughts were those planted by Stephen King's *Children of the Corn.* His mother had never allowed him to watch that movie while growing up in a cornfield. Those images were not conducive to a healthy, young Kansas mind. And Lenny had found this assumption to be true when he'd finally seen it in his University of Texas dorm room just last week. His roommate had rented it. It had not been Lenny's choice.

Now, as he stood on the porch, he wondered where "he who walks among the corn" might be. Had the professor really killed him? Or was the dead state trooper out there still? Was *he* walking among the rows just beyond the porch, waiting for cowardly Lenny Bender? His imagination coalesced into a fear that had him looking in every direction. He stepped from the porch and scampered to the back of the pickup, brushing the bumper with his blue-jeaned thigh hard enough to embed a rust red streak into the fibers. By the time he reached the passenger-side door of the station wagon, he'd freaked himself out so badly that a Sunday morning crow, looking for an early meal, made him squeal when it flew a few feet above his head. He gasped in much the same way as he'd done while watching *Children of the Corn*.

Once inside the station wagon, he slammed the door, breathing hard, trying to regain composure though the puke-encrusted seat was a gentle reminder of his cowardice. He snapped open the glove box, thinking as he did so that a blue-red spark might shoot from its black depths and abruptly cause Lenny to abandon his effort. Cautiously, he stuck his hand in; the dagger's blade was quite sharp; he was not interested in the pain that it might cause. He was a coward, a paranoid and scared little boy who should have never gone hitchhiking.

His hand shuffled across a folded piece of paper, a small book and the haft of the dagger. He grabbed all three items and set them in his lap. The folded paper was a map that charted southwestern highways through Texas, New Mexico and Arizona. The professor had highlighted in yellow Interstate 40 as it ran through the top half of the three states. In Arizona, the highlighting continued south from Interstate 40 through Flagstaff and ended in the city of Sedona. The professor had drawn a yellow circle around Sedona and Lenny guessed that this was his intended destination.

The book was about an inch thick and a bit smaller in width and height than a regular sheet of notebook paper. The cover was worn and felt like cloth. There was no title. When he tried to open the book, all of the pages seemed stuck together except for the center spread. Strange symbols were written on one of the two center pages. He closed the book to reveal an image of a dagger embossed in gold on the back cover. A star, much like the one on the Cubit, was etched in the dagger's haft. He rubbed his thumb across the star's edges; it felt warm.

His attention shifted to the dagger in his lap. It, too, had a star embedded into the haft just above the blade. It, too, felt warm in his left hand. He moved the dagger into his right hand and a pulse of energy moved up his arm and into his shoulder where the bullet wound still throbbed. A tingling sensation massaged his collarbone; it kind of tickled. He shoved the book and map into the glove box, closed it, then rubbed his shoulder; the throb decreased. The pain was subsiding. He still could not lift it easily without accompanied pain but there was no denying that it felt better.

When he exited the station wagon and ran to the house, he didn't notice that the red star centered at the top edge of the Cubit was glowing and that lying on the ground behind the station wagon, encircled by the star's red light, was the crow which had frightened him just minutes before. It writhed in the red glow until Lenny entered the house, then became stiff and still as the red star on the Cubit also died.

Janine finished cleaning the blood from the professor's chest and moved his legs and arms into a comfortable position on the couch. The bullet hole still oozed and she quickly mopped stray dribbles with the washcloth.

"This thing just might do the trick," Lenny said in the doorway. "It has some…" Lenny struggled for the right word. "It has some kind of electricity in it. It helped my shoulder."

"What are you talking about?" Janine rose from the professor's side and studied the dagger in her son's hand.

"I don't know. I felt a kind of electric tingle that went all the way up to my shoulder. Look, my arm moves a lot better now." Lenny raised and lowered it twice. "It is still painful but at least it moves."

Janine pulled back the collar of his T-shirt. Had she blinked, she would have missed it. And even after some of the flesh at the edge of Lenny's wound seemed to magically stitch itself back together, Janine could not believe it. She rubbed her eyes.

"Let me see that," she asked, stepping back. When Lenny gave the dagger to her she studied the haft's smooth, white surface. The top and bottom of the haft were fatter than the middle and were capped in gold. It was chiseled in such a way that it had five sides. A star embellished one of the sides just above the blade which curved seven inches in length to its very thin point; glistening in the living room's lamplight, it revealed no imperfections. Janine cupped the dagger in her hand but felt none of what Lenny had described as electricity. She waved it through the air a few times, first overhand then underhand not knowing why she did so.

"Mom." Lenny pointed at the professor whose face had become pale. "Give it to him."

She placed the dagger in the professor's unconscious right hand but she could not get his fingers to wrap around the haft. The red jewel in the star started to glow. She snatched it back, and felt its warmth and electricity.

"Do you hear that?" she asked Lenny.

"What?"

"That noise—that hum."

"No," Lenny said. "No hum."

But Janine heard it.

Mmmmmmm...

The dagger's glow began to pulse with the sound.

Mmm...Mmm...Mmm...

And then Janine, for reasons she would never understand, moved over the professor's chest and positioned the point of the dagger above the bullet wound. How shoving a sharp object into this man's flesh was going to save him, she didn't know. But it seemed to make sense. Slowly, she inserted the blade a quarter of an inch into the bloody wound. Lenny gasped and rushed forward, but was propelled backward by his mother's left arm.

"Not now Lenny," she urged.

"But you're..."

"Shhh!!" She turned to her son. "Do you want me to kill this man?" She didn't wait for an answer, "Then be quiet."

A full inch of the blade disappeared into the professor's chest. The farther the blade went, the brighter the star jewel glowed. Janine wondered how close the blade was to the man's lung; she wondered if she was cutting away vital arteries or veins. She was schooled in first aid but not surgery. Down the blade went through flesh that presented only minor resistance. The red jewel grew brighter.

And then the dagger met an obstacle that Janine was afraid to push through. The blade was in at least four inches and filled the bullet wound at the skin's surface completely. She believed she had struck bone since only the slightest nudge of the dagger met with staunch resistance. The jewel blazed red. Her arm trembled. The professor stirred, said something unintelligible, a mumble with no meaning.

Janine began to draw the dagger out of the wound but as she did so, she felt a gentle tug as if the man's body did not want the blade to be removed. She lifted with more force.

One inch emerged—two inches—like a medieval sword from a fleshy stone.

Three inches—four.

Both Janine and Lenny gasped simultaneously. Clinging as if magnetized to the point of the dagger was a half-inch, misshapen piece of metal. The bullet was coated in blood and was blunted from its impact with the professor's body. With the blade and bullet out of the professor, the jewel in the dagger's haft faded and the bullet dropped onto the professor's shoulder where it rolled, creating a narrow trail of blood toward the center of his chest.

Janine snatched the bullet, rolled it between thumb and index finger, then dropped it into the plastic bowl of red water. She wiped the professor's chest, rinsed the washcloth several times, then wrapped the blade of the dagger with the washcloth.

"I don't know, Lenny," she said, expecting questions. "I just don't know. It is a miracle. In the name of Moses it is a miracle." She turned to face him. "I'm going to guess that your friend here will recover, but he's going to need some rest. He's lost a lot of blood and I don't think even this has the power to replenish it."

After dumping bloody water into the bathroom sink and placing the bullet next to the sink's faucet, Janine retrieved a blanket from the hall closet and draped it over the professor. The color was returning in his face and this satisfied her belief that he would recover. She took her son by the hand, placed the dagger in the pocket of her housecoat, and headed for her special room, the one she kept under the house.

Janine and Michael had agreed on the internal basement shelter the day after a Category 3 tornado had destroyed the north end of Pickett's Crossing. It had missed their farm by just a few miles. Had the tornado taken a different track, one to the south of town, much of their crops and perhaps even their home would have disappeared into the late June summer afternoon.

The only discussion they'd had was not if they needed a shelter but where it would be located. Most storm shelters were external but Janine had seen in an issue of *Family Circle* how internal storm shelters were economical, safe, and could double as an added room when not being used to protect the family from imminent harm. If the Benders were to decide on an internal shelter, they would have to build an addition onto the house. The cost, with the addition, would be nearly double that of an external shelter. And this is where their discussion—which was never an argument but a "discussion"—had heated by the smallest degree. Janine and her husband never fought but the added investment which would essentially add two rooms to their house was one of those rare moments when discussion neared the intensity of an argument.

Could they afford it with a ten-year-old child whose complex move into adolescence was just around the corner? Certainly, the weather could never be predicted. Tornadoes aside, drought could hit and decimate their crops. Or perhaps their crops would become infested by some of the diseases or insects that Michael had read about in *Agricultural Digest*. They needed the extra $10,000 as an investment that would always be available for such "just in case" circumstances.

Janine had always wanted an addition. The house seemed just a bit too small, especially with Lenny requiring more and more privacy as he grew older. She had discussed the prospect with Michael on several occasions and Michael had always told her, as he did when the idea of a storm shelter arose, that they needed to be frugal, watch their expenditures. Disaster could strike anytime and they had to be ready for it.

But the Bender farm had been prosperous for five straight years. Their newest venture—that of raising AKC registered black Labradors—was starting to show a profit. It was time to stop thinking about all the bad that could happen and do something for themselves.

This is where Janine's side of the "discussion" had won out. They had waited so long for something bad to happen that they were not enjoying the good while they could.

Had Janine known that within the next ten years, her husband would be dead and much of the Bender assets would be sold, she would have put the money that an external shelter would have saved them into an account that, today, would be of great use. Some amount of savings would have helped her run from this collection of bad memories and move some place special, a place she often thought of as paradise. A place with sandy beaches and ocean waves where small-town friendly people knew you by name. A place far from here that was, just like in the *Wizard of Oz*, somewhere over the rainbow.

Janine gazed at the snapshot photo of a scene from the *Wizard of Oz*. The professor and Lenny were both fast asleep upstairs. It was just a little before dawn and she could not get back to sleep. Her mind was preoccupied with the picture. Dorothy was leaning against Auntie Em's wooden wagon wheel singing about rainbows, pretty little bluebirds, and why oh why can't I. Janine sympathized with Dorothy. Why oh why couldn't they? Dorothy was stuck in a world of grown-ups and rules. Janine was stuck in a world of alcoholic control. And just like in the *Wizard of Oz*, along came a professor to offer them both the hope of miracles. She didn't know what the professor's name was upstairs but doubted very seriously it was anything close to Marvel. The man upstairs, however, had something even the Wizard did not, a magic dagger. One that could draw bullets from bodies. One that, by its simple touch, could heal and certainly kill. The professor's dagger was as marvelous as anything in the world of Oz and perhaps, just perhaps, it could help Janine fly from here, just like pretty little bluebirds, to her own Oz—to her own paradise.

The storm shelter, which doubled as Janine's private room, was adorned with several pictures in frames that depicted images of what she believed to be paradise. Along with the movie scene from the *Wizard of Oz*, there were pictures of sunny warms places, each showing sandy beaches and crashing tidewaters. One was a shot from a beach just outside of Cancun, Mexico. Another depicted a shoreline along the African Mediterranean coast. A third was a beach along the southern end of Australia. All totaled, there were nearly a dozen framed "Janine paradises" all of which she knew were unattainable beyond a miracle.

On the other walls of her room hung an array of biblical renderings, artifacts and icons. Most referenced Moses and the exodus from Egypt. There was a swatch of Hebrew cloth, stone recreations of the Ten Commandments, a picture of Moses standing before the split Red Sea, the words "Let My People Go" scribbled on a tapestry that covered no window, an autographed picture of Charlton Heston, and many dime store novelty items that had some part of the scripture from Exodus inscribed on them.

Against the wall adjoining the paradise picture collage and opposite the narrow set of steps that led up to the storm shelter's floor-framed door was a three-drawer wooden dresser that she had refinished back when things were good. Atop the dresser was a tall mirror framed in the same dark-stained oak as the dresser, a small lamp with a shade that was printed with a repeating pattern of angels, and three framed pictures: one of Michael, one of Lenny and one of the three of them together with their prize-winning, and most beloved Labrador, Betty.

Janine rose from her bed, a double-sized mattress that took up two-thirds of the space in the room, and stepped to the dresser. She grabbed the picture of her family, ran a finger across the outline of her husband, tickled the chin of Betty, rubbed the shoulder of her son. The Janine in the picture was not the Janine she now stared at in the mirror. Though it had been only five years since the picture had been taken, the changes in her face were three times in age. She would be forty-two in three months but the lines under her eyes, the crinkled forehead and a full head of gray hair made her look much, much older. Physically and mentally she was forty-two but her appearance was frail. Her aged look was one of the reasons why she had become reclusive. Albert was the other.

She gazed over at the miracle dagger lying on the mattress at the foot of the bed and thought about Albert, about escape, about paradise. It could be used to cure but could it also be used to kill? Better yet, would it recognize Albert for the scumbag alcoholic he was and somehow fling itself into the demon's heart? She could not do it herself. She was a Christian lady.

Thou shall not kill, the picture of Moses seemed to say to her.

But was wishing for death the same as committing the act? Was it right to free oneself by killing others? Moses had, hadn't he? He'd slain an Egyptian slavemaster who was beating a frail Hebrew worker. He'd killed all of the Egyptian first born. He'd directed Pharaoh's army into the Red Sea and drowned them. Not to mention all of the people his Israelite army massacred on the way to the Promised Land. In his Exodus, Moses had killed many.

So it was right, then, to kill for freedom. With her Bible as rationale, she would not rot in Hell—instead she would be free to find Heaven. Still, she could not, by her own hand, thrust the dagger into any person. Even if Albert was asleep (which was the only time she felt that it might be possible to kill him) she could not. Even if she found out that it had been Albert who had killed her husband, she could not. Even if Albert threatened her once again, with wife-beating ramifications to her threats of leaving him, she could not.

She stared into the mirror, searching her own slate gray eyes for an answer. She looked at her hands, already spotted and wrinkled well beyond her age. Were these the hands of a killer? Were these the eyes that could forever withhold the truth about the murderer she would become? Further, how many times had she stood in this exact spot, gazing at her reflection and wondering *What If*? She'd never done it. She never could do it.

But then there was the dagger. And again there was that feeling of knowing without knowing how you knew. The dagger was the key to her salvation.

She stepped to the edge of the bed, grabbed the weapon, unwrapped the washcloth. She moved the haft from hand to hand, caressing its smooth surface, thumbing its fine craftsmanship, gazing at the golden star that was jeweled in red in only one of the five points.

A knock on the storm shelter's door above her, broke her from the trance.

"Yes?" she said.

"Mom." Lenny's voice was a whisper above the heavy wooden door. "I can't sleep. You mind if I come down?"

Janine wrapped the washcloth around the blade of the dagger and set it on her dresser. She, again, stared into her gray, sad eyes—searching. Perhaps Lenny could tell her more about this dagger, about the red stars. Perhaps with his help she would be able to do it.

"OK," she said. "Come down."

The first thing Janine did when her son reached the foot of the steps was pull him close to her. With a gentle hug she asked him about his shoulder. Lenny had changed shirts into one which pictured Grave Digger, the monster truck he'd raved over through his teen years. This jerked a tear from the corner of her eye. It was the same T-shirt he was wearing in the family picture on her dresser.

"My shoulder is still sore, but I'll live," Lenny said.

Janine pulled the collar of his shirt forward to reveal red inflammation underneath a large band-aid. She peeled back the band-aid, was satisfied that the bullet wound was not infected and replaced it. "How's your friend?" she said.

"Well, I wouldn't exactly call him my friend…" Lenny stepped back from his mother's embrace. "He's still sleeping. He was mumbling something before I came down. Probably just dreaming, I guess."

"Come over and sit down. We haven't talked in a good while. You don't write or call much." Janine stopped short of sounding confrontational as she and Lenny sat at the foot of the bed. "Anyway, it's really good to see you."

"I dropped out of school." Lenny stared at his socked feet.

Janine was not surprised, but she felt his withholding of information up until now added another degree of detachment between them.

"Agricultural science just isn't my thing," he continued. "Besides, without Dad…" He looked up and into his mother's eyes. "I mean it was him who wanted me to follow in his footsteps, to take over the farm some day." Though he tried, Lenny could not fight back the welling tears.

"I know." Janine caressed her son's hand between both of hers. She was upset with her son's decision to leave college but knew that he was right. After all, there was not much left of the farm for him to follow in the footsteps of the man who had built it. "If it is the will of the Lord then so be it. How long has it been?"

"Dropped out before the beginning of last spring semester. It was hard to study and work and stay interested in agriculture all at the same time."

"What are you doing now?" Janine remained supportive.

"Doing now?" Lenny looked confused, tired.

"In San Antonio—you working?"

Lenny hunched forward and stared at his feet as if trying to think of something to say. Janine was beginning to feel that a change of subject was necessary.

"I, uh—well I was just laid off from this construction company." His feet dangled an inch off the floor and he shuffled them back-and-forth as he spoke. "They were good people but the work just dried up."

"What happened tonight?" Janine said, squeezing and pulling his hand as to nudge him into looking at her. He turned. A slight tremble emerged in the corner of his mouth.

"I had a really horrible dream," he said.

"No. I mean with the professor and all."

"That's what *I* mean. Before I came down here I was dreaming about it. At least parts of it…the really bad parts. Stuff that didn't even happen. At least I don't think it happened—I mean—oh hell. I don't know what I mean." He looked up at the walls where Moses' picture stared down at him. "Sorry. I didn't mean to say hell."

Janine pulled him as close to her as his body language would allow. "Tell me. What did you dream?

Lenny's eyebrows curled inward, helplessly. His lip trembled more briskly as he said, "I have to kill myself."

Inwardly, Janine gasped but she didn't want to show such shocking emotion in her son's time of need. "You know this from your dream?" she said.

"From the professor."

"The professor told you to kill yourself?"

"Yeah, I know. Why would he do that? Hell..." He looked up at Moses and the split water walls of the Red Sea behind him. "Heck, we saved his life. He saved my life. That thing was dead but it was alive. He killed it after that dead thing shot us. And the Cubit. I didn't touch it, I swear. But he said I did. And now I have to kill myself. I have to kill myself with that dagger."

"Whoa. Hold on." Janine double-clutched his hand. "Let's take this one step at a time."

Lenny's eyes suddenly boiled with intensity, fear and shock. He stared straight through her. "I saw *Me*, mom. I saw *Me* in my dream and I was dead. I looked just like me but it wasn't me. It was a dead Lenny trying to kill me. An anti-Lenny. An evil Lenny." He clutched his mother's elbow with his right arm while his left hand remained clasped within hers. "That was the dream part. The dead trooper was real. But they are connected. They are both a part of that—Cubit. Whatever you do, don't touch it." He squeezed her arm tight enough to constrict the blood flow. "Stay as far away as you can. It's evil, mom. It wants to destroy the world."

Lenny collapsed onto his mother's lap. She caressed his temple and forehead as his eyes fluttered in a fight between consciousness and sleep. The revelations he'd unleashed in the past couple of minutes were too much for her to even try and comprehend. All she knew was that her son needed her. Something traumatic had taken his mind and had ripped it apart and now his dreams were keeping him awake. And they had to be dreams. Dead people didn't shoot guns.

She eased Lenny onto the bed and snuck a pillow under his head. He'd finally fallen asleep. She stretched out beside him and draped one arm across his chest, felt his racing heartbeat that seemed to skip a beat or two. Her own eyes blinked with exhaustion. Her mind raced with scattered pieces of information. Dead people. Lenny committing suicide. A magic dagger.

Paradise. The Cubit.

Lying beside her son, Janine fell asleep thinking about the small wooden box in the back of the professor's station wagon, the red star on its top edge, and how it had drawn her to it—how it had wanted her to touch it.

Albert Stine was pissed off. He could not believe that he'd been caught cheating. How dare they accuse him of doing something like that? How could they know he was counting cards? They couldn't read his mind. They were going purely on the word of the dealer. And how the hell could she know? The stupid whore was just tired of losing, that's all. If he ever saw her outside he'd teach her a lesson or two about treating men with respect. Damn bitch!

Albert swilled from a pint of Jim Beam then quickly chased it with a swallow of Diet Coke. His foot had mashed the accelerator with the thought of the casino blackjack dealer and he eased it up, looking into his rearview mirror for cops as he did so.

He'd get her, he thought again. No fucking woman was going to get the best of Albert Stine.

Kansas State Route 22 was nearly deserted of traffic. Occasionally, a sedan or van packed with Sunday-dressed families would buzz by in the opposite direction and Albert would giggle. Church was as useless to a man's soul as were women. Both wanted to save you. Both wanted to turn you into something you weren't. Both wanted to meddle in your life, ask too many questions, then leave you feeling guilty about being a man.

He thought of the casino dealer and his foot reacted against the gas peddle. How dare she meddle in his life? How could she have known? The technique was sound. Jimmy Jacks had guaranteed him that no casino in the country would ever know. Jacks had gotten away with counting cards at the blackjack table forever. There's no way *that* casino bitch could have known. And now he was banned for life from gambling at the Sandbox and it wouldn't be long before the word on Albert Stine spread.

"Shit!" he grumbled, swilled whiskey, chased it. He pounded his fist against the steering wheel of his blue Monte Carlo and half a shot of Beam spilled onto his lap. He ignored it.

He snapped on the radio, having pawned all of his CDs to get enough chips to play that one last hand of blackjack. Nothing but gospel and sermons. Angrily, he snapped it back off.

Being mad was not uncommon for Albert. And the more he drank the more pissed off he became. By the time he reached the Bender farm front road, he'd finished the pint and had worked himself up into such a furious frenzy that a mere infraction on his patience by anyone would set him off. He was going to sell the farm; that much he'd already decided. With the cash he would buy his way back into Vegas. Tons of rich farm land meant tons of cash. Perhaps even six figures. He could live well on that kind of dough—more dough than that bitch dealer would make in a lifetime.

And Janine? He'd take her with him. She'd often talked about paradise. Vegas was the perfect paradise. She'd have much to do. If she wanted to continue fixing people's clothes she could do that. There were plenty of people in Vegas who'd lost some portion or all of the shirt off their backs. If she got tired of that, she could become a dealer. She'd be popular. Players would love a kind, naive country girl, one that didn't accuse them of cheating, one that would treat men with respect.

It was close to noon when Albert stopped his car along the Bender's front road short of the house. He tapped his fingers on the steering wheel, anger welling, wishing for another bottle of booze. His breaths became an anxious imitation of an animal ready to fight.

Parked alongside Janine's truck was a station wagon that Albert had never seen before and he immediately jumped to the conclusion that Janine was seeing another man. Made sense too. Every time he left for Vegas, she never said one word to him. She never asked him why he spent so much time there, never asked him to stay home with his wife, and, quite frankly, seemed to urge him to leave by helping him pack and opening the front door as he left the house. She never called him in Vegas or tried to keep tabs on him in any way. Didn't all women do that? Didn't all women question where you were going and what you were doing and how long you'd be gone? Yeah, all women except those that were whoring around on you. The last thing those women wanted was you anywhere around them. Guy was probably from out of town. Probably someone wanting to romance the farm from under her. Probably that Markson character. He'd offered Albert a criminally low price for the farm the last time he'd thought of selling it. But Markson drove an Explorer not a station wagon. Still, covert actions required covert camouflage and this Markson was pretty sneaky.

Albert backed his Monte Carlo along the front road to a point behind the barn so it could not be seen from the house. He would not need a weapon. His courage came straight from the bottle. Besides, he'd already eclipsed the point of level-headed reasoning and this gave him the strength of ten Alberts. He felt he could chew bullets and spit nails even if those bullets were being shot at him.

Slowly, he moved to the barn, hunching a bit as to make his 240-pound frame a bit less revealing. He slid his back across flaking red paint as he stealthily moved from beyond the south wall of the barn and out into the open. The sun blazed his forehead and sent bumper metal reflections from the station wagon and truck into his eyes. He wiped away sweat, shielded his face with the palm of a hand and shuffled, still hunched, to the station wagon where he squatted by the driver's door. He peered through the window for evidence of its occupant, certain that he would find something to finger Markson as the adulterer. What he found was more confusing.

Blood, shattered glass, and something that looked like dried puke smeared the front seat in a macabre mosaic that pulled a small squirt of Jim Beam from Albert's stomach into his throat. Suddenly, the front door of the house opened and Albert dropped immediately. Breaths intensified. Sweat rolled down his forehead and into his eyes. He heard a man's voice then the door closed.

This verified his assumption that his wife was an adulterer. His anger became immense. He gripped rock from the drive path so intensely that when he released his grip and rose to his feet, several pebbles remained stuck to the pads of his fingers.

He sidestepped to the back of the station wagon. His adrenaline pumped energy that he did not know he had. He rose, planted his feet, eyed the five porch steps that he would easily leap over and chose a spot next to the door handle where he would plant his shoulder. He would catch them by surprise.

Out of the corner of his eye Albert saw what he thought was a laser beam, the kind that centers a target in a scope. It painted the side of his face with a red dot that pulsed across his cheek.

Markson had a rifle?

Wondering if he'd be shot as he did so, Albert slowly rose and looked for the source of the light. In the back of the station wagon he saw a wooden box. At the top edge of the box a small, bright, red star glowed.

Janine awoke to the sound of shattering glass. She quickly rolled from the bed and onto her feet. Lenny was up a few seconds later. Although his eyes appeared rested they remained shadowed by disquiet and bewilderment. He immediately went for the dagger lying on her dresser.

"He's coming," Lenny said, unwrapping the washcloth from the dagger's blade. "I knew he would. Just like the professor said."

"Who's coming?" Janine knew his answer before he said it.

"Me."

The boards in the roof of the storm shelter squeaked as heavy footfalls walked through the kitchen above them. Quickly, both climbed the stairs, Janine in the lead. She slid the floor door's latch and raised it only far enough to see into the kitchen. Broken glass scattered the vinyl floor in front of the refrigerator. She continued out of the storm shelter and laid the floor door back on its hinged legs. Lenny was quickly out behind her.

"Good morning!"

Janine and Lenny turned simultaneously to the voice behind them.

"Sorry about the glass. I can't find a broom anywhere." The professor sat on the couch with a glass of milk in his right hand and a chocolate chip cookie in the other. He'd wrapped the blanket around his shoulders and his bare chest revealed the red circular bullet wound which looked like it had nearly healed. "These are really very good." He waved the half-eaten cookie in front of him. "I was very hungry so I took the liberty. I hope you don't mind."

Lenny had unconsciously raised the dagger when he'd turned. He lowered it to his side, finding that his right arm functioned quite well.

"Ah, I see you found my dagger." The professor took another bite of cookie, laid the rest on one knee, shifted the glass of milk from his right hand to his left and took half the contents down in one drink.

"You gave it to me last night," Lenny said, shifting the point of the dagger downward in a less offensive position. "You don't remember?"

The professor returned the milk to his right hand. White froth remained on his gray-peppered mustache. "Lot's of things I don't remember and many I would love to forget."

"I heard that," Lenny said while moving toward the professor. "Your arm still not quite right?"

"Very sore. Can't move it for nothin'." He attempted a simple arm raise and lifted it two inches off his thigh before it collapsed. The half glass of milk splashed but did not spill. He looked from the milk to Janine. "But I'm alive," he said to her.

"It saved your life," Janine said. "Fixed Lenny's shoulder too."

"The dagger—Yes, I know."

"But how?"

"Lots of questions. And I have many answers. But first, the cookie and milk." The professor took another bite of cookie, dropped a large chip onto his bare chest, grabbed the stray piece and plopped it into his mouth. "I wanted to thank you for saving my life," he said, finishing off the cookie and milk in succession. "Janine is it?"

Janine moved closer to her son. "Who are you?"

"Cower. Christopher Cower." The blanket had shifted from his shoulders; he pulled it up and back into position. "Do you have a shirt I can borrow?"

"Lenny," Janine said. "Could you grab a shirt for Professor Cower?"

"Preferably a button-up," Cower interjected. "Easier to get my arm in." He grinned.

Lenny set the dagger on the small end table near the head of the couch. "I believe this is yours."

"Keep it, Lenny…" *You'll need it.* He didn't say it but it was implied in the way his voice trailed off. The knowledge was exchanged in the two men's stares. Lenny left the dagger on the table and went to fetch Cower a shirt.

Janine bent forward to inspect Cower's bullet wound. "It's healing nicely," she said. "Lord works in mysterious ways."

"Funny you should say that." Cower stared sternly but kindly. Their eyes were a foot apart.

Janine looked away and toward the dagger, the red star. "What is it…I mean what does it mean?"

"The dagger?" Cower picked up the dagger and set his empty glass in its place. He twirled the dagger like a baton between the fingers of his left hand. The long blade sliced close to his wrist as he expertly maneuvered it.

"The red star," Janine corrected.

Lenny returned with a plaid shirt that was a bit too heavy for June weather. Cower accepted it gratefully, dropped the blanket from his shoulders, then easily placed his left arm into the shirt. Lenny came around the back of the couch to help him with the other arm. Cower winced as Lenny manipulated the shirt onto his back. He left it unbuttoned.

"And I want to know why you wanted me to kill myself," Lenny said.

"I think you know the answer to that," he said to Lenny then added to both of them, "You know much about the Bible?" Lenny stared at the dagger on the table, the blade, how it shimmered in the light from a window behind the couch, a light that grew brighter as the rising midday sun erased barn shadows.

"Old Testament, mostly," Janine said.

"Good." Cower sat back into the couch. "Then you know what I mean when I talk about the five books at the beginning of it?"

"The Pentateuch," Janine said. Lenny looked bewildered.

"Please, sit down. This might take a while."

Lenny went to the kitchen for a couple of chairs and returned. Both mother and son sat. Cower cleared his throat and seemed quite calm for a man on the run. "Genesis, Exodus, Leviticus, Deuteronomy and..." he began.

"Numbers," Janine finished. "So the star represents the Pentateuch. Each of the points of the star represents one of these books." She said it as a matter of fact and not a question.

"Something like that," Cower said. "The five books. The five ages of creation. The five signs of the Apocalypse."

Lenny interrupted, "I thought there were seven signs of the Apocalypse."

"In some Bibles," Cower answered as if correcting one of his students.

"There's only one Bible." Janine said in a tone that was hinted with accusation of blasphemy.

"What makes you say that?" Cower leaned forward. "Because someone told you so?

"Who are you?" Janine huffed. "A professor? A professor of what? Ancient history?"

"The Torah and Qur'an are bibles are they not? They just give a different account of what is considered to be right and what is considered to be wrong. Now if we're talkin' Christianity then..." Janine sat stiff. Lenny shuffled his feet. "Then I gotta say that there are more versions of that Bible than any Qur'an or Torah. Isn't that what organized religion is all about in this country? Different interpretations of the Book?"

"So what Bible have you been reading?" Janine said, knowing that whatever he said would be dismissed by her own knowledge of the facts.

"One that would give another account of what really happened in those early days of man's ascent into God's own image." Cower suddenly shot a left hand forward and grabbed Janine's left, clammy wrist. "I know that faith is the strongest force on this Earth. I don't mean to even attempt to persuade yours differently. What I give you is knowledge. You want to know about the star, the dagger and, no doubt, the Cubit. What I have to offer is an explanation that will not make sense to someone unable or unwilling to accept possibility."

Janine said nothing.

Cower continued, "What would you say if I told you the world was created in five ages rather than seven days?"

"That's not how I know it," Janine said.

"Exactly!" Cower released her hand as gently as he'd grasped it. "Five ages to create life. Five ages to kill it. Depends on what you believe."

"Is that the Bible you're talkin' about?" Lenny said while pointing at the front door. "That book I found in your glove box? It had a picture of *that* on the back cover." Lenny moved his hand from pointing at the door to pointing at the dagger that was still clutched in Cower's left hand.

Cower nodded. "A Bible perhaps few have ever even heard of," he said.

"It explains all of this?" Janine asked.

"Only if you believe," Cower said, again as a teacher talking to a pupil. He shifted slightly on the couch, revealing a small splotch of bloodstain on the couch's middle cushion. "Genesis was about the creation of life but it was also about the creation of death. Exodus introduced us to a great savior but it also introduced the Antichrist. With every Good there exists an equal and opposite Evil."

"The Cubit," Lenny said. "How does that fit in?"

"Arc of the Covenant," Cower quickly responded as if in anticipation. "For every Good there exists an equal and opposite Evil."

"So there's another Arc?" Lenny scratched his wounded shoulder.

"Perhaps I should fetch the book. It'll explain everything."

"I'll get it," Lenny offered.

"I need the fresh air," Cower countered, pushing himself up gingerly from the couch. Lenny snatched the dagger from Cower's left hand and helped him to his feet. "I'll be right back."

Professor Cower stretched then slowly shuffled to the front door. The sun's rays, shining through the living room window, reached the couch, signaling that it was close to noon.

Janine had lost track of time in the interim between Cower's departure and the scream that now brought both her and Lenny to their feet. She'd been thinking about the many sermons that Pastor Kindle had used to post his own interpretation of the Good Book. She'd been questioning all that she'd come to know as right, according to the Book, and Pastor Kindle. *For every good there is an equal and opposite bad.* Isn't that what Cower had said? Did this mean that whatever Pastor Kindle had said was only half truth? She'd never seen anything in the pastor's performance that equaled the magic in the dagger that Cower had introduced into their household. Janine knew a lot about the Bible, at least the one that was generally considered as the documented truth. But she wondered: Was there another story?

The initial reason why she bolted upward to snatch the loaded shotgun leaning near the front door was that she wanted some answers and she needed Cower to answer them. Ancillary to this was a concern for Cower.

"Holy shh..." Lenny looked at his mother. "What was that?"

Neither knew. Neither questioned. Both headed out of the house, Lenny clutching the dagger in his left hand, Janine clutching the shotgun in both.

Outside, the sun blazed with a strength that immediately fostered sweat on Janine's forehead. She hunkered down not really knowing why she did so. The shotgun felt safe in her hands. Lenny crouched, similarly, behind her. He held the dagger by the haft, underhanded, blade curled upward, as if he were going to a rumble.

Janine peered across the drive, the front road, the acres of uncultivated, top-grade farmland. She did not see Cower anywhere. She did see that one of the barn doors was wide open. Footsteps littered the ground in a path from the back of the station wagon, through the rocky parking area, across a small stretch of access road, through an area that had been used a few years ago to feed chickens, and into the barn.

The Cubit, Janine thought. *The anti-Arc of the Covenant*. But why would the professor take the Cubit to the barn?

To hide it, of course.

And what about the scream?

Cautiously, mother and son stepped from the porch to the Ford and toward the back of the station wagon. The Cubit, as she expected, was gone.

Lenny continued along the footstep path while Janine stopped for a moment to inspect the car. She poked her head into the cargo bay, saw pebbles of shattered glass and a few drops of what looked like blood and she remembered how the Cubit had beckoned her.

A little of that memory flooded into her vision and she jerked backward, knocking the barrel of the shotgun against the tailgate with such force that she nearly pulled the trigger on a gun pointed at her chin.

The glowing red star. She could see it as plainly as if she'd been suddenly transported ten hours back in time. It had pulled her toward it with inescapable energy.

Janine shook her head but the image of the star did not rescind. And by coincidence or pure mystic luck, lying by her feet near the left rear car tire was a book turned face down; a magic dagger was etched in the center of its back cover.

She knelt, released her hand from the barrel of the shotgun and snatched at the book, stumbling forward as she did so. She dropped the shotgun as she lost her balance and fell onto all fours. Tiny rock edges dug into her palms and knees and she quickly rolled onto her butt.

"Mom. You all right?" Lenny said, standing a few dozen feet from the open barn door near a small blackened crater created by one of Janine's recent dynamite tree-stumping efforts.

She grabbed the book and shotgun and rose from the gravel in one swift motion that was much too easy for a woman that looked her age. She shoved the book into her housecoat pocket and ran to catch up with her son not knowing that, when she'd fallen, she'd ripped her housecoat pocket. The book fell from the hole without her knowledge.

Sweat rolled a salty sting into her eyes and she absently looked down, her vision blurred, into the tree-stumped crater. An empty, pint bottle of Jim Beam was lying in the hole. Alerts sounded in her head. She'd dynamited this tree stump just a few days ago, which meant that someone had put the bottle in the crater since then. And she knew only one man that preferred his Beam in a small bottle that he could easily integrate into the take-a-shot-and-chase-it-with-Coke cocktails *he* preferred.

"Albert's here," she whispered, pointing at the empty bottle.

Lenny shook his head as if he did not believe what he'd just heard. "What?"

"Bottle of Beam. Has to be his."

"But I don't see his car."

Both walked toward the open barn door, a little added caution in each step. Forget that his car was nowhere in sight; what if Albert had come home early? What if he'd lost so much in this excursion to Vegas that he'd had to pawn his car and had gotten a bus ride back? What if by chance, he'd shown up right when Cower had gone out the door to fetch his Bible? What if Albert had been drinking, had believed this man was sweet on Janine and had decided to take matters into his own hands? What if *that* was the scream they'd heard?

Lenny led his mother through the open door and into the barn. His grip was death-tight on the dagger. Janine had raised the shotgun to her shoulder; her finger touched the trigger.

The barn was of average size. You could get a couple of tractors in and still have plenty of room to work and move around. Inside, stalls long empty sat unattended along the far wall. Old bales of sour hay were stacked ten feet high to the right. An old John Deere that was missing much of its engine occupied most of the left side of the floor. Beyond the tractor and at the back wall was an area where all of the hand tools were kept.

As Janine entered the barn's shadows she did not see the man lying in the rotten hay as quickly as did Lenny. Lenny ran toward the stall at the back of the barn. In that same instant, Janine saw motion in her periphery to the left. She also realized that the professor's footsteps swooped around the open barn door and disappeared behind the engine-gutted tractor also to her left. She tiptoed the path, looking ahead while keeping an eye on Lenny and the man lying in the back of the barn.

Behind the tractor was the Cubit. It rested among a scattering of tools. A shovel and hoe were propped against it. On the floor in front of the Cubit was Albert. He was quite dead. A pitchfork had been planted through his neck, its tines secured in the dirt floor under him. Into one eye socket a stick of dynamite had been jammed three inches deep. There was plenty of blood, both on the dead man and on the thing that kneeled over him, which now looked up with what looked like flesh in its mouth. Janine leveled the shotgun.

It was Albert. But it couldn't be. Albert was skewered and dead on the ground. The thing that looked like Albert dropped what it had been gnawing and Janine saw what looked like a pinky fall onto the still corpse of the real Albert.

"Janee," it said. "Whoring on me, Janee?" Its voice was much deeper than the real Albert's. Its red eyes possessed an intelligence greater than Albert's. It plucked the pitchfork easily out of the ground, shook it a few times to get real Albert's neck off of its tines then pointed it at Janine. "Whoring on me?" it repeated.

It lifted the pitchfork in the air as if it were about to throw it and Janine pulled the trigger.

The light from the barn door illuminated only the first third of the barn's interior. Small slivers of sun sliced down through unsealed cracks in the barn's roofing boards, creating a dancing montage of thick shadow interspersed by sunshine spotlights. Lenny was under one of these spotlights as he knelt down to find Cower struggling with shallow breaths. He turned the professor gingerly onto his left side. Cower's face was a mess, looked like it was broken in many more places than just his nose. He was not conscious. He was pretty close to dead, Lenny thought. And that's when he saw Albert eating Albert.

It seemed like a very long time but the numbness that locked him into place lasted only seconds. In a fraction of that moment, his body had decided that it was no longer time to run from trouble. It was time to face up to his responsibilities. His mother was somewhere over there for crying out loud. He had to at least save her.

But he couldn't move. Even when the thing dropped its food and called his mother's name, his knees remained locked. Even when the limp head of the real Albert dropped from the pitchfork's tines to a dirt floor mired in blood, his body said No!

It took the blast from the shotgun to get Lenny moving. The Albert beast suddenly lifted and flew backward into the Cubit where it bounced off one sharp wooden edge. As it rose, Lenny rose. As it moved again toward his mother, Lenny stepped away from the professor. Lenny bolted forward with the intention of thrusting the dagger through Albert's face but was held back by a hand that darted from shadows.

"No," Cower groaned. "You can't win one-on-one. You don't have the skill. You gotta surprise it." He pulled Lenny's denim pant leg, urged him to calm down. He could barely move from his fetal position. "The dagger. Into the...into the neck. It is the only way." A bit of bloody spit oozed from his mouth.

His mother screamed then appeared from behind the tractor, her hand on the barrel of the shotgun as she ran out of the barn. Behind her rushed the thing that looked like Albert, moving but not quite running, with a smile large and cunning spread wide on its face. Lenny shook his leg to break free from Cower's grip.

"Please, Lenny—" Cower moaned then went silent. He released Lenny's pant leg.

Albert exited the barn and Lenny gripped the dagger tight, took two giant steps toward the barn door with as much courage as he'd ever known, then froze in his tracks. The Cubit glowed red from behind the tractor. It filled the barn with maroon shadows. It emitted a soft hum that became inaudible when a shotgun blast echoed outside the barn.

The star on the Cubit blazed in dark red before the wooden top started to rise.

Crimson, darker than the red in the star, escaped from the Cubit's top edge. The crimson grew wider and deeper as the top panel of the Cubit rose as if hinged. It radiated an energy that drew Lenny to it.

What had Cower told him? This thing was the anti-Arc of the Covenant?

From within the Cubit rose—something. It used its hands to hoist itself through the open top. It then crawled out as a shadowy crimson outline before the Cubit slammed shut. The blaze from the Cubit's red star blinded Lenny and he lost sight of whatever had crawled out and into the shadows. Lenny shuffled back several steps, swiped the dagger out in front and around himself, sliced haphazardly at nothing he could see. The light from the red star on the Cubit died out. The barn returned to a mixture of dark shadow and sunshine spotlights.

Lenny continued fumbling backward, hoping like hell there was nothing behind him. And then movement through a few sunlight strokes that disappeared, reappeared, and disappeared too quickly for Lenny to understand. The barn grew brighter, at least in Lenny's vicinity, as he neared the rectangular patch of light that fell onto the dirt floor from the open barn door. Suddenly, something smelled very bad. And then a voice.

"Ya haf to keel ya'self," it said.

Lenny was fully immersed in the sunshine that fell through the door and his irises contracted. The barn's interior turned black. But instead of running, he waited. He knew what he would see. He was brave but afraid. He wanted to run but he stood right there.

And then the face of the beast from the box poked itself into sunshine. Something that looked like Lenny was within arm's reach and Lenny yelped like a little girl.

"S'prise," Lenny said to himself, then two hands shot into the sunshine and yanked the real Lenny into darkness.

Janine was in panic as she raced from the barn, tripped over the tree-stumped hole, dropped the shotgun which fired on impact with the ground, ran to the house without it, closed and locked the door behind her, and headed for the storm shelter bedroom. Instead of entering the shelter, she closed the floor door and hid in the kitchen.

Right behind her came Albert. He easily kicked in the front door and headed straight for the storm shelter.

"Ya down dere?" Albert grumbled, lifting the door back onto its hinged legs. He cackled two brash belts of laughter then started down the steps.

A second or two elapsed.

"Where you? We talk. We move on to Vegas. Me, Cubit, you, dead."

Janine slammed the floor door closed then raced to the couch and began sliding it the twenty feet it would take to reach the door. The couch was sturdy and heavy. She only hoped she'd have enough time.

Four steps from the storm shelter, the floor door cracked open. Janine saw Albert's bloody eyes within; when Albert saw her he grinned in recognition. She dropped the couch and leapt as far up and as far forward as she could, landing squarely on the floor door. She heard his body tumble down the steps and she rushed back to the couch, sliding two legs across the door just as his fists beat from underneath. The couch jumped from the pounding; Janine doubted it would be enough. The only other heavy piece of furniture in the room was a cherry wood china cupboard her mother had given her years ago. Without concern for the plates and cups that toppled and broke against each other, she pushed the cupboard across the wooden floor, scratching wax as she went, to a place on the floor door next to the couch. The added weight appeared to silence his efforts.

"You die, bitch," the beast Albert hissed and punched the door. A board in the floor door rattled, loosened. "You and pain, guarantee."

Janine ran from the house. She knew what she had to do and she had to do it quickly.

She retrieved her shotgun from the yard where she'd dropped it, expelled the empty cartridges and loaded two more from her housecoat pocket. She slid, SWAT-like around the open barn door, shotgun held ready for anything.

"Lenny?" She questioned the darkness.

No answer.

"Lenny. Are you okay?"

She couldn't see much but she heard something that sounded kind of—squishy.

"Lenny—that you?"

At the far edge of the rectangular patch of sunlight that fell from the barn door onto the dirt floor was the dagger. Its haft lay in shadow but its blade glistened blue steel in the sunlight. Without hesitation, she rushed to it, retrieved it, then slipped into the darkness. It took her eyes a moment to adjust. She blinked then squinted. Lenny was at the back of the barn near one of the center stalls. Cower's body was lying in a fetal ball two stalls to the right.

"Come on Lenny!" she yelled. "You gotta help me. We gotta blow that damned Cubit back to hell, while we have a chance. I don't know how long that thing in the storm shelter's gonna stay there."

She lowered the shotgun and walked briskly toward her son. Lenny was bent down, his back to her. "Lenny?" she said, stepping more cautiously the closer she came to him. Lenny turned.

But it wasn't Lenny. As much as that thing in her room was not Albert, the thing that now faced her was not her son. It wiped something from its face with the sleeve of its Grave Digger T-shirt. Beyond it and inside the stall was what looked like a slaughtered animal.

"Mommy," the not real Lenny said.

Janine took a half step toward her son, almost hypnotically, then changed direction and ran quickly behind the tractor where the Cubit and the dynamite she used for tree-stumping were located.

"No Mommy," the Lenny-thing said. "Come here!"

Janine hunkered behind the front end of the tractor. She saw Lenny moving through shadow, walking briskly and confident toward her vantage.

Her one hand gripped the dagger tighter; the finger of the other tickled the shotgun trigger.

To her left and just ten feet ahead was the Cubit. Behind the Cubit was the tool shed. In the tool shed was the dynamite.

From the right, Lenny sauntered into full view, apparently not knowing or not caring that she was there. She unloaded both shotgun shells into it.

At first, she felt the joy that is often accompanied by victory. When she saw her son's arm blow off of the right shoulder she could not believe she had just murdered her son. The second shotgun blast hit Lenny in the same location, serving only to decimate the flesh that used to be its arm. The combined blast sent Lenny to the ground and Janine bolted forward, dagger held haft up and blade down.

But it was her son. How could she drive this dagger into her son? She hesitated.

The Lenny thing turned to look up at her. It had crazy looking red eyes that were flecked with silver, as if the mind behind them belonged solely to someone or something else. Some of the shotgun pellets dotted its cheek and only part of the ear remained. Then its face turned down into barn hay.

This was not her son. Lenny was that slaughtered animal she'd seen it eating. This was everything that Lenny wasn't, all packaged in something that looked just like him. This horrific resemblance needed killing...

Janine thrust the dagger through the back of its neck. The star in the haft blazed as she thrust again and again, not realizing that with each strike, the thing that was once Lenny was aging rapidly, turning to old flesh and bone in concert with her efforts. Then, as if all the moisture had been removed from its body, the Lenny thing's chest imploded, turning to dust. She stepped back. The star in the dagger blazed so bright that most of the interior of the barn turned some shade of red. Within seconds, her son turned completely into a misshapen pile of bones.

She quickly raced to the tool shed, snatched up ten sticks of dynamite, a bag of caps and a plunger. She moved in front of the Cubit, did not look at it but only the ground beneath it, then began jamming sticks of dynamite in every soft place she could jam them. She jimmied the final stick into a spot behind the Cubit, being careful as she'd done with all the other sticks not to touch its wood surface with her hand. That's when Albert stepped through the barn door. She quickly hid behind the tractor.

"Real slow," the Albert thing said. No weapon was visible. "Gonna kill 'ya real, real slow."

She took one step forward, revealing herself from the safety of the tractor. Albert was next to the professor's body, toeing it for life signs. It saw her and immediately reacted.

"JANINE!"

It was the creepiest and most insane sound she'd ever heard. It was yelled and screeched and slurred in rage all at the same time. Albert was three times as large as Lenny. Even if she could retrieve the dagger before the Albert thing caught up to her, she knew that there was little chance in easily dashing the anti-Albert aside with a few quick dagger thrusts as she'd done with anti-Lenny. She stepped back behind the tractor and began wiring up the dynamite sticks. There was only one way out of the barn and she planned to take everything and everyone with her.

"Mind me," anti-Albert said. "Get ready. We got good lovin' ta do."

Anti-Albert was a few feet from the tractor when Janine finished wiring what would be one mighty explosion. She closed her eyes and plunged the dynamite. But nothing happened. She'd been squinting so hard, thinking that her body was about to be blown into small fragments, that opening them was painful. She looked from anti-Albert, who now turned and started after her, to the one wire she'd forgotten to attach.

She was out of luck. Out of distance. Out of hope. The entire evening had flown by so fast. There was no time for wondering about life. It was a time for dying. She attached the last wire.

And then, just as quickly as it had taken her to write her life away, the professor suddenly leapt from the shadows to her right. Cower wailed, "RUN!" as he and the anti-Albert thing fell together into the bone pile that had once been an evil incarnation of her son.

Janine ran, the shotgun forgotten behind her, her son now convincingly dead in her mind, her new husband hopefully dying between the hands of Cower. Once in the house, she stood before the decimation of the couch and china cupboard, and a storm shelter door that was ripped into pieces.

Why she jumped into the shelter, she didn't know. If she hadn't, she would have surely been ripped apart by the blast that swept from the barn and through the house. From Janine's vantage on her back at the bottom of the staircase, her head throbbing from the impact with one or more of the steps, she saw what she believed would be the last thing this reality had for her.

A vision of everything that had been hers and Michael's and Lenny's blew past her in a destructive wave of fire and rubble.

The Cubit
PART II

THE CUBIT: PART II

PARADISE LOST

SUNDAY, SUMMER 2008

Much has been said about the small island town of Port Aransas. Tales too tall to believe are common. As with most stories that are passed on through generations, facts are changed as dozens of storytellers add personal nuance. Like the story of what many in the town refer to as the "great white summer." Fishermen will argue that *Jaws* was much more than a blockbuster movie in the 70s. Most will argue that Peter Benchley based his story on actual events that took place right here, along the beaches of Mustang Island more than a dozen years before the construction of the Corpus Christi shipping channel.

And then there's the most popular tale of pirate Jean LaFitte's treasure. As he did in so many coastal towns along the Caribbean Sea, LaFitte left a mark on Port Aransas that is so powerfully convincing it goes beyond legend. It is a part of Port A's history, so much so that the story accompanies many of the town's tourism brochures. The legend provides for much marketing hype that has brought more than just a few to the island in search of immediate wealth. Somewhere buried in the thirty-mile stretch of beach sand, LaFitte is said to have stashed a great wealth, plundered by he and his crew throughout the infant days of the United States.

More recently, there is the not-so-tall tale of corporate and political corruption—nothing that had been proven so far, but the evidence was so apparent a blind man could see it. Onshore table gambling had never been allowed in Texas, but the powers that be were pushing for a new casino on the island. Their argument was simple. Legalized offshore gambling thrived in Gulf States like Louisiana and Mississippi. Port Aransas was an island therefore it was "offshore." Port Aransas was also a major summer vacation spot and a popular winter retreat. And to help move the tall, illogical argument forward, Port Aransas was now run by a bunch of bumpkins who would let anyone do anything as long as *they*, not the island, could profit from it. This new political structure had already usurped the power once held by the island conservationists by allowing new construction on protected marine life habitats. How would the town grow if the damned sandhuggers always got in the way, they'd argued.

And just as it was with any policy or procedure or law, once you gave special interest latitude, the road to social change was already mud on the boot—or in the case of Port Aransas, sand in the toes. Once wealthy island residents began raking in the cash, progress and backhoes would be forever linked. And tearing up a small part of the beach for a casino would seem like necessary evolution. All you needed was money, influence and a few toughs who could happily offer the choice of blackmail or bribery or something much, much worse.

Billy Jo Presser believed Chancey Lett came to Port A to ruin his island by using such corruption as a tool and he was going to prove it. However, unknown to Billy or anyone else on the island, Lett's arrival and the accompanying controversy had nothing to do with the building of a casino. It had everything to do with myth, legend and lore.

It had taken him only a few minutes to place his robotic starfish inside the canister tube of the drive thru at the Port A branch of the Big Texas Bank. He now sat in his vintage 1963 VW Bus, a hundred yards from the bank, manipulating the joysticks on a computer console that, hopefully, would move Shoe up the tube and into the bank.

Shoe's video eyeball revealed a plastic tunnel of dull sunshine capped by darkness, but the drive-thru tube schematics pinned to a corkboard above the computer monitor showed that at the tube's apex, a ninety-degree turn would enable Shoe's entry into the teller window. Moving Shoe beyond that point would require Billy's accurate memory of the bank's interior.

In his periphery, Billy saw the city police cruiser before it pulled into the parking lot of the Treasure Trove Inn. He remained in the back of the VW Bus and calmly watched the cruiser as it passed a full lot of June vacationers' vehicles. Billy's VW was parked at the rear of the lot nearest the bank and as the cruiser passed, it slowed. Officer Keadle knew the vehicle. Billy knew

Officer Keadle. And even though Officer Keadle looked right at him, Billy knew that the sun's reflection off the VW's windshield effectively hid all occupants within. It was not unusual to find Billy Jo Presser's classic VW parked anywhere within Port A's city limits. He owned and operated one of the town's best seafood restaurants and was renowned for some of the best catering this side of Texas. Officer Keadle would suppose, incorrectly, that Billy was inside the Trove conducting business. The cruiser passed without suspicion.

Billy returned his attention to the computer monitor. Shoe had already halved the distance to the top of the tube. Apparently, the adjustments he'd made to the robotic starfish's five feet where working better than he'd anticipated. He studied the schematics that he'd obtained rather effortlessly from the manufacturer's web site and coupled them with his memory, a skill he'd honed from his two years at MIT. He was superb at memorization. The talent had saved him both academically and socially more times than he could recall.

He'd gone into the bank pretending that he was interested in some long term investments that went beyond his restaurant. Just as the Big Texas Bank slogan promoted, "Meet the friendliest people in Texas," Billy was quick to find the helpful services of the bank's executive assistant, Stephanie Drake.

For three days Billy visited the bank with questions about investments he'd supposedly heard about from restaurant clientele or from Internet research he'd conducted. Each day his mind's memory machine logged as much of the apparent distances to points beyond Stephanie's desk. Last Thursday he'd been fortunate enough to witness the changing of the tellers and had seen the interior of the teller window through the open door. It was pretty much what he'd anticipated. It looked very similar to the pictures of teller windows he'd found at the drive-thru tube manufacturer's web site: a chair where the teller sat, a waist-high shelf that ran the width of the window, and most importantly, the plastic, not wire, version of Drive-Thru Tube's Model #DT9000. The wire version would have made it next to impossible for Shoe to crawl down once inside the bank. The plastic version, unlike the wire version was totally encased, making the crawl within a solid tube much more manageable than along four stainless steel cage wires.

The way Billy had figured it, Shoe could breach the exterior of the bank through the tube then crawl down the interior section of it and onto the teller shelf. He'd have to take the chance that no obstacles would be lying on the counter shelving which would impede Shoe's movement to the wall. Once down the wall and onto the floor, Shoe would have to crawl under the teller door. Billy had the approximate height of the opening in mind from his visit

Thursday but until Shoe tried it, he'd be unsure. Then it was onto Shoe's destination: Stephanie Drake's desk.

Not only did Drake's desk sit pretty much in the middle of all the action, the surface was covered by an assortment of sea creature ornaments in celebration of Port A's "Sea Life Month." Beyond the conventional selection of real sand dollars and seashells and the kind of fake seaweed you can get at Wal-Mart, there was a SpongeBob Squarepants plush toy and several of his cartoon plush friends sitting around the plastic seaweed as if they were talking to each other. More importantly, several of Drake's ornaments were starfish and were anchored to the wooden sides and legs of the desk. Thanks to Port A's celebration of the sea and Drake's creativity, one more starfish ornament would not make a difference. The starfish motif made perfect camouflage.

Shoe scaled the tube, crawled through the dark transition between outside tube and inside tube, then crept downward and onto the teller's counter. The progress lasted more than thirty minutes during which Billy did not move his eyes from the computer monitor.

As Shoe settled onto the teller counter and squirm-crawled in a clockwise direction, a coin tray became visible in Shoe's video eyeball and on Billy's computer monitor. There were no coins in it, of course. Still, the coin holder could prove immovable. Shoe's delicate construction could nudge a few ounces and no more. Billy had already wasted too many hours trying to increase tension strength in the robot's five starry legs but repeatedly found that anything heavier than a half a can of Budweiser only served to pop the water vessels that served as the lifeblood and mechanical motion for the starfish.

Billy thumbed the joystick forward, gently, as the first orange-yellow bands of Texas dusk pierced the VW's interior. Glare made the video monitor hard to see, revealing dusk specks that he had not wiped clean in some time. His hair twinkled in a banded blonde array that fell to his shoulders. A bead of sweat rolled into one eye.

One starfish arm nudged at the coin tray. Graphic bars in a pop-up window on the computer monitor rose into the yellow as tensile pressure rose against Shoe's extremities.

Billy pressed the joystick further. Graphic bars rose from yellow to red. The coin tray didn't move.

Orange sunshine wrested beads of sweat from the nape of his neck and they collected in a half moon of dampness above the Pat MaGee's Surf Shop logo on the back of his T-shirt.

Just a little more, he thought. He'd reengineered Shoe just for this possibility. If the robot was going to break, it would have already done so.

Just a little more.

He pressed the joystick ever so lightly. The pressure bars lifted, bright red and maxed out. And then, suddenly, the coin tray flew off the counter making an audible cling-thud as it hit the carpet below. Shoe scooted quickly forward as the pressure bars returned to normal. Billy released the joystick. On the counter where the coin tray had rested was a circular imprint left by what Billy guessed was a can or glass of Coke. The syrupy residue had anchored the coin tray until Shoe's last desperate push forward had freed it from the sticky connection.

Billy wiped sweat from his neck, moved Shoe to the teller room wall and started the robot down, keeping in nearly perfect sync with the sun as it dropped toward the Texas horizon. As the sun's glare left the VW's windshield, Billy maneuvered Shoe to the floor. The computer monitor now showed the gap at the bottom of the teller room door. There was about an inch of clearance. Shoe would fit, but just barely.

The interior of the bank was still visible but would not be for long. Billy guessed that he'd have about forty-five minutes before all dusk turned to black. He would not be able to maneuver the robot in darkness. Fortunately the path to Stephanie Drake's desk was a straight line, about twenty feet ahead. The loop pile carpeted floor would provide good traction for the starfish's tiny tube feet and as Billy had calculated the night before, the trip to the desk would take about twenty minutes to traverse and another ten would be needed to climb to a position on the side of the desk. That left about ten minutes of "wiggle room."

The view on the monitor was like a scene from the movie "Land of the Giants." The castor of a chair was a black spherical rock. Trees of finely carved chair legs towered on four corners. Twenty feet seemed like twenty miles in this video world of Giants.

Shoe reached Stephanie Drake's desk in a little under twenty minutes and started its ascent to an undecorated spot that would provide a great view of the bank vault, Mitchell Bone's office, and a cluster of three chairs where those waiting to speak to the bank manager would sit. If evidence was to be gathered, this would be the most likely place to record it. The evidence Billy hoped to gather would tag Mitchell Bone, in collusion with Chancey Lett, as a liar, a cheat and someone who didn't give a damn about the small island community. He and his bank had emblazoned "Meet the Friendliest People in Texas" all over billboards, newspaper inserts, the town's trolley and the trolley stop benches, and the island ferries, but the truth of the matter was that Bone didn't give a damn. His "friendliness" began with a crooked grin and a small hand that he used to welcome people and their money into his bank.

His eyes were peevishly small and his toupee was horribly fashioned giving his entire "friendly" appearance a childish indignation that most people could not see through.

Except Billy.

He knew what Mitchell Bone really meant to do. Gambling in Port A would not place it on the map as the "Southern Las Vegas." Gambling in Port A would destroy a hometown atmosphere that made it a beach-laden vacation haven unlike any other. It would destroy the island's marine sanctuary and change one of the Gulf's best fishing locations in ways Billy and many deceived fishermen could not imagine.

A door opened and voices murmured outside of the VW, breaking Billy's concentration. Two doors slammed shut and he watched the back end of a Chevy pickup roll away from the parking spot next to his. The Chevy's headlights snapped on as the truck left the parking lot and Billy turned back to the monitor. Darkness veiled much of the bank's interior.

He punched a set of commands on the computer keyboard to place Shoe in a standby record mode that would fire up once light returned to the office the following day. Tomorrow, he would check the collected evidence that Shoe was programmed to transmit to his apartment atop the restaurant.

Mitchell Bone had little time left in Port A. The residents would run him out of town once they saw what Billy knew he'd find: connections to crime syndicates, bribery of local officials and other flavors of coercion.

Billy took the usual detour on his way home. Even though night had fallen, activity on the beach, especially in mid-June, would have only slightly diminished. Weekenders from Corpus would have already taken their tanned bodies back to the city but locals and those from Rockport and Aransas Pass across the channel were rarely done by nine-thirty. There was an ambiance to the surf after dusk that was more enticing than the hot Texas sun on sandy brown beaches, especially for those who lived their lives under it. Vacation pamphlets never touted this as one of the island's great treasures and Billy was grateful for this ignorance.

He drove Alister Street to Avenue G where Pat MaGee's remained brightly lit. Inside, several people roamed about, shuffling through a large selection of shirts, shorts, shells and shoes that each hoped would make the perfect souvenir. As he turned onto Avenue G toward the beach, he saw Coolie and Sweets outside, talking and pointing at a selection of boards. Billy slowed to a stop.

"BJ," Sweets yelled. "Coolie wants a new ride but he ain't got the cash for it." Sweets pointed at a freerider that sparkled fluorescent green under the surf shop's canopy.

"Ugly," Billy acknowledged. "Girls'll run away when they see his skinny legs on that thing." He grinned. Coolie was always looking for a new surfboard. "Besides, since when did you find three hundred bucks?"

"Just lookin' and dreamin', man," Coolie countered. "Sides, I got into some cash just the other night."

"Yeah," Billy said. "And what bank did you rob?" He couldn't help glancing back at the computer monitor where minutes before he'd used it to commit a felony.

"No, man. It's not like that. Yo' mamma paid me good for some good lovin'."

"A dollar won't even do a down payment," Billy said.

All three of the surfers laughed. Sweets walked toward Billy but traffic behind pushed the VW onward.

"You two still comin' to the luau Tuesday night?" Billy said.

"Hell yes," Sweets said. "We'll be there a couple of hours before it starts if the swells they're predicting show up." He stopped at the curb as Billy's VW moved slowly forward. Someone hit their horn behind the VW. "Up it, Eastcoaster," Sweets added and threw both arms in the air.

"See you tomorrow," Billy said.

"Right on," Sweets agreed.

"Later," Coolie yelled and turned back toward the fluorescent board to dream.

The coastal dunes showed in silhouette under the waxing moon that was three-quarters dark. A salty breeze ruffled his hair as a coyote howled somewhere close by. Drifts of clouds interrupted sparse moonlight, shifting silhouette to darkness in intermittent spurts. Between the dunes, Avenue G split the natural barriers and Billy saw the comforting froth of white surf. The car that had honked behind him shot by in the no-passing lane and the driver, an apparent male tourist and his female companion, scowled at him. Billy paid no attention. Off-islanders always seemed to want to get places much more quickly than the locals. Billy was used to it. Besides, he was already aware of Officer Keadle's police cruiser which sat just beyond the last dune in wait for those who didn't have patience. Keadle's blue and red rollers lit the quiet night and the guy that had passed him, which Billy now realized was the same Chevy pickup that had been parked beside him in the Treasure Trove's parking lot, came to a stop a few hundred feet from the beach. Billy waved at Keadle as he passed.

Several cars slowly roamed the wide beach in opposite directions. Many more were parked closer to the shoreline but would soon have to move as high tide crept inland. Several tents stood along the beach but they, too, would soon move since county ordinance prohibited camping overnight in all but the state park campground a few miles to the south. Up ahead was the Horace Caldwell Pier. Billy passed it, slowed to dodge a group of fishermen, then parked on the north side of the pier where many of the local surfers gathered. The surf was lame this Sunday evening and no one was out.

The sound of crashing waves pulled him from the VW to the surf and he stepped into it knee-deep. Moonlight glittered atop shallow breaks. There was a magnetic pull to it all that only surfers understood. Riding waves was the only place left on the planet that one could find complete solace. Man and nature together as one. And Mitchell Bone wanted to destroy it all. If Bone's plans went through, the surf culture in Port A would die. Plans were to build the casino on the south side of the pier where some of the better surfing on the island could only be found. He'd spent the last two years in Port A, on the beach, at the pier, and now it was all about to change. Unless he could find evidence at the bank, Coolie, Sweets, Bottlenose, CrabMan and he, BJ, would have nowhere to surf. And Billy could not let that happen. None of the local surfers could let that happen. It was the reason why they were having the luau: to protest and hopefully convince voters that a casino was wrong. Even Officer Keadle had promised to show up. He was one of the few officials that Bone and his bank had not coerced. Keadle had lived his life in Port A and Billy knew he was not about to let any amount of money change his native community.

At the end of the pier to his right, several silhouetted fishermen stood two hundred yards from the shoreline, casting and reeling against a blacker ocean background. Tiny poles in tiny hands fought against fish and surf. To Billy, they looked like statues in a black and white cartoon made by animators stuck back in the 30s. Simple up and down motions. An occasional shift from one point on the pier to another. Just a bunch of easily drawn frames, repetitious, and not difficult to create even for a child. Almost mechanical. As fishing, to Billy, seemed to be.

Far off to his left, the south jetty of the channel that serviced Corpus Christi Bay was hidden except for the marker lights at the head of the jetty and several fishermen's lanterns that pockmarked the length of the rocky passage. Joel Canton stood near one of those lanterns, Billy suspected. He'd be reeling in tonight's catch of speckled trout and redfish that he'd want to sell to Billy at his restaurant the following morning. And Billy would buy whatever he had to offer. He always did, regardless of the health of the fish.

Joel needed the money. Fishing is all that he did. Fishing is all that he knew. He was poor because of it. Half the time, Billy would chuck the fish in the trash but he would always buy, for prices that easily exceeded what he spent for larger quantities from the local companies.

And that's how it was in this little island town. People helping people. People taking their time to get from one place to another. People dreaming about things they would never afford. People unlike Mitchell Bone and his greedy desire to destroy it all.

Before returning to his VW, Billy noticed that one of the jetty lantern lights, just a starry dot against the night, abruptly turned black.

Joel's hands were much older than he. They'd pulled in enough Texas Gulf sea life to feed a small country. Scars from hooks and sharks teeth and fillet knives and bar fights riddled the valleys between the veins. They were strong and weak at the same time. They could reel in a fourteen-foot Marlin or snap a man's arm who'd looked at him the wrong way after he'd pounded an assortment of Jack Daniels and Stroh's, but they could never caress the soft cheek of a woman or hold the nimble hand of a child.

Both his bar fighting days and marriage were over. He'd never had any children. Women and kids had always been second to fishing. Nothing to him had ever been more important than fishing. And every time he threw out a line he regretted his selfish history. Tonight was no exception.

He jerked his fishing pole and the line snapped, toppling him against his lantern which rolled, broke, and died immediately. There were no curse words left in his vocabulary—really wasn't a need for any anymore—so he sat on the jetty rocks wondering how he was going to afford another reel of fishing line and, more importantly, another lantern. He had a dozen fish in his basket—not enough to buy a new lantern. He exhaled against the Gulf breeze which tossed his unwashed breath back in his face. Slowly, he collected his gear and his catch and made his way from the jetty toward the shoreline. He'd walked it a thousand times and remembered the rocky uneven path as a blind man remembered his own home's interior. Tonight that memory would be quite valuable since it was almost impossible to see his footsteps without the lantern. He slipped a couple of times but nowhere as many as he'd slipped up in life.

THE CUBIT: PART II
EVIDENCE

Stephanie Drake was a consummate depressant on Monday. It was the job that made her so. Even in a "beach town" it was hard to relegate the weekend as a memory for what would dictate the rest of the next five-day span. And to her that's what life now was. Weekends and the five-day span. And the catalyst to the depression was always Monday.

"Sea Life Month" lay spread across her desk. She'd taken a little pride in most of the adornments since more than half of the objects had been dictated. Even in creativity, she'd been shackled. She didn't like sharks, but there one was, doubling as a stapler. Chomp…chomp… here's the report you wanted Mr. Bone. Chomp…chomp…here's your loan application Mr. and Mrs. Jones. The stapler never worked right—it always took two chomps (and sometimes three depending on the number of pages) to get the Jaws-like stapler to do what it was supposed to do.

But she had SpongeBob. His cheery, plastic face always made her smile.

She fell back into her chair, a hard, wooden, decorative piece of furniture that was more show than function. Her ass went numb during the day as did her mind, especially on Monday.

Carol stood behind her as if appearing from nowhere. She dropped a stack of papers on the desk that the Jaws stapler couldn't handle. "Bone's got some heavy investors coming in this morning," she said.

"What time?" Stephanie said. Stephanie and Carol had not liked each other since the day young Steph arrived.

"I don't know for sure," Carol said. Stephanie spun in her uncomfortable chair to look at Carol who had chosen a complimentary wardrobe of sea life patterns on her skirt and blouse. "You're the exec. assistant."

Stephanie mustered a smile, the same one she used each time that a natural smile could not surface. "This morning is what Bone told me." The surname was absent but she had not meant to sound so reproachable, especially to Carol, the bank's most senior employee and holder of numerous "Employees of the Month."

"Just be ready," Carol said. Stephanie thought Carol treated her like an unruly child that often needed a swift kick since the "real world" was still only concept.

"Got it covered," Stephanie said, holding back a dictionary of words that begged for release. "I just wanted to know if he'd given you any…" She struggled for patience. "I just wanted insight into the arrival time."

"You're the exec. assistant," Carol reminded her. "*You* should have all the information."

Carol's emphasis on "You" meant that it was *you*, a young pretty thing fresh out of college that got the job of executive assistant instead of *me*, a dedicated employee who *deserved* the title—and raise.

Carol was another of the reasons that made Monday and the four days that came after it so hard to deal with. The woman turned and stepped quickly toward her post, one she'd occupied for twenty-five years, behind the teller's counter. Stephanie ignored her and riffled through her preparation of the day's clientele.

Not all of the bank's employees were as hateful as Carol. Many, in fact, were quite friendly. It was easy for most of them to serve the bank's mantra as the "Friendliest People in Texas." For Carol, it was all fiction.

"Good morning, Stephanie," said Barbara Wallace as she spun the dials on the bank vault to open it. Her smile was genuine.

"Good morning," Stephanie acknowledged and returned the smile.

Chester Kalimaris, one of the bank's loan officers, came up from behind her and gently patted her shoulder. "How was the weekend?" he asked, smiled, and continued toward his office next to Mitchell Bone's.

"Fine, fine," Stephanie said, trying to sound appreciative. "Lots of sun and sand."

"Never any shortage of that around here," Chester said. "You all settled into the apartment now?"

"Just a couple of scattered boxes, but mostly, yes." Barbara walked over to her as Chester entered his office.

"That offer is still open you know," Barbara said. "Anytime you want to do a girls-night-out just say so. Corpus has a great night life."

Stephanie appreciated her, and Chester's, kindness. They understood how Carol got under peoples' nerves, especially those that Carol believed had stolen her promotion.

As the rest of the bank's employees shuffled in, Stephanie sat at her "Sea Life" desk and began thumbing through the stack of papers that Carol had dropped in front of her. All of them dealt with the acquisition of funding by Mitchell Bone's greatest new customer and friend, Chancey Lett. There were documents of collateral security originating from Las Vegas, several pages of reports from the three major credit bureaus, a list of real estate interests in Sedona, Arizona, and much more. All tolled, Chancey Lett was worth more than a hundred million dollars according to the net worth total revealed in summary on the last page of the stack. No wonder Mr. Bone had been in such a pleasant mood these past few weeks. His bank was about to open its largest account in history. The proposed Mayan Casino would make this branch of the Big Texas Bank much richer and Bone would rise in whatever circles bank managers rose into.

It was shortly after nine o'clock when the day's first customer, a local lady who owned a small coffee shop on Alister Street, strolled in and toward Carol who remained busy at her window and did not look up. Mrs. Black, owner of Black's Café, moved to Barbara's window instead and Stephanie saw Carol almost grin. Seniority kept her in the job. Friendliness certainly did not.

Stephanie fired up her computer and began going through the daily routine of account checks and balances but her mind soon wandered and the columns of dollar signs became apparitions. She typed methodically while the cast of SpongeBob characters on her desk beckoned for attention. Patrick the starfish, Gary the snail, Mr. Krabs and, of course, SpongeBob were lined up along the left corner of her desk. They were *her* addition to the sea life motif.

Who lives in pineapple under the sea...

The dollar signs and decimals blurred. Her typing slowed.

SpongeBob Square Pants.

She stared at SpongeBob's bucktoothed grin and couldn't help smiling.

Absorbent and porous and yellow is he...

The theme song took control of her thoughts.

SpongeBob Square Pants.

If nautical nonsense be somethin' ya wish...

"SpongeBob Square Pants," she murmured.

Then drop on the deck and...

"Flop like a fish," she said a bit louder.

"Miss Drake!"

Her mind was suddenly wrenched from daydream. Mr. Bone was standing in front of her. He smiled but only because of the two other men that were standing beside him.

"The SpongeBob song," the man with the greasy hair said. "I love that show." He plucked the SpongeBob toy from Stephanie's desk. "Aye, Captain," he said to it.

"Miss Drake," Mr. Bone said, the tension across his forehead tentatively easing. "This is Chancey Lett." He pointed at the man who held SpongeBob. "And this is his..."

Stephanie stood and shook Lett's free hand.

"This is Mr. Lett's head of security," Mr. Bone continued.

Stephanie turned her body to acknowledge the large man beside Lett but he offered no hand as greeting, did not smile and only looked cautiously around the bank. His face was pockmarked with scars, some tiny, some long and hard. He carried a satchel that was brimming with papers. He gazed at Stephanie without emotion.

"Don't mind him," Lett said. "He always looks like that. It's his job." He returned SpongeBob to his lifeless companions on Stephanie's desk, leaned forward and placed a hand to the side of his mouth. "A job I could never do. I smile too much," he added, thumbing toward his bodyguard and producing a wider grin that was strangely comforting.

Mr. Bone returned the conversation to business. "Miss Drake. Would you please gather Mr. Lett's documents together and bring them to my office?"

"Mitch," Lett said. Stephanie had never heard anyone call Mitchell Bone that. "You are too much business sometimes."

"Sorry Mr. Lett. I just thought that...well you have a flight out in just a few hours."

"Chancey, my man. Please. Mr. Lett sounds too formal."

"Ah, yes, Mr. Chanc..." Stephanie had never seen Mitchell Bone squirm before either. "Yes, Chancey."

"Nice meeting you Miss Drake." Lett was used to being in control. It was obvious by the ease of his conversation and the sweat that suddenly appeared below Mr. Bone's toupee forehead. "What is your first name, dear? Miss Drake is quite amorous if not mysterious but I prefer first names."

"Stephanie."

"Wonderful," Lett said, his smile never faltering. "Stephanie Drake. Well it's good to meet you Stephanie Drake."

Mitchell Bone swayed impatiently. His smile, having been a part of his face for the entire introduction, must have been agonizing to maintain.

"This way, Mr.—Chancey," he said.

Lett and his bodyguard followed Bone to his office. Stephanie collected the papers that Carol had given her and followed the trio inside. She didn't look behind her but could feel Carol's cold stare.

Bone sat behind his red mahogany desk, the trophy from a long horn steer positioned on the wall directly above him. Stephanie set the documents on his desk and turned to exit.

"Miss Drake," Bone said. "Would you mind helping Chancey's…"

"Assistant," Lett interjected. "He's my bodyguard, assistant, and encyclopedia of self-defense knowledge. But Assistant will do just fine."

Bone's cordial smile returned. "Would you mind assisting Chancey's assistant with an addition to our vault?"

"Of course."

"Thank you," Lett said as she and his bodyguard turned in unison. "If all of Port Aransas is as charming as you then I know my investment will come back to me tenfold."

Stephanie left the office, waited for Lett's bodyguard to follow, then closed the office door behind him.

"How can I help you?" she said.

"Outside," the bodyguard said, pointing. His voice was exactly how Stephanie expected it to be. Man of few words. Matter-of-fact. Deep and without inflection. The long scar etched above his lip and deep into his cheek seemed to damper any hope of a smile. He led her out of the bank's entry without offering the door.

Outside, the bodyguard opened the rear hatch of a black Hummer that was parked in front of the bank doors, pulled out a hand dolly, then muscled a wooden crate that was about the size of a large television set. The bodyguard's thick arms stretched wide to wrap his hands around the width of the crate as he hunched into the rear of the Hummer. Slowly he slid it out, teetered it on the Hummer's tailgate, then, very gently, lowered it onto the dolly. He didn't grunt even though the box seemed heavy and was awkward to handle. He didn't sweat even though the Port A sun had already warmed the island to ninety degrees. He didn't say a word even when Stephanie asked him what was in the crate. He did smell, however—body odor and Aqua Velva.

The bodyguard dollied the crate toward the bank and Stephanie shuffled forward to hold the doors open. Once inside, he rolled the crate directly into the vault without her help, as if he'd worked inside banks and vaults all of his life. Safety deposit boxes lined most of the vault walls but there was a small space toward the back about the size of a large coat closet that the bodyguard set the crate into.

"Yes. That will do just fine," Stephanie said, knowing that it would be useless to ask the bodyguard to move it. He followed her out of the vault and stood there as if protecting the crate, both hands clasped together in front of him, his concentrated stare passing over Stephanie and toward the front of the bank.

The door to Bone's office cracked open slightly but the two men remained just beyond. Stephanie heard the muffled end of their conversation.

"Well it's coming up for a vote on Saturday. I think we have the numbers," Bone said, his voice barely audible. Stephanie inadvertently craned her neck in that direction.

"I hope so," Lett responded. "There's a lot of money to be…"

"Miss Drake?" Carol interrupted her concentration on the conversation. She stood behind her.

"…up their beach," Lett continued.

Carol intentionally distracted her. She desperately wanted to put Stephanie in her place, wanted to tell all of the bank employees that Miss Drake was eavesdropping but, perhaps because of the importance of the client visiting today, she refrained.

"…a million dollars…" Lett said whose voice was again suffocated by Carol's incessant intrusion.

"Don't you think Mr. Lett's assistant might like some coffee?"

You ask him, Stephanie thought. *He's not much of a conversationalist.*

And before Carol could become any more annoying, the door to Bone's office swung wide open.

"I understand," Bone said, following Lett out of the office. "But I can assure you that I have all the vot…" He looked a bit startled when he noticed Stephanie and Carol both staring at him. "You ladies have work to do?"

Carol immediately turned and went back to her position behind the teller window. Stephanie turned her attention to her desk. Lett smiled at her.

"You have every right to be curious, dear," he whispered, bending closer as if what he said was secret. "Lots of changes coming your way." His grin widened. "Lots of changes for lots of people." His complexion was flawless, tanned, strong. "I will see you again very soon, perhaps in a much less intimidating atmosphere."

"Nice meeting you," she said.

"My pleasure." Lett walked confidently, his black Ralph Lauren suit glistening within the rays of sun that marked his exit from the bank. Bone was right on his heels. The bodyguard took up the rear.

Stephanie turned back to the open vault; her gaze landed on the crate. It looked out of place within the sterile, symmetric feel of the deposit boxes that lined the walls. It emitted an electric buzz that she'd never heard in the month since she'd started working at the bank.

She thought about Lett and his charm, his bodyguard and his smell, Mr. Bone and his greed-driven groveling, SpongeBob and his friends.

A customer entered the bank and went right to Carol's window. Carol mustered a smile and took the woman's deposit.

Stephanie tried not to think about Carol.

The Surf Side restaurant was actually located a couple of blocks over from the surf. It was close enough that beachcombers could easily stop in for a quick afternoon snack, and far enough from the tourist trap seafood restaurants lined up on Cotter Avenue that it was considered by the Port Aransas tourist brochure to be: "a quiet dining experience away from the busyness of fishermen, fishing boats, and overpriced dinners."

Billy Jo Presser lived atop the restaurant in a two-bedroom apartment-like space that was plenty large enough for a single guy and his robot hobby.

The place had a small bathroom with a standup shower, a center space that was both his living room and bedroom, and a third room that served as both his lab and his office—he called it his "lab-office." In the center space was his bed, one five-drawer, tall dresser with a second-hand lamp on top of it, a brown bean bag chair, and an old, white end table, the kind you buy in a box and assemble yourself. A coffee pot sat on the end table. There was no kitchen but he did have a small, dorm-sized refrigerator where he kept cold water, an occasional beer, and leftovers from the restaurant.

He'd been up since seven o'clock even though his restaurant would not open until eleven-thirty. Running a restaurant was replete with paperwork and Billy used Monday mornings to gain any early-in-the-week advantage over a chore that would otherwise overtake him by Friday. His quarterly tax statements were coming due and he needed to get his employees withholding information organized. He did not complete the tax processes; he was too impatient for this financial mandate. Besides, every time he'd attempted to do his own taxes, the idea of giving his money to the government always fired him up so much that he'd never been able to complete, accurately, all of the necessary forms. The town's only CPA handled this task for him. Still, the CPA needed organized information and Mondays were the only days when forms that started with a "W" came anywhere close to Billy's hands.

By the time he'd finished organizing Uncle Sam's needs it was nearly nine-thirty. He'd already downed a half a pot of coffee and stood from the paperwork to grab a fourth cup. The "paperwork" desk in his lab-office was small. It had been a grade-schooler's homework station before Billy had purchased it from the child's mother at a yard sale for only twenty bucks. It had two drawers that sometimes stuck and a space under the desk top that was only slightly wider than his two knees pressed together, an uncomfortable piece of furniture to say the least. Why had he purchased such an uncomfortable workspace? He loathed paperwork. Subconsciously, he had decided that buying something uncomfortable and barely usable would decrease the likelihood that he'd be spending much time using it.

Paperwork aside, the small desk did serve a much better purpose. It provided for a great assembly station when soldering his robots. His soldering iron and coil of solder, his small jewelers hand tools, and his eyepiece magnifying glass, once positioned on the desk top, left him plenty of space on his workbench to assemble one robot. Unfortunately, on several occasions, he'd forgotten to secure paperwork inside the tall file cabinet next to his small desk before working on his robots, and had burned away small corners of important documents with the soldering iron.

He shuffled the employee paperwork into its appropriate manila folder and jammed it into the top drawer of the file cabinet. A folder full of merchant receipts for supplies and food, plus the utility bills remained on the desk, but the blinking green status light on one of his computer hard drives vied for his attention. Shoe was busy recording a day in the life of the Big Texas Bank. Every time the green light blinked, more evidence against Mitchell Bone was being stored. Billy itched to watch as the evidence was received, a nearly synchronized vision of what was going on in the bank at that very moment. He took a step toward the computer then gazed back at the folder of bills to be paid, reminding himself that Mondays were for paperwork and that to allow distractions would mean that the rest of the week would be agonizing, especially since he'd be occupied with protesting and surfing and collecting evidence.

Billy refilled his coffee cup and returned to his lab-office to pay bills, review inventory and create a list of supplies and food he'd need this week at Surf Side. By eleven o'clock, much of the paperwork had been completed. He'd have to put another hour into it Tuesday morning but for now he needed to get downstairs, and prep the restaurant. "Sea Life Month" always increased activity for all businesses in Port A, especially for the seafood restaurants.

Downstairs, Jerry, from Devries Seafood Supply, was talking to Kale

Jurgenson, Billy's restaurant manager. Kale turned as Billy approached.

"How many are we serving at the Trove, Thursday?" Kale said as Billy walked up to the two men. "Jerry says the Specks are running fat and delicious right now."

"Fifty adults and a few kids," Billy said. "What do figure, Kale?"

"I'm thinkin', with the increased business inside and this catering gig… about two to three hundred pounds of Speck should get us started. But I'd like to get half now and a fresher half later in the week. Order might go up by then."

Jerry appeared quite pleased.

"And shrimp?" Billy asked.

"A hundred pounds at least," Kale said, "but we get that from Brigade's across the channel."

Jerry's face lost its happy salesman appearance. "I can give you a better price on the shrimp," he said.

"And quality?" Kale asked before Billy could do so. "We still remember that last 'deal' you gave us. Shrimp were puny compared to Brigade's."

Jerry was silent.

Kale smiled. "But the speckled trout you guys get is still some of the best on the island."

"Especially when the Surf Side fixes em' up," Jerry added. "OK, then. But promise me you'll keep us in mind. We *do* pull in some pinky-sizers to rival Brigade's. I'll add a couple of pounds to your order, no charge."

Billy left the two men dealing, and headed into the restaurant.

Kale was one-of-a-kind when it came to restaurant managers. He was always on time if not early, had a good relationship with most of the wait staff, cooks, and suppliers, and was just, generally, a nice guy. He'd come over to the island after completing a year at the restaurant management school in Corpus, but much of what Billy liked about Kale could not be taught in class. He was people-oriented, a personality trait that one could only be born and raised with, a trait that was absent from so many so-called restaurant managers. Billy was lucky to have him, and he'd told Kale this more than once.

He was also lucky to have his head chef. Unfortunately, Pedro Melindez would loose his work permit this summer unless Billy and he could find a way to meet the immigration requirements for renewal. They had already applied for his admittance into a culinary school, and if accepted this would get him another couple of years in the United States, but, as in any catch-22 situation, going to school meant providing some sort of permit or proof of citizenship, and you couldn't get a permit without showing evidence of need, such as attending school.

"Mí jefe," Pedro said from the kitchen when he saw Billy cross in front of the service counter. "Buenos días."

"And good morning to you," Billy replied. Pedro slipped through the kitchen's swinging door and stood offering his handshake while smiling a set of bright white teeth that were augmented further by his dark Mexican skin.

"We will be busy today, yes?"

Billy nodded. "Sí. And all the rest of the month." He returned Pedro's smile which always seemed to lift the spirit, even on Monday. "You ready for it?"

"Estoy…" They released hands. "Estoy preparado for sure, dude."

It didn't quite come out as surfer talk (especially with the Mexican accent) but Pedro continued to try. It was his attempt to fit in. Not only was he doing a great job at learning the English language, he'd also made great strides in matching the island culture. Both men chuckled.

"Cool beans, dude," Billy replied and shot Pedro the surfer's hang ten hand sign.

Pedro's three middle fingers curled inward but the thumb and pinky still had trouble remaining outstretched. He had to push them outward with his left hand. "You rock," he said.

"What's the lunch special today?" Billy asked. "Something smells wonderful."

"Carib…Carry-bean…" Pedro struggled with the word. "Island shrimp platter," he said instead.

"Caribbean shrimp platter?"

"Sí. Pineapple and sweet apples and Gulf shrimp. Light and…" Pedro thought for a moment… "tasty. Will not make you feel fat when you walk the beach in a bikini."

"Great advertisement! You hooked me…except for the part about wearing a bikini, but I sure don't mind looking at them."

"We are the same, mí jefe." Pedro winked then returned to the kitchen.

Alicia and Candice were busy placing the tables, sweeping the floors around the tables and changing light bulbs. The waitresses pulled up the wooden blinds on two walls of storefront windows and the interior of the restaurant came to life. Texas sunshine immediately warmed and lit the entire space. Surf Side could serve about a hundred people, if you included the stools at the small bar near the entrance. While the weekdays tended to fill only half of the restaurant, weekends needed every chair, even in months that weren't celebrating Sea Life.

Two waitresses would probably be enough until four o'clock when the early dinner crowd began, but Billy decided to remain in the restaurant just in case. He enjoyed helping prepare meals, serving dinners and chatting with diners. His volunteerism was one of the reasons why he and those who worked for him got along so well. There wasn't a thing he'd ask someone else to do that he would not do himself.

A dozen people entered when the restaurant opened. An hour later, at least thirty people were enjoying the diverse menu that the Surf Side offered, including a happy array of diners feasting on Pedro's Caribbean shrimp special. Billy served a few guests then took up a position behind the bar since Alicia and Candice were inundated with alcoholic beverage orders. Billy made a mean margarita and several requests, an unusual amount for Monday afternoon, were tended by his talented hands.

Around three o'clock, as the afternoon lunch-goers dwindled, a man whom Billy did not know entered the bar. He was much too large for the stool on which he sat. A large scar traced the flesh above his lip.

"Bar opens in an hour," Billy said to the large man.

"You're here," the stranger said, staring at the bottles of liquor behind Billy. "Jim Beam and Coke."

Billy was the consummate bartender gentleman. He welcomed all newcomers to his restaurant regardless of policy. Still, he felt that this man was trouble. Intuition was his best angel for thought. If he'd told the man to leave, he believed that the bar stool on which the man sat would quickly take flight. He turned and grabbed a bottle of Jim Beam.

"Don't mix it," the man demanded. "Shot and chaser."

Billy poured a heavy shot into one glass and filled another with Coke. He placed both on the bar in front on the man.

"There any good surf around here?" the man asked. The question caught Billy off guard, not so much that he'd never been asked it, but more so because the man asking it did not look to be the surfer type.

"Yeah," Billy said a bit too cautiously. "Down by the pier."

"You surf there?" the man said, knocking back the shot and Coke in swift succession.

Warning bells sounded in Billy's head. *The controversial casino*. Perhaps he was being paranoid but the man's demeanor and direct question were too coincidental to deny.

"Yeah," Billy answered. "I surf there a lot."

The man pushed both glasses forward in a nonverbal request for seconds. "You...*Dig* the small waves there, don't you?"

Instead of an answer, Billy replied, "You ever surfed?" He filled both glasses then pushed them toward the man.

Instead of answering, the man said, "I've always wondered what was so special about this damned island." He swallowed the Jim Beam and then the Coke. He'd been sizing up the restaurant, never giving his full attention to Billy until now. "Good fishing—that's about all. Surf, well, it sucks."

"You're not a surfer," Billy said.

The man's thin grin showed no reaction. "Says you." He wiped a drop of whiskey from the scar on his cheek. "Nothing ever breaks above five feet around here. You call that surfing?"

"Every wave is a good wave," Billy countered. "All *surfers* know that." Generally, Billy maintained his cool, especially in the restaurant, but this guy was getting under his skin. He was dissing Billy's great love. He was dissing Billy's home waves. When the man asked for another shot, Billy refused to serve him.

"That'll be eleven-fifty," Billy said and removed the glasses from the bar. He expected a right cross at that moment. Instead, a grin too wide for his face spread above the man's square chin without showing teeth. The scar above his lip lengthened diagonally across his cheek into what looked like a fleshy, bald caterpillar. The pupils of his eyes changed color, a deep crimson, perhaps—Billy wasn't sure. The stare seemed to caress his very soul. Billy blinked.

"Expensive," he said. "Too expensive for a shit-hole restaurant on a shit-hole island that couldn't attract flies even if its roads were made of shit. What this town needs is a little excitement. What you need is to find some other surf—before it's too late."

The man dropped a twenty on the bar, turned from the stool, and walked through Candice who could not grab the margarita glass that fell from her tray and crashed to the wooden floor. Billy watched the man climb into a black Hummer then pull out of the parking lot, nearly swiping a few parked cars as he left.

"Who was that asshole?" Candice said as she came around the bar to get a broom.

"An asshole," Billy acknowledged, trancelike. "I don't think he likes surfing."

"What?" Candice gazed at her boss who still had not looked at her.

"That guy. He's trouble. And he's probably brought a whole lot of it with him."

"Brought what?" Candice began sweeping up the remains of margarita glass.

Billy turned to her. "Ah…sorry. That guy's probably with the casino people."

"Definitely asshole," Candice said. She dumped the shattered glass in the trash and asked Billy to make her two Mega-Margaritas.

Billy mustered a smile. "Coming right up." Some of the dozen or so diners had turned when the glass had shattered. They now returned to their plates. A lady with a wide-brimmed, frilly hat motioned for Candice.

Billy made the margaritas as his concern increased. He should have expected that "muscle" would accompany any gambling venture. The man knew something about Billy Jo Presser, knew that he was a surfer and probably knew that he was the protest organizer.

The intimidation had begun.

Lantern globes cost fifteen dollars and a reel of twenty-pound test line was another six or seven. Joel did not have twenty dollars worth of fish to sell Billy. The one fish that did survive, a nice twenty-six-inch redfish, might get him five bucks, and a generous five bucks at that. Short of begging, Joel was out of cash; his meager welfare money was spent.

And so, that is why he waited outside until the afternoon crowd at the Surf Side began to dwindle: to beg. That's what his life had really come down to after all. Joel Canton was one of the best fishermen this side of the Gulf, was renowned for helping capture the great white shark that terrorized the island back in 1972, was the hero who saved a woman's life during the floods caused by Hurricane Alicia in 1983, and was a self-proclaimed Port Aransas historian. He'd lived here all of his life, never having to ask for anything no matter how hard things got.

But, anymore, things were just too hard. His hands ached incessantly. His knees were not as flexible as they'd been just a year ago (a condition most locals called a "hitch in the giddyup"). He was slowing down both physically and mentally. Even the fish he'd pulled in last night, a good fifty pounds worth of redfish and speckled trout, did not survive the night.

Joel sat at the curb far enough from the Surf Side that he would not be easily seen, but close enough for him to determine the number of people inside. He stood up, took one step toward the restaurant and stopped. Another customer emerged from side door. It was the same guy who'd pulled up in a black Hummer just a few minutes ago. The man was stocky with short dark hair and looked alarmingly similar to the man who'd taken his wife from him a long time ago. The man who jumped into his Hummer and haphazardly sped out of the Surf Side parking lot, nearly sideswiping a parked Monte Carlo, looked like Bert Nookle's twin.

But of course that couldn't be true. Bert Nookle was one of a kind and had died several years back. Joel had gone to the funeral. Bert Nookle had been his "best friend." They had been a part of the crew that had captured the murderous great white. Bert had been the captain (who not so coincidentally looked a whole lot like Robert Shaw who played Captain Quint in the movie *Jaws*). Joel, who looked nothing like Richard Dreyfuss, had been the first mate. Both of them had ended the Great White Summer of 1972.

The man behind the wheel of the Hummer gave Joel one quick scowl as the black vehicle sped past. It was Bert Nookle reincarnated! Or perhaps Joel's eyesight had also finally found old age. He'd never thought that fifty-five years of life labeled a person as old. It all depended on how much life had been lived in fifty-five years. In Joel's case it was at least a hundred and ten. Old—and a beggar.

Joel halved the distance between where he'd been sitting and the side entry door to the Surf Side when he realized that he was just too good for begging. He couldn't—wouldn't stoop that low. There were other ways to make a few bucks; he'd just not thought things through. He'd figure this out. Survival was his middle name.

Joel left the parking lot, rubbing his belly because he was hungry and because the scars were there—the scars from 1972—and they began to itch.

"Later, Mr. Presser," said the bartender. Jelanie was his real name; his surf name was Gelatin.

"Have a good evening," Billy said, smiled, shot him a hang ten, and then rushed up the stairs to his apartment. The man with the scar over his lip had invigorated his desire to see what Shoe had recorded. He tossed his keys on the bed and headed straight to the computer. He would not be able to review everything tonight; there was just too much of it. His intention was to move through the data randomly in hopes that something would quickly catch his attention.

For sight, Billy had equipped Shoe with one of the newest mini-micro cameras, the kind used by covert operators—detectives and such. He'd ordered it through the mail; he still didn't trust the security features of the internet enough to release credit card numbers into the vastness of fiber optics and hackers. The camera was programmed to snap stills every ten seconds then send the images over radio frequency to the receiver in the back of Billy's computer. Its implantation into the robot's mechanics had been easy. Shoe's ears, however, had not.

Since continuous hours of video would eat up massive storage space Billy had not only opted away from video streaming he had installed an extremely sensitive microphone, unidirectional and twice as powerful as any other listed in *Popular Mechanics*. Audio was lenient with hard drive space and a good microphone would provide all the evidence he needed. The challenge had been with feedback. For some reason, the small motors in the starfish robot's legs (all five combined) caused the mic to squeal unexpectedly. He'd had to rework the motor configuration to allow for the microphone's sensitivity. This had added another two weeks to his timetable, giving him and his island that much less of a chance to thwart the casino efforts.

As luck would have it, the added two weeks had conjoined with the arrival of Chancey Lett.

Lett, it was rumored, was a Las Vegas casino boss, very rich and very connected. How he'd become interested in fucking up Port Aransas no one knew beyond what some editorialists in the local paper had suggested: he had family in Corpus Christi (false), he and the governor where tight as oil sheiks (false); he was a greedy, self-centered bastard that would sell his mother's farm if that's what it took to remain at the top of the food chain (most likely true). He was also rumored to be a collector of fine antiquities, thus the reasoning behind the name of his new casino venture: The Mayan. But beyond all of that, Lett was perhaps best at finding greedy people and greedy governments looking to fill their pockets: all Lett asked was that they look the other way, drop an influential vote or two—but of course, this was all rumor. And that's what Chancey Lett pretty much was: a rumor. There had been nothing beyond rumor written in any of the papers, not the island's *South Jetty* nor the city's *Corpus Christi Daily*.

Greedy people—looking the other way.

Billy's computer and monitor were crammed into the opposite corner from his "paperwork" desk; the robotics workbench separated the two. He switched on the monitor and opened up Shoe's programming interface. Status bars indicated that Shoe had begun recording at 9:01 in the morning and had ended at 6:15 in the evening, numbers that were slightly off from those Billy had set, a minor problem he'd deal with later. The robot had transmitted more than three thousand frames of video and over nine hours of audio. Billy tapped the keyboard and a window full of thumbnail images cluttered the space. He scrolled through several dozen shots that depicted little more than three chairs, an open vault and the bottom two-thirds of two office doors. Occasionally, legs that were blurred by the camera's inefficient auto zoom shuffled passed. Then, at 9:38:10: something interesting. For the next several frames, thumbnail images showed three sets of legs standing in front of Stephanie Drake's desk. Billy double-clicked the first of this sequence, synchronized the time with that of the audio feed and clicked "Play." An image filled the computer monitor, one every ten seconds, while the audio narrated the scene.

The legs belonged to Chancey Lett, Mitchell Bone and a third man whose name went unannounced. Stephanie Drake's voice was background noise but easily heard with the microphone's sensitive pickup.

Don't mind him, Chancey Lett's voice said. *He always looks like that.*

Once the formalities of introduction had ended, the three sets of legs, visible from the middle of the thigh down, disappeared, then two frames later reappeared, a few feet more distant, in front of Mitchell Bone's office door. Stephanie Drake's legs joined them. All faces were turned away and only their bodies from the neck down could be seen. One frame had them entering the office; ten seconds later, Stephanie was walking out of the office.

How can I help you? her voice asked.

Outside, was the answer. Though the person that said it remained hidden, Billy had a good idea who it was.

More than thirty video frames later Stephanie stood, once more, in front of the starfish robot. Ten seconds later, she was in the vault; standing in front of her was the man who'd accosted Billy back at the Surf Side, the thug who'd preferred his Jim Beam straight. He gripped an empty hand truck. Beside his leg was what looked like a wooden crate; Shoe's angle from the desk did not reveal any more than an inch or two of it as the edge peeked into the video frame from beyond the vault door.

Yes. That will do just fine, Stephanie's voice said. The thug remained silent.

At that moment, an office door squeaked open and Lett's voice sounded hushed through the computer's speakers. The sensitivity of Shoe's microphone had enabled the recording of his whispers to Bone beyond the doorway. The men did not appear in the time-synced video grab of a partially opened office door but their voices had been captured with clarity that made Billy smile.

Well it's coming up for a vote on Saturday. I think we have the numbers: Bone's voice.

I hope so. There's a lot of money to be lost. Remember, your cut in this could pretty much buy this island: Lett's voice.

Most of them know nothing about it. They don't know where and they don't know when: Bone.

That won't be enough. Lett.

I told you…

…now I'm telling you! We're going to stack the deck. Let's just say for

now that those that vote our way won't be able to pass up a chance at a million dollars.

I'm beginning to think that...

You're not in this to think, Bone. Let me and Sedona do all of the thinking.

There was a long pause and then more dialogue as the next video frame appeared on the monitor. Bone followed Lett out of the office.

I understand, Bone said. *But I can assure you that…*

Lett ignored him, opting instead for a few pleasantries with Stephanie, then in the next minute, Lett and his bodyguard thug left the bank.

Billy slammed his fist against the computer hutch and nearly crushed his keyboard. The vote was no doubt the one that, by town referendum, was not supposed to take place for another month. The concerned conservationists and fishermen had been pushing for a delay and a month was all they'd been able to wrangle from a town council well stacked with profiteering business interests. What Bone and Lett were planning had to be illegal, Billy thought. He'd remained a quiet distance from everything political at M.I.T. but common sense told him that much. In the least it was unethical. Bone, however, sat on the town council as did most of the influential residents, including the *South Jetty* publisher, Nole Kilpatrick, which meant that information was controlled. Lett was going to "stack the deck," whatever that meant. Unfortunately, before any honest powers became wiser, the construction of the Mayan would be underway.

But not if he had anything to say about, Billy thought. And he didn't need no stinkin' newspaper. He could make flyers and distribute them all over town. He also had the luau tomorrow night, one he'd worked hard to organize in an effort to protest the casino. He'd tell the townspeople of the impending change of plans and let them burn the appropriate demigods at the stake. At least he'd get the word out about the vote so that there would be no stinkin' deck stacking of any kind.

Shoe had done its job. Billy had done his job. Perhaps he'd never be able to use the recording in a court of law (he'd committed a felony just to get it), but the information had, minimally, enabled him to delay connived plans. Still, the audio could be useful in the future. He'd been politely threatened earlier in the day. Who knew how far these men would go. Having a little bargaining chip could help.

Billy reversed the video and audio sequences back to where the three mens' legs first appeared, set the timer for twenty-five minutes and clicked record. It was ten minutes before eleven and the Surf Side would be closing down at the top of the hour. He stood with the intention of heading downstairs to help with the cleanup, but dropped back onto the metal chair; one of the video clips grabbed his attention. He paused the recording.

Mitchell Bone's legs stood along the right edge of the frame, Chancey Lett's were in the middle and the bodyguard's were to the far left. Lett held a leather satchel and something was sticking out of it. Billy drew a marquee around the satchel to zoom in on it. The top inch of two sheets of paper became visible but the zoom made what was written on them hard to understand. On the first sheet was drawn what looked to be some kind of hieroglyph: the troubled stare of a man in a mask; and beside the mask, appearing much fuzzier in the zoom, was what could have been a spear or a sword—a weapon of some kind. The hieroglyphs reminded him of some of the ancient temple drawings he'd seen on the History Channel.

The top paper partially covered a single word on the paper underneath it. Billy could not decipher the entire word; the zoom made the letters almost illegible.

A word puzzle, Billy thought. Seven words. The first letter was probably an 'L' although it could have been an 'I.' The third letter was easy: a capital 'F.' The fifth and sixth letters were the same; Billy thought they were 't's.

"L-F-tt-"

The word was written in an old style Calligraphic cursive that reminded Billy of the writing on the Declaration of Independence. Very colonial. He mentally went through every letter of the alphabet and tried them in the empty spaces but nothing worked.

It was eleven-thirty when he decided that his brain, at this time of night, was not going to decipher either the word puzzle or the hieroglyphs. He printed the zoomed image, restored the record settings and left the computer to its task. He took the printout to bed with him, studied it further, then set it next to the coffee maker before switching off the lamp light.

L-F-tt-

His brain wouldn't let it go.

THE CUBIT: PART II

NO MAYAN FOR MY ISLAND

Though his bed was extremely comfortable (one of those adjustable types that uses a number) Billy's sleep had been restless. He'd even forgotten to set his alarm. Most days, he was up by six. The morning sunrise was his addiction.

He woke with the image of the Port Aransas public library in his mind. The word puzzle, the hieroglyphs and the library had connected in his subconscious. The idea of research had pumped its time-consuming curiosity into him once again—a feeling he'd not had since Cambridge.

It was a little after eight o'clock when he swung his feet from the bed, snatched the empty coffee pot, walked it over to the refrigerator and filled it with the water pitcher from inside. His mind raced with the to-do list in his head. He went through the coffee-making motions but paid no attention to what his arms and legs were actually doing. He realized that he spilled water while filling the coffee maker reservoir only because the water fell onto the printout he'd left there last night. He quickly mopped the water with the tail of his T-shirt before it smeared the ink.

L-F-tt-

"You won't keep your secret long," he said to the paper. "That's why man invented the public library."

Billy had no internet service to his restaurant. He'd never seen the value in such an investment. He'd known too many users who'd spent too much time with too little to show for it. Besides, if he wasn't working, he was surfing, in the Gulf, where no connection to the wired world was necessary. The public library had internet; that's all he needed.

He started the coffee and went to his lab-office. Paperwork that needed to be finished beckoned. Just one hour and it would be done.

He pushed it out of his mind, opting instead for the computer. It took him only thirty minutes to finish the flyer he would distribute around town. It read:

Don't let big money interests destroy our Island Paradise.
VOTE NO for the Mayan
Saturday, June 22

Simple. To the point. Nothing flashy except the eye-catching red lettering he'd used.

He printed the flyer just as the hard drive status light flashed the start of another day's worth of robotic data collection at the bank.

He opened the program interface and watched video frames as they were received every ten seconds. Again, the same three chairs, the bottom two-thirds of Bone's office door and the vault. The lights in the bank had not yet been turned on, but enough sunlight fell through the windows to see that the vault door was open but only a couple of inches, as if it had been left that way all night which, of course, could not be true. Suddenly, the lights in the bank came on and one of the bank tellers approached the vault door, swung it wide open and went inside. Her name was Carol, he thought. The video frame showed her hand on the vault wheel and one foot inside. She then disappeared but never reemerged from the vault. He watched three minutes worth of static images that did not change then decided he'd been wrong. Maybe she hadn't gone in the vault. Maybe she'd just looked inside. That was the trouble with capturing ten-second images: you always had a ninety percent chance that you'd miss something.

He turned off his computer screen, showered, then put on his normal wardrobe of surf culture: boardies, a beach shirt with Mr. Zoggs prominently displayed and sandals. His brown eyes and shoulder length blonde hair completed the stereotypical islander look. He snatched the flyer and the printout of the word and picture puzzles and headed outside.

Downstairs, Kale met him at the side entry door apparently distressed.

"No specks, man," he said, almost imitating the Cheech and Chong accent. "All of the Specks never came. Devries Seafood didn't deliver all that we asked for and the price was much more than Jerry had said it would be."

"How much?" Billy said, hoping to calm Kale down.

"Ten bucks a pound." Kale could hardly say it. "And we only got fifty pounds."

"That ain't gonna do it, is it?"

"Not with the catering gig at the Treasure Trove Friday…not even close."

Billy smiled. "That's not going to do it even without the catering." He pointed at the restaurant. "Look around—see what can be done. We'll just have to raise our prices a bit."

Kale nodded.

"Pedro inside?" Billy asked.

"Sí," Kale said. "I'll check for food in Rockport for starters."

Both men entered the restaurant. Billy turned toward the kitchen and Kale walked to the hostess podium to make a few phone calls. Billy entered the kitchen to find Pedro cleaning shrimp near the sink at the back.

"Mí jefe," Pedro said, moving his hands under the sink to rinse shrimp.

"How creative are you?" Billy said.

Pedro wiped his hands on a towel. "Creative? Yes I am very creative. Always trying out new specials."

"We might run a bit short on food this week. Cutting back a tiny bit on our very large portions might help."

Pedro dropped the towel and walked toward Billy. "Mí jefe. I can make masterpieces with very little comestibles." He opened his arms around his belly which was not very large; his thin frame looked as if it needed more nourishment. "And people will still feel very full. When you are from a town like Chiapas, you learn to estiramiento lots of things."

"Estiramiento?"

Pedro smiled. "Stretch. We stretch lots of things. Two pounds is four pounds easy with a few potatoes." He looked at Billy's hand and pointed at the papers he held at his side. "Wayeb?"

Billy lifted the paper and looked at it.

"Wayeb," Pedro repeated. "This here. Unlucky days." He stepped closer and touched the image of the face in the ceremonial mask.

"What's so unlucky about them?" Billy asked.

"Nothing stops the underworld." Pedro bent forward and whispered as if he didn't want anyone but Billy to know. "Evil can cross over."

"Serious?" Billy chuckled. "I mean…really?"

"By my father's honor." Pedro bowed slightly. "He told me. A Mayan symbol for the last five days of the year. That's Wayeb. You should stay indoors on those days."

Billy pointed at the weapon pictured next to the Wayeb. "Anything you know about this?"

Pedro studied it for a few seconds and said, "No…Not sure. And what is this?"

Pedro grabbed at the corner of the flyer and Billy let him have it. "The town vote for the casino is Saturday and I wanted everyone to come out and vote No."

"I have not heard of no vote." Pedro handed back the flyer.

"Not many people have. They've been keeping it a secret."

"I will come out and vote if you want me too, Mí Jefe. You know I'll help in any way I can." Pedro returned to his preparation of today's new 'leaner' menu.

"I wish that you could," Billy said. "You still need to get your work permit in place. It will be a few years before you're ready for citizenry."

"And I thank you for all of your help." Pedro nodded.

"No problem." Billy waved a hand and shook his head. "And I thank you for yours." He turned to leave and added over his shoulder, "What are you cooking at the luau tonight?"

"Sí," he said, grinning. "Grilled crab cakes and island-marinated vegetables…a leaner version of them."

"Island-marinated?" Billy turned around as he started through the kitchen door.

"It's a secret sweet and spicy sauce that combines a couple of old Mexican recipes." Pedro said it as if he were making an advertisement.

"Mmmm…" Billy licked his lips. "If I don't see you before, I'll see you there."

He left the restaurant with Kale still on the phone, trying to cut a deal for tuna.

Billy had gotten a lot of unexpected information from Pedro, primary research that he'd not intended to conduct. Mayan symbols? Were the papers simply a collection of decoration swatches showing interior design ideas? He'd become so critical—of everything— scrutinizing all of society much more than he used to. As was reflected on his flyer, he hated the influence that big money had on people without big money. But these were just decoration ideas, that's all. The only secrets Lett and his followers held was the vote. All they wanted was the casino. There were no other conspiracies. Right?

Billy now wondered if the contents of Lett's satchel held nothing fantastic—mere architect's sketches perhaps. The Wayeb symbol was nothing more than decoration for the new "Mayan" casino.

Outside, Billy got into his VW, but before he closed the door, Joel appeared as if from thin air.

"Billy. Hello." The old fisherman almost gasped. He looked as though he did not feel well.

"You okay?" Billy stepped back out onto the asphalt.

"I think I had some bad fish for breakfast. I've had bad trout before and got over it. I'll just have to be more careful with the catch."

"Can I get you something? Medicine?" Billy started for the restaurant but Joel grabbed him—a fisherman's grip—firm but not uncomfortable.

"Well. Yes. Yes you can." Joel burped and turned away from Billy. "Sorry." He rubbed his stomach. "It's just that I busted my lantern and I don't have the money to buy a new one. I don't have any fish to sell either."

"How much is it?" Billy reached into his pocket.

"Now you know this is only a loan," Joel said. "I will pay you back as soon as possible."

"A loan."

"Thirty dollars?"

Billy peeled off a ten and a twenty. "Here," he said. "An interest-free loan."

"I will pay you back double in fish. Thank you. I really hated to ask…"

Billy waved away the explanation. "No big deal. I know you're good for it." Joel put the money in his coveralls pocket. It was ninety-five degrees out and Joel was wearing coveralls, but Billy had rarely seen him dressed in anything else. Occasionally, he even wore a different set of coveralls. "Make sure you come out to the protest tonight. There'll be some good eating."

Joel rubbed his belly. "Hopefully, I'll be ready by then."

Billy got back into his VW Bus, waved to Joel, and drove off.

Around ten o'clock, he pulled into the empty parking lot of CopyKatz. Business appeared slow. Inside, the clerk was helping a customer at the copy machine. "Be right with you," she said.

For most of the population of Port A, everyone knew everyone else. Small towns were like that—knowing everyone else's business while maintaining what others thought of your own. But if you lived in Corpus Christi and were currently working a summer job on the island, chances were few people knew you. Billy did not know the CopyKatz clerk.

The clerk came around and behind the counter. Billy laid the flyer in front of her. "Fifty of these, please," he said, grinning cordially.

"Cool," the girl said. She wasn't tall but she was very cute. Her dark, red hair looked natural. "Full color is ten cents a copy." She read the words on the flyer. "Vote no for the Mayan. What does that mean?"

"You from the island?" Billy said, knowing the answer.

The clerk continued her chore. "Naw. Going to school in Corpus. And you?"

Billy smiled. "You are the curious type."

"Pre-law," she said. "Professors kind of instill that curiosity thing in you." She fidgeted with the copies for a few seconds as they sprang one-by-one from the copier. "You're an islander. One of the good ones. Not one of the real nasties around here. They are just plain snobs." Her lip curled and she thumbed her hand in the direction in which the rich that she talked about lived. Billy knew exactly what she meant. They often ate at his restaurant.

The copier ended its operation and the clerk plucked Billy's stack of flyers from it.

"That's five dollars and thirty cents with tax." She entered the numbers into the cash register.

Billy gave her the exact change and invited her to the protest luau. "Good eats," he said and smiled. "Hope you can make it."

"Yeah. I'll give it shot. Bye…eh…mister." The clerk shut the cash register door.

Four guys plucked all but ten of the flyers from his hands. Billy knew he'd find energetic volunteers at Pat MaGee's.

"Yeah, I'm helping," local surfer J.J. White said.

"I'll hit the hotels and ranches," said CrabMan, one of the surfers that Billy regularly hung out with.

"I'm going to cover the pier," Billy told them. "I'm curious to see the fishermen's reactions."

The other two surfers that offered to help were Shana Greathouse (and some would say she had one), and Peter Jennings, spelled just like the news anchor from ABC; he got a lot of crap for having a name like that. That's probably what made him so…touchy.

"That tropical storm has turned inward, Billy. You hear about that?" The manager of the store tapped his shoulder. Bottlenose was his surf name. Nobody knew his real name, not even Billy who was his best friend.

"No." Billy turned. "I haven't been paying much attention to the news lately."

"Yeah, I figure. The luau is eatin' up your time." Bottlenose read the flyer; immediately, his face turned red. "This fuckin' blows, you know? I mean, it really blows. Makes me want to pound some politicians." Bottlenose could certainly put a pounding to anyone he chose. He was built like Charles Atlas.

"We'll pound 'em with the pen," Billy said. "And when they lose they can blow us all the way back to Vegas."

"He-he," Bottlenose replied. That was about as close to laughter as the big man ever got. He had a great sense of humor, but whenever he found anything to be funny it was always a short *He-he*.

Billy raised his voice intentionally to catch everyone's attention. "Tonight should be a good time. Starts at nightfall. A dozen local chefs have entered the cooking contest including my very own Pedro Melindez."

A short round of clapping began, then quieted.

"Come hungry. Bring a friend. A few protest signs might even be appropriate." Billy grinned while applause again rose; this time it included some of the patrons near the surfboards at the back of the store.

"And remember everyone," Billy continued in true political fashion. "Vote No to the Casino. No Mayan for my Island. No Mayan for my Island."

And that became Billy Jo Presser's rallying cry for what would hopefully become a small island protest against the intrusion of bad money and manipulation into their paradise.

After a short chant of "No Mayan for My Island" settled down, everyone departed for their designated assignments. Billy left his VW at Pat MaGee's and took off on foot for the pier. It was less than a mile away and he felt that a brisk walk in the fresh Gulf air would open up his mind. Everything was getting a little crazy. Timelines had sped up. The vote was this Saturday and he grimaced at the thought of how "undercover" the whole thing had become. Trust was becoming an issue. He hated scrutinizing everything. One of the reasons why Port A appealed to him was because of the feeling of trust within a community, a kind of trust that allows car doors to be left open and a back door unlocked. You had to be careful when tourist season peaked because of off-islanders, but other than that Port A cared for itself.

And then came Mitchell Bone. The false smile. The clammy, tiny handshakes. But as much as he wanted to, Billy couldn't hang all the blame on Bone even though he was a major contributor to a change in trust that had begun when outside influences were allowed to control island interests. Some of the "rich" people that the CopyKatz clerk had talked about included many of these outside influences. These people were more into their own positive cash flow and would easily, and without guilt, leave very little to the Port A community. That's why they were down the island a few miles, out of the city limits. God help them if they ever had to pay a little bit of the tax money to help support a community which provided the vacationers who rented their time and spaces.

Billy crested the first set of barrier dunes to a wave of Gulf breeze that slapped his hair into his eyes. He inhaled deeply. The heat of the day combined with the pure salt smell of the Gulf yanked a breath from his lungs. He gasped twice more.

Second to the trust of an island community, its culture was as big a reason why he'd chosen Port A after dropping out of MIT. The beach. The sun. The waves.

He'd gotten really sick of the New England culture, especially around the campus in Cambridge. At MIT, and in much of its community, everybody acted as if they were better than you, had been more places than you, had more education than you, had more stuff than you. It was too competitive. And the competitive culture naturally created an aura of mistrust. That's how it was at MIT. He couldn't trust people. He'd experienced students plagiarizing his ideas on many occasions. Where was the trust in a culture like that? He'd even had a professor claim one of his robotic components to be his own design. That's when he'd had enough. The professor had held credentials that Billy could not litigate against.

His parents hadn't been too happy about his departure. Both his father and mother were educators. Having one of their sons drop out of college was against their academic religion. His own savings had been enough to get him started in Port A. His parents had provided nothing.

He crossed a second set of dunes and headed for the shoreline. The brown sand was Texas hot. If you weren't from Port A or didn't visit often, you probably weren't aware of just how hot it could get. That's why whenever Billy saw a beachcomber without sandals cursing, he knew that person was an off-islander.

The beach grew crowded as the sun neared its daily peak. Its width could hold many people plus a two lane sandy road of slow traffic, which made for a great weekend cruising spot. The beach roads were, most times, packed on Friday and Saturday evenings.

And that's about as much of the outside world as Billy wanted on *his* island. A casino would not only change the tradition of cruising the beach, it would change who was driving in those cruise machines. Instead of high school kids with hot rods and four-wheel drives, there would be pimps in long Cadillacs, drug dealers in slightly larger Cadillacs, and lots of people with lots of money and lots of outside influence.

Billy walked the shoreline toward the pier a few hundred yards ahead. He studied the waves as he sloshed through the soupy froth. The warm water invited him in. Breaks were uneven. The onshore winds were beating them down, dumping them in big uneven chunks. He thought about the tropical storm Bottlenose had mentioned. Storm swells could make for some superb surfing later in the week. The storm didn't need to hit the island; the best surf was when the storms remained a hundred miles out before turning north like so many of them did. The strong side of the storm whipped around some knarly waves once it was up the coast.

A couple off-islanders raced up the sand without sandals as Billy walked in from the shoreline toward the pier entrance. "Damn that's hot," the fatter man said. Billy chuckled.

The cost to get on the pier was three bucks but no one ever charged the regulars. It was just one of those "island" things. He posted a flyer at the entry to the pier and one at the bait shop.

On the pier, he talked with many people; most he knew—most didn't realize that the vote was this Saturday. He handed out all of the remaining flyers except one. This last flyer he posted on the railing at the end of the pier. All of the locals said they would be voting. Many of them said they'd attend the protest luau.

"You're gonna love my dish," said a voice from behind.

"Burgess," Billy said, acknowledging the voice. "I only wish I could be a judge. Pedro would certainly get high marks."

"What's he making?" Burgess, who worked at the Terrapin, looked like the chef from a can of Chef-Boy-Ardee. He didn't have the hat on but it was easy to imagine.

"He hasn't told me. Secret I guess," Billy teased, remembering Pedro's "island-marinated" menu. "I'm just glad that there's going to be such a great spread from some of the local best."

"My contribution will be *my* best." Burgess didn't have a French accent either, but again it was easy to imagine.

Billy left Burgess on the pier contemplating his dish for the night, waved good-bye to several people, exited the pier and continued down the shoreline toward the channel. The local newspaper was another half mile up and across the dunes. He'd originally intended to return to his VW before visiting the newspaper but the walk felt good. It gave him energy. And the energy would come in handy when he confronted Nole Kilpatrick. The *South Jetty's* responsibility was to tell its citizens of important items affecting their community. Billy wanted to find out just how much money Kilpatrick's silence cost. What was the sanctity of Port Aransas worth?

He reached the offices of the *South Jetty* a little after noon. Kilpatrick was conveniently out.

"You guys know anything about the vote on the casino proposition coming up this Saturday?" Billy said to the lady at the front desk. He didn't know her name.

"Proposition vote?" she said, still sitting. "No. I haven't heard about that."

"When's Kilpatrick get back?"

"Mr. Kilpatrick may not return the rest of the afternoon." Billy couldn't tell if she was lying or if that is exactly what Kilpatrick had told her to say. "He's a very busy man."

"I bet," he said, defensively. It was that lack-of-trust thing intruding upon him again, making him suspicious. "Can you tell me where I could find him?"

"Mr. Kilpatrick doesn't tell me where he goes, Mr…." she grabbed a pen. "And your name? I'll leave him a note that you were here."

"That's okay," Billy huffed. "I'll catch up to him later."

"Would you like to make an appointment?" The lady flipped through the appointment book.

"No," Billy said and left the building, not meaning to slam the screen door so hard.

Billy returned to Pat MaGee's by walking the beach and chuckling at apparent vacationers. He tossed out to sea several broken sand dollars, wondering again if the tropical storm would create the knarly waves Port A usually lacked. He'd not caught a good one in a while. He'd told Coolie and Sweets that he might do some surfing before the luau but the way things looked now, he wouldn't get much more from this surf than a sunburn. The surf did, however, provide the white noise catalyst that calmed his mind and prompted reflection.

L-F-tt-, he thought. *A puzzle. Seven letters.*

Wayeb. Five unlucky days when Evil can cross over.

And that damned bodyguard goon son of a bitch.

The waves crashed and foamed around his feet. He stood for a moment, trying to cancel out the screaming children behind him and the parents who screamed after them.

Just what the hell had the bodyguard put inside the Big Texas Bank vault? A crate? Full of what? Valuables? Illegal secrets? Shoe could not see the vault's interior well enough to gather much of anything. Would Stephanie Drake know? All of the puzzles were driving him crazy. His analytic cogs were overloading. He needed some answers. The library would provide only so much. He would have to go back to the bank and talk with Stephanie Drake. He'd invite her to the luau. Perhaps while "unwinding" she would reveal further clues. He also needed to get into the vault and check it out—personally. The only way he could do that was to rent a security box.

On his way back to Pat MaGee's, he decided to visit the bank before heading for the library. He returned to his apartment and Kale caught him at the front door as Billy shoved a meager coin collection that his father had given him into a small backpack.

"Looks like the local fishing companies are going to be doing much less business than usual," Kale said. "There's a report of dead fish in the catches."

Billy slung the backpack onto his shoulder. "What's causing it?" he said.

"Red Tide was the general consensus."

"Anyone gotten a hold of Walker?" Billy snatched his checkbook from his lab-office and met Kale at the doorway.

"Well—I'm not sure." Kale's voice was calm but it came in gasps. "I could call him."

Billy led Kale out and closed the door. Kale's expression as he watched Billy lock it was one of astonishment, but that's the way the new "suspicious Billy" had to proceed.

"I'll tell you what," Billy said, leading Kale down the steps. "I'll give Walker a call. I've been wanting to talk to him for a month now. Just keep on looking north for supplies and try not to break the bank. Whatever it is won't be around for long."

"You think it's a spill?" Kale released the rumor that had apparently been nagging him. "While talking with the fishing companies, I got the feeling that, though everyone was saying 'Red Tide,' most were thinking 'chemical spill.'"

"All I can say is, I hope not." Billy walked to his VW. "It's a slim possibility but only slim. Let's stick with a more reasonable reason. I'll call Mark. He'll know what it is." He tossed his backpack to the passenger's seat and slid under the steering wheel. "How's business?"

"Good…considering." Kale looked at the restaurant.

Billy rolled down the VW's window. "Good," he said. "Pedro got everything he needs?"

"He hasn't said otherwise."

After a quick wave, Billy drove off. Typically, he would have stayed and fixed the problem himself, but his days of micromanagement were just about done. Besides, Kale could manage. Kale would *have to* manage, at least until they closed at seven. Tonight would be an early night for Surf Side. Everyone would be at the luau.

It was hard for Stephanie to believe it possible.

Carol had said very little all day long. It was kind of creepy, like the way you feel when you know someone's going to come up behind you and yell, "Surprise!" At any moment, Carol would do just that. She'd catch Stephanie off-guard as she studied her computer monitor. And then without warning, Carol would blurt out, *Surprise, Miss Drake! And tell me... how does it feel to have stolen my promotion?*

But Carol never surprised her. She conducted business behind her teller window and escorted people to their security boxes in the vault without grunt or grimace. Almost robotically. It was very creepy.

No one had seen Mitchell Bone. He'd not called Stephanie to reschedule several appointments all of which she had already cancelled and apologized for before lunch. Now, it was shortly after one o'clock and his next appointment was due in ten minutes.

Stephanie dialed Bone's cell number. It was at least the tenth time she'd done so. Again, all she heard was his answering service. Again, she left him a message to call her.

Carol walked passed her desk with one of the owners of the Mustang Ranch just south of town—a Mr. Farber, if Stephanie remembered correctly.

Both she and the young man entered the vault. They were in there for what Stephanie believed was a long time—ten minutes perhaps. Then she escorted the owner to the front of bank and waved good-bye.

It had been like that all day. Everyone Carol had led into the vault had remained in there with her for at least ten minutes. There must have been a dozen of them, and every one of them was an owner of some business or property that had needed financial help from Mitchell Bone. Stephanie knew all of them. Several had cancelled appointments with Bone earlier in the day. Each of them had done business with Big Texas Bank within the last month.

So what if everyone in town suddenly wanted to look inside their security boxes, she thought. Coincidence, that's all.

But Carol acting the way she did—that was different. She just wasn't right at all.

"Hello."

The voice surprised her. She jumped in her chair.

"Sorry. Miss Drake? It is Miss Drake?" Billy stood behind her. "I didn't mean to scare you."

Stephanie smiled with a small bit of embarrassment.

"Stephanie," she said. "Or Steph if you like." She thought about his name for only a moment. "Billy Jo Presser," she added.

"Just Billy," he said. "I'd like to check out one of your security boxes."

Yeah, you and a dozen other business owners, she thought. "Go ahead and have a seat," Steph said, pointing Billy toward one of the three red chairs that Billy had already seen in a hundred image snapshots.

He looked over the numerous ornaments occupying her desk then leaned far forward as if analyzing one of the starfish that decorated the sides of the desk.

"These are really nice," he said, smiling. "We all got to do our part for Sea Life Month, eh?"

Steph moved the paperwork for security box rentals in front of her. "So how's the seafood restaurant business going?" she said.

"Better than ever. Having a theme month was a brilliant idea—one of the few our council has had of late."

"And people are more into doing beach things." She knew that Billy was a local surfer. She picked up a pen. "Will that be a small or large box?"

Billy hoisted his backpack onto a knee, unzipped it and pulled out four thin blue books: the entirety of his silver dollar coin collection. "What will these fit?" he said.

"Small should do it." She checked the appropriate box on the rental agreement. "You should have a pretty good turnout at the luau tonight," she said.

"You want to join me?" He put the backpack on the floor but left the coin albums in his lap.

"I'm not much of the protester type," she said, wanting to go.

"Doesn't matter." He leaned forward. "You don't have to do any protesting. Just being there is enough. Besides, it'll be fun; a peaceful protest with lots to eat. I'll introduce you to some of my friends."

"What's your address?" she asked.

'That's OK. I'll pick you up."

"No," Steph smiled and tapped the rental form with her pen. "I mean for the rental. Your address?"

"Will you go?" He said it as if her answer was a prerequisite to him renting the security box.

"Sure," she said, perhaps too quickly. "Now let's see some identification."

Steph finished with the paperwork, handed Billy his driver's license, stood up with a hand on a set of keys that she'd pulled from her desk drawer and asked Billy to follow her into the vault; she'd not been inside since yesterday.

The crate was still where Chancey Lett's bodyguard had left it. It was about two feet wide on all six of its cubed sides. Its boards were darkened with age, appearing almost rotten in places. The top of the crate was securely attached. No seams in the crate existed that might reveal its contents. There were no hinges, screws or nails…only wood. Steph felt its *chill*, smelled its ancient dusty moisture. She walked into the vault not realizing how much distance she'd given it.

To the left of where the crate sat was a deeper room of about ten-feet squared; most of the security boxes lined these vault walls. A small stainless steel table sat in the middle of the room. Steph stuck both keys into one of the smaller box doors about halfway up the right side wall, opened it, and pulled out the drawer inside.

"Here you go," she said, handing him the drawer and one key. "I'll be outside. When you're through, just slide the box back in and lock the lock."

"This won't take long." Billy dropped the coin albums into the drawer, replaced the drawer into the security box and locked it. "All done." He clapped is hands together as if dusting them off.

"It's just that we're not supposed to be in here while the renter is going through their box. It's personal courtesy."

"You've been quite courteous already," Billy said. After a short pause, he added, "What's up with that crate? It seems a bit…"

"Out of place," Steph finished. They walked together toward the wooden cube. "The guy who's building the casino—It's his."

"Maybe some valuable artifact that they are going to use as decoration?"

Steph had not considered that. It made sense. They both gazed at the crate for another dozen seconds then Steph led him out of the vault. "Probably just decoration," she said.

Carol looked up from her teller window. Her eyes followed Steph and Billy as they walked back to her desk. She continued to stare at them as Billy pulled out his checkbook.

"The box is fifteen dollars a month." Steph said. "First and last month's rent due at the time of rental."

"I'd also like to try one of your short-term CDs," Billy said. "A thousand dollars."

"Really?" Steph was surprised. "OK. Well let me get the paperwork."

"Don't you just hate that?" he said, grinning.

"CDs?" Steph placed a form in front of her.

"Paperwork," Billy clarified. "I hate it."

Steph started writing on the form. "Unfortunately, a necessary evil," she said and looked at Carol who, still, was staring.

Billy signed two papers, and wrote a check. "I'll pick you up at...say eight-thirty-ish?" Billy stood. "Where do you live?"

"Paradise Cottages," she said. "Number 10."

As Billy left the bank, Carol went into the vault, reappearing only moments later. She glared at Steph then toward the front door of the bank. Billy disappeared around the corner.

Billy thought that the creepiest thing about his visit to the bank had nothing to do with the crate in the vault; it was the way that the bank teller had stared at him on his way out. It was something in her eyes, dark, almost lifeless, set in an expressionless face, as if painted on by a very unimaginative artist. She could have doubled for a mannequin except that her neck had turned as Billy had walked passed. He thought he'd heard her spine cracking. That teller had been the same woman whom Shoe had videotaped going into the vault earlier that morning.

He got into his VW and headed for the library but his concentration was not on the questions he would try to answer there. Carol the teller's stare kept intervening. It reminded him of the encounter he'd had with Lett's bodyguard at the bar the day before. He'd remembered being consumed for only a fraction of a second by the depth of the big man's lifeless eyes. And somewhere deep inside the pupils there had been fire. That's when he'd looked away. He'd felt that if he'd stared for only a second longer, the bodyguard's eyes would have swallowed him. Carol's eyes would have, too, had he been close enough to her and had he had the courage to stare into them for only a second longer.

And then there was the crate. There had been something coming from within it—something invisible—an energy that repelled and attracted erratically. He'd felt suddenly weak the moment he'd entered the vault, and the closer he'd gotten to it, the stronger the attraction and repulsion and his weakness became. Its energy again reminded him of the bodyguard. He, too, had had an invisible force about him—something that pulled Billy in toward his dark stare but also repelled him at the same time, as if some sort of spiritual battle between the man's demonic intent and Billy's soul had been played out right there in the Surf Side restaurant.

Shoe had appeared to be functioning better than expected. Billy had seen no water leaks and was pleased how well the little robot blended in with the thematic environment of sea life on Steph's desk. Billy had worked on Shoe's stealth for many weeks and this, too, was functioning better than he'd anticipated. Nothing mechanical could be heard. The water propulsion system had worked tremendously well. If only the guys back at M.I.T. could have gotten a hold of Shoe. They'd tear the little robot apart trying to understand, again, how Billy Jo Presser had managed to pull it off. To them it was always another "breakthrough" in robotic kinesiology; to Billy it was just a hobby that constantly needed tweaking.

And then there had been Steph. She'd looked much prettier today than she had last week. Perhaps she had worn less makeup which had allowed the light skin tone of her rounded cheeks, chin and nose to pop out in natural nakedness. Perhaps it was the way she'd styled her dirty dishwater blonde hair that, instead of lying in curls on her shoulders, had been much straighter, falling behind her back just inches below her neckline. Perhaps Billy just liked the simpler look of the native islander, one who cared less for how everybody else thought a bank manager's executive secretary should look—one who had dumped the flashy business suit for a more relaxed slacks and blouse wardrobe. For whatever reason, Billy had found his heart racing just a little bit louder, his cheeks flushing just little bit brighter and his desire growing just a little bit stronger. He'd been happy that she had accepted his invitation to the luau. As he pulled into the library parking lot, he envisioned their evening together and how it might very well turn into something more romantic in the future. He could always hope.

The library was dead as was usual during weekday afternoons. Only one person strolled through the stacks at the back of the reference section and Billy supposed that it was the summer librarian. He didn't know her. Most summer librarians were college students from Corpus who'd found Port A to be the perfect place for an internship in library and information science: They'd spend the day amongst the stacks and the evening amongst the waves and get college credit for it. What a life.

The girl, who appeared to be no older than twenty-one, looked over at Billy as he entered the reference section, pulled out the computer printout from his front pocket and sat down at a computer station. She did not offer any immediate help.

Thanks to Pedro, his first search was easy. Instead of combing through screens of information about ancient civilizations in hopes of finding a picture of the ceremonial mask, he simply typed "Wayeb" into a Google search.

Just as Pedro had said, Wayeb was a term used by the Mayans that denoted the final five days of the calendar year. Their calendar contained eighteen months of twenty days each. Each of these months was named for a seasonal or meteorological event or animal. Wayeb, however, literally meant "days without souls." Mayan culture warned that on these five days it was best to stay inside, to comb one's hair often and thoroughly so as to cleanse any evil spirits that may have hidden within the strands, and to pray that none would be born on such unforgiving days. These were the days when evil was allowed to cross into the mortal world without boundary or limit. Unsuspecting mortals who did not heed the warnings were often found to be maimed, dismembered or missing.

Billy scoured the many links that Google presented about Mayan culture. There was little else about Wayeb other than what Pedro had told him; however, he did come to understand the Mayan calendar as a whole a little better. He'd never examined anthropology or ancient peoples while at M.I.T. therefore much of the information he now scrolled through was new to him: for example, the Mayan Calendar Round. A picture of it showed a circular piece of golden metal inscribed with many colorful symbols of ceremonial masks, animals, and nature. The Calendar Round dated a complete Mayan cycle that started more than 26,000 years ago. What Billy found to be most interesting was the calendar's end date: December 21, 2012, a day that was just around the corner.

Several links led to cheaply designed web pages full of prophetic warnings that on December 21, 2012, the world would end. Dozens of books had been written about the End Date, most calling it the alpha and the omega—the beginning and the end.

One web page read: "According to Mayan calculations, the current cycle of the world is due to end in December 2012. There is some disagreement over whether the end of the current cycle of the world will involve the end of the world itself."

Another read: "The Maya messengers, renowned for their architectural, artistic, mathematical and scientific achievements, left a calling card as a series of superhuman-sized stone monuments and pyramids with precise calendric computations. Planted with great intention, these dates were left to ensure that future generations would be alerted to the coming end point of this great 26,000 year cycle."

For this date, connections were made to Revelations in the Bible, the Muslim calendar, the birth of Buddha, North American Indian tribes, a rare astrological alignment of Earth, Sun and the Milky Way, interdimensional shifts, pole shifts, reversed magnetic fields and just about every apocalyptic catastrophe the mind could imagine. The amount of information ranged from spiritualistic nonsense and foreboding to doctoral theses on zero time and its conjunction with the year 2012. From pure nut cases to philosophical doctorates (and sometimes it was hard to tell one from the other), what was known as the Mayan Prophecies was thoroughly documented.

Not that any of this had anything to do with Chancey Lett, the crate in the Big Texas Bank vault or the building of a casino, but it was fun to read. It had been a while since Billy had become so engaged by research that time seemed to stand still. An hour had passed in the blink of an eye. His concentration was broken only by the librarian; he suddenly realized she was standing next to him. He did not know how long she'd been there.

"Strange," she said. Her voice made her sound ten years old. Billy shifted in his seat.

"Excuse me?" Billy scowled. He did not like people reading over his shoulder.

"I'm sorry," the girl squeaked. "It's just that my professor always tells us that it's very rare that two people will research the same piece of information on the same day in a public library." She smiled apologetically. "In college libraries it's common, but not in public libraries."

The scowl remained on Billy's face. He had no idea what the girl was talking about.

"Those links," she said and pointed at the computer screen. "Another guy was in here this morning searching for the same information."

The scowl left Billy's face and was replaced by a squinted question mark. "And why is that unusual beyond what your professor says?"

The girl did not answer. She turned away, her head drooping, as if she'd done something bad. Billy turned back toward the computer screen. Interruptions greatly disrupted his research methods. After all, he did not take notes—that was not his way. He memorized much of the information but to do so accurately he had to go without interruption.

He started a new search, concentrating this time on the word puzzle: *L-F-tt-*

He entered the word, leaving spaces for the unknown letters, into Google. Results included pages by a man name Jay L. Fitt, the law offices of Lavrey, Fitt, and Fitt, a book on How to be Fit in Fifteen Days by an author named Joe Fitt, and screens filled with other useless clues. What he did come to understand is that there are a lot of people named Fitt.

But there was only one LaFitte. And there he found, on the fifteenth screen full of results, the answer to his puzzle. Jean LaFitte. He clicked the link which went to the Wikipedia online encyclopedia.

Jean LaFitte...circa 1780 to 1826. The year of death had a question mark next to it. He'd been a pirate in the early days of America, had aided troops against the British at the Battle of New Orleans, had engaged in slave trade and, though actual accounts differ, robbed ships as they came through the Gulf. He later became active along a neutral strip of lawless land from Spanish held Texas to Louisiana. He is believed to have died in the Yucatán but no one knows for sure where or when, the Wikipedia entry claimed.

As he continued to move through screens of information he found that, basically, Jean LaFitte—a.k.a. Lafette or La Fite—was a conundrum. Accounts had him being born in many different places including France, Spain, and Haiti. He worked the Mississippi delta in slave trade, which was a highly acceptable and respectable means of living back in 1809. Some would have called him a pirate—others, including himself, referred to him as a privateer, a man who understood the politics of three countries well and used that knowledge for profit. When politics changed in the Monroe years, LaFitte was hunted down by the U.S. Navy; he burnt down his own town (which was in Galveston, Texas at the time) and slipped out into the night. What happened to him from there is as much mystery as the rest of his life. Some say he moved to Charleston, South Carolina where he raised a family and moved west. Others have him disappearing to Mexico in the Yucatán, perhaps up near Cancun.

Of great interest to Billy were the *similar* accounts of LaFitte's actions during those last days of his Gulf empire. Once LaFitte had escaped the U.S. Navy, most accounts merged into one theory. He moved south and regardless of where he ended up—the U.S., Mexico or some island in between—most were certain that he'd taken his loot with him and had buried it at one or more locations throughout the Gulf. Most scholars concur that LaFitte's treasure had been worth in excess of a half a billion dollars in an 1810 economy. He would certainly have been a multibillionaire today.

And then it struck Billy suddenly, unexpectedly and rather off-guard: Treasure map?

He picked up the printout with the tops of the letters of Jean LaFitte's name now easily understood. It was only a sliver of evidence: only the top five percent of the page and not much else. It was in the calligraphic script of that time period but that style could have been duplicated easily.

So what Billy came to understand in almost three hours of memorized searching was that the two papers in the satchel carried by the bodyguard were, number one, related to the Mayan culture and number two, related to Jean LaFitte. The only connection to Port Aransas was the one account of LaFitte moving to the Yucatán in his last years. The treasure map idea was intriguing but, really, was it realistic? What Billy had uncovered was not mystery…it was easy to see. Chancey Lett was going to build a casino and name it The Mayan. He had collected information pertaining to all things "Mayan." The Wayeb symbol is Mayan. Jean LaFitte, perhaps, ended up in Mayan territory. If Shoe could have jumped off the desk and wrenched open the satchel, the robot would certainly have taken pictures of many more documents pertaining to both the interior and exterior décor of Lett's new venture. All Lett had in the satchel was a wish list of Mayan artifacts to decorate the casino. One of those artifacts was in a crate, stored in a vault of the Big Texas Bank, Port A branch. There was no conspiracy here. Mitchell Bone was doing exactly what Mitchell Bone always did: grovel and brownnose and answer yes-yes-yes if a buck was to be made in it. Lett wanted to use his vault to store what appeared to be some very valuable artifacts. One piece was in there now. More would be coming in the future. The satchel was full of the descriptions of these pieces. Lett was "renting out" space in the vault for these items.

Nothing more. Nothing less.

And the idea made Billy angry. He mashed the Exit key on the library computer keyboard and stood. He snatched the printouts from the table and headed for the door. On his way out, he saw the librarian, who spoke like a ten-year-old, hiding behind the comic book rack. He waved good-bye to her though he knew it would not help her nerves. He'd been a bit brash but that's how he was when it came to research. The librarian had been an innocent bystander.

At ten minutes to five, Steph got a phone call from Mitchell Bone.

Now? she thought. Minutes before it was time for her to leave the bank and prepare for the luau and, finally, Bone calls.

"I want you to pick up an investor from the airport Friday afternoon," Bone said.

She hesitated as if she was really going to say: *No! Are you out of your fucking mind!*, but instead she said, "Yes. Of course, Mr. Bone. And what should I do with today's appointments?"

After a short pause, Bone said, "Stick them in where you can and call them back. As for tomorrow, cancel them all. I'll be tied up with other interests."

Canceling his appointments for tomorrow meant that Steph would have to work after five o'clock. "Yes," she said reluctantly. "I'll cancel. The new appointments will be in the computer calendar."

Bone hung up without gratitude and this burned Steph. One part of her job responsibilities was to aide Mitchell Bone in his daily activities even if, on occasion, those activities entailed after hours work—but of all the days to have to work overtime. She took a deep breath and counted to three before calling Bone's first appointment for the following day.

By five-thirty, most of the staff had said their good-byes; some frowned in recognition of Steph having to stay late, others patted her hand in sympathy. Only she and Carol were left in the bank. Carol said nothing as she went to the vault, entered briefly then reappeared and closed the vault door. She yanked the handle and spun the cylinders on the four lock dials. She never looked at Steph. She never said good-bye to anyone. It was very programmed. She left the bank moments later, leaving Steph all alone.

Billy arrived at the Surf Side around five o'clock. Business was slow in the day's transition from lunch to dinner. Only one man sat at a two-seat table near the window at the back of the restaurant. He was busy with a plate of boiled king shrimp, one of Pedro's specialties. A handwritten sign on a dry erase board hung from two small hooks in the hostess station:

SURF SIDE RESTAURANT WILL CLOSE, TUESDAY, AT 7:00.
JOIN US AT THE LUAU ON THE BEACH INSTEAD.
PEDRO'S DISH IS FOR SURE TO BE THE BEST!

Billy chuckled. Candice's work, no doubt. She had a great way with words and people. He didn't see her immediately.

"Slow," she said, appearing suddenly behind him. "Been like this all day." She wiped her hands with a towel; she'd been washing dishes. "Pedro's getting ready—packin' up in the back." She thumbed in that direction.

"You the only one here?" Billy looked around at empty tables that were well lit by sunshine that beat down on the tinted large bay windows. The guy eating the shrimp had a large pile of casings on a plate next to a nearly equal-sized helping of fresh king shrimp. Like a machine, the man peeled, dipped and ate the shrimp then discarded the casing on the appropriate pile. He had gone through two dozen large, pinky-sized shrimp already and he showed no signs of slowing.

"I am," Candice replied. "Alicia went home around two-thirty. Lunch was weirdly slow, like, bizarro slow." She rolled her eyes then walked away from Billy toward the shrimp-eating machine. She turned and whispered as she left, "He'll eat all of today's profits with his all-you-can-eat coupon." At the table, she dropped off an additional bottle of Surf Side Cocktail Sauce, a wonderful elixir of flavor that Billy hoped he might package and sell one day. Candice was cordial and talked with the customer for several minutes before heading for the kitchen. As she passed Billy she quietly said, "I think he's full."

Billy followed her into the kitchen and immediately saw Pedro at the back of the room. He lifted up a small plastic milk crate that was full of cooking utensils and turned to a hallway that led to the rear service door. He saw Billy and looked up.

"Getting mí cooking gear packed up," he said. "This will be a good time?"

It took a moment for Billy to understand what he meant. "Sí, indeed," he said. "Great food. Great people. On the surf. Not a cloud in the sky. What a wonderful day for a protest." Candice began washing dishes to his right. "You need some help packing?"

"If we were feeding more people then yes," Pedro said. "But only one hungry shrimp eater. I think I will be OK." He hugged the crate, which didn't appear to be heavy, freed the right hand and moved his fingers and thumb into an OK sign. "I guess everyone is waiting for the big beach party to eat. Nobody hungry has been in here for today."

"Kale around?" Billy asked.

"I think he went to market up d'coast to find a supply man." Pedro entered the hallway and Billy could hear the hallow acoustic of his voice. "This is going to be fun," the voice said, fading.

Billy followed him out the back door; Pedro was loading the crate into the trunk of a small Fiesta. "You'll never get all you need into that small box on wheels," he said.

"It is a little crowded, yes?" Pedro closed the trunk gently. It barely latched.

"You can borrow my VW if you'd like. There's a lot more room."

"Really? Mí jefe!"

"However, I'll need to borrow your car to take care of some things before my date tonight."

Pedro fell silent and a smile slowly emerged from the right corner of his mouth. The left cheek remained stationary as the right corner stretched high, revealing six teeth.

"Señorita, eh?" Pedro seemed pleasantly surprised. "That will be very good for you. We all need a compañero. Is she from here?"

"From over at the bank. She's the executive secretary. Stephanie is her name."

"Esecute…esecutive?" Pedro tried to say it.

"Executive secretary," Billy corrected. "She's the manager's assistant, basically."

"Like I am your assistant, basically." The smile still captured the right side of his face.

Billy thought for a moment. "Yeah. Something like that…basically." He returned the smile though not as brightly. "Here's the key to the VW."

"Here is the keys to my little car."

Billy looked at the small Fiesta, which, for a beach car, had only a small amount of rust on it. "Cozy."

"Cozee?" Pedro said.

"Comfortable," Billy added.

"Sí. She is that. Muy cómodo."

Pedro walked toward the parking lot where Billy had left his VW. Billy was not concerned that Pedro would see his computer surveillance equipment. Pedro knew Billy's hobby was robotics. Pedro had met Shoe shortly after Billy had built the starfish and shortly before the hydraulic systems in the robot had failed for the first time. All of the digital components in the VW, should he see any, would only fascinate him. Besides, the equipment was mostly out of sight behind cabinet doors that Billy kept locked.

Billy pulled the latch on the Fiesta's trunk and set Pedro's crate of cooking utensils on the pavement beside the car. He grabbed the set of large bowls sitting in the passenger's seat and set them on top of the crate.

Pedro kept the car in good, clean shape; it was very "beachy." Traces of brown sand scattered the floorboards and the car had that sea smell: it kind of smelled fishy and salty and wet all at the same time. With the artificial sweet odor of Hawaiian Tropic suntan lotion mixed in, the car smelled very beachy. Atop the car was a surf rack that could hold two long boards. Billy had never seen Pedro surf and didn't remember seeing the surfboard car racks until now. Perhaps he'd taken up the sport and just hadn't said anything.

Billy moved the driver's seat back and climbed in. It was less cramped than he thought it would be. He started it and drove off, adjusting the rearview mirror as he did so. Looking into the mirrored reflection, he saw Pedro park the VW near the restaurant's back door and easily load the bowls and crate.

And then, suddenly, Billy felt very dizzy. A nauseous tightening of his stomach made him stop the car before leaving the parking lot. He grabbed his belly. The view of Pedro and the VW in the rearview mirror became very blurry. He placed the car in Park and just sat there, staring at the mirror, watching as the vision in it started to change.

At first he thought it was the heat, the sea smell, the Hawaiian Tropic lotion and the cramped car all working against his intestines. But the nausea wasn't in his stomach—it was in his mind.

He shook his head as all of his senses became involved in some strange altered vision.

It was suddenly dark outside. He felt that he was driving very fast. Tires screeched. In the driver's side mirror he could see two sets of headlights blazing very close to his bumper. Shots were fired and the rear window blew apart. In the back of the car, which was much too large for a Fiesta, was a wooden box…a crate.

"Pull the fuck over," someone yelled.

Billy blinked and turned toward the voice to his left.

And just like that the vision disappeared. His mind and senses jolted back into reality but still swirled with the experience of being in another place at another time. Momentarily, Billy was lost. His mind said "someone is firing a gun at me" while his eyes read "Pedro is packing my VW." The nausea subsided. His breathing eased.

It had been like a really bad nightmare, one which you awaken from screaming, or punching at the wall or falling out of bed. For an instant it had seemed so real. He'd seen something that was not a part of his memory. He'd never experienced being shot at or even driving a car much beyond a few miles over the speed limit.

But the vision had been so real.

Pedro waved at him in the rearview mirror then disappeared through the back door of the restaurant. Billy shook off the chills that raced across his spine and placed the Fiesta in Drive, then cautiously peeked back into the rearview mirror half expecting to see headlights, shattered glass, the sound of gunfire, and a crate.

A crate?

No…more like a cube. It was nearly two feet across in all dimensions. Some kind of energy from it attracted and repelled at the same time. It was something to be avoided but was also the object of much desire.

The altered vision had lasted a mere second but Billy had memorized the entire event. In the altered vision, not much of the cube had been revealed. It had hidden itself in shadow as window glass rained around it.

But it *was* the crate in the bank vault! Billy was sure of it.

Like a projector stopping on a single frame from a movie reel, Billy's mind captured the memories of the image of the crate in the altered vision and the image of the crate in the vault and made a mental comparison. Whatever the reason for the altered vision Billy didn't know, but he was pretty damned certain that the crate in the vault of the Big Texas Bank was a part of it.

Perhaps the crate had even caused his vision. He'd gotten within a foot of it. Maybe it had infected him somehow. The crate contained some kind of hallucinogen, perhaps. Maybe it infected *anyone* that came too close. Maybe Carol had been infected too—that's why the woman seemed catatonic. She'd been too close to the crate on too many occasions and was now the proud owner of one hefty helping of mind-altering drugs.

And then it hit him—Chancey Lett's box contained drugs. It made the most sense of anything he'd guessed so far. There were no Mayan artifacts or pirate artifacts or any other kind of decorative ornament for a new casino. The bank was a front for the distribution of some kind of hallucinogen.

Perhaps he couldn't "prove" a conspiracy to stack the vote but, if he could show that Chancey Lett was a drug runner, the "Mayan" would have no chance and gambling would move onto the next unsuspecting Texas town. Mitchell Bone would be ousted. The island would return to normal.

Billy turned down Avenue G, looked over at a relatively quiet Pat MaGee's and headed for the surf. Officer Keadle's cruiser sat in the same spot where he'd pulled over the impatient couple the night before. Billy waved at him as he passed, but Officer Keadle did not respond. Apparently, he hadn't recognized that Billy was driving Pedro's Fiesta.

Out on the beach road Billy found traffic to be light. Many off-islanders were packing up and heading out as Billy drove by. Perhaps it was a good sign. Perhaps most people were heading home to clean up and get ready for an evening of luau entertainment and great food.

The beach side where the proposed *Mayan* casino would be erected and where some of the only good surfing in Port A could be found was slowly transforming into a small Bedouin city. Billy saw the tents and the tractor trailer flat beds near the pier in the distance. Three surfers were out trying to grab what meager waves washed in. He supposed that Sweets and Coolie were two of the surfers. A new tent suddenly sprouted among the others, its red canopy a stark contrast to the subtler beach prints around it. *Enjoy Coca-Cola* was emblazoned on its surface. By the time Billy parked near one of the flatbed trailers, all of the tents that would be needed for the luau had been erected. There were twelve tents for the cooks and another nine or ten for amusement games and refreshment.

A man on the flatbed behind Billy moved a set of speakers around a tangle of wire and set them down, one on top of the other.

"Everything going okay?" Billy asked the young roadie.

"You bet," the dark-skinned kid said. "We gonna rock this house, gonna tear the place apart."

"When's the band due?"

"Got me, man." The roadie kid stopped what he was doing and lit up a smoke that he pulled from behind his ear. "I'm supposed to have all this shit together by six."

"Need any help?"

The roadie kid inhaled deeply and blew a large cloud of smoke. "Naw. Jacksie will be back in a second." He pointed at Billy with the cigarette pinched between two fingers. He smiled and added, "But I appreciate ya askin'," then puffed and blew another large Marlboro cloud.

It appeared that everything was on schedule for a seven-thirty start. The cooks would begin at that time. By eight-thirty, all the dishes would be completed. Judging would begin shortly after that. Five locals agreed to be taste judges; however, their collected opinion would not be final. Half of the cook's score would come from a vote by the luau guests.

A country beach band would provide the entertainment. They called themselves *Knights in White Satin* however it was rare to see them in anything other than shorts and T-shirts or no shirts at all. The "White Satin" probably described the extreme bleached blonde hair of all five band members.

Billy made his way through the small tent city, shaking hands with the workers, thanking each for their volunteer efforts and donation of tent usage. Many of the volunteers, Billy knew. Most told him that they understood what they were doing was for a good cause. All of them were vehemently against gambling moving in anywhere near their great little island town.

Closer to the surf, two men and a woman were busy digging a wide, shallow hole. They looked to be in their late teens or early twenties. Beside the hole and anchored in the sand under the skinnier man's knee was one of Port A's tourist brochures. It was folded to the panel that described Jean LaFitte's legend and the treasure that was buried somewhere on the island's beaches. As Billy walked past, he gazed down into the hole. It was about three feet wide and three feet deep, a perfect size to bury a crate full of drugs from Las Vegas, he thought.

"Don't touch it, man," the skinny guy said.

"Yeah," the girl giggled. "If you do, it'll pull you in and you'll become part of it forever and ever."

Billy stopped and turned around. He was about five yards from the hole.

The other guy, who was as large as both of his friends put together, slapped the girl on her forearm. "Shut up," he groaned. "That's not part of the legend."

"Oh yeah it is," the skinny guy said. "Why you think no one's ever found it? Because they became part of it!"

The fat guy reached down into the hole. Billy saw something glisten silver in the sun under his hand. The girl pushed him and he fell headfirst into the hole. The skinny guy and the girl laughed hysterically.

"Not right, man," the fat guy said, pushing himself out of the hole. He wiped sand from his eyebrows and forehead. His frown turned into a half smile. "Just for that, I ain't sharin' the treasure." He opened his hand.

"Whoa," the skinny guy said. "Look at that."

The three friends craned their heads forward. Billy bobbed his head for a better view as well.

"Is that a nickel?" the girl said. "It kinda looks like a nickel."

"Great find, Columbo," the skinny guy added. "Don't spend it all in one place." He giggled.

"No. Wait, man," the fat guy said. "You ever seen a nickel like this?"

Billy couldn't see what the fat guy held in his hand though it was certainly shaped like a nickel.

"Yeah. My dad's got a collection of them in his attic," the skinny guy said. "It's a buffalo nickel."

"That ain't no buffalo. How can you say that's a buffalo?"

"Let me see it," the girl said and opened her hand.

"Forget you. Find your own treasure," the fat guy said.

Billy thought again how ridiculous off-islanders could be. The whole idea of buried treasure was made up—a marketing gadget—a mystery based on historical speculation. There was no treasure to be found here: not by any fat guy and his two friends and not by any visiting hoodlum from Las Vegas. How could Billy Jo Presser, M.I.T. genius and dropout, have ever even considered that Chancey Lett was here to dig up treasure? The Nevada hood wanted to spread his illegalities to the Gulf Coast. Drugs and gambling and, most likely, prostitution is what Lett and Bone wanted to peddle. These things were their treasure.

The trio started to dig again. The tide was slowly moving in and would cover their hole in the next thirty minutes. The three looked like a pack of dogs digging for bones.

"BJ!"

The voice startled Billy. He turned to see Coolie standing behind him with the fluorescent green surfboard he'd been caressing outside of Pat MaGee's two nights before.

"Surf sucks," he said. "But the board's got grab, dude. I mean it might not be the pertiest thing but it's a swell grabber sure enough."

Coolie was skinnier than the guy digging the hole. His sternum and ribs etched uneven trails under the skin of his chest. His arms had little meat to them but the muscles he did possess knew how to maneuver a surfboard. He was strangely pale for someone who spent most of his time in the Texas sun.

"How'd you afford that?" Billy asked. He walked up to Coolie and ran his hand across the tacky waxed surface of the board.

"I told you. Me and yo' mamma. She pays well." He snickered. "No really, dude. Bottlenose said to take it out for a spin. Said no one but me was lookin' at it. He's had it there since spring. Wanna' try it on for size?" Behind Coolie, Billy saw Bottlenose and Sweets roll into the shallow soup. They wiped muddy froth from their hair and face as they approached.

"What's with the corpses?" Bottlenose said, thumbing toward the three treasure hunters. "They're tearin' up the hang."

Bottlenose had his own language. "Corpses" was a term he used for off-islanders from Corpus Christi and "hang" meant a beachside surfer's hangout. In complete contrast to Coolie's thin frame, Bottlenose looked as if he'd pumped weights most of his life.

"Hey," he yelled at the corpses. "Stop diggin' on the hang. Get out of here."

"We're just looking for LaFi…" the fat guy started to say.

"Out!" Bottlenose took a step toward them and they quickly stood and began walking away. "Fill the damn hole back in. You come in to someone's house, you gotta leave it the way you found it."

The triumvirate quickly complied then rushed away toward the pier without another word.

"So what's this I hear about the fish around here?" Bottlenose said as the four surfers walked to the spot where the hole had been. His voice dropped an octave lower as he added, "Damn corpses anyway."

"I don't know," Billy said. He slipped off his sandal and wiped his bare foot through the moist, cool, loose sand where the hole had been. "What have you heard?"

"DuPont went and dropped another load of industrial cleaner into the gulf."

"Really? I haven't heard that. Do you believe it?" Billy looked into Bottlenose's turquoise eyes, wondering if the surfer was serious or simply playing around. He turned to Coolie and Sweets. "I guess not if you're out there swimming in it."

"Whoa, man." Bottlenose lifted his hands in defense. "It's only what I heard not what I believe. I mean if DuPont had gone and screwed up again, don't you think we all would know about it?"

All four surfers looked at each other knowing the answer. Billy shook his head.

"I heard it was an underwater heat vent," Coolie said, stroking the green fluorescent fin of his borrowed board.

"I heard it was a red tide," Sweets added. "I also heard that there's absolutely nothing wrong with the water and the fisheries are creating a panic to drive up the prices."

Bottlenose looked at Sweets and smiled. "Now there's a logical answer!" He clapped Sweets on the back. "Let's go catch a sulfuric acid wave." He grabbed his board and turned his head around toward Billy. "You coming? Surfin' sulfuric is the bomb, man!" He grinned.

Before Billy could answer, he heard Pedro shout to him from under one of the tents. "Mi, jefe!" Pedro waved a spatula over his head to get his attention.

"Maybe some other time, Bottlenose," Billy said. "I'll see you tonight?"

"Wouldn't miss it." Bottlenose ran into the surf and paddled out to where Coolie and Sweets had already taken the lead.

Billy took a step in the direction of Pedro's voice and something squished up through the wet sand between his first and second toe. He bent down to pick it up.

It was shiny and looked like a nickel. But that was no buffalo etched into the surface. It didn't look American at all. A wave of surprise and confusion consumed him. The design on both sides of the coin looked exactly like the symbol he'd researched earlier in the day, the same one that was on the sheet of paper carried by a Las Vegas hood in the Big Texas Bank of Port Aransas. It was the face of Wayeb.

Steph finally finished Mitchell Bone's appointment calendar realignment at a quarter to six. She'd made contact with fifty percent of the phone calls; she'd left messages with the others. The late afternoon sun cast shadows across half of the bank's interior. She stood into one of them.

She clicked off her computer screen and looked across the top of her desk to see that everything was mostly in order. She rotated SpongeBob a quarter turn to the left. She readjusted Mr. Krabs arms so that his claws were resting on his hips in a stance that depicted determination. Patrick she left as is, his pointed, starfish head and face smiling at her. The toy made her smile, too.

She rose and stretched and grabbed her small purse, and turned to exit the bank when a very low hum stole her attention. It came from within the vault. She turned toward the steel door unconvinced that she was hearing anything at all.

Mmmmm—it was very low and nearly inaudible, sounding much like a boy's chorus exercising their voices before a performance. If the bank wasn't so quiet, she probably wouldn't have heard it.

Mmmmm…

And then a red glow—just under the edge of the vault door. It undulated, maroon in color, the low hum accompanying its pulsing glow in perfect synchronicity.

Mmmmm…mmmm

The red, thin line from under the vault door seemed to creep slowly through the bank shadows toward her. But, of course, that could not be. The seal of the vault door was tight. No air or water or light could enter or escape.

She stepped away from her desk while watching the red line of light that could not possibly exist. Feeling backward with one hand for the teller windows she knew she would run into, her flat rubber heels briefly slid on ceramic tile flooring and she turned toward the counter for support.

And just like that, they were gone.

The hum…the light…gone.

The bank was deathly quiet. Steph shook her head as if clearing it from dizziness. This was just her imagination, right? It had to be. The vault was airtight and blast proof. And why would there be light coming from *within* the vault?

And that strange hum.

Steph convinced herself that what she'd just seen was only imagination brought on by stress that had been agitated by Bone. She looked across her shoulder to the bank's sunlit entrance. A luau awaited her out there—and she needed it.

She reached for her purse, which she'd dropped on the teller counter during her slide across the tiles, and realized that she was standing in front of Carol's window. The counter on the other side of the glass was a mess. Dozens of papers had been left scattered in small piles. Steph knew several of the names written across what appeared to be signed security box rental agreements. All were owners of real estate and businesses within Port Aransas. Steph had just cancelled appointments with each of the names that were written on the dozen or so applications.

That was her job, not Carol's. Unless her responsibilities had been subverted, she was in charge of security box rentals. Perhaps Bone didn't want her to do anything but run errands for him any more. Perhaps Bone was circumventing her gatekeeping by going through Carol instead. Why he would do that, she didn't know. Maybe Steph was on her way out. Maybe she needed to start looking for another job. Maybe another job was in her best interests, one where creepy bosses and creepy clients and creepy employees were not standard regimen. And there was the crate, of course. She certainly needed a job where glowing, humming, creepy crates didn't drive a person's stress to the point of hallucination.

Pedro told Billy that the *Knights in White Satin* were stranded in their broken down van just over the causeway from Corpus. The band had phoned the restaurant shortly before Pedro had left and had asked if someone could come pick them up. Billy had set the band up for the evening. He was their contact. So he agreed to pick them up. He quickly calculated that driving out and back would give him enough time to return to the restaurant, settle the evening's business and take a shower before his date with Steph at eight-thirty.

But another calculation kept rolling through his mind as he took the VW's key from Pedro, walked to his vehicle and got in. What were the mathematical laws of chance that were related to coincidence? He remembered studying something about the subject while at MIT. He remembered reading that the laws of chance predicted that coincidence would occur sooner or later. He remembered reading that without coincidence the world would be even more surprising.

So what mathematical law could explain how the Wayeb symbol on the paper from the bank had caused Billy to print that symbol out so that he could investigate it at the library, which caused Billy to have the printed paper in his hand while talking with Pedro in the restaurant that morning, which caused Pedro to recognize the symbol as being the Mayan Wayeb, which gave Billy needed information for further research, which somehow (and this could have been a separate coincidence within a coincidence) connected Mayan history to the mystery of Jean LaFitte, who supposedly buried treasure somewhere along the Gulf Coast, perhaps by the pier in what is today Port Aransas, which was being excavated by a group of "corpses" from the city in a location where Billy found a coin that had the symbol of Wayeb stamped onto its surfaces.

What were the chances?

Coincidence?

Or—and Billy (a proud scientist) had a tough time thinking of the possibility—was it metaphysical?

Something that could not be explained.

As Billy drove the VW out of town his mind tried to comprehend what it could not explain. He rolled the silvery coin between the fingers of his left hand, glancing down periodically then back out onto the straight, flat, Texas road. Dry waves of heat lifted from the asphalt, pulling his vision into them. The horizon ahead turned hazy, wavy and blurry—a Texas mirage induced by the sun.

And suddenly he was thrust into that altered reality again.

He was in another car, at night, moving very fast, was being chased and shot at, and the crate from the Big Bank of Texas was there with him. The Texas dirt around him transformed into fields of corn that slapped at his windshield. There was an explosion and a bright orange ball of fire blazed behind him.

Billy suddenly felt very ill. He grabbed at his stomach and pulled the VW to an abrupt stop on the side of road. An old Oldsmobile station wagon blasted its horn and sped by as Billy stepped from the vehicle, grabbed his knees, and gagged. Just a small amount of spittle dribbled onto the steamy asphalt. He stood, looked around to gain composure. He saw no cornfields. No one was chasing him. There were no gunshots. But the station wagon that had just passed him and was slowly fading into the hazy horizon suddenly backfired. Billy reactively ducked. But there were no bullets. It was all just another illusion…a hallucination brought on by casino bosses and bank vault drugs.

He'd been shot at in his illusion and a car had backfired in reality.

What mathematical law could have explained that?

It was all just coincidence.

Janine Bender arrived in paradise by cab an hour before nightfall. She wore the same sunglasses that she had worn back when she was living with Albert. The lenses were very dark for a reason: it provided great camouflage for black eyes and bruised cheeks delivered by open-handed slaps during drunken rages.

She'd found out about Port Aransas (or "Port A" as the brochure she held in her hand read) from a lady who'd asked her to adjust a wedding dress back in Kansas. The lady's daughter had become pregnant and the dress needed a little "letting out." The lady had lived over in Chucktown and had been good business for Janine from that wedding day on—until Albert had driven her away. Albert had driven everything away.

Except paradise.

Not even Albert could erase such longing. Not even if he was still alive.

But, of course, Janine had been the only survivor—at least that's what the doctors and nurses at the hospital had told her shortly after she'd awakened. They'd also told her that the barn had been completely destroyed and that much of the barn debris had hit the main house. Her home had been condemned.

Many of her material memories she'd left behind. Two duffel bags carried what was left, and she'd packed them lightly and tightly so that she could carry both to the bus stop. A friend in Kansas City had helped. They'd gone to high school together. Beth Blandford had been a year ahead but they'd kept in touch, even after Beth had moved to the city shortly after graduation.

As she stepped from the Corpus Christi White Cab onto Alister Street, a jolt of fear accompanied the force of a strong Gulf breeze that whipped through her grey hair; she peeled blowing strands away from the front of her face.

"Thank you," she said to the cab driver. The driver set her two canvas bags on the sidewalk.

"My pleasure, señora."

Janine handed the driver his fare plus three dollars. She didn't have a lot of money but cabbies worked for tips, right?

She stood there with two bags of life and déjà vu slamming her psyche from all angles. As the White Cab slowly disappeared down Alister Street in the direction of Corpus Christi, that intense feeling of loneliness consumed her. She cried, briefly, then wiped away the tears.

It was when her eyes regained focus that she realized she *was* in paradise. Alister Street looked just like it did on the brochure: very quaint with a touch of—but not too much of—commercialism. It really didn't look much like a "vacation town" at all.

She'd worn shorts and a light blouse all the way from Kansas City. It had been a scorcher in the city when she'd left two days ago. Though Port Aransas was hotter, the Gulf breeze at least made it bearable.

She pulled a piece of paper from her blouse pocket and read from a small map, one that Beth had found online and had printed out for her. Her new home was a one-bedroom apartment located off of Alister Street. Appropriately, the name of the rental complex was Paradise Cottages. She quickly realized that not only was she on Alister Street but the place where the cabbie had dropped her off was Paradise Cabins. The sign in front of several one-room buildings across the street said so. The cabbie had misunderstood her. According to her map, her true destination was on the opposite end of town, and though she would have loved to walk the streets of her new home (Paradise Cottages was only a couple of miles away), her sacks were a bit too much to carry such distance. A small, brown sign with a green trolley car etched in its center was directly across the road. *Trolley Stop* the sign read.

"Can I help you? You look lost."

Janine looked over her shoulder at a tall, slender woman whose very long, black hair covered much of the front of her body. "I'm new in town," Janine said, not really knowing what else to say.

"Yes," the lady said. "You don't have to be a fortune teller to see that." She smiled a perfect set of bright white teeth.

Behind and above the tall woman was a shop, presumably hers. The sign above the front door read: *Marcy Can See Your Future*.

"Marcy?" Janine asked.

"Yes. You have the gift of E.S.P.," she grinned pleasantly and turned to her shop sign. "And the gift of logical deduction."

"I am…"

"No. Don't tell me." Marcy the fortune teller whipped around dramatically to face Janine, closed her eyes and held her hands out toward Janine's shoulders. "You are a traveler looking for a place to stay." She opened her eyes with a smile.

"That obvious?" Janine returned the smile.

"I saw the taxi cab drop you off." Both women chuckled. "Would you like something to drink?" Marcy said and bent forward to grab one of Janine's bags. Her long hair touched the sidewalk behind the bag.

"Yes." Janine picked up the other bag. "Yes. That's very nice of you."

And that is how Janine made her first new friend in her long imagined paradise where a total stranger helped another, no strings attached—just a simple, friendly gesture that is common to inhabitants of paradises. Loneliness, for the moment, was forgotten.

The two women talked for more than thirty minutes but could have gone on for hours. It was Marcy who brought the conversation to a close.

"You want to catch a luau?" the fortune teller said, her hands on the end table that separated the two chairs in which the women sat.

"Well, I need to check in with my landlord. I think he's expecting me today." Janine thought the inside of Marcy's shop was just as she'd imagined a fortune teller's would be. Dark. Lots of things hanging from the ceiling and door frames. A round table in the main room covered with black silk. A deck of Tarot cards. Even a crystal ball. And in Marcy's waiting room, where the two now sat, the craft of her alchemy was advertised heavily. What Janine hadn't imagined a fortune teller's shop to contain was a fortune teller who went against all of Janine's stereotypes, and Janine had many, most of which were a product of her Christian beliefs. Marcy wasn't creepy or crazy or un-Godly in the least. She was a single mother whose daughters played soccer for the local youth group but were currently spending a summer month with their father who lived in San Antonio. She was a very active member of the community and prided herself for having attended every community council meeting since she'd moved to Port A five years ago. Her activities also included protesting the construction of a proposed casino.

"Let's give 'em a call," Marcy said. "I can take you over after the luau or if that's not good for the landlord, you can always stay in my extra bedroom upstairs."

Janine thought for only a moment. She did not want to be lonely her first night in paradise and a luau actually sounded quite exciting. What a better way for her to relax and separate herself from the past than with a beach party.

"All right. Let's do it," Janine said and patted Marcy's hand on the end table. "Sounds like fun."

Close to sunset, Billy turned onto the beach road from Avenue G and looked over at his passenger. She was much prettier than the *Knight's* singer, though that guy was perhaps one of the "prettiest" men he'd ever seen. She smelled much better too: a peachy fruit smell that slowly consumed Billy's nostrils. The *Knights*, in contrast, had smelled like men who'd spent too much time sweating in the sun.

Steph had chosen a halter top with dolphin prints and a pair of red shorts that were invitingly snug but not too tight. From her earlobes dangled small silver dolphins that jiggled as she laughed. She wore very little makeup and Billy was glad. Beaches and cosmetics were not meant for each other. The purity of the ocean and sand made lipstick and eyeliner and rouge seem blasphemous. Her hair was pulled up into a single pigtail that fell through a hole where the strap of her ball cap connected at the back of her head. The ball cap announced that Pat MaGee's was "Your Surf Shop Stop." The guy riding a shortboard above the lettering looked a lot like Bottlenose.

Beyond Steph's silhouette, the ocean's azure light continued to fade and was increasingly consumed by the red-orange hue of the Texas sun which closed in on the horizon opposite the Gulf's skyline. Scant rays of sunlight that were interrupted by shadows of distant buildings pierced the driver's side window and intertwined with Steph's smooth cheeks, strands of light and dark blonde hair and the silver dolphin earrings. Her entire face twinkled as she turned to Billy.

"What were they like?" She smiled as she had been doing ever since Billy had picked her up. "Were they…knightly?"

"Well…I would say they were more Nightly with an 'N' than Knightly with a 'K'. Not too much nobility with a group like that. I'd describe them more like dark and surreal. They've got an interesting concept on life."

"How so?" Steph shifted in the seat so that her tanned leg draped closer to Billy's hand which rested on the long stick shift.

"Freewheeling," he said. "They told me that they had even considered naming themselves the Freewheelers but some of the band members thought that would associate them with trucker music."

"Trucker music?"

"Yeah. My thought exactly. What the heck is trucker music?" Billy replied. Steph let out a quick giggle. "They don't really have a home. They call Earth their home and 'freewheel it' across the country from one 'Earth gig' to another."

"Hippies?" Steph suggested.

"Kinda. Perhaps a better term would be New Age Hippies or Millennium Hippies or something similar. They don't do drugs and don't eat processed foods although the lead singer told me that if he had a choice he'd go with the drugs since any amount of marijuana could not be compared to the chemicals the food companies use in packaging."

They laughed together. Ahead, a bon fire blazed near the surf and glowing lanterns denoted each tent farther up from the shoreline. Some of the *Knights* were atop the flatbed trailers tuning instruments. Several dozen cars and trucks were parked along the beach road and several more were headed toward the luau from the opposite direction. Another half dozen advanced in a slow line behind Billy's VW. To Billy, this was a great sign that the protest would pull more people than he had hoped. The gathering was not to officially start for another twenty minutes or so and already more than thirty vehicles appeared headed for the party.

Billy parked near the flatbed trailers in the same spot where he'd dropped the *Knights* off earlier. They'd told him that they'd save the parking place for him so that he could "be right up near his freewheelin' brothers." As he excited the VW, Richard, the band's lead singer and leader immediately recognized him and yelled out, "My brother!" The three other band members yelled out simultaneously, "Brother!" Billy and Steph approached Richard who leaned his acoustic guitar against one of the four-foot speakers and kneeled to the floor of the flatbed.

"This is Steph," Billy said.

"Excellent, man," Richard replied, extending his hand which Steph took and shook. "She's everything you said she was."

Billy had not said anything about Steph to the singer while driving them to the beach. He blushed but in the waning light it was hard to detect. "Yes. She is…uh…and more."

Steph beamed brightly. The luau bon fire which had gradually risen in height fifty yards behind them cast an angelic halo around her head. She released Richard's hand and grabbed Billy's arm. She turned him, a little flabbergasted, and together they walked toward the tents.

"Hang with ya later, brother and sister," Richard added behind them. "We're gonna rock this place into the wee a.m."

"What did you say to him?" Steph asked quietly.

"I, uh—" Billy tried to think of what he would have said to Richard had he said anything at all. "I told him that I had this really cool chick…"

"Cool chick, aye. I guess that's the language he understands the most." She grabbed his forearm with both hands and drew closer to him. "Very nice of you to say so."

"Very pretty is what I should have told him." Her ball cap had tilted askew while exiting the VW and he straightened it, positioning the brim above the fire reflections in her eyes. He placed his right hand on both of hers and felt the cool dampness of sweat.

"Mí jefe!"

Pedro approached them with open arms.

"Mí jefe and his señorita. Buenos días."

"Hey Pedro." Billy removed his right hand and Steph released his arm as if she suddenly felt that the touch was inappropriate.

"No please," Pedro pleaded. "I did not mean to intrude."

"That's okay," Billy said. "You weren't." He motioned toward Steph. "This is Stephanie Drake."

Pedro shook her hand with both of his. "Esecutive secrary," he said.

Billy swallowed hard and turned to Steph. "Yeah. Uh, I told him that you were the executive secretary at the bank."

Steph smiled, flattered. "You've said much about me."

Billy turned back to Pedro. "How's the dish?"

"Increíble." Pedro smacked his lips. "The best crab cakes in Texas."

"We'll be the judge of that," Billy teased.

Pedro led them through an aisle of tents; exhilarating smells assaulted them from all sides. There were soups and stews and skewers and slabs of meats and seafood and vegetables of great variety and spiciness. From one tent came a sugar sweet maple and pineapple aroma; from another came a pungent waft of jalapeno pepper, chili powder and garlic. Pedro's cooking tent was last on the left next to the Budweiser keg tent. Billy asked for two cups of beer as he passed and handed one to Steph who swallowed half the contents in one motion.

"Thirsty," she said, wiping the foam from her lips and burping a tiny amount of air.

"Would you like a crab cake to go with your cerveza?" Pedro offered.

"Yummy," Steph quickly replied. "I'm starved."

"An you, mí jefe?"

"Of course," Billy said. "These look a little different than the ones you make at the restaurant."

"Yes. Like I say already. It is a secret Mexican recipe mí madre give me many years ago."

Steph cut a wedge out of the round patty with a plastic fork. The piece was so moist it barely made it from the plate to her mouth without crumbling. "Oh my!" Steph savored the bite. "What is that…it tastes like…"

Billy forked a piece into his mouth. "Like honey mustard?"

"Well, yeah. Sort of."

Pedro smiled. "It is a spice that is found in the Guatemalan rain forest. It has a mustard and honey taste but it is not. It's a little peppery too, you think?"

"Amazing," Steph said while dividing an even larger chuck from the cake with her fork.

On the table skirt below the dish of crab cakes Billy noticed a piece of paper tacked to the fabric. It was a flyer that read:

NO MAYAN FOR MY ISLAND

The lettering was bold and black and centered in the middle of the white paper. As he looked back down the aisle of tables, he saw that each table skirt around each tent's table also had the same sign.

Steph finished her crab cake and followed Billy's gaze. "No Mayan for My Island. What a great slogan," she said. "Who made that up?"

"Well, Mr. Presser here did." The voice came from behind them, near the beer table. Port Aransas police officer Jim Keadle approached with a cup of beer in one hand. "The kids over at MaGee's told me what you said this morning so I thought I'd get some more practice using my new computer and printer."

"Wow," Billy said and stepped closer to the officer. "They look great."

"Nothing fancy." Keadle reached for a crab cake. "May I?"

"Sí," Pedro quickly offered. "Sí, señor."

"I'm not much of an artist. Took me all morning just to figure out how to make the letters large and bold." He belted one quick, gruff laugh. A piece of crab cake dropped from the corner of his mouth to the sand. "Scuse me." He took another bite. "Hey. This is really good, Pedro. You gotta be one of the best chefs in town."

Billy clapped Pedro on the shoulder. "That's a good sign, my friend. Officer Keadle is one of our five judges tonight."

"And I am another," Mark Walker said as he strolled up to the group now gathered at Pedro's table. He wore a brown polo shirt with the name *University of Texas Marine Science Institute* stitched into the chest.

"Hello Mark," Billy said and offered his hand.

"Great signs." Mark grabbed a plate and served himself a crab cake. "I wish I would have thought of it."

"Keadle did them up," Billy said.

"But the slogan is yours," Keadle added. "No Mayan for My Island!" He raised his voice and repeated, "No Mayan for My Island! No Mayan for My Island!"

A small group began to chant. Soon, everyone around them chimed in. The slogan rose through the crowd like a wave. Even the *Knights* picked up on it and over the microphone yelled: "Come on everybody. Let's get it up. No Mayan for My Island. No Mayan for My Island." More than fifty people joined in and the slogan became a rising roar.

And as a perfect segue, the *Knights in White Satin* began their first set of the evening singing a 60s song entitled "Signs."

Sign, sign everywhere a sign
Blocking out the scenery breaking my mind
Do this, don't do that, can't you read the sign

The protest was on.

An island breeze that rushed through Janine's hair was all that she imagined it might be. The cool, warm chill, sea salt smell and gritty texture flowing across her ears and neck was a stark contrast to the moist corn mash sensations that permeated all of Kansas even on the windiest day. Unfortunately, those same corn mash memories carried the baggage of horror and sadness—of that insane day nearly a year ago. The thought of Lenny's death made it hard to completely succumb to the beauty of her new paradise.

Marcy downshifted her Jeep Wrangler as she approached Cotter Avenue. She turned right. A sparse offering of restaurants and motels changed into residential housing as they drove toward the coastline. A small, green, street sign denoted that the "South Jetty" has just ahead. An arrow on the sign pointed in the direction they now traveled.

As much as Janine had tried to erase them, she realized that *controlling* her nightmare memories' unexpected push toward consciousness was about all that she could manage. She saw Lenny's bloody face instead of the tiki hut-style home that passed on her right. A huge cargo ship moved through the channel in waning sunlight to her left but visions of the Albert-thing chasing her to the storm cellar interrupted her exasperation at the vessel's enormity. Having lived in Kansas all of her life, she'd never been so close to such a large ship, but instead of being enthralled with fascination, she temporarily wept. Crying was something she had not been able to control. Only time would cure that, at least that's what Beth Blanford had told her.

"Honey?" Marcy patted Janine's shoulder.

Janine sniffed. "Just something in my eye. Sand I think."

"The island breeze has a way of doing that to a person. Here." Marcy gave Janine a handkerchief. It was silky and black with red lace sewn at the edges. Janine wiped both eyes. "What do you think so far?"

If Janine told her what she was really thinking at that moment, Marcy would toss her out of the Jeep in hopes of never seeing the kooky woman from Kansas ever again. Instead she said, "It's amazing how huge that ship is."

Marcy looked toward the channel. "You never seen a cargo ship before?" Before Janine could say anything, Marcy answered her own question. "Of course you haven't." Again she patted Janine's shoulder.

"The closest I've been to the ocean was on my honeymoon," Janine said. "Michael took me to Myrtle Beach but they don't have big cargo ships nearby. Lots of fighter planes flying overhead but not a lot of ships."

"I'm guessing Michael is no longer in your life."

Marcy slowed for a walking group of people who appeared to have already started their party evening. Two of the group of six swayed into the road. Marcy lightly hit her horn. "Sorry," one of them yelled.

"He died a couple years back," Janine said.

"I'm sorry, honey. Any children?"

Janine delayed her answer. Visions of Lenny's death pounded for conscious release. She subdued the vivid imagery.

"Yes. He died as well."

"Oh…honey...I'm so sorry. Just tell me to shut up. I didn't mean to bring up bad memories."

Janine blotted a fresh tear with Marcy's handkerchief. "That's OK. Really. I need to deal with it anyway. You didn't know."

Marcy frowned in disgust of her own rudeness. "I could beat myself for that."

"No really. I'll be fine. See. No more tears. All gone." Janine handed back Marcy's handkerchief.

"You just hold onto that," Marcy said. "You never know when sand may blow unexpectedly into your eye again." She smiled lightly. "We'll leave that behind us for tonight. The luau will help. Let's just say 'To Hell With It All' and have ourselves a great time."

"Deal," Janine replied.

"Well, let's get this party started." Marcy reached between the seats and pulled out a CD that she loaded into the Jeep's console. "You like Cher?"

"Sure. I haven't heard something from her in a while."

As Cher began to belt out the lyrics to *Gypsies, Tramps and Thieves*, Janine realized for the first time how much Marcy resembled the dark-haired diva. And when Marcy began singing along with Cher while licking her top lip with the tip of her tongue, Janine was sure that a star was sitting right next to her.

Joel Canton watched the luau fire grow from a spark to a blaze as he prepared to launch his first cast of the evening from the south Port A jetty rocks. With the thirty dollar loan from Billy, Joel had replenished his fishing reel with new line, had replaced the broken globe of his lantern, and had bought some milk, bread, potatoes, a dozen cans of half-priced baked beans and a Milky Way candy bar. He'd stashed the remaining two dollars and change in a coffee can he kept under his cot back at his one-room, clapboard home—or as many in town referred to it: the Canton Shack. It wasn't a shack, though. He kept it pretty well. But compared to many of the high-priced homes around this summer vacation town, his was smaller than many of their garages. And he liked it that way. A small house meant little needed maintenance which meant more time to devote to the Gulf.

Joel was feeling particularly lucky tonight. The official beginning of summer was just around the corner and his "fishin' senses'" always fired on all cylinders around this time of the year. He unwrapped the top half of the candy bar, took a small bite, squeezed off a bit of the nougat between a forefinger and thumb and molded it over the fishing hook. It was his secret bait, guaranteed to pull in the biggest speckled trout that might have the misfortune to be in the vicinity of Joel Canton, master fisherman.

Though he was a good half-mile from the growing crowd on the opposite side of the pier, he heard the chant of dozens of people protesting the construction of the casino. Then the band began to play. Sometimes noise was a good thing—sometimes it wasn't. It all depended on how the fish were feeling.

He cast his line a good twenty yards into the darkening water which lapped gently against the jetty rocks. The sun had already dropped below the horizon and only a thin red glow remained beyond the dunes. Overhead, multicolored bands of blue to gray to black spread across the sky. Stars slowly twinkled into existence. The Big Dipper was the first constellation he recognized. He found the pole star by following the dipper's cup, down toward the Gulf water horizon. Lights from freighters and cargo ships twinkled in the black below the pole star.

How he longed to be out there again. He wished he were riding one of those points of light on the water looking up at the points of light in the sky, navigating by the pole star, just him and his boat and the stars. It was beyond a man's intelligence to describe just how that felt. Spiritual, was not good enough. Otherworldly, was too "Hollywood." It was like trying to describe Heaven: no one really knew but everyone had their opinion.

His fishing pole jerked and Joel let out a little line. He tugged lightly and the fish struck. He whipped the pole upward and felt the power of the fish in his fingers. Slowly he reeled it in, the combined force of the struggling fish and the Gulf current working against the strength of his forearms and wrists. All at once, the fight stopped. He'd lost the fish and that was rare. Perhaps he was not going to be so lucky this evening after all. He turned his reel to recapture his line but as the hook drew close to the jetty rocks, he saw that he had not lost the fish after all. A speckled trout the length of his forearm floated toward him. Its spasms kept it slightly submerged and as Joel pulled it up onto the rocks, its fight completely stopped. It didn't flop. It was barely alive. Joel wriggled the hook free and a small chunk of nougat and several drops of blood fell to the rocks.

Joel was not lucky. Of the last nine fish he'd caught over the last four days, eight of them had been ill or dead. He dropped the trout back into the water and watched as the fish struggled momentarily before flipping over on its side. Its motionless, floating body crashed against the rocks in shallow waves.

At that same moment, a horn caused Joel to look up and toward the shore. Over on the beach road, two jeeps, almost identical in size, headed in the direction of the pier. They were a good hundred yards from him but Joel knew who was driving both. The lead jeep had emergency lights attached to the roll cage though they were not turned on. Tall radio antennae whipped from either side of the Marine Institute vehicle. Mark Walker was driving.

The jeep behind Walker's had two people on board. He knew who was driving that jeep not so much because he could actually see her but more so because he knew of no other topless vehicle in town whose occupant's hair blew in such a long stream. It was Marcy the fortune teller, another in town whom Joel could call a friend.

The dead trout was gone, having apparently floated out of his lantern's halo of light. Joel turned off the lantern and packed his gear. There would be no good fishing tonight, luck or no luck.

And he was going to ask Walker why.

"When were you born?" Marcy asked as she turned down the volume on *I Got You Babe*.

"November thirty," Janine replied.

They had turned onto the beach road just a few minutes ago and were following another jeep that looked a lot like Marcy's. She'd said that the man driving was named Mark Walker. He was a marine biologist from the marine institute and she'd read his palm and flipped Tarot cards for him on a couple of occasions.

"Sagittarius." Marcy grinned. "That explains your positive outlook on life and your adventurous spirit to experience things beyond the physically familiar. Like Port Aransas."

Beyond the physically familiar, Janine thought. If Marcy only knew just how right she was.

"Yes," Janine said. "I guess you might say that. I *have* become much more adventurous in the last year or so."

"You religious," Marcy said as a statement rather than a question. She turned toward Janine, her hair flailing in twisted strands about her face.

"You mean do I believe in God?"

Marcy's grin spread into a smile. "Don't we all?"

Again, Marcy broke Janine's fortune teller stereotyping. She'd never considered that mystics could believe in God. "Well, I've met a few who don't." She thought of Albert Stine.

"I know what you mean," Marcy intervened. "People just don't want to believe." She shifted down a gear as the jeep approached the pier and a crowd that looked to be in the hundreds. "For instance, I can tell a person many things about them just from one piece of information: the day they were born."

"That's information that only God knows."

"You are religious," Marcy said. "That is good. Where we are headed needs lots of faith and a heavy dose of belief for us to survive."

Janine looked around at the small tent city, the lights, and the white foam of crashing waves in a background of watery darkness.

Marcy patted Janine's hand as she parked. "No, dear. Not the luau. Our future. Mankind's future. We are headed into the Age of Aquarius and only the faithful will survive."

Marcy exited the jeep as Janine sat there, wondering why Marcy had felt the need to tell her such things. There were dots that Marcy, apparently, wanted her to connect but she could not find the right path. Somehow, Marcy sensed in Janine the one thing that had saved her from the beast a year ago. Faith. Marcy was a fortune teller—a mystic. She told people things they wanted to hear as a gimmick and she made a living doing so. No crystal ball could tell the future and no lifeline could describe the past. It was all just gimmick. But Marcy *did* know that Janine was a religious person and that her faith had guided her to safety so far. Whatever the Age of Aquarius was, Marcy certainly believed that Janine would be a part of it.

Marcy walked to the passenger side of the jeep and grabbed Janine's hand. "You are a survivor, my dear." A chill raced along Janine's arm. Marcy had said exactly what she was thinking. She was a survivor—a survivor in paradise.

Together, they approached the tents at the gathering's top end where a band full of blonde-haired, scantily-clothed young men gyrated to *Proud Mary* atop a tractor trailer flatbed. Janine's father had driven a tractor trailer flatbed to haul construction materials when she was just a kid but she'd never seen one used as a musician's stage before.

Rollin...rollin...rollin on a river...

Marcy sang along with the band as the women made their way among the tents. The crowd was shoulder-to-shoulder as dozens of people piled chunks of food onto plates and into mouths. Around a huge bonfire closer to the water, at least a hundred people drank and danced. Teenagers ran through the dark surf behind the dancers, chasing footballs and Frisbees, though Janine wondered how in world they could see what they were throwing or catching.

"Try this," Marcy said. She handed Janine a plate of shrimp and chunks of pineapple. A light red sauce was drizzled on and around the food.

"Oh my," Janine exclaimed. "This is…Wow."

"Tasty?" the man behind the tent table asked.

"Yes. Very, very."

Marcy introduced Janine to Pedro Melindez. "He is the chef at a restaurant just down the street from me," she said. "One of the best we have in town."

"Gracias, Marcy." Pedro nodded his head with respect. "I have much more. Would you like to try my crab cake?"

Janine had never eaten crab before. In fact, up until the moment she placed the Caribbean shrimp into her mouth, she'd eaten seafood on very few occasions, one being the evening she and Michael had arrived in Myrtle Beach for their honeymoon. She'd not been too crazy about the seafood buffet that night. The shrimp had been particularly unpleasant. But what rolled across her lips and tongue now was pure delight, having only the faintest hint of the sea distributed among the wonderful flavors of pineapple, coconut, and what she thought was a peachy, appley, orangey flavor with a hint of pepper scattered throughout. She took the forkful of crab cake that the chef now offered to her. Again, her taste buds exploded with delight. Though the crab cakes had more of a seafood taste, the flavor was in stark contrast to the shrimp she'd just swallowed. The mixture of the two tastes, one right after the other, was very pleasant.

"Wow," Janine said again. Pedro smiled, proudly.

"Are you visiting our tiny island?" Pedro asked.

"Just arrived today." Janine swallowed. She realized that Marcy was not standing near her any more. A group of five men stopped at the tent and plucked shrimp and crab cakes from the serving dishes. "Hey, baby. Wanna dance?" the ugliest of the five said. They were all unshaven and looked as if they had not washed in weeks. Janine guessed they ranged in ages between forty and sixty. They smelled fishy and this turned Janine's stomach and her attention away from the food and the men.

"Beat it scalawags," Marcy said, appearing from behind Janine with two cups of beer. "Go jump in a lake…or perhaps an ocean would be better for the likes of you."

The ugliest man elbowed his nearly-as-ugly counterpart. "Hey. If it ain't the wacko gypsy. You cast a spell on us, Madame Ruminski?"

Marcy handed Janine both beers then slipped a pair of fingers into her halter top between her breasts. She pulled out a pinch of sand and tossed it at the ugliest man. "Your catch in the sea tomorrow will deny you food or funds. Now, back off before I take your boats, too."

Janine gawked at Marcy's incantation and was even more surprised when the ugliest man flinched backward, tripping over his nearly-as-ugly companion and into the arms of the three other men whose mouths hung open with shrimp sauce smeared across their lips. The men seemed to want to run but did not want to show the apparent fear that suddenly resided in them. Instead, all five quickly sauntered away, keeping an eye on Marcy until they disappeared into the crowd.

Janine's expression remained quizzical. Marcy turned to her and belted out two short laughs. "Haa…Haa!" Pedro joined in almost simultaneously. Janine sipped from her beer to wash down the remains of the crab cake and grinned but didn't laugh. Marcy took the other cup of beer but didn't drink from it until her laughter had subsided.

"Amazing what a little sand and a whole lot of superstition can do for a lady," Marcy said. "Those toads are infamous for causing trouble on the island. Don't let their rudeness turn you off to our little slice of heaven."

"Sí. They are problemas," Pedro agreed. "They cause trouble even at the Surf Side."

"Surf Side?" Janine questioned, taking another sip of beer and looking toward the crashing waves. Marcy had downed her entire cup.

"Where he works," Marcy said atop a tiny burp. "Oh, pardon me."

"Well, thank you, Pedro, for a wonderful little meal," Janine said. "And to answer your question—before we were so rudely interrupted—I am from Kansas and I am new in town. I think that I will be staying here for quite some time."

Pedro shook her hand with both of his. "We are happy to have you. I would be glad to show you mí isla. Yes?"

Janine looked puzzled. Marcy translated. "He wants to show you around his island."

"Oh, yes, thank you," Janine said, her hand still clasped between Pedro's. Of the few Spanish words she knew, thanks was one of them. "Gracias. Gracias."

Marcy chaperoned Janine toward the bonfire, around a crowded sandy dance floor full of gyrating bodies that had found some way to dance to AC-DC's *Back in Black*, then strolled to the left toward the pier away from many of the partiers. She stopped, slipped off her sandals, and stepped ankle-deep into shallow waves. Without a word, Janine followed.

"Beautiful, isn't it?" Marcy stared at the clear, black sky. "And to think we are all a part of that wonderful vastness. Just starlight, Janine. We are all just starlight." She pointed upward toward the constellation of Gemini. "The twins are bright tonight. They always help guide us through the summer months. They helped guide you here tonight."

Janine had been following her finger, trying to understand where Marcy was pointing. "What do you mean?"

"The stars guide all that we do." Marcy lowered her gaze and looked into Janine's eyes. "We all have a destiny, Janine. It is written before we are born. The stars are our escorts on this wonderful journey. You have been through much. I can see it in your eyes and you've come to this island looking for solace, for peace, for rest." Marcy hesitated for a moment, perhaps in search of Janine's soul. "Do you believe that it was coincidence that you were dropped off at my doorstep? Do you believe that it is coincidence that you are here with me tonight at this wonderful luau? Will it be coincidence when, tomorrow, you will become entangled in the nets of this island?"

Janine had to look away from Marcy's stare. She turned her attention back toward the stars. "I don't understand," she said under her breath.

Marcy placed her hand on Janine's shoulder. "You have come to this island for solitude but this island is troubled right now. It will be tested in the days to come. It has great secrets to unveil upon the world, secrets that men should not witness."

Janine turned back toward Marcy's stare. She thought it was odd that the fortune teller talked about the island as if it were a living, breathing thing.

Before Marcy could finish her revelations, a voice from behind yelled, "Fruitcake!" It was the five ugly men. "Beware, beware, we're all going to die!" They didn't approach the women but instead continued on toward the pier. "Gypsy slut!" another yelled out.

Marcy turned back toward the water. "Men like those are the reason; men who have no understanding of what is good; men who only take but never give; men like those will be the end of us all."

Both women were silent for what seemed, to Janine, like several minutes. She became lost in the sea of brilliant starlight that reminded her of Kansas evenings just before harvest. It made her think of Michael and how he'd roll out of the fields, climb off of his John Deere and squat on the porch as the last of the heat and light fell across the western horizon. They'd sit there for minutes that seemed like hours and do nothing but stare into the heavens and sip fresh lemonade. She'd caress his shoulders and they'd kiss once or twice as the Dog Star blazed brilliantly overhead. No words were spoken. All that was heard were sounds of the light breezes brushing through cotton and corn, the occasional squeaky hinged barn door when the wind hit it from the south at just the right angle, their shallow, even breaths and the once or twice smacking together of gentle lips, and the tinkle of ice cubes in glasses of lemonade.

Marcy suddenly turned toward the pier, breaking Janine's reverent silence. Out of the gray shadows and into the bonfire haze strolled a man with a grizzly, silver beard. For a moment Janine thought it was the ugly man. He carried a fishing pole and a darkened lantern. He gazed at the beach sand as if being particularly careful not to trip over hidden obstacles.

"Joel!" Marcy yelled. "Hey Joel!"

He looked up.

"Joel. I have someone here I'd like you to meet."

Joel stopped, lowered his fishing pole's grip to the sand and stood there as if using the fishing pole as a staff. Marcy grabbed Janine's hand and led her out of the water.

"Joel Canton, meet Janine…" Marcy hesitated and looked at Janine.

"Bender," Janine added and reached out a hand to shake. "Janine Bender."

"Hello Marcy," Joel said, acknowledging Janine with a quick gaze but no handshake. "The fishing is not getting any better." His voice had the sharp edge of concern.

"I've heard," Marcy said as Janine lowered her hand. "It'll pass though. We're just going through one of those…things."

Janine could not see him very well in the limited light but what was unveiled of Joel Canton was a man who was not much cleaner in appearance than the five men who had accosted her earlier. His face, though, had a warm, gentle appeal that was ruggedly handsome. What really sparked her curiosity about the fisherman was what she saw in his eyes. There seemed to be a world of suffering attached to his pupils, as if his life had gone nowhere near as planned. The tiny, sparkled, firelight reflections added a strange, inspirational hope to the weary gaze. Like herself, this man had ended up at this moment in time, having never meant to make this particular journey. Was it coincidence that had brought her to the island? Was it coincidence that had her standing in wet sand, looking at a strangely magnetizing man whom she'd never met before? Or was it fate, like Marcy had implied?

Joel, without a particular reason, let his fishing pole drop to the sand and offered his freed hand to Janine which she took. "Joel Canton," he said. "Do I know you?"

Janine curtly smiled. “I really don’t think so. I’ve never been to Port Aransas before.”

“I see.” Joel looked puzzled. “Janine, did you say?” A very small curl of a smile hinted at the right edge of his mouth.

“Uh-huh.”

Joel continued shaking her hand, gently, as if it were fragile. She felt a rough sandy grip that was firm and strong, one that might easily wrestle the largest fish out of water, yet his fingers around hers offered a pleasant sensation of kindness.

“I…uh,” Joel said, releasing the handshake. “I saw Walker heading in and wanted to ask him about the fish.” He turned his attention to Marcy but kept peering at Janine from the corner of his right eye, as if her image would suddenly disappear if he looked away.

“Let’s go together,” Marcy said, smiling, and apparently happy with what she saw in Joel’s expressive response. She picked up his fishing pole and Joel reached his hand forward to grab it. “I’ll carry it for you and the lantern too if you wish.”

They were his greatest means for life support and in every other circumstance Joel would have fought hell and high water to protect his fishing pole and lantern, but, almost hypnotically, he handed their custody over to Marcy whose smile now gleamed.

Joel’s senses swam in a sea of memories. He tasted the salt of the water and of his own blood that ran in a swirling mixture from his forehead across his mouth. The sun was unbearably hot that day. It was the summer of 1972. The sailboat’s boom had just swiveled into his head and he had not ducked in time. Bert Nookle was screaming, “Big Fuckin’ Fish! Big Fuckin’ Fish!” And then Joel had passed out.

When he’d awakened, the boat was near shore and a towel was wrapped around his head. Bert was at the wheel. The shark was in tow.

Unlike in the movie, the captain of the boat did not die and the shark was only twenty feet long, but still large enough to break every record from here to Galveston Bay. Also, unlike the movie, three barrels shot into the Great White had been enough to swamp and kill it. They’d hauled the shark to the docks over by the inlet where the Corpus Christi Channel would one day be built and a hundred cheers from fellow islanders greeted them. Bert had announced, “We got the son of whore” and had clapped Joel on the shoulder with one meaty hand. “See what the bastard did to my mate.”

No one except Bert and Joel's wife, Jane, had ever known the real story. It was Bert who had single-handedly captured the Great White. And the scars across Joel's stomach had indeed come from the shark but not because the killer had bitten him. He'd been careless in moving the shark out of the water and had slipped on the docks. The shark had fallen on top of him and two of its teeth had buried into his belly.

After that day, he and Bert's friendship had slowly taken a turn for the worst. Joel's shame had prevented him from revealing his own truth and Bert had used it as a strange kind of blackmail. The two had been heralded so much that Port Aransas history had written the Nookle-Canton story into the summer of 1972. Joel had gotten a new charter boat and a huge touring business out of the lie. The sudden success had prevented any revelation. The sudden success had driven him into the Gulf with his charters and his fame and his own sad false glory. It had also driven Jane away.

Bert and Jane left the island a year later. A simple note had been left on Joel's bed. It had been attached to a stapled compilation of legal papers. The note had read:

Dear Joel,

I cannot live with the lie any longer. Bert has asked me to marry him and that is that. I wish things had been different. I wish you had come home from the Gulf more often. I once loved you Joel but all you are to me now is a memory.

Please sign these papers and return to the address below. Please do not contest this. I want nothing from you. I have never wanted anything from you more than YOU.

-Jane
P.S. If the lie is to stay a lie then sign these papers quickly.

That P.S. had been the most disturbing. Joel had been convinced that Bert had written it. It was a strange kind of blackmail, one that would allow him to keep his charter company but lose his wife.

Bert died ten years later. It was 1983, the year of the Big Wind. A week before the high tides caused by Hurricane Alicia devastated Joel's charter and nearly drowned much of Port Aransas, he had gone up to Galveston to see his old friend buried. Jane had been there. She'd stood near the preacher clad in black wardrobe that covered every inch of her body. Her veil had disallowed his vision of her face. After Bert's death, she moved into her parent's home in El Paso. He'd not seen her since, leaving nothing but the memory of that black, lace veil from the funeral, a masked memory so strong that he'd forgotten her beauty and what once was their love.

Until now. Until Janine.

Joel was mesmerized by the resemblance.

The five smelly fishermen made their way past the turnstile, past the small bait shop and souvenir stand and onto the weathered boards of the Horace Caldwell Pier. They stumbled and cursed and annoyed just about anyone who cared to notice they were there. This wasn't the first time the five men had ventured onto the pier looking for trouble, and after their confrontation with Marcy the fortune teller, their determination was more abnormal than usual.

"Hey, Baby," said the smelliest of the five, whose name was Jacque. "How 'bout a five-on-one, eh?"

The person whose long hair had instigated Jacque's rudeness turned from the pier railing; the hair rained across his thin chest. "Pardon me?" the wiry man said.

"Good God, Peter," Jacque said to one staggering buddy. "You ever seen a man with chick hair like that? What a fuckin' girl."

Peter pointed at the long-haired man. "Hey bitch. I think you need a goddamn hair cut." He pulled a gutting knife from a sheath on his belt.

The man dropped his fishing pole and ran from the pier. Peter ran after him, knife held point forward and glistening under the pier lamp light, until the man bolted through the turnstile. He sheathed the knife and turned back toward his four smelly friends.

"What about that?" he said to them snickering. "I wasn't gonna' charge him for it."

The five laughed together then continued stumbling out toward the end of the pier. The walk held slim pickins for the five. Most people were over at the luau which, from the pier, blazed brilliantly three hundred yards across the water from where they stood. They prodded a drunk who'd passed out but they were unable to awaken and harass him any further. Other than that, only two other people were on the pier. Both stood together to the right of the T that formed at the end. Both were looking back toward the luau. Both were outlined in a dim halo of red-orange light that, somehow, had reached them from the luau's bonfire across the water.

The five smelly men turned together at the T and staggered toward them. All but Jacques stopped when the larger of the two men turned to face them. The smaller of the men stayed where he was, leaning on the railing, smoking a cigarette and gazing out over the water. Before Jacques said anything, the figure leaning against the railing exhaled a lungful of smoke. "It's Jacque, isn't it?" he said without turning and looking.

Jacque took another step forward. Either out of curiosity or just plain stupidity he replied, "So who the fuck wants to know?"

"He does," the smaller shadow said as he puffed the cigarette and thumbed in the direction of the larger shadow.

Jacque looked up and for the first time realized just how large the larger shadow was. The orange-red glow was at the large shadow's back, outlining it, giving it depth and breadth and menace. Near where the eyes should have been were two circles of scarlet red that undulated and swirled and pierced Jacque's gaze until the smelly man had to look away.

"If you guys are looking for trouble," Jacque said, "look no further." He turned to see that his buddies had not moved any closer. "Come on you faggots. These guys ain't nothin' but hot air."

And then the smaller shadow flicked his cigarette into the waves below and flinched, his chin rising quickly up and down as if he'd just nodded agreement to some unspoken question.

In one swift motion that was much too fast for Jacque to challenge, the tall shadow stepped forward, snatched Jacque by the neck with one hand and lifted him off the pier. Jacque's toes were ten inches from the wooden planks when his eyes fell upon the bodyguard's hell-red stare. He uselessly wrenched at the grip on his neck with both hands. Jacque reached around and snatched a small whittling knife from his back pocket, flicked it open with his thumb, and buried it into the arm of the shadow. Jacque's four companions stood frozen as their friend dangled like a doll from the bodyguard's grip. It wasn't until Jacque stabbed the bodyguard's arm a second time and the dark shadow walked to the railing of the pier to effortlessly throw Jacque into the Gulf that all four ran.

Jacque's scream could be heard for a full two seconds before everything on the pier went silent except for the footfalls of four smelly, drunken fishermen.

Billy looked over Mark's shoulder and out toward the pier. He thought he'd heard something—a scream perhaps. At this distance, all that could be seen was the pier's long dark line that stretched for more than two hundred and fifty feet out and twelve feet over the Gulf.

"I doubt it's the Red Tide," Mark was saying. "I've done samples from here down to Mustang Point and no buildup of algae is present anywhere."

Billy reset his vision on Mark who sat in the sand to his left. Steph sat to his right, stroking her toes through the sand. They were a dozen feet away from the bonfire. Several empty paper plates that were slathered with a mixture of sauces and sand, and a couple of empty beer cups lay at their feet.

"Chemicals?" Steph said. It was the first thing she'd added to the discussion.

Mark looked at her, scrutinizing, the way he would have done a student who'd just suggested to his class an unexpected but quite intellectual observation. "What makes you say that?" he questioned, as he would have a student who'd made such an observation.

"Rumor mostly," Steph quickly offered. "Nothing scientific. Just... ehh...conjecture." She'd become more relaxed after the three beers she'd had. "People talk. And inside a bank where businesses sometimes live or die by rumor, I hear the fear in many that the Big Spill has finally happened."

"I've heard that rumor," Billy said, remembering what Kale had told him earlier. "Any justification to it, Mark?"

Mark weighed his answer with more care than he had when answering Billy's suggestion of a Red Tide. The Big Spill was a rumor that had often surfaced in the five years he'd been studying the marine life around Port A and never had that great fear materialized. Everyone knew there were ample opportunities with DuPont Chemical just north of the island but never had there been documented proof.

"I don't think so," he finally said.

"But it's a possibility," Billy added.

"You know me, BJ. All answers are valid until there is proof to the contrary."

"Or no proof at all," Billy said.

"We've had this discussion before," Mark said, shifting in the sand and crossing his legs while staring out over the dark waves. "A lack of proof equates to mere theory. Without tests of the hypothesis, there can be no sound answer."

"Said just like a true doctor of marine biology." Billy looked over at Steph. "What do you think about that?" he asked her.

Before she could answer, Officer Keadle appeared behind them. He held three full cups of beer between the outstretched fingers of both hands.

Each of them snatched one. The off-duty officer then squatted and slowly sipped a bottle of water he'd carried in the waist band of his shorts. Billy downed all of his beer in one gulp. Steph sipped hers, a beer buzz already roaming through her body. Mark sat his onto the sand as if waiting for Steph's answer before drinking any of it.

"I think…" she sipped some more beer. "I think that not everything has to be proven to be believed."

Billy smiled half glad and half shocked. A slight chuckle accompanied his glee when he turned to look at the astonished stare on Mark's face. "Interesting choice of words," Billy said, patting her shoulder a bit more passionately than he'd intended. "Don't you think, Mark? I mean, just because you can't prove something doesn't mean it can't be *believed*."

Mark shifted uncomfortably. "Belief is a lazy cop out. You can believe all the rumors about chemical spills that you want to, but until my test tubes collect the samples that my microscopes find to be tainted, all that the believers are doing is making themselves and anyone who will listen to them, paranoid."

"I'm not paranoid," Billy said. "But I am worried."

"You think there's a spill, Billy?" Officer Keadle asked, genuine concern apparent in his voice.

"Not if the good scientist here says there isn't." Billy reached forward and gave Mark a hearty jab with an open hand to side of the arm. Billy knew this discussion always stoked Mark's compassion with science. About proof, Billy felt pretty much the same way but he pretended not to just to drive his friend's gullibility. "I'm worried about Mark though. He's going to drive himself crazy thinking about not worrying about something he can't prove or believe in."

All three looked in silence at Billy. Then Mark smirked, then chuckled, then laughed. "I don't know what you just said but I suspect you're right. I can't argue with an intellectual equal."

"Equal?" Billy questioned, sarcastically.

Mark sipped some beer. "Why don't we check it out tomorrow then. I'll take the helo down the coast and we can pull some representative samples from several buoy locations."

"Free helicopter ride?" Billy said and whirled his index finger in the air like a rotor. "And a chance to do some experiments with the good doctor? I'm definitely in."

Keadle laughed because he knew the men's strange sense of humor. Steph laughed because everyone else laughed and because the beer had oiled her senses.

The *Knights in White Satin* returned from a break and started their second set of the night with their own version of the Moody Blues' *Knights in White Satin.* Their licks on the guitar strings nullified any of the original artist's haunting melody. It sounded more like Nirvana meets Blink 182 and raged with the teen spirit of a rock show.

The subject of Gulf pollution and the growing fish kills transformed into a discussion of the impending casino vote that had been silently placed on Saturday's town agenda. Officer Keadle, though off duty, left the trio to settle a small scuffle that had broken out among some drunken dancing teens near the makeshift flatbed stage.

"No Mayan for My Island—I like that," Mark said. "I wish I'd of thought of it."

"Won't mean a hell of beans unless we can get enough people together to quash this absurd 'silent' vote," Billy countered.

"I don't remember reading anything about it in the *Jetty*."

"That is disturbing," Billy said. "I went to see Kilpatrick today but his secretary told me he was out."

"Out of his freakin' mind," Mark added, smirking. "He's got a responsibility to print in the public interest."

"That is what is so disturbing." Billy leaned forward. "What is in the public interest is what Kilpatrick says it is. If he's been lured to the dark side, he'll not jeopardize the casino and whatever kickback he's probably getting."

Mark leaned back and set his hands in the sand behind him so that his arms supported his weight. He unfolded his legs and stretched them toward the Gulf waves which were slowly crashing closer as high tide moved in. "What can we do other than hang posters and protest on the beach?" he said.

Steph let out a tiny burp. Billy and Mark grinned and looked at her simultaneously as if another line of wisdom was about to be revealed.

"Go door-to-door," she suggested, stretched out her legs and propped herself onto her arms in much the same way that Mark had. "I can go around after work tomorrow and the rest of this week if that's what it takes."

Again, Billy looked at her as if she were the smartest person among them. Mark said that he could cover a portion of the north side of the island near the marine institute and hit the restaurants around the jetty. Billy said that his surfer buddies could pound the pavement along Alister and Avenue G. Steph offered to remind those she met at the bank and then take whatever area that was not already covered after work. Billy offered to join her and she quickly agreed.

"Not gonna work," slurred a voice from within the sound of crashing waves which were now a dozen feet away. Into the dimming bonfire glow appeared CrabMan, one of Billy's surfing friends. "Not gonna waste time. They gonna be a casino. Not gonna stop it."

"Crab," Billy said, looking up at the thin man whose red skin melded into the orange-red flickers from the fire. "You're not giving in are you Crab my man?"

"Useless, Presser." CrabMan slobbered, his spittle making his Ss sound snakelike. Rally Panini, a.k.a. Crabman, strode into the middle of the group's half-circle without looking at either Mark or Steph. His scowl was menacing, as if he were trying to pick a fight with Billy. CrabMan had never called Billy by his last name. When Billy started to stand, CrabMan pushed him back down to the sand.

"Hey!" Mark yelled and rose to a knee.

"Sit down," CrabMan growled, keeping his gaze on Billy. "You no want this."

CrabMan could not have weighed more than a hundred and thirty pounds wet. His arms were thin, his legs spindly. He'd gotten the nickname CrabMan because his skin always looked sunburned. A thin goatee made him look a lot like Shaggy from the Scooby-Doo comics except that his hair was nearly blonde-white. To Billy's knowledge, he'd never been in a fight in his life.

"You want a bunch of mobsters to come in here and take our surf away?" Billy said, trying to reason with a man who'd apparently downed too much beer, too much smoke, too many pills or a combination of the three.

"Stay out of my buzzyness," CrabMan countered.

And then, suddenly, Steph flopped forward toward CrabMan's legs. "Look out!" she yelled.

In CrabMan's hand was a short, broken piece of driftwood about four feet long. He'd had it hidden behind his back and he now brought it out and lifted it high over his head as if he was about to chop a log in two. At the end of the piece of wood was the point of a polished nail, one that had apparently been freshly driven into the wood to serve as a weapon. Steph grabbed one of CrabMan's boney ankles as the nail point glistened firelight for a fraction of a second before starting its downward motion toward Billy's head.

"No!" Steph yelled again as Billy rolled to his left.

Out of nowhere, a hand snatched the arm that held the wooden weapon and in one swift motion, wrenched it free of CrabMan's grasp. CrabMan did not scream even though his arm went backward in an inhumane twist that should have broken it. He continued staring right through Billy as his striking arm was forced into his back. Officer Keadle's thick forearm wrapped under

CrabMan's chin and he held the surfer in a choke hold as he kicked the makeshift weapon into the surf.

"What the hell have you been smokin', Panini?" Keadle said. A small group of luau onlookers had gathered near the commotion. "Nothing to see here," the policeman said to the crowd. "The man's had a bit too much for one night." He lowered his voice and spoke into CrabMan's ear. "Isn't that right, Panini?"

"Screw you," CrabMan slurred.

"That's it! A night in the pokey is in your immediate future."

As Keadle escorted CrabMan away from the crowd, the angry surfer peered down at Billy. "Stay out, Presser. You need some other surf… before too late."

A strange crimson glow flickered in CrabMan's pupils, firelight reflection perhaps. This coupled with what he'd said sent Billy's mind in search of…

Lett's bodyguard—the goon at the bar yesterday.

Those had been his words, though they'd been much less slurred and much more threatening.

He'd had that same hidden rage.

He'd stared with those same crimson eyes.

Out on the pier, the big shadow that had thrown Jacque the smelly fisherman into the Gulf watched the scuffle on the beach. The smaller shadow puffed from a cigarette and blew a perfect circle of smoke. "Keadle's gonna be trouble," he said to his bodyguard. "Take care of it."

The bodyguard scowled, loathing the need to take orders from a man such as Chancey Lett. But, for now, it was necessary.

The illusion had to be maintained for a few more days, at least until the excavation began and the beach revealed its hidden treasure.

Joel found Mark near a tent serving fish kabobs shortly after Mark had left Billy's company. Janine and Marcy talked in low voices behind him, chitchatting about the people they'd been watching on the beach. Joel approached Mark from behind and tapped him on the shoulder.

"You sure that's safe to eat?" he said, scowling. Burgess, the cook that looked like Chef-Boy-Ardee, stepped forward before Mark answered.

"You got a beef with my fish, Joel buddy?" He pointed the two-pronged cooking fork he held in his left hand at Joel's face. A piece of fish fell from one of the points and landed on the pant leg of Joel's coveralls. Joel clenched both fists and squeezed hard.

"Wasn't talkin' to you, fat boy," Joel hissed. He kicked his leg forward to throw off the fish meat.

When Mark reached out and lowered Burgess's cooking fork with his hand, Marcy intervened. "Your kabobs are burning," she said. Burgess hurriedly turned to his grill and jabbed at the kabobs with his fork. "There's nothing wrong with the fish around here," Burgess said to Joel. "Why won't people listen to me?"

Joel's clenched fists relaxed. "They don't listen because the sea keeps popping up dead fish."

"The sea does that more often than most people realize." Mark entered the conversation. He finished chewing a piece of fish and swallowed. "Doesn't mean that there is something wrong."

"You got that right," Burgess yelled over his shoulder as he tended his meat. "My fish are the best. They don't float like yours do, Canton."

Mark stepped between Joel's scowling line of sight to Burgess. "Pay no attention," he said to Joel. "But he is right. There's nothing wrong with his fish or any other sea creatures being served here tonight."

"And how do you know that?" Joel peered over Mark's shoulder at Burgess who had found one of the luau's taste judges and was now peddling what he thought were superior cooking skills.

"Let's just say that there's been no evidence to the contrary."

"Every day for the past fours days I've had evidence to the contrary."

Marcy stepped up behind Joel and placed a hand on his shoulder. "Maybe the good professor is right, Joel. He's never steered the island wrong before."

Joel glanced at Marcy and saw Janine in his periphery. He suddenly felt very embarrassed that his anger had bested him. He'd not eaten a decent meal in several days and believed that his livelihood was dying. He'd had to borrow money just to get this far and that was something that had hit his pride hard. However, the sight of Janine eased his anger and his fear of failure. Jane had been able to do that, too. Ease his anger. Ease his fears. Just the sight of her had been enough.

Mark plucked a piece of fish from Burgess's table. The cook was too embroiled in his own self efficacy to notice. He handed it to Joel who did not take it. Janine took it instead.

"Aren't you hungry?" Janine asked Joel. She took a bite out of the one inch chunk of meat. “See—nothing wrong. It actually tastes very good and I’m not much for fish food.”

Joel opened his mouth as Janine brought the fish forward. It smelled like coconuts. She slipped it into his mouth and he chewed, never once taking his eyes off Janine as she smiled and licked her fingers. His stomach groaned for more.

Burgess turned to them. “Hey. I thought you hated…”

Janine cut him off. “I know one of the chefs on the island,” she said purposely loud. “His name is Pedro and his food is…” she looked at Marcy who added: “el mejor de todos. Only the very best.”

Janine grabbed Joel’s arm and led him away from Burgess who scowled discontent before turning back to his food preparation.

At Pedro’s tent, Joel spent the next ten minutes eating better than he had in many weeks. Pedro had kept the food hot and fresh and plentiful. Joel didn’t say a word until he’d had his fill. Mark had not accompanied them, saying that he’d had to get back to the institute to continue monitoring the sea for contaminants “to keep the island safe” as he’d put it.

“I guess Mark was right,” Joel said, belched silently and excused himself. “Nothing at all wrong with this. It must be my bad luck.” He looked at Janine and measured his words. “But I think the ole’ tide is turning.”

Marcy nibbled on a few hunks of pineapple. “Since you guys like Pedro’s cooking so much, why don’t you check out his restaurant. If you think this is good, the food *there* is much more delicioso.”

“Gracias,” Pedro said. “It would be my pleasure.”

“And my treat,” Marcy said. Janine started to protest but Marcy cut her off. “I insist. Think of it as my welcome wagon gift to you as a new member of our community.”

Janine nodded.

“Joel?” Marcy asked.

“I usually don’t eat in restaurants,” he said.

“And?” Marcy prodded.

Joel looked at Janine and wrestled a small smile loose. “Will you join me for lunch tomorrow at the Surf Side?” he asked her.

Janine blushed but not so much that anyone could tell in the dim bonfire light. “Noon?” she said.

Joel nodded.

Marcy grinned, her task complete.

It was well past one o'clock.

Steph had increased her consumption of beer after the attack by the red-skinned surfer Billy had called CrabMan. It was as close to such brutality that she'd ever been. It had messed up her adrenal glands something horrible and the only way she had to stifle the tremble was to drown it in alcohol.

You need some other surf... before too late.

Before what was too late? She'd always assumed that the surfer crowd hung together, especially when it came to issues that threatened their way of life. But the look in the skinny red man's eyes had been as far from camaraderie as anyone could get. The surfer had meant harm. If given the chance, the surfer they called CrabMan would have driven the nail as far into Billy's skull as his meager weight and strength would have allowed. CrabMan may have been high, but Steph believed he'd been driven by power, menace and hate. A killer's instinct. She'd seen it in the red swirl of evil that beamed from each eye's pupil.

The luau fire was now nothing but embers. The *Knights* had packed up thirty minutes ago and had left with the assistance of Billy's chef, Pedro, who had volunteered to drive them to their motel using Billy's VW. A few stragglers wandered the beach under a night sky that was partially obscured by a moon that glowed one quarter full. The lunar surface seemed much closer through her beer-goggled vision, so close that she reached out with one sandy hand as if to caress one of its pockmarked craters.

Billy was behind her. He'd slid one leg to either side of her and his body now provided a backrest for her to lean against as they both sat in the sand, their butts wet from the licks of high tide that had rolled in an hour ago and had helped douse the luau bonfire.

"What's it like?" she said, her hand still grasping for craters that were miles above her fingers.

"Cold, I imagine," Billy said, gazing from her elbow to her hand to her outstretched fingers. Her milky, untanned skin glowed in lunar light. He wrapped his arms gently around her waist and she openly accepted his timid embrace. "Probably can't breathe very well either. But I understand that you can hit a golf ball a hell of a long way."

Steph giggled, lowered her arm, and wrapped her hand around one of Billy's at her waist. "No, silly." A tiny burped escaped. "'Scuse me," she said as Billy giggled with her. "I mean what's it like to ride a wave?"

"Well," Billy said, pausing for just the right words. "It's like this." Then he suddenly stood, drawing Steph up onto her feet as he did so. Her head spun momentarily as blood quickly rushed from head to toes. He took the arm that, moments before, had beguiled the moon with angelic grace and led her into shallow surf that licked at her calves. Lunar light revealed soupy, wave break froth at her feet. "Look out there." Billy pointed at the Big Dipper which now sat at the ocean's horizon. "Ever wonder what it would be like to grab a hold of the Big Dipper and swing from its handle?"

Traveling to the stars was a playful illusion that Steph had often considered but she'd never imagined swinging from them. Her beer buzz augmented the fantasy. She suddenly felt light on her toes. Waves slapping at her legs seemed to lift her though she was actually sinking into the receding sand.

"Here," Billy said. He ran one hand up each side of her body, gently stroking her flesh from hip to shoulder. An excited chill raced through her as he lifted both of her arms and pulled them out to her sides like wings.

"OK," she said. "I know this part. This is when the Karate Kid stands on one leg and kicks the snot out of the bad guys." She started to lift one leg and chuckled.

"If you can pull off a one-legged stand on a surfboard I'll fly you to the moon," he said and gently lowered her leg with an open hand. His warm touch on her thigh teased out goose bumps. "Now crouch down a bit."

Together they squatted. Four arms stretched in unison. Billy's chin rested on her shoulder. His cheek was so close to hers that the goose bumps racing across her flesh puckered up to kiss his. A rush of sea breeze carried splash and wind into their faces. They licked salty wetness from their lips simultaneously.

"It's like this," he whispered in her ear. "You are about as close to God as any one person has right to be. Do you hear that?"

Steph fell silent, her giggles withheld for the sounds that Billy wanted her to hear. Wind. Waves. Crashing. Splashing. And Billy's shallow breaths in her ear. She closed her eyes and imagined flying toward the Big Dipper's handle, wondering if the vastness of space smelled like salt water. When she opened her eyes she expected to see the Dipper's cup within arm's reach. She expected to grab hold and swing from its handle.

And then Billy kissed her—lightly—a peck at the corner of her mouth. She tilted her head back into his chest and moved her mouth toward his. The kiss lasted a full minute though it seemed, to her, like an eternity. She wrapped her hands around the back of his head and he wrapped his around her waist. Together they stood in sand and surf, flying through the heavens and swinging from the stars.

When Billy's lips moved from hers, her eyes blinked open, wearily, knowing that to look at him would forever end the passion of the first kiss. She expected to see Billy gazing down upon her, his face silhouetted against the moon, his eyes searching for the desire that was certainly apparent in her own stare. But he wasn't gazing affectionately at her. In fact, he wasn't looking at her at all. His attention was guided toward the ocean. He watched the waves with piercing concentration as if they were the most important thing in his life.

The serenity of the crashing sea and its gentle tug at her legs was broken when Billy quietly exclaimed, "What the hell?" She moved her head forward from the comfort of his bare, hairless, chest and followed his gaze. The waves broke four feet high and thirty feet out. She could see them clearly under the moonlight. They curled and broke unevenly which was not odd for the surf at Port A. What was odd was their color. Under the stark contrast of white hazy moon glow, the ocean appeared red, almost crimson. The top of the waves clearly reflected an iridescence similar to looking through a glass red marble. It sparkled like champagne. And when the waves folded and crashed, a red froth rolled toward the shoreline. Steph looked down at her feet. Billy had already started to bend forward.

"What is it?" Steph said, bending from the knees beside him. She ran her hand through the water, following Billy's lead. The froth in her palm was pink and bubbly. She threw it away quickly, as if it were burning through her flesh. Billy sniffed a palm full of red froth then dropped it into the surf.

"Let's get out of water," Billy said not waiting for her to answer. He tugged her arm lightly, leading her onto the wet, sandy shore. "Smells funny. Could be an algal bloom of Red Tide."

Steph sniffed the palm of her own hand. It smelled like the air around the Ingleside DuPont chemical plant; it stung her nostrils and added to the intoxication she already felt. She wobbled, taking two quick steps backward in the sand in an attempt to regain balance and tripped. Billy snatched her forearm before she hit the sand and pulled her toward him. Her eyes drooped and slowly fluttered shut. The last thing she remembered before passing out was the overwhelming desire to take a shower.

Billy carried Steph to his VW and gently set her upright in the passenger's seat. He swiped the hair that had fallen across her mouth and nose and pushed it behind her head. He was certain she'd passed out from the alcohol. The algae from Red Tides was only toxic if you ate the sea life that was exposed to it—at least that's what he'd heard. He'd not known anyone who directly or through word-of-mouth had died from Red Tide.

But what if it wasn't Red Tide? What if the worst had finally happened?

What if the outlandish rumors were correct? What if the disaster that DuPont said could never happen—had? He looked at his feet, suddenly wondering if the flesh was still attached. It was. He looked at Steph's legs, touched them lightly as she squirmed under his fingers. No discoloration. All the flesh was intact.

He gently closed the VW's door and locked it, then leaned Steph's body toward the open window so that she would not slouch to the left and possibly into the steering wheel. When he turned around to face the ocean, he was shocked to see someone surfing. When he started to rub his eyes in disbelief, the polluted smell on his hands caused reconsideration.

Somehow, the surf had almost doubled in the time he'd walked from the water's edge to place Steph in the VW. The surfer rode atop what appeared to be an eight-foot wave. It was impossible, of course. There had rarely, if ever, been eight-foot waves along this part of the Texas coastline unless some tropical storm or hurricane had stirred up the Gulf. But there he was, too large to be a woman, silhouetted against the thumbnail moon at the horizon, riding the curl of a monster wave that did not break for what seemed like a full minute. The shadow of the surfer raced across the backdrop of the moon like a witch on a broomstick, the bloody red wave's sparkling iridescence falling to either side of the board as it sliced though the water.

Billy looked at his feet again—sniffed his hands.

Chemicals?

Hallucinations?

Too much to drink?

When he looked up again, the surfer was gone. The eight-foot waves had fallen back to three. The moon was still there, glowing near the horizon, and the waves still sparkled in crimson, but the surfer was nowhere to be seen. Billy waited several minutes without avail.

The surfer. It must have been his imagination, by intoxication.

Still, the ocean *had* turned red.

The bodyguard lay flat on his surfboard and pushed himself toward the pier as Billy's VW left the beach. Red laps of water splashed into his eyes, nose and mouth without effect. Once Billy was out of sight, he ditched the surfboard and swam to shore. Walking at the water's edge to the underside of the Caldwell pier, he found what he was looking for. Jacque the fisherman's body floated face down, and was tangled in a swirl of shallow water between the pier's pilings. The body's broken neck beat against one wooden piling as waves rushed in. The bodyguard hoisted the dead man onto his shoulder with less difficulty than Billy had carrying Steph to his VW, and strode to where he'd parked his black Hummer a hundred yards away. He tossed the limp baggage into the backseat and drove off toward the Port A branch of the Big Texas Bank.

THE CUBIT: PART II

DOMINION OVER THE FISH... THE BIRDS... EVERY CREEPING THING

When Steph awakened, several thoughts raced through her mind in rapid succession. The first was that she needed a shower. The second was that she was not in her bed. The third was that Billy had kissed her. She touched her lips.

She was still wearing the halter top with the dolphin prints but a towel, the color of Texas sand, was wrapped around her waist. She slowly peeled away the Velcro strap that held the towel's hem together expecting to see bare skin. She found that her red shorts were still on and still damp. She wiped her hands across the bed sheets and they were damp as well.

"I hope you don't mind," Billy said, emerging from a room to her right. "I wanted you to be comfortable but I didn't want to..." his words trailed off.

Steph shifted to the edge of the bed, swung her feet over the side and rubbed her eyes. Her halter top loosened and nearly fell off before she grabbed the knot and pulled it tighter. She caught Billy staring at her and when she looked up, he turned his attention away as if embarrassed.

"The bed is wet," she said, standing while she refastened the Velcro hem of the towel around her waist. "You didn't have to do that. I could have slept on the floor."

Billy turned his attention to her. His cheeks blushed a timid pink. "To be honest," he said, "that's where I laid you down first." He pointed to the tan, carpeted floor at Steph's feet. "But I couldn't just leave you there. You'd have woken with creeks and cricks in parts of your body you didn't know existed. I figured a hangover would be enough to cope with the workday."

"Oh shit!" Steph said, looking sporadically for a clock.

"It's just after eight," Billy said. "And don't worry about the bank. I called them a few minutes ago and said you'd be in a little late." He smiled and took a step closer. His hand reached for her shoulder and she allowed it to settle just below her earlobe. The gesture reminded her of his breath in her ear as waves slapped at her legs less than seven hours ago.

"I'll take you back to your place so that you can get ready. If you'd like, use my shower. I've got a shirt and shorts you can wear. It might make you feel better. We can stop for a quick bite downstairs."

Billy was a gentleman. There was no other way to put it. He was a kindhearted, considerate, surfer gentleman. He'd not taken advantage of her, had sacrificed his bed, had notified her workplace, had offered her his clothes and wanted to feed her breakfast before escorting her home. What man is his right mind would ever do that for a woman? Was one kiss worth all of that?

Or did Billy just want to get in her pants? Isn't that what all men wanted? That's how her two previous "relationships" had treated her. The phone calls and favors had come fast and furious until she'd given in. But *they* had been college creeps, and this was...well, not just any man. He'd not even minded that her wet body had dampened his bed sheets and mattress. He could have stripped her clothes off first but this man, who was not just any man, had more respect for her.

"And don't worry about the bed," Billy continued as if reading her mind. "It will dry. Won't take long either. This isn't the first time a body wet from the surf has slept in it." He moved his hand from her shoulder and patted his chest.

She smiled. "OK, it's a deal. As long as you let me wear what you wear when you surf."

This brought a quizzical look to Billy's face that lasted a mere second.

"Deal," he said. "But only if you go surfing with me in it tomorrow."

Quickly, before considering any other obligations, she accepted. An opportunity to ride on the ocean toward the stars and the Big Dipper's handle would easily place her job on hold. Though she'd be late today, she'd still ask for tomorrow off. Or perhaps she'd just call in sick. Mitchell Bone didn't seem to give much of a shit any more. Carol was doing most of his loans and she'd been relegated to gopher: an errand girl—a job she'd not signed up for.

Billy walked to his dresser, pulled open the second drawer and snatched a pair of boardies. From the third drawer he grabbed the first shirt on the stack. He handed both to Steph then escorted her toward one of the only two other rooms in the apartment.

"Hope you don't mind the mess," he said. "Haven't had much time to clean things up."

There wasn't much of anything to mess up, Steph thought, then saw the stacks of papers strewn across the desk in his lab-office as she passed it. The office was about half the size of the front room and was packed with stuff. There was the desk with papers on it, a computer and a printer on a second smaller computer desk, a bookcase with at least a hundred or more titles orderly shelved, a stack of boxes all the same size that reached from the floor to the ceiling in one corner, and a card table about four feet squared in the opposite corner. On the table was a small chest of drawers, the kind that tinkerers and craftspeople use to store small items such as buttons or beads or small electronic components. Something that looked like a starfish sat in the middle of the table and scattered around it were tiny screws, some thin wires, and what looked like small computer chips.

Billy snapped on the bathroom light and motioned for her to enter. "There's a new bar of soap and a towel in the closet there." He pointed to a door in the wall beside the shower. "Hope you don't mind the shampoo. It's the Dollar Store brand."

"That'll be fine," Steph said, consumed by the masculinity of his bathroom. "Thank you." She closed the bathroom door.

Pedro whipped them up a quick plate of huevos rancheros which Steph downed hungrily as she watched Billy and Kale in a concerned discussion at the Surf Side bar. Billy would put a forkful of egg into his mouth then respond to Kale. In the ten minutes it took Stephanie to eat all of her eggs, Billy had managed to eat only three or four bites. She handed her empty plate to Pedro, who quickly bowed, and told him how wonderful the eggs had been. "Could I get a glass of water from you?" she asked.

"Sí señorita. Un momento, por favor." Pedro plucked a clean glass from a rack behind the front counter and filled it from the waitress island. "Did you have a good time last night?"

Steph had not considered it until now. She was wearing Billy's clothes, had come down from his apartment and was eating breakfast with him. How that must have looked to Pedro and Kale. But she did not think that Pedro would be so rude as to imply such thoughts and assumed that he was talking about the luau. In truth, she really didn't care what anyone thought.

"I had a wonderful time," she said and smiled. "You are the best cook on the island—maybe all of Texas."

"You are too kind," Pedro said. "You come to the restaurant later and I will fix you something muy especial."

"More special than last night?" Steph smiled. "That'll be hard to beat."

"Gracias," Pedro said and again lightly bowed.

Steph finished off half the glass of water as she sauntered over to the bar. Kale was saying something about dead tuna and Billy was asking why.

"Nobody knows," Kale said as Steph stepped closer.

"Hi, hon," Billy said. "Kale, meet Stephanie Drake."

They shook hands and Steph could tell that Kale's mind was not open to anything except restaurant business. He politely smiled, then turned back to Billy and the discussion.

"I'm heading out with Mark today to test for chemical spills," Billy said.

"Dear God in heaven." Kale's face turned pale. "You don't think…does Walker think…?"

"He doesn't know what to think. He's pretty sure it isn't Red Tide but then again he couldn't say yes and couldn't say no. That's why we're going out a few miles to grab some samples. I think everyone wants to know what's going on."

"Businesses are gonna drop like flies around here," Kale said, insinuating the Surf Side but not saying so. "What'll we do in the meantime? Without fish, we're…"

"Dead in the water," Billy finished. "We have enough in cold storage to get us through a couple of days."

"What we have in the freezer isn't the big worry." Kale leaned forward on the bar. It was clear that he'd not shaven in a couple of days. "I think we both know that once word gets out, no one will want to eat anywhere near the Gulf Coast."

Billy stuck a forkful of eggs in his mouth. More than half his serving remained on the plate. "Let's just continue business as usual. No 'word' has gotten anywhere further than those in the business. We'll just have to hope that it's something short term and that DuPont hasn't gone and screwed up."

"Hope and faith," Kale said. "You can't really serve that on a plate with cocktail sauce."

Billy turned to Steph. "We gotta get you home or else the bank is gonna be absent its best employee for not only tomorrow but today as well."

Kale shook his head, knowing the conversation had ended, and headed for the telephone near the waitress station.

Steph left her cottage apartment a little before ten o'clock. She'd quickly changed into her neutral bank attire—nothing too dressy but a little more than casual. She noticed as she left that someone had rented the cottage next to hers. The light inside the kitchen window was on and the "For Rent" sign had been removed from the front lawn. The cottages were not connected to each other (which was one of the features that had convinced Steph to rent here) but their separation was less than six feet; wooden fences at either end of the narrow alleys prevented passage. A small lot of front yard accompanied each unit. Parallel parking was available at the curb.

After a drive of less than five minutes, she parked in the Big Texas Bank lot in a space farthest from the front door. This was Mitchell Bone's policy. The parking spaces closest to the bank were to be left for customers.

When she entered the bank, no one said a word to her. Not even a *Hello*. Everyone seemed extraordinarily busy. Carol, sitting behind her teller window, had a line of six people waiting for her. Barbara Wallace sat at her desk near the front door and was talking with a family of five. The children were well-mannered, sitting with their hands clasped at their waists as their mother and father looked over a papered stack of account information. Chester Kalimaris had a young couple in his office, probably working on a home mortgage. Mitchell Bone's office door was closed and Steph assumed that he was not in.

She sat at her desk to see that her computer was already running. The screen was Microsoft blue. There was no sign that it had been used but she assumed that Carol had accessed it—she was the only other employee that knew the password.

She checked her email. Nothing more than a half dozen spam messages appeared. She checked her telephone voice mail. There was only one message; it was from Billy and had been recorded just moments before she'd arrived at the bank. It said:

> *Hi Steph: Sorry I forgot all about setting up a time for our surf date tomorrow. I'm assuming the water will be fine but I'll find out more on that today. I'm not concerned. But, anyway, I'll call you later on in the day. I don't have your home number so I'll*

try you at work. Or you can call me at the restaurant. Talk to ya soon. Ciao.

Not concerned? That's not what she'd thought as he'd driven her home. He hadn't said much, the discussion with Kale apparently reverberating through his mind, the concern for his business and only lifeline in jeopardy. He'd given her a short peck on the lips, the kind of kiss that a son gives to his mother, not passionate at all and done more so out of absent obligation. His message seemed like an apology for his earlier lack of attention.

Steph pulled a manila folder of paperwork from her desk and quickly noticed that it was not as thick as she'd left it yesterday. She looked over at Carol whose attention was on her own computer monitor. The owner of Island Ice Cream was at the window. Her name was Misty Percy.

Steph thumbed through the short stack of loan applications in the manila folder; she'd placed Percy's there after canceling Bone's appointment with her before leaving yesterday—she was sure of it. The paperwork was not in there. The next four people in line after Percy were each loan applicants whose names she knew from Bone's appointment book. Each owned some business or property in Port A. None of their applications were in her folder either. When Steph looked up from her search, Carol was staring straight at her. What might have been a curt grin spread from the left corner of her mouth. Steph grimaced in response. A lack of sleep and a nagging hangover, coupled with the idea that Mitchell Bone had not informed her of any change in customer relationship management—and the simple fact that she hated Carol—was more than she could handle. Even though she'd been late this morning and even if her confrontation of Carol would make for some interesting drama in front of the bank's loyal customers, she stood, slamming the manila folder shut.

Carol, as if desiring the aggressive encounter that was about to take place, walked from around the teller counter, never removing her grinning stare from Steph. Misty Percy joined her at the end of the counter and together they walked to the vault where the door was only slightly ajar.

Steph rounded her desk, took three steps toward the two, began the confrontation with "Hey…" and then fell silent. Before Carol reached for the vault, it opened. From within emerged Chancey Lett and his bodyguard. They escorted a third person whom Steph did not know. By the way he was dressed, Steph thought that he could not have been a business owner. His clothes were ragged and dirty and looked damp as they clung to his body around the shoulders and thighs. A waft of dead fish emerged from the vault with him.

"We'll see you for the vote Saturday, Jacques," Lett said. Jacques nodded and passed Steph without a word. His smell grew worse as he bumped her shoulder, then he walked out of the bank, feeling the vacant space in front of him with both hands as if he was blind. "Miss Drake." Lett turned his attention to her. "How good to see you again. Miss Percy, here, would like to check out a security box today. Could you help us help her?"

Steph wanted to ask each of them a question. To Misty Percy she wanted to know why the town's favorite ice cream shop owner was now dealing with Carol for her banking needs. Steph had always been her customer rep. She wanted to ask Carol why she'd taken documents that were not rightly hers and why she'd been nosing around on her computer. She wanted to know who had given Chancey Lett the authority to direct business at the Big Texas Bank, Port A branch, when that was Mitchell Bone's job. She also wanted to ask him just where the hell Mr. Bone was anyway. Finally, she wanted to ask the bodyguard what had given him the right to take anything off of her desk. In the breast pocket of his pinstripe blazer was her toy Patrick the Starfish, his purple, pointy-headed face peering from the cloth as if trapped and wanting escape.

"Do you mind?" she said to the bodyguard. "What gives you the right?" She pointed at Patrick not caring that the man was at least a foot taller and almost twice her width.

Lett either did not know of his bodyguard's improprieties or mocked surprise. He pointed at the toy and opened his hand. The bodyguard hesitated, his eyes roiling with what Steph imagined to be boiling blood, and reluctantly pulled Patrick from his pocket. Lett snatched it from his hand and gave it to Steph.

"My apologies," Lett said. "I just don't know what gets into him sometimes." He glared at his bodyguard as if chastising a child for improper behavior.

Misty Percy interrupted. "I'm sorry to intrude here." She looked quizzically humored but annoyed at the same time. "I have to get to my shop. Can we get this business over with?" She snatched the security box key from Carol's hand and motioned for Steph to follow her into the vault. "I am sorry, Miss Drake. I should have known that the good service I've received at this bank is because of you. This woman's got issues." She thumbed at Carol who stood right beside her.

Misty Percy was an energetic young entrepreneur that reminded Steph of Billy. Sharp, eager, and unwilling to accept bullshit when the truth was a much easier sell. Steph smiled and led Misty into the vault. Together they walked to the wall where, yesterday, she had escorted Billy. Misty's box was right above Billy's. Behind them, Lett, his bodyguard and Carol stepped into the vault. Carol pulled the door closed.

"What are you doing?" Steph said. "Our policy."

Misty removed her key but had not yet opened her box. "Do you mind?"

And then the crate behind Lett and the bodyguard started to glow. A nearly inaudible hum, an undulating energy, seemed to come from inside. It was just as she'd remembered from the day before. The crimson glow from under the vault door. The hum.

"We'd like to show you something," Lett said. "It is quite beautiful and unique. The only one of its kind."

Misty stepped closer to Lett, halving the short distance between them. "Would you mind doing this at some other time?" she said, mounting frustration apparent in the way she held her clasped arms together. She looked down at the white plastic watch on her left wrist. "You make me late and I'm taking my business elsewhere."

Lett smiled, making his tanned face come to life. His dark eyebrows and hairline scrunched a forehead that had only begun to wrinkle with age. "This will only take a second. You see, I'm building this casino and I wanted to get your opinion on a piece of art that will be displayed inside. Being the business intellectual that you are, I think that your thoughts will be most valuable."

"Do you see that?" Steph said, pointing at the crate.

Misty followed her finger. "What? What is it?" she said.

"It's glowing—the crate."

Lett intervened. "Don't be ridiculous," he said. "Nothing in there glows." He looked at his bodyguard and Carol then back at Steph who had taken the two steps necessary to stand shoulder to shoulder with Misty. "Perhaps you're still a bit…tired—from last night. You were up mighty late."

"And just how the hell would you know that?"

"A matter of logical deduction. I saw you at the luau. You called in late for work…or should I say your friend called you in late. Billy Jo Presser, isn't it?"

"And that's none of your damned business."

"Calm down, Stephanie," Lett said, holding his hands out as if to ward off an attack. "We wouldn't want to cause a commotion in front of our fine customer here. Mitchell doesn't know anything about your tardiness. We'll keep it just amongst ourselves."

"Former customer," Misty blurted out. "Former customer." She stepped to where Carol stood in front of the vault door. "The door, please."

Lett nodded and Carol stepped aside.

Misty looked over her shoulder at Lett and flipped the security box key a bit too aggressively for him to catch. It clanged when it hit the steel vault floor. "And don't count your chickens, gambling man. No one on this island has given you permission to build anything yet. Whatever is in that crate you can cram it up your ass." She exited the vault and Carol pulled the door closed.

"Now where were we?" Lett said and rubbed his hands together. "Ah, yes. The Cub…" He stopped mid-sentence. "The crate," he continued.

"I don't care what's in there," Steph said, standing her ground. "You're not building any damned casino on my island if there's anything I can do about it."

"But you can't do anything about it." Lett motioned with a hand toward the bodyguard who went around the back of the crate and pushed it toward Steph. Lett quickly stepped aside as if the wooden container carried some contagion.

The crate grew a brighter crimson revealing a glowing star etched into its surface near its top edge. The hum grew louder. Steph wondered if it was just her imagination since Misty had not apparently seen or heard any of it.

"I'll scream," Steph said.

But she didn't. Her wide eyes and her confused mind became transfixed on the wooden cube that glowed and slid closer to her as she stood motionless. Her jaw hung open and a tiny drop of saliva hit the vault floor at her feet.

"Our Father who art in Hell," Lett said.

"Hallowed be his name," Carol added.

Without knowing it, Steph added, "Thy kingdom come. Thy will be done. On earth as…"

And suddenly, she saw a bright light.

After dropping Steph off at the bank, Billy headed for the beach road to check the surf before hooking up with Mark whom he'd arranged to meet in thirty minutes. He turned onto the beach road three miles south of the marine institute and parked. Few vacationers had yet to wander this far from the pier. A mother and her daughter walked the wet sand looking for sand dollars and shells. A fisherman stood knee deep in shallow waves casting into the surf. A small group of teens toed a large mound of sargassum weed that had yet to be removed by the town's public works.

"Whoa. Neat. Hey, finder's keepers, losers weepers," one of the male teens in the group suddenly exclaimed. He'd found something hidden beneath the sargassum. His four friends circled around as the teen lifted the nose of a surfboard from the wet sand and rotated it sideways to inspect the board's broken fin; it was nearly twice as long as the boy was tall. "Aww, man," the teen said. "The tail's broken." The only female in the group added, "And the nose is chipped, too. Lotta work ahead to get that ride back in shape." The boy nodded dejectedly, dropped the surfboard and the group moved on to inspect the next mass of weeds. In Port Aransas history, there had been many reports of small treasures found washed ashore within the sargassum. Billy suspected the teens were looking for their own small claim. The surfboard, apparently, wasn't worth their hassle.

He walked over to the broken surfboard; it reminded him of last night: a surfer on an eight foot red wave silhouetted against a nearly full moon. It reminded him of the surf's smell: almost toxic. He remembered having felt very weary, his vision blurring, much in the same way he'd felt when the hallucinations of gunshots and speeding cars had grabbed hold of him outside the restaurant and then again as he'd headed out of town to pick up the *Knights in White Satin*. He remembered the coin with the Wayeb symbol that the "corpses" had found buried in the sand. He remembered—coincidence.

Was this the board the night surfer had ridden? Was it just coincidence that, along the many miles of Mustang Island shoreline, he'd chosen to stop right here? Of course there was no way he could determine if *this* was *that* board. Hell, he couldn't even say for sure that what he'd seen had been real.

Upon closer inspection, he could not determine the manufacturer of the board. He was damn good at matching board designs with the many he'd stored in memory but this one was not in his mental catalog. The board was wooden and much too heavy for a man under two hundred pounds to handle.

He kicked at the sargassum mound expecting to find a mass of sea life now dead from the toxic red water he'd waded through the night before. All he found was a dead sea trout with one eye and two dead starfish. He stepped into the surf, cupped a handful of white, frothy water and sniffed it. Sea salt. Nothing extraordinary.

He walked several hundred yards up the coastline in the opposite direction that the teens had traveled, looking for dead fish, discolored sargassum, or red water—anything that could verify his experience after the luau. A seagull hopped on one leg across the wet sand, its single webbed foot stamping impressions, a tangle of flesh stuck to its beak. It moved toward him like a feathered Pogo Stick with eyes.

"Seen any red tides?" he asked the bird. "Anything fishy at all?" He snickered at his own weak pun. The bird hopped twice. “A simple yes or no would be fine.” The bird blinked, craned its head from side-to-side, hopped once more, then opened its beak and let out a wail so loud that Billy stepped backward to ward off a possible attack.

But the bird didn’t attack. Once the screech subsided, the bird toppled over on its one good leg. Its eyes and beak remained open, frozen in a last moment’s gasp for life, then it fluttered once before dying.

Billy cautiously approached, toed the dead bird then knelt beside it. Surf rolled in and filled the gull’s open mouth.

And then it occurred to him. He’d seen very few seagulls. He’d not really noticed since seagulls were such a part of the ocean beach tapestry as to be interwoven to the point of irrelevance. He looked up, across the beach, in both directions, and out over the surf. One or two birds flew here and there. There were no flocks.

Billy decided to take the bird with him to the marine institute but did not want to touch it. He returned to where he’d parked, grabbed the broken surfboard and a handful of sargassum, placed them in the back of the VW and drove to where the dead bird now bobbed in shallow surf. Quickly, before the ocean could steal his evidence, he grabbed a roll of paper towels, ripped off two sheets to protect his hand, ran from his VW and snatched the bird by its dead leg. When he returned to the VW, he rolled paper towels around the carcass and dropped it next to the pile of sargassum, then drove off toward the marine institute, the sun shining bright white over a birdless blue sky.

Steph had recited the Lord’s Prayer on many occasions as a kid. Her parents were not strict Catholics but the Lord’s Prayer had been one of the uncompromising ceremonies they had always held true to. Years of Mass had engrained the Words into her soul.

She remembered the part about the valley of the shadow of death and the part about not being led into temptation, but the word “Hell” was not in there. Neither was there any allusion to the Dark Lord or the Devil.

Steph chanted, “For thine is the kingdom, and the power, and the glory, for ever and ever. Amen.”

And into the light emerged Mitchell Bone.

“What’s going one here?” he said, standing in the vault’s doorway. “We just lost a good customer because of you knuckleheads.”

The crate sat inches from Steph’s hand. Her fingers tingled. She quickly stepped backward.

"Carol," Bone continued, agitated, his voice controlled so that the encounter would not create a scene. "You've got a line of busy customers waiting for you. I suggest you take care of them."

Carol looked at Lett as if needing permission, then strolled past Bone in her slow, methodical, unhurried way.

The bodyguard repositioned the crate to where it had been when Steph entered the vault.

Lett said, "Timetable has been moved up. There won't be enough unless we work through the day."

"Enough what?" Steph said. She noticed that the crate no longer glowed nor hummed. "What's in there anyway?" She pointed at the crate.

"The future Stephanie," Lett replied. "The future."

"You buying influence, Mr. Bone?" Steph asked. "You letting *him* buy the vote?"

"Relax, Stephanie," Lett said. "It's nothing like that. Tell her, Mitchell."

Bone hesitated. He looked out into the bank lobby where several people were now looking at the vault. "We'll talk about this later," he said to Steph. "Now…please...back to work. We've got a lot of new accounts today. The promotion has gone over better than we'd anticipated."

"Promotion?" Steph questioned. "I didn't hear of…"

Lett intervened. "If you'd have been to work on time then perhaps you would have."

Steph glared at Lett. Bone glared at Steph and motioned for her to leave. "Later, Miss Drake."

When Steph emerged from the vault three people were waiting in the three chairs around her desk. She replaced her angered, confused frown with a friendly, customer-service-smile. "How may I help you?" she said.

Bone, Lett and the bodyguard entered Bone's office and closed the door.

"We'd like to take advantage of the promotion," one of the customers said. "We'd like to rent a security box."

The University of Texas Marine Science Institute sat on more than seventy acres of prime island beach-front real estate just below the south jetty of the Aransas Pass Shipping Channel which linked Corpus Christi Bay to the Gulf of Mexico. It was uniquely positioned among the large range of marine environments nearby—from the Gulf to the internal bays and inlets—making it a preeminent research institute for coastal zone ecosystems. Ironically, it was founded in the 1940s by a scientist who had come to the island to investigate an enormous fish kill.

Though the institute had summer programs for its marine biology degree, enrollment was down this year. Billy had no problem finding a parking spot near the main building. He grabbed the paper-toweled bird and mound of sargassum and entered the tan brick building under a marquee made of metal and painted silver. It read: UTMSI. Inside, a security guard sat behind a semi-circular desk, reading the current edition of the *South Jetty* newspaper. When he saw Billy, he folded the paper and stood.

"Mr. Presser," he said.

"Hello, Dave," Billy replied. Dave had been the institute's chief security guard for nearly twenty years.

"What'cha got there?" He pointed at Billy's hands.

"Presents for Mark."

"You guys gonna find out what's killing all the fish?" Dave was an old islander, close to sixty, and had probably started as many rumors as he'd spread in his lifetime.

The seagull had stiffened. Its open beak poked at the palm of his hand. "What have you heard?"

"DuPont, a'course. Ain't they the ones what get the crap all the time anyway? Hell, since I been here there must'a been two dozen of them make-believe chemical spills. Not a one of'em ever panned out."

"Well, if it's any consolation, we really don't know what's going on." Billy had the notion to ask Dave if he'd seen any suspicious bird behaviors then quickly decided not to chance the start of any more rumors.

"Good luck with this one," Dave said. "Sure is a mystery, ain't it? And I love a good mystery. Like this fella Chancey Lett." He pointed at the front page of the newspaper. "What a mystery man he is, eh?"

Billy did not have the time nor the desire to discuss Chancey Lett and his brute force. "Mark?" He questioned. "You know where he is?"

"Out getting measurements from the instrument room on the pier. 'Least that's what he said he'd be doing around the time you arrived." Dave sat back down and flipped open the newspaper. "You know your way, Mr. Presser. Ya'll have fun figuring out the mystery. If I was ten years younger I'd be beggin' to tag along."

Billy smiled, acknowledging the old man's desire, knowing Dave had probably never touched a research instrument in his entire life.

The UTMSI main building's central purpose was for tourism and outreach education. The corridor walls were lined with examples of Gulf sea life and each was accompanied by easily read descriptive text. Painted onto a concrete beam that supported the corridor ceiling were the words "UTMSI is your Window on the Sea." Billy turned right at the end of the corridor, went through a set of double doors that connected the main building to the central lab complex and headed for the entrance to the research pier. Mark came through the door just as Billy arrived.

"You about ready?" Mark said. He wasn't much for ritualistic greetings. "Sargassum?" he added, pointing at the sea weeds Billy held in his hand. "I did a run on that this morning."

"I figured you might have." Billy shrugged his shoulders. "But I bet you didn't find one of these." He dropped the sea weeds into a nearby trash bin and unrolled the seagull.

"Dead bird," Mark said and lightly chuckled. "I wasn't looking for any but thanks anyway."

"Something's messed up with this bird." Billy pointed at it.

"Yeah. He got a foot bitten off."

"No," Billy said, annoyed. "This sucker did something I've never seen a bird do. It let out one hell of a squaller then collapsed, right there in front of me, as if it had a heart attack or something."

"Maybe it did. Birds have heart attacks."

Billy never considered heart attacks as being deadly to any species other than human. "Hmm…well maybe," he said. "But maybe not. You wouldn't mind running a test or two on it would you—maybe after we get back from our ride? I've got a feeling about this."

"A feeling? Now that's scientific." Mark grabbed the bird by its one leg and carried it without the paper towels to a lab room on the left where he dropped it in a stainless steel sink. "But I certainly can't deny my favorite roboticist his gut feeling." He smiled, which was a rare expression coming from Mark. "Come on. Lacey's got the bird ready to go."

"Bird?" Billy thought about the dead seagull.

"Helicopter." Mark's smile faded, returning to an expressionless norm that resembled a man who was always thinking about solving some problem: a concentrated absence that pushed eyebrows together and delayed acknowledgement of others around him.

The two men walked together to the main lobby, Mark wearing his usual blue jeans and polo shirt with the institute's logo stitched into the chest, Billy wearing the same surfer's wardrobe that he'd had on the night before. They waved at Dave simultaneously, and exited. As they passed Billy's VW and turned the corner around the main building, Mark said, "You know you should really think about getting yourself a new ride. That thing looks like it came out of the 1950s."

"More like 1963," Billy said. "It's cheap on gas, easy on maintenance and a classic. Besides, you know me. A non-conformist wouldn't be seen dead driving around in a new Jeep Wrangler."

The quip on his own vehicle almost put the smile back on Mark's lips but his concentration on the helicopter a hundred yards ahead kept his mind narrowed and task-oriented. The rotors on the Long Ranger sprang to life as the men approached. A woman emerged from the copter. She stood tall and lean and her skin glowed a deep tan that had been coated in lotion that made it look slippery. Her blonde hair had a long, think braid stitched around each temple. She reminded Billy of Bo Derek, but much taller with a slight touch of Hispanic heritage molding her face.

Mark nodded. "Lacey. This is Billy Jo Presser," he said, his voice rising as the blades chopped the air above them.

Billy and Lacey shook hands. "I thought Mark knew how to fly one of these things," he yelled at Lacey.

Lacey laughed. "Are you kidding? There'd be no safe place on the island."

"Good to know you, Lacey." Her hand slid from his grasp and she ducked around the front of the copter to the pilot's seat. Mark emerged from the rear of the copter and offered the open door to Billy.

"Everything looks in order," he yelled. "Let's head out to sea."

Billy climbed in and Mark took the passenger seat in front of him. As the copter lifted off, Billy was reminded of how few birds he'd seen earlier. Their scarcity became more pronounced as the copter gained altitude. They were in the air fewer than five minutes when Mark observed what Billy already knew. "Where in the hell are all of the birds?" he said. "No gulls, no pelicans, no anything."

"There's a couple over there," Lacey said, pointing out over the nose of the copter to a point near the pier directly below them.

Mark craned forward for a look. "What I meant to say is that there are abnormally small populations of birds flying about today." Mark frowned at Lacey who was not looking at him.

Billy also leaned forward, his knee clanging into the collection kit that held a dozen plastic jars, each resting in its own square pocket. The kit reminded Billy of the thing strapped around the neck of vendors who walked through ballparks selling cans of beer. "I'm glad it isn't just me," Billy said to Mark.

Mark turned in his seat. Sunlight flashed across his smooth cheeks, enhancing his youthful complexion. "You didn't say anything because you wanted to see if I would come to the same conclusion."

"I admit it," Billy agreed. "Looking for a little corroboration of an observation, that's all." Conversation with Mark always stimulated upper-level thinking. "And now that you've substantiated my observation, perhaps you will look at my one-legged avian offering with more curiosity."

Mark stared at Billy as if looking straight through him. Billy knew that the cogs of his left-brain dominant colleague had kicked into high gear. "Yeah," he said, absently, almost hypnotically. "Very strange indeed."

Lacey interrupted. "First bobber dead ahead," she said.

An ocean science buoy bobbed in calm water two hundred feet below the hovering copter. The number 12 was emblazoned in black on the side of its pyramidal structure.

The man with the receding hairline dropped a copy of the *South Jetty* onto Steph's desk. It had been folded to the second page. Filling the bottom half of the page was an ad for the promotion that Steph, until now, had not heard of. In bold title lettering it read:

OWN YOUR PIECE OF THE FUTURE
ENTER FOR THE CHANCE TO WIN 10 ACRES
ON MUSTANG ISLAND

Under the title, Steph read the details of the contest. Apparently, Lett was using his huge cache of cash to sponsor a contest that tied the rental of a Port A Big Texas Bank security box to a chance at winning ten acres of land yet to be developed south of town. The value of the land was estimated to be worth more than a million dollars, according to the ad. Basically, what a person needed to do to "enter" was to rent a security box from the bank and either store collateral worth $5,000 in it or add $5,000 to an existing or new account. Inside each rented security box was an "official entry" to an "official drawing" that would be held at the end of June. The contest was a win-win situation. Pay a small monthly charge for the security box, keep your valuables safe, increase a cash investment of $5,000 with a competitive interest rate and receive a chance to win a million dollars worth of real estate that was sure to be of greater value once the Mayan was operational. Stephanie assumed that the large investment requirement of $5,000 was meant to attract only those who had the monetary means necessary to do so. The bank wanted to increase its influence on the island but it did not want lower income investors involved. Only upper class individuals were eligible.

"Miss Drake," the balding man said. "We pooled our resources and have $5,000 to open a savings account...and to, of course, rent a new security box. There are no rules in the contest against pooling money is there?"

Steph did not know. She hadn't even heard that a contest existed. If her assumption was correct, if the contest was meant to lure only the wealthiest, then she also assumed that pooling cash was prohibitive to entering the contest. To allow pooling would mean a hundred low income individuals could enter with fifty dollars each. Perhaps pooling was allowed but within limits. In any case, she did not have an answer for the balding man or either of his younger, eager male amigos.

Steph set the newspaper on her desk and started to rise. "I'll verify that for you, Mr....?"

"Rodriguez," the man said. "Manny Rodriguez."

And then Steph fell back into her chair. Everyone in the bank except Carol turned toward Mitchell Bone's voice that thundered from his office as the door opened.

"That was not a part of the deal!" he yelled. "I'm flying her in tomorrow. She owns half the interest in this venture. We'll see what she says."

Bone emerged from his office, disregarded the stares and tromped toward Steph's desk. The three investors flinched as Bone angrily told Steph that she would be going to the airport tomorrow instead of Friday as had been previously arranged. He turned away without waiting for a response then left the bank, fists clenched, his stride, aggressive.

Steph had wanted to say: *But I'm going surfing tomorrow. Dammit, Mr. Bone. I was going to call in sick and go surfing. What the hell are you doing to me?* Instead, she maintained her customer service smile even as Lett and his bodyguard strolled from Bone's office, seemingly indifferent toward Bone's response or the multitude of eyes that were on them.

"Mitchell works much too hard," Lett said to Steph directly and to her three customers indirectly. "I think he needs some time off." He smiled that perfect white-toothed smile that Steph was beginning to hate. "I'll see *you* later." He pointed at her then he and his bodyguard left the bank.

"That was fun," Manny Rodriguez said, sarcastically. "Perhaps our investment at this bank is not such a smart idea."

"We all have our bad days," Steph said, absently tapping the ad in the *South Jetty* on her desk. "If you are still interested in entering the contest, I'll verify the rules on pooling." Steph didn't believe that Mr. Rodriquez was serious about taking his business elsewhere. The chance at a million dollars was too tempting. He was playing her like any smart perspective customer would. Besides, his two male co-investors had not said a word the entire time and had actually frowned when Mr. Rodriquez had threatened to leave.

"Yes," Mr. Rodriguez said. "I suppose you're right." He dropped $5,000 in cash on the newspaper that Steph's fingers absently tapped. "Put it all on number 123."

The stack of cash was tall, mostly made up of twenty dollar bills. "Number 123?" she asked.

"We'd like to rent out security box 123." He peeled an extra twenty dollar bill from his shirt pocket and shoved it toward Steph, then turned to each of the men sitting beside him. "Right?" Each nodded without a word. Steph was beginning to wonder if either of them could even speak…or at least speak English. Mr. Rodriquez had never intended to leave. Mr. Rodriguez and his amigos were gamblers. They wanted to place their bet on the number 123 even if it meant moving someone else's items to another box. And if there were rules against pooling, they did not want those rules to get in the way of their shot at a million dollars worth of real estate. Bribery was totally appropriate.

"You hold onto this for just a minute." Steph handed all the money back to Mr. Rodriguez. "Let me verify the status of the contest and of security box number 123." Mr. Rodriguez maintained his smile but Steph knew that he was not happy. She also knew that he would sit tight, his gambler's blood roiling, until she had an answer for him.

She asked Barbara Wallace who was still busy with the same family who'd she'd been helping since Steph entered the bank. Barbara didn't have an answer. Steph asked Deli Clayton and one of the newer tellers, Francis Gerts. She had not dealt with any money pooling issues related to the contest and told her to ask Carol. Instead, Steph went to Chester Kalimaris' door and knocked. Chester asked her to come in. A man and a woman sat in padded chairs near his desk. Steph asked to be excused then asked Chester if he knew any of the details about the contest. He politely said that he didn't and referred her to Carol.

Mr. Rodriguez watched in anticipation as Steph emerged from Chester's office. The wad of money rested in his lap. Beyond him, at the teller window in the far corner nearest the vault, Carol waited on a line of five people. Standing frozen for a complete second, Steph measured the situation. So what if there was a rule against pooling? No one had told her. Her job was to satisfy the bank's customers. She could not get in trouble for that. Regardless, anything was better than having to deal with Carol, to ask any favors from that woman—even if it meant being reprimanded by Bone.

She returned to her desk and asked that Mr. Rodriquez be patient with her as she looked on her computer for a list of open security box numbers. She found that nearly half of all the boxes had been rented when, just yesterday, the number had been less than a third. The bad news was that Misty Percy had rented out box number 123. The good news was that Misty had stormed out of the bank a half an hour earlier, relinquishing her box number and a chance at one million dollars in real estate to Mr. Rodriquez and friends.

"You're in luck," she told the triumvirate. "No rules against you and number 123 is open for business."

She pulled out the necessary paperwork as Mr. Rodriquez placed the $5,000 stack and the twenty in front of SpongeBob.

"Take her down," Mark said to Lacey, then turned to Billy. "It'll take about three hours to sample each of the buoys down the coast and do a point-source check inside the shipping lane."

"I've got three hours," Billy replied. "We want to be thorough—a no-questions-asked complete survey."

Mark nodded approval as the copter's floats settled in calm sea a dozen yards from the buoy. To Lacey he said, "We'll be here for a few minutes, Lace. You can go ahead and cut the engine." She did so and the copter blades' circular motion slowed. "Billy," Mark added. "If you'll hand me the jar labeled 12, I'll go ahead and collect the sample."

Billy looked through the carrier of jars. They were neatly arranged in numerical order from top down and left to right. He snatched the one in the lower corner and joined Mark who has already out of the copter and standing on the float. A light breeze made the direct sunlight tolerable.

"Nothing visually odd," Mark said, kneeling and pointing at the water. "No alga blooms, no chemical streaming. Smells just like the Gulf always smells." He took the jar from Billy, filled it with sea water, spun the jar lid tight, and handed it back to Billy who replaced it inside the copter. "I'm going to go ahead and check the buoy data while we're here."

"Can't you do that back at the institute? These things do have RF don't they?" Billy wondered how Mark was going to get over to the buoy. His jeans and polo shirt would make for an uncomfortable swim.

Mark stood. "Yeah," he said. "But there's nothing like getting your hands dirty." He clapped his hands together as if brushing off invisible sand. "Besides, I haven't done an inspection on this buoy in over a month. As the closest one to the institute I always think I'll get to it later. But I never do." He grinned mischievously and added, "Feel like going for a swim?" Before

Billy could answer Mark turned to his pilot and asked her to throw him the tow line.

Lacey shifted in her seat to reach behind her, showing both men how beautifully proportioned she was from the rear. She caught them both staring at her as she emerged with a coil of fluorescent orange rope.

"Not bad, huh?" she said to both of them with a smile. "The water. It looks just fine."

"Fine indeed," Mark said to her and caught the rope when Lacey tossed it to him. He walked to the end of the float where Billy stood. Both men knelt.

"I know what you're thinking," Mark whispered to Billy as he looped one end of the rope through a hook in the float. "We're all business. I assure you."

Billy stripped off his shirt and dropped it on the buoy. "All work and no play?" he whispered back. "You can do better than that."

Mark gently shoved Billy who fell backward into the water. "Hey. You're right," he said. "A little play never hurt anybody." Lacey sat inside the copter with her long legs dangling outside the passenger door. She laughed.

Billy's insinuation had embarrassed Mark and Mark had retaliated. These were small victories for two men who lived their friendship through a silent competition that continually measured wits, intelligence and, occasionally, humor. He swam the short distance to the buoy then climbed onto it. The buoy nearly capsized, but Billy's knack for balance, a skill he'd honed as a surfer, righted the buoy before it toppled. Mark tossed him the rope and Billy tied it off. "All set," he shouted. Mark pulled the rope through the hook in the copter float then tied it once the buoy was close enough to step onto.

The buoy was a three-meter discus that housed an onboard computer. Four yellow, steel tubes provided pyramidal framing and rose from a circular platform a foot over Billy. Three long antennae rose several feet farther above the top of the steel frame. Within the framing, the PC was housed inside a protective, water resistant box. Mark stepped onto the buoy and pulled a key from his pocket which he used to open the PC cabinet. A pelican landed on top of the buoy and looked at the men as if expecting to be fed.

"Strange," Mark said as he punched a series of squares on the PC's touch screen. At first, Billy thought Mark was referring again to the scant bird population, but realized that Mark had not even noticed the pelican.

"What is it?" Billy said, craning his head forward to see what Mark was reading.

"Wave data here. There must be something wrong. It's impossible."

Billy looked at the graph on the computer screen. "That big spike in the curve. Does that mean what I think it means?"

"Eight feet," Mark said, confused. "We had an eight foot wave here last night."

Billy's heart pounded; it felt as if it would burst.

"But that's impossible," Mark reiterated then noticed that Billy's hand shook. He looked up to see that Billy stared, trancelike, at the coastline which was at the horizon a mile away. "What? What is it?"

"I saw this guy last night," he said without looking at Mark. "I thought maybe I'd had too much to drink or that toxic water was making me see things."

"Toxic water?" Mark followed Billy's stare toward the shore. Only a few birds were visible near the Caldwell pier. Dozens, if not hundreds, usually inundated the walkway in search of kindly vacationers that tossed bread and chips and other assorted food scraps.

"Smelled funny, last night, and it was red," Billy said, almost hypnotically.

"When were you going to tell me this?"

Billy looked at Mark with distant eyes. "I thought I was hallucinating. I mean…" He hesitated. "I mean it was like the other visions I had. Unreal."

Mark patiently listened as Billy recounted his strange slips from reality the previous day, and his suspicions about the contents of the crate in the Big Texas Bank vault. When he finished, Mark said, "You got any evidence?"

"I'm working on that," Billy replied but did not reveal how he'd infiltrated the bank with his robot. He felt that Mark was trustworthy enough with the information he'd offered, but breaking and entering was an act best kept secret. At least for now.

"And what about the surfer you say you saw?" Mark asked. "You know who it was?"

"Not a clue. And I didn't stick around to find out. I had to get Steph home. Besides, like a said, I didn't think it was real."

Mark closed the computer box and locked it then stepped back onto the copter's float. Lacey still sat with her legs dangling out of the copter's passenger side door. Billy was unsure if she'd heard any of their conversation. "Let's get going," Mark told her then turned back to Billy. "Would you mind if I take a sample of your blood when we get back in? If there's some drug or toxin in your system perhaps I can detect it."

Billy stepped onto the float and Mark untied the buoy as the copter blades spun above them and the pelican took flight, nearly decapitating itself. "Yeah. No problem. Even though you aren't a medical doctor." He managed a smile.

As the men climbed into the copter and Lacey flew it into the sky, the buoy floated back to its mooring point where, nine hours earlier, Chancey Lett's bodyguard had ridden an impossible wave.

Janine had sworn that, after Michael, she'd never love another man. She'd certainly never loved Albert. Their marriage had been a lie from the start.

So she found it a little disorienting that she'd dreamt of Joel Canton.

Joel was with her back in Kansas. He'd come to her home (which was now demolished and the land it stood on sold) and he'd strolled through the front door with a stringer of fresh fish dangling from one hand and his fishing pole in the other. This, of course, was not logical since nowhere within a fifty mile radius was there a place to fish in Pickett's Crossing, Kansas. But dreams were never logical.

He'd called her sweetheart. It was if they were married. It was as if Michael had returned to her in the body of Joel. He'd even kissed her in the dream. Her sleeping heart had recaptured that fleeting feeling of what once was love.

And that's when Albert had appeared from her storm cellar room, a dagger with a long, thin blade clasped in one hand. He'd *risen* from the cellar as if floating to the surface from Hell.

The dream had been so vivid that she smelled the fish in Joel's hand and the Jim Beam on Albert's breath. And then Albert had attacked.

That's when she had awakened in Marcy's guest room. It was a quarter past eleven.

She'd not slept for ten hours since the first night she'd stayed with Beth Blandford back in Kansas City. In fact, it was rare that she slept much at all anymore. Memories of Lenny and the thing that had looked like her son haunted recesses of subconsciousness so deeply that, not only did she have sleeping nightmares, she often found herself fully awake and catatonic, visions of the Lenny-thing, the professor and Albert flashing like a slideshow in front of her open eyes.

"Are you awake, hon?" Marcy's voice asked from behind the guest room door; it was open just a couple of inches.

"Yes. Yes, I am awake. Come in."

"You gave me a horrible fright last night." Marcy sat at the foot of the bed as Janine rose to a sitting position. "Do you often scream in your sleep?"

Janine flushed with embarrassment. "I am sorry. I used to do it a lot more."

Marcy patted one of Janine's feet. She started to say one thing then apparently changed her mind. "There's a clean towel in the bathroom if you want to freshen up before your date."

Date?

It took her a second to remember. She'd agreed to have lunch at the Surf Side with Joel.

"What time is it?" Janine asked before noticing the clock on the wall to the right of the bedroom door. The clock's face was black and had Tarot card prints positioned where the numbers should have been.

"You have about forty-five minutes," Marcy said. "I didn't want to wake you. I figured you must have had a terrible nightmare and did not sleep well." Marcy stood and handed Janine a robe made of black velvet that was trimmed in red lace. "Also," Marcy added. "Your landlord said everything is a go for you to move in tonight. Mr. Agey can be a hell of a nice guy when he puts his mind to it."

Janine slipped on the robe. It felt soft and slick on the bare skin between her bra and panties. "Thank you, again," she said. "Really…you've gone way beyond Good Samaritan. I'm a total stranger. You don't know me from a psycho killer. I cry without reason and scream in my sleep. Marcy, the fortune teller, you're something else."

Marcy smiled and placed an open hand on each of Janine's cheeks. "And the King said, 'For I was hungry and you gave me something to eat, I was thirsty and you gave me something to drink, I was a stranger and you invited me in.'" She kissed Janine's forehead.

Marcy's knowledge of Bible verse comforted her. "You are with the righteous, Marcy. Your inheritance will be grand."

"If you're talking about life after death, I can wait a while for any kind of inheritance." Though Marcy was at least a dozen years younger, she seemed quite motherly at this moment. It was contradictory to Janine for a fortune teller that looked like Cher to quote scripture. But Marcy's care went far beyond mere appearance. Humility was her greatest strength—as was her gift for prognostication. Marcy winked at her. "Forty minutes," she said.

When Janine finished her shower, she found that her guest room bed had already been made and her two sacks of life lay on top of the black and red bed sheets. All of her possessions were still in the bags. Marcy had not dumped them out nor had she, apparently, gone through them.

Janine chose her most valued blouse from inside one sack. She'd made it from scratch the day before she and Michael had gone on their Myrtle

Beach honeymoon. It was made of soft white cotton and had subtle patterns of prairie grass and wheat stitched into it. She'd carried only two pairs of shorts with her in her sacks of life; one nearly matched the tanned stitching of the wheat pattern in her blouse. She slipped it on.

She descended the steps to the first floor that served as Marcy's shop. An aroma of coffee filled her nostrils.

"In here," Marcy said from a room down the hallway that paralleled the staircase.

Janine entered a small kitchen. This room, unlike most of the others in the house, was decorated in cool pastels. The sunlight from a single window over the sink provided great warmth, both visually and across her skin. Marcy handed her a cup.

"Coffee's on," she said. "I didn't know what you wanted in it but there's cream and sugar and regular milk if you prefer that. I don't have any sweetener. Never really trusted those chemical substitutes."

"Black will be just fine," Janine said and filled her cup from the pot on the kitchen counter. She sat next to Marcy in one of the four chairs around the kitchen table.

"You look wonderful," Marcy said. "Here. I've got the perfect island accessory for you." Marcy handed Janine a ponytail scrunchie the color of sand and water. "Made it myself."

Janine was thrilled. She thought it was the perfect accessory, not so much because it matched her own self-made top or the color of her gray hair but that it had been made by hand.

Marcy noticed how proudly Janine held the gift. "It's nothing really. Nothing like what you can do. Your top is beautiful. This came from a kit my daughter got for Christmas last year."

"How did you know I made this blouse?" Janine flexed the scrunchie between the fingers of both hands.

"Remember the sign outside? Marcy sees all."

"Come on…no…really."

Marcy grinned. "My mother was a seamstress. Retailers can't hold a candle to the precise subtleties of a hand-made piece of clothing."

Janine twisted the scrunchie and pulled a tail of hair through it. Her face cooled from the absence of hair at her temples.

"Looks perfect," Marcy said. "Scrunchies are a Godsend for us ladies with long hair who have to tolerate the Texas sun."

Janine sipped coffee while Marcy looked at her, adoringly, for several minutes as if she was trying to sketch every nuance of Janine's face into memory. Janine broke the silence.

"So tell me about...Joel."

Marcy's elbows were on the table and she placed her chin in her hands. "I thought you'd never ask."

Marcy told her what she knew about Joel, about his charter boat company and his wife that had both left him many years ago. She told her about the summer of the Great White and how history had placed Joel within its context. She did not know Joel's truth so her recount was much in the way most Port A islanders understood Joel today: a man who'd lost everything when he'd lost his wife, a man whom the island owed a great debt for the capture of a shark that could have easily killed lives and the livelihood of one of Texas' great vacation destinations.

"You'd better be getting over there," she said, ending her story. "It's just a couple of blocks away. I've got an appointment at noon or I'd walk you over."

"No, that's fine. Just tell me where to go."

Janine walked from Marcy's shop and stood in the exact same place where she'd exited the cab the day before. Marcy stood at the front door like a mother seeing her child off to school and waved. When Janine turned, she nearly ran straight into Mitchell Bone. "Excuse me," he said to her then walked up the steps to greet Marcy with a handshake. He stepped inside and Marcy closed the door.

They'd flown all the way down to South Padre Island, landing near each of the science buoys along the way. The round trip had taken more than two hours and a full set of twelve jars now held the contents of sea water from each of the locations.

The flight had held no surprises: no red seas, no alga blooms, no dead fish—nothing that sparked curiosity in Mark remotely close to the data he'd found at Buoy 12. Billy, however, had noted that the farther south they'd traveled from the Port A coastline, the more "normal" *his* observations became. The bird populations had returned. The public beaches were crowded with summer vacationers. There were sailboaters and jetskiiers, and parasailers, and surfers.

But beyond his visual observations, Billy had also *felt* different. He couldn't really explain it, but being away from Port A filled him with the sense of freedom, as if somehow, Port A had become a cage filled with unknown fears and the helicopter had freed the three of them from an invisible entrapment. Now, as the copter again approached Buoy 12, the fear-filled loneliness of a caged animal returned.

"One more stop and we'll head in," Mark shouted to Lacey. "Let's head out another mile or two along the shipping lane."

Lacey guided the copter out to sea, flying over a huge tanker headed in toward the jetty.

"It's the Energia," Mark said, turning half around in the passenger seat so Billy could hear him. "Chemical tanker out of Campeche, Mexico, headed for the DuPont plant. This thing can probably hold ten million gallons of trichloroethylene, enough of DuPont's sully solvent to mess up life along the coast for many miles and for many years."

A thousand yards past the tanker, Mark told Lacey to set down onto what Mark described as a water trail. "The tanker's empty so they've probably released their bilge already. There could be a few hundred thousand foreign aquatic tag-alongs. We've got a good opportunity to log the introduction of foreign populations into our marine ecosystem."

Lacey landed softly as she'd done twelve times already, and Mark asked Billy to hand him a metal case that sat next to the orange fluorescent tow line. Mark pulled from the case a glass jar that, Billy assumed, would more safely hold what might be found here.

"Grab the rope and join me outside," Mark said to Billy as he slipped on a pair of gloves which he'd not used while collecting the samples at the buoys. Both men stepped out onto the float. Mark unsealed the glass jar, tied the rope through the eyelets at the top of the jar, then slowly lowered the jar into the water.

Looking over his shoulder, Billy observed the defined edges of what Mark had called the "water trail." The stream was a good hundred yards wide from where the copter sat and narrowed to a point behind the Energia which had become much smaller at this distance. Multicolored bands of some surface slick twinkled on the top of the water: a prism of pollution.

"What the…!"

Billy turned his attention to Mark who was reeling in the seawater sample. As the jar emerged from the surface, a twenty-five-inch-long sea trout bobbed up from the sea with it. A huge air bubble followed. Then another fish, this time a tuna. More bubbles. More fish. By the time Mark had the glass jar in his gloved hands, the sea was bubbling up dozens of fish in a five foot circle. To Billy, it appeared that the water was boiling but no steam rose to the surface, only dead fish.

Then Billy noticed the contents within Mark's glass jar: hazy, red water, the same color as the eight foot wave he'd seen the surfer ride the night before.

Let's get out of here, Mark was saying. *Billy!*

But Billy couldn't move. He couldn't stop staring at the bubbling water that had now doubled in circumference and was not only spitting out dead fish in numbers, but had also turned a crimson red.

The Canton Shack's plumbing was a mess. Sometimes it worked—most times it didn't. Today it was cooperating but only in thin streams as Joel tried to wash the fishy filth from his body. The shower stall barely allowed enough room to turn around in. It needed cleaning. The water was room temperature as he did not have a water heater. It had broken earlier in the spring. Still, it was very refreshing, particularly since the day would certainly break a hundred degrees and his one-room house had already reached the high eighties.

No. Joel Canton did not have much. He struggled each day of his life. Each day he was one more bad piece of luck away from becoming Port A's most beloved bum. The only things that kept him in from the streets were that he owned his house, as small as it was, and his friendships with a few key people on the island. Marcy was one of them. Billy was another. Officer Keadle also lent a hand from time to time. Keadle was a great handyman and Joel hoped that he'd have some time to look at his water heater before winter set in.

Joel dried himself, pulled the shower curtain closed, and considered cleaning the stall. What if Janine dropped by unexpectedly? It was just a hunch. He'd not invited her but she *had* hand-fed him fish. No one had touched his lips like that in over twenty years. A touch like that deserved an invitation. But his "Shack" was such a mess.

He dressed in his only pair of jeans. Coveralls were not the clothes of a man going on a date. Besides, his coveralls smelled like fish and seawater. He had one brown, collared shirt which he'd never worn and as he slipped it over his head he realized how new it still smelled. He made his bed and put his dirty clothes in a cardboard box inside his makeshift closet—these, too, were chores he rarely made time for. But he kept thinking about Janine.

Before looking at the bedside clock that Marcy had given him last Christmas, he tried to guess the time: 11:30. The clock's face featured a magician and his hands pointed out that it was 11:40. Not bad. Marcy had given him the clock because, as she'd said, in that fortune-teller way she possessed, "You may one day find that your internal timepiece has busted a spring."

He tapped his forehead with an index finger. "Still working fine," he said to the clock magician, thinking of Marcy, and grinned.

He walked the half mile to the Surf Side, thinking of the perfect seafood dish he could order for Janine. He'd never eaten there—though he'd supplied the restaurant many pounds of fish over the past year—so he was unfamiliar with the menu. The restaurant's chef, Pedro, had cooked up some fine finger food the night before and he assumed that his full course meals were just as tasty. Personally, he loved redfish, but he didn't know if Janine would like it. She'd eaten shrimp at Pedro's luau table so that was a guaranteed winner, but, perhaps she'd want to try something different. But what? He was unsure. One thing was certain though, he was thinking about it way too much.

He arrived in the parking lot of the Surf Side and to his dismay, the Black Hummer he'd seen two days ago sat in the handicap parking space nearest the front door. The Hummer's driver had reminded him of Bert Nookle and that memory was the last thing he needed on his first date since Jane.

Candice met him at the door as he entered. There were no other diners. Janine had not yet arrived.

"Joel!" Candice said, surprised to see him. "After all this time you've finally decided to visit our little slice of the sea." She looked around the dining area where tables sat in empty solitude under spotlights of sunshine that streamed through the bay windows. "Really, the food ain't bad," she added. "I don't care what the locals say; there ain't nothing wrong with the fish. But you see how rumors can bring bad business. And we ain't the only ones."

Joel nodded. "I'm meeting someone here for lunch," he said. "Could I get a table over there." He pointed at a table for two built into the far wall away from the bay window sunlight.

"Well…let me check our reservations." She pretended to look in the book on the hostess podium. "You're in luck. No reservations. Follow me sir." She grabbed a menu and led Joel to his table. "Want to start with something to drink?"

"Not yet," he said, politely. "I'll wait for my…"

"A date, huh?" Candice lightly chuckled. "Well you ole' dog." She slapped the table in front of him. "I'll bring over a couple of glasses of water to tide you over until she gets here."

"That'll be fine," Joel said, trying his best to follow proper restaurant manners. He didn't care much for the sit-down, have a waitress, napkin in the lap, leave-a-tip etiquette of indoor dining. It just wasn't his style.

Joel studied the interior of the Surf Side and was impressed by the collection of assorted fishing artifacts that decorated the walls, particularly the large blue marlin nailed to the wall over the entrance. The thing looked to be thirteen feet across, easy.

And then, into his solitude and discomfort, someone yelled.

"Pedro don't know nothing!" The voice came from the kitchen. Joel started to rise but Candice intercepted him with two glasses of water. She tried to calm the situation.

"Everything's just fine, Joel," she said, setting the glasses on the table in front of him. "Just a little misunderstanding with a food order. Appetizer, perhaps?"

"No…no thank you," Joel said looking beyond Candice toward the blue marlin. Underneath the big fish, Janine walked in. "Here's my, eh…date now."

"He's concerned about fish," Pedro said to Chancey Lett. "He went to the ocean with de science man from college. But over that, Pedro don't know nothing!"

Pedro's back was to the sink. The hallway to the rear exit was to his left. He did not feel cornered until the bodyguard stepped in front of the exit. That's when his voice had risen.

"Calm down, hombre," Lett insisted. "We're just inquiring." Lett nodded for the big man to step back. "What I really came to tell you is some great news that concerns *you.*"

A paring knife rested in the sink within arm's reach behind him but Pedro had not even given the weapon a thought. "Yes?" he said as a question.

"I know you've been wanting to get into the culinary academy. I know that you need U.S. clearance to do so." Lett grinned like a friend might before playing some physical prank. "Your cuisine was so wonderful last night. I'm convinced of your ability to get through such a challenging program of study. I'll push through your green card quickly and you can start school next fall."

"You can do this?" Pedro said, his nerves calming.

"The only thing we need to do is make the case that a similar position such as yours can not be filled by an American worker who is willing and able to take the job. I'll serve as witness that this is true. There might be someone willing to do a gourmet chef's job, but few are able. Once you get the card, getting into school will be a cinch." Lett still grinned.

Pedro answered, "Yes," thinking that if he said *No*, the bodyguard would not like it.

"Of course we'll need a second recommendation from a respectable source. Your boss would be a superb choice."

Pedro nodded.

"Why don't you bring Mr. Presser down to the Big Texas Bank around, oh, say, six o'clock tonight? We'll take care of all of the necessary paperwork then."

Pedro nodded again, considered the bodyguard, and wondered how he was going to ask his jefe for such a favor. "I'll see you at six."

"Excellent. And don't forget to bring boss man. We'll need him, too. You'll be enrolled at The Julienne Academy before you know it."

Kale came into the kitchen at that moment. "Hey Pedro. You seen…" he started to say.

"Excuse us," Lett said and turned. "We were just leaving." Lett was about the same height as Kale but much stockier. The bodyguard, of course, made everyone look small. Kale stepped aside as the casino men exited.

"They were looking for Billy," Pedro said, still shaky.

"Yeah," Kale answered, bewildered. "Seems like a lot of people are."

They were safely on land now, but there had been moments when Billy thought the sea was going to open up and swallow them, helicopter and all.

Before Lacey had gotten them airborne, the sea had begun churning so fiercely that the copter shook as if caught in a hurricane. It had bubbled up hundreds of fish and had spewed forth a large diameter of red water, a small sample of which Mark had sealed in a jar and had placed in its metal container. By the time the copter's floats had been released by the gurgling ocean, it had looked as if God had dropped a big eyedropper full of red death right there in the Gulf. The water immediately below them had turned into a bloody, thick red pool that had spread out from its center to encompass a good hundred yards. Dead fish had been everywhere, so many in fact that Billy had believed he could have walked across them. By the time the copter had risen a couple hundred feet, the outward, increasing diameter of the red death had stopped. It was as if one small circle of the Gulf had suddenly hiccupped, bringing to the surface a blood-colored substance and a whole bunch of dead sea life.

Mark had been completely silent the entire way back. He'd stared at one corner of the windshield for the majority of the return flight. Billy had supposed that Mark was anxious to get to the lab and find out what it was in the Gulf that had suddenly done something Mark Walker had never seen the Gulf do. But Billy believed that Mark was also truly scared. Billy didn't have the proof but, perhaps for the first time, Mark had used belief over truth in coming to the conclusion that something was disturbingly wrong with the water around Port Aransas.

Mark thanked and dismissed Lacey then carried the metal container with the jar that held a sample of what he called the *Blood Drop* and asked Billy to grab the twelve plastic samples they'd collected near the buoys. It was the first thing he'd said to Billy since the anomaly had developed. Now, he mostly babbled to himself.

"I really don't know what it is, Billy," Mark said as if Billy had asked him a question. "It could be a vent. Yes. It must be." He led Billy from the helicopter to a side of the laboratory accessible only by the entry card he held. "Just a bunch of alga and dead fish. Why dead fish?" He shook his head and shrugged his shoulders, still talking to himself but having the presence of mind to lead Billy through the lab and to a station where, in the sink, the dead, one-legged seagull still lay. He pulled the jar from its metal container and set it next to the sink.

"You still going to take my blood?" Billy asked, trying to gain his colleague's attention.

Mark turned from the sink and stared through Billy, his eyes still wandering in the curiosity of science. "Blood," he said and blinked. "Yeah… yes…yes, of course. What do you think of this?" He pointed at the glass jar.

"You mean what's my take on all that crazy shit that just happened out there? What the hell was that, Mark?"

"Heat vent, probably." He snatched the jar full of red water and moved over to one of the lab's microscopes.

"You know that ain't right, Mark. A heat vent causes the water to heat. That water wasn't heated."

"Well…maybe not always." Mark slipped on a pair of lab gloves.

"Maybe not always what—what does that mean?"

Mark turned and pounded the air with a clenched fist. "Maybe," he said, maintaining his patience but struggling to do so. "Maybe the heat dissipated on its way to the surface. Maybe this is another kind of heat vent that isn't hot and perhaps should be called a cold vent. Maybe we've uncovered a never-before recorded event in the Earth's oceans and maybe it'll be called the Walker-Presser Gulf Event to all of those who study it afterward."

"So you *don't* know what it was."

Mark dropped his arm to the table and opened the glass jar with one gloved hand. "No," he said. "I really don't."

Mark tested the contents of the jar five times in an attempt to eliminate false negatives, to make sure that what his microscopes were telling him was the truth. The cold, boiling water had looked like blood…that's why Mark had called it the blood drop. Now, his analysis confirmed that it not only looked like blood…it was blood—at least blood mixed with seawater. The blood was aquatic, probably composed of the fluids from the fish that had bubbled up with it. Knowing this, though, did not provide any answers. Mark admitted that nothing like this had ever happened, at least not to his knowledge, and he offered an educated guess for its existence. "A violent eruption deep in the ocean could have changed the water pressure so dramatically that the blood was squeezed right out of them, just like orange juice."

"The water isn't very deep just a mile or so out."

"Yes," Mark said. "I know. But at least it's the start of a hypothesis." He grabbed Billy's wrist. "Come over here. Let's see if anything is floating around in you."

Mark took a syringe full of Billy's blood. After mixing it with other chemicals and numerous passes under the microscope, he found that it contained a slight trace of alcohol but no toxins, neither industrial nor natural.

"I guess that whatever is in the crate in the bank vault isn't narcotic after all," Billy said. "I guess I wasn't hallucinating last night. I mean, your instruments confirmed the big wave, right?"

Mark shook his head. "Well, if anything in there is narcotic, you certainly weren't affected by it, at least that's what your blood says. And, yes, the instruments recorded the wave but I have yet to eliminate the possibility of a malfunction." And then Mark's eyes glazed over. Absently, he added, "Maybe it was because of the hurricane." He pointed.

Billy followed Mark's finger toward a muted television. The Weather Channel crew offered an update on tropical storm Antiago which, just an hour ago, had been upgraded to a Category 1 hurricane. The track of the storm had moved from the northern tip of the Yucatán peninsula and into the Gulf.

"Hurricanes have produced many anomalies," Mark said, staring as if hypnotized by the hope that a hurricane could explain everything.

"If that thing hits us, *we'll* be the only anomaly," Billy said. He patted Mark's shoulder as Mark leaned toward the Weather Channel. "But it'll turn. They always do. Besides, it's much too far away to provide causation." Mark nodded, and Billy continued. "If you find any *real* reasons to explain all of this, give me a call."

Mark shook his head to disengage his attention with the Weather Channel. "The fish are all right as a whole. It's just these strange anomalies. I really don't think there is anything in the water." He grabbed the first buoy sample they'd collected at marker #12 and poured several samples into small test tubes as Billy headed for the exit.

Nothing could have prepared Janine for it. It was supposed to be a simple lunch with a newfound friend. She'd sipped twice from her glass of water and had thanked Joel for meeting her just as the restaurant's kitchen doors swung open. Sudden shock crept up her spine and she hunkered further into the dining room shadows, as an animal might upon seeing its predator.

She'd hoped he was dead but there had never been any proof. They'd assured her that no man could have survived such a blast. But that was just it. The man who walked from the kitchen and back into her life was no man. He was a monster. He was Albert Stine.

He sniffed the air as if the hunter had just detected its prey, then followed a shorter man with slick hair out of the restaurant.

Joel was gawking at her. She didn't look at him but she knew that he must be. Her paradise had become purgatory—again.

"Are you okay?" Joel was saying, but the buzzing shock that scrambled her mind made hearing difficult. He grabbed her forearm gently, but she jerked away and gasped, startled. "You look like you seen death itself."

She now turned to him, wondering how he knew. "Death," she whispered within a sigh.

Joel patted her hand. "If it's of any account, I don't like them much either. They're trying to take over the island."

Candice returned and asked what they wanted for lunch. Joel ordered for both of them. He chose redfish for himself and a sampler platter for Janine that was not on the menu but could be created by Pedro just for her.

By the time the meal arrived, Janine had regained much of her composure. She asked Joel what he'd meant—that *they are taking over the island.*

Joel told her what he knew. When he'd finished, Janine was not surprised that Stine was part of such gambling conspiracies. What she did not understand is why God in Heaven had placed her here at the same time.

Mark remained shaken up. Part of the reason for his chattering nerves was that he was actually excited about the chance at a new discovery. Having your name attached to new phenomena was every researcher's dream.

But a deeper feeling of self-doubt was what had really done the trick. All of that blood and all of those fish had roiled and boiled to the surface in one big clump. They'd splashed life's last breath all around the helicopter floats and his feet, slapping at his ankles, nearly pulling him into the blood drop. The memory of it had simply screwed him up. How could he be afraid? He was a doctor of marine biology. Finding reasons for mass fish kills was one of the field's greatest priorities.

He finished testing the buoy #7 sample and still he'd found nothing alarming— nothing that could be argued as a reason for fish kills or blood drops.

He went to the sink to clean up and noticed the one-legged seagull that lay in the sink's right-side basin. It had rolled free from its paper-toweled enclosure. Its face was twisted in apparent surprise and shock, its eyes wide open, its beak stretched into one last scream; even the talons on the one good dead leg pointed straight out in a kind of sudden death surprise.

Maybe the bird *had* died of a sudden heart attack. He'd seen humans who'd stiffened in similar ways.

He plucked the bird from the sink and carried it to a sterile station to dissect it. He first inspected the bird for evidence of unnatural death. The bird was so stiff it felt as if it were stuffed. The talons on the one foot stretched out so widely, he wondered if it would stand by itself.

He tried it.

The bird remained upright for a half a second before falling over with a thud. Mark shrugged then began the dissection.

He was quick to find the reason for its death, and when he did, he stumbled backward. The bird had no heart—at least not anything that resembled a heart. An indistinguishable mass of flesh was all that remained. It was as if something had grabbed hold of it and had squashed it in its grip.

And then he heard the crash of breaking glass beakers and turned to find Lett's bodyguard staring at him.

Joel was relieved to see that the color had returned to most of Janine's face. For a few moments he'd thought she might pass out. Joel only knew of the casino men from what others had told him. Apparently, from her reaction to them, Janine knew more than he did, and more than she was willing to tell.

He was unsure if she'd liked any of the items on the seafood platter. She'd toyed with one butterfly shrimp, nibbling at its fat edges but never consuming the whole thing. She completely avoided the crab legs or anything else that required any physical strategy beyond picking it up and eating it. The icy glasses of water seemed to be her favorite; she'd consumed five of them in the time it took for him to explain the casino men and devour his meal of redfish.

"So the vote needs to pass for them to do anything," Janine said.

"From what I've heard," Joel replied. He eyed the crab legs in front of Janine. "Do you mind if I…"

Janine waved her hand. "No. Please. Go ahead. They look…" she paused as if searching for a word that was more courteous than she felt. "They look good."

"Did you like the shrimp?" he asked while snatching one of the two meaty legs and the crab shell cracker.

Her stare still wandered though Joel could see she was trying to concentrate on their conversation. "It's all good," she said, looking directly into his eyes. "I'm just not hungry. In fact, I really don't feel very well at all. Would there be any way you could help me back to my place? I've not even seen it yet."

Joel released the crab leg in mid crack. He put it and the cracker on his empty plate. "I'd be happy to," he said, and then for no other reason than pure honesty, he added, "I really like your hair tie. It's very unique."

Janine almost smiled. The left edge of her lip tweaked upward but the rest of her mouth remained motionless. "Thank you," she said. "Can we go?"

As they left, Candice told them that Marcy had already paid their bill. Pedro was behind the bar sipping from a small glass of what looked to be cola. A bottle of Southern Comfort sat near the glass.

"Thank you for a great lunch," Joel told him, while gawking at the big blue marlin nailed to the wall above his head.

Pedro looked up as if dazed, nodded once, returned to his drink.

The two walked a few blocks to Alister Street and waited for the next trolley. Janine remained quiet except for telling him where she lived. Joel wondered if her silence was because of something he'd done or said.

"This will get us close to Paradise Cottages but we'll need to walk about a half a mile or so," Joel said, sitting beside Janine on the trolley stop bench. "That place is relatively new and out beyond where the trolley goes right now."

Janine shifted on the bench to face him; her cheeks flushed all at once. "I know one of those men, or at least one of them looks a whole lot like someone I know."

Joel didn't respond. If Janine was going to tell him something, he was all ears. She'd been way too silent for too long.

"There are a lot of bad memories associated with that man," she continued. "He's one of the reasons I came to the island. Now it seems he's found me." The trolley approached before she could say any more.

They stepped onto a trolley filled with a dozen people, most of them visitors to the island. Janine did not continue her revelations amongst the strangers but her pain was apparent to Joel from what she'd already said. One of the casino men was after her. She'd not even seen her new residence and already her dreams for this island, her new home, were shattered. And for that reason, Joel did something he'd not done since losing his wife to Bert Nookle.

"Would you go fishing with me tomorrow?" he said, hoping that such an adventure would calm her nerves. A little boy no older than five who was holding his mother's hand and sitting at the back of the trolley looked up as if to say: *Come on lady. Are you kidding? He said fishing. He said fishing.*

Janine stared at Joel for the longest minute, weighing the question. She looked at the little boy who could think of no other answer and said, "Yes. That sounds like fun." The little boy smiled.

"The trolley starts at eight. Would that be too early?"

Again, the faint hint of a smile touched the left corner of her lips. "We'd want to catch the first worm, right?"

"I'll come pick you up on the first trolley over."

Janine shook her head. "How about if I meet you at your place? You've been much too kind already." She covered his hand with hers. "Where do you live?"

Regardless of his home's condition, he couldn't hide from her, and quite frankly didn't want to, especially now that he felt the need to watch after her, to protect her from the casino men.

"Well, it ain't much," he said, apologetically, feeling the dampness in the palm of her hand across his knuckles.

"I don't need much," Janine said.

Joel explained where he lived, thumbing over his shoulder with the hand that was not held by Janine in the direction of the Canton Shack. The little boy who liked to fish sat concentrating on Joel's explanation as if he was trying to understand the directions with the intent of joining them in the morning. The boy's mother had to jerk his arm to get his attention when the trolley stopped at their corner.

"Fishing," the boy said as he passed them. "Dead fishing." He waved his small hand as his mother tugged him off of the trolley.

The boy's observation reminded Joel how angry he'd become at the luau. He'd yelled at Mark and had almost duked it out with fat boy Burgess. Fish equaled food. Fish equaled cash. Dead fish meant that Joel would end up on the streets, in the soup kitchens, begging for pennies from Corpus Christi strangers. But right now, right here on this trolley, just a dozen minutes after he'd seen Janine's expression of fear from the presence of a man who apparently threatened her, Joel Canton did not care about himself, his livelihood, or fish. And this was an epiphany for him and his soul. Until this very moment, he'd not really considered loneliness, and the idea of growing old without anyone to care for or to be cared by. As he sat on the trolley with Janine's moist, warm hand over his and the air blowing waves of heat across his cheeks as Alister Street passed them by at thirty-five miles an hour, he began to realize that Joel could no longer be the most important person in his life. He began to realize that self-salvation is a useless concept when uncoupled with instances of care and consideration for others. In the end, he'd not cared about Jane, and Bert had not cared about him. It was Joel's own lack of compassion about anything other than catching the Great White of '72 and every other fishing excursion he'd taken since then, that had made him what he was today. The only one that would ever need protecting was himself. The only food that was important was what he could obtain for himself. And ever since his meager charter boat company had gone bankrupt some twenty years ago, any time Joel had gone fishing it was always by himself. He had never let anyone into that world. It was *his* world. The only thing left. The sea, and all it had to offer, was his self-salvation. The sea was his love and nothing else could ever receive whatever passion was left in the fisherman's soul.

At least not until now.

"Last stop," the driver yelled. This shook Joel from his thought trance. He smiled at Janine but not so widely that his teeth showed.

"Can I walk you home?" he asked, slowly standing.

One busy 7-11 sat on one corner and several new construction projects occupied the other three. Hammers and saws and men shouting orders punctuated the landscape. Janine peered up and down both streets at the crossroad as if looking for something specific and said, "Well. Since I don't even know where I live, most definitely yes."

Joel had not released her hand and he used it to gently guide her off of the trolley and onto the street. Together they strolled along unpaved sidewalks, like a pair of teenagers setting out for experiences unknown, like two youthful innocents who were no longer alone.

The last mortal vision that Albert Stine had seen took place at Pickett's Crossing, Kansas, almost a year ago. It had found him though he'd thought himself well hidden in the barn.

The last mortal emotion Albert Stine had felt was fear. It had been an odd sensation: being afraid to such an extent. Albert Stine, until then, had not been so scared in his life.

It had been *him*!

It had ripped the flesh from mortal Albert Stine's face with the strength only matched by something that was as evil as itself.

The real Albert Stine, the evil one that was in gambling debt up to his ass to a Vegas shark named Chancey Lett, the one who vociferously enjoyed his Beam shots and Coke chasers, the one who, even as a mortal, had Hellishly slapped his wife on one occasion or two, had created a cubited replica that was so horrible even Evil could not live in its presence.

The replica, the one that many on the island town of Port Aransas now referred to as Chancey Lett's bodyguard, had made quick work of the mortal (as much as he deserved the right to be called such) Albert Stine. The death had been quick and easy. But it had taken some time to devour so much human flesh.

From that day forth, the new Albert Stine had been on a quest. It had taken nearly a year for all of the pieces to come together, for it to procure the entirety of Stine's personality—to become Albert Stine. And now it was only days away from seeing the dark prize come to life.

The Cubit would change this world—this time—just as it had for eons.

He'd still not seen that former bitch of a wife Janine but he knew she would be here. All of the players would be here, like stars aligning on the Galactic Center.

Joel Canton.

Chancey Lett.

Janine Bender.

Alixel.

And, of course, Jean LaFitte.

Together, they would help him rule a new age that would last 5,000 years—an age full of chaos and catastrophe: the Age of Hell.

There had been some minor interruptions in destiny's plan. Some of the islanders were troublesome but manageable. The key right now was the vote for the casino. It would be the reason he'd need to start digging up the beach and reveal what lay underneath: the last piece. Control of the future.

Chancey Lett was one of his biggest problems. The gambler had a kind of sixth sense, one that was not easily led, one that was manipulative, sly and heartless in its own right.

Lett had not been cubited. Stine needed him mortal for now. The cubited dead could emulate their mortal selves in many ways but interacting convincingly with the living took time that Stine did not have. Lett would push the vote through and Stine would get his bulldozers.

The bank promotion had really been Stine's idea but he'd consciously let Chancey have the credit. The vault provided a safe and secure environment to change the needed key people and the contest provided a reason to get them near the Cubit.

Bone had told them in his office earlier that day that almost forty new security box accounts had already been recorded. For Chancey Lett (and Stine), that was not enough; Lett had told Bone this. They'd need additional numbers if the vote for the casino was to be guaranteed, he'd said. Bone didn't really understand how a contest would guarantee a vote, but the man was easily manipulated. Most greedy mortals were. Bone thought that the crate held some valuable artifact. In a way, he was right. What he didn't know was that it was the artifact that would guarantee the vote by changing the voters.

Billy Jo Presser was an extreme nuisance; he'd sparked a rally that had threatened the vote's guarantee. But really, all that had done was cause Stine to make a little adjustment in plans. Those who would be cubited sooner rather than later now included a surfer, a policeman, and a publisher. Though it would have been nice to have Billy's spiritual strength on their side to expedite things, Presser would simply have to die. Pedro had told him that Billy had gone out with the "science man from the college." Other than that, Billy's chef "did not know nothing."

Stine arrived at the marine institute looking for Billy thirty minutes after Billy had left. What he did find though was Mark Walker: another nuisance that had to be eliminated.

It was nearly two in the afternoon when Billy pulled into Pat MaGee's. Not only would Bottlenose help him find some used plywood to cover up the windows at the restaurant should the hurricane hit, he might also provide some insight into the maker of the beautifully strange surfboard Billy carried from the back of the VW through the front door of the surf shop.

"Yo, BJ," Coolie said from behind a counter that displayed board wax and sunscreen lotion. "Dude. That 'cane's a headin' in our general direction."

Billy set the nose of the surfboard on the floor and said, "Saw it on the news just a few minutes ago. Nothing to be overly worried about yet…just cautious."

"What'cha got there?" Coolie came around the counter to check out the board. "Never seen one like that before. It's a freakin tree!"

"You ever seen wood like that?"

Coolie rubbed his hand across the board's glassy surface then lifted it from Billy's grasp. His thin frame had trouble with the board's weight. "Not balsa for sure. Thing is huge on weight. Must be at least nine feet."

"You know anyone who makes these long wooden rides anymore?"

Coolie shook his head. From behind both of them, Bottlenose added, "Neither do I." His eyes were filled with wonder. He took the board from Coolie and held it in his muscular grip with much greater ease. "Christ! This baby is at least fifty pounds. Beautiful. Vintage. And the wood. Definitely not a pop-out."

Coolie continued rubbing the board's surface as Bottlenose held it. "You know what it's made of?"

"I got a guess," Bottlenose said. "Seen a similar design off the Yucatán coast in Mexico several years ago." The board had three distinct colors: the outside edges were reddish brown, the nose and tail were dark brown, almost black, and the center stringer was a blonde tan. Bottlenose traced the edge of the board with one finger. "This could be a lot of things. Most people would guess mahogany by its color. But when you match it up with this wood," Bottlenose tapped the board's nose with his hand, "you've got to consider the board's origin. It's my guess that all of these woods came from southern Mexico. And it's my guess that these woods are all quite valuable…and rare. The nose is perhaps Chechen. The edges I'm sure are Cocobolo. The center is…hmmm." He rapped the center of the board with his knuckles. "Definitely not hollow."

Billy got to thinking about the red wave rider, the surfer's silhouette against the moon. "Who rides a board like this? None of the locals. Corpses perhaps?"

Bottlenose took the board to the back of the shop where the surfing museum still had not seen today's first visitor. Billy and Coolie followed. "A corpse with a long wood board…nah. I mean those mainland surfers wouldn't know what to do with a beauty like this." He set the surfboard face down atop a pair of sawhorses he used to demonstrate board waxing. "But I'll tell you one thing. The guy riding this board is probably huge…at least his weight is huge…and his strength…and his courage. Can you imagine what would happen to the ol' noggin if this piece of lumber came down on top of it?" Bottlenose inspected the chip in the nose of the board. A good inch wide and two inch long chunk had been busted out of the nearly black wood surface. "Amazing. Huge amazing."

"How's that?" Billy asked, leaning forward to inspect the chip.

"You can't chip a board like this...at least not with anything less than a jackhammer." He suddenly rose and studied Billy quizzically. "Just where did you get this anyway?"

Sweets, Shana Greathouse and Peter Jennings entered the shop together. They made a beeline to where the three men stood.

"Hey, man," Sweets said. "New addition to the museum?"

"Slick," Shana added. "You wanna take me for a ride on it Bottle?" Shana had never been shy about showing her desire in public for Bottlenose.

"Not mine," Bottlenose said. "Ask BJ. It's his board."

"How much did that run you?" Peter asked then saw the chip in the nose. "Aw, man. The value's already been robbed."

All four surfers gathered around the board, staring from it to Billy in silence, waiting for him to fill them in. Billy felt the need to lie, to raise his reputation by fabricating a cost and a place of purchase. Surfboards promoted status. He'd already obtained much symbolism on the island. A board like this would solidify it for years to come. However, to claim ownership would mean that he'd have to ride the monster in front of all those that would lift him to local stardom. Bottlenose was right. A board like this smashing down against his head might kill him.

"It didn't cost me anything," he admitted. The four surfers remained silent but their quizzical stares mixed with sudden disbelief. "I found it."

"Found it?" Coolie questioned, his voice rising two octaves. "Who finds a board like this? I mean, come on."

"On the beach," Billy continued. "This morning. Just a couple of miles south of the pier."

"Well, it *is* busted," Peter interjected.

"Not so much that it couldn't be fixed," Coolie added. "Right, Bottlenose?"

Bottlenose shrugged his shoulders. "Gotta be worth a grand easy. It would be worth patchin' up. It wouldn't be the same though. Hell, there'd be no way of finding any wood like this around here. The integrity would suffer. It would take a great laminator. Might serve better as a museum piece."

Billy had to agree. He wouldn't be using it. Too heavy. Too long. It would kill him for sure. And it wasn't like it cost anything. "All of your boards are in such good condition though," he said to Bottlenose. "You sure a board with a broken nose and tail fin could find a place among such mint condition pieces?"

A big question mark surfaced across Bottlenose's expressive face. "Broken fin?" He stepped to the tail of the board, brushing past Shana who beamed with pleasure. "This fin ain't broke."

But it was broken. At least it had been when the teenage boy had found it on the beach. At least it had been when Billy had inspected it. The last two inches of the fin had not been there. Billy was sure of it. Coolie stepped aside as Billy moved toward the fin.

"I'm tellin' ya," he said to Bottlenose. "This thing was broken this morning."

"Well it ain't broke now," Coolie said.

Billy leaned in, inspecting both sides of the fin, looking for a crack that wasn't there. What he did find shocked him more than the idea that he'd imagined it all. At the very tip of the fin etched in deep red across the dark brown, almost black, wood surface was the Wayeb symbol, the same Mayan icon that had been on the papers carried by Chancey Lett's bodyguard and had been etched on both sides of the coin the Corpus Christi visitors had found in the sand. He could not hide his surprise from the others. They were all staring at him when he rose from the board.

"You gonna faint or something?" Shana said.

Billy shook his head and absently reached into the front pocket of his shorts, the same shorts he'd worn the day before. The coin was still there. He pulled it out and let it rest in the palm of his open hand and said, "This is what those corpses dug up in the sand yesterday." He gave the coin to Bottlenose who drew it closer to his eyes for inspection. "Now look at the fin."

Bottlenose did. "Same thing," he said. "So?"

"Strange coincidence don't you think?" Billy said.

Bottlenose flipped the coin back to Billy. "Yeah, but there are a lot of those in the world aren't there? Really, I don't see anything special about it. What I'm more concerned with is you thinking the fin was broke. You sure you're okay?"

There had been a lot of shit that had happened to him in the past twenty-four hours, so much so that he wondered he if was merely dreaming, that suddenly he'd wake up in bed, his shorts still wet from an evening of surfing, a huge knot on his head from where his surfboard had crashed down causing a concussion. If anything made sense, that did. There'd been glowing vaults, strange crates, menacing bodyguards, visions of displaced time and space, and of being chased and shot at. He'd witnessed red tides and eight foot waves, blood drops and massive fish kills. Birds no longer flew on an island famous for its avian complexity. How could a person explain such things? Easy. He was dreaming.

"Yeah, I'm fine," he said. "It's just been a long couple of days. Very stressful."

"I know what you mean, bro," Bottlenose said, comforting. "You've taken on way too much, fighting those bastards from Vegas and all. Shit, your business can't be doing that hot either with all this rumor of chemical spills. And now we got a hurricane whirling up our ass."

Coolie interjected, "But that's a good thing ain't it? It'll miss us and shoot up the coast and leave eight foot waves in its wake. Talk about knarly, dudes and dudette. Like, Port A will be the greatest surf spot in the lower forty-eight."

"Always one to look on the bright side," Shana said. "Won't do us much good if that Vegas asshole gets his way. We won't even be able to walk on our own beach."

Billy stepped back from the surfboard and dropped the Wayeb coin in his pocket. "If you want it you can have it," he told Bottlenose. "I'm not much into the long board rides. And as for the rest of you. If we're gonna keep our surf and ride Coolie's eight foot swells this weekend, we're going to have to make sure the vote is on our side. The *South Jetty* ain't helping us. In fact, other than the luau last night and what we can do by pounding the pavement, lots of islanders aren't going to know the ramifications of the vote. They may not even know that a vote is going to take place."

"What can we do?" Peter Jennings said.

"Knock on doors," Billy replied. "I'm going to print up some door hangers. Can you guys help distribute them?"

Simultaneously, all the surfers shouted, "Hells yes!"

"Excellent. I'll be back around five o'clock then." Billy started out the door then turned to face Bottlenose who was still examining his new museum piece. "You still have a bunch of that used plywood out back you saved when you tore down the old board shaper's shop?"

"Yeah," Bottlenose replied, not looking up from his new museum piece.

"You got enough to where I might borrow some in case that storm breaks our way."

"Should be enough for MaGee's and the Surf Side."

"Nice. I'll see you in a couple of hours then."

Coolie, Sweets, and Jennings gave him the thumbs up. Shana was too busy staring at Bottlenose's biceps.

Billy stopped at the CopyKatz on his way home. He hoped that the girl there would have no problem throwing something together for him in an hour or two. He figured a couple thousand door hangers would probably do the trick. Luckily, the copy shop was not busy and the girl was happy to oblige though she was not certain she could print and cut two thousand hangers in such a short time. But she did promise that when five o'clock came around she'd have as much done as possible. She didn't like the idea of the casino either and the pavement pounding sounded like a great idea. In fact, she offered to help which Billy gladly accepted.

When he arrived at the restaurant, Candice and Kale were sitting at the bar drinking ice water. Their expressions were as if someone had just died. As he entered, they did not look up. There were no diners.

"What gives?" Billy asked.

"Our jobs," Kale mumbled.

"And by that you mean…"

Kale swirled a finger through the ice in his glass. "You know how many people we've had in here since noon?" He lifted his hand from the glass, showing two fingers. "You know how much fish I was able to purchase today?" The two fingers curled inward to form a zero. "You know how long we can stay in business this way?" He returned his hand to the glass of water. "We can't. No one can. The Wharf and the Tarpon have already closed their doors. Now we got this damned hurricane to deal with. I've pretty much given up, Billy."

Billy moved to the bar and stood where the Vegas bodyguard had just two days before. "Where's Pedro?"

"Left about an hour ago," Kale said. "He didn't seem too happy. He said something had suddenly come up that he had to deal with. I didn't figure we'd have much business anyway."

"You're right," Billy said.

"What do you mean?"

"We can't stay in business this way. We're gonna have to close shop. At least until all of this rumor and the storm passes."

"What if it isn't rumor?" Kale sipped some water and looked into Billy's eyes for support. "If they find chemicals, Port A will be a ghost town."

"Mark's working on that. We didn't find anything today that would point a finger at DuPont." Billy told him only part of the truth. Talking about one-legged birds with heart attacks and blood spots full of dead fish would not help calm his manager's nerves.

"They denied it, you know." It was the first thing Candice had said since Billy had entered. "It was on TV earlier. That Chagnard fellow—you know the one with the crazy blue eyes—he was on the afternoon news and said that there was no reason to think DuPont would ever be so irresponsible. He reminded his audience that DuPont had had a clean record since the disaster in Galveston and that their safety program budget had swelled into the millions since then. He pretty much guaranteed the public that DuPont had nothing to do with the fish kills."

"Well there you have it," Billy said.

"You trust that weasley-faced press agent?" Candice said. "Man, I wouldn't trust him as far as I could throw him."

Just then, a couple of obese men entered the restaurant. Each of them easily weighed more than three hundred pounds. "Damned nice to see something open on this island," the one with the rosier cheeks said. "What's the special today? Got any buffets? Any all-you-can-eats? We're starved for seafood and lots of it."

Candice leaned forward and whispered. "Looks like we're two diners too late for closing. And they ain't gonna make us any money that's for certain." She mustered a smile and added, "So who's cooking?" then escorted the men to a table in the center of the dining room.

"You go ahead and do an inventory," Billy said to Kale. "See what we can store on ice and what won't last four or five days. I'll cook these guys up something. I don't think they're going to be too picky. They seem more into quantity than quality."

"We won't be able to save much," Kale said and chugged down the rest of his water. "We got the reputation of freshness. Perhaps we can cook some of it up and refrigerate it for stews and platters."

"Good thinking. And we'll need some signs about the closure."

"I'll take care of it. The sooner the better before we lose any more money." Kale nodded toward the two fat diners.

Carol had screamed at Steph, and everyone in the bank, all twenty-three of them, had turned toward Steph's desk.

"No fucking pooling!" she'd yelled.

At least three people in the teller lines had gasped. One of them, a mother with her young son, had covered her child's ears. That had been almost four hours ago and still Steph could not get the memory of the uncontrolled outburst out of her head.

Steph stared at Patrick the Starfish. The toy had an expression of surprise, a gasp planted on its plastic face as if SpongeBob had said something shocking or stupid, as if a twisted bank teller had just yelled in a cursive slang that was not indigenous to the bottom of the sea.

"Screwed up," she whispered to the starfish. "This has been one screwed up day." Steph signed.

Business at the bank, however, had not been screwed up. The million dollar real estate promotion had been nothing less than a major success. More than a hundred new accounts had been opened so far and there were at least twenty more prospects standing in line at the teller windows or sitting with bank reps at desks. Carol had directed most of the new business away from Steph since her outburst and she'd not allowed Steph into the vault. This had pissed Steph off. How had Carol gained so much unofficial control? Steph had been tempted on several occasions to test her, to enter the vault just to see what Carol would do, but Steph wasn't that brave. Anyone who would scream such language in a place of business with a couple dozen customers around didn't have all of their marbles. Carol's proverbial cheese had slid of the cracker and who knew what she was capable of, the least of which would certainly entail another foul-mouthed tongue lashing. It was as if Carol had become the guardian of the vault, a sentry placed conspicuously and menacingly at its door. Only Carol and customers would enter and each time she went in Steph swore she heard that low hum though no one else in the bank seemed to notice.

Patrick the Starfish's gasp lured her into an imaginary conversation. In its dopey voice the toy said:

I don't know about you, but the crate in there sure is creepy.

"I agree," Steph said in a hush so no one in the bank would notice her talking to the toy.

I wonder why that big ugly fella pushed it at you?

"I'm not sure," Steph whispered.

He's sure is ugly. He's got Squidward beaten by a mile. And he stinks, too. The inside of his pocket smelled like Mr. Krab's crabby patties.

Steph considered the Mr. Krabs toy, leaning against the side of her computer monitor, who now entered the conversation.

The only thing that stinks around here is you, Patrick. My patties are the best tasting and smelling crab cakes in all of Bikini Bottom.

Apparently, you haven't tried Pedro Melindez's crab cakes, Steph thought but didn't say.

But we're not in Bikini Bottom, Patrick said. *We're in the Big Texas Bank, Port A branch, where you can get a security box and a chance to win a million bucks worth of real estate all in the same day.*

Don't you think that's a little weird, Patrick?

Yeah, Mr. Krabs, but it's workin'. The bank's pulled in at least a half a million dollars in new accounts.

Patrick, you're an idiot. The bank doesn't care about the money. They just want to get as many influential people as possible into that vault and close to that crate. You never were able to put two and two together.

Four, Patrick said and giggled. *I got an A in math.*

You're enough to make a crab pull its hair out.

But you don't have any hair, Mr. Krabs.

I know that you idiot.

Hey, now. Wait a minute, Mr. Krabs. Do you hear that?

Hear what?

That hummy noise coming from the vault.

That's not a hummy noise. It's the telephone ringing. Starfish are so stupid.

Steph was shaken from her daydream daze. She had no idea how long the phone had been ringing. She snatched the receiver.

"Are you going to do any work today Miss Drake or are you just going to play with your toys?" It was Carol's voice, and when Steph looked up and over at the teller window, Carol had the phone to her ear and was glaring at her. "Mr. Bone is on line one. Would you mind picking it up?"

Steph did not reply but instead cut Carol off by pressing the blinking button on her handset.

"Yes, Mr. Bone?" she said.

"Carol tells me you allowed some customers to pool their money. Would you mind explaining yourself?

Steph wanted to respond in many ways. She wanted to tell him that Carol was insane. She wanted to tell him that the crazy bitch had screamed "Fuck" right in front of his beloved customers. She wanted to explain that Carol had taken command of his bank and was not allowing Steph to take part in any transactions. But instead, she replied, "I'm sorry Mr. Bone but I didn't know the rules of the contest."

"If you'd gotten to work on time that would not be an issue."

Carol was grinning but not looking at her. She escorted another customer into the vault and closed the door.

"I…" Steph started to say but Bone cut her off.

"I'm counting on you to pick up our investor from the airport tomorrow. I want you to provide her with every amenity she requests. Can I trust you to do this one small thing?"

"Yes. Of course, Mr. Bone."

"Her plane arrives at two o'clock. I expect you to be there at least a half hour early in case the flight arrives early. Take your car and the bank will reimburse you for the expense. She'll be staying next door at the Treasure Trove.

"I'll take care of it," Steph said and Bone hung up.

In a way, Steph was relieved. She'd not need to go to the airport until the afternoon which would allow plenty of time to spend with Billy. However, if she called in sick, what signal would that send? How could she be sick and escort this woman all in the same day? How could she explain herself? The short answer was: she couldn't. She had to make a choice. Surfing and Billy weren't as important as her job, were they? She was only three years outside of adolescence and the irresponsible tingle associated with immaturity still pulsed vibrantly within her. For responsible, mature adults, there was no choice. But recently, her responsibility had been shanghaied by a crazy woman named Carol. Was she still Bone's executive secretary? Did her job no longer require her to keep tabs on Bone's daily schedule? Had she been relegated to nothing more than a chauffeur? Would she still have a job by week's end?

The hum from the vault and shrill ringing of the telephone engaged her senses simultaneously. She picked up the receiver expecting Mr. Bone, but it was Billy. He wanted to know when would be a good time to start their door-to-door protest campaign, something Steph had forgotten all about. She suggested five-thirty and Billy said he'd pick her up at her apartment.

As she hung up the phone, Carol emerged from the vault. Professor Nelson followed. The professor looked dazed, as if bright headlights had just blinded him. When he walked past Steph, she said to him, "Hey Professor Nelson. How are you today?"

The man continued past without acknowledgement, seemingly catatonic, as if only one thought occupied all of consciousness. She wondered if he was thinking about the Lord's Prayer, or at least the version that Carol and friends had come up with. She wondered if he'd touched the crate. She wondered if *she'd* touched the crate. She looked at her hand then down at Patrick.

There's something creepy going on, the toy said. *And you are right in the middle of it.*

It took the two men an hour and a half to eat what Billy had termed "The Super Platter." None existed on the menu but it was what the men wanted and it was one of the easiest things to make. No special sauces. No extravagant presentation. Just pounds of shrimp, scallops, and redfish and almost a gallon of seafood gumbo that Pedro had simmering in a large crock pot. Kale had placed signs on the entry door and in one bay window an hour ago.

Along with the Super Platter, Billy cooked up much of the fresh seafood remaining in the refrigerator freezer. There really wasn't a whole lot left; Kale had not been able to purchase much this week. Billy stored everything in plastic containers and filled the shelves of the refrigerator. By the time he'd finished cooking and cleaning up, the two men had paid their fifteen dollars each and had left a measly tip for Candice which she'd been quite angry about. He had called Steph and had arranged to pick her up at five-thirty, and he'd also tried to call the marine institute several times but had gotten no answer, not even from Dave, the security guard. Billy knew Mark well enough to believe that his colleague had simply gotten so involved in his blood drop research that every other outside intrusion had been blocked by his concentration. But Dave not answering—that was a different story. It was part of Dave's responsibility, especially in the summer months when activity at the institute slowed. Billy made a mental note to stop by and check the place out while distributing the protest door hangers later that evening.

He closed and locked the door of the restaurant. Kale and Candice had left ten minutes ago. It was nearly five o'clock. He stood outside the restaurant reading the sign that Kale had created:

The Surf Side will be closed until further notice. Please keep our island in your prayers.

Sufficiently vague with a bit of helplessness mixed in. Was it the rumor of bad fish or the threat of a hurricane that had caused this restaurant to lock up? In either case, the Surf Side had closed for reasons beyond its own control. When would it reopen? Only God knew the answer.

Billy slid behind the wheel of his VW Bus and headed for the CopyKatz.

It was like an itch that she couldn't scratch: the feeling, the intuition, that she would not have a job by the end of the week. The feeling was that Carol had somehow taken over her position and Mitchell Bone had let her freely ride with the opportunity. He was never around the bank anymore; he'd been in his office a total of four hours since Monday. There had been no scheduled meetings beyond those with Chancey Lett. Mr. Bone just wasn't himself. Granted, he'd never been what you might call "kind" but recently he'd become "unkindly." This whole thing with the casino and the money power that came with it had turned the greedy man's head into opportunistic mush. His bank had brought in more than a half million dollars worth of business. There should be celebration. There should be pats on the backs of all the employees. There should be bonuses and time off for excellent work. But he seemed not to care. And the only one taking advantage of the situation was Carol.

So Steph made the decision at five minutes to five that she would not come in for work tomorrow. And the investor she was supposed to chauffeur back to the island? Screw her. Screw Bone, screw Carol, screw this whole damned thing. She could find another job. Perhaps Billy could help. She'd waitressed herself through college; she could waitress herself until something better came about. One thing was certain though: she was not going to be pushed around any more. She was going to scratch that itch with insubordination. She'd leave the investor hanging at the airport just out of spite.

Few people remained in the bank. Stealthily, Steph dropped her three cartoon toys in a grocery store plastic bag. She added to the sack, her favorite pen, a diet book entitled *Skinny Bitch* that Misty Percy had let her borrow a month ago, and a print out of all the people who had taken out security boxes and had gained an entry into the million dollar real estate contest during the day. She thought the list might come in handy though she did not, at this time, know how. It served as a log of all those who had been in close contact with the crate in the vault and might prove to be valuable as the vote on Saturday approached.

She stood to exit, following Chester Kalimaris who drug his feet as if he'd just pulled a sixteen-hour shift, and made it to the bank's double doors before Carol spoke out from behind her. The voice was close, not more than a few feet away.

"Miss Drake," Carol groaned. Steph did not immediately turn around. She snuggled her plastic bag full of evidence closer to her side. "Miss Drake!" Steph slowly turned only partially around to the right, leaving her left side and the plastic bag unexposed.

"What is it now?" she stammered with apparent indignation.

"What's in the bag?" Carol's eyes boiled red, as if she hadn't slept in years. She pointed.

Steph's nerves kicked up several notches. "My toys," she said. "You apparently don't like them so I'm getting them out of your face."

"Give them to me." Carol took a step closer.

"I will not!" Steph took a step backward. She felt the need to run.

"I think you're a liar."

"Back off, bitch." But these were not Steph's words, though she wanted to say them. These words came from behind her. Chester came around and stood between Carol and Steph. "You've been riding Miss Drake all day long," he continued. "I don't know what's gotten into you but," he turned to acknowledge Steph, "WE don't like it. Bone's going to hear all about it, I guarantee you that."

"You're fired," Carol said to Chester.

"On what authority?" Steph had never seen Chester this angry. "You're just a simple teller."

"I'll make it happen," Carol countered.

"Well you had better bring an army because that's what it's going to take."

And just like that, Carol shut up. She smiled very widely, which was quite disturbing, but she shut up. She turned around and walked back toward the vault as Steph and Chester exited.

"Thank you," Steph said, stepping off the sidewalk and onto the asphalt parking lot.

"I don't know what's gotten into that woman," Chester replied. "Hell, I don't know what's gotten into this entire bank. Everything has gone... crazy."

"My thoughts exactly." Steph could have continued a conversation on the subject but she really didn't know Chester that well. At least she knew she wasn't the only one in the bank that was annoyed by the sudden changes.

"We'll take care of it tomorrow," Chester said and gently patted Steph's shoulder. "And for the record, I really like SpongeBob. I watch it with my kids just about every day."

Steph smiled. "Again, thanks."

Chester turned toward his car which was parked at the opposite end of the lot as Steph climbed into her Chevy Cavalier. Chester's small addition of noble fortitude had made the end of the day somehow palatable. And thank goodness for that. Had Carol gotten a hold of her bag, Steph could have been arrested for stealing confidential records.

Chester exited the parking lot ahead of her and as Steph followed his Mercedes' taillights, she saw Pedro Melindez out of the corner of her eye. He walked across the parking lot toward the front of the bank. She thought about turning around but considered the papers she'd taken from the bank and decided that giving Carol another chance was not smart. Instead, she continued on toward her Paradise Cottage apartment and an evening date with Billy Jo Presser.

The clerk at the CopyKatz, whose name was Rachel, said she wouldn't mind distributing a hundred door hangers to the residents around the copy shop. She'd managed to print and cut 1,411 hangers which was, as she'd said, "a production record for me this summer." Billy thought that her enthusiasm to work so diligently toward the cause was based as much in her attraction toward him as it was in her passion to save the beach, perhaps more. She'd not stopped smiling from the moment he'd entered her shop.

At Pat MaGee's, Bottlenose had already made a place in the surfboard museum for what he had named "The Yucatán." He'd not yet set the board on display, wanting first to polish it and create its history. Each board in the museum had some kind of history to it. Most were factual; many were based loosely on fact. The Yucatán would most likely have a plausible but totally fictitious history created for it that did not include surfing at night on red waves.

Billy had kept 311 door hangers and had distributed the rest, giving each surfer a designated island area to cover. Shana had said that she would double-up with Bottlenose but Bottlenose had reminded her that he'd have to manage the store until closing. Billy had chosen the area around the marine institute for himself and Steph.

At a little past five-thirty, Billy turned into Paradise Cottages and parked behind Steph's Cavalier in front of the cottage next to hers. Steph greeted him at the doorstep, grabbed his hand, and guided him toward his VW. Billy got the impression that she did not want him to see inside her cottage. Perhaps she'd not had the time to straighten up. Women were funny that way.

Before driving off, he saw Steph's neighbor through that cottage's front window. The woman sat at her kitchen table, her head down and resting across folded arms. She was crying.

Billy parked at the marine institute. Two other vehicles were in the lot near the front door: Mark's Jeep Wrangler and Dave's old Buick Cutlass. He left the door hangers in the VW and he and Steph entered the building. Dave was not at the front desk. Though this was not necessarily unusual (Dave could be making the rounds) his chair was flipped over and several papers, including the edition of the *South Jetty* he'd shown Billy earlier, were strewn in a mess on the desk; a few sheets of paper lay next to the toppled chair.

"Dave?" Billy shouted out. "Hey!" His voice traveled down corridors to the left and right leaving a hallow echo behind.

"What is it?" Steph asked. "Who's Dave?"

"The security guard."

Billy collected the messy papers into a pile and set the chair upright. He led Steph down the corridor to the right, trying not to alarm her though he felt alarm was of optimum concern. Through double doors and down another corridor toward the research pier, he found the wet lab door open.

"Mark?" he said to the open doorway. "Hey Mark. You in there?"

Inside the lab, Billy's feet crunched across broken glass before he found the one-legged seagull opened at the chest and pinned back to allow for examination. He knew enough about avian anatomy to understand that all of the bird's organs were not in place. Mark had apparently removed its heart.

At a second station, Billy found Mark's toxicology report on the buoy samples and reviewed each. Only minor pollutants had been recorded; nothing out of the ordinary. At the bottom of the last page, Mark had hand-written: *The Water is Safe*.

Steph stood wild-eyed beside him. "He must have left in hurry," she offered.

Billy considered this but even in haste, he could not believe that Mark would have left the lab in such disarray. "Perhaps," he said. He pointed at the reports. "Toxin tests are negative. The water is safe as far as Mark was able to find."

"That's good news," Steph said. She managed a smile though her pressed eyebrows bared concern. "Maybe he's gone to the paper."

Billy turned to her again surprised at how easily she deduced what seemed to be quite obvious. He nodded. "That makes sense. He's probably at the *South Jetty* right now. We'll stop in there as we pass out the hangers."

Billy and Steph walked at a comfortable pace; the weather was too muggy for anything expedient. Near the institute were several residential apartment complexes and some of the richer homes on this side of the island. It would take them a good hour to cover the ten square blocks. They'd unload half of the door hangers in this area alone.

Billy took one side of the street and Steph took the other. On some occasions, the occupant of the home or apartment met them at the door. Seldom, had any of those people even heard about the impending vote and its ramifications.

For forty-five minutes, they pounded the pavement, lobbied to those who would listen and slipped their cardstock hangers on doorknobs. What they didn't notice was that CrabMan, who'd gotten out of jail that morning, was following them. He lurked in whatever shadows the bright sunny day offered, emerging only after Billy and Steph moved on to the next block. His sole purpose was to remove every door hanger the two had delivered. Once in awhile, he got caught by the occupant or a neighbor and, for the most part, he'd just ignored them. But that was not the case with the owner of the house on 25 Cotter Avenue. That man got all bent out of shape and CrabMan had to put him down. Crab's strength had grown immensely in the past twenty-four hours; he'd not really tried to break the guy's jaw but it had been so easy. One right cross and the owner had fallen backward into his home. Crab had simply pushed his legs inside and had closed the door. He'd be long gone by the time the man woke up and called the police. But even the police would not stop him. Not any more. In fact, the police were busy on the other end of town doing the very same thing behind Billy's surfer buddies though there had been no occasion when any occupant of any resident had needed to be silenced as Mr. 25 Cotter Avenue had. People trusted the police, right? No one would question an officer's intent to remove "garbage" from doorknobs.

With about a hundred hangers remaining, Billy and Steph came across the *South Jetty* building. Kilpatrick was not there and the rude receptionist told them that she didn't even know who Mark Walker was.

"I don't believe her," Billy said as they left and walked toward the next section of residences.

Steph stopped suddenly and pointed. "Hey. Isn't that Crab…what's his name?" Billy followed her finger. "He just ducked behind the newspaper building."

"Are you talking about CrabMan?" Billy clarified.

"Yeah. The guy who tried to stab you last night. He was right there."

Billy handed his short stack of door hangers to Steph and told her to stay where she was. The idea of being followed unnerved him, especially if the follower was someone who had tried to slash him with the point of a nail.

Slowly, he walked thirty yards to the front side of the *South Jetty* building and stealthily craned his head around the back corner. He found nothing more than a few broken wooden pallets sitting within an overgrowth of seagrass and weeds. He looked back in the direction where Steph still stood and raised his arms in confusion. At that moment the *South Jetty* receptionist appeared, seemingly out of nowhere. She stood between his line of vision with Steph, hands behind her back, her black, thick horned-rimmed glasses slightly askew.

"What the hell do you want anyway?" she hissed. "I told you. No one is here. If you keep poking around, I'm gonna have to break your arm."

Billy shook his head but not because he intended it as any kind of acknowledgement. It was purely involuntary; a shake of disbelief. Had she really just said that? Didn't she really mean to say that she was going to call the cops? She stood five-foot-nothing and probably couldn't break the lead in the point of a pencil if she tried. But break his arm?

Steph was yelling something at him.

Cat?

Hat?

She's got a hat?

No. What Steph was trying to tell him was that this crazy woman had a *bat*, which she now produced from behind her back: a 35-ounce aluminum Louisville Slugger. Before Billy could say a word, she swung for his forearm, missed, and landed the head of the bat against the brick face of the *South Jetty*. The force was so great that a spray of brick chips and dust peppered Billy's bare legs and arms. She'd made a fist-sized divot in the wall and dented the bat.

"Jesus…" Billy moaned and quickly stammered backward.

"Even He ain't gonna help you now, Presser," the tiny receptionist snarled and swung the bat again, missing his head this time by only a few inches. Wind whirred by at incredible bat speed.

And just as suddenly as the receptionist had appeared from the building, Steph was there with a two-by-four. She swung the lumber hard and fast as the receptionist lifted the bat high above her head in an axe-chopping motion. The bat flew from her hands and ricocheted off the wall. A clear, sharp cracking noise accompanied the lumber's impact with the woman's swing. Either the board had broken or the receptionist's arm had. Steph dropped the two-by-four as Billy grabbed her hand and both of them ran from the building and the receptionist whose arm had already swelled with a deep purple bruise. When they reached the spot where Steph had dropped the door hangers, both turned in unison. The receptionist was gone. Gulf breeze had scattered several of the hangers and she and Billy collected them. "What in God's name is going on around here?" she said, gasping slightly from the exertion of the run.

"It's not just me then." Billy brushed the sand from his door hangers.

"What do you mean?" Steph, again, looked toward the *South Jetty* newspaper building before following Billy toward the next block of residences.

"I've lived on this island for more than two years now and I've seen some crazy shit." He hesitated, hoping that Steph did not mind his choice of words. "Like last year when the Spring Breakers went bonkers on the beach, flipped a couple of cars over and set them on fire. They had to bring the riot police in for that. The next day they pulled a car from the channel with four teenagers in it. Witnesses said that beer cans were floating all around their dead faces. We even had an axe-murderer living here up until the end of last fall. The loon had chopped up his family in Vermont then had decided to take a permanent vacation on our island. He would have never been caught had the murderer not videotaped the entire slaughter. And then of course there's the occasional drug runner that gets nabbed offshore and a whale or two that have beached themselves on the south end of the island." Billy noticed the concerned frown on Steph's face and continued. "But you've got to understand. A place like Port Aransas is meant for those who want to get away from it all. Civilization as they've found it just doesn't cut it anymore. They come to the island for its peace and tranquility, for its wonderful Texas hospitality, to dream, to get away from the doldrums of life and the despicable people they've found in it. Unfortunately, a place to escape from rote living also attracts wayward transients. Port A is perfect for those that want to hide from their pasts, be they good or bad."

"Is that why you came to the island?"

"Yeah."

"And what were you escaping from?"

Billy stopped. He looked directly into Steph's eyes and said, "I'm not a bad person. I just couldn't live in a city that rewards achievements in intellectual theft and bribery."

Steph smiled. "I know that…I mean, I know you're a good person. It's in your eyes."

Billy returned the smile then continued walking. "But ever since that Chancey Lett fellow came to this island, everything seems…you know… off."

"I've gotten that same feeling," Steph said. "That receptionist back there. She reminded me a lot of Carol. Just kind of whacked out. Like someone took away their true personalities and replaced them with…" Billy stared in anticipation. "I don't know. Like something programmed. Like they've been replaced by robots. And there's more."

"More?"

Steph looked at the door hangers in her hand. "Come on," she said. "We're never going to get these things done. I'll try to explain as we finish up."

Steph recounted her day at the bank in small chunks. It seemed to Billy that she could not find all the right words in one long explanation and needed the breaks supplied by their distribution of door hangers to each side of the street. Each time they'd covered a block and came back together, Steph would add more to her story until, finally, when all the door hangers had been distributed and they had returned to the marine institute, she'd told him everything. From her encounter with Lett, Carol and the bodyguard inside the vault to Carol's cursed outburst, to the hypnotic way each new account holder exited the vault after Carol had taken them inside, to her decision to surf instead of work, she tried to explain what she meant by "controlled" and "robotic."

"I don't blame you for not wanting to return to such a situation," Billy said, wiping fresh sweat from his forehead. "Now I've got a bit of a confession to make to you."

But before he could tell her about Shoe and how he was using the starfish to record evidence which would substantiate Steph's claims, security guard Dave's Buick Cutlass suddenly roared to life. The two of them stood at the entrance to the marine institute's parking lot as the car sped past, bottoming out as it exited the lot and turned onto the street. Dave was driving but ignored them, instead staring straight ahead as if every motion was programmed, as if he too had become what Steph had termed "robotic."

Billy decided to take the beach road back to her place. Coincidentally, it was at about this same time yesterday that they were on this same stretch of sand but had been driving in the opposite direction toward the luau.

What a difference a day made.

She'd been so excited just twenty-four hours ago. She'd had a job. She'd had growing friendships with people to whom Billy had introduced her. She'd felt the spark of romance and of desire that she'd not experienced since leaving college. She'd ridden imaginary waves to imaginary stars and had felt on top of a world that she could control.

But control was the last word she'd use to describe her emotions now. Nothing, really, made much sense. Hell, she'd carried on a conversation with a bunch of children's toys—how much more absurd could you get?

A woman trying to use Billy's head for baseball practice?

And how about Carol? If you wanted a definition for absurd, you could stop right there. And wasn't it absurd that she, Stephanie Drake, a woman who'd graduated in the top ten percent of her college class and had been voted most likely to succeed, had even contemplated ditching work for pleasure let alone had decided to go through with it? Work had become absurd. The people she worked for had become absurd. Residents of the island had become absurd. Really, the only sane thing left was Billy. Thank God for Billy.

Shortly after Dave the security guard had nearly run them over, they'd gone back inside the institute, again looking for Mark. Dave's desk had been as they'd left it, but the broken glass had been cleaned up from the lab and all of Mark's toxicology results had been missing. Even the one-legged bird that had been dissected (and had turned Steph's stomach upon seeing it) had been removed. Billy had assumed that Mark had returned to the lab and guessed that he'd probably taken off for Corpus where the media was more influential.

Rays of waning sunlight peppered her legs as she absently gazed at the only thing that currently made sense to her. Billy's silhouette filled her with protective comfort, as if he were the eye of the storm, a harbor in the tempest. He did not smile. His furled eyebrows denoted a man whose mind moved in calculated complexity, as if he was trying to answer some unwieldy equation or solve a complex mystery.

"I've infiltrated the bank," he said after a long stretch of silence.

Steph shifted in the seat toward him. "What do you mean?"

"Well, you know how much I trust that Vegas fellow and Mitchell Bone."

"Like, zero?"

"Yeah, even lower." He mustered a quick grin. "I figured that if I could get some evidence, any evidence, that would undermine their attempts to destroy our beaches and bring in the sloth of people a casino would attract, it would be worth the chance of being caught. Hell, if the casino comes in, the island will change and I'd lose everything anyway. Instead of the peaceful tranquility I talked about earlier, this island would become the place that people would want to leave, myself included."

"So you broke into the bank?"

"Not exactly. I am…or was before I left MIT…a roboticist—a creator of mechanical toys if you will."

Steph remembered the table in Billy's apartment and the tiny parts that rested on it.

"I used you," Billy said and lightly blushed. "And I apologize. But your desk is right in the middle of everything. It provided great camouflage. And it was the best vantage point for Shoe."

"Shoe?" Steph's mind raced with visions of robotic sneakers.

"My starfish robot. He's attached to the side of your desk. I got him in via the drive-through tubes. He's equipped with audio and video capture devices. Any suspicious thing Bone does within Shoe's perimeter, Shoe will record."

Steph tried to remember everything she'd said and done in the past few days. Had Shoe recorded her, too? She suddenly felt embarrassed and intruded upon. A small hint of anger that began to unease her mind was quashed when Billy added, "There's something wrong about that bank. That crate in the vault. Whatever it is, it is not what Lett or Bone or anyone else claims it to be."

"I thought I was loosing my mind," Steph said. "I've felt its…"

"Power," Billy finished.

Steph thought about that for a moment. Power. The power to attract and repel at the same time. The power to invade the subconscious. The power to turn people into controlled, robotic drones. But that was ridiculous, wasn't it?

"How?" Steph said. "Why?"

"I don't know. At first I thought perhaps Lett was running narcotics and using the bank as a distribution channel. I thought that I'd been affected by whatever drugs were in the crate—yesterday when I came to see you, to check out the security box." He paused for a moment then confirmed exactly what Steph was thinking. "And yes, that was just a ploy to get into the vault. Again, my apologies."

"So what do we do now?"

"Shoe has limited energy life so I've been a bit selective in turning him on, but given all of the information you told me earlier, I'm certain that tonight should be a good opportunity to move him closer to the vault, to get a better angle of the crate. Perhaps I'll get lucky and there will be some after-hours activity worth recording as well."

"I wish you could get the robot into the vault. That's where the real action is taking place."

"A starfish would look a little out of place in such a sterile environment, even if the vault door was left open over night. Luckily, much of the bank has the Sea Life theme running through it. Shoe mixes in quite well. I'm thinking the teller window closest to the vault should give me a good angle once the vault is opened tomorrow."

"That's Carol's window. That'll be perfect." Steph thought of all the juicy tidbits the robot could record from that vantage. "Can you fill me in tomorrow?"

"Mix business with pleasure?"

"If you get what you—what *we* hope to get, business will be pleasure."

Billy turned from the beach road onto Paradise Lane, drove past several new construction projects and parked in front of Steph's paradise cottage. He walked Steph to her front door. "I'll pick you up around, say eight-thirty-ish?" Billy said.

Steph nodded and kissed him on the cheek. She peered deeply into his brown eyes. "We're going to get through this. We'll figure it out. And the island will return to some kind of sanity."

"*We* will," Billy said and left.

Before Steph entered her cottage, she noticed that her new neighbor had poked her head outside her front door. The woman looked to be in her mid-fifties. Her face was emotionally twisted in what Steph thought was a combination of sadness and fear, the ashen cheeks wet as if she'd been crying for hours.

"Hello…" Steph said but the woman quickly ducked back inside and closed her door.

Billy felt apprehensive about how much information he'd given up to Steph. Really, how well did he know her? Was it so wise to admit a felonious crime, especially a crime committed at her place of employment? She was the bank manager's personal secretary. She was *that* close to someone who could put him away for life, if not longer.

She'd revealed herself. Her revelations had threads within his own disbeliefs. They shared a common crazy enigma. But could he believe her? Did he believe her? Did he have a choice? The proof was in the pudding, as the old saying went. And he was going to prove something one way or another.

His VW sat in the very same parking spot he'd parked in three nights before. It was nine o'clock. The Treasure Trove lot was nearly empty, providing no inconspicuous cover, but the bank was not vacant. A black Hummer, a grey Mercedes and a white Ford Ranger dotted with lots of rust were parked in the handicap spots nearest the front door. He knew the owners of all three vehicles and questioned whether he'd be able to accomplish his primary goal: to stealthily move Shoe from Steph's desk to the teller window closest to the vault. The night, however, would certainly not be a total loss, not with Lett, Bone and the woman whom Steph hated named Carol inside. Shoe could certainly steal some valuable info from them.

When Billy snapped on the computer console, ten seconds elapsed before the RF transmitter connected to Shoe's receiver. Five seconds later, the first video image scribbled black and white across one of the station's two monitors.

Again, a horizon of perception appeared. Closest to Steph's desk, the top two-thirds of two empty chairs was visible. Beyond the chairs, most of the last two teller windows, all of the vault door and a truncation of Bone's and Kalimaris' office doors were shown in panoramic pixels.

Black and white scan lines temporarily blurred the video images as a block of RF interference suddenly passed between Shoe and Billy. When the blur reassembled, Billy saw Lett, his bodyguard, Bone and Carol. Their knees came into view first and as they neared the vault he saw each clearly. He snapped on the console's audio system.

"…can't keep using the bank like this," Bone was saying. "This is my bank, dammit! Our deal did not include such indiscretion." Billy turned up the volume.

"A half a million dollars, Mitch," Lett replied. "I made you half a mill."

"What about Alixel?" Bone said. "She's as big a part of this. You seem to have forgotten her. I've certain promises…to you…to her."

Carol intervened. "It's time you made a choice, Mitch. Are you with us or against us?"

"She'll be here tomorrow," Bone continued as the four of them entered the vault. The door remained open though Billy could not see them or the crate inside. Voices became mumbled, incomprehensible.

And then one, sharp exclamation erupted.

"NO!"

The shriek was squeaky high, the sound of a woman's scream from a man's throat.

Almost simultaneously, a gray aura of pixels spread from the right side of the screen. Billy knew that later, when he reviewed the recorded video on the color monitor at home, the gray glow would reveal its real crimson color.

Lett's bodyguard appeared in the vault's doorway from the left, disappeared to the right then reappeared, pushing the glowing crate toward the left.

Another girly burly scream erupted, this time causing the speakers in Billy's computer console to crackle.

"SHIT!"

About thirty seconds elapsed in silence. Only the gray, pixilated, undulating glow was visible. To Billy, it was like watching an Alfred Hitchcock film interspersed with an intentional director's pause to build tension. And he felt himself fortunate and unfortunate all at the same time. Having a color monitor would have made what he saw next horrifically realistic.

He clearly remembered how gruesome the black blood running from Janet Leigh's body to the shower drain had appeared. He'd been only twelve when he saw *Psycho* for the first time. Even in black and white (or more appropriately, because it *was* in black and white) the violence of the shower scene had been, up until that time in his young life, the most disturbing thing he'd ever witnessed.

But this was different. What he now saw was real. The black drool that leaked across the floor into the vault's doorway from the left was, without question, blood. It flowed slowly, its thick viscosity, clumpy. And the grey glow that most certainly emanated from the crate within, spread outward, seemingly magnified by the increasing blood flow.

And then Mitchell Bone's head rolled into view. Everything scary from the pubescent memory of Janet Leigh and Anthony Perkins was forever dashed. When a hand appeared in the doorway from the left, snatched the head as if it were a deformed basketball and crushed it, Billy fell off of his stool wondering about his own sanity. Something was terribly wrong with Shoe, he thought. Its video eyeball was malfunctioning. What he just saw could not be real. Something had intercepted the RF signal and was feeding him cinematic Hitchcock propaganda.

He rolled onto his knees, never taking an eye from the monitor, flooded with self-denial.

That's when the bodyguard's face filled the monitor. The video started to shake as Shoe was plucked from the side of Steph's desk.

"You're next," the bodyguard said.

Then the monitor went black.

His mind raced. Visions spun. He was certain he was, again, hallucinating. Memories of false images from yesterday raced forward. Gunshots. Someone telling him to "Shut the fuck up." He was nauseous. He was puking. And then there was the red tide, incredible waves, and a surfer who rode a board made from the rarest of woods. Birds with one leg screeched in sudden death—*but that had been real, hadn't it*? Fish boiled in blood bubbled to the Gulf surface at his feet—*but that had not been imagination, right*?

Then there was CrabMan. And that crazy bitch from the *South Jetty* who'd tried to take his head off. That *had* been real. The bat had missed his head by inches and if it hadn't been for Officer Keadle, CrabMan's crude nail weapon certainly would have planted deep into his flesh.

Was he going mad?

And then there came a knocking. He grabbed his head between both hands.

But the knocking only grew louder.

He wanted to scream but could hardly breathe.

Knocking. Between his hands. Within his head.

"Anyone in there?"

Billy quickly removed his hands from his head, looking at his palms as if they'd just spoken.

"Hey!"

The driver's side door of the VW deflected inward as three more short, pounding knocks assaulted exterior metal. The door handle was yanked but he'd locked it. It was Officer Keadle.

Billy slipped belly flat to the floor and snugged up against the shadows behind the passenger seat. A flashlight beam wandered through the windshield, probed the inside like a stage spotlight looking for an actor. The monitor above him was still on but it now only revealed blackness. The light beam disappeared; silence took its place. Then the crunch of shoe on gravel moved toward him.

Bang! Bang! Bang! came Keadle's fist again, this time right beside him. Billy almost yelped.

"Presser! Hey, Presser!"

The flashlight beam reappeared, probed near his feet, crawled across the floor toward his head, stopped momentarily then went out. The passenger side door handle was tried but he'd locked it too. He'd locked all the doors, including the rear hatch which was now handled without success. A full minute later, Billy heard Keadle open and close a car door. An engine revved. Tires crunched gravel. Headlights passed through the windshield, briefly lighting the VW's interior before exiting the Treasure Trove parking lot.

Slowly, Billy rose from the floor, peered beyond the passenger seat and through the windshield. The Big Texas Bank and three cars were in the distance, their shadowy outlines visible under two street lamps and the quarter moon. Keadle was gone.

He decided to wait a few more minutes, just in case the VW was being watched. So he sat in the driver's seat, keys in the ignition, waiting for heartbeats pounding against his ears to subside, waiting for his intuition to signal it was safe, waiting for fear to dissipate.

But none of that ever happened. In fact, his heart now nearly exploded, his fear culminating toward a plateau that would be hard to step down from. Everything was not okay nor would it ever be again.

From inside the bank a dull crimson glow emanated through two sets of windows. Red halos around the panes were interrupted by several short blasts of bright white, as if someone was shooting photographs with a gigantic flash bulb.

And then the bodyguard suddenly appeared in the window to the right, his tall, wide silhouette outlined by the crimson glow behind him. Billy couldn't see his eyes from this distance but he knew the man stared straight at him.

You're next, he'd said.

Maybe not, Billy thought. Maybe I have all the evidence I need. Bone had been murdered and Shoe had sent the recorded signals to his computer. Billy was afraid, but he was also confident. The mixture made him nauseous.

He shot the bodyguard his middle finger then drove off with fear and courage fighting for control of his stomach…and soul.

Janine's nightmares had become reality. They had followed her from Kansas to Texas. And she'd been crying ever since Joel had left her more than eight hours ago. Her new cottage apartment had been a blur. Thankfully, the former tenant had left a full roll of toilet paper in the bathroom. More than half of it was now gone. Matted wads lay on the bed beside her; several others were scattered on the carpeted floor. Still more were on the kitchen table where she'd done most of her crying.

The medical doctors and psychiatrists had told her that none of it had been real, except for the part about the barn exploding. Dynamite had not been stored properly, they'd said. The explosion had taken the life of the man she'd claimed to have had a "magic dagger." That man had been an imposter. The real Professor Cower had been found murdered in his upstate New York home; he'd been stabbed repeatedly through the heart.

The dynamite had also taken the life of her son. No one had eaten anyone. The psychiatrists had been particularly concerned about this part of her psychosis. They'd been incapable of actually visualizing such a gruesome scene let alone considering that it had been real. People just didn't eat people, they'd told her. People just didn't eat themselves. How could they? It didn't make sense. It wasn't logical, and if it wasn't logical, how could it have been real? At least that's the argument they'd made.

As for Albert Stine and the thing she called a Cubit, they'd found no trace of him or the box in the rubble. The doctors had reasoned that they'd simply been evaporated. Anything too close to an explosion that large would disintegrate, they'd said.

But those logical, well-reasoned, highly educated men and women had been wrong. They'd kept her in the hospital under "close observation" for three months before releasing her to friend Beth Blandford. And for what? To convince her that her reality was all in her mind, that she was living in a nightmare from which she could not wake up? Damn those people. Damn their accusations. Damn them for making her partially accept their own false reasoning. She'd started to believe that, just perhaps, it had all been her mind's way of explaining the loss of those closest to her. She'd haphazardly stored the dynamite and her carelessness had caused their deaths, they'd said. It had been all her fault but her mind had denied it with such an elaborate story as to make her appear insane. Once she'd accepted the diagnosis, basically admitting that she'd inadvertently caused the deaths of three people, they'd let her go. She would not be arrested. There would be no trial. That was part of the deal. Sixth months of probation in the care of Beth Blandford had been her penalty. There hadn't been a court in the country that would have convicted her of anything based on the lack of evidence but she could no longer sustain a life in bed under doctors' microscopes. So she'd signed the paper.

They'd been wrong, of course. The snot wads around her were evidence.

She was afraid to go to sleep and now wished that she'd had enough courage to ask Joel to stay with her. A Christian woman didn't do such things though. But God made concessions for frightened Christian women, didn't he? If God had again placed Stine in her path then he must have also provided for her protection.

Marcy?

Joel?

Her eyes now red and swollen with misery fluttered. Fear kept them open. Fatigue closed them. Bare bedroom walls and the mirror that sat on the furnished bedroom dresser flashed on and off until fatigue finally won.

It didn't take long for the real nightmares to return. Albert and the Cubit sat atop a huge pile of sand. Behind them, clouds blacker than oil whirled in anger. Bolts of lighting skittered and clashed. Around Albert, sprawled out in the hundreds at the foot of the sand pile were dead people. She knew one of them, Marcy. And half way up the sand pile, lying dead on his back with a stiff hand reaching for Albert's leg was Joel. His skin was charred as if struck by lightening.

"Rise," the Albert thing said. "Rise and join me my dear, sweet wife."

The Cubit began to glow. Crimson light flooded the star at the top edge of its wooden surface. Slowly, its lid lifted on hinges that weren't there. A bolt of lighting careened into the opening as if the Cubit had pulled it, unwanting, inside. Dark, bloody crimson grew in a giant halo and from within it rose a figure dressed in a black wedding gown, its face turned away toward the ocean. The black lace was shredded at the hem. Patches had been ripped from the arms and neckline. Something red drooled haphazardly, as if an artist had flicked brushes full of paint across the gown's surface. When the figure stepped from the Cubit it turned. Janine's own face stared back at her, the cheeks sunken, the teeth gone. And the Cubit slammed shut.

This brought her out of the nightmare screaming. Someone was pounding on her cottage door. She jammed the bed sheet in her mouth to stifle her cries.

"Hey!" the door-pounder yelled.

It was the Albert thing. It had come to take her away. It had come to make her part of its dead world. It had come to make her its wife. She bit down hard on the bed sheet. Blood sprouted from her lip.

"You all right in there?" the pounder yelled.

She wanted to hide but there was no place that the Albert thing could not find her: in Kansas, in Texas, under her bed, it didn't matter.

And then the door opened. She'd forgotten to lock it. Why had she forgotten to lock it? Dear God!

"Ma'am," the voice said from beyond the open bedroom door. "You in there?"

The shadows of the approaching visitor, stretched into the bedroom's doorway. A board creaked. It was all she could do to keep the scream down.

But it wasn't the Albert thing. It wasn't even a man. Had she not been so panicked, had she not just awakened screaming from another nightmare, she would have heard the soft voice of a concerned woman. It was her neighbor. It was the woman who'd waved at her earlier in the day.

But the revelation was too much for the scattered remnants of logic to comprehend. Reality and nightmare were one in the same.

And she fainted.

Just after midnight, they massed a hundred strong within the bank. The Cubit had been efficiently busy. Each of the contest entrants, those that had entered the vault with Carol during the day and had been introduced to the seamless, wooden crate inside, now stood in cubited glory—like drones. Like robots. Each understood its task. Just as the cubited Mitchell Bone had "recycled" the real Mitchell Bone, so too would each of these new Port Aransas residents. By the time Saturday rolled around, the cubits would act pretty much like their human counterparts, except of course, when it came time to vote. All cubits would vote one way.

That's how Albert Stine had planned it. The influential would vote for the casino. The influential would influence others to vote for the casino. The vote would pass and the bulldozers and backhoes would get busy. The ancient treasure would be uncovered. The final piece would be in his grasp. The beginning of the end of the world was only days away.

The crimson glow from the Cubit faded as Professor Nelson crawled from its depths. He was the last for this evening and like all those that had emerged before him, he looked and acted as if he'd risen from the dead—which was not far from the truth. He assembled in ragged disarray, stumbling over one of Stephanie Drake's customer chairs, as he moved toward the front of the bank.

Without a word, Stine opened the bank's double doors and the walking dead spilled out into the parking lot. Some stumbled and fell, a comical sight for Chancey Lett who, after all, was the only human in the bunch and therefore was the only one with a sense of humor.

In the distance, Stine saw four cubits enter Officer Keadle's cruiser which sped off toward the south end of town. Nole Kilpatrick also arrived with a van that held fifteen cubits. His receptionist was with him. A half a dozen got into Stine's black Hummer, seven stumbled into the bed of Carol's

Ford Ranger, but none got into Bone's Mercedes. The cubited Bone could not drive yet. Such a complicated skill, like so many others, would be acquired over the next day or so.

The rest of the cubits lurched and staggered into the dark shadows around street corners en route to recycle their human counterparts. Within twenty minutes, only Lett and Bone remained. They reentered the bank; the cubits had left quite a mess, especially in the vault where its sterile interior remained splattered by the cubited bank manager's feeding on bone and flesh.

THE CUBIT: PART II

A DAY AT THE BEACH

At 3:35 a.m. Thursday morning, the NOAA upgraded Hurricane Antiago to Category 3. Antiago had left the Yucatán coastline off of Merida and had entered the Gulf shortly after two o'clock. A Category 3 hurricane in the Gulf during June was not unusual. What was odd, which Jim Cantore reiterated during the early morning Weather Channel broadcasts, was that in less than thirty minutes the storm's sustained winds had gone from a hundred to a hundred and thirty miles per hour, a rarity unmatched in the history of the tropics, especially since the hurricane's diameter was less than fifty miles across. Stranger still was that Antiago had made an abrupt turn of nearly ninety degrees, a dogleg to the west that set it on course for the southern Texas coastline. Cantore made the comment that it was as if Antiago had suddenly connected with some invisible Texas magnet. And because everything in Texas was big, he joked that a magnet from the Lone Star state might just be large enough to have caused such a sudden shift.

For the fishing industries around Port Aransas the idea of a hurricane slamming into them was far from funny. The industry had already suffered from a massive fish kill that was yet to be explained. A hurricane would certainly decimate what was left. But the wrath of Mother Nature was nothing compared to the terrible evil that was slowly transforming the people of Port A. Reports of screams had come into the police dispatcher throughout the night. There had been at least twenty calls and Officer Keadle had been sent to respond to each.

After sunrise, another twenty or so witnesses stopped by the *South Jetty* with stories ranging from worrisome, to outlandish, to horrific. The newspaper receptionist recorded each with a smile and told each storyteller that publisher Kilpatrick would review their accounts for possible publication as soon as he returned. "Look for your story in Monday's edition," she lied to each resident.

Around the same time that Billy Jo Presser's alarm sounded Thursday morning, a flatbed tractor-trailer rolled onto the beach close to where the *Knights in White Satin* had entertained luau guests two nights before. The red lettering on the Kenworth cab read: *Reed's Excavation*. Chained to the lowboy was a Caterpillar backhoe.

Billy dressed and headed out the door. Minutes later he stopped next to the trailerless Kenworth on Alister Street a mile from Paradise Cottages. The lettering on the cab's door made him think of the impending vote Saturday. He glared at the Kenworth driver as if the driver was the sole reason for the mayhem that had turned a wonderful island getaway into a trap from which everyone could not get away from fast enough. Billy had not meant to scowl, but he did; it was a menacing scowl, a threatening scowl, one that tested the Kenworth driver's patience. When the light changed, the driver flipped off Billy then spun eight of the Kenworth's ten tires which bolted the cab from the light.

Car horns blared behind him while Billy continued staring at the space emptied by the screeching truck cab, but he paid them no attention. He couldn't. His mind was too engaged with visions of *his* beach, with hills of excavated sand and scooped-out holes. Huge machines surrounded him with metal teeth and ribbed feet, and at the center of the mayhem was the bodyguard. He stood directing the destruction, his hands to the sky, a black storm boiling behind him.

"Asshole!" a passing driver yelled. This shook Billy from trance. When he looked up the light had already changed back to red. A black Hummer pulled up beside him but he couldn't see beyond its tinted windows. Again, the light turned green and again the car horns blared from behind. The Hummer's window slowly lowered.

"Hi cutie," the girl in the passenger seat said. "You want to join us?" the driver added. Both girls giggled then the Hummer peeled away.

It was as if he was back in Cambridge taking a test or engaged in research. Once his mind locked it was hard to disengage. Like a computer stuck within an exponential equation, his brain could not stop its processes until some answer was complete. But these thoughts had no solutions, at least none that would enable him to keep his sanity.

Billy blinked and shook his head then finally set the VW in motion.

When Billy pulled up to the curb outside her cottage apartment, Steph was rubbing Janine's temples. The two women stood together on the narrow lawn.

"How can I ever thank you enough?" Janine repeated. Steph had stayed with her until she had fallen asleep just four hours ago. Circles of exhaustion rang both of the women's eyes. Steph pushed stray gray strands away from Janine's forehead.

"You go on now and get ready," Steph said, smiling. "You and Joel are going to have a great time." She turned toward the VW and waved at Billy. "Are you sure you don't want a ride? Billy won't mind."

Janine grabbed one of Steph's hands and gently massaged it. "You've done enough," she said. "Besides, a morning trolley ride into town might just be what the doctor ordered."

Steph, who was a couple of inches taller than Janine, bent forward and kissed her forehead, turned without another word, walked briskly to Billy's VW and got in. She waved from the window as Billy drove off.

Janine had found a third friend, but more importantly, her neighbor had found her—screaming in the night, paralyzed with fear. She'd found her and they'd talked, and she'd stayed there until Janine had finally fallen asleep.

Janine had said nothing about seeing Albert. How could she? A stranger could never understand. So, instead of telling her neighbor that a dead man—who ate people and had killed her son—was in Port Aransas and would soon kill her too, and instead of telling her that Albert would probably kill anyone even obscurely close to her, all she'd said was that she'd had a really bad dream. And she had. She'd become the demon's wife.

Miss Drake (Steph, she preferred to be called) must have wondered how any nightmare could make a person shake so intensely or why nearly a full roll of toilet paper lay in scattered wads throughout the kitchen and bedroom, but she'd asked no such thing. Steph had brought her a glass of water, had combed Janine's hair and had placed a damp washcloth on her forehead, and had repeated, "Everything is going to be okay. Everything is going to be okay." Steph was cut from the same good people stuff that Marcy was, the same Paradise Island hospitality. The same care. And Janine felt fortunate that God had chosen her new friends so purposefully.

The thought of Marcy reminded her that she'd left her "sacks of life" in the fortune teller's guest bedroom. She'd been so frazzled after seeing Albert that she'd not even considered them on the trolley home with Joel. The same clothes that she'd worn to the Surf Side were now heavily wrinkled and damp with tears (particularly in the cleavage hem of her blouse). She'd need to stop at Marcy's on her way in to town.

Janine slipped Marcy's scrunchie on her head, brushed what wrinkles she could from her blouse and shorts, and pulled her cottage apartment door closed. She twisted the knob to check that it was locked. The smell of Volkswagen exhaust still lingered as she set out for the trolley stop at the end of the road.

It was a quarter past eight when she boarded Thursday's first trolley run.

"Welcome back aboard," the driver said, though Janine did not remember him from the previous day. When she offered him the dollar fare, the driver waved his hand. He was a small man with a small face. His age appeared close to hers. "You can get a monthly pass that will save you at least fifteen bucks."

Janine looked at the bill, turned it over in her hand to see if something like snot or tears was awash on its surface. She noticed a curious look from the passenger sitting three rows behind the driver. "Okay," Janine said. "But the fair today is one dollar. That's all I have."

The driver suddenly blushed with embarrassment. "No, no," he said, now waving both hands. "I don't mean to be a salesman. I just thought, ya know, being new to the island and all, you just didn't know."

Janine smiled, her wall of suspicion crumbling.

"Carl," the woman three rows back exclaimed. "Can we get going already? You know I have to be at the docks by eight-thirty. Hands on the wheel please." The twenty-something woman scowled at Janine.

Janine handed the bill to Carl. "Thank you," she said. "I'll take your advice when I get to town." She walked past the dock lady without looking at her and sat in the very rear of the trolley. A young boy, no more than ten years old, sat unescorted two rows up to the left. His attention was connected to the white iPod earplugs stuck into both ears. His head bobbed to the digital, pre-teen beats.

She stepped from the trolley ten minutes later, and stood a block from Marcy's shop. The boy with the iPod exited the trolley with her, paying little attention to anything except the beat between his ears. Janine walked the short distance and when she stopped and turned to climb the three-step rise to the shop's front door, the iPod kid ran right into her, nearly knocking her down.

"Hey!" she exclaimed, rubbing her shoulder. The iPod kid did not look up but instead continued staring at the sidewalk, his head bopping, a tiny bead of Texas sun sweat trickling across his forehead. "Pay attention to where you're going."

The iPod kid took two more steps and his head stopped bopping. He stood there, motionless, as if his feeble brain could not continue without the accompaniment of digital juice. She was less than a dozen feet from him when he looked up with a bewildered expression, one often found on the face of habitual sleepwalkers who've awakened in places far away from the bedroom. He turned toward Janine.

She gasped, took a shuffled step backward, tripped on Marcy's first step and fell into a sitting position onto the third. Something swirled within the iPod kid's eyes. Pools of crimson and silver sparkles, filled with stupidity and intelligence—repelling and attracting all in the same instant. They were Albert's eyes in the face of a ten-year-old boy. The morning's warmth did nothing to prevent the vertebrae-freezing chill that raced to the back of Janine's head.

The iPod kid stared as if he didn't comprehend, like a little boy who'd seen a toad for the first time, had found a sudden attraction for such a little boy thing, and was considering what to do about his newfound discovery. Then, like an automaton, the iPod kid resumed his position on the sidewalk, not looking at Janine but instead again at the sidewalk. She heard the beat of a new song throbbing from the earplugs. The iPod kid's head resumed its beat-throbbing movement and he continued along the sidewalk, not stopping at the next intersection where a car patiently waited for him to cross, then turned in the direction of the beach.

Of course she'd imagined it.

Right?

A lingering aftereffect of last night's dream.

Right?

Something that the doctors in the psycho ward would have called residual dementia.

How could a person eat themselves, one of the doctors had said. That's just not logical. And if it isn't logical it didn't happen.

How could the iPod kid have the Albert-thing's eyes? It wasn't logical.

So, it didn't happen.

She slowly rose, rubbed the soreness in her shoulder and butt cheeks, turned to the front door and knocked. Knocked again. And again. She desperately wanted to change. Beyond presenting herself to Joel as unkept, the clothes she wore were battered memories of last night's fight against logic.

She twisted the knob and found it locked. Moving around to the back of the shop, she approached the back door while looking around to see if others were watching. She remembered that this door opened into the kitchen and that Marcy had said she usually kept it unlocked. It was.

"Hello," she whispered then raised her voice. "Hello?"

When no one answered she entered the kitchen then climbed the steps toward the guest bedroom, found her two sacks of life where she'd left them on the bed, opened one, and spilled its contents. Folded blouses, shirts, and shorts unraveled into a pile on the bed. She shook the sack to release a book which dropped on top of the clothes. Etched into its red, back cover was the image of the magic dagger.

The book was all that she'd salvaged from the piles of her former life. After being released from the psycho ward, she'd convinced Beth Blandford to take her back to Pickett's Crossing just one more time. The doctors had demanded that Beth do no such thing. They'd said that if Janine ever returned to the cause of her dementia they'd have no choice but to try her on manslaughter charges for the death of her son. They wanted to protect her, they'd said. But what they hadn't said was their real, illogical reason: They didn't want such an experience to tip her psychopathic scales in the direction of murder. And Beth would be her first victim.

Among the heaping piles of weed-overgrown barn, cars, house, dirt, and corn, Janine had found the book jammed into the vacant hole of a tree she'd dynamited near the barn years ago. Investigators had never recovered the book; it had been hidden two feet deep. So what had led her to it? What had made her stick her arm into a space that no human had a right to do so? Perhaps it was because within five minutes of exiting Beth's car, she'd tripped and had landed within a foot of the hole and had *heard* it—a nearly inaudible hum.

But that was illogical. Books didn't hum.

And then the depths of the hole had begun to glow, taunting her residual dementia, testing the reasoning of logical doctors. *And if it was illogical, it did not happen.*

Beth had seen nothing, of course. And when Janine had stuck her arm in and had pulled out the book, Beth had asked her why she'd stashed it there. *It's my personal diary*, she'd lied. Something so sacred as a widow's diary could never be questioned. And Beth hadn't.

Janine massaged the book's leathery surface; she touched the point of the dagger with care and reflection, remembering its power to heal. She'd never been able to read the book's entire contents since all of the pages were stuck together except for the center spread. But it was on these two pages that the book's magic was revealed. She flipped it open.

The left page was completely drawn in what appeared to be pencil. Pictured were temples that were not Egyptian pyramids, but resembled them in structure. There were strange animal/human hybrid creatures written along the page edges. Some had bodies of mammals, birds and reptiles sporting human heads. Some images were completely glyphic and indiscernible. But her favorite image was the magical one—the one on the right side. It was that page's single entry: a bird with wings of fire. It swooped majestically from the center binding at the top of the page, a trail of dust or wind following close behind. It seemed to dance on the page and to Janine appeared to be smiling. But her fascination with the drawing's beauty was unmatched by the magic of its existence. It had not been there when she'd recovered the book from the stump hole. The Bird of Fire had drawn itself into the page over the last six months.

But that was illogical, and if it was illogical, it did not happen—it did not exist.

But it did! And as she stared at the drawing, another minute stroke of the heavenly pencil added one more tip to one more flame that engulfed the bird's wing.

She wiped the pads of her fingers across the delicate paper surface and closed her eyes, to see, again, the face of Professor Cower whose anguish from the bullet planted in his chest would quickly fade when Janine stuck the thin blade of the dagger into the entry wound. Professor Cower, who had brought the book and the dagger into her life. Professor Cower, who, according to detectives, also did not exist.

She closed the book and dropped it back into the linen sack. She snatched a pair of shorts, a green t-shirt that read "John Deere," and went to the guest bathroom to freshen up and change. When she switched on the light she found a Post-it note stuck to the bathroom mirror. It read:

Janine: Went to see a man about a loan. Make yourself at home.
I'll catch up with you when I get back.

- Love, Marcy

"Okay, Marcy," Janine said to the note. "We'll catch up when you get back."

And boy do I have an illogical story to tell you.

She removed the note and began washing the wrinkles from her face.

Joel stared at the magician's hands and tapped two fingers against the paint-peeled metal railing that constituted the foot of his bed. The clock, Marcy had given him. The mustached man on the clock's face pointed out that it was nearly eight-thirty. A black top hat with two little rabbit ears poking out of its brim was painted on the clock face near the six o'clock position. The magician's long minute hand closed in on the top hat, inching closer to the six as if the mechanical magician was about to perform one fantastic illusion but was taking forever to pull it off.

Joel had never wasted so much time staring at a device that ticked so much time away. And this clock wasn't one that slowly eased through sixty minute cycles either. The clock that Marcy had given him was an antique. Its minute hand actually jerked forward for each minute that passed with an audible click. With each forward jerk-click movement, Joel's fingers strummed the bed frame metal faster.

Janine was supposed to be here by now. The trolley would have picked her up by eight. The ride was no more than ten minutes.

Jerk-click!

Had she decided against it? Had she decided that Joel was the bum that everyone had said he was? Had she decided that there was no future with a man who lived in a one-room shack, a man who had no job and little means of support?

Jerk-click!

And after all the hard work he'd put into cleaning up the place last night. He'd scrubbed the mold from the shower stall. He'd scraped the rust from the bed railings where his fingers rapidly tapped. He'd washed his clothes and the linens, had hung them to dry overnight, and had gotten up early to fold the clothes and dress the springy, oblong bed mattress.

Jerk-click!

He'd expended a great deal of time thinking about how this day might unfold. What fishing lessons he'd teach her. How he would teach them. If he'd get any closer to her both physically and mentally.

Jerk-click!

He wondered if she'd free her mind and trust in his confidence. Why had she come to the island? What was in her past? Why was she running? Who was chasing her and for what reason?

Jerk-click!

The magician's minute hand jerk-clicked onto the top hat when Joel realized, again, that all he'd been thinking about was himself. Poor Joel. He'd cleaned his shower and washed his clothes. Poor Joel. He'd spent time thinking about teaching someone something new. Poor Joel. Janine was not yet here because Poor Joel was… poor.

But what if he was wrong? What if none of this had anything to do with Poor Joel? What if her tardiness had everything to do with the casino men? What if one of them had found her on the trolley? She'd acted so frightened at the restaurant. What if the casino men had harmed her? What if it was because of them and not Poor Joel that Janine was not here? Or worse, what if he, Poor Joel, the man who'd sworn against a life of solitude less than twelve hours ago found that the woman who could have saved himself from himself had been taken from him by these men?

Jerk-click!

The magician's hand revealed no secrets and provided no answers as the clock clicked to 8:31. Joel's hand stopped drumming and started trembling. He tried to look away from the magician but he couldn't.

"Please let her be all right," he said to the clock.

"Joel," the clock seemed to say. "Hello, Joel?"

He sat upright on the bed, glaring curiously at the magician whose mustache revealed no lips.

"Joel Canton?"

But the voice, he realized, was not coming from the clock; it was coming from beyond his screen door. He turned to see Janine as she walked along the pebble-dirt sidewalk toward him. When she reached the screen door, she repeated his name. "Joel. There you are. Are you okay?"

He smiled, relieved, and almost leapt from his bed spring.

"Welcome," he said exasperated. "I…eh…" He pushed the screen door open. "Come in." He shot a quick scowl at the magician, at the clock. Janine followed his glare.

"Sorry," she said. "Are we too late?"

Joel's immediate urge was to swipe the clock from its place on the wooden milk crate. Instead, he grabbed the circular metal timekeeper and offered it to Janine.

"Clocks are so overrated," he said. "But this one is more a keepsake than anything else." Janine gave the clock a curious stare but did not take it from his hand. "Marcy gave it to me," he continued. "She said that my old fisherman's intuition might some day leave me. This ole thing is supposed to, you know, help me keep track of time."

"The rabbit is out of the hat," Janine said, smiling.

Joel looked at the clock face. He'd never given the clock enough of his time to realize that some mechanism inside pushed a rabbit out of the magician's hat at thirty-five minutes past each hour.

"Uh, yeah," he lied. "That's what I've been waiting for. The magic trick."

Janine continued smiling, her eyes filled with a childlike wonderment. "I don't think I've ever seen anything like it."

It was an awkward moment, Joel holding the clock in the palm of his hand not knowing of its mechanical magic, Janine staring at it having moved no more than a foot into his home, Joel trying to avoid the assumption that he'd been patiently waiting, using the clock as a guide that had summoned all kinds of false conclusions.

Janine grabbed the clock and reset it on the wooden crate end table. "That Marcy is one special lady," she said then grabbed Joel's open hand and added, "so what are we fishing for today?"

Her hand felt like melted butter in his rough, wrinkled grip. "Whatever the sea offers." He led her farther into the Canton Shack and together they sat on his bed which squeaked in stress from the unknown added weight. "How have you been? You look tired."

She released his grip and lightly tapped his knuckles. "I've never been able to sleep well in a new bed."

Joel suddenly stood. "Is it the casino men? Are they bothering you?"

Janine stood beside him. "No. Really, it's the bed." She looked at Joel's mattress. "Shouldn't we get going? I'm really excited to learn sea fishing."

His ex-wife Jane had always wanted to learn how to fish in the Gulf but for many reasons, every time the idea had surfaced, she or Joel had always been busy with some other more important task. For Joel, the charter fishing boat company had overridden any leisure time the two could have spent together. From the day that "Jaws" had been captured, the charter had been his number one priority. But it hadn't lasted. The charter had slowly gone bankrupt, giving Joel plenty of time for leisure and for sea-fishing lessons to anyone who asked. But by then it had been too late. Jane had already separated from Joel, though not legally but certainly in mind and spirit. Bert Nookle had stolen her away. She'd left Joel a Dear John and had moved to Galveston. He'd not taught anyone to fish since.

"Yes," he said to Janine, again relishing her striking resemblance to Jane. "Yes, I'll get the gear."

Joel disappeared into an adjoining room he'd created using a shower rod and bed sheets, the space in his small home that served as his bathroom and closet, and returned with his fishing rod. In the corner at the foot of the bed next to the wooden crate end table and the magician clock was a small, dorm-room-sized refrigerator which sat atop an empty wooden spool, the kind used to store coils of telephone and electric pole wiring. From within the dingy white door, he pulled out the remainder of a Milky Way candy bar and slipped it into his coveralls. "Special recipe bait," he said in response to Janine's curious stare. "Bet you didn't know fish had a sweet tooth?"

Janine shook her head.

"Well then, let's get started."

"Where's the tackle box and the stringer?" Janine asked.

Joel giggled. It was the first time he'd done so in a long time. "We won't be needing any of that commercial mumbo jumbo. All that's really needed is a pole, some strong line, and just the right bait."

"You sound like Huck Finn," Janine said, smiling.

"Ah, yes. Of the Mississippi Finns. Clever boy that one. Don't know how he ever got them kids to whitewash his fence."

"You mean Tom Sawyer," Janine corrected.

Joel's eyebrows furled for a moment. "Sawyers. Yeah. Dammit if I don't get them kids confused. Ornery rascals, both of them. If it weren't for Becky, they'd both of ended up in the pen."

Janine grabbed Joel's free arm and locked her elbow around his. "And *they* kept *her* out harm's way," she said.

Joel understood. He would protect *her* and she would keep *him* out of trouble. Just like Becky and Tom. Just like Samuel Clemens might have imagined his young characters as senior citizens. "Shall we, Miss Thatcher?" Joel said, snuggling her elbow within his own.

"Lead the way, Mr. Sawyer."

It had all of the purity and innocence of the first American love story. Two people, young at heart, newly acquainted, strolling arm-in-arm, without the cares of the complicated world they lived in, under a perfect sun, with only scant white fluffs of marshmallow-cotton clouds breaking the heat in spurts that carried light, salty breezes into the faces, noses and lungs of the youngsters. Their outer skins belied their inner youths. They were giddy. They talked about nothing important which was the most important conversation any newly coupled humans could engage in, the kind of conversation that rarely happens more than once, a conversation of probing, one without political, economic or social underpinnings. Babbling some would call it, nonsense others might say, but it was this very collection of babbling, nonsensical talk that connected men and women like glue. Nothing material ever came of talk like this. It could not be labeled. No price tags were attached. Its channel was spiritual, and for every couple it was always different since the only understanding that could be deciphered was done by the human soul.

That's how it was for Janine and Joel, alias Becky Thatcher and Tom Sawyer, as they strode across dunes that protected Port A from the ocean surges of the Gulf.

Janine coddled Joel's arm as if it were a valuable piece of Venetian sculpture. His coveralls smelled of Tide detergent. A couple of stains were visible across the chest and lap. She had the overwhelming urge to slip her free right hand into the coverall's right breast pocket. In fact, as she and Joel crested the final dune to the visual and auditory beauty of the crashing beachhead waves, Janine fantasized about jumping into the coverall pocket. She would be safe there. Albert would never find her. In the security of Joel's pocket, the nightmares could not reach her. She'd have Joel's heartbeat to comfort her and the Milky Way candy bar would prevent starvation.

"And that cloud looks like a bunny," Joel was saying as she stared at his pocket. She looked into the sky. To her, the cloud looked more like a dog with really long ears but she didn't say this. Instead, she continued their nonsensical conversation by referring to another cloud, closer to the horizon where the south jetty stretched its long rocky finger into the Gulf.

"A mushroom," she said and quickly wished that she hadn't. It broke the mood. The connotation of a mushroom cloud brought the real world smashing back down upon her. The unimportant conversation that came only once in a lifetime had ended.

And to make matters worse, at the bottom of the last dune where the beach road stretched north and south a hundred yards away from the water break line stood the iPod kid. Nothing much had changed about him since he'd cornered her back at Marcy's front porch. His wavy blonde hair jumped to the seemingly pneumatic drive of his head as it beat like a piston back and forth, chin to chest. The white iPod ear plug wires drooped and tangled around his left arm which carried the digital music box. A white pickup nearly hit the iPod kid as he stumbled hypnotically, his head down and thumping, across the beach road toward Joel and Janine.

"Ted Lavender," Joel said of the boy. "Is that Ted Lavender?" Janine shrugged her shoulders. She, of course, knew very few people on the island, but she realized the question was not meant for her.

At the base of the last dune, the iPod kid and Janine and Joel stopped and stared at each other. The iPod kid looked up from the sand, his head still thrusting to beats in his ears. He looked quizzically at Janine and quickly dismissed her. They were a good ten feet apart but Janine could still sense the crimson sparkle that reminded her of Albert. Again, she felt the urge to jump into Joel's coverall breast pocket.

"Is that you, Teddy?" Joel said. "You okay, kid?"

The boy who was apparently Ted Lavender did not seem to know his own name, but to Janine it appeared that he recognized Joel. Little Teddy's head stopped beating though the music still thumped in muffled volume from the iPod earplugs.

"G-G-G…" little Teddy's lips began to pronounce. "G-G-Gee…"

"Joel," Joel said. "Remember me, kid?"

"G-J-J-Joel?" Teddy's eyebrows curled inward with an expression of concentrated study. "F-f-fish," he continued. "We… caught…a…fish… Joel."

Joel took a step toward Teddy. "Son? You look tired."

Teddy pointed at Joel's fishing pole. "F-fish," he muttered. "Fish… are…dead. Teddy…are…dead."

Janine didn't know if Joel saw it but at that very moment the crimson and silver swirls and sparkles that occupied the center of Teddy's black eyes suddenly brightened and twisted in a moiré of chaos. Then, without reason, Teddy belted out a scream so viciously loud the white pickup truck that almost hit him moments before stopped abruptly on the beach road and the driver looked back through the cab's window. Teddy threw both hands in the air and ran between Joel and Janine, brushing both with both of his shoulders. He raced up the dune, screaming.

In his sudden maniacal rush, Teddy had dropped his iPod and it now rested at Joel's feet. He picked it up and dropped it into the breast pocket where Janine had imagined roosting. "I'll get it back to him the next time I see him," he said with the same quizzical stare that Janine imagined was sketched across her own face. "Lord knows I wouldn't know what to do with the thing."

They walked on toward the south jetty within the Nueces County State Park without another shared word.

At about the same moment that Janine stepped onto the jetty rocks for the first time in her life, Steph stepped onto a surfboard for the first time in her own.

"You can swim can't you?" Billy said grinning but totally serious. "I mean, you look as though you can handle the surf."

Steph had chosen her two-piece, baby blue bikini on purpose. It revealed the fine lines of her abdomen and the sleek curves of her legs and buttocks. She had always been very athletic, a self-indulgence that only once included team play in high school where she was named All-State as a setter for the volleyball team. She'd been offered an athletic scholarship to Texas A&M but had opted for an academic scholarship only. Succeeding in business meant, to her, a devotion to studies that did not afford much time for practice and play.

They were a couple of miles south of the jetty. No one was on the beach except the two of them. Billy grabbed her waist with a gentle but instructional force and told her to kneel. They were not yet in the water. Her first lesson was what Billy called a "dry start." A nine-foot Malibu surfboard rested in the sand a dozen yards from the breaking, foamy surf. Billy had dug a small divot in the sand so the board's fin could lie safely during the lesson. She stood on its waxy surface about a third of the way up the board from the tail.

"I swim like a fish," Steph said, squirming silently with delight between Billy's soft hands; his grip of her flesh reminded her of their luau date—and flying to the moon.

"Good." Billy guided her down onto the board, his hands still clasped just above her hips. "You never know when the surf might test you."

The board's waxy surface grabbed her navel and the very faint hairs that surrounded it as Billy continued his instruction.

"This is the most important maneuver. You can surf all day with your belly to the board but that ain't surfin'. You need to stand. It's called the pop-up."

Her face was against the board. Billy's legs straddled each side of her waist. It was hard to concentrate.

"Once you paddle into the wave, you need to pop-up onto the board in one smooth motion. This entails pushing on the rails while swinging your knees inward and planting your feet in a crouched position. Use your knees as shock-absorbers, kinda like you would if you were water-skiing."

Steph turned her face from the board and into the sun. Billy's head silhouetted the blazing orange circle in the sky. "I've never water-skied," she said.

Billy was smiling at her, his long arms draped toward each side of her body. "Ever slid across a patch of ice in your sneaks?"

Steph remembered that, as a kid, she had. "Yeah. About ten years ago."

"You remember falling?"

Steph *had* fallen. It had been in Colorado while visiting her uncle who worked at Wal-mart. She remembered how much it had hurt her tailbone. She nodded while looking up at him.

"So the next time you tried to slide, your balance was controlled by your knees. The knees kept you from falling on your ass."

Steph knew that Billy was serious about his surf instructions, but at the same time he was so cute and timid and caring. It was hard not to giggle. Funny thing was, what he said was accurate. After she'd fallen and had busted her tailbone, after the tremor of pain had fizzled out of her spine, after she'd wiped the cold tear from a cheek that was rosy with embarrassment, she'd stood, that competitive, athletic attitude roiling within her young soul and had tried again. This time she'd not fallen. This time she'd controlled her balance. And only now did she remember how she'd done it. Her knees had kept her from falling on her ass.

"Yeah," she said in revelation. "Okay…I get it. Balance. One foot in front of the other. Knees bent. I can do that."

Billy leaned forward to within inches of her upturned lips and said, "Let's see it." He pulled upward on her waist, his hands firmly entrenched against her hips, and, naturally, as if she'd done it a million times over, her knees came forward, her feet swung inward, and she popped-up. Her feet planted incorrectly as one straddled each rail but she quickly shifted them, her right foot moving forward, her left moving backward just as if she was back in Colorado sliding across the icy Wal-Mart parking lot.

"Goofy-footed," Billy said a little surprised. His hands moved off her waist. "You sure that feels comfortable?"

"It's how I safely slid across the ice. Doing it the other way made me fall."

"Let's see it again."

Steph dropped onto her belly and quickly popped-up, this time planting her goofy-footed stance with near perfection.

"To hell with that lesson," Billy said. "You sure you've never done this before?"

"Never."

"Ever done any kind of water sport?"

"None."

Billy's mouth hung open. Then, like a true stereotypical surf dude he said, "Whoa! Too totally cool. You are one righteous babe. Whatta'ya say we catch one?"

Steph gleamed with pride. She really had never done any type of water sport beyond swimming laps in a public pool. And up until now, she'd never really had the desire. But Billy filled her with such positive reinforcement; she felt she could ride the Hawaiian pipeline.

Twenty minutes later she realized that duplicating in the water what she'd done on land was much more difficult. Riding the surf was in no way analogous to sliding on ice. They were only thirty yards out and the surf was less than three feet on average but she had yet to successfully pop up. She'd ridden several waves belly-to-board but that wasn't surfing. Still, Billy provided encouragement.

"Remember to keep the knees bent. It's one fluid motion. If need be, pop to your knees then stand." Billy sat on his board, legs draped over the rails and pointed. "Here comes a good one. Now start paddling."

Steph started stroking the rising water just as Billy had directed her a dozen times already. Her arms moved faster as the board lifted onto the growing wave. This one looked to rise higher than any she'd attempted so far. Billy yelled out.

"Whooo...Yah-yaa! Hang it baby! That's one knarly wave!"

She sped forward. Wind and spray pelted her cheeks, cooling the heat supplied by the sun's water surface reflection. The wave began to crest and she maneuvered into the curl. She quickly pressed against the rails, pulled her legs inward and planted her knees onto the board's waxy surface. Billy would tell her later that the whole event lasted less than five seconds but to her it was a lifetime. Her speed increased and she fought the water's attempt to throw her off. Seemingly far away she heard Billy yell, "Do it!"

And she did.

In one swift motion, she released the rails and popped up from her knees to the same goofy-footed stance she had perfected in the sand. For a fraction of a second she was surfing. For a fraction of a second she was flying. For a fraction of a second she felt as if the Big Dipper was within mortal reach and she now understood the freedom from reality that Billy had described as they'd waded in the surf at the luau. It only lasted a fraction of a second but the memory of it etched deeply into her subconscious. It *was* possible to tame Mother Nature if only to be humbled within a fraction of a second.

When she fell, she dumped forward into the curl, a picturesque wipe-out. She felt the ankle strap tug and stretch as the board fought the wave's attack on its buoyancy. She gasped in a mouthful of water only because she was smiling so widely in victory as her face hit the wave. When she surfaced she coughed, laughed, and screamed.

"Yah-yaa!" She pumped her fist then grabbed the surfboard.

Billy, sitting on his board twenty yards out, pumped his fists in response. "Yah-yaa!" he answered.

Her success had released some locked energy. She paddled effortlessly toward Billy over surf that, minutes before, had denied her the right to stand against the ocean. These juvenile three-foot waves were miniscule. She could surf these, she thought. She could stand atop them and ride them to the shore. She had conquered a curl twice their size. Yah-yaa!

As she neared the spot where Billy sat waiting, she pushed the nose of the board forward, swung her thighs across each rail and planted her butt, straddling the board.

"What do you think about that?" she gleamed.

The tail of her board touched the tail of Billy's. Her right knee stroked the surface of his thigh. Billy's exuberant expression allied with the tranquility she felt streaming through her body.

His mind swirled with a mouth-opened, astonished wonderment that Steph had ridden the elusive, rare, five-foot Port A wave. There was jealousy in the thought, one reserved only for Port A surfers who rarely saw such surf let alone was afforded a chance to ride one. She'd stolen what was reserved for veterans.

But she was *His* girl.

Right?

His girl had ridden the five-footer.

And he, the veteran, had been paramount in her success.

He'd ridden the wave with her. His mind's energy had helped her pop up. His muscles had involuntarily gone through the motions with her. Pushing, curling inward, fighting for balance, standing, looking around, feeling proud, conquering Mother Nature. If only for a fraction of a second. If only for a fleeting moment.

He'd fallen head first with her. He'd swallowed salt with her. He'd yelled *YahYaa* with her. And now, her body and board were connected to him by something greater than physical restraint. It was, metaphysically, cosmic.

There was a stream near Pickett's Crossing. Michael had taken her there one week after they'd met. It was about an hour east of "the crossing" over in the lowlands in a valley near the Missouri River. In stark contrast to the flat brown landscape of agricultural Kansas, the Salt Creek River was nestled amongst evergreens, oaks and maples, and smelled not of the dry dust but of cool wetness, of wildlife that slithered and swam, of mist on tree leaves and branches.

He'd brought a lunch; they'd been the best peanut butter and banana sandwiches she'd ever eaten.

"Those shoes won't work out here," Joel said.

Even now, as she slipped off her sandals and stepped onto the Port A south jetty rocks, the taste of peanuts and bananas lingered between her taste buds. The wet spray of aquatic life engulfed her nostrils.

Michael had said pretty much the same thing twenty-two years ago. Her future husband had held her hand, had guided her across smooth, wet boulders—some round like bowling balls, some flat like concrete steps—toward a very large rock that sat in the middle of the stream. Her feet had grasped the wet surface; cool water had cascaded through her toes. She'd lost her balance only once but Michael's reflexes and strength had saved her.

"You seem to have done this before," Joel said as he tried to maintain his grasp of her hand. She released it and moved quickly forward. The jetty rocks were ten times larger than those she'd crossed in Kansas but none matched the size of the big "picnic" rock where she and Michael had sat for hours, soaking up the sun and eating peanut butter and banana sandwiches.

"Janine. Hold up."

It was Joel's voice just a dozen feet behind her.

"Janine?"

The long stretch of rocks that narrowed to a point several hundred feet in the distance locked her attention. She thought that if she stood on the very last rock at the very point of the jetty it would be like walking on water, as she'd done in Kansas, as she would now do in the Gulf. She imagined Michael standing at the point of the jetty, his arms held out, a picnic basket draped around one forearm. The smell of salt water and peanut butter and bananas teased her forward.

"Janine!"

The jetty rocks were fifty feet wide at the beachhead but only five feet wide at the point. Waves crashed at the base of the jetty near the beach but the jetty rocks were totally awash at the point.

Janine was already a third of the way out. The jetty rocks had already narrowed by ten feet. Though there was a flat path intentionally created on top of the jetty for visitors and fishermen to easily traverse, Janine chose to walk the rocks about midway down from the path to the water.

"Janine! You can't go past that sign!"

Janine looked up and to her left. She read:

No trespassing beyond this point.
By order of the Nueces County Sheriff's Department

But she kept on going. Michael was out there waiting for her. He'd taught her how to walk the rocks. She wasn't scared.

"Janine! Please stop! Fishing won't be no good out there!"

Fishing? Who said anything about fishing? She and Michael were going to have a picnic. Then she and Michael were going to be married and have a son and a farm with cows and chickens and corn and a barn perhaps—and a pickup truck. And they were going to live happily ever after.

Janine's heart started racing and she picked up her pace. Michael was waiting. A chance to start all over. Out at the point. Out on the Salt Creek River picnic rock where they'd first made love. Where Lenny was conceived.

The jetty had narrowed to twenty feet. The pedestrian path had ended at the sign. More rocks were Gulf water wet. A splash or two pelted her calves. She slipped and reached for Michael who still waited another two hundred feet ahead, but without the strength of his hand, she toppled backward.

For a second she thought that she'd find her balance as she moved her right foot backward but when her bare toes found nothing but the space between two boulders, she fell, her body angling for the rocks and water below, a collision that would certainly bash body and bones.

And then Michael was there, grabbing her hand, prohibiting what would have placed her back in the hospital under the microscopes of logical, intellectual idiots. Her right arm flailed sporadically as her left arm tugged in the opposite direction.

"Are you crazy?" Joel said, wrapping an arm around Janine's waist, his fishing pole dropped and forgotten behind him. He balanced her on the slick rock that challenged their combined weight. "I mean… It's dangerous out here. That's why the sheriff put up that sign."

Janine turned to him. She smiled and cozied into his grasp. "Michael. Thank you, Michael." She looked up. Somehow, Michael looked like… "Joel," she cried. "Oh my God! Oh my God! I…I…"

Joel coddled her tightly then, and together they sat. Gulf water froth lapped their legs and feet, leaving brown rivulets as bubbles popped and drooled onto the rock. Her tears dropped into his overall's breast pocket, moistening Teddy Lavender's iPod. They remained like this for a good five minutes. When Janine stopped crying, she lifted her head and looked out toward the point of the jetty. Michael, of course, was not there.

"The Gulf can play some funny tricks on a person," Joel said, his arm draped over her shoulder. "I've seen things."

Janine wondered how he could read her mind. "Really?" she said, still looking out at the point. "Me too." She wiped away what was left of the salty tears moments before her face was again moistened by salt water spray.

"What did you see?"

"Loved ones."

She turned to him.

"My wife, particularly. She'd visit me right here on these rocks."

"Did she die?" Janine asked, wondering if the deceased and the jetty had some ghostly connection.

"To tell you the truth, I don't know. I haven't heard from her in many, many years." He released her shoulder and brought both arms forward to rest on his lap.

"I saw Michael," she said. "He was my husband. He died in a farming accident years ago." She, again, looked out at the point. On the horizon appeared the small dark outline of a ship. She guessed correctly that it was headed for the jetty though it would be hours before it reached them.

Joel followed her gaze. "Why are you here?" he said without looking at her. "Do those men from the restaurant have anything to do with it?"

Janine looked directly at the side of his face. Fluffs of grey hair that were longer and thicker than most men his age stuck to the Gulf moisture on his cheek. His eyes remained on the horizon.

"Does your husband's death have anything to do with it?"

Janine's mouth hung open. She imagined that Joel could hear her thumping heartbeats which had not yet calmed, beating out an alien language of fear and anxiety.

"Are you running?" He now turned and their eyes locked.

She needed to tell someone. Keeping it all inside had become unbearable. It tore through her emotions as if they were made of papier-mâché. But could she trust him…this stranger…with the darkness locked up inside?

"I don't know how he found me," she finally said.

"The men from the restaurant," Joel concluded.

Janine shifted on the rock to turn more comfortably toward him. In her periphery she saw his fishing pole where he'd dropped it on the jetty. In the distance she saw few people on the beach which her mind absently recorded as something strange. "The big man," she said. "He used to be…I mean, you could say we're divorced."

Joel's eyebrows rose. "Your ex is chasing you?"

She needed someone to trust her, to listen to her revelations, to help her release some penned-in misery. But telling Joel, or anyone, a dead monster that ate people was a part of her reality would certainly end any chance for friendship.

"Yes," she said. "Yes. He must be."

Joel's stare did not leave her even as a seagull suddenly crashed into the jetty rocks a dozen yards away, its body flapping momentarily before dying and rolling into the water. "Why?" he asked.

Truthfully, Janine wasn't really sure. "He killed my son and now I think he wants me gone, too. Clean up any evidence."

"What!?" Joel's grey eyebrows lifted into his forehead. The stray hairs that stuck to his cheeks fell from skin that suddenly filled with wrinkled shock. "We should go to the police. Keadle will help us." Joel licked his lips. "He killed your son?"

Janine patted his hand. "Shhh." She placed a finger to her lips. "That won't do. The police don't believe me. They think I'm…" she paused for the right word. *Crazy* wasn't it nor was *Insane*. "They think it's all in my head—that I imagined it."

"You saw him do it…kill your son?"

"Yes. Almost a year ago—a very long year ago."

"So if you saw it, how could you have imagined it?"

It was bound to happen. No matter how the conversation would have started, and no matter how hard she tried to control the information, sooner or later what she saw would become the principal question. A dead man… eating flesh…a thing straight from hell itself, chasing her, wanting her dead, Joel dead, the world dead.

"There was an explosion," she revealed. "Debris knocked me out. The doctors said it was a head injury. I was in therapy for several months but…"

"But it wasn't your imagination."

Janine cried. "He chopped Lenny up." Her head fell to his chest again. Tears welled into fresh pools on the pocketed iPod. "He's an animal from Hell."

Joel patted her head. "Shhh," he soothed. "He's not here now but I am."

She looked up and he stroked her forehead, one rough fingertip following shallow wrinkles. She tried to smile—a dim glimpse of hope—but couldn't. Joel was a brave man but only human and no match for Albert Stine.

"Besides," Joel continued, "I've got a cure that heals all wounds… Fishing."

At the end of the jetty where the ghost of Michael Bender had lured his wife into the Gulf, another seagull dropped suddenly from the sky, its wings lifeless and stiff, and plopped into the water.

They sat on their boards beyond the break for what seemed like hours though it had only been twenty minutes or so since Steph had conquered the surf. The silence was nearly absolute. Save for one or two gulls Billy saw fall awkwardly from the sky, no beach life was present. He'd seen no fish surface and none had bumped his submerged, dangling feet. Though they were surfing far from where most visitors chose to enjoy the Port A beaches, mid-June always promoted some kind of activity for miles down the Mustang Island coastline. It seemed odd that no one was walking, playing, or sunbathing for as far as he could see in either direction. Apparently, the fish kill supposition had made it into public knowledge with such negative grace that even the locals were not taking chances. Apparently, Mark had either not contacted the media with the lab results from the samples they'd collected yesterday, or the media had not listened. There were no contaminants in the waters along Mustang Island. Though he'd not yet seen any fish today, he also had not seen any dead fish. And no crimson waters. And no blood spots. But newspapers sold better when the news was negative.

In such complete silence, with nothing but the intoxicating splashing, lapping water surges slapping past he and Steph, it was hard not to think about the bloody end to the life of Mitchell Bone. He stared out at the horizon where a ship slowly grew in size as it crept closer inland and wondered: he'd not seen it first hand; they were video clips transmitted by Shoe; they could have been manipulated; someone could have jacked into the frequency and could have fed him any lies they wished. Chancy Lett and the bodyguard came to mind. But why would they have him believe such a thing—that Bone was dead, that Bone had been murdered, that he'd had his head ripped from his body?

Of course, the images could have been real. The ramifications of such reality were still beyond his comprehension, as was so much that had gone on in the past few days. All he'd intended was to collect evidence that could have been used against the construction of the Mayan casino. What he'd uncovered was…

"Did you move Shoe?"

He looked at Steph, curiously, as if she'd been wandering through his thoughts.

"You said you were going to move your robot to a position where it could see better into the vault."

Billy drove his surfboard closer to her. "I did," he almost whispered. Steph looked around. "At least I tried."

"What do you mean?" She emulated his whisper.

"Shoe never made it to the teller window."

"Did it break down or something?" Steph's disappointment became concern. "What will happen when they find it in the middle of the floor?"

"It's not in the middle of the floor." Billy looked back toward the horizon. "Quite frankly, I don't know where Shoe is. I lost his signal."

"Well that sucks…doesn't it?"

Without looking at her, Billy said, "I saw something. Shoe saw something."

"The crate? What? Can we use it against them? Can we use it to take down Bone?"

"He was murdered," he said bluntly.

"What!?" she pushed her board against his. "Who? Who was murdered?"

He looked into her eyes, hoping that truth and not dementia would shine through. "Your boss. Mitchell Bone. That big fella took his head off."

Steph stared at the churning water as if it were some crystal ball that enabled her to see what Billy was describing.

"I saw the head," he continued. "It rolled right into to vault's doorway. There was a tremendous amount of blood."

"How do you know it was Bone?" Steph said.

"I saw it!" He'd not meant to sound so harsh and Steph flinched. "Sorry." He touched the rail of her board just behind where her left thigh straddled its surface. "Lett's bodyguard did it. One minute Bone was arguing something about indiscretions, the next minute he was directed into the vault along with the bodyguard, Lett and Carol. Then there were screams. The head just rolled into the doorway; the bodyguard picked it up and crushed it. He grabbed it like a bowling ball through the eyes and mouth and just squeezed."

"We have to report this?" Steph grabbed his arm. "Did you report it? You have the evidence?"

"Yes, I have the evidence. It should be stored on the computer back home, though…" he took a deep breath, "…though I'm not in a hurry to look at the footage just yet."

"Give it to the authorities."

Billy grabbed her hand and gently petted it. "Do you think that would be such a wise idea? Breaking and entering a financial institution will certainly draw me five-to-ten in the state pen."

A fish suddenly darted between their boards. It was the first one he'd seen all day and it startled him. He released Steph's hand.

"I was thinking more in the line of the press," he continued. "I might be able to get certain protections through them. Besides, all I have is the video. There's been no body found yet. No crime has been committed until the victim is found."

Steph shook her head. "Well, we'll have the evidence when the body does show up and that will be the end of that for the Mayan." She swirled her legs through the water, contemplating. "You think the body is in the vault?"

Billy flinched a short grin. "That would be my guess. But how could we know? Are you going back to work there?"

"I decided yesterday that you were more important."

Billy's grin turned up a notch but he was not yet able to smile. Though he didn't agree with her decision he was flattered. "You quit your job to go surfing." He shook his head. "I know a lot of guys around here that have made that choice a dozen times."

Steph blushed. "Not to change the subject but I will be needing a job."

"Waitress?"

"You're good at reading minds."

"Maybe. Some equations are just easier to complete than others." Another fish, or perhaps the same fish, darted between their boards, this time brushing aggressively against Billy's calf. "I think I can find something for you, that is, once all of this fish kill frenzy subsides and business gets back up to speed again."

"Thank you. Now that's one problem solved. What about Bone? Can you get Shoe running again?"

Billy recalled the face of the bodyguard on the video display in his van. "I doubt it. I think the bodyguard may have…terminated him."

"Then we're stuck. If the body is in the bank vault, it won't be there for long. For all we know it's already been moved."

"I was thinking of tipping off Officer Keadle but I'm not really sure how to go about it without making myself suspect."

They floated for several minutes, each contemplating their next move. Billy had the evidence to rid the island of the future malaise a casino would certainly bring. Now all he needed was a headless body. Shoe was certainly of no use any more. The bodyguard had taken care of that. He wondered now if he could talk Keadle into opening up a security box. Perhaps Keadle would see something suspicious inside the vault. Perhaps his suspicion would cause him to demand that the wooden crate be opened. There he would find, among other incriminating evidence, Bone's body. All Billy would then need to do is hand over the video and Chancey Lett would be nothing more than a bad memory.

Steph suddenly grabbed his board and swung it toward her. "I think I have a possible answer. Not sure it will work. I don't even know her. But it's worth a shot."

At that same moment, the fish that had been swimming between them surfaced, flipped onto its side, and floated. Billy thought he saw a strange crimson light swirl within the fish's eye just before it blackened into a cold stare.

He could not remember the last time someone cried on his shoulder. It was certainly before he'd met his wife. By the time he and Jane were married his rugged, sea-faring, fisherman persona would not have permitted such displays of caring and emotion. His shoulders were meant to handle the laborious task of pulling in the day's catch. They held the weight of responsibility, of being the man of the house, of bringing home the bread. If you wanted to cry in front of him, he'd lend you his hanky, a fishy-smelling accessory he kept in his back coveralls pocket, but you could not have his shoulder. Besides, nothing good every came from crying. It was a weakness, with the sole purpose to make others sad and depressed. It was a waste of energy that was better channeled into something productive and worthwhile like making a living for your family so that they had a roof over their heads and food on the table.

At least that's the way he used to think.

Years without Jane and hours with Janine had changed all that. He now questioned the sensibility in it all. How many years had he wasted? How many opportunities? Certainly "love" had taken a backseat. Realistically, though, had he ever known what the term "love" really meant? He loved an orange sunset as much as he loved watching grey-black thunderheads roll in under the same orange horizon. There had been a time when liquor and leisure had been loves…the feeling of knuckles to jaws…a pool stick used as a weapon. And then there was fishing, the Gulf, the vastness of the unknown. What measure could one give to such things? He loved them all. But he'd never really "loved" Jane—at least not in any way he could understand. Jane had never soaked his breast pocket with more salt than the average flipping, flailing redfish that had slipped the hook before the net. No woman had ever cried on him. What value was there in it?

Crying.

Tears.

Janine released her fear and depression onto his coveralls. A pool of salt as large as the palm of his hand encircled the right breast pocket. He gently grabbed her shoulder and set her up straight. As much as some internal desire wanted him to, he could not find the courage to wipe away the remaining stray tears on her cheek.

"Sit here," he told her. "I gotta get my fishing rod." He questioned her ability to hold herself upright. "Good with that?"

Janine managed a flickered smile. She placed her hands onto the rocks for balance.

"You settle," Joel said. "I'll be right back and then we'll get us the big one. A fish that could feed the whole island."

Janine nodded as he rose to his feet. He stole glances back across his shoulder as he moved away, fearing that she might suddenly leap forward and into the surf. But for the entire two minutes that it took him to retrieve the fishing pole and return to her side, Janine did not move. Her arms remained rigid, her hands clasped to the rocks as if any relaxation would cause her demise. He reached into the salty, tear-stained breast pocket and fished around Ted Lavender's iPod for the chunk of Milky Way.

"A fish with a sweet tooth," he said to her. "Quite funny if you think about it."

He could not deter her attention from whatever locked her thoughts.

"Fish cavities," he tried.

Nothing.

"How many fish does it take to make a full set of teeth?"

No response.

"Thirty-two." He laughed but she didn't.

A minute of silence followed.

"I never caught him," he said, abruptly, not really knowing why. "It's all a lie."

Janine looked up and over.

"My life is a lie."

She stared at the Milky Way wrapper that covered half a bar.

"I don't know how he did it but Nookle pulled that son-of-a-bitch in without my help. I was knocked out of it the whole time. And then a couple years later the big movie came out. We were the heroes but I had nothing to do with it. I used the public's ignorance for gain. Hell, *Jaws* was the talk of the country. And Bert and I were the real-life counterparts. But I had nothing to do with it. I only wish…" He hesitated. Janine still stared at the wrapper of the half of candy bar which Joel now opened. "I only wish it never would have happened." He grabbed the fishing hook and baited it with a round ball of Milky Way that he'd rolled between thumb and forefinger. He licked his fingers and offered the rod to Janine.

She quizzically stared at it as if it were a precious form of art, but said nothing.

"I'm running, too," he said. His grin was slight and concerned—reinforcing. "We're all running from something: people, our hearts—" He swallowed. "Death."

"Joel?" It was the first thing she'd said since drowning his breast pocket. "Do you…?"

The fishing rod, offered within Joel's knurled hands, and a sticky ball of candy wrapped around its lined hook, waited for her to take it.

She continued, "Do you trust me?"

The question seemed impossible for him to answer, but he was quick to understand that her question was directed in response to his own revelation, information that was meant only for those that people trust. Janine, a woman he'd known for little more than two days, was the only person to whom he'd ever confessed the history of "Jaws"—and the confession of love—though Joel still struggled with that concept.

"I wish I knew what the hell was causing all of this," Billy said, kicking at the dead fish with his naked heel. "It's so frustrating."

"And where are all of the birds?" Steph added. She'd seen only one or two in the few hours they'd been surfing.

"I know. Weird. One thing's for sure, whatever it is ain't in the water. At least not in any water around this island."

Steph watched the fish bob out of sight then said, "I think that if we can run Lett out of town, everything will return to normal. Everything seems to have started going badly when he arrived Monday."

"With the crate," Billy added.

Steph considered this. She remembered the strange power it had emitted when she'd been accosted by Lett, Carol and the bodyguard as they'd recited their own dark version of the Lord's Prayer. The strange glow. The nearly inaudible hum. Every time Carol had taken another customer inside the vault to set up a new security box, the person had changed, had become almost robotic.

"So what was your idea?" Billy said. "How can we get into that vault?"

"I suspect that with Bone out of the picture, Lett and his cronies will take charge of the bank, at least until we can uncover evidence."

"With them in control, that seems pretty impossible. I could ask Officer Keadle for some help."

"What if they've gotten to him?" Her question seemed to throw a wrench into Billy's reasoning. Apparently, by the way his eyebrows suddenly squashed inward with an expression of befuddlement, he'd not considered that possibility. Steph had grown use to his expressions. It was easy to determine just by looking at his face when he was deeply calculating, when his thoughts were, to him, well-reasoned, and when, like now, his well-reasoned thoughts had suddenly met with some cognitive obstacle. "My idea concerns this investor from Sedona, the one I'm supposed to pick up today at the airport."

Billy's expression suddenly turned into that "deep calculation" mode. "Bone said something about that last night. Alixel, I believe is her name. But how can she help? And besides, I thought you said you didn't work for the bank anymore."

"Alixel won't know that."

"But what if she's in on it? What if talking to her would be no better than talking to Lett?"

"Not sure yet. We'll have to feel it out. Perhaps she's an innocent investor being manipulated just like Bone was. Maybe her head is meant to roll at some point in time as well." Steph's feet were suddenly tickled by a tiny mass of bubbles that rose from beneath her and moved between her toes. The little bubbles popped at the water's surface. She shivered.

Billy looked up at the sun that bore heat down from its apex onto his face and shrugged. "When are we supposed to pick her up?"

"We?"

"Of course. We're in this together now. It's up to us to stop him. It's more than just the casino. It's murder."

She was glad to hear him say that. It made her decision to quit the bank comforting. It made her decision to come to Port Aransas worthwhile. She'd left some friends back in College Station but few were those that she had truly bonded with. That's how it was when you were a valedictorian in your college class. A closed-minded attitude toward anything but educational success tended to alienate many who were only in college for the social party ride into adulthood. Now, she had Billy Jo Presser, an intellect in his own right but a real beach "dude" to boot. *They* were going to figure all of this out. *They* were going to put Chancey Lett in his place. *They* were going to the airport. A few more bubbles running through her toes added to the tingly sensation streaming through her emotions.

And then someone screamed.

Simultaneously, both of them turned to the shriek near the shoreline. Steph's board collided with Billy's and she dumped into the water. Her board shot out from under her but her ankle strap kept it from slamming into Billy's head. Her board fell into the water upside-down and Billy helped her right it. She draped both arms over the board, her legs kicking in the water for balance, and floated as she saw someone crest the top of the nearest dune and run down its slope toward the surf, tripping once in the sand and leaping back up in a brisk jackrabbit motion. A second person topped the dune a moment later. Something flashed in this person's hand, a metallic glint of bouncing sunrays. The words in the screams of the person being chased became clearer as the figure neared the water.

"Billy!"

They floated a good thirty yards out and the crashing, splashing water made the words sound muffled, but Steph was sure that they were:

"Billy, help me!"

Steph knew this person. It was the chef from the luau. It was Billy's chef, Pedro.

"Pedro?" Billy yelled out. "Pedro, is that you?"

Pedro stopped at the surf perpendicular to where Billy and Steph floated out beyond the breakers. He turned and pointed at the figure chasing him who had now halved the distance as Pedro stood there.

"Sí," he yelled. At least to Steph that's what it sounded like. Perhaps it was "oui" but she didn't think he spoke French. But as he yelled the same word repeatedly, it became clear.

"Me!"

And that didn't make any sense either.

"Me! Help, Billy! Me!"

Pedro took off, running along the shoreline for another fifty yards before heading back up into the dunes. Right on his heels was…

Steph blinked. The sun glinting off the metal object that the assailant held temporarily blinded her. Billy started paddling in toward the shoreline as bubbles began racing between her toes and thighs, and across her breasts. These were big bubbles, at least ten times the size of the small tickly ones that had teased her moments ago. And these bubbles were red.

"Billy!" she screamed. "Billy, help me!"

What Billy saw on the shoreline was impossible. Pedro was yelling. "Mí jefe" is what it sounded like. Pedro said that a lot. But that's not what he was saying. "Me!" he was screaming. And for good reason. Pedro was being chased by…

Himself.

Billy blinked. He thought he was hallucinating again. The sun—it was playing mind games with him.

"Me!" the first Pedro yelled again, then ran into the dunes.

And then from behind him…

"Billy, help me!"

He turned to see Steph immersed in the same phenomenon that had mesmerized him and Mark the day before. She roiled in an expanding blood spot. Dead fish popped to the surface around her. Some were as long as her small feet which now flailed against the water's surface. Some were half the size of her surfboard which, to Billy's horror, freed itself from Steph's grasp leaving her alone in the middle of the boiling mess. Somehow, the board's ankle strap had slipped free.

He quickly paddled to the middle of the blood spot, grabbed one of Steph's arms at the elbow and paddled with his free arm away from the bubbling surface. He stroked and pulled and yanked as the blood spot expanded, seemingly wanting to take both of them down into its crimson depths. Steph's body bounced repeatedly against the red death that floated in mass around her. His one-armed strokes became labored and he released her, guided her hands to his legs where she clamped on tightly, and paddled with both arms, towing her free from the blood spot.

She gasped and choked and spit. Her hair was red and she submerged to wash the color from it. Horror and shock coupled in a singular expression that told Billy that he'd have to get her to shore immediately. He pulled her body up onto his surfboard where she lay draped over the nose.

"Everything will be fine," he consoled but she said nothing. Drool clung to her lower lip and stretched down to the surfboard in a slight, wind-blown arc.

He began paddling toward the shoreline but stopped after two strokes. The second Pedro was just now disappearing over the same dune where the first Pedro had gone. But it wasn't the Pedros that caused him sudden distress. It was the bodyguard.

He stood just beyond the waterline, the surf rolling to within inches of his sparkling, polished black boots but never touching them, as if the water was afraid, as if the black boots were poison. He wore a three-piece black suit that must have felt extremely uncomfortable under the hot Texas sun. In his hand was a starfish. Billy assumed correctly that it was Shoe. The bodyguard raised the tiny robot over his head and squeezed in much the same way as he'd done Mitchell Bone's head. Then in one aggressive thrust, he slammed Shoe into the beach sand and crushed it with the heel of one boot.

From beyond the dunes, a gut-rattling shriek echoed out in agony. "AGHHH!" Some Spanish gibberish followed. Then complete silence. The bodyguard smiled which was creepy in its own right.

"You're next," he said, not yelling, but just loud enough for Billy to hear.

Steph started gasping and coughing again. "Billy," she said. "Yes. I'll be okay. You can't go in—not with him there. He'll kill us both."

Billy eyed Steph's surfboard still floating in the mass of bloody water and floating fish. The blood spot had stopped bubbling, still, he really didn't want to swim into that mess. "We'll wait for your board to clear then paddle up the coast toward the pier. He's not going to touch us if there are witnesses."

"Yes," Steph coughed. "*We* can do that."

So they both were liars. The only difference in them, as far as Janine could tell, was that Joel had, moments ago, revealed a part of his soul that had been eating at him for many years. Shame, jealousy, loneliness—he'd pretended to love but had never really known how to love. His encounter with the great white shark had changed his life and, for a brief moment and perhaps for the first time ever, he'd felt comfortable enough to open up to someone who just happened to be, for all accounts and purposes, a complete stranger. His heart lay on his sleeve, vulnerable to whatever Janine decided to do with it.

She, on the other hand, had continued her lie. Her heart remained hidden behind memories that were much fresher than "Jaws." While Joel bargained for truth by bartering his own disgrace, Janine had nothing to offer in return. It was a matter of belief and sanity. How could he believe her? Professor Cower. The magic dagger. Albert and the Albert-thing. People eating people. Lenny! He would think her insane. He would call in the white coats. She'd be returned to the sterile environment where logical men made illogical decisions. Unless…

Unless she trusted him. Unless he trusted her.

"Let's see if you can get this hook in the water without snagging me," Joel said.

Janine took the pole from his hands. A courteous smile remained on his lips though she could tell he'd tensed by the concern revealed by his thick, salty eyebrows. Nobody touched Joel's pole. Nobody. But he trusted *her*.

She had no idea what she was doing. She'd never fished in her life. As she started to swing the pole forward in a motion she'd seen portrayed in movies and television, Joel gently, but with authority, grabbed her shoulders.

"You and my…" he started. "You and the pole are both headin' into the surf if you cast like that. You gotta find your balance. Why don't we try to find a flatter spot?"

"I can do it," Janine said, not fighting the strength of Joel's vise on her shoulders.

"You've never done this before," Joel said, understanding the truth. He released one shoulder and grabbed her left thigh directly above the knee. This sent sensations into her bones that she'd forgotten existed. "Move your leg forward and bend it a little." He guided her leg then lightly karate-chopped the back of her knee. "Yes. Like that. Now move your other leg behind you a bit. You want to get your weight behind the cast so the hook finds a spot beyond the breakers or else all you'll be doing is playing cast and reel with the surf."

"Can you show me first?" Janine felt uncomfortable. The weight of the pole, which was at least two feet longer than she was in height, had suddenly gained fifty pounds in her hands.

"I trust you, Jane." Joel's eyes bugged. "I mean…"

"I know what you mean." Somehow, his slip gave her confidence. She was as important to him as Jane had been, perhaps even more so.

Her first cast was lame at best. The hook traveled farther in the air than it did into the water. The line slapped the water and Joel helped her reel it in. The Milky Way nougat ball was gone.

"I got enough for about five more casts like that," he said and baited the hook with fresh candy. "Go out to the side a bit. Not so much over the head. You should be able to feel the Milky Way."

"Feel the Milky Way?"

"Yes." He moved behind her and grabbed her arms, then rocked them back and forth while remaining attentive to where the hook was at all times as it swayed behind them. "I can feel it. Can you?"

What she was feeling was certainly not what Joel was referring to. He was, basically, hugging her. His strength felt protective. Her spine shivered. They moved on the jetty rocks in some strange, stationary slow dance to the music of the Gulf. She closed her eyes.

"Can you?" he repeated.

"Yes," she said, trying not to swoon.

"You feel the hook?"

"Yes," she crooned.

"Okay…ready?"

"Yes," she repeated, drowning in emotion.

"Excellent!"

She opened her eyes as he released her arms and stepped onto a rock behind her. There she stood, the fishing pole in her hands, her weight evenly distributed by her bent-knee stance on the jetty rocks, the line from the pole strung out in front of her that disappeared well beyond the crashing surf some hundred feet away.

"Now take your finger and press the line against the pole," Joel directed.

She did so.

"You'll be able to tell if you get a bite when the line tugs on your finger."

"It's tugging now," she said, excited. "It's tugging now!"

Joel giggled. It was quick and nearly silent against the crash of the waves but Janine definitely heard it. "That's the wind you feel," he said. "Catching the wind is pretty easy. Feeling the fish…well, I think you'll know the difference when it happens."

She'd not remembered any of it, her first official fishing task, which was depressing and not so at the same time. Somehow, her mind and body had not connected. She wanted both experiences repeated. His touch. Her cast.

The sound of a distant horn, from the ship that had only been a speck on the horizon almost an hour ago, displaced the experience. It was like being on the Mississippi: wet spray in the face, the paddle-boat whistle, fishing in the "mud", Tom Sawyer her educator, warning her of dangers while reinforcing her actions. She was Becky Thatcher, and Tom would keep her safe. No monsters could get to her, not on the Mississippi, not with Tom's strong hands wrapped around her. No monsters had ever penetrated Trust between two people. Evil was undefined.

"I have something to tell you, Joel, and I hope that you can trust me," she whispered, not knowing if Joel had even heard her. "I am not insane."

Joel stepped forward but did not touch her. "Look!" he shouted, pointing. "You got one!"

"I saw him last night," Steph said.

"Saw who?" Billy continued paddling ahead. They were near the Caldwell Pier. The bodyguard kept pace along the shoreline. Only two people occupied the pier—not enough, Billy suspected, to deter any harm that the bodyguard might have in store for them.

"Pedro." Steph looked tired, haggard. She had the body of an athlete but Billy supposed that most of her athletic maturity was not attained in the water. "He was headed into the bank. When I was leaving, I saw him."

Billy stopped paddling and pulled up to a sitting position on his board. Steph did the same. The bodyguard stood and stared at them. The pier was less than fifty feet away. The two people on the pier, an elderly couple, looked down and waved. Steph stared as if dumbfounded. Billy returned the wave but did not think about the action; instead, he wondered why Pedro would have gone to the Port A branch of the Big Texas Bank. He wondered if Bone's death had anything to do with it. He wondered if the bodyguard had anything to do with it. He wondered if the wooden crate in the vault had anything to do with it.

"Do you know why he was at the bank?" Billy said, absently, still waving at the elderly couple on the pier who had stopped waving at him and had turned their backs.

"No." Steph stared at the bodyguard. Her breaths were shallow. "He might have wanted to enter the contest."

As their boards carried them under the pier and to the other side, Billy considered this. "Do you remember ever seeing Dave come into the bank?" he asked.

"Dave?"

"The security guard from the marine institute. The one who almost ran us over yesterday."

"No," Steph said. "I didn't see him but then I wasn't in the bank all afternoon. I did take a short break for lunch."

"And that crazy bitch from the newspaper office. You ever see her in the bank?"

"Nope." Steph paused. "What are you getting at?"

"It's got to be in that crate," Billy said, not looking at her but only at the nose of his surfboard. "I think we both agree that whenever someone goes into that vault, they come out somehow…different. You called it 'robotic'."

"Not everyone," Steph said. "You went in and came out okay. I've been in several times and came out okay."

"But you said that when you went in with Carol, and the fellas from the casino they pushed the crate at you. Did you ever touch it?"

"I don't think so."

"Are you sure?"

Steph stared in silent contemplation. "I don't know," she said. "Why?" Her eyes welled with sudden concern. Billy pulled her board closer to him and patted her hand.

"Nothing, really. I mean, you feel just fine, right? You don't seem 'robotic' to me."

Steph jerked her hand from Billy's grasp and examined it as if it were infested with some invisible disease. “You think the crate has some kind of contagion?” she said. “You think I contracted it?”

“No,” Billy said. “—I mean, yes.”

She stared at him as if he were crazy and purposely let her board drift away from his.

“No, I don’t think you are infected,” he clarified. “And yes, I think there may be a contagion, something distributed by touch. Nothing airborne.” He paddled to her and pulled her close. And before the surprise left her face, he kissed her, lightly, quickly. “And if you are, then we both are.”

And then there was laughing, deep and guttural, emanating from the shore.

“Sweet,” the bodyguard growled. “Sweet. Sweet. Sweet.” His voice was two octaves below baritone. He stepped into the water and started toward them. Ten feet in, the breakers hit him in the chest and face but his body broke through as if the water had no force at all.

“Holy shit,” Steph said as the bodyguard took his first stroke into the water and began swimming.

“Time to paddle out of here,” Billy suggested and laid belly to board. Steph got into the same position and both of them started paddling farther out and in the direction of the jetty.

The bodyguard kept pace, his black boots beating the water behind him, his black wardrobe a mass of soaked weight that promoted the image of a hungry shark moving in for the kill. Billy’s arms tired and he suspected that Steph’s were reaching exhaustion.

Still, the beach remained vacant of sunbathers. No witnesses. Out beyond the jetty, a ship cruised inland, its horn sounding the approach, but it was still too far away to provide witness. Billy believed they had no other choice but to head for the shore and take their chances on land. Certainly they could run faster than they could paddle.

“I can’t go on much more,” Steph said, her voice hushed and choking on splashes of seawater.

“Let’s head in,” Billy said. “We’ll have to run.”

“I can’t,” Steph said. “I can’t make it.” She started falling back as the boot-driven shark closed the distance. “Billy!”

“Hold on,” Joel said. “Feed a bit of line.” He showed her how to do so.

Janine had felt the unusual pressure across the pad of her finger but she’d not reacted. She’d been thinking about telling him everything.

"That's it," Joel said, excited. "Can you tell? You hooked a big one, now let's reel the sucker in."

Again, his arms were around her waist, his hands on her forearms.

"Crank it slowly. Don't want to rip out the fella's lips."

She did so, still contemplating insane revelations.

"Now slow down a bit. This one's a fighter. My God, Janine. First time out and you bested the best."

She cranked on the reel as Joel directed but her mind still wandered. *I am not insane*, she continued to think. *Trust me, Joel, I am not insane.*

"That's it," Joel teased. "Yes. That's it."

And then, Janine whipped the fishing pole in an upward arch; her elbows knocked Joel backward. She had tired of the fight. She had something to say…something important. It was much more important than fishing.

When the hook came out of the water, no fish was attached. The fishing line vaulted high, much in the same way as it had when she'd tried to cast the line the first time, only now the hook was moving in the opposite direction. The sun glinted off the tiny piece of metal just before Janine ducked.

"Agghh!"

She turned to see Joel with a hand clasped to his left ear. A tiny spot of blood drooled through his middle and fore fingers. Joel stared as if in disbelief but instead of scolding her, he said, "Well, there's a first time for everything. Never been hooked in the ear before."

Janine released the fishing pole as if it were diseased. It dropped to the jetty rocks and settled between the cracks. "Oh…Oh…I…"

"Well you hooked one, my dear, and a big one too."

"I…"

"And I just love Milky Way."

Janine reached out to coddle his bleeding ear. The hook had fully penetrated the lobe.

"No worry. You just settle." Joel reached into the back pocket of his coveralls and pulled out a knife which he used to cut the fishing line. Then, with gentle strokes, he used the knife to slowly saw the barbed end of the hook which dangled just below his earlobe. In seconds, the metal was severed and he removed the hook. He now held the two pieces of fishing hook in one hand and the knife in the other.

Janine blinked.

It couldn't be!

"I just love this thing," Joel said. "Sharp as Hell. Can cut through anything."

"What…Where…" Her face turned ashen.

Cupped in Joel's right hand was an exact duplicate of something the doctors had told her didn't exist. In Joel's hand was the magic dagger, the one that had removed the bullet from the professor who had never visited her on a night that never happened.

No, she wasn't insane.

"How?" she said to Joel. "How could you have that?"

Joel turned the dagger in his hand. It had the same impossibly thin blade, the same jeweled handle. But at the same time it was different in a way that went beyond the build up of what might have been red rust or dried blood on its surface. He dropped the severed fishing hook, and the two pieces disappeared between jetty rocks.

"I found it," he said, giving the dagger a sudden reverence that was dictated by Janine's awe.

"May I?" Janine held out her hand. Joel passed the dagger with much less thought that he had his fishing pole. She quickly studied it, traced the haft's edges with her fingers and drew the artifact closer for inspection. A red jewel occupied one point of a star. But something was different. It nagged her. Something about the jewel. Something that told her this dagger was in every way the same dagger that had entered her farm house a year ago except for the red jewels. This was that dagger…but it wasn't.

"Proof," she said. "This proves that I am not insane."

"My knife?" Joel said, surprised.

"A magic dagger," Janine corrected.

Joel smiled. He held his earlobe to stop the blood flow and just stood there, his eyes searching hers as if measuring her truth.

"I only told you part of the story, Joel," she began. "Now it's time to tell it all. I am not insane and you can trust me on that account."

They sat on the jetty rocks and Janine recounted everything—withheld nothing. She explained every gruesome detail. She told a story that could rival the fiction of Stephen King. Joel remained silent and only nodded a few times throughout her explanation. When she came to the end she said, "Unbelievable, isn't it?"

"I, uh…" Joel said, again looking into her eyes as if looking for her soul. "I don't know what to say."

The dagger, which Janine had set on a rock in front of them suddenly twitched. A metal-to-rock scraping sound accompanied the dagger's shuttering. It was as if the dagger was cold and shivering…

…and alive.

The jewel in the haft began to glow, creating a red halo around the trembling artifact.

"Help!" someone yelled, and together Joel and Janine looked out into the surf to see two surfboards heading toward them, and the black, splashing outline of a swimmer in close pursuit.

The shark closed to within ten feet by the time Billy reached Steph. Three more strokes and the bodyguard would have her—would have them. Without warning, Billy grabbed the nose of Steph's board and flipped it over. Steph went into the water at the same moment that the bodyguard's hand grabbed her ankle. She tried to scream but water filled her mouth. No strength to fight remained in her exhausted arms. She quickly went under.

Billy lifted the nose of Steph's surfboard. Then, in one forward thrust, he hurled the back of the board at the bodyguard. The board's fin missed Steph's struggling, submerged head by fractions of an inch and struck the bodyguard in the face, ripping open the flesh of one cheek and causing the black shark's grip to release its hold on human prey. Billy grabbed Steph's flailing hand and pulled her torso to him; the added weight almost toppled him. Steph coughed up seawater as she struggled to hold tight to Billy's surfboard while Billy began back-pedaling. In a disturbing display of rage, the bodyguard did not simply push Steph's surfboard aside as most angry humans in pursuit of homicide might, but instead, proceeded like a shark, attacking the surfboard with all of its energy, beating the fiberglass into small pieces as if the surfboard was the appetizer to the object of its aggression.

Though Billy distanced himself and Steph by more than a dozen yards while the bodyguard destroyed the surfboard, he knew that it would not be enough. The jetty rocks were another thirty yards away, the shore, forty. The bodyguard's powerful strokes would certainly have them in his grasp before they could escape.

"Billy!"

The shout came from behind him.

"Over here. Swim hard!"

Billy had already stroked for almost two miles. As fit to the water as his muscles were, the combination of time, distance and, now, weight, sucked any hope from his determination. The voice of imperative direction, which he quickly determined was that of Joel, served only to exacerbate the dilemma. Steph barely hung to the end of the surfboard. His arms felt like thick glue.

The bodyguard had satisfied himself with the destruction of the board and now resumed his efforts toward them, his boots pounding the waves like fins, his black menace swiftly engaging them like a predatory torpedo.

Billy stopped paddling, his hope swallowed by the reality of his physical limitations. He, sitting on the surfboard, and Steph, draped across its nose, drifted with the rise and fall of the current while the bodyguard closed the distance, an eerie, wide grin of incisors predominant under the fresh red tear that pulsed across the flesh in his right cheek. The image of Mitchell Bone's decapitated head reemerged in his mind. He glared, hypnotized, at the bodyguard's hands and each hand's powerful stroke; he imagined how easy either appendage could snatch his noggin from his shoulders, an index and forefinger through his eye sockets, a thumb stuck in his mouth—just like a bowling ball. It would be a matter of seconds before he and Steph met the same fate as Bone. The bodyguard had them.

And then…he didn't.

And then, as if some spiritual entity snapped its mystical fingers, the entire scenario changed. A force field developed though Billy knew such a thing did not exist.

The bodyguard drew back. The final swim stroke that would have landed on Steph's flesh was averted by…

Billy looked over his shoulder. On the jetty, an aura of crimson light that engulfed a twenty-foot circle glowed and grew. The halo of red light raced across the water and, seemingly, attacked the bodyguard. It produced a reaction of nauseating madness from the black-skinned shark. The bodyguard writhed and retreated, swimming with equal aggression as he'd used in his assault. As the crimson halo expanded, the bodyguard swam faster, keeping just beyond the halo's outer rim until, at the edge of the pier, a good hundred yards away, the halo disappeared and the bodyguard returned to the shore.

Janine grabbed the dagger, her right hand's grip swallowing the glowing, crimson jewel. The weapon buzzed her entire arm, inducing reverberating chills that raced past her elbow and into the back of her neck and down her spine. Crimson colors peeked between her fingers. Four red rays escaped, looking much like thin laser beams. Without knowing why, she lifted the dagger over her head and yelled as loud as she could, directing her bellow at Albert who was little more than a speck of inhumanity crawling to the shore near the pier.

"Back to hell, you son of a bitch!!"

The glow from the jewel faded as Janine lowered her arm, opened her fist and, again without realizing it, spun the dagger atop the palm of her open hand in two complete circles before grasping the haft with the blade pointing down and at her side.

"Mother of God!" Joel whispered, more to himself than to Janine. "What in the name of…"

"…everything Holy," Janine finished. "Well he's not. He is a demon."

Joel looked perplexed. "Who?" he asked. "And where did you learn to handle a knife like that?"

"Dagger," Janine corrected. "A magic dagger." She lifted the dagger from her side as if praising it. "A magic dagger that performs surgery and wards off demons."

Billy and Steph floated on one surfboard near where Janine had dropped her fishing cast just moments ago. "Joel," Billy yelled out. The crashing waves against the jetty rocks made the word sound hallow. "What the hell was that?"

"A demon," Janine repeated under her breath.

"Come on in here," Joel said to the surfers, waving his hand as if reeling in a fish.

A few minutes later, the four of them sat together. The dagger lay behind Janine, its magic seemingly gone from the moment that had encapsulated her. Each person occupied one rock. Jetty spray splashed around them. The cargo ship that had been on the horizon at the start of the day now entered the jetty behind them. Its horn shrieked as if sounding the beginning of some great change which the four would later refer to as the "moment of great enlightening."

Janine started the conversation. She knew about those things which had brought them together: the dagger and Albert. She told them everything she'd told Joel. She opened up her soul to the possible ridicule of more strangers. Evil came from the Cubit, she explained. Albert came from the Cubit. He'd murdered her son and her life.

Janine's was a crazy story of insanity—but it was only slightly worse than the delusion of Billy's revelations who now told the group all that he had discussed with Steph: what he'd seen in the vault, the day on the coast with Mark, blood spots and dead seagulls and the creepy secretary of a missing newspaper publisher.

Steph added her facts about robotic security box recipients and the crazy bitch known as Carol, the bank teller.

Joel added the connection to Steph's word "robotic" with the mannerisms of little Teddy Lavender.

"Anyone seen Pedro?" Billy said after Joel had finished. He looked at Steph. Both Joel and Janine shook their heads. "Well we have. In fact there are two of them." He turned toward Janine. "Didn't you say that while you were in Kansas, you saw…eh….” Steph frowned in disgust in much the same way as she had when Janine had told the story moments before. “Didn’t you say you saw your son eat himself?”

“Yes—but that’s one part of my memory that I still question. People just don’t eat themselves.” She hesitated. “Do they?”

“Following the logical path of reason, the answer is absolutely: No!” Janine frowned and Billy took her hand. “But nothing around here is logical anymore. I’ve—” He gently stroked her flesh with his thumb. “*We’ve* seen too many things that cannot make sense to logic.”

“Zombies!” Joel suddenly added to the discussion. “The walkin’ dead.”

Billy glared, a compiled expression of *Are you crazy?* and *You have something there!* all mixed into a confused frown. “I just don’t know, Joel, but I wouldn’t use the word zombie.”

Steph leaned forward. “Billy and I have a plan.”

Billy looked quizzically at her.

“There is another player in all of this and she has yet to make her appearance.” She told Joel and Janine of the investor from Arizona and the plan to meet her at the airport. “Maybe Alixel can shed some light. In the meantime, I don’t think any of us should be left alone.”

“I agree,” Janine said quickly.

Joel covered Billy’s hand which still rested on Janine’s. Steph solidified the pact by topping their hands with hers.

“I’m scared,” Janine said while reaching with her free hand for the dagger.

“With that,” Joel said, nodding at the weapon, “I don’t think you have anything to worry about.”

THE CUBIT: PART II

REVELATION

The dunes now held no innocent magic. That morning, as Janine and Joel had walked toward the Gulf, the scattered, uneven heaps of sand had posed as obstacles to anticipated beauty. The water, the surf and the melding of their naive souls had shadowed all of the troubles that the "real world" dictated. Cresting one dune only to be confronted by another had increased the anticipation. She'd seen the ocean only once before. She'd never gone fishing. She had been Becky Thatcher and Joel had been her Tom.

But as they headed back in from shore—from the madness and revelations that had shattered what could have been Janine's final break from her year of insanity—all she could think about was death, demons, and the demise of *her* Paradise. The dunes no longer stood in the way of beauty; they now protected her from the ugliness of certainty. Insanity had been an unwanted but convenient excuse to forget her past, but the south jetty of the Corpus Christi shipping channel had provided the setting for a reality that, in a few abrupt moments, had made her past inconveniently true and more complex.

As she and Joel traversed the sand away from the heat and the confusion of the morning, Janine questioned her belief in choice. Perhaps, in the end, no human being had such luxury. The decisions of every soul were preordained.

God was the director. Her decision to arrive in this Paradise was not hers. Her decision to break from the past was really the most insane idea she'd ever held. You couldn't run from destiny. You couldn't choose to stand on the sidelines while Evil played out the antagonist's role. She was *meant* to be here. She and Joel, Becky and Tom, and the roles *they* would play in the days that followed were already written into destiny's script. What she had to do was accept it. What she had to do was believe. But to help her mortal ineptitude, and to help forward God's plan for her, she would have to understand the mysteries that had been revealed.

"Careful," Joel said as they crossed the final dune between them and the asphalt surface of Cotter Avenue. "That little ball next to your foot will grab hold if you aren't careful."

Janine looked down. An inch from her open-toed sandal was a tiny, unassuming, egg-shaped cactus that had no roots. It sat atop the sand like a prickly grenade.

"That sucker can smell human flesh and will snag you in a way that makes fishing hooks feel good." He touched his ear.

Janine casually avoided the tiny cactus, her attention more on the curiosity of Joel's dagger which she still held in her hand.

"This is in so many ways the dagger I used to pull the bullet out of the professor's chest," she said, raising the thin blade toward the sun's glinting, midday heat. "But it isn't. And even if it was *that* dagger, how in God's name could you have it?"

Joel only shrugged his shoulders, sensing that her questions were not meant for him to answer. He twiddled his fishing pole, nervously, between the fingers of his left hand.

"Which can only mean that there's more than one of them. Where did you get it? And please don't tell me Kansas."

"On the beach," he said. "Or more appropriately, in the beach."

"In it?"

Joel hesitated as if embarrassed by what he would say. "A few years ago I went on this…craze, I guess you might call it. I went treasure hunting. You see, I've always had this fascination with pirates." He paused for some expressive response from her, but Janine said nothing as she avoided another tiny, human foot-hungry cactus. There seemed to be many more of the spiked plants than she'd remembered on their way out to the jetty. "In particular, I've always had this thing for Jean LaFitte. A fascinating character if there ever was one. He made the Gulf his home during the early part of the nineteenth century. Some say he wasn't even a pirate. Some say he was more a profiteer in a day when Spain and America were at odds and slave-trading was a way of life."

"The dagger," Janine said, a bit too impatiently. The history of Jean LaFitte was not one of the mysteries she was interested in solving. Her impatience surprised Joel.

"Yes…well. LaFitte, it is said, had a huge treasure which he took with him when he was forced out of Galveston in 1820. Some say he took it to the Yucatán where he used the wealth to build a new life. Others say he lost it in a massive hurricane that nearly destroyed his ship. Then there's the myth that his treasure is buried right here on Mustang Island. I went digging around for almost a full year back in '95 in search of the myth. The only thing I ever found was that knife…eh…dagger."

"Where?" Janine stopped and looked back toward where the ocean was now hidden beyond the dunes.

"By the pier," Joel said, pointing. "Pretty much near the spot where I met you two days ago at the luau."

"How far down was it?"

"You mean how much did I have to dig to find it?"

Janine nodded.

"Couple of feet was all. Digging too far that close to the pier would have brought the badges out."

"Didn't Billy say that the casino was supposed to be built in that area?"

Joel nodded.

"And Albert's one of them," she said more to herself than to Joel.

"What was that?" Joel asked.

"It's just that Albert is playing bodyguard for the man in charge of bringing the casino to Port Aransas."

"Okay."

"And they are planning to build it where you found the dagger."

"Yeah."

Janine saw the confusion in his stare. She smiled.

"Oh, I don't know. Just running some of the facts through my head. It's just that everything seems so 'convenient' if you know what I mean."

"Convenient?" Joel said. "You mean as in how convenient it was that your dagger came to life just when that…what did you call him…ah, yes—I think it was demon. Just when that demon nearly killed Billy and Steph?"

She raised the dagger at arms length. "Strange. There are so many mysteries. But we're going to figure them out. Aren't we? As long as we stay alive that is."

"I wouldn't worry about that zombie if that's what you're referring to.

You have the ultimate in zombie radar devices right there in your hand."

"I suspect that he is not the only *zombie* around here. From what Steph was saying, there may be hundreds more."

"Now that's an idea a person could lose sleep over." Joel covered her hand with his and she released the dagger into his grip.

"We'll pick up some polish," Janine said. "It's quite beautiful once it's all shined up."

They walked in silence the rest of the way to Joel's Canton Shack. Janine kept a weary eye out for anyone who looked suspicious though she wasn't quite sure what "suspicious" really looked like. The iPod kid came to mind—little Teddy Lavender. He'd certainly acted inhuman, or as Joel had put it, zombie-ish. What continued to trouble her, though, was that there might be "zombies" out there that didn't act zombie-ish. And worse—what if the dagger did not warn them? Just because it had gone nuts when Albert had gotten too close didn't mean that it would protect them from what could be hundreds of these things. If they looked human and acted human and nothing could tell her or Joel any different then they had little chance of surviving. And being torn apart and eaten—the way poor Lenny had been—was a horrific thought. She'd not come this far to die like that. It just wasn't in God's plan. It could not—must not—be her destiny. She had to believe.

But believing was hard, especially when she and Joel turned onto the pebbled path that led to the Canton Shack and found the screen door ripped from its top hinge and flailing askew on its single, twisted bottom hinge. The screen mesh had been ripped as if sliced by a knife. Joel immediately pushed Janine behind him, lifted the dagger in a defensive posture, and dropped his fishing pole. The dagger's haft did not glow but Janine was unsure if this was a good thing.

Cautiously, Joel stepped into his home. The first thing his toe touched was the clock that Marcy had given him for Christmas. The glass face was broken and in shards on the floor. The magician's hands were bent at odd angles. It did not work.

"Stay here," Joel said to Janine.

"No," she insisted. "We're in this together."

They entered what looked to be the aftermath of a tornadic storm. Joel did not have much, but whatever material belongings he owned were in mass disarray. All of his clothes and linen were scattered everywhere. His mattress had been flung from the bed spring, torn open and disemboweled—pieces of foam and fluff sat like brown snow on the floor, the bed spring, the window sill, his makeshift bookshelves and tabletop spool, his tiny refrigerator which had been turned upside down, its meager contents emptied and mixed in with the mattress stuffing. The curtain that had served as a divider to his bathroom-closet lay in a balled mass on the shower stall floor. His fishing lamp was busted and lay in ruin around the balled curtain, as if someone had thrown it against the shower stall wall.

"They're looking for this," Joel immediately concluded, referring to the dagger. "I don't have anything else of value. And from what I've heard and seen, this must be worth a fortune."

"Maybe," Janine agreed. "But whoever *they* is might also be looking for something else. We have to get to Marcy's."

The foursome had made an arrangement to meet back at Paradise Cottages later that evening. The hope was that Billy and Steph would gain additional knowledge from the woman whom all of them knew only as Alixel. Meanwhile, Janine said that she and Joel would make their way back to Janine's cottage.

Billy and Steph had a long walk ahead of them. Traversing a mile in the surf had not seemed so exhausting—at least not up until the time that Albert had entered the water and had chased them from the pier to the jetty. The water had provided relief from the unrelenting heat of the Texas sun. And the joy that had been shared by both he and Steph, the innocent moments together in the surf and Steph's victory over the five-foot wave, had made time slip away. But now, as they trudged barefoot along the wet sand at the Gulf's perimeter, minutes seemed like hours and the hot sun stripped them of energy. Worse, though, was the concern for the wide and deep footprints that paralleled them. Albert's, no doubt. His destination was certainly theirs: Billy's VW.

"Do you believe her?" Steph said. "I mean really."

Billy walked a good thirty paces before he answered. His mind's logic fought the apparent reality that Janine's revelations had conjured. But the facts spoke for themselves. And no matter how hard he tried to reason away the events of the past two days, no matter how hard he tried to calculate an explanation using what had always been the reliable scientific methodologies solidified through academic study, the truth seemed apparent.

"It sounds absurd," he said, finally. "But until we find out what's in that crate, whether it be Janine's Cubit or something more realistically sane, I can't ignore the possibility."

"Even if that means there are dead people walking amongst us?" Steph absently kicked a broken seashell into the surf.

"Yeah. Even if it means that. Even if it means that the Pedro we saw running and the Pedro we saw chasing and the scream we heard from across the dunes when the one had caught up with the other means that the real Pedro is now dead. Even if it means that we have to consider, based on Janine's storied past, that the one Pedro ate the other. Even if it means that we could go crazy thinking about what all of this means. We have to consider the possibility."

"So we have to find Pedro."

Billy nodded. "And we have to find out more about what's in that bank vault."

"Until then we have to assume that anyone could be something they are not."

Billy stopped walking as did Steph. He turned to face her. "That could lead to paranoia."

"I'm already paranoid," she said, looking back toward the pier which, in the distance, was no more than a shadowy line atop the surface of the water. "I'm already thinking about what I'd do if I saw myself holding a knife. I'm already wondering if I could outrun…me. And if I couldn't escape, then what would it be like to be eaten alive?" A tear welled in her left eye. "This can't be real, can it? I want you to tell me that it can't be real." Her lips twitched as the tear fell onto one breast.

Billy pulled her to him; her chin rested on his naked shoulder. Wet streams of salt trickled down his spine. She sighed, trembled. "I wish I had an answer," he said.

Billy's back was to the distant pier. Up ahead, along the shoreline and still a good thousand yards away, he saw the vague outline of his VW. He also saw what he believed was Albert though at this distance the figure could have been anyone. The bodyguard would be at—and certainly be in—his vehicle within minutes. Albert would destroy it, Billy was certain, the way he'd destroyed Steph's surfboard.

Steph suddenly yelled out.

"Look!"

Billy turned around to see that a vehicle was approaching along the beach road, a Chevy van, circa 1979, that had a medieval retro-paint job slathered across the body's copper-colored surface. He recognized it immediately. It was the *Knights in White Satin*.

As the van slowed to a crawl beside them, the driver leaned out the window. His bleach-blonde hair was knotted in a ponytail. "What's up with all the lame activity around here dude and dudette?" It was Richard, the band's vocalist and leader.

Billy avoided the formalities. "Can you give us a lift to my v-dub?" He pointed toward the gray outline which now appeared to merge with the bodyguard's.

"No problemo. Hey, you saved our butts. Right? Right…"

Billy led Steph to the opposite side of the van where one of the painted knights on the van's metal split in half as the band's drummer opened the sliding door and offered his hand. "Enter, me lady," the drummer said, his white mustache and beard manicured in a way that reminded Billy of the face on the cover of a pack of ZigZags. "Let us escort thee to thine own divine providence." The drummer's smile was one that could easily be contagious under other circumstances.

"Please hurry," Billy said as he sat on a bench seat next to Steph. The drummer sat behind them with the group's guitarist. Behind the guitarist were two cases shaped like the musical instruments he played.

"Gunnin' it now my friend," Richard said. "Like what's up with this island, man? I thought this place would be the bomb but it's nothing more than one giant crater of boredom."

Billy saw that Albert had now reached his VW and was attacking the driver's door.

"Whoa, Bill," Richard said. "That dude's fuckin' up your ride."

"Faster," Billy replied.

"On it my man." Richard looked over at the bass player sitting in the passenger seat. "You still got that punk bat, Dillon?"

Dillon leaned forward and pulled a short wooden bat, the kind you might get as a baseball game souvenir, from under the seat. Billy saw the word *Mud Hens* emblazoned in the grain. "Holy crap," Dillon exclaimed, his voice as deep as the chords he played for the band. "That motha' punched right through the window." He looked at the small bat, as if suddenly questioning the success of its intended use.

Albert had beat several dents into the driver's side door of Billy's VW, and was reaching through the window he'd busted when the *Knights'* van diverted his attention. He stepped away from the vehicle, his wrinkled black shirt, pants and boots riddled with streaks of dried sand, and clenched both fists.

"Hit him," Billy said. Steph looked at him with a shocked but confederate stare.

"What?" Dillon replied, smacking the fat head of the small bat in the palm of his hand.

"That tiny toothpick ain't gonna help us one bit," Billy said. "Believe me. He'll rip us all a new asshole."

Richard glanced over his shoulder at Billy. A short, quick grin spread from the corner of his lip then was gone. He whipped his head back around and his white-blonde ponytail followed in an arc that Billy seemed to see only in slow motion. In fact, the next few minutes all came at him in slow motion. "Bon…zai…" Richard wailed, though his words came out as if they'd been recorded and were being played back at half speed. "You…muth…a…fuck…ah…"

The *Knights'* van jumped as Richard hammered the gas pedal but to Billy the jump was more like a tiptoe. He felt the additional g-force that pressed him into the van's seat and he saw Steph's head jolt backward in unison with his own, but the moment seemed to last forever, the way a momentary dream seems to endure for hours, the way he'd felt when he'd left the Surf Side on Tuesday and then when he'd pulled over in the breakdown lane of Route 361 on his way to rescue the *Knights* that evening before the luau. His mind had blurred into slow motion then as he'd somehow been transported to that other dimension where he was being chased and shot at, where someone was telling him to "Shut the fuck up!", and where he'd puked into the shattered pebbles of windshield glass.

A dream that seemed more like a memory.

Richard's hands yanked the van's steering wheel to the left, but the motion seemed incredibly slow. "Come…here…you…muth…a…," he snarled. Through the windshield, Billy saw that the distance between them and Albert was less than twenty yards. He noticed that the speedometer read fifty-five. But time seemed to stand still. It came at him in still-framed succession.

Snap!

Richard clamped down on the steering wheel, his knuckles showing white.

Snap!

The bass player named Dillon dropped the bat and grabbed the dashboard.

Snap!

Someone screamed, though he was unsure if it was him, Steph, or one of the band members behind them.

Snap!

Albert stood to the left of the van's hood. Impact was a nanosecond away. He did not flinch. He did not try to avoid the van. He just stood there, grinning, his eyes filled with the crimson swirls of dark insanity that Billy remembered from the Surf Side bar.

Snap!

And then, suddenly, the slow motion stopped and the reality of the impact sprang catastrophically alive. When the van hit Albert it seemed as if the Chevy had actually hit a wall. Richard fought for control of the steering wheel as the van fishtailed to the right, its rear bumper missing Billy's VW by inches. Dillon's head lurched into the windshield and made a sickening thud! He grabbed his nose which was now bloody. Both Billy and Steph plowed shoulder first into the headrests of the front bucket seats and the drummer behind them flew up and over their seat and landed behind them, his ZigZag beard planting in the small of Steph's back. The van spun 180 degrees before coming to a complete stop. A cloud of sand enveloped them and rained in through the open windows. Everyone coughed for clean air.

"Holy shit!" Dillon said. Billy didn't know if his exclamation referred more to the impact with Albert or the blood in his hand.

"Are you all right?" Billy asked Steph whose spine looked uncomfortably arched with the drummer's head behind her.

"Oww," she moaned. The drummer shifted and pulled himself up and back into the seat behind them. She rubbed the place where his beard had scratched her skin then stretched the muscles.

"Some divine providence," the drummer said. "Weren't nothin' divine about that. What the hell did you hit?"

The sand in the van trickled down—brown sparkles under a Texas sun—and as the cloud dissipated, all six of them stared out the windshield with anticipation.

"That big mutha fucka," Richard said, shaking the disorientation from his head. "Didn't I? Or was it a fuckin' freight train?"

Buried in the sand just a few feet away from Billy's VW was the outline of Albert. The body was pressed into the sand face first. His black clothing made it appear as if someone had poured a shadow into the beach. Albert did not move.

"Is he dead?" Dillon said.

Billy and Steph stared at each other, knowing the truth.

"You ran right over him." It was the first thing the guitarist said since Billy and Steph had entered the van.

Richard stepped out of the van. Dillon exited and slid open the van's side door with one hand while he pinched his nose with his right and tilted his head back. The blood flow slowed, trickling in thin rivulets across his cheeks toward both ears. Outside, Billy moved around to the front of the van where Richard stood, gawking at the dent and smashed left headlight.

"Shit," Richard said. "I thought for sure he'd jump out of the way." He turned toward the shadow planted in the sand. "I killed him. Holy shit. I killed him." He looked at Dillon and the drummer and guitarist who stood behind him, then gazed out across the dunes, up and down the beach road and out into the surf. The reality of what he'd done was gaining self-importance. "We gotta get outta here."

Billy grabbed Richard's shoulder, feeling the soreness in his own as he did so. "Just get back into your van and drive away. You probably saved all of our lives not to mention the v-dub. I'll call the authorities as soon as I get into town." Billy looked over Richard's shoulder at Albert. "To tell you the truth, I don't think you killed him."

"Holy shit," Richard repeated. "Of course I did."

"No you didn't," Dillon confirmed. "Look!"

One of Albert's boots suddenly shifted in the sand. The heel turned downward and the pointed tip turned up, which looked physically impossible.

"Broken leg," Richard said. "I broke his leg."

The other boot followed the motion of the first, heel turning down, toe twisting up. Now both feet were pointing in the wrong direction, looking much like two shark fins in the sand.

Billy pushed Richard toward the Chevy. "Get out of here," he urged. "You didn't kill him, but you probably pissed him off something horrible."

Richard's expression was one that reminded him of how Steph had looked as they sat on the jetty rocks listening to the impossible stories told by Janine. He apparently did not believe what was occurring but could not question its reality.

"Man," the drummer said. "We gotta move, bro. If we didn't kill him already, we ain't gonna get another chance."

One of Albert's arms lifted from the sand, then the other, and the shadow which was no longer a shadow did a push-up. Albert's face turned upward toward them. His eyes boiled in crimson red and emitted a glow that developed a faint, crimson halo around his head.

Everyone scattered at that instant.

The *Knights in White Satin* almost tripped over each other as they raced for the open van doors. Billy and Steph bolted for the VW.

Albert rose to his knees making the pointed toes of his boots, still turned in the wrong direction, seem even more anatomically incorrect.

It took four turns of the ignition key to get the *Knights'* van started and with each unsuccessful turn, Billy saw through his own windshield how much more concerned both Richard and Dillon became. They watched Albert—who now rose onto his backward pointing feet—reach down, grab his left leg just below the knee and twist it in a clockwise motion. Impossible as it may have been, and as sickening as it was to watch, the lower leg turned 180 degrees under a knee which could not have possibly supported such a motion. He applied the same technique to the right leg then stood up straight, his eyes beaming hatred at them.

The Chevy tires spun, causing the van to fishtail. For a moment, Billy thought that Richard was going to drive it right into the surf but a second later, control was regained and the van sped away down the firm, wet sand at the surf's edge.

Billy had a similar problem getting his VW to start. He turned the key twice before it came to life. By that time, Albert was three steps from the back of the vehicle. The crimson glow from his eyes filled the VW's interior as he grabbed the rear bumper. Billy stomped the accelerator to the floor and for a split-second, he thought that Albert had them, that his strength was too much for the meager vintage horsepower of the four-decade-old vehicle. The VW spun in place, not moving an inch and Steph screamed.

"Go! Go! GOOO!"

The VW suddenly broke free, causing Billy to struggle with the steering wheel for control. As they sped away both looked back, almost knocking heads between the bucket seats. Albert stood in the center of the calamity, shards of broken windshield, headlight and van reflector scattered at his feet. He held Billy's rear bumper in one hand.

Marcy was not home but her back door was still unlocked. Janine and Joel entered into the kitchen and Janine led the way upstairs to where she'd left her sacks of life. Nothing appeared out of place but to Janine that meant nothing. She thought that those that had devastated Joel's place could have found what they were looking for at Marcy's without destroying property.

When she entered the guest bedroom, she was still unconvinced that her sacks, and the book that rested within one of them, would still be there. She knew that the book held dire significance. Pages just didn't write themselves. But her sacks *were* there, untouched, just like she'd left them. She grabbed the bottom of the sack closest to her, felt the impression of the book inside, opened it, dropped in the dagger, then pulled the sack closed and draped its pull-string around her hand. Joel grabbed the other sack and slung it over his shoulder.

"You want me to carry that for you?" he asked. She said nothing, only shaking her head instead.

She headed down the stairs and Joel followed. "What is it?" he said.

"Your face looks..." She turned to him as her foot hit the last step at the bottom of staircase and scowled unintentionally. "...twisted," he concluded.

Janine paused, one foot on the landing, one foot on the last step, the sack and its contents weighting her left arm with what she now believed was salvation. She stepped to the landing, looked up at Joel who towered three steps above her, and was suddenly stricken by memory. Of Kansas. Of Michael. Of Lenny. Of her own special room that doubled as a storm cellar against tornadoes. Of Spirituality and God and Paradise.

Then, for reasons she could not understand beyond divine intervention, Janine thought about *The 23rd Psalm.* She stared straight through Joel and back into time, to that place, in her home, and at the framed page of scripture mounted on her "Paradise" wall. She read aloud:

"The Lord is my Shepherd; I shall not want.
He maketh me to lie down in green pastures:
He leadeth me beside the still waters.
He restoreth my soul:
He leadeth me in the paths of righteousness for His name' sake.

Yea, though I walk through the valley of the shadow of death,
I will fear no evil: For thou art with me;
Thy rod and thy staff, they comfort me.
Thou preparest a table before me in the presence of mine enemies;
Thou annointest my head with oil; My cup runneth over.

Surely goodness and mercy shall follow me all the days of my life, and I will dwell in the House of the Lord forever."

Joel stood frozen for a full minute. "Christian woman," he finally said. "That could come in handy." Then he joined her at the bottom of the stairs.

The storm cellar wall faded from memory and was replaced by Joel's concern. "We need to go to the Surf Side," she said not looking up. "The shadow of death. We'll find it there."

"Shadow of death?" Joel questioned.

"Yes."

Janine headed into the kitchen and out the back door before Joel could say anything further. He followed.

They found that the Surf Side had been broken into. The glass from the side entry door was in pebbled shards; webbed, sharp edges still clung to the aluminum frame. Joel swept Janine backward with a gentle but forceful stroke of his left arm. He dropped his sack to the pavement and it crunched atop the broken glass pebbles.

Shadow of Death.

Janine's words kept nagging him. He'd met many *Shadows of Death* in life but none that even closely resembled those that had been suggested to him in the past hour. People didn't eat people…sharks did. But as the Psalm that Janine read revealed, he—Joel—was with her. His rod and staff would comfort her. In fact, his rod and staff would beat the crap out of anyone that laid a finger on Janine. Janine should fear no Evil as long as Joel walked with her through the Valley of the Shadow of Death.

"Stand back," he said, now reinforced with a will reserved for protectors and guardians and saviors, and stepped into the shadows. The hostess podium had been toppled but none of the tables in the dining room ahead had been touched. The bar immediately to the left, however, was in shambles. Liquor, and the bottles that had housed it, lay scattered on the floor in a pooled Technicolor mess one-inch deep. Wine glasses and shot glasses and beer mugs and the mirror behind the bar had been swept to the floor, adding to the glistening reflections of moisture and crystal. The only two items that had not been destroyed sat atop the bar: a full bottle of Jim Beam less one shot that sat within a jigger next to the bottle. Joel dismissed it but when Janine entered behind him, she gasped.

"He's been here," she said.

Joel knew. "Albert?"

"He used to drink that fire juice and then hit…" Janine quickly looked away.

"He hit you?"

"He tried to kill me." She still had the sack hanging from her left hand and it looked as if the weight was taking its toll on the muscles of that arm.

"Why don't you put that down? Or I could carry it for you."

"NO!" she yelled, then placed a finger to her lips. "Shhh…he might be here," she said to herself.

She turned toward the kitchen and Joel rushed in front of her, again using his gentle strength to force her back. He eased through the swinging double doors to find a kitchen so dimly lit that it was almost impossible to see.

He searched for the light switch and flipped it up with a forefinger. Nothing happened. The only illumination into the room came from the open swinging doors and this was so dim, Joel's shadow was quickly eaten by the darkness beyond six feet. An intruder could easily be hidden.

Joel grabbed a broom which leaned against the door frame to the left and took a step forward.

"If it's Albert," Janine said from behind, "that broom will be of no use."

Joel looked at the wooden handle then quickly slammed it against one raised leg. It snapped almost completely in two and Joel had to wrestle with the rounded end to separate it. What remained would serve as a spear, the edges of the splintered wood shaped into a jagged point.

"Still," Janine warned.

Joel stepped forward and disappeared into the shadows just as a loud THUD! echoed above them from Billy's apartment.

They traveled the length of the island on Route 361 in silence. Off to the left, Steph noticed that, for the first time in two weeks, clouds were rolling inland and it looked as if the island would finally get some welcome wet relief. It was fitting, she thought. The dark days were on the horizon.

Billy's blonde hair whipped in disarray as wind swirled into the now-shattered driver's side window. Since they'd left the beach in such a panic, they'd had to stop at Steph's apartment to get some decent clothing before heading to the airport. She'd given Billy a yellow T-shirt with the words *Mary Kay* stamped on the chest; it was the only clean shirt she had that fit him.

Steph still trembled from the experience on the beach; she clenched her jittery hands and sucked in one deep breath. Dried tears of fear rested on both cheeks. "What in the name of God…"

Billy gently grabbed her hands and stroked the knuckles. "Not God," he said.

For a moment, she almost yanked free of his grasp. Somehow, his touch no longer excited her. Gone was the simple innocence of their first kiss at the luau. Gone was their shared victory over the five-foot wave. Funny, how the walking dead did that to a person, how the threat of death ripped desire from the soul. It was a fleeting moment…his hand, ugly, menacing, as if it were made of the same dead flesh that had decimated her surfboard, had punched through the VW window, had withstood a direct hit from a speeding Chevy van, and had ripped bolted metal from the back of the VW as easily as one might peel a banana. His hand was Albert's hand and it would kill her! For a fraction of time that almost sent her over the edge, she almost jerked away and screamed, "Stop this fucking car!" She almost screamed and then she almost puked.

And then the moment subsided. Billy was Billy again. His touch, though not full of anticipated desire, was reassuring. She glared at him knowing her face had turned green; her lips trembled and the tears rushed uncontrollably.

"I'll pull over," he offered.

She moved her hands over his, sniffed and mustered a smile. "No," she said and patted his hand. "I'm fine…really. We can't be late."

"We have plenty of time."

She shook her head. "What if they get to her first?"

Billy's eyebrows raised, again in that calculator-that's-lost-a-transistor expression of confusion, but he said nothing.

When they arrived at the corner of 361 and South Padre Drive where Billy would turn right toward Corpus Christi, Janine noticed him staring into his rearview mirror. His gaze remained even after the traffic light turned green. Vehicles zipped by them, the drivers blaring horns and shouting obscenities. He continued staring, oblivious, through a complete traffic light cycle. What was most troublesome to Steph, though, was the way his face shifted with expressions that ranged from curiosity to fright, as if the mirror contained some projected suspense movie that glued him to its screen. When the light, again, turned green she gave his shoulder a gentle but forceful shove.

"Green means go," she said.

The kid was no older than an average college graduate. His hair was dark and straight with no wave to it whatsoever; it almost touched his shoulders but not quite. His twin looked *almost* like him, except the twin's eyes were red, its hair a molted tangle and it smelled so bad a word for the stench was not in the English language.

Billy watched the smelly twin eat its primary through the looking glass of his VW's rearview mirror. He knew that the dead and the dying were both Lenny Bender, the son of the woman who had revealed this small piece of an insane story back on the jetty rocks. And Billy realized that his previous visions, Tuesday—the one outside of the Surf Side when he'd been transported into a chase scene with police and gunshots and someone named "professor", and the one that had caused him to pull over and puke on Route 361 while en route to pick up the stranded Knights in White Satin—were all pieces of Janine's story. A woman he'd never met...a story that could not be true...a vision of the past revealed to him in the future.

The mystic part of his reasoning that he'd always cloaked in a veil of scientific denial leaked into his consciousness, and as he'd always, habitually, done, he tried to push it aside; he tried to ignore it; he tried to reason it away. But this time it wasn't going to work. He knew it, and that's what made his rearview mirror, now a wide screen of projected magic, so much harder to resist. He looked into the past. He saw someone eat themselves.

No, Janine. You're not insane, he thought. *The world is.*

And then the vision blew apart, scattering across the rearview mirror surface like shards of glass. Twisting. Twinkling. Bouncing against the edges of the mirror's frame then reforming into another image that occupied its center. A book. And an image of Janine's magic dagger embossed into its surface.

Steph shook his arm. Someone else yelled, "Asshole! Get off the damn road!" He looked away from the mirror.

A passenger on the back of a Harley Davidson, a woman in black chaps and tattoos, flipped him off as the motorcycle passed on the left then sharply turned right onto South Padre Drive in an aggressive move that nearly clipped the VW's front bumper. A police cruiser quickly crossed the median from the opposite direction and its lights swirled into action, following the motorcyclist into the Go-Mart parking lot at the corner of the intersection.

Billy peeked back into the rearview mirror, slyly, the way children do from under the covers when they know monsters are chasing them. And that's exactly what he saw.

He'd not realized it, and had no idea how long they'd been following behind, but there they were: Officer Keadle and Crabman, sitting in the front seat of a brown Chevy Impala, one of Port A's unmarked state trooper cruisers.

"You're right," he said to Steph. "Looks like others are interested in the airport arrival." He grabbed her arm. "Don't turn!"

They traveled across the causeway to the mainland with Keadle and Crabman two cars behind them. It wasn't until they reached the traffic light at the intersection which led to the airport terminals that the Impala pulled up beside them on the left. Crabman, in the passenger seat, turned toward Billy, his head twisting on a neck that seemed disconnected, a skull with no spine, like a child's toy doll with a head that spins a full 360 degrees with little more than the twist of a hand. Crabman's eyes were huge, doll-like, the whites completely encircling the center crimson color Billy now associated with those who had been changed. And the thing that used to be Crabman, which looked in almost every way just like the real Rally Panini, grinned. Its lips curled up into its cheeks impossibly deep and a set of bright white incisors appeared. The big, round eyes atop a half moon of teeth that were etched into a face painted onto a spineless skull reminded Billy of John Carpenter's *They Live*. It was as if Billy had that special pair of sunglasses through which he could see the beasts that had taken over the Earth's population.

And then, just as Keadle stomped the accelerator to race toward the terminal ahead of them, Crabman's teeth parted to reveal a cavernous, black pit—no tongue, no gums, no throat, just emptiness—and he bellowed forth the sound of diseased laughter. It was of such a piercing high pitch that Steph covered her ears. Even as the cruiser raced out of sight, the maniacal craziness remained, as if it were trapped inside the VW, a foul entity that could drive a person insane.

Billy's apartment door stood wide open; bed sheets fluttered across the threshold. Inside, the mattress had been toppled and, like Joel's mattress, had been gutted with a knife. Chunks of foam that had been ripped in handfuls were scattered everywhere, including the wooden porch where Janine and Joel now stood.

Something fell to the floor inside and shattered. Joel crept into the open doorway; he held the makeshift broom-handle-spear defensively in front of him. The porch boards creaked as he stepped from them, alerting the intruder.

And then he saw him—Pedro. The Surf Side cook poked his head from the recesses of Billy's makeshift lab-office.

"Pedro!" Joel immediately said, while lowering the broom-handled weapon in confidence. "Who the Hell did this?"

But it took Joel only a fraction of a second to answer his own question. This was not Pedro. It looked like him, but it was not him. It was the other one. The *dead Pedro*, as Billy had called him; the one that had eaten the real Pedro. Joel raised the point of his spear.

"Back, you zombie," he warned. "Now you just back on into the bathroom where I'm gonna lock you up until the authorities get here."

The cubited Pedro stared for a moment, animal-like, its eyes roiling in crimson and silver. It looked past Joel to Janine who stood in the doorway, her sack of life in one hand, the dagger which she'd pulled from it in the other. The haft of the dagger glowed a dull red but nothing with the magnitude it had when Albert had approached the south jetty in pursuit of Billy and Steph.

Pedro rushed the door, zeroing in on the dagger as if the weapon was what it had been looking for. It paid no attention to Joel who plunged the point of the broken broom handle into its lower back, piercing one kidney. The cubited Pedro wailed in agony but did not stop its forward assault toward Janine. When it reached her, Janine twirled the dagger in the palm of her hand in one complete circle then slashed out at Pedro's throat. She opened a small slit just under the chin which immediately gushed a stream of blood that was much darker than normal human blood. The cubited Pedro flailed past Janine, grabbing its throat and the wooden spear which still protruded from its kidney, and hit the deck railing with all of its forward momentum. Through the railing it went and plummeted twenty feet to the hard, sandy ground below. Joel ran to Janine, checked that she was uninjured, then looked out over the deck to see the Pedro cubit rise to its feet, one broken arm dangling, the broom handle now pushed completely through its body and protruding from its stomach, a mess of black blood coating the skin, then limp run in the direction of the beach.

"I cut myself," Janine said.

When Joel turned, he saw that Janine was holding her wrist; blood leaked between her fingers. "I guess I'm not as good with that thing as I thought I was."

"Ah, Jesus," Joel moaned then snatched one of the bed sheets from the open doorway and quickly tied a tourniquet around her forearm.

"That's not the man who fed me Caribbean shrimp two nights ago." Janine swooned as she grabbed one end of the bed sheet, covered the bloody wrist slit and mopped up stray rivulets of red that flowed on her skin along the same lines as the blue veins underneath.

"He's one of them," Joel said. "An Albert. A cubit. Just like BJ said, the Pedro that served you shrimp has become his own dinner."

Janine dropped to the wooden deck. Her blood continued its relentless escape from her wrist, drooling down her fingertips and dropping through the divisions between the six-inch deck boards. "Joel," she said in a weeping squeak that usually accompanied throats without moisture. "Why?" She blinked. Red drops as large as dimes fell from between her forefinger and thumb. Joel clasped her wrist between both of his sea-beaten hands but the blood flow continued, leaking over and through his grasp, his strength useless against Janine's heart which pumped the life from her across flesh and wood and the sandy hard ground that lay beneath.

Joel crouched over her, wondering: *What if she bleeds to death right here in front of me? What if I lose her like I lost Jane? What if...*

And at that same moment, as Joel considered the consequences of a life without Janine, the blood flow stopped. In fact—and Joel would forever remember it—the blood that had escaped down both his and her forearms and the blood that freshly pooled atop Billy Jo Presser's porch suddenly reversed like a rewinding video. Janine's blood hungrily returned to her wrist. Streams and drools flowed back through Joel's fingers and disappeared under his palm which had not loosened its clasp of her right hand. She blinked and then her eyes flapped wide open. Crusty remnants of crimson adhered Joel's hand to her wrist and when he peeled it free—a Saran Wrap crunchiness accompanying the movement—the wrist slit was in the process of closing. The red mouth of open skin and veins actually stitched themselves together right then, in a matter of seconds that should have taken days, the skin folding, a plump hill of flesh protruding, the final remnants of blood deterred by the closing mouth.

And then it was done. There was no scar. It was as if the flesh had never been severed. The only evidence that remained stained the porch wood, the sandy ground below, and Billy's bed sheet.

"Why?" she repeated, her voice nearly a whisper. Joel hugged her body to his chest. The wrist may have miraculously healed but her body remained as limp as any bled animal. "The shadow of death…I see it."

"Nonsense," Joel countered.

"The valley. I'm going there, Joel. Oh…it's so beautiful."

Her breathing slowed and she gasped. At that same moment, a gush of wind exited the apartment through the open door as if the place was belching forth some unwanted gas. It knocked Joel to his knees and he tottered at the edge of the porch, Janine against his chest, the rail splintered from where Pedro had slammed through it. Had a second blast followed, he and Janine surely would have fallen. Janine rolled from his grasp and reached for the apartment's open doorway, her eyes drooping, her strength depleted. Through the doorway floated two pieces of paper. They curled and twisted like feathers before landing on the porch where Janine's blood stained the wood. They were the copies of the snapshots Billy's robot had taken of Chancey Lett's satchel. On the top of one printout someone had written the word "Lafitte." The Mayan symbol known as "Wayeb" was at the top of the other. Janine pointed at the symbol and said, "The valley of the shadow of death."

Steph and Billy stood in the terminal, reading the list of arrivals. She could not remember if Mitchell Bone had ever told her the flight number nor which airline Alixel was to be flying in on, however, she knew the plane would be coming from Arizona, most likely Phoenix, around two o'clock. Unfortunately, there were three flights due to arrive from Arizona around that time but none precisely at two. All of the flights were on Southwest Airlines; the one closest to the top of the hour was scheduled to arrive at 1:55. The flight number was 33. She and Billy headed for Gate 15 with an hour to spare.

The fear she'd experienced while walking the shoreline—the idea that anyone at any time could easily be one of the living dead—now resurfaced, but she didn't cry this time. Her acceptance of the nightmare had grown to exclude tears but it was impossible to subdue the adrenal rush, the anticipation that at any moment any one of the hundreds of travelers might suddenly turn on her.

A man bumped her shoulder and she wondered if he was one. A trio of flight attendants simultaneously turned and stared at her and she wondered if they had touched the Cubit. So many people…so many chances…so much adrenaline.

And then there was the idea that she, herself, a Steph-cubit, might appear at any moment. Had she touched it? Had Albert and Chancey and Carol initiated her? What would happen if that were true? If she saw herself, she would surely go mad.

Inadvertently, she latched onto Billy's arm and hugged it close to her hip. He smiled reassurance, a gesture she knew he realized she needed.

Near Gate 10, a large group of at least thirty people had assembled around The Pecos Bar. None of them were eating or drinking—they were just standing there, looking into the bar's dining area.

"…has grown in strength to a Category 5…," Jim Cantore was saying, "…and has taken an unprecedented turn while picking up speed. I have never in my twenty-five years seen such a meteorological event."

Bustling talk ensued among the onlookers as a graphic appeared on a large, flat screen television mounted on the bar's dining room wall. *Hurricane Antiago*, was written above a satellite image of a storm that was not very wide but had a clearly defined center. A solid red line traced the storm's path from a town called Merida in the Mexican Yucatán. In only two days, Antiago had traveled more than five hundred miles and was set to make landfall in southern Texas by Friday morning, if not sooner. A shaded triangle depicted the storm's possible collision with the coast; it spread for hundreds of miles and included all of Texas and parts of Mexico and Louisiana. The most probable landfall, depicted by the red line, was drawn straight to Corpus Christi.

"We now have the latest from the hurricane center in Miami," Cantore continued, "and you're not going to believe this. Sustained winds of 175 miles per hour. The pressure at the center of the storm has fallen to 890 millibars.

That's a drop of twenty millibars since the last reading just an hour ago.

"The mayors of dozens of coastal cities have ordered immediate evacuations but there is a concern that many could be stranded in the storm's path if this very unusual and sudden shift in speed and direction continues."

As Steph and Billy stood within the growing crowd, they did not notice that Keadle and Crabman were seated near Gate 15 and were staring straight at them.

Janine stowed the dagger and the two pieces of paper in her sack before she and Joel boarded the trolley. She remained physically weak, but the strength of her faith had returned, having been in hiatus since the doctors had convinced her that she was crazy. And she knew that it would take more than faith and more than the dagger to save herself from the likes of Albert. The dagger had apparently been unable to detect Pedro as it had done Albert and, therefore, she could no longer trust it as a "warning beacon" as Joel had suggested.

They sat in the same two seats they'd occupied the day before. Five people sat in front of them. Joel immediately snatched Janine's right hand and gently, as if it were made of fine crystal, cupped it between both of his. "Look!" he exclaimed, pointing. "It's Marcy."

Janine followed his finger to the front of Marcy's home. Marcy walked along the sidewalk in front of her shop then slowly climbed the three concrete steps to her front door. Her movements were stoic, straight and without freedom, without personality, without individualism—robotic. The fortune teller had so much grace in her gait; it was a quality that Janine admired (along with her old Cher tapes and her brutally honest way of making sexist men squirm). But her grace was absent and Janine considered the obvious reason.

When Marcy entered and closed the door, Joel said, "I hope not." He knew what she was thinking and was probably thinking the same thing himself. "Do you want to stop and tell her you retrieved your bags?"

Janine's denial was unwavering. If Marcy had been cubited, she didn't want to know. "No!" she replied with more volume than was necessary. Three of the five riders turned with expressions of anger.

Five minutes later, the three angry trolley riders exited. The two remaining passengers still had not revealed themselves. They sat on opposite sides of the same row, three back from the front. The one on the left had short, dark hair with a neck and ears that were either very tan or were Hispanic.

This person wore a white baseball cap and seemed to be male though it was hard for Janine to tell. The one on the right was certainly a woman. She wore a blue bonnet over a head of curly silver hair. Her sun dress, which flowed over the left edge of her seat and into the aisle, was light blue with white flower prints that were trimmed in red and orange. Someone's grandmother perhaps…a little old lady returning home from a day of shopping. The two remained seated, neither moving an inch (and Janine knew it because she kept staring at the backs of their heads) even after Joel reached up and pressed the *Stop* button.

Janine hesitated, waiting for the two riders to exit. This was the last trolley stop but neither moved.

"We're here," Joel said rising, Janine's hand still held within his. He led her forward, passing the strangers who paid him no attention. But as Janine passed, both turned to her simultaneously.

Skulls. Janine expected them. Fleshless jaws parting, cackling out some belligerent rants, telling her it was a ridiculous waste of energy to believe that they could be stopped, that she or her lying God could change the course of fate, which of course was the end of the world.

But that's not what happened. Both looked up and both smiled. The tan male was a teenage Hispanic and the old lady in the bonnet was surely someone's kind grandmother; you could tell by the geniality conveyed by her cheery face. Nothing dead could ever smile with such absolute kindness. Janine returned the smile; she couldn't help it.

"Be careful, Janine," the grandmother warned. "They are everywhere."

The Hispanic boy nodded in agreement.

Janine stood mesmerized. The two strangers knew her? That couldn't be.

Janine.

She blinked.

Janine.

She looked to the front of the trolley.

"What is it?" Joel said while tugging her arm.

She turned back toward the two passengers. Neither made any expression of recognition. Both stared at the seats in front of them as if Janine and Joel were invisible. Janine shook her head and followed Joel without looking where she was going. When she passed the trolley driver, he reached out and grabbed her arm. It was the same driver who had given her ticket fare information that morning.

But it wasn't. His eyes told her so.

"You fuckin' bitch," Carl, the driver snarled, sounding strangely like Albert. "When I get my hands on you death will be a blessing."

Joel punched Carl's forearm ten times before the driver released her. Both quickly jumped from the trolley.

"Your boyfriend will suffer greatly and I promise to show you every fuckin' minute of it," the cubited Carl howled before making a U-turn back toward the center of town, his eyes swirling in a chaotic mix of crimson and silver sparkles.

Standing at the corner of Route 361 and Paradise Lane, Janine and Joel waited for more than five minutes. And though they were both thinking about Carl's rants, the big reason why they could not move was because of the steady flow of traffic that streamed in one long line, a flow of traffic that was escaping the town of Port A.

From the periphery, Billy saw them first. While he stood there calculating how much time it would take for the hurricane to hit the island given Cantore's meteorological data, he almost turned all the way around but caught himself. He whispered to Steph without moving closer to her. "Do you remember the gate number for the two-ten flight?"

She continued staring at the television. "That flight is from Tucson. She wouldn't be on that one."

"The gate number," Billy insisted. "What was it?"

"Thirteen." She now turned to him.

"Don't turn! Keep looking at the TV." She did so. "Keadle and Crabman are near the ticket counter at Gate 15. We are going to pass them as if they aren't there and head down to Gate 13."

"But what if…"

Billy interrupted. "Gate 13. We'll talk then."

Billy watched from the corner of his eye as they walked past Gate 15; Keadle's and Crabman's heads turned in unison but they didn't rise. Billy doubted they would. Alixel was their target. Had they wanted Billy and Steph, they could have taken them during the drive from Port A. Billy additionally hoped that both men—who were, of course, no longer men—would believe that he and Steph were at the wrong gate and would consider them a non-threat to their goal. How he and Steph would steal Alixel away from them, he had yet to determine.

Billy settled for a seat that faced the terminal aisle and away from Gate 15. Steph sat to his left, Billy's body hiding hers from the stares of the two cubits. Billy asked, "What do we have—about thirty minutes?"

"Yeah. The airport clock is over there." Steph pointed toward the clock but realized that she was also pointing toward Gate 15 and quickly lowered her arm. "Sorry. I'm not use to this Sherlock Holmes meets Stephen King shit."

"Agreed. So how do you figure we distract them long enough to sweep Alixel away?"

Steph looked at him as if the question was the dumbest thing he'd ever said. "I don't even know what she looks like."

"Too much chance," Billy mumbled. "Not enough facts. This is going to be tough but we've been going by the seat of our pants since this morning. Maybe that's our new strategy. Maybe the most logical is the illogical: wait and see what the hell happens next." He grinned, uncomfortable with the idea of inaccuracy.

And then a curious thought occurred. What if she didn't arrive at all? What if there was no Alixel? What if they were left to deal with this "crisis" all by themselves? If there had been an evacuation ordered, planes may not be allowed to land. Apparently, the idea had not been a concern of Keadle and Crabman. They believed that Flight 33 from Phoenix would arrive as scheduled and that Alixel would be on board. But they were dead…what could they know?

Billy looked out the terminal's tall windows. Planes were landing. He could see them taxiing in from the runway. He could see passengers disembarking several gates away. The flow of traffic at Corpus Christi International Airport was a vibrant tussle. Many of those that had just arrived joined the growing arc of people that stood outside The Pecos Bar and now blocked half of the terminal aisle. Most of those people had expressions of surprise, shock and fear from the Weather Channel's revelations. Two men, who had just arrived moments before, turned immediately and ran back toward their gate, their business suits fluttering as they fled with what appeared to be panic.

The airport's public address system announced:

Southwest Flight 33 from Phoenix now arriving at Gate 15.
Southwest Flight 33 from Phoenix now arriving at Gate 15.

And then after a short pause, continued with:

Due to the evacuation declaration of Mayor John Richardson, all inbound flights will be diverted from Corpus Christi

International Airport beginning at four p.m. central time. Please see your carrier's flight information desk concerning diverted arrivals.

The evacuation announcement repeated and when it finished, for the smallest fraction of time, the entire airport went silent, which to Billy seemed impossible. Everyone stopped talking, walking, working, and waiting. At that very moment, time switched onto a path of an alternate thread. Life would never be the same for every person that heard that announcement. And then, in a sudden rush, half of those who stood outside The Pecos Bar rushed away. There was tripping and falling and cursing. One man punched another. A child cried. Billy noticed that Keadle and Crabman watched with delight. Their dead faces brightened with pale glee for the melee.

"What do we do now?" Steph asked.

"We wait."

One-by-one, passengers entered the terminal through Gate 15. None looked like Alixel, or at least none looked like the person Billy had already pictured in his mind as Alixel.

"That her?" Steph pointed.

"No," Billy said. The woman was too thin, and her hair was blonde though she did have a nice tan. Billy thought Alixel would be an extravagant specimen of womanhood, with a walk that spoke of riches and a body sculpted by the money she possessed. Alixel would not have blonde hair, he thought. Red hair seemed inappropriate as well. Alixel's hair would be dark. Her skin would be dark. But no one who exited Gate 15 looked like that. In fact, once the door was closed Keadle and Crabman stood there studying the passengers for Alixel who, apparently, was not on the flight.

Chatter among the airport's new passenger arrivals increased. Most had been told of the impending hurricane and the conversations Billy could hear now centered on how possessions could be saved: homes, cars, computers, little Johnnie's brand new tree house. The chatter and confusion was so intense that neither Billy nor Keadle and Crabman noticed that Flight 20 from Tucson had arrived and was now disembarking through Gate 13 behind them. Steph grabbed Billy's sleeve, turned him around and said, "How about her?"

Alixel did not look exactly as Billy had imagined but her appearance was close, and though he had no proof that it was her, his instincts told him the truth. Her figure did appear as if it had been sculpted by wealth and she did wear some extravagant clothing that flowed with Southwest colors and prints, but her hair was much longer than the Alixel drawn in his head. Two orange-red streaks traced along the temples through hair as black as night. The streaks flowed back above the ears, down her neck and ended an inch short of the full length of her mane which stopped at the waist. Her skin was very dark and Billy guessed accurately that she was, indeed, of Native American descent. She wore no make-up which surprised Billy, but her natural skin tones did not need it. High cheekbones, a small rounded nose and lips that were full in the middle but thin on the ends highlighted her beauty. She stood with hands on hips just inside the gate's doorway, a small bag that was not a purse hanging from one forearm, and blocked other passengers who maneuvered around a woman apparently upset that no one was there to greet her.

Quickly, Billy and Steph moved in her direction. The two men that had started fighting shortly after the public address warning were now back at it and, this time, the fight went out of control. People gathered around the two men. There was blood. There was screaming. Two security officers appeared. Billy did not plan it; all he'd had to do was wait. Fighting was never logical, but it now provided the perfect opportunity.

"We're here to escort you to your hotel," Billy said to Alixel, thinking that he should bow but not knowing the reason why. He'd forgotten that both he and Steph were still wearing beach clothes.

"What are you!" Alixel demanded. "Certainly not my chauffeur."

"You are Alixel?" Steph questioned. "You've come to Port A because of the casino?"

The woman paused, scanned Steph from head to toe, then added, "And what are you? Of course I'm Alixel, but what are you? And Port A?"

"Port Aransas," Steph grunted. "Where the casino will never be built."

"Where is my chauffeur?" Alixel demanded.

"We are they," Steph countered. "And if you'll follow us, we'll get you to our lovely island A.S.A.P."

Both security officers were now engaged in the scuffle between the two men.

"Please," Billy said in an urgent but consolatory voice. "We need to go—Now!"

Alixel measured him, his clothes, his woman and his statement. "Yes," she said. "These heathens are not to be trusted." Billy thought that she looked directly at Keadle and Crabman but there was so much commotion, her stare could have been directed anywhere.

Together, they scurried into the terminal aisle. Keadle saw them. Crabman turned as well, his red, not-sunburned skin a bit paler, his lithe body a bit lither. Both advanced, pushing through the crowd, dodging the melee caused by the two men, their sole, combined purpose aligned. Keadle threw a woman and her child to the floor. Crabman rammed a man whose glasses flew from his face and landed in the makeshift ring of the wrestling combatants. A baby in a stroller whose mother had been distracted by the fighting sat between the hunters and the hunted but this did nothing to divert them.

Three Corpus Christi police officers entered the confusion. One grabbed Keadle. "Jim!" he said. "What's this about?" Keadle brushed aside the officer's hand with such force that the officer's shoulder dislocated; the officer screamed. Crabman rammed the baby carriage with his thigh and as the carriage toppled and the baby screamed, a second of the three police officers righted it, coddling the basket with both arms and smiling at the screaming infant. The third officer, a heavyset man three times the size of Rally Panini, tackled him at the waist and both went down.

Billy, Steph and Alixel quickly walked away. Down the escalator they went, briskly, not running, past the security checkpoint and baggage claim areas, and exited the airport through swooshing electronic double doors. They stood for a moment on the sidewalk under the concourse before turning toward the parking lot.

"My bags," Alixel exclaimed.

"Our associates will get them," Billy answered without thinking. He looked over his shoulder. No one followed.

Steph sat on the floor of Billy's VW as the trio raced above the speed limit toward Port A. The evacuation was apparent. Many vehicles moved in a concentrated line in the opposite direction. Several flashed their headlights.

"Please roll up your window," Alixel said to Billy.

"Not an option." His candor was emotionless.

"Why?"

"Broken."

"Why didn't you get my bags?"

Steph broke in. "Listen. We've gone through a whole lot of hell just to get you this far." She saw Billy shaking his head. "Billy told you that we've taken care of your luggage. All we ask is that you bear with us. As you can tell, our island is not in the best of ways right now."

Alixel turned in the seat, her long hair whipping in the wind that rushed through Billy's window. She scowled. "Who are you people? You aren't my designated drivers. Lett and Bone are not such fools."

"Actually," Billy said before Steph's increasing aggravation became unmanageable. "Steph was told to pick you up."

Alixel turned to him. "In clothes such as these? How ignorant. You don't know who I am do you?"

"Alixel. From Sedona," Steph said. "An investor who wants to help ruin Port Aransas."

"I really don't think any of us has much to say on that issue." Alixel nodded toward the evacuating cars and campers and trailers and trucks.

Steph leaned against the computer console which had been closed and locked since the night Mitchell Bone was murdered. "Hurricane Antiago or Hurricane Alixel. Either way, the island is doomed."

Alixel scowled. "The wealth a casino would bring to this island is immeasurable."

"And wealth to you no doubt. Wealth to you and Lett and Bone..." Billy was shaking his head again. His eyes, peering through the rearview mirror, told her to behave. Alixel picked up on this.

"Let her speak her mind. I've heard worse I'm sure. The lack of knowledge always manifests in ignorant behavior."

"How well do you know Chancey Lett?" Steph said, holding back the aggression that boiled like a knot in her stomach.

"Well enough to know that he knows how to manage casinos and make them profitable."

"And Mitchell Bone?"

"Don't know him other than through phone conversation."

Billy now shook his head with greater urgency.

"He's dead," Steph said. "Murdered by Chancel Lett's bodyguard."

Alixel's expression, which had remained smug and dictatorial, like royalty in the presence of pagans, changed for the first time. She could not hide her surprise and concern which molded her face into something truly compassionate. "When?"

"Last night," Billy said, still uneasy with the release of such knowledge to a total stranger whom they had no reason to trust.

"Why wasn't I told sooner?"

Steph crossed her legs. Her feet pressed against the opposite side of the VW's interior. "Murderers don't reveal themselves," she said.

"I mean the police." Alixel scowled again at Steph.

"The police are in on it," Steph said, apparently pleased that her *ignorant behavior* pressed Alixel's buttons.

"Take me back to the airport."

Billy said, "You'll not get a flight out. The city is being evacuated. Please, please give us a chance. There's a lot more going on in Port A than the murder of one man."

"Yeah—hundreds," Steph mumbled.

"Steph," Billy pleaded, looking in the rearview mirror. "Not now." He smiled at Alixel. "Where are your reservations?"

"The Treasure Trove," Alixel replied through a mouthful of hair that had blown across her lips. She pulled it free and brushed it behind her with long fingers.

"Figures," Steph grumbled. "Right next to the bank."

Billy and the Treasure Trove's manager, Nigel Felino, had created a wonderful working relationship from the first day that Billy had opened the Surf Side. Billy supplied professional catering and reasonable prices. Nigel provided group meals as part of business conferences. But beyond the business side of their relationship, they just liked each other. They shared many common interests, including surfing. Nigel had never surfed before he'd met Billy. Now the hotelier could not get enough of the sport.

As chance would have it, the Treasure Trove also served as one of three hurricane shelters on the island. The first floor and an underground basement were strengthened by reinforced concrete and steel that engineers claimed could withstand, minimally, a Category 4 hurricane. Though evacuations were always the first line of defense against casualty, the hurricane shelters had been established after several lives were lost when Hurricane Andrew had decimated southern Florida. No one wanted the same thing happening in Port Aransas.

Few cars were in the parking lot when Billy's VW stopped under the canopy at the hotel's front door. As he stepped onto the asphalt and looked over at The Big Texas Bank, a sudden rush of fear snatched his heart. A black Hummer and a white Ford Ranger were parked near the bank's entrance. There were no other vehicles. In fact, since the bank and hotel were neighbors, the combined empty spaces between them magnified the sense of impending calamity. The thickening gray clouds overhead only added to this depression. Though he saw no activity through the bank windows, he felt someone was watching and rushed around the front of the VW to help Alixel out of the vehicle. She may have acted the prude but Billy still remembered *his* manners. He held her hand as she stepped down, then helped guide Steph around the stick shift and passenger seat. He hurriedly urged both of them toward the hotel's door. A bellboy met them inside.

"I'm sorry, sir, but we are not taking any guests at this time. There has been an evacuation ordered."

Billy did not know the kid who, most certainly, was not a resident of the island. "Yes. I know. Where is Nigel…eh, I mean Mr. Felino?"

"Doing a room check upstairs." The bellboy pointed at the ceiling.

"I have a very important person here I'd like him to meet. She will be staying at the Trove and I want to make sure her accommodations are the best."

"Can I tell him who's asking?"

"Billy Jo Presser. We're friends." Billy reached into his pocket. "And please hurry," he added while handing the kid what change he had. One of the coins fell from his hand to the floor as the bellboy turned to fulfill his request. It rolled on edge and fell flat next to Alixel's brown leather shoe. She picked it up. Her jaw immediately dropped, then instantly settled back into her stoically painted face. Steph did not see the sudden expression, but Billy did. "What?" he said to her.

She offered the coin in the palm of her hand. "Interesting piece. Where did you get it?"

It was the coin with the Mayan mask pressed into it. "Found it on the beach. Oddly enough, I found it where you and your investors will be digging footers for the casino."

"You know what this is, don't you?"

Billy plucked it from her hand. "Mayan symbol called Wayeb."

Alixel appeared shocked at his knowledge. "You know what it means?"

"Bad times are coming."

"Yes, but that's not what I'm referring to. It means you found…"

"Billy!" Nigel appeared from within an elevator on the opposite side of the lobby. His accent was thickly Italian as was his moustache. "What brings you to my Trove under such stormy conditions?"

It means I found what? he wanted to say but minded his manners.

"Alixel. This is Nigel Felino, owner and operator of this hotel." She gave the coin to Billy and held out her hand, palm down, as royalty might do when hands are expected to be kissed. Nigel happily engaged the knuckles with his lips.

"It is my honor. I have a wonderful premiere suite ready for you; unfortunately Antiago seems intent on ruining our evening. But you know hurricanes. Most can never make up their minds where they'll end up until the last moment. You are welcome to stay in the penthouse but if Antiago does decide to visit our island, we'll need to get you into the shelter." Nigel had been so enamored by Alixel's presence that he did not release her hand until now. He bowed and she smiled, something that neither Billy nor Steph had seen her do. "Your bags?"

Alixel turned to Billy. "They're on the way," he said, knowing that the airline would hold them until Nigel called.

Nigel escorted them to the front desk where the bellboy stood at attention. "Would you please hand me the card key to 322?"

"I'd like a different room," Alixel said. Nigel appeared upset but for only a second. Steph huffed and shook her head. Billy shrugged his shoulders.

"Room 322 is our best suite," Nigel said with a smile.

Alixel replied with silence.

"Steven." The bellboy turned to Nigel. "Please see that 321 is ready for Miss…Alixel." Steven quickly scuttled to the elevator and disappeared. "While Steven is preparing your suite, please join me for a cup of coffee. My family shipped some wonderful flavors from Sicily that are still very fresh."

The Treasure Trove restaurant was small but enchanting. It became apparent to Billy that most of Nigel's staff had already left the island as Nigel handled the brewing of the coffee himself. He poured four cups and set them on the square table in front of each of them. He poured a quick stream of cream into his own cup and said, "So, tell me something, Billy."

Of all the things Billy could have said, his mind still remained wrapped around Alixel's comment about the Wayeb coin.

It means you found…

He pulled the coin out of his pocket and dropped it on the table. Alixel, who'd been looking at the front glass doors of the hotel and had not touched her coffee, turned her attention to the clinking metal.

"You ever seen anything like this before?" Billy said to Nigel who snatched the coin and turned it over in one hand while he sipped from the coffee cup with the other.

"Never. Looks like play money."

"I found it on the beach where the casino is supposed to be built." All three of them flashed a glance at Alixel. "Alixel tells me that I found…what was it you were saying?"

Steph glared at Alixel who did not give her the pleasure of acknowledgement.

"Wayeb," Alixel replied. "Like you said, Billy Jo Presser, you found a coin with a Mayan mask on it."

Billy shook his head. "But *you* said there was…"

"Bad days are coming," Alixel interrupted, frowning, her hand with its long fingers tapping the table to the right of the coffee cup saucer.

Nigel smiled to break the sudden tension. "So let me get this straight. You found a coin on the beach with markings that stand for bad luck. Now, that's what I call coincidence."

"Not bad luck," Alixel insisted. "The symbol is one that demarks the five bad days at the end of the year. Unlucky days. Evil days."

Nigel's smile wavered. He paused to find a grin then added, "Whew, glad we're in the middle of June." Nigel tried to hide what Billy could see was growing uneasiness. Alixel was good at propagating such a response from people. "But I guess you can't get more unlucky than a Category 5 hurricane hitting you square in the face, can you?"

Steven walked into the restaurant. "Room 321 is ready, Mr. Felino."

Nigel stood a bit too quickly. His thigh hit the edge of the table and coffee spilled onto the table from all four directions. "My apologies," he said and quickly turned to escort them to the elevator. Billy knew that Nigel had had enough of them. His urgency betrayed his good manners.

Room 321 was the size of an efficiency apartment. The bedroom was sectioned off and could be made private by closing its door. The living area highlighted the suite. It was larger than Billy's entire apartment. Its cool blue, aqua and green colors were in stark contrast to the southwest warmth that Alixel was adorned in.

"So now what do I do?" Alixel said, sitting on the loveseat. Billy and Steph sat across from her in a pair of cushioned, high-backed chairs. "I invited you two in so that you could help me work this out."

"The bank is right over there," Steph said, thumbing in the correct direction. Her dislike for Alixel had not diminished a bit. "Why don't you go see for yourself? I hear they have a great deal on security deposit boxes."

Billy peered angrily. "Steph. Remember that we need her help." He looked at Alixel. "As you've probably already surmised, the investment you planned to make is pretty much in the can. Bone is dead, Lett is a murderer and there's one hell of a storm headed this way that will surely put an end to any hopes of a casino, no vote needed. But there is more." Steph opened her mouth but Billy's look backed her down. "First, I need to know something." He took a breath. "Tell me what it is about the coin that disturbed you so much."

"You won't believe me." Alixel sat rigid in her seat. For some reason, she kept staring at the front door and spoke without turning away from it. "That coin is part of a great treasure. If you found the coin, you found the treasure."

Steph couldn't help herself. "What!?" she said, slapping her head and leaning forward. "Treasure? There's no treasure. It's some lame excuse to tear up the beach. To hell with the casino, there's a treasure to be uncovered."

"LaFitte," Billy said and grabbed Steph's hand, which had moved from her head and was now pointing at Alixel.

Alixel turned away from the front door. "You know a lot, Mr. Presser."

"Billy," he interjected.

"What else do you know?"

"About LaFitte?"

"About LaFitte." Alixel leaned forward and a string of jeweled turquoise slipped from her cleavage and onto her blouse's patched brown and tan prints. Something glistened within the strand but Billy couldn't quite make it out.

"He was a trader who amassed a large amount of valuables—gold, silver, jewels—and buried them somewhere along the shorelines of the Gulf Coast…or so the story goes."

"A good story," Alixel said. "One that is quite true. What else do you know about him?"

"From my research, I found that some regarded him as a pirate and some believed him to be a patriot. He helped in the War of 1812 but also dealt in slave trade. I understand he became quite rich and influential, so much so that President Monroe had to, I guess for a lack of better words, do away with him. Research suggests that he fled to the Yucatán where he used his great wealth to support a luxurious way of life. Mythologies talk about him burying his treasure then disappearing without a trace."

"Research?" Alixel sat up straight. The turquoise necklace flopped against her firm breasts. "So you are a scientist?"

"Roboticist," Steph corrected.

Alixel shunned Steph's addition to the conversation. "Do you believe in God?" she asked Billy as if it were a completely normal question for one stranger to ask another.

"You mean in a Christian God?"

"What's the difference? Either you believe in the *mythology* of a spiritual higher-being or you do not."

"I don't understand."

"Of course you don't. You're a scientist through-and-through. I've known many scientists. They are the ones who would destroy the sacred lands of the great Southwest. They do not follow faith. Facts are the only things that mean anything to them. I take it from your research that you found enough facts to support your belief that LaFitte found a life in the Yucatán?"

"Not really. No one knows what happened. There are only theories." Billy squinted, trying to make out what looked like a cross hanging from Alixel's neck. "I have faith. Believe me. In the last few days, it has been greatly tested."

"Then you are one of the fortunate." Alixel grabbed the silvery pendant that dangled on a string of turquoise and gently stroked it. "LaFitte's treasure is buried on this island and from your discovery, I'd say it's buried quite close to where you found that coin. By the way, the coin is perhaps fifteen hundred years old and worth more than this entire hotel."

Billy patted his pocket to make sure the coin was still there. "So you're telling me that Chancey Lett never intended to build a casino. All he wanted was the treasure."

Alixel nodded.

"He needed a reason to dig up the beach."

Alixel nodded.

"And you were going to help him do it?"

She shook her head this time. "Not for the same reason."

"Then why?"

Alixel suddenly looked at the front door, her face contorting into an expression of grave concern. She moved her hand from her necklace to her waist. Incredibly, her belly began to glow. Billy shook his head and rubbed his eyes but that did not diminish the fact that between Alixel's fingers, a dull red hue—much like what he'd seen coming from the hand of Janine on the south jetty rocks—grew in magnitude.

A knock echoed outside and down the hall. The knock became louder, insistent. Then someone kicked in a door, splintering wood.

Alixel stood, still holding her belly. "We have to go…Now!"

Alixel led them out of the room and to the stairwell which was, thankfully, the next door down from suite 321. Steph followed Alixel and Billy took up the rear. He looked back down the hall one last time before closing the stairwell door. The room that had been invaded was 322. Albert stepped from it into the hallway as the stairwell doorknob silently clicked.

Mark Walker followed Joel and Janine from the trolley stop to Paradise Cottages. Their appearance, for Walker, was an unfortunate result of bad-timing. He'd been sent to search both Steph's and Janine's cottage apartments. He'd expected them to be vacant. However, as Albert had ordered, if Janine *was* home, killing her would not be an option, at least not by anyone other than Albert himself. He could do as he liked to Steph, Albert had said, but Janine was to be left alone. Of course in Mark's cubited mind, not much made a whole lot of sense. Since killing his twin the day before, the development of Mark Walker's physical and mental attributes had been a slow process. For some reason, the word "bloodspot" kept revolving through his thoughts like a programmed glitch stuck in an endless loop.

Mark maintained a distance that would not attract their attention and when the couple entered Janine's cottage, he jimmied the lock on Steph's door and entered undetected. "Whada hewl is da blow spoot," he mumbled incoherently, the vocal chords still unable to mimic Mark Walker. "Whada is dat?" He closed Steph's door with visions of helicopters and one-legged birds rolling aimlessly in his dark mind.

"I thought you said he was dead." Steph pointed out the glass window of the VW's rear hatch. They'd made it successfully down the staircase and to Billy's vehicle but the ignition of its engine had apparently alerted the hunters. From out of the hotel ran Carol, Albert Stine and Mitchell Bone.

"He is," Billy yelled, adrenaline pumping into his throat and head, making his temples throb. "That man isn't Bone." He sped from the parking lot as the hunters ran toward the bank.

"Where are you taking me?" Alixel demanded.

"Quiet!" Steph countered. "We don't have time for this."

"I have something to show you and some friends for you to meet," Billy said. "Then I have one hell of story to tell, one that I think you already know about."

"What about them?" Steph said, thumbing back in the direction of the bank.

"No worries. Alixel will protect us."

Alixel sat on the floor, legs crossed, in a position that reminded Billy of a Native American ceremonial gathering. "I don't know what you are talking about."

"Of course you do." Billy glanced over his shoulder as he drove down Alister Street away from his restaurant. Much of Port Aransas had already evacuated. He dodged what traffic remained by turning down side streets. His intention was to double-back in hopes of losing any pursuit. "Somehow, you knew to avoid your original room assignment. Plus, you have one of the daggers."

"Daggers? You are insane. You are both insane."

"The only things insane around here are all the dead people walking about."

Wind-whirl whipped through the broken window; the VW's clickety-clack engine revved with increased RPMs.

"I thought you were a scientist," Alixel said.

"Yeah. Me too. But you don't go through our last seventy-two hours without seriously questioning everything you know." Billy turned onto Avenue G and continued toward the beach.

"Then you do believe in a God."

"Really. I don't see what my spiritual preference has to do with…"

"It has everything to do with it!" Alixel almost screamed, then just as quickly calmed down, her voice evening out into one of monotonic reflection. "We will not survive this unless you understand that."

Steph turned all the way around to face Alixel. "You know what's going on here! You know!"

"Of course I know," Alixel confessed. "Why else would I be here?"

"So your deal with Mitchell Bone…"

"I don't care about that weasel. All I'm concerned with is the treasure." Alixel's legs remained crossed, her voice even and matter-of-fact. "You told me, Billy, about Wayeb. How did you…" She hesitated. "Why would you even care about such a thing?"

"Because Lett cared."

"I don't understand."

Steph took the cue. "You! Don't understand?"

"Steph!" Billy urged. "To make a long story short," he said to Alixel, "I took some pictures at the bank. One of them was of a document that Lett was carrying. The document had that symbol, the one on the coin, written at the top."

Alixel unfolded her legs. "You must show me this." Her voice peaked with a hint of excitement.

"That's where we're headed. I got something else to show you too, something I haven't even looked at yet, something I'm not too sure I want to relive."

"And that is?"

Billy stared out the window at the growing thundercloud darkness that suffocated the horizon. The wind had kicked up since he'd turned onto the beach road and back toward the Surf Side, and the VW shook sporadically with each gust. "Mitchell Bone's death," he finally said.

"Shoe got that?" Steph added.

"I'm thinking, yeah, and if so, it might give us some more clues about the Cubit."

Alixel curled up onto her knees and crawled forward. It was an action that took both Billy and Steph by surprise. It was an action that drew her down to their level. Those of power and wealth did not crawl on hands and knees. "The Cubit?" she said, her mouth agape with surprise. "How do you know?"

"Janine," Billy said. "One of our friends whom you will soon meet."

Billy raced past a backhoe, a bulldozer and two yellow dump trucks that were parked near the pier. He turned on Beach Street and a block from the Surf Side, it became evident that the building had been vandalized. The glass door to the restaurant lay in shattered disarray on the sidewalk and parking lot, allowing wind gusts to invade the interior. Some of the window blinds rapped against glass; stray papers whirled inside. Behind the restaurant, the wood railing around his apartment porch deck was missing half the horizontal boards and the door to his apartment stood open; a bed sheet fluttered from it. Billy parked the VW behind the restaurant so as not to be easily seen. All three of the occupants exited simultaneously and when Billy came around to the passenger side of the VW, he could not help but to look at Alixel's stomach. Her blouse sagged at the belly and could easily hide the haft of a weapon. He looked at the restaurant then back at her stomach.

"No," Alixel said. "They are not here." Billy looked up, embarrassed. "Besides," she continued, "the glow does not promise nor preclude Evil. Caution will always be the best course of action."

"Stay with her," he said to Steph. "I'm going to check the restaurant." Five minutes later he returned, shaking his head without a word. He led them to the back of the restaurant where they encountered a large, irregular, brownish-red stain and several smaller brownish-red circles in the sandy dirt under the porch.

"Blood," Alixel said.

In the dirt near the steps was the imprint of a human body. Broken wooden boards lay scattered in all directions. Billy quickly ran up to the deck and stopped above Steph and Alixel who were peering up at him through the deck board spacing. There was dried blood on the ground below but none was on the deck itself. His attention turned to the sound of breaking glass from within the apartment. The bed sheet that was stuck in the doorway suddenly took flight, fluttered quickly into his body and wrapped around him. He screamed quietly and quickly. Alixel and Steph bolted up the steps to his side and Steph pulled the sheet free, releasing it to the Gulf wind. It flew from the deck, over the edge where the horizontal boards were now missing, and onto the ground, covering the imprint of the missing body.

Alixel entered the apartment first; one hand rested against her stomach. She tip-toed through torn mattress foam, busted pieces of furniture, and shards of table lamp glass. Billy quickly followed, disregarded the mess and went straight for his lab-office. Paperwork lay everywhere. All of the parts to all of his robotic endeavors had been swiped from the table and were mixed into a stew of destruction. His computer monitor had tumbled from the table face-first; he stepped over broken pebbles of its display screen. The computer itself appeared unharmed but the disks that held the data from the bank were missing as were the printouts he'd intended to show Alixel. He plowed through the paper heap but could not find either of them.

"How could they know?" he said, kneeling, with wads of invoices and cancelled checks in both hands.

"Whoever did this was not looking for evidence of a murder," Alixel said. "They are looking for one of these." She lifted the fold in her blouse with one thumb to reveal what looked like a belt buckle and pulled from a hidden sheath exactly what Billy had expected to see: a dagger that looked just like Janine's. The blade was long and thin and Billy wondered how it could have been so comfortably nestled against the curvature of her waist. "Did you have one of these?"

"No," Billy said. "But I know who does."

Janine was embarrassed. Balled toilet paper knots of dried snot lay on the kitchen table. Several created white, dotted trails from the front door to the bedroom and bathroom. She kicked the few at the door's threshold, then dropped her sack against the wall just inside the door. Joel set the one he carried next to it.

"Nice place," he said, smiling. "Much nicer than mine or Billy's."

"I didn't get a chance to tidy it up. If I'd have known you were coming…"

"Nonsense. I'm honored that you invited me in. Been a long time since a lady has done that to Joel Canton."

Janine smiled then. Most people only knew his rough exterior but to Janine, Joel was perhaps one of the kindest men she'd ever met—next to Michael. She knelt to pick up the tissues on the floor and had grasped a half a dozen before Joel grabbed her arm by the bicep.

"Really," he said. "The place is fine. Don't trouble yourself. You've had too rough a day to worry about a used roll of toilet paper. Come over here and sit with me. Relax. I imagine we'll be having company in short order. This would be a good time to recharge the batteries."

Having company? She wondered if he meant Steph and Billy and Alixel, or if he meant *bad* company. She wondered if he thought they were in danger. *She* certainly thought they were. Two apartments had been destroyed by dead, desperate crooks. Yes—bad company was on the way and it would arrive in short order.

She followed him to the couch and together they sat on two of the three cushions. She dropped the collected wads of stiff tissue on the third cushion and Joel immediately grasped the empty hand. He stroked it with each of his ten rugged fingertips, turned it over to look at the wrist and the scar that was not there. "How?" he said. "I've cut my hand with that thing before. Sharp bastard, it is. But I healed up just like any regular human." He gazed into her eyes that were suddenly filled with apology.

"I don't know how, Joel, but I can assure you that I am human and that whatever that dagger is, is beyond human."

"We can certainly agree on that." He traced the invisible cut with one finger. Janine saw that he was fighting with the decision to ask his next question. "Your blood. It flowed backward. The cut sucked it right back in. You know…I thought you were going to die right then and there. I thought for sure I was about to lose you."

Janine's eyes fluttered with fatigue. "Nonsense. I am honored that you saved my life. It's been a long time since someone has done that to Janine Bender." She thought of Michael as she said it.

Joel pulled her close. A kiss was the next step. Janine had fought that desire since walking toward the beach hand-in-hand, he as Tom Sawyer and she as Becky Thatcher. Michael was the only man she'd ever kissed, at least passionately. She wondered if Michael was looking down upon them at that very moment. She wondered if it was okay. And then her mind, in its need for rest, wondered if Becky had ever kissed Tom. She wondered if Becky had ever loved another man. She wondered if Becky and Michael would have ever made it as husband and wife. But, of course, that notion was crazy. It was just about as crazy as Janine kissing Joel.

Unfortunately, the chance or the choice never came. From outside her cottage apartment bellowed a scream so loud it shook her bones to the marrow. "The dagger," she cried and pointed to the sacks by the door. Joel stood, took one step forward, and then froze as the unlocked front door swung slowly open. Mark Walker stood in the frame and he looked quite mad.

"Whey is nit?" Mark slurred. "Whey is na dugger?"

"Mark!" Joel said, a welcome and friendly tone to his voice. "What did you find out about the water? Is it poisoned?"

Mark stepped into the room. Both sacks lay by his feet to his left but he did not notice them. "Fuc na wader!" Clouds had thickened outside, hiding the waning Texas sun but what little light remained glistened off the butcher knife that Mark held in one hand. He lifted it and shook it at Joel. "Na dugger! I won nit."

Joel stepped between Mark and Janine and looked at the sacks. Mark's red, silver swirling orbs followed.

"Na dugger!" he said and cackled. He turned completely around and reached for the first sack as Joel leapt for the butcher knife. Joel's weight carried both bodies through the open door and out onto the sidewalk.

"Joel!" Janine screamed. She bolted for the sack that held the dagger but as she reached it, Joel came flying backward through the door and crashed into her shoulder which sent both spinning and sprawling onto the carpet. Before either of them could recover, Mark snatched one sack and emptied its contents on the floor. The book flopped onto a pile of clothes, opening to the center spread where the invisible pencil had made its notes. The cubited Mark stared at the book, seemed to marvel at the drawings for only a second, before grabbing the second sack; he emptied its contents over the book. The dagger dropped onto the pile and rolled off toward Joel. The two printouts from the bank fluttered in a sudden rush of air and floated, twisting and turning, out the front door. Joel and Mark reached the dagger at the same moment as Mark slashed at Joel's face with the butcher knife. The sharp edge cut across his neck and blood immediately pulsed from the wound.

Janine's torso lay sprawled on the carpeted floor, her legs on the kitchen linoleum, her feet touching one kitchen table leg. When she saw the butcher knife open Joel's skin, she kicked outward in an attempt to quickly rise to her feet. The action sent the table skittering across the linoleum; used tissues from the top of the table rained down around her. She swept the white rags aside, curled to her knees and held out her arms as Joel collapsed into them. Blood rained across her bare arms. She covered his hand which covered the wound but the combined pressure was not enough to slow the bleeding.

"Agghh!!!" Mark screamed. "Na dugger is mine!" He held it in one hand above him, a victorious acquisition, a prize of great sacrifice, a tool for torture and for killing. He glared down upon them, a master to slaves.

Joel's body seemed to pump into Janine's hand as much blood as she'd dropped onto Billy's deck boards. Joel's blood, however, did not know reverse. It drooled from their clasped hands down both forearms, dripped from both elbows and onto the carpet and kitchen linoleum where it remained without hope for restoration.

"You, fitherman. You cwap uv da iwand. Die, fitherman, die!"

Death stood in her doorway just as it had done more than a year ago. It wailed crazy, nonsensical rants and threatened her with ideas that went beyond human knowledge. This cubit would chase her as the Albert-thing had, ultimately placing her back in an insane asylum where she would never have the chance to convince anyone that she had ever been sane. This thing, an abomination to all that was Holy suffocated her front door with its presence; storm clouds roiled behind it; Gulf winds whipped through its matted clothes. It screamed again, some wail of hideous victory, then coiled forward and slashed down with the dagger.

And Mark, who was no longer Mark, suddenly froze. The bump of flesh surrounding his Adam's apple opened to reveal a shiny point of metal. The dead man gurgled and the dagger dropped from his hand, bounced across Janine's head and settled on the blood-stained carpet.

Its eyes melted.

Its face disappeared.

The body collapsed, morphing into fleshless bone right before her eyes.

Behind the dissolving cubit stood a woman with long, dark hair that was pinstriped in red along the temples. Janine thought for moment that it was Marcy but this woman was too short and looked nothing like Cher except for the long, dark hair.

"Janine!" Billy yelled and stepped through the doorway. Steph followed.

The stranger swiped the dagger—which she had just driven through Mark's neck—across one thigh before slipping it into its sheath at her waist. What remained of Mark's body looked as if it had been dead for twenty years. The boney toe of the corpse's foot rested on Janine's leg and she kicked it away in disgust. Joel gurgled.

"He's lost a lot of blood," Janine said to Billy.

"Where is it?" the stranger asked, ignoring Joel's plight. The dagger rested on the carpet just beyond the spread of Joel's blood. When the stranger bent to pick it up, Janine kicked it farther away.

"Billy," Janine begged. "Don't let her have it."

Billy bent over them. "This is Alixel. She is friend not foe." His gaze went to the blood covered hands clasped against Joel's neck. "Joel. Can you hear me? Joel?" Joel's eyes fluttered, battling consciousness. "It'll be all right. You're going to be fine." He turned to Alixel who had grabbed Joel's dagger and was studying its haft. "He is isn't he?"

"Creation of man," Alixel said to the dagger. "At last I have found you."

"Joel," Billy urged. "Can you help him?"

Alixel knelt over Joel who remained cradled and now unconscious within Janine's arms. Janine was hesitant. She wanted no one touching Joel, especially a complete stranger. But her resistance faded as soon as Alixel grasped her hand and smiled.

"Please," Alixel said, in a pleasant, motherly tone. "Or else he's going to die."

Alixel's touch sent chills into her blood-coated arm. A tremor raced into her neck and she swooned as if she'd just been touched by God. Her hand was peeled away for her; she had no control of those muscles. She shook her head, trancelike, denying Alixel's intent.

"Please," Alixel repeated.

When Janine released her grip, Joel's hands fell from his throat, flopping one to each side of his body, and the blood bubbled from the diagonal cut below his chin. Janine reached forward but Alixel intercepted the hand, caressed it, nodded, smiled. She brought forth the dagger and angled it down, as if she was going to make Joel's wound even deeper. Though it frightened her, Janine allowed her to continue without protest.

The haft of the dagger began to glow. Janine's concentration on it at this point was microscopic. She remembered how one of the red points had glowed incredibly loud when she'd performed a similar ceremony for Professor Cower. She'd stuck the blade of the dagger into the professor's chest. She'd performed surgery with it. She'd pulled a bullet from him. She'd sealed the wound.

Alixel set the dagger lengthwise across Joel's neck and set it there, pressing the blade into the wound. The bubbling blood immediately stopped its flow. Stray, crimson rivulets wrapped and rolled, twisting around the thin blade, hungry for its shiny surface. And then, in one swift motion, as if again slicing open Joel's throat, she swiped the dagger away. All of them watched the miracle of healing. Joel coughed. He gurgled as if trying to breathe water. He spat up a small drop of blood and his breathing regained a regular, deep rhythm. His eyes fluttered. The slit in his neck folded, stitched, closed and became scar tissue in a matter of seconds. A sticky mass of blood remained and when Janine wiped it away, the wound was gone. Alixel stepped away.

Lightning raged in Port Aransas for the first time in more than a month. Its singular white disturbance illuminated the open door to Janine's Paradise Cottage apartment. The flash was so bright that it blocked out what remained of the day. Thunder quickly followed, a boisterous revelation of things to come, a malevolent screech that introduced the first day of summer and, seemingly, the rebirth of Joel Canton. The sight and sound echoed through the room and in the foreground, silhouetted by the flash of light, Janine saw the tears racing down Alixel's cheeks.

Joel had awakened and Janine stroked his temples as she watched Alixel stumble to the couch and collapse onto the tissues she'd left on the cushion. "I'm okay," Joel said. "*She* needs your help."

Janine left him with Billy who knelt to take her place, holding Joel's head as the fisherman slowly rose to a sitting position. A light rain began to fall and Steph closed the door and toggled the light switch which illuminated a small lamp on an end table in the corner opposite the couch where Janine now sat next to Alixel. Alixel's head lay limp against the backrest. Joel's dagger, which she'd used to save his life, rested on the cushion between them. The tears had stopped flowing but remnants remained stained on her cheeks. Janine gently dabbed them with one of the tissues she'd used to wipe away her own tears.

"Why are you crying?" Janine said. "You saved his life."

Alixel rolled her head toward Janine. "So many have been lost and I'm so tired." Alixel looked to be half Janine's age but her eyes expressed an epoch of existence. "We don't have much time. I can feel them coming."

"Who?" Janine said.

"I think you know who."

"No. I mean, who are they? What are they? Why are they here? What is the cubit? What are…?

Alixel extended her index finger to Janine's lips. "Shhh," she hushed. "It may be better that you do not know. Bad things happen to those who know."

That tingly sensation from Alixel's touch again raced into Janine's body. "Bad things have already happened to me," she said when Alixel removed her finger. Janine looked at Billy, at Steph, at Joel, who had all inched closer to their conversation. "Bad things have already happened to all of us because, like you said, we know. We just don't know why."

"The why is…" Alixel smiled the kind of smile that a mother expresses just before sending her first born off to war: a smile to comfort, to reassure, to provide hope, to exonerate what future sins her child must perform for the sake of all that is good. "The why is the end of world." Another fresh tear sprouted and dropped onto the pendant hanging from her turquoise necklace. To Janine, the pendant looked like Christ's cross but this one had four parallel cross members instead of just one.

Since the day that Professor Cower had entered her life Janine's world had become a nightmare that she could not wake from. She'd questioned her memories, her sanity, her faith, and her reality. Now she would find out why. Alixel was about to tell her—tell them—how painfully real a nightmare could be.

Once Janine had finished with the introduction of her friends, Alixel sat up straight, took a deep breath and like a teacher to her students asked them a question.

"How many of you have read the Bible?"

Janine's hand quickly rose. Billy's followed. Steph and Joel's hands rose to about shoulder high.

"And so you know of the Book of Revelation?" All four nodded. "It is a prophecy of the end times, of the rising of the Antichrist, of the consumption of the world by fire. Only the purest of men and women will survive such catastrophe. Those who have not prepared themselves spiritually will suffer in ways unknown to human existence."

"The Apocalypse," Janine said.

"Not really," Billy interjected. "It all depends on how one reads the term. *That* connotation is more a recent definition supported by evangelical nutcases trying to sell fear for salvation and a heaping mound of cash on the collection plate."

Alixel smiled, her tears aborted, her brown eyes suddenly alive as if the teacher had just found her "A" student.

Billy continued, "But quite literally it means something like: the revealing to selected individuals of sacred information kept hidden from the masses, or perhaps, more specifically, the unveiling of God. So the Book of Revelation is the Apocalypse according to John: the unveiling of information about the milestones that precede the return of God. To Christians, of course, God is usually manifest in the body of Jesus Christ."

"It's all in the interpretation," Janine said. "I interpret it as the end of the world."

Alixel patted her hand. "There are no wrong interpretations as much as there are no right interpretations. That's the true power of faith. However, no sacred text reveals everything. The Qur'an, the Torah, the I Ching, even my people's sacred texts do not tell the whole story, because, as Billy has alluded to already, some information is not meant for humankind."

"Your people?" Janine asked.

"I am Hopi by ancestry."

"So…Alixel…that name is Hopi?"

"Yes. It means Princess."

Steph chimed in, "And what are you the princess of?"

"For now, let's just say that I am the Princess of Rebirth. But that is another story."

Billy got the discussion back on track. "So the information not meant for mankind…you're going to tell us it has to do with this thing called the Cubit."

"Everything in this world has an opposite and opposing force," Alixel explained. "One cannot exist without the other. How could a person know the splendor of birth without knowing the heartbreak of death? It is a universal constant. There's no good without bad, no cosmos without chaos, no yang without yin. Alpha has its omega—the beginning always has an end. Throughout Earth's history, humans have ad infinitum found ways for speaking to their spiritual plateau—their God. They built alters, and temples, and complete religions around this one obscure need. They do this because they lack information and therefore, no matter how hard they try, all constructions for portals to Gods are inherently human and riddled with error. The only way of connecting with God is by the use of something created by God. Your soul is one good immaterial example, but too few in history have ever mastered this knowledge. They are known as prophets.

"There does exist several material objects that have served as portals. The Arc of the Covenant, for one. Though the Bible alludes to its creation by the hand of Man, this is only an interpretation. The Arc was created by that which it has a connection with: God. As Dr. Belloq from the Indiana Jones movie so eloquently put it, 'It is a radio for talking to God.' But, as I said, everything in this world has an opposite and opposing force."

"The Cubit," Billy guessed. "A radio for talking to the Devil."

"The Devil, again, is a Christian construct. Let's just say that the Arc is to Good as the Cubit is to Evil."

"And what emerges from the Cubit is Evil in its purest sense," Janine said, confident by experience.

"Yes. One touch and from it emerges the anti-you, a construction of all the Evil that resides within your human vessel."

"Albert Stine," Janine moaned. "He is the Devil himself."

Alixel still had a hold of Janine's hand and again gave it a light patting. "You might be more right than you imagine. Stine has his sights set on visions of grandeur. His desire is to be the Antichrist.

"You mean from Revelation?"

"The references in the Bible are not of the Antichrist, Janine. That is the interpretation. As is the interpretation that there have been other Antichrists in the past. Nero nor Napoleon nor Hitler were Antichrists. The only thing those men had in common was the possession of the Cubit. There can be only one Antichrist and there can be only one time in history that he or she can be born."

"*Can be* born," Billy questioned. "Does that mean we have a chance?"

"There's always hope, Billy, just as there is despair."

"So all that Nostradamus crap is just…crap?" Billy said.

"Not necessarily."

"So he was a prophet?"

"No. Definitely not a prophet. I think you misunderstand my use of that word."

Complete silence ensued for several seconds which gave the lightning and thunder a chance to showcase its anger outside. Joel, still weak from the attack, leaned back against the couch at Janine's feet and she stroked his thin hair with her free hand.

"No one person is a prophet," Alixel said. "At least no one mortal is a prophet. That would be an oxymoron. *People* are prophets. Groups of people, entire subcultures in an era of existence are prophets. These are the groups that frighten men. These are the groups that men destroy. These are the lost cultures, those that are now extinct or are very close to becoming that way. A prophecy is created by the collective. Some are false prophets. We call these religions. False prophets are fearful of the true prophets and, with great hypocrisy, slaughter those who present a danger to them."

"Were the Jews prophets?" Janine said. "After all, six million died at the hands of the powerful Aryan dictator."

"Perhaps," Alixel said. "They did reveal knowledge of the Arc in the Old Testament. How that knowledge was gained will always be one of the great mysteries."

"Unless it's all just mythological story-making," Billy said and immediately regretted doing so.

"After all you've seen," Janine said. Her hand stopped stroking Joel's head. Joel's eyes, which had been slowing closing, fluttered open then closed again. "You're not just dreaming as I was not dreaming the night my son died."

"That's okay," Alixel intervened. "The scientific way can lead to many false prophecies. Closed minds lead to closed intelligence."

Billy cleared his throat. "I deserved that. It's hard to agree on unproven truths."

"But you have proof," Alixel said.

"No one would believe me."

"I can think of many who would."

"The Jews," Billy quipped.

"Not all. And not all Hopis and not all Mayans, and not all within the Roman, Greek, Egyptian or Chinese empires."

Steph moaned and rubbed her stomach. She'd been kneeling while listening intently but now dropped back onto her buttocks and scooted over to the far wall next to the pile of clothes that had been dumped from Janine's two sacks.

"You okay?" Billy said.

"I don't know. Maybe just hunger, but something alive seems to be boiling inside my stomach."

"I've not had a chance to do any shopping," Janine said.

"No worries. I'll be fine. Just exhausted and hungry."

"So what's the deal with these?" Janine said, returning her attention to Alixel as she pointed at Joel's dagger lying between them.

"Creation Daggers," Alixel said. "They can save us."

"It's the only way to kill those things?" Billy said.

"It's the only way to make sure they are gone and don't come back. One strike with a Creation Dagger to the base of the skull and lights go out for good."

"So throwing them in a meat grinder won't do the trick."

"The Cubit can make more."

"Christ. I hope I never touch the damn thing."

Steph moaned again then suddenly rose and ran to the bathroom. A minute later she returned. "Sorry. My stomach just ain't feeling right. Perhaps I should lie down."

"Please," Janine said. "Use my bed. You might have to clear away a few wads of toilet tissue."

Steph disappeared into the bedroom but did not close the door.

Janine grabbed Joel's dagger from the cushion and traced the star pattern on the haft with a finger. "Quite beautiful," she said. "The red jewel glows just like yours." She nodded toward Alixel's waist.

"Jade," Alixel said. "A very rare red jade." She pulled her own dagger from its sheath.

"Created by the hand of God, no doubt," Billy added.

"As a matter of fact…" Alixel did not finish the testimony but instead continued with the description. "There are five points on the star, one for each Creation. Each dagger and each jaded point represents one of these creations." She pointed at the red jade in the star's left arm in Joel's dagger. "The Creation of Man." She pointed to the red jade in her own dagger. "The Creation of Religion. The top of the star represents the Creation of Good and Evil." To everyone's surprise, Alixel reached to her waist and pulled another dagger from a second hidden sheath, displayed it, and pointed to the jade in the top of the star. "The star represents the story of the Fifth Age."

"Fifth Age?" Billy said.

"The last of the Mayan's great 26,000-year cycle. In it there has been or will be the Creation of Good and Evil, the Creation of Man, the Creation of Religion, the Creation of the Antichrist and the Creation of the End. The five points of the star. The first three have already happened. The last two will take place in the future at nearly simultaneous points in time."

"Wait a minute. I've heard of this: Mayan prophecies of destruction, galactic alignment, the end date. A bit like Revelation don't you think?"

"John's revelation is not prophetic; it is a warning."

"And the Mayans were prophetic." The condescension in Billy's voice again raised its ugly head. "So you're telling me that on December 21, 2012, the world will come to an end."

Janine's face melted into an expression of panic.

"That is an interpretation," Alixel said. "The Mayans mark the end of the Fifth Age as the beginning of the next great cycle. The Alpha of the Omega. It doesn't have to mean that it is the destruction of the world."

"There you go again." Billy quickly raised and lowered his hands. "Talking in riddles. First, it's that the Antichrist *can* be born, not will be born. And now you're saying that there may or may not be an end to the world. So which is it? I get that there can be no thing in existence without its opposing opposite, but when you're talking about prophecy, the truth will eventually present itself. Either we're all going to die or we aren't. Both ideals cannot exist simultaneously. You might think that to be more of my scientific closed-mindedness, but come on."

"Billy. I think we have finally found agreement." Alixel grinned, the thin corners of her lips rising into her rounds cheeks, making the center of her lips plump outward. "And it is up to people like us to direct the outcome." She twirled her daggers majestically in the palms of her hands. "What we need are these."

"So there are five of them," Janine interjected.

"There are," Alixel said.

"Then that explains it."

"Explains what?"

"The dagger that Professor Cower brought into my house. The one I used to save his life. If I'm not mistaken, the red jade in that one occupied the left leg of the star."

"Professor Cower!?" Alixel's smile quickly morphed into an expression of surprise. Her eyes lit up. "How do you know *him*?"

"He brought the Cubit to my home a year ago. He's the reason I'm here."

"That man's name sends shivers down my spine."

"He's dead," Janine said. "He dynamited the Cubit and blew himself up."

"And now Albert has the dagger and the Cubit." Alixel almost whispered this to herself while shaking her head.

"That's four of them," Billy said. "So where's the fifth?" He paused, then quickly added, "No—wait a minute. In the ground. By the pier. Where all the heavy machinery is. LaFitte's treasure. That's the reason you're here."

"Cower is the reason I'm here as well," Alixel said. "He took the Cubit from us and I have to recover it."

Harsh winds kicked at the kitchen windows. Lightning continued in short spurts but the loud cracks of thunder had subsided somewhat. Joel had fallen asleep and began to snore quietly.

"Cower was an anthropologist from one of the state universities in New York," Alixel continued. "His interests were Hopi mythology and the Mayan classical and post-classical eras. And so, about five years ago, while exploring some of the underground dwellings at Chichen Itza, Cower found the dagger he brought into your home."

"So how do you fit in?" Billy said.

Alixel shifted on the couch uncomfortably. "I trusted Chris. He came to Sedona a few years before his Chichen Itza expedition to help us keep the Red Rock Anasazi ruins safe from private development. An anthropologist's claim that there was a historical importance to the land and the Anasazi who once lived there was much more convincing than a bunch of protesting Indians. He provided evidence that kept commercial interests out. Unfortunately, he also uncovered wall etchings that would eventually bring him back to Sedona, an etching that matched what he would find at Chichen Itza."

"The dagger—the creations," Janine said.

Alixel nodded. "He brought the dagger to me and started asking questions that I could not answer so he went looking for the answers himself. That's when he found the Cubit."

"Your people knew of the Cubit?" Janine said.

"Yes. We are its guardian."

"You are a prophet then."

"I am not. My people were chosen."

"To protect information not meant for the mass of humanity."

"And not a very good job of it. Cower took the Cubit."

Billy said, "I thought you couldn't touch it, you know, without becoming one of those things."

"That is true. And what your next question should be is 'if the Cubit makes an Evil duplicate of you, why aren't there two Cowers running around, or two Alberts, or two of anyone who touches it?'"

"Because they eat the original," Janine said.

"And take the place of that person in the world," Alixel continued, "complete with all their personality traits and memories and intelligence. The fortunate thing is that they are easy to spot early on in the transformation. It takes time for a cubited human to mature into its previous self. Their personalities will be awkward, they may have trouble speaking and their memories may be scrambled."

"And Professor Cower?"

"There is only one way to survive a cubited duplicate. You have to kill it with one of the five daggers, to the base of the skull, just like I did with that." She pointed at the remnants of Mark Walker. "If you are fortunate enough to have a dagger and know how to use it, you become immune to the effects of the Cubit."

"So Cower had the dagger," Billy said, "but how did he know what to use it for or even how to use it correctly?"

"That, I'm not sure. There would have been no knowledge of such use within the Anasazi sacred grounds."

"Perhaps he found it in the book," Janine said.

Alixel's eyes widened. "Book?"

Billy remembered the visions he'd seen in the VW's rearview mirror. "Are you talking about a book that has one of your daggers etched on its surface?"

Janine looked surprised. "How could you know that? No one has seen it since the day my farm blew up."

"I can't explain it. I had these visions—like dreams, almost. There were bullets, and screeching tires and that book with the dagger on it." He also remembered that the person driving the car in his vision was probably Professor Cower though he did not tell them this. He was trying to piece it together himself. He was trying to piece all of this together. His calculator brain was smoking with too much information, puzzle pieces placed by the hand of mythology and not reason; faith and belief were two of the largest pieces that he just couldn't find space for quite yet. He knew that once he allowed belief to take the place of reason, all that he'd ever known, everything he'd been taught, all the science, would no longer make sense. The door to Illogic was open; he had one foot inside already. Denial kept his other foot safely in the land of Reason.

And as if reading his mind, Alixel said, "You're slowly coming over to our side. Now you're having visions. Pretty soon you just might become part of the prophecies yourself. Is it so hard to accept?"

Janine offered, "Would you like to see it?"

Billy's mind twisted at that very moment. If Janine had in her possession what he'd denied in his visions then—the land of Reason suddenly felt very far away.

"Oh my," Alixel moaned. "Oh great father. You have the Codex? You have the lost Book of the Djed?"

Billy thought that she had said "Dead" and immediately skepticism roared back to life, but when Janine pulled it from the pile of clothes by the front door and he saw the dagger blazoned on its back cover, he knew that he could no longer base his decisions solely on scientific methods. Science had no explanations for those who "saw things" but here was proof, an irony really. He'd found proof that illogic actually existed.

Alixel could hardly control herself. She quickly stood and met Janine halfway to the couch although the distance was less than four feet. "May I?" she said, sheathing her two daggers and holding out both hands. When Janine gave the book to her, she held it as if it were made of wet rice paper. Her eyes were so large she could have doubled for an anime cartoon at that very moment. She shifted the book to one hand and stroked the gold embossing with a forefinger, starting from the haft of the dagger and moving slowly down to its point near the bottom of the book's back cover.

"The Book?" Janine said. "Is it valuable?"

"It has no value," Alixel said.

Billy knew it before he said it; he was beginning to believe. "A work of God."

Alixel nodded. "In a way. The message is Holy but most of the writing was done by the hand of man."

"Like the Ten Commandments," Janine said.

"Like the Ten Commandments," Alixel agreed. "But not Hebrew—Mayan."

"I've looked at the center pages but I was unable to open any other parts," Janine said. "I think the pages have been glued together."

Alixel simply patted her arm then sat on the floor and placed the book on the carpet. Janine sat to her left and Billy sat to her right. Joel snored behind them. Lightning flashed in the panes of the kitchen window. There was no thunder.

To Janine's surprise, Alixel easily opened the book to its first page. "They were stuck together. How…" Alixel simply shook her head, reminding Janine how futile reason had become.

The first page was blank. Its edges, and those of all the pages in the Book of the Djed, were parchment brown. Alixel lifted then turned the page slowly, carefully, as if it would disintegrate between her fingers even though it had a crisp, heavy texture that prevented it from bending. She would handle each page the same way. On each page she would reveal a colorful mass of symbols that she said was an alphanumeric language few people understood. The hieroglyphs on each page would be clustered around that page's central theme, usually a drawing that told a story which Alixel, from the beginning, now revealed.

"This is the story of the Fifth Age," she said, pointing to a pair of drawings that looked remarkably like the Cubit and the Arc of the Covenant. "It begins with the Creation of Good and Evil. The Fifth Age is the only one of all five that contains both. In fact, our current 26,000-year Great Cycle is the only one in which an *Age* contained both. The four that came before were either good or bad, paradise or chaos. It is said that the extinction of the dinosaurs began an Age of chaos. The Ice Age was an Age of chaos. There were also Great Cycles of Eden, or Heaven as the Bible would call it, when the tranquility of life ruled."

"So why now?" Billy said. "Why is *this* Age different?"

Alixel turned the page. The answer was evident. "The Creation of Man," she said. The theme across this spread of pages depicted men's faces in ceremonial masks, of men hunting, of men fighting. One of the drawings was of what looked like men hanging from trees by their necks. At the bottom of the right hand page was the scene of what must have been a massacre: human body parts were graphically revealed in red.

Alixel turned the page and Janine gasped. On the left side of this spread, among the mass of hieroglyphic encryptions, were the drawings of a tree, a snake, and of a naked man and woman. "Did the Mayans know the Bible?" Janine asked.

"No. They did not," Alixel replied.

"Then how…"

"Some things are not meant for us to know," Alixel reminded her.

On the right, the same man and woman were now clothed and there were two children at their feet.

"The Mayans must have had access to the Bible," Billy said, again questioning the factual and mystic connotations.

"The Spanish did not invade the Yucatán until the early 1500s. It would have been impossible." Alixel countered.

Janine interrupted by grabbing Alixel's hand. She guided it to the edge of the page, urging her to move forward. From that point on to the center of the book, each of the next six pages depicted man's struggle between Good and Evil. There were pages where supreme beauty was the central theme and there were pages that were graphically horrific. There were symbols depicting fire, and water, and earth, and wind and rays of light that Alixel told them stood for a fifth element, man's psyche which, she said, was the source of the this Age's great confusion. "Those were the stories of the third creation: Religion," Alixel said of the pages she flipped through.

"We don't have a chance," Billy said and leaned back against the wall with his hands over his head.

"How can you say that when there's so much love in the world?" Alixel said. "Remember that this is the Age of both good things and bad things and given those odds we'll always have a chance. The second half of the Book of the Djed should reveal this."

She turned to the center spread which was drawn in a way unlike any of the other pages. The language appeared Mayan but the symbols were recently drawn with what looked like pencil.

"This is a diary," Janine said. "Don't you think? It looks like the professor was archiving the discoveries he'd made."

"Cower didn't do this," Alixel said. "The center is saved for the hand of only one."

"No!" Billy grumbled, throwing his arms up against the wall. Joel stirred but did not awaken. "That's going just a bit too far."

"It's the truth," Alixel said. "These are the words of God, and he's telling us how to save the world."

"Yeah? Well he left off one big chunk of information." Billy pointed at the right hand page which was mostly blank. "Is that the part we're not meant to know? I mean, come on, how are we supposed to save mankind if God doesn't tell us everything?"

"He will, in time, as 2012 draws near."

"She's right," Janine said. "The last time I looked, these weren't here." She pointed at three numerals that were stenciled in under the Bird of Fire; the numerals were no larger than those written in an average textbook. The first two were well-defined but the last one looked as if it was still being created. The numerals were 666.

"The mark of the beast," Janine said, her mouth remaining agape.

"An interpretation," Alixel reminded her. "Not necessarily true."

"So what *does* it mean?"

"We won't know until the message is complete. Then we can use the key to decipher the exact time and place of the raising of the Djed on December 21. These two pages and the key will also reveal instructions for the ceremony that must take place if the next Great Cycle is to usher in 26,000 years of paradise, rid us of Evil and destroy the Cubit."

"The key," Billy huffed. "And I suppose we have to go looking for that as well?"

"Actually, no," Alixel said. "You remember that printout you told me about? The coin you showed me? The symbol of the Wayab is a part of the key and it is right here." She turned a page. Then turned another. Her gentle caress of the pages turned into an aggressive pursuit for something she could not find. She flipped back to the center and again turned the page. She brought the book up to her face so that her nose was an inch from the binding then lowered it. "It's gone. It's been ripped out."

"It must have somehow torn free in the explosion," Janine offered as explanation.

"Which means that Albert not only has the Cubit and Cower's Creation Dagger…" Alixel began.

"…he also has the key," Billy added. "That's what he was carrying to the bank along with what must have been the location of LaFitte's treasure…"

"…and the fifth dagger," Janine concluded.

"He'll try to kill us to obtain our daggers," Alixel said with sudden revelation. "This has been his plan all along. With everything in his possession, he will lead the next Great Cycle into pure chaos."

A blinding flash of lightening stabbed through the kitchen window and thunder crashed immediately overhead. The lights in the apartment went out.

"FEMA is going to be all over this place in the morning." Chancey Lett growled at Albert. "We've got to get it going now!"

Albert drove the black Hummer toward the beach, loathing Lett more and more with each street he passed. He would have killed him already if only he'd known how to operate a backhoe; somehow that knowledge had been lost in his transition. All Lett could think about was greed and the power from money it gave to individuals. What the casino boss didn't understand was that the real power was not in the riches one held in their hands but the soul they possessed inside. Once you had the soul, you had the power. An individual's life force was invaluable. Fortunately for Albert and all of the demons that had ever existed, either real or conjured, nearly all humans were oblivious to that one Truth—as Albert had been before the Cubit.

The new, improved Albert had recovered the Cubit and Cower's dagger once he'd awakened after the explosion on the Benders' farm, and had taken the artifacts to the casino boss who had forgiven him his gambling debts. Albert had used Lett's greed to manipulate everything that had happened since then. The promise of LaFitte's treasure had been the lure. The priceless dagger had been the bait.

Now everything was set. He had the key, he had the Cubit, and the Book of the Djed and all five daggers were in the same place at the same time, an occurrence that had not happened since the beginning of the current Age. After a year of waiting, he was merely moments away from killing Lett, taking the dagger which Lett kept strapped in a sheath above his ankle, and using it on the rest of those who would unknowingly secure his destiny. Albert would take his rightful place as this Age's fourth creation and would direct the outcome of its fifth.

No one else was in the bank when it happened.

The birth of death began as it always did: the top of the Cubit cracked open—a lid on a crate. Deep crimson fired from within, splattering the interior of the bank vault like blood in a massacre. Slowly the lid rose on hinges that weren't there. A hand pushed the lid upwards, and an arm slowly rose from the depths of the Cubit, making short, jerky motions as if what was inside was ascending a staircase. A crown of light hair, which was less blonde than bloody, appeared. The head was bent forward and the long strands of hair hid the face. As was the case with all cubited humans, this one was reborn as an exact duplicate of its living counterpart at the moment the Cubit was touched, and so the pantsuit on it looked awkward, giving it the clean look of a new corpse freshly prepared for burial.

It stepped from the Cubit and looked briefly around, confused, then stumbled as it took its first few steps. Its previous mortal memory guided it out of the vault and to a desk where, in life, it had spent much of its daylight, and it sat in a chair to gaze across the barren wooden desktop. Something was missing, it thought. Something that, at one time, had made it laugh.

"Pat-twick," the cubit slurred. "Pat-twick the stawfish."

State trooper Andy Collar had never been as busy as he was the night that Hurricane Antiago sat on the doorstep of Corpus Christi. Weather reports said that the hurricane had sped toward Texas "at a rate impossible to meteorological science" and might hit any time in the next two hours; however, even that number was a "guesstimate" since every calculated movement of Antiago so far had been inaccurate. Its path through the Gulf, its lateral speed toward the coastline, its tight circumference, its internal wind speeds—all had teased forecasters into believing they actually knew what they were talking about. Even the shape of the storm was irregular, with the front end of the storm producing only tropical storm strength winds while the back of the storm raged with the intensity beyond a Category 5.

There had been so few troopers and so many terrified people that Andy and his partner had split up, each taking a cruiser in an opposite direction. Andy had been charged with organizing the officials of Port Aransas in hopes of moving whoever remained to safety; word was that there were still a couple of hundred people on the island. Andy had grown up in Port A for a short time, mostly before he'd turned thirteen not a dozen years ago, so he knew many of the people and, so his lieutenant's theory went, would have a better chance at organizing them. But theories went out the window when panic was in question. Regardless of his associations, getting two hundred people to agree in the few hours remaining before the hurricane hit would be difficult.

As he neared Port Aransas from Route 361, he did not notice the new construction just beyond the 7-Eleven to his right. If he had looked in that direction and if the lightning would have flashed at just the right moment, he might have seen a large number of people organizing near an apartment complex a few blocks away.

Instead, he continued into town, passing under the blinking yellow traffic light at the corner of Avenue G. Pat MaGee's looked abandoned. He remembered that, in his youth, the owner of surf shop had placed a small prefabricated storm shelter in the lot behind his store; it was one of those newfangled shelters that doubled as a room addition. He briefly wondered if anyone was in MaGee's shelter and made a mental note to check it after going through town.

Alister Street seemed deserted. The street lights still functioned but few homes appeared occupied. Where these so-called couple of hundred people might be, Andy could only guess. He cruised by the Surf Side Restaurant but it was too dark for him to see that it had been broken into. He cruised by the University of Texas Marine Science Institute and found one car, an old Buick Cutlass in the parking lot. He turned back toward town and cruised by the ferry station. Both ferries were moored. No one was in the control tower.

He decided to cruise along the beachfront and headed toward the south jetty back along Cotter Avenue and, again, passed the marine institute. There, stumbling along the side of the road was a young woman in a business suit. He rolled to a stop and lowered the passenger window with the automatic switch.

"Ma'am," he said. "Excuse me, ma'am." The woman took three more steps before turning to his voice. Her hair and clothes whipped violently in a gust of wind that shook the trooper's cruiser. "Can I ask what you are doing out here?"

"Pawadize cottagey," she mumbled and pointed toward the south side of town. "I am at pawadize cottagey."

Andy thought the woman was drunk. "Would you mind getting in? It's much too dangerous out here."

"Pawadize cottagey," she repeated.

The woman looked as if she'd been in a horrible fight. There were clots of blood in her hair and her face was streaked in crimson and dirt. Her lips were purple as were the circles around her eyes. He leaned across the seat and opened the door. "Get in, please."

The woman stumbled into the seat but Andy had to lean across her to close the door. She smelled as bad as she looked and Andy kept the window down to keep from gagging.

A minute later, he turned onto the beach road at the jetty and headed south. Lightning and thunder flashed and roared with increasing frequency. The winds knocked the cruiser sideways on its springs. It was raining but, oddly, not in unison with the storm's other hammering elements.

"Who wibs in pine-papples unner da sea?" the woman said. Her neck muscles were unable to withstand the wind that slapped against her face; the back of her head beat against the seat's headrest.

"Excuse me, ma'am?" Andy said. "Who what?"

The woman turned toward him and her eyes blazed blood red. Tiny silver irises sparkled with each lightning strike. "A pine-papple unner da sea. You know."

"I'm sorry, but I don't understand…"

She started humming a strange verse that somehow seemed familiar to Andy. Her head found the muscles necessary to make it sway to the sound. Her hands lifted in front of her and she tapped the dashboard with dissonant rhythm. "Who wibs in a pine-papple unner da sea?" She repeated the question while tapping and humming.

"Ma'am? I think you've had a bit too much to drink. Where is your home?"

It was then that Andy passed the Caldwell Pier to find several pieces of heavy machinery and a black Hummer parked a hundred yards from the shoreline. A backhoe started up as he came to a stop. He switched on his flood light and aimed it at a large man who was approaching the car. "Not a very good evening to be moving around machinery," Andy said to the man.

"Agreed," the man said from ten feet away. He wore a black cowboy hat and black boots. In fact, his entire wardrobe was black. A fresh cut was etched into his face near a scar that looked like it had been there awhile. "If you don't mind, could you turn that thing off?"

Andy flashed the flood light toward the backhoe but the driver was hard to see. He appeared to be wearing a business suit which, to Andy, seemed odd: a man in a business suit atop a Caterpillar?

"That's my boss," the man said. "Wants to get his machines farther inland before that 'cane hits."

"Spund Bob!" Andy's passenger suddenly yelled, giggling. "Spund Bob Sparepanths!"

To Andy, the woman seemed to be more of a priority than these men. Besides, how far could they take such large machines even if they were thieves? The hurricane would stop them cold.

"You guys taking shelter?" Andy yelled over a boisterous clap of thunder.

"Treasure Trove," the man said. "We're staying at the Treasure Trove."

"Spund Bob Sparepanths; Spund Bob Sparepanths; Spund Bawwwb… Spare-panths!"

"Yeah. Good. Be careful." Andy switched off the floodlight and slowly pulled away. The woman next to him was driving him crazy. He said to her, "Where did you say you lived?"

"That way," the woman pointed. "To my pine-papple unner da sea."

Andy doubted that he'd ever find her home.

The lights went out the moment Steph woke up. She'd been having a horrible nightmare and the clap of thunder that now brought her out of bed had been part of it. She was on the beach. Albert was there with her. So was the Cubit. Just Albert, herself and the Cubit. As if these three things were all that remained in the entire world.

Albert stood against fierce winds and driving rain. In his hands were five daggers. He screamed something at the black clouds above but thunder drowned out the meaning. Then the Cubit opened and something emerged. Lightning flashed and she thought she saw…BANG!

Steph squealed as she sat straight up in Janine's bed. Her hands shook and she clasped them together, hoping the tremors would subside. She swung both legs to the floor and felt her way through the darkness. Blasts of lightning helped her find the door.

When she peaked from the bedroom toward the kitchen she, at first, did not understand what she was seeing. Her mind remained scattered from the nightmare. She still felt nauseous. Perhaps she was still asleep. Perhaps what she now saw was more of the dream, one in which you wake up only to enter into another nightmare.

There were faces looking in at her; a dozen of them were pressed up against the kitchen window. When the lightning flashed, she could see them plain as day: Professor Nelson, Chester Kalimaris, Jacques the smelly fisherman, Dave the security guard, and Misty Percy. Misty had been with her the day that Chancey and Albert and Carol had cornered her in the vault. Misty had been determined to take her business elsewhere.

Steph stepped from the bedroom and into the short hallway that quickly opened into the adjoining living space. The eyeballs of the window faces followed her; lips were squashed against the glass; cheeks were bloated. Lightning revealed Misty Percy's sparkling white incisors as the woman started chewing at the glass, creating a squeaking screech not unlike fingernails against chalkboards.

Thunder clasped.

Squeaky-squeaky.

Joel, Billy, Janine and Alixel were all sitting in the dark on the floor next to the couch.

Squeaky-squeaky.

Alixel drew two daggers from her waist. Janine had one dagger which she rolled between the fingers of one hand.

Squeaky-squeaky.

They stared at the window that Misty Percy was chewing at. Suddenly, the front door blew inward at the same moment that the combined face weight collapsed the kitchen window.

Several dozen people loafed on the lawns outside Paradise Cottages. Andy stopped short of the mass. "Is this it?" he asked, feeling a bit fortunate that the drunk had led him to many of the people he had been ordered to help find shelter. "Is this your home?"

"Who wibs in a pine-papple unner da sea?" the woman repeated for the hundredth time.

"I DON'T KNOW!" Andy yelled. He'd been listening to the jibber-jabber for much too long.

"Too bad," the woman said, then reached over and grabbed Andy's neck with one hand. Her strength was overwhelming; the fingertips dug into flesh. Andy released his holster snap, drew the revolver, pointed it at the woman's head.

"Stop!" he gurgled. "Stop or I'll shoot."

And then he did. But the bullet simply sped through her forehead without effect. The woman knocked the gun from his hand with her free hand then squeezed harder. Blood squirted everywhere, darkening the windshield and pooling on the dashboard. A moment later, the woman ripped Andy's esophagus and carotid arteries from his neck. His head lolled on torn muscles and flopped against the driver's side window.

"Spund Bob," the woman said and exited the cruiser.

Mitchell Bone came through the doorway first. Janine was to be left unharmed, he'd been told, so his assault was directed at Joel who had not completely recovered and was therefore easily knocked backward from Bone's momentum. A sharp point of metal severed Bone's Adam's apple and Bone's strength quickly vanished. Janine yanked the long blade of her Creation Dagger from the back of Bone's head and kicked the disintegrating corpse onto the carpet now marked by Joel's sticky-dry blood.

More of the living dead rushed into the room and clambered into the kitchen across fragments of glass and mushy, rain-soaked wads of toilet tissue. Billy kicked a young woman with big incisors in the stomach with no effect. Joel, still lying on his back, flung a leg out at the same woman, collapsed her knee, quickly got to his feet as the woman fell. Several other intruders stumbled over the woman in a heap.

"To the bedroom!" Janine yelled. "Hurry!"

Billy snatched the Book of the Djed and shoved it into the waistband of his shorts. He grabbed Steph who stood there comatose, led the group into Janine's bedroom and slammed the door shut. Janine immediately threw a table lamp against the bedroom window and both shattered on impact. Billy locked the bedroom door and slid the end table in front of it.

Wood split in the bedroom door frame. The interior wall surrounding the door looked as if it would implode at any moment. Plaster cracked. Something snarled.

One by one, Billy helped his comrades out the bedroom window. He pushed Steph through last, hurriedly grabbed the bricked window opening, sliced open the palms of both hands on jutting glass and pulled himself up as the bedroom door caved in. Like roaches freed from a dark crevasse, the cubits rushed into the room, lunged at Billy's flailing feet and screeched in unison at their prey's escape.

As she passed her own bedroom window, Steph almost lost consciousness. What she saw was simply too much for the mind to comprehend. Her legs went limp and she would have fallen had Billy not been there to snatch her up by the armpits.

"Come on," he encouraged her. "We have to get out of here."

"I—I—," she pointed at the window. Billy looked but the face was no longer there. "I saw me. Oh, my God!"

"You're here, Steph. You're with me."

"I'm dead," she said, not hearing him. "Please, Billy. Don't let her eat me."

There were four cottage apartments per building. Steph's was one from the end. A wooden, tall fence blocked any escape other than beyond that last vacant apartment. Behind them, the mass of cubited townspeople flooded into the narrow passage from the opposite direction. Misty Percy led them, snarling her white incisor sneer while limping and lunging on the knee that Joel had kicked in.

Ten feet from their escape in the opposite direction, Carol, the bank teller, blocked their passage. Alixel, however, made quick work of her, brandishing both of her daggers with a whip-whirl motion between her fingers that brought both blades forward, piercing each of the dead woman's eyes. Carol scratched at her face, stumbled backward, and toppled sideways which opened the kill shot to the back of her head that Alixel engaged immediately.

Out from the back of the cottages the five of them ran, rain pelting their faces, wind knocking them back, lightning flashing like light bulbs over the main event. Steph suddenly screamed, the terrifying memory of her own face looking back at her, the thought of her as a cubit overwhelming, the dire need to get as far away from her own apartment overriding the safety provided by those with the weapons that could save her life. She jerked free of Billy's grasp and ran to the front of the building where three dozen dead citizens loafed for something to do until they saw her. Simultaneously, they turned. Steph's Cavalier and Billy's VW Bus were parked beyond them. A police cruiser sat idling in the middle of the street. To get the hell out here she'd have to go through the blockade. Fortunately, she hesitated long enough for Alixel and Janine to catch up. Billy and Joel were a few yards behind.

"You'll not make it," Alixel warned. "Their strength will rip you to shreds. Stand behind me."

Steph stepped backward as Janine joined Alixel to form a three-daggered offensive front and like a wedge through the front lines, they met the mass of cubits head on.

Alixel's prowess with the daggers was understandable but what really amazed Steph was the way Janine expertly dispatched four cubits with four quick strokes. Jacques the smelly fisherman who smelled a lot worse now, lunged at Steph but Janine buried the blade of her dagger to the top of his head. The fisherman's grasp locked onto Steph's T-shirt and as the body fell, it ripped the shirt and bathing suit top from her shoulders. She stood naked from the waist up. And that was just too much for her to take. She bolted from the protection of Janine's fight, slipped Billy's grasp who tried to stop her, screamed because she thought that one of the dead men had tried to grab her bare breasts, dodged several lunging attempts to take her down, and leapt over the hood of her Cavalier like a cop chasing a speedy drug dealer. Her athletic fortitude had helped salvage her life but when she opened her car door, none of that really mattered. She could not scream fast enough. Her cubit snatched her arm and yanked her into the car; her forehead cracked against the roof and her neck snapped from the force.

Billy heard her scream but he knew it wasn't really Stephanie Drake. This scream was one of pleasure, of victory, not one of absolute horror. Steph's body disappeared into her car as if she were the victim of some giant, maniacal vacuum cleaner. Her body was then propelled from the car and when she hit the asphalt, her body convulsed several times before it was pounced on by her cubit. The feeding that ensued was something Billy wished he'd not seen. He tried to look away, and he eventually did, but the few seconds that it took to understand what was really going on was enough to ingrain the memory of dismemberment forever. He stood, stupefied, until his bicep was almost torn by the grip of a large Hispanic man.

"Drop!" Alixel screamed, and Billy's feet obeyed. He dropped to the ground as Alixel lashed out with both daggers. One severed the Hispanic cubit's hand at the wrist and it remained clamped to Billy's bicep until he rolled on the wet grass and swatted it away. Alixel's other dagger sliced open face flesh, then with two more slashes she dropped the cubit to the ground beside him.

Alixel really was amazing. There must have been thirty or forty of those things surrounding her and her daggers moved faster than the lightning flashing above her. Rarely did a cubit actually touch her. While kneeling on the wet grass, Billy witnessed the fury of the blades, fingers flew in the air, an ear launched skyward, some thing's limb flopped onto the asphalt without a body. In one instant, he thought Alixel was done for, a group of cubits surrounding her in a mob that he couldn't see through. A moment later, tracers from lighting reflected on steel arced through the darkness, a blur of movement that Billy's eyes could not adjust to, the death strikes of two daggers dropping the mob in a matter of seconds.

Janine held her own as well. With one dagger, she was able to fend off at least a dozen cubits. The weapon twirled in her hand and between fingers like a baton and she knew exactly when and where to strike with it.

By the time Billy got to his feet, most of the living dead that had surrounded them lay on the ground; many were dismembered. The few that remained were inside Billy's VW, apparently hiding to avoid Alixel's blades.

"Come on," Alixel said. "Now!" She quickly peered inside Steph's Cavalier then ran to the police cruiser which was already idling. Billy took a step in that direction and froze. Steph was there, right in front of him, wearing the pantsuit that made her look so professional. Her hair was a bloody mess; her lips dripped with carnage.

"BJ." she gurgled. "My wittle BJ. Let's go thurfing and maybe I give you thumb. I know you wan me."

He should have lost his mind at that very moment. Everything started moving in slow motion just as it had back on the beach right before the *Knights* had slammed into Albert Stine. Steph reached out for his neck. She pursed her lips. She grinned so wide, the piece of flesh hanging from the corner of her lip fell onto her breasts.

"I know you wan me," she repeated.

Her hands never made it to his throat and he would have let them, too. He would have done nothing to stop the kiss that the Steph cubit had planned for him. She would have grabbed his neck and placed her lips against his and he would have simply melted into insanity. But Janine made sure that didn't happen. In fact, the thing that finally made everything in his mind move at normal speed once again was the blade that suddenly emerged from the Steph cubit's mouth. Billy quickly backed away while yelping a short, girlish cry and the cubit fell at his feet. Janine twirled the dagger in a circle before bringing it down to one side. She grabbed Billy's arm and raced with him toward the police cruiser. She tossed him in the back then turned around.

"Joel!" she yelled.

A lot of what was now happening reminded him of the summer of the great white back in 1972, and as Joel stood leaning against the cottage apartment building, watching the struggle that unfolded before him, those thoughts overwhelmed him. He was afraid, an emotion that he'd never been able to admit.

Just as he'd not admitted to what he'd actually done to capture the shark—which was nothing. He'd been knocked out cold from the sailing mast.

Just as he'd not admitted that his false assurance made possible by his false heroism was the reason that his marriage had broken and the reason why he'd sworn to never love again.

Just as he'd not admitted that no real man could live off of lies and that pretense would someday come back to bite you in the ass.

Just as he'd never admitted that he'd stripped himself of his own manhood and that was the reason why Joel Canton took to living and hiding and being scared in the confines of his tiny shack near the shore.

He'd known Mark Walker so well and when he'd come through Janine's cottage door and had attacked him, Joel had been afraid. When they'd scrambled to the bedroom, Joel had been the first one out the window. When he'd seen the Steph cubit looking out at him through her own bedroom window at the same moment Steph had been running with him to escape—well—that's when the cowardice had really took control. But the final stroke had been Janine. He had convinced himself that love was, again, possible. And to love a woman meant to protect a woman. He would become her hero and save her from the beast she was running from. No one would harm the woman he loved. No one would be her great white shark, not while Joel Canton was around. He was her Biblical staff and rod!

But it wasn't he who would be the hero and it was hard for him to admit that. As he leaned against the wall, watching her prowess with the weapon he'd found on the beach, knowing that she could have single-handedly killed the great white terror of '72, whatever mental and physical strength remained in him drained, leaving behind a coward.

Janine stood by the police cruiser yelling his name but he couldn't run to her. He was ashamed of himself. What a joke he was. Joel the Joke they would call him. The great pretender.

As several cubits emerged from Billy's VW Bus, Joel turned toward the back of the apartments and ran there to hide.

Blood covered the front seat but Alixel did not seem to care. Janine, however, felt queasy and her stomach churned further when Alixel switched on the police cruiser's windshield wipers. The swooping motion of wipers over blood reminded her of what she'd just done.

"It was necessary," Alixel said. "They were already dead."

"You were something else," Billy added from the back seat.

"What about Joel?" Janine said to Alixel. "We just left him there."

"He ran from us and we don't have the time."

"I could have..."

"I need you," Alixel demanded. "*We* need you."

It became evident as the trio sped in the cruiser toward the beach that Hurricane Antiago was close to making landfall. Alixel wrestled the steering wheel as whips of wind attempted to throw the car sideways. When she turned onto the beach road, the handling difficulties intensified. The rain had increased in density and speed. Some wind gusts practically shoved the police cruiser onto two wheels. In the distance, a single light blazed near the Caldwell Pier.

"We don't have time," Alixel repeated more to herself than to the car's occupants. "Hold on." She gunned the accelerator and took the police cruiser to a speed that was just under her loss of its control.

Nearer to the pier it became evident that Lett was operating the backhoe and Albert was directing the dig. Albert stood atop a tall pile of sand, lighting striking wrinkles into the sky behind him, wind ripping at his black clothing, his cowboy hat somehow remaining tacked to the top of his head, and Janine was reminded of her nightmare in which she had become his cubited bride. As they approached, Albert turned, his silhouette acknowledging their presence; he then shuffled out of sight down the back side of the sand mound. The light on the backhoe went out.

Alixel switched off the cruiser's headlights as she parked the car near the hole that had been created. Lightning provided short snapshots of the depth of the hole. What was at the bottom could not be seen from within the car. Beyond the hole sat the backhoe. Its digging arm was frozen, the bucket flexed, its metal teeth stretching toward the hole. Alixel switched on the cruiser's flood light.

Lett, still wearing his business suit, sat slumped within the cab of the backhoe. Blood covered the white shirt and tie. His face was buried in his chest. Behind him, also in the cab, stood Albert. He held a dagger in his hand that began to glow in unison with the two daggers in Alixel's belt sheath, the one in Janine's hand and a red halo that started to expand from the depths of the hole. Alixel doused the floodlight then both women exited the cruiser, leaving Billy inside.

"Protect the book," Alixel said to him then closed the door.

The women scaled the sand pile and stood at its apex; sand skittered into the hole from the weight of their feet which struggled to counteract the soft ground and mighty wind; the daggers hummed a gentle rhythm that was nearly inaudible.

At the bottom of the excavation, LaFitte's treasure lay scattered from the haphazard digging by the backhoe's operator. Wooden chests had been splintered open and small silver coins, much like the one Billy had found, littered the sand pit's floor. Gold, silver, ivory and copper statues from ancient civilizations poked their bodies up from deeper in the sand. Faces of Maya, faces of Egypt, faces of China were all present and looking up at the women as if pleading to be set free. Sticking straight up in the sand, apparently lodged into something that remained covered beneath it, was the fifth dagger. The red jade that symbolized the Creation of the End glowed with the same brilliance as the other four.

"Janine, my wife. You've finally returned to your loving husband," Albert said in a soothing tone that served only to raise Janine's alarm further. He remained partially hidden within the backhoe cab. Even the lightning was afraid to reveal his face. "And Alixel—princess of hope, guardian of despair—great fucking job you've done. I've got to admit, though, that without you none of this would have been possible. Your faults have been my gains. I was once just a simple country fuck with no money and a bad Jim Beam habit. And look at me now. I have the Cubit and the key and soon I'll have all the daggers and the recipe book which will tell me how to secure myself at the top of the sand pile." He laughed and the thunder acknowledged his pleasure with a pounding barrage.

"Three against one," Alixel yelled and pointed her daggers in his direction. Janine followed her lead, lifting her dagger to create three halos of red-jade light.

"Seriously?" Albert said and threw Lett's body from the backhoe cab as easily as one might toss an apple. He sat behind the controls. His face became visible above the glow of his own dagger. "You don't think I'd come to a fight empty-handed do you?"

At first, Janine thought that what she saw was an after-image created by the glowing daggers. She'd stared at them too long and now three red circles occupied her eyesight. It made the surf, which had moved inland more than fifty yards since they'd arrived, appear spotted. But when the fourth, fifth and sixth spots formed in the surf, she realized that it was something totally different. The spots in the surf did not glow. Under the rampant flashing thunderstorm, the spots looked like blood. Each bubbled as if boiling. The blood spots grew wider and the crimson turned darker. From each emerged a dozen cubited residents of Port Aransas. They rose heads-first and in unison, as if the sand were lifting them as a singular unit. When they'd risen to waist height, each walked forward, rigid, unwavering, even though the surf bashed their backsides. When they came to shore, Alixel turned to Janine.

"You ready?" Alixel said. "We'll have to do this together. You know what's at stake."

The world, Janine thought. Alixel never said it but she knew. *God's destiny for her was to save the world.*

She gripped the dagger with a strength that made it glow brighter and stepped forward just as the bucket of the backhoe passed within inches of her face and swatted Alixel into the bottom of the sand pit.

"Now that's better odds," Albert cackled wildly.

The cubits from Billy's VW had followed Joel behind the apartment building and were now hovering outside Janine's bedroom window, unable to figure out how to pull their new bodies up and in. Joel cowered on Janine's bed, hugging her pillow. He stared at the broken window, listened to the grunts and shrieks and guttural breaths of his pursuers. He could do nothing except wait. Sooner or later, the cubits would understand that going through the window to get him was not their best approach. Pretty soon, they would be rushing through the door. And they'd rip him apart. God help him, they'd rip him apart more ruthlessly than would any shark of any size.

Glass shards broke underfoot outside the splintered bedroom doorway.

Crunch!

Joel hugged the pillow closer, as if he could hide his entire body behind it.

Crunch-crunch!

He started crying and moaning his former wife's name. "Jane…" he bawled. "Oh, dear, Jane."

Crunch-crunch-crunch!

Snot and saliva and tears drooled over the pillow and onto his coveralls.

And the crunching stopped.

And Joel stopped.

The cubits outside the window still bustled with discontent. He sniffed and stared and mopped his eyes with the soaked pillow then blinked.

"Joel," a hushed voice said from beyond the wall. "Joel. Is that you?"

Joel nodded but did not answer.

Her hand appeared first, curling into the doorway across the broken frame, the nails painted black as they always seemed to be. "Joel. We've got to get out of here."

Marcy shuffled quietly into the room. Her attention was on everything at once. She looked back to the hallway, then in at the window, then over to Joel. She stepped to the edge of the bed.

"Take my hand," she said. "Quickly!"

Joel reached out to her, dropped the pillow, and allowed her strength to pull him from the bed. She tiptoed through the bedroom doorway and Joel followed, tiptoeing the best way he knew how. She rushed to the open front door, wind kicking her in the face, thunder raging overhead and Joel did not release her grip. She paused at the front door's threshold then released Joel's hand and ran as fast as she could to Billy's VW.

"Come on!" she urged.

Her strength had left him and Joel found that he could move no farther.

"Joel!" Marcy yelled louder.

He stared at his legs wondering why they wouldn't move. His pounding heart made his entire body shake.

"They're coming—Hurry!"

To his left, emerging from the side of the apartment building, scuttled no less than eight cubits. One of them was little Teddy Lavender. "Dead fish," Teddy said, his hands out and grasping at nothing. "Joel, take me dead fishing." The taller, older cubits ran past little Teddy but Joel paid them no attention; he couldn't take his eyes off the boy.

"Dammit Joel!" Marcy's hand was again pulling him forward; she'd run back to get him. "We…are going…to die!"

Jacques the smelly fisherman, missed ripping Joel's arm off by a fraction of an inch as Marcy yanked him from the doorstep. She pulled Joel with her, the cubits at their heels, toward the VW. She entered through the passenger's door, yanked Joel inside, reached over and slammed the door against Jacques' hand, gasped as two fingers fell to the floor board, and pulled the door closed. The cubits attacked the VW as Marcy started the engine and pulled away. Teddy Lavender's tiny hand reached through the busted driver's side window and grabbed Marcy's throat. She couldn't breath. She beat the tiny arm but it would not loosen its grip. The VW rode in a circle as Marcy tried to gain control of the steering wheel. Her face turned purple. A drop of blood sprang from a tiny finger that ripped at the flesh under her chin.

"Jo–aghhh!" she moaned.

At that moment Joel's cowardice disappeared completely. Another of his friends was about to die and he just couldn't let that happen anymore. The urge to run became the fortitude to fight. He reached across Marcy and, with every ounce of energy his proud fisherman's body could muster, slammed his fist against the tiny arm which broke at the elbow. He pried the fingers from Marcy's throat and tossed the limp limb out the window.

"Go!" he yelled.

They drove no more than two miles before the VW's engine abruptly quit though the gas gauge read a quarter full. They'd made it to the beach road and could see the glowing commotion near the pier in the distance.

"What the…" Joel said and jumped out. He walked to the back of the VW and lifted the engine cover. Something had been drug underneath the VW and pieces of it had lodged in the engine. Body parts, it looked like: tiny, thin body parts.

"What is it?" Marcy said.

"Nothing." Joel dropped the engine cover before Marcy looked inside. "We'll have to hoof it. You much of a running woman?"

Marcy smiled. "Anything you can do, Joel."

Alixel lay motionless atop LaFitte's treasure. Both of her Creation Daggers were now mixed in with the mass of coins that pictured the Wayeb symbol. Sand fell into the pit and covered her feet.

"You know," Albert said to Janine. "The neat thing about having this Antichrist job is how quickly you pick up on things. You pull a lever and you bury a princess." The backhoe arm swooped across the mound of sand and Janine leapt from it as the bucket pushed more into the pit. The cubits that had emerged from the surf formed a circle around the excavation.

Janine could have escaped but, for her, that was not an option. Revenge and rescue had taken control. She ran at the backhoe, ducked under Albert's attempt to swat her with the machine's metal arm and jumped up onto the side of the cab. Albert kicked her in the face and she flopped backward and onto the sand at the feet of one of the cubits. The cubit kicked the dagger from her hand.

"I've been meaning to tell you something, my love—something I've waited an entire year to say." Albert, standing in the cab, loomed above her. "I used to be a pretty decent guy. Never could control that Beam addiction though. That's what Mikey used to say. 'That Albert Stine wouldn't be such a bastard if he'd just let loose of the bottle.' But you see, as much as ole' Mikey was my friend, he always had something that I never would…you know, because of the drink and all." Albert stepped down off of the backhoe. He pointed his dagger at her. "So I took what I could not have." He laughed. "Mikey didn't die in no combine accident. You've always known that haven't you, hon? Of course I killed him. How else was I going to get the farm? How else was I going to get you? I just wanted you to know that he suffered immensely before he died. Bleeding to death without legs and arms is a hard way to go. As you will shortly find out."

Rain pelted Janine's face so hard she could not see Albert clearly as he knelt down, the dagger in his hand. She scrambled backward, searching for her own weapon that the cubit had kicked out of her reach. Albert's dagger came down, the point angling for one of her sand-thrashing legs.

It wasn't until the backhoe arm knocked Alixel into the hole that Billy reacted. He'd been sitting there hugging the Book of the Djed to his chest, thinking about the slaughter in front of the cottage apartment building and how easy it was going to be for the two women to rid the world of the two men who had done so much harm. The women didn't need his help; the women could take care of business; Good would prevail over Evil.

But then the blood spots had appeared, and the cubits had emerged from within, and they'd walked as if on top of the water to the shore, and they'd surrounded the women and the sand hole and the police cruiser. The backhoe had taken care of the rest.

Several cubits stood near the cruiser but none attacked it. It was as if they were waiting for orders to commence with the killing. Billy decided to use the lull in their activity to his advantage and run to the aide of Alixel, but when he tried to open the car door, Antiago winds pressed it back upon him. The rain came down so hard that he could not see outside the car's windows.

Albert not only controlled the dead, but apparently the hurricane as well.

He crawled over the back seat and sat down in Andy Collar's drying blood. The cruiser's engine was still running and he flipped on the wipers but the rain fell too fast for the wipers to catch up. He knew it was probably a hopeless effort but he tried the cruiser's radio.

"Hello," he said into the handset. "Can anyone hear me? I'm in a state trooper's car at the Caldwell Pier and we need backup. A murder is in progress." He waited to the sound of static. "Hello. Anyone there?" He dialed through numerous channels only to receive the same static response to his requests for help. Then he switched on the cruiser's P.A. which crackled to life within the howling wind.

"Stop!" he shouted. "This is the police!"

Two things happened almost simultaneously and together they saved Janine's life. The pounding rain pelted her ear holes, making Albert's voice sound hollow, but Billy's voice was sharp and much too loud for any human's vocal cords: "Stop!" Billy yelled. This distracted Albert long enough for the second action that saved her life. Out of nowhere, someone rushed Albert, planted their shoulder in Albert's rib cage just below his dagger-wielding arm, and took him to the ground. Janine wiped rain from her eyes, kicked with her heels, rolled, and her hand came down on a dagger which she assumed was hers but was Albert's. A scuffle ensued on the ground in front of her; wet sand fishtailed into the air. One of the fighters was propelled backward and fell at Janine's feet, crumpled and broken. She toed the body face up.

Joel!

She tried to scream his name.

Joel!

His neck was bent at an odd angle. He gasped for breath.

Joel!

She knelt down to push the rain water away from his nose and mouth.

"Ja…Ja…," he moaned. "Jane-ine…I love you."

And then he said nothing else.

"JOEL!" she suddenly screamed, releasing an energy that had been roiling inside her for an entire year. "You son-of-a-bitch!"

Albert laughed as loudly as Janine screamed. He stood above them, his eyes blazing crimson. Silver streaks in his pupils danced with demonic delight. And then, suddenly, his expression changed to one of great concern. The dagger Janine held began spreading its bright iridescence in a halo around her. She found her own dagger and snatched it from the sand; its glowing haft added to her confidence and her rage.

And then she held nothing back.

She lunged from a crouched position, a cat toward its prey, the daggers held forward like tiny bayonets. Albert backpedaled into the sand pile and tried to climb it backward, his arms in the air as Janine slashed at them with both daggers.

"That's for Joel," she screamed and sliced off Albert's left hand.

Albert scaled the sand pile in retreat.

"And that's for Lenny!" she wailed while planting another blade into Albert's forehead. Janine released the dagger, and the haft, glowing brightly, remained between his eyes. He topped the sand pile and fell to his knees, grasping in vain at the dagger with his handless left arm.

"And THIS is for Michael!"

With one wide, swooping motion, she stabbed Albert in the back of the neck right below the skull. The silver in Albert's pupils spun erratically. The red irises bulged. The red jades in both daggers became so bright that life seemingly jumped from them. Albert's head began to shake. His teeth broke and flew from his mouth.

And then he exploded inside a bright flash of red light that blew apart the top half of the sand pile.

Marcy, who had sprained her ankle as she'd ran with Joel, was sitting a half mile from the explosion. She would later explain that something had split the dark clouds and had sucked the red ball of light into the heavens.

When the ball of light was gone, so were Albert and Janine.

Billy had managed to exit the police cruiser and join Alixel at the bottom of the excavation just before the explosion. When he reached her, she was already alert and had recaptured her two daggers. She nodded in the direction of the third dagger which still remained planted in the ground.

"It's not over," she said.

Billy grabbed the glowing dagger and it released freely into his hand like Excalibur to Arthur. When he looked up, Janine and Albert were no longer there but the cubits had formed a circle at the perimeter of the hole and were looking down at them. One of the cubits suddenly jumped and Alixel quickly stuck him in the back of the head as he landed beside her; the former owner of the Mustang Ranch withered at Billy's feet. Another jumped and Alixel made quick work of him as well. By the time the tenth cubit jumped into the hole, Billy realized what was happening. They weren't jumping in, they were being pushed. The wrath of Hurricane Antiago dropped them in one by one as if helping Alixel remove them from existence.

Slowly Billy and Alixel rose from the hole on the accumulating bodies of former Port Aransas residents. Billy had not used his dagger once. When they reached the top, a single cubit remained. It was Bottlenose, the owner of Pat MaGee's and Billy's closest friend. The Bottlenose cubit stood between them. Alixel stepped away.

"You have to do it, Billy," she said to him.

"But he's my friend." Billy remembered how he had almost let the Steph cubit take his life. He'd almost kissed it. How was he going to kill his best friend?

"It's not over," she said again. "There will be others that you'll have a harder time with." Alixel scaled the partially leveled sand pile and stood where Janine had destroyed Albert. "The future is in your hands."

Bottlenose attacked. Billy was thrown sideways by the storm's winds and he swung the dagger, haphazardly, not really wanting to stab anything. Bottlenose turned and lunged, and, again, Billy was aided by the hurricane which knocked Bottlenose down at his feet.

Billy looked up at Alixel and stood there mesmerized as Bottlenose, writhing in the sand, grabbed Billy's foot. He could almost see through her. He could almost see the backhoe's frozen arm behind her. He blinked and she faded further.

"You have to do it," she said, lifting both arms and both daggers into the torrent of rain and wind. "For all of us."

Billy brought the dagger down, the blade slicing into the back of his best friend's neck. Bottlenose released Billy's foot, then the body withered like a prune and lay motionless.

Billy looked back to the top of the sand pile in time to see the bright light where Alixel once stood. He covered his eyes and crouched to the sand. The hurricane's wind and rain raged around him with such force that he thought it would suck him into the sky.

Then it was over. Dark clouds remained overhead but the wind and rain had stopped.

Alixel was gone. The hurricane was gone. The bodies of the cubits were gone. LaFitte's treasure was gone. All daggers except the one he held in his hand were gone. He'd been clutching it so hard that when he now released it, the mark of the star from its haft remained embossed into the palm of his hand. And lying on the sand next to his hand was the key page that had been ripped from the Book of the Djed.

"Billy!" someone yelled.

In the distance he saw Marcy waving at him and watched her collapse to the sand a hundred yards away. Billy grabbed the key and the last dagger and drove the police cruiser to her rescue.

The Cubit

PART III

THE CUBIT: PART III

A NEW BEGINNING

Friday morning, Billy handed the Surf Side over to Kale Jurgensen. He'd made a deal with the young man: take care of the business while he was gone and he'd make him a partner when he returned.

He'd never found his VW Bus and figured that the hurricane had taken it; other cars had been swept from the island. One of the ferry boats had even sunk. Most of the buildings, however, had survived. The only property that had been completely destroyed was the Port Aransas branch of the Big Texas Bank.

The Cubit was gone.

By Friday afternoon, local authorities in Port Aransas reported that more than two hundred people had lost their lives. Tiny pieces had been found that were later identified as belonging to half a dozen residents but the rest had simply disappeared. Speculation was rampant. Evangelical leaders set on scrutinizing the casino that had never been built said that the sinners had been swallowed by the hand of God. Meteorologists had suggested a more scientific explanation. The bodies had been sucked up by a cyclonic funnel from the "hurricane of the century" and had been deposited somewhere in the depths of the Gulf. The Coast Guard had been dispatched and a search grid had been created but few believed it was worthwhile. Billy *knew* they were wasteful efforts. He knew what had happened to all of those people. But no one would ever believe him.

It's not over, he remembered Alixel saying.

But she'd said so many wise things that had made her seem so real. Had she been? Perhaps he would never know for sure. He had no proof and that was good because he had his belief to guide him. She existed, if not only in his mind and memory. She had saved him from himself and had put the world back on track for 2012. He now felt obligated to continue the effort. Her people, the Hopis, would help. It was, after all, his destiny.

You have to do it for all of us.

He opened the Book of the Djed and noticed that the center spread now fully revealed all three sixes and had begun auto-writing the next clue that would help humanity survive the End Time.

He slid behind the wheel of Steph's Cavalier, gave the Book and the key page to Marcy and was quickly consumed by tears that blurred his vision. The car smelled like Steph, but more saddening was that SpongeBob sat on the dashboard and smiled his porous, carefree smile. Marcy rubbed his shoulder.

The drive out of town was slow. Debris, the media, and emergency vehicles were everywhere. But no one stopped them as they continued along Mustang Island and the beginning of a long journey to Sedona, Arizona.

The border patrolman at Brownsville Crossing #22 suspected nothing. Why would he? Pedro Melindez was a Mexican national who lived just north of Chiapas and he had the papers to prove it. Besides, the vintage VW Bus looked a lot like the one the patrolman's father had owned.

Their conversation was in the native language. Pedro had only recently begun talking with any kind of clarity. Spanish had been easier than English. The border patrolman asked him *Where are you going?*

"Mí hogar," Pedro said.

And where is your home?

"Está en Chiapas."

That is a long drive and it is very hot today.

"Sí. Pero tengo agua."

You have water. Good. What else are you bringing to our country?

Pedro glanced into the rearview mirror while rubbing the arm that was now healed from his fall off of Billy's deck. The Cubit rested against his suitcase. He had not transformed enough to worry about looking suspicious.

He had, however, become aware that smiling was a very effective way of communicating with humans and Pedro had one of the best smiles around. He used it now. "Apenas yo y mis ropas," he said.

The border patrolman returned his papers but not his smile. *Be careful or the sun will make the end to your destination.*

The end, Pedro thought. It wouldn't be much longer.

Before rolling up his window and driving into Mexico, the cubited Pedro thanked the border patrolman and with a wide grin said:

"El extremo está más cercano que usted piensa."

THE END IS CLOSER THAN YOU THINK

Book Two
The Djed

The Djed

PART I

THE DJED: PART I
666
1945

"This war—*Your War*—will cost this planet over seventy million lives!" Alax's voice stumbled over the words. He felt nervous but absolute. Another mortar blast crumbled brick thirty feet above them.

Eva spoke up, something she rarely did, but she was a newlywed and her husband was being wrongly accused. "What do you know? Your information is as much a lie as all of meine ehemann's generals. And see what they've done to him." She grabbed her husband's arm and gently massaged it.

The bunker, now full of billowing concrete dust, reminded Alax that time was running out. The dust pulsed dull crimson and was enlivened by the red light that beamed from a crate on which Eva's husband sat. Alax had never seen anyone touch his boss with such compassion. "He is not the one," Alax said to Eva. "Look at him. How can *that* last another sixty-seven years? He is premature. His life is premature. This war is premature."

Alax's dialect was slowly transforming from consolatory German-Slavic to one which Eva had never heard before. "Imposter!" she grumbled and raised the Walther P38 loaded with a single bullet that had been meant for her. "Who are you? What have you done to meine ehemann? What have you done to Deutsches Reich?"

The red light from the Cubit and the thickening concrete dust filled the bunker with a crimson iridescence that danced in the short distance between Alax and Eva. As more explosions ripped the ground above them and more dust rippled into the room, the curtain of wispy red became so thick that the occupants could barely see each other. Eva's gun wavered, the hand holding it, indecisive. She looked between her husband's legs at the glowing crate then at his face which was twisted in a frozen expression of despair. His eyes suddenly popped wide open and he glared at Alax. For some reason, he couldn't talk but Eva knew what he wanted her to do. Still, it wasn't until the red light began emanating from Alax's waist that Eva pulled the trigger.

Alax was too fast—even for a bullet. He'd unsheathed the dagger and was beside Eva before the curling red dust could identify his speed. "He cannot be allowed to live," he whispered in her ear as the locked, steel bunker door shook from the fists outside that beat against it. "WE cannot allow such Evil to exist. It was a mistake to believe otherwise."

The Cubit hummed quietly as Eva jammed the pistol into Alax's ribs and repeatedly pulled the trigger on empty rounds. Her husband moaned, stirred. Dust flew from the bunker door as German feet, fists and exclamations demanded entry. The star in the dagger's haft and the one at the top edge of the Cubit blazed with such intensity that the entire room floated in a wavy sea of crimson.

"I'm sorry for you, Eva," Alax said, still whispering as if consoling and apologizing and asking for forgiveness all at the same time. "Innocence is Evil's greatest victory." He smacked Eva in the back of the head with the haft of the dagger and she fell forward onto the floor, kicking up a red cloud of dust when she landed. When he looked up from her body, Alax flinched. Hitler was standing there, suddenly not so weak, suddenly not so vulnerable, suddenly determined that it was not his time to go, that another sixty-seven years of life was not only possible but was his destiny. He kicked Alax in the throat with the point of his boot, then turned to the Cubit which now opened. Alax flailed backward, red dust clouds encircling his unbalanced withdrawal.

The top of the Cubit lifted on its hingeless edge and the light from inside deepened the crimson that enveloped the bunker. The bunker's door dented inward as heavy objects assaulted it. Hitler planted one leg into the open Cubit. "I'll be back," he said, the opening sucking at his appendage.

Alax raced forward, aimed the dagger's point, and jammed it into the back of Hitler's neck.

"NOOO!" the cubited fuehrer screamed, clutching at the hole in the base of his skull. "I am da one! I am da…"

The Cubit slammed shut, amputating Hitler's right leg below the knee before the rest of his body dissolved to bone. The bunker door bent further inward. Another explosion rocked the room from above. Alax sat on the Cubit, and gazed up at the shaking, dust swirls above him.

"Take us back, great Spirit," he said to the ceiling. "We are its keeper and none shall gaze eyes upon it until the time of reckoning, until the Raising of the Djed. Take us back and forgive me for my transgressions."

Alax lifted the Creation Dagger above his head then thrust it downward in a swooping arc that buried the blade into the star in the Cubit.

One of Hitler's generals broke into the bunker just as the last visage of Alax and the Cubit disappeared.

The Djed
PART II

THE DJED: PART II

"THAT'S GREAT, IT STARTS WITH AN EARTHQUAKE, BIRDS AND SNAKES..."
—R.E.M.

Sedona, Arizona, is a story about rocks, great monoliths jutting from ancient seabeds, ragged-edged spires shaped by the hand of God, majestic and magical to the mortals who have gazed upon them, who have felt the red rock vibrations resonate within their very souls.

Sedona is also a story about hope and heaven and those who would take advantage of such naiveté. Leylines and vortices, shamans and sages, crystals and dreamcatchers and incantations—all waiting for those who believe, want to believe or, like Billy Jo Presser and Marcy Ruminski, have come in search of the truth.

But revelations of truth are rare: sometimes it takes an act of God—a flood, a firestorm, a hurricane—to make mortals understand. The earth must open up at the very heels of those in denial...tempting fate. Tempting finality.

Such was the case on the first day after Thanksgiving at five past ten o'clock in the evening. The tremor that shook the red rock monoliths and left Billy and Marcy grasping at the city park bench served as a reminder to all of Oak Creek Canyon: something higher than man existed.

Billy and Marcy had been in Sedona for more than five months looking for answers and had, as yet, found nothing. Billy was beginning to believe there was nothing to find. Billy was beginning to lose all faith and had, increasingly, started doubting everything that had led them here in the first place. Nothing new had been added to the mystery and nothing old had been subtracted, since he'd almost killed the crazy woman in Las Cruces on the drive out. Wasted time and wasted money all because of a promise.

Marcy had just begun talking about her exhilarating day when the tremors shook her face, chattering her teeth. She grabbed the wooden bench boards, her long, red fingernails digging for support. The shallow Oak Creek, flowing under the city lampposts just a few dozen feet away, seemed to freeze as if in panic that the fault line underneath would suddenly open and swallow its timid flow of precious water. Car alarms blared from the direction of "The Y," a central hotspot where the city's two main roads intersected. Screams resounded as glass shattered in the distance.

The quake lasted less than ten seconds, causing Billy to release a tiny belch filled with the flavors of the milk and Fruit Loops he'd had for dinner. He gazed over the horizon, more to ensure himself that the sculpted Coffee Pot Rock was still there, that, indeed, God had not kissed it and Sedona goodbye by swallowing the majesty only He could have created. Billy placed a hand over Marcy's. Nightfall had dropped the temperature ten degrees to a comfortable seventy-five but, still, her skin was cold to the touch; apparently, her hands had been clamped so hard to the bench that the blood had raced away from her fingers.

"It's done," he said, gently patting her flesh. A thin, red dusty haze enveloped the numerous lampposts along the L'Auberge Resort front road and had clogged one of Billy's nostrils. He sniffed.

Marcy gazed toward the west, toward The Y, ignoring the dust and the quake to return to her revelations. "I found this woman who knows about the Cubit."

Billy released her hand and turned toward her, ignoring the sudden rush of emergency vehicle sirens that quickly grew from fade to furious as they approached the center of town behind them. "I don't want to hear it. I said, it's done." Marcy's long black hair glistened with specks of red silica. The dark, cosmetic applications to her eyebrows, and the ruby red lipstick reinforced her similarity to Cher. As she licked her lips, the match was indelible. "Look. We've been through this before. These damned spiritualists around here will say anything to make a buck. How many times, now, has someone told us they knew this or that about Cubits and daggers and death only to be found out as frauds?"

"Yeah. But Cooper seems legit."

Billy shook his head. "No. I'm tired of it. I just want to go home." A shrill memory echoed once again from his mind's deepest hiding places. Paranoia leaked into his rationality, causing beads of sweat to emerge precariously close to his brown eyes.

"You're doing it again," Marcy said, wiping away one salty runner on his forehead with her thumb, leaving behind a red rock streak of moistened mud. "You're thinking about that woman in New Mexico, aren't you?"

He nodded quickly, his chin rising and falling a fraction of an inch, his shoulder-length blonde hair slapping his cheeks.

"She was just some crazy ol' vieja pumped up on pills." Marcy said, trying to comfort him.

Up the creek, toward the exclusive L'Auberge Resort, a pack of vacationers ran along the asphalt access road away from the resort. "You are the end…the end!" one woman seemed to scream as she approached. She wore a collection of rich accoutrements that dangled and jangled around a much-too-tight black halter top that was just wrong, especially since the woman was a good thirty pounds beyond what her body was meant to carry. Designer flip-flops struggled with the weight and the speed of her descent down the uneven slope of paving. She tripped twice—the first time, she almost fell flat on her round face; the second time, she lost one of the flip-flops and shrieked when the asphalt touched her bare heel. After recovering the flip-flop, she jogged the remaining distance to where Billy and Marcy sat.

You are the end...

Billy shook his head. She really wasn't saying that was she? Of course not. None of it had been real. None of it! But Billy's denial was no match for the shock that had never really gone away. The drive from Port Aransas and through Las Cruces and the memory of lost friends had embalmed his neurons with cautious uncertainty that tiptoed on fragile rationality. He would never get the blood-washed vision of Stephanie Drake out of subconscious...or the bodiless head of Mitchell Bone…or poor Janine as she'd turned to face him just before blowing apart, just before the hurricane had sucked her into the sky. No matter how hard he tried, he would never forget Las Cruces, either, or the woman whom he'd nearly hit with the car. She'd screamed, just like the woman running toward him was doing right now. Damn, he wished she'd shut up. Damn the earthquake. If not for these things, Billy's decision to leave, this time, would have been irreversible.

"The end," the woman panted. "We have to get to the labyrinth and pray for salvation before the end." Her eyes spun aimlessly. When she stopped beside the bench, her sweaty hand grabbed the backrest behind Marcy.

"It's just a little tremor, hon," Marcy offered. "I'm fine. You're fine. Here, sit down."

A man who might have been her husband passed the bench. He was much thinner and a whole lot lighter on his feet. Six other resort guests ran with him. All stopped when he did. "Lana," he said. "We have to keep going. The labyrinth will only hold so many."

"Sit here," Marcy repeated. "No one is going to go anywhere. Besides, that tremor was only a warning shot meant to remind us of how fragile we all are." She scooted closer to Billy, placed her small, cloth handbag on her lap, and patted the empty bench space with her hand. "Labyrinths are meant to show us the path, hon, but not necessarily its outcome." Lana looked confused by the statement but Marcy's words seemed to calm her for a few moments. Lana sat and Marcy placed a hand on her shoulder. "See. No more rumble. We're all fine."

More sirens bellowed in the darkness from multiple directions as emergency crews descended on The Y. Billy saw a ladder fire truck race toward town along Highway 89 and wondered why a ladder would be needed for any of the small buildings in Sedona. The accumulative sirens and scant mixture of car and theft alarms reignited Lana's tension. She quickly rose and ran to the man, hobbling on the one heel that had touched the asphalt. On her face was an expression of what Billy could only describe as compliance.

"Yes," the woman said to her husband. "To the labyrinth. He told us this would happen just before the end. Did you call the kids?"

The man hugged his wife which drew the other resort guests closer. "I left a message on their cells," he whispered to Lana. "We'll meet them there." The husband glared protectively at the pack and snuggled Lana closer. Husband and wife quickly scuttled, clasped together, down L'Auberge Lane to its intersection with Highway 89, stopped, turned and looked in both directions as if lost, turned back toward Billy and Marcy and the pack, then headed right, toward Uptown Sedona.

The rest of the resort guests dispersed as fine red mists of dust settled across the shallow waters of Oak Creek. The lampposts, spaced a hundred feet apart, cast a fluorescent sheen on the water, turning the small shards of silica dust into red-tinted sparkles of light. The creek water snatched the starry points and churned them into its current, creating a long, wavy snake that twinkled and slithered in and out of shadow toward the center of town.

"Wiped clean by the hand of God," Marcy said as if in chant. She waved her hand out across the creek and giggled like a child. Billy perked up and turned, not realizing Marcy was still quite close to him. One red fingernail pressed against red lipstick. Fat sunglasses sat askew atop her head, and black hair at her temples looped around the arms. "Sorry. It's just so silly. I mean, those people. This isn't the end and you're not the end. We both know that the end doesn't come for at least a few more years." She stood. "That's why we're here: to find out how."

Billy crossed his leg, drawing his cargo shorts pant leg up and above his knee. "Any of your new knowledge make reference to earthquakes?"

"Come on, Billy. We all know earthquakes are precursors of bad-things-to-come."

"I'm glad you can make so much light out of this."

"Just trying to cheer you up and get you out of this funk you're in. We've got a job to do. Remember?"

Billy had known Marcy in only coincidental ways while living in Port Aransas. She'd been to town hall meetings often and had been a go-between friend for the poor fisherman Joel Canton, but other than that, her personality and added idiosyncrasies had been a mystery. In the past five months, though, he'd gotten to know her better. Marcy seemed to be the consummate optimist and she had used this sanguinity (along with innocent giggles) to help remedy his anguish. Today was not the first time he'd thought about giving up and today wasn't the first time she'd tried to cheer him up. It just seemed that each time, it was getting harder and harder to convince him that Sedona was where he should be.

"So, are you going to take me out for coffee like you promised?" Billy asked, trying as hard as he could not to smile.

"Only if Charleys is still standing." Marcy strolled off in the direction of The Y, toward the sirens that had decreased in number and in volume, her small plaid handbag bouncing against one hip. Billy sat for only a moment as the remnants of defeat faded, then quickly joined her at the end of the road.

When they arrived at the Y-intersection of Highways 89 and 179 just ten minutes later, cars stood still in all three directions. A new lamppost that had been anchored in place just a week before, had fallen and now blocked all passage as it lay across Highway 89 like a long, broken, railroad crossing arm. The shattered array of lamps at the top of the metal post were scattered across the far side of the road and the adjoining sidewalk. Charley had dodged losing his coffee shop by about twelve feet. Billy now understood the need for the ladder truck he'd seen earlier. The firefighters were using the boom of the ladder to raise the lamppost. They had just finished hooking everything up when Billy and Marcy stopped among dozens of other pedestrians who were curious as to the success of the emergency crews. Billy pointed at Charleys.

"It's still standing," he offered. "You think they're serving?"

Billy and Marcy pushed through the crowd and into the street, circling around a perimeter set up by the police. Most of the cars sat unoccupied, the drivers now a part of the gawking mass of pedestrians. A few parked rows of cars away from the intersection sat a VW Bus, late 60s model. With a different paint job and less chrome it could have doubled for the one Billy had owned in Port A. He'd loved that vehicle, but it had been swept away in the hurricane just like so much else.

"Come on." Marcy grabbed his elbow.

As they neared the coffee shop, the top side of the lamppost was winched in the air six feet. A police officer's hand suddenly jutted forth, pressing back against Marcy's chest. Marcy looked at his hand then at his face.

"Sorry ma'am," the officer said with a tepid, southern drawl. "Please stand back." He removed his hand though, to Billy, it seemed to have remained there an uncomfortable few too many seconds.

The truck ladder swung the lamppost toward the opposite sidewalk and crews quickly lowered it onto an area where pedestrians were slow to move out of its way. Cleanup crews assembled around Billy and Marcy and a street sweeper rolled across the broken glass in the street. In a few minutes, traffic began crawling through The Y while police directed the flow.

Billy and Marcy crushed shards of glass underfoot as both entered Charleys. Not only was the place serving, it seemed that Charleys was *the* place to be with standing room only. Chatter was overwhelming, no doubt centered on eyewitness accounts of the lamppost and the earthquake that had toppled it. The counter where coffee was ordered and where pastries were few behind the counter's glass enclosure was inundated with people drinking, eating and ordering.

"I thought the damn thing was going to drop right down on top of my head," said a lady who looked a lot like the Lana from the resort. "The glass flew like shrapnel. Got me here." The lady pointed at the back of one of her legs. Her flip-flop hung from the heel. A small, red line that looked more like a paper cut than shrapnel marked the skin above her Achilles tendon. Another woman who was listening to the story, gasped, covering her mouth with both of her hands.

"Starbucks is close enough for a walk," Billy suggested to Marcy. "Injuries are probably not so life-threatening over there." The wounded lady looked at him, started to say something, but instead turned to her friend, took her hand, and nudged further into the human mass.

West Sedona was pockmarked by alternating chunks of small retail shops, larger strip malls, ranch-style residential homes and essential city buildings. On one street corner sat a lot filled with all of the big national businesses whose signage challenged peaceful spirituality with monikers glowing in Wal-mart blue, Subway yellow and Home Depot orange. On the next street corner, an elementary school sat in recess for the Thanksgiving break, its playground filled with motionless swings, merry-go-rounds and basketball nets. For blocks of sidewalk further along, there was nothing but mom and pop shops carrying the essential experience of impulse buying. Everything under the Arizona sun could be purchased for those who thought, for just one instance, that this Native American Indian curio or that bottle of holistic remedy was perfect for themselves or for someone they loved. Sporadically thrown into the mix sat modern homes built of masonry and spackled with stucco, with roofs cascading red and brown Spanish tile, and landscaping akin to scaled-down versions of desert botanical gardens.

Because it was Black Friday (or perhaps because an earthquake had just awakened the curiosity of residents and visitors), West Sedona seemed overly active. It was closing in on eleven o'clock when Billy and Marcy reached the intersection of Airport Road where a bench for the city shuttle, Roadrunner, was full of shoppers. On the far side of the crosswalk, the neon glow of Starbucks green infiltrated the night. Most of the rustic stores they'd passed in the last block and a half had remained open to scattered foot traffic and slow moving vehicles, inviting, what Billy thought, were dozens of women just like Lana and the "shrapnel maimed" lady from Charleys. These were women who looked less like each other than they were psychologically connected: women who were more so predisposed to the same beliefs and controls only a "Lana" could understand, women whose massed knowledge (which by their own admittance was way too much) had been created by a recipe of big city pressure accelerated by dead economics. The Lanas that walked the sidewalks and sampled the wares of Sedona's small retailers wore flip-flops, shorts and tops that bared too much skin and were one size too small, and they all complained about the simplest of life's challenges.

While Billy and Marcy waited to cross the street, a Lana who had just emerged from Vor-Tech's Glass Menagerie ran haphazardly into Marcy. She held a green glass sculpture of what looked like a winged dog with two heads. One of the wings was broken. She held the body of the dog creature in one hand and shook the sharp edge of the wing at Marcy.

"Dammit," she growled. "Look what you made me do!" Marcy tried to ignore her, looking instead at the traffic light which had just turned yellow. "Hey," the Lana continued. "I spent good money for this and you just broke it."

In Vor-Tech's storefront window, Billy noticed that several glass sculptures were toppled over and broken. The hand of one of the store owners was busy setting many of the pieces upright. Another hand on the opposite side of the storefront propped a sign in the window that read:

EARTHQUAKE SALE.
50% to 70% OFF

The man who had placed the sign looked up at the commotion between Marcy and the Lana. He shook his head at Billy and pointed at the sign, then walked around his wife who continued to rework the storefront presentation. When he appeared at his shop's front door, Marcy turned to the Lana and said, "You clumsy duck. Get off my back or I'll break *your* wing."

For a moment, Billy thought that Marcy would really do it…break the Lana's arm. The act would have gone against everything Billy had come to understand about the fortuneteller. She had shown streaks of aggression but nothing that had ever neared physical violence. Marcy, from what he knew, would have broken the Lana with an intelligent array of metaphor and simile, anchoring on the psychology and spirituality of the person and not the skin and bones.

"Ma'am," the store owner said. "That piece was broken by the earthquake. If you'd like to return it, I'll give you a refund but don't go blaming others for what Mother Earth did."

The Lana turned, huffed, glared once more over her shoulder at Marcy who had not shifted her stance by a single inch, then flip-flopped off down the sidewalk.

"Sorry," the store owner said. His wife now stood beside him. "We get 'em every now and again. I guess you just can't please everyone."

Marcy relaxed and stepped closer to Billy. She grabbed his hand which sent a slivered happy chill into Billy's body. "You're a good person," she said to the store owner. "Thank you."

"No. Thank *you*." The store owner snatched his wife's hand in much the same way that Billy held Marcy's. "I just didn't want to watch you belt her, though the woman certainly deserved it. She gave my wife quite a fit. That's a five hundred dollar piece she got for fifty bucks. Even broken, it's worth twice that to the insurance company." He looked at his wife and grinned. "But I guess anyone like that is easier to deal with than the insurance company. Either of you interested in some great, glass shop, post-earthquake bargains? I was about to close up but if…"

Billy absently looked into Vor-Tech's storefront. "No thanks. We were just heading over…" And then he stopped mid-sentence. Words floated in saliva that had suddenly become too thick for his tongue to work with efficiently. Lying on a fabric-wrapped curio display was—what Billy swore was—what couldn't be. "What's that?" he said to the owner.

The man followed his pointing finger as his wife took the cue to grab the object from the display and bring it to Billy. "Lots of people look at it but no one has ever shelled out the cash for it," he said. "It will protect you from evil, or so the myth goes."

The owner's wife handed Billy a glass replica of a Creation Dagger, one very similar to the real thing which Billy had carried hidden in a sheath under his shirt since leaving Port Aransas, since killing his best friend. The very thin tip of its seven-inch, curved blade was broken off but the handle and the red star in the handle's haft was etched to near perfection. Except for the red star, the glass was clear and used the neon green glow of the Starbucks' sign to cast dancing sparkles of emerald onto Billy's face.

"That's why we call it the Glass Menagerie," the owner said, pointing at his shop's entry door nameplate. "All of our pieces tend to do that. It's usually the prism effect that gets to most peoples' wallets. Should I wrap it up for you?"

Billy's fascination must have been transparent. "How much?" he asked.

"I'll tell you what." The store owner smiled. "You hold onto it. If you like it, we'll talk price tomorrow. Besides, I have this strange feeling you might need it tonight." Billy looked up, the emerald reflections dancing into his open, gasped, mouth. "You know…to ward off evil. Like that woman." The man thumbed in the direction that the Lana had gone.

"But you don't know me from Adam," Billy said, his lips kissing the green sparkles.

"But I do." The owner snatched the glass dagger from Billy's open hand and gave it to his wife who disappeared into the soft light of the store's interior. "You are a gentle soul on a perilous journey that needs a little trust to help you along…to help you believe."

"You must be a fortuneteller," Marcy said, squeezing Billy's hand, encouraging him.

"Yes," the owner said. "I'll see you tomorrow."

His wife reappeared and gave Billy the dagger, which was now wrapped in a soft, purple velvet cloth. And then she did something that took all three of them by surprise by craning her head forward and up about six inches to kiss Billy on the cheek. "You'll know what to do when the time comes."

"You mean pay for the dagger?" Billy whispered not knowing why he did so.

"Yes, of course." The store owner's wife backed up to stand beside her husband. "Take care of her."

Billy quickly looked directly at Marcy's red lips then down at the wrapped glass dagger.

The Vor-Tech's Glass Menagerie proprietors waved farewell as Billy and Marcy crossed the street. Before entering Starbucks, Billy turned back to find that the store's interior was dark and the owner and his wife were gone.

Billy could not stop staring at the purple cloth that rested in the center of the circular tabletop.

"It really is beautiful," Marcy said. "How close is it to the real thing?"

"Spot on." He sipped from his glass of iced coffee and considered the real dagger sheathed near his heart under his shirt. "Except of course for the broken tip. And the star."

"The star?"

"The one in the handle. It is completely red." He pointed at the cloth. "The real thing has a star that is red in only one of the star's points."

"Is that significant?" Marcy sipped mocha latte and stroked the soft velvet with an index finger.

"Of course not. This isn't the real thing."

"I wish I'd been able to see one…to hold one. All I know is from what is drawn on the back of your book."

In the five months that they'd been in Sedona, Billy had never told Marcy the complete story. How could he? The memories were too insanely complex and upsetting. Foremost, he'd not told Marcy about the Creation Dagger he'd kept hidden from her because he was certain that to do so would endanger himself, Marcy and anyone else that knew of its existence. Trust wasn't an issue. Marcy had proven herself time and again and, if truth be told, had really helped save them all. She'd rescued Joel Canton from the mass of cubited Port Aransas residents and Joel had saved Janine Bender who had then killed the real antagonist, Albert Stine. He trusted Marcy but the Creation Dagger was much more important than trust. As far as he knew, it was the last of its kind, the other four having been swept away by Hurricane Antiago. And, since the Creation Dagger was the only thing he knew of that could kill a cubit, and, since he remained paranoid that any one individual he came across could be a cubit, the dagger remained close to him. He slept with it, showered with it and had even swum with it a month ago when he'd finally visited Slide Rock Park, a local recreational swimming spot.

Most everything else he'd explained, particularly those parts that were necessary for her to help him find out about Professor Cower, the man who had seemingly started this whole mess by carting the Cubit, one of the Creation Daggers, and the Book of the Djed halfway across the country en route to Sedona and had found his end in the middle of nowhere Kansas.

Marcy unwrapped the velvet cloth and the glass menagerie immediately began: tiny prisms of rainbow colors bounced in every direction. "There were five of them, right?" She tapped the dagger with her index finger, the red nail adding singular dissimilitude to the multi-colored sparkles.

Billy chewed an ice cube and spit a chunk back into his glass. "There were five but they're gone now." His attention momentarily shifted to the jingle of the front entry door as two men entered and sat two tables away. The Caucasian man wore a John Deere ball cap that nearly matched the color of the Starbuck's sign mounted on the wall behind him. The darker skinned man wore a straw hat with a brim wide enough to cover most all of his face.

"Well then," Marcy said. "I don't know how we're gonna save the world without them. Didn't you say some time ago that we needed all of them?"

Billy's mind pondered and prodded and picked. It was something about the two men who, instead of ordering from the waitress, began a discussion that caused the white man to glance over at Billy. Billy looked away, deciding that he was enthralled by the glass menagerie. "I did, but I just don't know anymore," he said.

Marcy stopped tapping the velvet cloth and slipped the finger through the handle of her coffee cup but did not drink. "Strange."

"What's that?" Billy traced condensation on his glass, unknowingly writing something similar to the letters that spelled out C-u-b-i-t.

"How we met. I mean it's been months and we haven't really uncovered much info. And just by accident, I found Cooper." Marcy giggled more out of perplexity than out of humor. It momentarily diverted Billy's growing paranoia of the two men.

"By accident?"

"Her van hit a huge pothole and she scraped the guardrail up on Boynton Pass Road. She popped a tire and her whole tour group was stranded there on the side of the road. I was actually right behind them and saw the whole thing."

"So you rescued them?" Billy smiled.

"Not really. I hit the same pothole. I was too busy watching her crash. That's why I'm without the rental now. I took out…what did Les say?…I took out the tie rod bar."

"Les?"

"The mechanic. Lester is his real name, but he markets his business with the slogan: *You get more with Les*." Marcy absently stroked the broken point of the glass dagger blade. "So we were both stranded. Fortunately, I've built a good relationship with Les who I met a few months back. He's a great storyteller, especially when it comes to Sedona mythology. Anyway, he brought his wrecker out in record time. I think Les has a shine for me."

That someone had a "shine" for her was not surprising to Billy. That Marcy felt the need to tell him so was. "You'll have to lay some of those myths on me some time," he said, dryly, then added, "Tell me about this woman."

"Les called for a ride to come pick us all up and on the way back into town we just started a bunch of small talk…you know, like where are you from?...what do you do for a living?…that kind of stuff. When I told her that I was currently unemployed and in search of answers to some of life's perplexing questions she said that she'd heard it all before."

The waitress again approached the two strange men but they waved her away. Billy now noticed that the man in the John Deere hat was mostly bald except for a thin flip of blonde-white hair that peeked down across his forehead from under the brim.

Marcy continued, "…and when I told her I was looking for stories about the Cubit and....well, you should have seen the look on her face."

Billy stopped listening to her altogether. The man with the Deere hat—now Billy realized where he'd seen him before. Billy interrupted. "Turn slowly like you're looking for the waitress and check out the guys that came in a few minutes ago. That's them. Those are the guys from Las Cruces. I'm sure of it. But that was five months ago."

Marcy's face twisted into an expression of distraught. "I thought we already went over all of that. Besides, if they had followed us here, we would have seen them before now."

"Please. Just humor me. At least tell me that Deere-hat man over there isn't the same guy from that Las Cruces restaurant. He's got that same bald head and wavy flip of hair. It has to be him. Who else looks like that?"

Marcy rolled her eyes and slowly turned and as she did so, Billy relived the entire experience, his brain's memorization engine flipping through static images that flashed quickly, like frames in a movie. It had been the day after the "Hurricane of the Century" had swept away the cubited population of Port Aransas and what remained of his life. They had fled toward Sedona in search of answers and had made a stop in Las Cruces, New Mexico. In Las Cruces, the crazy Hispanic woman whom he'd almost killed had attacked the bald man with the thin flip of blonde-white hair while screaming: *You are the End! You are the End!*

In Las Cruces, the hunters had shown themselves.

They'd needed gas and Marcy had been complaining about hunger, though how she could have had an appetite after living through such a massacre had been beyond Billy. He'd been nauseous for the entire ten-hour trek that Interstate 10 ran through Texas. He'd felt that he might puke at any moment. And there'd been that constant feeling that he was being watched...followed...chased, a feeling that he supposed would never go away. Stephanie's SpongeBob Squarepants toy, which sat in silent, smiling humility in the middle of the dashboard, had only served to increase his body's malign attacks but he'd been unwilling to move it, thinking that the toy also represented one final link to a somewhat sane world.

Though he wasn't hungry, he wanted to explore what living arrangements might be found in Sedona. They'd left in such a hurry, considerations for living had entailed nothing more than the acquisition of cash from two teller machines and a brief overview of credit lines and available balances. When he exited the interstate near New Mexico State University, he asked Marcy to be on the lookout for some sort of Internet café. From the exit ramp, a right turn onto University Avenue had them driving near the heart of the campus within minutes.

The transposition was numbing at first. On the right side of the four-lane road, the glass and brick majesty of college life pulled him like a magnet, refilled him with a passion that only those in pursuit of knowledge—those meant to pursue knowledge—could understand. On the left side of University Avenue there was poverty, some seemingly too extreme to have been erected just across the street from such academic dissimilitude. It reminded him of a couple of years back while he was still at MIT, when he'd visited Yale in New Haven for a lecture on nanotechnology. There'd been that grandiose aura of social importance on the east end of town and the entirely opposite state of welfare a block away. He'd remembered that when leaving his motel, to turn right meant textbooks and importance and safety, and to turn left meant illiteracy, self-loathing and danger. Complete opposites and a complete care-less attitude. Those who had so much to gain cared the least about those who had little to lose.

On the north end of the Las Cruces campus they entered an increasingly broken-down part of the neighborhood...a stereotyped area of the city where the unemployed reigned, where the lost hopes of immigrants were stenciled into the landscape as broken cars, tiny stucco homes, dirt yards, and many, many sad faces. Immigrants sat on porches that skewed to one side, some wearing broken straw hats, some chewing on the ragged brown reeds of grass that grew in scattered clumps between the cracks in the porch floorboards. But it was the children that really drew Billy's attention. They didn't run and jump and play. They didn't laugh with the delight of learning new things. There was nothing new for them to laugh about. And the sun—it beat down upon their tiny heads, browning further their Hispanic skin tones, a relentless heat that was already pushing ninety degrees at noon.

And Billy thought that he was in another country. He had to be. How could the land of the free and the home of the brave treat its people with such antipathy? Billy's country was made up of immigrants, wasn't it? It was the immigrants who had been given the opportunity to become the masters of the universe which now denied the hopes of these people…and their children. How could they? Had the powerful forgotten their past? Was materialism that strong a force? Had all hope and goodness been wrested from their souls? Had they become…

One of the children he'd been staring at suddenly jumped up and pointed straight at him. At that same moment Marcy yelled, "There's one." And then she screamed, "Look out!"

Someone was in front of the car and Billy mashed the brake pedal. He'd been driving just under the 35 mph speed limit but the Cavalier still took an agonizing two seconds to stop. The pedestrian stumbled backward and fell to the pavement. As the pedestrian disappeared beyond and below the car's hood, SpongeBob tumbled from the dashboard and onto Marcy's lap. The Book of the Djed, which he'd stashed under the seat, slid into view across the floorboard.

"Oh my God!" Billy moaned, his fists locked tight to the steering wheel. "Did I hit her?" He craned his neck forward.

Marcy sat motionless, neither a smile nor frown revealing how she felt, with SpongeBob's face planted between her knees. She absently swiped the toy to the floor and matched Billy's forward-leaning gaze.

Suddenly, the pedestrian popped up in front of the car. She was Hispanic, middle-aged, and Billy could see no blood on her. She was clothed in the same scant wardrobe as the residents on the left side of University Avenue: a torn, sweaty blouse, and ratty, off-brand blue jeans that had been cut off to make shorts. She was not wearing anything on her feet and Billy wondered how she could walk the asphalt's temperature without shoes—he wondered, for that matter, how she was even alive.

He grasped the car door handle with the intention of getting out and helping her but before he opened the door, the woman continued across the road, paying no attention to him, the Cavalier, or the delivery box truck that screeched to a halt before hitting her. The woman staggered between cars parked along the curb then tripped onto the sidewalk, supporting herself with the metal pole of a street sign that read *One-Hour Parking*. Nobody came to her aid. Nobody asked if she was hurt. The half-dozen bystanders that *had* stopped to gawk continued in the directions of their midday destinations.

"That was close," Marcy said, turning from the stumbling woman to Billy.

"I think I hit her." One of Billy's hands still death-gripped the steering wheel. His foot seemed cemented to the brake pedal.

"No," Marcy said, "but it was damned close." She grabbed his clenched wrist. "That's what the sun can do to you—daze and confuse." Billy was uncertain if the comment was meant for him or the woman. A horn blared behind them. "Come on. I saw a restaurant with an Internet sign in the window back there just before…" She smiled, comfortingly. "Head around the block. I'll show you."

The side streets around University Avenue were filled with just about every kind of store a typical college student could want, from used textbook dealers to small outdoor pubs to shops selling New Mexico State University Aggies mascot paraphernalia. Billy turned back onto University Avenue and parked behind the delivery truck that had almost hit the stumbling woman. When he stepped from the Cavalier he couldn't help looking back toward the center of the road, hoping that another woman would not be there sprawled over the asphalt under the baking sun, wondering how many others on the poverty side of University Avenue had failed to cross over to the land of plenty, wondering if anyone had ever been killed, wondering if anyone had ever really cared.

The food in the restaurant was exceptionally tasty and inexpensive; at least, that's what Marcy told him. Beans and rice and tortillas were the perfect ingredients for a multitude of recipes and, with his fork, Billy prodded several on the "Taste of Mexico" platter he'd ordered. He was a restaurateur, a sampler of all things edible, but for some reason, none of what he smelled or tasted was very appetizing. Marcy, on the other hand, wolfed down her chimichanga then proceeded to help Billy with his order.

While he waited for one of the three computer kiosks to become available, Billy watched the Saturday midday news on one of the two wall-mounted flat screen televisions. News anchors reviewed local stuff, mostly. Much of it was bad news as all TV news seemed to be anymore. More deaths at the Mexican border. More drug busts in homes not so dissimilar from those across University Avenue. He looked in that direction through the restaurant's storefront window. They were there, all huddled on their busted wooden porch looking at him. An entire family. Three complete generations. They looked at him and pointed, their mouths working on words that could not be heard. Then, one by one, they stood and walked into the traffic. One by one, their bodies were crushed by bumpers, grills and wheels. They didn't scream. The cars that hit them didn't stop. The bodies simply disappeared from his view beyond the frame of the storefront window. The oldest went first. The smallest girl was last. A BMW doing fifty missed her by a foot. A speeding 4-Runner missed her by an inch. She walked directly into the window and squashed her face up against it, her six-year-old incisors biting at the glass, squeaking out the garbled words: *You are the end...*

Squeaky...squeaky.

Her brown eyes bulging and her brown face bloating as it pressed harder into the glass. Breath and tongue and teeth.

Squeaky...squeaky.

And a tear.

Squeaky...squeaky.

"The end," a voice that was not the little girl's said. "The one at the end is open."

Squeaky...squeaky.

"Billy!"

He turned from the window when Marcy grabbed his forearm.

"The computer on the end is free. You Okay?"

Billy's breath and heart skipped in unison. When he looked back toward the window the little girl was gone. Across the street was an open field occupied by a single utility pole. "I...eh...yeah...Okay."

"You sure you don't want some food? At least drink some water." She pushed his tall plastic glass across the table until it touched his clenched fingers and followed his gaze. "I'm sure she's all right. You didn't hit her."

Billy forced a smile, then rose with the water in hand and turned toward the computer kiosk. "Let's see what Sedona has to offer," he said. Marcy followed him.

It took his mind a moment to adjust, to force out the squeaky teeth and moaning cries, to understand that what it had just logged was not real. He chugged half the glass of water then let his fingers fall atop the keyboard to tap haphazardly while his mind still wandered.

"That's not how you spell Sedona," Marcy said. Billy had inadvertently entered "the end" in the Google search box and the results listing was inundated with references to prophecy and the year 2012. "Here." Marcy pulled the keyboard away from Billy's hands. "You drink some more water."

Billy sipped as Marcy searched for rentals in Sedona. The water did have a calming effect and by the time he'd emptied the plastic glass, the daydream of the little girl and the squeaky window had moved sufficiently into subconscious that he could concentrate on the choices Marcy had saved.

"Most of them are six- to twelve-month leases," she said, scrolling. "How long are we going to be there?" Marcy shifted the sunglasses that sat atop her head so that they would act as an anchor against the long bangs of black hair that kept falling in front of her face. She quickly looked from Billy's blank stare back to the computer screen. "Don't know, do we? I'll revise to see if there's any places with monthly terms." A few minutes later, she found two units, though not in the same complex, that accepted monthly arrangements. One was an efficiency apartment; the other was a one bedroom house located across the street from the efficiency's street address. "Six hundred for the efficiency and nine hundred for the house," she said.

"We'll split the costs." Billy pointed at the computer monitor. "We're in this together after all."

Marcy smiled but did not look at him and Billy was struck, again, by her beauty, her tan cheeks, her long, jet black hair, her manicured fingernails on the keyboard. He thought for a fraction of time that, perhaps, they should room together. Logic said that it would be cheaper that way. Lust said that it would provide opportunity. But he wasn't brave enough to make her the offer. She was at least ten years his senior. She had children. She was a fortuneteller for Christ's sake. How could his science and her mysticism live in unison, rest in the same house—sleep in the same bed.

"I'll take the efficiency," he offered. "I'm used to tight living arrangements. Besides, a small place will force me to be outside, exploring, trying to find out why in hell we went to Sedona in the first place." He pulled out his wallet and gave her his credit card.

While Marcy made the reservations, Billy's attention wandered again to the television. The midday news had just ended and a commercial was telling him about flat abs and the breakthrough nutritional supplement that would guarantee them.

With a great body and healthy nutrition...
You, too, can be a star with Popstar.
The only nutritional supplement you'll ever need.
Brought to you by BETH Pharmaceuticals,
Bringing **E**veryone **T**otal **H**ealth.

"Lies! Lies!"

Billy jerked around to the front of the restaurant.

"Hijo de putas! Hijo de putas!"

It was the woman he'd almost killed. She picked up a salt shaker from the nearest table and threw it at the TV. The shaker broke against the wall beside the flat screen.

"This is what it does to you. This is what they'll all do to you," she continued, enraged. Then she locked her attention on two men who sat near the television. "You...You!" She pointed. "Killers! Murderers! It's all your fault!" She stepped toward then men then suddenly rushed forward, her bare feet slapping the ceramic tiling. "You are the end!"

The man sitting on the left, stood. His funky-looking flip of blonde-white hair that tried to cover increasing baldness flopped down between his eyes.

"You are the end of us all!" the woman bellowed, and when she was within arm's reach, the man shoved forcefully with both hands. The sudden, halting impact snapped the woman's head forward then backward as she fell against the edge of one diner's table. Beans and rice and red sauce flew against the wall above the computers. A basket of tortilla chips and the squat cup of salsa next to it jumped across the toppling table and dropped on top of the woman as she fell. The thud of her head against ceramic tiling mixed almost seamlessly with the crackling of broken tortilla chips. The woman's body went limp.

"What the hell!" The man grumbled at the manager who came running from behind the service counter. "Is getting attacked a part of today's special?"

"Lo siento," the manager said; he was young enough to be a student at the university. "They sometimes do that." He paid no attention to the injured poor woman as he turned his complete customer service training on the old Mexican diner whose food had just taken flight. "Por favor, señor. Déjame ayudarte."

Billy didn't know how long his mouth had been open but he now closed it. Marcy snatched both credit cards from the kiosk then took Billy's hand. "Come on. We've got what we came for."

"But the woman..."

"No sense in getting involved."

Marcy pulled him from the stool but he paused as he stepped around the woman on the floor. The woman clenched a prescription bottle that had opened upon impact with the ceramic tile. Several of the pills had rolled out and now soaked into the Mexican salsa pooled between her fingers. The pills looked exactly like the ones in the commercial: the Popstar pills.

And the man she'd been screaming at, the one who was apparently the end of us all, the one whose bald head and flip of blonde-white hair that had not been covered by a John Deere hat, was the same guy who now sat two tables away from Billy in a Starbucks that was five months and five hundred miles away from that day in Las Cruces.

"No," Marcy insisted. "Please, Billy. It's not good to live with such paranoia."

"But it is!" His voice raised one octave too high. Deere-hat man and his buddy both peered more intently at them. How much had they already overheard? Billy wondered. These *were* the same men, paranoia be damned. He lowered his voice. "Let's get out of here." He shoved the glass dagger toward her. "You take this."

"Why? So I can ward off evil? So I can protect myself from your paranoia? I'm a fortuneteller not a mystic." It was evident that Marcy had momentarily lost her optimism but she took the dagger anyway and slipped it into her cloth handbag. "The things I put up with. And I thought scientists were stronger than this."

The Starbuck's waitress asked Billy if he wanted another iced coffee before they closed at midnight. Instead of answering, Billy quickly stood without acknowledging the two men and exited.

Marcy said to the waitress, "Sorry, hon. Looks like we're leaving. Is Roadrunner still making the rounds toward Cottonwood tonight?"

"Yeah. I think so." The waitress snatched the empty glass and cup and set them both on her tray. "For Black Friday, I think the shuttle is running an extended schedule. Earthquake might have messed that up though."

Marcy dropped two dollars on the table before leaving. She looked back at the two men and, simultaneously, both tipped the brims of their hats. The flip of blonde-white hair fell farther down the forehead of Deere-hat man and for a moment, Marcy stopped and stared. When Deere-hat man smiled at her, she quickly left.

Outside, Billy had already crossed the street and was, again, standing in front of Vor-Tech's Glass Menagerie. The store was closed. The display stand in the storefront window that had promoted Billy's new glass dagger now featured a glass replica of the Mayan calendar round; the top edge was chipped.

"Maybe," Marcy said, coming up from behind him. Billy didn't turn.

Vehicle traffic remained robust with late night shoppers traveling in search of the perfect Christmas bargain. Pedestrian traffic, however, was sparse in this part of West Sedona; most of the three or four adjacent street blocks were lined with mom and pop shops that had extended their businesses two hours past the usual nine o'clock closing time but were now closed. Other than Starbucks, only bars and nightclubs remained open.

"Maybe what?" Billy continued staring at the round glass calendar, wondering if what Marcy had told him really was true. Paranoia had taken root so completely that he was now seeing things and connecting things and fearing things that weren't really there. He considered how unscientific it all was. He considered how much he really had changed. He hated to admit how powerful suggestion was, how coincidence was more believable than fact, how myth and magic were mightier than Mensa. He absolutely hated to admit it.

"Maybe we are being followed or watched or…whatever you want to call it." Marcy grabbed his shoulder. "I got to admit that the one fella did look a lot like the man from Las Cruces."

"Please don't patronize. It's bad enough as it is. I didn't ask for any of this shit. I'm really thinking of going back to Port A, the surf, the serenity. I gotta get back to the restaurant. Kale can't manage it alone. Damn it all!"

Marcy placed her second hand on his other shoulder. "Do you really think going back there without finding what you came for is such a good idea? I thought you said you were given a duty—a mission to accomplish. Didn't you tell me you were supposed to save the world?"

Billy spun around so quickly that Marcy's hands remained on his shoulders. Her face was full of shadows that illuminated then darkened as cars and trucks rolled past. Flecks of white headlights and red taillights flickered against her eyes. "You said what? You said what? That's crazy!"

Marcy shook him, lightly. "You saw all of those people…all of the people who were your friends…all of those people who you cared about—dead. You might not want to believe it now but it's true. They came back to life and Janine and Alixel killed them—just like you said. How do you explain…"

"I don't. I can't. I won't. We have found nothing here to substantiate anything. Nothing!"

"There's Cooper."

"You mean the woman who was saved by a mythological storyteller who doubles as a mechanic. Woo-hoo!" Billy threw his arms in the air and Marcy's hands fell from his shoulders. "*I've* got a story—you wanna hear it? It's about two people who traveled a thousand miles to spend all of their money and time looking for ghosts. Punch me now and wake me up and I'll tell you how this story ends."

"Ghosts." Marcy said just as the Roadrunner shuttle stopped beside them. Its double doors opened and the driver asked if they were going to get on. "It's funny you should say that. Cooper told me she knew Professor Cower."

Billy's mouth hung open in disbelief. "But he's not real."

"Yes, he is. I've been trying to tell you all night." She grabbed his hand. "Come on. I'll explain everything."

Sedona's Roadrunner shuttle service was an easy and convenient method for getting around most of the town and its sister cities of Cottonwood and the Village of Oak Creek. Billy had used it almost exclusively since arriving, mostly because of its convenience but also because Stephanie Drake's Cavalier was just too full of too many memories. Every time he sat in the damn thing he remembered Steph being yanked inside and her neck snapping against the roof, how the driver's seat had been splattered with Steph's blood and how hard it had been to clean before they'd left Port A, how Steph's cubit had mewled at him, taunting him closer with those damned eyes roiling with red and silver sparkles of insanity. Whenever he did get the courage to drive the car, he'd always make sure Steph's SpongeBob was with him, the square, yellow character sitting happily on the dashboard as if the toy was some kind of guardian angel. And he'd always cry—not a slobbering waterfall of tears, but the kind where the eyes moisten for a fraction of time before the mind pulls them back in denial.

The shuttle was understandably busy this Friday-after-Thanksgiving evening. Shoppers and intoxicated bar crawlers flowed on and off as the shuttle slowly made its way toward the city limits. Billy and Marcy had rented a couple of places just south of Boynton Canyon—the shuttle would drop them about a mile or so away.

Throughout the entire trip through West Sedona, Billy silenced each attempt Marcy made to explain what Cooper had told her about Professor Cower. He just didn't trust any of the shadowy people that filtered through the aisle and shuffled in their seats, especially the guy wearing a John Deere cap that had boarded three blocks from Starbucks; he'd sat right in front of them. And when he'd started to turn in his seat, Billy thought about the Vor-Tech store owner's wife.

You'll know what to do when the time comes, she'd said.

Take care of her, she'd said.

The real Creation Dagger snuggled against his left breast had seemingly warmed up, as if it had known that the man who'd turned to ask for directions *was* Deere-hat man from Starbucks. And when Billy had asked the shuttle rider to remove his cap, just to see that no blonde-white flip of hair was present, the man whose hair was dark and curly turned abruptly away before moving to another seat.

The Creation Dagger had remained warm all the way through West Sedona to the point that it caused his breast to itch. His baggy shirt was actually sweat-stained from the casual heat. He had decided that the dagger's warming was a warning not to speak of such things like Cooper and Cower and Cubit in public…that such information could be used by the Evil that the dagger knew was present even if Billy saw nothing and no one that caused him alarm. Until…

They were a block away from their shuttle stop when Billy first noticed the red eyes. They peered from the very last row where a bench seat spread across the breadth of the shuttle's interior. They didn't glow as much as they reflected—a color of red that matched Sedona's red rocks.

Glaring circles of rust.

The shadowy figure behind the eyes did not move as Billy and Marcy rose to exit the shuttle, but when they stepped onto the sidewalk at the corner of Dry Creek Road and the shuttle drove off, he saw the eyes looking at them in the rear window. He told Marcy to look, quickly, to reassure him that they really weren't eyes at all but just simple window glass reflections, but by the time she looked up, the shuttle was too far away to really see anything inside except for the dim glow of one overhead reading lamp. The farther the shuttle receded into the distant darkness, the more Billy's dagger cooled until, finally, it was only as warm as his heart.

The walk wasn't long—at least it wasn't anymore. In five months, he'd traversed Dry Creek Road dozens of times. He knew that the words "Sam is an anus" was finger-stenciled into the concrete sidewalk at the corner of Thunder Mountain Road. He knew that after that intersection, there was only scantly paved sidewalk and that the remainder of the journey would be dusty underfoot and a bit too close to the road for anyone walking near midnight. The light of the moon often helped the sparse streetlights in illuminating what flora or fauna hugged the shallow berm, but tonight, the moonlight was missing—only a fingernail sliver dodged in and out of sparse clouds. Cacti and the creatures that lived near them were scattered mere feet from them.

"Cower came here a year ago," Marcy said after ten minutes of silence. Soft Arizona sand crunched as they walked.

Billy didn't respond but instead looked up from the dirt he'd been staring at and out across the landscape. Even this far from Highway 89, a few acres of dry earth had been cultivated into square lots of Spanish style homes. On another acre or two resided small businesses: a dentist's office, a touring agency, a spiritualist shop. It was because of the vortices. It was because of the shamans. It was because of the marketing hype that Billy believed anyone in their right mind would spend so much to build such extravagance in the heart of such wasteland. And the farther Dry Creek Road stretched toward Boynton Canyon, the sparser the landscape became and the fewer more extravagant homes had been built. This place, this manmade oasis in the middle of scorched hope, really was the perfect setting for blasphemous artifacts such as the Cubit. If Professor Cower had found it anywhere, Billy thought, Sedona was it.

A car approached from behind, its headlights bouncing against red rock silica which projected sparkles of rust from the ground into Billy's face. When he finally turned to acknowledge Marcy's statement, the car was a dozen feet behind them and its lights snapped from high beam to low. In that instant, whatever reflections that had taken hold of Marcy's silhouette dimmed. For a split second, her forehead, cheeks and nose had glowed with an aura of rust; her eyes had been saturated with the color. She was looking right at him when the car passed and her eyes reminded Billy of the shuttle passenger in the rear seat—*its* eyes…rust red reflections…full of memories…of Steph…of death…of massacre.

The car tooted its horn and Marcy blinked as did Billy. Marcy said, "Your eyes. They looked just like…"

"I know. Yours too. Sedona red. Just like…" Billy pushed the bad memories back. He shook his head, grabbed it, stood near a tall saguaro cactus, the faint street light glow dropping the cactus' meager shadow of a sombrero at his feet. Marcy took the single sidestep that was necessary to stand beside him, grabbed his shoulder and gently massaged it. The grip felt firm, almost manly strong, but reassuring and pleasant.

"Okay," she said. "Enough about the Cubit. Let's just enjoy the walk."

Within thirty minutes they reached Gringo Road, a T-intersection which did not cross Dry Creek Road. To the right, Gringo Road skittered and curled into the shadowed distance. A small, twelve-unit apartment complex stood on one corner; Billy's efficiency was among them. A single-level, one-bedroom home occupied a sparse lot of land across from the complex in a space where Gringo Road would have continued had developers found the need. Marcy lived there. Both stood at the intersection.

"You feel like talking some more?" Marcy asked. "I could put on a pot of coffee. I think I've got a couple of donuts left over from this morning."

Billy knew that sleep would be impossible anyway and believed that, even though such a discussion might pull him too far back into the recent past, such a verbal release might just be necessary medicine. He'd been keeping it all down for far too long. Five months of repression could not be good for the mental soul. Most professionals by now would have prescribed a couch and psychiatrist—someone who would listen without prejudice. Billy thought that a fortuneteller and a donut might serve as the perfect substitution. Billy thought that—just to be close to her, to listen to her sultry undertones, to be infused by her girlish giggles, her soft tanned skin, the way her red lips undulated and her red fingernails played with whatever she held in her hands—she could, indeed, sooth his torment. He was so tired and susceptible. He could think of no better place to be right now than in her room, within her arms…soothing words and red lips.

"What flavor?" he asked.

Marcy turned; more rusty red reflections bounced from the streetlamp, to the ground and into her eyes. "What?"

"The donuts. What flavor?"

She giggled. "Chocolate frosted and maybe one or two jelly-filled."

Billy grabbed her hand, which was comfortably cool, and together they crossed Dry Creek Road. Before entering Marcy's temporary cottage, Billy glanced back toward his own rental in an apartment complex named The Getaway. Steph's Cavalier sat all by itself near the far corner unit that Billy now called home.

Though the small Spanish cottage (they called them casitas in Sedona) had been furnished, Marcy had added many personal effects, so many in fact that Billy thought she would need a small U-haul trailer to get everything back to Port Aransas when they left.

Port A. He'd had another sudden squirt of homesickness that had shown Marcy a side of himself few would ever see: a man with a lack of control, weak, susceptible to suggestion, and easy to manipulate—a man who mirrored just about every other man on this planet—a man who could be convinced of just about anything as long as a good illusionist was around who knew how to pull just the right magic strings. Men like these were married to the Lanas of the world. Men like these believed that lust was love and that a few clicks across Internet porno screens always found satiation for such misguidedness. Lanas were everywhere and so where men that Billy never wanted to become, men like his father who was not married to a Lana but, instead, had always been married to an office, clients, and money. Men like that meant growing up fatherless and no child deserved a life like that. No one!

"What are you thinking so long and hard about?" Marcy poured two cups of coffee and set them next to a white box on the kitchen's round, glass tabletop. Billy stared out the ceiling-high bay window onto a black night that, in the morning, would reveal the distant Kachina Woman rock formation at the trailhead to Boynton Canyon. Marcy sat and sipped. "Come here. Sit down. Have a donut. You'll feel all sugary better."

Her words made him think about what the Oracle said to Neo in the movie *The Matrix*.

Here, take a cookie. I promise, by the time you're done eating it, you'll feel right as rain.

He really wasn't the same man anymore. He actually felt as if he was inside a computer generated program, one that kept tossing his emotional well-being as easily as the Smith had tossed Neo the first time they met. Cookies nor donuts would ever make him feel right as anything again. He remained standing, his back to her.

"We've been here five months and nothing," he said. "Then all of a sudden the earth shakes and revelations come tumbling out. We've talked to dozens of people and have visited dozens of places only to find what we already knew. Sedona is a spiritual mecca where lost people come to try and hide from reality. That's why Cower came here. That's why anyone comes here."

"I don't think so."

Billy turned abruptly. "No!?" His voice was unintentionally aggravated and loud.

Marcy stared at the donut box; one finger tapped the glass top of the table. "No. I told you. Cooper knows something…really knows something. But, what does it matter now anyway? Seems like you've lost your belief in this whole thing."

Billy turned back toward the window panes. Something moved through the darkness outside. It was low to the ground: a prairie dog perhaps. He followed its rust red eyeball reflections as it scooted past shadowy short desert trees and cacti. "Do *you* still believe?" he asked.

"Of course I do. I've left my kids with my ex for far too long to no longer believe." Marcy stood and stepped beside him. "How can you just throw away all of what has happened? You saw it for yourself. You experienced it. You killed for it."

Billy couldn't face her because she was right. He did, however, find a distant comfort in seeing her reflection in the window. Another prairie dog's rusty eyes moved across the blackness in front of her image.

Marcy continued. "I know you have a hard time believing in fate, that events aren't merely coincidence. Even when the cosmic tumblers turn square up in your face you deny it. Now that takes guts." Billy wanted her to touch him but she didn't. He wanted to touch her but he couldn't…he just couldn't. "Think of it this way. What about all of those believers out there? What happens when you, the scientist, try to explain away what they feel is true in their souls. No matter how many facts and figures you give them, they don't listen—do they?"

Billy's head shook involuntarily.

"These people—these faith seekers will deny every piece of evidence you place in front of them no matter how convincing because, like you, they are so rooted and without an open mind that science does not connect for them just as faith doesn't seem to connect for you."

The memories started resurfacing and Billy, again, tried to seal them.

"You saw Steph as a cubit. You saw what Evil was within her. You saw the manifestation of her darkest half. You know this is what the Cubit does to people. Are you so blind as to disregard these accounts? Your own eye-witnessed facts?"

"No!" Billy turned away from the window and quickly walked to the adjoining living room. He sat on the couch which Marcy had dressed up with frilly pillows and a black comforter. He grabbed the sides of his head with both hands and stared at the hardwood floor. "Is that how you do it? Is that how fortunetellers and mystics and all of the John Edwards of the world do it? Grab a person's emotions, ask a few questions, spin answers into confusion, rearrange emotions and continue until a person starts believing?"

Marcy remained in the kitchen but she wouldn't back down. "You… saw…her. And *you* killed Bottlenose. And the sand pile blew up to the heavens. And Alixel…you told me she was some kind of God or something."

"No. No! I was wrong. It didn't happen. People don't eat people."

"And the Cubit isn't real even though you said you saw it in the bank's vault."

"I never saw anything but a wooden crate."

"And the Book of the Djed isn't real either. You never saw it write anything all by itself."

"Yes. Of course the Book is real. But I never saw…"

"And the daggers? You used one to kill Bottlenose. It burned a mark in your hand for Christ's sake."

That's where the argument ended since, as soon as she said it, Billy lowered his right hand from the side of his head. The pentagram that occupied the haft of the Creation of the End dagger scared his palm. Most of the fleshy pink star points were still easily distinguishable, especially the point in the lower right quadrant—the point in which a red jade had blazed brilliantly at the moment he'd driven the dagger into the back of Bottlenose's skull. He dropped his right hand to his heart where the Creation of the End dagger rested in a sheath under his shirt.

And then he cried. This time the tears came as an endless waterfall. He fell back onto the couch and grabbed a frilly pillow to cover his embarrassment.

Marcy came to him then. She pushed the pillow aside and covered his forehead with her lips. "I'm sorry," she said. "Why don't you stay here tonight? Being alone might not be such a great idea."

As if her permission had been the enabler, Billy felt himself suddenly falling asleep. He blinked twice, the tears rolling down both cheeks, and the last thing he remembered was her blurred, red lips and the cold touch of a red fingernail.

The second time that Cooper Reyes would actually see the walking dead was on Black Friday, the night of the Sedona earthquake. The eerie similarities between the two incidents—the one last year and the one that was about to happen, would have her questioning her very sanity.

An anonymous email earlier that morning had directed her to The Y. She was to sit in this exact chair at this exact table under the outdoor terrace of the Café Aus at two in the morning, or "shortly after the bars close" as the email had demanded.

"Hey Coop."

The voice from behind startled her. It was Luke, an Australian, and the restaurant's manager.

"We're shuttin' down. You want one more before I turn the key?"

Her sweaty glass of iced tea sat half full in front of folded arms. A lick of strawberry-blonde curl fell over one eye. "Got what I need," she said. "And, hey." She turned at the waist toward him. "Thanks for letting me hang out past closing."

"No worries. Your fella stood you up, did he?"

Cooper grinned. "Who says I'm waiting for a fella?"

"Good luck." Luke waved. "And be careful."

Cooper habitually waved in reply though her arm stopped halfway through the second wave.

Be careful, she thought. This was certainly a time to be careful. The anonymous email had implied danger and irrationality.

Situated just west of The Y, the Café Aus provided the perfect roost for anyone interested in people watching. Tonight was no exception. There were lovers and transients and professionals (with a few professional transients thrown in for good measure). The display of vehicles still cruising under the

Friday night lamplights were just as varied: clunker to classic to cavalier, including a flower-painted VW Bus that spewed blue smoke, and more than one Hummer floating on lift kits that were as tall as their tires were wide.

People watching had always been one of Cooper's favorite habits. She loved leading tours into Red Rock Country as much for the quirky habits and personalities of her tour groups as she did for the enjoyment of teaching them about this part of Arizona. The habit had been ingrained by her Psych 404 professor at Arizona State University nearly eight years ago. Dr. Doer had enjoyed giving her students assignments she'd called "people peeking" (her creative term for people watching), assignments that had helped her own research more often than it had helped student learning. But Dr. Doer had been an easy A as long as you fulfilled her survey requirements and mastered her four, thirty-page reports, most of which had been a permanent part of the Greek cheat filing system for some time. "People peeking," the doctor had said, "is an inherent gratification activity meant to ratify the abnormality of an abnormal life." Under that definition, everyone was abnormal and you couldn't walk a step without running into someone needing therapy, including yourself.

Cooper remained at the table for another thirty minutes before she began to feel uneasy. People peeking had all but dried up. Most of the pedestrian crowd had abruptly disappeared, as if some Morlock bellow had suddenly filled the evening with the threat of Eloi casualty. At around 2:45, she saw (and naturally started to analyze) a man who could not find his center of gravity. The guy was in his twenties and seemed to be a happy drunk. When he tripped into the iron railing that marked the café porch's perimeter and pushed off of the railing before stumbling momentarily into the street, Cooper almost stood.

"Naw," the man slurred. "Ya'll go on ahead. Ol' Digger'll be jess fine."

Cooper didn't know if the man was talking to her or an imaginary character, one that often springs forth from the intoxicated mind. She'd learned all about that psychosis from her substance abuse class. Drunks often made friends out of inanimate objects and people that just weren't there.

The man stumbled onward for another half a block, partially on the brick paver sidewalk and partially on the concrete road, before staggering into an alley between Charleys coffee shop and a branch of the First Arizona Bank where an ATM machine's blue signage traced the man's silhouette into the darkness.

Cooper had to laugh. She was nervous and, admittedly, even a little frightened. The comic tickle that teased the back of her throat relieved the tension when it finally surfaced. She raked short fingers through her short, strawberry-blonde hair and dropped the hand to her knee.

Not going to happen, she thought. *It's not going to happen because no one knows where it is.*

It was the reason why she was sitting here. *It* was the location of the Great Hall of the Anasazi, the place where the Cubit had been kept. The anonymous emailer had said that she could obtain a map here, tonight, at the Café Aus, after the bars closed. Apparently, it was just a ruse—just another jokester who was now happy to have pulled one over on Cooper Reyes, Sedona's answer for those who wished to find spirits within the red rocks.

She stood with the intention of leaving but, instead, sat back down when her bare knee rubbed against something that wasn't the table. She reached under the wrought iron top and yanked it free. Because it was wrapped within a plastic bag that read *Sedona Red Rock News*, Cooper thought that it was a newspaper. The clear tape that had fastened the bag to the table snatched three of her fingers and she struggled to pull the stickiness free. She untwisted the wire bag tie, unfolded the closure and looked inside—gently, carefully—as if something might jump out and bite her.

And that's when she heard the scream; it came from the direction that the stumbling drunk had gone. She thought that the man had finally fallen onto, into or through something. When the second scream echoed from the same direction, she decided that he might have hurt himself to a degree that necessitated some help.

She retied the newspaper bag, moved from the table and hopped the fencing, her short, athletic frame easily managing the iron railing's hip height.

Traffic was very light. She passed one old man walking in the opposite direction and wondered why he, too, was not investigating the screams. He didn't look at her; his eyes were locked on his feet.

She walked into the alley unalarmed for her own safety, her mind recounting every volume of first aid knowledge (which was necessarily broad for a guide who escorted ignorants through rattlesnake country) that might be needed to save a poor drunken man from himself. Only two dim halogens interrupted the vast shadows that filled the length of the alley. She had walked its one hundred yards in bright daylight on many occasions but never at night. It wasn't like there was anything to be afraid of—she wasn't in New York City for crying out loud—she was in Sedona, Arizona. The alley wasn't constructed of tall brick buildings and fire escapes and large smelly trash bins housing cats and rats and robbers. A Sedona alley was more like one you'd find in an old western movie, a shortcut for townspeople to get from one end of the town to the other. Cooper knew that at the end of this particular alley a person could turn left and walk a narrow passage en route to a small desert botanical garden one local resident had made from the land he owned.

She quickly moved to the end of the alley but stopped before stepping into the passage when she heard the argument.

"I won't let you," one voice threatened—and to Cooper it sounded like a threat: masculine, bold, forceful.

A second voice, female, retaliated. "You. Won't let? What can you do without the dagger?"

It was at that point when Cooper, again, remembered the first time she'd seen the living dead. Professor Cower had killed it with a dagger.

"The earthquake has done its job," the woman's voice screeched with an echo that reverberated within the passage. "The location of the Great Hall has been revealed. It's all just one more step toward the inevitable."

"Your death?" The male voice.

"Without the dagger? Without the Cubit?" The female voice.

"That no longer matters." The male.

"Liar. Are you now so lost as to wallow in a pit of denial?" The female.

"You know as well as I that Cower stole it. You don't have it either." Male.

"Oh, but we do." Female.

"We?"

And then the passageway lit up in what Cooper thought was a blaze of fire. She slowly stepped toward the passage, her back scratching against swirls of stucco wall, suddenly wondering if either of the two combatants in the passageway had anything to do with the anonymous email she'd received. When she reached the corner that, with one more step, would entwine her into the scuffle, she peeked forward; her cheek felt as if it were glowing.

Each combatant was dressed in costume, the kind ancient Mesoamerican warriors wore, complete with ceremonial headdress and mask. The one on the left had a face that resembled a wild, spotted cat, perhaps a jaguar. The one on the right wore a mask that resembled the sun embossed by the face of a featureless man. The sun face glowed with a brilliance that Cooper assumed was the source of the heat.

"You can't kill me," the jaguar said in its female voice.

"And nor can I die," replied the manly sun. "But I can sure make you remember what pain feels like."

When the sun stabbed the jaguar in the heart with a long, broadsword, Cooper covered her mouth to prevent the escape of an audible gasp. When the broadsword struck the second time, cleanly severing the head from the jaguar, she squeaked and quickly dodged back around the passageway corner. She pulled her iPhone from the pocket of her jeans and was greeted by the anonymous email that had brought her here. She wiped the message away with a forefinger and dialed 911. A second later, she hung up. The cops couldn't get involved. They'd confiscate what she'd found under the table and then where would she be? Back to zero.

Again, slowly, with a single eyeball, she braved the corner. The jaguar stood headless, leaning against the back wall of Charleys coffee shop. The sun warrior lifted its broadsword for a second strike and kicked the jaguar's head toward Cooper, a thick black-red blood oozing from the neck and splattering the brick paving in blotches of gooeyness as it wobbled to a stop a few feet from her. The sun warrior slashed downward but the woman jaguar, without her head, quickly dodged the blade and drew from her waist what looked to Cooper like…

A dagger! But not a dagger at the same time…at least not the same kind of dagger that she saw Cower use to kill the walking dead a year ago.

The headless jaguar thrust the glittering blade into the chest of the man in the sun mask. And Cooper squeaked again, her hand rising too slowly to squelch the sound this time. Both combatants turned simultaneously, the jaguar without a head, the sun with a dagger implanted near the heart.

"Ma'am?"

The voice came from behind. Cooper shrieked and dropped the newspaper bag. When she turned, the police officer's flashlight beam hit her square in the face.

"Ma'am. What's going on here? Who's with you in the alley?"

"I don't know who they are but they have weapons."

The officer's free hand dropped to his holster, releasing the gun strap. He grabbed the mic dangling from one shoulder and called for backup as he drew his weapon. "Stay here," he said.

But Cooper didn't stay. She'd seen enough. She snatched up the newspaper bag and ran back the way she'd entered. Behind her, three quick cracks of gunfire riddled the acoustics of the alley. And then a scream.

Cooper escaped the police backup by running into the tree line that paralleled Oak Creek. Her jeep was parked several blocks away. She could get there undetected but she'd have to follow the creek, atop uneven ground, between patches of city lamplight and complete darkness. She gripped her new treasure, believing that, if she tripped and fell or dropped the newspaper bag into the water, the Great Hall would be lost forever...again.

Slowly, she crept along the creek bank, slipping on the first rock her shoe touched.

THE DJED: PART II

THE DAYKEEPER

Billy's Saturday morning filled him with such panic that he immediately reached for his heart. As his eyes struggled to unglue themselves from the dried and crusty remnants of last night's sorrow, he saw Marcy with his Creation Dagger. She was washing it in the kitchen sink. When she noticed that he had awakened, she said, "Looks beautiful all shined up." Billy traced the outline of the real dagger under his shirt as Marcy continued. "Even if the point is broken, it's still quite a find."

Billy expelled one long, gasping breath then daintily swung his legs from couch to floor. He rubbed his eyes.

Marcy turned off the kitchen faucet and wrapped a hand towel around the glass curio they'd gotten from Vor-Tech's Glass Menagerie. She walked to the fireplace within the wall opposite the couch and held the dagger above the mantle where a collection of other Sedona novelties and collectibles had already found a home. Her lips and fingernails were still red but her long robe was jet black. It did not have frills; it did not have lace. The robe was light and airy—almost see-through. Imagining what was underneath the soft, thin cloth was easy to do since it clung to Marcy's body at the hips and hugged each breast with cuddly care.

"What do you think?" she said, never taking her eyes off of Billy as her arm remained stretched out to the side and above the mantle, the dagger resting in the palm of that hand.

Billy, in his early morning grogginess, thought about many possible responses, not the least of them was one that might have had Marcy forgetting all about the dagger with interests more tuned to showing Billy how accurate his X-ray vision really was. He also thought that a proper response might have had something to do with how the dagger in no way fit with the Native American worship motif she'd chosen to display above and around the fireplace. Twinkling glass menageries didn't seem to have a place among hand-carved peace pipes, feathered headdresses, symbols of ancient animal and planetary gods and one dreamcatcher. But what he actually said was, "Who needs a fireplace in Sedona, Arizona?"

Marcy set the dagger on top of a black wad of silk cloth right next to what looked to Billy like (and just might have been, knowing Marcy) a pair of testicles. She giggled. The dagger's broken point touched the balls atop the oval nibs as if it had been the dagger that had performed the castration. "It'll get chilly enough for it in another couple of months. Besides, fireplaces at any time of the year are so romantic. Don't you think?" She didn't wait for an answer. "What would you like for breakfast?" She strolled back to the kitchen, her robe taking its time to catch up with the back of her legs. Billy stood from the couch and pressed what wrinkles he could from his shirt and shorts, then walked to the fireplace. Somehow, the balls that looked like testicles turned his stomach when Marcy added, "How about a couple of boiled eggs?"

"Nothing for me, thank you. I've got some energy bars that need my attention across the street."

Marcy cracked and peeled two boiled eggs. Billy refused to watch her; the eggs' smell added an additional churning attachment to the testicles.

"How much do you think it's worth?" Marcy asked, a shaker of salt in one hand and a fresh bite of egg in her mouth. "If you don't want it, I'll be glad to take it off of your hands. If I can't have the real thing, might as well."

"Not sure. Without the broken tip, I imagine it might have gone for a pretty penny. At least that's what the store owner seemed to imply."

"It is curious why he just gave it to us." Marcy finished one egg and sprinkled salt on the second while walking over to stand next to Billy. The boiled egg smell was overpowering and melted away what visions of nakedness Billy had recorded. He turned away and walked to the bay window where, last night, prairie dog eyes had glared in at him. The box of donuts still sat on the kitchen table and he almost grabbed one, but then he saw Marcy. He'd never imagined what Cher eating a boiled egg might look like but now it was all too easy. White and yellow mush peeked through red lips as she chewed. "You might get him down to a hundred bucks," he said. "Perhaps offer him a barter if he's into the tarot card, crystal ball thing."

Marcy returned to the kitchen to wash her hands and pour a cup of coffee from the space saver coffee maker under one cabinet. "Hey. That's not a bad idea. Are you sure you want to give it up? I know how much those things mean to you."

She swished the egg from her teeth with coffee and Billy was, again, able to look at her without grimacing. "No, really. Go ahead. I think it was probably meant for you anyway."

"What do you mean?"

Billy glanced over at the glass dagger. It had captured a beam of sunlight that had found its way through a separation between the Venetian blinds that covered the window beside the front door. A rainbow band of colors bathed the rest of her collection with an aura that seemed almost protective, almost sacred. Even the balls that looked like testicles appeared angelic. "It fits perfectly there on the mantle, don't you think?"

Marcy nodded. "You sure you don't want something to eat?"

"Naa. I gotta get going. Today's shopping day; time to restock my own cabinets. You know me, always the consummate health food nut." He slipped on his sandals. "Thanks for letting me crash here last night and thanks for listening with a critical ear. Everyone needs a little hard love every now and then."

"I hope I wasn't too harsh." Marcy leaned backward at the hips across the kitchen countertop, her breasts pointing north of her chest.

"Like I said…" Billy went to the front door. "Slapdowns are a necessary part of any relationship." He opened the door. Marcy's voice followed him outside.

"We should do this more often."

Billy nodded. "I'll get a hold of you later. Maybe we can talk some more about Cooper."

He tried not to look at her as he closed the door.

When Cooper had finally gotten home last night, she'd anxiously opened the newspaper bag and had gently unrolled a current edition of the *Sedona Red Rock News* to find, buried within its pages, a sheet of brown parchment paper. She was certain that she would find a map; that's what the anonymous emailer had promised. But what was written on only one side of the parchment certainly was no map, at least not any kind of map that she had envisioned. Maps had arrows and Xs and recognizable geography that the treasure hunter was supposed to stitch and knit and decipher.

So she'd stuck the parchment to her bedroom wall with masking tape, had taken off her clothes, and had sat there in her underwear, staring at the three Mayan glyphs and ten scattered dots, trying to find some meaning to them by mentally connecting the dots in a dozen different patterns, trying to understand why two of the three glyphs looked so much like the sun and jaguar she'd seen in the alley behind Charleys. She'd sat and stared until she'd fallen asleep. Her subconscious had done the rest. Her resting mind had connected the dots.

When she awakened Saturday morning, she almost leapt from the bed and ran over to the small desk she used to do all of her business-related paperwork. The bottom drawer of the desk was the one she used to organize folders. From it, she plucked a larger, bulging, manila envelope that was labeled "Vortex," dropped it on top of the desk and pulled out much of its contents. Any time she'd run across information related to energy vortices she'd always stuff it into this envelope. The information didn't necessarily need to be Sedona specific (there were energy vortices all over the world) and that was probably the reason why it was so full. She'd often thought about organizing the contents better, using different envelopes for the different vortex locations, but had never quite gotten around to it.

She shuffled through flyers and pamphlets and pictures and personal experience letters from places like Tibet, the Egyptian pyramids, the Bermuda Triangle, Easter Island and the Incan ruins until she found what she was looking for and yanked it from the stack. A sticky note was attached. On it was written, "The immortality of the stars." Chris Cower had given this to her. Cower had written the note. The very thought of him made her shiver. Goosebumps popped out across the entire surface of her exposed skin. How could she have been such a fool? How could she have given that old son-of-a-bitch her body? He'd lied to her. He'd set her up. She angrily pulled the sticky note from the paper and haphazardly threw it.

The drawing on the sheet of paper was of what Cower had described as Sedona's leylines, patterns of energy that flowed through Red Rock Country. The patterns were in the shapes of two stars, one six-sided and one five-sided. Most of the named rock formations in and around Sedona marked the points of the stars. The two stars came together at a common location: the Airport Mesa, one of Sedona's most popular tourist attractions.

Cooper walked to the parchment paper stuck to her wall and held Cower's drawing out in front of her. The points in the drawing matched the

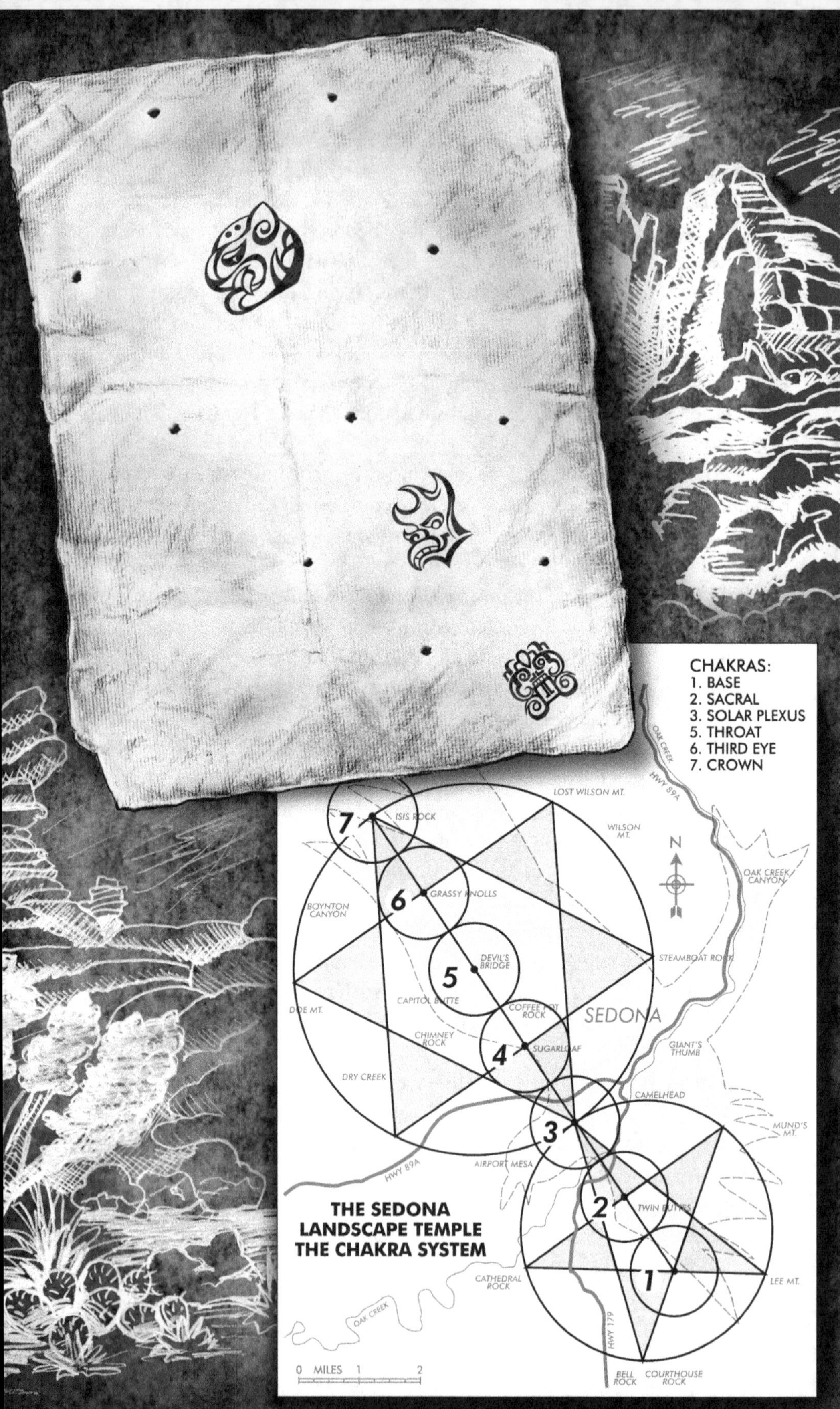

CHAKRAS:
1. BASE
2. SACRAL
3. SOLAR PLEXUS
5. THROAT
6. THIRD EYE
7. CROWN
LOST WILSON MT.
ISIS ROCK
WILSON MT.
N
OAK CREEK
HWY 89A
OAK CREEK CANYON
GRASSY KNOLLS
BOYNTON CANYON
DEVIL'S BRIDGE
STEAMBOAT ROCK
CAPITOL BUTTE
DOE MT.
COFFEE POT ROCK
SEDONA
CHIMNEY ROCK
SUGARLOAF
GIANT'S THUMB
DRY CREEK
CAMELHEAD
MUND'S MT.
HWY 89A
AIRPORT MESA
TWIN BUTTES
THE SEDONA LANDSCAPE TEMPLE THE CHAKRA SYSTEM
CATHEDRAL ROCK
LEE MT.
OAK CREEK
HWY 179
0 MILES 1 2
BELL ROCK
COURTHOUSE ROCK
1
2
3
4
5
6
7

dots on the parchment. She traced the two star patterns with a forefinger. As the pad of the finger touched each of the points, she named several of them: Steamboat Rock, Cathedral Rock, Twin Buttes, Lee Mountain, Airport Mesa.

So the Sedona leylines were actually a map? she thought. And all of this time, she'd had the map to the Great Hall of the Anasazi buried in an envelope in her desk?

Visualizing the two stars on the parchment, she determined that the Mayan glyph of the jaguar was centered inside the six-point star; the sun glyph was centered in the five-point star. The third glyph, one she had never seen before, was isolated all by itself in the lower right corner of the parchment. She sketched a mental diagonal line that intersected the centers of the two stars and the lonely third glyph, but that really didn't decipher anything. She supposed that the obvious might be the answer: the Great Hall was located at one of the two stars' ten points. But with that kind of reasoning, the intersection of the lines that connected the points could also be locations, or perhaps the center of the stars were locations, or the middle of the crossing lines, or…the number of possibilities could be dozens. Finding it would take forever, even if this was a map, even if this wasn't another diversion, even if this wasn't…

And then she thought of something that set her blood on ice. What if Cower had returned? Could that have been him last night, dressed as the sun? Had he left her the message and the screwed up map? Cower had used her once and he was using her again. Right?

She threw Cower's leyline sketch onto the bed then shook her head more out of shame than from a nonverbal refusal to believe that Chris Cower was even alive. She glanced away from the parchment to her flat belly and to the waistband of her white panties, remembering how he'd taken her, his sixty-year-old body desiring her thirty-year-old youth. She was forbidden fruit, the only kind of fruit that Chris Cower ate. Young lust. Right out there on the back porch where many of her private tour groups had feasted, where the spiritual energies of the masculine and feminine had pulsed through both of them, blinding them, taking them to places they should never have gone.

She walked the four short steps to the mirrored sliding doors of her closet and just stood there, all five-foot-four of her, never looking her own self in the face, the same forefinger that had traced star patterns on the parchment paper now tracing the tight lines on either side of her dark-skinned abdomen, her other hand snatching a firm grip of one hip and strong buttocks. She flipped strawberry-blonde curls from her forehead with one quick jerk of her head and this forced her eyes to lock on her own facial reflection. Her appearance was convincingly Hopi except for the hair which she attributed to her real

Puerto Rican ancestry.

"Is he here?" she said to her reflection. "God help me if he is. God prevent me from killing the son-of-a-bitch."

And as if God was actually going to answer at that very moment, her iPhone rang, its vibration causing it to skitter atop the lamp table beside her bed, its sudden shrill echo causing nerves to skitter up her spine.

She stepped quickly to the bed and sat, scooping up the phone at the same time. She did not recognize the incoming number. "Hello," she said.

"Cooper Reyes?"

The voice was only slightly familiar. "Speaking."

"My name is Marcy Ruminski. Perhaps you remember me from yesterday?"

"Of course. How are you? How's the car?" Cooper was only being polite. She cared much less for the condition of Marcy's vehicle and much more about the conversation they'd had on the way back from the accident, yesterday. She stared at the ten dots and three glyphs on the parchment.

"I suspect Les will get both of our vehicles back to us on Monday. Keep the fingers crossed." After a moment of silence, Marcy continued. "Listen. The reason I called is to ask you what your schedule might be like for the next day or so."

This was the woman who'd asked her about the Cubit. This was the woman who'd talked about Cower. Might she know something about this map? Might she even be involved? Their random meeting yesterday was just too coincidental. "I'm free for the most part," she said.

"My friend and I would love to exchange more info concerning some of the—"

There was a long pause during which Cooper thought about Cower, and Cower's book, and the Great Hall.

Marcy continued. "Well, I promised I'd call."

"Yes," Cooper said. "Why don't you and your friend come over to my house. I'll fix us up a good old-fashioned Sedona fiesta, one that's good for thinking and sharing and, well…understanding."

"Sounds great. Shall we say five-ish?"

"Five it is unless I hear otherwise from you. Need a ride?"

"Actually, we're only a mile from you. We'll walk over."

Cooper hung up, dropped the phone on her bed and just sat there, numb. A complete stranger knew Chris Cower, she thought. A complete stranger wanted to talk to her about a man she loathed. Her fingers drummed lightly against one thigh as she thought about the stranger named Marcy, about how they'd met, about what had been said.

Cooper had been traveling toward the canyon with a group to celebrate what she termed "Red Friday." Cooper had always despised the day after Thanksgiving and the way corporate America had turned it into some kind of shopping spree. So she'd created an alternative. Red Friday was meant for those who realized, as she did, that no day was *meant* for shopping and that every day provided another chance to reconnect with the beauty of the world. Red Friday was their (and her) deliverance from the madness that Madison Avenue had created.

She'd hit the pothole with one rear tire doing forty-five, which had immediately caused it to explode. Marcy had been behind her and had struck the same pothole with the same tire. Until now, Cooper had never really considered how convenient that had been. Who in their right mind would hit the same obstacle they just saw someone else hit? The natural reaction would be to swerve out of the way. It was almost as if the stranger had hit it on purpose.

Also convenient was that Marcy had known someone who could, with just one call on the day after Thanksgiving, send help that would have everything taken care of in less than an hour: Cooper's touring van and Marcy's rental each had their own tow truck; a separate van had been sent to escort the Red Friday tour group back to town; and Les, the mechanic, had driven them home himself.

Sitting in the backseat of Les' 1972 Chevelle (one that he continually had boasted as the best car ever made), Marcy had started asking questions. How long had she lived here? What did she do for a living? Had she ever heard of a Djed or a Cubit? Did she know of a man named Cower? Just like that. Right out the blue. A complete stranger. Had she met Marcy on Saturday instead of Friday, if she would have met her after the anonymous email and the incident in the dark alley, she probably wouldn't have told her a thing.

Why do you ask? Cooper had said.

A friend and I are trying to figure out a mystery that was left on our doorstep, Marcy had replied.

By Cower?

Yes. By Cower.

Because of Cooper's spite for Cower, and because her first assumption was that Marcy was some sort of undercover agent looking to put Cower away for life, she'd told the stranger that she'd known Chris Cower almost a year ago and that she hadn't seen him since.

The short drive from the accident to Cooper's house had not provided enough time for further details, but both had agreed that they should continue the discussion later. Cooper had given Marcy her number and Marcy had said she would call.

But that had been before the map and the earthquake and the headless jaguar. That had been before she'd seen the walking dead for the second time and had remembered how Cower had confronted his own Evil before leaving Sedona for good. That had been before, once again, the world had started turning upside down right on top of her.

One of the few times that Billy did drive Steph's Cavalier was when he needed to restock his kitchen cabinets. He would always purchase enough to last him several weeks so that the necessity to drive remained limited.

As he waited to turn left from Gringo Road onto Dry Creek, he looked past the smiling face of SpongeBob Squarepants to the front door of Marcy's casita where, less than an hour ago, he'd left a beautiful woman dressed in a scant, black robe, standing alone by her kitchen sink. Admittedly, he'd been as close as ever to acting on twenty-three-year-old urges, those that swallow common sense for the chance at fulfilling fantasies associated with younger men and older women. But to succumb would have opened doors that he was too paranoid to walk through. It wasn't so much the idea that Marcy was a friend and that to screw a friend meant forever changing a good relationship as it was the concern that to do so would reveal too much of himself. Too many psychological secrets were always revealed once climax was shared between two people. Moreover, he couldn't succumb because of the tacit pact he'd made with Alixel to never reveal that he possessed the Creation of the End dagger. Of course, he could have simply dropped his drawers and taken her with his shirt still on (a notion he'd already imagined several times), but he was always too paranoid, too shy, too chicken to attempt even that feat. At any time, he could have unclasped the sheath, storing it from sight before revealing himself, but that would mean that the dagger would be out of reach, if only for a moment, and he just couldn't let that happen. He would be unprotected and mentally naked, and this would dull any attempt to fulfill physical fantasies.

Billy's attention to the Cavalier's brake pedal slipped as he pondered, causing the car to creep into the intersection. It was the blast of the tour bus horn that simultaneously slapped his daydreaming and caused the muscles of his right leg to mash his foot forward. The bus swerved into a vacant left lane. Passengers' faces pressed against tinted glass as the bus missed the front of the Cavalier by a foot. Most of their expressions promoted surprise—gaping mouths, bugging eyes, lips drawn downward—but two of the passengers near the back of the bus flipped him off—city dwellers, perhaps, that were used to aberrant drivers that didn't pay attention. ***Boynton Canyon Express*** was emblazoned on the side of the bus below their faces. ***Feel the Vortex***, the slogan read. ***Escape the Rudimentary***.

Rudimentary, Billy thought. *Nothing about life will ever be rudimentary again.*

His first stop was Walmart where he always purchased inexpensive necessities for hygiene, house cleaning and cooking. He made quick work of this hated chore, speeding quickly through the aisles, wanting to leave the pack of humanity that was taking far too much advantage of Sam Walton's family heritage that promoted a plethora of Christmas marketing schemes.

The checkout line was long enough that he had the opportunity to (and, really, it was hard not to) gaze at all of the "temptation" items stocked on either side.

2012 Prophets Agree:
It's the End of the World as We Know It.

The bold headline that topped the most recent issue of *National Enquirer* was within arms' reach and he tried not to look at it; he convinced himself *not* to grab it. He *would not* avail himself unto the Walmart clientele that he, too, held enough mystical curiosity to read such nonsense. More so, he didn't want to admit to himself that his mind was full of enough uncertainty to even consider what the tabloid contained. He was not like these people. He didn't believe in such drivel, did he?

But the simple fact was, he really didn't know—not anymore. Even as a scientist he'd always understood that some things just couldn't be explained. As a protective mechanism, these things labeled "unexplained" he'd always stored safely away from consciousness. It was a seldom-accessed mind vault (at least it had been); its content was similar to that found in the X-drawer of the steel cabinet in Fox Mulder's office—unique collections of unique experiences, catalogued and waiting for evidence that could move them out of the unexplained vault and into reason. Education had helped him move a lot of that stuff out. Multiple experiences (also referred to as age and wisdom) had helped to empty it as well. But then there were the intangibles.

Regardless of your smarts or how long you'd lived, a person's degree of malevolence toward science or reticence toward mysticism always directly affected the contents of that "U-File," the mind's vault of stored anomalies. Some people could explain the existence of UFOs just as easily as they could a peanut butter sandwich; their U-File on this subject was empty.

Being a doctor or a dropout didn't matter. Either could produce evidence that supported their truth. But for Billy, such evidence based purely on faith and belief were different matters altogether. Faith and Belief always acted as temporary storage containers, as the intangibles, for all of his ideas that never quite made sense, ideas that could not simply be catalogued as real or unexplained. These were the ideas that never really made it into Billy's U-File but, instead, hung around outside like unwanted trash, waiting to be converted into understood knowledge or unexplained ignorance, perhaps never to find a proper home as either.

Marcy had plugged into that concept last night. She might not have realized it, but she had used it against him…or perhaps to help him. Billy had way too much information orbiting the U-File, in a place of suspended animation as it were, where the label was neither "reality" or "unexplained" but was instead being processed by faith and belief.

Someone grumbled behind him and Billy pushed his cart to fill the empty space ahead. He could now see that the lower half of the *Enquirer* contained several mug shots of world figures: Osama Bin Laden, Dick Cheney, Pope Benedict, Hu Jintao, and a man whose name was familiar but not the face: Richard Manson. Below the mug shots was written:

Would the Real AntiChrist Please Stand Up?

"Sick," the old woman behind him said. She hunched over the eggs and bread in an overflowing shopping cart and was staring at the *Enquirer*.

Billy blinked. "I agree. Such drivel."

The woman continued as if he'd not even spoken. "How could they even consider that poor Dick Cheney is the Antichrist when everyone knows it's Obama."

"You mean Osama."

"No. I mean our president, Obama Bin Laden."

Billy turned away from the woman, knowing full well that one of her belief containers had mistranslated some knowledge into her own reality. To her, the new president was the Antichrist and there wasn't a soul on the planet that would ever convince her otherwise.

"Grab it or go," the checkout girl urged since he'd not placed any of his items on the conveyor. The old woman scowled as if he, too, would soon be entered on her list of Antichrists.

His second stop was the Health Heaven Haven, one of the largest wholesome food store outlets in Arizona. "Fresh", "non-genetically engineered", "organic" and "natural" were words spread out in mass throughout the store—words that had become mantra to Billy since he'd left Massachusetts for island-living in Port Aransas two and a half years ago. His Surf Side Restaurant had been built on the idea of fresh and healthy and this business model had always separated his restaurant from most of the others on the island.

He drove into a crowded parking lot and absently wondered how Kale and the restaurant were doing. The last time they'd talked, about a month ago, Kale had told him that business was pretty much as usual. Kale had said that the restaurant had gone through several chefs since Pedro's "disappearance" but the new guy, also Mexican, seemed to be working out. Immigration was really the only concern.

Billy parked the Cavalier two spaces beyond the deepest row of cars. The lot, as large as it was, reminded him of those used for overflow traffic at ball games and amusement parks. A good portion of Sedona could shop at the "triple H" and still find plenty of parking.

"Let's see what Heaven has to offer us today," Billy said to toy SpongeBob. "Perhaps a Krabby Patty or two?" SpongeBob's eternal, two-toothed smile accepted the notion.

A sudden distant scream caused him to look up from SpongeBob and into the rearview mirror. Just beyond the parking lot's perimeter, he saw two people running around within a cloud of red dust. He quickly exited the car and looked back across the roof. Beyond and above the dust cloud, Sedona's Airport Mesa rose thirty feet to a flat surface where the airport's runway remained hidden from sight. What Billy at first thought was the sound of a distant propeller was actually the object the two people were chasing: a gas-powered, radio-controlled monster truck. It jumped and flipped a few feet off the ground then stopped. A boy picked up the toy and showed it to a man who was, perhaps, his father.

The tiny toy buzzing and the screams of human happiness resumed and resounded across the mass of motionless steel as Billy walked the lot toward Heaven's entrance, a squirt of extreme loneliness suddenly pulsing though him. Again, he thought of Marcy.

Inside of Heaven the crowd was as thick as it had been in Walmart but this crowd, of course, was different. First, there were far fewer children and, therefore, far less skittering, scrambling and screeching. Parents weren't yelling at unruly offspring and soft sounds of desert life were easily heard and enjoyed through the store's speaker system. Wide aisles were crowded but the shoppers in those aisles respected other shoppers by maintaining clear passages. Talk amongst the shoppers was not about bargains for unnecessary Walton emotional purchases but was centered on the information trade of health knowledge—of healthy bodies and healthy minds and how the ingredients of the items they handled could further benefit such perceptions. Just as there was in any crowded shopping venue, at least one disgruntled person could be seen and heard, arguing with a store clerk or their own significant others, but in the triple H, such displays were the exception not the rule.

Billy rolled his cart through familiar aisles, plucking from shelves and bins and refrigerator cabinets items that were easily prepared and mostly free of processed foods and additives. When he was satisfied that his collected goods would last him at least two weeks, he went to check out.

The lines were long but hassle-free. There were no shock-riddled magazine and tabloid covers, and no last minute, useless gimmicks except for a small display that promoted Clif Bars and PowerBars and other "natural" energy products. Billy snatched a few Clif Bars; the display reminded him that he might need a quick bite sometime in the future.

Back out in the parking lot, Billy loaded the Cavalier's trunk and noticed that the man and his boy were still out beyond the lot's perimeter but were no longer running around. The dust had settled. The mechanical buzz of the toy had died.

Curiosity led Billy's drive from the parking space toward them. As he approached, he noticed that the man, kneeling, held the truck chassis in his hands. The body of the toy sat on the dusty ground next to him. His boy stood there, analyzing the toy's guts as his father prodded it with a small screwdriver. They looked up when Billy stopped, the Cavalier idling.

"Need any help?" Billy offered.

The man, who looked to be Native American, turned to him and smiled. "Not unless you know anything about RC toys."

Billy switched off the ignition and stepped from the car. "Looks like you're in luck." He strolled from the parking lot's concrete pavement and onto red earth. Wheel ruts from the monster truck toy twisted crazy patterns underfoot. "I've fiddled around with a few of these in my days. What seems to be the problem?"

"I think we gave it a little more than it could handle," the man said, his accent matching his ancestry. "Jumped it over there but when it landed, the rock would not allow the machine any more rights today." His words were almost respectful and were in no way angered. The boy, who was also Native American, nodded agreement.

The man stood and handed the chassis and screwdriver to Billy who then prodded the plastic and metal components for only a minute. "The flywheel is busted. It needs replaced. You have any spare parts?"

The man shook his head. "They tried to sell us a repair kit with the truck but I thought it was only a pitch, you know, like how salesmen always push add-ins to up the price." Billy handed the chassis to him and the man followed the direction of the screwdriver as Billy pointed. "We should have listened." The man looked at the boy, then offered his free hand to Billy. "They call me Lax. My son is Aaron."

Billy grabbed Lax's right hand and immediately felt its strength as he shook it. "They call me Billy," he said. "Good to meet you." He released Lax's hand then offered his to Aaron. "And you too." Aaron, who looked to be a year or two away from adolescence eagerly accepted.

"He's got a tattoo in his hand," Aaron exclaimed. "I've never seen one there before."

If Billy had been paying more attention to Lax than to his son, he would have seen Lax's astonished expression. Billy did, however, hear the man gasp. "It's not a tattoo," Billy said to Aaron. "It's a…"

"Sign," Lax interjected. "A sign of divine protection."

Divine? Protection? Yes, Billy thought. *That's exactly what the Creation Dagger was.*

"A holy sign," Lax continued. "Where did you get it?"

Billy, for what seemed the hundredth time, traced the pentagram's pink edges, pressing harder as the pad of his forefinger passed over the denser flesh that filled some of the points. "Holy?" he mumbled. "A sign of protection?"

"Yes," Lax reassured. "The pentagram. Used as a seal to protect us from evil." When Billy looked up, Lax was staring directly at his chest. "To protect your soul."

Lax suddenly reached out and Billy stumbled backward, tripping over the body of the RC truck; he landed on soft earth as the truck's body, which had been launched skyward by the toe of his sandal, landed on his chest, an audible thud-click resounding as plastic bounced off of the haft of the sheathed dagger under his shirt. Billy gasped as much from Lax's sudden move as from the name emblazoned across the truck body's green surface: "Grave Digger" it read. The name meant something to him, though he couldn't remember ever having such a toy.

"Oh, please. Please forgive us. You are only trying to help. I didn't mean to…"

Billy waved his hand, the one with the pentagram burnt into the palm, then sat up. The Grave Digger truck body rolled from his chest and onto the dirt where it sat gutless and upright. "Nope," he said. "My bad. My clumsiness." He stood and brushed red dirt from his butt and legs. "You ought to go back to your dealer. I'm sure he'll help you fix it up in no time."

Aaron said, "We are sorry, Billy. Really. Maybe we can treat you to some maize and frijoles?"

"A custom," Lax added. "For disturbing your spirit." He patted his son's head while his eyes pleaded with Billy's. "Besides, you helped us. Maybe we can help you."

An onslaught of embattled thoughts kicked up a storm so strong in Billy's head an immediate response was impossible. *Help him*? How could complete strangers help him? And why had Lax tried to grab him? His heart? His dagger? What the hell did this man know about daggers and pentagrams and the powers of protection they represented?

And then it occurred to him. Something had happened in the past twenty-four hours. Something esoteric...something you couldn't get your hands on or wrap your mind around. It was like a locked door that was now open, a flood of circumstance and coincidence unleashed, a Pandora's Box of illogical continuity. Disparate pieces of some greater spiritual puzzle were suddenly rushing together and the keystone date had been Black Friday, the day after Thanksgiving, a day when an earthquake had shaken Sedona for the first time in over two hundred million years. He'd been in Red Rock Country for five months and had met no reliable sources who knew anything about cubits or djeds or daggers or the living dead...there'd been lots of myth-talk, superstitious mumbo jumbo and pure faith-mongering but nothing that he had found to have been of any use beyond pure entertainment. And now, just by chance, Marcy had met this woman named Cooper, stranded by accident, and Billy had met Lax suffering from a strangely similar predicament: an accident with a radio-controlled monster truck toy. Perhaps Lax could help, but Billy felt overly cautious. It was Lax's grab for his heart that had done it. Could he know what rested underneath his shirt?

"Help?" Billy finally said. "I don't even know you."

Lax looked at Aaron as if he were testing the boy to make a decision and put thoughts into words. Lax wasn't going to answer; he wanted his son to provide reason.

"Then that's where we'll start," Aaron said. "We'll help you know us so we won't be strangers anymore."

Lax smiled, his cheeks bulging dark skin, the corners of his lips rising into them. He clasped one of his son's shoulders with a hearty hand and they stood there on the red earth, the Airport Mesa rising behind them, saguaro cacti dotting the landscape, the sun almost directly overhead, a portrait that could have hung from thousands of walls in thousands of homes whose occupants loved the great Southwest but had never seen it.

"So, you will join us for dinner on the holy day." Lax said as if the decision had already been made. "We will pick you up tomorrow at five and we'll nourish our bodies as the sun touches the horizon. Where do you live?"

Billy was already speculative about having dinner with this man. He certainly didn't want him to know where he was living. "I'll meet you at The Y," he offered instead.

"He does not trust us," Aaron said to his father.

Lax nodded. "Yes. At The Y. Tomorrow at five. Look for my truck." He pointed at a white Ford Ranger that was coated by thin layers of red dust. Lax, again, reached for Billy but this time, he offered his hand to shake. Billy took it. "Forgive me," he said. "We'll talk about it tomorrow."

Billy drove away from the Health Heaven Haven parking lot dazed by expectation. He did not notice the green Cadillac that exited behind him nor the driver who wore a John Deere cap that was of the same green color.

The green Cadillac and Deere-hat man followed the white Cavalier all the way to Getaway Apartments. This wasn't the first time the stalker had followed its prey but it was the first time that Deere-hat man had made it evident that he was doing so. He did not maintain a division of at least two cars between him and the Cavalier. He did not continue on past the apartment complex when Billy pulled in but instead, turned into the driveway of the house directly across the street and just sat there, knowing that, at least, the car would be seen. Once Billy entered his apartment, Deere-hat man and his passenger, whose bald head was covered by the wide brim of a sombrero, exited the Cadillac and walked around to the back of Marcy's casita. They stood, together, in front of the same bay window from which Billy had tracked prairie dogs the night before and waited until Marcy opened the back porch door to let them in.

By far, the best thing about Billy's efficiency apartment was the stacked washer and dryer that sat in the corner of the kitchen. Sure, it reduced the elbow room when it came to cooking but, quite frankly, he'd fixed few full-course meals since arriving in Sedona. He'd simply lost the desire. Two years as a restaurateur had made him a pretty damn good cook but transferring that knowledge to this efficiency just wasn't practical. Perhaps it was the size of the kitchen. It contained a single tub sink, a small refrigerator, and an unusual two-burner stove that included, instead of an oven, a small microwave set into a narrow shelf under the burners.

And, of course, the Whirlpool stacked washer and dryer unit. Being able to do one's own clothes in one's own home was a luxury best appreciated by those who'd struggled through any extended periods of time without the ability to do so, as had been the case for him in Port Aransas. This convenience trumped all other household luxuries by a factor of one hundred...especially on laundry day.

The kitchen countertop was so small that he placed some of the plastic grocery bags in the sink, rustling a couple of bowls, dishes, and a spoon or two as he did so. He'd been able to slip the handles of most of the bags around both arms but there remained one bag of non-perishables from Walmart in the Cavalier. He decided to put off retrieving it until he'd stored the rest of the groceries and sat for a moment. He was quite exhausted. He'd not slept well. But mostly, his brain felt tired, the cognitive muscle overworked, the plentiful new data not stored, unsorted—scattered. It was moments like these that he had to stop forcing himself. Understanding would arrive; all it took was time and rest. Convincing himself of this simple relaxing exercise, however, was never easy.

After he emptied the shopping bags, he sat on the mahogany red sleeper sofa in the adjoining living room and closed his eyes, took a long, deep breath, felt his lungs expand to their fullest, then he slowly exhaled. The surge of oxygen relaxed his brain for a second or two and all of the collapsing memories and thoughts and confusions intertwined into one gray nothingness. He followed the calming exercise with three more before the blast of a car horn outside jerked him out of temporary solitude and reminded him to retrieve the last shopping bag.

When he opened the door and stepped out onto the welcome mat that read "God Loves You" (also furnished with the apartment), he saw a green Cadillac backing out of the driveway to Marcy's casita. From his vantage, only the tail end of the car was identifiable. The tags were from Texas and there were two occupants visible through the rear window. As the car sped away toward town, a flash of sun reflected into Billy's eyes and he raised his hand to shield the glare.

A ball cap, Billy thought. *The driver was wearing a ball cap*. The sun's reflection had somehow stamped the image onto his eyes like a flashbulb onto film. His imagination filled in the remaining pieces including the color of the cap, the insignia sewn into it and the color of the flip of hair that fell from under it. He ran from the front porch to the road, trying to catch a final glimpse of the retreating car before it was too far away for him to confirm what he thought he'd seen, but it was useless. What he did see was Marcy, staring out of her casita's front window. When he waved at her, she shut the blinds though he was uncertain if his wave had been what had caused her to do so.

More deep breaths, he said to himself. *You need a whole lot more. You're starting to connect imagination to reality and that's never a good combination if sanity is to be maintained.*

He sucked in hot, desert air that stung his lungs, then wiped sweat from his forehead and paced himself to the Cavalier where he grabbed the remaining Walmart bag and returned to his apartment. He set the bag on the throw rug near the door and returned to the sleeper sofa where he immediately began extricating the desert air from his body.

You are being followed, the hot air seemed to warn.

He took another deep breath. *No. It's a mirage*, the cool apartment air countered.

He exhaled. *Panic is your survival mechanism*, the fleeting hot oxygen maintained.

One more deep breath. *But calm is the only way you'll make sense of it all.*

He exhaled.

And then his heart skipped when the beating of knuckles assaulted the front door. When he opened it, Marcy was standing there, smiling, her painted red lips forced into a lie that her eyes betrayed. She glanced over her shoulder toward the road before she spoke.

"I have great news," she said and stepped into the apartment. Billy closed the door and, with an open palm, offered her a place on the sofa. Her short, white skirt hiked up above her knees when she sat, revealing tanned portions of thigh. "Cooper wants to meet with us."

It took a moment for Billy to comprehend. He was staring at Marcy's legs but he wasn't thinking about them. He was thinking about breathing. He was thinking about exhaling. Marcy crossed her legs and turned slightly sideways on the sofa, patting the vacant cushion to her right as she did so. Billy sat. "Cooper," he said. "You mean the local guide you found on the side of the road?"

"Not found…rescued." Marcy's smile was now much more genuine.

"Ah, yes. Rescued with your broken car and Les the mechanic. I remember now."

Marcy pushed him, her palm against his shoulder, as one child might do to another who was fooling them. "She wants us to come over to her house for dinner tonight. She might have some information that could be valuable."

"Professor Cower?"

"Yes. And probably much more."

"What does she want in return?"

Marcy leaned over and placed both hands, palms down, on Billy's shoulder then rested her chin on top of her knuckles. Her lips were inches from his ear. She lowered her voice. "Same as us…information."

Billy looked straight ahead. Nervous desire warped through him. Cautious tension kept his body rigid. "Who was in the Cadillac?"

Marcy drew back. Her smile faded but did not totally disappear. "I'm not sure what you mean."

"You didn't see the Cadillac parked in your driveway?"

"I heard a car but when I looked out, it drove away. I saw you out there. Is there something wrong?"

Billy forced a faltering smile. "No. I guess not. I just thought…" Marcy didn't say anything; she just kept staring at him, as if she were daring him to start up with his nonsensical talk again. "Oh…nothing."

"You didn't sleep well. Are you sure you're up for a meeting with her? I could go alone and bring back—"

Billy shook his head. "I'm up for it. I just don't know what I'd say to her."

"Tell her what you know of Cower. Tell her what you know of the Cubit. Tell her what you know of the Book of the Djed."

"No!"

Marcy blinked. "No what?"

"As I've said before, no one needs to know about it. I'm paranoid enough just having it here."

"You have it here, still? In the apartment? I thought you said you were going to move it to a safer place, like a bank."

"Changed my mind. I remembered how banks and I don't get along very well."

Marcy gently grabbed his forearm and Billy knew what she was going to ask before she said it. Marcy had been fascinated with the Book of the Djed since she'd seen it slide from under the Cavalier driver's seat back in Las Cruces. Just about once a month since they'd arrived in Sedona, she'd asked to see it. She was fascinated with its power to self-write and she was almost deranged in her desire to know what new etchings had been made to its center spread. He'd given in to her requests only twice, not really wanting to bring the Book out of its hiding place at all, but she'd not asked to see it since Billy had told her he was moving it, which he never did. Frankly, he was curious himself if the center spread had added anything new. Little of it had changed since they'd left Port Aransas; just a few more tail feathers had grown onto the bird at the top of the page.

"Yes," he said. "You can take a look. Actually, I wouldn't mind taking a peek myself."

Marcy nodded, grinned, giggled then pulled the hem of her white skirt forward toward her knees with polished red fingernails. Billy stood and closed the front window blind then entered the bathroom and closed the door. He opened the linen cupboard where he'd hidden the Book and the page torn from it that Alixel had called *the key*.

"Why do you do that?" Marcy said. "So you keep it in the bathroom. You don't have to close the door. We're friends, remember? On a journey together, remember?"

Billy emerged from the bathroom with the Book in hand. "And I'm a paranoid hypocrite, remember? It's just habit. Here." He handed the Book to her. "See, I trust you."

Marcy took it gently into both hands and set it on her lap. "I wish we could read the whole thing."

"Even if we could open it, I doubt we would understand. As far as I know, only one person can open and read all of the pages and she's…" Billy cleared his throat. "Go ahead."

Marcy pinched the leathery cloth cover between two fingers as if trying to open it to the first page. The attempt, again, failed. Instead the Book opened to the center spread, all of the pages in front of it locked together as one big leaf. She shifted it so its spine rested between her thighs. Billy immediately craned his head forward. Something substantial *had* changed.

The glyph of the bird at the top of the right-hand page seemed to have become darker, the black lines of fire streaming from its tail now thicker, denser, almost embossed. It even appeared that the first hint of another color had made its mark within the drawing—a few very thin lines of red traced one of the bird's fiery tails.

The three sixes under the bird had also changed. They were now larger, taking up twice the space they once had. They occupied the left half of the page about a third of the way down from the top and Billy was sure that they had moved from where they'd once been centered under the bird. But they had to have moved to make room for the new drawing that had been added to the right of the last six: three additional numerals, all smaller than the sixes…

999

"What does it mean?" Marcy asked. She turned the Book upside down. "Sixes and nines."

"Maybe Revelation had it all wrong. Maybe John the Apostle envisioned the numerals the wrong way. Maybe it means nothing that pertains to the Bible."

"The mark of the beast?" Marcy traced one of the upside down nines that now looked like sixes.

"And the mark of the upside down beast? The mark of the Antibeast."

Marcy spun the Book right-side up and almost simultaneously both of them said. "The Savior."

Billy grabbed the Book and closed it. "That would certainly make sense." He stood and walked toward the bathroom.

"How so?" Marcy asked.

"Revelation is not only the story of destruction, it's also the story of hope. That is, if you believe those kinds of things."

"But didn't you tell me that this Book was of Mayan origin? They didn't have access to Revelation or the Bible back then."

Billy stopped inside the bathroom door frame. "Alixel seemed to suggest they did. Or maybe the creators of the Bible had access to the Mayans, their culture, their beliefs, their spirit." He closed the door then appeared a moment later. "Honestly, I don't believe the numerals in that Book have anything to do with Revelation. It's just a coincide…"

Marcy stood with some kind of victorious grin spread across her face. "Coincidence, Mr. Scientist? You are coming over to the dark side. Soon you'll be saying that little green men are living on planet earth."

"Well, not exactly green. Walking dead is a better description."

She turned away from him. "We're to meet Cooper at her place at five. She lives about a mile or so up toward the canyon. We should give ourselves about thirty minutes unless you want to drive." Billy shook his head while Marcy went to the front door and stepped out on the welcome mat. She read from it. "God loves you."

"I'll see you at four-thirty," Billy said and waved good-bye.

Cooper Reyes lived near the trailhead to Boynton Canyon. She'd chosen the location for several reasons. Since the destination of most of her tour groups was the canyon, living where she worked provided quick access to all of the ceremonial grounds and spiritual planes that inundated the area. Additionally, her home's close proximity to the canyon provided shelter on days when unexpected storms caught her and her tour group by surprise. On rare occasions she also offered special, private packages to smaller groups, mostly couples, which included a southwestern meal that she prepared and served at her house. Though she enjoyed cooking and would have loved to have expanded such offerings, she was very choosey about the people she let into her home and, therefore, offered less than a dozen such packages a year. There were simply too many unappreciative head jobs out there who wanted more to fill up digital cameras than to really *experience* what Sedona had to offer: real, genuine, spiritual energy.

And that was the biggest reason why she'd chosen this place to live. Nowhere else in Sedona (or in all of Red Rock Country for that matter) was the spiritual energy as powerful as it was in Boynton Canyon. A vortex, it was called: an electromagnetic divining rod where humans connected with their inner selves and outer turmoil.

A place for cleansing.

A place for experiencing.

Her job (as she understood it) was to introduce "vortex virgins" to the experiences that could only be found in Boynton Canyon. That's what she called them: vortex virgins. These were people who had heard about the Sedona vortices, had read about the Sedona vortices, were skeptical about the Sedona vortices but were ignorant of how powerful such vortex energies really were. And like it was for any virgin, each experience was personal and unexpected. Some visitors left the canyon high on new-found purpose. Some totally freaked out, having felt what they termed an "invasion of their soul." Some left unaffected, unconvinced and closed-minded, their spirit forever locked away from any attempt to cleanse it. The former types of people were those to whom she might offer private packages—those that had taken with them something that needed returning: a gratitude for life and the opportunity to live it. The later types of people, those that could never believe, were those she maintained at a safe distance, often referring them to other tour guides when their return to Sedona was eminent. The third type of visitor, the ones that freaked out, she didn't worry about. They would never return anyway.

Because her van (the one she used to transport her tour groups) was in the shop and would not be ready until at least Monday, she'd had to cancel tours scheduled for the next two days. The popularity of the Thanksgiving weekend had made the availability of rentals scarce to nonexistent. But that was fine with her. Applications for the weekend groups had not looked at all promising. Both groups scheduled were completely comprised of vortex virgins from New York City, and with the memory of last evening's craziness still roiling through her senses, she thought that virgins from the city would increase her stress more than the two strangers who were coming over for dinner.

She started organizing her kitchen an hour before her guests were due to arrive. She usually kept her home quite organized but it had gone into slight disarray because of the distractions over the last couple of days. Though she would never admit it, she really was a clean freak—her psychology professor Dr. Doer would have most certainly diagnosed her as obsessive compulsive—not to the extent of Adrian, her favorite character on her favorite television show *Monk*, but a clean freak nonetheless.

Most of her obsessive cleanliness was centered on her kitchen, by far her favorite room in the house. She'd done all of the remodeling herself, following advice from numerous magazines and an occasional episode on one of the home improvement satellite channels. Southwest motifs were a part of every corner and wall, every wooden cabinet, the pots and pans, the floor and ceiling. Her countertops were her most loved renovations. Thick, white veins curled through granite the color of the red rocks at dusk, the veins like lost rivers feeding a barren land suffocating from heat. The island in the middle of the kitchen was topped by the same granite beauty. Iron skillets and grill pans and long chef's utensils dangled on black metal hooks above the island. They hung low enough that many of her private tour guests (particularly the men) had smacked their heads into them, but their height from the floor was more pragmatic to her short stature than accommodating to visitors. A small ceiling fan spun quietly above a gliding porch window which she had opened a few inches so as to circulate the smell of the desert without sacrificing too much of the air conditioning.

She had planned a similar meal to those she served all of her guests which included a combination of calabaza and poblano stew, chile rellenos, cheese enchiladas and a hearty mixture of marinated strips of chicken and beef and fresh vegetables all seared on the kitchen island's grill and served as restaurants do their fajitas: hot, sizzling and meant to be assembled according to one's own tastes. Her guests always loved her soups and entrées but they would rave over her salsa and tortilla chips, both of which she made herself. She'd cooked up a batch of chips just two days ago and felt no need to replenish the lot since she stored them in the refrigerator in air-tight brown bags to keep them fresh. The salsa, however, she would never store except for her own consumption. The salsa for her guests was always made the day of the meal.

Purple onions and fresh red and yellow tomatoes lay in chopped mounds on a thick, wooden cutting board that sat atop the island. She turned to the window and pulled several sprigs of cilantro from the small herb garden that also held vibrant, foot-high plants of dill, rosemary and thyme. She placed the cilantro on the cutting board, then went to the stainless steel, side-by-side refrigerator to get her secret salsa addition: chipotle peppers—not the store bought variety but those purchased straight from the Hopi reservation to the north of town. She'd befriended some of the Elders' wives back when Chris Cower had done the ole' misdirection two-step.

Once everything was chopped to chip-scooping perfection, she pushed the ingredients from the cutting board into a deep ceramic bowl with the back of the knife, sealed the bowl with plastic wrap, snatched another plastic wrapped bowl filled with marinating meats from the refrigerator and set the salsa in its place.

Across from the island and hanging between two framed prints that pictured Arizona Native Americans preparing meals with mortar and pestle was a flat screen TV. She turned it on with a remote intending to navigate to a soft rock satellite radio station but hesitated when the promo for News 5 at Five caught her attention.

"Sedona police remain baffled by the disappearance of one of its officers," the female news anchor said. "The complete story and all of the weather tonight on the Verde Valley's award-winning news hour."

Cooper's immediate reaction was one of self-concern. Had she been seen? And if she hadn't, would their investigation lead them to Luke at the Café Aus who would name her as someone who'd been curiously waiting, all alone, at a table just a block from the officer's last know location?

She tuned the TV to the soft rock station. Ironically, Lindsey Buckingham was singing *Trouble*. She dropped the wooden cutting board into the island's deep sink and pulled out a plastic cutting board from a cabinet door next to her right leg.

I should ruuuun...un..., Lindsey sang.

She rinsed the chef's knife then plucked a chicken breast from the meat bowl and began cutting thin slices.

On the double...

Red marinade oozed from the chicken and marred the cutting board which, coupled by Buckingham's lyrics, made it hard for her to ignore what she'd seen in the alley.

I think I'm in trouble.

If the police did tag her as a possible suspect (or at least a witness) what would she say? The entire truth was not an option. She ignored Lindsey's lyrics and absently kept slicing and thinking, moving the blade dangerously close to the ends of her fingers.

Tell me Miss Reyes. What were you doing at the Café Aus all by yourself so late at night?

I was waiting for a date that never showed.

A date? You mean a man?

Yes. Yes. A man. He stood me up.

Really? That's not what Luke told us. He said that you told him you weren't waiting for…how did he put it…oh yes, a chap.

I don't go telling everyone my personal business.

I see. And does your personal business include killing police officers?

Are you insane? Of course not.

You were in the alley beside Charleys last night weren't you?

Why do you ask?

We have a witness that saw you go in there.

You mean that drunk who almost ran into me?

So you were in the alley last night.

Yes. But it was only to investigate a scream I heard.

Tell us Miss Reyes. What did you see?

I saw the Sun chop off the head of a Jaguar.

Come with us Miss Reyes. You're under arrest for suspicion of being a crazy fuckin' nut case.

Cooper nicked the side of her forefinger which brought her out of the imaginary conversation. She'd drawn no blood but the red marinade spattered across the cutting board made it suddenly difficult to continue the food preparation.

What would she say? What lie could she create? Would they even suspect her?

She dropped the meat she'd already cut back into the bowl, resealed the plastic wrap, washed her hands, then turned to stare out the kitchen window.

And the doorbell rang.

Billy and Marcy easily found Cooper's house; it was the only one located at the corner of Boynton Pass and Boynton Canyon Road. They had agreed that Billy would do most of the talking: one, because Billy knew more about Cower and Cubits and such and, two, because Billy had "forcefully" suggested he do so. He wanted to control the conversation. He didn't trust Cooper. For all he knew she was a cubit. For all he knew, anybody could be one. He also thought that Marcy might say something that could jeopardize further revelations; she might freely give up something he'd told her without getting useful information in return—something that had to do with the

Book of the Djed or Hopi princesses or the walking dead. Really, the only information that Billy was interested in revolved around Chris Cower. If he could understand why Cower had come to Sedona, then perhaps he could understand why he was there as well. To save the world, was not good enough.

It took three rings of the doorbell before Cooper answered. She was shorter than he'd imagined and in many ways resembled the Hopi princess Alixel, except for the strawberry blonde curls that framed her face. Strong arms and legs extended from a T-shirt and shorts that blended southwestern pastel solids with the color of the hardwood floor and wall paint he saw within the doorway behind her.

"Hi Marcy," Cooper said. She shook her hand and looked at Billy. "And Marcy's friend?"

"Billy," he said and shook the tips of her small, unpainted fingernails.

Cooper led them inside. The juicy sweet aroma that had assaulted him outside was overwhelmingly delightful as Cooper closed the door behind him.

"That's fantastic," Marcy exclaimed. "Smells as wonderful as what Pedro used to cook up at the Surf Side. Don't you think so?"

Billy smiled. "As wonderful but without the sea."

Cooper looked curiously at Billy then escorted both of them into the living room where handmade Hopi and Navajo rugs overwhelmed the floor and walls. Thick beams of hardwood supported a high ceiling and lamps on long poles dropped down a foot from the beams but were not illuminated; the living room was lit solely by numerous tall windows and a sliding glass porch door through which Billy saw a skirted, round table covered by an umbrella. On the table were a couple of glasses, a pitcher and a setting of three plates.

Cooper led them to the sliding doors past a huge kitchen in which Billy saw a couple of bowls on the kitchen's center island which Cooper grabbed. Outside, an orange-red sun hovered an hour or so above Boynton Canyon's jagged horizon; the table umbrella had been adjusted to block its direct heat, casting a solid shadow over table and chairs. Cooper set the bowls of chips and salsa within the shadow.

"Go ahead and have a seat while I finish up the preparation," Cooper offered. "Some say my salsa is the best in town."

Billy and Marcy sat with their backs to the house and both immediately sampled Cooper's salsa as she disappeared through the sliding doors behind them. Marcy was right. Not only did the smells from the kitchen remind Billy of Pedro, so did the taste of the salsa. The thought of his chef and the memory of his murder briefly made him sad.

Cooper returned to the porch and switched on a round, plastic portable fan near the far corner where a three-step riser of stairs descended into the red earth landscaping. The stream of air circled the table, billowing Marcy's long hair and cooling sweat beads on Billy's forehead. Cooper sat, poured water from the pitcher into each of their glasses, grabbed a chip, slid it into the salsa and plopped the chip's triangular corner into her mouth.

"So why are we here?" she asked, bluntly. "Information sharing?" She chomped the rest of the chip and licked her thumb. "What could I have that would possible interest two visitors from Texas?"

How Cooper knew that they were from Texas, minutely jogged Billy's curiosity. He ignored it. "How do you know Professor Cower?"

"My. We are the in-your-face-type aren't we?" All three of them snatched chips and dipped together. "Nothing like getting right to the point." Cooper settled back on the chair's tan cushion. "We'll wait until after dinner to discuss that. There's more info than there is time before the food will be ready. Perhaps some small talk before we get into…" A small chunk of tomato fell from her chip and landed on her right forearm, and she kissed the chunk into her mouth. When she lowered her arm, Billy saw the tattoo of a djed stamped near her wrist. Cooper noticed this and ended her statement with, "…before we get into Cower and djeds and such." She drank some water then added, "I could make us some margaritas if anyone is interested."

"Maybe later," Billy said. He couldn't stop staring at Cooper's tattoo. The last time he'd seen something similar, it had been dangling from Alixel's neck.

"A gift from Chris," Cooper said to satisfy his curiosity. "And a bad decision on my part. Would you please excuse me? Dinner will be ready in a few minutes. I hope beef and chicken are a part of your dietary constraints. I forgot to ask if either of you were vegetarian."

"Sounds good to me," Marcy said.

Billy nodded agreement. "Thank you for inviting us. It all looks and smells wonderful."

Once Cooper was gone, Marcy proclaimed, "Cower told her about the Djed."

"I suspect. So she probably knows about the Book."

"Maybe she knows the significance of the numbers."

"Doubtful. They weren't there until just recently." Billy suddenly realized that the kitchen window was open when he heard Fleetwood Mac singing *Tell Me Lies* from inside the house.

"Will you tell her you have it? That info could be the bargaining chip."

"Shhh," Billy whispered and motioned with his head toward the window. He sipped water and watched a large hawk circle near the rocky

Kachina Woman spire in the distance; it dipped above and below the circle of the setting sun that had moved fifteen minutes closer to dusk. He raised his voice. "Did you get a chance to talk to the man at Vor-Tech's?"

"I did." Marcy nodded her understanding of his change of subject. "He wanted too much for it, so I gave it back to him."

"Really?" Billy was surprised. He'd been convinced that Vor-Tech's proprietor would have given it up for next to nothing. "How much?"

"Five hundred."

"Crap. That's insane. You try to barter with some of your fortunetelling skills?"

"He said he already knew his fortune, so I told him that he, therefore, must know that I wasn't going to shell out five hundred bucks for a broken piece of glass. It was strange, really. He was nothing like he was last night. His wife was much more bitchy, too."

"Maybe they had a bad sales day. Most of their stuff was probably busted by the quake."

"I didn't get that impression. Perhaps they just liked you better."

Billy played with the point of one triangular chip before grabbing and eating it. "Too bad. It looked great right next to your testicles."

Marcy laughed, hard. "Those aren't testicles. They're scaled down replicas of the ceremonial balls used in the ballcourt games. But I like your idea better."

Cooper poked her head out of the sliding door. "It's ready. Grab the bowls and glasses if you don't mind."

Cooper's rectangular dining table was big enough for six people. Only three places were set up, all toward the side of the table closest to the kitchen. Cooper sat at the head with Marcy to her left and Billy to the right from where he could look out through the sliding glass doors onto the porch. A half a dozen bowls and plates of southwestern cuisine sat in front of them. Smaller cups of salsa, guacamole, sour cream and chopped green onions dotted the festive food landscape. A woven wooden bowl held a warm towel where flour tortillas comfortably waited within. The next fifteen minutes was full of hearty consumption and small talk.

"What's the Surf Side?" Cooper asked Billy.

"It's a restaurant I own in Port Aransas. Seafood mostly."

"And quite a delicious place to visit," Marcy added. "Don't let Billy's modesty fool you."

Cooper tried a smile but it seemed a bit contrived. "Really? So how does my cooking measure up?"

"I was just telling Marcy outside how really great everything smelled and the salsa, as you said, is top-notch. You've grilled the meats to perfection. The chile rellenos…well, this is only the second time I've ever had any but, up until now, I've never thought a chile could taste so good." Marcy nodded as she stuffed her mouth with a rolled piece of tortilla that overflowed with a mixture of just about everything on the table. "I am curious though. Where's the beans and rice? I thought those were staples in the southwest."

"Fillers," Cooper said. "Without them, you get to eat more of the real entrées. Restaurants serve too much of the frijoles y arroz to fill you up and save on the expensive ingredients."

"Makes sense." Billy ate the rest of his chile relleno. "So tell me… where did you learn to cook like this?"

"In college. I lived a short stint with a sorority house where I was designated the house cook. You get really good, really fast with twenty stuck up bitches always hammering you with complaints." Cooper ate strips of chicken without a tortilla, moving the meat trough red marinade before forking it into her mouth. "So what's your story?" She pointed the empty fork at Marcy.

"I also have a business in Port A." The statement was muffled by the huge wad of food in her mouth. She swallowed. "A fortuneteller."

"Marcy Ruminski sees all," Billy said. "And she's quite good at it." Billy thought that he had sounded too callous. Even though he was beginning to believe in mystical influences, his baser instincts still protected him from total immersion. Last night's argument with Marcy hadn't helped. Perhaps, he thought, he should just keep quiet when the topic arose in the future.

"You can see our future?" Cooper asked.

"Perhaps." Marcy quickly replied. "Perhaps you should come over to my place some time and we'll test the waters."

"Not into tarot cards and such," Cooper said. "Never was much of an astrologer either. Fate is what you make of it, and if you're wrong, fate will steer you back on the right path."

"We have a lot in common," Marcy said, wiping her hands on a cloth napkin. "We just call them different things."

Marcy asked for some milk to cool the heat of the meal's chile undertones. When Cooper returned with the glass she said to Billy, "What do you know of the Djed?"

Billy wiped his hands and mouth. "So—who's cutting to the chase now?"

Cooper smiled, genuinely this time. "I thought that's how you wanted to play." She sat. "But we can wait until…"

"No. That's fine. Because, quite frankly, I don't know a whole lot about it. All I know is what anyone with a computer could look up on the Internet. I know that it is a reverent Egyptian symbol. It is connected with interpretations such as 'stable,' 'enduring,' and 'resurrection.' It represents the death and renewal of the yearly cycle. It is mostly known for its connection to the legend of Osiris—the murder of Osiris. Osiris is tricked into climbing into a wooden chest by the evil one, Typhon, so the story goes, and the chest is dumped into the Nile where it wanders into the sea and finds land near a huge tree. The tree grows around the chest until one day, the trunk of this tree, containing the body of Osiris, is cut down and turned into a pillar for the house of the king. I also remember reading that Osiris was born on the three hundredth and sixty-first day of the year, one of five unlucky days. As it was in Egypt. As it was for the Mayans."

"As it is for many cultures," Cooper concluded. "There seems to be a common connection to peoples who lived across impassible oceans in times when water navigation was in its infancy. Makes you wonder if all cultures are all a part of some greater…" She hesitated for the right word. "…some greater existence."

Cooper folded her hands and placed both elbows on the table, straddling her empty plate. Her statement reminded Billy of the images of the Bible's creation story as it was depicted in the Book of the Djed, as Alixel had explained to him on the night of the hurricane. He remembered not believing her. He remembered thinking that such cross-cultural connections were impossible.

A few uncomfortable minutes passed in silence as the diners finished their meals, then Cooper stared directly into Billy's eyes, never blinking, never flinching and with a threatening undertone said, "Since we are being so blunt this evening, I'll offer this: you want to know about Chris Cower; I want to know if you have the Book of the Djed."

Billy snatched a quick glance from Marcy whose eyes looked apologetically disdain. He thought Cooper must have overheard their conversation through the kitchen window.

"Wait," Cooper said, abruptly. "Before you tell me you *do* have it let us retire onto the porch for a bit of green tea and sunset." She scooted the chair from under the table and stood before either Billy or Marcy could answer. "I'll be out in a moment. Please." She offered her hand in the direction they were supposed to walk.

Outside, the fan still spun a cool breeze across the table but the umbrella was of no use any more; the sun had fallen below Boynton Canyon and twilight had taken its place. Billy collapsed the umbrella, looked over at the kitchen window which appeared to be closed, then sat beside Marcy.

"I don't trust her," Marcy said.

"What makes you say that? Because she doesn't like fortunetellers? Seems lots of people don't like fortunetellers around here."

Marcy slapped Billy's arm. "Enough with the fortunetelling thing." She rubbed the spot she'd just slapped. "I don't trust her because I think she's playing us. I don't trust her because, somehow, I think she's in on this with someone else. She might not be the bad guy but she's working for him. I think you've known me long enough to trust my intuition."

"Yes. Of course I do. But we've gotta give to get. You said as much yourself."

Marcy moved her hand from Billy's arm to brush red-painted fingernails though her black hair. She leaned back in the chair, prompting her chest to rise upward toward the waning light. "You're right. Just be careful. I wouldn't want to lose my favorite man."

Cooper appeared with a tray that held a ceramic pot decorated in bands of red, orange and brown, and three similarly decorated cups. Steam trickled from the pot's closed top. She sat with her back to the darkening horizon and poured each of them some green tea. "I hope you don't mind drinking it straight," she said. "It is the best way to drink green tea…you know without all of the artificial additions."

Billy didn't answer the question but instead said, "I do have it. And to tell you the truth, I really don't know why I have it. I guess it was sort of passed down to me."

"From Chris?" Cooper asked, sipping tea.

"From Janine Bender."

"I don't know any Janine Bender."

"No. You wouldn't. I only knew her for a few short hours before she was killed."

Marcy watched her tea steam but didn't drink it. "She was a wonderful person," she said. "Kicked around and beaten down. She just wasn't at the right place at the right time."

Cooper raised her hands, palms high, in an I-don't-know-what-the-hell-you're-talking-about pose. One red-haired eyebrow lifted up under a curl of hair equal in color.

So, Billy told Cooper the story of Janine Bender, at least as much of her story as she had told him. He recounted details about the destruction of her farm, about Janine's flight to Port Aransas to escape her husband, Albert, who had then followed her to the island. He told Cooper that Janine had saved Cower's life and that she had acquired the Book from him though he didn't tell her how since he didn't know himself. He left out parts concerning the walking dead and all of his friends that had been cubited, and when he had finished, Cooper looked directly at Marcy and said, "So what about the Cubit? You asked about that yesterday."

Marcy directed the answer toward Billy. "He knows more about that stuff than I do. I'm just along for the ride."

Cooper turned a stern look on Billy. "We are going to get nowhere unless we can all be totally honest with each other. You have to understand that the Book and the Cubit are interconnected. How well, I'm not quite sure, but I do know one thing. That Book you have possesses great knowledge and great power. With it, you can become invincible."

Marcy responded before Billy had the chance. "So that's why you want the Book? You're hungry for the elusive and quite fantastic delusion of immortality?"

Billy could not have said it any better. He nodded at Marcy then gazed expectantly at Cooper for an answer.

"It's not delusional. At least that's what Chris said."

"Chris," Billy replied. "Chris Cower, the good professor? He seems to be at the heart of all of this. Why don't you tell us about *him*?"

The final sliver of twilight drifted away from the horizon and Boynton Canyon's skyline became nearly invisible. Perhaps it was the sudden coolness that swarmed through the night air that made shivers crawl up Billy's spine. Perhaps it was the shot of adrenaline that pumped through him as his expectant ears waited for what would hopefully further define his own fate. Whatever it was, it froze his mind into a singular concentration. This is why he'd come here tonight.

Cooper began…

THE DJED: PART II

THE RISE & FALL OF CHRISTOPHER COWER

Professor Christopher Cower had visited Sedona on more than one occasion. The first time was in the fall of 2003. His purpose then was the same as it would be four years later: to provide argument against land developers who were driven to influence reservation and national park leaders that the Sedona real estate was useless without their investment. But in 2003, Cower's desire to help had been heartfelt, an altruistic effort, unlike the distractive lies contrived in 2007.

He'd come from a State University in New York—Cortland, perhaps, but Cooper could not remember exactly which one, though she did remember that the school had excelled in anthropology studies of which Cower was a professor. A Hopi Elder named Alixel had asked for his help.

And Cower had run off the developers, using archeological reasoning to reinforce what the Indians and naturalists already knew—that, basically, nature was not short on cash. But something else had happened while he'd been in Sedona in 2003, something that would forever change him and, apparently the fates of many, something that would eventually drive him back to Red Rock Country in 2007. Apparently, he'd found some etchings on walls within a burial site that no one had known existed. He'd stumbled on the site purely by accident, and to hear him tell the story, the accident had been predestined and had almost killed him; he'd literally fallen into it and had suffered a minor concussion, had passed out, and when he'd awakened, he'd found etchings on tomb walls depicting horrific scenes of mass murder and suicide. But the tomb also held something intangible, a spirit, and it had "infected" him; it had prevented him from mentally putting away the images and they had haunted him, forced him into a solitary pledge never to return to Sedona again.

Then in 2005, while hosting a prominent entrepreneur and former professor at his state college, Cower was, again, engaged with the memory he'd tried to quit. The visitor, whom Cower only referred to as "Dick," had engaged him in a conversation that had revealed many truths about the burial site he'd stumbled upon. Dick had told Cower the story of the great Anasazi tribe and of their sudden, complete disappearance and that what he'd seen on the walls in the burial site was sort of a final epitaph, scratched for infinity by one of the tribe's last survivors. This epitaph documented the true reason for the tribe's disappearance and served as a warning. According to Dick, the Anasazi had not died from plague or famine or tribal warfare and they had not been taken to the stars by extraterrestrials. The Anasazi had killed themselves. They had become possessed by an evil transformation that tempted all men, an evil that cared not for compassion unless compassion was a lie that would culminate in the true goal. Absolute Power. Absolute invincibility. Absolute control of the Earth and the Sun and the universe. This aberrant belief had embattled brother against brother and father against son. They had murdered each other, some taking their own lives in mass suicides so as not to be consumed by the evil that would guarantee them great suffering.

As an archeologist, Cower was staunchly curious as to the reason for such mass insanity that could destroy an entire population and Dick had helped him satisfy this curiosity. Dick had told him that the answers lay at the bottom of a hidden chamber that had yet to be uncovered in the Mayan ruins at Chichen Itza.

With directions from Dick, Cower had found a secret room in the ruins and had uncovered the reason behind the Anasazi's self-genocide. He'd also stolen two artifacts that led him back to Sedona in 2007. One of them was a Creation Dagger. The other was the Book of the Djed.

In the summer of 2007, Sedona had come under the influence of another powerful corporation. The multinational company, Phoenix International, whose industries included oil speculation, pharmaceuticals and gambling, among others, had tried to gain a foothold in Red Rock Country through false promises and lots of money. Phoenix International, locally led by a man named Chancey Lett, had wanted to build a casino on national park land that had been leased to the government in a hundred year deal from the Hopi Nation. Because of his success in 2003, Cower returned to Sedona to fight the impossible battle against corporate greed and corruption. But this, of course, was not the real reason he'd returned. His presence as a hero spokesperson and nature preserver was legitimate in the eyes of the Verde Valley residents but it served only as a distraction for the pursuit of his ultimate goal: to return to the burial site because he now understood that it was the entry into the Great Hall of the Anasazi in which he would find the mechanism that had caused the annihilation of the Anasazi and would eventually destroy the world.

The Cubit.

Cower had hooked up with Cooper because of her knowledge as a guide and because he'd lost the confidence of the Hopi Elder, Alixel, whom he'd joined in common cause four years before. Cooper also had a great relationship with both the Indian tribes and the Parks, having presented herself as an advocate for the preservation of all the beauty the Red Rock Country offered. He'd "hired" her to be his personal guide and companion spokesperson because of the respect she commanded in the community. He'd offered her more than money, though; he'd offered her knowledge. He'd shown her things that most humans would never see. And he had fallen in love with her.

Or so he'd said.

Cooper had never known if Cower had truly loved her. There had certainly been lust, but the lust had been mutual. With Cower in the heyday of his sixtieth birthday and Cooper in the heyday of her thirtieth, both had found solace in the comfort of each other's arms. He'd convinced her to get a tattoo (something she'd sworn she'd never do) because, as he'd said, the Djed was the protector against evil and the resurrection of the good. And she'd been convinced of this because he'd shown her the Book.

On the night before Cower had left, he'd told Cooper the story of the Book of the Djed: how it was an instruction manual to prevent the end of days; how it could be used to raise the Djed; how it could make a person invincible. He'd shown her the center spread and she'd seen an invisible hand sketch into a blank page the image of a fiery bird. She'd seen the flames virtually written onto the bird's wings right before her eyes. And she'd become consumed by it.

The following morning, Cower had gone, leaving no trace of his visit. It was only by pure luck that Cooper would see him one more time and that was the night she'd seen the walking dead for the first time. Cower had found what he'd been looking for all along. Cower had found the Cubit and the Cubit had created his evil twin, just like it had done to the Anasazi, just like it did to anyone who touched it. Cooper had seen him slash his own cubit with the Creation Dagger near Café Aus then had watched him drive off in a station wagon with Cubit, dagger and the Book, never to be seen again.

Or at least that's what she had thought then.

"I think he's returned," Cooper said, concluding her story. "I think he's back in town having fun at my own expense. And I think he might be following me around."

Billy immediately thought of Deere-hat man, but Janine Bender had sworn that Cower was dead, that he'd pushed the plunger that had blown up her farm and himself. "Why do you think that?" Billy asked her.

"Someone sent me an anonymous email yesterday morning that said they knew the location of the Great Hall and that they were willing to share the information with me. I only know of one person who would know the location of the Great Hall of the Anasazi."

"But you never saw him did you?"

Cooper hesitated. "No."

Marcy interjected. "Did you get the information?"

"Kind of..." Cooper looked out toward the canyon. The moon had grown one day closer to new. Only a tiny fingernail of it remained in the sky toward the southwest. Its absence of lunar light made the black night a stargazer's feast. Something streaked across the sky, a pinpoint of light that could have been a satellite or meteor. "I'll show you, but first you have to promise me something."

"I won't tell anyone of our conversation," Billy said.

"Thanks. But that's not what I was going to ask for, though I think our mutual confidence in this is paramount to maintaining our sanity in the eyes of others. I want to see the Book. I want to hold it."

Billy didn't hesitate. He'd known she would ask for it eventually. "We can arrange that," he said. Cooper's smile appeared and faded so quickly that Billy wasn't sure he'd seen it at all.

"Splendid," she said. "Follow me."

Cooper led them into the house, past the dining table still littered with uneaten foods and dirty dishes, and into her bedroom. Billy immediately saw the parchment paper taped to the wall. Below the parchment on the hardwood floor laid a copy of the local newspaper and the plastic delivery bag it had been wrapped within. "It's a map," Cooper said.

Marcy walked closer to the wall. "Doesn't look much like a map.

Looks more like it does outside: a bunch of stars clustered together into constellations."

Cooper looked surprised. "You're actually not far off." She walked to her desk and grabbed the Sedona leylines sketch. "Coincidence?" she said, showing them the paper. "Cower gave it to me a year ago and now this parchment shows up."

Billy walked closer and Cooper followed. His finger tested the texture of the parchment then traced patterns that connected the dots. "The Great Hall of the Anasazi is buried among the stars?" he asked, not looking at Cooper.

"Well…not precisely. But these dots do represent heavenly energies."

"Tell me more."

"I think this is the representation of energy lines across the face of Sedona and the Verde Valley. At least that's what Chris told me."

"Yes," Billy said. "I see them. Literally, it is a star map. One six- and one five-pointed star." He saw the puzzled look on Marcy's face and traced the two patterns for her to interpret. "So where is the Great Hall?"

Cooper shrugged. "At one of the points. At one of the intersections…"

"Or anywhere in between," Marcy interjected. "Some map."

"Marcy." Billy raised his voice. "Can we focus, please?" Cooper and Marcy moved away from each other and closer to Billy's opposite sides. "Is there any reason why one of the points might be a more reasonable choice than another? Do these two symbols have any meaning to the riddle?"

"Three symbols," Cooper said. "There are three symbols. Here…my mistake." Cooper grabbed the curled end of a slice of masking tape from the lower right corner where she'd repositioned it earlier. When she peeled it away, the third symbol appeared from underneath. "I know that this is a glyph that represents the sun or ascension and awareness, and this is a glyph of the jaguar, the ruler of the underworld, but I am not sure about this one."

"Wayeb," Billy immediately replied. "Dear God." Both women turned to him simultaneously. "This really forces back some uncomfortable memories."

Cooper touched his shoulder; it was the closest she'd been to him all night. "What does it mean? Does it give you any hint to where the Great Hall might be?"

"No. Not really. It's a Mayan symbol for the last five days of the year… of their year—bad days…unlucky days…evil days. Perhaps that's why it's drawn so far away from the star points. Evil must be kept separated."

Marcy said, "So maybe this isn't a map. Maybe it's some kind of calendar—some kind of countdown."

Billy's eyebrows rose. "Maybe it's both. Maybe it's neither." Cooper's hand was still on his shoulder when he asked her, "And you think Cower's involved? You really think he's alive?"

Cooper shrugged, retreated from the star map and walked to her bedroom door. "So when can I get a look at the Book?"

"Can I call you?" Billy said, following Cooper's nonverbal push to leave her bedroom. "Monday might be preferable."

The night was at an end. For some reason, Cooper seemed no longer interested in their company. She wasn't getting the answer she wanted, Billy supposed, but, quite frankly, he didn't have many; the search for answers was why he'd come to Arizona. But he did have one other piece of information he'd been holding back—something that could be used as a bargaining chip and could be added to the ante. If he was going to find out anything else from Cooper he'd have to play his one last card.

"There's been more written in the Book since you last saw it," Billy offered.

Cooper stopped and stood halfway between the dining room and the front door. "Chris said that would happen." She looked at her bare feet as they shuffled over the wooden floorboards. "More will continue to appear until 2012." Cooper's face turned to him and Billy was struck for the first time with how pretty she really was—not in a beautiful or gorgeous kind of way, and not in the sultry and seductive confluence that defined Marcy's entire body, but a pinch-your-cheek and glow-like-the-moon kind of cute. Even the stern look she gave Billy at that very moment he considered cute. "What is it? What's written there? And if you say something stupid like, 'You'll see when I show you the book' then we can say to hell with our newfound relationship."

Marcy walked to the front door and opened it, a silent retaliation for Cooper's aggressive ultimatum. She was shaking her head *No* when Billy said, "Sixes. Three sixes written under the bird of fire."

Cooper's expression changed in an instant. Now it was her turn to ask for answers. "What does it mean?"

"I think you already know what it means. A warning, perhaps. A premonition. A fortune." He looked at Marcy who stood in the open doorway.

Cooper's mouth hung open as her head absently shook in disbelief. Her eyes wandered across the floor looking for nothing that wasn't there. She, again, turned to face him. "You'll bring it to me on Monday, then; Monday at noon. You bring it here to my house and we'll go for a walk. In the meantime, give the star map some thought. You seem like an intelligent man. Maybe you can figure out if there's anything else to it." Cooper escorted him to the door. "I'm trusting in you. Please understand, beyond anything else, that all of these puzzle pieces we've been talking about are of no value apart. They must come together at the right time and in the right place—by us if we are to save the world; by them if they are to destroy it. The one with all of the cards in the end will win."

Billy didn't say anything; he only nodded. He was struck by Cooper's sudden attitude shift.

"And Billy," Cooper added as he and Marcy retreated from the doorway. "Be careful out there. The jaguar is alive in Sedona."

Cooper had learned much by eavesdropping through her kitchen window. The stolen knowledge had helped her control the flow of the conversation, had helped her make a deal, had guaranteed that she would actually hold the Book in her hands again. But it was what Billy had said at the end of the night that had really flipped her lid.

Three sixes had been written into the Book by the Hand of God.

Well, he hadn't really said "Hand of God" but Chris had suggested as much. And that's why she'd become so obsessed by it. The Hand of God writing clues in the middle of an ancient book that, if understood, would guarantee immortality in the Great Hall of the Anasazi.

She ignored most of the meal's dirty dishes, rinsing just a few and leaving them in the sink, something that she'd seldom done but her obsessive compulsive tendencies had refocused.

Sixes. She remembered Chris telling her his opinion about the sixes in Revelation. She remembered him telling her that they had nothing to do with the mark of the beast or even the Bible. She remembered him saying that the numbers served as a historical marker, that sixes had more to do with calendars that were unrelated to Western ideals or idols. He'd said that the meaning of the numbers 666 had not originated from the Middle East at all but from Central America.

She walked out onto the porch where the half-empty pitcher of water still sat and poured a small amount into one of the glasses though, in her absentmindedness, she was not sure, nor did she care, which glass she'd selected; Marcy's red lipstick faintly colored the opposite side from which she drank.

Monday was such a long time to wait, she thought. The Book was so close yet still too far away. What if something happened to him between now and then? What if something happened to this man who had, toward the end of the evening, began to feel *comfortable* to her? What if something happened to Billy? She might never see the Book again. And her dreams would forever haunt her. The idea of three sixes would remain an unsolved mystery until the end finally came. And she would die never knowing.

Damn Chris Cower for doing this to her. Damn Him!

She threw the plastic glass as hard as she could into the dark brush and heard it clunk off of some distant rock. Farther out, along Boynton Pass, a pair of headlights grew bright as they neared her house. When the headlights turned right onto Boynton Canyon Road, the single streetlamp at the crossroad flashed a shadowy green color from the passing car's metal surface onto the porch's wooden handrail and Cooper's right leg but she paid it no attention.

Sixes...

Three of them...

Did they have anything to do with the map?

Did the map have anything to do with the calendar?

Why was she driving herself crazy?

Obsessing. About the Book. About the Great Hall.

DAMN CHRIS COWER!

Cooper retired to her bedroom and sat on the edge of her bed, to stare at the parchment of dots and glyphs that made no sense no matter how many times she tried to entice the idea of sixes into it. She would eventually fall asleep in the same spot, collapsed to one side, her butt barely on the bed, her legs bent as if she was still sitting, her dreams an agonizing mixture of what she thought she knew and what really was fiction.

They hadn't walked more than a few hundred yards when the car approached from behind them. Billy was trying to understand how Marcy could have been so rude to Cooper and had just finished asking her if she just might be a little jealous, when the car's horn startled both of them. The car traveled another fifty yards then stopped, its red taillights blazing as the driver held a foot against the brake pedal. Marcy grabbed Billy's arm above the elbow and he stood with her on the side of the road, silent. When the Cadillac's door opened, no interior light offered clues to the driver's identity, though the shadows provided every indication that the driver was wearing a ball cap. When it looked at them, its eyes roiled like silver spheres covered in blood.

"I warned you," the guttural, masculine voice said, sending a hallow echo into the darkness that seemed to swallow Billy's spine. "You know what happens when you don't listen."

The dagger in its sheath under his shirt began to warm. His breast sweated. He looked down to see that his shirt was not glowing—at least not yet.

The shadow continued, its voice rising in anger. "If that bitch screws everything up, I guarantee you they'll all die." And then the shadow pointed at him, its red and silver eyes emulsifying into crimson blood spots. The shadow smashed its fist into the roof of the Cadillac, got back into the car, slammed the door closed, and sped off. A rooster tail of dirt carried into the air and dropped in a thin wave on Billy and Marcy.

"What the hell was that all about?" Marcy asked. "Do you know that man?"

"No. But that car looks like the one that turned around in your driveway. And did you notice the ball cap?"

"That guy from Starbucks. You can't be serious?"

"I'm just saying."

"I think it was some drunk who thought we were someone else."

"Maybe." But Billy really did think so. His dagger's warmth had warned him otherwise. He *knew* that the shadow he'd just witnessed was not only Deere-hat man but was also a cubit—the evil dead—but he wasn't going to tell Marcy this. She wouldn't believe him. He only hoped that the faith which Marcy thought she possessed equaled the courage he thought she might need should the Cadillac's driver decide to visit her. "Do you have anything to protect yourself with in the house?"

"Why do you ask?"

Billy pointed at the retreating taillights which quickly faded to black. "That was Deere-hat man and that was the Caddy that was in your driveway." He said it sternly, as if he wanted absolutely no argument.

"Billy Jo Presser. Why you caring fool. I've got a big walking stick but that's about it. Unless, of course, you are making me an offer."

Her smile eased his nerves for the moment before he understood what she meant. "I didn't mean *that*, but I am concerned for you."

"And what about yourself? Perhaps I should be the one concerned about you. It's you that has the Book of the Djed. Do you have any way to protect *yourself*?"

It might have been his imagination but, suddenly, all of the critters in the desert went silent; it was as if all of the hoots of owls and squawks of nightjars, the cries of prairie dogs and howls of coyotes, even the slithering of rattlers and scuttling of scorpions, had paused their nocturnal searches for food and water to await Billy's answer. It was as if their calm was warning him.

Don't tell her, the silence of the critters demanded. *Don't tell her you have the dagger.*

Billy placed his hand on his chest. "But he doesn't know I have the Book. How could anyone know I have it…well, except you and, now, Cooper."

"My point exactly."

The desert night was again filled with the sounds of wildlife struggling for existence. Billy resumed walking and Marcy followed at his right shoulder. "You really don't trust her, do you?"

"Neither do you. Isn't that what you said? You told me to keep my trap shut tonight because you didn't trust her."

"But she did give us some extremely valuable information."

"Assuming it's true."

"Why would she lie about having an affair with an old professor? It seemed to hurt her pretty bad."

"You haven't known many women in your life have you Billy Jo Presser? I've known some of the worst drama queens God could ever conjure up. Cooper wants what you have and like all women, she's bound to say or do anything to get it. Hell, she screwed an old man for information."

"Sounded to me like he screwed her."

"Yes. Well…all I know is if what she says *is* true and *if* the Book *is* an instruction manual for ending or saving this planet or for becoming immortal or for whatever, then I suspect you'll have your answer soon. Regardless, until Monday, or until you make up your mind if you'll actually show her the Book, I'd keep it in a safer place than your bathroom—some place like a bank vault."

Billy stopped and stood and glared at Marcy without saying a word.

"Sorry." Marcy corrected herself. "Perhaps a bank vault isn't the safest place either, come to think of it."

The rest of the ten minute walk home was silent except for the critters. Again, Billy thought he was imagining it, but it seemed to him like the animals were following them, as if an outer perimeter had been set up by packs of mammals and birds and reptiles and those packs were walking and hoping and flying and slithering in concert with each step he took. This imagination became even more believable when Billy and Marcy stopped at the crossroad of Gringo and Dry Creek Road and Marcy pointed at her casita and said, "I could hide it for you. There's lots of places to hide a book in there. Some of the floorboards are even loose."

And again, the night fell silent.

"Do you hear that?" Billy asked her.

Marcy paused. "No. I don't hear anything."

Don't give her the Book, the silence warned.

"Don't you think that's strange?"

Don't let her know you have the dagger.

"Yeah. It is strange come to think of it. So, what do you think?"

Don't trust her.

"I think that I'll keep a hold of it for now."

Don't tell her anything else.

"So, I'll see you tomorrow then?"

"Not sure. I've got to get a few things done. I'll stop over."

Marcy turned away and as she headed for her front door the animals began talking again. She looked over her shoulder and raised her arms in the air as if acknowledging nature's voices then entered the casita and closed the door.

Billy walked to his apartment and stood for a moment on the doorstep landing. Looking out in the direction of Cooper's house and Boynton Canyon, he saw what appeared to be a huge animal sitting on a large rock. At its distance from him, it was no bigger than a postage stamp and was illuminated by some unknown light source that provided a faint orange hue behind its black silhouette. He knew that it was a cat because of its tail. He knew it was a cat because of its ears. He knew it was a cat because it suddenly snarled loud enough that the echo reached him in less than a second.

What had Cooper said before he'd left her house?

The jaguar is alive in Sedona.

THE DJED: PART II

INVASION OF REALITY

Cooper was awakened by the pounding at her front door. It was ten o'clock. She would have rather taken a few minutes to work the kinks from her neck (sleeping sideways like she'd done had forced most of her upper body muscles into unknown configurations) but the pounding was relentless. It wasn't until knuckles began beating against her back porch sliding glass door that she rose, stretched one time, brushed both hands through strawberry curls and pulled her T-shirt down over her belly button. She took two steps then stood motionless in the bedroom doorway, her groggy-brained alarm clock bellowing shrill warnings that immediately engaged memories of headless jaguars and sword-wielding suns.

The police officer's silver badge bounced sunshine directly at her and she lifted her forearm, the one with the djed tattoo, to block the white pain from reaching her eyes. A second officer roamed the porch decking, looked at the water pitcher but didn't touch it, scanned the desert landscape as if looking for something in particular.

"Ma'am," the officer at the glass door was saying though his voice was muffled. "Ma'am. Could we speak with you?"

She tried not to look guilty even though she wasn't. Oddly, and only for the brief moment that it took her to walk to the door, she feared being taken in for questioning only because such an unexpected circumstance would mean leaving behind a table and kitchen full of dirty dishes. She slid the door open.

"I'm Detective Beets. This here is Detective Dreagan. Do you mind if we come in?"

Cooper looked over her shoulder at the table. "Can we talk on the porch? My house is a mess." Detective Beets' eyes were covered with stereotypical cop sunglasses (big, round and mirrored) but she knew he was scanning the home's interior.

"It's getting hot out here. Heat wave ain't over yet." He paused to entice a reaction from Cooper. When she said nothing, he added, "Okay then. But a couple of glasses of water would be nice."

Cooper opened the door and pointed. "Could you hand me that pitcher?" she said. Detective Beets did so. "I'll be right out."

As she filled the pitcher, she stared at the flat screen TV on the wall, remembering the news anchor's announcement, remembering that she might become a prime suspect. She'd done nothing but she'd seen everything. When she returned to the porch, the table umbrella was open and both officers sat under its shade. She poured them water and sat between them.

"Do you know why we are here?" Detective Beets said, removing his sunglasses. His face, in many ways, mirrored Tom Selleck's, right down to the bushy mustache.

Cooper didn't bite. "It's awfully early for a Sunday. I usually sleep in. Could we just get to the point?"

Sitting to her right, a younger Detective Dreagan removed his sunglasses (also cop-like). He was not as cheerful as his counterpart and he looked nothing like any cop she'd ever seen on TV. In fact, he looked more like a criminal. "You are Cooper Reyes, aren't you? The Sedona guide? One who wakes at the crack of dawn to lead droves of ignorants into our mountains and valley passes?" There was a silent pause. "And you usually sleep in on Sundays?"

Cooper's grogginess caused anger to form quickly. "I had a late night."

"How about Friday nights?" Dreagan said. "Are you up late on Fridays as well?"

Cooper turned away from Dreagan and looked straight at Beets. "So he's the bad cop, eh?" she said, thumbing with her right hand. "Why don't you tell me why you're here on a Sunday drinking water with me on my porch instead of inside a church where people need saving?"

Beets reached into his tan shirt pocket and opened the folded piece of paper he'd stored there; he flipped it onto the table. "Do you know this person?"

On the paper was an artist's sketch. Cooper thought she knew the face, but wasn't sure. She snatched the paper to study it further. "No," she said.

Dreagan again chimed in. "Luke says you were at his restaurant late Friday night."

Cooper continued staring at the sketch. The face was familiar but not the bald head. Even the neck, which abruptly ended at the paper's bottom edge, seemed a part of some recent memory.

"He says you were waiting for someone," Dreagan continued. "Is this that person?"

Cooper shook her head. "No," she repeated.

Beets said, "I suppose you've heard that one of our officers went missing Friday night?"

Cooper nodded. "It was on the news."

"We have a witness that saw the woman in that sketch leave the alley next to Charleys around the same time we last heard from the officer. Café Aus is just a block away from there and you were sitting outside."

Cooper nodded.

Dreagan snatched the sketch from Cooper's hands. "So did you see this woman or didn't you?"

Beets said, "Please excuse Dreagan. The officer that is missing is his best friend."

"I must have left the restaurant before any of this happened," Cooper said, dreamily, since the identification of the person in the sketch preoccupied her mind.

"That's what Luke told us," Beets said.

"Or we would be here arresting you right now," Dreagan added.

"My friend stood me up," Cooper said. "That's all I know. That's all I saw."

"And who is this friend?" Beets asked. "Perhaps he knows something."

"Who says I was waiting for a man?" Cooper stood. "Doesn't matter anyway. It was just another spiritualist who wanted to arrange a personal tour into the canyon."

Dreagan stood and Beets followed. "His name?" Dreagan demanded.

"Chris Cower." Cooper said. "Now, if you don't mind, I have some cleaning up to do. I'm a very busy woman, preparing to lead droves of ignorants into our mountains and valley passes." She glared at Dreagan who returned his sunglasses to his nose.

"Cower," Dreagan said. "How do you spell that?"

"Just like it sounds." She spelled it for him anyway.

"We'd like to ask you more questions should the need arise," Beets said.

Cooper nodded. "Good day, gentlemen."

Once the police cruiser was out of her driveway and down the road, Cooper collapsed onto her couch. The dishes needed washing, her kitchen needed cleaning, her home needed a good hour or two of her attention. But that was now impossible since her mind was overwhelmed with a singular revelation: the person in the sketch, with a lot of long, dark hair drawn in over the bald head, was the woman to whom she'd served dinner last night. The woman in the sketch was Marcy Ruminski.

Billy had intended to ask Marcy if she wanted to walk with him to the library but she wasn't home. Even though she could be annoyingly callous sometimes, he did enjoy her company. Marcy always put a different spin on his thoughts and though it was hard for him to admit, he liked that part of her—always challenging him, and, always doing what women were good at: changing their minds.

He knocked on her door several times and even went around back to peek into the back porch window just in case she hadn't heard him. It was well after noon so he doubted that she was still asleep. "Marcy," he shouted. "Yoo-hoo."

He stood on the porch another three minutes before giving up. When he turned to exit, his attention was drawn to dozens of dark red circles that stained the wooden porch floorboards. Blood, perhaps. There were six large circles about an inch in diameter and many smaller dribbles. He immediately thought about the cubit in the Cadillac and he hoped that Marcy had been correct: that the man had been drunk and that he and she had been misidentified. The blood could have been left by an animal or…there were many possible explanations including ones that discounted any blood at all. Still—

I warned you. You know what happens when you don't listen, the cubit had said.

Billy started his walk along Dry Creek Road, trying not to think about Marcy and their journey home last night which was, of course, impossible. Every vehicle that approached from behind made his skin crawl just a little and, for each vehicle, he stopped, stepped away from the road and waited as it passed, ensuring himself added safety even though he knew that if anyone would have wanted him dead, he would be dead already.

If that bitch screws everything up, I guarantee you they'll all die.

In the thigh pocket of his cargo shorts, he carried a small spiral notebook and mechanical pencil. Earlier that morning he'd jotted down information according to Cooper and his intention now was to do a bit of research, check out her story, ensure himself that she was not a liar. He'd have a couple of hours before his planned dinner date with Lax and his son.

Sedona's public library was conveniently located at the end of Dry Creek Road, about a block from the intersection with Highway 89. Also convenient for Billy was the fact that the library had decided to open on Sundays for the holiday month, something that it had not done before but was experimenting this year thanks to a grant from some local bibliophiles.

Inside, the library was quite busy. Over in the children's section, a group of youngsters sat in a circle as a woman read to them. To the right of the children were computer kiosks but every one of the ten computers was occupied. To burn time while he waited, Billy sat in the reference section where local newspapers hung from wooden poles that rested inside a square rack. He grabbed the pole that held last Wednesday's edition of the *Sedona Red Rock News* and sat at a square, wooden table to read it. Much of the usual small town community news occupied the first section of the newspaper, including stories in which gossip was given a degree of credibility by having it published and promoted. Some community members complained about street construction and the "crooked" way construction contracts were granted. Some congratulated Christian leaders for merging gaps between the local spiritualists and God. The Village of Oak Creek didn't like the fire station that was going to be built there. Cottonwood was worried about increased traffic without the law enforcement necessary to enforce the increased traffic. A few articles devoted column inches to the Thanksgiving holiday season, to shopping, and to recipes.

But it was the front page of the sports section that changed Billy's quick scan consumption to full immersive reading. The bold headline drew him in:

Llama Lunatic Mountain Bike Race Begins Monday

The City of Sedona and the Village of Oak Creek announce the first annual Llama Lunatic Mountain Bike Race to be held on Monday, Dec. 1.

In cooperation with the National Parks Service and sponsorship by BETH Pharmaceuticals, the race will traverse a loop marked by the Llama Bike Trail. National race professionals will be challenged by sharp natural benches, slickrock, big drops and, perhaps, a cactus or two as they traverse the relatively new trail around Bell Rock and Courthouse Butte and up the challenging rise of Lee Mountain.

> "This is an event we've been working on for a couple of years," said Gin Arropo, mayor of Sedona. "The beauty of Sedona's autumn will bring in dozens of prominent athletes from all over the country which will be a holiday boon for local merchants."
>
> BETH Pharmaceuticals, manufacturer of the popular Popstar health pill, has guaranteed a purse of over $50,000 to participants.
>
> "BETH Pharma pledges to bring everyone total health," said the company's president, Richard Manson. "We can't think of a better cooperative effort to bring this mission to these superb athletes and to the people of Arizona."
>
> Stretches of the Llama Trail will be cordoned off for spectators along the entire route. The National Park Service reminds you that if you visit any of Sedona's beautiful natural parks to "Take what you bring and leave what you find." Please visit our local adventure merchants for further information.

BETH Pharmaceuticals. Las Cruces. The Popstar pill. The crazy Hispanic lady he'd almost killed. Deere-hat man. Short chunks of memory collided into a maelstrom of coincidental circumstance. He quickly snatched his notebook and pencil and scribbled the connective keyword sentences, one after the other, on a blank page in the center of the notebook. On the last line, at the bottom of the page he wrote the same name he'd seen on the front page of the *Enquirer* at Walmart—the name of the president of the corporation that owned BETH Pharmaceuticals: Richard Manson.

Two of the computers were now vacant and Billy quickly returned the newspaper to its rack. The monitors were only a couple of feet apart and when he sat at the end of the kiosk, the person to his left, a middle-aged woman who did not wear makeup, looked at him and grinned, then returned to her pursuit of keywords that included cacti, first-aid and poison.

He'd intended to begin his research for anything related to vortices and Sedona but found himself more curious about BETH Pharmaceuticals and the odd connections he was making to that company and recent experience. He opened up Google.

BETH, which was an acronym for Bringing Everyone Total Health, was a relatively new company, having become public just three years ago. It manufactured only one product: the Popstar pill. It was the subsidiary of a much larger corporation: Phoenix International. Its ownership was ninety percent in the hands of one man: Richard Manson.

The Popstar pill was the brand name for what many in the industry were calling "the wonder drug." Clinical trials stated that the pill "reacted with the body's chemistry to negotiate a truce with the urge to eat non-nutritious food." Apparently, the Popstar pill had been shown to reduce obesity by "reprogramming the mind to hate bad foods and initiate satiation of caloric intake." Basically, the pill told the body to choose healthy food over junk and to stop eating once caloric intake reached what the body considered enough, not what the mind thought was enough. This, of course, was a panacea to the health industry and a dogmatic attack on those companies that dished out quick, preservative heavy menus. The fast food industry had unsuccessfully lobbied against the FDA's approval of the drug and the Popstar pill had landed in select communities across the country which, in a year, had shown dramatic decreases in obesity rates. Southwestern cities such as El Paso, Las Cruces and Tucson had quickly risen atop the nation's list of healthiest places to live.

Richard Manson, a former professor of biochemistry at Arizona State University had "discovered" the pill. Manson, the biography read, had made his mantra of bringing everyone total health shortly after recovering from a serious surfing accident when he was a teenager. He'd been a fat kid then and he'd always blamed his obesity on the accident, claiming that a healthier body and mind would have prevented it. To fund research, Manson had become a speculator in oil and other natural resources. His savvy investment decisions had soon made him one of *Forbes* richest men in the world, thus allowing him to pocketbook the Popstar pill's development. Today, Phoenix International and subsidiary BETH Pharmaceuticals were preeminent sponsors for several national health- and athletic-related organizations and activities, including the Olympic Games, the X-Games, a bunch of school systems and dozens of charities.

Billy scribbled the information into his notebook then added a single word at the bottom of the notes: Coincidence? He flipped three pages forward. Before going to bed last night, he'd dumped his memory of the dinner date with Cooper into the notebook. Along with notes about Chris Cower's past five-year history, he'd sketched out a reasonable facsimile of Cooper's map. Ten dots were arranged on the notebook paper but he'd not connected them to form star patterns because doing so, he thought, might lock his mind with an answer to the map that might not be correct. Perhaps the dots weren't meant to form stars; he'd wanted to keep his options open.

He'd also stenciled in the three glyphs in approximately the same location that he remembered them: Jaguar, Sun, and Wayeb. He wasn't a very good artist, at least not with pencil on paper, but his memory provided a satisfactory rendition of the symbols. If he saw them on the computer screen, he'd make the connection.

On the notebook page following the map were several words on individual lines. He'd kept the list short since one search term often led to tributaries of links.

He opened up a new browser window and typed "Sedona vortex" into the search box. Results included links to web pages representing some of the local businesses, including a reference to Cooper Reyes. He clicked that link. The web page that appeared was a directory listing that included contact information and a brief description:

> Specializing in one of the most profound vortex sites in all of the United States, Cooper "Clairvoyant" Reyes is your local guide into Boynton Canyon. Hikes into the canyon are arranged by special request only.

"Clairvoyant," Billy whispered aloud. The woman beside him who was concerned with cacti hunkered forward as if she thought Billy was watching her search habits. He jotted down the contact information into his notebook and added the keywords "Boynton Canyon."

The next link he selected took him to an online pamphlet that defined the four main Sedona vortices and the energies they resonated. There was a vortex at Cathedral Rock which resonated with "feminine energies," one at the airport which resonated with "masculine energies," one in Boynton Canyon that provided energetic "balance," and the last was at Bell Rock which offered energies that satisfied all three.

Masculine energies, according to the online pamphlet, resonate with people who are self-confident, who take charge of their own lives, who take appropriate risks. The feminine energies strengthen one's compassion, kindness and consideration of others. Balance weighs the two gender-specific energies equally and resonate in those who do not take action without considering the harm they may cause, while at the same time, deter others from taking advantage of them. Balance, Billy read, was the hardest to achieve and because so few had gained this plateau, its absence in the world was the reason for so much suffering.

Billy wrote in his notebook an additional word, separated by an equals sign, beside the words *Boynton Canyon.*

Boynton Canyon = Balance

The next link Billy chose surprised him almost as much as had Cooper's link and her clairvoyant nickname: Vor-Tech's Glass Menagerie. The web page was an online store with which one could order many of the pieces sold at the brick and mortar counterpart. Billy typed "dagger" into the store's search box. The glass Creation Dagger immediately appeared. The proprietor had even added an engaging green glow around the picture of the dagger that made Billy think of his walk to Starbucks two nights ago. The dagger in the photo on the web page was not broken. Its price was five hundred dollars which, to Billy, was confusing; Marcy had told him earlier that when she had talked to the store's owner on Saturday, five hundred dollars had been his quote…for a broken dagger. Surely, Marcy had simply made a mistake. Vor-Tech's owner (Calvin Alvery, the web page noted) and his wife had been so insistent that Billy take it, they'd pretty much given it to him.

Within the web page's menu along the left side, Billy chose the link "Our Philosophy." Every paragraph he read matched perfectly with his first impression of the couple he'd met. Calvin and his wife, as the philosophy read, promoted the Chakra as the centerpiece of all human existence. The word "Chakra" was hyperlinked for each instance it appeared and when Billy clicked it, he gasped. The cactus woman beside him stood and walked away.

A thorough explanation of the Chakra's human energy systems was wrapped around a small thumbnail image of what was labeled "The Sedona Landscape Temple." It contained two stars, one six-pointed and one five-pointed. He expanded the thumbnail with a mouse click and the two stars, superimposed over a terrain mapping of Sedona, filled the screen; except for added information about the Chakra, it was the same as the sketch Cooper had showed him the night before. Quickly, he flipped his notebook to the page where he'd rendered the memory of Cooper's parchment star map. On the computer monitor, a line connected seven points of intersection through the two stars and each was labeled with one of the Chakra energies.

Billy plucked one of the scrap index cards sitting next to the monitor and used it as a straight edge to connect the dots and create the stars in his notebook. He drew a diagonal line through the center of the stars, similar to what was on the monitor, and extended the line to the lower right corner of the notebook page where it intersected the Wayeb symbol he'd drawn there.

Once he'd finished, he set the notebook and mechanical pencil down on the table and stared at the geometric shapes. The points of the stars and the intersecting diagonal line now provided place names for sixteen different geographic locations, but nothing provided clues as to the location of the Great Hall of the Anasazi. What stood out most was the lonely Wayeb glyph which now had the extension of the diagonal line through its center. He ran his index finger along the line he'd drawn, starting from the jaguar, tapping each of the three glyphs, then repeated the action in the opposite direction, running his finger up the page and to the left. He did this finger-tracing three more times before deciding that, perhaps, the line represented a directional marker.

He sent the Chakra map from the computer to the library's printer, closed the web browser window, then opened up Google Earth and directed the program to center over Sedona. Using Google Earth's straight line tool, he drew a diagonal line with the mouse on the computer screen across the face of Sedona in the same direction as he'd drawn it in his notebook. Grabbing the lines lower right endpoint, he extended it, then zoomed out of Google Earth's satellite image to reveal all of Arizona, extended the line, zoomed out, and repeated this process until all of the southwestern United States was visible. He really wasn't surprised to find that the further he lengthened the diagonal line, the closer to the Gulf of Mexico it grew until it intersected with Port Aransas, Texas.

"Shit," he said a bit too loud. One of the librarians at the circulation desk glared at him. In the children's section, several of the kids' mouths opened in astonishment. The woman reading to them placed a finger to her lips. Billy mouthed the word *Sorry* but didn't say it.

Out of curiosity, Billy zoomed out of the satellite image once more, knowing what he'd find. Fully extended, the diagonal line he'd drawn began in Sedona, crossed through Port Aransas and ended at the ruins of Chichen Itza in Mexico where Cooper had said that Chris Cower had found the Book of the Djed.

"My God," Billy whispered but was, again, too loud. The woman reading looked over at the circulation desk. A librarian headed in Billy's direction.

"Sir," the librarian said. "If you can't keep your comments to yourself, you'll have to leave." She looked at his notebook and then the computer monitor as if she expected to see something unsavory.

Billy cancelled Google Earth and the screen was filled with his previous search that concerned BETH Pharmaceuticals. "I am sorry," he said. "I get carried away sometimes."

"Well, just keep it down or you can carry yourself…" The librarian pushed her glasses up the bridge of her nose and squinted at the computer. "You a teacher or something?"

Billy shook his head. "No. Why do you ask?"

The woman reading to the kids glared at both of them. The librarian lowered her voice. "That Popstar pill is pretty popular among the schools around here."

"How so?" Billy said, and when the librarian did not immediately respond he added, "I'm not a teacher but I am a researcher. Can you tell me more about it?"

Their conversation was beginning to annoy not only the circle of children and their reader, but also the five other people who sat in front of the computers around them. The librarian motioned for Billy to follow her. He closed out his web searches, snatched his notebook and pencil, and plucked the printout of the Chakra star map as he passed the printer. Billy stood near a line of two people who were waiting to check out books as the librarian disappeared into a small room then reappeared with a handful of newspapers.

"Here," she said. "These should provide you with information." She handed him back issues of the *Sedona Red Rock News*. "Frankly, I don't think our kids need it, but you can be the judge of that. I've never thought a pill was any substitute for good old-fashioned child rearing. Parents are just lazy."

"Thank you," Billy said. "I'll return them in a few minutes."

"Take your time. We're open 'til five."

Billy returned to the reference section and began reading, his notebook opened to his entries concerning the Popstar pill. The six newspapers dated back to the previous summer, around the same time Cooper had said that Chris Cower had changed her life. He read that BETH Pharmaceuticals had made a proposal to the city in which the school system would receive, free of charge, the Popstar pill as part of Sedona's mandate to reduce its student obesity population, which had dramatically risen since 2001. The schools would also receive grant funding to improve, and in some cases rebuild, athletic facilities and cafeterias. A heavy stipend would be included to better transportation, in-school technology and textbooks. The proposal came at a time when the city was considering a new school levy against businesses that would have raised the tax rates by, at least, six percent, so it was no surprise that many local business owners supported the effort.

There had been heated arguments in city council meetings mostly due to the fact that Phoenix International was asking for something in return: the release of some national park land on which it would build a casino. The property release would garner extra funds for the city's coffers but it would also disrupt a chunk of land near Lee Mountain that had been preserved since the days of the first settlers who had used the mountain pass to move across the Arizona mesas. Some council members had been accused of accepting "pleasantries" if the proposal were to be accepted. The controversy had finally culminated in the proposal being placed on the back burner for further consideration and the school levy did not pass.

When Billy finished, he returned the newspapers to the librarian. It was a little after four o'clock. "Thank you," he said. "You helped a lot. But tell me…did the school levy pass this year?"

"No," the librarian said, removing her glasses to wipe a smudge with the tail of her blouse. "But BETH Pharma is still involved with the city. Even though their proposal hasn't been accepted yet, they still remain true to some of the promises they'd made in connection to its acceptance. The company gave some money toward rebuilding the high school football stadium and..." The librarian replaced her glasses. "...and it did give the library a bit of funding. That's why we've been able to open on Sundays."

Billy was quick to pick up on the librarian's frustration. "But at what cost?"

"At what cost indeed." She nodded. "It's an uncomfortable catch-22. I hate the idea of this wonder drug but I also love my library. I figure it won't be long before the proposal is accepted. BETH will buy its way into the community."

The librarian's disclosure was familiar. Billy had faced similar circumstances in Port Aransas. Money was always the great influencer, whether it was for the purpose of building a casino on environmentally protected land, or building a front hold into the nutrition decision-making of a public school system.

His denial of coincidence was pretty much decimated, but what was more significant was that he was willing to accept it. Science was his passion and had driven his reason for almost ever. But that was over...over and done with. His parents, of course, would not approve. They would question his sanity just as he had always questioned those who'd been dead set on mythological and spiritual mumbo jumbo. He just couldn't lie to himself anymore. He had to apply the unexplainable more to destiny than to theory. He had to rely on instinct regardless of what facts suggested. He had to believe that he was now living the planned life, one according to the unknown, unseen and unproven greater being.

He realized all of this on the Sedona Roadrunner shuttle as he traveled Highway 89 from the library toward his meeting with Lax. He'd connected the dots, literally and figuratively. He'd been "given" the Book and the dagger for a reason. He'd been led to Sedona for a reason. He'd met Lax, and Cooper and, even, Deere-hat man for a reason. He hadn't just stumbled upon information; he'd been led to it. He'd been manipulated by the hands of either Heaven or Hell to have come this far, to be sitting on this shuttle, on this day, four years before the Mayans predicted that the world would end, realizing that, really, there wasn't a damn thing he could do about it. He absolutely knew that Lax would further his path toward destiny, that Cooper would, that Marcy would, that, perhaps, even the Roadrunner shuttle driver would.

He could almost feel the puppet strings attached to his hands and feet. He hated the idea but it was comforting as well. Did he have free will? He wondered. Did anyone really have it? He could jump off the shuttle and bust his brains all over Highway 89 at any time he chose. Wasn't that free will? He could screw destiny at any moment. Wasn't that free will? The puppet strings were invisible and they had no power to hold him back, and if that's the way he was meant to go, then so be it.

He caressed his chest and the sheathed dagger. He rubbed the star that had been burnt into his hand. He stared at his research notebook page which he'd opened to the star map. A line connected three towns. He'd now been in two of them. He'd collected artifacts in Port Aransas and was sure that he'd find more in Sedona. And he was now certain that destiny would take him to Mexico. Like a character in a fantasy video game, he was stuffing his gunnysack with items that would be necessary to win a final battle. He even knew that fated date: December 21, 2012. If only he knew whose hand was on the joystick. If only he knew which button, the red or the blue, the joystick operator would press next.

The shuttle stopped at the light at Airport Road. It seemed to Billy that this corner had been rather "fated" for him in the past few days. Vor-Tech's was on the far corner to his left. Starbucks was on the near corner to his right. Near the top of Airport Road was the Health Heaven Haven where he'd met Lax and where, according to his recent research, there was one of Sedona's renowned vortices. He thought for only a moment about exiting the shuttle and visiting Calvin at Vor-Tech's; he thought that he should verify Marcy's story. But he didn't. Vor-Tech's was not open and Marcy wasn't a liar. She'd just made a mistake, that's all. But Billy was beginning to wonder; his effort to even consider it was proof. Still, it made no sense why she would lie about such a simple thing. Marcy was an oddity, but she was the only person he could trust. Characters in fantasy games had to collect characters they trusted as much as they had to collect artifacts for salvation.

The shuttle reached The Y a little before five o'clock and when Billy stepped from the shuttle doors and onto the sidewalk, he immediately heard the quick tapping of a car horn to his left. Traffic filled the intersection that connected Highways 89 and 179 and, through the moving melee, he saw a white Ford Ranger on the far side of the road. The small truck was parked along L'Auberge Lane just yards from where he and Marcy had been sitting when the earthquake had shaken his destiny forward. Again, Billy was not surprised. The quaint connections with present and past and coincidental markers with physical constructs were all a part of spiritual momentum. He even giggled. Where else would Lax have been parked?

Once he'd crossed the intersection, Lax's son opened the passenger's door. It creaked a cry of rust infestation and stuck momentarily before Aaron pushed it to its full extension.

"Hello, my friend," Aaron said, his smile comforting and encouraging. "Jump in."

"We are glad you accepted our invitation," Lax added as Billy yanked the door closed.

The front seat was a tight fit but Aaron's thin body made it possible to manage. His poncho tried to tangle the stick shift, adding a degree of difficulty to the truck's navigation.

They headed south along Highway 179 for just a few minutes before Billy said, "Why did you invite me to dinner…I mean really?" He couldn't stop thinking about his sudden revelation with destiny and this made him impatient.

"Are you hungry?" Lax offered, instead.

Billy thought about it. His stomach had not mentioned it to him since his mind had been too preoccupied for it to listen to anything else except the tidbits of research with which he'd been overwhelmed. "Yes," he said. "Yes I am."

"Then that's why we invited you to dinner. Hungry people need to eat."

Billy let it go. Instead, he followed along. "So, what's for dinner?"

Aaron rubbed his stomach. "Maize. Frijoles. Arroz. Pan de horno de pozo. And vanilla flan for desert."

Billy smiled because of Aaron's play between Spanish and English. "Pan de horno de pozo?"

"Pit oven bread," Aaron translated.

"Really? I had some great fajitas last night," Billy offered. "The meat was grilled to perfection but not in a pit oven."

"We don't eat meat," Lax said. "Our ancestors did—they had to. But we are given better choices today."

"Vegetarians," Billy said.

"No," Lax responded without malice and with total contentment. "Respect."

"Well, that certainly puts a new spin on things."

"Indians that don't eat meat." Lax laughed. "Yes. The world is changing—ever changing."

"And I suspect that is why I was invited tonight." Billy's stiffness within the confines of the truck's cab eased and his shoulder and arm relaxed against Aaron.

Lax lifted a heavy eyebrow, his dark-skinned cheek still bunched from his laugh. "You know more than you think you know." He down-shifted as he slowed the truck for a right turn. Aaron's knees accommodated. "Corn and beans and rice and pit oven bread…a magic elixir. Makes a man think about where he's going. Makes a man think about what he's done. Cleans a man out." He laughed again.

They drove along a curiously titled road called Back O' Beyond. To his left rose the grandiose spires of earth known as Cathedral Rock. To his right, and moving closer to them the farther forward the truck traveled, was Oak Creek. Lax passed what seemed to be the last house on the road, drove at least another mile, then parked in front of a single-level, Spanish-style home, reminiscent of just about every other home in Sedona. Billy was surprised only because he'd had the image of the old western in his mind, one in which John Wayne or Clint Eastwood rode into Indian country only to find teepees and smoking fires and food cooking in the sunshine.

"We don't eat meat and we don't live in teepees," Lax said, his smile still strong and vibrant. "But we still love our bows and arrows." He patted Aaron's head twice. "We'll show you."

Lax's home might have looked like something right out of the new millennium from the outside but inside, tradition reigned. There was no clutter. There were no pictures, no paintings, no floor coverings, and it appeared that the room Billy entered (which he assumed was the living room) housed just two electrical components: an air conditioner and a ceiling fan that spawned four light fixtures.

The room was not empty, however. Billy guessed that Lax was a craftsman, schooled in the fine art of woodworking. The couch and easy chair and two small end tables had either been purchased on a reservation or Lax had built them himself. The arms and legs were whittled into compelling logs of intricate patience and had been stained so that the chunks that had been sliced away appeared darker and deeper. The walls, too, were not completely bare. The bow and arrows that Lax had mentioned in the truck hung above the couch. A quill held six arrows. Eight more arrows were attached to the wall in an intersecting pattern that resembled an asterisk. The bow was decorated with six feathers. Again, all of them looked as if they'd been carved by hand.

"Welcome to our teepee," Lax said. "Aaron. Would you please check the fire?"

Aaron disappeared around a corner of the room to the left. When Billy followed Lax to the couch, he saw that the corner around which Aaron had gone beheld an anteroom that was too dark to see through. He guessed that more of the house existed beyond the chamber but its darkness masked any possible confirmation.

"Please, have a seat." Lax offered the easy chair with an open hand. "Tell me what you think. It's Aaron's first piece."

The chair had hand-stitched, brown upholstery that wrapped around the seat and backrest. Its arms of wood twisted into a knob at the end of the arms' length, as if the craftsman had taken individual branches and had turned them clockwise upon one another, similar to a strand of braided hair. The legs of the chair were formed in the same knurled pattern. When Billy sat in it, the comfort consumed him, seemingly wrapping itself around the perimeter of his backside.

"You are one with the chair, yes?" Lax asked.

"Amazing." Billy patted the twisted arms. "I've not seen or felt anything like it."

"He learns very fast. Aaron will be a master craftsman one day." Lax sat on the couch which was made in much the same way as the chair. "It is of learning that I asked you to come here today. It's the reason why you came to Sedona. You are here but you don't know why you are here."

"Yes," Billy said. In front of him was the dark anteroom. His attention was drawn to it as Lax continued.

"What do you see?"

"I don't know what you mean."

"In the darkness. What do you see?"

The more he stared at the dark chamber, the further his consciousness seemed to be consumed by it. He began to feel lightheaded, as if his brain's neurons had suddenly sprang from the top of his head and now floated an inch or two above him.

"I see…"

The darkness twisted, forming lighter shades of shadow across the blackness. And then a face, hazy at first, took shape.

"I think I see a woman," he said.

"Who is she?" Lax interjected.

The face drifted within the anteroom's darkness and formed into…

"It's Alixel," Billy sighed. "But how can that be?" He turned away from the image just for a second and when he looked back, the face was gone.

"She still lives here," Lax said. "Her spirit has never left."

"You know Alixel?" Billy continued staring into the darkness but the face did not return.

"She is my sister. She said you would be coming."

Whatever part of him that seemed to have separated from his body now dropped back into place. He could actually feel its invisible weight. “Then you know all about…If you and she are siblings then…She told me that I was supposed to save the world…And that means…”

“It means that I am also here to help you fulfill that destiny.” Lax scooted across the couch to within arm’s length of Billy. “Your hand…let me see it.”

Billy turned in the chair to offer Lax his right hand and presented it palm up.

“I knew it was you when I saw this yesterday,” Lax said. “A sign of divine protection. And there is only one way that you could have received this mark. You have it, don’t you?”

Billy said nothing as Lax traced his palm with one fat finger.

“You have the Creation of the End dagger.” Lax lifted the finger and pointed at Billy’s chest. “I can feel its energy. It has been lost for so long and now it may be the only thing left to prevent an age of chaos.”

The last person to see the dagger, besides his best friend whom he’d killed with it, was Alixel. It seemed almost prophetic that her brother would be the next. Billy slowly unbuttoned his shirt to reveal the dagger’s white haft and the star etched in it that duplicated the pattern burned into his palm. He reached for it but Lax grabbed his wrist.

“No,” Lax demanded. “Keep it there. The next time it is unsheathed will be the moment it saves your life.”

Billy’s hand hovered over the dagger. “When?” Billy whispered. “Do you know?”

Lax settled back into the couch. He shook his head. “Only the Great Spirit knows that answer. But I can tell you this…” Aaron walked through the dark anteroom at that moment. Billy buttoned his shirt. “The jaguar will try to get it from you and you cannot let that happen.” He turned to Aaron. “How is the fire, son?”

“Smokin’,” the youngster said and grinned. He watched Billy reattach the last button of his shirt. “It’s ready for him.”

“Let’s cook, then,” Lax said then looked at Billy. “Follow us.”

Aaron returned to the anteroom abyss and Lax urged Billy to follow. As he entered the dark chamber, Billy was overwhelmed by a feeling of supreme serenity, as if the small, dark space was filled with all of the world’s answers, as if he were walking through dark heaven. On the far side of the room, Aaron lifted what appeared to be a tarp that hung from the top of a doorway. A flash of light appeared then was gone as the tarp fell back in place. Billy’s hand wandered forward, connected with the makeshift door, swung the heavy obstruction to one side and entered what was certainly a kitchen. Lax followed.

Again, Billy was greeted with the accoutrements of modern day home living. The kitchen was not much different than Cooper's in that it contained many high-end appliances. What the "front" room lacked for efficiency, the land behind the tarp excelled. The most fascinating thing about the space, however, was its glass walls. From the floor to the ten-foot ceiling, sunshine gathered in abundance. Only the corners of the kitchen were not transparent. It was, in all ways, a solarium. Greenery sat and hung in pots and packages everywhere. The smell was pure nature.

Lax pointed as he described some of them. "Basil. Oregano. Parsley. And these over here…almost impossible to find in America." The plants he now tickled with all of his fingers ranged in size and raggedness. Some had flowers. Some looked almost ill. Some looked too deadly to even touch. None of them was familiar to Billy. "This one gives the body defense against water-borne viruses. This one soothes rashes caused by allergies. This one just makes everything come out according to plan. Kind of like the frijoles but much prettier." He chuckled. "And that one over there provides the mind with the ability to awaken to possibilities outside of experience."

Billy walked over to a small tree that stood about five feet high. Small pods that looked like twisted pasta shells hung from several limbs. He lightly touched one of them. "Sounds like a narcotic," he said.

Lax huffed. "A word used by law enforcement to control a person's attempt to break the bonds of the natural world."

"You grew up in the 60s, I'll bet."

Lax just smiled.

Beyond the glass, the home's backyard patio had been laid with bricks that looked as if they'd been formed and fired by hand. Brown and beige and tan and sand colored the earth's floor in artistic patterns that made sense only to those who gave them concentrated effort. Beyond the perimeter of the brick paving and straight ahead from where Billy stood behind the solarium glass wall was a circular indentation in the ground that spewed smoke.

"You are a cook," Aaron said, tugging at Billy's short sleeve. "Come on. I'm hungry."

Aaron led Billy through an opening in one glass wall and out onto the pavers and Billy immediately gasped. The glory of the solarium and the fine craftsmanship of pavers and furniture were miniscule compared to Cathedral Rock which towered before him, its twin spires of sedimentary history nestled between mounds of abutments that were many yards higher. Billy's head craned at an angle greater than forty-five degrees so as to encapsulate the magnitude of such beauty. "My God," he said.

"Our God," Lax added. "But I think that deserves a little latitude."

"There's not much difference as far as I've been able to tell."

Lax shuffled sideways to where Billy stood in amazement. "We are learning, aren't we? Alixel would be proud."

Billy thought of responding but he knew that it was unnecessary. Their silent bond had been secured. And he knew that he'd finally arrived in Sedona.

The food cooked in a clay pot that was buried in the ground. Aaron taught Billy how to cook bread in it by sticking discs of dough against the sides of the pot with a heavy glove. It took only minutes to bake and when the dough was cooked, it fell to the bottom of the pot where it was plucked free with a long, metal fork. Beans and rice and a heaping helping of grilled fresh vegetables and herbs from the solarium sat on a hand-crafted wooden table. There were no plates and only a single wooden spoon occupied each of the food bowls. The procedure for eating in the Lax household entailed the immediate use of the fresh pit oven bread stuffed with whatever assortment of fillings a person wanted. There was no waiting. Since the idea was to eat the bread while still hot, Billy could be eating while Aaron waited for another disc of dough to cook. They took turns, basically.

"It seems that every time I have dinner with someone, the food just keeps getting better," Billy said, catching a strip of green pepper that fell from bread as he nibbled it. He plopped it into his mouth. "Cooper's peppers were good but not this good."

Lax backed away from the clay pot with a disc of baked dough clasped in the claws of the long fork. "Cooper?" he said, his big eyebrows furled with concern. "Cooper Reyes?"

Billy nodded and took another bite.

"She's bad news," Lax continued. "She tried to steal the Cubit."

Billy had just stuck the last chunk of bread into his mouth and now he choked. Aaron came around behind him and slapped his back.

"Of course we know about the Cubit," Lax said. "We are its protectors."

When Billy could breathe again, he drank some water. "She said it was Cower who tried to steal it. Chris Cower."

"He didn't try. He did. But she helped him. Do you know where it is?"

"I used to but the hurricane swiped it away in June."

Lax shook his head. "No. It didn't. It returned to Mexico. It returned to the land of our forefathers. As did the daggers. Our great mother of nature has a way of correcting earlier mistakes." Lax ate his piece of bread without stuffing it. "But we made a big mistake trusting that man, and we'll likely pay for it in the end."

"If you know where it is, why don't you just go and get it?"

"That's your mission Billy Jo Presser."

Billy thought about the notebook he carried in his cargo shorts front pocket, about the map he'd drawn in it, about the line connecting three cities, about his own premonition that he would eventually end up in Mexico. "Chichen Itza," he whispered to himself.

Lax stopped chewing and took a moment to stare at Billy. "You should understand what you will be getting into."

"I already do. That thing killed all of the people I cared about."

"The Cubit doesn't kill anyone. It makes people kill."

"Either way…" Billy sat down in one of the wooden chairs. The sun painted the horizon with the same desert colors as it had the night before. Cathedral Rock glowed within its iridescence. "Alixel told me that there is only one way to kill a cubit." He patted his chest and the dagger. "I saw her use two of these. She sure could take out those damn things."

"One of the daggers was mine," Lax said and sat beside Billy. "We thought that she might need them both." When he broke off another chunk of bread, steam escaped from a hidden pocket and the sudden heat made him drop the bread onto his poncho. When he plucked the bread from his lap, his finger caught the tail of the poncho, and he accidentally lifted it as he brought the bread to his mouth. For an instant, Billy saw an inch-wide scab just below Lax's dark-skinned rib cage, as if he'd been recently stabbed there. He pulled the poncho down, ignoring Billy's stare. "Now they've all returned home as well, except yours, of course."

"That leaves you defenseless," Billy said.

Lax huffed and smiled. "Aaron. Could you go and bring us some dessert, son?" Once Aaron had finished his last bite of stuffed bread and had disappeared into the solarium kitchen, Lax added, "How old do you think I am?"

Billy shook his head and lifted both shoulders. "If you lived in the sixties…fifty-five, maybe."

"I'm more than five times that age, as is my sister. We come from a long line of the ageless. We are never defenseless. Some would even call us invincible, at least up until the time that we accomplish what the Great Spirit has placed us here to do."

Billy really wasn't surprised. He'd given up questioning the fantastic. The energy drain wasn't worth the effort anymore. He accepted what was said as fact and considered Alixel's fate. "So your sister's purpose was to kill Albert Stine?"

Lax shook his head. "If you remember, it was Janine Bender who killed that beast."

It took him mere seconds to realize the correct answer. "Me," he said. "She was there to save me."

"We all have a greater purpose in this world than we can possibly know. She gave you a *chance* to further your own understanding and you took it."

Billy watched Aaron shuffle through the kitchen behind the tall, glass wall. "And your son? How old is he?"

"He's not my son. We can't have children. I adopted Aaron from the Hopi Nation when he was just a baby. He's grown up thinking that I am his father, though."

"I understand," Billy said as Aaron returned with their desserts. "Vanilla flan. That really looks good, Aaron." Billy sliced a chunk of the molded sweetness. A creamy, white filling oozed out. "So if I'm supposed to be going after the Cubit, it sure would be nice to know more about it." He looked at Aaron, suddenly concerned that perhaps that information was not meant for him, at least not yet.

Lax forked a bite of dessert into his mouth and pushed a stray dribble of vanilla filling into the corner of his lip. "That's okay. He already knows. The oral tradition is still quite strong in the Nations."

Once everyone finished dessert and Aaron had retrieved a fresh pot of white tea, Lax sat back in his chair, gazed out over the Sedona sunset, and began…

THE DJED: PART II

THE STORY OF THE CUBIT

(AS TOLD BY A DAYKEEPER)

The Cubit, simply put, is the manifestation of Evil in the Age of Jaguar. It is the physical construct of Evil. It occupies space only so man can understand it, since it is man that it desires. It symbolizes that which drives men mad, that makes the innocent arrogant, that attaches value to materialism. It makes man use the club not for survival, but for power and lust and greed. Man's faulty genetic code harbors that which the Cubit empowers. Fortunately, the absolute influence of the Cubit to control all of life has been kept, for the most part, in check. Good has prevailed. It is the only reason why we are sitting here today, discussing such things, instead of ramming steel blades into each others' chests, instead of dropping warheads on our neighbors' houses.

Still, the Cubit has infiltrated this world in great degrees. The history of man is replete with names associated with the very essence of it. These hopeless humans were those that the Cubit had complete control over. A bully is evil, his genetic code tripping into a need for suffering in concentrated ways, but pure Evil desires the destruction of everything. The real Cubit, the one that represents itself as an innocent wooden crate, desires a human that can change more than schoolyards at recess. The real Cubit desires men with power, men with aptitude, men willing to give their very soul in pursuit of every deadly sin. You've heard of these men. Christians call them Antichrists.

Islam calls them Al Mahdi. And, of course, there are dozens if not hundreds of pseudonyms. They are the supreme beings of everything awful, memorialized in mythology, dreamed about in nightmares, realized in places all across the world and throughout recorded time.

And this is Evil's greatest accomplishment, not so much that men exist of such malignity but that men should think that Evil exists at all. It is with the Age of Jaguar that Good and Evil was created, thus giving moral superiority to those who think their Good justifies those atrocities they bestow upon those they categorize as Evil. Just think of all the death and suffering we can attribute to this Age's third creation: Religion. I can justify my God as being more righteous than your God and if you don't believe me, I'll kill you, or have my followers kill you, or have my country kill you. A man who holds the power of the Cubit in his hands can change thousands. A man who holds the power of the Cubit in his hands can control an army. A man who holds the power of the Cubit in his hands can end the world as we know it, thus ushering in the next Age as one of pure chaos, when there will be no hope, no mercy, no love—when murder will be an acceptable means to an end and only the worst of humanity will survive. The Jaguar will be dead, its position as guardian of the underworld gone with it, and the retched population of the underworld will eat upon this earth.

Much of the Cubit's history has been lost in time. The destruction of great cultures almost always included the destruction of their knowledge so as to 'prevent such Evil' from spreading into those who have conquered them. That is why the oral tradition is so important. One can destroy what I write but cannot take away what I remember, and I as long as I tell stories before I die, knowledge is saved. The knowledge of the Cubit in my time, I now pass onto you, so that you, too, will not let the world forget.

The Cubit is uniquely adept at masking its influences, usually destroying everything human so as to silence any transfer of its existence. You, Billy, have seen this as the consumption of human flesh. Those that have been 'cubited' devour their primaries just as Evil consumes Good so as to hide itself, so that no warning can be made, so that Evil is accepted as normal. If this process of transformation is allowed to continue unabated, you can imagine how quickly an entire culture could be consumed. And so was the case with the ancient Maya.

My story begins with the name, Samaal, which in Yucatec Mayan means 'tomorrow.' It should be comforting to know that in the presence of Evil, no matter how consuming that Evil may seem, there will always be at least one who will survive to record the history; there will always be at least one whose charge it is to destroy those men who have come under the

Cubit's greatest influences and help prevent Evil from consuming the next population by hiding the Cubit from temptation. Samaal was this man in the ninth century. Samaal was in Chichen Itza when that city fell to the influences of the Cubit.

For many years, the Maya of the Lower Peninsula and present-day Guatemala migrated north. The city of Chichen Itza not only became one of the first great immigrant cities in this hemisphere, it also became the center for trade from cultures outside of the Mayan civilization. Thus, Chichen Itza became what might be analogous to an early Rome or New York City, governed and socialized by an extremely diverse population of customs and histories, which, unfortunately, is the perfect breeding ground for Evil's influence. The more diversity a population has, the easier it is to create dissension, to blame another culture as being the 'bad' culture and to morally lift one's own culture up as being supreme.

But great diversity is also essential to the exploration of human consciousness and the shattering of barriers that tend to prevent the progression of the mind. Though Chichen Itza eventually destroyed itself, it became the center of knowledge for the growth of agriculture, architecture and astronomy…particularly astronomy. The Mayan calendar and the end date that you know so well were edified in the years of the Great City and Samaal had a lot of influence in these developments. That's because, like myself and my sister, Samaal was a Daykeeper, an ancient warrior of the mind if you will, tasked to keep record of all time for all time to come—tasked to guard the Cubit.

Chichen Itza remained prosperous until the Cubit was discovered during the construction of the city's observatory, Caracol. A renowned architect of the time, Ka'at, stole the Cubit from a hidden chamber in which Samaal had placed it. It was not long until Ka'at became very powerful in a city that had no single leadership. Ka'at ruled with might and fury, introducing human sacrifice as a means for control. The Cubit offered Ka'at the power of the universe but ended up destroying him and all of his people. The Maya of that time disappeared from the face of the earth. Scientists, today, can only speculate as to what happened to them. There are also some pretty wacky claims by others concerning creatures from outer space. But we know what happened to them. Samaal passed the knowledge forward, preserving it in writing within the observatory vault from where the Cubit had escaped his protection, and preserving it in the oral tradition as he passed this knowledge onto another Daykeeper.

The Mayans killed themselves as the Cubit's influence spread among them quickly and with intentional malice. Very few escaped this total, self-cultural, massacre. Samaal was one of them and he fled with the Cubit.

The Cubit disappears in history for several hundred years, during the time of the Dark Ages. It reappears right here in Sedona around the thirteenth century. It is guarded by Eka, an Anasazi Daykeeper, and is kept in the Great Hall, a place of worship but forbidden to those uninvited for fear of certain death.

Now, if this story is starting to sound familiar, it is. Daykeepers can only maintain the historical record and can *attempt* to prevent the Cubit from influencing man, but we cannot undo the aberrant genetic code that makes man repeat his own mistakes. The Cubit again finds solace in the possession of the son of the Anasazi ruler and, again, an entire population slaughters itself. The atrocities were cited on the walls of the Great Hall before Eka fled with the Cubit when, again, the Evil is lost in time.

My sister and I became involved in the eighteenth century. Our charge was not only to hasten the capture and protection of the Cubit but also to destroy those who had gained maniacal power over even larger populations of people. The world had expanded tremendously since the days of the Anasazi, and now the Cubit, through one man, could endanger millions.

Alixel was responsible for Napoleon Bonaparte. She 'dispatched' the dictator on the island of Elba in the year of 1821 then took the Cubit across the Atlantic with the intention of returning it to its safe-haven under the ruins of the Caracol observatory at Chichen Itza, but her ship was intercepted by a gang of pirates in the Gulf of Mexico led by captain Jean Lafitte. He commandeered the ship and enslaved Alixel but did not find the Cubit stashed in a hidden cargo hold. When he returned with his new prizes to his home fort in Galveston, Texas, one of his shipmates stumbled upon the Cubit; it was not long before the shipmate's cubit shared this secret with the island of pirates.

Lafitte, who took a shine to my sister, believed her to be a princess of the ancient Maya and gave her that Mayan name, Alixel. He was very protective of Alixel; his men were not even allowed to touch her. But this, of course changed as the men changed. Not touching Lafitte's female treasure only instigated the deed from a growing cadre of cubits.

Late one night while Lafitte and Alixel were sleeping, a band of cubits placed the Cubit in bed with Lafitte and it changed him, his cubit crawling forth to take immediate charge of the dead around him. As you know, my sister is quite talented with her Creation Dagger and she quickly dispatched dozens of them. Lafitte, however, took the Cubit and fled the island on the stolen French ship which he had renamed *The Pride*.

The story from here gets somewhat sketchy since my sister was no longer around to record the Cubit's successive history with Lafitte, but we do know this: the next time the Cubit appears, it is in the possession of Adolph Hitler and I am sent to retrieve it and kill the fuehrer. The Cubit is transported back to the Great Hall where it is kept protected from temptation until the arrival of Chris Cower. From that point on, you probably know more than I do.

"Lax is my real name but you can call me Alaxel or Alax or Lax. My sister preferred Alaxel. She gave me that name. She felt that if she was going to be known as a Mayan princess, then I should be known as a Mayan prince. Honestly, I prefer Lax. It's easier to say and has a kind of ring to it, don't you think?"

"Amazing," Billy said. "Truly amazing."

"And every bit the truth."

"No one's going to believe me, you know."

"The story's telling is not meant to make believers out of mortals. It is told so that it is not lost."

Up on the smaller of the two Cathedral Rock spires that now radiated sunset red, perched a bird that was unrecognizable at its distance. Billy knew that it was a bird only because he had seen it land there just moments before Lax had finished his story. It flapped its wings, just tiny flips of feathery arms against the waning sunlight, then leapt from the spire and plummeted toward the ground, disappearing into the shadows created by the majestic rock. Moments later, Billy watched it reappear, flying low to the ground but now half the distance from where it had fallen and heading straight at him. It bellowed a sharp squawk and this caused both Lax and Aaron to turn toward the noise.

"Osi," Lax said to Billy. "Short for Osiris, the Egyptian caretaker of the underworld. He's been hanging around ever since the earthquake."

"He likes our pan de horno de pozo," Aaron said and stood to add a piece of dough to the earthen oven that still steamed with warmth.

The bird, which Billy knew was a hawk when it flew two feet over his head, landed at the apex of the house's roof where its talons slipped momentarily on clay tiles before it righted itself and screeched once again.

"Una momento, por favor," Aaron said to the bird as he slapped a disc of dough into the oven. A couple of minutes later, he produced a round of fresh bread clasped in the claws of the long metal fork and waved it at Osi. "Come and get it," he yelled. The bird dropped from the roof and dove at Aaron who flipped the bread into the air for Osi to snatch with huge talons.

The bird flew off into the growing darkness and landed close enough for Billy to hear its squawks of delight as it feasted.

"Why didn't you call the bird Jag?" Billy asked. "You know…short for Jaguar."

Lax leaned forward, the hint of a grin tickling the left side of his face. "I don't understand. Osi is a good name, don't you think?"

"I mean…You said that the Jaguar was the guardian of the underworld. Why use an Egyptian namesake? The word 'Cubit,' too, is also connected with Egyptian history. For that matter, so is the Djed. I'm confused why these Mayan artifacts reference Egyptian ideas. It is historical fact that the two civilizations could have never intertwined. Each was dominant during a different epoch of evolution. Not only that, but they had this gigantic body of water separating them called the Atlantic Ocean."

Lax's grin widened. Aaron remained near the pit oven where he continued to cook more bread for the bird. "Perplexing isn't it? Man is too attached to time and space to really understand that all things are connected by everything that came before, everything that currently is, and everything that will ever be. Jaguar and Osiris and the Chinese Yama are only words. It's the concept and the construct and the comprehension that is universal, not the words. I think that, one day, you will understand. It is a transcendence that few ever attain."

Aaron tossed a fresh disc of bread like a Frisbee into the darkness. Osi squawked its gratitude.

"Until then," Lax continued, sitting straight up in his chair with a new, concerned look on his face, "beware of everything that wants to prevent that knowledge from finding you. Remember I told you that the Cubit has lived in Sedona for many years. In that time, more men than Chris Cower have chanced upon it—more men than Chris Cower have touched it. Fortunately, none of them have been the messiah of death but all who are not the messiah are his servants. And they roam everywhere, in all parts of the world, occupying positions of control and influence and change. Some of these cubits lust for power that is only a delusion; it will always be the case that they exist only because the messiah of death, the Antichrist, allows them to do so. They exist to serve His ultimate fate: the end of the Age of Jaguar and the beginning of an Age of Chaos."

"Who is it?" Billy asked. "Who is the Antichrist?"

"Evil clouds that knowledge from even the Daykeepers. But he lives… now…today. And he awaits the omega point: December 21, 2012."

"Is it true that this…" Billy hesitated, thinking that the word *man* was now incorrect. "Is it true that this *thing* needs the Cubit and the daggers and the Book of the Djed to complete the transference?"

"Alixel told you this." Lax didn't wait for an answer. "Yes. And the necessary ceremony must be done in the right place and at the right time. That's why, other than for protection, you must never give up your Creation Dagger, particularly since it is the Creation Dagger of the End that will either save the world or end it."

"Where?" Billy said. "When?"

"Only the Book of the Djed and Great Hall of the Anasazi can tell us that."

"And where is that?"

"I can't tell you…at least not yet. But when the time is right, we'll go together. And it won't be long. Chances are, I suspect, you'll figure it out for yourself before that time. If so, I warn you that there are many out there who desire its location. The Evil from the Cubit remains in the Great Hall and still produces a mighty influence over mere mortals and the cubits that roam Sedona. The energy of false promises can seem overpowering."

Aaron threw the last piece of cooked bread into the consuming darkness that was now lit only by the house's solarium and the dying embers in the ground under the pit oven. Osi squawked with delight one final time before its wings could be heard pushing the air as it took off to search for meatier snacks.

Cubits, Billy thought but didn't say it.

"Yes," Lax said. "I guarantee you that at least one has been keeping its eyes on you. It wants what you have and will wait until the right time to get it. It will use those around you to get it. And it cannot be killed without that which you carry close to your heart."

An unrelenting silence fell over the triumvirate as Billy sat and stared at Cathedral Rock, its spires somehow darker than the pure moonless night behind it. Again, he was amazed by the absence of any nocturnal rumblings, just as it had been the night before—just as it had been when the Cadillac had stopped in front of them and the shadow with the ball cap had emerged.

He was now convinced that he'd been followed ever since leaving Port Aransas. Deere-hat man was a cubit and it was waiting for the perfect moment to make its move.

"Could I get a ride home," Billy finally said.

Lax stood. "I thought you'd never ask."

He descended a steep staircase that spiraled. The steps were made of red rock sandstone, the edges of which were so sharp that to fall would mean certain death, not only from the multitude of serrations the human flesh would endure but also from the distance the body would bounce toward the staircase base. He had to take each step at an angle and had to use his trailing hand on the steps behind him to maintain balance. Dust and tiny pebbles that had not been disturbed in quite a while skittered under his feet, making the descent even more problematic.

Light was provided from two directions. Up above, the disc of the sun shone dead center through the hole he must have climbed down though Billy did not remember doing so. Below, a much redder light glowed from some hidden source, making the bottom of the stair pitch questionable at best.

His heart pounded so vibrantly that he thought he heard drums beating somewhere beyond the below. The intense hammering in his chest pressed the sheathed dagger against a torn, white button-up shirt and it flexed the fabric in rhythm with his body's pulsing blood.

A voice infiltrated this noisy solitude.

You must save the world.

He stopped on a step and looked around at the dark round walls that were only a few feet from his face.

Now!

The staircase chamber trembled. Dust and pebbles rained down on top of him. His hand lost its grip on the steps behind him and his foot slipped. Down he went, his back scraping the sharp edges of steps that were few compared to the distance above the floor that he thought he'd been standing. He fell only a couple of feet, which didn't make sense, but he was happy to be alive.

He stood and waited as the dust settled around him. Red clouds swirled and twisted in a mixture of blue sunshine from above and the hidden red glow which now appeared to be emanating from a squat opening directly in front of him. He walked the five steps to the opening, his head at the same height as its archway, but stopped before stooping and passing through it. On the walls on both sides of the opening and across the arch was scrawled the glyphs of a history long dead. The story of their own self-extinction pictured men decapitating men and women torturing babies. Animal glyphs of all breeds scattered away from the doorway, away from the human massacre.

Cower, Billy whispered to himself. *This is what Chris Cower found. The Great Hall of the Anasazi.*

But Billy was too scared to pass through the opening. He didn't like the crimson red aura that pulsed beyond it. It reminded him of temptation. It reminded him of the Cubit.

And then his hand started to itch—the one with the star burned into it. He absently scratched it as he tried to find courage but the palm's irritation was relentless, becoming uncomfortably hot. When he opened his hand, he found that one of the star's scar points glowed—the one in the lower right quadrant—the point that referenced the Creation of the End: the fifth point. He lifted his hand in front of him, palm pointed toward the opening, and the red heat from the scared star became a beacon of white light that ripped through the archway, dousing the crimson aura that undulated within.

Then he stepped through, his hand blazing courage, and he screamed. Staring him in the face was…

Himself. And he grabbed him.

Billy's eyes flickered open, or at least that's what it felt like. For all he knew, his eyelids might never have even closed. The room was so dark.

"Billy."

It was Lax and he was standing right next to him in the anteroom just beyond the kitchen solarium. Billy shook his head, the twisted image of himself burned into consciousness.

"I…saw…me," Billy mumbled. He turned to face Lax's dark outline. "I was there," he continued. "A staircase. An opening. Drawings on the walls of horrible death."

"Sit down for a moment," Lax led Billy out of the anteroom and to the couch.

"No. I'm all right." Billy looked back into the darkness. "But why?"

"That room is our place of worship. Spirits come alive in there. All homes of the true Hopi have them. It is a place we go for answers."

"I didn't ask any questions."

"And those are the answers that are most beneficial."

"I don't understand."

"You will."

Aaron came through the front door then. "Truck's ready for departure," he said.

Lax took Billy's right hand, which was still warm from his experience, and led him out of the house. "It's been a long night, now it's time for rest."

Though he was only ten, Aaron drove. Lax sat beside him, his eyes wary with anticipation as his adopted son successfully operated the stick shift between his bulky legs.

Billy was squashed up against the Ford Ranger's passenger side door so much so that he had to hang one arm out the open window. His body sat at a slight angle. He closed his eyes for a moment but quickly opened them since the memory of his garish face remained planted just behind his eyeballs. Cool Sedona breeze helped alleviate the psychological pain delivered by Lax's spiritual anteroom, but it was not enough to sooth the fear that his evil twin would forever haunt him. Every time he closed his eyes, Bad Billy would be there. Waiting.

Other than a few instructional directions from Lax to his son concerning the rules of the road, they drove in silence the entire way to the corner of Dry Creek and Gringo. Aaron parked beside Stephanie's Cavalier.

"Yours?" Lax asked, pointing at the car as Billy opened the door and almost fell out.

"It belonged to a good friend of mine. I don't drive it much."

Lax shuffled from his place in the middle of the cab and closed the passenger's side door. His thick elbow rested within the window opening. "Don't let your memories haunt you," he said. "Life is too short."

Billy was unsure if Lax was talking about Stephanie Drake whom he'd never met, or the vision of Bad Billy whom he'd never seen. Perhaps Lax was simply offering a final piece of humanistic wisdom. Regardless of the intent, Billy thanked him for all of the knowledge that he'd learned and all of the wonderful food that he'd eaten. When he asked if they'd be getting together again anytime soon, Lax did not provide a straight answer. Instead, he ended their evening with humor.

"Watchum' for bad men, Kemo Sabe," he said, playing the role of Tonto. "May the five elements keep you safe."

Billy watched the truck pull out of the lot and head back toward town. Across the street, Marcy's casita rental appeared unoccupied. No lights were on inside. Again, he wondered why she would have lied to him about the cost of the broken glass replica of a Creation Dagger. Again, he thought of the Cadillac and the shadow wearing the ball cap that had groaned obscure warnings. Again, he wondered if the red drops on Marcy's back porch were blood, and if so, from what animal. Again, he wondered if Marcy was safe.

But he wasn't going to let his thoughts haunt him…which was better said than done.

THE DJED: PART II

THE VORTEX

Cooper thought that the last time she had wasted so much of one day was back when Chris was here. They'd spent an entire Sunday doing absolutely nothing except talking and cooking and eating and exploring each other's bodies. She'd taken no phone calls, had not been concerned about giving tours into the canyon, had done absolutely no work of any kind: no house cleaning, no landscaping, no home maintenance—she'd not even left the house, and that was odd, considering how much staying indoors for long periods of time drove her crazy. But it had been a Sunday when she'd thought she was falling in love. At the time, it had been worth it but in retrospect—knowing now what she didn't then—the day had been a total waste. It had been Chris Cower's greatest deception.

Yesterday had been kind of like that—without the sex, of course. After the good and bad cops had left, she'd sat down on her couch, staring at the walls, thinking about nothing and everything all at once. She'd been excited and doubtful and afraid. She'd spent hours reliving the Cower experience, believing that, if she put enough thought into it, she might remember one small piece of the complex Cower puzzle…just one, that would help her understand why she was sitting like a vegetable contemplating it at all. She'd thought about Billy, wondering if he, too, had some hidden agenda—wondering if he, too, would figuratively screw her. And she'd given Marcy a considerable amount of contemplation. From the moment she'd met the red-fingernailed fortuneteller, she'd thought that something was fishy. Woman's instinct had waved the warning flags, and that instinct had been justified when good cop Beets and bad cop Dreagan had shown her the artist's sketch. Had Marcy Ruminski been dressed up in the ceremonial Jaguar costume? Had Marcy Ruminski driven a dagger into the chest of a ceremonially masked Sun? To think of such things was insane. To have seen such things meant insanity. Besides, Marcy Ruminski could not have been the Jaguar…the Jaguar had been decapitated.

Crazy, incomprehensible thoughts like these were what had sterilized her body for all of Sunday after the cops had left. Finally, as late evening had approached, she had picked her lazy ass off the couch and had cleaned up the remains of a dinner that had been stewing behind the porch window glass sunshine for nearly an entire day. Her sleep had been restless and filled with all of the confusion her wasted-day mind-fuck had bestowed upon her subconscious. But it had all been worth it.

When she woke Monday morning, she felt cleansed…her mind somehow fresh and ready to tackle anything. If the cops showed up again… no worries. If Marcy came hunting for her with a dagger…no problemo. The only thing that could really screw up the day would be if Billy did not bring the Book of the Djed. Her newfound outlook on life really centered on this singular anticipation. It wasn't every day someone would come bearing the gift of eternal life.

She removed the star map parchment from her bedroom wall and rolled it up inside the newspaper just as it had been delivered to her. She then grabbed her Swiss Knife from a dresser drawer; she never went into the canyon without it. She took the newspaper and knife and set them on the dining table as she went to the kitchen to grab a couple of water bladders and some energy bars. From the utility room, she plucked two small backpacks from the nail on which they were hanging. Just before she closed the utility room door, she snatched a pair of men's hiking boots from the floor. She'd stored six pairs in various sizes just in case one of her private tour participants forgot that climbing rocks and walking among desert wildlife was not something for which sneakers—or heaven forbid, flip-flops—were created.

All of the items needed for the hike into the canyon she massed onto the dining table before dressing in cargo shorts and a light cotton shirt that buttoned at the chest. Then she sat and waited. Her intent was to take Billy into the canyon so that if there were any aggressors that wished to follow them with the intent of stealing the Book, they would be on her turf, in a place she knew like the back of her hand, where nooks and crannies and caves and corners made for easy hiding places from those who didn't know they existed.

She drummed fingers across one dark-skinned knee that was crossed over her other leg. It was five minutes before noon and her tension continued to build. She stared at the door.

Was that a knock?

No, just some rattling car as it passed in front of the house.

Okay, what about that? That was definitely a knock.

No. That was a car door slamming.

Why did he drive? He said he would be walking.

Maybe it isn't him. Why don't you get off of your ass and see?

She nodded at the notion and went to the front window. Outside, just beyond the driveway, was an unmarked police car. Cooper immediately recognized the two cops that emerged and now confronted Billy.

Up until the point that the two cops stepped out of their car and asked him his name, Billy Jo Presser was having one heck of a good Monday morning. He'd slept rather well, considering his mind's status before going to bed. Serene, was the word that kept coming to him throughout breakfast. He'd had a serene sleep, the mind at ease as if a mighty weight had been lifted from it. His apartment had a serene comfort level to it: homey, bright and inviting. Even the air outside smelled of total serenity. The heat wave that had taken hold of Sedona since Thanksgiving had cooled down to a more seasonable seventy degrees. Clouds had even returned to the Verde Valley. If the animals could sing, he thought, today would be the day they'd reveal such ability unto the world.

The last thing Billy did before leaving the apartment was grab the Book of the Djed from its hiding place in the bathroom. Shortly after renting the place, he'd found that one of the shelves in the bathroom's linen cupboard had been loose. He'd lifted the shelf from the recessed cupboard to find that the paneled wall inside was also loose. Behind the paneling was the cupboard's two-by-four framing and a horizontal board provided a perfect roost for the Book. He'd kept it and the Book's key page hidden there ever since.

His walk to Cooper's house included a skip or two. He was afraid of nothing, was concerned about nothing, and looked forward to a day full of discovery. Such connectedness that he felt all the way up to the point where he turned the corner from Boynton Canyon Road to Boynton Pass, he likened to surfing…not the water and the wave, but the absolute serenity one feels while mastering Mother Nature for a fraction of a moment. He was king of his domain and nothing was going to drag him down.

Except Detective Dreagan.

Apparently, the two cops had been sitting and waiting and watching just a block from Cooper's front door. Billy had absolutely no idea why they were there and his serene attitude, at the moment, really didn't care. But Detective Dreagan had a way of getting under a person's skin and it took three sentences for Dreagan to prove it.

After confirming his name, Dreagan said, "Hello. I'm Detective Dreagan and this here is Detective Beets. Did you and your girl kill my friend?"

Beets grabbed his partner's arm and attempted a serene smile. "Hold on, Dreagan." He acknowledged Billy with a quick glance then turned to glare sternly at Dreagan. "Forgive him," he said to both Billy and Dreagan. "My partner here has had a difficult day and is sorry for what he said…right?"

Dreagan backed down from his aggressive stance. His eyes fluttered. "I apologize," he offered, but Billy wasn't buying it. It was the cop's smug delivery and his youth that belied his sincerity.

Beets handed Billy a piece of paper. "Do you know this person?" he asked.

Billy unfolded the artist's sketch of someone who looked a lot like Marcy without hair. "Why do you ask?"

"Calvin Alvery says that you and this woman were at his shop last Friday night."

The name sounded familiar. *Alvery...*

"He said that he gave you and this woman a weapon."

"Weapon?" Billy said, still trying to remember the name.

"A glass dagger. One with a broken point."

"Yes. Oh, yes. The owner of Vor-Tech's. He gave us the dagger because of the earthquake."

Beets pulled a second piece of paper from the same shirt pocket as he'd stored the first and handed it to Billy. Dreagan stared indignantly, a smirk pulling the left side of his face into the shape of doubt. Billy shuffled the paper over the face of the Marcy-looking sketch. It was a photograph of a broken-tipped Creation Dagger that looked in every way like the one Calvin Alvery had given him—except for the red stain covering the dagger's broken tip. "Is this the dagger he gave you?"

Billy suddenly felt extremely uneasy. He thought about the real dagger he kept near his heart. He thought about the Book of the Djed which he'd stashed in his short's waistband behind his back. He thought that if they frisked him, he'd be thinking much more about lawyers and courtrooms and jails. He thought that, perhaps, he shouldn't say anything else. Thankfully, at that very moment, the conversation was interrupted when Cooper yelled to him from her front door. "Billy!?"

Dreagan immediately turned to her and yelled, "This doesn't concern you. Get back into your house." Cooper remained at the doorway.

Beets continued. "Is this the dagger he gave you?" he repeated more forcefully.

"How would I know that?" Billy offered. "He gave us a piece of glass that looks like what you have there in the photo, but I can't tell you if that is it."

"Where is the piece he gave you?" Beets asked.

"Marcy has it…had it. She returned it to Vor-Tech's, Saturday."

"Marcy. You mean the woman in the sketch?"

Billy nodded.

Dreagan walked quickly toward him. "Can you tell us where she is, and mind you, your answer will determine if we put you in handcuffs today or tomorrow."

Billy ignored Dreagan. "What is this all about?" he asked Beets. Neither of the detectives noticed Cooper as she walked up behind them.

"Yes," Cooper added. "I'd like to know as well."

"Ma'am!" Dreagan almost yelled. "I told you to get back in your house!"

Beets waved his hands in the air, in a let's-all-calm-down motion. "One of Sedona's police officers went missing Friday night," Beets said to Billy. "A witness saw the woman in the sketch at the scene. Your friend, Cooper here, was near the scene when it happened. That weapon was found near a puddle of blood and was catalogued as evidence, but disappeared from the police cruiser's trunk that same night."

Cooper walked over and stood beside Billy. "Sounds to me like someone wasn't doing their job very well," she said and glared at Dreagan.

Beets' nice-guy approach changed at that moment as he snatched away the papers in Billy's hands. "When we find this woman Marcy," he grumbled, "we'll return for both of you. A missing police officer is not to be taken lightly and we will go to the ends of the earth to find out just what happened. We suspect that both of you are involved and when we find the proof, you'll be spending a lot of time in the Arizona pen."

Billy was about to tell them that the dagger from the crime scene could not be the dagger he'd been given by Calvin Alvery because *that* dagger had been sitting on Marcy's fireplace mantle when he'd awakened on her couch Saturday morning. But before he could say another word, Cooper interjected.

"Good luck with that," she said. "Come back when you have evidence. And don't try to pull anymore of that psychological crap on us because you both stink at it."

"Don't leave town," Beets said.

"Your asses are ours," Dreagan added.

Then both turned away, got back into their car, and spun a rooster tail of dirt that would have covered them both had Billy and Cooper been standing behind it.

"I don't know," Cooper said as if anticipating what Billy was about to say. "I don't know what the hell is going on but your friend is hip deep in it."

She walked back toward her house and Billy followed. "Why would they think that you have anything to do with it?" he said. "You only met Marcy a couple of days ago, right?"

"Right."

"So?"

"So nothing." She stopped at the front door which she had left wide open. "Remember the star map? I got it near where the policeman disappeared. Coincidence, that's all." She walked into the house then pointed at Billy's feet. "Nice hiking boots. They'll do. Come on."

Just who in the hell was Marcy, anyway? Billy had known her in only bits and spurts in the two years that he'd lived in Port Aransas. They'd gotten to know each other because of Joel Canton. Marcy had befriended the poor fisherman and had introduced him to Billy after one of the city council meetings. But other than an occasional run-in with her in the town, a few dinners served to her at his restaurant, and the connection to Joel, he really didn't know Marcy at all. She was separated from her husband or divorced—one or the other. She had two kids, she'd said, and they were staying with their father while she was here in Sedona. She never talked much about her kids and, quite frankly, Billy suddenly wondered why. All mothers talked about their kids…they talked about them all the time. But Billy couldn't, in the past five months, remember her talking about them at all.

And her hair. In Port Aransas it had been long and luxurious, Cher-like, but now she didn't have any at all, at least that's what the cop's sketch had shown. Maybe she'd never had any hair. Maybe she'd worn wigs. Her hair was false—just like her kids were false; just like her reason for being in Sedona was false. At least that's what he was beginning to believe.

Billy's head hit the roll bar of Cooper's jeep as she turned onto an access road that would take them to one of the trailheads into Boynton Canyon. He bounced in the seat, its springs squeaking under him. While in the bathroom before they'd left, he'd placed the Book of the Djed in the small backpack that Cooper had given him. He now held the backpack with one hand between his legs as he grasped the roll bar with the other.

"Marcy killed a cop?" he said to himself, intentionally out loud.

Cooper, who had said little until now, glanced at him, her sunglasses hiding her expression. "It would seem so. She had the dagger, according to you. A witness saw her at the crime scene. Pretty cut and dry if you ask me."

"I thought I knew her better than that."

Cooper bounced up and down. "How much does anyone really know someone else? We're all liars to some extent."

"What makes you say that?"

"Years of reading textbooks. It's a psychological necessity—a part of the classic fight or flight mechanism. We lie to survive." They reached their destination and Cooper stopped the Jeep in a small cul-de-sac that was occupied by two other vehicles. She turned to Billy while dusting off her shirt and dropped her glasses on the dashboard. Her strawberry blonde, curly hair mixed conspicuously well with the fire that burned in her green eyes. "So tell me, Billy. Did you lie to me? Do you have the Book and is it in that backpack between your legs?"

Her face was inches from his nose as he nodded. "I have it," he said, remaining close to her face, her small nose, her pert lips. "Now tell me. Are you going to steal it? Is that why you wanted me in Boynton Canyon so that you could bury my body in some dark rattler's nest?"

A curt smile grasped her lower lip. "Why, Billy. Haven't you figured it out by now? The Book means nothing without you. Besides, I think you have way too much untold information for me to be burying you anywhere."

Her head moved slightly closer and for a split second, Billy thought that she was going to kiss him, but she backed away while opening her door and jumped out with backpack in hand. She walked to the beginning of a line of trampled earth that snaked its way around a tall, thin, rock formation that, with enough imagination, looked like what the sign at the trailhead professed it to be: Kachina Woman. "Are you coming?" she said.

He joined her and, together, they started up the trail. "Why did you want to bring me out here? You could have looked the Book over back at your place."

"You don't like my company?" She kept walking without looking at him. Kachina Woman towered above them as they traversed the path around it. "I don't like the idea of not controlling my space. You saw those idiot cops, snooping around, looking for a reason to arrest anyone they find the least bit suspicious. The Book surely would ignite a curiosity I don't want them to have. The last place the Book needs to be is locked up in an evidence room somewhere, just waiting to tempt a lowly clerk into stealing it. Then what would we have: no way to save the world."

"And no way to live to an eternity," Billy added.

Cooper stopped then. "Okay. Yes. That's right. We use it to raise the Djed and we live for an eternity. But that's what's necessary for the world's salvation."

"Is that really what you want? To save the world? Or to save Cooper Reyes?"

"We have a long way to go don't we? I don't trust you and you don't trust me, simply because we are innately both liars. I suppose we'll both have to live with that. Perhaps, the time will come when all that changes. Until then, let's just pretend."

"Pretend?"

"Yeah. Pretend we like each other. That'll make our journey into the canyon much more pleasant. Besides, the energies here don't like negativity. I've had a few tourists succumb to some pretty nasty visions just because their minds were pretty nasty thinkers."

"Okay." Billy gazed up at the head of the Kachina Woman rock formation. Sunshine broke through chunky white clouds directly above it and cast a rainbow aura around the bulbous rock. "We can be friends but I'm not gonna hold your hand."

Cooper laughed. It was the first time he'd heard her do so. It wasn't as alluring as Marcy's laugh was; in fact, it sounded a bit too brash, hoarse, and annoying. She even snorted. "Deal," she said and walked away from him.

It was at the first crest of rock when Billy heard the drumbeats for the first time. Cooper had been leading them forward and Kachina Woman was no more than three hundred yards behind them when Billy stopped and listened. The path snaked its way between rock formations in front of him. The drumbeats seemed to be coming from within the canyon. They weren't very loud at all; in fact, Billy, at first, thought that it was his heart beating.

"What is it?" Cooper asked.

"Drums…I think."

"I suspect you'll hear, and see, a lot more than that before the day is over."

"Vortex energies?"

"Yeah. They are gonna stick to you like glue." Cooper waited until Billy stood beside her. "There's something about you that I haven't felt from anyone else, especially now that we are near the canyon. You exude energies, almost as if you are a vortex in and of yourself."

"Flattering."

"No…Serious. If I was going to come on to you, I would have kissed you back in the Jeep. I'm simply stating a spiritual fact."

"Isn't that what you'd call an oxymoron: a spiritual fact?"

"Smart guy, huh? That will certainly be useful later on."

She turned away and continued her lead, her steps bouncing, her short frame agile, her strawberry blonde hair now denser and darker since the sun was mostly hidden behind clouds and shadow had taken control.

Cooper had not been pulling his leg nor was she hitting on him. She was quite serious. Billy almost undulated with it. She could even see the aura of energy that doctored his body with electrical sparkles. It was alluring and fanciful and, to be truthful, arousing. But, it wasn't the physical nature of the energy that was getting to her—it hadn't been for Chris and, for the most part, it wasn't for Billy, though she had to admit that he was quite attractive. It was something else entirely, something that the two of them had in common. Something like…

And then all of a sudden it hit her. The Book of the Djed. That one wasted Sunday that she'd spent with Chris a year ago had been filled with the same feeling she was now getting from Billy. An intoxication, really, as if someone had put a roofie in her water. That was the day that she'd seen the hand of the Great Spirit write man's destiny into the center spread of the Book: a bird of fire, one of death and of life. The Hopi called it Mochni but it was better known as the phoenix.

Cooper was becoming so excited, she trembled. She even stuttered when Billy asked her about the Yavapai Indians he saw within a narrow ravine as they'd pushed farther into the canyon.

"What are they doing?" he said.

"M-m-medicine wheels," she mumbled. "B-b-building medicine wheels for worship."

"You're shaking," he said, touching her shoulder.

"T-t-took a chill."

And when he touched her, the trembling stopped. She actually saw the red sparkles of the aura around his right hand suck a wisp of something out her body. When he removed his hand she saw the star burned into his palm. One of its points glowed, undulated, but for only a second. As her trembling faded, so did the red point of the star. She'd seen the star before. It looked just like the one that was etched in the haft of Chris Cower's Creation Dagger.

"You've touched one," she said, pointing. "You've held it in that hand."

Billy looked in the distance as the Indians knelt in front of the markers they had assembled out of rocks and twigs and dirt.

"Do you have it?" Cooper added. "You have it don't you. The Book *and* Chris' dagger; you have them both. That's why I feel…that's why you have such energy."

"No," he said. "Only the Book—as I promised."

"A lie?" she questioned.

He stepped in the direction of the worshipping Indians. "I don't have Chris' dagger," he said, absently.

"No," she said and tried to grab his elbow but missed. "They don't take kindly to interruptions."

But as he continued in their direction, the three Yavapai that had been kneeling, stood up. One even waved him forward. And drumbeats…Cooper now heard them. She'd experienced drums beating in the canyon before, but this was somehow different, louder, rhythmic, meaningful. She followed a dozen feet behind him but stopped short of the ceremonial ground as Billy reached it. The three Yavapai gave Cooper a kindly but stern gaze, then turned their backs to her and stood in a short line, blocking her sight of Billy. Billy remained hidden behind the Indians for ten minutes while the aura of sparkling energy that had encapsulated his body filled the space beyond the Yavapai; their bodies were temporarily engulfed by it just before the energy blaze weakened and died. Billy emerged between them, walking slowly as if dazed, but surefooted. When he finally stood beside her, the Yavapai returned to their own ceremonial labors.

"Chris Cower is not the stalker," he said, dreamily. "Cower is dead and gone."

"Stalker?" She shook his arm. "Billy?"

And then he came out of the trance. "It's Deere-hat man."

"Deere-hat man? Who's that? How do you know? What did you see?"

"Come on," Billy said, taking her arm. "Let's not disturb them further. Lead the way and I'll try to explain."

He'd not been in control of his thoughts or his actions; that's how he explained it to Cooper. But before he could tell her what he saw within the medicine wheel, he had to explain the rear view mirror, the one in his VW

Bus, back in Port Aransas. He'd had visions within it, of someone screaming at him, of being chased, of being shot at, of puking. And now he understood what it all meant. Now he understood that what he had envisioned in Port A, and now in much greater detail because of the medicine wheel, was the end of Lenny Bender's life. Creepier still, was that he had envisioned it *through* Lenny Bender, as if he was Lenny Bender. He could feel the bullet nick his ear before webbing the station wagon's windshield. He could smell the acidic stench of a hamburger and fries as it coated Chris Cower's arm. He could hear the sirens of the police cars as they rammed them, metal-to-metal, from the left. And he could see…

He could see inside the state trooper's car. He could see the officer in the front seat, the one on the passenger's side, the one with the radio microphone in front of his lips, the one screaming through the P.A.: *Pull the fuck over, Professor Cower! You ain't got no escape this time! We'll make sure of that!*

It was their stalker! It was Deere-hat man, except, in his medicine wheel vision, he was wearing a state trooper's hat—at least he was wearing it until the wind blew it off. And that's when Billy had been sure. That's when, through Lenny's eyes, Billy had seen the thin flip of blonde-white hair as it slapped against a mostly bald head. And its red eyes with swirling silver sparkles…raging red eyes…crazed red eyes…dead red eyes…eyes and hair and body that had been dead for a long time.

Billy (as Lenny) relived the confrontation with the burnt creature that had been one of Deere-hat man's accomplices as it stood over him, as its charred flesh crumbled into his gaping mouth.

Billy (as Lenny) relived Janine's use of the dagger to magically pull the bullet from Chris Cower's chest.

Billy (as Lenny) relived touching the Cubit, feeling its energy, watching the blue spark of temptation snatch away any chance for future survival.

Billy (as Lenny) relived dying. He relived seeing himself as a cubit. He relived the pain of being eaten alive.

But the worst thing Billy relived was being Lenny's cubit, of eating flesh that was not dead, of feeling no remorse, no guilt, no life. He relived the experience of being stabbed with the dagger by his own mother, of molting into ash and bone. And he experienced…

Floating.

As Lenny Bender's cubit, Billy had become all of the nastiness cubits' encumbered. But after Lenny's cubit finally settled into a heap of bones, Billy had relived a spiritual release, as if Lenny's soul had been imprisoned within the cubit and then rose from the ashes to witness the Bender farm's destruction, to witness Chris Cower as he fell onto the dynamite plunger that incinerated all.

"If you believe that Cower has anything to do with anything going on in Sedona today, you can forget it," Billy said in closure. "I guarantee you that nothing could put all of his pieces back together again."

"Then who in the hell gave me the star map?" Cooper said more to herself than to Billy.

"That crazy bastard that has been following all of us, I suspect—the one that has been manipulating everything. The one who chased Lenny and Cower into the cornfield. The one who followed Marcy and me from Port Aransas. The one who punched a poor Hispanic woman in Las Cruces. The one who is in Sedona, who wears a green ball cap with the words John Deere sewn into it and drives a Cadillac."

"The one who probably has something to do with the missing police officer," Cooper added.

They had been walking for an hour without rest, but now both of them stopped and stared at each other. The canyon, in that time, had closed in around them, the red walls becoming taller and redder on either side. They were now engulfed in complete shadow. Blue skies had become gray clouds. A chill of wind skirted past, whipped up the ground, and dashed its dirt against the canyon walls.

"What do you mean?" Billy asked.

"I saw it all. I wouldn't dare tell the cops that, though. They'd think I killed him. At first I thought that I was imagining things. But listening to you now—well, I guess anything is possible. Still, it's not every day you see two life-sized kachinas going at each other, and one of them loses their head, and can still walk, and can still plunge a dagger into the heart of the one that just cut off its head."

"You're not making much sense."

"There was a man and a woman, dressed up like a jaguar and the sun, in the alley on the night that the star map was delivered to me, on the night that the police officer disappeared. One had a broadsword and the other had what looked like a Creation Dagger, but it sparkled too much. Anyway, the woman dressed up like the jaguar had her head chopped off by the man in the sun costume. I don't think I'll ever forget that damned jaguar head as it rolled toward me and I know I'll never forget watching that headless woman stab the guy in the chest with the dagger."

"Then what happened?"

"I don't know. I ran just when the cop showed up. I heard him scream as I got the hell out of there."

"Did you see Marcy anywhere around there?"

"I think she was the jaguar and she had the dagger that dickhead Beets showed us in the picture."

"How can that be? You said the jaguar's head was chopped off."

"How can it be that you saw all the shit you just told me?"

And then an absolutely horrifying notion came to him, one that knocked his knees right out from under him and caused him to fall to the red dirt canyon floor. Cooper sat with him, suddenly understanding as well. He opened his mouth but she said it first.

"Marcy's a cubit!"

Billy shook his head in denial but thought that there could be no other answer. It made all the sense in the world, except that, Marcy didn't act like one—at least, she didn't act like what Billy thought a cubit would act like. "Shit," he moaned. "If she can pull it off then we are totally screwed. Who knows what person out there is one of them." He glared curiously at Cooper.

"No way, José," she said, bringing both hands out in front of her. "I'm all pure woman. I'll prove it to you if you don't believe me."

The temptation was almost too good to turn down but Billy thought that now was not the time. He had to agree, though, that screwing someone would be a damn good way of finding out who was a cubit and who was not, but the idea of choosing poorly made his skin crawl.

"As far as Marcy's concerned," Cooper said, "there's one good way to find out if she was at The Y, Friday night."

"And that is?"

"Pull her hair."

Cooper, at that moment, reminded him of Stephanie Drake and how she'd seen logic so simply. Billy smiled, that inkling of sound reasoning tickling his fancy. "First chance I get, I will. You better believe it." He looked around and up and down. "Is this a good place?"

"Good place for what?"

"You know what I mean."

"Good place to prove I'm a woman?"

Billy reached out and gently pulled a lock of her curly red hair. "All woman…like you said." This made her laugh and, again, snort. "I'm talking about the Book."

"Excellent place," Cooper quickly replied while grabbing the hair that Billy had just released. "Give it to me."

Her breaths came fast and furious. She felt totally and completely turned on. Billy's energy and his honesty overwhelmed her. Every word he spoke was nuanced in her mind with sexual connotation. That's how Chris had done it to her. That's how Billy was going to do it to her. She wanted to prove that she was all woman. She wanted to rip her clothes off right then and there. And when he touched her hair she thought that she would bust. A snort of laughter escaped because there was absolutely no way she could hold back the air that was building in her lungs, air filled with words that she knew should not be spoken but she said them anyway.

"Give it to me."

And when Billy did, her desire magnified beyond what she was mortally capable of maintaining. When Billy handed her the Book, the energy that pulsed through Boynton Canyon centered on her, raged within her blood, fused with her brain. All of the power of all of the ages consumed her. Her life flashed before her, every piece of it, every person in it, every place she'd been to, every touch her fingers had ever stroked—all in the span of an instant. She saw the Book's center spread…the phoenix bird undulating under her fingers, the sixes and nines twisting and turning and becoming nines and sixes and sixes and nines. She even felt the grooves that the Great Spirit had carved into the very fibers of the Book's papery texture, grooves that now beheld clues that would save or end everything.

Her heart beat faster. The clouds bunched down around her. The canyon walls fell on top of her. But Billy was there, his body thrown over her like an invincible cloak, protecting her from the deluge of her growing insanity. Billy was there on top of her and he held a weapon. He held a Creation Dagger. And he plunged it downward.

When Billy dropped the backpack from his shoulders and unzipped its main pocket, he heard something but ignored it. When he grabbed the Book and pulled it free, he heard it again and looked around. Part of his outer body experience in the inner body of Lenny Bender had included the young man's obsession with Clint Eastwood. This synthesis into his own consciousness had Billy looking to the cliffs on both sides, looking for those outlaws who would have been tailing Eastwood in every spaghetti western he'd ever starred in. He looked for glints of reflected metal. He looked for, and listened for, falling rocks. A hiccup or a cough or a tactical word of some kind would have determined the source of the sound, but there was none of that. The noise he now heard for the third time didn't even come from the towering rocks encircling him. The sound, actually, came from his feet.

He handed the Book to Cooper and she opened it at the exact moment that the rattler struck. Because she'd been sitting with her right hand on the ground for support, that arm was easy pickings for the diamondback. It struck her twice before quickly slithering away. When Billy looked at her arm, the djed tattoo was now punctured four times, one snake fang incision occupying each of the tattoo's four crosses. There was very little blood but an immense amount of swelling. The snake had struck her brachial artery and the poison was working very quickly. She swooned and fell and the Book toppled and closed beside her body.

Billy quickly yanked the backpack from Cooper and furiously searched its contents. A newspaper was in there as was her water bladder. He turned the backpack upside down and a Swiss Army knife dropped at his knees. It was good to have such a valuable tool but Billy had no idea how he could use it against four venom holes. He knew that to cross cut the skin and suck the venom from the body was one survival method that he'd been taught as a Cub Scout too many years ago, but the way that Cooper's arm was swelling made him believe that he could cut and suck all day and she would still die.

So there was only one option.

He didn't know if he should stab the snake bites with the point of the Creation Dagger or simply set the long blade across the wounds as Alixel had done to the cut across Joel Canton's throat back in Port A. He opted for the later and immediately understood that it was the correct decision as crimson light spewed from the dagger and from his hand. He placed the seven-inch blade on top of Cooper's mounding, puss-filled skin and the magic did its thing. It was amazing to watch. Lenny Bender's view of his mother pulling the bullet out of Cower's body was of no comparison. The dagger's blade actually sucked Cooper's arm. It sucked the infiltration of poison from the wounds. It sucked the mounded skin full of infection and venom and spit long rivulets of moisture from the very tip of the blade and onto the red dirt ground below. In a moment that was quicker than a moan, the dagger had completed its task.

Billy studied the dagger still resting in his palm. The last and only time he had unsheathed it was to kill his best friend and that had been five months ago. Now, at this moment, sitting between majestic canyon walls with a women he'd met only days ago, squirming at his knees, venom and blood splattered around her in broken Rorschach patterns, and a bird squawking an echo of resolution from some hidden recess, he considered how valuable it must be—it was the last of its kind. It was the Creation of the End. It had blazed brilliant red while sucking the life back into Cooper, but now only twinkled a timid glow from its haft. Curiously, and this is why Billy kept staring at it, the haft was positioned in his hand in exactly the same way he'd held it when he'd killed Bottlenose, when the star in the haft had burned its likeness into his palm. The fifth point, the one in the lower right quadrant which continued to undulate a faint red aura, was precisely aligned with that same point in his hand.

In quick succession, his experiences from the Yavapai medicine wheel and from Lax's ceremonial anteroom flashed before him. He saw himself as Lenny Bender creeping through barn shadows, looking for his mother, only to find his own cubit and his own death. He saw the low, arched entry into the Great Hall of the Anasazi decorated with massacre and fleeing animals, and he remembered the light that had blazed from his hand, from that single point, the fifth point, the point in the lower quadrant, the one that symbolized the end. He remembered that light, penetrating the darkness, revealing his own ghastly face, a warning, a threat.

Cooper moaned and this brought Billy out of the trance, but he continued staring at the dagger, which had now stopped glowing altogether. He continued staring at it because something kept his mind boiling with calculation. He continued staring at it because the dagger would not let him go. Cooper's star map did point to the location of the Great Hall and now Billy knew exactly where it was.

He looked curiously at the canyon walls then quickly returned the dagger to its sheath and the Book of the Djed to his backpack. The thought of Eastwood-hungry outlaws became nervously prominent because, somehow, he knew that they were being watched.

The three Yavapai Indians that had shown Billy the light, disappeared from the cliff's edge shortly after Cooper regained consciousness. They made very little noise as they returned to their medicine wheel and added a new centerpiece to the circular alter. It was not dead but was frozen in coiled infamy. The centerpiece was the rattlesnake that had bitten Cooper Reyes.

"Phoenix," she moaned. "Sixes. Nines. Dagger."

Cooper's eyes flickered and fluttered and Billy wiped sweat from her forehead with the back of his palm. She sat up, her hands propped behind her for support. He fed her water until she coughed. The intense energies that had taken control of her were now gone.

"Damn," she said. "I've seen that happen to those I've brought in here but it's never happened to me—not like that anyway."

"You've never been bitten by a rattler?" Billy said while pointing at her arm.

The lower part of her right arm throbbed as if it had fallen asleep and was just now coming back to life. She lifted it into her lap and studied the tattoo. When she touched it, a blaze of pain shot up her arm. One red circle occupied each of the djed's four crosses. Each puckered a tiny smear of blood. "Rattler?"

"You don't remember."

"I thought it was the vortex. I thought I was having an experience."

"You had an experience all right." Billy offered her more water but she waved it away.

"Two bites in the main artery. I shouldn't be alive."

"But you are." Billy took a deep breath. "You're right about this canyon. Mysterious. It has the power to take life or give it."

"No." Cooper shook her head. "It doesn't work that way. You must have done something." She saw her Swiss Army knife lying on the ground. "My knife…" she began, then reconsidered the snake bite: four holes and nothing else. "But you didn't use my knife did you?" The top button of Billy's shirt was loose and Cooper saw the hint of leather strapped to his chest. She pointed.

Billy grabbed the pointing finger and gently lowered it to her lap. "I know where the Great Hall is," he said.

Cooper answered with an astonished expression.

Billy looked around them. "Being out here in the middle of nowhere is suddenly making me very nervous."

He helped her stand. "You should be," she said. "You know where the Great Hall of the Anasazi is, and you have the Book of the Djed and a Creation Dagger. Who wouldn't be nervous?"

A camaraderie was born between them in the hour that followed. There was no denying that the masculine and feminine energies alive in Boynton Canyon had much to do with this transformation, but it was more so because Billy had saved Cooper's life, and in doing so, threw off all doubt about her true intent. The dagger had not only sucked the venom from her, it had sucked out a bit of her very soul that Billy's energy was able to taste, to sample, to judge. He *knew* that her desire for the Book had been driven by Cower's deceit, his false promises, by the unseen and unknowing, by her true want for human survival. The professor had been the real false prophet, guaranteeing her a life of power and immortality: a false prophet with a false promise set on a slick stick like a carrot before the horse. Cooper's strength and intelligence had been no match for mortal lies combined with whatever ancient influences on mortals that the Book and the dagger, together, possessed. Cower was dead, but his manipulation of her remained cold inside and this was apparent as they talked.

To raise the Djed…that's what all of this was about: raising the Djed and immortality. Cooper didn't know how to perform the ceremony but she knew that the Book and the dagger were necessary. Cower had never surrendered any specifics. The Book would explain, he'd said. And the dagger…well Cower had admitted that he'd never known exactly what to do with it (other than to kill cubits) but he knew that it was important.

Billy told Cooper where the Great Hall was located: in the fifth point, a representation of the fifth element, and the fifth creation. It was located on her star map and she reached into her backpack as he explained. He assumed that whoever had given her the parchment had meant for her—and most likely both of them—to find the Great Hall and this scared the hell out of him. When she unrolled the map from within the newspaper and looked at the ten points that imagination could easily connect into six- and five-pointed stars, she pointed where Billy had intended her to point: Lee Mountain, symbolized on the map as the fifth point.

Of course, Cooper had needed to know how he knew. Magic and logic, he'd told her— the two greatest forces and foes man had ever been challenged to understand.

First, he told her about magic, about Lax, about his own visit to Lax's house, about the anteroom, about his visions within the anteroom and how his palm and the star burned into it had lighted the way. He told her how, after he had saved her life with the dagger, the fifth point in its haft had connected with his skin, as if it were trying to tell him something.

He told her about logic, about Chancey Lett and the acquisition of Port Aransas beach front property under false pretense, about how Phoenix International wanted to acquire land for the same said purposes on Lee Mountain, which, logic would suggest, meant that something there, too, was hidden in the earth and was the real target of interest.

According to Billy, logic and magic were manifest in the Book of the Djed, particularly its center spread. The very existence of the writings was the magic. Trying to understand what they meant was the logic. The phoenix, he reminded her, was the symbol of birth and of death, of giving and of taking and logic would dictate that its place in the Book meant that Phoenix International was part of the big puzzle.

Cooper suggested that the second set of symbols in the Book, the three sixes, must therefore mean that Phoenix International was the Antichrist. Billy admitted that he'd already considered that connection up until Saturday, moments before they'd had dinner together, when he and Marcy had opened the Book to find the added triple nines. If the phoenix represented the antithetical hypocrisy of life and death, Billy said, then what must three sixes turned upside down mean? Antichrist and savior? Perhaps, in that sense, one could read into the symbolism that Phoenix International was the world's savior, but Billy said he was not ready to go that far, particularly because of the corporation's connection to oil, pharmaceuticals and gambling.

Billy then told Cooper more about magic, about Lax's other revelations, about Daykeepers and their responsibilities, about their immortality, about ancient civilizations that were destroyed by the Cubit, about Napoleon and about Hitler. And he furthered his ideas concerning logic by telling her about Jean Lafitte, about finding Lafitte's treasure in Port Aransas where Chancey Lett had wanted to build his casino, about the Creation of the End Dagger that he'd found within Lafitte's treasure and how he had used it to kill a good friend, the same dagger that he'd kept covertly hidden, the one that he'd used to save Cooper's life.

Logic and magic. Good and Evil. Antithetical hypocrisies meant to live together in the Age of Jaguar, in the age of Mankind where absolutes could never exist.

Between them, while sitting in Boynton Canyon under increasingly cloudy skies, Billy and Cooper came to understand beyond a doubt that they were in this thing together, and that, just perhaps, they always were. They came to understand that the only way to survive was not alone and that the cubit that had been following them had been providing tiny clues, had been pushing them on toward the Great Hall, had wanted them together, had wanted Billy and Cooper and the dagger and the Book for the purposes of immortality. And they *knew* that this cubit, be it Deere-hat man or Marcy or both, would eventually create that chance.

It was only at the very end of their conversation that both realized the presence of the Yavapai Indians who now revealed themselves on all sides of the canyon walls. There were at least a dozen of them. As Billy and Cooper continued their journey out of the canyon, the Yavapai followed, taking up positions in front of and behind them but always maintaining their distance among the red rocks. Nothing could harm them with the Yavapai present, they thought. Nothing could harm them until they were out of the canyon.

It would be dark soon and a storm was brewing. It was Cooper's idea to have dinner at Café Aus. She didn't feel like cooking and Billy said that he had nothing substantial in his apartment. Besides, he'd said, his kitchen was much too small for entertaining.

The temperature had dropped to a more seasonable sixty degrees. Many of the people who sat en masse around Billy and Cooper in the restaurant's outside patio wore light jackets.

"You cold?" Cooper asked.

"Not a bit," Billy said, chewing on a tortilla chip he'd just dipped into salsa. "I'm quite comfortable. Really." He studied the chip. "You know. Your salsa is the best I've ever tasted, but I gotta admit, this ain't bad. Kind of fruity and crunchy."

"Luke…he's the owner…added a bit of his own country to it. The sweetness is from the muntries and the crunch is macadamia nuts."

"Muntries?" Billy grabbed another chip and dipped. "That flavor would be excellent on redfish."

A waitress had taken their order but Luke brought their entrees to the table and set them down.

"I see you found your mate," he said to Cooper, smiling. "You know, a couple of the local blue heelers have been snooping. I hope I didn't put you in a wrong way by telling them your name."

"No…no," Cooper returned his smile. "Everything has worked out just fine."

"Wheew! Never thought of you as a killer." Luke chuckled but when neither Billy nor Cooper replied, he said, "Can I refill your dipping bowl?"

Billy handed it to him. "You have a recipe for this that I could steal off of you?"

"How about I give you a sack of some to carry with you after the supper, no charge?"

"Sweet." Billy said, as Luke wandered away from them to acknowledge the finger gesture from a diner two tables away.

Cooper devoured her plate of mango chicken. Billy finished his plate of the same order but it took him twice as long since his attention was drawn to the crowded patio. She sat there drinking water and considering his nervous tension while he slowly forked the last chunks of chicken into his mouth.

"What do we do now?" she asked.

Without looking at her, he said, "We go to Lee Mountain." Then he pointed out toward the street at a line of tables that were loaded with at least a dozen young men who wore the commercialized outfits of professional mountain bikers. "Isn't that Richard Manson?"

Cooper turned in her seat. Among the cyclists, sitting at a table next to the patio's iron fence and all the way over to the left corner, were four people dressed in casual slacks and shirts. She knew all of them. "Yes. And that's Bill Tate, Cheryl Mokier and Pat Roberts, three of our city council members."

"Uh-huh," Billy said. "And you don't think that's kinda strange?"

"In what way?" she said but was quick to answer her own question. "You mean Manson? He's the president of Phoenix International."

"We were just talking about that back in the canyon."

"Okay."

"And now here he is."

"Okay."

"Sitting with city officials."

"I still don't get where you're going."

"He sponsored the bike race that has a course that runs through Lee Mountain. He wants the property to build a casino. He's sitting with council members of the city which can grant those rights. They are violating the open meeting law statutes."

When Billy said that, all four of them turned in unison. Only Manson was smiling. In fact, with the low light conditions in that part of the Café Aus patio, that's all Cooper could see of his face: white teeth curled up into a smile. Of the council members, all she noticed was their eyes. It was hard not to. All three sets glowed crimson red. She shook her head, quickly, as if trying to erase a vision that couldn't be real. She blinked and so did the six red eyes, then Manson and his friends turned back toward their meals.

"Did you see…" Cooper pointed and Billy quickly grabbed her finger.

"Yes. And that means it won't be long before the decision about Lee Mountain is made. A three-to-two vote is guaranteed."

"We'll have to go tomorrow then."

Billy let go of her finger. "No. Tonight. We can't wait any longer. I suspect you have the gear necessary for a night hike?"

Cooper nodded.

"Hopefully we can take them by surprise."

"Who?"

"Whoever it is that has been waiting for us to bring the Book and dagger and ourselves to the Great Hall."

Manson and the three council members rose from their chairs at the very moment a streak of dry lightening lit up the sky. The foursome blinked in and out of sight for a split second, then started walking in Cooper's direction. She sat stiff and turned her face away as they approached. The three council members walked by without a word, but Manson hesitated as he stepped behind Billy. "We know who you are..." he whispered, looking straight ahead at Luke who was standing there with Billy and Cooper's check in one hand. "...and we know where you live." Manson then thanked Luke for a wonderful meal and followed the council members into the restaurant through the patio's double doors.

"Richest man in the world," Luke said. "In my restaurant. What a hum dinger, don't you think?" He handed the check to Cooper.

"Hum dinger," Cooper repeated. "He's a real hum dinger all right."

Lightning flashed again. This time it was accompanied by a spine-jerking clap of thunder that shook the entire restaurant.

Dry lightening creased the night sky in greater magnitude and quantity as Cooper parked in front of Billy's apartment. One streak caused the sky to brighten so intensely that Billy saw SpongeBob, seemingly quivering, sitting beyond the Cavalier's windshield.

"I'll pick you up in about an hour," Cooper said as Billy exited the Jeep. "Dress warm and don't forget the essentials."

"Already packing them." Billy patted the backpack strap on the right side of his chest and the sheath of the dagger on the left then waved as the Jeep exited the parking lot and headed up Dry Creek Road.

Across the street, it seemed that every light was on in Marcy's rental casita. Shadows moved behind drawn blinds. He thought about going over there. He thought he needed to know if Marcy was a cubit. But then he denied the act. He denied the want for knowing. It was better that way. If she *was* a cubit, she would try to kill him. If she wasn't a cubit, she'd soon find that he had left and that it was time for her to return to her children. If neither was true and she was dead, then it really didn't matter and whoever it was casting the shifting shadows inside the casita would certainly be unfriendly—

—Just as unfriendly as his apartment now became as soon as he opened up the front door, switched on the light, and found that someone had absolutely destroyed the place. Food and drink and clothes and the guts and broken bodies of furniture and appliances and cabinetry were combined into such heaps that he could not tell which piece once went where. Plasterboard walls were torn from wood framing and large chunks lay within the massacred contents of the room. His attention was drawn abruptly to the bathroom where he'd stashed the key to the Book of the Djed when something shattered from within its dark recess.

He slipped the backpack onto both shoulders before moving toward the bathroom. His first step landed on a protruding nail that could not penetrate his hiking boot's thick sole. A small chunk of sofa stuck to the boot and Billy had to shake his leg to get it off. He pulled the dagger from its sheath. It did not glow but it was warmer than the sweaty palm of his hand. He stood frozen and waited for a full minute that was filled only with the nocturnal meanderings of the desert beyond the apartment's open front door. He then rushed into the bathroom and slapped a wall switch that illuminated one single bulb in a light fixture filled with two others that had been broken; the sounds that he'd heard were fragments of busted bulbs falling to a floor filled with the rubble of broken sink porcelain, shattered slivers of mirror, a broken toilet seat and tank and a twisted array of towels and other linens. He tried to gain access to the linen cupboard but the mess on the floor prevented him from moving the bathroom door.

"Billy!" Marcy screamed. "Billy. Oh dear God you're alive." He peeked out from the bathroom to see her standing in the front doorway. She saw the dagger in his hand, gasped, and pointed. "You have it! I knew you did. I just knew it. Hurry," she urged. "My house!"

When she turned to run, Billy yelled, "Wait!" Marcy stopped but didn't turn around. "Wait a damn minute! What the hell is going on here?!" He moved quickly through the busted room to where Marcy stood, her back to him. She turned then and Billy expected the worst, had the dagger ready to plunge it into her if necessary. She still looked like Marcy. She still wore red lipstick and black mascara. Her luxuriously long hair was as jet black as it had ever been and he reached forward, grabbed a tangle of it and yanked, hard.

"Ouch!" she screamed. "What the hell?"

"Just wanted to make sure you were you."

"Who else would I be?"

Billy had a thousand questions. Where had she been? What had she been doing? Was she a murderer? But the opportunity was truncated when she turned and ran, yelling out, "Please hurry. Someone is in my house."

Billy stood, indecisive. He had to get the key, if it was still here, but when he watched Marcy cross the road toward the casita, he saw the green Cadillac pull into the driveway. Marcy entered her casita and a fat bolt of lightning blasted the sky, killing all of the lights everywhere: the ones in her house, those in Billy's apartment, and the few that lined Dry Creek Road. The only electricity remaining existed in the jagged bolts of blue that swarmed overhead. There was no thunder and there was no rain—just bursts of blue and white, as if a very old black and white movie was being flash photographed with a twenty-first century digital camera.

Someone was getting into the Cadillac. He took one step and…

Flash!

Another shadow appeared from behind the house. Billy walked more briskly. He stepped out into the road…

Flash!

The Cadillac rolled out of the driveway, its headlights dim. It turned south toward town, carrying occupants that remained hidden in the…

Flash!

The driver wore a ball cap but the passenger—he couldn't see more than its black outline. Someone also sat in the back seat: a third shadow that…

Flash!

He heard a shriek from inside the house and immediately crossed the road. Slowly he moved up the driveway, his senses alerted to every nuance within the black night, every slither, every slough, every…

Flash!

This blue light carried an immense and immediate crack of thunder that dropped on top of him like an anvil, causing him to jump two inches off of the driveway pavement.

Billy circled around back. When he stepped onto the porch and looked through the bay window, the absence of lights inside made it impossible to see anything. Even the double Flash! that now illuminated the landscape did nothing more than…

Wait. There was someone…lying on the floor. The blue light infiltrated the window, outlining a body, and then it was gone.

He went to the sliding glass door and shoved it open on squeaky rails that caused his teeth to grind. When he entered, the body on the floor did not move.

"Billy?"

He looked at the body, confused by the source of the sound of his name.

"Billy? Is that you?"

The voice came from further inside the darkness.

"I think you are too late. They killed them."

It was Marcy's voice, but he couldn't see her. Even when the next blue flash struck and snuck into the house through the sliding glass door and bay window panes, all that was visible was the body on the floor. He knelt toward it then fell back on his ass.

Flash!

It was Detective Beets! His teeth were clenched between lips that were fat and puffy. His eye, the one that looked up at Billy, had been abused to great extent. Blood that looked blue-black in the flash of lightning oozed from the socket and drooled into his creepy grin.

"Billy. Help me."

"Where are you?" he said.

"In the bedroom. Please…"

Billy stood and walked cautiously brisk to where he remembered her bedroom to be located.

Flash!

He saw the doorway but not the second body that lay across its threshold. He tripped and fell on top of it.

Detective Dreagan.

Two more quick lightning strikes revealed that Dreagan's body had been torn into a couple of pieces. The detached leg was the part that he had tripped over. The head seemed to be attached but only by a thread of tissue.

"They were looking for the Book," Marcy said from within the bedroom. "Those cops just got in their way."

Billy, again, rose from the floor. "Who?" he said. "Who was looking for the Book?"

"Deere-hat man," Marcy's voice responded. "You were right. Oh God, you were so right."

More lightning, flashing through a window to his left, revealed Marcy's bed and Marcy who was sitting on it in a shadowy, cradled position. Billy shuffled toward her while looking around the room. "Are you hurt? Did they hurt you, too?"

"No," she said. "He didn't hurt me but said that he would unless you gave them the Book and the dagger."

Billy sat at the foot of the bed, his backpack to Marcy whose feet stretched out to touch his waist. "Well, they're not going to get 'em. And you aren't going to be harmed, not with me by your side."

Her arms suddenly encapsulated him. He felt her added body weight against the backpack. Her hands roamed down over his shoulders and grasped both of his breasts; one of them stroked the dagger from tip to top. Her breaths, deep and furious, blew into his right ear.

"My hero," she moaned. Her breathing heaved against him. "We can get through this together."

He lowered his head to look for her roaming hand that had found the haft of the dagger under his shirt. Her lips were now on his ear; their moisture leaked across the lobe. She whispered.

"It will soon be over and we will be free." Her hushed and excited breaths increased. Billy raised one hand to her head, caressing the hair that he knew was jet black. She was there for him. She had always been there for him. And then her fingers pulled forcefully on the haft of the dagger.

Flash! BANG!

Billy jerked forward, his hand still twisted within her hair. His arm fell to his lap and in the blue flash, he saw…

Her hair. Her wig. Long and luxurious. Just like Cher's. She clamped onto his back as he rose in sudden shock. He tried to pry her hand from the dagger but its vise-like grip was unrelenting. Together, they fell to the floor and rolled on top of the pieces that once were Detective Dreagan. Billy beat at the appendages around him. He shoved with buckled legs against the shadowy body that covered him. Lightning struck the ground outside the bedroom window, igniting a fire that illuminated the darkness within the bedroom and someone who was not Marcy…but was.

Except for the bald head and the fresh, red scar that encircled her entire neck.

"Give me the fucking dagger!" Marcy's cubit growled. "Give it to me or she dies!"

The combative force of both of their hands against the haft of the dagger sent it reeling out of its sheath and through the bedroom doorway. The Marcy cubit rose up on knees that were straddling Billy, and brought both of it its fists, clasped into one fleshy hammer, down.

Billy rolled. The cubit's fists slammed into the floor before it flipped forward out of the bedroom to search for the dagger. Billy groped the floor. His hands found Dreagan's arm and when he tossed it aside, the entire appendage came loose, flailed across the room and shattered the bedroom window. Heat from the lightening fire wafted into the room.

Billy rose to his knees to find Marcy's cubit towering over him, its black outline framed dead center within the bedroom's doorway. "You putrid excuse for a human," the Marcy cubit exclaimed. In its hand glowed Billy's dagger. Then the cubit leapt at him.

He jumped out of the way as the cubit fell to the floor. Billy blinked. Heat from the fire outside sucked the moisture from his eyeballs. He blinked again. On the floor, two shadows fought for the possession of the dagger: the cubit and …

Cooper!

Her arm wrenched at the dagger that the cubit was not willing to give up. Both shadows stood, wrestled, turned and twisted in all directions, then fell through the shattered window and disappeared from view outside. A screech followed that was louder than the thunder that hammered the darkness. When Billy crawled to the window and stood, he saw Cooper raise the dagger for a second strike to the back of the Marcy cubit's bald head. The cubit convulsed on the ground for an impossibly long second before succumbing. Its head fell off of its re-stitched neck then all of its flesh turned black, molting and melting and disintegrating, the lightning fire behind it providing visual evidence of the cubit's final writhing existence.

Billy jumped through the window and stood beside Cooper in time to see the green Cadillac that sat, idling, at the Boynton Canyon Road intersection. Farther up the road, a pair of headlights from an old Ford Ranger raced toward the Cadillac and within the truck's headlights Billy saw the occupant in the Cadillac's back seat.

It was Marcy Ruminski.

THE DJED: PART II
BREATHE

They'd left Marcy's casita shortly after Lax had arrived and Billy had returned to his apartment to retrieve the torn page from the Book of the Djed that he'd hidden there. Billy had almost forgotten about it, but Lax had reminded him of its need. The death and destruction they'd left behind for the Sedona authorities to figure out.

Now, the three of them sat at the small, wooden table in Lax's backyard, which provided a spectacular view of Cathedral Rock and the lightning bolts that cracked the black night behind it.

"Where's Aaron?" Billy asked.

Lax's legs were crossed and he leaned back against his wooden chair. "Dropped him off at a friend's house on the way out to see you two. I didn't think that he was mature enough yet to witness exactly what cubits are or what they are capable of."

Billy and Cooper sat next to each other on the opposite side of the table from Lax, watching heaven's light display for several silent minutes when Billy finally said what they both were thinking. "You knew."

Lax sat up, his legs uncrossing. "I knew," he said, his voice deep but calm. "I knew that the woman you call Marcy had been cubited. I didn't know that her primary had been kept alive."

"I thought Daykeepers were all-knowing," Billy said.

"We know what we have experienced and since we live so long, that knowledge encompasses quite a bit." Lax then looked directly at Cooper. "I must apologize to you."

Cooper shrugged. "Why?"

"I saw you Friday night, around the corner, watching. You witnessed me taking off the Marcy cubit's head.

"The sun kachina," Cooper said to herself.

"Yes."

"So why all the ceremonial garb?"

"Because it's tradition for two invincible warriors. And to protect my identity."

"Whatever." She dropped her hand on top of Billy's.

"I thought you were like the professor," Lax continued. "I thought your spirit was not clean."

"None of our spirits seem to be clean." Cooper sat back in her chair as blue lightning played with the strawberry red colors in her hair, her fingers drumming against Billy's knuckles. "We all have a little bit of cubit in us."

Lax scooted closer, his face an expression connoting solemn thought. Both of his elbows slid across the wooden round tabletop and he craned forward. "Young wisdom," he said, studying her. "It never ceases to amaze me. This world truly does have a future." He glanced quickly at Billy whose attention had also been drawn away from the unique display of nature in the night to the center of the table. "I think you two are the perfect choices."

Cooper stared at Lax. It was almost impossible to turn away. His slate gray eyes pooled hundreds of years of experience; the irises were magnetic. "What do you mean by that, old man?"

"I mean that when I tell the story of 2012, it will include wisdom and youth and, I might say, a great sense of humor."

Billy interrupted. "So what's our next step? We were thinking that we have to act quickly, before Phoenix International gets ownership of the land.

"Wisdom requires patience," Lax said. "I don't think Phoenix International is going to be buying anything anytime soon. You saw what happened when they tried to buy beachfront property in Texas."

"Hurricane," Billy quickly responded.

"Makes you feel enlightened knowing nature is on our side, doesn't it?" The dark skies lit up with multiple strokes of dry lightning that illuminated the entire face of Cathedral Rock. "Do you even know why you desire to venture into the Great Hall?"

"It's why I came to Sedona," Billy said.

"And you?" Lax asked Cooper.

She hesitated. "I think...well, I used to think that it was to become immortal."

He grabbed Cooper's free hand and she let him. "Nothing ever dies," he said. "We exist in this flesh to complete cycles that have no beginning and no end. Unfortunately, we are told otherwise. Humans lie because they don't understand. Science lies because it doesn't understand. Faith makes excuses for the lies and packages misunderstanding in convenient collections of knowledge that is distributed as argument. Like you said, every one of we mortal beings have a little cubit in us and that, Cooper, is why death even has a definition. Death has a materialistic understanding, one that can be used against passion and hope and love. It is a bargaining chip."

Billy asked, "So why *are* we going to the Great Hall?"

Lax released Cooper's hand and sat back in his chair. "To make sure that the definition of death does not become the definition of life. And to save your friend."

"Marcy?"

"Yes. There can be only one reason why she has been allowed to... live."

"The Book," Cooper said.

"And the dagger," Billy added.

"And the future," Lax concluded. "What did Professor Cower tell you about immortality?" he asked Cooper.

"He said that to gain immortality, you have to raise the Djed, and the only way to do that is by conducting a ceremony in the Great Hall with the Book and the dagger."

"He was wrong," Lax said.

"About immortality?" Billy asked.

"He was wrong in his understanding of what immortality means. And he was wrong about the location in which immortality is gained."

Cooper stood then and walked to the perimeter of the brick-laden patio. The pit oven that had cooked bread for Billy and Lax and Aaron and the bird called Osi was at her feet. She looked at it, curiously. "So the reason we are going to the Great Hall is to find out the location where the raising of the Djed is supposed to take place?"

"Young wisdom," Lax said. "And now there is an innocent life at stake. The use of death against love. Even if we thought we had a choice, we do not...not if Marcy is to live."

"And the Book will tell us?" Cooper added.

"The Book will tell us where it is that the Djed can be raised," Lax confirmed.

Billy stood then and joined Cooper, placing his arm around her shoulder. Lightning was now only sporadic, providing little illumination.

"You have done this before," Billy said to Lax, his back to him, Cooper's head leaning into his arm. "If you are hundreds of years old then you must be protected by the Djed. Just like your sister was. But I saw her die."

Lax now rose and joined the couple at the patio's perimeter. He stood a few feet away as a thrust of desert wind careened into them. "She had completed her purpose, as I will soon complete mine." A second, mightier gust of wind billowed Lax's poncho open; the Djed amulet hanging from a leather necklace, jumped out from under it and bounced against his chest. He turned to them then, the amulet twinkling though there was no light source to provide such reflection.

"Only one more exists," Lax said. "And it is for you Billy Jo Presser. You are to be immortal until *your* journey is complete. The Djed will protect you from all harm as it has all Daykeepers. Daggers and bullets and even the Cubit are of no consequence once you, too, have raised the Djed."

What would it be like to live for a hundred years? Two hundred? Five hundred? The complicated answer to that question kept Billy awake.

His true destiny had now been outlined for him and this "journey," as Lax had put it, would begin shortly. First, though, Lax had demanded that each of them rest. They'd have no chance against Evil without sleep, he'd said. Tomorrow morning, they would go to the Great Hall to save Marcy and to find out where the journey would take them next.

Billy looked up at the dark ceiling. Aaron's bed was comfortable but small. His bare feet dangled out from under the bed sheets and beyond the edge of the mattress by several inches. Lightning still played a minor role in illuminating the small bedroom, and with each faint flicker that entered the space through one single-paned window, Billy looked at his feet, wiggled his toes and thought about growing older.

Fear and fantasy dominated the conversation in his head. One thought centered on Superman, the comic book icon. Would he be able to leap tall buildings in a single bound? Would he be able to stop a speeding locomotive? He wouldn't be able to fly would he? Of course not. That fantasy was pure fiction.

Perhaps he'd be able to fearlessly ride the treacherous waves off of Tahiti. Better still, he fantasized about riding waves in the wake of a monstrous hurricane, one that would lift the surf fifty feet above the ocean's surface.

He'd become something like Silver Surfer, and would ease his surfboard into every port of call that necessitated superhero intervention. Bad guys wouldn't have a chance against Captain Daykeeper.

He giggled while staring at the square of window glass glow and then sat straight up in the bed. His toes retreated under the sheets and he massaged his legs.

Immortality. The meaning was beyond comprehension. A fantasy and a fear. Lax had said that bullets and blades would not harm him. But he had also said that immortality had an end. A few hundred years. Or longer. Or sooner. It all depended on when Billy completed his journey, which really meant that he wouldn't be immortal at all. According to Lax, nothing began and nothing ended. In a world like that, immortality had no meaning, and that had been Lax's point all along. So what would the Djed do for him other than bounce against his chest for the rest of his not so immortal life? He'd be able to sling Creation Daggers like a whirring buzz saw and take out droves of cubits, of that he was sure. It would probably make him a lot wiser, more spiritual, and reduce the stress in his life…it would probably eradicate the stress in his life. If a bullet and a blade couldn't kill you, what the hell was there to stress about?

Oh, nothing—except the end of the world.

That thought caused him to get out of bed and walk to the window. His breaths, now deeper and heavier, quickly fogged the glass. He wiped his hand across the moisture then started a simple doodle with one finger: a star, just like the one in his hand…just like the one in the dagger. A star was important for saving the world. He didn't know why or how, but he knew.

Another heavy breath nearly erased his finger art but its smudgy, wet edges remained. A flash of lightning redefined it further. And then it moved. Billy blinked and rubbed his eyes with both fists but that didn't make the star on the window pane stop moving; its top point which Billy had draw straight up, turned a half circle and now pointed straight down. The fifth point, the one that represented the Creation of the End, the one that was burned prominently into his hand, was now resting in the ten o'clock position. Billy continued to stare at it, the fifth point, as it began to glow a dull crimson; then it undulated, the crimson strengthening then weakening, bright to dull, in perfect rhythm with his heart.

Mmm…..mmm….. Mmm…..mmm…..

That sound…he'd heard it before.

Mmm…..mmm….. Mmm…..mmm…..

It had come from within the bank vault at the Port Aransas branch of the Big Texas Bank.

Mmm.....mmm..... Mmm.....mmm.....

It had come from the Cubit!

As impossible as it seemed, the pulsing fifth point drawn into the window glass broke away and fell to the window sill where, as an animated triangle, it continued to glow and hum. Billy picked it up. It was tiny, about half the size of a guitar pick, and its edges were very sharp. They sliced into the thumb and forefinger of his right hand, causing a thin line of blood to emerge.

Mmm.....mmm..... Mmm.....mmm.....

Billy's attention centered on the pulsing triangle of red. It was like staring into a looking glass—a crystal ball shaped like a triangle—and in it he could see...

A face. But it was so small he couldn't make it out. He did, however, hear what the face was saying. Mixed in with the numbing humming, were the words:

We are the creation of the end. Follow with me to your destiny.

And then the tiny, unrecognizable face disappeared and was replaced by giant balls of fire pelting a tiny rendition of the earth. Billions of people screamed from within the fiery triangle, and Billy woke up.

Their breakfast was very simple: some berries, bananas, small corn muffins and tea. Billy never said anything about the dream. He never said anything about believing that it was not a dream, that he thought what he'd seen might be prophecy. He did ask to clarify what an upside down star signified. He'd always believed it to be the sign of Satan, though that could easily have been misguided by blockbuster movie theatrics.

Cooper was the first to react. "Just another way man has defaced divine symbols for use in scare-tactic strategies." She ate the last piece of her banana and tossed the peel onto the patio's wooden table. The skies were much cloudier today; they drooled in gray at the horizon.

"A pentacle," Lax explained, "turned upside down means nothing. It all depends on which way the top point is pointing.

Cooper nodded. "Top point to the north and you invoke positive energy, protection of the spirit from the underworld and the divine principle. Top point to the south and..."

"Just the opposite," Billy finished.

"Satan is a religious icon for negative energy," Lax added. "It is the ignorance of materialism which clouds a person's natural ability to deny ego and accept the divine that rests hidden, and always ready to be unlocked, within each of us."

"Is that what we'll find today," Billy said. "Our divine selves?"

Lax snatched all three empty wooden bowls from the table, stacking them one inside the other, and stood. "I suspect we'll find both. There's a little bit of cubit in all of us." He grinned at Cooper. "We should probably be on our way."

"I am curious about something before we go," Cooper said. "You've never asked to see the Book. I think that's a bit strange considering how valuable it is."

A half a dozen corn muffins remained in a tray on the table. Lax grabbed the tray with his free hand and jettisoned the muffins out into the desert landscape, then set the empty bowls on the tray. "The Book is of tremendous value, but not for me…at least not anymore." Osi appeared out of nowhere and landed among the tossed corn muffins. The giant hawk ate one of them in a hurry then offered its gratitude with a sharp screech. "You're welcome, my friend," Lax said to the bird.

All of their gear, packed into three backpacks, sat near the solarium kitchen door. Once Lax had finished inside, they prepared for the hike that would take them to Lee Mountain. Though the star map had already served its purpose, Cooper stuffed it, still rolled in last Friday's edition of the *Red Rock News*, into her pack. Billy double-checked that the Book of the Djed and the key were safe and secure in his pack then zipped it up and followed Cooper and Lax around the side of the house.

"Ironically, Phoenix International has provided us a bit of camouflage by sponsoring the bike race today," Lax said as all three climbed into the Ranger. "It'll take us right to the Great Hall under Lee Mountain."

They weren't on the trail more than ten minutes before a light rain started saturating the ground. The organizers of the Llama Lunatic mountain bike race had done a wonderful job of flagging off a pedestrian traffic lane from the main course, but because of the terrain, the two paths were adjacent and in some places, intersected. Pedestrians had to remain attentive to avoid being run over by racers. What some spectators probably had not considered was the rooster tail splashes of red mud that pelted their bodies in turns and in areas where puddles had formed. Some of the spectators (women included) reveled in the mud and rain, having taken off their shirts to write explications across their bare chests. Others, who were certainly tourists, stood rigid, frowning at their red blotchy clothes; one family looked absolutely miserable and Cooper tried to ease their pain as she walked past.

"What's done is done," she told the father of the triumvirate. "You'll need to soak those clothes as soon as you get home or else Sedona will forever remain in the fibers." The man glared at her. The mother asked if they could leave now. Their boy, who was no more than eight years old, smiled, his face dotted with mud. "Who's your favorite rider?" Cooper asked him.

The boy pointed at the bicycle that was heading in their direction. "Cobra Diego," he yelled. "He's in the lead and ain't nobody gonna catch him." Cooper instinctively backed a few steps as Cobra skidded across the bike path, sending a fresh tail of red mud over the head of the boy and into the faces of his mother and father. The mother wiped the mess from her mouth and exclaimed, "That's it! I'm outta here." She shoved past Cooper who was amazed to see that the woman was wearing flip-flops; she slipped on a rock and almost fell.

"Come on," the father said to his son. "We better help her or she's gonna bust her butt." The boy looked totally crushed as he watched his favorite racer disappear around the next turn, but he grabbed his mother's hand and all three headed back down the hill toward the trailhead.

Lax and Billy, who had continued on when Cooper had stopped, waved at her from the rocky turn that Cobra Diego had just managed. After three additional racers passed, she stepped out onto the course and headed up the gentle slope to meet them.

They stood a few yards away from the course as rain continued to mist the area. Clouds broke at one point and, for a few minutes, a rainbow appeared in the direction that Lax said they should go, which was straight ahead, across a wide, flat plain filled with multicolored autumn brush and cacti, toward the base of Lee Mountain about a mile and a half away. To their right, the bike race continued along the west rim of Lee Mountain, snaking its way up treacherous slopes, across flat and rugged ground, around corners where the racers disappeared momentarily before reappearing to continue their slippery journey toward its apex. To their left was a set of smaller hills that had not yet gained prominence in the presence of the more sensational red rock monoliths promoted in the area.

As they descended a short slope to flatter land, Lax explained that it was in this plain where trailblazing pioneers had moved between Arizona and Utah in the late 1800s. The mountain was actually named after one of these men who settled nearby.

"I'm sure it came with great cost," Cooper said as she scraped mud from the bottom of her hiking boot with a broken juniper tree branch. She handed the stick to Billy who followed the same procedure.

"All men have a right to the land," Lax said. "But not when that right is defined by self-serving policy." Lax took the stick and cleaned his boots, using Billy's shoulder for support. "You are right, though. White men pioneered on the backs of dead natives. The policy was called Manifest Destiny—to settle in the name of American progress. But we all know who the real Americans were then and still are today. Progress for America by killing Americans. That tune sounds familiar, doesn't it?"

"One that doesn't make much sense," Billy offered.

"And never will," Cooper concluded.

Once their boots were a pound of mud lighter, they started across the plain, following Lax's lead. Rain continued but it was light, and unlike on the hillside, the ground beneath them now was stitched with enough autumn tobosa grass that their boots did not collect much of the earth. Considering that the terrain was densely populated with desert flora, the trek was not encumbered: they walked a trail, it seemed, though no footprints or other signs of passage was present.

Throughout the hike, Cooper kept thinking about their conversation the night before, about the idea of immortality and the implications for those promoted to its promised hierarchy. She wondered if Lax was telling them the truth. It certainly wasn't inconceivable that it had been Lax all along who had wanted them and the Mayan artifacts together in the Great Hall. That thing around his neck could be any one a thousand lookalikes sold at any one of a hundred shops in the Verde Valley. This could all be one big ruse to find out for himself exactly where the real Djed could be found, she thought. He'd then kill them both with the help of his accomplice, Deere-hat man. He'd kill them, then kill Marcy and flee to Mexico…to Chichen Itza where Cooper suspected the Djed lay in wait. Lax had told Billy that he would become immortal only to gain his confidence. Just as Cower had used her own ego against her, Lax was using Billy's against him. The promise to live forever could not be ignored by mere mortals.

They stopped once for rest and water and this is when Cooper had to ask. "Why should we trust you?" Billy looked shocked, as if he'd never even considered such blasphemy.

"I've given you no reason," Lax said, simply.

"Then this is as far as we go." Cooper looked to Billy for support. "Right?"

Billy suddenly seemed defeated and helpless. "But we do trust him… don't we? We've come so far."

"I'm not Marcy," Cooper grumbled. "*We* haven't come far at all. I was taken on a carpet ride to the Land of Liars before. It's not happening again."

"Please," Lax pleaded. "This is unnecessary. I can prove that I am who I say I am."

"A Daykeeper?" Billy asked.

"Yes. I can tell you what is contained on just about every page of the Book except the center page, the one that is being written by the Great Spirit, and the pages that will be revealed by the key."

"What do you mean?" Billy asked, taking one step away from Cooper and one step closer to Lax.

"The center page reveals clues that guide the end of the Age of Jaguar. The key reveals where to find the Djeds and how to seal the Cubit forever."

"The Djeds…plural?" Cooper said, suddenly feeling a bit ostracized.

Lax wiped accumulated mist from his forehead. "Right now, the key reveals three locations. The first is of the Great Hall itself where the revelations are made. The second is Chichen Itza where my sister raised her Djed."

Cooper looked confused and Billy clarified. "Alixel."

"The third location revealed by the key is where *my* Djed was raised." Lax tapped his chest where the bulge of the amulet pressed up against his wet poncho. "Puerto Morelos."

"Where's that?" Billy asked.

"In Quintana Roo…on the Riviera side of the peninsula. It's a small fishing village very much like your Port Aransas."

Billy pulled his backpack from his shoulders and started to unzip it.

"Stop!" Cooper demanded. "What are you doing?"

"I'm going to see if he's lying."

Cooper stepped to him and gently but firmly grabbed his hand. "He could have opened it last night while we were sleeping."

Lax's face spread into that cavernous grin of his. "Wise but paranoid," he said to Cooper. "I guess there's only one way to find out then. Billy, you know what to do."

Cooper released Billy's hand and he gave the pack to her. "What's he talking about?" she asked him. "Wait…you don't mean…"

But before she could finish her sentence, Billy had already unleashed the Creation Dagger and plunged it into Lax's ribs, then quickly withdrew it. The seven-inch blade was coated in Lax's blood; the dripping point hovered over the crimson hole in Lax's poncho. Cooper looked across the landscape, wondering if she should cry for help. Up on the rim of Lee Mountain, the ant-sized shadows of bike racers continued up the slope in earnest. Then, appearing out of nowhere, flew the hawk Lax had called Osi. She ducked, slipped forward, and fell to her knees. She'd never seen a raptor that big. It continued to hover overhead while Lax's body proved its immortality.

While the dagger remained an inch from the wound that it had just inflicted, the blood on its blade jumped from the metal surface and onto the hole in Lax's poncho. It was as if the blood had suddenly been frightened by the reality of being pulled out of its home and was now desperate to return. Every ounce of it drained in a thin rivulet from blade to body. The blood splotch soaking the surrounding fabric followed in retreat. The magical procedure lasted only a minute and when it was over, Lax lifted up his poncho. Cooper then realized that Billy had struck Lax in the exact same location that she'd seen the Jaguar stab the Sun last Friday night. The wound had already started stitching itself, sucking any remaining blood around the vertical opening until nothing but a thin scar remained.

Billy returned the dagger to its sheath and said, "Believe?"

Osi screeched above them, circled once more, then flew off in the direction they were headed.

At the far end of the plain, Billy was surprised to find a cemetery. It would have been hard to detect from just about any vantage point, even one that looked out over the plain from high up on Lee Mountain. The headstones, about a dozen of them, were located behind an outcropping of rocks from which short but bushy broad juniper trees had grown. From the ground, the rocks hid the headstones. From above, the juniper trees provided camouflage.

In addition to the flora that seemingly guarded the cemetery, an obviously angry mass of fauna encircled it as well. Billy counted ten rattlers before he'd even crossed the rocky barrier into the cemetery. Skittering across the rocks themselves were more scorpions than he'd seen since coming to Arizona. There was even a coyote sitting and watching them on a short rocky shelf a hundred yards above them. But none of that mattered since, as Lax led them forward, all of the desert creatures parted as if they were either scared or respectful of his presence. The only threat to their passage into the cemetery came from one stray rattlesnake that slithered up behind them and tried to snag Cooper's foot. Osi again appeared as if out of thin air, swooped down, and snatched the reptile within its giant talons. It took to the sky and disappeared beyond the mask of the juniper trees, the snake writhing into a question mark.

The headstones were chipped and eroded; some had fallen over; some were broken in several pieces. Billy read from the five that still offered legible epitaphs.

Ole Man Jacobs d. under his tractor Oct. 1886

Robert Kenny d. Apr. 1900 Typhoid Fever

Mamie Baker d/o Ben and Ella d. shortly after birth

Wife of G.W. Johnson d. on Lee Mt during the Civil War

Unknown Child d. 1865 Starved to Death

Lax continued through the cemetery then stood by a mass of one- to two-foot sandstones that lay in scattered, half-circle disarray.

"Over here," Lax said. "The earthquake opened up the door to the well."

Billy stepped onto the scattered stones and Cooper followed. They helped each other across the stones' wet surfaces until they stood beside Lax. The rain began to fall more aggressively as Lax pointed at the shadowy hole in the ground.

"The well," Billy said. "I saw this well in the vision."

Lax nodded. "Remember—both of you." He waved a finger. "Remember the purpose of the Great Hall. It served to imprison that which was the mechanism for the creation of Evil. And it is protected by the Jaguar—the undertaker of the underworld."

Billy took the lead. Gray sunlight was the only source of illumination and this provided a glimpse at only the next five steps below his descent. Just like in his vision, the stairwell spiraled downward and each step was as narrow as the width of one foot. As fascinating as it was to be actually living a dream, he felt his concentration could not chance a state of wonderment since, with each step, his footing was challenged not only by the tapered steps and their sharp edges, but also by the running water that cascaded from the opening above and washed a slick residue under his boots.

This staircase seemed to be much deeper than it was in his dream-vision. The farther down he went, the darker the well became until, at one point, only the next step could be seen. He stood there for a moment and Cooper's hand fell on his shoulder.

"What is it?" she asked, her voice hollow as if she were speaking from inside a tin can.

"I can't see the steps."

From above, Lax urged him onward. "You know where they are. You've walked these steps before."

"Yeah. But I fell that time," he said, referring to the dream-vision.

Water rolled down the steps at an ever-increasing rate, flooding the sole of his boot as he stepped downward once more. The light from above disappeared altogether but the well did not become completely dark; below, a dim red glow lit the bottom. The red hue provided a view of the rest of the staircase but grew only faintly brighter by the time he finished the descent. He helped Cooper and Lax down the remaining steps and the three of them looked up at the twisting staircase, at the rain water which was now tumbling down and splashing profusely. Red froth collected at their feet and within minutes, the water had risen above their ankles. To their right was the source of the red illumination. It peeked through a stone obstacle that blocked the arched doorway. The obstacle's seal, however, was too tight to allow the deluge of water an escape. It now rose to their knees.

"This wasn't here before," Lax said and quickly sloshed over to the doorway. "Give Cooper your pack and help me push this out of the way or we're all going to drown. And Cooper…keep the pack out of the water. I don't know if the Book has ever survived submersion but I don't want to find out now."

She took Billy's backpack and held it with both hands over her head as the water rose to her waist. Billy and Lax wrestled with the stone obstruction, wrapped their fingers into a narrow crevice, pulled with combined force to the left.

The water rose to their chests.

They tried rolling the stone to the right.

The water rose to their shoulders.

The weight of the water was now draining their strength. Together, they pushed as hard as they could.

The water covered their mouths.

Briefly, Billy looked back at Cooper. All that remained of her was two arms sticking straight up with his backpack clamped between her fingers; short curls of hair swirled within the rising water. He turned then, and with every ounce of strength he could manage, pushed through the water and into the obstruction. The stone toppled backward and the immediate rush of escaping water sucked them through the arched doorway. Billy fell on top of Lax and Cooper fell on top of Billy. Cooper gasped for air, her face inches from his.

"The pack ain't wet," she said and coughed, then crawled off of the body heap with Billy's backpack in her hands. She offered her hand to

Billy, then Billy helped Lax to his feet. Water continued rolling through the doorway, hitting the round stone obstacle and cascading off of it to each side. The streams rushed into small slits that had apparently been carved into the rock walls of a long corridor in which they now stood.

"The underworld," Lax said. "She is quite thirsty today."

"And very pretty," Cooper added.

Billy turned around to see Cooper standing in the middle of the Great Hall; it was a two-hundred-foot-long, twenty-foot-wide, twenty-foot-high corridor that dead-ended into a stone wall. Her entire body reflected shades of red that fell from the high ceiling. Her silhouette mixed dark shadow within the red hues and she looked kind of demonic.

"It's a chemical brought up from the Yucatán," Lax said and pointed toward the very top of the walls where a rounded shelf of rock housed the chemical source of the red light; the shelf was continuous, as was the light, and ran the length of the corridor along both walls. "It was produced from a combination of plants that are now extinct. The chemical reaction is self-replicating; it never goes out and never needs to be reenergized. It would have been invaluable in today's resource-hungry world."

Billy thought of some of the chemists back at M.I.T. that would have sold their mothers for a chance to be standing where he was now. Ancient Mayan plants now extinct, providing perpetual light for an underground corridor built by the Anasazi.

And, suddenly, that didn't make sense to him. "Wait a minute," he said. "Are you implying that the Anasazi visited the Mayans? That can't be. There's a three- to four-hundred-year difference, not to mention a couple of thousand miles that separates the two cultures."

"I am not *implying* that at all." Lax sucked in a deep breath in a way that made the air seem precious.

"Unbelievable." Cooper gasped. "Look at these walls. I'm no archeologist but this looks like a convergence of ancient Mayan and old Native American writing."

"No." Billy shook his head. "Really? The Mayans were the Anasazi?"

"Not precisely," Lax corrected. "But the surviving Mayans had to migrate somewhere. Remember what I told you about Samaal and Eka?"

"The Mayan and Anasazi Daykeepers?" Billy answered. "The influence of two cultures colliding. The transference of knowledge."

Cooper stroked the walls, fingered the striations. "You are supposed to be the next one aren't you?" she said to Billy. "Don't you see? You are supposed to be the next Daykeeper. Lax is passing the knowledge on to you right now." She looked at Lax. "You are a clever one aren't you, my

Hopi friend—if you really are Hopi. My guess is that you and your sister are descendant of the last surviving Anasazi."

In the red luminescence, Lax's big, fat grin made his teeth look bloody. "She's sharp, Billy. I'd hang on to her if I was you."

"But you're extinct," Billy said.

"Nothing ever dies," Lax reminded him.

Billy turned his attention to the wall's deep etchings of pictographs and glyphs that told stories with lost meanings. Hunters stalked bison. Lizards swirled around twisted trees. There were many four-legged creatures and orbs that Billy guessed represented celestial objects. As he walked along the corridor, the simple pictographs began to transform into the kinds of glyphs one could find in the ruins of the Maya. Deep chiseled etchings of frogs and serpents and men with fantastic headdresses merged with the more simplistic pictograph scratches. The farther he walked, the more transformative the drawings became until there remained only Mayan glyphs.

He stood near the end of the corridor and looked back toward the well opening. The wall drawings presented a chronological move forward in history, but at the same time told of a recession in intellect. The Mayan glyphs closest to him were meticulously crafted, some chiseled into three-dimensions all stacked in rows one on top of the other. But as the corridor continued toward the well, the drawings lost their third dimension and became scattered, simple depictions that reminded Billy of something he might find in a kindergarten class.

When he turned back around, Lax and Cooper were waiting for him in front of a narrow vertical opening of about five feet wide that split the dead end wall from floor to ceiling. Billy stood there for a moment longer because of the sound he heard behind the wall.

A humming noise.

"Hey. Do you guys hear that?" he asked as Lax and Cooper disappeared into the vertical slit. Billy followed.

When he emerged on the other side he gasped, the one breath seemingly stuck in his open mouth. The temple face in front of him really didn't look like anything the Anasazi might have constructed. It looked Mayan. A rectangular door carved an entrance through the middle of the temple face and it glowed a dim white. To each side of the door stood a statue of a jaguar-headed human; their noses pointed down toward the doorway which was a couple of feet shorter than the statues were tall. Ceremonial accessories of feathers, small animals, carnivorously sharp teeth and a slithering snake were chiseled across their bodies. The walls to the left and right of both jaguars were filled with glyphs set in horizontal rows. Some of the glyphs were stained in red, some in blue, some not at all.

"What does it say?" Cooper asked Lax, pointing at the glyphs beside the statue on the left.

"In a roundabout way, it says we better not enter unless we want our souls ripped from our bodies and sacrificed to the underworld."

"Wonderful," Cooper moaned.

"And on this side?" Billy asked.

"It names the Daykeepers from history. We are the only ones whose entry is guaranteed safe."

"Then I'm good," Billy said, studying the glyphs, their arrangement, their representative iconography. "Where am I?"

"You aren't a Daykeeper yet. You still have quite a demanding journey ahead of you."

Billy wondered what it would take to get his representation chiseled into the temple wall. What labors would he have to accomplish to be awarded with such reverent gratitude? The thought scared him. He should have known that the ascension toward immortality just might kill him in the process.

Cooper walked over to that side of the temple. "So, you are inscribed into the last row?" she asked Lax.

"It's not written in such linear terms nor is it written to be translated as English," Lax explained.

Billy interjected. "That would go against everything the Mayan culture believed in: no beginning and no end, just one long, unending cycle. Kind of like all of the 'begots' in the Bible: a lineage of ancestry without chronology dating back to the beginning of human history. The importance is that one came before and one came after and not when those links were created."

Above and in front of the temple face and attached to the ceiling, was a row of what Billy thought were stalactites. Inverse conical sandstones, their sharp points hovering directly over his head, seemed almost like teeth and when Billy realized that an equal set of conical shapes stood upright across the entire base of the temple, he was sure that is what they represented. Lax verified his assumption.

A single sandstone step sat in front of the doorway like a welcome mat and Lax now stepped onto it. "Let us enter the mouth of the underworld," he said. "The Wayeb Chamber awaits." And then he stepped through the doorway.

THE DJED: PART II
YA'AXCHE'

As it always has been and as it always will be, spiritual ceremonies and mystical ruminations remain central to all human cultures throughout time. For the Maya, the sacred ceremony Ya'axche' represents the center of life on earth and is the connection between Heaven and the Underworld. Only the wisest of men are allowed to perform the ceremony which has, as its central symbol, the Tree of Life: the ceiba tree. Found in all parts of the Yucatán, Central America and the Caribbean, la ceiba is fundamental to survival. Its wood is used to build shelters and canoes and containers, and provides a base from which are constructed handicrafts and wondrous artwork. Within the tree's numerous seed pods grows a cotton-like fiber with which clothes are made and the seeds, themselves, provide fertilizer for crops. As one of the largest trees in the tropics, its gray-white trunk, which is inundated with protective thorns, rises several feet before branching into a canopy of leaves and seed pods high above the ground. The most striking part of the tree, and that which is considered connected to the underworld, is its roots. Standing tall and thick above the ground, the tree buttress roots are often taller than the height of a human. It is at these roots where X'Tabay waits for unsuspecting men.

Legend has it that X'Tabay is a deadly spirit of the night; she is the goddess of suicide. During a full moon, she awaits unsuspecting male souls as she sits atop the ceiba tree roots, stroking her long black and beautiful hair, her body and eyes so seductive that men are helpless to deny her advances. This deceitful, dark spirit sings tones of increasing sensuality, luring her victims into her embrace. Men cannot escape as her arms turn into thorny branches, her face into razor-sharp spines, and her mouth into a cavernous pit that devours them alive.

For Cooper, it was the ceiba tree, standing in the center of the temple's ceremonial chamber that first caused her to gasp. Its twenty-foot tall, four-foot thick, white trunk rose into the ceiling where it spanned out into a canopy of many leafy, pod-bearing branches. The tree seemed to continue straight up through the sandstone where, from above, very dim rays of daylight found spaces within the dense canopy and provided dull illumination throughout the vast chamber. Cooper knew the ceiba tree very well. She'd grown up understanding its tremendous material and spiritual value in Puerto Rico. At an early age, its use was required learning, particularly since her hometown was named after the tree.

For Billy, it was the woman tied to the ceiba tree roots about thirty feet away, that first caused him to gasp. In almost every way, she resembled what legend described as X'Tabay. Marcy's long black hair flowed over a thin sheet of cloth that covered most of her body. Her eyes, though open and staring straight at him, did not appear conscious of the reality around her. She sang a soft hum through slightly-parted red lips, a sensual tune that locked Billy's attention. Her body was tied to the tall roots with lashings of vines that prevented all movement except for her head.

"Marcy?" Billy said and took one step forward but was held back by Lax's arm. She continued staring at him, her soft hum never changing its harmonic pitch. Lax glanced around the chamber, at the numerous shadows that hid the depth of the red sandstone walls on all sides.

"Go ahead, Presser," a hidden voice echoed from their left. "X'Tabay wants your young soul. And she wants to know where the final Djed will be found. Show her, or she will die."

A spear flew through the air from the shadows and missed the middle of Marcy's forehead by a couple of inches; it impaled the tree root directly above her head and a feather tied near the spearhead, swooped down over Marcy's glassy eyes. It fluttered each time a humming breath emerged from her lips.

"To the Cubit's throne with the Book," the voice urged. "Hurry!" Another spear flew overhead and struck the tree root to the right of Marcy's head.

Lax and Billy walked cautiously toward Marcy.

"Not you, Daykeeper," the voice demanded. "Just the boy."

"Go on," Lax said. "I'll join you shortly."

Billy looked at Lax curiously, but did as he was told. As he neared the tree, he realized that a square pedestal made of stone sat at Marcy's feet. Billy guessed that it was what the voice had referred to as the "Cubit's throne" since it looked a lot like the Cubit, right down to the red star that was centered and glowed just an inch from the stone's top edge. A green John Deere ball cap sat on top of it. Billy slapped the hat from the pedestal, then pulled the backpack from his shoulders. From inside, he grabbed the Book of the Djed and the single page that had been ripped from it. He had no idea what he should do with them except to set them on the Cubit's throne, which he did.

"Go ahead," Deere-hat man said from the shadows. "Open it. Do your thing. Show us the way."

Billy opened the Book to its center spread. The strokes of heavenly lead depicting three sixes and three nines had become thicker; the tail of phoenix bird of fire had become more colorful with swirls of red and orange and yellow. He picked up the stray page and examined the symbols that were written on one side, trying to understand what he should do next. He dropped the key page on top on the center spread but nothing happened. He tried to turn a page in the Book and couldn't.

"Hurry up, boy," Deere-hat man grumbled.

"He can't do it," Lax said. "Only Daykeepers can, or have you forgotten that too, cubit!"

"I'll drill her in the forehead," Deere-hat man said. "I swear it."

"Yes. Of that I am sure."

Lax quickly walked to Billy's side and turned the page. Billy immediately noticed the serrated remainder of the key page sticking a half an inch up from the binding. The page that was visible included sketches in three of its four corners. In the top left corner was the face of the temple that he now stood inside, complete with two Jaguar statues and the glyphs etched into the walls beside them. In the bottom left corner was drawn a structure that looked a lot like an observatory. The sketch in the top right corner looked like a sinkhole and Billy guessed that it was located where Lax had said he'd acquired his Djed in Puerto Morelos, Mexico. The lower right corner was blank.

"This is why the key is so important," Lax whispered to him. "Without it, we would never know the fourth location and you will not know how to seal the Cubit forever."

Lax took the key from Billy and when he placed it into the Book, it automatically re-stitched itself to the serrated edge, becoming whole and firm again.

At that same moment, the chamber shook once, as if the God of the Underworld was either overly pleased or massively pissed off that the Book was again whole. Dust rained down from the dark ceiling. Seed pods from the ceiba tree dropped like tiny grenades. Leaves fluttered to the floor all around them. Much of the falling debris nearly struck Marcy's defenseless body but she did not flinch, the drug within her so strong that it blocked all thought of self-preservation. Billy, wanting to protect her, stepped around the Cubit's throne but, again, Lax's hand came down across his chest.

"No! Not yet," he urged. "You have to be strong, Billy. The ceremony is incomplete."

Lax's strength knocked Billy backward and he tripped and fell, hitting the back of his head on the hard, sandstone floor. A seed pod struck him in the nose.

"The dagger," Lax demanded. "Give me the dagger!"

Blood ran from Billy's nose and into his mouth. His vision blurred from the force of his head's impact with the floor. Lax wanted his dagger, but Billy couldn't give it up for anything. Even Lax had told him so. It was all that could protect them from the cubits. It was all that could save Marcy. It was all that could bring him…

The chamber's trembling stopped and Deere-hat man showed himself. His three cubited accomplices who had been hiding in silence, also appeared: the three city council members that Billy had seen seated with Richard Manson at the Café Aus. Councilwoman Cheryl Mokier grabbed Cooper and Councilmen Bill Tate and Pat Roberts rushed to either side of Lax, grabbed the big Indian, and wrestled him to the ground. Billy didn't have to see the flip of blonde-white hair to know that the man now standing over Lax, wearing a feathered serpent headdress, was the cubit that had been stalking him every since he'd left Port Aransas.

"Ain't living forever a total thrill?" the Serpent said to Lax as he stood over him.

Lax no longer wrestled against the strength of the two councilmen cubits. "Evil never wins," he said to the Serpent. "And your pretension as Lord of Reincarnation is blasphemous."

"Is that so?" The Serpent grabbed a large chunk of sandstone that had fallen during the tremor and dropped it on Lax's chest. The crunch of ribs reverberated throughout the chamber but Lax refused to cry out. "Immortals can feel pain, can they not? At least your kind of immortals can." He picked up the stone and dropped it on Lax again. "Can they not!" he yelled. Then he turned to Billy. "Come on, boy. Show us what you got. Complete your destiny or the next throw crushes his face."

Billy wiped the blood from his nose and sat up, still woozy from his fall. He didn't know what to do. Cooper screamed, "Kill him!" and was immediately slapped to the floor by the cubited councilwoman.

And then something peculiar happened. It felt as if he were suddenly back in the dark abyss of Lax's spiritual anteroom. A memory surfaced that was not his. A voice emerged in his head that had been a part of another time. Thoughts of a boy now one-year dead, became Billy's thoughts. When Lenny Bender had been faced with a moment of truth in a Kansas cornfield he had thought about Clint Eastwood. And now, so did Billy.

You gotta start living or you gotta start dying, the voice suggested.

The dagger's warmth quickly grew against his chest. His hand itched. The star in the top edge of the stone throne pedestal began to brighten. Billy looked at his palm. The fifth point blazed with crimson light. The dagger against his chest became so hot that he had to free it. And then...he understood!

With the Creation of the End Dagger in his right hand, the star in its haft perfectly aligned with the scar it had burned into his palm, he approached the Cubit's throne and thrust the dagger's point into the glowing red star in its top edge. From above, the light infiltrating through the tree's canopy that had been merely miniscule suddenly blazed bright white, sending a beam down onto the Book. The key page acted as a filter, using the light from the tree to stamp an image into the page that followed it. The fourth location. Billy blinked once, a snapshot planted in memory, just before Deere-hat man, feathered serpent headdress and all, snatched the Book from the pedestal and raved, "That's it! That's it! After all of these long, long years." The cubit grabbed Billy's hand and tried to wrench the dagger from his grasp.

That was when the light above the tree died and the earthquake started.

The Serpent screamed when a boulder crushed his foot, having not fallen from above but thrown by Lax who had freed himself from the retreating councilmen cubits. The Serpent released Billy's hand and Billy immediately withdrew the dagger, slashing out at the back of the Serpent's head but missed it by inches.

Out of the chamber, the Serpent ran with the Book of the Djed in hand as rocks fell all around it. The cubits that had pinned Lax quickly followed. The cubit that had held Cooper was now under Cooper's foot. She waved at Billy who threw her the dagger and Cooper quickly planted it in the back of the cubit's skull.

Another large rock hit Lax and he groaned loudly as he fell onto his back. He tried to protect his face, but it was futile.

Up against the ceiba tree, Marcy remained unharmed. The broad canopy above her deflected much of the debris that pelted Billy and Cooper and Lax.

"Over here!" Billy yelled to Cooper. "We have to get him under the tree!"

With dust and sandstones falling at her feet, Cooper ran to Lax's side and, with Billy, wrestled the big man up across the stone pedestal and rolled him against Marcy's feet. The four of them remained under the protection of the Tree of Life until the earthquake subsided.

"Did you see it?" Lax moaned. "Do you know where the Djed is to be raised?"

Billy knelt at his side and wiped red, sweaty mud from his brow. "I saw it but I am not sure what it is. You have to help me. You have to stay awake."

Lax grabbed his hand. "You will," he said, his voice hushed. He smiled then, that big grin parting his face from cheek to cheek. Then he closed his eyes. "Find the Gormen," he whispered. "The Gormen will be waiting for you."

"Who?" Billy squeezed his hand. "What do you…"

"Billy. Remember what I told you about immortality? You too will serve like us, to protect from man what he should not know. But first you must fulfill your own fate."

"What do you mean?"

Lax coughed up blood. "Find the Gormen. Find the Djed. Assume your destiny." Then he blinked once and exhaled with words that faded as did his body. "Tell Aaron I do love him so."

And Lax lay still.

From above them came a screech that tore through the chamber's acoustics. Billy and Cooper looked up to see a giant bird roosting in the canopy of branches that were now bare except for a few leaves and seed pods. The Djed remained hidden underneath Lax's poncho but it now became so green-white bright that the edges of the four crosses were easily discernible through the fabric. The green-white aura quickly encapsulated Lax's entire body and Billy felt its energy pulse beneath him. The aura rose, sparkles of green diamonds swirling within it, until it connected and was absorbed by Osi. The bird, now wrapped inside green-white light, flapped its wings twice, sending a wave of energy downward that Billy would forever remember as being pure spirit. It then hopped the branches up the tree canopy and disappeared from sight.

"Billy?"

It was Marcy's voice.

"Billy? Where am I? I feel so…"

"Stay here with her," Billy said to Cooper. "I'll be right back."

Billy exited the Wayeb Chamber to find that the stalactite teeth had fallen from the ceiling and were now in broken ruins as was much of the corridor in front of him. At the far end, the opening to the water well had collapsed and was sealed shut. The remaining plant chemicals that provided eternal light from above cast the crumbled path into broken red shadows that only served to enhance the sight of its destruction.

Billy turned back toward the temple and noticed that both of the jaguar statues had suffered little, if any, damage. The glyphs noting the dire warning on the left wall had been chipped by falling debris. The glyphs on the right, those that enshrined the names of Daykeepers, had been saved except for…

Billy walked to the wall and just stood there, trying to remember…

The last row of glyphs had changed; he was sure of it. He knelt and leaned closer. One new glyph had been added—one that looked just like a bird. Its sharp beak and piercing eyes seemed to be looking at something and Billy followed its gaze. Poking out of a short pile of sandstone rubble was the corner of the key page from the Book of the Djed.

"It must have torn free," Billy said to the bird glyph. "Thank you." He snatched it, returned to the chamber, and told Cooper that the well had collapsed and that they were sealed inside.

"No." Cooper shook her head, then led him to the back side of the broad tree trunk where long spikes rose to the ceiling like rungs in a ladder. "We'll follow his spirit. We'll follow the Great White Hawk."

Though Cooper knew that she would be a suspect in the deaths of Detectives Beets and Dreagan, it was not the primary reason she wanted to go with Billy to Mexico. She hated the idea of just picking up and leaving her life behind. She had a good job, a great reputation (at least up until recently), and she really loved her house. But everything had changed. All that she'd experienced in the last four days had taken her life on a different path. To be with Billy was something she was meant to do. Cooper was unequivocally convinced of this. Besides, there was absolutely no way in hell she was going to miss watching Billy "raise the Djed."

After they had escaped the Wayeb Chamber by climbing up the ceiba tree, they had returned to Lax's home with the hope of finding Aaron. They needed to tell him what had happened to his father, but Aaron was not there and none of them had any idea where he might be. So Billy left him a note:

Aaron:

Your father has joined the Daykeepers in Heaven. I believe you knew that this day would come. Please do as your father has asked of you. Your home is now among the tribe of men. Take care.

-Billy

All three of them now sat in Cooper's home at her dining table. Marcy had just finished telling them her story: about how it had all started in Port Aransas. As he'd done with many other business owners on the island, Mitchell Bone had lured her into the vault at the Big Texas Bank where she had come in contact with the Cubit. That same night, while she'd been asleep in her home, her cubit had paid her a visit. It had been a nasty looking thing, she recalled, having been out of the box for only a few hours. It had snarled at her and had cursed and had threatened to tear her apart. The only reason it had not, was because it had been on a steel chain leash; its handler had been the one whom Billy had named Deere-hat man, the one with the flip of blonde-white hair—the Serpent who had drugged her and had tied her to the ceiba tree.

We have your daughters, the Serpent had threatened. *If you ever want to see them alive again, you'll do as I say. Your cubit, here, is quite thirsty for your flesh but it can be appeased by snacking on your offspring. You wouldn't want that to happen, now would you? I can assure you that it would be a most horrific and painful death for both of them.*

So, Marcy had been told to: *Keep an eye on Billy. Make sure he gets to Sedona. Find out if he has the Book. Find out if he has the dagger. And never forget that we will be watching. Never forget the innocence of your daughters that will be brutally ravaged if you even hint any of this to that young prick.*

"I'm sorry, Billy," Marcy said. "But that thing Cooper killed at the casita would have eaten my daughters."

Billy, who sat to her left, massaged her shoulder. "What else could you have done? Your daughters are safe now."

Cooper smiled at the shared compassion but knew that it was time to move on. "We have to figure out what to do next." Billy and Marcy nodded. "I think we already know where we are headed."

"Chichen Itza," Billy confirmed.

"And we have to lay low. It won't be long before they find Beets and his buddy in pieces at Marcy's. I figure we'll all be suspects."

"I'm not going to Mexico," Marcy said. "I have to see my daughters. I have to go back to Port Aransas. I have an entire life that I was forced to leave behind."

"Can you prove that?" Billy asked, his hand still on her shoulder. "I mean, can you prove that you were being blackmailed with the lives of your daughters?"

Marcy had apparently already considered the possibility. She turned her head to Billy, her eyes still swimming with the remnants of the drug she'd been given, her lips still full and beautiful even though they were scratched in places. She leaned forward and kissed Billy on the forehead. "The authorities are looking for a woman with a bald head." She draped fingers through her long, black hair. "They really don't have any other proof than an artist's sketch made by a drunken pedestrian. Besides, I think they will be quite interested in the goings-on of a couple of their city councilmen. I suspect they were the ones that destroyed your apartment and they certainly helped my cubit in the slaughter of the two detectives."

"So what are you saying?" Billy said.

"There really is no other choice. You both need to continue with your own destinies. I have mine to contend with. I'll stay here as a diversion while you and Cooper get a big head start. Your names will be suspect, for awhile, but I figure their investigation will soon stray away."

Cooper asked, "Where will you say we've gone?"

"To Port Aransas, of course. That would be the most logical place… at least it would be for Billy. It also has the added benefit of getting local authorities involved with the threats made to my daughters."

All three of them stood simultaneously. "We'll need to get going immediately," Cooper said. "Before our names get placed on a computer. Getting into Mexico will be impossible then."

"We can't fly and we can't take your Jeep," Billy offered. "The Cavalier. We can make it to the border by nightfall."

Cooper packed as much as two suitcases could hold then locked up her house, hoping that she would soon return. The three of them walked the wet road to the intersection of Dry Creek and Gringo.

Billy went to his apartment to get as many of his personal effects as he felt was needed, then placed them in the trunk. Cooper was already in the passenger's side front seat and was playing with SpongeBob, grabbing his rubbery hand and shaking it. He then hugged Marcy long and strong, and whatever desire he'd had for her in the past completely vanished as their embrace sealed a friendship of love that would last forever.

"Be careful," Marcy whispered in his ear. "You come back to Port A once this is all said and done, okay? You promise?"

Billy nodded. "Marcy," he said, releasing her. "We couldn't have done it without you."

"Nor could I have without you." Marcy turned away and did not look back, even as Billy pulled out of the parking lot and beeped the horn.

The last thing he would remember of Marcy Ruminski would be her long black hair as if shifted and shuffled behind her through the casita's front door.

The Djed

PART III

The Djed: Part III

Welcome to the Jungle

(Friday, ten days later)

At sunrise, Evan jumped from the Cessna two thousand feet higher than usual. His boss had demanded it. The added altitude would give them ten more seconds of freefall.

His new helmet-mounted camera wiggled a bit as air rushed past at a hundred and ten miles an hour, but that was of less concern to him than the accuracy and comfort of the earplugs which he'd added to the helmet's interior within the last week. They were experimental, of course, as was so much of what he did for his boss. Richard Manson demanded perfection from untested inspirations, a bear of an attitude to have, especially if one served as his right-hand man.

Today, Manson had decided to take his sky surfing prowess to the Gulf of Mexico. Below them, there was nothing but water, dark blue and hard, a sheet of bone-crushing liquid that looked intimidating even from this height. Manson's intent was to have fun, defy death, and in the process, get some knarly footage that could be used to pump up the next X-Games for which his company was a major sponsor. As his cameraflyer, Evan knew exactly which angles would not only portray sky surfing as the ultimate in extreme sports, but would place Manson dead-nuts center as the single most important influence in getting the sport accepted, once again, into the competition. If this old man could do it, anyone could. Age-defying beauty, Manson had called sky surfing, and in the process had called out all of the young bucks who still thought the sport was too dangerous.

Today's experiment included synchronization to music. Manson thought that the old-school method of adding music to action only after the action had ended was boring and bogus. Anyone with a few dollars worth of computing muscle could simulate the sky dance with flash cutting and mashup mixes. What Manson was interested in was the real thing, a sky dance on a sky board set to real-time music. The grabs and side slides and barrel rolls and inverted flips would all be orchestrated in flight to the fast-paced, in your face, feels like flying into space lyrics of R.E.M.'s *It's the End of the World As We Know It*. The only way this could be accomplished was if the cameraflyer (Evan) and the sky surfer (Manson) were both listening to the same tune at the same time. Manson would perform as the cameraman repositioned himself for the sweetest angle, one that rocked to the beat and rolled to the rhythm.

To accomplish the synchronization, Manson had "borrowed" one of Steve Jobs newest gadgets: a wireless, waterproof iPod. The two CEOs had always acted as if they were best buddies but few-to-none had ever believed it. The rich did what they needed to do to remain rich and if acting all chummy was a part of that ritual then that's what the public got. What Jobs got was a heavy investment from Phoenix International and media blitzes every time Manson showcased one of Apple's products. Manson got brand association and influence with the young pop group. It was hip to be on the Apple bandwagon and Manson was about the hippest old dude on the planet.

Almost fifty seconds had elapsed since they'd jumped and Evan stepped off of the bottom of Manson's board, the camera pointed at his boss who soared upside-down, just as R.E.M repeated the chorus which magnified what he believed would be some of the best sky surfing footage ever. The actor and the cameraman were in perfect sync, married to the performance, a director's dream. With the red-orange sun ball rising atop the horizon and the indigo marble of water twinkling underneath, no studio in the world could have provided a more perfect setting.

Evan pulled his chute as Michael Stipe rolled on with the words *Slash and burn, return, listen to yourself churn*. Immediately, his body jerked hard as his relative speed went from a hundred and twenty to ten miles an hour in a second. Evan looked around for Manson, expecting to see his infamous phoenix-painted canopy nearby; Evan always added this extra footage for outtakes that included some pretty hilarious gestures from his boss.

But the parachute was nowhere on the horizon.

Evan looked up, then down. Manson was below him and his chute was not open. In another six seconds, the man would hit the surface of the Gulf traveling at over a hundred miles an hour. Evan angled his head down at the receding dot that was Manson and adjusted the zoom ring in his helmet camera. From fifteen hundred feet up, he knew that he'd only capture Manson's small, white dot of a splash as his body hit the water but, considering that he'd never been told of his boss's intent, he'd not rigged anything more powerful.

Suddenly, Stipe's voice stopped on the words...*a tournament of lies.* Below him, a ripple no larger than that made by a pebble in a pool, encircled the white, frothy center where Manson had landed. Two hundred yards away and speeding atop the water was their chase boat.

Evan angled his parachute toward the pickup zone and when he was a hundred feet from splashdown, the music returned...*of the world as we know it, and I feel fine*. To his left floated the shattered remains of Manson's skyboard and a few feet farther out, Manson, whose arm was in the air and waving.

Evan missed his own landing on the chase boat's deck because he was too busy filming Manson's rescue; instead, he landed softly in the water just a dozen feet from the deckhand's struggles to pull Manson's body up and onto the boat's rear platform. His camera was still zoomed way in and it captured the essence of Manson's screams.

"God-damn, that was great!" Manson bellowed. "Wasn't that great, fellas?" All three deckhands nodded in unison while one of them fished the chute pack off of Manson's back and another helped him stand on legs that were twisted in physically impossible directions. Evan swam to the boat's rear platform and pulled himself aboard. "You get that, Van? Christ that's gonna make some good Youtube." Manson removed the iPod earplugs.

"Totally banananonkers," Evan replied. His language was often this kind of twisted amalgamation: combining two words into one; in this case, bananas and bonkers, which really meant crazy and irrational. He removed his pack and pulled in the canopy and stringers from the water's surface, then took off his helmet cam and stood beside Manson.

Manson pushed on the joints in his legs until they were, again, straight. "That was like hitting concrete," he said to all of them, combing back short, silver hair with his fingers. "Just think what a mile-wide asteroid would have done sixty-five million years ago. Those dinos didn't have a chance."

The sky surf was only ancillary to the real reason why Richard Manson had come to this location, twenty-five miles offshore from Mérida, Mexico, where the alleged dinosaur-killer asteroid had struck. His vast oil exploration resources had recently found that such a speculation was, perhaps, fact. Perimeter demarcations and unusual sea bed densities had been detected three thousand feet under the very spot where the chase boat now floated.

Geologically-speaking, such an impact and the associated heat should have compressed the earth with such ferocity that oil pockets could have formed underneath ground zero. Richard Manson was convinced that it had.

"Dinos didn't have a chance," the youngest of the deckhands replied to Manson. He was a wiry man of about twenty years; Evan really didn't know his age. Manson never asked about ages when Evan brought in new hires, though his boss did tend toward the younger crowd. The deckhand's name was Jessup or Jester or—it might have even been Jesus—all that Evan could remember was the *Jes*. The young Hispanic had been a part of Manson's "executive team" for only a month and he had yet to earn any brownie points, mostly because Manson had not yet trusted him enough to assign him duties other than piloting the chase boat and ordering take-out. For the time being, Jes was a Yes Man, something Manson loathed.

"What did you say?" Manson asked Jes, his silver eyebrows uncurling into sharp edges.

"The dinosaurs didn't have a chance. The asteroid wiped them out just like you said."

Manson ignored the response. "And what about your hair? Didn't I tell you never, NEVER! allow it to grow below the neck?"

"Yes, sir."

"So why are you still standing in my face? Cut it!"

Jes looked around at the other deckhands, then at Evan. Manuel, who had been a part of the executive team for more than a year stepped forward, taking Evan's non-verbal signal to do so. "Cut him," Evan told Manuel. Manuel was twice as wide and twice as heavy as Jes and he easily escorted the youngster to the front of the boat.

The thrill of the jump had seemingly dissolved from Manson's immediate memory. Evan could tell by the way Jes had so easily pissed him off. "What's next on the agenda, Van?" Manson asked.

Evan quickly walked to the boat's cabin to retrieve his iPhone. Beyond the cabin, through the front windshield, he saw Manuel, with scissors in hand. He turned away and returned to Manson, opening up the cell phone and scrolling through the day's appointments as he managed the boat's rocking motion. "The sheik will be in Mérida at…" A scream and then a splash from the front of the boat interrupted him for a moment. "He'll be at the Tower for breakfast at nine," Evan continued, watching in his periphery to the right as Jes's body floated face down, a trail of new blood streaming across the shallow, choppy waves, the blade of the scissors still stuck in his neck. "At noon you have lunch with the team from Explorer One. They will update you on their recent core drill results. The mayor of Mérida also asked for the pleasure of your company today though I don't have him scheduled yet. And…excuse me for a moment. There's a message here from Bartholomew." Evan listened to the message. "Bartholomew says that our guests have arrived."

This brought a huge smile to Manson's face. His attention transformed again from all business to all fun. "Excellent," he beamed. "Isn't that excellent?"

Evan did not say *yes*; he only nodded and watched Jes's head bounce against the chase boat's rear platform.

"I want to see the footage you grabbed today. We'll put together a Youtube clip tonight then get it out as soon as possible. Make sure Jobs knows. Call him personally. Maybe the son-of-bitch will finally make some time to talk face-to-face. It's been too long. We gotta get sky surfing back on the X-Games map."

Again, Evan avoided the word yes. "Done," he told his boss. "And Jes?"

Manson squinted, the sun now blazing across the early morning Gulf. He thought about it for only a moment, looked down at the deckhand's floating body, then said, "Too bad. I almost liked him." He walked away toward the boat's cabin, his legs still wobbling at the joints, the boat's rocking motion making it even harder for him to maintain balance. "Sharks gotta eat, too," he added, then started the boat's engine.

Entering Mérida was no different than entering the other, few, major metropolitan cities that had intervened in their drive from Arizona to the Yucatán. Mexico had seemed inundated with these kinds of topographical short stories that emulsified globs of poor around centers of wealth. Cardboard boxed walls provided shelter for most citizens that couldn't afford, by wallet or by wiles, the scrap plywood squares of existence that dotted the brown perimeters leading into the cities of gold. Mexicans ran naked, peed naked, lived naked, outside the invisibility of progress. If, by airplane, one flew into the progress, you, as an average tourist, would ignorantly dodge this true flavor of Mexican reality, an experience that now had Cooper wishing for Nexpa.

Not all of Mexico was as depraved as it was on the outskirts of the big cities. In smaller towns, the lack of greed and fruit of labor combined to form a self-sufficient unit of people, animals, plants and possessions that were wondrously symbiotic. Taking too much advantage of any one of these meant that the whole community suffered equally and, in this regard, was self-regulated. Nexpa, a surfing spot on the Pacific Ocean, was one such town.

Billy had suggested that they stop for a day or two to "chill out." He'd said that they should take Lax's advice about preparing the spirit for battle, and Billy had taken the advice one step further. He'd explained how rest and relaxation was the elixir of life. You either lived it or you searched it out and stuck it into your 365-day calendar at some point to prevent insanity. And, according to Billy, there was no better way to rest and relax than to jump on a seven-foot long board of fiberglass and attempt to ride it atop ten-foot swells of salty extreme, as were the waves that pounded the Nexpa shores five peaks at a time.

Yes, Billy had become quite a philosopher in their ride south of the border. During the long, dry stretches of roads leading to Nexpa, the spirit and the soul and the self had been popular topics. He'd talked about good versus bad, right versus wrong, and love versus hate. These were men's words, Billy had suggested. They were created for social control. Their abstractness was intentional, to be easily manipulated by those who demand that life be led not for the purpose of spiritual oneness but for the purpose of conformity. Those who held such reins of power wished only to make us slaves to our own emotions by using these brilliantly orchestrated words. Billy had even brought up the conclusions of Dr. Carl Jung, at least those that he wanted to remember from his Intro to Psychology class back at MIT. Cooper had been impressed with the accuracy of his memory and though he'd not quoted verbatim, he'd presented the essence of Jung's thoughts as they pertained to one's psychological turmoil.

When an inner situation is not made conscious, it happens outside as fate. The individual remains divided, unconscious of his inner opposite, and the world acts out the conflict, tearing the individual into opposing halves.

Opposing halves. Of all that he'd said, those two words had stuck in Cooper's mind, reverberating, reiterating and reinforcing her recent experience. She'd seen the physical manifestations of such psychological premises. After all, that's exactly what the Cubit was all about: it ripped the opposing half right out of you and then presented that pure Evil to you at your bedside, during black nights full of nightmares that detailed the agony of being eaten alive, of being literally consumed by your darkest half.

Mérida was like that, too: opposing halves—the haves and the have-nots; a juxtaposition so evident it was blinding. Of particular magnitude was the monstrous Phoenix Tower that beamed its materialistic might of steel and glass reflections onto the timid block and stucco facades of the centuries-old buildings around it. Simple shops and single-story homes stuffed with families cowered under its forty floors of new world order.

Cooper leaned forward as far as her seat belt allowed, her forehead not quite touching the windshield or SpongeBob's incessant happy open arms and happy open grin. She'd asked to remove the toy from the dashboard only once in their ten-day adventure, but Billy had adamantly denied the request; he had apparently anointed the character to the iconic position of guardian angel and had demanded that its removal would "alter their good luck." She'd moved it from directly in front of her face to the middle of the dashboard so that she could see the road ahead without staring between the toy's spindly yellow legs but she had not removed it—not once.

SpongeBob's hand caught in a strawberry red curl as Cooper gazed up the side of the Phoenix Tower, watching as the morning sunshine was snatched away by the building's girth. On the shadowy west side of the tower, the word BETH was anchored in bold blue letters above the fortieth floor windows. "Where do you suppose he is?" she asked while settling back into her seat.

"Maybe we're not looking for a man." Billy straightened the toy arm that had tangled in Cooper's hair. "Maybe we're not even looking for a person." He maneuvered the car very slowly through the deluge of pedestrians that apparently found jaywalking through moving traffic to be a perfectly viable option for getting around town, and did not divert his attention from them until he stopped at the next intersection. Just ahead, sunshine awaited just beyond the tower's sharp shadow. He looked at SpongeBob and then at Cooper. "Maybe we're looking for a group of people. The Gormen kinda sounds like a tribe or some other collective." The traffic, again, began its slow creep through the pedestrians and Billy returned his attention to the front of the car. In Cooper's opinion, he was being way too cautious. If he'd just pick up the pace the pedestrians would get out of the way—at least that's what the cars in the left lane were doing—and they could get the hell out of this city and on toward their destination. "So I've been trying to think of all of the words that begin with 'gor' and perhaps uncover some kind of clue as to the origin of Gormen. For example gorilla men, but that doesn't make sense to me. I don't think they have gorillas in the Yucatán do they?"

"No. I don't think so."

"How about gore men, like in a violent group of men who shed blood?"

"Why would Lax want us to hang out with a group like that?"

"I don't know. There's just not many words that begin with gor."

Cooper thought that Billy was putting way too much effort into this line of thinking, but she didn't tell him that. She honestly believed that the Gormen was a single individual. "How about gorgeous?" she offered with a smile.

"Gorgeous men..." Billy chuckled. "I think we came to the wrong city for that."

The sunshine returned in full force, blazing heat against the side of Cooper's face. Unsure of what the pedestrians might do, they had rolled up their windows before entering the city. Cooper now rolled hers halfway down. "Why are we even concerned about this guy...or this group of guys? We already know that Chichen Itza is our current destination, don't we? The star map and the Book and even Lax said so."

Billy turned to her then, uncaring of the woman and her two children that quickly ran away from the front of the car. "Because Lax said that we should. What do we do when we get to Chichen Itza? We know that there's a secret chamber but where? I gotta believe that whoever or whatever the Gormen is knows the answer. I gotta believe that Gormen knows a lot more than we do."

"Okay. So, I ask again: Where do you suppose he or they are?"

"Gorilla men!"

"What?"

Billy pointed toward Cooper's side of the street. They were now a block passed the Phoenix Tower plaza. The buildings on this end of town looked as if they'd been recently restored. Historical in stature, they included the only multi-storey structures Cooper had seen so far. She guessed correctly that these were public buildings, housing government entities, religious sanctuaries, and a rather profound number of museums. The building that Billy pointed at was the History Museum of Mérida. A banner above its entrance read in both Spanish and English:

December is the Month of the Gorilla Men

"Coincidence?" Billy asked, a curt grin capturing the left edge of his mouth.

"What in the world does that mean? There are no gorillas in Mexico, at least none that haven't been brought in for zoos."

"You hungry?" Billy didn't wait for an answer. "Yeah. Me too. They gotta have some fresh tortillas around here somewhere."

Cooper really didn't want food but she knew they weren't going to eat anyway. "You mean like inside the History Museum of Mérida?"

Billy nodded and immediately began looking for a place to park.

—∞—

The concept of coincidence really didn't compute for Billy anymore. He now saw the world as a never-ending collection of checkpoints where markers to future "coincidences" awaited his eventual arrival. Things that people said and how they acted, objects and places that intervened in daily routine, even his dreams, were all there to move him forward, to help him step into and through the next arm of the maze toward the end, whatever that was.

Such was his new attitude that was quite comforting and frightening at the same time. All he had to do was keep on moving forward, accept intuition, and keep his eyes and ears open for the signs, regardless if they were filled with good intent or malice.

Like *Gorilla Men.*

It was ridiculous to even consider that one of the final pieces of advice passed on to him from a Daykeeper would have anything to do with gorillas. *Gormen* was an amalgamate of gorilla men? He just didn't see it. Neither did Cooper. Maybe the Gormen was a single individual. Maybe it was a group of savage tribesmen. But gorillas? Intuition couldn't even remotely confirm such an idea. Intuition did, however, roar an *it-just-can't-be-coincidence* alert when he passed the history museum and saw the banner, not because it had anything to do with the origin of the word Gormen but, more so, because he and Cooper had been talking about it at the exact moment they had driven passed the Phoenix Tower, owned by Phoenix International, the corporation that seemed to have been following him ever since Port Aransas. They had been discussing the Gormen in the shadow of the tower and then, as soon as they'd emerged into the sunlight, there it had been: the red banner with the black words *Gorilla Men.*

How could he not stop?

Billy was surprised to find an underground parking garage within a block of the museum. When he got out of the car, he grabbed his backpack from the back seat and slung it over his shoulders. The backpack had now become as much a part of his daily routine as had the dagger which he still kept sheathed against his heart. Inside the pack was the page from the Book of the Djed that had fallen free during the Serpent's retreat from the Great Hall. He'd thought of simply folding it for easier transport in his pocket but something—that intuition thing—had told him not to, that he should keep it free of creases and protected from nature and man.

Together, they emerged from the parking garage into a mass of pedestrians that was only slightly less crowded than those roaming around the Phoenix Tower plaza a block away. The sun quickly drew sweat onto his forehead. Cooper's curling bangs moistened and stuck to one eyebrow. He'd not walked more than ten steps when the incessant collisions with others' shoulders prompted enough caution that he removed the backpack and cradled it in both arms in front of him. Few of the Mérida Mexicans looked directly at him but those that did forced an extreme discomfort—a feeling as if he was intruding, as if he, alone, was responsible for all of the repression that imperialism had bestowed upon their land. His white skin and the Phoenix Tower were inseparable according to these pedestrians' expressions. Whatever the tower meant to them, which was most certainly loathing, Billy had caused it. None of them looked at Cooper like this. Her dark, Puerto Rican complexion prompted indifference in most (and hungry grins from a few men), but none looked at her with loathsome contempt.

They were twenty yards from the entrance to the museum when Billy noticed that the long, tall shadow from the Phoenix Tower was slowly creeping toward them. To the left of the tower, the sun's orange ball moved in a slow rising arc that would, very quickly, find a hiding place behind steel and glass. For each step forward and another shoulder bumped into, the shadow gained two steps on them in the opposite direction. Billy looked around as if he might find the source of this manifestation, as if he'd see some guy sitting atop a trash bin with a remote control in his hands, twisting joysticks and thumbing knobs that careened pedestrians into him, slowing him, so that the tall shadow that was also being manipulated could catch him, and Cooper, before they gained the safety of the museum.

Billy freed his left hand from the backpack and grabbed Cooper's forearm, his fingers wrapping around the four rattlesnake fang scars in her djed tattoo, and led her double-time through the crowd. Some Mexicans cursed at him in Spanish; others parted like the red sea for the American who suddenly looked as if he'd run them over if they did not move.

The tower shadow and he and Cooper were now equidistant from the three steps that led up to the museum's front door, over which dangled the *Gorilla Men* banner. The shadow seemed to speed up the closer it approached and appeared darker than shadows had a reason to be; it ate up the cars and bicyclists, the sidewalks and the people, the plaza's squat, imported palm trees and other non-indigenous plants. Billy was now running, Cooper in tow behind him, the pedestrians jumping out of his way. Only a small sliver of orange sun glow remained just to the left of the big BETH sign above the tower's fortieth level. Now in front of the museum, Billy leapt the final three steps, pulling Cooper up and away from the shadow that snatched at her heels, trying to eat her, too. They entered the museum as the eclipsed sun enveloped the rectangular doorway in darkness. Automated lighting flickered on in the museum's small front lobby.

"Help you?" a Hispanic guard said. Billy's breaths rushed conspicuously fast. The guard had, no doubt, seen his share of suspicious characters.

"Gorillas." Billy took two deep breaths in an attempt to calm himself. "There aren't any gorillas in Mexico."

The guard, who wore a standard blue uniform trimmed in red piping, looked at him as if he were insane. "Perdón?"

"The banner. It says you have gorillas."

"Amigo," the guard said but was only being polite. "We no have gorillas. We have statues." He pointed. "This is a museum not a zoo."

"Yes, of course," Billy said. "We came to see the statues." Billy stepped forward, still panting.

"No puedes entrar!" the guard demanded, holding his arm out like a traffic gate.

Billy looked at Cooper. "You can't enter," she said.

"Why?" Billy said to Cooper then looked at the guard. "Why?" he repeated.

"The bag." The guard pointed at his backpack. "What is in it?"

Billy hugged the pack closer causing the guard's eyebrows to rise further. "Research papers," he said. "I…" he looked at Cooper. "…we are from the university."

"Universidad? Que uno?"

"Cancun," Cooper said.

"I have to look in," the guard demanded. "O no puedes entrar."

Billy looked past the lobby and into one of the large display rooms where he could barely make out the large statue of what could have been an ape. Closer to him and just beyond the counter that the guard stood beside were two stanchions, standing hip high and separated by about five feet: metal detectors. The Book's key inside the backpack was suddenly secondary to his concern for the dagger which would certainly set off an alarm.

"Fine," Billy said. "Then I will wait here. My research is much too important for just anyone's eyes."

The guard obviously did not understand everything Billy had just said except the part about waiting. "Wait outside," he said, pointing to the dark, shadowy entrance.

Billy opened the backpack and pulled out his small notebook, the one in which he'd scribbled information from the Sedona Public Library, and handed it and a pencil to Cooper. "You remember what we are looking for?"

he said to her. "Gor…Men."

Cooper nodded though Billy could tell she was confused; still, she played along. "Of course," she said and handed the notebook to the guard who flipped nonchalantly through pages that were certainly gibberish to him. He actually didn't even look at the pages; his attention squared on Billy and the backpack.

Cooper walked through the metal detector as Billy turned toward the door. He took several cautious steps, looking over his shoulder only once to see Cooper enter the room with the apes, and the guard whose expression was of anger, before walking into the rectangle of Phoenix Tower shadow.

—∞—

Cooper had rarely been separated from Billy since they'd left Arizona. Even during their three-day layover in Nexpa, she'd not been out of ear shot for more than ten minutes at a time. Until this very moment, when she saw Billy disappear through the museum's entrance and into darkness, she'd not realized how important his company had been, how comfortable she felt around him, how much protective energy he provided. She'd gotten quite close to him in Nexpa. He'd taught her how to surf and she'd taught him a thing or two about making really great Mexican salsa. They'd snorkeled together, had ridden horseback together, had swum in the lagoon together, and had eaten every meal together. And when the days were done, they'd watched three beautiful sunsets together while nestled under a lean-to made from the branches and leaves of nearby plants. It had been during moments like these, with the waves crashing in soothing loud bunches and the colors of the Pacific dusk illuminating wide, white beaches and the salty, gritty wind tickling every hair on their bodies, that Billy had talked about life. His thoughts had been so deep at times that Cooper didn't understand what he was talking about. But the words, though sometimes unintelligible to her, were full of wisdom—the wisdom from a mortal who'd recently discovered that immortality was within his grasp.

Cooper had indeed fallen for Billy, but it was an emotion unlike any she'd ever had before. It felt a little bit like a girlish crush, a little bit like sibling friendship, a whole lot like life-saving gratitude, and, with a pinch of lust thrown in, it was all very surreal. She cared about him…a lot. And when he disappeared from view, emotional alarms went off that made her think she might never see him again.

She stood there, in the anthropology room filled with artifacts but no people, her eyes fixed on two statues behind velvet ropes that did, indeed, look like gorillas, wondering that if she screamed right now, would Billy even hear her.

The guard was watching. She didn't turn in that direction but she felt his gaze at her back. She opened Billy's notebook more for show than for purpose, and flipped through the pages, wondering why he had left her. Several pages were filled with lists of words: BETH Pharmaceuticals. Las Cruces. Popstar. Crazy lady. Deere-hat man. Richard Manson. On another page was written her phone number and the words Cooper Clairvoyant Reyes. A smiley face was sketched next to her name.

She wasn't very clairvoyant now, she thought. *She didn't even know why he had left her, unprotected.*

On another page, he'd sketched a reasonable facsimile of the star map, had connected the dots to form two stars, had drawn a diagonal line through their centers, connecting the line to three tiny glyph scribbles of the jaguar, sun and Wayeb; beside the Wayeb glyph he'd written: Port Aransas. He'd told her that the Wayeb meant five evil days.

She knew some martial arts but she didn't have the dagger. And anyone could be a cubit. Especially here, in Mexico.

She flipped through a couple of empty pages, thinking about the dagger and then she turned toward the lobby, toward the guard who quickly looked away. The metal detector…Billy couldn't enter because of the metal detector.

You remember what we are looking for, he'd said. *Gormen.*

She walked to the side of the two statues; one stood slightly taller than the other, about five feet in height, and both presented bloated chests and thick arms that hung almost down to their feet which disappeared into square blocks of stone.

She was looking for the Gormen…or perhaps she was waiting for the Gormen to find her! Yes. That's it, Clairvoyant Cooper. Billy left you here not to find someone but for someone to find you!

Again, she looked behind her then around the room which displayed important artifacts against bland white walls. Acting like a researcher from Cancun University, she flipped through several more pages, looked at the gorilla statues, flipped through pages, looked at the statues. The notebook had lots of sketches in it; they weren't particularly artistic but she knew what they were: memories from the Great Hall of the Anasazi, including some of the cross-cultural glyphs from the corridor, the Mayan glyphs from the outside temple walls, the pedestal on which the Cubit once rested, and a drawing of the *fourth destination*, the one that the Book had produced behind the key page that Billy now carried in his backpack.

She looked at the statue then back at the notebook.

She could tell that Billy had given the fourth destination more artistic effort. The sketch in the notebook had been meticulously rendered, right down to the mortar joint lines between the limestone blocks of the structures presented.

She looked at the notebook then back at the statue and paused for a moment. What was that? At the foot of the taller gorilla? Something was written there. A Mayan glyph? She leaned forward, her body arching over the velvety rope that warned her not to do so. She blinked and the glyph seemed to move. She leaned farther forward, grabbing the stone at the foot of the statue for support. What was that? And then it occurred to her. She'd just seen that glyph while flipping through Billy's notebook. Still leaning forward, she brought the notebook to the foot of the gorilla and thumbed a few pages backward to the sketch of the Wayeb. It filled the entire page and was as intricately drawn as was the fourth destination. She moved the notebook next to the glyph on the foot of the statue to find that they matched.

Billy had been standing on the top step in front of the entrance to the museum for ten minutes, watching the melee of activity that partially rushed and partially meandered around the intersection where the modern façade of the Phoenix Tower plaza met the colonial Spanish restorations of all the city blocks around it. He hoped that, at any moment, Cooper would come strolling out with the answer to the Gormen question. Who was it or who were they? And why the hell had they stopped in the first place? It had to be more than stupid coincidence. They'd been talking about it and then he'd seen the banner—he'd seen the sign!

It was past noon and the plaza's numerous stone benches and plush, rolling landscape of green grass and cobblestone paths was littered with people eating, talking, and relaxing. It was too industrialized, too first-world, too American, Billy thought. No one seemed to care that the Phoenix Tower had gobbled up all of the precious sun. No one seemed to care about anything.

The sun's ascent finally found the top of the tower and the right half of shadow, that which was farthest from the museum, disappeared. The people that had been enjoying that side of the plaza suddenly stopped what they were doing and stood, almost in unison, as if they had been programmed to do so. Now immersed in sunlight, most of them walked off toward whatever chores or jobs or sightseeing they had scheduled for the rest of the day. Those that remained walked over to the dark half of the plaza and sat among those who, with few exceptions, had not moved. To Billy, it was an unnerving sight: the left half of the plaza was crowded, the right half contained only sunshine. It seemed that no one wanted to enter the plaza square that was sunlit, opting instead for every inch of real estate that marked its north perimeter. This made passage by foot or vehicle around the square almost impossible.

And that's when Billy saw him. Billy absolutely, and without hesitation, knew that it was the Gormen. The man stood in the center of the sunlit side of the plaza all by himself and, even at this distance, Billy knew that he was staring straight at him. He was huge and black, the dark skin protruding from khaki shorts and white shirt a stark contrast to the sun's glare. He didn't move. He waited.

Billy left the museum's front steps almost in a trance, not looking at anyone around him, holding tight to his backpack. Spanish exclamations came fast and furious; he was almost hit by more than one car as he crossed the intersection and stepped onto the cobblestone path that led from the street, through the plaza and directly toward the black figure. Billy was not afraid but he was cautious. The sun continued to rise and escape the south side of the Phoenix Tower and in his periphery, Billy saw that people evacuated in time with the movement of the sun-to-shade terminator.

As he approached the stranger, he began to realize just how damn big this man really was. Billy's first thought questioned how he'd ever gotten his massive arms and legs into his clothes. The second thought came almost as quick: John Coffey; the man that stood in front of him was almost as big as the character from the movie *The Green Mile*. He had been reincarnated right here in the middle of Mexico, his body a near splitting image (bald head and deep voice included) of the black savior falsely accused of murdering two little girls.

"Weird, ain't it?" he said to Billy. He waved one massive arm out in front of him, as if offering the plaza to Billy. "Just about every day—except Sundays when no one around here works—it's the same thing. When the sun gets over the tower and none of the shadow remains, everything returns to normal. Watch." The man folded his meaty forearms and looked to where the last remnants of shadow contained a sliver of pedestrian life. Once the sun was full overhead and for an additional five seconds, no one except Billy and the black man stood anywhere within the city block that contained the Phoenix Tower plaza. The black man counted: "One…two…three…" When he got to five he snapped his fingers, obviously already knowing what was about to happen. That's when the crowds stuffed at the plaza's perimeters began filing, again, onto the sunlit cobblestone paths and grassy knolls; the plaza returned to its average, everyday, out-of-place, industrialized, America business park. "Like a force field or something, ain't it?" the black man said, his slight southern drawl becoming more apparent. "I been around these parts for years and still I can't figger it out."

"Ritual?" Billy offered. "Respect for the sun god?"

The black man laughed one, big fat Hah! "I like the way you think. My name is…"

"Let me guess," Billy interrupted.

"If you say John Coffey, you gonna make me awful upset. I get tired of vacationers from the states calling me that."

"Well," Billy said. "I don't know what the hell they are thinking. You look nothing like him. John Coffey wasn't so handsome."

"Hah!" The black man's teeth blazed sunlit reflections. He reached out his hand and Billy released his stranglehold on the backpack, then slipped his right hand into the black man's palm where it was consumed by mighty fingers.

"I am Billy Jo Presser and you are…" Billy hesitated. The black man was staring at his hand, at the star that was burned into it. His expression turned from one of commandeering jocularity to one of reverence. "You are the Gormen?"

The black man's big lips were parted but no words came out. A few Hispanics passed on either side, giving wide berth to the two men still clasped hand-in-hand. "Who are you?"

"Billy Jo…"

"No. I mean, how do you know that name?"

"Lax sent me looking for you."

The black man released Billy's hand but did not stop staring at his palm as Billy's arm fell to his side. "Alax," he whispered to himself. "My dear friend Alax. He's dead isn't he?"

Billy replaced his right arm against the backpack. "He would not call it that but, yes, he is no longer a part of this world. How do you know that?"

The black man didn't answer the question but instead said, "Alax always messed up my name. It's not Gormen, it's Gordon. John Brown Gordon."

"The abolitionist?"

"Maybe in a past life. Today I'm a guide. And as good timing would have it, I'm your guide. It's what Alax wanted." And then both of them turned simultaneously toward the museum. "You hear that?" John said.

"Cooper!" Billy yelled and then ran.

Cooper lost her balance, the rubber sole of her right sneaker slipping on the vinyl tile flooring. Her right hand slid to the left across the foot of the statue and intersected the Wayeb glyph she'd been studying. The glyph jumped from the stone to her hand and for a moment, Cooper thought that she was hallucinating. She blinked, but the glyph did not go away. It sat amongst the knuckles and veins on the back of her hand.

"Very nice," a hallow, deep Mexican accent said from behind her. Something rubbed her butt which was prominently displayed in her bent-forward position. "It's against the law to touch such things."

Cooper quickly pushed off of the gorilla statue, nearly toppling it over, and turned around. The man was quite close to her and his breath smelled of beans gone bad. She immediately realized that the glyph drawn at the foot of the statue had not been drawn there at all. It had been a shadowy reflection of the man's earring: a Wayeb glyph dangled from his left earlobe.

"I'm a researcher…" Cooper started to say.

"Yes. From the Universidad. So I've been told."

The man was big but not tall, thick but not fat and he *was* much too close to her. She felt cornered. Beyond the man's shoulder, she saw no guard, no people, only the rectangular entry doorway that was still filled with Phoenix Tower shadow.

"You know what they do with lawbreakers in Mexico, don't you, researcher?"

"I haven't done anything wrong," Cooper demanded, standing her ground even though her fear was skyrocketing. "I'll scream."

Her threat did nothing more than bring a grin to the Mexican's mouth. "Why would you do that? I am a guide, sent to help you find what you and your boyfriend came looking for."

Cooper stepped sideways then backward to open up space between her and the man with the Wayeb earring. "Gormen?" she asked.

The man continued to grin but his eyes had that moment of confusion that one could see only if one was staring intently into them, as Cooper was doing right now. The eyes' split-second consternation was accompanied by cloudy swirls of silver and red flecks that were nearly hypnotic. "Gormen," he said. "I will help you find Gormen."

Cooper knew she was in trouble and she knew screaming would not help her but she screamed anyway. Not only was she certain that this man was not the Gormen, she now understood that the guard was in on it too when he closed and locked the museum's front door. The big man in front of her grabbed her, covered her mouth with one bean-smelly hand and pushed her up against the gorilla statues.

Why had Billy left her there? Why had he left her unprotected?

On the fortieth floor of the Phoenix Tower, high above the plaza, Richard Manson opened his eyes and looked out at his building's long shadow while thumbing through his iPhone. He pressed a couple of screen images and turned to Evan, who stood near the pile of lobsters that had been picked clean by the sheik and his entourage a half hour ago. Evan thought Manson was going to ask him about the sheik's bad manners, about how the man's pompous attitude was probably not the best business sense one could bring into a meeting with Mr. Manson, but that's not what he asked.

"You think we could build a tower tall enough to see the Gulf from here?" he said.

Evan opened the office door and several bus persons took the tray of red carcasses and empty wine glasses. "Allamah has one in Abu Dhabi that is said to look out across the Persian Gulf all the way to Iran."

"Fucking ass," Manson said. "He's a fucking ass. I'm not sure I should be doing business with such an ass tool like that."

"That's not why you want his alliance."

Manson gritted his teeth so hard, the screech was almost deafening. As much as he wanted to, Evan didn't cover his ears. His frankness often pissed of his boss but it was the reason why Evan was his right hand man… his Watcher. It was his responsibility to watch out for Manson particularly where stupid humans were concerned. Manson slammed the iPhone onto the oak desk but didn't break it this time.

"Van!" he raged. "Shit!" He turned back toward the window and looked down at the plaza. "He's made contact," he said in a more evened tone.

"Yes," Evan said.

"And Manuel?"

"Removing one of the trouble spots as you asked."

"Don't kill her," Manson warned. "If he kills her there will be hell to pay."

Evan took this literally. He'd seen way too many people who'd met the hellfire that Richard Manson could put on flesh and bone. "Manuel can be trusted."

"You can't trust things like that," Manson turned from the window.

"They live for the sheer delight of causing as much misery as possible. I should know."

"Of course."

Manson picked up the iPhone and started pressing the screen with one finger. "Any luck with Jobs?"

"He won't return my calls."

"Why do I put up with these goddamned assholes?"

"Because you need them."

Manson looked up and smiled, but it was not the kind of smile that made one feel all good and happy; it was a smile that only added to the uncertainty that Manson innately created. "When are we going to look at the footage from this morning?"

"Anytime you want. I quickly zipped through some of it. I think you'll be very pleased."

"This outta get Jobs attention. We need him for the X-Games. We need the influence."

Evan nodded.

"When Manuel returns, call me and we'll set something up."

Evan nodded again and left the office.

As soon as the door closed, Manson returned to the tall glass window, gazed down toward the History Museum of Mérida, then closed his eyes. He tasted refried beans though he hated them and stunk like the ocean though he'd showered since returning from the Gulf earlier in the day. But these were palatable inconveniences that came with his projected experiences, especially when those experiences included the rape of puppets.

She'd killed two of them. She'd taken Billy's dagger and had thrust it into the back of the cubited head of Marcy Ruminski and the councilwoman named Cheryl Mokier. That act had made her feel strong and fearless. The dagger had filled her with a sense of overwhelming comfort, an assuredness that nothing could harm her as long as she wielded the magical weapon. Invincibility was the furthest thing from her mind now.

Mr. Bean Breath's eyes boiled red; thin swirls of silver occupied the pupils. His hands covered her mouth while the other wrenched at her thigh, trying to pry her legs apart. The guard came around to her right and pulled her right knee in that direction. Her struggles caused her back to scrape against the rough edges of the gorilla statues. When she looked up, the worn simian faces ignored her, looking directly over the top of her curly hair to the locked entry door.

"Tengo ganas poonta," Bean Breath cackled. "Tienes ganas?"

The guard pulled and fully flexed her leg but fell backward when his hands grabbed her shoe and it came off. "Chinga usted chorra poonta," he yelled from the floor.

They were cursing at her, she knew that much, and she was sure that she was going to be raped. If only she had the dagger. If only Billy had not left her. She kicked with the leg that the guard had released but it was useless. The big Mexican's hand grabbed the button of her blue jeans and yanked, hard.

"Leave some for me, Manuel," the guard pleaded.

Suddenly, the museum's front entry door broke wide open. Sunshine infiltrated the space and Manuel turned, loosening his grip enough that Cooper kicked off of his chest, dropped to the floor and rolled away. Her head smacked against the plaster wall and dazed her long enough that she doubted the vision she saw standing in the doorway. It was big and it was black, its head barely clearing the doorway's top frame. Manuel was big, but this thing was twice his size. The guard scrambled to his feet and ran in the opposite direction of the advancing black behemoth. Manuel was not such a coward; cubits never were.

The black man said nothing as he entered the anthropology room. Manuel, on the other hand, would not shut up. He spewed so much Spanish so quickly that Cooper could not understand a word of it except, *Geechee*, which she knew was a derogatory term associated with skin color. He screamed it over and over again, particularly as he was lifted off the floor and thrown against the wall opposite from where Cooper laid. Manuel's neck and right arm broke on impact but he stood anyway, his head lolling to one side, his arm dangling because the humerus was sticking an inch out of his skin just above the elbow. He ran like that at the black man, his head bouncing up and down against the shoulder which supported an arm that flapped uncontrollably. When he was a foot away, the black man stepped aside and, behind him, stood Billy with the dagger out and ready to strike. When Manuel saw him—saw the dagger—he immediately flipped and flopped away from Billy who slashed at the back of Manuel's head, missing the kill spot and slicing off a quarter-sized chunk of the cubit's cheek and the earlobe from which the Wayeb earring dangled. Manuel left his pieces on the floor and ran out the front door where he quickly disappeared into the crowd. Billy spun the dagger two full circles across the palm of his hand then sheathed it in one smooth motion.

"Dammit!" Cooper yelled. "Don't ever leave me like that again." Her adrenaline had soaked into every bodily function and now, as the intensity of the moment faded, all of that energetic rush caused her body to tremble. She stared at the earlobe chunk on the floor—the Wayeb earring—thinking how close she'd just come to being…

And then she cried.

Billy came to her, knelt beside her, pulled her shoulders up against his chest, allowed the tears to soak his breast while John searched the rest of the museum for the guard without success.

"Time to leave," John said, the depth of his voice echoing through the room.

Cooper gawked at him as if she'd never seen a black man before.

"John's the name, ma'am," he said to her, offering his hand. "You know me as the Gormen."

They'd left Mérida and were now heading east toward Chichen Itza along the *autopista*, a four lane government highway that was inundated with toll stops where Mexican soldiers with carbines stood at attention, waiting for anything suspicious to pass their lines of sight, waiting for anything that would mercifully cause them to move from their stoic, sentinel stances. One toll stop featured a soldier still in adolescence who stared at the car as Billy handed the attendant fifty pesos. Billy averted the boy soldier's threatening stare, realizing that the soldier probably wasn't even looking at him with John stuffed into the Cavalier's back seat. The soldier pointed at them, said something to another soldier ten feet away, and both soldiers smirked. Billy wondered what would happen if they suddenly ran to the car, guns pointed forward, yelling commands in Spanish. What if they searched the car? What if they searched him? How would he explain the dagger? A simple stare or a big black man might be all the instigation they needed. He left the toll stop, his attention on the side view mirror, but nothing military followed.

John fit in the back seat of the Cavalier like a size twelve foot in a size ten shoe. He looked uncomfortable, but John had made do, his big body slung out across the entire width of the seat, his head in one hand that was supported by an arm that rested within the open window. Wind beat at his eyebrows; his checks flapped a bit when he turned his head in just the right direction. He rubbed his bald head with his free hand then let it fall forward onto the headrest behind Billy. Billy jumped.

"Sorry," he said. "Not many places to put the meat hook back here." Billy saw John looking at him in the side view mirror. "They act as if they never seen a blacky before, don't they?"

"They probably haven't," Billy said. "Particularly one as big as you."

"I suppose you're right. Seems like every time I come through here, they get younger."

Cooper turned to him. "You visit Chichen Itza often?"

"Used to. I serve as a private guide mostly in Mérida where I run a scuba dive shop. The really special people, though, I used to take on tours through several of the ruins around here, from Uxmal to Chich to Ek Balam."

"Special people?" Cooper asked.

"Yeah. Those that really wanted to learn. Them that wasn't scared to experience new things. The kind that didn't take advantage of God's graces. They were rare but they were the best kind of turistas."

"Hablas Español?"

"Solo Un Poquito. Y Tú?"

"Yes. Of course." Cooper turned back around and absently reached out to tweak SpongeBob's arm which sat directly under the rear view mirror. "I know what you mean by special people. I ran tours through the red rocks of Sedona and met some people you wish you could just through back. No respect at all."

Billy asked John, "What made you stop?"

"Takin' people to the ruins?"

Billy nodded.

"Too much danger in it anymore." John pushed himself up in the seat as much as headroom would allow. "This whole place has changed. Foreigners have infiltrated and bunkered themselves in. They take and take and don't leave nothin' but bad spirit and bad people. They've turned the locals into bad people. It's a you're-either-with-me-or-against-me mentality and it's led to a lot of mistrust. It's becoming just like the Middle East where you don't know if your neighbor is the one's gonna blow your head off from one day to the next. All depends on if you follow this new religion of greed the resort and oil industry thugs have created."

"Looks pretty subdued from what I can see," Cooper said, watching endless swaths of flat Yucatán jungle bush pass along both sides of the car.

John looked out the window. "Naw. It's out there. You just can't see it. It doesn't look like what you imagine. It's not about big buildings and lots of roads. It's in the small villages, those that have homes built of rocks and food supplied by the jungle. It's something inside." He pounded his chest and it made a solid thud. "Promises and lies. It's one of the reasons I took up the dive shop business. Only place to get away from these crazy vibes is to drown'em…with some good scuba gear on, of course."

"Is that how you met Lax?" Billy said.

"Lax?" John was still looking at him through the side view mirror reflection. "You mean Alax…yes. And his sister. They came down a couple of years ago wanting me to guide them into Chich though I wasn't sure at the time why they needed me. They seemed to know the layout of the joint quite well. Of course, I know better now. I was their camouflage, their diversion, their legitimacy for being there and for doing what they did. And to set up a future that would lead you to me."

Billy didn't have to ask. John saw the question in his eyeball reflections.

"Yes. I know why you are here. You came to get one of them amulets that hung around Alax's and Alixel's necks. You came to tell stories. You came to remember."

"And why are you here?" Cooper said, again turning to him.

"What…you don't know? I'm a black man in a brown man's country. I'm here to stir the shit up. I'm here to pick fights and throw them damned dead things against walls. I'm here because of a promise, one without lies, one that will hopefully end all this bad vibe shit forever."

"You're here to protect us." Cooper said. "Like you did for me in the museum."

John looked into Cooper's eyes but didn't say anything. Then he looked at the back of Billy's head and brought his big hand up to his mouth, patted the fat lower lip, and looked out the window.

"No," Cooper said. "That's not it at all, is it John?" John wouldn't look at her. "You promised to protect *him*. How could you have known he was going to bring extra baggage?" She turned back around. "I'm not supposed to be here, am I? I mean, according to the way this whole story is written, I don't get more than a movie extra's role."

Billy was watching John's expressions in the mirror as Cooper revealed what was obviously true. He remembered how close Cooper had been to death, how he'd just left her in the museum because of his own selfish desire to find the Gormen. "She's the reason I'm here," Billy told John. "Without her, your promise would not be worth squat."

"I know that," John said. "But there'll come a time when a decision has to be made. Just like it was in Gulf One and Two. In the pit of battle, some live, some die."

"I tell you what," Billy said. "You watch my back and I'll watch hers. I'm not asking for any favors but I'm not gonna lie to you either. Having a bodyguard such as you, one who has apparently spent some time fighting wars, definitely makes a stranger in a strange land feel at bit more at ease. But if it comes down to it, I'll not leave Cooper and we'll, *together*, have to deal with it—that is, if you are to uphold your promise." Cooper looked hard into Billy's face but Billy kept his eyes on the road ahead.

"Alax said you would be strong," John said. "My promise is to protect you, Billy, to make sure you get to where gettin' needs be. And that's what I'm gonna do, at least until you don't need me no more."

Another toll stop loomed ahead. A military Jeep with a soldier stationed behind a machine gun sat parked on the right side of the road. Directly above the soldier's head and attached to a thick, overhanging pole was a green highway sign noting that the road to Chichen Itza veered right immediately after the toll stop. As the Cavalier passed the Jeep and the soldier turned to look at them, Billy knew that if the soldier suddenly decided to spray the car with machine gun bullets, John would leap between the seats, between him and Cooper, and take round after blazing round while Billy watched Cooper shred into pieces beside him.

Cooper was thinking about Manuel, his cold hands, his bean-smelly breath, his Spanish gibberish, his piece of earlobe and the attached Wayeb glyph which she had snatched from the museum floor and now carried in the pocket of her khaki shorts, when John said, "I hate them gawd-awful things. Harder to kill than a dug-in Taliban on the cliffs of Khyber."

"You served in Afghanistan?" Billy asked.

"And Kuwait and Iraq and, if truth be told, Iran and Pakistan, too."

"We're not at war there."

"You sure? Lies of the heart. Lies of the media. Lies of presidents and pastors. We believe what we hear."

"Army man," Billy interjected.

"Marine," John quickly corrected. "Semper Fi—Hoorah!" He lifted his arm quickly and accidentally punched the car's roof, creating a dent. "Sorry. Got carried away." He fiddled with the roof's new irregularity.

"They got cubits in Iran?" Billy asked.

"That what you call them things? Cubits? We call 'em Mu'bä 'round here: poor souls that have just been buried and are unable to move peacefully to the afterlife because they are called forth by someone on earth to obey whatever commands the master makes; they're flesh eaters…zombies basically."

"And you believe there are actually dead people walking around and eating people?"

"Yes, and so do you—so do these Mexican Mayans who live their lives drowning in such mystic BS. That's why they're so easily manipulated by the greedy ones. Every tree and flower and bug and rock has some meaning and some purpose and something to do with life and death. Drink too much alcohol and the Mu'bä will become part of your nightmares. Sleep with your neighbor's wife and the Mu'bä will come take you away. Fight the industrialists and the Mu'bä will kill you and your entire family."

Both Billy and Cooper said in unison, "Sounds familiar."

The rural road to Chichen Itza was much narrower than the more modern four-lane highway they'd traveled on from Mérida. Every time a truck or bus or any vehicle that was larger than the Cavalier passed in the opposite direction, Cooper cringed, her legs stiffening, her thumb pressing harder against the piece of Manuel that she'd stashed in her pocket. Scattered intermittently along the right side of the road were old women riding on the back of three-wheeled bicycles that their old men pedaled, their short, stocky legs easily maintaining momentum regardless of the size of their women. A large vehicle approached head-on at the same time they were trying to pass one of these bicycles and Cooper closed her eyes. The Cavalier shook when the truck passed and when she opened her eyes to look in the side view mirror she saw that the old man and his passenger had not even flinched even though she swore she'd heard the bicycle's rusty handlebar scratch her door.

No one said a word for a good fifteen minutes. Cooper used the time to consider her own safety as their journey moved them closer toward what she was beginning to regret, particularly since John had basically told her, had told both of them, that Billy's life was more important than her own, and that if it came down to it, John would let her die. Why he had saved her from Manuel she could only guess, but she figured it must have had something to do with Billy's survival as well. Perhaps keeping her alive was for no greater purpose than to keep Billy happy. John couldn't sacrifice her if Billy's emotions would also be sacrificed. How could a brokenhearted Daykeeper save the world? It was a flimsy basis for denying insecurity but it was all she had. Her big gamble, though, was the feeling that Billy really *did* care for her in the same way she cared for him which promoted a dilemma. If he cared so strongly for her, he just might sacrifice himself to save her and then where would they be? All of their lives wouldn't be worth shit and John's promise would be null and void.

She looked over at him and became absorbed by his tanned, strong chin that had not been shaved since Nexpa, his dirty dishwater blonde hair that was wavy and waving through the wind that wiped within the car. He looked at her and smiled and she averted his gaze for a moment to hide a blush. His hand crossed the invisible divide between the bucket seats and dropped atop hers which still played with the earlobe that Billy had sliced off.

"He approves," Billy said, his voice hushed. She thought, at first, that

Billy was referring to John, but when he nodded toward the dashboard, she realized that he was talking about SpongeBob's happy grin. Of course, its frozen expression of toy joy approved of everything but its happiness did have a contagious way of making things seem okay in the midst of imminent gloom. Perhaps, this was a secondary reason why Billy clung to it so much. The primary reason was certainly Stephanie Drake.

He'd told Cooper about Stephanie during their layover in Nexpa. Her memory had been deeply rooted and was particularly attached to surfing. She'd known this because on at least three different occasions while he was teaching her to surf, he'd called her "Steph." Finally, she'd asked him why he kept calling her that and, after admitting he hadn't even realized he'd said Steph's name, he'd told her about the bank, the beach, her horrible death. He'd told her all about Steph on their last night in Nexpa while they'd been huddled under the hand-woven lean-to, watching the surf rise and fall like clockwork in front of a sunset that was more purple than red. Cooper had known then that Stephanie Drake would forever be a part of his soul and that the chance of losing another person he cared about would, for a long time, make him cautious in a way that would prevent him from telling her how he really felt.

The car slowed as they entered, Ikil, a small scrub of a town turned tourist hotbed with one of the Seven New Wonders of the World just up the road. A huge concrete speed bump made Billy almost stop the car completely. The wheels crawled over the yellow-painted obstruction, giving a few of the locals a chance to market their wares while following the car's slow advance. In their pleading hands were maps and trinkets and facsimiles of artifacts that were sworn to have healing powers and protective powers and reproductive powers.

Ikil was not very big but it was very crowded and in most ways resembled nothing of the bush jungle they'd traveled through so far. Apparently, the Mexican population had somehow gotten it into their heads that foreigners loved bright pastel colors and they loved them plastered onto everything, but Ikil had gone a little overboard. The town's main thoroughfare made Cooper think of a highway stop along Interstate 95 at the border of North and South Carolina. *South of the Border* it was called, the tourist trap of all tourist traps. That place proved that even Americans believed that Americans loved bright pastels. And like that American version of a Mexican town, Ikil had its share of small shops, pressed side-by-side, on both sides of the road. Above and surrounding them were many bold neon signs that promised luxury, entertainment, and spirituality all at "rock-bottom" (Ikil businesses apparently also knew that Americans loved the word "rock bottom") prices.

Though the signs were dormant in the afternoon sunshine, Cooper imagined what the pastel-ridden, mile-long stretch of shops would look like under them at night: unnatural, industrial, over-bearing and materialistic. What had John called it? Lies of the mind?

Billy, like Cooper who was also too engaged by the touristy feel of the town, did not see the second speed bump. It was not painted like the first one and when he hit it, even at the slow pace they traveled, all three of them jumped off their seats, the Cavalier's springs wining with the sudden impact. SpongeBob fell to the floor and Cooper quickly replaced it on the dashboard. John fell forward, his torso wedging itself into the floorboard space behind Billy's seat. He pushed himself up, but when the car's rear wheels contacted the speed bump, he fell back in.

"Sorry," Billy said. "Those things come out of nowhere."

"Topes for dopes," John murmured as he rolled back up and into his stuffy position across the rear seat. He rubbed his bald head. "That's what they call 'em around here. And damn, that one was really topey. I don't remember them puttin' one in the middle of freakin' Main Street." Another young merchant ran up to the window where John's head glistened in the sun. He tried to hand John a flyer and John bellowed, "Get outta my face! Váyase!" The flyer fluttered from the boy's hand, flapped through John's open window, and fell to the floorboard where his head had just been. He reached down and picked it up. Then he laughed. "That boy's got some business savvy. Maybe it was him or his old man that put that damn tope there in the first place. This flyer, here, promotes something about undercarriage car repair. And this flyer..." John shuffled the two pieces of paper he'd plucked from the floor. "Why, this ain't a flyer at all. It's a computer printout. Why would a kid in the middle of Mexico have a computer printout? Why would a kid in the middle of Mexico have a computer?"

Billy stopped the car for a plentitude of pedestrian traffic. "Can I see that?" When John gave him the paper, it took Billy only a second to realize that the paper must have been under the driver's seat all of this time; it was a computer printout from the Big Bank of Texas, Port A branch, and the names listed were people he knew, people that had owned businesses on the island, people that had been cubited.

Car horns urged him forward. Billy had not realized that he'd been idling there, right in the middle of downtown Ikil, thinking about the list of names for a full minute after the pedestrian flow had passed. More local youngsters approached the car as Billy lowered Steph's computer printout onto his lap and eased off the brake. The boys shouted Spanish at him but he didn't understand a word of it.

Canton Andrews, Madeline Black, Charlotte Broughton...

Slowly, the traffic crawled forward until it crossed the town's third speed bump, painted yellow, then gained momentum as the view became less American modernized and more Mexican rural. Most of the traffic turned left at a beautifully sculptured wooden sign that read "Sacred Cenote." An arrow painted in pastel red, orange and yellow pointed the way. An "Enjoy Coca-Cola" sign dangled underneath it.

Lewis Kennedy, Nole Kilpatrick, Jeffrey Lemmon...

Another hundred yards up the road, a half a dozen not-so-modern motels, in various phases of reconditioning, sat only partially occupied. They looked much older than the buildings within Ikil, having somehow been left out of the loop when Ikil went the way of the Western world. None of them had paved parking lots and only one of them had seen a fresh paint job in at least a decade.

Professor Theodore Nelson, Dr. Shasta Preston, Manny Rodriguez...

As Billy passed the last of the buildings, the memory of faces attached themselves to the names. So many people had died. So many people had been cubited.

John broke his concentration. "Turn left up there."

A dirt road led into dense bush and thick trees and Billy turned onto it. The road was in desperate need of repair and Billy had to use its entire width to slowly navigate the craters, some so huge that he could have parked the car in them.

"Where are we going?" Cooper asked.

"A friend," John said. "We can't go into Chich in the middle of the day. We'll have to wait for nightfall."

"But isn't that dangerous?"

"Yes. That's why it's good to have friends, especially those that have worked at the site for as many years as he has." John, for the first time since they'd left Mérida, rose to a sitting position. His back hunkered forward and, with his head lowered against the dent in the car's roof that he had punched earlier, he shuffled against the bucket seats, his chest filling the space between them. "So you gonna tell us about the printout? When I handed it to you, you looked like you seen a ghost."

"Mu'bä," Billy said. "A couple a hundred of them…from Texas."

"You got a list of the walking dead? How'dya manage that?"

"I didn't. Steph did."

John looked perplexed.

"We killed most of them before we left the island. The hurricane got the rest."

"We? You mean you and this Steph?"

Billy swerved to miss a crater that wasn't very wide but was deep enough to disable the car. "Long story. If I have time, maybe we'll get into it."

"You're the Daykeeper," John said. "That's what you do."

"I'm not one yet."

John's hand came around Billy's left shoulder and dropped, his fingers delicately but firmly massaging the meat. "I'll get you there. I'll get you both there." He purposely grinned at Cooper but did not hug her. "Here it is." He pointed with a finger that still rested on Billy's shoulder.

There were actually three buildings spread out in a wide one-acre plot that had been cleared of plants and rocks. All three of the buildings looked similar in size and construction, with walls made of irregularly shaped limestone boulders and simple gable roofs made from the trunks of the trees that suffocated the perimeter of the clearing. The density of the jungle around the plot helped shade the open area. Billy parked beside a rusted, old Chevy Impala that was propped up under the front axle by two large rocks; its wheels were missing.

A window made of Plexiglas was centered in the front door of the building nearest them and within it, a head quickly appeared then disappeared. John pulled himself out of the back seat of the Cavalier as a man with intense gray hair, a worn, scraggly cowboy hat, and more wrinkles than Billy had ever seen on one face, emerged from the building with a shotgun in both hands but not pointed at anything in particular.

"A hundred pesos says ya can't hit the side of a taco stand with that thing," John teased.

"You know I hate fucking taco-th," the man said, his accent a mixture of Mexico and Texas that lisped behind the two front teeth that were missing. "You bring me a new toy to play with?" He pushed his gun in the direction of the Cavalier but did not point it at the car. Billy and Cooper exited and Billy walked around to stand beside Cooper.

"Chill," John told Billy. "He's not referring to Coop. He likes the car."

"Another trip into the ruin-th, Johnboy? It-th the only time you come thee me. Been a coupl'a year-th now."

"Chich ain't the same as it used to be, my friend."

"Got that right. Who-th the gringo-th?"

"Tourists," Billy quickly answered.

"Really," the man said. With the barrel of the shotgun, he tipped a crumpled bend in his cowboy hat, uncovering an abundance of wrinkles in his forehead. "Where from?"

"Texas," Billy said and looked at Cooper. "And Arizona."

"Thun-of-a-bitch!" the man said. "Thun-of-a-fucking-bitch! Did you tell 'em to thay that, Johnboy?"

John waved Billy and Cooper closer. "This here is my friend," he said to them. "He's really quite gentle unless you do him wrong." The man nodded and then smiled, revealing the dark hole where his two incisors once existed. "Honestly, I can't tell you his first name since I don't know it myself, but I've come to know him as Strykor. At least that's what we called him in the Gulf."

"You guys served together?" Billy asked.

"We didn't therve any whore," Strykor said. "We killed a bunch of mother-fucker-th though."

"Strykor's from Texas, too. Galveston, isn't it?"

"Damn thtraight. Was an oil drillin' man before them peckerhead-th in Iraq thtarted thcrewing everything. You drill oil, thun?"

Billy shook his head. "No. I used to own a restaurant."

"Yeah?" Strykor said. "Plannin' on thtarting one in Ikil?"

John interrupted. "He came to see the well."

Strykor's eyes popped a bit more open. "Really? And what-th your thtory muchacha?"

"They both came to see the well," John said. "I thought you were going to get some new teeth? You sound like a damned snake."

"Thhhh…" Strykor hissed, his tongue firmly pressed against the open space. "And ready to thtrike. Like old time-th, eh buddy?"

"This guy just couldn't be killed," John said to Billy and Cooper, thumbing in Strykor's direction. "That's why the captain always sent him in to do the dirty stuff."

"Don't give me all the glory," Strykor said. "You got yourn." Strykor walked casually to them, an odor following him like Pigpen dirt that wafted over Billy the closer he came. Strykor smelled acidic and unwashed and a bit like tree bark that's been freshly ripped from the trunk. "What do ya want for it?" he asked Billy.

"Want? For what?" Strykor tapped the hood of the Cavalier with the barrel of the shotgun. "You want to buy my car?"

"Naw. Ain't got no money." Strykor squinted and his face wrinkles rolled into new positions. He studied Billy, his head lolled backward, the missing incisor hole a black rectangle until his tongue moved behind it. "We trade in theeth part-th."

A little spittle launched from the tongue-in-tooth hole and landed on

Billy's cheek which Billy, on instinct, refused to wipe away. Disgust for this man's spit could upset him to a point that he might suddenly relive one of his glorious, covert missions in the Middle East. Instinct also told him not to ignore Strykor's request. Billy had had no intention of selling Steph's Cavalier, at least not up until this point in time; John had said nothing about it, had in no way prepared him for such a quandary. He'd not even known they were going to meet such a man as Strykor, let alone be subjected to a decision that would leave them all without a means to transport them farther, toward the fourth destination, wherever the hell that was. Even though reason told him that John would interfere with any attempt by Strykor to harm him, instinct told him that such an intervention would not be necessary. If only he had the right answer. What was Strykor really saying? This was a test—it had to be. *We trade in theeth part-th.* Trade? Cooper grabbed his elbow.

"Can you get us safely to and from the well?" Billy asked Strykor.

"Doe-th a dog thit in the jungle?" Strykor said, studying Billy's face.

"What's in the well?"

"We'll find out together, I th-pothe."

"And I suppose nothing is free around here."

"You got that one right, gringo."

"The car for your guidance, then."

Strykor didn't smile but Billy could tell he'd said the right thing since, after he'd said it, Strykor pointed at John with the shotgun and said, "Th-arp gringo. You brought me a th-arp Gringo, Johnboy. Now let-th eat!" He slapped Billy on the back then slung the shotgun over one shoulder. "What would you make on a hot mother-fucker day like thi-th, rethrant man?" he said to Billy as he walked away.

Instinct told Billy the answer. "Snake, I suppose."

Strykor laughed, his boisterous bellow echoing within the acre of jungle he called home.

Billy had eaten snake on two occasions, both while back in college, which, ironically, was before he'd moved to a state known for its slithering inhabitants. In Cambridge, it had been "a thing to do," something different, something daring, something not affordable to the "average" person. A good section of rattler could cost upwards of fifty dollars a plate and, prepared well, was worth the money, more for bragging rights than for the purpose of nutrition.

Billy hadn't paid for it. His parents had been visiting on both occasions and had insisted. They liked doing what others did not have the opportunity to do—at least his father always did. Billy suspected his mother just went along for the egotistical ride, not really enjoying such "upper class" snobbery but supportive of her husband regardless of how she really felt. Billy remembered how wonderful the snake had tasted. When prepared correctly, it tasted just like chicken, just like Strykor's snake did on the eve of their journey to Chichen Itza.

They sat on four shaded tree stumps around a fire pit that had been carved into the limestone ground between two of Strykor's buildings. "What's that sweet taste?" Billy asked the cook. Strykor stirred the fire then grabbed Billy's stick and stabbed another portion of meat he pulled from a wooden bowl. He gave the reloaded meat stick to Billy and Billy immediately stuck it in the fire. John asked for a refill and soon both sticks of rattler were hissing in the open flames.

"A theecret," Strykor said. "Caribbean thnake. What about you, honey?" he said to Cooper. "You like my thnake?"

"It's good," she said, chewing slowly, a half piece of blackened snake still clinging to her stick. "It would go really good with my salsa."

Even Billy could tell she was lying. She ate the snake but was in no way enjoying it. She drank way too much water even though it looked muddy.

"You don't have to like it," Strykor said. "Unfortunately, I haven't made it to the thtore recently. When we get back from the well tomorrow, we'll get thum thtuff for your thal-th…your thal-th—" He spit all over his chin. "Your thal-tha."

"Teeth," John said. "Get some goddamn teeth and you can yell out salsa from the top of your lungs."

Strykor suddenly stood and quickly walked into the cottage he called home. Billy thought that John had just pissed him off and that Strykor had gone to get his gun, but when he returned all Strykor had in his hands was another wooden bowl of marinating snake. He sat on his stump and said nothing for the longest minute.

"More," John said. "And this time don't be so stingy." Strykor reloaded John's stick but still did not say anything. "What the hell's wrong with you? I've never known you to be this quiet."

"Thalsa," Strykor said under his breath as if he was really trying to work on that one word. "Thalsa," he repeated a bit louder. "Salsa."

"Whoa," John said. "How'd ya do that?"

Strykor grinned then and all three of them looked at his mouth, squinting simultaneously. The black rectangle of missing incisors was now filled with two oversized blocks of white that hung over his bottom lip. "Carved 'em myself. What'da ya think?"

John's lips puckered because he was struggling so hard to keep his laughter inside. His eyes, which were quickly moistening, rolled in Billy's direction and Billy was certain he would bust at any moment. His expression tickled Billy so much that when John finally did release it, Billy started laughing, too. "You sound much better," John finally managed, wiping his eyes, "but you look like…you look like…"

"I know," Strykor said. "Bugs Bunny." And then he started laughing. "Carved 'em out of a coyote's ass."

Cooper, who didn't seem to know how to react, added her own small bit of shy laughter but, again, it was a false response meant to please the status quo.

"Come on, Coop," John said. "Liven up."

But Cooper stopped laughing and just stared at her meat stick.

John snickered through the last bites of his second helping and pointed at what was left of Cooper's meal. "Ain't ya gonna eat that?" he said, and before she could respond, he plucked the last bite from the charred stick and plopped it is mouth.

What in the hell were they going to do without a car? Cooper was not about to be stranded in the middle of the Yucatán jungle. She had survival skills, but come on!

Throughout their entire meal, that's all she could think about (along with an overwhelming feeling of dehydration and a careless attitude about the color of the water she drank). Billy was going to give up their ride for a guided tour into Chichen Itza? And what about John who seemed to go along with all of it? Billy had a destination and it wasn't "Chich." Chich was a place for raising a Djed of the past, not of the future. And another thing: why didn't the big son-of-a-bitch give a shit about her? She was beginning to second guess her belief that he would keep her alive if for no other reason than to keep Billy happy. To hell with cultural excuses; women in Mexico remained among the low rungs of the social ladder—but not women named Cooper. She wasn't cooking anything and she wasn't cleaning anything and she wasn't bearing his children but she still demanded respect, dammit! She still deserved some fucking protection!

His buddy Strykor was no different. She didn't like his crappy snake meal…so fucking what! Why didn't he offer something different? Some goddamned tortillas would have been just fine. Why didn't he have any goddamned tortillas? All Mexicans had tortillas! And those teeth. Stupid. What was so goddamned funny about teeth that looked like Bugs Bunny? And if he said the word salsa or thaltha (or whatever and however he called it) one more time, she'd scream…she'd absolutely lose her fucking mind!

But it was when John took the food from her stick without asking, whether she liked what was wrapped around it or not, that had been the final straw. Her mind did flip. Her anger exploded. Fucking sexists! Goddamned them all!

Then Cooper passed out.

At about the same time that Cooper fell into Billy's lap, Sedona councilmen Tate and Roberts met with Evan at an outside taco stand a couple of miles away in Piste. Tate was round and fat. Being cubited only intensified his voracious hunger. He ordered five more fish tacos.

"Manson is pissed as hell you fuckers let Cooper get away," Evan said. "Now we've got to do this the hard way."

"Blow me," Tate growled. "It was your piss ant Mexican dumb shit that got his head all broke."

Evan punched him square in the face. Tate's fat, squishy forehead easily absorbed the blow. No one at the taco stand, not even the American tourists, paid any attention. Tate rubbed his face then dug into his refried beans with his fingers.

Unlike Tate, Roberts' cubit had maintained some of its primary's self respect. It even wore a coat and tie and polished shoes. "They hooked up with another missionary Marine," Roberts said.

Evan slammed a fist on the makeshift wooden table, causing Roberts' glass of cheap wine to topple on the table. "Strykor!"

For a cubit that was only a couple of month's fresh, Roberts had transitioned particularly fast. Its expression mimicked a real person's surprise. "We knew that was going to happen, didn't we?" he said. The waitress brought Tate's five tacos and he immediately dug into them, smearing their contents all over his face and table. "Disgusting," Roberts added and sipped the rest of what had not spilled from his wine glass.

"Yes," Evan said, ignoring the pig sounds that emerged from Tate's feeding. "But only after the transformation." He reached over and slapped the half eaten taco from Tate's hands. "Listen, you pathitiful fool! Remember why you are here."

"The Serpent screwed up," Tate said through a mouth full of slop. "Not me."

"You all screwed up. That book ain't worth jack shit without the key." The cubits stared at him expressionless and frozen, as if some internal springs had died and needed rewinding. "You work for me not that Serpent idiot. You remember that or hell will feel like heaven once Manson gets through with both of you."

Tate picked up another taco and began chewing. "We gob it cobbered."

Evan, again, slapped that taco from his hands. "You have nothing covered. Manson has it covered and you fucked it up."

Roberts said, "I thought we were going to take them in the well."

"*We* are not going to take them anywhere. The Serpent will do our bidding for us. Has Manuel made contact with him yet?"

"The camp is all set," Roberts said. "We'll roast all four of 'em."

"Stupid! Both of you are the dumbest…" Evan looked around the outdoor restaurant and lowered his voice since everyone was now looking at him. "You will not hurt Presser. Even the Serpent knows that if Presser dies there will be no *raising* of anything except your heads from your shoulders."

"No cares," Tate said, grabbing for another taco. "The Cubit will make more of me."

"I wouldn't be so confident if I were you. Even the Cubit has a master."

"Like I am the master of this taco," Tate said and took a bite.

Evan knew it was useless to talk any further. Roberts, perhaps, would still be of some use but Tate was a lost cause; he'd make arrangements for his disposal later. Right now, Evan had to do what the two cubits had not been able to do: recover the key to the Book of the Djed. The Book and the key and Presser had to be together on December 21 or else Manson was going to destroy all of them. Evan took a deep breath, snatched Tate's taco from his hand and dropped it on the table. "Leave," he said to both of them. "You have work to do, don't you? The camp? Remember? You fuckin' idiots."

The two cubits left Evan to stare at the remnants of Tate's slop. A waitress came to the table and apologized to Evan for no reason as she cleaned up the mess. "Agua, por favor," he said to her and a moment later she returned with a plastic bottle of water.

To rule in the New World. That had been the deal. Manson had promised that when all of this was over, Evan would have everything he could ever want. He'd have his choice of cities, of the people in them, a chance to be somebody. He'd be able to make all of the decisions and not just wander in the shadows as he'd done his entire life. He'd finally have respect and admiration and if anyone disagreed with him then, well, he'd make sure they never disagreed again...in a similar way that he was going to make sure Tate would never disagree again. Unfortunately, you couldn't really threaten a cubit, but the people that remained after 2012…they would be flesh and blood and controllable. If the world as it existed today was any indication, he'd be able to control masses with just words, his words, the things he believed in, the things he desired—the way Manson controlled the cubits: with promises. The Serpent, like all cubits, was simply a pawn in Manson's great scheme. All cubits thought, in their cubited little brains, that they were in total control.

Promises…

Promises for errand boys.

Kind of like how Evan was an errand boy but dramatically different. The latitude that Manson gave him with disagreement showed how much Manson needed him. All cubits needed human counterparts, at least all cubits that expected to remain hidden from human discovery.

"La cuenta, por favor," Evan said to the waitress with a wad of pesos in hand. Without the diversion of Tate's gluttony, he now found the young woman to be extremely pleasant but he was too damn shy to ask for her. He certainly had the money and she certainly would give herself to him. That's just the way it worked around here. Still...

The time would come when money would no longer be necessary. Demanding was so much easier.

The last of the sunlight had disappeared an hour ago and all Billy was left with was an oil lantern, a hard cot, a sparse room, Cooper who rested on a second cot beside him, and his thoughts.

Strykor could not have apologized enough. He'd taken his hand-carved, coyote-ass teeth out and had kept repeating, over and over, "Tho thorry. I'm tho thorry." Apparently, Strykor had thought he'd brought all of them water that he'd distilled for drinking. Accidentally, Strykor had grabbed one of the tumblers in which he kept well water, stuff that he had not boiled, stuff that he used for washing his hands and wiping his face.

Cooper had drunk all of it and there was no telling how many parasites had entered her body, Strykor had said. He'd thought that the snake marinade had masked the odd taste of the well water and so, Cooper had not known any better. He'd also said that the parasites could easily turn a person insane, could knock them out cold, or both. Fortunately, Strykor had been prepared. He'd said that he'd made the same mistake himself only once and the madness that had ensued had been so bad that he'd never wanted to take such chances again. Since then, he'd kept plenty of what he'd called "antidote," which was a prescription from the pharmacist in town. It would work quickly, he'd promised. She'd feel some nausea when she awakened, but the parasites would be gone and so would the madness. She'd be ready to travel by midnight, the time Strykor had set for their excursion to Chichen Itza.

Except for one young man who had maintained a revolving occupancy in the last cottage in the row, Strykor's "motel" had been vacant for quite some time. This was the same cottage that Billy and Cooper now lay in. Strykor had said that the young man rarely came around on the weekends and never before midnight since he worked long hours at the ruins. The cottage had only a single room. There was no bathroom; the shithouse was out beyond the cottage at the end of a path that had been chopped through the jungle. Strykor had dissuaded Billy from going out there after dark without him, and had urged Billy to "take care of business" before the sun went down.

The stone walls of the cottage had two openings: one for a door made out of tree limbs that were tied with strips of bark, and one for a window that had no glass—just a screen to keep insects out. Beyond the screen, a full moon broke through shuffling clouds and its white luminance fell angelically on Cooper's sleeping face.

When she'd passed out and had fallen off her tree stump into his lap, Billy had been quite concerned. He'd thought he'd seen blood smears at the corners of her lips but John had assured him that it was nothing more than Caribbean snake marinade. Still, the memory of concern remained strong and he hated it. It made life much more complicated when you cared for someone else, especially when recent experience reminded him how Steph had been so heinously taken from him, how her cubited naked body had been one of the scariest things he'd ever seen, how she'd mewled for him to come closer. How she'd demanded a kiss.

The soft pitter-patter of rain rustled the roof's natural construction and jostled some of the jungle bush outside the cottage. The moonlight still roamed intermittently through the window and Billy stood, momentarily glanced down at Cooper when she softly moaned, then walked to the window. More clouds than clear filled the moon-glow horizon and Billy figured they'd have a wet hike ahead of them. To the left were the other two cottages; John was in the center cottage and Strykor was at the end. Between them, glowing embers from the fire pit sizzled whenever a raindrop found them. To his right was jungle. Even with the moonlight, it was hard to see very far into it. A path had been cut into the jungle but it curled away to the right so that the shithouse could not be seen from the window. There was, however, something else sitting along the path. It wasn't predatory. In fact, it wasn't even animal. He opened the cottage door for a better look, blinked, looked right then left, blinked again. It was still there. The VW Bus was still there.

He walked to the head of the path with only enough caution to prevent him from tripping over the tree roots underfoot, his gaze centered on the VW's round, broken headlight. The vehicle sat in a small clearing to the right of the path and as he neared it, he kept telling himself that it couldn't be his VW, the one from Port Aransas, not all the way out here. Besides, the hurricane had taken it, hadn't it?

His heart hammered harder. The VW's driver's side window was missing and when he looked through the opening and into the vehicle's interior, he saw cabinets, just like the ones he'd built into his own VW, the cabinets where he'd stored his computer equipment, the computer equipment that controlled his robot, the robot that had infiltrated the bank, the bank that had housed the Cubit, the Cubit which was the reason why he was standing here in the first place.

He walked around to the back of the vehicle to find more evidence. The rear bumper was missing and when he bent down to look under the VW, moon glow revealed that the brackets that had held the bumper were twisted wrecks of metal, as if something had literally ripped the bumper right off of it.

Albert Stine's twisted image flashed through memory, how he had held the VW by its bumper, how he and Steph had escaped only because the bumper had torn free.

Billy slowly opened the rear door panel and crawled inside. The cabinet doors were open and empty. Still, Billy was convinced that this was his 1963 VW Bus. For final confirmation he tapped the floorboards with his knuckles and a small door popped open on spring hinges. He flipped up the door and found what he expected to find: electronic parts. The compartment contained a couple of solar batteries, some replacement solar cells, a small remote control, a tiny robotic insect that he'd given up on repairing and a Ziploc containing various circuit board components. Billy pulled up the tail of his shirt and piled into it the compartment's contents. When he pulled out the Ziploc, a can of Budweiser rolled into view. He looked at it curiously, not remembering when he'd put it in there, then shrugged and plucked it out, sticking the can into a pocket in his shorts before closing the floorboard door.

He shuffled backward through the VW's rear panel and stepped out into the light rain while juggling the contents in his shirt tail. Quickly, he returned to the cottage where he squatted and spread everything out onto the limestone floor. He removed the beer can last and set it among the pile of components. Rain drops rolled down the Budweiser label. He snatched up the can, flipped open the tab, and took a long swallow.

How in the hell did his VW Bus get here, he wondered, licking foam from his lips. Coincidence, for him, just didn't exist anymore. But thinking about it right now made his head hurt, so he turned to the electronics and the solace they represented, turning each piece in the palm of his hand, examining it, remembering what purpose it served. He'd not gotten to play with his robots in so long. The excitement made him giddy and, coupled with the beer which he now finished in one gulp, Billy felt right at home in the middle of the Yucatán jungle.

Both John and Strykor had machetes though Cooper wondered why. The purpose was not for trailblazing; the path they walked seemed as if it had been traveled frequently. She assumed that the machetes were meant for something in the jungle that she could not see, which was very unsettling.

She'd awakened about an hour before they'd departed. Her stomach had ached something horrible but the crazy thoughts had gone. She'd become so angry, so quickly and if she'd had a gun, she probably would have shot them all. A shiver of that thought had accompanied her awakening and when her eyelids had finally unglued themselves, she'd found Billy toying with scattered pieces of electronic components on an earthen floor within a circle of broken moonlight. He had been giggling, and his head had bounced back and forth as he'd assembled some of the pieces into objects that were, apparently, making him very happy. His giggles combined with her lingering thoughts of murder had only made her nausea worse.

Billy had told her what had happened and how apologetic Strykor had been, and as they'd prepared to leave the makeshift motel courtyard en route to Chichen Itza, Strykor had treated her like a queen, asking her time and again if there was anything she needed, anything at all, to just "thay it and it-th your-th." All she could think of at the time was to request that he reinsert his makeshift incisors so that she could understand him.

But Strykor said very little during their journey to the ruins. His only commentary was in response to Billy's question concerning the resident of the cottage in which she'd slept off the poison's influence. "Yes," he said to Billy. "Pedro is his name. He traded a box of artifacts he said he'd recovered in Texas for a job at the ruins. I helped him return them to the well and gave him a place to stay."

John, too, said very little. He warned them about some of the surrounding plants, particularly the skinny tree that leaked poison which he called the chechen negro. Getting some of its sap on the skin would guarantee misery, he said. Oddly, a tree that always grew right next to chechen negro was the chacah, a tree that provided nectar which neutralized the chechen's poison. John stopped them for a momentary explanation he felt was necessary to ensure that Billy and Cooper knew what to look for in the future.

The canopy of the jungle wasn't very high but it was very moist. Light rain earlier in the evening had now turned to pure mist and, in the full moon shine, it cast an eerie blue hue against everything, dripping that blue sheen downward, a surreal curtain filled with dire consequence. Visibility increasingly diminished the farther they walked; at one point, Cooper lost sight of Billy's backpack when she stopped for only a second to assure herself that the tree closest to her right arm was, indeed, the chechen. If it had not been for one swooping sound of a machete against bush, she might have lost her way.

An hour into the journey, they emerged from the jungle into a clearing that revealed a white road of inlaid limestone (which looked blue under the current conditions); John called it a *sacbe*. About a hundred yards ahead, at the other end of the sacbe, loomed the misty outline of a squat pyramid centered among two other shorter, rectangular structures. Strykor put his hand out to stop their forward progress.

"The Nunnery," he whispered. "There will be a guard stationed just around the corner and a second one should be walking the perimeter."

As if on cue, a guard appeared in front of the pyramid, walking right to left, the misty haze wafting behind him as he moved. Strykor sidestepped to the cover of wet bushes and trees and the rest of them followed. He dropped his backpack from his shoulders then removed his boots, his shirt and pants. Underneath, he wore what Cooper assumed was the dark blue uniform of the Chichen Itza guards. He shoved his outer clothing into the backpack, slipped back into his boots and inspected the blade of a commando knife that he then stashed in a strap around his calf. "They know me," he said to Cooper. "But just in case." He took out his fake teeth, handed them to her along with his backpack and machete, then ran off along the edge of the jungle bush. He continued, stealthily, to where the jungle's camouflage ended halfway to the ruins, then he stood straight up and walked casually, as if he had every right to be there.

When Strykor waved an arm, John stood from cover. John whispered, "Coast is clear." John told them to leave the machetes and they moved quickly to where Strykor stood.

And then, all four of them jumped when a small dog appeared, seemingly out of nowhere. It started barking incessantly at the intruders. When Strykor flicked a small rock that hit its hindquarters, the dog only momentarily quieted, ran into the shadows, then returned, barking even more aggressively.

Strykor snatched a much larger rock and Cooper grabbed his hand.

"Not that way," she insisted. Strykor hesitated, the endless folds of wrinkled face flesh scrunched prune-like into disbelief. "You said you'd do anything for me. Don't hit the dog."

Strykor dropped the rock just as someone shouted, "Parada! Quién es eso?" John yanked both Billy and Cooper backward and into the space between two of the stone buildings. A flashlight beam missed revealing them by half a step.

Cooper peered from her hiding place and out beyond the centuries-old buildings. Strykor was out of sight and just beyond the moonlight blue misty corner of the ancient building and to the right. Billy stood behind her and John was next to him, his dark skin a perfect complement to the shadow in which he stood. A little déjà vu attacked Cooper's senses. It had been exactly two weeks ago that she'd stood in another alley, hidden beyond another corner, listening to the conversation of two other people she did not know.

Most of the Spanish she understood though Strykor's lisp made the conversation harder for Cooper to decipher. Strykor apparently didn't know the guard but the guard accepted him as a co-worker. Strykor's additional lies included statements pertaining to him arriving late for work, a request of the guard to not tell the boss, an offer of two hundred pesos to forget they'd even seen each other, and a question concerning who was watching a *caracol*, though she had no idea what *caracol* meant.

"Julio y Pedro," the guard said. The dog started barking again. "Perro! Tranquilo!" the guard yelled and did something that made the dog yelp. The dog ran past the space where Cooper hid. It looked at her and for a moment, she thought the dog was going to give them away, but it kept running, tail between its skinny legs.

"Grathia-th," Strykor said. "Buena-th noche-th."

Billy kept shaking his head. Pedro *was* here and, according to Strykor, had brought with him the Cubit.

"What is it?" John said, his deep baritone whispering like a bass drum in his ear. "You act like you just saw a ghost."

"Yeah," Billy said. "More like, heard a ghost."

"Don't deny intuition. It's about all we have left."

Strykor popped his head around the corner and Cooper yelped. "Come on," he said. "The Caracol i-th juth around the corner."

Cooper handed Strykor his fake teeth. "Please," she said. "What you have to say right now might be too important to be misunderstood."

Strykor grabbed the teeth and his backpack and reset both, then stepped cautiously along the perimeter of the Nunnery's colonnade of structures, leading the group between a square building on the right and the short pyramid on the left. The moon and the mist really screwed with Billy's pre-conceived notions of the great city of Chichen Itza. It certainly looked nothing like the pictures on the internet or in any brochure, pamphlet or flyer he'd ever perused. Not only was everything blue, it was shadowy blue, eerie moon-white blue, misty wet-to-the-bones blue. His right hand ran across the mortared limestone blocks of one of the oldest buildings in the city, the twenty-foot tall Iglesia, and the faces carved into them stared back with what Billy thought were shocked expressions of open-mouthed men who were gasping because of the superstitions they attached to blue nights. Even with the protection of two Marines, he could not help the chills that raced through every nerve in his body. He'd read (in some of those pamphlets and on some of those web sites) that to visit Mayan ruins in the middle of the night invited malevolent ferries into the human spirit, ferries that could easily drive a person to madness, ferries that would never leave until the body they infested was dead. Perhaps that was the chill he felt: ferries scratching their way into his soul, clawing at his very essence, anchoring themselves there forever. Perhaps the ferries were the only thing that could kill an invincible Daykeeper apprentice, and a whole legion of Marines couldn't do a damn thing about it.

When they rounded the far corner of the Iglesia, they came upon a large, vacant plot of land that had once served as a great Mayan center for trade. On the far side of the open area, stood a building that looked nothing like the ones he'd seen so far.

"Caracol," Strykor said, pointing at it. "The well is in the Caracol."

To Billy it looked almost like a modern day astronomical observatory. The dome had partially crumbled, leaving only four window openings in the front half and a big hole in the back; in the blue haze, the entire structure, the dome and the three platforms it sat atop, seemed to glow with invisible energy. Strykor and John both looked in directions that Billy did not: to the far left where jungle infiltrated the marketplace square, to the near right where rows of stone columns that no longer supported roofs stood next to the Caracol's second-level platform like frozen soldiers awaiting long forgotten commands, and behind them where the scrawny dog sat silent in the shadows, sniffing the air and watching.

Strykor adjusted his teeth before he spoke. "When I say go, we all run to the platform with the standing columns. Stay low, silent and quick." Strykor looked around and made some hand gestures that probably meant something to John then returned his gaze to Billy and Cooper. "Ready…Go!"

Strykor left the cover of the Iglesia first. Cooper and Billy followed in quick pursuit. John took up the rear and the scrawny dog followed him. As if it had understood everything Strykor had said, the dog stayed low, was quicker than all of them, and didn't make a sound. By the time the foursome had dashed across the fifty yards of open space, the dog was already sitting between two of the limestone columns, waiting and wagging its tail. All four of them took a different column, positioning their bodies so that if someone was perched above them, they could not be seen.

"Pedro will help us," Strykor said. "Not sure who Julio is but I'm sure Pedro can create a distraction. He's done it before."

"The Pedro from your motel?" Billy asked just to reassure himself that he already knew the answer.

"Yeah. The one who owns the VW you broke into." Someone appeared in one of the dome's windows. "Never mind that now. Pedro can settle with you later." Strykor squatted and pressed up against his column, and the rest of them followed his lead. He placed a finger to his lips.

It was, indeed, Billy's chef that now stood in the domed observatory window. The last he'd seen of Pedro was on the beach in Port Aransas. He'd heard Pedro scream. He'd thought Pedro was dead. But there he was, standing within a rectangle of darkness, his incessant grin still beaming incessantly white teeth that sparkled even at this distance.

And if Pedro's presence wasn't shocking enough, below him, laid into the dome's stone structure, was a pattern of blocks that looked exactly like the Wayeb.

Life was without coincidence. Life was without control. The Wayeb had been a part of his very soul, following him, marking his progression, verifying his journey. The face represented Evil's infiltration into the world; it occupied the top of the key to the Book of the Djed that was now stored in the pack on Billy's back; it had been inscribed on the fin of a mystery surfboard Billy had found on the Port A beach; it had been imprinted on the coins found in Lafitte's treasure on the night of the hurricane; it had been the title of the chamber that had housed the Cubit in the Great Hall of the Anasazi; it had dangled as an earring from the rapist that had tried to hurt Cooper in the History Museum of Mérida. And now, here it was, like a stamp marking the proverbial X.

Under the inlaid Wayeb face was a doorway into the dome; Pedro disappeared from the window above as people emerged from it.

People...In the middle of the night...Appearing from within a building more than twelve hundred years old.

And not just one or two people, but dozens. They labored when they walked; at least one of them dragged its left leg like a dead stick. A couple of them tripped and fell from the top platform, down a dozen stone steps, to the intermediate platform just above Billy's head. One of those that had fallen, a woman, slowly rose and staggered in his direction, her flip-flopped feet skittering recklessly across the limestone mortar joints. She stopped and stood just above him. Apparently, she didn't see him or didn't care that he was there, even when the scrawny dog took off back in the direction of the Iglesia. More people filled the Caracol's platforms. More fell down the hard steps. More filed onto the open marketplace grounds. And none of them made any sound whatsoever.

"Mu'bä," John moaned.

The woman standing above him suddenly took one errant step forward and fell straight down onto the top of one of the columns, her head cracking against its surface, her body twisting in the air and toppling to the floor at Billy's feet. Her face turned up to him; it was slathered with blood that appeared gray in the light blue misty hue. Billy knew the woman. Her name was Madeline Black. In fact, when Billy started concentrating on the faces of all the twenty-five or thirty people that had emerged from the observatory dome, he realized he knew most of them. They had at one time been residents of Texas but had made the mistake of applying for a security box just to enter a contest at the Big Texas Bank. And every one of them was listed on Stephanie Drake's computer printout that John had found under the Cavalier's front seat.

Across the open marketplace square, the cubits wandered aimlessly in multiple directions, seemingly lost, walking as if drunk, as if they'd just been reborn as something beyond dead—not really zombies, not really Mu'bä. Still, the blue mist that wafted around them made Billy think of the classic George Romero living dead movies. Even Michael Jackson drifted into thought, and how, even at two years old, the *Thriller* video had made such a psychological impact on him.

Broken Madeline Black, owner of Black's Café in Port Aransas, Texas, rolled onto her side and grabbed Billy's foot. Billy couldn't help yelping which caused all of the wandering cubits to turn around.

John grabbed his arm. "Gotta get," he said.

Strykor and Cooper had already taken off, hunkering low against the first stone platform of the Caracol; Strykor's commando knife was out and ready. Billy unsheathed the dagger and held it in front him in similar fashion.

"Ain't gonna need that just yet," John said.

Billy stared at him long enough to replenish his trust then replaced the dagger, even though the cubits were moving in on them, and followed John up the first set of steps. Ahead, two cubits (Lewis Kennedy who had owned the Mustang Ranch and Charlotte Broughton who had been a Port Aransas real estate agent) writhed on the steps. When Cooper stepped over them, Charlotte grabbed her ankle. Strykor quickly separated the arm with his knife and Cooper swatted the severed appendage from her leg which then tumbled down the steps a few feet from Billy, the fingers still grasping for a leg that was no longer there. The foursome ascended the remaining steps two-at-a-time and stopped in front of the doorway that led into the dome. Pedro appeared within the internal darkness.

"Hola," Strykor said to him. Pedro only nodded then disappeared.

Billy stood there, dazed and wondering. Had Pedro really survived? Certainly, a man like Strykor would have known better. If a cubited Pedro had shown up looking for residence at his makeshift motel, the Marine, with all of his training in covert operations, dealing with the worst kinds of people this world had to offer, would have detected something fishy. A cubited Pedro would have slipped up at some time during the past five months and Strykor would have put it down. But the two seemed too conspiratorial for that. They actually seemed chummy. Strykor and Pedro in collusion. Strykor and Pedro.

And then a thought sunk Billy's heart right down into his stomach. What if both Pedro and Strykor were not "alive?" What if both of them were actually…

"Watch out!" John yelled and pulled Billy to one side. Out from the dome's doorway stepped a man dressed as a guard. It wasn't Pedro and it didn't struggle with its body's functions as did the mass of cubits that now were fumbling up the first set of steps behind them.

"Parar!" demanded the guard whose name was Julio. He had a pistol and he waved it at the heads of all four trespassers. "Manos arriba!"

Cooper immediately raised her hands. Strykor, who had stashed the commando knife behind his back, raised only one. John lifted both of his arms and urged Billy to do the same. Half of the cubits behind them had completed their awkward ascent of the first platform and were now attempting the second flight of steps. One of them raised its arms.

Poor Julio never saw it coming. As Strykor slowly brought his knife out from behind him, gunfire rang out from within the dome's shadowy doorway. The bullet exited Julio's head just above the nose and he fell forward, tumbled down the steps and took out five cubits like a bowling ball crashing through pins. Smoke curled from the barrel of the pistol that Pedro had fired.

"Hurry!" Pedro said. "Before they catch us."

Billy walked straight into an interior wall of a secondary dome that was built inside the Caracol's outer dome. The parallel domes created a five-foot wide passageway that wrapped in a circle within the entire structure. Billy rubbed limestone dust from his nose and turned left, following John whose enormous body in the narrow passage prevented him from seeing that Pedro led Strykor and Cooper ahead of them. A quarter of the way around the passage, the shadows began to glow in the same blue hue that had been cast by the full moon across the entire city of Chichen Itza. Halfway around the inner dome, he stopped and stood and looked up just as John and Cooper were doing. The full moon, hidden behind sparse clouds, was centered within the dome's broken opening.

Pedro and Strykor had entered the core of the Caracol through an opening in the interior wall to his right. Except for the viewing platform from which ancient astronomers had peered into the skies through the windows at the top of the dome, the entire core was filled with a single spiraling, stone staircase. It curled down from the viewing platform forty feet above him, which, along with the dome, had been sheared away over time. Four of the dome's stargazing window openings still remained, one of which Pedro had been standing behind a few minutes ago. The winding staircase, during "regular" visiting hours, would have ended at the floor but tonight, a large hole had been opened and the stone steps disappeared into it.

The well, Billy thought. Lax had told him that this was where Alixel had raised her Djed, that this was where the Cubit had been kept by Samaal back when the Mayan civilization eradicated itself, that this was the secret well that housed the secret room in which Professor Cower had stolen the Book of the Djed.

It was like walking down the center of a giant snail. The experience was eerily similar to his descent into the well at Lee Mountain in Sedona, except that these steps and this stairwell were much wider and much older and seemed to have been constructed with much greater effort.

He was at least as far down the stairs as the Caracol's dome was high before he saw the red light; it dimly illuminated the end of the spiral steps. Pedro stood at the base of the stairwell and when Strykor joined him they walked together out of sight, as if right through some wall that Billy, from this distance, could not see. John was a few steps below and in front of him and his bald head shined with a mixture of the red glow emanating from the bottom of the staircase and the blue hue from the opening above. Billy looked up. The faces were small but recognizable: Port Aransas cubits. Six of them hovered over the opening and, to Billy, it looked as if they were considering the ramifications of an attempted descent. They were learning quickly, Billy thought. Stumbling down the Caracol's platform steps outside had served as lesson number one. Still, one dumb cubit stepped into the opening and toppled forward, bouncing ten feet down before coming to rest in a twisted heap. It twitched, its back arching upward, and tried to stand on limbs that were no longer useful but, instead, rolled down another six steps.

When Billy got to the bottom, the first thing he saw was the jaguar. Cooper yelped a hallow echo that seemed to spiral upward toward the cubit faces which were now very small. This statue was different from the two that had stood majestically outside of the Wayeb Chamber in the Great Hall. This jaguar stood menacingly on all four legs just inside a wide cut that had been made into the side of the well wall, its sneering face and saber-like teeth a purposeful greeting of dread and discontent for any and all trespassers. Red light blazed from two red jade eyes that had, at their centers, swirling twists of silver that reminded Billy of cubits' eyes, of the insanity that twisted inside their twisted minds, of the insanity that would surely snatch his own soul and store it here, in the underworld, if he continued staring into them. But Billy couldn't will himself to look away and it took John's tug on both shoulders to finally free him from the trance. As he and John joined Cooper in the sacred room Billy wondered if the statue had anything to do with all of the people he now saw carved into the limestone walls.

Circular in shape, the room had no corners, its forty-foot ceiling a dome of carved rock. Much of the room that was closest to him was illuminated in that same red jade glow provided by the jaguar's eyes, but farther back, the room was hidden in shadow. All around him and chiseled into the wall were dozens of Mayans, some in complete ceremonial outfits, some bare-naked. There were men and women and children and they rose from the flat floor all the way to the apex of the dome, a Michelangelo-like rendering of the people who existed a thousand years before the Italian Renaissance artist was born. The people in the wall were not happy. In fact, they looked absolutely miserable, scared and suffering. Billy looked over his shoulder at the jaguar statue and thought, again, about his own soul.

Billy, Cooper and John stood shoulder-to-shoulder. Strykor and Pedro stood together twenty feet in front of them in the center of the room, their faces turned away. When Billy stepped forward, John's meaty hand grabbed his shoulder.

"What are you doing here?" Billy asked Pedro.

"Doing what you and your fellow Daykeepers failed to do," Pedro said not turning around, his Spanish accent completely gone, his voice sounding nothing like the Pedro, Billy once knew. "We're keeping Evil in its place… for now."

"We?" Billy asked.

Strykor's head shifted from what he was looking at directly in front of him to the shadows in the back of the room to his left.

"Strykor and me and a whole lot of others," Pedro said, again talking as if someone else controlled his mouth.

"You son-of-a-bitch," John said to Strykor. "After all we've been through."

Strykor still said nothing and continued staring at the shadows.

"Don't blame him," Pedro said. "Actually, all of you should praise him. He helped me return the Cubit to its proper place."

At that moment, Pedro stepped to the right and turned. His eyes were red and swirled with silver just like those in the jaguar statue. Strykor, however, did not move, his attention seemingly frozen. Billy leaned forward.

Behind Strykor and beside Pedro was a stone pedestal that was nearly identical to the one in the Wayeb Chamber of the Great Hall of the Anasazi. It differed only by the Cubit that sat on top and the three glyphs on its front face. Engravings of two Creation Daggers were chiseled in opposing directions, their seven-inch blades dipping down at forty-five degree angles, the tips coming together in the center of the pedestal. Below the V-shape created by the daggers was a Djed—or at least it appeared that a Djed used to be there. Unlike the daggers which were carved in the same three-dimensional style as the Mayan occupants within the domed wall, the Djed seemed to be missing. The shape of the Djed remained, its center column and four crosses recessed into the stone, but it was empty, as if something had pried the Djed from it.

Pedro stroked the top of the Cubit's wooden surface. "It's the end of the world as we know it," he chimed. "And I feel fine." He laughed loudly, once, then added, "To bad Strykor doesn't feel the same. When I saw my cubit for the first time, I was also absolutely terrified."

From the direction that Strykor was staring stepped…Strykor. The folds in the face of the cubited Strykor were much more pronounced than were those of its primary. The cubit, apparently, hadn't had the time, or know-how, to carve its own artificial incisors and when it spoke, it lisped so badly it was almost impossible to decipher.

"Thha-pri-thh, Thh-trik-thor. Drop-th ta yor-th knee-th an' make-th thi-th eathy on aw uff uthh." The cubited Strykor stepped fully from the shadows carrying a broadsword with a blade that was as long as his leg.

The fight that ensued ended so fast that none of them could have reacted even if they had wanted to. The real Strykor stabbed hesitantly at the cubit with his commando knife. This provided his cubit an opportunity to chop off the thrusting arm, impale the attacker in the chest, and decapitate the Marine, all in swift, succinct motions. The body fell in three pieces to the limestone floor next to the Cubit's pedestal. The Strykor cubit then backed John off with the sword and wrenched Cooper from her grasp of his arm. She screamed as the cubit pulled her in tight and, using her as a shield, shuffled backward to the jaguar statue. Billy stood by himself a few feet in front of the Cubit; John was between him and Cooper.

"Billy…poor Billy," Pedro said. "You came all of this way based on the lies of an Indian and a nigger. What did you actually think you'd find here other than death?"

"I didn't think I'd find you." Billy's hand moved to his chin to scratch nothing that itched; he just wanted to get his hand closer to the dagger under his shirt.

"Life is a fuck in that way. You never know what you're going to get." Pedro grabbed the lid on the Cubit. "You know what's in here?"

"Evil, of course," Billy said, still nonplused by the way Pedro talked as if someone else controlled his mouth and vocal cords.

"Evil? How simplistic. Evil isn't in here. Evil is in you. Evil is in all of us. You think Alax was almighty pure and honest and good? You think Johnboy here is some kind of fucking angel? He's murdered more innocent lives than there are sinners forever frozen on these walls." He raised his arms and looked around the domed room. He picked up on Billy's confusion. "Ah. I see. They didn't tell you, did they? They didn't tell you the real reason they brought you here."

Billy ignored the deception. "How do you know Lax? Even in life, you'd never been to Sedona."

"What do you mean 'in life?' This is life. I can dance." He shuffled his feet and shook his scrawny butt. "I can laugh." He whaled one short guffaw that rebounded throughout the room. "I can even cook one hell of a Caribbean shrimp platter just like I did back at the Surf Side. Life is what you make it. Mine holds a more realistic future than the one you follow so blindly, one cooked up by the goody two-shoers of the world. What you fail to understand is that everything exists to feed on something else. Politicians feed on your fear of taxes. Pastors feed on your false sense of morality. Cancer feeds on the body. Maggots feed on death. Right down to the microscopic and macroscopic levels, this consumption is eternal. You're a scientist Billy Willy. Certainly you understand that something always has to be feeding on something else, or else how could life exist at all?"

"Who are you?" Billy said. "You might look like Pedro but you talk like…"

"I talk like one intelligent son-of-a-bitch that would never deceive you as your so-called friends have." Pedro stepped away from the Cubit and halved the distance between himself and Billy. "Go ahead. Ask him. Ask the abolitionist what his promise to Alax really was."

Billy turned toward John as Cooper grunted, "Don't listen to him," before her mouth was sealed by the Strykor cubit's hand.

"I brought you here so that you know where the Cubit must stay for an eternity," John said.

"And…" Pedro urged.

"And nothin'."

Pedro continued. "And that, as a Daykeeper, he'll have to remain a prisoner in here for the rest of his immortal life. Go on…tell him."

John looked at the red-glow-gray limestone floor. "Alax said that to keep the Cubit out of the likes of people such as this asshole, you'd have to remain close to the ruins."

"Not close. In the ruins."

John shook his head and looked up. "No. That's not right. Alax never stayed in the Great Hall. He was never a prisoner there."

"And neither did his sister. And see what happened. Those two shirked their responsibilities and let the Cubit get out. It's because of them all of this shit is even happening. So you see Billy: raising the Djed is nothing more than a prison sentence, one that continues for an eternity. Now who wants to live life like that, hmm? No loves, no adventures, no children. If you want to know where Evil comes from, I gotta believe you've found it." Pedro pointed at John. "He wants to take everything human away from you."

"No," Billy demanded. He stuck his hand under his shirt. "I don't believe you."

"I don't give a shit what you think you believe, but the truth remains. Johnboy brought you here so that the process of immortality could begin. You raise the Djed and come back here for an eternity." He pointed at the domed wall. "At least you'll have company. I think there might even be a couple of Daykeepers in here that pretty much lost their minds and the jaguar added them to his collection. So, shall we get started?"

"Started?"

"Processing you for immortality." Pedro looked at John who again looked down at his feet. "Hah!" Pedro laughed. "Son-of-a-mother-fucker. You really do suck, Johnnie. You know that, don't you? Why, you didn't even tell him that… You were too much of a coward to let him know about…"

Suddenly, the top edge of the Cubit began to glow red. The box looked as if it were trembling atop its pedestal. The lid, which had no hinges and no hasp, very slowly started to rise, the crimson from within growing brighter the farther it opened.

"Well I guess we'll have to put the induction of Billy into the land of immortality on hold for a bit," Pedro said. "Looks like another of our island friends is coming out for a visit." He offered an open hand toward the Cubit as if he were some kind of model on a TV game show. "Isn't it beautiful? Isn't it just like every movie and every novel and every fantasy adventure you ever saw or read? The Cubit, returned to its proper place, returned to where it will usher in the End of Days…the alpha and the omega. An oracle satisfied, one that has nothing to do with the Bible, or the Torah or the Qu'ran or any of the fucked up religions this world has suffered under. This oracle was set many ages before such foolish notions such as Man was ever conceived. It is the oracle of the beginning and the end, of a complete cycle in which hope and love have screwed up everything. The universe feeds upon itself—there is no hope in that. Everything that lives, also dies and is reborn again and again and again."

The lid on the Cubit stood straight up and crimson light streaked from inside, creating deeper shadows toward the back of the circular room, further detailing the stone-frozen Maya that were forever entrenched into the wall. The intensity of the Cubit's red light magnified the three-dimensional depth of the suffering faces that seemed to cry out for salvation.

Billy's attention was drawn to the figure etched into stone at the domed apex of the room. He wondered if that man had been a Daykeeper and had lost his mind while guarding the Cubit as Pedro had suggested. He wondered if he, too, would become part of the suffering mosaic. He wondered if Pedro and whoever it was manipulating him was telling the truth. Immortality meant living no life whatsoever.

It was Cooper's muffled scream that returned his attention to the Cubit and the two hands which flopped up from the inside, the fingers curling over the edge. Its shoulders, which inhumanly appeared before the head, were too wide for a comfortable emergence but that didn't matter. Its bones were like jelly and squished through the top of the Cubit with ease. When its head sprung from the shoulders, the cubit stood from the box, a bright red aura encircling its entire body, and crawled carefully down to the floor. It turned around and Billy gasped, his dagger becoming so hot that he had to pull it from the sheath.

"Your buddy, Crabman, used to be a great surfer," Pedro said to Billy. "But those days are over. He makes a much better Mu'bä don't you think? Hell, this is your fourth rebirth isn't it, Crabby? And the more we return the faster we learn."

"Da more we weturn da faster we wearn," repeated the Crabman cubit.

Billy waved the dagger underhanded, the curved blade pointed forward.

"The only thing you are going to do with that is give it to Crabman," Pedro said.

"I'll give it to him all right," Billy warned.

"We can make this easy or we can make it hard. Give him the dagger and then, won't you be so kind as to give him the key as well. It's in your backpack, right?"

"I don't know what you are talking about." Billy waved the dagger at him.

"Sure you do." He lifted a finger toward Strykor. "Hand them over or your girlfriend's head comes off."

"She's not my girlfriend. She's just a hitchhiker we picked up on our way over."

"Now who's a liar?" Pedro lifted his arm over his head. "One last chance."

That's when John reacted. He spun around with the dexterity of a man a hundred pounds lighter, crouched, slung one leg out, and smashed the back of the Strykor cubit's knee with the heel of his boot. The cubit only flinched but loosened its grip on Cooper enough for her to drop to the floor. John took off from a three-point stance like a massive lineman after the quarterback, snatched the dagger from Billy's hand, and pounced on Pedro. Billy ran to Cooper as John missed Pedro's kill spot in the back of the head, brought the dagger up and thrust downward for a second attempt. The Strykor cubit swatted Billy aside and grabbed Cooper by her curly hair, pulling her up and into his grasp once again. When Billy rolled to his knees, he saw John plant the dagger in Pedro as Crabman lifted the Cubit from its pedestal. Pedro screamed one last time, "Take her fucking head off," before succumbing to the blade.

Billy looked at Cooper whose head was between Strykor's hands. Her eyes told him what they both knew was about to happen. He yelled, "No!!!" then took one step in her direction and saw in his periphery the flying box of wood just before the Cubit knocked him cold.

He didn't know how long he'd been out but he suspected that the sun had risen somewhere above him; it was the pinpoint of light at the apex of the dome that made him think so. The one inch twinkle of white was the only source of illumination other than the shadowy fraction of light peeking in from the stairwell beyond the jaguar statue; the twinkle peered down at him from the eye of what Billy had believed was the stony, etched reverence to some past Daykeeper. The beam fell directly on the center of the Cubit's empty throne like a spotlight. John sat, leaning against the pedestal's two daggers and empty socket where a Djed had once been carved, his knees drawn up to his chin, his big forearms clasped together around his shins. His head rocked ever-so-slightly back and forth, lightly tapping the stone with his bald skull. He hummed a melody that was distantly familiar but was too low and broken in volume for Billy to identify. Halfway between his feet and John's distant stare was the Cubit. It sat upside down on the limestone floor. Next to it was Billy's backpack; it had been unzipped and the contents dumped. Lots of individual electronic parts and his notebook lay scattered in front of him. The Book of the Djed's key page, he assumed, was gone.

When Billy cleared his throat, John looked up. "I'm so sorry," John said. "I couldn't save you both. I had to choose. I had to choose you. It was a promise and I couldn't break my promise again."

"Where's Cooper?" Billy stood.

"They took her."

"They have the key, too."

"I'm sorry, Billy. It's just that…"

The bone-ash remnants of Pedro lay just beyond the dimmest part of the overhead spot of light. "Here," John said, uncurling from his fetal position to reveal the dagger clasped in his left hand. "You're going to need this."

The Cubit was at Billy's feet and when he leaned forward to grab the dagger, he understood what John meant. The Cubit had knocked him out; it had touched him. John looked from the box to Billy and then to the dagger. He nodded. "When?" Billy asked.

"I don't know. No one ever knows. That's what's so damned scary."

Hearing such a mountain of a man even say the word "scary" was scary. Billy returned the dagger to its sheath. He'd always known that its blade would one day become paramount to his salvation but he'd never really thought about coming face-to-face with his own cubit. Living vicariously through Lenny Bender's grotesque murder had been horrific enough. His imagination immediately began searching the dark recesses within the room.

"Not yet," John said. "Been sittin' here watchin' it."

"Can it open turned upside down?"

"I figure the Cubit can do any damn thing the Cubit wants."

"So we just sit around and wait?"

"Course not." John stood, pressing the dust from his shirt. "They took

Cooper and we are going to get her back."

"How do you know she's still alive?"

John stepped around the Cubit and patted Billy's shoulder. "Because… you are."

"I don't understand."

"Get your stuff and let's get out of here. If we seal it in then maybe it'll be trapped here as well."

Billy looked at the Cubit and thought about what his Evil half might look like, imagined it poking its head out of the toppled box, wondered what manifestation of malfeasance an anti-Billy would master. He swept all of the electronics and his notebook back into his pack, slung it over his shoulders, and followed John past the jaguar statue; it's eyes were dead, the snarling face no longer as menacing as it had been a few hours ago.

The stairwell was drearily lit by the shadowed opening fifty feet above them. John led the way, never talking his eyes off the steps above and in front of him. Billy, on the other hand, kept staring back down, watching for red glowing clues that would signal the emergence of the dead from the Cubit.

"Be careful," John said. "Watch where you're going, not where you been. Falling from here might take your life and I really wouldn't want that." He stopped about thirty steps from the top and urged Billy to take the lead. "If something comes, I'll be ready."

When they exited the well, Billy couldn't help looking down once more. A red hue glowed at the bottom but he wasn't sure if its source was from the reignited eyes of the jaguar, the reincarnation of life from the Cubit, or just pure imagination.

John grunted beside him. "A little help."

John grasped a thick pole of wood and was using it to slide a slab of limestone that was a bit larger than a standard-sized door across the floor and over the stairwell opening. Billy grabbed a second pole and pried it under the slab. Together, they muscled the stone forward, covering only half of the entry into the Cubit's chamber. John led him to a second, equally-sized piece of limestone and they pushed it to where it interlocked with the first stone, completing the camouflage that had, with few exceptions, kept the Cubit secret for hundreds of years. Both dropped the poles when they heard Spanish chatter from beyond the dome. Apparently, a couple of guards had found last night's casualties.

John led Billy into the inner hallway created by the overlapping domes and moved clockwise, away from the footsteps that shuffled toward them in the same direction. They walked when the guards walked and stopped when the guards stopped and entered the center of the dome. Billy pressed his face up against the wall to hear them questioning each other just beyond its nine-inch thickness, then reenter the inner hallway to move, again, in their direction. John yanked his arm and shook his head at the rectangular doorway that opened onto the platform outside. Together, they ran.

Guards roamed near Mayan structures that were distant enough for Billy and John to go unnoticed. They quickly scuttled down the Caracol's three sets of steps and Billy saw what looked like blood but no body parts. Within another minute they were crouched under cover in the jungle bush just beyond a large pile of stones that Billy guessed had once been a part of the observatory. When he looked up, the face of the Wayeb that had been inlaid just below one dome window stared down at him, and Billy wondered how much the Wayeb truly knew about the future.

They retrieved the machetes they'd left in the jungle and razed a trail back to Strykor's motel in a different direction than they'd come. The bush was still wet and this made chopping messy. About thirty minutes into the trek, Billy finally asked. A lot of the things the Pedro cubit had said hadn't made much sense and his preoccupation with the information had nearly caused him to severe a chechen negro twice.

"That didn't sound like the Pedro I knew," Billy said, slashing at a knee-high plant that had triangular leaves with prickly edges."

"Most likely, it wasn't." John dodged a crop of bushes and urged Billy to do the same.

"How's that?"

"It's like glossolalia. You ever heard of that? Back in Georgia, it happened a lot, particularly in those backwoods churches. Most people called it 'speaking in tongues.' Words come out of the mouth that aren't their words but are thought to be channeled through the greater God." John stopped and turned around. "In this sense, we are all just vessels that think we are in control of our own condition when actually we are just tools…a means to an end. What you heard from that guard in the well were words spoken by his real master."

"The Devil?" Billy's mouth worked faster than his mind had to reason.

"I wouldn't call it that. Devil's too simplistic. Devil's too Catholic. Whatever is out there that's caused the world to know Evil…that's really what we're talkin' about. And with cubits, you can always tell when it's happening."

"How?"

John turned back toward the jungle and resumed slashing at plants that were taller than his waist. Up ahead, a small building sat in a ten-foot wide clearing. "Their eyes," he said. "They turn all red and swirly-looking. That's when their master is in control."

"How do you know this?"

"Alax…and experience."

"He never told me such things."

"I suspect Alax never told you lots of things. How long did he know you?"

"A day or two."

"A lifetime of knowledge in a day or two…unlikely, particularly since we both know how old he was."

"So my destiny is to become immortal and sit in that god-awful secret chamber with all of those god-awful people chiseled into the walls just so the Cubit doesn't get out and screw up the world more than it already has?"

They'd made it to the clearing and the smell from Strykor's shithouse blew into their faces as a gentle breeze changed direction. The path to the motel cottages wound through the jungle ahead of them. John stopped once again.

"I'd say that your destiny, right now, is to save your girlfriend. What you really gotta learn, Billy, is to focus on things you can control. Concentrate too much on the end and you'll lose the now, and then your destiny will certainly take a turn for the worst."

"How do I save her when I don't even know where she is?"

"I think I know. It's just a hunch but a good one. The sacred cenote near Ikil is infamous for Saturday night partying. It's a closed invitation kind of thing…a rave kind of deal. They got lots of drugs—some really bad ones. Los Zetas—a paramilitary group that are enforcers for the Gulf Cartel—hang out there to deal heroin. Some say they even make sacrifices to the cenote but that may be more scare tactic than reality."

"Sounds like the perfect place for cubits to hang out."

"Yes. And a perfect place to recruit them."

Billy looked at his machete's fat blade. "Not much use against a force like that," he said. "Got any machine guns or tanks or missiles?"

"Faith," John said. "You gotta have faith." Then he stepped into the shithouse and closed the door.

In her mouth was a foul-smelling rag that, for all she knew, could have been an ass wipe for any one of the several dozen men and women that she heard talking and screaming and laughing around her. She kept her eyes closed and tried to refrain from gagging.

"When do we get to do her?" The voice was Mr. Bean Breath from the museum and he was much too close to her.

"Keep it in your pants," another voice said that she also recognized. "Anything happens to her before I say, and I'll cut it and your floppy head right off."

Rocks skittered close by. Deep breaths that were distant moved closer to her face. A hand swept through the curls on her forehead and wiped away the cool moisture. "Cooper. Wake up, Cooper."

She sat against what her spine thought was a tree. Her arms were bound behind her. It wasn't raining but she could smell mist. She continued her act though the stinky cloth in her mouth was nearly unbearable. *The voice...who was that?*

"They're coming for you, Cooper. Fret not."

Who in the hell was that?

"Not as luxuriously sexy as Marcy, but you make a fine X'Tabay nonetheless."

The Serpent! That's exactly who knelt in front of her. She heard his voice fade and more rocks skitter so she opened one eye just a fraction of a slit. Her head leaned too far forward for her to see anything more than two legs below the knees walk away from her. A second set of legs moved closer and she immediately smelled the beans. "Sexy," the rapist said then licked her forehead sweat. "And tasty."

For another hour, she continued acting as if she was unconscious when, suddenly, music started playing. Its volume went from low to loud as the beat turned furious. The music was American heavy metal that sounded as if it was being covered by Mexican artists. It was an odd mixture, listening to *Sweet Child O'Mine* being sung by a pseudo Axl Rose Mexican imitator. The guitar licks were spot on but the voice…it just didn't quite work.

When someone screamed right in front of her, she finally opened her eyes and lulled her head back against the moist, round root of a ceiba tree. She guessed that it was around noon but dense clouds masked the sun's true direction. Under the gray light she watched what she thought was some kind of party rave. She sat bound in a jungle clearing thirty feet from a small fire around which four men gyrated to the Mexican Rose. All four of them wore green uniforms that looked like those she'd seen the guards wearing at the autopista toll stops. Pistols were strapped to their waists on gun belts and all of them waved long sticks of charred meat above their heads. One of the men fired his automatic rifle into the air every time Mexico Rose screamed "Sweet Child O' Mine."

To the left and farther away from the fire were dozens of people, stamping the dirt and twisting their bodies to the hidden source of music. Few of them had any rhythm; in fact, it looked almost as if none of them had any control of their muscles whatsoever. Some fell to the hard dirt and others fell over those that had just fallen. They laughed and screamed and cried and yelled. Two men were kissing at one point during the song, then suddenly they were beating the shit out of each other as *Sweet Child* ended and a non-AC/DC version of *Dirty Deeds Done Dirt Cheap* began.

To her right and much farther away, she saw several people gathered around what looked like a sinkhole, or *cenote* as they called it in Mexico. From where she sat, she could barely see the cenote's far side limestone wall as it curved raggedly inward, about fifty feet in diameter, toward the numerous onlookers who gathered around a platform that had been built at the forward perimeter. In front of and over the heads of the onlookers, an axe appeared that quickly swooped down and out of sight. The group chanted as a headless body was thrown into the cenote. The head was then lifted up by the hair, the chant became louder, and the head was thrown into the cenote as well.

Cooper looked down when one of the chanters saw her looking at him. She closed her eyes but it was too late. A minute later, he was beside her.

"You like what you see?" Cooper remained motionless. "Come on, love. I know you saw it." A hand grabbed her chin and gently lifted her head. "Don't worry, Cooper. We're not going to throw you in…at least, I'm not going to throw you in." She opened her eyes. The man was rather skinny but athletic at the same time, Cooper thought—something like an endurance athlete—a distance runner, perhaps. His black hair was about as straight as any she'd ever seen; it was trimmed around his forehead in a half-moon from temple to temple; its length stopped at the earlobes. His eyes were pure gray. Not one speck of any other color occupied any part of the irises which only made the pupils look much, much darker.

"Allow me to introduce myself. I'm Evan Santinal and I'm here to protect you." He reached forward and loosened the knot on the smelly twist of cloth in her mouth. Immediately, she spit it out. "Here." Against her lips, he tilted a plastic bottle filled with purple liquid; the word *Gatorade* occupied the center of a label that, besides that one word, was inundated with Spanish. "If the taste is anything like the smell, this will seem like god-juice." Cooper drank half of the contents in one gulp; the man named Evan had to pull it away from her. She coughed. "Manuel wants to do some very unheard-of things. I think he's a bit cookoo—well, I know he was a bit cookoo in real life. The shit he used to do to women…Sad." Evan took the smelly rag from her face and threw it away as if it were a disease. "What do you think of him? Do you want me to kill him?"

Cooper's tongue still played with threads from the shit smelling mouth rag. She spit but the thread only launched as far as her cheek. Evan wiped it away. "He's already dead," she said.

Evan smiled. "Aren't we all?" He turned his attention to the gathering by the cenote. Manuel emerged with an axe from the center of inhumanity. His head still flopped to one side, bobbing up and down on his right shoulder as he strutted toward them. "You're a psychologist. What's your diagnosis of such a bumbling fool?"

Cooper gasped and as soon as she did, she regretted it. It seemed that this reaction was exactly what Evan wanted.

"Yeah. We know," Evan said. "We know everything." He smiled.

"Fuck you," Cooper squawked, her throat unable to enforce the vocal strength that her mind demanded.

"Fuck seems to be the pivotal word here, doesn't it?" Manuel walked up to her, holding the bloody axe like a trophy. "What do you think Manuel?" Evan said to the grungy Mexican who smelled less like beans and a lot more like the rag that had been in her mouth.

"Fuck is good," he moaned, apparently excited by the mere mention of the word.

"Billy's gonna make you wish you never existed," Cooper grumbled.

Evan turned toward Manuel and yanked the axe from the cubit's grasp. He held it awkwardly, as if he'd never held an axe before. "Bring it on," he said, his skinny face puckering into an expression of fortitude that was so much a lie Cooper almost laughed. He planted the blade into the tree root well above Cooper's head. "In fact, if he doesn't show his coward ass and 'make me wish I never existed,' Manuel will make a permanent part of you between his legs."

She looked at Manuel who grinned with a sour looking set of teeth that were set at an angle in his lolling face. Her memory of his aggression made the skin crawl up the back of her neck. "And if I tell you to kill that ugly bastard, then what?"

Evan knelt in front of her and gently grabbed one of her strawberry curls. "You really have no idea what's happening here do you? I can only hold these monsters off for so long. I take one out and it just comes back to life. What I really need is the dagger. With it, I can put all of these creatures in hell for good and you'll never have to worry about any of them fucking you or your boyfriend. I really mean that…from the bottom of my heart."

"You're not one of them," Cooper said, jerking her head away from his touch.

"Correct. Like I said, I'm here to protect you." Manuel suddenly reached forward and touched the top of her head. Evan punched away the forearm. "Not now, you stupid ignoramus." He returned his attention to Cooper and smiled. "But I'm not gonna be able to for much longer. They are more like zombies than they are given credit. Living flesh absolutely drives their desires banananonkers. I hope your boyfriend shows himself pretty soon."

"And if he does show?"

Evan bent closer for a whisper. "Then I'll take the dagger and get rid of Manuel for you. You'll never have to worry about him again…except, maybe, inside your nightmares, but I can't do a damn thing about that."

She nodded in the direction of the man with the flip of blonde-white hair who was dancing with a couple of degenerate cubited women. "And what about the Serpent? I'll bet he's the one that tied me up like this. He's got some kind of fetish for women and ceiba trees. Will you take care of him as well?"

"No can do." Evan looked over his shoulder. "He's the boss man. He's the one that set you up. He's the one that's been setting all of this up. If it wasn't for him, none of you would even be here and I wouldn't have a job. He wants Billy…and not just his dagger."

"Why would he want Billy?"

"You're a smart girl. You can figure it out, can't you?"

Cooper remembered their encounter in the Great Hall. "He took the Book."

Evan nodded.

"He already knows the fourth location."

Evan nodded.

"So why doesn't he just show up and raise the Djed himself?"

Evan shrugged.

"And why does he need the key? I saw that Crabman thing take it from Billy's backpack. The key has already revealed all he needs to know." She watched the Serpent walk toward her."

"Perplexing isn't it. I wish I could tell you. I wish I knew. Maybe you should ask him." Evan stood.

"I see she's awake," the Serpent said. "Hello delicious."

Cooper scowled.

"I mean you really do look delicious sitting there all tied up to the ceiba tree. Tantalizing, don't you think?" Manuel hungrily agreed. Evan simply nodded and smiled. "Marcy was tastier, but you'll do."

"Shove it up your ass," Cooper growled.

"Temper…temper. Anger makes the meat sour."

"Who the hell are you anyway?"

"The boss man. Like Evan said."

"You've got everything you need. Why don't you just leave us alone?"

"But I don't have everything. If I had everything, you would be dead."

"So my death is important for raising the Djed?"

"You give yourself too much credit. You're nothing but a pawn—a goddamned, no good poonta. You were used by Cower. You were used by Billy. Now I'm using you. That's really the only purpose you serve. It's your only value in life. Evan may say he's going to protect you, but we both know that's a lie. He's a really good liar." Evan, again, nodded.

"If he's a liar then you aren't the boss man," Cooper said. "You must be a pawn, too. We have a lot in common."

The Serpent slapped her. "You tie your tongue or Manuel will be the very least of your worries." He turned away from her and called over one of the men dressed like a soldier. "Give her a taste," he said. "The experience will set her straight."

The soldier, whose forearm had the injection point tracks of a junkie, presented a hypodermic needle and knelt beside her.

"Feed her Djed," the Serpent ordered.

The soldier reached around the root of the tree, plunged the needle into one of Cooper's rattlesnake scars and emptied the amber fluid into the djed tattoo. The effect was almost immediate.

"How do you like the taste of heroin?" The Serpent asked. "It is the elixir of life."

John's faith would have to be strong enough for both of them. The man was big. The man was strong. The man was a Marine, schooled in tactics that Billy had only seen portrayed in the movies where actors playing Rangers and Seals and Green Berets almost always reminded their fellow soldiers—and the theatre's audience—that the trained mind was more powerful than any arsenal of weapons. Still, it was hard to see how two men with no firepower could rescue a woman held hostage by dozens of trained killers. Billy's faith eroded even further when he stepped from the shithouse path to the cottage clearing to find that the Cavalier was gone.

"It's close enough to walk," John said when he saw Billy's concern.

"It'll take a couple of hours but I wasn't going to suggest the car anyway."

"It's not that," Billy said. "It's just that..."

"Sentimental value." John walked over and stood in the spot where the car had been parked. "A concept that's of absolutely no use to us right now."

Billy shrugged. He couldn't help his emotions. The car had been such a part of his life for over five months, even if it had just sat in the parking lot outside his Sedona apartment. Of course, it wasn't the physical construct of the car that had mattered most; it was the value association to lost friends and a lost life. Port Aransas had been the last place he'd ever expected to live. He'd built a business from scratch and had connected with nature in ways that most people would consider fairytale. But more than that, the car represented freedom: freedom to have chosen Port Aransas in the first place; freedom to have had the courage to drop out of college and decimate his parents' hopes for him; freedom to start a new life, to accept the desire for another person into his soul, to ride the waves of Mother Nature. The car represented the freedom to flee when these freedoms were taken from him. The car represented freedom from *this* God-forsaken place.

"Wait," John said. "What's this?"

Billy walked over to where John was pointing. A little yellow hand stuck up from the ground. Billy knelt and scooped away the dirt around SpongeBob's smiling face. He plucked the toy from its burial prison and blew dust from its yellow, sponge body. He wanted to hug the toy right then and there but thought the timing was a bit inappropriate. John smiled, perhaps even expecting a joyous embrace, then waved for Billy to follow him into Strykor's cottage.

The interior of the cottage was a complete mess. It wasn't destroyed like his apartment had been; it was simply a pigsty and it smelled like one, too.

John walked to a waist high refrigerator that was brown dirty and littered with magnets promoting all things military, from the USMC logo and several bulldogs, to antique pinup girl magnets—the kind that might have been distributed during the World Wars though Billy didn't think refrigerators were very popular back then. "We'll need to eat and reenergize before we tackle the impossible."

"You kind of sound like Lax...eh, Alax."

"Naw. I think he got that idea from me." He opened the refrigerator and pulled out a couple of Mason jars filled with liquid slurry surrounding what were likely indigenous meat chunks. "Not sure what it is but if he can eat it, so can we." To his armload he added a milk jug that was hand-labeled *CLEEN* and a block of yellow cheese that thankfully looked as if it had been purchased rather than handmade. "Grab the tortillas and let's go start us a fire." He pointed to the round metal table that was cluttered with tools and towels and bowls and cups and a bag of ten-inch tortillas.

"You seem to know Alax quite well," Billy said. Next to the tortillas was a soldering iron and a circuit board that was about the size of a pack of cigarettes. He looked at the board curiously before taking it and the tortillas, then followed John outside. "Did you guys serve in a war together or something?"

"We both served, but not together." John placed the food and jug on one empty tree stump then walked to the back of the cottage and brought out an armful of wood which he dropped onto the black ashes inside the fire pit.

Billy set the tortillas on the same stump, removed the backpack from his shoulders, dropped the circuit board and SpongeBob inside, and went to grab a second armful of wood. "You handle a Creation Dagger pretty well," he said from the back of the cottage.

"Is that what you call them things?"

Billy added his wood to the pit. "John. I'm not that stupid. You saw me use it on that thing from the museum and you never said a word. You asked for it in the Chichen well as if it was yours. You knew exactly how to use it."

"Yeah…well. I used to have one of 'em." He sat on one of the stumps then reached down to where a notch had been carved into the wood. From it, he plucked a small tin with the rusty words *Altoids* printed on it. He opened it and grabbed one of the matchsticks inside, then struck it against one of the limestone rocks surrounding the pit and threw it onto the wood pile.

"What happened to it?"

"Cower."

Billy sat, hard, onto a tree stump.

"I see you know the name. Son-of-a-bitch tricked me and I had always thought that was impossible. Sucker like that humbles a person."

"He took it from you? How could anyone take anything from you?"

"Don't remind me." The fire grew to a gentle blaze. "Throw me that cheese and a tortilla will ya?" Billy flipped him the cheese but took out two tortillas from the bag before passing them. "Cubits ain't the only twisted shits in the world—don't you ever forget it." He broke off a chunk of cheese, waved it at Billy's face and slapped it into Billy's open hand. He saw the burnt star scar in the palm but didn't say anything about it. "The really bad thing was that the ass was so damned nice and honest-like. I mean, he really could have sold ice to Lucifer. Where I come from, you don't come off trustworthy then betray it. With people like that, even *you* can't save this world from itself."

The fire grew hot enough to cook in; Billy handed John the jars of mystery meat and two of the charred sticks they'd used to eat snake the night before. John wrapped a big chunk of cheese with one tortilla and shoved the whole thing into his mouth. He peered at Billy from the corner of one eye as if he knew what was about to asked. While turning the cap on the Mason jar he said, "Alax told me. In fact, the promise I made to him did include protecting you, but that wasn't the big promise." He sniffed the contents of the jar and shrugged, then fished out a couple of meat cubes and stuck them on his stick. He did the same thing with Billy's stick and set the jar on the ground. "Whoever was behind Pedro's eyes was correct in one way. 'Processing you for immortality,' as he so gracefully put it, took one giant step this morning."

Juice ran down Billy's stick as he stared at John who would not look at him. "I'm to raise the Djed." Billy said.

"Mmm hmmm. Won't do you no good unless..." He lowered his stick into the fire. "You gotta meet and beat that which no man ever wants to confront." As he grabbed Billy's hand and urged it and the stick toward the fire, he stared hard into Billy's eyes. "My promise was for you to touch the Cubit. You have to confront your worst fears, those which make up the darkest part of your very soul. You have to face your own cubit and *You* have to kill it."

The memory of Billy's vision from Alax's anteroom came thundering back into his head. *Bad Billy* had been waiting for him, beyond the doorway, in the darkness. He shivered at the thought of being eaten alive like Lenny Bender had been, like Pedro had been—and Steph...the flesh had been hanging from her lips...she'd wanted a kiss...and that had taken him over the edge. "I don't think..." he mumbled. "How can I possibly..."

"You have no choice any longer."

Billy dropped his skewer, his fear quickly transforming into anger as he gazed into the fire. "You! You took me there. It's all your fault. You motherfucker!" Billy's fist flew and connected with John's jaw with such force that the Marine fell off his stump; his stick of meat skittered across the ground. Billy looked at his hand as if it didn't belong at the end of his arm.

John pushed himself to a sitting position. "I guess I deserved that. But you gotta remember. At least we sealed it in there and it doesn't have any place to hide. You'll have the upper hand."

"I don't want the upper hand. I don't want any of this."

"Christ, Billy!" John stood and for a moment Billy thought he was going to return the punch. "Grow up and accept it. You think your own cubit is bad...wait 'til we get to the party tonight. At least cubits aren't among the living. What you should really be afraid of is real humans, especially these."

Billy's stick had caught fire. The meat cubes on it had burned so badly that the black chunks fell into the flames. He tossed the stick aside. John walked around the fire, picked up the stick he'd thrown when Billy punched him and snatched the jug of water. He washed the dirt from his meat cubes, sat back down, and resumed cooking them. "I get the feeling that Alax never had the chance to tell you how important it is that you don't give up."

Billy stared into the fire, unresponsive and pouty.

"Answer me one question. Why aren't you dead?"

Billy was tempted to look at him, but his concentration on the flames had promoted a vision of Cooper Reyes with flesh hanging from her lips.

"He could have killed you in Texas."

Cooper's mouth sucked up the hanging flesh and Billy could almost hear the slurping-sucking noise it made.

"He could have killed you in Arizona."

Cooper's mouth was smeared with the blood from her own sinew.

"All the way through Mexico, he could have sent any dozen men who would have killed you for a couple a hundred pesos."

Cooper puckered her gruesome lips.

"In Mérida. In the museum. In Chich. In the well."

Cooper wanted a kiss.

"BILLY!"

Billy shook away the fiery trance.

"Why aren't you dead?"

Billy turned to him then. John peered sternly, like a professor waiting for an answer before resuming his lecture.

"I had the Book."

"Gone."

"I had the key."

"Gone."

"I still have the dagger."

"You didn't in the well, remember? You gave it to me, which means you were defenseless, without the key and without the Book. Strykor's cubit could have easily taken Cooper out then you."

"But he didn't kill either one of us."

John pulled the stick from the fire and gave it to Billy, who wrapped a tortilla around one hot chunk and pulled it from the stick. He didn't eat it; he just held it for a moment as he tried to understand. "They need the Book and the key and the dagger to raise the Djed," Billy said, thinking out loud, again turning toward the dancing orange flames. "The Djed provides immortality. But a cubit is already immortal in the sense that it cannot die. Unless you stab it with the dagger. So if a cubit gets a hold of the Djed…" He looked at John, astonished that he knew the answer. "The dagger cannot kill it."

John nodded.

"They didn't kill Cooper because they wanted the dagger. They want me to bring them the dagger."

"They want *you* to bring *you*."

"A trap?"

John ate his meat chunk and chased it with a piece of cheese.

"You're getting warmer."

"Dammit! Just tell me. Okay? I have a destiny…fine. I'm supposed to be some kind of Daykeeper…fine. I live for an eternity, telling stories or I live in a dark-domed well with a bunch of creepy stone carvings and a pet rock jaguar…whatever. How I'm supposed to save the world is irrelevant since you aren't going to or can't tell me anyway. But all of this is mute if they…if he…" Billy's eyebrows lifted. "Deer-hat man? The Serpent?"

"Of course. But that doesn't answer the question."

"Was it the Serpent who was staring at me through Pedro's eyes?"

"No. Someone much more powerful. The cubit you call the Serpent is only a self-serving pawn, just like the rest of the cubits."

"Who?"

"Not totally sure but he wants you alive…for now."

And then the answer to the riddle came to him; it simply popped into his head as if it had been trapped in a bubble that had just burst. "I'm the only one that can become a Daykeeper. I'm the only one that can raise the Djed. The recipe includes the Book, the key, the dagger and me!"

"Hallelujah!" John bellowed at the clouds above him. "Now you've got the *who* and the *with what* now all you need is the *when*, *where*, and *how*."

"Jesus…we're not going to spend the whole afternoon playing twenty more thousand questions are we?"

"We could and I probably would if I knew *all* the answers. I like playing these intellectual games with you. Stimulating."

Billy huffed. "I think I know the *when* and I have a clue as to the *where* since the Great Hall showed it to me."

"When?"

"December twenty-one."

"And what grand piece of reasoning tells you that?"

"The end of the Mayan cycle. The winter solstice. The turn back toward the living. And, it begins the five-day cycle of the Wayeb when the underworld is given a chance to enter into our own."

"Impressive! You know a lot more than I gave you credit for."

Billy jammed his entire wad of tortilla-wrapped food into his mouth and immediately grimaced. "What the hell is that?"

"Iguana, I suspect. Not Strykor's best effort."

And that's when Billy, for the first time, saw real sorrow attack the big man's expressive face. No doubt he was thinking about his friend. Billy actually thought he saw a tear on the far side of John's face but he scratched that cheek so fast, Billy wasn't sure. He slapped John on the back as he chewed then stooped to his right to grab his backpack. "It's not very good but I'm starving," Billy said. "The cheese helps considerably. I wouldn't mind another piece."

While John assembled more food for the fire, Billy reached into his pack and pulled out his notebook. "The *where*," he said while flipping through the pages. He folded the notebook back along its metal spiral spine and presented the page where he'd sketched the image he'd seen in the Book, noting the fourth location. John wiped iguana juice from his hands and traded the notebook for the cooking stick that now held two more pieces of meat and what looked like small onions. Billy stuck it in the fire. "Recognize it?"

"You weren't an art student, I take it."

"Funny man." Billy smirked. "Robotics, actually. I can do some pretty fine mechanical drafts but that necessitates a table, square and a few other drawing utensils. As for freehand. Well, there you go."

John studied the sketch until the food was cooked. He turned the notebook upside down and sideways several times, said, "Hmm" at least twice, then swapped the notebook for the fresh tortilla wrap Billy had made for him.

"Anything?"

"Yeah," John said, studying his tortilla. "That looks like El Castillo in Tulum…at least part of it does. Don't know what that chicken scratch to the right of it is supposed to be." He took a bite. "Hey. The onion sure changes the flavor."

"You sure?"

"About the onion?"

Billy scowled.

"Yeah, yeah…I know." He chuckled. "Not a hundred percent. If that is El Castillo, it is pictured from an angle that looks in from the ocean."

"The Serpent saw it. He must also know."

"Most likely." John finished his food and swilled from the water jug as Billy took his first bite. "You keep calling him the Serpent. Why is that?"

"It seemed more fitting than Deere-hat man."

John's eyes rolled. "I don't think I want to know. But I think you should know."

"What? More revelations you've been holding back from me?"

"Daykeepers are supposed to figure these things out for themselves."

"I will as soon as you tell me."

"Why Billy. The answer, like every other answer so far, has been staring you right in the face ever since you started to believe. You need to open up your mind much more in the future." He handed Billy the water jug. "Here. You better clear your throat so you don't choke."

Billy drank water even though he hadn't eaten anything in several minutes.

"He set up that entire ordeal in Texas. He used Albert Stine who used Chancey Lett who used Mitchell Bone. The excavation of the beach was solely for the purpose of recovering the dagger which you now possess. And all of the other pieces just fell into place for him after almost two hundred years."

"Who?"

"Someone who knew Alax's sister quite well."

"Who, dammit!"

"Captain Jean Lafitte, of course."

Evan didn't think Mr. Manson gave him as much credit as he deserved. Dealing with all of these ignorant peons, whether dead or alive, took all of the willpower one man could muster. He would have much rather been skydiving or scuba diving or splicing and dicing extreme footage on his gigantic Mac system back in Mérida—secluded, by himself, the only challenges being those that his own mind and imagination placed in front of him. He so hated people: all of them. He was introverted to the max and this made dealing with morons so much less pleasant. He had zilch people skills and zilch patience. Even the avatars in World of Warcraft had more spine than these simple-minded freaks.

But he had to maintain the illusion. The pirate had to continue to believe that he was in control of the entire situation. The pirate was the boss and what he said was the word. Unfortunately for Evan, following the commands of a two-hundred-year-old pirate was one of the most unpleasant chores he'd ever been given. Every time the inverted ponytail bastard returned to the peninsula, Evan's imagined future utopia seemed to slip farther away.

The pirate's reasoning was all screwed up. Evan didn't like the way that he'd used Billy's friend, Marcy. He should have simply sent his minions in to take what he wanted. These stupid mind games drove Evan crazy but the pirate seemed to get off on them. He'd done the same with Chancey Lett and Albert Stine and who knows how many other people in the past two centuries. Now he was working on Cooper. Was it really necessary to pump her with heroin? Was it really necessary to put her through the hell of watching all of these addicts rave and rant and revel in their perceived almighty drug lord power trips? There had to be an easier way. But then, again, Evan wasn't one of them. He was much smarter. He would bide his time and get his just reward. Soon, he would be the boss and if the pirate was lucky enough to live that long, Evan would introduce him to Davey Jones' Locker, whether Mr. Manson agreed to the deed or not.

"Evan. I said get your ass over here!" Lafitte stood near an unmarked box truck which had pulled in off the dirt road a few minutes ago. He'd just opened the rear doors. "Rapido!"

Evan took one more look at Cooper. The effects of the heroin were evident. Her open eyes were glassy, she smiled a goofy grin, and her head lolled to one side, kind of like the way Manuel's head was now permanently attached. Evan giggled short and sweet, not because of Cooper's situation but because of Manuel's. He absolutely hated that smelly-assed cubit and couldn't wait to execute Manson's orders to erase the problem; its failure at the museum was, after all, the entire reason why he was standing here in the middle of the jungle taking orders from a power-tripping dead pirate. He casually walked to where Lafitte stood. Without warning, Lafitte hauled off and slapped him.

"Thirty cases of beer! Thirty!" he wailed. "Not twenty-nine. Not thirty-one. The Zetas are precise in what they desire." Lafitte looked behind the stacked boxes that were labeled *Coors Light*. "How many kegs?" he asked the truck driver. The short, chubby Latino looked at his manifest.

"Ocho," he said and flinched as if Lafitte was going to slap him next.

Lafitte glared at Evan who was rubbing the hand print on the side of his face. "At least you got that right. You really make me wish I'd a saved Pedro. He was much more efficient and unquestionably loyal."

"But he's dead now isn't he?" Evan couldn't help it. Perhaps he was a glutton for punishment. Lafitte swung at him again but Evan dodged the blow.

"Get this shit off the truck and into place," Lafitte ordered. "And would somebody please turn that fucking music off? They'll be here shortly and they like their own tunes."

Tonight's rave at the sacred cenote was a cover for the drug deal that was about to go down. Everyone knew it, the local policia, the Mexican gobierno, the citizens of Ikil. But it really didn't matter. These were Los Zetas and they'd be well packed. They'd bring enough firepower to knock out a platoon if need be. Besides, many of the recipients of tonight's exchange would be local, state and government officials, all non-cubited non-law abiding citizens of the country's corrupted underbelly. Money was to be made and power was to be dealt during a moiré of fanatic partying by both the living and the dead. And that's exactly how Lafitte liked to play it. The goal to raise the Djed was important to him since it would ensure his ever-lasting menace to the world, but it was not a priority. He had until December twenty-one and he'd use every last day, leaving absolutely no room for error. Above all else, Evan hated this patience the most. It unnerved him. Evan wanted to get shit done and move on. If Lafitte would only play it like World of Warcraft. You have a goal which garners you power and you go about collecting all the pieces necessary to attain that goal. If it had been Evan, the game would have been solidly in his hands a year ago. Cower had possessed most of what they'd needed—But no! Lafitte had to play his stupid fucking mind games and the key had gotten separated, and the Kansas woman had disappeared with the Book, and Albert had disappeared with the dagger and…

"Shit!" Evan yelled. Lafitte stood behind him.

"If you can't do such simple tasks, I'll find someone who can. Strykor looks like a willing and able subject."

"He's an idiot," Evan said. "He just came out of the box this morning. He can't even tie his own shoelaces."

"Then perhaps Billy, when he shows up."

"He's not gonna help you do anything except stick a dagger into the back of your head."

"Not that Billy, dumb ass…the one in the well." Lafitte laughed then, mostly because of the expression on Evan's face. "He'll make a wonderful concierge, don't you think? Even as a cubit he'll be much smarter than you. You should know by now that I've only kept you alive because of your knowledge concerning 2012. I suspect Billy knows as much if not more. And, given time, so will his cubit. Then I'll have the pleasure of watching you replaced. Until then, please try not to screw anything else up?" Lafitte whistled and two of the men dressed in military uniforms came over to the truck to help unload it.

It was so hard for Evan: taking this kind of abuse and receiving no credit. Manson would surely see his sacrifices. Manson would surely reward him. But he'd have to wait and patience was not his greatest virtue.

It really was impossible to get his head wrapped around it all. Ice in the spine…that's what it felt like: a creepy, freezing, alien tiptoe up his vertebrae. His brain looped through theatrical tones that had tied current circumstance to his meager mortal memories.

You are the one, Neo.

Mos Eisley Spaceport. You'll never find a more wretched hive of scum and villainy.

You gonna draw them pistols or whistle Dixie?

I'm sorry, Dave. I'm afraid I can't do that.

How could he be the one if he was dead?

He had one dagger, one machete and one Marine. How in God's name was he going to save Cooper and save his ass and save the world?

He sat on the floor of the cottage formerly rented by Pedro's cubit, his backpack at his feet, the notebook flipped open to the sketch he'd made of the fourth location…of what John had identified as El Castillo. John said that they would be leaving in a couple of hours which would allow them enough time to walk to the sacred cenote and arrive after nightfall. In the meantime, rest was priority one.

Better said than done.

SpongeBob's yellow hand poked out from between the pack's zippered pocket. He lifted the pack's flap and SpongeBob's big smile and blue eyes caused him to grin and grimace in rapid succession. He dropped the flap. Lifted the flap. Saw the happy face. Dropped the flap. It was a goofy attempt to try and humor himself but it was working. Billy finally smiled and pulled the toy out.

"What would SpongeBob do?" he asked it. "Something totally off the wall, no doubt. Something that made no sense whatsoever. Something that would have nothing to do with responsibility." He moved SpongeBob's hand as if in salute against its sponge head.

"Aye, captain," he mimicked the toy's voice. "You think any Mexicans have ever seen a walking sponge before?"

He moved the toy back and forth across the floor, imitating a walk. "How could they Spongy?" he said in his own voice. "They're too busy getting stoned and killing innocent Daykeepers."

He set the toy down and pulled the circuit board from his backpack. He'd been curious as to why a recluse in the middle of the jungle would have such a thing but, until now, hadn't had the chance to give it much thought. He set the circuit board on the floor beside SpongeBob and said, "Hey Sponge. Meet your new partner in crime." He tried to think of a superhero kind of name for the circuit board and drew it closer to read the manufacturer's stamp on the top edge. *Zogg's Boards*, it read. Billy blinked then turned the board over in his hand, examining the soldered components. He'd always purchased his electronic components via mail order from a place called *Zogg's*. It was a small Mom and Pop shop outside of Cambridge with which he'd stayed in contact once he'd moved to the island. The irony of the name and its association to the infamous surfboard wax, plus the always reliable and inexpensive components had made him a permanent customer.

And then he remembered that the computers had been removed from his VW. Apparently, they were somewhere in Strykor's cottage. He picked up SpongeBob, searching its big blue eyes for inspiration. He examined the circuit board, dumped out the rest of the electronic parts from the backpack, thought about his computer surveillance equipment, wondered if it had been salvaged. His mind whirled, the icy infiltration that had grabbed his spine now melting. An idea was emerging. It might not be much but…

"Nautical nonsense, my ass," he said to the toy. "You're a genius!"

She was no longer bound but that really didn't matter. Heroin controlled her. She tried standing only once but the euphoric buzz was too much. She fell back against the ceiba root and slid to the ground. The tree was her only salvation, now. Its thick trunk and broad leafy canopy above provided a false sense of security from the melee that danced without music in psychedelic terror all around her.

What was real and only imagination coalesced into one big fat mind fuck. It seemed that night had fallen but she really wasn't sure. It seemed that the fire had grown from infant to inferno, but again, her sweaty eyeballs could not gauge any truth. Instead of considering the reality of the brutal sacrifices that raged around the fire and on the platform of the cenote farther away, she stared at her forearm, at the djed tattoo, at the pinpoint incision that the hypodermic needle had added to her flesh's landscape. Men screamed for salvation but she ignored them. Women pleaded for second chances and she clasped her ears with both hands, drawing the djed tattoo closer to her face.

In the flickering firelight, the djed tattoo did things no tattoo should do. It became animated, dancing with the heavy metal schizophrenic pace of *Chop Suey*. The four snake fang scars turned into snake fang imaginations, launching themselves at her face, stretching the forearm's epidermis beyond anatomical reason. She tried to grab the elastic illusions with her left hand but the skin fangs sank quickly back into veins.

"That-th creepy. Th-kin fang-th."

The Strykor cubit's folded, wrinkly face hovered over her. Toothpicks were placed between its cheeks and forehead like lean-to poles to keep the skin from folding over its eyes—but, of course, this too could have only been her imagination. Strykor walked away and Manuel took his place. "You're sexy," he mewled. Manuel's face had molted since the last time she remembered seeing it; white splotches pockmarked its entire surface as if a thousand rattlesnakes had planted two thousand fangs into it. "I just hope they leave enough for me." His panting increased as his shoulders turned his broken neck toward a caravan of military vehicles that rolled into the clearing and parked a good distance from her. Blurry men dressed in blurry uniforms carrying blurry guns jumped from the vehicles. "Manuel!" someone screamed, and the smelly cubit left her there to struggle with the heroin's effects.

Music, which had been silent for quite some time, resumed with a Mexican covered version of the Backstreet Boys' *Larger Than Life*. The heavy metal versions of pop were bad enough, but even in her drug induced fantasia, she thought that the vocals that now infiltrated her brain could have easily driven a straight person insane.

Night took control of the party thirty minutes later. At least a hundred people danced around a huge fire to her left and the boy band cover songs kept coming. The effects of the heroin had diminished quite a bit in the short time span and Cooper attributed it to the small quantity she'd been given. Regardless of her recovery, she continued acting stoned. On several occasions, soldiers stood in front of her, yelling Spanish expletives while gyrating too many body parts too close to her face.

To her right, around the sacrificial platform of the cenote, drug deals were in the process of completion. At this distance, she couldn't actually see the money trade hands but the exchange was evident. Large plastic wrapped cubes that twinkled in the firelight went one way and cloth satchels bulging at the seams went the other. Vehicles entered and vehicles left; all tolled, Cooper witnessed the transfer of too many pounds of heroin for too many paramilitary-supporting pesos.

Once most of the deals had been made, she overheard a conversation between a bearded militia man and the Serpent; most of it was in Spanish but she understood the gist of it though the connotation was disturbing. Apparently, the Zetas were ready to start their target practice and the militia man was asking the Serpent how the game was going to be played tonight. *Duck shoot*, is what Cooper had translated and that was the confusing part. Moments later it became evident.

All of the Zetas took up positions near their vehicles. All of them had cash that they tossed in small wads onto the hood of one Jeep; a bet of some kind. To the right, the sacrificial platform remained faintly illuminated by the firelight and was unoccupied. When the Mexican covered version of 'N Sync's *Bye Bye Bye* began, one of the Zetas took a kneeling position and brought his pistol up, clasped in both hands. From the dancing pack around the fire, one man suddenly ran to the right toward the cenote. When he was a few feet from the sacrificial platform, the Zeta soldier fired. The man flinched and fell on top of the platform. The other Zetas howled and took chunks of cash from the hood of the Jeep. Apparently, the kneeling soldier had lost the bet. A second Zeta remained standing and set his scoped rifle against one shoulder. Money flooded the Jeep's hood as another cubit (a woman that Cooper recognized as one that had stumbled down the steps at the Caracol) ran toward the cenote. The moment the cubit stepped on the platform, the Zeta fired his rifle. It lifted the woman off her feet and she disappeared over the far edge. A split second later, a splash resounded and the rifleman turned and snatched the cash from the Jeep's hood.

The game continued but Cooper could no longer watch. She lowered her head but flinched every time a shot was fired. She counted two more splashes before the bearded leader of the Zetas grabbed her chin. He was kneeling in front of her and smiling. Cooper tried to continue her act but the man was wiser.

"Not interested in our game play, chica?" he said. Cooper thought that the man was strangely attractive for a murderer. His hair and beard were well-groomed and his teeth were straight and white. "You don't need to fear me or any of this. I will be taking you with me at the end of the night. You'll be quite comfortable in my mansion on the hill." He gently twisted one of his fingers through one of her red-haired curls. "Fresas. Beautiful." When he released her hair, he waved the hand and another soldier appeared with a syringe. "This will help you enjoy the rest of the night. We'll see you in a couple of hours."

The soldier dumped another hit of heroin into the vein in her arm and her eyes returned to glass just as another shot-splash crashed into her ears.

When they were available, Billy and John followed trails that had been cut through the jungle by some of the local tribes. For the most part, though, they had to chop their way toward the sacred cenote. Billy was getting good at trailblazing and he was obtaining a great education from John about the indigenous plants of the Yucatán. At one point, Billy amazed even John by pointing to a small tree that stood chest high. Small pods that looked like twisted pasta shells hung from several limbs. "This one here provides the mind with the ability to awaken to possibilities outside of experience," he said.

John grinned. "Maybe you should give some to your sponge toy. I'd say the little fella will soon be experiencing some major outside possibilities." Another trail appeared just ahead and John cut a path to it. Together they stood on the trail which was one of the widest so far—about six feet. The faint sound of music trickled through the bush. "You really think it'll work?"

"I may not be a military man but I've watched my share of westerns." Billy patted his chest. "Alixel was able to take out a couple dozen cubits but she had two of these and there were no real live Mexican mobsters to deal with. Even Clint Eastwood knew when to say when."

John's eyebrows perked up. "This ain't no movie western."

"Maybe not. But they got something in common with Marines and survival. You know what it is?"

"SpongeBob." John smirked.

"Come on, John. You need to open up your mind. The answer is staring you right in the face."

"Okay. All right. I get it." John scratched his chin and acted as if he really was giving it some thought. "I give up."

"A distraction. You get the enemy going one way while you plant the bomb, or rob the bank, or break your buddy out of jail."

"Or save the girl."

Billy nodded. "Or save the girl."

"But a toy? How in the hell is a sponge toy going to create a distraction?"

"Well while you were resting back at the motel, I was busy with…"

At that moment, Rally Panini, alias Crabman, emerged from the jungle. "Goddammit you're hard to track down," he grumbled. Even as a cubit, he was still unnaturally red and impossibly skinny. John could have screamed loud enough to knock him over. "How's the bump on the head treating you? Ya'know what happens when you touch the Cubit." He snickered.

"Why don't you stay dead?" Billy said, waving his machete.

Crabman pointed at the back of his scrawny skull. "Kill point. Remember? You gotta get to the kill point." He took a step toward them. "And you gotta have a dagger to do it."

Billy waved his hand in a come-and-get-it motion. "You want the dagger? I'll give you the dagger."

Crabman took another step. He was less than ten feet away. "I overheard you talking about distractions and I gotta tell ya: I agree."

Just then, Bill Tate fell from the tree in which he'd been hiding. His weight had snapped the branch where he'd roosted and he tumbled onto the path, crushing bushes and flattening small plants as his fat body rolled onto the trail. He stood, stumbled once, then said, "Tada! Now hand over the blade." He pulled a small pistol from his pocket and pointed at Billy.

"You won't hurt me," Billy said. "You need me."

"You know. You're right." And Tate turned the gun on John and fired. The caliber of the weapon was small and when it only grazed John's left bicep, he ran remarkably fast to Tate and took his head off with one swipe of the machete. A second gunshot rang out from behind and John spun around while grabbing at his back as if trying to scratch a relentless itch. A blood spot grew from a bullet hole that had entered his shoulder blade just to the left of his spine. Pat Roberts stepped from the bush on the opposite side of the trail as John fell. Smoke trickled from the barrel of his much larger caliber rifle.

"What'cha gonna do, Billy?" Crabman said. "What'cha gonna do when they come for you?"

The cubit's eyes started to glow—crimson red irises with swirling silver pupils—and Billy wondered who was behind them. The master of all Evil was now staring straight at him and Billy took the opportunity to tell him exactly what he thought.

"I know who you are," Billy said. "You're a bumbling fool who likes to play with pirates and little boys. And you're a coward. Why don't you come out of your hidey hole and face me like the Antichrist you are. Do I frighten you that bad?"

"Suffering," Crabman said, his voice now very similar to the Pedro cubit from the Caracol's well. "It's all about suffering. Janine suffered. Joel suffered. Stephanie suffered. Marcy suffered. Cooper and John are suffering. All of your friends, everyone you know has, are, or will suffer. My 'hidey hole' is in your mind and I think I'm playing with it quite fantastically. Look at him. He's dying. Doesn't that frighten you? I'd hope it does considering that, without him, you have absolutely no hope left."

Roberts came up from behind and stuck the barrel of the rifle into Billy's backpack. He shoved hard, forcing Billy to drop his machete and stumble toward Crabman.

Who lives in a Pineapple under the sea?

The sound came from within the backpack. Roberts looked at it, curiously.

SpongeBob SquarePants!

The force applied by the rifle's barrel wavered.

Absorbent and yellow and porous is he.

When he longer felt the barrel pressed against him, Billy spun around, blocked the barrel with his left hand, and punched Roberts in the jaw. The rifle fired and Crabman jerked backward, grabbed his face, and fell onto the trail. Billy never realized how hot the dagger had become as he unsheathed it, flipped it in the air to readjust his grip on its haft, and kicked Roberts who fell to the ground face-first. Billy jammed the seven-inch blade into the back of Roberts head then turned toward Crabman.

"You won't be coming back again," Billy growled as he stood over the writhing cubit, one of its eyes now missing. "Your suffering ends here." One, quick, downward thrust and Rally Panini morphed into bone and ash seconds later.

"Gunshots," John moaned. He kicked dirt while his hand wandered across the hard ground. "They'll be coming." He tried to crawl but his strength was fading as fast as the blood that flowed from the bullet wound. "T-t-t—take cover."

Billy replaced the dagger and ran to John's side. He tried dragging the big man by the arms but lacked the strength.

"Your-s-self," John pleaded. "Not m-me."

"Shhh," Billy said. "You have to protect me, remember? You have to keep your promise." He scooted John's body so that it was parallel with the trail then rolled him into the bush. A sharp embankment helped John's forward rolling momentum as Billy pushed from the side until his body came to rest beside a ceiba tree about twenty feet from the trail. The tree's buttress roots were tall enough to hide them, but moving John's body to the backside of the trunk seemed impossible.

"I need you to help me," Billy urged. "Come on. Push!"

And John did. With what little strength remained, John crawled as Billy pushed and yanked and pulled until they were nestled in between two tall roots.

John's breathing came in rapid pulses. His eyes were closed and Billy wondered if he was even conscious. "We're going to get through this John Brown Gordon. You hang in there with me, you hear?" The front of his shirt was soaked in blood and Billy pressed the palm of his hand against the wound just as three men came walking down the trail toward them. He hunkered over John, hoping that his body would hush John's breaths.

The men spoke Spanish and their vocal inflections told Billy that they were confused about what they'd found on the trail. All three of them chambered their guns. Feet shuffled into the bush on Billy's side of the trail. The rustle of plants stopped no less than five feet from him. "X'Tabay," the man said. "Donde está usted, X'Tabay? Tengo algo para usted."

Where are you X'Tabay? Billy understood that much. And then the man fired his gun into the tree, sending chips of wood down on Billy's hunkered head. Another voice yelled at the gunman and he responded, again to the tree, by yelling "Vete al infierno!" then he fired two more times and shuffled away.

It took a full ten minutes before Billy felt it was safe enough to curl up from John's body. John's rapid breaths had transformed into wisps of inhalation so shallow and weak, Billy feared it was too late.

"John," he whispered. "John." He lightly slapped both of his cheeks and lifted one eyelid though he did so more because he'd seen doctors do it and less because he really knew what a rolled eye in the socket really meant. After checking his pulse at the throat, Billy knew he had to act immediately.

He stretched John out at the base of the tree and flipped him over. The entry wound had produced much more blood than the exit wound. He drew the dagger out and, for no reason whatsoever, kissed the star in its haft, gazed up at the ceiba tree's canopy, and looked for hope, looked for a giant hawk. He stuck the dagger's blade gently into the hole and the single fifth red point in the star immediately grew bright. John jerked and Billy almost thrust the point too quickly at an angle which could have severed the heart. Not wanting to take the same chance again, he inhaled deeply then buried the dagger in one swift motion, all seven inches of it. The dagger grew so bright and so hot so quickly that it literally blew Billy off of John's body, knocking him back into the ceiba tree roots where he fell onto his butt. Billy looked back toward the trail and throughout the jungle. He thought that the gray clouds overhead coupled with the waning sunlight would have made the blazing spectacle that encircled John's body easily visible for at least a mile. But no one came and Billy just sat there, watching, as the blade did its thing, reworking and restructuring and re-stitching human flesh while slowly rising, inch by inch, out of John's back. The point tottered on his shoulder blade for an impossible second, the entire dagger erect and defying all physical laws, before its light blinked out and it tottered off of John's body to the ground.

"Am I in heaven?" John said while slowly rolling onto his side and blinking. "Ah shit…Ain't no way in hell."

It was very garbled with intermittent static but Cooper swore she heard SpongeBob. The soldier had filled her with twice the heroin she'd experienced the first time around so the voice, she believed, had to be imaginary. But voices and visions were two different things altogether. Not only was she hearing the damn thing, she was seeing it, too. SpongeBob stood just inches from her left leg and looked at her. She tried to swat it away with her knee but it backed up on its eight metal legs, which really freaked her out.

"If nautical nonsense be something ye wish," the eight-legged SpongeBob said.

She blinked and tapped her ear against one shoulder. It didn't even sound like the SpongeBob captain…it sounded like Billy.

"SpongeBob SquarePants!"

"What the fuck is that?" It was Lafitte and he was standing halfway between the assembled Los Zetas and Cooper. The modified SpongeBob toy scuttled away into the dark bush, repeating its name in Billy's voice as if stuck in a loop.

SpongeBob SquarePants... SpongeBob SquarePants... SpongeBob SquarePants

"Hey! Come back here." Lafitte turned from the toy and yelled at the good-looking murderer with the trimmed beard and white teeth. "Captain Teigas. Surveillance!"

SpongeBob SquarePants... SpongeBob SquarePants... SpongeBob SquarePants

"Atención!" the paramilitary captain yelled. "Federales!" He pointed where Billy's voice reverberated relentlessly.

SpongeBob SquarePants... SpongeBob SquarePants... SpongeBob SquarePants

Lafitte grabbed the captain's arm and the captain looked at the hand as if he'd just desecrated a priceless object, but when he looked up and into Lafitte's glowing eyes his expression immediately changed. "It's not the government," Lafitte said in a voice that was not his own. "It's that fuckin' kid. Remember, don't kill him."

"We won't, mi jefe," the captain said, looking away.

"Your life in the jungle will never be the same if he dies," Lafitte warned.

Captain Teigas ran with his scrambling platoon, yelling orders not to kill the intruder and guaranteeing every one of them what horrible consequences awaited for disobeying.

Several dozen ravers remained around the fire, dancing hypnotically in complete oblivion of what was taking place around them. Gunfire and screams of aggression went unnoticed. Cooper watched Lafitte join the dancers, his ponytail flip of blonde-white hair whipping back and forth as he maintained a pretty good hip-twisting rhythm to the boy band beats.

And then a hand grabbed her from behind which almost caused her to swallow her tongue as she gasped. She turned to see a familiar black face. She really didn't think the face was real so she just smiled and slurred, "Why, he-wo b-yout-ful. Ya come ta join ma rave?" The whites of John's eyes became tracers that twisted and swirled.

"Be still," he said. "We've come to rescue you."

"Why? Am havin' such good times." She giggled. "Did yooo see Spund boob?"

"Hush," John repeated.

"Spider Spund boob," she giggled again.

Gunfire and commands were moving closer. John stepped around the ceiba root and cradled Cooper in his arms. She kissed his cheek and said something that was meant to express her appreciation but it didn't come out that way. She giggled once more and slapped the bicep that Bill Tate had grazed with his .22 caliber pea-shooter. John grimaced and whispered, "Please, Coop. Hush."

"Why you big black chaco-, choca-, shocolate thing you."

John ran with her into the bush unnoticed by everyone except Evan who had been standing and watching the entire rescue from within the cenote's sacrificial platform shadows. He kicked one bullet-riddled cubit into the cenote water and smiled as John disappeared with the bait that Evan had let off the hook.

Billy sat in a thick mangrove tree as the soldiers ran under and away from him. His face and arms were painted with mud, something John had added as camouflage, which made his fingers' manipulation of the tiny joystick slippery whenever sweat rolled a dirty wash down his wrist and into his palm. The tree had been chosen for its angle to where Cooper sat, but it was not a good roost for determining his robot's whereabouts once it ran from the clearing. He had mind-mapped a path for the robot he called SpongeMod, and felt comfortable that the range of his wireless joystick would be efficient enough to provide John the time he needed. He had not anticipated the audio recording malfunction and was happy when SpongeMod finally shut up.

Strykor had indeed scavenged his computer equipment, and Billy had been able use the parts to modify Stephanie Drake's SpongeBob toy with an ability to create a diversion. The hardest part had been the legs. Bipedal motion would not have worked. Fortunately, Billy had been working on a new spider-like robot while back in Port Aransas. The parts for that creation, he'd found in the floorboard compartment of the VW Bus. Once the leg mobility problem had been solved, everything else was pretty straightforward. SpongeMod was one creepy looking robot, John had told him. Billy had agreed. It would certainly accomplish its mission as a diversion.

Billy thumbed the controller and looked to where he thought SpongeMod should be. There! At the edge of the clearing. He pressed the red button and the robot started rambling again, repeating its name in Billy's recorded voice.

SpongeBob SquarePants... SpongeBob SquarePants... SpongeBob SquarePants

Billy walked the robot to the center of the clearing near one of the military Jeeps, then snatched his backpack from a tree limb and dropped the controller inside. John appeared under him, Cooper cradled in his arms seemingly unconscious. "Let's get," he whispered.

"Getty yap," Cooper moaned, but not loudly. "Yee-haw."

Billy dropped from the tree and the three escapees ran off into the jungle.

Evan heard the giggles recede into the shadows as Captain Teigas and his men surrounded the annoying toy.

SpongeBob SquarePants... SpongeBob SquarePants... SpongeBob SquarePants

Lafitte entered the small circle and screamed, "GODDAMMIT!" Then his foot came down and crushed SpongeMod. He punched the captain then left the circle to rage internally elsewhere. Captain Teigas drew his .44 Magnum, pointed it at the back of Lafitte's head, then turned it down toward the toy that still would not shut up. He emptied all cylinders into it.

Evan sat and laughed. He was beginning to understand how patience and manipulation were, in fact, quite exhilarating, almost as much as dropping from the sky at a hundred and twenty miles an hour.

He still had a week. While Lafitte continued to try and satisfy his own selfish goals, all Evan had to do was wait.

THE DJED: PART III

LA CALMA QUE PRECEDE A LA TORMENTA

(SATURDAY MORNING, ONE WEEK LATER)

Billy had been sitting on the vacant Puerto Morelos beach and staring at the ocean for the past two hours, smelling, tasting, listening, thinking. It was like being back in Port Aransas…almost. He'd risen before the sun, he'd walked down to the beach, he'd found himself the perfect seat in the sand, and his mind had been taken away. The wind that blew his hair into comfortable disarray was unlike Port A's in that it had no sea smell to it. He'd run his toes and fingers a dozen times through sand that was white and not Port A brown. He'd sat just beyond the high tide's farthest reach and had relished the cool aqua-white water that looked so much more inviting than the green Gulf. Birds were different, too, as were the creatures that ran through the soupy froth looking for early daybreak snacks.

He wiped sandy fingers on his T-shirt that was silkscreened with the words Pat MaGee's across the chest. He'd found it under the driver's seat of his VW Bus a few days ago and hadn't even questioned why it was there. Really, none of the whys even mattered anymore. It was easier to accept what was offered and appreciate each gift. They had so little time left. Tomorrow was the winter solstice.

Like the calm before the storm, the past six days had been full of wonderful serenity, particularly since none of them had spent the time worrying about a future they couldn't control. Billy had seen it in both of his comrades. Cooper tended to make funny faces in response to lighthearted comments and had, on occasion, spontaneously danced outside local restaurants that broadcast live or recorded Mexican music. She'd stick out her tongue and give just about anyone the raspberry for no other reason than to draw laughter from those on the receiving end, especially children. She'd even done her hair differently, having set it in a more greased-back version of something right off a retro Annie Lennox *Sweet Dreams* album cover.

John, too, had transformed during the days they'd been in Puerto. He smiled a lot more and Billy swore that he'd lost a few pounds, though on a frame like his, it was not evident to those beyond friends. The wound near his heart and the one in his bicep had healed completely and there wasn't a day that went by that he did not thank Billy for saving his life.

John had also treated all of them to the wonders of the sea. Though they had not known it then, he had been preparing them. Over the first three days in Puerto Morelos, he'd taken them offshore to some of the best dive spots he'd visited in the past. They'd marveled at the barrier reef, a sunken ship, and an underwater cave which they had entered only once and for only a short time. They'd not become professional divers in that short time frame but they'd learned enough—at least John had said they'd learned enough to get them to the third location denoted in the Book of the Djed: a cenote they'd finally visited last Wednesday.

A local friend of John's, Sebastian Bondager, had driven them to the cenote which was located just off the coastal highway about halfway between Puerto Morelos and Tulum. As a half Latino and half Scottish retired divemaster, Sebastian knew just about every place there was to take a tank of compressed air throughout the Riviera. If there was a point of interest and it was under water, Sebastian knew how best to get there, what dangers to avoid, and what features were most notable. But as far as the third location was concerned, Sebastian had never heard of it. The cenote they'd visited didn't even have a name, at least none that was publicly popular.

The morning sun was now a good ten degrees above the horizon. Local weather reports had forecast a couple of beautiful days ahead and Billy was going to take advantage of every last ounce on this final Saturday. He looked around for a seashell to toss back into the water but there were none. The barrier reef two hundred yards offshore effectively limited such surfside collectibles. The reef was also the reason why there was no sea smell. According to Sebastian Bondager, the reef blocked the passage of algae and, therefore, few feeding fish could be found between the barrier and the shore. According to Sebastian Bondager, Puerto Morelos was special in many ways and he'd told them as much as he'd driven them to the remote cenote.

Cooper had been sitting in the back seat of the smoky Chrysler Caravan and had been quietly talking with John about the revelation he'd laid on her that morning concerning the man she'd known as the Serpent.

"How can anyone live for two hundred years?" she'd asked him.

"We both know someone who lived much longer," John had reminded her.

"But the Serpent—Lafitte? Surely someone would have busted his cover in that amount of time."

Sebastian, whom they had only met that morning, had become interested. "Jean Lafitte?" he'd questioned in a peculiar accent that merged Scotland with Central America. "Of course he lives. Mu'bä never die. They attach themselves to a place and never seem to leave."

Billy, who had sat in the passenger seat, asked, "So you've seen it… um, him?"

"Many times, but more recently just yesterday. Ain't never seen a Mu'bä drive before but by God that's what he was doin'."

"In Puerto Morelos?"

"No. Over in Playa del Carmen." Sebastian had huffed then, shaking a head of old skin that was sun baked and crackly. "You'd think a ghost would be ridin' a motorcycle or something but not this one. Drivin' a damn Chevy."

"Cavalier?" Billy had asked.

"Yep. How'd ya know?"

"What color was it?"

"Why the hell should that matter?"

"Just curious."

"White, it was. And he had passengers. A Mu'bä driving a damned Chevy with passengers. And I thought I'd seen it all."

It had been confirmation and hadn't surprised any of them. All of the players were where they should be. Billy needed the Book and the key. Lafitte needed Billy and the dagger. Tulum was the setting and Sunday was the date prescribed.

The cenote had been located near a highway rest area. Such rest areas in Mexico were unique (at least along the stretch of road that connected Cancun and Tulum) in that they not only provided a place to use the bathroom, but, at many, you could also take a quick dip in a nearby cenote. Sebastian had parked at one of these rest areas but the cenote they were headed for was not the one populated by weary travelers. They took their scuba gear with them in a different direction, led by John, through pleasant-looking plants that towered and flowered all around them. About a half a mile from the highway they came across a big hole in the ground. It was only ten feet wide and the only reason Billy knew it was there was because of the thick rope that dropped into it.

"There's a limestone shelf below where we can assemble before the dive, but we'll have to gear up here," John told them.

"How do you know about this?" Sebastian asked.

"Don't you really want to know how *you don't know* about it?" John replied, smiling. "It isn't the case that you can't teach old dogs new tricks, eh?"

Once they assembled below ground, Billy was greeted by some of the most beautiful water he'd ever seen. Somehow, it was illuminated from below, casting a sapphire glow against dark cavern walls. When he slid into the water, he felt as if he were standing somewhere man was never supposed to stand—either that or he was in a place granted to only those few humans who had passed the test, who'd gotten it right, who'd deserved such otherworldly payback for well done deeds. It was as if God's hand was wrapped around a blue sapphire and he was about to dive into its depths, to find what lay at the center of life.

John submerged first and Cooper followed him. Billy and Sebastian took up the rear. Parts of the journey through the underground caves necessitated their flashlights. Other areas were faintly lit from above. At one point, Billy swore he could see the tiny feet of several bathers as they waded far above him.

Stalactites and stalagmites were everywhere. Coral stuck to some of them and Billy took extra care not to disturb them. Fish and other aquatic life were sparse but he identified at least one catfish which surprised him. Cooper pointed at it, then chased it like a curious child for a few seconds until it zipped out of range.

They were in the water for almost thirty minutes before John's flippers started to ascend. Billy broke the water's surface moments later and was surprised to find two other people already in the chamber that housed another Cubit throne pedestal. The smell of pot was strong though neither young male diver revealed its source.

"You guys scared the crap out of us," the teen with bald head and flimsy mustache said.

"You're trespassing," John told them. "This cenote is governed by the federals."

"No way," the second teen with a crappy short haircut said.

"Way," John said. "Historically preserved and banned from all that don't have permission."

"Says who?" baldy said.

Billy spoke up then. "The penalty is death."

That, and John's massive size, had been enough to take the young divers' paranoia over the edge. "Sorry man," crappy haircut said. "We won't tell nobody." They were in the water so fast, they forgot to re-seal their bag of dope and it scattered into the ripples as their heads submerged.

The chamber, like that under the Caracol, was domed but the apex was only a few feet higher than John was tall. Unlike the well under the Caracol, there were no etchings on the walls, no jaguar statues, no Cubit. It was a dark and dank place that was filled only with chunks of ceiling that had fallen over time, the Cubit throne and the surrounding water.

"Not so glamorous as the places we've already visited," Cooper said. "If I was going to hide the Cubit, this would be it." Sebastian looked at her curiously, but didn't say anything.

The pedestal was a clone of the one at Chichen Itza. A star was centered at its top edge. Two three-dimensional glyphs of Creation Daggers were etched at an angle below the star, their points touching in the middle of the pedestal's face. Below the points was the hollowed home of a Djed amulet now raised.

"Alixel got hers in the well," John said, pointing at the vacant Djed outline. "Alax got his here, in the cenote."

The journey to the third Wayeb Chamber in the cenote had been quite spectacular. Standing in the blue sapphire under the earth then diving into it had made the trip worthwhile. Even the looks on the faces of the pot-smoking teens would have been worth an admission. But the Cubit throne and the etchings on it and the domed room and the feeling that Evil was all around them really wasn't special anymore. He'd been there and done that two times already. He knew the routine. It had been a different story for Sebastian who thought he'd seen and done everything there was to do along the Mexican Riviera, but for John, Cooper and himself, nothing had been added nor subtracted from the mystery of the Djed, the Cubit and the end of time.

On Thursday, Billy had gone off by himself to do some sketching. He'd chosen three locations in the town to do this. One was on the beach where he now sat. Another was at a metal table under a metal umbrella just up the shoreline near a pier where numerous snorkeling and dive boats moored themselves between excursions to the reef and points beyond. The third location was in the town's center square, just a block or so from the pier. This had been his favorite place to sit and think, and to scribble into his notebook everything about the Book of the Djed that he could remember. He'd spent the entire day doing this and most of the second half of his notebook was filled with such memories. Though he wasn't particularly good at it, doodling was a way to get the creative juices flowing. Doodling was an exercise in memory recall. Doodling, he thought, just might reveal someone, some thing, some clue, or some direction in which he should proceed that he had not yet thought of. What the hell was going to happen Sunday? What was it that he was supposed to do? "Why" may have been relegated to uselessness (he knew why he was going to Tulum) but "How" (in this case, raise the Djed) certainly remained an important mystery that could not be ignored.

The hardest parts of the Book to remember where those that Alixel had shown him on the night of Hurricane Antiago; he'd never been able to look back upon these pages since he'd only been able to open the Book to its center spread. While sitting on the beach Thursday, he'd scribbled into his notebook the random images of the Story of the Fifth Age, starting with the Creation of Good and Evil. On one notebook page he'd drawn a miserable replica of the Arc of the Covenant. On the opposite page he'd drawn a much better rendition of the Cubit. Under the metal umbrella by the pier he'd logged what he remembered about the Creation of Man, drawing scattered images of quirky masks and stick figures hanging from stick trees. Sketches of massacred pieces of human body parts inundated an entire page in his notebook and he was uncertain if these memories were from the pages that Alixel had shown him or were more so from his actual accounts of the glyphs he'd seen written on the entrance to and on the walls of the Great Hall of the Anasazi. He'd then relocated to the town's square to finish his doodling exercise that covered the Creation of Religion, the Book's center page spread, the key, and the page noting the four locations. While sitting on an unnaturally green patch of grass, he'd taken greater effort to draw much more stylized renditions of Adam and Eve and snakes and the proverbial tree of knowledge, which, in his notebook, looked a lot like a thick-trunked, buttress-rooted ceiba tree.

Before finishing his doodling exercise, he'd decided to take a brain break and eat a late afternoon lunch at one of the numerous restaurants that surrounded the town square. Le Café D'Amancia was a small, open-air coffee shop that had become his favorite in the short time he'd been in Puerto. The fare was tasty and inexpensive and was served by a friendly family that offered salutations to every customer regardless of creed or color. The family's dog even added to the shop's uplifting atmosphere as it often lay sprawled across the floor in front of the counter, offering a reticent grin as customers happily avoided its tail and legs.

Sitting at one of the shop's small tables with a fresh cup of Oaxaca-grown black coffee in one hand and a mechanical pencil in the other, he'd begun sketching out the remaining pieces of the Book of the Djed. The bird of fire he meticulously scratched in lead, its streams of flames quite elegant for a hand not given much credit for its knack at artistic improvisation. But it was the sixes and nines that had kept him seated inside the coffee shop for more than an hour. He'd kept tracing them over and over again until he'd finished his fifth cup of coffee, carving such deep impressions into the paper until, at one point, it had finally torn.

The recreation of the key page was the easiest to render. It had contained only two glyphs: a Wayeb mask and a thumbnail version of a Creation Dagger, both set at the top of the paper, and both of which he'd encountered numerous times since Port Aransas.

Jazzed on an extreme influx of caffeine, he'd returned to the town square patch of grass to finish his writing exercise: the recreation of the four locations, each taking the space of one corner of the notebook page that immediately followed the key. These sketches, except for the last, he'd recreated directly from experience. The fourth location, he had recreated from the previous drawing that he'd shown John.

Once he'd finished, he'd sat there, flipping back and forth through his notebook, absorbing the images, adding a flick of the pencil here and erasing any extraneous parts that didn't make sense. But it was the sixes and nines that continued to attract him the most. Perhaps, he'd thought, his incessant attention to the center page was based on the same obsession that had consumed Cooper: the idea that these images had been drawn by the hand of God coupled by the curiosity of what would be entered next. These were clues, signposts, warnings. The bird of fire certainly alluded to the antithetical idea of birth and death. But it also encapsulated an ancillary meaning, one which he and Cooper had believed identified Phoenix International as serving some importance. The sixes and nines, too, were antithetical if for no other reason than one was the mirror image of the other. But what ancillary meaning did they serve? What was it about them that he wasn't getting? Was it as simple as Antichrist versus Savior? Did the Bible have anything to do with it? Did Mayan history have anything to do with it?

And his thoughts had centered on that one idea: Mayan history…Mayan chronology…The Fifth Age. Did sixes and nines have anything at all to do with the Mayan calendar? If so, the ramifications of such coincidental (not an amiable word for him anymore) occurrence both in pre-classic Mayan culture and that of Christianity would be incredible.

The first tourists of the day finally showed up on the beach and yanked Billy from his thoughts. The young couple quickly ran into and out of the surf, screaming because of the water's chill. They walked past him and waved, and

Billy returned the greeting. The index finger on his right hand was moist and sandy and, again, he wiped it across his Pat Magee's T-shirt. As he watched the couple saunter up the waterline, he noticed that he'd absently written three sixes and three nines into the sand.

Cooper saw Billy on the beach thirty minutes before she decided to go down and sit with him. He acted just about the way she had felt all doped up on heroin back at the sacrificial cenote. He stared at nothing and everything, the morning breeze pushing sand in his face, a stray spoonbill hoping around his legs, plucking the ground with its long beak. He was writing something in the sand but not looking at it, as if in a trance. She knew exactly how he must be feeling: lost, separated, distant, consumed by every feeling associated with every person who'd known the battle was coming but was uncertain of its outcome.

His spell broke when the couple wearing the matching purple swimsuits showed up. He didn't notice that she was standing right behind him and gasped when she spoke. "Billy…sorry. Didn't mean to startle you." She saw the sixes and nines in the sand but didn't say anything. "What'cha thinkin' so hard about?"

He patted the sand to his left and she sat there. "Oh, nothing and everything."

"Anything to do with numbers and a Book?"

He looked hard into her eyes; the intensity of the stare reminded her of Nexpa, of their three days of escape from madness. "Perhaps. What have you been up to?"

"Pretty much the same as you, I suppose. Soaking it all in. Enjoying the beauty of the world. Enjoying this little patch of paradise." She dipped her toes in the sand. "I can see how Tony dumped his entire life for one in Puerto Morelos."

"Tony?" Billy turned his attention back toward the ocean. Cooper thought that she'd seen a tinge of jealousy in his reaction.

"A California businessman I met near the pier yesterday. He and his *wife*…" she purposefully added a little bit of emphasis on that word and Billy smiled without looking at her. "…they left great jobs, a great home, just about everything they knew, and moved here about a month ago. He's starting up a small bakery just north of the square."

Billy gently grabbed her wrist, massaged the multiple scars from snakes bites and needles. "We'll have to visit him once he gets it up and going." His expression attempted reassurance and she was thankful for that even though they both knew the truth. "You ready for a walk? We've got about an hour before John and Sebastian meet us by the old lighthouse."

She didn't say yes; she simply stood without releasing his hand. They brushed sand from clothing they'd purchased in town and Billy kicked sand from his blue Keds which, last Thursday, he'd proclaimed was the best find any westerner could have made in the Riviera. He led her to the water's edge and they began walking.

"Could you live here?" Cooper asked. "I mean, there's not much to do."

"I know where you're coming from but I think a wily person could find plenty if they wanted to. Our scuba expeditions are proof of that. Besides, I think what makes this place so alluring to people like Tony and his wife is the very idea that you don't *have* to do anything. As long as you can feed yourself, the rest lies in the hands of God's good graces."

"God?"

"Yeah," he smiled. "The Great Spirit. The Holy One. Zeus. Whatever you want to call it. Whatever it is that ensures that such complex creatures on a complex planet don't completely destroy each other."

Cooper stopped and stood and yanked his hand, pulling his attention to her. Her new hairstyle did not move with the wind nearly as much as Billy's dirty blonde waves did. "Are we going to die?" she asked.

Again, his intense stare sent Nexpa-like chills into her very soul. "On the eve of immortality?" he said. "Let's hope the Great Spirit does not know the term irony." They started walking again. "Truthfully, I don't think anyone can be sure. We'll try to avoid any obvious mistakes. That's why we're heading out to sea today. We can't expect the cubits to think of everything, especially an incursion by sea. It's a good plan. It should give us the early advantage."

"You know they aren't all cubits. There was one named Evan and he's definitely among the living. I think he let me escape."

This time Billy stopped and stood and squeezed her hand. "Let you? How?"

"He was standing over by the platform among all of those bodies." She coughed. "He was standing there while Lafitte and all of the soldiers went chasing after your robot. And when John freed me, he didn't say a word."

"And you think that's odd?"

"Don't you? I mean, the only reason I was there was to lure you in."

"And you did. Sounds to me like he's got different priorities."

"He told me that Lafitte was his boss."

"But you said he let you go. Maybe his real boss is someone else."

Cooper must have looked as confused as she felt.

"Look," Billy said, his voice even and soothing. "We can't waste energy asking ourselves 'why.' I think it's logical to assume by his action that Evan doesn't work for Lafitte. Why he would pretend to and why he would let you go is irrelevant, in my opinion. I do suspect we'll see more of him, though. I suspect he'll be at the Castillo vying for the Djed and the dagger and not for the purpose of helping Lafitte. He either wants them for himself and his own immortality or he is doing the bidding of his real boss."

"Real boss?"

"Phoenix International." They started walking again and Billy explained his hunch based on the Book's center spread. "The bird of fire is symbolic for the corporation; I think that assumption is correct. But I also think the bird of fire is a warning. I think it is a clue. The mythological bird lives in cycles; it dies and is reborn within a fiery blaze. Life from death. The alpha from the omega."

"And the sixes and nines? Does the phoenix have something to do with that?" More people started to appear on the beach the closer they came to the pier. They stepped over thick ropes that tied small fishing boats to metal anchors in the sand.

Billy continued. "That whole center page, once it is completely written, is going to present us with a story that is reliant on each clue but, at the same time, each clue will be a story unto itself, each also having multiple meanings that warn and reveal and exemplify. Stories within stories. Innuendo on top of innuendo."

The pier was growing quite busy as early morning snorkelers assembled beside their assigned boats. Billy led her up the beach, past the twenty-five-foot-tall vacant lighthouse that sat at an angle as an icon for the town. He shuffled through confused vacationers, leading Cooper by the hand through the melee until they found a small green patch of grass in the center of the town square.

"Still think you'd want to live here with Tony?" Billy asked while squatting.

Cooper nodded. "Just got to time your daily activities, I guess."

"Yes, well, about the numbers."

Cooper raised her hand. "Wait. Let me take a stab at this. The sixes represent Evil, a.k.a. Phoenix International. The nines represent Good, a.k.a. Billy and Cooper and company."

"Maybe. But the mere fact that they are turned upside down is symbolic imagery denoting extreme ends like the phoenix is symbolic for life and death."

She could see it in his eyes. "But that's not all, is it?"

"No. At least I don't think it is. I keep going back to the reality that so much of all of this revolves around the Mayan end date. Therefore, the symbols must also incorporate Mayan culture or history or something."

"Sixes are from the Bible."

"Well, maybe when John wrote Revelation, he was reading them upside down."

Cooper's eyes popped wide then. "You really are grabbing at straws now, aren't you?"

"Am I? Really?"

"What you're saying is that the Maya and the Christians had something in common before the Christians ever came to the Americas."

"Yes."

"That's cra…"

"Crazy? I used to think so, too. Now I don't ask why and it makes believing so much easier."

"So, how are sixes and nines interrelated?"

"That is the sixty-four million dollar question and one I can't yet answer. But if we survive this thing tomorrow, I'll be bound and determined to figure it out, starting with what is really at the heart of this entire drama: the Mayan's calendar which has given us December 21, 2012, as the end of days."

A voice interrupted from behind. "Anyone mention end of days?" John stood in the middle of the sunshine, casting a giant shadow over both of them. "Might as well get it on. Sebastian's got the boat hummin' and waitin'. Shall we?"

They weren't going to let rest and relaxation slip away too soon. Sebastian had planned an afternoon filled with fishing and scuba diving before they would head south toward their rendezvous with destiny.

His boat, a restored thirty-five foot Sea Ray, had an upper captain's deck and a lower bedroom cabin that was loaded with everything life at sea could need, including two beds, a toilet, and a small kitchen nook he'd built that contained a gas grill, a small sink and counter, and a short refrigerator. He'd spent quite a penny on the boat ten years ago after selling his "dirt" home for the one at sea and he hadn't regretted it for a second. He'd said that living at sea was like being reborn and he was determined to prove it to Billy and his friends before Sunday morning.

They spent an hour diving about a half a mile out, exhausting one complete set of tanks to explore the waters at a safe depth of about forty feet. Billy was amazed at the sights and sounds of underwater life. He'd spent so much time atop the water, always attempting to stay one step ahead of the surf's need to dunk him under, that he'd never really given the life below his board and feet much thought. The multitude of colors was beyond amazing. And he could hear them. As strange as the experience felt, he really believed that the schools of tropical fish were trying to communicate. Perhaps it was only his imagination; after all, everyone wished they had a little Dr. Doolittle in them.

But that fantasy was enlivened when the bottlenose dolphin showed up. Cooper would later tell him how absolutely awestruck she was with the mammal's antics and incessant devotion toward garnering Billy's attention. It was as if the dolphin had been his long lost friend, only now finding him after so many years apart. It talked to him. It hugged him. It kissed him. If dolphins could love, then this one loved Billy. What really screwed with him, though, were the emotional feelings he shared with the dolphin—human emotions that made him think of Stephanie Drake. And he would forever swear (but keep it to himself) that the dolphin, indeed, *was* Stephanie Drake in every way that Osi, the giant hawk, had become Alax.

Nothing ever dies, Alax had said. *We exist in this flesh to complete cycles that have no beginning and no end*. Billy had thought at the time that Alax had been referring strictly to human flesh. He now understood better.

The encounter with the dolphin pretty much destroyed Billy's and Cooper's desire to fish for the rest of the day. Sebastian and John understood their sudden intimate relationship with the sea, but they argued that they still had to eat. Certainly, God would never reincarnate man into the body of a yellowfin tuna, Sebastian suggested. To turn man into something man ate? He wasn't buying it. But Billy wondered. The Great Spirit often delivered lessons in forms not easily understood.

John and Sebastian fished while the boat slowly sailed south toward Tulum. When dusk took control of the colored shadows that twinkled off of the water's surface, Sebastian dropped the sails and anchor while John cleaned their catch. Once the tuna steaks were cooked and sizzling on the gas grill, the four of them sat on the long foredeck and ate. Billy and Cooper had opted out on the fish though its spicy aroma was certainly tantalizing. Cheese, bread, a helping of fried potatoes and several pieces of fruit were good enough for them. In fact, Billy wondered if he'd ever eat seafood again and how such a change in attitude would affect his ownership of the Surf Side Restaurant once, and if, he returned to Port Aransas.

The shoreline abutting the Tulum ruins remained a good distance from their anchor point; still, El Castillo's unique shape and height was discernible in the waning sunlight, especially since tourism had demanded that spotlights be placed around its base. The half moon sat directly above the pyramid and the Big Dipper was circling around from the north.

"Just like it was when Stephens and Catherwood discovered it in 1843," Sebastian said. "Just like it was when Samaal fled from it." All three of them turned to him in unison. Sebastian grinned, knowing he had their complete attention. "Ah. I see you like stories. Very good."

"Samaal," Billy said. "What do you know of Samaal?"

"Just an old myth, really; one that includes a vicious tyrant."

"Even better," John's deep voice added with an air of menace. "And appropriate." He nodded toward the shore.

Sebastian flung his legs over the deck where they dangled as an invitation for the rest of them to do the same. Billy and Cooper did so but John remained where he was, leaning on his side with an elbow propping him up.

"Story goes that Samaal was a great leader of the Maya in Chichen Itza. Now, scholars'll tell ya that the kind of culture that ran things in that big city had no single leaders, but they be wrong. Samaal was one of 'em and he ruled with an iron fist. Ballgames were won and lost on his behalf. Hundreds lost their heads."

Billy interrupted. "Are you sure about your story?"

Sebastian looked sternly at him. "You heard different?"

It wasn't the time for argument, Billy thought. Besides, how could you argue against myth? He'd already learned that lesson. "No. Sorry. Go ahead."

"Yeah…well, you see, this Samaal was beginning to piss a lot of people off. Tyrants can't maintain control forever. I think we can all agree with that." Cooper shrugged so that only Billy could see; her eyebrows curled with an expression of what-the-hell-is-he-talking-about. "There was an uprising and they threw Samaal out of the city—sent him packing as it were.

"But Samaal wasn't the type to just accept defeat; he was too power–hungry. Besides, he still had a lot of followers, military types and such. So he did what every good tyrant does: he relocated. He wanted revenge and he was determined to get it. He created this city by the sea, built up the walls to prevent attacks, and trained a new army. But none of that mattered. Sometime in the thirteenth century the neighboring cities came together and forced Samaal and his followers into the sea. In their retreat, they sailed from the Castillo right across this very spot. Unfortunately, Samaal's concentration on land battles had caused him to ignore the rules of the sea. Poorly built boats took on water and sunk right here, right below us. Legend has it, his ghost and that of his crew returns to Tulum every winter solstice, which of course, is tomorrow morning."

"You're so full of shit," John said, sitting up. "Now you know very well that ain't the right story. Why do you go and carry on so?"

"Better story than believing some damn box made Mu'bä out of everyone and Samaal was some hero who built the Tulum walls to ward off zombies."

Billy looked into the dark water knowing but not knowing how he knew. "It was the final battle for the possession of the Cubit," he said. "Samaal was trying to protect it; he was trying to keep it out of human hands. And he must have fled from Tulum using the sea as an escape."

"Cubit?" Sebastian said. "That what you guys were looking for in the underwater cave?" He took their silence as confirmation. "Ain't no such thing."

"So you've heard of it?" Cooper asked.

It was Sebastian's turn to remain silent.

Billy said, "That's okay. You don't have to believe."

"Tell them a different story," John suggested. "One that's true. One that will help them survive. Tell them what you know of Jean Lafitte." John moved over to the edge of the boat next to Sebastian, swung his legs over the water, and gave his friend a big squashing grip on the left shoulder. "Sebastian was just a little kid in these parts when the Nazis came looking for Lafitte and his treasure. You're interested in the oral tradition aren't you Billy?"

"Yes. Very." Billy understood what John inferred. As a future Daykeeper, Billy would be spending a lot of time listening to first-hand accounts of historical experiences. "Go ahead."

He was hard to follow at times, particularly since the farther back in time (and memory) Sebastian went, the more Scottish his accent became. It was almost as if he was reverting back to his childhood days. He cried and cursed and yelled out loud, which made all of them cringe since the scream was loud enough to have been heard onshore. He explained.

Obsessed with antiquities, the Nazis arrived in Puerto Morelos in 1939, looking for the legend of Lafitte's treasure. What they hadn't expected to find was Lafitte, himself. This discovery, of course, put a whole new spin on their collective curiosity and, like Nazis were prone to do back then, they started accusing the local fishing community of hiding the immortal and his secrets from them. They'd decided to make an example out of the uncooperative natives; the first victim had been Sebastian's mother.

Sebastian recounted in child-like detail, what he remembered of that day. He'd only been five at the time so the horror of the event had rooted so harshly that his only memories of his mother were those that included her being whipped while swinging from a chechen negro tree, the black sap oozing down her lashed and opened skin, blistering it further, making it bubble; he recounted how he'd knelt in front of her, praying for his father's return from the sea; he remembered his mother's glistening eyes, staring vacantly at nothing when, finally, her body had given up the fight.

They'd never captured Lafitte in Puerto Morelos, he explained, but instead, had chased him from the Yucatán, through the Gulf and all the way to Texas. Soon afterward, Germany had invaded Poland, starting the Second World War.

When Sebastian finished, Billy said, "You do know that they must have taken the Cubit."

Sebastian just stared at the water.

"I'm sorry for your pain," Billy continued. "If it's any account, the Cubit has been recovered. What we're here to do tonight is make sure it never gets into the hands of such Evil again."

"What if I had actually done it?" Sebastian whispered. He looked at Billy, the boat's running light adding a green hue to the left side of his face, his eyes saddened and deeply hollow from almost eight decades of pent up sorrow. "While I knelt there watchin' my mother slowly die, I held my father's dagger secretly in my hand. I was gonna end her suffering. But that SS Nazi bastard had gotten in the way. He'd stooped down and had looked me right in the eyes and I could see the horrible man that he really was. All I had to do was thrust quickly forward and the magic of the dagger would have ended the war before it ever started. If I had only killed him, he'd of never followed Lafitte and would have never returned to Germany with the Cubit. If only…"

"You can't change the past," Billy offered, patting Sebastian's trembling hand. "And you can't blame yourself for the future. What is…is. All we can do is go forward." Billy's next action was his immediate response to intuition. He reached up and under his T-shirt, drew the Creation of the End dagger from its sheath, and held it tightly so that it would not fall into the water. "Is this it?" he asked Sebastian. "Is this the dagger?"

Sebastian's tears told him the answer.

Such a coincidence would have had Billy's mind swimming for days back when coincidence really mattered to him. That the dagger he now possessed had, at one time, been the property of Sebastian's father, was far from mere happenstance; it had changed hands from Sebastian's father to

Lafitte and Lafitte had buried it in the sands of Mustang Island where Billy had recovered it.

A complete circle—earth-bound objects marking time's passage but never really becoming a part of such linear ideology.

Nothing ever dies.

Perhaps that three-word blink of wisdom applied to much more than the flesh of men and dolphins and birds, Billy thought. Perhaps even the inanimate was never truly inanimate. Daggers and boxes and books—all a part of this *Living Planet* that was always long with surprises.

He sat on the foredeck looking up at the stars as he'd been doing the entire night. The solstice officially started at 6:04 a.m. and he guessed that another thirty minutes remained before they would depart. The plan was to scuba from here to the shore so that they would arrive at El Castillo a good half hour ahead of the event. John had figured the whole thing out using Marine savvy to stage the surprise. If they could at least get the jump on Lafitte, perhaps snatching the Book and key away from him, then all bargaining would be in their favor. It really depended on how much Mu'bä muscle or paramilitary force Lafitte had decided to bring with him. It depended on how much of his real-life arrogance and, therefore, self-confidence remained. A pompous attitude would be to their advantage.

The first slivers of twilight snatched an inch of the night sky above the ocean's horizon and turned it dark blue. Behind him, John and Cooper appeared from the cabin below. Sebastian followed a moment later. Billy sat up and Cooper joined him while John and Sebastian prepared the scuba gear.

"You ready for this?" Cooper asked him.

"As I'll ever be." He draped one arm around her. "You know you don't have to go. It'll be safer out here with Sebastian."

Cooper grabbed his hand and massaged the starry scar in its palm. "You have the gift of foresight. What do you think I'm going to say to that?"

"Stick it up my ass?"

She grinned. "Well, maybe not in such flowery terms. Who knows? I might be the one that saves *your* life." She reached into her pocket then grabbed Billy's hand and brought it to her lap. "Here," she said. "The woman who sold it to me said it helps energize your nahual." She placed a necklace strung with tiny beads shaped like tiny animal heads into his hand. "Besides, you'll need something to hang your new amulet from."

"Nahual?" Billy asked.

"Your spirit animal. The one that protects you. The one you were born with."

"And which one might that be?"

She rubbed a couple of the beads between her fingers. "I'm only guessing but for you, I suspect…"

"A dolphin?"

"Is that what you think?"

Billy nodded, once.

"Then a dolphin it must be." She took the string of beads and placed it around his neck. "May the force be with you."

Billy's eyebrows rose with surprise.

"Yeah. I know it sounds corny but it's about the only thing I could think of." And then she kissed him for the first time, her lips connecting with his for only a moment, as if she did not want any passion to interfere with the importance of their situation. When she pulled back, Billy stared into her eyes, searching for some truth about her future, prodding for answers about her safety that were not forthcoming. Realizing that this chance for their spiritual bonding might be their last, he pulled her close and kissed her deeply, exchanging a hidden energy that only his soul with hers could provide.

"We're ready," John said.

When he released her, he immediately turned and looked at the shoreline. Twilight had begun its crawl across the land, dimly illuminating the seaside structures. El Castillo's pyramidal outline remained prominent, but it was the building to the right of it that drew Billy's attention. Maybe it was the way the nighttime spotlights were directed at it, but the small building sitting on a hill all by itself like a beacon to the sea, glowed a greenish-blue aura. Cooper and John confirmed the anomaly and Sebastian reminded all of them that this might have been what Samaal had seen while escaping from Tulum.

"Oh my God," Billy suddenly said. He jumped up and ran to his backpack where he'd kept his notebook. "It is. That's it!" All of them gathered around him as he flipped through the pages where he'd recreated the Book of the Djed. "Remember this?" he asked John, showing him the sketches that he'd made.

"Yeah. The fourth location. El Castillo."

"No," Billy said. "This here." He lifted the notebook and pointed it toward the shoreline. The haggard sketch and the view of the ruins matched almost precisely. "It's not in the pyramid," Billy said. "The fourth location is in that building." He pointed at the sketch then at the same building glowing above the beach. "The one where Samaal must have kept the Cubit. The one that still has its residual spiritual aura."

"Temple of the Wind God," Sebastian clarified.

"If you're right," Cooper added, "then Lafitte will be looking in the wrong place."

John smiled. "Advantage, good guys," he said and started gearing up. "Come on. Winter's almost here."

THE DJED: PART III
666
2008

Evan didn't trust cubits and he never would. How could the dead be trusted? All you had to do was consider Richard Manson. He was a multi-billionaire because he couldn't be trusted. But dealing with just one power-tripping cubit was one thing; Manson, at least, had some appeal to him, some savvy, some moxie, some real cojones. But these others…especially Lafitte and his goonball helpers Manuel and Strykor. He couldn't wait until Manson gave him the word.

Under the early twilight, his iPhone screen illuminated one side of his face as he texted a reply to Manson who was incessantly demanding updates. It had been easy for Evan to ignore his boss's micromanagement tendencies while in the jungle—he'd legitimately used the "I'm losing your signal" excuse just about every time he'd had the chance—but here, standing atop the tallest structure for dozens of miles, he could not.

His stomach ached. He hadn't eaten a decently prepared meal in days. The crap these cubits consumed was too close to rotten for him to stand so he'd had to fend for himself, often snatching quick bites from roadside stands as the "strike force" (Lafitte's terminology) moved quickly from location to location. If it wasn't for the BETH pills that he popped at a rate that was thrice the recommendation, his body would have certainly retaliated in more extreme ways than simple stomach cramps.

He typed "Not here yet" on the iPhone and the response was almost immediate.

Hes got 2 B there. Time is wasting.

"Yeah. Yeah." Evan whispered to the phone.

"What-th that?" the Strykor cubit asked. It and the Manuel cubit stood too close to him on the top platform of El Castillo.

"Fuck off," Evan growled. "And pay attention. They should be here any minute."

"Evan!" It was Lafitte's voice bellowing once again from inside the pyramid's chamber.

Evan reluctantly followed the voice into the chamber for the third time in ten minutes. This second-hand man shit wasn't all it was cracked up to be. "Lafitte," he said.

"Don't mock me piss ant. You haven't let the whores get passed you have you?"

Evan stifled a laugh. "You serious? How the hell are three people whose destination is this very chamber, gonna get passed three guards on the top of the tallest building that has absolutely no other access to it than a bunch of stone steps that provide no cover?"

"A dumbshit human like you is bound to make it happen. After all, you *did* lose their tail yesterday, did you not?" Lafitte stooped against the empty chamber's far wall, looking out a small rectangular opening, the Book of the Djed with the key sticking out of it held in one hand. He didn't wait for an answer. "Winter will be rising any minute. If he isn't here by then, Captain Teigas is going to make a filet out of you and feed it to his men."

"He'll be here."

"Goddammit! Get out of my face."

Evan returned to the top of the pyramid and looked out across the shadowy ruins. Beyond the city's sixteen-foot-high perimeter stone wall patrolled the Los Zetas. Several were stationed at the two watchtowers. Lafitte had asked for their assistance and Captain Teigas had agreed on the condition that Cooper would not be harmed and that she would be his after all was said and done.

Behind Evan, offshore, a channel of blue cut by the ancients slashed the dark reef that was becoming increasingly visible below the water. A boat sat at the distant horizon and as daybreak continued its ascent, the boat's comforting shadow set against a cobalt blue background made the insanity of his current company even more detestable. Thankfully, he'd have to suffer them for just a few minutes longer.

Unknown to Lafitte and his "strike force," the harbinger of their demise already awaited its final orders. It hunkered in the shadows just inside the doorway of the building next to them. Manson had ordered Evan to release Billy's cubit from the well of the Caracol and Evan had stuck it in the trunk of the stolen Cavalier. For Evan, the funniest part about it all was the idea that Lafitte had been driving around for the past six days, acting the part of the big honcho, obsessed with the idea that he would soon rule the world, thinking that after two hundred years his search for immortality was only days from reality, while all along, in the trunk, smoldered the rotten stink of the freshly born dead, a scent that his own inhuman cubited senses had never detected. No one had ever thought of looking in the trunk…why would they? Once they'd arrived at Tulum, Evan had simply let it out. Now, all it had to do was follow its own destiny. All it had to do was compete the circle, kill the Daykeeper and take his place in the world. The part about ripping Lafitte to shreds was just an added bonus, offered as an incentive by the true ruler of the world, by the cubited monster that had manipulated everything just to see fate turn in his favor.

Evan smiled as his phone rang. It was Manson. Unfortunately, Evan had no new information to calm his boss's increasing rage.

Billy surfaced just north of his intended destination. He was alone. The scuba tank weighted him uncomfortably as he removed his flippers and crawled from the surf to the jungle perimeter, scuttling quickly to avoid detection. He sat in the tall, wet grass, the tank behind him, and slipped it off his shoulders. Sporadic breaths seemed impossible to control but he took a moment to concentrate, to breathe, to absorb the good air and expel the bad.

Before dropping into the water, Sebastian had offered him a handgun but Billy had refused. Billy had told him that guns would not help him fulfill his duties. He had the dagger, he'd said. He had himself. He had fate on his side. Sebastian had simply grunted, his intimate personal knowledge of Nazi psychosis evident in that single, brash response. Now sitting below a cliff of limestone, alone and uncertain of his own faith, Billy wondered if he should have accepted it. A Creation Dagger could do a world of damage at close range but a gun…he might not be able to kill them with it but he certainly could have backed them off.

His breathing exercise was subsided by the rising twilight. He had less than twenty minutes, tops. Cooper and John had agreed to run the distraction, acting as if the true fourth location *was* the pyramid. They were to obtain the Book and the key and bring them to Billy in the Temple of the Wind

God before the winter solstice arrived. How they would attain this goal was unknown but John and Cooper had both sworn on their lives that Billy would have what he needed in time.

Billy put on his Keds and took off up a path carved into the cliff, keeping low, using the sparse, waist-high grass as camouflage until he reached a broken section of limestone wall, a remnant of one of the city's buildings that had been decimated long ago. To his left, the center of the ruins appeared as scattered dark outlines except for the Castillo which remained illuminated by the spotlights around it. Closer to him, and sitting all by itself, was the Temple of the Wind God. It still pulsed with an aura that continued to fade as daybreak neared. To his right, three shadowed outlines of paramilitary guards sat inside the defense wall watchtower; a match was lit and a cigarette was shared as the men talked. Billy scanned the landscape one more time before running quickly through the fading darkness.

The hill on which the temple sat was made of solid, uneven shelves of limestone and as Billy shuffled up its short slope, he slipped twice, his rubber-soled Keds finding no traction against the early morning ocean spray moisture. Pebbles skittered down the limestone shelving and Billy fell flat on his stomach, the dagger strapped to his chest pressing uncomfortably into his flesh. He remained motionless for a full minute, listening for the guards, before continuing across the limestone and into the small temple structure.

It was cramped and dark inside, the entire chamber no more than twenty feet squared. A single window pointed east, in the precise location where the sun would soon rise. Billy guessed that the temple had been built for that very purpose: to mark and honor the beginning of winter. Below the window was the dark outline of a stone pedestal into which must have been etched the markings associated with the Cubit's throne though he could not see them.

He stood, staring out the small window, the invisible ocean mist filling his deep breaths with salty sea, the sun creeping higher to where Sebastian's boat waited, wondering what he was supposed to do next. Time was running out.

Rocks skittered outside and Billy quickly turned around. "John," he whispered. "Hurry. The sun is almost at the horizon."

But it wasn't John. And it wasn't a soldier. And it wasn't anything that Billy had expected. He could smell it before it entered the chamber.

"Hi," Billy's cubit slurred.

Evan was never going to allow Lafitte to take the Djed. His orders were to get the amulet and bring it back with him to Mérida. He'd already seen John and Cooper surface in scuba gear along the public beach just to the right of the Castillo. He'd watched them dodge in and out of the thin tree line just below the pyramid. With every move they'd made, Evan had distracted the Manuel and Strykor cubits so that they would not see what Evan was allowing to happen. When the two intruders started up the pyramid steps, Evan smiled. He would now have self-gratification. It was time for a little payback.

He casually walked around to the back side of the Castillo platform where the two cubits stood looking at the brightening horizon. Evan pointed. "What's that? Down there!" Both cubits leaned forward and with two swift kicks, Evan sent both of them off the platform and down the jagged east face of El Castillo. Both bodies tore into scattered chunks as they continued down the ocean cliff wall before splashing as pieces into the white foam surf. He then ran into the Castillo chamber where Lafitte paced back and forth and told him that company was coming up the face of the pyramid.

"Something ain't right," John told Cooper. "This is too easy."

"Maybe you're just too good," Cooper responded, following him up the steps of the pyramid. "Wait! Did you hear that?"

"Sounded like something falling off the top of this thing." He didn't stop his ascent. "Come on. We don't have much time."

Billy had not accepted Sebastian's offer of a handgun but Cooper had eagerly taken it. She now held the 9mm Beretta in front of her, a loaded clip of ten shots ready for action. John had told her that bullets couldn't kill these things but the handgun made her feel safe nonetheless. She kept an eye on their flanks as John concentrated on their ascent. In the dark twilight, many soldiers paced aimlessly beyond the perimeter wall, but none paid them, or anything else inside the ruins, any attention.

At the top of the pyramid, they stepped carefully to the rear of the platform where Cooper saw Sebastian's boat set against the rising sun, a postcard perfect picture of man and sea combined. Down below, she saw what looked like human body parts bouncing against the watery cliff face. She was pretty certain that one piece, a head, looked a lot like the Mexican that had tried to rape her. "Poonta that," she said with a hushed breath that John, with hand signals, told her to quiet. She plucked Manuel's earlobe from her pocket and threw it at the floating, thrashing body parts. The Wayeb earring twinkled dim reflections before joining Manuel's head under the sea.

John led her back around to the front of the pyramid's chamber and, together, they walked inside. Cooper had the Beretta clenched between both hands in her best police woman pose and when she saw Lafitte, she aimed the pistol at his head. Lafitte was standing on a stone pedestal that, in shape and size, looked a lot like one of the Cubit's thrones except that there were no markings on any side of it. A rectangular window was above the pedestal and Lafitte's arm rested inside its recess. He held the Book of the Djed in one hand. To the left of him, standing in the shadows, was the real human who called himself Evan.

"I have been waiting almost two centuries for this day," Lafitte said. "It has been my life's pursuit."

"But you're dead," John said.

"It's all a matter of perspective, or haven't either of you figured that part out yet?"

Cooper stepped forward, the gun heavy.

"I'll throw it into the surf," Lafitte warned, the Book inching closer to the window opening.

"Where's Billy?" Evan asked.

"He's right outside," John lied, thumbing at the doorway behind him.

"Bring him in or the Book is gone," Lafitte demanded.

John reached over and gently pushed Cooper's gun-clenching arms down. "Let's be reasonable here," he said. "We only have a few minutes remaining and then no one will have a Djed with which to do anything."

"Evan," Lafitte said. "Go get our boy." He stepped down from the window and set the Book on the stone pedestal. The light in the window continued to brighten. "Hurry up!" he yelled.

Evan left, then reappeared moments later. "He's not here," he said. "They lied."

Suddenly, John bolted forward as Lafitte grabbed the Book and tried to throw it through the window. John's shoulder connected with Lafitte's rib cage and the Book careened off the edge of the window, flipped across the pedestal, opened up enough for the key to flutter free, and landed on the floor, face down. Though Lafitte's cubit was half John's size its strength was at least double. It pushed John to the floor and grabbed the Book as Cooper aimed the pistol at its head. In one quick snap of the wrist, Lafitte threw the Book at Cooper, knocking the gun from her grip. Cooper grabbed the Book and yelled, "I got it!"

Lafitte backed up and stepped on the pedestal. "And I've got the key," he said, raising the page from the Book toward the window. "Now let's try this one more time. Where the fuck is Bill—"

Four quick claps of gunfire erupted from behind them. Evan held Cooper's gun in both hands. The first bullet missed, but the next three struck Lafitte in the face, piercing both cheeks and his forehead. Lafitte toppled from the pedestal and his head cracked against the stone floor.

"Hurry," Evan urged. "Time's almost up."

Billy had nowhere to run. His cubit cornered him. He drew the dagger from its sheath and held it defensively in front of him.

"Gooood," his cubit moaned, its eyes blazing crimson with silver swirls twisting at their centers. "We need that."

"We don't need anything. You need to die."

"Come on, little brother. You've already seen what is about to happen." The cubit sounded nothing like him. The cubit sounded exactly the same as Pedro's cubit had sounded in the Caracol's well. "You give me the dagger and I rip you to pieces."

Billy blinked and so did the cubit, then he stepped up onto the pedestal, and the cubit stepped forward.

"You really don't think I'm going to let you stab me in the back of the head again, do you?"

"Again?" Billy asked.

"Dammit, boy. You sure don't learn easily?"

"Who are you?"

"I'm you, of course."

"I don't believe it."

"Doesn't much matter what the fuck you believe." The sun was moments from appearing above the horizon. The window behind Billy's head began to glow with the same crimson aura that now emitted from the dagger in his hand. "We'll raise the Djed together then I'm going to eat you…alive if possible…dead if necessary. Doesn't really matter. What matters is that you'll be gone, the prophecy will turn in my favor, and the world as you know it will come to a screeching halt in four years. That's what should be believed. That's what reality really is. Thanks to you…and me."

Evan ran in front of them as a dozen soldiers appeared through openings in the city's walls. "I don't trust him," Cooper whispered to John. "I don't care that he shot Lafitte. Just watch him." John nodded and followed Evan into the Temple of the Wind God. Captain Teigas shouted orders, demanding that his men not shoot and to remain at a distance from the temple.

Inside, two Billys stared at her. One held a glowing dagger; the other had glowing eyes. The small window behind them blazed in the same crimson color. "Hurry," Evan said. "Give him the Book."

Cooper walked quickly to the pedestal and gave Billy the Book and key page then stepped back to stand beside John who stood beside Evan.

"Go ahead Presser," Billy's cubit said. "Do your thing."

Billy fumbled with the Book in one hand and the key and dagger in the other. It was evident he hadn't the slightest idea what he was supposed to do.

"Just like Alax did in the Great Hall," Cooper offered.

Billy looked at her, at all of them, as crimson infiltrated the entire chamber. He set the Book of the Djed atop the stone pedestal and immediately, the star at its top edge lit up. Below the star, only the three-dimensional image of a Djed was etched into the stone; there were no daggers. Billy opened the Book to the center page and gasped. Cooper shuffled forward but remained two steps behind him. She had to see it. She had to know what God had written there since the last time she'd looked.

The three sixes and three nines had morphed into five of each number. The phoenix above the numbers was now drawn with fiery bold reds and oranges and yellows. Below the sixes and nines, a third symbol appeared at that very moment; as she stared at the parchment brown vacant space, the outline of a Djed was drawn there, the spiritual lead creating the outline, in one long stroke that took a full minute to complete. Billy held the key but he was unable to turn from the center page to reposition it in its proper place. Instead, he handed the key back to Cooper then grasped the Creation Dagger in his right hand, making sure the star in its haft and the one burned into his hand were properly aligned. He jammed the seven inch blade into the pedestal star at exactly the same moment the crimson red ball of the sun appeared in the small window. His teeth clenched so tightly that Cooper thought the incisors would snap in two. He seemed to want to scream but his jaw would not open. He stared straight ahead, his eyes glued to the crimson ball of solar divinity. And Cooper looked down.

The Djed that had been etched into the pedestal stone popped up and out. It didn't fall to the floor, but instead stuck to the stone surface as a ghostly, holographic image, and began crawling up the face in concert with the rising sun. Up the pedestal it rose, passed right through the implanted dagger and

Billy's hand, and flopped on top of the pedestal. As the sun consumed the entire breadth of the window, the holographic Djed positioned itself over the drawing in the Book. The sun's red blaze combined with the Djed's green glow and morphed the hologram into a solid sacred amulet. Then, all at once, as the sun rose above the window opening and its spectral light diminished, all of the occupants within the temple rushed for the Djed amulet in a twisted heap of living and dead flesh. Evan punched Cooper and she fell backward, the key still grasped firmly in her hand. She watched as Billy grabbed the amulet, pulled the dagger from the stone and haphazardly slashed out. The blade sliced a thin, long incision into Evan's cheek, continued onward in a sweeping arc, and planted in the back of the neck of Billy's cubit. Billy released the dagger and his cubit fell to the floor, writhing and grasping at the back of its head, trying to pull the dagger out. It kicked and moaned and molted, its red eyes blinking out as it quickly turned to ash and bone. The dagger rolled from the desecrated mound and Evan snatched it. He still had Cooper's gun and he now waved both of them at John who stood just within his reach.

"It's over," he growled, blood gushing from the slash in his face. "You've done your duty for your Godless country. Give it to me now." He didn't wait for Billy's response as he planted the dagger into John's shoulder. "Don't think. Just do it. Do it now!"

At that moment, Lafitte appeared in the temple's doorway. The three bullet holes in its face oozed a red that was darker than rust. Flesh that had exploded outward from the bullets' impacts with cheeks and forehead flapped against its blazing crimson eyes as it tried to speak. Every word was followed by the whistle of escaping air through the torn cheek holes.

"Yhoo whooren't going to keep it fooor yhooself, Efoon."

Cooper had fallen to the left of the doorway and she kicked Lafitte's knees as John punched Evan in the face with his elbow. Evan flailed backward, his nose busted, and the gun fired, nipping Billy's earlobe. In the same motion, John pulled the dagger from his shoulder and flicked it at Lafitte but missed the falling body. The dagger fell to Cooper's side and she used it to stab Lafitte in the leg.

Suddenly, outside, automatic gunfire erupted all around them. John grabbed Billy who grabbed the Book and both of them swept Cooper from the floor, jumped over Lafitte's body and ran out of the temple. Los Zeta soldiers were firing at something that was returning their gunfire to the right. Down the slippery limestone shelf all three fled. The soldiers saw them and repositioned their guns. Chips of limestone erupted at their feet. When the triumvirate got to the bottom of the temple hill, they saw Sebastian who was crouched behind the chunk of wall that Billy had used for cover on his way into the ruins. Sebastian fired a quick blast from his automatic and two soldiers fell from their positions.

"Come on, dammit!" Sebastian yelled. "You Nazi bastards ain't gonna kill her this time."

Cooper took the lead, running onto the sandy beachhead where Sebastian had anchored his boat just offshore. She rolled the key and stuck it under her shirt then dove into the water with the dagger in one hand. She waded there, watching as bullets erupted in multiple sand explosions all around Billy who fell; John scooped him up and continued running toward the water, the blood from the dagger strike to his shoulder smearing Billy's face which he closely coddled. Several soldiers appeared on the knoll and Sebastian took out two of them before diving into the water to help John with Billy's limp body.

Cooper pulled herself up onto the boat then helped John as he wrestled with Billy's body in the water. Together, they rolled Billy onto the boat's rear platform where Cooper saw three blood spots from the bullets in his chest. As soon as Sebastian was aboard, he turned the boat toward the channel in the reef and throttled forward. Behind them, Captain Teigas stood on the beach, firing his gun angrily in rapid succession over his head.

Richard Manson stood in his fortieth-story office looking out the window but not seeing anything except Evan who lay sprawled on the floor in front of him. His vision was partially blocked by the pieces of flesh that flapped around his eyes.

"You failed, Evan," he said trying not to whistle but unable to control the results of Evan's gunshots to his face. Evan pleaded for his life but Manson, through the eyes of Lafitte, was having none of it. He yanked the gun from Evan's grasp and placed the barrel against the forehead of the human who used to be his assistant. "Your footage of our jump last week absolutely sucked and Jobs hated it," he added, then emptied the clip into Evan's brain.

A minute later, Captain Teigas appeared in the temple doorway. Manson watched as Teigas walked forward, almost robotically, and stepped around the sunshine that infiltrated the room through the small window. Teigas lifted his automatic weapon and hesitated for a moment before pulling the trigger.

Manson's vision of the temple room vanished. In his hand was an iPhone that presented a digital slider which he now turned off. His anger was immense, the Djed was gone, but he still had alternatives. He always had alternatives.

And four more years.

He dropped the iPhone onto his desk and looked down upon the people who littered the Phoenix Tower plaza below.

"Soon," he said.

Below deck, Billy woke to the friendly smiles of three friends. He immediately placed his hand on his chest and Cooper grabbed it, patting the knuckles. "Blood," he said.

He tried to sit up but was unable without the help of John. "We thought we lost you but we forgot," Cooper said.

"Forgot?" Billy whispered. She patted his chest and Billy grabbed her hand. At that moment he felt the beads around his neck and the weight of the Djed amulet hanging from the necklace. He lifted his shirt and saw three scars where the bullets had entered his body. The Djed amulet hung centered between them.

"Immortal," John's deep voice verified. "The bullets just squirted right out."

"The Book," Billy said. "And the key and the dagger?"

"Right here," John offered. He pointed to the foot of the bed.

Billy leaned forward, grimacing. The Book was intact as was the key page. The seawater had not affected either.

He picked up the key page and examined it; he'd always assumed it was necessary for raising the Djed but it had not been. The small glyph of a Creation Dagger and the glyph of the Wayeb had not changed since the day he first saw them sticking out of Albert Stine's briefcase. The key's purpose, he thought, was for something else yet to be discovered.

He opened the Book to the place where the key had been removed and stuck the page against the bound serrated edge. It quickly stitched itself together. He then flipped the pages backward to the center spread to examine the three symbols now drawn there: the colorful bird of fire at the top of the page, the new Djed addition in the middle of the page, and the bold and heavy imprints of sixes and nines between them.

"There's five of each now," Cooper said. "What does it mean?"

"Locate a Mayan date converter and I think we'll find out."

Finally, the Daykeeper opened the Book to its second half and stared with his friends at the story of the fourth creation.

The Creation of the Antichrist.

Book Three
0-Time

0-TIME
PUSH*

Sunday Evening, December 19, 2010

His entire life had been built upon this one moment. Almost twenty-five years in the business and finally Michael had landed the big one. But he wondered: Was *Fox News Morning* really worth getting his head chopped off?

He climbed the last set of steps in a packed auditorium of classic rock enthusiasts who sat and stood and sang and danced in a tangled array that strangled the building's 16,000-person capacity. Across the floor, more than a thousand fans jockeyed for territory using elbows and hips and an occasional fist or two. Michael loved Bad Company, had grown up with them, but entertainment was not his primary reason for being here. Obtaining the drug was.

He'd been assigned the story two months ago, mostly because of his work on a documentary back in 2009. That film, aptly named "Bringing Everyone Total Health," had won Michael Arden a couple of video journalism and film awards and the sheen of notoriety had never really worn off. Because the documentary had focused on a similar subject—illicit substances—and the fact that Michael had worked for Fox as an intern some twenty years ago while attending college in Australia, his name had surfaced on a *Fox News* tip sheet. He was now scheduled to go live with Ben Reely in less than thirty-six hours.

Michael found his seat near the end of the last row in the section and tried to enjoy the show as he waited. He could sing most lyrics to most songs (karaoke had given him ample opportunities to practice), and when Paul Rodgers stood alone under a single hazy spotlight at the front of the stage and struck the first chord of *Burnin' Sky* he almost became absorbed.

The sky... is burnin'... I believe my soul's on fire...

You are... I'm learning... the key to my desire...

The key to a desire, Michael thought. How appropriate. PUSH* was the newest designer drug that had become so popular and elusive at the same time. Its value—and desire—was attributed to the very fact that it was so hard to get, a case study of supply and demand in action: reduce the availability and increase the cost of ownership, just like Cabbage Patch economics. Strange thing was, considering that the pill was so hard to find and so expensive to get once you found it, the teen sitting to his right didn't look like he could afford burnt toast. He kept repeating, "Are you ready, man? Are you fuckin' ready?" This was a telltale sign of PUSH* anticipation—of the Timeout; the euphoric rush hadn't yet taken hold but it was about to, guaranteed, sometime around ten o'clock.

Michael's contact was to meet him before the Timeout near the southwest emergency exit stairwell. Instructions had been relayed to him by a student from the university who'd had "reliable" knowledge that a PUSH* event was going to take place on campus during the concert. The student had also known how to obtain the drug though the details of his contact had never been forthcoming.

"Man, are you fucking ready?" the teen beside him repeated. Michael stared awkwardly at the kid whose wiry black hair was covered by a Bad Company ball cap. When Michael stood, none of the three teens to his right offered any kind of etiquette as he stepped on their feet and toppled one bucket of popcorn before exiting the aisle.

"What's your problem, old dude?" the girl at the end of the aisle asked without looking at him. She flipped long, blonde hair backward and it cascaded halfway down the seat's backrest.

"This is gonna be great," Michael said with only a little enthusiasm, scratched his days-old beard and brushed back short salt and pepper streaked hair. He was in his late forties but he wasn't old. Besides, he knew more about Bad Company than any teen in the place could hope to know.

"What-ev," the girl replied and turned away to caress the thigh of the boy sitting next to her. They both sang in unison.

Love you, baby, anyway.. oh, yeah...

Michael leaned against the concrete back wall of the Pan American Center next to the emergency stairwell and gazed at the mass of people swaying and singing and holding lighter flames that flickered in unison to the internal flow of sound waves. The crowd and the darkness made the auditorium seem much smaller than it was during brightly lit New Mexico State University basketball games, many of which Michael had attended. High above the floor, the basketball scoreboard's color monitor provided on-stage camera close-ups.

The sky... is burnin'... I believe my soul's on fire...

You are... I'm learning... the key to my De-Siiiii-rrrrrre...

Michael looked at his watch and then into the shadowy stairwell. Ten short concrete steps angled down to a dark landing which twinkled in stage-lit multi-colors every time the spotlights jerked in his direction.

After Bad Company finished *Burnin' Sky* with a solo lead guitar volley that shook the floor, a hush fell over the crowd. Lighter flames filled the darkness in such multitude that a majority of the fans could be seen underneath the butane-fueled glow. It was almost ten.

From his pocket, Michael pulled out his Flip camera and thumbed it on. He looked down at the small video screen and turned the camera's angle toward the row of popcorn-eating teens. But it wasn't the PUSH* pill's affect on the crowd that he suddenly found to be newsworthy enough to record. It was Bad Company. Michael knew all of their albums and thought he knew all of the songs they might have covered, but *Push It* by Salt 'N' Pepa? He never remembered Bad Company, a group that was the veritable definition of classic rock, performing pop-hit dance tunes. Without a synthesizer the song was thankfully less dance and more rock. The bass guitarist hit the synth notes, giving the intro an aggressively dark feel.

Oooh, baby, baby
Baby, baby
Oooh, baby, baby
Baby, baby

As backup vocals urged the crowd to *Push It Real Good*, a hand reached out from the stairwell shadows and landed on Michael's shoulder. He dropped the Flip and it immediately died when it hit the floor.

"Down here," a gruff voice whispered. "You still have time to experience it."

Michael grabbed his camera and followed the dark figure down to the stairwell landing. There was enough shadow to hide their transaction but not enough to fully mask the face of the pusher. The brim of the pusher's Bad Company ball cap, which was nearly identical to the one the teen boy was wearing, darkened half of his face. The one eye that stared at him sparkled with stage-reflected silver specks. The pusher opened a leather-gloved hand to reveal two white, oblong pills resting in the palm.

"Five," the pusher said, his lips parting ever so slightly below a thin brown mustache. Oddly, and probably because of the limited light and Michael's own paranoia, the pusher looked familiar to him.

"You were supposed to be here *before* the Timeout," Michael said.

"Four-fifty then. Pretty soon it won't be worth nothin' and I didn't come all the way out here just to go home empty-handed."

Ah, push it – Push it real good.

Michael took a wad of ten fifties from the pocket where he'd not stashed his broken camera and peeled off one of them. He grabbed the two pills and dropped the money roll in the open palm.

"Who's taking the other one?" the pusher asked, shoving the fifties into the shadows surrounding his body. "You only need one."

"Really?" Michael said, faking surprise. "I thought double the dose meant double the pleasure."

The pusher turned toward the performance and his face totally disappeared into shadow. "You've been misinformed," he said. Again,

Michael was confronted with déjà vu, particularly now that the pusher's back was to him.

"No refund then, I guess," Michael offered.

The pusher's dark head shook denial. "Well," he said. "Song's over in a couple of minutes. Don't you want the experience?"

Michael looked at the pills in his hand. A small asterisk was branded into the middle of each. "I thought these things were supposed to take me through to the end of the concert."

"Again, you've been misinformed. This is a *special* high—meant to last for five minutes."

"Pretty expensive five-minute high." Michael paused when the pusher didn't respond then added, "Do I know you?"

The shadow quickly turned back around. A half-faced grimace and menacing bloodshot eyes told Michael that he'd reached some limit to the pusher's patience. "I don't know anyone and you don't know me. That's how I play it. Get it?!" He pointed one leather finger at Michael's face. "Now less than two minutes. The cost per second keeps rising."

"Thanks for nothing," Michael said and the pusher's finger dropped immediately downward, the entire gloved hand quickly encapsulating Michael's wrist.

"I don't give a shit what you do with it," the pusher growled. "Cram it up your ass for all I care. What I do give a shit about is You ever asking Me for such favors again." He threw Michael's arm aside and quickly walked down the staircase toward the concourse. Without turning he added, "Push it real good, news man," then he laughed once before disappearing beyond the stairwell.

The silhouette and especially the laugh—Michael was sure he knew the pusher and it made him extremely uncomfortable, elevating his paranoia to new heights. The memory of ghouls scratched his subconscious.

He shoved the pills in the pocket with the Flip camera and walked back up the stairs to gawk at the crowd. Regardless of the heavy grunge-like dance beat that Bad Company had found for the song, nearly everyone stood frozen. Few sang and there were no lighters. The girl whose feet he had trampled gazed hypnotically forward, lips parted and emotionless, until the end of the song when she and, seemingly, the entire crowd yelled in unison: "Push it!"

Then, as quickly as one might flip a switch, the auditorium resumed its rock concert revelry as fans jumped and screamed and lifted dozens of people above outstretched arms who were then shuffled overhead down the rows of seats to the waiting fans on the floor. Within a few minutes, at least thirty people had been transferred from the perimeter of the auditorium to the security wall surrounding the stage. Each was then lifted across the wall by security personnel and rolled onto the wooden stage floor, one on top of the other, until a mass of humanity lay in a pile at the band's feet.

Paul Rodgers said something pertaining to rock and roll and orgies, then the band rolled into its next song: *Feel Like Making Love*.

Fifteen minutes later, Michael parked in the employee lot in front of the Biochemistry Building on the opposite side of campus. Mid-December weather in Las Cruces occasionally required a coat but tonight it was unseasonably warm. Still, Michael couldn't shake the annoying chill that had snatched his spine during the concert and when he stepped out of his Explorer, his entire body shook.

Programmed, he kept thinking. The crowd had acted as if they'd been programmed. Not doped, not hallucinogenic, not euphoric, but programmed. To him, the ramifications were horrifying. Up until tonight, he'd assumed that PUSH* had been the desire of individuals looking for a unique, perhaps once-in-a-lifetime experience. Cost, Michael had assumed, prohibited its use in mass beyond a small group of partygoers out for a night on the town. But that had apparently changed. Not only was the drug being used by thousands of people looking for one shared experience, its price had fallen dramatically. It must have. Even though Michael had forked over nearly two hundred and fifty bucks for one, there was no way all of those Bad Company fans could have paid that much for a high that would last only five minutes. Not so many thousands of them. Not all at once. Teens who could barely afford popcorn could not fork over such fortune. Besides, there weren't enough shadowy pushers in staircases to service such demand.

The front of the Biochemistry Building was brightly illuminated by two halogen lampposts. Like most of the architecture on campus, sandstone blocks colored in three southwestern tans rose two stories up and were capped by an A-framed roof of interlocking Spanish tiles. Manicured sparse lawns filled with hedges and cacti bookended a short concrete staircase in front of the building's double glass doors. Fred's Land Rover sat directly in front of the steps next to the handicap space.

Michael had known the chemist for nearly twenty years, ever since he'd moved from Sydney to Las Cruces. Fred had been his welcome wagon, per se, had introduced him to Southwestern culture, to the University, to solid leads for engaging assignments, particularly documentaries. Frederico Fernandez was his full name and he claimed ancestry (though many times removed) to Lisa Fernandez, the Olympic gold-medal softball pitcher. Fred had been raised in the Mexican Yucatán and had gone to school in Cancun for a short time before transferring to Arizona State University back in the early eighties. A few years later, an engaging doctoral opportunity at NMSU had brought him east at about the same time he'd acquired his U.S. citizenship. Since then he'd become renown, at least regionally, for his work in pharmaceutical biochemistry. Some of his early research had eventually been transformed into the popular drugs Viagra and Ambien. Michael had often teased Fred about that—about having been responsible for the "boner pill" and about how many times Fred must have experimented with the drug on himself.

Currently, Fred was working with a grant from the state to study the biochemistry of the popular BethStar nutritional supplement. The supplement's dramatic affect on the health of the local Hispanic poor (shown quite convincingly in Michael's 2009 documentary) had sparked the state's curiosity. BethStar's cost was practically free when all subsidies and federal discounts were applied and (also due in large part to Michael's film) there had been case studies earlier in the year that documented the supplement's positive influence on several school districts in Arizona. Sedona, for example, had absolutely flipped its once dismal rank as one of the least healthy school districts to one of the best. New Mexico had wanted to know if the drug was safe enough to distribute within its own troubled districts. That's why they'd awarded Fred with a five hundred thousand dollar grant plus new electron microscope equipment.

Though BethStar research demanded much of his time, Fred's hobby was PUSH*. He'd become so interested in the drug, particularly since Michael had been freelancing the story for Fox, that he'd been staying late in the lab trying to untangle its mysteries, trying to help his friend gather proof. But Fred had recently come to an impasse and that's why Michael had gone to the concert: to acquire the drug and bring him a sample of it during Timeout. The hope was that the pill would still be active under the microscope and Fred would be able to isolate the reaction. Michael only hoped that the PUSH* he'd acquired would be adequate, given that its effects had lasted only five minutes.

Michael ascended the three steps and looked to his left. His Explorer and Fred's Land Rover were the only two vehicles parked in the lot. Lampposts cast intermittent spotlights in circular halos at the lot's four corners and it was near the one closest to him, the lamppost to his left, that he'd thought he'd seen something. He stared at the darkness, at a short, weeping elm tree shadow rising just beyond the spotlight, at its trunk which seemed to be just a bit too fat. Suddenly, the trunk decreased in width, as if the added shadow saw him looking and ducked for cover.

"Hello," he yelled at the tree. "You wanna see what this stuff is made of too?" He tapped the pants pocket where the PUSH* pills rested, knowing that if someone actually was hiding behind the tree they wouldn't answer him anyway. "Yeah. That's what I thought."

This was not the first time his paranoia had been this extreme. Attention to his 2009 documentary had also produced several seedy characters, the men he'd called *ghouls*. Back then, as now, he'd stayed away from home, had lived in numerous motel rooms until he'd been assured (by Fred mostly) that the ghouls had gone—assuming they'd existed in the first place.

A long, green painted hallway greeted him when he entered what seemed to be an empty building. Fred's lab was at the far end about two hundred feet away. The hallway was illuminated by only half of its fluorescent fixtures and this made its length an interspersed highway of light and shadow. Closed doors on either side of the hallway loomed vacant and foreboding. If one could hide behind a tree outside, Michael thought, certainly another could snatch him from behind one of those doors. He tried in vain to shake the feeling as he moved forward. A ten-foot walk under fluorescent comfort was followed by ten feet of stepping through unsavory darkness and by the time Michael stopped halfway down the hall and turned around his mind was back at the concert with thoughts about the pusher, about the staircase. He gasped when, at the end of the hallway, he saw someone staring into the building through one of the entry doors he'd just entered—a shadowy outline of head to glass and an arm raised to a forehead.

"Shit!" Michael jumped and turned to the muted voice that suddenly echoed from the end of the hallway in the opposite direction. "Where are you!?" Fred's voice exclaimed. When Michael pivoted back toward the entry doors the shadow was gone.

He moved swiftly but carefully across slick vinyl tiling through dark and light until he reached the end of the hallway where he found himself in a familiar atrium filled with a dozen student science models and experiments, each displayed in glass cases that were illuminated by bulbs connected to photovoltaic cells. Twenty feet overhead, a glass ceiling enabled the sun to recharge the cells during the day. Some of the displays moved; some invited user interaction with buttons or levers that were labeled *Push*.

Something shattered beyond the closed door to his left and Michael quickly walked to Fred's lab. He entered without knocking. "Fred," he said as he swung the door open. "Special delivery." Unlike the hallway and the atrium outside, the lab was brightly lit from all directions. Michael saw his friend kneeling on the floor at the far end of the room. Fred waved a hand over his head without turning around.

"Good," Fred yelled, his Mexican accent only slightly apparent. "My impatience is causing clumsiness."

Michael walked between two long, tall counters where a dozen students could demonstrate their knowledge of chemistry at stations demarked by metal stools, stainless steel sinks, microscopes, and trays filled with a variety of glass beakers, tubes and slides. Beyond the lab stations, the room was sectioned off by another counter, this one semicircular, which ran from one side of the room to the other. Atop this room divider sat six computer flat screens and keyboards. Post-it notes, grouped by color, stuck to the countertop around each screen. Notebooks and plenty of pencils, pens and other researchers' necessities lay neatly scattered between the screens. Cushy, black fabric executive chairs, the kind that have smooth rolling wheels, sat behind three of the screens.

Within the semicircular counter was the expensive equipment, the centerpiece being the new electron microscope that the BethStar research grant had funded. It's thick, silver metal tube body was bolted into the floor and it rose six feet above two adjacent white tables. On the table to the left of the microscope sat a flat screen color monitor and several silver-faced control boards sporting a half a dozen rotary knobs meant for fine-tuning the equipment. The table to the right was twice as wide as the one on the left and it held twice as much of the same technology. The silver softness of the knobs plus the multitude of colorful lights that flashed on and around the setup reminded Michael of a video gaming "den" that a roommate in college had assembled many years ago.

Fred knelt in front of the microscope with large pieces of a broken glass beaker in one hand. "Bring it on in," he said, still not turning to acknowledge Michael. "We don't have a lot of time."

Michael walked to the left and around the end of the semi-circular counter. "We've run out of time actually." He pulled one of the pills from his pocket. "I think these things only lasted five minutes."

Fred dropped the broken glass into a clear plastic bowl and stood. He motioned with the bowl toward the wall behind Michael. "Grab the broom for me."

Michael snatched the handle of an electrostatic broom, handed Fred the PUSH* pill then rolled the broom across twinkling glass, the tiny pieces clinking as the static-charged rollers sucked them in. "I got ripped off," he said. "Two hundred fifty bucks for nothing."

"Two fifty!" Fred shouted. "For five minutes? That is a rip." He set the bowl of glass on the table to the left of the electron microscope. "We better get it in for analysis then. Wouldn't want to waste your investment."

Michael placed the broom against the wall and walked with Fred to a prep station behind the microscope. Fred crushed the PUSH* pill into a petri dish and added a small amount of clear solution from a beaker next to it. He swirled the mixture with a glass rod. "Something strange happened tonight," Michael said over Fred's shoulder.

"There's more of them and they are watching," Fred said and turned. Tired brown eyes peered narrowly from within brown-skinned wrinkles. "The closer we get to your date with Fox, the more it seems to be obvious and the more sleep I lose because of it."

Michael had intended to tell Fred about the way the Bad Company crowd had reacted to the Push, about how they had seemed programmed and controlled, but this response from Fred altered his intent. "Why do you say that?"

"Seen the same SUV parked out in the lot for the past six days straight."

"How do you know it was the same one?"

"New York tags with only three numbers: six-nine-nine."

"They ever talk to you?"

Fred poured some of the solution onto a glass slide. "Are you kidding? Why would they jeopardize any discovery? They're hoping I uncover their evidence for them."

"Federales?"

Fred nodded. "Of course. They can't figure it out. They need patsies. If we uncover what they need, I'm sure we'll be talking to them directly."

"What do you mean? What do they need?"

Fred placed the slide into the electron microscope and tapped on one of the computer keyboards to the right of it. "The same thing we do: evidence of who's making the stuff."

"You can tell the manufacturer by looking through a microscope?"

Fred smiled though Michael could tell that it was forced. "With this bad boy, definitely. Some molecules are uniquely associated with the labs that produce them. If we're lucky, we might even uncover bioengineered DNA that could link a chemical further. Take that for example." Fred tapped the computer's flat screen monitor. The recorded interaction of some chemical he'd previously placed into the electron microscope moved under his hand. "Just like a fingerprint. This construct is associated with BETH Pharmaceuticals. Nowhere else will you see such artistic blends of the bonds inside the BethStar supplement."

"Our wonder vitamin."

"Sí. The very same one you did your documentary on."

Michael touched the screen and the image grew larger. "You know that's what got us into this mess in the first place."

"Mess?" Fred forced another smile, this one more genuine than the first. "Your awards for the documentary and a great assignment with Fox because of it, and my half-a-mill grant and brand new equipment because of it and you call that a mess?"

"I was referring to the scary men you mentioned. I tried to tell you but…"

Fred turned his attention to the computer display and tapped instructions. "It's not the first time we've seen scary men following us around…is it? Daring discoveries takes grande cojones and we've got a pair of them."

"Are you sure they are government?"

"Sure?" Fred turned and looked at him. "Who else would they be?" A moment of silence caused Fred's eyebrows to wrinkle. "Wait. You mean those *pill men* are back? The 'ghouls' you say murdered the Smiths? I thought we agreed that they would be forever sanctioned to the Halls of Andar."

"Yes." Michael looked away, embarrassed to have brought up such bad memories. "But they are back. I think one of them sold me the PUSH*."

Fred shrugged and shook his head then returned his attention to the display where he tapped and stroked until the microscope started humming. The forced silence told Michael that this wasn't the time to go there, back to the summer of 2009, back to the "alleged" murder. The official story had been that the Smith family had been deported. But that's not what Michael had witnessed. Men from BETH Pharmaceuticals *had* brutally murdered all of them. No one had believed him, not even Fred. His good friend had done what good friends do. He'd supported Michael but he'd never really believed. How could he have? How could anyone have?

Michael had called the murderers *ghouls*; it was the best description he'd thought of at the time since they'd acted a lot like the adversaries in the online world Runes of Andar, a game that he and Fred often played. They'd looked like men, masking themselves in human form, but they'd acted like demons—heartless, unforgiving things that could not be killed.

Smith had not been their real last name. For the documentary, Michael had agreed that it would remain anonymous for fear of reprisal against other family back in Mexico. It had been the dramatic change in The Smiths' health that had become an unexpected highlight of the film. Father Smith had lost dozens of pounds, had reduced his blood pressure to one resembling an overactive teenager and had flipped his metabolic rate completely around. He'd done it in three months without the dietary or exercise changes that would have required a monetary investment that he, nor any of his Hispanic community, could have afforded.

The BethStar supplement had done it; Michael's documentary had just about proven that much. But the reason The Smiths had been murdered had not been because of their proof of the supplement's effectiveness—BETH Pharmaceuticals had loved that media attention; they'd been killed because of what the supplement had done to them after the documentary had been completed. Father Smith had insisted that he was being controlled and he'd wanted Michael to help him tell the world about evidence he'd had that named the men responsible. But Michael had been too late. And he'd seen it all…the pitchfork…the decapitations…the massacre. He was not crazy.

As if reading his mind Fred said, "I unfroze the one with the pitchfork last night."

Michael leaned toward him. "You really have no sympathy for my paranoia, do you?"

"I do. Oh yes, I do. That's why I've added a bit of challenge to the game." He turned from the microscope and locked onto Michael's stare. "I had a feeling that this Fox assignment might cause those memories to resurface so I did a little reprogramming. I want you to get online as soon as possible and follow this clue: Pitchfork Man knows where the magic chest is that holds the magic elixir that will, when consumed, erase that ghoul from the Runes forever."

After the documentary had been released, Fred had suggested that Michael try to psychologically erase the supposed ghouls from memory. The trick, Fred had said, he'd learned while still an undergraduate at ASU: take characters from your life that most disturb you and place them into computer game worlds where they could be manipulated at will. Fred had created two adversaries for Michael in the Runes of Andar. One, resembled the ghoul Michael had said he'd seen kill Father Smith. The other, Fred had called Decapitator which described Michael's memory of the second murderer. Fred had frozen these new adversaries inside of clear glass and had placed them in what was known in the online world as the Hall of Andar where they would forever remain out of action, out of reality and, according to the psychological exercise, out of Michael's mind. But Fred had changed the game. Since he'd anticipated Michael's relapse, Fred had apparently created a way for Michael to permanently destroy one of his greatest psychological nemesis.

"I don't know, Frederico," Michael said. "The memory is pretty deep but I'll try anything, particularly if you think it will help."

Fred smiled then returned his attention to the microscope. "Let's see here," he said, taking two fingers and stroking them in opposite directions across one computer display. An image under his fingertips grew in size. It looked, to Michael, like dozens of black and white curly tentacles swirling haplessly in fluid. Fred pointed at it. "As I suspected. Similar but not the same as BethStar."

"Not the same?"

"There's something in there but..." Fred touched the image display and the black and white tentacled mass broke apart as the microscopic eye zoomed toward an atomic level. Thinner, worm-like tendrils occupied this level of magnification and Fred gasped as one hair-thin worm swarmed across another, making it disappear. "They're eating each other," he said. "Makes sense. I'd have done the same thing."

Michael watched as several dozen microscopic worms became three. "Explain," he asked.

"If I was to create a biological agent that needed to hide itself...what genius." Fred answered Michael but didn't. His fascination with the video image was absolute. "Look. There goes another one."

"What?" Michael said, trying to understand.

"Look! Munch...munch...munch. Now there's only two." Fred saw the confusion in Michael's eyes. "Let's look at it at a million times magnification."

Another couple of taps on the flat screen and a turn of one rotary knob and Fred produced a moving image that looked like a collection of eight octagons all connected to each other; it formed an eight-sided ball of intelligent simplicity that was nothing less than ominous. It rolled and twisted and latched onto everything it came across, destroying all life without challenge and without equal, until nothing but *it* remained. It hovered and pulsed at the center of the microscope's lens as if threatening the eyeballs that looked at it.

"Uhh..." Fred mumbled.

"Do we have it?" Michael asked.

Fred looked away from the screen and stared at the far wall, at its white sterility. "Have it? And more. Shit. BETH Pharma is the maker. This octa... this octa-nano. It's beautiful don't you think?" Fred walked away from the microscope and sat in one of the three rolling chairs behind the semicircular counter. He spent almost five minutes shuffling through screenfuls of recorded video. "Watch," he said. His hands were frantic as fingers darted from keyboard to computer mouse. "There." The flat screen display became filled with dozens of similar octagon balls. "In the BethStar supplement they hover around certain DNA chains. These are parked near the genes that regulate the human metabolism."

Michael offered a guess. "Bioengineered molecules created by BETH Pharmaceuticals?"

Fred nodded. “Created by BETH without a doubt but these aren’t molecules. They’re nanobots.”

Michael knew about nanobots only peripherally from science news articles he’d run across. Cancer researchers were heavily endorsing nanobot use in terminal patients who had agreed to sign away their bodies as platforms for live experimentation. Microscopic robots is what they really were, tiny machines that could be programmed to hunt down and destroy cancerous cells, hard to detect intelligence that could be programmed to do just about anything.

“So what we have here,” Michael said, “is some pretty darn good evidence connecting BETH Pharma to PUSH*.”

Fred nodded again. “That’s what we have.”

“You have recorded evidence?”

“It’ll take a few hours but I think I can splice together all you’ll need for your report. There’s a bunch of BethStar data that I’ll have to sort through but the video of the PUSH* was just completed. The microscope records everything. Manson is finally going to get his just desserts.”

Fred was referring to Richard Manson, the CEO of Phoenix International and purportedly one of the richest men in the world. BETH Pharmaceuticals was just one of the corporation’s numerous subsidiaries. It had been back in college as an undergraduate that Fred had met Manson, had discovered that Manson had been plagiarizing research material and had turned him in. Manson was now a billionaire because he was a cheater and Fred hated cheaters. Proving Manson’s insidious nature had been a big reason why he’d worked so hard on the BethStar and PUSH*.

Suddenly, Fred’s face flushed with concern. He walked to the microscope control screen and sat down; the octagon ball had disappeared. “Damn thing must have destroyed itself,” he said and tapped controls that reversed the recorded video. Sure enough, all of the eight sides of the nanobot ball collapsed in upon themselves, stacking and dissolving until nothing but a single octagon remained. The microscopic stop sign twinkled two times then faded to black.

“Fox is going to go fanatic over this,” Fred continued. “In the PUSH* pill, BETH Pharma has apparently created nanobots purposefully programmed to perform an assignment then kill themselves. That’s the interaction users call the Timeout. Whatever these things have been told to do, which I’m guessing is some kind of manipulation of the pleasure centers in the brain, they do it within a certain time then erase themselves as evidence.” He swiveled in his chair. “Those BethStar pills supplements must do pretty much the same thing. Until tonight, I’d always seen those octa-nanos hanging around the

DNA molecule, but most of my thoughts have been focused on understanding which chromosomes these nanobots prefer to hover near."

"Those that would make an unhealthy man healthy," Michael said.

"Yes. It would appear that the same nanobots in PUSH* also exist in BethStar but are programmed for different functions."

Michael asked the obvious question. "So why don't BethStar nanobots kill themselves?"

"Why, indeed." Fred hesitated and again stared at the white walls. "Perhaps PUSH* is an experiment. Let me offer a hypothetical, one that you can use on Fox if you dare."

Michael nodded.

"Let's suppose that there is this powerful company owned by powerful men who have decided that the human race just isn't the best that they think it could be: too many sick people around sucking the life out of the economy via the health care system; too many immigrants crowding the halls of clinics where True Americans should get first dibs. Now suppose this company created a way to help alleviate not only the strain on the economy but also the poor health conditions of thousands—maybe millions—of people. I'd think they'd get some considerable support from some pretty influential people."

"Government," Michael interjected.

"Certainly. It's a win-win situation. The company gets to distribute its new chemical to the masses and the government takes the credit for completely transforming the health of a nation. Thing is, this company isn't completely honest. Helping people with weight control and dietary choices is only ancillary to their *real* intent."

Michael's memory flashed back to the concert, to the swarms of people that stood like robots. "Programming," he offered.

Fred nodded. "Since the company believes that the human race should be changed much further beyond simple health issues, they create a way to manipulate so much more, particularly the brain. Their miracle cure is really a mass distribution system for nanobots meant to...well, who knows what."

"And the PUSH* connection?"

"Simple. Use a subsample of the population to find out just how effective their nanobots can actually control the mind. Once you have your confirmation, destroy all evidence of the experiment. Then, when the time comes, with all those 'legitimate' BethStar nanobots still alive and circulating through the population, flip the switch."

Michael frowned with a lack of seriousness. "Flip the switch."

"Yeah. Turn everyone into ghouls or something."

"I think you've been playing around in the Runes too much."

Fred smiled. "Great thing about computer games is that it helps people think logically. Though hypothetical, you gotta agree it's logical."

"It's fantastic. What about all of the regulations attached to pharmaceuticals?"

"A powerful company with powerful influence…remember?"

As much as he hated to admit it, Fred's scenario resembled one that had been roiling around in his mind ever since Father Smith had been murdered. Whether he'd have the guts to say it on Fox was a different story. Ben Reely was a controversial host that loved the sensational but a conspiracy to control the minds of the masses? For now, he decided not to go there. "I'm taking off for El Paso at ten tomorrow morning," Michael said. "You think I could swing by to pick up something by then?"

"Plan on it." Fred tilted back in his chair and offered a hand to shake. "Be careful," he said, gripping Michael's hand forcefully, his voice tired and serious. "We're less than thirty-six hours away and I imagine the Federales are getting anxious." He stared hard at Michael's face. "Once you have the evidence, I don't think there'll be any stopping them."

"Stopping them?"

"From wanting to acquire it. They have a nation to protect after all."

"But I'm going to spill the beans on national television. That's all the proof they should need."

"Government doesn't necessarily work in the citizens' best interests; you should know that by now. Our evidence may be their leverage against the company—against the entire industry—but it may also raise concerns of collusion between the government and BETH. It all depends on what you say on national television. The Feds won't want to take that chance. They'll want to make up their own stories."

"So you'll make a backup copy then, just in case?"

"I will, but that doesn't make the idea of scary men kidnapping you any better, does it?"

"I can hold my own."

Fred stood. He'd not yet released Michael's hand. "Are you sure? Those ghouls really screwed your head up the last time."

Michael looked at Fred's clenched knuckles, felt his comforting but urgent grip that seemed to suggest that he and the chemist might never see each other again. "I thought we already took care of that. Like you said, it's got to be government."

Fred didn't speak another word on the subject, but his stare said it all. He didn't believe Michael. He didn't believe his best friend would ever get over it. He released Michael's hand. "Find the magic chest. Find the elixir. Destroy

Pitchfork Man. We'll get rid of those bad memories together, forever."

Michael left Fred sitting in front of his computers and reentered the atrium outside the lab. He immediately looked to the far end of the hallway where the double glass entry doors glowed in dull halogen white but no one was there. The perspective felt spooky and as he walked toward the doors he had the distinct feeling that he'd suddenly been transported into one of those Hitchcock movies where hallways elongated the more you tried to escape them. Dark shadows hiding inside empty lab classrooms now seemed more plausible than ever and as he weaved down the hallway, he moved from one side to the other so as to avoid all of the closed dark doors.

Michael was followed back to the motel by the same SUV that Fred had seen parked outside the lab building. He knew it was the same one because of the license: New York tags reading six-nine-nine. When he turned at the Holiday Inn and parked in front of his motel room, the SUV drove another hundred yards before it turned around and parked in front of a closed Dairy Queen across the street. When Michael slipped his key card into the door and entered, the SUV's headlights went out.

His first order of business was to ask the front desk for a wake-up call. An eight o'clock start would give him plenty of time to stop by the lab before checking out and driving an hour to the El Paso International Airport where he was to take the 10:55 flight to Laguardia. Fox had arranged everything and their reward would be much more than they'd bargained. Michael had been hired to cover the black market robustness of the drug, how it was acquired, and how it was used. He'd promised Fox that he might even get them a laymen's understanding of how the drug actually worked within the body (thanks to Fred). But what he'd found, what Fred had found, had been much more fantastically profound.

After talking to the motel's front desk he opened his cell phone and selected "Fox News" from the list of recent calls. Before connecting, he thought about the room, about the SUV outside, about tapped landlines and hidden bugging devices. He exited the room to find that the SUV was still across the street, its tinted windows unrevealing of the occupants inside. He purposefully ignored the vehicle and walked around the wing of the motel, out of sight, where an ice maker and Coke machine offered late night refreshment. Even at one in the morning, someone at Fox was quick to answer the call.

"Charlotte White, please," he said to the phone. "This is Michael Arden."

"Just a moment," an operator replied.

Michael peeked through a dense, landscaped population of transplanted cacti. The SUV was still there, still silent, still waiting.

"I'm sorry but Ms. White is not available at this time. Would you like to leave a message?"

"Yes. Thank you." A moment later a request for his recorded message was followed by a beep. "Charlotte," he said. "Tell Ben Reely that I have evidence connecting BETH Pharmaceuticals to PUSH*. I'm bringing it with me. I'm sure you'll want to expand our segment to include it. I'll call you with more before leaving tomorrow morning."

As soon as Michael reappeared from beyond the motel's west wing, the SUV's lights snapped on and the vehicle drove slowly out of the Dairy Queen parking lot. He stood and stared but could not see whether the occupants were Fred's government men or were, more likely, another set of pharmaceutical ghouls just like the ones he'd met more than a year ago.

The acronym BETH stood for *Bringing Everyone Total Health*. It had been an easy choice for the title of his documentary, more so because the title's meaning was antithetical to the real theme he'd worked on capturing: health systems are not made to help the poor. It had only been coincidence that some of the poor he'd documented were The Smiths. The family of seven had connected his film to the pharmaceutical company.

Michael had spent months recording everything. A university grant had helped a great deal but good equipment and good assistants had been a bit more expensive than twenty thousand dollars. He'd made the best of it though, stretching dollars everywhere, but it had caused the on-location filming to take forever.

The documentary had revealed some really harsh consequences to the lack of health care. Michael had not been selective. He'd gone where the poor were—white, black, red or brown—and in every case except one, the drama of lost limbs and lost lives had played out with "emotional intensity." That's what the critics had called it: emotional intensity. It certainly had not been the happiest film of the year…at least not until the end. That's where The Smiths had come in.

The Smiths and many of their neighbors had been experiencing dramatic improvements in their health. Michael's investigation had revealed that the BethStar supplement had supposedly been the reason. Its distribution, though, had been controversial. Father Smith, like his neighbors, had been told in a letter that the supplement was part of the government's new health program for the poor. Each week for three months, Father Smith had received an unmarked packet of pills, enough for the entire family, at his doorstep. He'd never saved the packaging and had never met the distributors.

BETH had claimed that a legitimate request had come from the university and that researchers from the school had distributed the supplement, but the university had denied ever having an association with the company. Still, the pill had made its rounds. Fortunately for all parties, The Smiths' community had improved so much that most had been willing to put blame aside and concentrate on the positive outcome, the one revealed in Michael's documentary.

Michael saw the ghouls only because Father Smith called him a week after filming had been completed. It was a Friday, late at night and two days before the beginning of summer. Michael was sitting behind his computer editing footage when his cell phone rang.

"Mr. Arden. I have a need to talk at you." Father Smith requested. "I have been with Juanita." Juanita was not his wife's name. In all the time he'd spent with the Smith family, Michael had overheard them call each other by name only twice. Father Smith had called his wife Sienna and Sienna had called her twelve-year-old son David, but other than that, the kids were always either "mijo" or "mija" and Father Smith was always "Papa."

"Who's Juanita?" Michael asked.

"Mi amigo."

"Did she take the pill, too?"

"You no unnerstand. I could not help me. I could not stop." Father Smith's voice became urgent with impatience.

"Okay. Hold on for a second." Michael saved his work and stood from the computer. He walked to his screened porch door and looked toward the dark outline of the Organ Mountains several miles away. "Tell me what's up."

"What to call it?" Father Smith said. "A fair? I had a fair."

A fair, Michael thought. A fair what? But that's not what Michael asked. He knew Father Smith was trying to tell him something that he didn't have the English to properly explain. "You had a fair with Juanita?"

"Sí. But I didn't want to. I was, how you say, maniplated."

It was then that both words came to Michael at once. Father Smith had had an affair with Juanita but only because he'd been manipulated to do so. It sounded like an excuse that thousands of men used every day. Why he'd called Michael to confess was rather odd. "That's not good," was all that he could come up with.

"Sí. And they will make me do it more. Help me, amigo."

"Who? Who will make you do it more?"

"The pill men. Please come. I think they will be here."

Michael had taken one of his four digital cameras with him, hoping to capture something that might have explain how the BethStar supplement had found its way to the Smith family. If the *pill men* were there when he arrived, he'd hide outside and record everything. Unfortunately, the battery in the camera he'd hastily selected was not charged and that error would serve as one of the biggest mistakes he'd ever made, particularly since what he could have recorded would have verified every last gory nuance of the story he would later tell Fred and anyone else that would listen.

It was around ten o'clock when he arrived at the Smiths' two-room, HUD-funded home. The *pill men* were already there so Michael stood outside a window and watched.

"What are you going to tell him?" said the pill man who would soon become known as Pitchfork Man.

"Nada," Father Smith insisted as his entire family cowered behind the protective breadth of their Papa.

"Liar! You called Mr. Arden just a few minutes ago."

Father Smith genuflected. "You make me take Juanita. You make me sin."

Pitchfork Man cackled only once but it was deep enough and loud enough to shake the window glass just inches in front of Michael's nose. "Sin? Are you serious? I was only doing you a favor. One woman forever is not the best recipe for any human man. Believe me. I know."

"The pill," Father Smith said. "I am better but I am not."

Pitchfork Man shrieked once again. "Now that's the best illegal immigrant conclusion I have ever heard."

That's when Father Smith presented the pitchfork he'd been hiding behind his back. "You go away," he demanded.

"We will," Pitchfork Man said. "As soon as you are dead."

Michael did not see the second pill man until that moment. The Decapitator, as Fred would name him, walked forward, appearing from the left of the window just a few feet from where Michael stood outside. The Decapitator held a machete.

Michael almost intervened. He almost screamed *Stop!* But Father Smith's sudden assault with the pitchfork dissuaded him for the one fraction of a second that probably saved his own life. When the heads and blood started redecorating the Smiths' wooden floors, Michael gasped and the pill men ghouls turned toward the sound at the window.

Michael had run then, his fear welling to such extremes that he had not gone home. If they *had* seen him they would have known where to find him, so he'd stayed in motels, moving from one to another until the investigation had been completed. The Smiths' house had been thoroughly cleaned and no Smiths had ever been found. The assumption had been that they'd been deported but Michael had never been able to acquire such evidence and he'd never seen the ghouls again…

Except in dreams where bodies and blood would be anchored for many months to come.

Little children's blood. Little children's screams. Pitchforks and machetes and decapitations.

The Holiday Inn wakeup call came as scheduled moments after Michael jerked straight up from another nightmare. The smell of copper overwhelmed him as it often did when the memories of the massacre manifested as dream. He grabbed the phone and dropped it back in the cradle without answering it then squashed the tip of his nose with the palm of his hand, hoping to erase the invisible smell of blood.

He quickly packed and showered then called Fred three times without getting an answer. He opened his laptop and attempted to contact Fred through email, Facebook and Twitter, again without success. He tried to remain calm but emotions boiled too fast. Thoughts of pushers in staircases, shadows behind trees, black tinted-glass SUVs and remnants of the nightmare culminated in a mad rush to leave the motel and find Fred as soon as possible.

As he drove toward campus, Michael told himself that Fred was just fine. This wasn't the first time his friend had ignored him. The chemist often locked his mind into research so completely that all other distractions became insignificant. Even when Michael had tried to tell him about the Smiths, Fred had not returned his call for almost a full day. Even when Michael had tried to tell him about the ghouls…

Michael mashed the Explorer's accelerator pad.

When he arrived on campus he found the parking lot in front of the Biochemistry Building to be just as empty as it had been the night before. Fred's Land Rover still sat in the same spot and Michael parked beside it. He stepped out onto asphalt and that coppery smell left over from the nightmare assaulted him once again, reminded him once again, jerked his panic strings once again. As he entered the building, his entire body trembled.

The green hallway was no longer interspersed with bands of white and shadow but this did nothing to ease his nerves. Closed classroom doors infused further anxiety and he could not help calling out as he quickly passed each one. "Fred?" he said. His sneakers squeaked against the vinyl flooring. "Frederico? It's me."

At the opposite end of the hall, bright sunlight warmed the atrium and revealed the multitude of student experiments that had the word "Push" labeled somewhere on them. Michael turned toward Fred's lab. The door was open but the room was dark.

"Fred?" he asked again. "Come on. Don't be messing with me."

Michael snapped on the lab room lights and was immediately overwhelmed by the degree of destruction he found inside. The countertop stations used by students had been swept clean, the beakers and slides and microscopes now scattered in broken ruin on the floor. Michael crunch-stepped slowly forward, his eyesight locked on the tall electron microscope that had recorded the evidence he'd come to collect—that, apparently, others had also come to collect. All of the computer flat screens were missing from atop the semi-circular room divider and from the tables adjoining the microscope. They weren't scattered on the floor as was so much else in the lab; they were simply gone.

Michael inched his way around the room divider already convinced that he'd see Fred's body lying behind it, but only found more destruction: chairs were toppled and broken and mixed in with pens and papers and textbooks and keyboards, one of which was snapped in two pieces. And there was blood. Just a drop or two but it was definitely blood.

"Fred?" Michael moaned, his voice now more sad than urgent. All of the evidence against BETH Pharmaceuticals no longer mattered and the thought made him remember last night, made him remember calling Fox and telling them he'd found damning proof, made him remember that the black SUV had pulled away the moment he'd hung up. He'd caused this, he thought. The ghouls had not wanted him. They'd only used him. His cell phone call had been intercepted and the black SUV had come for Fred, had taken Fred, had taken the evidence. Michael caressed the hard, slick metal of the electron microscope thinking about what could have been, hating his own selfishness. After all, it was he who had gotten Fred into this mess in the first place.

Under a scattered array of paper on the table to the left of the microscope, Michael noticed that something had been written on the tabletop itself. He pushed the papers aside to find four words scribbled in cursive Sharpie black.

The Ruin of Arden

At first, Michael thought that whoever had destroyed the place and had taken Fred had also left him a chilling reminder. *We have ruined you, Michael Arden*, the note seemed to imply. But the handwriting was Fred's, he was sure of it. His friend had left him one last clue.

The Ruin of Arden

That's how Fred had always responded when he'd gotten the best of Michael during play in their online game world of The Runes of Andar. Fred would slay an ogre and say, "And that will lead to the ruin of Arden." He'd rescue a beautiful princess and say, "And that will lead to the ruin of Arden." He'd find a magic chest and say…

Michael gasped. Somewhere behind him a beaker rolled off a counter and smashed on the floor. He turned not really seeing anything. He turned while thinking that he had to get to his computer. He ran from the lab thinking that he had to enter the Runes because Fred had told him to, because Fred had said that he'd left something there that would forever rid him of the ghouls.

Oh Fred, he thought. *I'm so sorry. Please be all right.*

But when Michael exited the Biochemistry Building and walked past the rear hatch of Fred's Land Rover he saw what looked like a handprint—a red handprint outlined against the tinted glass from the inside. And when he looked into the hatch he found that Fred was nowhere near all right. Fred's body lay mangled, bent, twisted and dead.

The drive to the El Paso International Airport was worrisome and frenetic. The police would no doubt find Fred's body and start an investigation that would lead them to Michael which, after all, had been the point of killing Fred in the first place. Take the evidence, off the scientist, and set Michael up to take the rap. Clean and efficient. Just like Federales might do. Just like anyone—or anything—trying to conceal the truth might do.

But for the entire fifty mile journey from Las Cruces, Michael wondered. Had they *really* gotten a hold of the video that Fred had promised to assemble for his report? Fred was a pretty sharp cookie; he would have left Michael something. He would not have died in vain. Those four words—*the Ruin of Arden*—would have meant nothing to his killers but to Michael, they connected straight up with the conversation he and Fred had had the night before.

Pitchfork Man knows where the magic chest is that holds the magic elixir that will, when consumed, erase that ghoul from the Runes forever.

A magic elixir that when consumed would rid him of the ghouls.

A video that when watched by the world would destroy BETH Pharmaceuticals forever.

The proof was in the game. The proof was in the Runes of Andar.

It just had to be.

Monday morning traffic at the airport was light and Michael quickly found an overnight parking garage space near a skywalk that led directly to his gate. He only had fifteen minutes before boarding would begin. In preparation, he'd turned on his laptop a few miles back to alleviate the time it would take to start it up.

He snatched his garment bag and laptop case then dashed into the terminal just as his cell phone rang. He didn't answer it. He didn't even pull it out of his pocket to see who was calling. He already knew. It was either the New Mexico State Police, who'd already called twice, or *Fox News*, who'd called once every ten minutes since he'd left Las Cruces; his message the night before had ramped up their curiosity. But Michael wasn't about to make the same mistake twice. Someone would be listening in, someone who didn't mind torturing people for truth, someone who could kill quickly and cleanly, someone who drove a black SUV. Fox would have to wait until he arrived in New York to get the skinny on conspiracies and cover-ups and murders—that is if Fred had actually hidden the evidence in Andar.

Gate 10 wasn't crowded. He sat with his back to a window overlooking the tarmac, opened the laptop and found a connection. The thought that someone in the airport might intercept the wireless signal was insignificant to his overwhelming desire to know. Paranoia had to take a backseat…at least for the next five to ten minutes. Still, he looked up from the screen as his login was accepted. No one paid him any attention. No one, apparently, had followed.

Michael met up with Fred's avatar immediately and the look of the quirky, bearded, beer-bellied character that in no way resembled Fred made him cry. A little girl sitting four seats to his left stared at his tears, her demeanor consoling of a complete stranger. Fred's avatar (which Fred had named FredRod) didn't talk and didn't move. It just stood there in the middle of the Halls of Andar waiting for its master to provide direction which now, of course, was impossible. Michael placed both his avatar (which looked a lot like Elvis and was named simply, Mikey) and FredRod into "lock up mode" which was a method in the game where one player could take a fellow player's avatar along for the journey even when both players were not logged in.

"Let's go find Pitchfork Man," Michael whispered. The little girl who'd been looking at him so solemnly suddenly turned away and placed her newly shocked expression into the upper arm of her mother.

It wasn't long before Mikey and FredRod found their nemesis. Its red body and four legs crouched near a golden chest at the bank of a virtual river.

Fred had done a number on Pitchfork Man, creating a thing that was part human, part dog, and part devil. It stood on its hind legs with pitchfork in hand as they approached.

I'll take that chest now, Michael typed.

Over my dead body, the red devil dog thing sneered.

At that moment, FredRod broke away from lock up mode and began acting on its own. It was as if Fred had just logged in and was now controlling his own avatar. But Fred was dead. The only explanation Michael could think of was that Fred had programmed his avatar to take action once it had arrived at a certain point in the game…in this case, when it was in proximity to Pitchfork Man.

Stick that fork up your ass, FredRod shouted then spit a ball of fire that rolled across the screen and engulfed the creature. FredRod ran to the right, shouting obscenities and drawing the attention and action of Pitchfork Man in that direction.

A diversion, Michael thought. The magic chest now sat unprotected and Mikey quickly ran to it, tapped it, pushed it, rolled it, but could not open it. To his right, FredRod and the devil dog were engaged in all out war as pitchforks and fire rained around them. Michael remembered that, sometimes, magic chests in The Runes of Andar necessitated magic words to open them and he typed in all the obvious choices: *abracadabra, open sesame, your mama is a goon* (that's one that Fred had made up some time ago) and then, finally, of course…

The Ruin of Arden

The lid to the golden chest sprang up and a small window popped open on the laptop screen entitled: The Elixir. A complex web address filled with only numerals and slashes was written at the top of the window; below it was a message from Fred.

> *Use this address only once as it is set to erase the file once the site is accessed a single time. You'll only get one chance to download it. Take care, my friend. I'm beginning to believe in ghouls.*

FredRod screamed and Michael turned his avatar just in time to see the red creature pull three pitchforks out of FredRod's beer belly, chest and face. It turned toward Mikey, the pitchfork tines dripping with FredRod's green blood. *Skewer*, was the single word it said before taking its first step towards Michael's avatar.

Michael silently repeated the web address over and over, his lips moving without speech, which made the little girl sitting four seats to his left squirm even further into her mother's bosom. The mother looked up then, saw the weird man mumbling to himself, considered her daughter's fright, and moved to the opposite side of the Gate 10 waiting area.

Michael looked up when the airport's intercom exclaimed, "Flight 699 for Laguardia now boarding at Gate 10. First-class and those needing assistance only please." When he looked back down at the laptop screen, the devil dog had already pierced Mikey's Elvis-looking face with three pitchforks and as his avatar fell and faded, the small window with Fred's message and the magic chest disappeared.

Michael repeated the web address in his head two more times before he closed the laptop and walked to the gate. He repeated the address in his head another dozen times as he walked the boarding ramp onto the plane. Once he was seated (Fox had gone all out by providing first-class airfare), Michael closed his eyes and saw the web address printed in white behind his eyelids. When he opened them, a large man wearing a black suit, black fedora and dark sunglasses was staring at him.

"I think you are in my seat," the man said, his voice somehow familiar. "Three A?"

Michael looked at his ticket stub to find that he was in the right seat. He showed the stub to the man who smiled and said, "My bad. So many numbers and they all look alike, don't you think? An eight looks like a three, a six a nine. It all depends. I must have remembered it all wrong." He pulled his own stub from his pocket. "Yep. Eight A. My apologies." The man smiled then moved along the aisle to sit five rows directly behind Michael.

As much as he wanted to, Michael didn't turn. As much as he thought he knew the man, he just sat there and again closed his eyes. The web address numbers reappeared but now Michael was uncertain if the threes, eights, sixes and nines were accurate. And though it was impossible to believe, Michael was sure that such confusion was exactly what the man in black had intended all along.

Michael's mind held the secret and paranoia had now taken complete control.

The plane landed on-time a few minutes after eight o'clock. Michael was one of the first to exit. He didn't look back. He had no idea where the man in the black fedora was and, quite frankly, didn't want to know. It had taken him the entire flight to calm down, to reassure himself that he'd be safe, that no one could possibly know what he'd found. The observations about numbers from the man in the fedora and sunglasses had just been a coincidence, that's all. And once he found the *Fox News* escort who was supposed to be waiting for him at the arrival gate, it wouldn't matter anyway. He'd sleep at Ben Reely's house if that's what it took. No one touched Ben Reely.

The Laguardia terminal was predictably packed. Many chauffeurs and tour guides held signs above their heads that advertised the names of people they were supposed to meet. "Arden" was not written on any of them.

As panic started to creep back in, Michael stood in the midst of the human mass and took several deep breaths. An onslaught of *What Ifs* assaulted him as people shuffled around, scowled at him, mumbled a few obscenities at him, bumped purposefully into him. He saw the man in the black fedora several yards away where an escalator promoted a means toward an exit, and as the man descended the moving staircase, his head turned just before the fedora dropped out of sight. The distance made it impossible to determine but Michael was certain that the man was staring right at him.

"Sir?"

A hand dropped onto Michael's shoulder and he jumped.

"Sorry," the voice said. "Didn't mean to startle you." Michael turned. "Are you Mr. Arden?"

The *Fox News* chauffeur was young and sharply dressed. Brown hair slicked back with way too much gel gave his Italian complexion a stereotypical mafia look. He held a dry erase board with the name "Arden" written on it.

"I am," Michael said. "You are from Fox I take it?"

"Yes. We have a room ready for you at the Rockefeller Center Hotel. Mr. Reely would like you to call him as soon as you settle in. Here's the number." The chauffeur handed Michael a slip of paper. "He said it's urgent."

"Yes. He would say that."

The chauffeur's face scrunched with curiosity but he asked no questions. "Please follow me," he offered and led Michael toward the escalator where the man with the fedora had previously exited.

Outside, Michael saw black SUVs everywhere—or at least in Michael's state of mind they seemed to be everywhere. The Fox chauffeur led Michael toward one of them.

"Excuse me sir, but could you spare some change?" A little girl no older than the one he'd frightened inside the airport in El Paso stood hip-level beside him. Her clothes were ratty as was her hair. Michael thought she could have popped right out of a Charles Dickens novel, minus the London accent. He gave her a dollar and the girl quickly ran off. When he turned around, the chauffeur was gone but the rear door to an idling black SUV stood invitingly open.

"In here, Mr. Arden," a voice that sounded a lot like the chauffeur's said from within.

And Michael got in.

Michael had been in the City many times during his twenty-plus years of living in the United States so he knew, immediately, that the SUV was heading in the wrong direction.

"You're driving toward the Bronx not Manhattan," he said to the driver whom he thought was the slick-haired young man who'd met him in the terminal. When the driver did not respond he added, "Hell-ooo…The Rockefeller Center Hotel is in Manhattan and I've got a few important phone calls to make, remember?" When the driver still did not respond, Michael tapped his shoulder. "Goddammit, man. I said…" The driver didn't have to turn around. Michael saw in the rear view mirror that the driver was not the guy who'd met him at the gate. He saw that the driver was the man from the plane, the one who had worn a black fedora. And, since the driver was no longer wearing his sunglasses either and Michael was only inches from the driver's face, he also realized that the man was the pusher he'd met in the Pan American Center stairwell…the one who had sold him PUSH*. He knew this because of the eyes, those bloodshot red orbs with pupils that danced in silver swirls.

"Let me out of this fucking thing!" Michael screamed and drew back to punch the driver's head but the handgun that now appeared in the pusher's hand shut him up immediately.

"I think you have something we need, Mr. Arden," the pusher said. "I think that you'll be more than willing to give it to us within the next hour."

We, Michael thought, knowing the answer was not *Fox News*. "Who the hell is We?"

"Relax. Sit back. Enjoy the ride. I'd hate to have to shoot you in a non-vital but very painful area of the chest. Blood and leather don't mix well, don't you think? Besides, there'll be plenty of time for blood later." Then he laughed, once, sounding a whole lot like the ghoul who'd skewered Father Smith.

Michael settled back in the seat and the gun's barrel was removed from his line of sight. "I know you don't I?"

"Of course you do. Everyone knows me. I am what nightmares are made of." He snickered.

Michael tried not to look at the pusher's mirrored reflection. "You killed Father Smith, didn't you?"

The pusher didn't hesitate. His immediate answer seemed filled with great joy. "Yep!"

"And Fred."

"Yep!"

"And you work for BETH."

"Yep!"

"And the PUSH* pill is an attempt to control people."

"Yep. Oh, Yep!"

Michael knew there could be only one reason that the pusher was so willing to confess such information. "If you kill me," he said, "a hundred newspapers will have the evidence in hand by the morning."

The pusher looked directly at him in the mirror and Michael couldn't help staring at the maniacal red eyes, the crazy silver sparkle swirls within the pupil reflections. "I'm not going to kill you."

Michael looked through the window, gazed at the New York City skyline and thought that this might be the last time he'd ever see it. "You'll have to 'cause I ain't talkin'."

"You can say that now, but…"

The pusher turned onto a road that paralleled the East River where shadowy warehouses dotted the landscape. Many of them looked abandoned and broken, standing as enigmatic symbols of the country's economic downturn.

"What. No canvas bag over the head?" Michael said. "No gag in the mouth? No duct tape around the wrists? What kind of henchman are you anyway?"

"You watch too many movies Mr. Arden. Real ghouls don't play that way."

Michael gasped.

"Yes." The pusher snickered again. "And might I say that's a splendid word for us."

The pusher parked in an abandoned lot at the end of the warehouse row and the pusher opened the SUV's back door. The pusher did not forcefully grab him and offered no instructions. Its physical presence coupled by the memories it had planted in Michael's head was enough. It turned and walked toward a set of large warehouse doors and Michael got out and followed, remaining at a distance that covered the pusher in a moiré of darkness which mixed inside a soft fog now rolling in from the river. For an instant, Michael thought he saw the pusher transform into the red devil dog avatar from the

Runes game world. Its long tail whipped foggy swirls as it slid open the warehouse doors and in that instant, Michael knew that his life had really ended back in June of 2009, back when logic had been replaced by visions that could not have been real…just like the devil dog pusher was right now: a fog-swirly red mass of unreality that beckoned him forward into dark recesses where no man should ever venture.

"Please," the devil dog mirage said and disappeared into the building.

It wasn't until he was inside that Michael smelled the gasoline and oil, and when the warehouse doors closed behind him the odor tripled in intensity, offering Michael's breaths no relief. He swooned momentarily.

"Back here."

The interior of the thirty-foot tall warehouse was drearily illuminated only by city light glare that infiltrated down through glass panes positioned at the top of all four walls. A brighter slit of light blazed through an open office door at the far corner of the vacant warehouse floor. The pusher's silhouette, which no longer resembled that of a devil dog avatar (if it really ever had), stood beside the door.

Michael slipped several times on the oily warehouse floor. Dizziness overwhelmed him. An ounce of the coffee he'd consumed on the airplane hiccupped into his mouth. The pusher nudged the door further open and Michael entered.

Satanic ritual was the first thing he thought, except only one person was wearing a hooded cloak. The room was rather large, about fifty feet squared, and was occupied by several individuals standing in a semi-circle around a pentagram that had been chiseled into the concrete, oil-stained floor. A steel office chair sat in the middle of the pentagram; above it hovered a bright lamp that was suspended from the ceiling by a single cable. Behind the occupants were dozens of flickering candles set atop cardboard boxes that varied in height. Michael did not need to be asked. He knew where he was supposed to sit.

"I like you, Mr. Arden," said the hooded figure directly in front of him. "You've made my life so much easier."

Easier, everyone in the room repeated simultaneously.

"But I dare say that you have one more thing to do for me." The figure dropped its hood and Michael immediately recognized him. He'd seen Richard Manson in the media many times, particularly since his documentary had made such a rock star out of him. "Tell me, Mr. Arden. Where is it?"

Where is it? Where is it? Where is it? the ritualistic clan said.

The intense gasoline vapors tickled his gag reflex but Michael held it back. He mustered a smile. "You can't be serious," he said boldly even though fear and the feeling of faint wrestled his courage. "You think all of this hob-goblin bullshit is gonna scare anything out of me? Go ahead and kill me, sacrifice me to your demons. Fold me in half like you did Fred... whatever...but you're going to go down nonetheless." He turned toward all of the occupants in the room and added, "All of you are going down."

Going down, they all repeated, their eyes forward and glassy, their unified voice reminding Michael of the crowd at the Bad Company concert.

Manson walked over to him and knelt. His face was fickle. "I think you already know that if I'd wanted you dead, you'd be that way already. But as I said, I like you. Your documentary did so much for me and my...future. If anything, I should offer you a reward."

"Good. Then let me go."

"Naw." Manson's smile curled upward. "I had something else in mind."

Michael turned to his left where the pusher stood at attention by the office door. In one of its hands was a pitchfork. "We found your nanobots," Michael exclaimed and hiccupped another half ounce of coffee. "And we have the proof. The richest man in the world is gonna end up in prison and your little scheme at mind control will come to an abrupt end."

Manson's smile instantly vanished. "We?" he grumbled. "Are you including that dead wetback? Fernandez had been a pain in my ass for far too long, but killing him before now would have only directed attention to me. He got me kicked out of ASU and that would have been cause for motive. But none of that matters now. Destiny is pretty near complete."

"You're a cheater and Fred found you out." Michael said. "You steal other's ideas and make them your own. Is that how you came to be so rich? How pathetic." Michael's willpower to throttle the puke at the back of his throat quickly eroded as the gasoline vapors continued to assault him.

"What is pathetic, Mr. Arden, is the human race." He walked casually over to the pusher and snatched the pitchfork from its hand. "Useless," he said and thrust the pitchfork through the person standing next to the pusher; when he pulled it out, the body fell. "Pieces," he continued and skewered the next in line, stepped back, and swatted the body to the floor. "Of shit." Another of the semicircular group took all four tines of the pitchfork in the chest without any attempt at salvation. None of the five remaining people said anything and none of them moved as Manson continued.

"God." Another fell.

"Hates." And another.

"Every." Stab.

"Last." Skewer.

"One of you." Manson had to shake the last person's body from the pitchfork.

Eight people lay dead on the floor, their combined blood drooling into one thick rivulet that found the outline of the pentagram and filled its grooves until the entire concrete engraving turned red. Michael shuffled his toes backward to avoid the sticky runners. His stomach took a leap that he could no longer control. Bile and coffee dripped from the corner of his mouth.

"I have this theory, Mr. Arden," Manson said as he returned the bloody pitchfork to the pusher. "Please feel free to use it at your leisure. I won't blame *you* for plagiarizing."

Michael wiped his mouth. "You forgot to stick that pitchfork up one more place. Here. Give it to me and I'll show you what I mean."

Manson grinned. "Everything feeds on everything else," he said. "All the way up and down to the nth degree, the only way anything can survive is if it consumes something else. Nothing lives in total absolution. Molecules eat molecules. Atoms destroy other atoms. It's natural selection…survival of the fittest…Darwinian ideals applied at the macro- and micro-levels. Even subatomic particles look over their shoulders wondering what, in time, will kill them." He pointed at the pile of dead bodies. "All I'm trying to do is accelerate the process, clean up this human infested world, change the status quo."

The vapors and the blood and the insanity spewing from Manson's mouth became overwhelming. "You're just another superior race nut job," he said. "And like history has shown to the nth degree, you'll end up destroyed and forgotten. I'll make sure of that."

The pusher now moved forward, lowered the pitchfork, and aimed one of the tines at Michael's left eye. A single drop of blood oozed down onto Michael's cheek.

"Tell us where Dead Fred left it," Manson demanded.

Michael swooned when the bloody pitchfork point touched his flesh.

"Pretty please?"

Michael woke to the knock at his hotel room door. The alarm clock beside him read 7:04. He jolted from bed wondering why he hadn't asked the front desk for a wake-up call. He always asked for a wake-up call, but he couldn't remember doing so last night. In fact, he couldn't remember a lot of what had happened after the moment he'd apparently passed out. He sat up and immediately touched his left eye. The bloody cold pitchfork tine remained as a deep subconscious impression.

The knocks on the door became fervent. “Mr. Arden?” a woman’s muffled voice urged. “Your limo is waiting for you.”

“Be right down,” he shouted, his dry morning voice unable to enunciate effectively. He swung his feet to the floor and realized he was still dressed. Next to the bed was his overnight garment bag and laptop case. How he or they had gotten there, he could only guess.

He rubbed his eye again and then gasped at the thought of what he might have said, of what he didn’t remember saying. Had he told Manson? Had he revealed the dark web site address that Fred had left for him?

Use this address only once as it is set to erase the file once the site is accessed a single time. You’ll only get one chance to download it.

He was scheduled to be at Fox Studio in less than half an hour. There was simply no time to find out.

He wet his hair and wiped himself down with a washcloth before dressing in the only suit he owned. Such a formal look was abnormal for Michael Arden but the information he was about to share with the world needed a professional look behind it to help believability.

Knocking returned to his hotel door; this time a man’s voice, one Michael recognized, exclaimed, “Are you all right, Mr. Arden? Can I be of some assistance?”

“Right there,” Michael shouted. “Be right there.” He grabbed his laptop case and looked inside to find his computer but his research notes were gone. In the rush to leave Las Cruces, he wondered if he’d even put them in there. Didn’t matter, he thought. Most of the information was safely stored in his head. He straightened his tie and opened the hotel door to find the same guy who’d met him and lost him at Laguardia. His slick hair and clothes had not changed from the night before.

“So good to see you, sir,” the chauffeur said. “I don’t know how I lost you last night.”

Michael waved away the apology. “My fault, not yours. I guess I just wanted to see the town.” The chauffeur offered a hand toward Michael’s laptop case. “That’s okay. I’m good.” As they walked the hall to the elevator Michael added, “The studio is just a couple of blocks down 6th Avenue. I could have walked, you know.”

The elevator opened and both men got on. “After last night, no way,” the chauffeur said. “I took one hell of a lip beating for letting you out of my sight. Mr. Reely told me if it happened again I’d be pounding the pavement.”

“Again, my apologies.”

The chauffeur shook his head. “Not necessary. Just another learning moment for a greenie fresh out of college…at least that’s what Mr. Reely told me."

The short drive gave Michael little time to think, to repeat the dark web site address over and over in his mind. He quickly scribbled a scripted speech on a note pad he'd taken from the hotel as he tried to shrug off the thought of last night, of all of those people who had just stood there, catatonic, mumbling simple words in unison. They had accepted death so easily. He forcefully shook his head in an attempt to shake the memory.

"Everything okay?" the chauffeur asked, his inquisitive eyes staring in the rear view mirror.

"Just getting my thoughts in order. I want to make sure Mr. Reely gets everything he asked for."

"Funny." The chauffeur returned his attention to the road as he turned into the Fox Studio parking garage. "That's exactly what Mr. Reely said about you. And I gottta say, between you and me, I've never seen *that* man so…oh, what's the right word…anxious."

"He and me both."

Michael followed the chauffeur through an array of elevators, escalators and doors until they arrived outside the studio where Michael was invited inside by the wave of the chauffeur's hand. "Good luck," he told Michael. "Not sure if I envy you or not." The chauffeur walked away before Michael could respond but he knew what the young man meant. An interview on live television with Ben Reely was enough to turn the nerves of any unsuspecting "greenie."

Stepping through the final threshold and into the *Fox News* studio was like stepping into a television. Glamour occupied every inch of the massive space, from wall to wall and floor to ceiling. Rows of boom lights pointed in the three directions where studio sets had been assembled. Some of the lights flashed bright and dull white then alternated to other lamps covered with red and blue gels. The test sequence continued for another minute before the center bank of key lighting snapped on, sending a sharp beam down onto the central news anchor desk where it was swallowed by the suffocating presence of neon.

Studio techs and production assistants swarmed the floor. One, a thin, short man who was no older than the chauffeur, grabbed the lapel of Michael's jacket and clipped on a tiny mic. "Where's the transmitter?" Michael asked.

"In there." He pointed at the lapel mic. "Microtransmitters are the way to go these days." He gave Michael that *What are you a dinosaur?* look which portrayed ignorance and generational difference both at the same time.

A woman in a pinstripe pantsuit and wearing a wireless headset grabbed his elbow. Michael jerked. "Sorry," she said. "Didn't mean to startle you."

Her grip was demanding and with it she pulled him toward the spectacle of light surrounding the anchor desk. "We go on in ten minutes. Show notes are already sitting on the desk. Can I take that for you?" She pointed at his laptop case.

"I'll keep it if you don't mind," he said. "Is there an agenda? Any question prompts from Mr. Reely that I should be aware of?" They stopped next to the anchor's desk and Michael absently stared straight into the boom lights then quickly turned away, a circle of white eradicating his focus.

"Been some time since you've been in a studio," the woman said as a matter of fact.

"Yeah. And certainly nothing close to this." He followed her lead toward the chair behind the right side of the desk as his vision slowly returned to normal.

"You know the agenda, Mr. Arden," she said. "BETH Pharmaceuticals and the connection to PUSH*."

"Okay. But what's he going to ask me?"

"Trade secret." The woman smiled. "Not our policy to reveal questions beforehand. Makes the show spontaneous and that is what our viewers tune in to see." She released his elbow and gave it two, quick, consoling pats. "You'll be fine. Have a seat. See if it fits you."

Michael sat and nodded and the woman walked into the thinning mass of set techs. In front of him was a manila folder. When he opened it, he gasped. All of the notes he'd thought he'd left in Las Cruces, all of his research and talking points pertaining to PUSH*, were in there. Someone had taken them from his laptop case. Michael quickly shuffled through them, finding that several sections were missing, particularly the parts that offered connections between PUSH* and BETH Pharmaceuticals.

"Five minutes," a set hand yelled, bringing Michael out of his daze and back into the theater of live television.

He closed the folder and gazed across the glass desktop, marveling at its sterility. There wasn't a single smudge on it except the ones his palms had left when he'd first sat down. In front of him, nestled within the desk below the glass top, was a flat screen monitor showing the current Fox broadcast feed. He scooted his chair backwards to test its wheels and noticed what looked like a miniature version of an iPad attached to the side of the desk between the two chairs. On its screen, several windows blinked time codes and showed different parts of the Fox set. Anchored below the small iPad was a leather pouch, its top flap secured by Velcro and hiding what was inside.

Michael scooted forward, his knees easily filling the molded inward angle of the desk. A control room occupied the far left corner of the studio and through its tinted glass wall he saw a man looking at him and giving him the thumbs up. A red light atop the studio pedestal camera closest to him blinked on and Michael looked straight at it then back at the man in the control room who was now shaking his head.

A bustle of people entered the studio to his right. One person dabbed Ben Reely's face with a soft brush while another held a thin stack of papers out in front of him from which Reely was silently reading. A third person was asking him questions and Reely gave quick, short sentence responses. All four of them stopped a dozen feet from the anchor desk and Reely peered up from his preoccupation. He stared at Michael and smiled almost mischievously. Reely dodged his triumvirate and walked toward Michael with his arm and hand extended.

"Mr. Arden," he said, smiling. "I can't tell you how great it is to have you on our show." He grabbed Michael's hand and gave it a hearty shake. "Brilliant work you've done, or as they say in Australia, bonny work."

"Enough to convict?" Michael asked.

"It all depends on that *proof* you say you've found. You did bring it with you?"

Michael tapped his head with one finger. "It's on the Web."

"Excellent." Reely's smile grew impossibly wide. "We've been given twenty minutes on today's special. I'll segue you into it. Just be ready to type the address into the control panel."

"You mean the little iPad?" Michael pointed to his side.

"You could call it that. It gives us a way to control some of the broadcast from the anchor's desk. We'll be able to jump right on the Internet." He turned toward his three assistants who stood silently behind him. "My idea," he said to them and pointed triumphantly at his chest. "Better than a chalkboard."

The assistants again surrounded Reely and Michael felt the growing weight of uncertainty drop like an anvil. The one piece of damning evidence that no one except Fred had seen was about to be revealed for the first time—right in front of millions of people. But if the address was wrong, if he'd remembered it incorrectly, if the threes and eights and sixes and nines had gotten jumbled somehow, what then? All Reely was interested in was the shock and awe associated with taking down the richest man in the world. All Ben Reely wanted was to make people famous, particularly Ben Reely.

Michael turned in his chair to study the iPad controller so that when the time came, he'd know how to type on it. His knee bumped against the leather pouch under the controller with enough force to open a tiny section of the Velcro flap. Poking out was what looked like the hammer of a pistol. He swung his elbows onto the desk and tried not to look down at it.

A gun? he thought. *In the studio? Next to Ben Reely? Were his interviewees that dangerous?*

He slipped his right arm off the desk and extended one finger. The cold metal touch of notched rills confirmed that it really was the hammer to a gun.

"What do you think?"

Suddenly, Reely was sitting beside him. Michael snapped his arm up so fast that his knuckles smacked the top edge of the desk. "Think?" he mumbled.

"Yeah. Our set. My set. What do you think? Nothing like the good ol' days that you grew up with, eh?"

"Nothing like it…that's for sure."

Reely recognized Michael's tension. "Relax," he said. "We're going to make history today. You know. The BethStar pill is connected to PUSH* is connected to BETH Pharmaceuticals. Your message said that you have evidence to prove this." After a moment of silence that lasted forever on the big studio set, he added. "Right?"

Michael nodded.

Reely's smile eroded. "We're taking a big chance here, having a guest who has such damning proof without ever seeing it ourselves."

"You'll get it," Michael said. "I can guarantee you that."

The studio set emptied and the man behind the tinted glass wall of the control room held up one hand. "Quiet on the set," he said through an intercom overhead. "Live in three…two…one." The red light on the pedestal camera opposite Reely illuminated. Reely's expression switched to one of great concern as he looked into the camera. He began.

"Is the world coming to an end? Volcanoes and comets and floods, oh my! Perhaps the end of the world will not come from Mother Nature at all but from man himself. We've all thought of that ugly reality: nuclear warfare, genetically engineered pestilence, climate change." Reely placed sarcastic undertones to the last two words and lifted his eyebrows for a camera close up.

"What if I told you that there is a pill out there that can pretty much do the same thing…turn the world upside down?" There was a scripted pause as Reely turned camera right. "Tonight we're going to talk about the real possibility that man will indeed cause the end of his own reality not by fire and brimstone, but by mind control. You heard me right…mind control." Reely again switched his attention from one camera to another. "It's called PUSH* and with me today is my friend and award-winning documentarian, Michael Arden, who knows all about it. Michael has been working on what has been a—what would you call it—undercover assignment for Fox News."

He turned toward Michael and the camera light opposite him illuminated.

"Undercover," Michael said, a bit of his forgotten Australian accent strangely resurfacing. "Yeah. You could say that." He forced a smile.

Reely jabbed a middle finger against the glass desk top and tapped it twice. "Could the PUSH* pill lead to mind control?"

Michael took the cue. "It already has."

Reely's face lit up. "I'm sure everyone out there has heard about the drug but you've uncovered the dark underbelly of what PUSH* is really all about."

Michael hesitated because he was confused. Where was Reely going with this? Michael decided to stick with his prepared script. He opened the manila folder in front of him and looked down. "PUSH* is a new designer drug that has grown dramatically in popularity over just one year. I was able to obtain some of it and with the help of a good friend…" Michael swallowed hard, "…we uncovered some interesting properties hidden at the microscopic level."

Reely intervened. "We should tell our audience that your purchase of the illegal drug was okayed by the authorities for the purpose of this assignment."

It wasn't the truth but Michael wasn't going to say so, not in front of a few million people. He continued his script. "Perhaps a bit of background is called for before I go into the full results of the investigation." He paused for Reely to add some sensationalism but he didn't. "Unlike everything else out there, PUSH* provides a timed high…some would say a euphoric high. You purchase the pill knowing that at a certain time on a certain day, zing—the push begins. No more sneaking to the bathroom stall or cowering in the concealed confines of your car, the PUSH* pill is auto-magic, delivering a healthy dose of enhanced reality. And you never have to awkwardly excuse yourself from the party."

Reely again tapped the glass desk top. "So what are the chemical reactions that cause this enhanced reality?" He'd apparently already read the contents of Michael's folder and knew the appropriate moments to lead the discussion. His cue segued into Michael's script several paragraphs ahead and Michael had to turn to the next page. The red lamps on all three cameras reminded him of the massive audience. Instead of reading any further, Michael closed the manila folder and looked at the center camera. The man standing behind the control room glass smiled.

"There are no chemical reactions, Mr. Reely," Michael said. "So how do you explain the high? I'll tell you. I'll tell all of you. It's nanobots." He turned and grinned at his host then slapped the table. "That's right! I said nanobots." Michael took pleasure in the way Reely's shoulders and face jerked with surprise as the studio lights and cameras caught the host's unusual reaction, a first for the morning news show. Two seconds of dead air filled the studio before Reely responded.

"Nanobots?"

Michael blinked as his eyes glued to the key light above the camera in front of him. His vision blurred and he looked down to where the iPad controller pulsed an array of colorful digital meters. A digital alpha-numeric keypad appeared below the meters and Michael dropped his hand to the little screen, touched the digital "H", then slid his finger further south to where the hammer of the gun protruded from its Velcro-strapped holder. Absently, he wondered what kind of firearm was inside and what it might feel like to hold it.

"Nanobots," Reely repeated. "Can you tell our audience what they are?" He waved his hand toward the cameras, beckoning Michael to look up in that direction.

But Michael didn't. For some reason he couldn't wrench his attention from the gun. "You know what the hell they are," he grumbled. "You tell your damned audience since you already read all my notes."

Real concern now fell on the entire studio crew. In the control booth, the production director asked his staff to cue up a commercial break. The cameramen gawked at each other. The pantsuited woman who'd led Michael to his chair stood at attention, a clipboard in one hand, near the emergency exit.

Reely began explaining nanobots to the best of his ability and this caused Michael's anger to grow though he didn't know why, nor could he control it. It was as if a switch had suddenly rerouted the emotional centers of his brain. Not only was he growing angrier, his desire to hold the gun grew irresistibly prominent.

"You uncovered a signature, a link," Reely said. "Isn't that right? One that can prove the manufacturer of this illegal drug?" Reely's eyes now locked onto what was at the center of Michael's attention. "BETH Pharmaceuticals—right? You have the proof. Go ahead and bring it up on the control pad there."

Michael pulled the Velcro strap.

"Mr. Arden knows the location of an Internet site where proof can be found that links the maker of the popular BethStar supplement to the supplier of PUSH*." Reely turned to the center camera but his preoccupation with his guest was apparent.

To Michael, nothing but the gun really mattered anymore. He heard Reely's words but they were gibberish undertones to what he believed was a hushed voice in his head.

The gun is pretty, it said. *The gun is fun.*

"Mr. Arden."

The gun can set you free.

"The web site, if you please."

The gun will shut him up.

The last well-reasoned thought that Michael Arden managed was a hunch: he'd been pushed. Then he drew the gun from its sheath, a nine millimeter Beretta. He'd never fired such a gun but it sure felt pretty and fun and free.

Richard Manson sat in his Manhattan penthouse apartment, watching *Fox News Morning*. He sipped hot coffee through a straw and lightly stroked the screen of a miniature version of an iPad, one very similar to that which was now a part of the Fox News studio set. He moved a digital slider all the way to the right then tapped the screen to close the display. The screen's image faded from the control application to a single geometric shape, an icon that looked a lot like a ball made out of stop signs.

0-Time Predicate

Saturday Afternoon, December 17, 2011

Cooper's concern for Billy was greater than it had been in quite some time. Nexpa had been the perfect hideout as the world had evolved three years closer to the 2012 end date. No one had come looking for them. No one had ever questioned why they were there. Their story could have been like many: people who had found their own tropical paradise and had liquidated former lives in exchange for it. They'd lived in the moment not thinking about where they were headed or the tumultuous saga of how they'd arrived.

But just a few moments ago, Billy had brought up the subject of the Book of the Djed for the first time since they'd settled in the small beach town. He'd said that he wanted to show her something connected with the Book and Sebastian's Island, something that he'd been working on since they'd left the island so long ago. Cooper wondered if it might have something to do with the cliff caves and the dolphins and Billy's obsession with them during the few months they'd lived there.

She relaxed in a beach chair near Billy's Surf Shop and stared at the tranquility of the Pacific Ocean. Billy would soon return from running a few errands and then, perhaps, he would tell her. He would confirm her fears that the time had finally come. The time for leaving was now. The time for fighting, once again, was about to begin.

"Hey," a young man with a horrible goatee asked her. "You know when Billy is coming back?"

She looked at the sunburned man but heard nothing except her own thoughts.

"Ma'am?"

She remembered waiting for Billy to return from the cliff caves.

"Hello?"

She remembered how the newest Daykeeper had battled with such newfound responsibility.

"Knock, knock. Is anyone in there?"

A neuron door opened and flooded her with memories she'd so carefully locked away—of Sebastian's Island and the journey through Mexico they'd made to Nexpa.

0-Time: Predicate

The Tulum Terrorists

Back at the end of 2008, Billy Jo Presser, John Brown Gordon, Sebastian Bondager and Cooper Reyes had fled from Tulum in Sebastian's Sea Ray, wandering and wondering in which direction they should go. Fortunately, Sebastian had provided a solution.

"My secret island," Sebastian had said the first day on the water. "No one will ever find us there."

But by the third day, with no island in sight, Cooper had begun to worry as had John. Cooper had retained her opinion that Sebastian, a man whom she'd known for just a short time, was a bit crazy—that perhaps his aging mind no longer had the capacity to reason, that his island was merely fabricated self-hope. John had not been so kind. Thankfully, he'd vocalized what Cooper had been thinking.

"Have you flipped or something?" he'd finally said. "We've been at sea for three days and supplies are running short. Don't you think it's time for the truth? Hope can only take us so far."

Sebastian, however, had not wavered. He'd insisted that the island was real. He'd told the incredible story that the government had given it to him twenty years ago for services rendered. While working in the Gulf as a contracted professional diver for the NOAA, he'd accidentally discovered a sunken treasure worth several million dollars, a fortune found that the administration had not wanted to go public. His incentive to keep quiet (the NOAA had called it a "reward") was something Sebastian had always dreamed about: a secluded place where, when the world finally went to total shit, he could survive.

Sebastian and John had argued at length…about the island, about their survival, about Sebastian's sanity. Billy, on the other hand, had not cared about any of it. From the time they'd left Tulum, he'd remained in the boat's cabin, had eaten very little, had spoken even less. His singular focus had been on the artifacts they'd collected, particularly the Book of the Djed. Cooper had thought that he'd examined every page at least a hundred times, perhaps trying to decipher it, perhaps only doing what Daykeepers did.

But Cooper had believed Billy's greater dilemma had centered on thoughts of immortality. He was supposed to save the world and coming to grips with such responsibility was enough to devastate any human being's sense of meaning. Cooper had tried several times to comfort him, to let him know that she was there for him, that she would do anything to ease his troubled mind, but Billy had kept such conversations at a distance, always politely thanking her but never going any further than that.

It was only when night had fallen on the third day and John had finally threatened mutiny that Billy had emerged onto the boat's forward deck. "We can't go back," he'd said. "We have to disappear."

John's big, black hands were curled into the fabric of Sebastian's shirt just below the neck. Had Billy not appeared at that moment, Cooper believed that John would have thrown Sebastian overboard.

"That's what I've been trying to tell you," Sebastian yelled at John, his voice quivering with anger and fear.

John, still holding tight, turned, lifting Sebastian's body from the deck as he did so. Cooper walked over to stand beside Billy.

"There's nothing we can do until it is time for us to do it," Billy said, his expression one of certainty unlike that which washed Cooper's face with dread.

"What the hell are you talking about? What the hell do you know?" John insisted.

"I'm a Daykeeper."

John released Sebastian and patted the wrinkles he'd created in Sebastian's oversized T-shirt.

"Lax would be disappointed in you, John," Billy continued. "Where's the faith? Where's that unquestioning acceptance to go forward—that knowing without really knowing how you know? Isn't that what Lax taught you? Isn't that what has gotten us this far?"

"Blind faith," John said, his voice shallow and spoken as if not wanting to be heard. "And we're all gonna die because of it."

"No." Billy waved a finger at him. "Because Sebastian is telling us the truth." He pointed to the horizon where a faint, blue star nibbled at the dark edge of calm water.

Sebastian really *did* have an island. Whether the government had ever "given" it to him or not, really didn't matter. Cooper and her friends would be safe and secluded for as long as the supplies lasted and, according to Sebastian, he'd stashed enough over the past two decades to provide for himself and one other person for at least three years.

The blue "star" they'd seen from the boat was a solar-powered marker that Sebastian had installed and it guided him through the island's only natural channel. After they'd docked (Sebastian had built a pretty rugged ten-foot pier), the first thing Sebastian did was to switch off the marker at the insistence of Billy even though Sebastian vehemently guaranteed that the island's secrecy had never been discovered.

With flashlights, Sebastian guided them to the one-room "hut-home" (Sebastian's words) he'd built. It was a beauty, he said, that could only be appreciated in daylight. Sebastian and John slept upstairs while Cooper and Billy slept in the storm shelter bedroom that Sebastian had built below the hut-home. The plans for the dual-use underground shelter had been acquired from a magazine many years ago. Sebastian said that he'd had to augment the construction material, trading out concrete for rock, but that the shelter had withstood a couple of hurricanes already, including "Nasty Wilma" that pretty much decimated the northern Yucatán back in 2005. Sebastian said that he'd had to rebuild the hut-home back then but that the shelter had done its job.

Cooper and Billy slept in the same bed the first night (there was only one rollout in the storm shelter), and though Billy quickly fell asleep, Cooper stayed awake until a couple of hours before daybreak. The bed was so small that roll-around room did not exist. Billy shifted only once during the night and this brought his face within inches of Cooper's. They'd kissed for the first time just four days ago but that had been before Billy had become a Daykeeper. Now, Cooper wondered if such intimacies existed for Daykeepers. She wondered if they were allowed. She wondered if she'd ever kiss him again. And so, she nudged forward and pecked one of his lips with both of hers. It was a stolen kiss, one that Billy would never remember, and the very second after she rolled away, she felt guilty, selfish and sad.

Could a Daykeeper love? she wondered.

That thought traveled with her into sleep where it incubated until she awakened to find Billy gone. A rectangular patch of light had replaced his small half of the bed and she stretched her arm to cover its warmth. Somewhere above her, she heard the harsh clatter of hammer-on-wood. Her internal watch told her that noon was somewhere close.

She climbed the steps of a ladder made of bamboo and emerged into the hut-home's single room. Repurposed furniture furnished the space. There was a dresser, a couple of end tables, footlocker, and two sleeping bags—one lying open and unzipped on the floor and one neatly rolled up and tied next to a flat, white pillow. Another hammer swing connected just yards beyond a constructed wall of remnant pine wood boards that looked as if they'd been collected from commercial discard piles. The craftsmanship was undeniable. Whatever goo it was that connected and sealed the discarded boards drooled down across wood knots, splits, and deformations. Sebastian had, apparently, taken recycling to a new level.

Cooper stuck her finger against one hardened drool, then against another. She smiled as her finger rolled. One drool at a time. Plucking. As if the entire interior of Sebastian's hut-home was one great harpsichord. Plucking. As if she could actually generate a sound. But the only response was the hammering, outside.

That's when John entered. The rectangular sunshot, blazing through the hut-home's makeshift, recycled timber door, became apparent only because John's monstrous silhouette occupied its center. "Hungry?" he said.

Cooper nodded and John presented her with a coconut shell filled with what Cooper thought was sushi—pink niblets surrounded by green sprigs that looked nothing like the flora she'd cooked up in Sedona. "Fish? For breakfast?" she asked.

"Closer to lunch," John offered. "Fish will be a part of many meals to come."

Cooper prodded the coconut bowl with an index finger, pushing the chunks of fish aside, opting instead for the greens and moist shreds of coconut she found underneath the meat. The memory of Billy's soulful encounter with a dolphin the evening before they'd gone into Tulum and his subsequent refusal to eat tuna, still prominently lingered and her stomach resisted the flesh.

"Okay," John said. "But you'll have to come to grips with the idea sometime, soon. Billy seems to think we'll be here for a few years."

"What's he eating?" Cooper asked, using her fingers like a spoon to scoop up and eat everything but the fish.

"He's not. At least I haven't seen him eat anything."

Cooper gave John the bowl and John ate one chunk of fish before turning away as if suddenly embarrassed. "Sorry," he said over his shoulder. "But I don't think I'm gonna become a vegetarian anytime soon. Sebastian has a pretty good stash of protein alternatives. We'll wrestle you something up that's more substantial a little later. There's more coconut salad outside if you'd like."

Cooper licked her fingers. "Yes. That stuff is really good."

"Sebastian is quite a chef—a much better one than I remember him being." John led Cooper outside. "Over there," he added, pointing toward a square table that was constructed of the same wood-plank remnants as the hut-home. A spread of bowls and plates sat buffet-style on its raw surface. Sebastian appeared from behind the left side of his hut-home then walked over and stood beside the table with a hammer in one hand.

"I need your help to raise a wall," he said to John before acknowledging Cooper's presence. "Merry Christmas, my dear. What do you think of my little island?"

Cooper had totally forgotten the significance of the day. "Haven't seen much of it beyond a dark cellar," she said. "Perhaps you could give me the tour?"

"Planned already. We'll take a walk together later on. Right now there's work to be done." Sebastian glanced at John who continued eating the leftover fish from Cooper's coconut bowl. "But you're going to need sustenance first." He set the hammer on the table and grabbed a plate filled with fruit, then invited her over with the wave of his free hand. "It's canned but tasty. I've added my own little touch."

Both Cooper and John joined him and she grabbed the plate, noticing that it was manufactured Corelle and not handcrafted from island resources as was everything else she'd seen so far.

Sebastian noticed her inquisitive expression. "Never could make a nice round plate," he said. "Besides, they were my mother's."

John set the empty coconut bowl on the table and grabbed Sebastian's hammer. "Let's do it," he said and together he and Sebastian walked over to the construction project while Cooper ate warm chunks of pineapple, mandarin oranges and grapes that tasted better than any canned fruit she'd ever eaten. It appeared that the two men were constructing an addition onto Sebastian's hut-home and as they pushed a fifteen foot wall frame upright and anchored it to the side of the existing structure, Cooper slowly turned in one complete circle to analyze her new surroundings.

Sebastian's Island could have been yanked right out of any one of numerous movies and television shows she'd seen. Around the clearing that

Sebastian had razed for living was a perimeter of thick tropical greenery that, for the most part, stood no more than thirty feet high. Several tree tops appeared to have been snapped off by harsh weather some time ago and Cooper guessed that most of the damage had occurred from Hurricane Wilma's wrath.

Behind her, shallow waves crashed against a wandering shoreline three hundred yards away. A natural jetty of flat and round rocks jutted another couple of hundred yards beyond the shoreline into the turquoise blue just a few feet above the water's surface, creating a point break that split the sea into two, white frothy halves. Sebastian had built his pier against the left side of the jetty and his boat calmly bobbed in the small inlet created by the peninsula of rock. A dozen seabirds flapped lazily around the boat, landing spontaneously to forage for forgotten human scraps with little success. Traversing the shoreline for as far as she could see to the north was a white sand beach that narrowed from several dozen feet nearest her, to almost no beach at all in the distance. Though it was only a dot of dark shadow from where she stood, something was moving along the beach at that far point.

She turned back toward the two men who were busy propping up the wall with boards set at an angle to it. "Has anyone seen…" she said, but was answered by John before she completed the question.

"Took off at dawn," he said. "Guess he couldn't wait for the escorted grand tour."

Cooper licked fruit juice from her fingers then dried them on the tail of a light blue T-shirt emblazoned with some fishing gear logo she'd never heard of which Sebastian had given her on the boat. She turned back to watch the dark spot at the distant shoreline and wondered if it was Billy, if he'd known that she'd kissed him and if that was the reason why he'd left so early. She thought for a moment that she should go to him and offer an explanation, to tell him that for one brief moment she'd become one of those people she'd grown to loath over the years. Love was not a selfish thing—at least it wasn't supposed to be—and she thought she should apologize for offering a promise that could not be kept, even if it had been manifest in the simple kiss of sleeping lips.

Could a Daykeeper love? she thought once more.

The distant dark spot on the shore suddenly rose and flew out over the sea.

They stopped working on the addition two hours before the early Christmas sunset so that Sebastian could show them at least a portion of his island. They'd almost finished the framing, moving at a casual and careful pace.

Billy had not returned all day and Cooper could tell that both men were concerned though they'd not said a thing about it. Perhaps, like her, John and Sebastian thought that an island tour would give them an excuse to look for him. It wasn't so much that she feared for his life (Lax as a Daykeeper had lived hundreds of years) as it was for possible injury; he still had mortal bones that could break and mortal skin that could bleed…at least, she thought he did. A Daykeeper wasn't Superman—that much Lax had made perfectly clear back in Sedona.

The more plausible answer was that Billy just wanted to be left alone. Knowing him even for a short time had revealed to Cooper how intensely obligated he could be to those he cared about most. He'd risked his and John's life to save her from rape and torture and there was no greater proof than such practiced self-sacrifice. Sooner or later he'd explain to all of them what he'd meant when he'd said that there was nothing they could do until it was time to do it. For now, Cooper thought, even Billy did not yet know an answer and time, alone, was the only remedy.

The three of them walked the sandy northbound stretch of beach for more than thirty minutes before stopping at about the same place where Cooper had seen the tiny shadow fly offshore around noon. White sand collided with flat rocks that sloped in a gradual rise of about twenty feet before flattening off to form a cliff face against the water that continued further north for as far as she could see. Red and blue flowers grew sporadically along the rocky ledge as if they'd been intentionally planted there for the sole purpose of warning.

"There's two small caves down along the rock face," Sebastian said. "Perhaps he's in one of them."

Cooper and John turned in unison toward Sebastian.

"Don't tell me you haven't been looking for Billy. I know I have."

Cooper shrugged. "Why there? Why a cave?"

"You'd know if you were sitting in one. It's the first discovery I made when I came to the island twenty years ago. You can see them better from over here."

Sebastian led them to the water's edge where sandy waves washed over flat rocks. Walking knee-deep in frothy water, Cooper saw that the short cliff face curved in a long, inward arc for at least another half a mile. Midway along the arc were Sebastian's caves. The two squares of darkness were within a dozen yards of each other, one etched into the cliff slightly higher and at more of an angle than the other. Both of the caves were about six feet high and the floors of each were no more than five feet above the sea but far enough so that the calm waves did not enter. Since the flowery edge of the cliff was just a few feet above the top of the caves, climbing down and into them seemed possible.

"They're not very deep," Sebastian said, "but a man, or woman, can get lost in them nonetheless. I've nodded into daydream in the one on the left several times, particularly at sunrise when the view is absolutely extraordinary. Gotta be careful, though. You certainly wouldn't want to fall asleep with an approaching storm. Wash your ass right out."

At that very moment, in the square blackness of the more northern cliff cave, a pair of milky-white feet appeared in stark contrast to the cave's dark interior. Billy's torso and head remained in shadow as his white legs shuffled forward and his toes gripped the very edge of the rock-faced floor. When he jumped head first into the water and disappeared for more than a minute, Cooper gasped.

"Don't fret," Sebastian said. "Done it many times myself. There's a jagged little set of steps leading back up into the cave. You just gotta watch the slippage. Wet rocks can be awfully dangerous, and some of the rocks are really sharp."

But Billy didn't swim toward the rocks. He swam away from them, moving into an offshore current that Cooper was sure would take him out to sea. Again, he went under.

"Sebastian?" Cooper pleaded.

John draped one beefy arm around her shoulders. "He'll be fine," he said staring at the water. "We just have to have a little faith."

Cooper thought about the night before, about how John had seemingly lost his own faith and had almost thrown Sebastian overboard, about Billy, his interdiction—he'd saved them all, again.

When Billy surfaced moments later, he had three friends with him.

Bottlenose dolphins.

Two months passed on Sebastian's Island before Billy told all of them what he finally understood. Until that day, he'd said nothing at all about djeds or cubits or the prophecies they represented, and on the single occasion when Cooper had approached the subject, Billy had left the homestead for a week, reappearing only because of the island's first torrential storm since they'd been there.

For the most part, she (along with Sebastian and John) had let him be, requesting nothing more from him than his company and an occasional demonstrated seafood recipe made famous by the restaurant he owned in Texas. Cooking seemed to lighten his mood but not wanting to eat anything that he considered to "have a face" tended to make his meals vegetarian.

In the two months before his revelations, Cooper and her compadres (a term she'd come to regard as two men without Billy) had gone about the business of survival, a duty made rather routine by Sebastian's many years of planning and stockpiling of resources. The addition to the hut-home had been finished in three weeks but living had certainly not been all work. During those months, Cooper had explored the island on days when her compadres had chosen to scuba dive offshore, and she'd become comfortable knowing just about everything the mile-and-a-half landmass had to offer.

Occasionally, she had snuck over to the cliff caves and had parked herself in seclusion to watch the fanciful drama of Billy and his dolphins. Their interaction was incredible. Billy would dive for chunks of time, remaining underwater longer than what Cooper perceived to be humanly possible, only to resurface with one hand on the fin of a dolphin. Stranger still was that one of the dolphins was pink. Cooper had never seen a pink dolphin before and she swore that Billy talked to it…talked to all of them. She couldn't exactly hear what was said from her secluded distance but every time his mouth moved, one or more of the dolphins either shook their heads or squawked in a way that only dolphins could.

On the day that Billy returned with the answers, Cooper and her compadres had just begun a new project which had as its goal the creation of a plumbing system that would pipe water from the shore to a desalination device that Sebastian had brought to the island. The project would take months to complete, Sebastian said, but would be necessary if they were to survive without returning to the mainland for as long as Billy had suggested they should.

Billy cradled the Book of the Djed in one arm. It was the first time any of them had seen it since Tulum. His presence, scruffy beard and all, reminded Cooper of Moses who had just returned from Mt. Sinai with stone tablets bearing the Ten Commandments.

"I'm putting all of you in danger," he said. "I've got to leave the island."

Outside the hut-home an hour after dusk, all four of them crowded around Sebastian's custom dining table on top of which he'd lit two fat, wax candles. The gathering had the aura of a séance at the beach, complete with sea salt breezes and the soothing crash of lazy waves. Billy placed the closed Book near the table's center so that the flickering candle flames would reveal what he was about to show them. Cooper couldn't help but to wonder what might happen if one of the candles toppled onto the Book. Would it burn? Would everything for which they'd endured be destroyed by clumsiness? As she pushed the candle closest to her a few inches farther away, the four rattlesnake fang scars embossed into the djed tattoo on her wrist seemed to ripple under the candle's yellow-orange glow.

"Don't worry," Billy said, noticing Cooper's apprehension. "I don't think fire likes it. I know water doesn't." He touched a corner of the Book to one of the candle flames. A puff of white smoke quickly appeared and dissolved and Cooper thought she heard something moan. "Yeah," Billy said and set the Book down again. "Not your imagination. Damn thing makes noises." He dropped a hand to cover the Book's leathery cloth face and cleared his throat.

"First off, let me say that the page in the Book with the symbols of the phoenix, the sixes and the nines, and the Djed is not the center of it as I had always thought. There's twenty pages in all so there is no 'center page.' The glyphs are on page ten and the key is page eleven. We already know that the first ten pages tell the story of three Creations: Good and Evil, Man, and Religion but the second ten have remained mostly blank. There was that odd moment back in the Great Hall when the Book and the key page somehow reacted in a way that temporarily showed me where I was supposed to raise the Djed, but those markings have since disappeared. There has been additional writing though—a fourth drawing on the page of symbols written directly under the Djed that appeared back in Tulum. In fact, while sitting in the cave over the past month, I watched its creation, saw each stroke of the invisible pen, marveled at how it was even possible. Frankly, the completion of this fourth symbol is the reason why I've been such a recluse. It was only today that I realized what it and the other symbols might mean—what they are, together, trying to tell us. I haven't gotten the entire story straight but let me share what I think is true."

Billy opened the Book to the page of symbols and looked directly at Cooper.

"You remember that we talked a bit about this back in Puerto Morelos," he said to her. "I think we got a lot of it right. The symbols in sum are the amalgamation of opposites, but each is its own puzzle." He pointed at the bird of fire written at the top of the page and Cooper immediately realized that more color had been added to it since the last time she'd seen it. "Here we have the phoenix. Pretty simple translation, right?" Cooper and John nodded. Sebastian just stared.

"Birth and death," John said, his bald, black head shimmering a sweaty sheen in the candlelight glow. "Resurrection from self-created fire. Immortality."

"Yes," Billy said. "Maybe even a symbolic representation of the Daykeeper, of something or someone that lives on forever though not necessarily always in the same form."

Cooper leaned forward still aware of how close her elbow was to the candle nearest her. "It that respect, it could also represent the Antichrist," she said. "Daykeepers and Antichrists would be considered opposites, right?"

Billy nodded and smiled in silent approval of her logic. "And to tell you the truth," he said, "I think the entire page is representative of the last two creations—of the Antichrist and of the End— and all the symbols are trying to tell us who the Antichrist is and how to prepare for the End. All along, I've been thinking that these Antichrist and End stories would be written into the second half of the Book when all along it's been staring me right in the face."

"Who?" Sebastian interjected. "Who is he?"

Billy patted Sebastian's hand which had gripped one of the candles at its base and was nervously shaking it so much that hot wax spilled onto his fingers. He jerked his hand away and the candle almost toppled.

"Bear with me," Billy said, returning his attention to the Book. "Not only is the phoenix a representation of opposites, I also think it's a hint for how the world is supposed to end. Consumed by fire perhaps, which would conveniently support predictions set forth in the Bible and other religious texts. What kind of fire, I'm not sure but it'll be *my* mission to find out."

"And stop it?" Cooper asked.

Billy slowly shook his head. "That's a part of this story that I'm just not sure of quite yet." He said nothing for what seemed like an eternity but was only a couple of seconds. Cooper got the impression that he was considering such a massive obligation: to save the world. He shook his head again as if trying to remove an unwanted thought then moved his finger down the page to the five sixes and five nines. "So here we have another direct link to a Biblical inference of the Antichrist but we also have that symbol reversed, again opposites." He looked at Cooper. "You'd mentioned the idea that the nines might represent the opposite of Antichrist, a kind of anti-Antichrist. I think this ties in well with the phoenix's multiple meanings. I also think that the bird and the sixes, which are nines which are sixes, promotes the clue that phoenix is the Antichrist."

"You mean the city?" John asked.

"No. Not the city. If you look at the newest symbol here..." Billy pointed. "What do you think *that* looks like?"

Cooper, John and Sebastian all leaned forward. The page's new symbol was written in gray, pencil-like strokes with no added coloring. It was centered on the page directly below the Djed symbol. Another two inches of space remained at the bottom of the page where a fifth symbol might easily fit. John and Sebastian spoke in unison. "Bethlehem," they said.

"Looks like a star to me," Cooper added and thought about what she'd just said. "Yeah...okay...the one that hovered over Jesus' manger." She touched the drawing, traced its eight points, gave added attention to the top and bottom points which were longer and thicker than the others, felt the pencil lead depression of the star's blazing center under her fingertips.

"For some, it's also the symbol of chaos," John interjected. "Particularly those that don't believe in Jesus Christ."

"What makes you say that?" Billy asked.

"My tour of duty in the Middle East. Lots of chaos around there... bunch of suicidal fruitbags to tell you the truth." John cleared his throat. "Well, you know what I mean."

"Chaos," Billy confirmed. "And its exact opposite, the Djed symbol written right above it which means new life and prosperity. But I think the chaos star, like the other symbols, has multiple meanings; it's a clue to understanding who the Antichrist is for one. Do any of you remember someplace else you may have seen this symbol—say, stamped on a pill?"

Sebastian's eyes suddenly widened. "Yeah. I remember. It's on that new wonder drug health pill. They been integrating that stuff into the Yucatán schools for the last year or so. It's called...uhh."

"Popstar," Billy said. "Manufactured by BETH Pharmaceuticals, which is owned by..."

Cooper gasped as John smiled a strange knowing kind of grin. "We were there just a couple of months ago," John said. "Phoenix International. Their office tower back in Merida. I always thought that place was bad news."

"A corporation is the Antichrist?" Cooper asked.

Billy touched the chaos symbol, then the five sixes then the bird of fire. "Is it really so hard to believe? And here we are right in the middle." He touched the Djed drawn in the center of the page then swooped his hand up and down across the Book. "We're getting in the way. We're surrounded. We are the Djed. We are the one thing remaining in this world's Pandora's Box."

"Hope," Cooper suggested.

Billy nodded. "But there's something else—something else about the chaos star...about the Popstar pill, perhaps. I'm just not quite getting it."

"Maybe you aren't supposed to," Cooper said. "At least not yet. You told us that we would have to wait here on the island. Maybe you'll know then."

John stood and looked toward Sebastian's bobbing boat. "Why *do* we have to stay here? All those looking for us have probably given up the search by now."

"I doubt that," Billy said. "But that's not the reason." He pulled the Creation of the End dagger from its sheath around his chest and placed it on top of the open Book. "The daggers. They are a conduit."

"A conduit for what?" John said.

"One that connects all five of them together." Billy stood and walked one pace to stand beside John. His short, blonde beard wiggled in the sea breeze and he placed his hand on his friend's thick shoulder. Cooper and Sebastian now stood and stepped to either side of John and Billy. Cooper grabbed Billy's left hand while her stomach churned with a sinking psychological potpourri of fear, courage and the unknown. There was a word for it that she'd learned in college, but the term escaped her. She remembered it having something to do with sour butterflies.

"When I left Port Aransas," Billy explained, "all of the daggers except for that one had been swept away by Hurricane Antiago. I remember Alixel telling me that my dagger would be extremely important…that I should never let it out of my sight. It, of course, kills cubits, but there's something else. There has always been something else. Now I think I know. I think my friends helped me understand.

Cooper shot a quick glance toward the cliff caves. "So that means they can see you, too," she said. "That means they know where we are."

Billy squeezed her hand. "No," he said. "If that were true, they would have been here already." His beard bobbed against her cheek.

"Why not, then?"

"Because I have something they don't." He pulled the Djed amulet, still hanging from the beaded nahual necklace she'd given him, from under his shirt and let it bounce with a single thud against his chest. "Protection. As long as I wear this, I'm invisible to them."

"Immortal and invisible," John said. "A hell of a combination. So, if you can't be seen with the amulet on, why is it that you think you're putting us in danger?"

"What if it comes off accidentally?" Billy said. "I just can't take that chance. If they find us on this tiny island, we'll have nowhere to run and the whole thing will be over."

Cooper suspected they all knew what he meant. *The whole thing*…as in *the whole world.*

Sebastian came around to face Billy. "So, you're just leaving us? You're not gonna take my boat."

Billy shook his head. "No. You're going to take me back to the mainland then return. It's just the way it has to be."

"I won't do it," Sebastian growled. "It's a death sentence. The police will certainly still be looking for you…for all of us."

"That may be true but the death sentence you speak of will be more certain if I stay."

John intervened. "Billy is of another…" He searched for the right word. "He's something that can't be killed."

"No," Cooper said in a huff. "That's not true. Lax died for us."

The table shook because John's knee involuntarily flexed anger. Both candles wobbled flame light. "Alaxel and his sister were my best friends," he said. "They saved me a dozen times. They saved the world a hundred times. None of you, not even Billy, knows what it means to be a Daykeeper. If Billy believes it's time for him to go, he goes. If Billy says the rest of us should stay, then it's in our best interests to follow the suggestions of one that has been chosen."

"Where will you go?" Cooper asked.

"I can't say. If, by chance, some of them do find this island, that knowledge would be detrimental to all of you."

A nervous chill made Cooper shiver and she huddled against Billy. She suddenly realized that staying on the island for any length of time without Billy wasn't going to work for her. She'd left Sedona because of Billy, had risked her life because of Billy, was now hunted by the police because of Billy and, above all, it was Billy who was the Daykeeper. He could protect her from anything, but not if she was here and he was gone. If the cubits did find the island, John nor Sebastian could save her. Only the chosen one, the invisible one, the invincible one with a special dagger could do that. "If you're leaving," she said, "then so am I." She felt his hurried breaths against the top of her head and he rubbed her shoulder.

"That won't work," he softly said. "The journey will be long and filled with too many…"

Cooper remained stern. "You can't stop me. Besides, you need me."

Billy stepped away and looked directly into her eyes. John and Sebastian stared curiously. "Yeah? How so?"

"Think about it. Since your entire involvement in this…destiny of yours, there's been one commonality." Billy shrugged as a curt little smile engraved the bearded whiskers around his mouth. "A woman. Since discovering the

Cubit in Port Aransas, there's been Stephanie, Marcy and me. We are your yang or yin, whichever you prefer. You've not gone it alone. You weren't meant to go it alone."

"So now you're a Daykeeper, too," Billy said.

"No. But I know how one thinks. I know that a budding Daykeeper can't see all of the future and needs someone—an extra set of eyes, another brand of instinct, a feminine knowledge, a…"

"A person who doesn't accept 'No' for an answer," Billy finished. "I can't see the future but I can feel it in the same way I feel that my presence here puts everyone in jeopardy. Perhaps you're right. Perhaps you are meant to be my sentinel. One less person on the island would ensure that food and water would be plentiful."

Cooper smiled, knowing that his reasoning was working in her favor until he lifted a finger.

"But you have to know that we'll all, eventually, meet the Antichrist. If you come with, you just might meet him sooner than planned and if that happens, who knows how that will affect the End."

Cooper didn't like the sound of that, and by the looks on the men's faces, neither did they. More disturbing though, at least for Cooper, was that the dolphins had seemingly voiced their concern…or, perhaps, confirmation… or approval. Maybe their sudden chatter in the shadowy distance was merely coincidence. Maybe, there had been no chatter at all and what she'd heard were wind tricks playing mind games with her ears—like the sound she now heard coming from behind her. A soft, undulating hum that was very familiar.

When she and the rest of them turned, proof of the sound manifested itself in the open Book lying on the table. The Djed, written in the middle of the page of symbols, glowed a green aura that pulsed in concert with the hum. The dagger, which Billy had set on top of the Book, suddenly spun in a half circle like a compass needle, the dagger's haft nearly knocking over one candle, its long thin point stopping on the page's newest addition. The chaos star changed at that moment, morphing from a dreary pencil-gray drawing to one that blazed with crimson light.

And from the direction of the cliff caves, three dolphins bellowed in such a way that Cooper actually thought *she* understood them. They were crying out for her salvation.

They couldn't come ashore in Tulum or Puerto Morelos and going farther south would put them in Belize. Rounding the Yucatán peninsula past Merida (and they certainly couldn't disembark there) would mean consuming too much of Sebastian's limited fuel supply. Really, they had one choice: Cancun. As a tourist trap (particularly in February), the city would provide them with ample cover. Billy and Cooper would pretend to be on their honeymoon. They could hop on one of a hundred 'touring' buses and, if lucky, get at least as far south as Calakmul where they would need to find transportation for the rest of their journey. Sebastian gave them enough pesos so that they could pay for the silence of just about anyone willing to take them across the country to the Pacific Ocean. The plan sounded pretty straight forward but there were way too many people, and cubits, that could easily trip it up. Cooper didn't know if Mexico had all-points bulletins and an aggressive internal investigation bureau such as those that blasted Most Wanted posters across the States, but just one chance encounter with a Mexican who'd heard of the American ransacking of Tulum might be enough to spark curiosity. Hopefully, the pesos would quiet such questions.

For the journey to the mainland, John had opted to stay behind. He thought that his stature and color would draw too much attention. "Besides," he'd said. "Who's gonna look after the island and the Book?"

Cooper never questioned why Billy had decided to leave the Book of the Djed on Sebastian's Island. She figured, as he must have, that it was the safest place for it. As much as he'd reread the thing, he probably knew it by heart. It was comforting, though, to know that John would be its keeper. The Book still had much to tell them. For now, it would reveal no more. For now, Billy had said, the Book would stay in limbo.

Cancun's many deep sea fishing excursions offered Sebastian the opportunity to blend in. He guided his Sea Ray into port behind some of the more popular fishing boats because he knew too many of the captains of the smaller, lesser known and more private seafaring groups. He docked only long enough to say two quick good-byes then departed as stealthily as possible.

"Hola señor y señora. A beverage?" The female resort employee startled both of them. "Very pretty shirt, señora."

Cooper looked at the same baby blue T-shirt she'd worn almost every day for the past month. The fishing equipment logo sporting a reel and a rod was stained in a couple of places and she thought it looked anything but pretty. "Agua," Cooper said. "And one for mi esposo."

After the employee walked away, Billy said to Cooper, "That's weird."

"What's that?"

"Hearing you call me your husband."

"Not as weird as it was saying it."

They shared a quick chuckle before walking toward a huge plaza and the twenty-story resort hotel that stood behind it. An Olympic-sized pool occupied the center of the plaza; four much smaller, square pools and two round, bubbling spa tubs surrounded its perimeter; palm trees were everywhere. It was close to midday and it seemed that at least a hundred or more vacationers were either eating or drinking something while sunbathing. Two young kids ran past, one boy chasing another, and their mother quickly followed, tripping over her clunky flip-flops and bellowing much louder than Cooper thought was appropriate. It provided Cooper with momentary confirmation for a decision she'd made long ago: no children.

"Agua, señora?" The female resort employee stood behind them with a tray topped with two sweaty glasses of water. A lime slice and a tiny umbrella protruded from the lip of each. Billy immediately grabbed one of them and plucked out the umbrella, then raised it over his forehead. "At least my nose won't get burned," he said to the employee. "Gracias."

Cooper chuckled again, lifting her own little umbrella over Billy's head. "And one ear, too," she said. The employee stood silent, her polite smile wrinkling with an apparent lack of understanding, then turned and walked quickly away as if she'd suddenly decided that these two turistas were just a bit loco.

Cooper liked Billy's newfound sense of humor. He'd not been so droll for such a long time that she'd figured his stoicism was all a part of the transformation. It gave her hope that becoming a Daykeeper had not totally wiped out the personality that had drawn her to him in the first place. Of course, a more likely reason for his up-beat attitude was to establish the façade of a couple in love and, perhaps, for the purpose of simply setting Cooper's nerves at ease. Their journey could end at any moment. It would take just a single recognition and the plaza was filled with hundreds of chances.

"Cheers," he said and tipped his water glass against hers. "To the power of agua and lime." He downed the water in two big gulps then squeezed the lime slice against his teeth as if he'd just shot a few ounces of tequila. "Yummy. Now, let's find ourselves a bus."

Cooper finished half of her water and they both set their glasses on an empty, umbrella-shaded table as they walked around the perimeter of the plaza. No one paid them any attention until they came to the glass entry doors at the back of the hotel where Cooper noticed the female employee who'd served them. She stood beside an outdoor bar and was talking to a man whose dress looked resort official. The girl was grabbing her own arm and looking in their direction. It was then that Cooper first noticed the wristbands attached to each person who entered and exited the hotel. The resort official looked up but Cooper had already shuffled Billy through the door. "We don't have a wristband," she whispered as she led Billy by the hand.

Now that she was aware, the lobby of the hotel seemed filled with a sea of evergreen wristbands. Each adult had one wrapped above their right hand. Behind them, she noticed the resort official who now stood at the back door, craning his head to look over the crowd. Instinctively, she hunched, yanking Billy's arm down with her, and led them around a corner and into a hallway to the left. She pulled him into the hotel's private Business Center, closed the door, and moved to the side so that anyone looking in through the door's glass pane would not see them. Thankfully, no one else was in the small space that housed two computers, one printer-copy machine and an unusually large number of potted plants that were all crowded next to the room's only window.

"What is it?" Billy urged and Cooper placed a finger to her lips.

"I think the manager is following us," she whispered.

"I don't think that…"

The door opened and Cooper shifted one foot forward and both hands up so that she could defend herself. She probably scared the living shit out of the old man that walked in, and her aggressive posture was probably the reason why he turned around and quickly stumbled out.

"Cooper," Billy said. "It'll be all right. We'll find a way out of here."

"Blind faith," she said and immediately regretted it.

Billy only smiled and massaged one of her shoulders. "It's the only way to fly."

The new, calm and collected Billy was as alluring as it was annoying but she'd learn to deal with it. Right now, she'd have to go on blind faith.

Billy released her shoulder and sat down in front a computer flat screen. He began typing and Cooper wondered if he was trying to find a way out. She stepped behind him to see that he was searching the internet on the keywords "mayan calendar."

"What are you doing?" she asked, still wondering about the manager, thinking that the old man she'd just scared out of the room had located him and both were now shuffling toward the Business Office.

"I want to know what the sixes and nines mean," Billy said, clicking on a link that read "Mayan Calendar Tools."

Cooper was frustrated. How could Billy be so complacent? He'd drilled caution into all of their heads back on the island. He'd said that they would have a rough time just getting out of Cancun let alone to the other side of Mexico. Now all he could do was surf the Internet? Blind faith was one thing and perhaps it *was* the reason why the manager never walked into the room, but blind faith was not going to get them through the lobby or onto a bus without a Sol and Sand Resort wristband.

On the computer screen popped up a conversion tool that would take a Mayan calendar entry and convert it to a Gregorian date. Billy entered 6-6-6-6-6 and pressed *Submit*. The date that appeared was the year 623 B.C. He entered 9-9-9-9-9 and the calendar tool calculated it to be 622 A.D.

As Billy continued searching the Internet for further possible keyword relationships, Cooper suddenly had an idea unconnected to Billy's efforts—one that had to do with saving their butts. The color of the wristbands were the same green shade as were the fronds of one of the room's potted ferns. The fronds were long and some were about as wide as the wristbands. She walked to the plant and broke one off, then wrapped it around her wrist. It could work, she thought. As long as no one gave it close inspection, it might be enough to get them through the lobby and even onto a bus. She tore the frond to make its length just right. Now all she needed was something to connect the ends…some tape would do the trick but she could find none in the room. She did find several discarded paperclips in a wastebasket next to the printer-copier. As she bent over to pluck them out, the machine started up. Out came several sheets of paper that Billy grabbed as he stood.

"Here," Cooper said. "Give me your right hand." Billy moved the papers from his right hand to his left and presented her with his arm. She curled a frond around his wrist and connected the ends with one paperclip. "What'da ya think? Good enough to get us past a bus driver?"

"Absolutely. How did you…ahh, what does it matter. It's genius."

"I'd swear we *were* married, Billy Jo Presser, because you're annoying the hell out me."

Billy smiled and kissed her on the forehead just as the door opened and a resort official (not the one that had followed them from the plaza) looked in. Cooper quickly wrapped her arms around Billy's waist to hide the second frond she'd not yet attached around her own wrist. Billy's right arm dangled at his side and the young man looked directly at it. "Perdón," he said. "Buenos tardes." He smiled and lightly nodded before closing the door.

"Good enough," Cooper said. "Hopefully, the bus driver has eyes like that kid's." She attached her frond wristband in place and, together, they left the room.

Cooper kept a lookout as she dodged scrambling children and felt comfortable that they both had safely made it unnoticed to the front door. Outside, a line of three people waited to board a tour bus destined for Valladolid.

"Señora!" It was the voice of the girl who'd served them water.

Cooper didn't hesitate. She shuffled Billy outside and they rushed over to the Valladolid bus. The door had just closed and Cooper lifted her wrist to the tinted, double glass panes. When the doors opened, Cooper asked, "Bus to Valladolid, señor?"

The Mexican bus driver quickly glanced at both of their arms and waved them inside. "Bienvenido," he said. "There are several seats to the front."

Cooper sat in the second row seat against the window and watched as the girl water server came through the hotel's front door. The girl stood, confused, never really considering that the couple she was looking for had just hoped on the bus that idled right in front of her. She walked in the opposite direction as the bus pulled away.

"I'm glad you're with me, Coop," Billy said and sat next to her. "You've got a sharp eye. For some reason, mine isn't as sharp as it needs to be. Preoccupied, I guess." He stroked his short, untrimmed beard. Lighter blonde streaks were beginning to weave into the curly mass. "I think it might have something to do with what I found online. Gives me a bit of the shivers to tell you the truth." The Caucasian couple sitting directly behind them looked up and Billy lowered his voice. "Later," he added. "Once we get on the autopista."

Valladolid wasn't as far south as they would have liked to have traveled but anything was better than the near confrontation they'd left in Cancun. They were thirty minutes north of the town when Billy finally pulled out the copies he'd printed. Also in his hand was an engraved pen that read: *Sol and Sand Resort. For the Best Sun in the Riviera.* He used it as a pointer.

"I didn't have a lot of time to go very deep into the search but it wasn't necessary," he explained, unfolding the papers and laying them flat against his legs. "Searching the Mayan converted date of 66666 produced 623 B.C. and another search on that date immediately presented a long list of hits." He moved the pen across the top of the first page as he read:

> *As the birthplace of the Lord Buddha - the apostle of peace and the light of Asia was born in 623 BC - the sacred area of Lumbini is one of the holiest places of one of the world's great religions, and its remains contain important evidence about the nature of Buddhist pilgrimage centres from a very early period. Lumbini, in the South-Western Terai of Nepal, evokes a kind of holy sentiment to the millions of Buddhists all over the world, like Jerusalem to Christians and Mecca to Muslims.*

"The birth of Buddha," Cooper said. "Okay."

Billy circled the word *Buddhists*. "More importantly, it is the birth date of a religion, one of the most influential in the world today. Curiously, I also found the name of Buddha's mother." Billy shuffled to the next page and circled another name: *Maya Devi*.

"Coincidence," Cooper offered but Billy only grinned. "You're saying there's a connection between Buddha's mother and the name of the Mayan civilization?"

"Perhaps, but we'll not go there." He shuffled the pages again and continued. "The Mayan date conversion for 99999 produced 622 A.D. and a search on that date led to an immediate result." He pointed at some more text and read:

> *In 622 AD, the Prophet Mohammed and his followers moved to Medina, starting a wave of conversions that swept the Middle East by fire and by sword.*

"The birth of Islam," Billy added. "Another great influential religion."

Cooper was truly astonished and Billy reacted to her revealing facial expression.

"Yes. Pretty amazing, isn't it? You take a number revealed in a Christian text, plug it into the Mayan calendar calculator and get Buddhism. You flip that same number over, plug that in, and you get Islam. Then you consider the New Testament source of the sixes or nines, depending on how you look at them, to be the Book of Revelation and that the number's reference is to the mark of the beast and…"

"Antichrist." Cooper finished the sentence and her mouth remained agape.

"More like anti-Antichrist. Those were your words, remember?"

"Yeah, but I was just assuming the symbolism of opposites. What you're saying is that the Bible pegged Buddha and Mohammed as Antichrists."

"No. I don't think so. Antichrist as used in Scripture refers to someone or something that is the opposite of what Christ stood for and in the most generic sense, that means Good against Evil. The followers of Buddha and Mohammed regard their saviors as Good prevailing over Evil as well."

Cooper shook her head. "There's a lot of evangelical nutcases out there that would disagree. If this ever got out…I mean, if anyone ever really believed what you're saying, they'd use it as a platform to argue that these religions are Evil just because they believe that sixes are a direct Biblical reference to the person who will bring about the end of the world."

"I know, and that makes me very nervous. Lots of false prophets out there who will derive from Scripture whatever they want just to make sure that money keeps flowing. Man has created meaning in the world of religions and as long as man demands that one religion is the true one and all others are Evil, there can be no reason. For radical thinking Muslims, Christianity is the Antichrist, the Evil that will destroy the world."

"So Buddha and Mohammed were anti-Antichrists, meaning they were the liberators of Evil."

"Yes. Just like Jesus. Just like Lax and his sister."

Cooper gasped. "Daykeepers?"

Billy stared out the bus windshield, saying nothing until Cooper closed her mouth. "Now you know why I've been preoccupied. What do you say when you've just confirmed that you are supposed to save the world?"

Cooper grabbed the paper stack and refolded it, then wrapped her hand around Billy's leafy wristband. "You say—thank God."

They exited the bus in the middle of a town square that had Cooper believing she'd just been transported to Spain; its colonial influence was everywhere: a pastel-infused architectural mecca dotted by a half a dozen Catholic churches and cathedrals. The streets and buildings and people looked clean, healthy and well-maintained. The central square landscaping of squat trees and broad green shrubs was well-manicured, the center fountain sprayed a refreshingly clear blue stream of water, and the four sidewalks that spoked toward the center fountain were completely clean of trash, dirt and even bird droppings. Tight asphalt roads were filled with tricycle bikes and mopeds that zipped by with happy Mexican couples; the sidewalks along the streets had the occasional peddler but for the most part were unoccupied by the extreme bartering atmosphere common to many Mexican tourist destinations.

"What do we do now?" Cooper asked.

"We find something to eat and look for another method of transportation. It's a bit more than a thousand miles to Nexpa, a good two-day's drive at least."

"How about a cab?"

Billy shook his head. "No cabs. Too big a chance. If I were the Mexican police, I would have definitely made sure every cab company in the peninsula had descriptions of the American banditos."

Cooper removed her makeshift leaf armband and stuck it into the pocket of her shorts. "Not banditos. Honeymooners. Remember?" She pointed beyond the water fountain to the opposite side of the square where a Dominos offered a juxtapositional reminder of yet another outside influence on a town whose people were destined for infinite assimilation. The pizza shop's blue and red logo blended quite well with the décor of the buildings around it. "I haven't had a slice of pie in such a long time." She took Billy's hand and led him almost trancelike toward the fountain.

Situated around the water fountain between the four sidewalk pathways were four wood and wrought iron bench seats. Sitting on the bench closest to their approach was a dark-skinned man whose head was turned away and looking down at a sheet of paper on the empty seat next to him. The man wore a black fedora with a little yellow tassel sewn into the crown that didn't dangle as much as it lay there like a multi-fingered octopus. He was busy with a highlighter, marking lines on the paper that traced an orange path across a map of Mexico. When they got to the opposite side of the fountain, Cooper said, "You notice that man over there? Looks like he's heading in the same direction we are."

"What?" Billy craned his head to see through the jutting fountain water, having apparently not noticed what Cooper had seen.

Cooper yanked his arm and lowered her voice. "Grab us some pizza while I talk to him. Maybe he can help lead us in the right direction. Wouldn't hurt to ask."

"Ahh…Well sure. Like I said—you've got the sharp eye." He started to walk away and added, "What'll you have?" The man in the fedora looked up for just a moment then returned to his highlighting activity.

"Extra cheese," she said and waved her hands in a downward motion that told Billy to *Shoosh.*

Cooper walked back around the fountain with casual steps, as if she was admiring every landscaped detail, then softly sat at the far end of the bench seat. The man didn't look up and continued highlighting with a left hand that seemed to not understand how to draw. Very, very slowly, the man marked over one of the east-west highways on the map, the hand jittery, like a two-year-old struggling to remain inside the lines of a coloring book masterpiece.

"Perdón, señor," Cooper said.

The man did not look up. His highlighter line was almost to the Pacific Coast.

"Señor. Excuse me."

"Yes." The man sounded impatient and unwilling to be disturbed. The single word response had no Spanish accent whatsoever.

"I'm sorry but I couldn't help noticing your map there. Funny thing. I'm heading in the same direction. Are you from the States?"

The man's head snapped up in one swift motion that caused his fedora to fall off his head. He was mostly bald underneath, the skin there a much whiter shade than the rest of his face. When he saw Cooper, he blinked; a grimace of being inappropriately disturbed quickly faded into a full grin of pearly white teeth that cracked his tanned features. Cooper was immediately struck by how colorfully Latino his skin was compared to the American-looking facial structure. It was as if he'd painted himself Mexican. He replaced the fedora then straightened his cotton white, button-up shirt collar.

"Sí, señorita," he said, a Spanish accent now apparent. "The state of Tijuana."

Cooper didn't bother with a corrective translation. "Do you speak very good English?"

"Sí." The man dropped the highlighter on the map and gave his full attention to the pretty woman sitting next to him. "What do you have for me?"

"Well. You see. My friend and I don't really like tourist traps and such. We like to explore a country by traveling the roads ourselves, picking up rides where we can."

"Tourist traps?" the man asked.

Cooper pointed and the man looked toward one of the groups that had exited the bus with them a few minutes ago. Those five people, Cooper thought, were the epitome of distinguishable American tourists, with their multiple cameras and smartphones and big, floppy hats: a confused and bewildered herd that was much too obnoxiously loud.

"Sí. Comprendo," he said, turning back to face Cooper.

"We're going in that direction." Cooper pointed at the map. "Do you know where we might find a ride?"

"For you and your amigo?" The man pointed in the direction of the Dominos entrance.

"Sí."

"How much money you got?"

The question raised an immediate mental alarm. The last thing you ever wanted to tell a foreign stranger in a foreign country was how much money you had. So Cooper dodged the question with one of her own. "How much would it cost to travel the road you marked?"

"I can take you for…" The man grabbed the orange highlighter and wrote 3,000 above the line he'd drawn. Cooper wondered if he was serious or if he was just trying to find out how much money she really did have."

"Three thousand pesos?" she asked.

The man pointed at Cooper with his highlighter. "Plus three thousand para su novio."

"He's not my boyfriend," Cooper said. "He is mi esposo." It was a protective reaction, one that meant, *I need your help but don't fuck with me because I have a husband who might not care for your shit so much.*

The man leaned forward. "Still three thousand more…and some pizza."

Billy walked up from behind with a large, boxed pizza between both hands. An edition of *USA Today* was folded on top.

"Billy," Cooper said. "This is…I'm sorry, but I never got your name."

"Julio," the man said. "Your new amigo." He pointed at the box in Billy's hands. "A slice, por favor?"

Before leaving the town square, the man who said his name was Julio ate half of the pizza himself, acting like he owned the keys to their salvation which, Cooper thought, he just might. He said very little while he sat there, staring at Billy for the most part, while slowly chewing as if cheese pizza was the most miraculous food on the planet. Cooper thought that he was sizing them up, trying to scab all that he could: free pizza, perhaps some cash, and a sense of power over two stupid touristas. She could have guessed what he would say before finally standing. "One thousand pesos and I'll get the car." He belched and asked Cooper for the rest of the bottle of water she'd only half consumed, then held out his hand toward Billy. Cooper shook her head.

"You'll understand if I say no," Billy said.

The man lowered his hand. "Do I know you?" he asked, maintaining a Spanish accent that now sounded a bit flawed. "I think I have seen your face before."

Billy hesitated for only a second. "No. We haven't met." He reached into his pocket and pulled out a single hundred peso bill. "Six thousand pesos is quite a lot of money. Are you sure you want us to just walk away? How about a hundred as down payment? The rest when we get to our destination."

The man snatched the bill and quickly walked away.

"You know we're never going to see that money again," Cooper said, watching the man's black fedora and yellow tassel until it disappeared in a mass of tourists gathered around the town's twin-spired, Colonial Catholic Church.

"A bet," Billy said. "A bet that you were right when you saw him in the first place." He grabbed the newspaper he'd purchased inside Dominos and sat, unfolding it to the life section. "We really don't have a lot of choices."

The man who said his name was Julio returned ten minutes later with a small, two-door Fiat. Cooper squeezed into the back and Billy sat in the passenger side bucket seat. The beige interior of the car was exceptionally clean except for many small pebbles of glass that were strewn across the carpeted floor. Cooper had to swipe a few from the seat to protect her legs from the tiny sharp edges.

"Small car for a small deposit," Julio said, glancing back at Cooper through the rear view mirror before turning toward Billy. "About a hundred pesos worth."

The Fiat turned from the town square and snuck in between two buses that were headed out to the autopista. From beyond the car's open windows, Cooper heard someone scream and then a pair of police sirens. She turned in the seat to see a crowd rushing from the town square toward the Catholic Cathedral. When she turned back around, Julio wasn't looking at her but she could see the reflection of his big set of white teeth, grinning.

They'd pulled off the main autopista about five minutes ago and were now traveling on a dirt road that was apparent only because there were no plants growing on it. The jungle had gotten thicker the farther south they'd traveled and Cooper was now reminded of the place she'd been taken and held captive by the paramilitary cubits after the encounter at Chichen Itza, a jungle filled with foreign prickly flora and withering trees like the one she'd been tied to until Billy and John had saved her. She'd been so drugged that everything had pulsed: the plants, the sky, the stoned cubits and pseudo army force, the horrible henchman who'd smelled like rotten beans. It was kind of like that now—a pulsing strangeness, a misplacement in time, a smelly feeling that she should be anywhere else but here—except the responsible drug at this point was pure, white paranoia and not a forced dose of dirty heroine. It had been Billy's question and Julio's answer that had really pumped the panic.

"Why did we turn off the highway?" Billy had asked. "That was a quicker, easier way."

"Easy, yes," Julio had replied, pushing his fedora an inch up his forehead and wiping sweat beads from both eyebrows. "Quick, maybe. But not the safest way if you do not want attention. This way is one without so much attention. I have amigos with gasoline this way. We will need five hundred pesos. You have five hundred pesos?"

The chance encounter with Julio in Valladolid, the commotion in the town square, a turn onto a road less traveled with Julio's friends waiting somewhere along its path, and now prodding for more money. If that wasn't enough to enliven Cooper's paranoia, there was always the *USA Today*.

Oil Magnate Murdered in Cancun

CANCUN, Mexico—One of the most influential billionaires in the oil industry was found dead in his Cancun hotel room early Wednesday morning. Mexican officials said that Sweden-born Handel Klosch was killed execution-style with a bullet to the back of the head.

Though not a household name to most people, Klosch was well known in the financial markets where his portfolios included majority holdings in five of the most powerful oil industry corporations. His net assets placed him as the world's second richest man with a net worth exceeding 60 billion dollars. Only Richard Manson, CEO of Phoenix International and its subsidiaries, is worth more.

"There have been a lot of murders here in the recent past but most of those had to do with drug cartels," said an officer of the Mexican police in the Quintana Roo. "This is a first for this type of execution."

Police said that there were no witnesses and no further clues have been uncovered as to who the murderer might be, but that an investigation is ongoing and is in cooperation with law enforcement officials from Sweden.

Cancun officials said that tourists were not in danger in any way as the murder was directed at a specific target. They say that Cancun remains one of the safest vacation destinations in Mexico.

The paper had shuffled between the bucket seats and had fallen, face up and open across the floor's center hump as soon as they'd reached the autopista outside Valladolid. Cooper had not wanted to pick it up. She'd not wanted to let on. She'd not wanted to spark any suspicion. So she'd read it from where she sat, not leaning over but squinting quite hard. An assassin had been in Cancun on the same day that they had arrived from Sebastian's Island. And she'd wondered every minute up until this very moment. Had the assassin snuck onto the tour bus in Cancun, too? Had he been riding with them all that time? Had he heard any of their conversation about Antichrists and saviors and such? She couldn't remember seeing Julio anywhere until they'd arrived in Valladolid. And how in the world could he have gone from the bus to the town square fountain bench with map and orange highlighter so quickly?

White, paralyzing, head-screwing paranoia. That's all it was. All she needed was a little blind faith, just one crunchy bite of that fleeting fix called belief. Besides, Billy had already put the puzzle pieces together—he must have. He'd not said anything up until now because there was nothing to say. Daykeepers were too sharp to have ever let an assassin take them this far into danger…to a point of no return. To disappear. Mission not accomplished.

"Amigos," Julio suddenly said; the abruptness caused Cooper to involuntarily squeak. "We are almost there. Give me the pesos. These guys are not ones who should see gringos with cash."

Cooper was taken by surprise when Billy's hand appeared from the right side of his bucket seat. Five paper bills were between the fingers. She took them and waited.

"Cooper," Billy said. "Do we have that much left?"

"What!" Julio said just one octave below shouting. "I am to get six thousand."

"We don't have that money on us. It's at our destination."

"Not a good place to tell me that. Not a good time either. These men. I only hope…"

And then the Fiat rolled into a clearing that was at least a half a mile big in all directions. A small village was assembled in the middle of it. The Fiat crossed a one lane, wooden bridge over a small stream that curled like an angry snake around the left side of the town's wooden buildings from which people emerged as the car approached.

"Here," Cooper said. "I have the five hundred pesos." She handed the bills that Billy had given her to Julio. "You said they were your friends, didn't you?"

"Sí," Julio said, sweat now rolling in one, long dirty bead from his eyebrow to his chin. "But not all of them."

When they parked in front of the first building, a middle-aged Mexican woman and two children greeted them with respectful curtsies. "Buenos noches," the woman said. "Como estas?"

"Bien," Julio answered. "Donde es Hondo?"

"Él está en el agua." The woman pointed to where the stream widened a hundred yards away. Several people were in the water wading and splashing about. She saw the five hundred pesos in Julio's hand and smiled almost hungrily.

"Gracias," Julio said and walked toward the swimmers.

"Buenos noches," Cooper and Billy said to the children. The children politely smiled but didn't say anything, hiding, instead, behind the woman's long skirt.

Cooper wondered if they should follow Julio. Billy had the remaining cash that Sebastian had given him stashed somewhere on him, and she wondered if moving from where they stood to a much more secluded watery hole (where a quick and easy drowning could transpire) was such a good idea. She wondered if the woman and her children would even care. She wondered if they were actually in on it. The look in the Mexican woman's eyes had that appetite for something she'd rarely seen: money.

Billy made the choice by grabbing her hand and walking ten steps behind Julio. She was nervous but she felt safe at the same time. Billy was a Daykeeper. He had a magic dagger. She didn't know how many men, women and small children it would take to overwhelm such a weapon, particularly when wielded by a skilled hand, but Billy could certainly overpower the ten men who stopped cooling themselves and turned in unison as they approached.

"Stay here," Julio said, dropping an open hand by his side without turning around. "I will introduce you."

Cooper and Billy stood and waited. Billy's hand rested near his heart where, under his baggy shirt, the dagger was sheathed. Julio walked into the water and talked to a short, stocky man with a goatee and pointed at them and talked some more and pointed some more. Then he gave the man the five hundred pesos which the man gave to one of his fellow swimmers. Cooper couldn't quite tell from their distance to him, but she thought she saw him smile. Then the short man with the goatee pointed at them and waved them over.

"Would you like a swim, amigos?" the goateed man said. "Por favor… please."

They had no change of clothes and Cooper really didn't want to get wet, but to do nothing might seem rude. Fortunately, Billy intervened. He walked briskly, as if he and the men in the water, who now moved toward the muddy bank, were long-time friends. He flipped off his sandals and entered the water without missing a step. He held out the hand that had been pressed against his heart.

"Mi nombre es Billy," he said.

The goateed man took his hand and shook it twice then released it. "I am Hondo." He looked at Cooper and added, "And you, señora? The water is very fresh."

A couple of the men who were now out of the water stared at Cooper, their stances rigid. Billy leaned closer to Hondo and whispered something that made the man laugh out load.

"That is okay, señora," Hondo said. "You do not have to get wet." And then he laughed again. "Welcome to Hondo. This is my town."

Hondo said that the gasoline would not be delivered until the morning. He said that his little town was a popular destination for many travelers who wanted a taste of *real* Mexico and that it was not uncommon for him to sell a few hundred gallons a year. It was also not uncommon that Americans visited from time to time (though much more rarely than Europeans) but there were also "others" who were not as pleasant and grateful of Hondo's hospitality and the town, especially the men, had to maintain caution. For this, he apologized and offered all three of them a place to stay, free of additional charge. He also said that he was sorry that Cooper wasn't feeling well but that he understood and he knew that her *malestar*, her "discomfort," would soon pass. Apparently, Billy had told Hondo that she was on her period (which she wasn't) and that getting in the water would reveal such embarrassment. Billy was a clever Daykeeper but Cooper wished he'd come up with something a little less invasive.

Throughout the rest of the evening, the people of Hondo were so friendly Cooper wondered why Julio had suggested that they might not be. She thought, perhaps, that Julio had never even met them. If the townspeople were his "amigos" they certainly didn't play the part. They treated him less amiably than they did either her or Billy. In fact, at one point, right before nightfall, she'd overheard the woman they'd met coming into town talking with another woman as both kneaded fresh masa for the fire. Cooper's Spanish was excellent but the woman talked with a Mayan dialect that was hard to follow. She swore they'd been talking about Julio, how they didn't like him, and how Hondo should keep his guard. One of the stranger things they'd said had to do with something Cooper had a lot of trouble translating.

The stranger had a bleeding face.

Maybe they'd meant that he sweated a lot, or that he liked sweet wine, but Cooper was sure she'd heard the word *sangria* in the sense that it meant *to bleed.*

It was now close to midnight and, again, Cooper was lying next to Billy though not in the same bed. Christian values were strong in Hondo; a man and a woman did not sleep in the same bed except for the single purpose of procreation, and that's how they prepared their living quarters, both for themselves and occasional travelers. She rose from a springy but surprisingly comfortable thin mattress and walked to a window covered by fine screen mesh. Again, she was transported back to Chichen Itza, to Strykor's little cottage that also had screens for windows, to the accidental ingestion of unfiltered water and the unsettling effects it had caused her digestive system. If she'd only known before leaving Sedona what she would eventually get herself into. Would she have ever left in the first place? Dead cops aside, she could have talked herself out of any accusation. She'd been well-known and well-supported by the Sedona community. They would have never charged *her* with murder.

But that's not why she'd left and, really…the real reason slept right behind her. For Cooper, falling for any man seemed, just a few months ago, impossible. So many of them had screwed her over in too many ways, including her ex-fiancé—but that had been so long ago and so distant as to be unreal. Kerskker was the reason why she'd never returned home to Puerto Rico. He was the reason why she'd ended up in Sedona. He was the reason why she'd even changed her last name.

Billy mumbled something that sounded like "sangria" and Cooper shook her head. He said it again and this time it sounded more like "Sedona." She needed rest. The lack of a solid night's sleep was making her see things and think things and hear things that just weren't true.

But Cooper didn't return to the springy mattress. Instead, she went outside.

The road that had led them into town meandered through the middle of a dozen or so handmade buildings that resembled, in many ways, the Old West towns of the American late-1800s, except that these buildings were made of jungle woods instead of milled lumber. There were no hitching posts and no swinging-door saloons (not in such a highly Christian enclave as this) but there were several oil lamps hanging from ten-foot posts that, together, created enough light along the length of the main street to erase half of the shadows. She didn't see anyone but she heard what sounded like someone crying, someone young—a girl.

To her left, the half-moon twinkled atop the stream where the town's men had initially met them. The girl moved at the river's edge and then splashed. By the motion of the shadowy arms, it appeared that she was bathing. Cooper left the comfort of yellowy lamp light for the much fainter blue shade of moon glow and stepped cautiously, unable to see all of the obstacles that lay at her feet. The warm jungle air became mildew moist as she neared the crying girl.

"Señorita?" Cooper queried, "Estás bien?" Startled, the girl shuffled backward out of the water and fell onto the muddy bank. She didn't try to run but she did cower as Cooper approached. The closer Cooper came, the more Cooper realized that the girl was one of the two who, with their mother, had greeted the Fiat upon arrival. She was about twelve-years-old Cooper thought, and she was wearing a full-length dress that looked identical to her mother's. The lower part of the dress clung to her waist, hips and legs. Her Mayan dialect was hard to follow since it was mixed with a lot of sobbing remorse.

"Please don't tell my mother," Cooper thought she said.

"I won't," Cooper replied, hoping that the words were coming out correctly. "I'm Cooper. What is your name?"

"Ladia," the girl whimpered. "I don't know what is happening."

"What do you mean?"

The girl looked down at her wet dress and Cooper moved closer, taking careful steps so as not to upset her any further. In the dim moonlight, the patterns in the girl's dress were solid patchworks but their true colors were muted by shadow. There was an irregularity though—a splotchy dark stain encircling the girl's crotch and Cooper immediately understood. Ladia had just begun her ascent into womanhood and she was scared to death. Anger and helplessness combined in Cooper's mind. Where was Ladia's mother? Why hadn't she told her daughter of female adolescent expectations? Bleeding for no known reason would scare the hell out of anyone, man or woman.

Cooper sat next to Ladia, gently grabbed her hand and, when the girl did not jerk away, massaged one of the knuckles. "Where is your mother?" Cooper asked, still struggling with the girl's native language.

"Dead," Ladia said.

Cooper's translation could not have been accurate. Ladia must have meant that her mother was *Gone* or *Not here* or even *My mother doesn't care about me*. "My dear," Cooper said. "You don't mean that."

"Yes. She mean it." The response in English came from the shadows over Cooper's shoulder. Both she and Ladia turned to find the woman who Cooper had assumed was Ladia's mother. "Her madre killed by the jungle. I am su tia…how you say…aunt."

Cooper went straight to the point. "Ladia is having her first period and she is scared as hell." The woman gave her a curious look. Perhaps, Cooper thought, it was her use of the word *hell*. She rephrased it. "Ladia is upset."

The woman quickly shuffled to Ladia, kneeled on the opposite side of the girl, looked down, then engulfed Ladia with a giant hug. She stroked the girl's long hair and repeated, "Lo siento, Lo siento." She was sorry that she had not been there. A few of the woman's tears caught the moonlight and sparkled. She looked at Cooper and grabbed her forearm. "Gracias. Muchas gracias, señora," she said, and then suddenly jerked her head toward the town's yellow, lamp lit glow.

Cooper turned to see a boy running out of the building in which Billy was sleeping. A second later, Billy emerged, grasping his chest. "Thief!" he yelled, as the boy disappeared into the town's shadows.

The boy thief had taken Billy's amulet while he slept. Fortunately, Hondo and a couple of the town's men had been rustled from sleep because of Ladia. They caught the boy immediately and Hondo lifted the short youngster over his head. Hondo's words were angered and aggressive. When Hondo dropped him, the boy walked slowly back toward Billy who still stood in the doorway of his guest's home. Both of the boy's feet shuffled through the dirt as if the short trek across the main road was the absolute worst moment in his life. The boy did not look up the entire time and when he finally stood toe-to-toe with Billy, his gaze remained that way. He offered Billy's amulet with both hands and Billy quickly grabbed it and lassoed the necklace over his head.

"What do you say, niño?" Hondo demanded.

The boy's English was horrible. "I sow-ry."

Billy grabbed the young boy's chin and lifted. He couldn't have been much more than five years old. "Why," he said. "Por que?"

The young boy's dark, brown eyes seemed to hold a magnificent young boy secret. "Es hermoso. Se ilumina."

Hondo translated. "He said it is beautiful. He said it was glowing. It is the reason he took it because he has never seen such a thing."

All of the men in the town were now gathered behind Hondo and the boy. Cooper walked over to Billy's side while Ladia and her aunt stood next to one of the men who, Cooper thought, was Ladia's uncle. The man looked at Ladia's blood-stained dress which now looked much more macabre in the lamplight glow. His misunderstood anger caused him to run at Billy and Cooper.

"Parada!" Ladia's aunt yelled and rushed up to her husband's side, whispered in his ear, then pulled him back to where he stood next to Ladia and stroked her head.

A dozen men, a dozen women and almost twice as many children were now standing along the main road, hushed and gawking. Only the sudden squawk of some unseen jungle bird broke the silence. And then Hondo stepped forward. "Que es?" he said, his big brown eyes bulging with a wonderment saved only for little inquisitive boys. He stroked his short goatee and repeated, "Que es?"

A second man who was quite large and carried a machete walked up and stood beside Hondo. "Es, es…" he mumbled, pointing at the hanging amulet.

The amulet was glowing very faintly which pulled the two men's heads forward like a magnet. The rest of the townspeople moved closer, forming a half circle audience twenty feet away from Billy and Cooper. A moment later, Ladia came through the crowd and stood with Hondo. "Yaxche," she said, reached out, and touched the amulet which Billy allowed her to do. Its green glow intensified.

For Cooper, the girl's word for the amulet was an epiphany. *Yaxche*. She'd never put it together until now. *Yaxche*. The tree of life. The ceiba tree. The single most important icon of life and death and renewal for the Maya and so many other cultures of Mesoamerica. *Yaxche*, with its four crosses, like branches, like arms, grasping for freedom, reaching up to the heavens, asking for salvation. Just like the *Djed*! The same symbolism but from an entirely different culture, from an entirely different part of the world. But the same world. Intertwined. As one.

Ladia fondled one of the Djed's glowing crosses. Then Hondo reached forward to do the same. The man with the machete dropped the blade and Cooper could tell that he, too, wanted to touch it. The townspeople, together, took a step forward. The boy thief crawled between Hondo and his fellow townsman and stood beside Ladia, followed Ladia's hand with his own, touched the glowing amulet.

And then all of them, Hondo, the machete man, Ladia, the boy thief, all of the townspeople—even Cooper—gasped and jerked backward, as if they'd just been hit with static shock. The green glowing Djed amulet hung in the middle of Billy's chest right against his sternum. Just to the right of it and under his shirt at a point that marked the center of his heart, a new light appeared, one that was no bigger than a quarter and glowed crimson. The red light softly hummed, as if it were attempting the start of a lullaby.

Mmmm... mmmm... mmmm...

"Diablo," the boy thief mumbled, stepping back into the legs of Hondo. "Diablo."

Cooper knew that the object glowing atop Billy's heart was his Creation Dagger. She also knew that such a glow meant a cubit was somewhere near, and she could tell by the look on Billy's face that he was thinking the very same thing. Both of them stepped backward and both started analyzing each and every face that encircled them. Anyone could be a cubit...even the little boy thief.

And then, suddenly, Julio spoke from beyond shadow in the direction of the stream. "The Americans are wanted by the policía and the policía have come to get them," he shouted in English. "They are the terrorists of Tulum. They will kill all of you!"

The jungle seemed to rustle from all directions and Cooper remembered how Ladia's aunt had told her that the jungle had killed Ladia's mother. The crimson glow of the Creation Dagger doubled in intensity as the green glow of the amulet faded completely. Everyone except Billy, Cooper, the boy thief, the man with the machete and Hondo ran for the shadows like ants escaping extermination. The boy thief repeated, "Es el hombre! Es el hombre!" and then continued jabbering so quickly it was hard to understand. "It's the man who told me to," Cooper translated. "He told me to steal it or he would kill my mother."

"Que?" Hondo said. "Who will kill your madre?"

The boy pointed toward the stream. His voice trembled. "El Diablo."

They were a couple of dozen yards away and the darkness hid his face, but Cooper knew that Julio was a cubit, and she was now convinced that he was also the Cancun assassin. His two red eyes peered like openings into hell, the silver sparkle pupils visibly dancing even from her distance to them. The voice was no longer Julio's, but she'd heard it before…back in Tulum; it was the voice of the Antichrist. It was Phoenix International's Richard Manson. Billy had been right. As soon as the Djed amulet had been removed, Manson had been able to locate him and was now going to use his cubit assassin to get rid of more than just some oil industry billionaire adversary.

Hondo's friend bent forward ready to strike, machete in hand. Hondo pleaded with him not to go, tried to hold his friend back, but the man pushed Hondo away. "You will not kill my wife," Cooper heard him say, realizing at that moment that the man was the boy thief's father. "I will kill *you*."

The boy's father lifted the machete over his head as he walked from the town's yellow glow into the jungle dark shadow. The cubit remained by the stream, its red eyes dancing together a few inches in all directions as if its body was swaying with anticipation, like an animal preparing to pounce.

And then there were two quick pops: bullets exiting a silenced barrel. The shadow of the machete fell from the man's hand a second before the man fell himself.

"No!" the boy screamed and started to run to his father but Billy grabbed his arm and held him back.

A third pop exited the cubit's gun and Hondo flinched, grabbed his stomach, and fell face first. Billy dragged the boy with him into the guest house and Cooper followed.

"It's no good, Daykeeper," Manson snarled through his cubit. "You're just another useless pile of shit."

Once inside the building, Cooper looked through the screened window as the cubit grabbed the fallen man's machete and began hacking, bellowing "Billy" for each of the half a dozen whacks he gave the body. The dead man's son struggled to escape but Cooper held him down. It was then that she realized, Billy was standing in the middle of the town's main road, his Creation Dagger glowing between the fingers in his clenched right hand.

The cubit held the bloody machete in one hand and a pistol with a long silencer in the other as it walked into the yellow light like an outlaw gunslinger. The electric sparkles in its red eyes swirled blue lightning but it was the thing's face that shocked Cooper the most. She remembered what the two women had said earlier in the evening. She remembered they'd said Julio had a bleeding face. Now she understood. Julio was not a Mexican cubit. He'd painted his face and now the cosmetic was rolling off the skin like melting, burnt butter. Underneath was a white man whom Cooper did not know—but Billy apparently did.

"Chester Kalimaris," Billy said. "But how can it be you? You died in Port A."

"You should know better, Billy," the cubit said. "You should know by now that nothing ever dies. We just get rid of the trash." The cubit fired a silenced shot straight at Billy's heart but the amulet knocked the bullet aside. "How can you care about all of these human clumps of crap?" He lowered the gun and raised the machete. "Like that stupid little boy. I wanted him to get the dagger, but the stupid little fuck can't even accomplish that simple chore. Fortunately, he got the ancillary prize and now here we are. So you give me the dagger and the Book, and I won't make a butcher's shop of this entire town."

"I'll give it to you," Billy said, his voice controlled and matter-of-fact. "Right to the back of the head."

The cubit laughed. "Not with no arms you ain't." He sliced the air with the machete in one giant X-motion and started walking toward Billy.

The Creation Dagger's glow created a red aura that extended about ten feet from Billy's hand. When the cubit came to the perimeter of the aura it stopped and lashed out with the machete only to miss Billy's face by a couple of inches. He raised the pistol and…

From the jungle, all hell broke loose. Three bright, white beams engulfed the town from three different directions. A voice on a PA demanded that everyone drop their weapons. The cubit turned and fired two shots at the voice and one light blew out. When the cubit ran, Billy turned, sheathed the dagger, and kneeled beside Hondo who was writhing on the ground in a fetal position, both hands clasped against his stomach. Billy wrenched one of the arms free and dragged him into the guest house where Cooper and the boy hunched for cover.

"Policía," Hondo moaned. "Hide. Rápidamente!"

Cooper had not realized that the small guest house had a second room until the boy showed them. Following an order from Hondo, the boy slid open a false door that had looked like it was part of the back wall and motioned for Cooper and Billy to go in, then knelt next to Hondo as sirens and gunshots and men screaming obscenities swarmed closer to them. The crevices between the vine-strapped wooden false wall provided enough light for Cooper to see the two policemen when they entered the room beyond the wall. Both wore bullet-proof vests and held assault rifles with flashlights tied to the barrels. They acknowledged Hondo who lay bleeding from the stomach, his hand covering the bloody shirt.

"El Diablo," the boy said to them.

One of the policemen knelt beside Hondo, pulled off a glove and held the palm of his hand against Hondo's forehead. "Where is he?" he said to both the boy and Hondo. "Where is the devil?"

"He killed my father," the boy cried in his particular Mayan dialect. "He's going to kill my mother."

Hondo spit up a small runner of blood that streaked his goatee. "Shot me. Careful. The gun is silent."

"He's an assassin," the policeman said. "We've been tracking him for the past day. He stole a car in Valladolid—killed the owner. He took two hostages with him. We saw them outside. Are they still here?"

Hondo rolled his head. "Don't know. They run into the jungle." The policeman rose from his knees and Hondo grabbed his arm. "Who is he? What is it?"

The policeman looked at the boy. "He *is* el Diablo."

Semi-automatic gunfire erupted outside. A whistle screeched from the opposite end of town. Both policemen quickly stood and ran from the building and as soon as they were gone, Cooper and Billy came out of hiding.

"They leave, amigos," Hondo grunted and spit up more blood.

Billy quickly moved to Hondo's side. The dagger was already in his hand. He ripped Hondo's shirt open where the bullet wound in his abdomen anxiously pumped out crimson life. Cooper pulled the boy to her side and with him, watched the miracle of the Creation Dagger.

About four inches of the dagger's blade disappeared into Hondo's belly, the star in its haft again blazing red light as the sharp steel sank. Billy twisted the dagger back and forth, bunching the belly flesh in one direction then the other. To Cooper, it looked like the wound had become painted lips, two red strips of flesh puckering up against the blade as if it was sucking on a straw. Gently, Billy pulled the blade up through flesh that did not want to let go. Then in one swift motion, he yanked the blade up and away. The bullet vaulted, smacked the ceiling with a hollow thud, and clinked onto the floor somewhere to the right of them. The blood stopped flowing and Cooper watched the skin begin to reattach itself, the puckering lips morphing into scar tissue.

The shuffle of approaching footsteps outside made Cooper and Billy run back behind the false wall. The same two policemen reentered and the boy immediately placed his hand on Hondo's stomach. It was one of the smartest, most mature things Cooper had ever seen a five-year-old boy do. The child had seen a miracle, had watched the miracle man perform the feat, knew that the miracle man was hiding for a reason he cared nothing about, knew that if the police saw the miracle of the self-healing wound they might stick around long enough to find the miracle man, and the boy was having none of that.

"Hijo," the policeman said in Spanish. "Have you seen el Diablo? He came this way."

"No," the boy whimpered and covered Hondo's stomach with his body as if he was giving the man a hug.

"Stay here. We will send help."

Next to her, Billy had turned away from the false wall and was holding both hands tightly against his chest. The dagger had not stopped glowing and he was trying to diminish its discovery by the policemen.

And then, suddenly, a voice. Just a foot beyond the exterior wall. El Diablo. The cubit formerly known as Julio. Chester Kalimaris.

"Billy," the voice said assuredly, soothingly. "I found you once and I will find you again."

The cubit's voice was so close to Cooper that she stumbled backward. Whether from memory or now, in reality she could see its red eyes and the silvery pupils peer right through the dark, exterior wall. She took a half step forward as if hypnotized and a machete sliced through the wall, its point stopping less than an inch from her left breast. The cubit punched the wall then started tearing away the jungle wood in big chunks. Billy pushed Cooper behind him and held the dagger to ward off the attack. In seconds, the exterior wall was demolished enough that the face of the cubit and most of its machete-wielding torso was visible through the wall's jagged edges.

"Chester?" Billy said.

"So good of you to recognize my face," the cubit responded, grinning, the brown goop of face paint drooling across the lips, the eyes uncomfortably big and red and roiling.

"Manson!" Billy said.

"I usually go by Richard, but Chester Manson or Stephanie Manson or

Albert Manson…they'll all do. Even Billy Jo Manson. Yes, you'd like that. Billy Jo Manson, just another cubited son-of-bitch."

The dagger's red glow intensified, the outer edge of the aura pushing the cubit backward until it stood six feet away. That's when the barrage of bullets hit it. The first rounds knocked the machete from the cubit's hand. The next several dozen rounds found some part of the cubit's upper body. For a moment, Cooper thought that the cubit also wore a bullet-proof vest since the force of each round only nudged the thing, but when several shots ripped through its face, the cubit went down. Cooper and Billy ran back inside to find Hondo and the boy standing there with two large blankets. Hondo wrapped one around Cooper's shoulders and the boy gave the second to Billy who sheathed the dagger and wrapped himself. Together, they exited the guest house, walking quickly but not running, Cooper and Billy hunched over to hide their faces. Policemen ran past and joined the other dozen lawmen that had swarmed the guest house. Ladia, her aunt and her uncle waited at the end of the main road directly under one of the yellow, hazy oil lamps and shuffled the four of them into their home as screams and gunfire erupted outside.

Early the next morning, Hondo's men scouted the entire perimeter plus a mile and a half before reporting that the Devil had escaped. None of the policía had remained either; their singular purpose had been to capture a billionaire's assassin. If Hondo ever really cared what Cooper and Billy might have done, what the policía might have found out about them, Hondo never asked and no one ever said so. His response to the his new friends was total reverence. Billy had saved his life.

At the funeral, they found out the names of the young boy who wasn't a thief and his dead father. Not far from the town, they stood in an impeccable, well-maintained plot of cleared jungle. No signpost said so but it was Hondo's cemetery. There were six markers made out of various materials, none of which looked anything like stereotypical headstones. One marker was a bulbous four-foot clay pot that displayed a colorful array of blossoms and jungle greens. Another was a simple cross made of two hand-shaved wooden stakes attached appropriately. All of them memorialized the name of the deceased written somewhere on the markers.

The newest addition was Ernesto Ordero. His marker was his machete, the blade clean and sparkly and planted in the ground. A rectangular cut of tree bark served as the nameplate that was firmly attached around the handle with yellow twine. The women cried. The men did not.

Billy wiped a tear from Cooper's cheek while she gently massaged the shoulder of the young boy whose name was Vincente. Vincente had become extremely attached to both of them, particularly Billy. The boy had seen a miracle and, to him, only one thing in this world could perform miracles.

Ladia's aunt and uncle said that they'd care for the boy. The boy's mother had also passed away some years ago but it had not been in Hondo. She'd fallen ill while visiting American relatives and was buried somewhere in Arizona. Ladia would have a new brother and that pleased her immensely.

Hondo's injury was completely healed as he showed the entire town after the funeral. He told them of Billy's power, delivering his oratory just like a king on a thrown from some great city in the past.

Hondo returned their five hundred pesos, had drawn them a crude map routing them away from as much "trouble" as possible, and offered two motorbikes to take them "wherever God had intended." It would be a trade for the Fiat which, as stolen, could not be driven in the daylight of law enforcement. The police would no doubt return to Hondo for the car but by then, Hondo said he'd "get rid of it" for new motorbikes and perhaps a little bit more.

Billy confessed that he'd ridden a motorcycle only once in his life and that had been a catastrophe. He'd gotten the foot pedals confused and had failed to brake as the bike had gone headfirst into a wooden fence. Driving all the way to Nexpa, he said, would be quite a challenge.

Cooper reassured him with a curt, mischievous smile. She'd ridden bikes many times, especially trail bikes around Sedona. They'd start out slow, she told Billy, and by the time they got to the asphalt autopista, any spills he might take would be of less impact on dirt.

What Hondo had given them was a pair of hybrid 400cc Hondas that would ride well both off-road and on. They were very popular bikes in the Yucatán and Hondo warned them of this. Any nonattendance and they'd be without transportation.

After a few last good-byes, Cooper and Billy had been on their way. The townspeople had revered both of them as they'd rolled out, the tropical February wind whipping across their motorcycles, their destination, Nexpa.

The ride to the Pacific Ocean had been filled with lots of moments that continued to bind Cooper and Billy. There were moments when nerves had sharpened as they'd ridden through small towns and villages, many of which looked trapped in time three generations back. They'd stopped only once for fuel and that had gone without a hitch though the gas attendant, who had spoken enough English to complete the sale, had given their motorcycles a hungry glare.

There had been moments that had made her wish she was riding *with* Billy instead of beside him. He'd still not shaved the blonde beard and it had grown long enough to thump in the wind with gentle grace. His hair had grown beyond shoulder length and had she been sitting behind him, it would have slapped her face caressingly. She'd thought of hugging him, her arms wrapped just below the dagger, the lower tip of the Djed amulet tickling her knuckles and the wind rushing past, snuggled together as one invincible force, easy riding their way across a foreign country.

There had been lots of *Easy Rider* moments on their ride to Nexpa where a motorcycle and miles of road was salvation. Throttling up to an easy fifty-five and settling in with a friend at your side and a future uncertain, riding away from schedules and clocks and unrealistic demands, away from places to live and homes to buy and money to spend, away from people whose words of trust weren't worth one second of an *Easy Rider* experience. With metal and motor beneath you and the rest of the world by your sides, you were saved.

They'd never run into the assassin and the only real trouble they'd encountered had been on that first night when they'd slept in the Camécuaro National Park. A park ranger had awakened them, wanting to know what they were doing; sleeping on park tables was not allowed and motorcycles were not allowed in picnic areas. The ranger had been on the verge of arresting them when a woman had appeared out of nowhere. She'd told the ranger that her son and his fiancée had been accidentally locked out of their RV, which had been a good enough explanation for the ranger.

The woman and her husband had been from Wyoming and said that they were "taking in the rest of what life had to offer." They'd given Cooper and Billy a place to sleep and a locked chain for the bikes. They'd fed them well the next morning and had asked no questions. Handshakes were the good-byes.

Cooper had never known their names and they'd never asked for hers or Billy's. It had been strange, having conversations with pronouns only. But they had been good people, the ones you find when not looking for any, just like most of the residents that they would be living with in Nexpa.

They'd arrived in the beach village near the end of the second day, just in time to see the not-so-rare purple sunset that Cooper had engrained into memory the first time they'd visited after leaving Sedona. Billy's friends, Jerry and Debbie Hunter, had found them a place to stay and Billy had made a down payment from the pesos that Sebastian had given them so that such an arrangement would continue until the world called him.

0-TIME: PREDICATE

IN LIMBO

Saturday Afternoon, December 17, 2011

It had taken almost three years of sedentary living in Nexpa for Billy to understand one irrefutable truth.

Daykeepers were not superheroes.

He often remembered that night back in Lax's Sedona home when he'd tried in vain to sleep in Aaron's bed. With his feet poking out beyond the short mattress, he'd imagined himself invincible, or at least the Daykeeper kind of invincible. He'd imagined himself as the superhero Silver Surfer, a god-like entity that traveled on a surfboard and could change the universe, for the good or bad, with just a thought.

But it wasn't like that—being a Daykeeper. It wasn't like at all. He couldn't leap tall buildings, fly in cool bat things or surf in any other way than he'd been taught. Being a Daykeeper was like being the one. You just knew it. You didn't have to prove it. You didn't want to prove it. By its nature, being the one was a very lonely venture. Laying low, was the priority. Just because you knew that some very influential people were actually dead replicas of their living selves didn't mean you went around telling everyone. A person couldn't save the world from a locked, padded cell. And a person couldn't do it from a small surf town on the Mexican Pacific either. But his time to leave was coming. Daykeepers were good at knowing about time. There was this inner presence, a second heartbeat in a way, that started thumping louder the closer that time moved toward moments of novelty. With five days before the winter solstice, Billy knew it wouldn't be much longer.

"Dinner still on for six?" Cooper's voice snapped him from thought. "There's a college bowl game on if the reception holds."

When Billy looked up and over, the sun blazed an orange circle into his eyesight. He blinked and slid the sunglasses from the top of his head down onto his nose. He'd gotten rid of the beard a long time ago but he'd kept the shoulder-length hair. He grabbed a wavy strand of it and pulled it from his ear hole.

Cooper's hand rested on the tail of Billy's newest surfboard which stood upright in the sand next to a dozen others. She stroked its waxy surface. "Feels ready for a ride. You planning on a jaunt in the surf before dinner?"

"Got a couple of newbies going out for lesson number one." Billy touched the board, touched Cooper's fingers. "You like?"

"Green and yellow," Cooper said, studying the board and Billy's hand. "Not my choice of colors but you did wonders with them."

It was another one of those moments: Cooper so close to him when circumstance could easily turn into a kiss. "Thank you," he said and stepped back. "I should be done in plenty of time for the feast. D'you say football was on?"

Cooper nodded. "You've got about two hours. You need me to help you close up?"

Billy's Surf Shop had been around for almost as long as he'd been there. When they'd arrived in Nexpa, he'd initially tried waiting tables and bartending but neither position had really been "him." Just as he'd done with the Surf Side back in Port A, he'd started the business slowly and now had more than a dozen boards for sale that he'd shaped himself. Another dozen or so (some he'd bought, some he'd made) he rented out and used when giving surfing lessons, two services he'd added to his board sales just a year ago.

The "shop" was in two parts. A twenty-foot long wooden building that had no front wall or doors served as a place to showcase his boards and rental service during open hours. The structure was about seven feet deep and resembled an outdoor closet. The main shop was a one-room, thirty-foot-square wooden building about a dozen feet away. It had a small covered porch with a single wooden bench and a couple of potted indigenous plants hanging from hooks that were screwed into the rafters. Three wooden steps led up to the porch and the front door.

Inside, a meager assortment of salable beach paraphernalia sat on a couple of shelves that were stacked three-high between sixteen-inch cinder blocks. Most of the sale items were original works created by Nexpa residents. The most popular were the rope bracelets and necklaces that had small pieces of coral and sea shells woven into them. Billy sold lots of those. The artist was an old woman who lived alone a few miles off in a village not so unlike Hondo. Next to the makeshift bookcase and sitting atop a square, fold-out card table was a couple of stacks of affordable surf clothing, including a depleted supply of Billy's own handmade boardies. The rest of the vacant area inside the main shop he used to store his boards when the shop was closed.

Billy grabbed a sign that read *Surfboard Rental* and pulled its stake from the sand. "Thanks, Cooper. Grab a board and I'll meet you inside."

They completed the shop closing just as Billy's surf lessons showed up. Both the girl and the boy were in their early teens and Billy thought that they were related in some way though he couldn't remember how. Billy handed each a long board and grabbed his newest green and yellow creation, then stood on the porch with them while he locked the shop door.

"We'd each like to get a pair of Billy Boardies, too," the girl said.

Billy looked at both of them, then at his key, then at the door he'd just locked. He shook his head. "Yeah, sure. You want to wear them now, I suppose." Both teens nodded and Billy reopened the shop, took their money and gave them two of the last three pairs he had. He told them he'd wait outside while they changed if that was all right with them. After giggling for a few seconds, they both agreed.

Outside, Cooper and Billy set the noses of the three surfboards in the sand. "For some reason, dinner and a football game sounds a lot more inviting than the surf," Billy said to her.

"I know what you mean. Younglings."

"I'll see you at six," he said as the teens emerged in their new surf shorts.

"They're not like yours," the young girl sniveled and pointed at Billy's waist.

"Good-bye," Cooper said and left Billy to his challenging tasks.

There'd been much interest in Billy Boardies thanks to someone's YouTube video that showcased its unique style and features. Almost fifty percent of beach visitors now requested a pair. Since he and Debbie Hunter created each by hand, supplies were limited. Such rare value placed on a piece of clothing—and the YouTube video—was one of the reasons Billabong had contacted him about licensing the shorts. They'd even drawn up artist sketches of how the shorts would be marketed.

The "Aussie" shorts with the "Kangaroo Pouch"

The licensing didn't have to include rights to Billy's Velcro-enhanced pouch invention but they did ask for permission to modify the design, with Billy's approval of course.

If Billy had been stateside and none of this Daykeeper stuff had ever taken place, the thought of such a deal would have had him reeling. He would have had a restaurant and a popular line of clothing, distributed, basically, worldwide. We would have been the successful business man that his father had never believed he'd become. M.I.T. degree or not, Billy could have proven that some decisions were best left to the decider.

But, of course, the Cubit and daggers and such had changed all of that. Ironically, it was because of his dagger that the need for a unique boardie had surfaced.

Shortly after arriving in Nexpa, Billy had realized that surfing would be an issue. Having the Creation Dagger in his possession was a necessity but surfing with a sheath and a weapon in plain sight wasn't going to work. Never surfing for as long as he was going to be in Nexpa wasn't going to work either. Plus, even if he tried surfing with it sheathed under a shirt, the dagger could easily slip free, particularly on a wipeout, and Billy's surfing style was a bit too aggressive to take such a chance.

So, he'd created a pair of shorts into which a sheath was sewn inside the waistband. The daggers were very flexible as had been evidenced when Alixel had revealed hers back in Port Aransas. She'd pulled two of them from some hidden sheath at her waist. The seven-inch blades had apparently been flexible enough to wrap around the outside of her waist. Billy thought he could create something similar.

The whole idea had originally come to him while he'd been sitting in the cliff cave about a month after landing on Sebastian's Island. There'd been lots of time for thinking back then. The cliff cave had proven to be the perfect sanctuary. He'd thought that if he'd only had the right material and the skills of a seamstress, he could create a pair of shorts in which he could comfortably carry his dagger. Debbie Hunter had been the answer for the seamstress and Nexpa had provided the material.

A working version of the shorts was revealed in the summer of 2009.

A pocket made of some nearby plant fibers had been stitched into a wide waistband. Into it, Billy had easily placed the dagger blade, its length wrapping as expected around his waist. Debbie had sewn on a flap of material that could be slipped over the haft to hide it. Additionally, she'd sewn on a special Velcro-type of strap, one that he'd invented (again from indigenous plant material) that was a hundred percent more waterproof than standard Velcro. The strap, which snaked around the base of the blade, was used to hold the dagger in place. The new waterproof Velcro was also used as a closure for one right-side boardie pocket into which Billy could stash the Djed amulet while he surfed.

The design had been perfect, at least for personal use, but it had garnered a lot of attention. Just the over-sized waistband on a pair of boardies was enough to spark interest. Soon, people were wondering how they could get a pair. As Billy's Surf Shop business grew, inquisitions about his boardies grew two-fold. People asked: *Why such a wide waistband? It's cool but does it serve another purpose? You're carrying something in it aren't you?*

Of course, Billy would have never revealed what he did carry. He told the inquisitors, instead, that the waistband's width was for the purpose of holding a pouch.

Pouch?

Yes. A storage pouch into which you can store stuff like keys, a credit card, or even a small flash drive or cell phone.

Wow! That sounds useful. But won't stuff get wet or lost?

Not with my new-fangled Velcro-type waterproof closure.

Really? No water will get in and a wave ain't gonna knock it loose?

That's right.

Where can I get a pair?

Well, we're working on completing the design.

Aw, man. That stinks. I'm leaving tomorrow.

Lots of people left without a pair of what would become Billy Boardies until the Christmas of 2010 when Billy revealed his, and Debbie's, modified creation. By the following summer, at least one person every day was asking about them. Since then, they'd sold more than five hundred, all via Billy's Surf Shop.

It *was* a great opportunity. He could realistically make millions. It was all about the marketing. It was all about coming out of hiding, about making "laying low" less of a priority. He couldn't hide any longer. YouTube had found him. Billabong had found him. His apprehensive second heartbeat had found him, and it was thumping just a bit too loudly.

The two teens had not been as much of a pain in the ass as Billy had thought they were going to be. Once the girl had gotten over the fact that Billy was not going to show her what he carried in either his "pouch" or his pocket, they'd settled quite nicely into the lessons. Both had successfully ridden at least a half dozen waves and both still gleamed with pride.

Billy waved both of them good-bye and locked the shop door. The December sun was already lounging atop the Pacific horizon which meant he had about a half an hour to wash up before riding out to the Hunters.

Billy's home, a bungalow, was a short walk from the shop. He slipped on a sandy brown, short-sleeved button up, one that Billabong had sent him as a "thank you" though Billy had yet to agree to anything. He'd thought of selling it at first but when he'd tried it on, the comfort and color were just too him.

He kicked sand with his sandals as he strolled fifty feet from the shoreline past the Island Ice Creme Shoppe and two small community buildings where surfers and other penurious beach lovers could stay. The community building accommodations were short on amenities like running water and indoor bathrooms, but there was a shared bathhouse that provided these necessities. The bathhouse intersected Billy's path home and as he walked past, a woman with blonde hair wrapped inside a turban-rolled towel emerged. She turned toward the community building closest to her known as the Cheap Beach Pad and Billy saw that she was wearing a pair of his boardies. Her shape filled the shorts quite nicely and Billy smiled. What a great advertisement, he thought. She could sell a thousand just by standing in them.

The woman partially turned to where Billy could see that one eye was on him. He continued staring for a second longer and the woman smiled, the corner of her lip turning upward in her partial silhouette. He quickly nodded and turned away. Did he know her, he wondered? Had he sold her the shorts? Certainly, he would have remembered.

He continued past a few more beach shops, waving at those people he knew, before arriving at what had become his Nexpa home since riding in with Cooper on motorcycles back in February of 2009.

Unlike those Big City tourists trap beaches, Nexpa did not have an Atlantic Avenue or a Pacific Avenue or any avenue that was filled with modernity. The Mexican jungle came right up to the beach and just enough of it had been cleared as to provide living and travel for a few hundred residents and guests. Billy's place was located in a cutout of what the local sheriff, Ron Buck, had described as medicinal plants. Who needed pharmacies when Mother Nature provided cures, Buck had told him. It was all about understanding Nature's recipes and Buck had taught him plenty. Billy had often wondered if the gathering of such knowledge was something he was "supposed" to do rather that something to satisfy pure curiosity. A Daykeeper would need to know how to use Mother Nature as a remedy.

Ten wooden steps led up to the small balcony of his bungalow. The whole wooden structure sat atop four, thick, tree trunks that had been shaped into six-foot-tall pillars. It had been built shortly after back-to-back tropical storms had whisked away an infant Nexpa back in the 70s.

He climbed the ten steps, then turned and looked in both directions, out over the jungle where darkness was quickly consuming most shadows. Tikis flamed in multitude along the beach, marking places where people gathered. About a hundred yards off the coast, waves broke in glorious harmony, each reflecting a prism of soft reds and oranges as the sun fell below the horizon behind them. Three hundred yards to the left where the shallower Rio Nexpa lagoon emptied into the ocean, some Saturday night locals were setting up for their own celebratory get-togethers. Two oil barrels simultaneously blazed into life on opposite ends of the lagoon and Billy could hear, even from his distance to them, the whoops and hollers of a good time.

Inside his bungalow, Billy had all that he needed to live a comfortable life on the beach. Unlike the community buildings where blonde-haired babes stayed at little cost, Billy's pad had all the necessary amenities: indoor plumbing, a great bathroom, and even a much desired window AC unit which was not currently running. The temperature outside was a comfortable seventy and Billy raised a couple of windows to let the night air in.

He slipped out of his new Billabong shirt, sniffed it a couple of times, and decided it was fresh enough to wear to the Hunters. It smelled like the beach as did most things around him. After a quick shower (the water pressure was wonderfully strong for a municipal system in such a small village), he strapped the dagger around his chest and buttoned up his shirt to cover the Djed amulet that dangled above his breastbone. He left his boardies to hang dry over the shower curtain rod and slipped on a pair of khaki cargo shorts.

The Hunters lived five miles out, across the Rio Nexpa about halfway to the neighboring town of Caleta, which was the more highly commercialized beach destination in the area. Most of Nexpa's residents got their supplies from Caleta, and the Mexican postal system had a regional office there where needs not supplied by Caleta could be mailed from online purchases.

Billy and Cooper still had the two hybrid 400cc Hondas that Hondo had given them, but Cooper's tended to break down quite often. Billy's, on the other hand, had performed magnificently, requiring only the standard maintenance procedures that had kept it running smoothly and reliably.

He locked the front door, descended the ten steps, and went around to the back of the bungalow. A small, aluminum tool shed housed his motorcycle and he spun the combination dial on the locked door until it opened. The shed was just big enough for the bike so it took him a few minutes to finagle it out. As much as hybrid motorcycles were valued in these parts, only one person had ever tried to steal his; the kid had been caught with a pair of bolt cutters and a snapped lock by Sheriff Buck a couple of years back. Buck was a good friend now. Billy had taught him to surf and Buck had told him about Nexpa's indigenous plants, plus a few good pointers when it came to profiling would-be thieves like the one who'd tried to steal his bike. Dinner at the Hunters always included an invite for Ron Buck.

The ride along the state's coastal road felt a bit sticky, particularly as he crossed over the river and its marshy tributaries. Billy hadn't worn his helmet but he rarely did. He'd figured a while back that Daykeepers really didn't need them. An accident wouldn't cause him death, not with a motorcycle, not with anything, really—not if he was fated to save the world. The only thing that could kill him…well, he'd given that a lot of thought. Just about every time he'd gone for a ride he'd thought about it. And his thoughts always circled back, as they did now, to the dolphins near the cliff caves on Sebastian's Island. How he'd been able to hold his breath for extreme extents of time while diving with them. The wonders of the coral caves they'd shown him. The marvelous turtle that lived in one of them and the colorful schools of fish that lived in the others. He'd gone under for twenty minutes at a time. The threat of drowning had become irrelevant.

As for bullets, his body had already proven that such lethal bits of hot lead could not kill him. They hadn't when he'd been shot three times while escaping from Tulum. They hadn't when he'd confronted Chester, the cubit assassin in Hondo.

But, what if he came off his motorcycle doing sixty? What if his body ripped into pieces? Would his Daykeeper invincibility stitch the parts back together? Mend a crushed skull? Reshape a human body that had been deformed by speed, metal and asphalt? He couldn't drown, but as far as he knew, he still bled, still felt pain, still considered his body just as fragile as any mortal's. Perhaps Daykeeper invincibility was more associated with avoiding such calamities in the first place, having a sixth sense, as it were, knowing that danger was around the corner long before taking any of life's turns.

The Hunters had a pretty nice ranch-style home. They'd built it themselves after relocating from Minneapolis twenty-five years ago. They'd never had children so leaving had been easy, particularly since both had grown tired of nine-to-fives, unholy traffic and people en masse. On the day that Jerry had turned thirty (Debbie was just a year younger), they'd moved to Nexpa, had purchased land and had started a new life. Hunters Restaurant was one of the more beloved in town, both by locals and visitors. Aside from the curiosity that the restaurant's name implied (some visitors thought that the restaurant served locally hunted animals), the food was downright tasty, the service impeccable, and seasonal favorites always kept patrons coming back for more. Jerry had emptied his savings account to buy the place and restore it from the rundown taco joint it had been, to *the place* to eat while in Nexpa. Hunters Restaurant was where Billy had started his first job and where Cooper still waited tables.

But not tonight. Never on Saturdays.

The Hunters, though savvy entrepreneurs, had decided long ago that Saturdays on the beach were special. Even if it meant closing the restaurant on what could be its busiest night, they'd vowed not to conduct business and, instead, spent Saturday evenings relaxing, or entertaining, or engaging in some sort of recreational activity, or all three. There'd been complaints—running a business was never short on those—but the Hunters had stood fast and now people simply understood.

Tonight, the Hunters had planned a mid-December barbeque. Jerry loved grilling outdoors in the winter, a feat that had been much too challenging back in the Minnesota suburbs. He'd invited the regulars (Billy, Cooper and Sheriff Buck), but had also invited a recent visitor to Nexpa with whom Jerry had an affinity: they'd both grown up in Minneapolis. It wasn't unusual that the Hunters entertained strangers at their home. Much of the couple's popularity was due to their very open personalities. Jerry and Debbie could start a conversation with the most introverted person on the planet.

Three vehicles were parked on the Hunters' long, two-car wide, graveled driveway. The Ford SUV was Jerry's. The old Chevy Caprice police cruiser was, of course, Buck's. The third car, a new, white VW Beetle, Billy didn't recognize and assumed it belonged to the invited stranger.

In front of all of the vehicles was Cooper's motorcycle. The kickstand had broken off a week ago so Cooper had leaned it against the Hunters' garage door. As Billy rolled his bike up to Cooper's and dropped his kickstand, Debbie opened the front door and stood in its frame. Above her head and beyond the Spanish tile roof of her home, a white rush of smoke ballooned then disbursed above them. Billy smelled the prominent odor of charcoal lighting fluid.

"Just in time to watch Jerry ignite the house," she said, looking up. She wore a loose-fitting top with repeating patterns of barbeque utensils woven into it. She waved.

Billy half-jogged around the jungle landscaping, along a ten-foot-long clay tile path and up three short steps to stand next to Debbie. "Aren't we looking festive today?" he said more to her top than to her.

"Just arrived today. I tell ya, before the Internet, getting anything like this would have taken weeks…maybe months."

Billy grabbed one of the top's sleeves, covering the print of a spatula under his thumb. "In this case, perhaps it should have taken years." He smiled then leaned backward to ward off Debbie's fake punch.

"Got a couple of other things to show you, too," she said. "Come on in."

Billy followed her into a wide, open living area that consumed half of the house. Since they entertained so often, the Hunters had needed such an area and had added it to the building plans more than two decades before. It was not always the case that guests had the option of congregating outside; on rainy days, the large room accommodated a dozen people comfortably.

A seventy-five inch flat screen TV, sitting on a short, metal and glass stand, occupied the center of the wall on the right; tower audio speakers stood like bookends on either side of it. Under the TV, an Xbox 360 and a DVD player sat idle on the TV stand's one shelf. Football pre-game highlights and commentary was on. The volume was comfortably low.

Opposite the TV was one long, brown couch that was so cushy it swallowed your backside. It was Billy's favorite place to sit while watching a game or, for some get-togethers, a movie. Jerry's chair, of course, was the room's one recliner. It sat to the side of the couch nearest the front door. The positioning was purposeful so that Jerry could welcome people as they arrived.

At the other end of the room was a long, skirted table topped with an assortment of bowls, plates and glasses. Beyond the table, Cooper looked in through a sliding glass patio door. The left side of her faced glowed from the barbecue fire that blazed near her. She waved.

Billy followed Debbie outside to where three men stood in a half circle around a brick stove, staring at the flames as if engaged in some Neolithic ritual. An assortment of patio lights on wooden poles illuminated other corners of a backyard that had been cleared of most of the jungle perimeter.

"See anything interesting?" Billy asked the group. All three turned in the same direction.

"Worshipping the God-fire known as Barbeque," Jerry said, the flames whipping two feet high behind him. He might have been in his mid-fifties but

Jerry looked nowhere near the half-century mark. In fact, Billy thought he looked even younger than usual, as did Debbie. Both had noticeably fewer gray hairs and Billy assumed they'd gotten color treatments.

"Really?" Debbie said. "Was he the one responsible for burning down Rome?"

"Coulda' been. Coulda' been," Ron Buck added. "But that must have been one wild cookout." Buck, who was a good six inches taller than anyone else, stood beside Jerry. His height had, a dozen years ago, garnered him a basketball scholarship back in Arizona where he'd studied criminal justice. Today it served as a great intimidator when it came to confronting suspicious individuals. "I heard you got some steaks from Omaha. Those damn things are great."

"Omaha steaks and burgers and dogs," Jerry confirmed. "And a Gardenburger or two." He offered a hand toward the stranger standing on the other side of Buck. "This here is Duncan Swallow. He's from Minneapolis, too."

The stranger was fresh-out-of-college young. His wardrobe, a forest green Polo button-up and a pair of tan Dockers, would have been more appropriate for a casual business dinner date. Swallow's hair looked plastered on, the short, black strands matted to his head with copious amounts of gel. He looked quite out of place in the Mexican jungle.

Billy walked over and shook his hand which was leafy fragile and absent of much strength. "Good to meet you," Billy said, hoping that he'd not injured the man's hand. "Minneapolis, eh? Sure is a different kind of December there."

"Too cold," Swallow said. "No barbeques."

"One of the reasons we're here," Jerry added and looked at Debbie. "We have something in common."

"Yes," Swallow said, dryly. "Of course." Billy thought that if he'd have to converse with Swallow for much of the night he'd be bored out of his mind.

An odd moment of silence was broken when Cooper looked into the house through the patio door and announced that the game was about to start. "You want to get the munchies ready?" she said to Debbie. Billy immediately offered his assistance and the three of them went inside.

The kitchen was right next to the entertainment space. Billy helped separate chips into bowls. "What's up with that guy?" he asked Debbie.

"Shy. Real shy. It's one of the reasons I invited him. That kind of person just needs to be around some friendly people."

"Said like a true therapist," Billy responded.

Cooper grabbed an empty serving tray and started assembling crackers and cheese. "She's right," she said. "Psychologically, it's helpful."

"That college education sure comes in handy," Billy teased.

"It has been with you." Cooper grinned.

"I bet. I'd be a great case study."

Debbie shook her head. "You're not shy."

"No," Billy said to her. "I'd be a case study in many other ways."

"You mean like the obsessive compulsive way you have for cherished heirlooms?" Debbie said.

Locally, there were only two people who knew Billy had a Creation Dagger: Cooper and Debbie Hunter. Showing her the dagger had been necessary as they'd created Billy's first pair of boardies. The size of the sheath sewn into the waistband had to fit perfectly. Billy had told her the dagger was a family heirloom passed down through generations and that estate wills had required each inheritor "to keep it on their person for as long as they should live." It could never be sold, Billy had told her, and the only way it could change hands was when Billy died and he, too, left it to a future generation. Such a unique story was easily sold and Debbie had wanted to share it with Jerry, but Billy had asked her not to. Part of his ancestral responsibility, he'd told her, included as much secrecy as possible. Only for "special" reasons could anyone know he had it. It was written just like that in the estate wills. Debbie's knowledge, he'd told her, had been for a special reason.

"I guess keeping it close to me would seem a bit compulsive, but it is the will of the past." He touched his baggy Billabong shirt where the dagger rested underneath.

"That's a great shirt," Debbie said. "From the Internet?"

"From Billabong. A present of sorts."

"I wonder if they make women's sizes?" She inferred but didn't say: *Billabong had not offered a freebie to Billy Boardies' other designer.*

"If the deal goes through," Billy said, "I'm sure you'll have all the clothes a young lady would need."

Debbie grabbed the bowls of chips that Billy had assembled and led him to the living room table. "How exciting. Have you made a decision yet?"

"No. I'm teetering."

"Teetering?"

"Yeah. Right on the fulcrum."

"Of becoming rich?" Debbie set the bowls on the table and Cooper added her tray of snacks.

"That's not it," Cooper said. "It's the responsibility for the business end of it. We're in Nexpa to get away from responsibilities, right?"

Billy knew what she meant. "The times they are a changin'."

"So you're leaning toward Yes," Debbie said, crunching into a cheesy Dorito she'd plucked from one bowl.

"I think that if I have the opportunity, I'll take it. What's your opinion? The design is part yours, too."

"You know what I think. Damn the torpedoes. Full speed ahead."

"You're still okay with forty percent?"

"And you know I think that's still too much."

Billy grabbed a cube of cheese as Buck and Swallow came in from the backyard.

"You ready to go for it?" Buck said while walking around to the side of the table where Billy stood. For a moment, Billy thought he was referring to the Billabong deal, and in that same moment he almost said Yes, but Buck pulled a twenty dollar bill from his pocket and laid it on the table next to the cheese and crackers. "Arizona by three," he continued, referring to the game on TV.

Billy looked at Debbie instead of Buck and said, "Yeah. I think I'm ready."

By halftime, everyone had a full plate of barbecued goodies and sides. Jerry sat in his chair and Billy sat in his usual spot at the end of the couch next to Jerry. Cooper balanced a plate of food atop her bare knees to Billy's left. Next to her, Buck chewed on a hot dog bite. Duncan Swallow sat stiffly on a cushioned fold-out chair, a full plastic cup of untouched beer siting of the hardwood floor between his feet. Most everyone had let Swallow be. His shyness or introvertedness or whatever was just too chronic. Billy thought that he looked even pastier now that he was inside and away from the fire.

"Deb. Come on," Jerry said. "Sid-down. Game's about to start."

Debbie was doing what Debbie always did: making sure everyone had their plates and cups full before she satisfied herself. "You got what you need?" she asked Swallow.

"Yes," Swallow said and nodded.

Buck had a burger in his left hand and he waved it toward the kitchen. "We got other kinds of brew in bottles in the fridge. Don't seem you're getting along with that one." The burger-in-hand swooped down to point toward Swallow's cup of beer.

"This is fine," Swallow said. "Unfortunately, I have to be going."

Debbie had taken one step toward the kitchen with the intent of gathering a selection of beer bottles for Swallow to consider, but she now stopped. "Going? The game is just getting good. And you haven't touched your plate."

Swallow looked at his hands that were grasped to the sides of his paper plate as if he was contemplating disagreement. He *was* touching the plate, the confused stare seemed to say. "I'm sorry." He handed the plate to her but knocked over his beer as he stood. "I have to be going." He stepped over the puddle of frothy liquid without looking at it. "Got to take care of a phone call." He walked in front of the TV and Jerry stood while Debbie grabbed a couple of dish towels to mop up his mess.

"Sorry you have to leave so soon," Jerry said and opened the front door. "We'll have another one soon, I'm sure."

"I'll see you later," Swallow said, his voice monotonic, then he left.

Jerry closed the door. "I gotta say. I'm not unhappy to see him go."

"He's just uncomfortable with strangers," Debbie countered.

Buck took one of the last two bites of his burger. "Back in Tucson, we got a word for the likes of him."

"Oddball?" Billy quipped. He'd not yet touched his veggie burger but had made ample progress with his salad greens.

"Similar." Buck wiped ketchup from his thin mustache. "We call 'em a Grum."

"Grum?"

Buck finished his burger. "Gloomy and awkward," he said while chewing. "Kinda like a Goth without all the black dress."

"That about sums it up. What's his deal anyway?"

Debbie finished filling her plate and sat where Swallow had been. "He's got business in Caleta," she said.

"What kind?"

"He didn't say."

Buck stood. "Anyway. I'm gonna have one of those beautiful Omaha steaks and savor the thought of an extra twenty in my pocket."

"That six-and-a-half-foot frame can sure pack it in," Jerry said, sitting back down in his chair and grabbing his plate from Billy.

"God, howdy!" Buck replied.

By the third quarter, Arizona was still up on Arizona State by three. Billy really didn't follow any specific college football team and, in fact, really hadn't gotten into the sport at all until he'd come to Nexpa. Jerry had turned him onto it. His giant TV screen and frequent barbeques had helped Billy acquiesce.

Billy had made the bet with Buck because Buck was from Tucson and his alma mater was the Arizona Wildcats. Billy wasn't an Arizona State Sun Devil fan but his mom had graduated from there and as far as he knew, still worked as a researcher in the chemistry department. Everyone had eaten plenty and they all now relaxed as the game, which had become very defensive, trudged forward.

"You all ready to see what I got today other than those great meats and this fantastic party top?" Debbie suddenly asked. "I promise not to interrupt the game too much."

"Absolutely!" Cooper quickly replied. She'd not been paying much attention to the game. "More clothes?"

"From the states." Debbie grinned and left the room for a couple of minutes. She returned with an unopened cardboard box that, to Billy, was just about the size of the Cubit.

"You haven't even opened it yet," Cooper said. "How can a person get new clothes and…"

"I wanted to share the new clothes experience. I thought at least one of us would appreciate it." She scowled, teasingly, at the men.

"I'm interested if the box is from Victoria's Secret," Jerry said.

"Jerry Hunter!" Debbie walked over to him with the box. "I told you *that* stuff was for Christmas. Now give me your knife."

"Uh-huh. Yeah. I got'cha," Jerry winked at Billy and Buck, then pulled a small pen knife from his pocket and used it to open Debbie's box. Debbie set the box on the floor away from the front of the TV.

Most of the things she'd ordered were for her use at the restaurant: a pair of comfortable shoes, two aprons, two tops that could be worn on any occasion, and a pair of orange capris. The orange pants came out of the box last and Debbie held it by the waist out in front of her. "What do you think?" she asked Cooper. Jerry responded instead.

"Orange? How many orange things you got?"

"None," Debbie said without looking at him.

Cooper dropped from the couch and crawled over to her. She touched the capri's short legs. "You'll look hot in this," she said.

"Oh no!" Debbie said, surprised. "Look." Cooper leaned forward to look inside the capri waistband. "It's the wrong size."

"A six," Cooper said. "You've lost some weight recently. You sure?"

Debbie smiled. "Thanks for noticing. Been on a new diet. Still, a six ain't gonna cut it. I'm more like a ten."

"Come on," Cooper said.

"Scouts honor." Debbie handed the capris to Cooper. "They do seem to be more your size, don't you think? Sure would hate to pay for postage to return them."

Cooper's expression turned into a half-and-half frown-grin as one corner of her lips turned up and the other turned down. "You didn't get this for you," she said. "You got it for me."

Debbie collected all of the clothes and shoes and put them back in the box. "I guess you caught me. Consider it an early holiday present. When I saw it, it just screamed Cooper!"

"They *are* me, aren't they?"

All three men agreed simultaneously.

The football game ended just after nine and Billy had to surrender the last twenty dollar bill in his pocket. Arizona had covered Buck's three-point spread by a touchdown. Buck helped Debbie with the last of the cleanup while he happily told everyone how he might spend his brand new Andrew Jackson.

"You going to give me a chance to win it back?" Billy asked.

"Another bet Billy boy? You might want to choose another sport."

Debbie was standing near the kitchen sink when she suddenly grabbed her stomach and leaned forward.

"You okay?" Billy asked. "Was it something you ate?"

"No," Debbie said, her breath shallow as whatever churned inside her momentarily zapped her strength. "It's happened before. I think I'm still going through the change. Cramps are horrible." She took an empty glass from the kitchen counter, filled it with tap water, grabbed a red prescription bottle from inside one cabinet door, and struggled with its safety cap.

"Here," Billy offered. "Let me help." He took the bottle, opened it and gave it back her. Debbie tapped the plastic container until one, white, oval pill rolled into the palm of her hand. In the fraction of a second before she consumed it and the water, Billy thought he saw a familiar mark stamped into the pill on one side. It looked just like the fourth symbol that had appeared in the Book of the Djed right before he'd left Sebastian's Island nearly three years ago. A star. It was perhaps a bit too personal to ask, even though Billy and the Hunters were great friends, but he couldn't help it, especially since Debbie's condition seemed to improve dramatically within seconds of consuming the pill. "That's some prescription you have there. What is it? I've never seen anything work so quickly, except maybe Alka-Seltzer."

"Alka-Seltzer doesn't work for what ails me," Debbie said, avoiding the question. She sealed the bottle and quickly placed it in the cabinet as if she expected Billy to snatch it back for further inspection. "So. With that drama out of the way, what do you say we call it a night?"

It was unlike Debbie to end an evening of entertainment so abruptly, but it was getting late and all of them were working on Sunday. Jerry and Cooper had been out back cleaning up and they both came into the house. "… like a Mexican platter of some kind," Cooper was saying.

Jerry stepped into the kitchen first. "Hey, hon. What do you think of a vegetarian Mexican platter at the restaurant? I mean something unique; not just beans and rice…" He understood what was going on immediately. "You going through an episode again?"

"Not anymore," Debbie walked gingerly to him. "We were just calling it a night. Busy day ahead tomorrow."

Cooper patted her shoulder. "You can take the day off. We can handle a Sunday crowd."

Debbie shook her head. "It's not like that. I'm fine. Really. I'll see you in the morning."

Jerry escorted the three of them to the door. "You still coming over for Christmas dinner?" he asked.

"As usual," Billy said and Cooper nodded.

"You know you're always welcome, sheriff," Jerry said to Buck.

Buck thanked him. "I'll be cooking again for the guys back at the station. I've never been able to trust them with a good old American turkey and sweet potatoes."

Behind Jerry, Billy saw Debbie turn off the television. She smiled and mouthed the words *I'm okay*, then Jerry waved good-bye and closed the door.

Billy was certain of it, now. The creeping crawl of fate snatched at his heels. It told him not to be surprised. All that weird coincidence crap didn't matter anymore. Shit happened…for a reason.

For nearly the entire time he and Cooper had been in Nexpa, life at the beach had been simple, if not storybook, particularly if compared to their lives just before Nexpa. When almost three years is filled with sun and sand and surf, coincidence and fate become irrelevant. You don't think about the long-term consequences of your daily actions. You don't think about tomorrow. You live in the moment, you welcome Time, and you never wish it away.

But in the past day or so, that had changed. Billy had felt it more than anything, not really finding material proof until tonight, until Debbie had her "episode." He'd only gotten a quick glimpse but he was positive that the mark on the pill matched the one in the Book. The Bethlehem star. The chaos star. Which meant that Debbie was taking the supplement. Which meant that Billy, again, had to start thinking about the road ahead, about his purpose.

He had intended to tell Cooper about the pill once they'd gotten back to Nexpa but the motorcycle ride home trumped that decision. He decided, instead, that they would live in the moment, at least once more, when the simplicity of hair flapping in the wind and an occasional bug or two in the teeth tempted greater meaning. He wouldn't spoil that for her. He wouldn't spoil it for himself. Who knew if they'd ever ride motorcycles together again?

Cooper saw it on his face the moment she parked her bike against a small palm tree outside Hunters Restaurant where she lived in a room upstairs. "What is it? You worried about Debbie?"

Billy switched off his motorcycle but remained seated. "I am."

"But there's more, isn't there?"

"Have you ever thought about life after Nexpa?"

The question made Cooper frown. "I try not to." She walked over and placed a hand on his back. "Why do you say that?"

Billy fiddled with the handlebars then looked directly into her eyes. "We can't stay here forever."

Cooper's hand moved from his back to his shoulder. Two of her fingers lightly stroked his neck. "We've had this discussion. It's all about choice, right?"

Billy reached up and grabbed her hand, cupped it, gently placed it atop the Djed amulet inside his open shirt. "Choice," he said, looking at her hand. "What a deceitful idea."

She moved her hand, still in Billy's grasp, up his chest to his neck, then used his chin to tilt his head, and lips, toward hers. "I don't know. Being able to choose your friends is very comforting."

"You are," Billy said. "My closest friend."

A string of firecrackers exploded in rapid succession behind them and both turned to see three young men off in the distance near the shoreline. They were throwing the lit strings at each other. Small dots of yellow flame popped around their shadows.

"Bad choice," Cooper said. "What idiots." The explosions had caused her to release Billy's chin and he now started the motorcycle.

"I'll stop by for lunch tomorrow, then, maybe, we can do something later."

Cooper scowled at the men on the beach. "Yeah. We can do that."

"I'll see you mañana."

Cooper nodded then walked away and entered a side door to the left of the restaurant.

Billy traveled the short distance to his bungalow, parked the bike out front and ascended the porch steps two at a time. Inside, he dropped into a recliner that Jerry had given him last Christmas and stared at the open window across from him. In a lot of ways, he felt bad for not telling Cooper about the pill. They were so close, to withhold information seemed deceptive. All he was trying to do was to protect her, to provide her with a little more storybook before the world came crashing in.

He touched his shirt where Cooper's hand had been and massaged the amulet. He'd been so close this time. He'd almost given in to temptation. He'd almost reached up to grab both of her cheeks. He'd almost kissed her more passionately than any previous meager peck he'd planted. He'd almost thrown caution to the wind, had almost swept her off her feet, had almost taken her here, to his bungalow, to his bed.

But something wasn't quite right about making love to Cooper. Something was missing. Love, perhaps. This wasn't the first time he'd sat alone thinking about loving Cooper but, tonight, the feelings were intense. He could imagine himself as Silver Surfer or Aquaman or some other mostly invincible superhero, but he couldn't fathom what love meant. There was nothing to compare it to. You were just supposed to know it when it happened. Was that why he was just sitting, numb, he wondered? Was he now "knowing it" and was such knowledge something that he was afraid of?

A blast of tropical moisture blew in from the window as a rogue storm rolled in from the ocean. He stood and closed both open windows and looked toward the bathroom where his custom boardies hung from the shower curtain rod. Billabong, Debbie's pill, the confusing notion of love—something was brewing and he wondered what new surprises lurked ahead.

The wait was short. When he walked to the bathroom, he noticed that his shorts had been moved on the curtain rod. As sure as he was that Debbie's pill was Phoenix International's health supplement, he was also sure that he'd hung his shorts crotch side in. Not only were they now sticking out, the cloth flap that wrapped around and concealed the haft of the dagger was hanging freely, like a limp tongue. He always tucked that in. Someone had been in his bungalow.

He turned, mouth agape, to the windows he'd just closed and was convinced. Fate *was* snatching at his heels.

0-TIME: PREDICATE

DAWN OF THE OVERCAST

Sunday, December 18, 2011

How long could a woman wait? For the right man…forever. At least that's what Debbie always said anytime the subject of Billy arose between them. She was right, of course. Cooper had told her quite some time ago about Danny Kerskker and Debbie's advice had always intentionally reminded her of this bit of her history with men. Billy, of course, was nothing like Kerskker but was more like that scumbag's polar opposite. Still, it was a lesson well learned—maybe, so well learned that some distaste for all men had hardened her soul.

Why had she let the firecrackers distract her? Why hadn't she snatched him up? Why hadn't she kissed all the delicate parts of his face? Why hadn't she thrown herself at him?

A lesson well learned.

Why hadn't their great friendship ever evolved into something more romantic?

A lesson well learned.

And why was she beating herself up about it for the umpteenth time?

Danny Kerskker.

"Dammit!" she said a bit too loudly and almost dropped a bowl of chili as she came through the restaurant kitchen's swinging door. A dozen diners looked up from their Sunday morning brunches. She stood there for a second, embarrassed, and shook it off. It was the third time that morning she'd almost dropped something because of her mind's preoccupation.

She delivered the plate to an old man sitting alone. "Got any firecrackers?" she thought the old man said and looked at him dumbfounded. "Crackers. You got any crackers? I can't eat my chili without crackers. Saltines work the best."

"Sure," she replied. "Crackers."

"And some extra cheese."

"Okay."

"And how about some Kerskker?"

Again she stared at him, speechless. He hadn't just said that. He didn't want Kerskker. How could he?

"You living on this planet today, young lady? Can I get some ketchup, too?"

She looked at the bowl of meaty chili that the old man had not yet touched and considered why anyone would add ketchup to Debbie's homemade special. "Crackers, cheese and ketchup. Got'cha." She turned to walk away.

"And make it snappy. My food's getting cold."

Not only had her mind been consumed by thoughts of Billy throughout the morning, the entire breakfast and brunch crowd had not been the friendliest. Even a couple of the regulars had regarded Cooper with much less warmth than usual. Cold stares from people she knew had been a unique, and unwanted, experience.

When Cooper entered the kitchen to grab some extra cheese, Debbie had just finished chopping vegetables for use in side dishes throughout the rest of the day. Chunks of green peppers and onions sat in a pile under a chef's knife that she held in one hand. She wiped away an onion tear with the back of the other hand. "Can I talk to you for a sec?" she asked.

"Sure." Cooper walked over.

"Something on your mind today other than my health?" Debbie said.

"Oh. I don't know."

"It's Billy again, isn't it?" Cooper nodded and Debbie set the chef's knife next to the vegetable pile. "It's unlike you to mess up so many orders."

"I'm sorry. But last night after we left…"

"Same old story, right? Close, but no cigar?"

Cooper nodded.

"It'll come, if it's supposed to. And I think it's supposed to. Great relationships take time."

Tad, a young waiter from St. Louis who had been working at the restaurant since the summer, peeked in through the food pickup shelf and said, "Hey. There's some old man out here complaining that his chili is getting cold, but he's just sitting there looking at it."

"He wants to put ketchup in it," Cooper said to Debbie.

Debbie turned from the cutting board and grabbed an empty soup bowl that she filled with more chili. "The customer gets what the customer wants. Here." She handed Cooper the bowl. "Piping hot chili all ready to be customized with Heinz."

Cooper asked Tad to hold up for a moment as she gathered a small plate of grated cheese and some saltine crackers. She handed it and the ketchup to Tad. "If you wouldn't mind taking that to him," she asked. "I'm going to take a quick break."

Tad nodded and left, then Cooper headed for the kitchen's rear exit. Debbie waved the chef's knife at her. "Lunch with be starting in a few," she said.

As soon as she was outside, she looked out toward where the firecrackers had interrupted last evening. There were lots of beachcombers and no apparent idiots among them. A little further to the left was Billy's Surf Shop, but she couldn't see it from the restaurant because a line of fat trees and stout plants blocked the view. Billy had said he'd be over for lunch and she stared in the direction of the shop, hoping that he would appear from between the trees right now, while she was taking a break. She wanted to tell him she was sorry for last night. She wanted to tell him it wasn't right for her to expect…

And then Billy was there, on the beach, but he was running away from her toward the surf. He didn't have a surfboard but the woman behind him did. Even from Cooper's distance to them it was easy to discern the woman's beautiful body. The woman and Billy met at the waterline and Billy pointed at the offshore swells.

Why would he have lunch with me when he's got that eye candy to look at? she thought.

To her right, a small rental car pulled into the sandy parking lot and five men got out. They shouted obscenities at each other as they entered the restaurant. "What's up sweet lips?" the last one said to her. Cooper turned back toward the beach but Billy and the woman were gone.

As if the day wasn't going bad enough already, now the Jackass Gang graced the restaurant with their own style of revelry. A couple of them were dressed in leather. They were older than teenagers but definitely not yet adults. They gave Cooper hell, told her she'd screwed up their orders when she hadn't, dumped salt and pepper from the shakers onto the tabletop, threw food, disrupted other customers…it only took them a half an hour to run everyone out and send Tad, almost crying, to the beach for an extended break. A couple of the verbally-assaulted local diners found Sheriff Buck over by the Nexpa lagoon and Buck entered the restaurant a few minutes later.

"Pay your bill and get out," Buck demanded.

"What if we ain't finished?" one leather-jacketed delinquent said while standing.

"You're finished," Cooper interjected and moved closer to Debbie who stood at the cash register.

Two more delinquents stood and the leather-clad leader added, "Yeah?" He pointed a finger at Cooper and took a step toward her. "You gonna have the honors, sweet lips?" He snickered again and all of his comrades added their own simple-minded grunt orchestra of approval.

"Pay and leave the beach or spend the night with me," Buck said, sliding his nightstick from its belt loop.

The leader wagged a finger and one of his men dropped a crumbled wad of bills on the table. "Go ahead. Count it if you don't trust me."

Cooper took a moment to collect herself then walked confidently, with Buck by her side, to the gang's table. She grabbed the wad of bills and counted, pulling each one free from the mass and smacking it down on the table. "You're twenty short not counting the tip," she said.

The leader smirked. "Oops. My bad." He pulled two twenties from his own pocket and tossed them onto the bills that Cooper had counted. "Keep the change. Maybe use some of it to get your boyfriend a haircut." The entire jackass gang laughed, then, one-by-one, stood. "See ya 'round, Cooper Reyes," the leader added, then snapped his fingers and the gang left.

"You know him?" Debbie asked and took the crumpled money from Cooper.

"Never seen the jerk in my life." Cooper said. "Wouldn't be too hard for someone to find out my name. He's just coaxing me."

Buck holstered his nightstick. "Well, let's hope he's not succeeding," he said to Cooper. "You don't need any of that action."

"How did he know Billy was your boyfriend?" Debbie asked. "You can't find that on the Internet."

Cooper shrugged her shoulders but Buck added his learned opinion. "Observation. You can learn a lot about a person just by watching them."

"They're watching me?" Cooper said. "Why?"

"Well, I didn't say that they were; I only suggested that…"

"Why would a pack of complete strangers be watching me?"

Debbie opened the cash register and put the Jackass Gang's money inside. "They're just getting their kicks," she said. "It's all a part of some need to be in control."

"Not in my town," Buck said. "I'll show them control from behind a set of iron bars." He grabbed Cooper's shoulder and turned her so that he could look her in the eyes. "They come anywhere near you, don't hesitate to call. I don't care if it's just a bunch of name-calling, I'll find an ordinance to charge them with. Besides, we don't need their likes in a beach town this close to Christmas."

Buck left the restaurant and a few minutes later Tad returned, having seen the Jackass Gang leave. He assured Debbie that he was fine now and Cooper asked if she could take off for a half an hour or so.

"By all means," Debbie said. "As long as you don't go chasing after those fellas."

"Scouts honor," Cooper replied. "Billy was supposed to come over for lunch. I'm going to check up on him, then I'll be right back."

"You don't think those guys…" Debbie said, but when she looked up from the cash register, Cooper was already gone.

The Jackass Gang had not visited Billy so Cooper didn't say anything about them. She didn't ask about the woman she'd seen with him either. She already felt an odd tension between them and Billy's lack of attention for her only magnified it. He kept staring out the surf shop's front door, watching the waves crash in bunches.

"What's on your mind?" she asked and offered him the can of Red Bull she'd been sipping on since arriving.

He took the can, drank a little, gave it back to her. "Busy day. Lots of good surf. Lots of business."

"When did you want to hook up and talk about the Book? Didn't you say you had something to show me…some kind of connection?"

Billy finally turned his attention to her. "Yes. Of course. Maybe tonight, if you're not busy."

"I'm off at six."

"Good. So, we can make it a date?"

Before Cooper answered, Billy's attention turned abruptly, again, toward the surf. Cooper saw her way out at the last break. The woman shredded the waves flawlessly and dumped halfway to the beach from where she'd started which was still a good fifty yards out. Cooper lost sight of her until she appeared right outside the surf shop thirty minutes later. A bunch of teens were passing a football along the surf line while listening to a portable stereo. When Cooper and Billy emerged from the surf shop together, there she was, sitting on the wooden bench in front of the shop window. From the teen's portable stereo blared Duran Duran's *Rio*.

And when she shines she really shows you all she can...

The woman stood and smiled and held out a hand for Billy to shake which he quickly did. Her body and hair was Barbie doll perfect and she wore a light blue cover-up over a solid aqua string bikini.

"When were you going to show me where to ride?" she asked. "I mean, you are the beach pro around here."

That she was hitting on him became immediately apparent. The woman quickly glanced at Cooper's scowl but her smile never faltered. "You were out just a few minutes ago," Cooper said to the woman and looked at Billy's hand which she had not yet released.

The woman cupped the hand tighter within both of hers. "Yes. But beach pros know where all the *right* spots are." A silent pause was filled with *Rio* lyrics—*You make me feel alive, alive alive*—then she added, "It's Billy, isn't it?" She squeezed then released Billy's hand.

"Yes," Billy said. "I see that you have your own board."

"I do. But I'd rather try one of yours. Gotta have the complete Nexpa experience."

I tell you something I know what you're thinking...

Cooper was getting rather annoyed with the song and the Barbie Doll surfer wasn't helping matters.

"Of course." Billy said, his smile widening. "Let's look at what I have. Do you go short or long?"

"Depends on who I'm surfing with." The woman licked her lips though Cooper knew from the pink shade of her lip gloss that they needed no moisture.

Billy and the woman left Cooper standing there as they walked across the sand toward Billy's rentals. The woman didn't look back but she did send Cooper a couple of body signals when she wiggled a quick hip shake and shuffle against Billy's body as Duran Duran played on. It took Cooper the entire five-minute walk back to the restaurant to get that "seductively cuddly moment" out of her head, but she couldn't silence those damned lyrics…

Her name is Rio and she dances on the sand.

It wasn't until eight o'clock that Cooper finally gave up. Billy wasn't coming over. It was the second time that day he'd stood her up and he'd never done that before. Had her denial of his eager eyes the night before done more damage than she realized? And as bad timing would have it, that…woman… had showed up. Such an easy temptation for a man shunned. Debbie had always told her that waiting for the right man was imperative. It wasn't right to think that Billy followed the same philosophy.

She stood from the love seat in her small apartment, walked to the door, turned the knob, released it, walked back and sat down.

He was supposed to come over to *her* place, wasn't he? she thought. Something must have come up. Billy didn't have a phone so she couldn't call him. Both of them had outlawed cell phones long ago, but Billy could have called her. Debbie had installed an extension to the restaurant's telephone line in her apartment. All he had to do was use the surf shop phone.

But he didn't.

In addition to the phone, Debbie had also furnished her apartment with a 24-inch flat screen TV and Cooper used the remote to turn it on. The reception was horrible and the broadcast feed was unreliable. Sometimes she got three channels; sometimes, she was lucky to get one. An independently owned transmitter in Caleta rebroadcast a satellite feed that would have been considered illegal in the states, but the technology it used was decades old. Still, it did provide local Spanish language channel most of the time and CNN and TNT, occasionally. Tonight, Cooper was lucky—with the broadcast quality of the TV at least. CNN was fuzzy but much better than usual. She locked onto the news stories as a distraction for her thoughts. The usual political banter occupied much of the content and Cooper's eyes soon fluttered with boredom.

> Jousting! A sport for the ages. But not many know of its modern day comeback. It's called "Full Contact Jousting" and its popularity has been growing over the last few years. Coming up after the break…an unstoppable knight from Puerto Rico, a rising king of the sport, and his ethereal blade. And he's challenging the knights in the United States.

Cooper sat straight up. *Puerto Rico? His ethereal blade?* Her vocabulary wasn't the greatest but ethereal, she thought, meant *something other than this world.* And he was from her Puerto Rico? She got up, went to her small, efficiency kitchen, grabbed a bottle of water from an open case on the countertop, and returned to the love seat. Another ten minutes passed before CNN finally satisfied its jousting teaser.

> He calls himself "Triple K" and he rules the full contact jousting playground in Puerto Rico. Some say he's invincible. Others think it's nothing but common day knavery. Triple K has not lost a joust, ever. He says he's invincible and destined…because of his blade.

The bottle of water fell from Cooper's hand, bounced on the wood floor and spilled its remaining ounce. A crane could not have lifted her jaw.

> Danny Kerskker is his real name. And this is his ethereal blade.

Could the day get any worse? Cooper thought. There he was in all of his putrid glory. Mr. Motherfucker who had almost ruined her life. The photo on CNN revealed an older scumbag (but a scumbag nonetheless) who now donned a metal helmet instead of a sailor's cap. His peevish eyes, prominent within the helmeted photograph, were more disturbing than she remembered them being that last night before he'd stranded her in Texas. He pulled from behind his back…not a lance.

Cooper stood and walked through the water she'd just spilled. She leaned forward, her face just inches from the TV. In Triple K's hand was…the clenched hand covered the haft but there wasn't another blade in the world that looked like the one that jutted from the enclosed fingers—seven inches, long and thin, the sharp edge curved ever so slightly. The news anchor explained that Kerskker's ethereal blade was not one that unseated horsemen. It was one that guaranteed he would do so. A sound bite from Kerskker followed…

> "You want me American gringos? I got the power of the Gods. I am the chosen."

Gods? Good god. He sounded just like some grandstanding pop wrestler. Still a fake. Still a liar. Still trying to be something more than his gutless, cowardice, self-loving self. Why he was staring at her, telling her this, from within some extraterrestrial choppy signal, was as enigmatic as if he was standing right there in front of her. Kerskker was in her apartment. He was spouting ridiculous promises that served to prop his ego above all else.

And I'm going to plant this sucker deep in Cooper's heart.

He'd not just said that, had he? She blinked as the broadcast signal turned into a bunch of indistinct squares. Then it went out altogether. Scan lines replaced Kerskker's face.

Cooper remembered a Twilight Zone episode that featured a deceased love that contacted his living counterpart using an 'ethereal' telephone line. Cooper wasn't dead but she felt the same ambiguity from that episode. Could the deceased horrify the living?

"You're dead!" she screamed at the scrambled TV and immediately thought about what she'd just said. Kerskker was dead. He was invincible. He was a cubit. And he had a Creation Dagger! This was something that she had to tell Billy. Right now!

And it was her reason to do what she had been arguing against all night. The walk was minutes but the shock of what she saw when she arrived at Billy's bungalow added an eon to the concrete slurry of mistrust her soul felt for all men. Cooper squatted in the jungle behind a wide tree trunk just yards from Billy's bungalow porch steps.

The woman, the one with the Barbie doll string bikini, stood at Billy's front door. She wore shorts now, but her ass still stuck out beyond the stitched enclosure. The woman suddenly turned as if she knew someone was watching, and Cooper squashed her body closer to the tree bark. Seconds later, when Cooper peeked from her hiding place, she saw the woman's ass bounce through Billy's front door.

No, Cooper thought. The day could not have gotten any worse… until now. She ran back to the restaurant as that damned Duran Duran song incessantly played in her head.

He'd been rude to Cooper but, really, how could any warm-blooded human male deny such beauty? At least that's what his libido kept telling him.

The woman was the same one he'd seen exiting the community bathroom the night before. When he'd asked for her name, she'd looked at the teens playing football and had said, "You can call me…Rio. Hell, you can call me anything you want."

He'd shown her his boards and she'd selected one of Billy's custom shapes and they had finalized plans for noon on Monday to surf the south side of the river mouth where swells sometimes reached five or six feet. They'd talked for a dozen minutes then Rio had walked off, her body rocking and swaying in sultry ways that had stopped the beach football players in their tracks. When Billy had returned to the shop, Cooper had already left.

It was now ten minutes to six. Billy finished moving his boards inside the shop, locked up, and headed home. He was a bit nervous about his date with Cooper. He wanted to show her what he'd been working on since arriving in Nexpa, a journal he'd finished just a few days ago that duplicated, to the best of his recollection, the exact contents of the Book of the Djed. He wanted to tell her about Debbie's pill. He wanted to tell her he was sorry for being rude earlier in the day. He wanted to talk about their relationship.

He scaled the porch steps and opened the bungalow's door to find a short stack of envelopes, both large and small, scattered on the floor under the door's mail slot. In Nexpa, the mail was delivered only on Sundays by a contracted driver in Caleta.

He gathered the envelopes and dropped them on the recliner, then went into the bathroom for a quick shower. When he was finished, he drew the dagger from the waist of his boardies, slung them over the shower rod to dry, and slipped on a clean pair of cargo shorts. He put on a short sleeve shirt, buttoned it to cover the Djed amulet, took the dagger with him to the recliner, then moved the mail and the dagger onto an end table next to the chair and expelled one long, thick sigh.

Women, he thought. Can't live with them; can't live without 'em; can't kill 'em. He chuckled, wondering where he'd heard that line before, then snatched a big manila envelope from the top of the stack. It was from Billabong and, most likely, contained another copy of the intellectual property rights release for him to sign. Billabong had sent him one a week for the past month and every one of them had arrived in a big manila envelope with a big blue cursive "B" stamped on the backside. He'd opened each of them only to peek inside, but had never pulled out the contents until now.

The release was ten pages long, was printed in small type, and included too many heretofores and whereases for him to make sense of it. "Yuck," he said to the paper. "I thought you guys wanted me on board. I can't read this. How do you expect me to sign it?" On at least three occasions, a Billabong lawyer had offered to help find Billy a local, legal representative but Billy had denied each attempt. Up until last night, Billy wasn't having any of it: no deals, no contracts, no notoriety. He was a Daykeeper whose top priority had been laying low, but now it seemed that destiny was catching his heels. Besides, there weren't any Daykeeper laws that said a Daykeeper couldn't make a little extra cash.

He dropped the contract, the envelope it came in and the next three smaller Billabong envelopes onto the floor for later consideration. About a dozen or so letters remained on the end table and he fanned them out, realized that most of them were junk mail ads for everything beachy, and grabbed the dagger. He'd not used it in so long (thank God) that to grip its haft felt awkward. He even had trouble lining up the star on the dagger with the one it had burned into his palm so very long ago. Anymore, the dagger had been more of a burden, really…having to lug it around everywhere, hiding it from those who would never understand its purpose…he'd even had to invent a special pair of shorts just to go surfing.

He put the dagger back on the end table where it rolled and shifted the stack of fanned mail to reveal the smudged corner of an envelope that wasn't much bigger than a postcard. He plucked it out. The return address noted Tempe, Arizona, but no sender's name appeared above it. He opened the envelope, unfolded the single sheet of paper inside, pulled off some of the hanging spiral notebook confetti, and read the hand-written note:

Billy:
I don't know where to start. It pains me to think about how separated we've become over the years. I want you to know that your father and I have divorced. I want you to know that I'm doing well but I have run into a bit of trouble that concerns you. It was by pure coincidence that a student in my class showed me the YouTube video of your surf shorts so, at least, I was able to get this letter moving in the right direction.

Please contact me or better yet come to Tempe. I need you Billy.

-Mom

Whatever oxygen that was in the room now disappeared. Billy could hardly breathe. He felt the thump of his heart inside both ears. He read the letter again.

…I need you Billy.

Full circle, that's what it was—life coming around full circle. This was the light bulb, the eureka moment, the tipping point, the keystone. A letter from his mom after more than five years of silence, delivered to a remote part of the Mexican jungle, on a day when everything simple seemed to be unraveling under the grimy hands of Fate…it really was just too much. Billy released the paper and it fluttered momentarily before descending lightly to the floor.

His parents had divorced?
His mom was in trouble?
And it concerned him?

His head pressed into the backrest of the recliner and he looked over at the end table, at the dagger, at the star in its haft, at the one triangular red jade that occupied the star's lower right leg—a symbol of the dagger, a symbol of the End, a symbol that was buried by heat into the palm of his right hand, marking him as the One. He looked at the back of his right hand, studied its veins, turned it over. The starry burn scar had all but disappeared, leaving the most prominent remnant, the triangular corner that marked the Creation of the End, as his palm's last commemoration. He touched it with his left index finger, thought about his mother, tried to remember what she looked like and that made him sad. A tear emerged and drained down his cheek, found the corner of his lips, tasted salty and coppery and sour, tasted like blood.

Billy pushed himself from the recliner and went to the bathroom where he opened up the mirrored medicine cabinet above the sink. He removed the meager contents, the two glass shelves and the false back panel. Beyond the panel, he grabbed two books. One of them was the small research notebook in which he'd logged so much of his Sedona, Merida, Puerto Morelos and Tulum thoughts. The other was the brown, leathery cover, perfect bound journal. It looked just like the Book of the Djed. Its contents duplicated, from memory, what was in the Book, page for page and symbol for symbol. It was something he'd been working on for almost three years. All of those days in the cliff caves—reading the real Book, snapping mental pictures of it, memorizing it, jotting down amateur renditions of the images in the research notebook—had supplied a need for him to recreate it a few months after settling in Nexpa. Writing it had been a mental exercise more than anything else, something to while away the silent nights, a way to remain connected to that which he knew he'd have to deal with sooner or later.

He returned to the recliner, set the recreated, leathery faux Book journal atop the unread mail next to the dagger, and fingered the cheap cover of the research notebook. Its contents were logged moments of time that he'd left for limbo three years ago. He remembered writing Cooper's name in the notebook back when he'd just met her and trusted no one. He remembered the Sedona library where he'd first learned of Richard Manson. He remembered the tiny plot of grass that he'd sat on in the Puerto Morelos town square, scribbling like a madman and wondering what sixes and nines had to do with anything. He remembered and his eyelids became heavy. Faces appeared in the darkness.

Steph. Janine. Joel. Alixel. Lax.

His eyes snapped open when someone knocked on the front door. He shook his head and rose from the recliner. A second knock was followed by a voice.

"Billy?"

It wasn't Cooper. The inflection was more like…he opened the door.

"Is this an inappropriate time?" the woman he knew only as Rio said. Her string bikini was gone. A flowery halter top and snug shorts had taken their place. A creamy peach scent wafted into the room.

"I…uh…" Billy said. "I was just doing some paperwork."

"You don't have a phone so I had to come over," Rio said as if the world was coming apart.

"What?" Billy said.

"I have to change our time tomorrow. Can we do it earlier, like, say, eight?"

Billy smiled. *Is that all you wanted?* he almost said, but her halter top changed his tongue's direction. "Sure."

"That's cool," Rio said, pointing at Billy's fairly reasonable facsimile of the Book of the Djed which rested on the recliner's end table.

Billy followed Rio's finger. "On the Internet you can get anything," he said. "It's just a little journal."

"You are a writer," Rio proclaimed.

"No more than the average Joe."

"But your name is Billy."

Billy looked left and right and up and down, all in the matter of one confusing second.

"So—Can I see it?" Rio took two quick steps into Billy's bungalow and Billy stepped laterally between her advance and the recliner's end table.

"Eight o'clock," he said. "I'll meet you on the beach."

Rio smiled but didn't immediately leave. "You have something I want," she told him, her voice as seductive as anything he'd ever heard. "I'll get it tomorrow."

When she turned to leave, Billy had to look away. "Tomorrow," was all that his lips could manage. Rio closed the door and Billy wobbled over to the recliner. Jerry had picked the chair out himself. It was like a glove, he'd said, just like the one in his own home. It could make any moment better. Billy fell flat into its thick cushions.

0-TIME: PREDICATE

THE PAST RETURNS

Monday, December 19, 2011

He jerked upward, instinctively knowing that he was late. He'd fallen asleep with the dagger and his mom's letter in his lap and now both fell to the floor. The sun had not yet risen high enough above the Mexican jungle ridges to touch Nexpa so Billy knew it wasn't quite eight o'clock, but it was close.

He folded his mother's letter and placed it in his journal, then returned it and the research notebook to the hidden pocket behind the medicine cabinet. A clock on the bathroom wall confirmed that it was fifteen minutes before his appointment with Rio. He had one Red Bull left in the refrigerator and he sucked it down as he headed out the door.

Outside, he immediately knew that something was wrong. Several plants had been flattened by something that had run over them. He followed a single tire track to the back of the bungalow, to the aluminum shed. The lock had been crushed—not snapped or beaten, but crushed. Parts of the thin metal door looked like an accordion. His motorcycle was gone.

Short on time, he decided to call Sheriff Buck from the surf shop but when he got there, Buck was waiting outside.

"Have you..." Billy started to say.

"Got 'em locked up right now," Buck said.

"Who was it?"

"Were *they*," Buck corrected. "The bunch of them came into the restaurant at lunch yesterday. Gave Cooper and Debbie and everyone in there a whole bunch of hassle."

Billy felt a twinge of regret for missing Sunday's lunch date with Cooper. "Where did you find it?"

"Over in the lagoon."

"In it?"

"Those jackasses must be the dumbest thieves I have ever known. Apparently, they took it sometime around three this morning and went gallivanting around town, taking turns on the bike, making all kinds of noise by riding it so hard it blew. They chucked it in the water in front of several witnesses."

"My bike blew up?

Buck gently tapped his shoulder. "Sorry, man. I'm trying to get the local magistrado to set a bail that will keep them locked up for a good bit… at least until after Christmas. Who knows what misery they could cause for vacationers on such an important holiday."

"Good. And shit! I loved that bike."

"I know you did, but like I said…sorry. You'll get justice."

"Thanks." They shook hands and Billy unlocked and entered the shop. He still had a few minutes before Rio was supposed to show and he wanted to give Cooper a quick call to, primarily, apologize for last night, but also to tell her about the theft so she wouldn't get the story from inaccurate gossip.

Cooper answered the phone. "Good morning, Hunters Restaurant."

"Good morning, Cooper." A short silence followed.

"I missed you last night," she said. "I mean it. I really missed you."

"Me too. I am sorry but…can we talk about it this evening? I absolutely promise I will not stand you up again. I'll stop by the restaurant right after you get off and we can head over to the lagoon. How's that sound?"

"I'll expect you at six-fifteenish sharp."

"There's something else. My motorcycle was stolen last night. Buck was here with me just a few minutes ago. He said some jerks came into the restaurant yesterday and harassed everyone. They're the ones that took it."

"Oh no," Cooper moaned. "Did you get it back?"

"They trashed it and threw it in the lagoon."

"I'm so sorry, Billy. I know how close the two of you were."

Billy thought that she had an odd but accurate way of putting it. He *had* become pretty close to the bike. "They're in jail now. I'm hoping I can, at least, get restitution from them. There were lots of witnesses."

"At least that's something."

Peaches! He suddenly smelled peaches. He looked up to see Rio standing outside a few yards beyond the shop, talking to Buck. Her odor was so thick he could taste its sweetness.

"Hello?" Cooper's voice intruded.

"Yep. It's something, all right. So, I gotta get busy now. See you after six."

He moved the phone's receiver from his ear to the cradle as Rio came into the shop and said, "What do you think?" She was wearing a pair of Billy Boardies.

She paid him for four hours of "surf lessons" though Billy was in the water with her for only half that time. Rio was a beast in the surf; she could have given him a few lessons. Some of her maneuvers were above professional and she did a trick that Billy had never seen before: a sort of kick flip with the board right at the apex of the wave curl. When Billy wasn't surfing with her, he laid on the beach, chilling, and watching all the other surf dudes (who, by no coincidence, had all migrated to the south side of the lagoon) hit on Rio. She teased the crap out of every one of them and Billy just chuckled. Anytime Rio came out of the surf, she would give him a big hug and a quick peck on the cheek before leading him by the hand, through all the other dudes who had wanted a chance. Though Billy knew it was purposeful, her ego boost refreshed him. She was the prize and Billy had won her—at least, that was the perception.

About a half an hour before noon, Rio came out of the water and sat beside him. The rest of the surfers waited a few more minutes, staring at their own loss, then most of them left.

"I really love my shorts," she said. "Very comfortable. But yours are different. You have something sticking out there at the waistline."

Billy felt a fleeting stab of embarrassment. He looked down at his crotch, thankful that the only thing "sticking out" was a small corner of the flap that covered the dagger's haft. He tucked it back in. "These are the original concept shorts. The design has changed considerably since then."

"I heard Billabong is interested."

"Really? How do you know that?"

"Surfers talk."

Billy eyed the two guys who still floated on their boards fifty yards out;

one of them was a local who knew about the deal. "Nothing is set yet. Just trying to get through all the legal stuff."

"You could make a billion off these things with the right marketing."

"Yeah? What do you know about marketing?" The question sounded rude but Rio shirked any insinuation it might have offered.

"I know that a good body in good clothing sells. Each one of those guys out there would have bought a dozen from me if I had only asked. Besides, I have connections."

"Are you making me a proposition?"

"I told you last night that you had something that I wanted."

"My shorts?"

Rio smiled and giggled and nodded. "I want your shorts, Billy Jo Presser." She pushed him, playfully, but her strength was much more than he anticipated and he rolled completely over next to the short surfboard she'd borrowed for the day.

"Hey, Billy!" It was Sheriff Buck and he stood right behind them. "Did she tell you yet?" "Did you tell him?" he asked Rio.

"Tell me what?" Billy said, looking around and up at Buck.

"I didn't think so," Buck said. "You promised me, little lady."

"Tell me what?" Billy repeated. Rio still said nothing.

"The guys who stole your bike are her friends."

Rio and Billy stood simultaneously. "I didn't say they were my friends," Rio explained. "I said we were living together at the Cheap Beach Pad." She thumbed toward the community building on the other side of the lagoon.

"No. I think you said they were your friends, and then you tried to 'convince me' that they hadn't done anything wrong. You tried to 'convince me' to let them go. Billy's the man that will be making part of that decision. Regardless of how you might successfully *convince* Billy otherwise, they did destroy public property and they'll have to pay for that. The magistrate needs to know if you're pressing charges, Billy. They demolished your bike."

He glared at Rio. "Yes. I'll be pressing charges. And I think you'll be going now."

Rio backed up a couple of steps. "I am sorry, but I tried to tell them…I tried to tell them to leave your fucking bike alone. I tried to tell them but they are morons."

"Did you know your moron friends were going to steal it last night when you came over?" Billy asked Rio. Buck looked quizzically at him.

"I told you," Rio demanded. "I told them to leave the fucking thing alone. Goddammit, won't someone listen to me?"

"Okay," Buck said. "Okay. No reason to get all bent. Just because they are friends doesn't mean you're their caretaker. You should know that the magistrado placed their bail at ten thousand dollars, each.

"WHAT!" Rio screamed. Whatever beauty she had was now completely covered in rage. "That's fucking insane! We don't have that kind of money!"

"I thought you had connections?" Billy reminded her. "You can turn my shorts into a billion dollars but your connections don't have a few Gs to bail your buddies out?"

"Yeah. Well, we'll see about all of this." Rio stormed off in such a fit of ugly incivility, she couldn't have sold her ass in a pair of shoestrings.

"You can come by the station in Caleta when you've secured the finances," Buck yelled after her.

"Ten thousand?" Billy said to Buck. "Isn't that a bit high?"

Buck lowered his voice. "It's not ten. It's only one for all three of them. I just wanted to see her reaction. They're her friends all right. She said she was going to tell you. She's a big time manipulator, that one."

"Ya think?" Billy said sarcastically. "She said she wanted my shorts."

Buck laughed so loudly Rio turned around and flipped him off, which only made him laugh harder. "You'll need to fill out some paperwork," he said with the sheen of happy tears in his eyes.

"Can't make it to Caleta today. Is it okay to come by tomorrow?"

"Yeah. I think that will be fine. You know, I could bring them to you. After all, you don't have transportation anymore."

"I was actually thinking about going over tomorrow anyway. I have some research I need to do on the Internet. Jerry lets me use his SUV for shopping. I'll ask him. But if that doesn't work out, I'll give you a call."

Buck walked off in the same direction as had Rio who now stood a hundred yards closer to the south side of the lagoon. Two young men stood beside her. One wore a leather jacket. The other…Billy was sure it was that strange fellow from Saturday night at the Hunters.

Duncan Swallow.

Last night had ended in a cloud of depression. Cooper had seen that woman in Billy's bungalow and Danny Kerskker had abruptly reentered her life. When she'd awakened Monday morning, a pool of dried tears that she'd not remembered crying stained her pillowcase. The depressive mind cloud had followed her into sleep and had turned on the spigot to a salty dam.

Billy's phone call had helped at first. He'd said that he was sorry and that they needed to talk. He'd guaranteed her that he'd see her after work.

Then, he'd told her about his motorcycle and about the Jackass Gang that had destroyed it, and her mood had shifted back toward melancholy. Total depression had returned when, right before Billy hung up, she'd heard that woman's voice.

What was she doing there? Cooper had thought. *Something had happened last night. The woman had seduced him.*

"Stop squinting," Debbie said to interrupt Cooper's thoughts. Cooper filled another salt shaker and set it on a tray with several others. "Whatever you're thinking about, you better stop. Your face is going to stick that way."

Cooper shook her head.

"Man troubles? Billy troubles?"

"Sort of. Well, maybe. Hell, I don't know. I think my imagination is getting the best of me."

"Don't let that happen. You have to talk to him. Tell him how you really feel. How can you *not* imagine something you are unsure of?"

"You're right…again."

"No," Debbie said. "He's right. For you. And if he's not going to make the first big move…well…you gotta claim your prize before someone else does."

"That's what I'm worried about."

Debbie gently grabbed Cooper's hand so she would stop working on the shakers. "You know what one of the biggest motivators there is when it comes to romance?"

Cooper shrugged.

"Jealousy. It makes you do things you would never have done before."

Cooper still stared, saying nothing.

"Yes. I saw them together this morning and, yes, that woman is a babe, but I've got to tell you…she was draping herself over him, not the other way around."

"I think that helps," Cooper said and then she told Debbie about seeing the woman on Billy's porch the night before.

"The mind fills in what the eyes don't see," Debbie offered. "You know what you two need? A vacation. You know the Giovanis. They've recently taken over the Mariposa Cottages outside of Caleta. Why don't I set something up for you—for both of you?"

Though the idea was odd (taking a vacation from a vacation town), Cooper thought Debbie was right. She had to get Billy away from Nexpa, away from his surf shop, away from that woman. "Okay. I'll see what he says."

"The sooner the better," Debbie added. "Temptation is a mighty seductive thing."

Cooper understood and asked Debbie to make the arrangements.

Around one o'clock, Duncan Swallow entered Hunters Restaurant. Tad waited on him. Swallow asked for coffee and just sat there, staring at the walls, until Debbie came out of the kitchen with a steaming cup in her hand and sat next to him. His gel-plastered hair didn't move an inch when he looked down at the hot, black liquid.

From inside the kitchen, Cooper couldn't hear what was said but she saw fewer than a dozen words move across Swallow's thin lips. He looked at Debbie only once, offering no expression that could help Cooper understand the conversation, then left without ever having touched his coffee. Debbie returned to the kitchen.

"I see your Minneapolis friend is back," Cooper said. "He didn't like your coffee. Maybe it needs ketchup."

Debbie's blank stare transformed into a smirk. "Yuck."

"He's a strange one. Swallow, was it?"

As if she knew Cooper was about to ask the question, Debbie said, "He was asking about Billy. He wants to go surfing."

"That guy? Talk about a fish out of water."

"To each his own, I guess." Debbie grabbed her stomach and grimaced. "Scuse me for a second. I need a bathroom break. Pipes ain't working well today."

"Again?"

Debbie looked at her once more before going into the bathroom. "When you get to be fifty-five, you'll know what I mean."

Billy met her at the restaurant at exactly six-fifteen, just as he'd promised. Cooper chose the orange capris that Debbie had given her and she was immediately rewarded when Billy's eyes rolled. He grabbed her hand and led her toward the beach.

The lagoon was a calm body of warm water that stretched from the shore inland in a two-hundred-yard-long irregular pattern and served as a favorite hangout just south of the town center. A purposeful walk would get you from the restaurant to the lagoon in less than ten minutes. Cooper and Billy meandered, taking their time to enjoy the sand and blackening night sky that still had not seen the moon rise. They paused often to talk to the visitors they already knew. One of them, a teenaged rookie surfer, asked Billy who the "hot chick" was that he'd been surfing with earlier.

"Her name is Rio," Billy said and Cooper's mind filled in the remaining lyrics.

"No shit," the teen said. "Very appropriate. I'd like to throw a few buckets of paint across that body."

"A lot of guys would," Billy said.

"She's a good surfer," the teen suggested.

"One of the best I've seen on this beach." Billy grabbed Cooper's hand and walked off, leaving a few more comments and questions hanging on the teen's tongue.

"You okay?" Cooper asked. She really wanted to ask him about his surf date with Rio but there was much more she thought they *had* to talk about.

"Yeah. Nice night," he answered, avoiding any connotation, and said nothing else until they were at the lagoon.

Several groups of partiers occupied spots along the lagoon perimeter. One group burned a camping-grade wood fire while another lit their party spot with a bunch of brush and trash stuffed into a fifty-five gallon oil drum. Most groups had not built a fire, opting instead for darkness. These groups were located near the shore, away from the fires, where they could enjoy the density of star lights above them.

Billy stopped short of the first group far enough away to avoid whispers and squatted in the sand. He flattened a space for Cooper and when she sat he said, "I got a letter from my mother."

Cooper said nothing.

"Doesn't that surprise you?"

She shook her head. "I got one better. Another Creation Dagger has surfaced."

"What!?" Billy's hand went to his chest were his dagger was sheathed under the button-up.

"And you know what's crazier than that?"

"I do. Debbie Hunter is taking the Popstar pill."

It was Cooper's turn to gasp. "What!?"

"Saw her take one Saturday night. Right before you came into the kitchen. She took it to help her stomach cramps."

Cooper immediately remembered how Debbie had suddenly doubled over in the restaurant earlier in the day. "You sure? There's got to be a lot of pills that look like it."

"Not ones with a Bethlehem star embossed in them. I haven't had the chance to ask her about it yet but I'm pretty sure. I'm thinking of going into Caleta tomorrow to double check some stuff on the Internet. I have to meet Buck anyway to sign some documents regarding the theft of the motorcycle."

"Your motorcycle. That's so sad. It was like a…a buddy to you."

"It had some history." Billy absently pushed sand between his toes. "You want to go with me? I called Jerry before I left the surf shop and he said I could use his wheels."

"You must be reading my mind. I've been thinking that we need a little vacation from all these vacationers. Why don't I arrange for us a little relax time? You can go over to the coffee shop, do your research and connect with Buck, while I do a bit of shopping. Then we can head over to the waterfalls. Their overnight cottages, I hear, are really nice."

"Spend the night?" Billy's toes stopped shuffling and sand sat atop the nails.

"If you want to."

"Yes," he said. "I want to." Billy sighed almost inaudibly and his toes resumed digging. "So what's the deal with the Creation Dagger? Where is it? How did you find out?"

The crash of the surf riddled the airwaves and Cooper had to raise her voice. "CNN was on last night and they had a special report about a man in Puerto Rico who has it." The group nearest them turned toward her. She lowered her volume. "It's Kerskker."

"Your Ex?"

"The fucker is a goddamned knight."

"Huh?"

"A knight. One of those jousting knights."

Billy leaned forward to stretch his legs. "Like you see at a dinner theatre?"

"No. Like you see in this new sport they call full contact jousting."

"Does that make any sense to you at all?"

"That he jousts or that he has a Creation Dagger?"

"Either…both, I guess."

"Makes absolutely no sense."

"Good."

Cooper gasped, again. "Good? How can that be good?"

"It's good because it means that I'm not the only one going crazy."

"The letter from your mom?"

"Yeah."

"What'd she have to say?"

"That she and dad got a divorce and that there was something going on that she needed my help with."

"Help with…what?"

"Letter didn't say."

"That's crazy."

"Like I said."

"What are you going to do?"

"I guess I'm..." He turned and looked hard into her eyes. "I guess *we'll* be leaving. The time was going to come sooner or later." Billy's stare shifted to the dark froth of crashing waves. He looked up and down the coastline as if this night's vision of it would be his last. "You know. Sometimes it really sucks being a Daykeeper. I'd much rather stay here for the rest of my life."

"Your mother needs you. Hell, this whole damn planet needs you."

"Do *you* need me?" he said, still looking at the waves.

She grabbed his right hand. "Is there any doubt?" When he turned to face her, that look was on his face again, the one she'd turned away from because of the firecrackers. "You were going to show me something...something you said you've been working on."

The group nearest them stood in unison and pointed at the southern sky. Cooper and Billy looked up to see a small light moving slowly from left to right near the horizon; it grew brighter as it traversed the constellations.

"What is it, man?" one of the six in the group said.

Meteor, Cooper immediately thought but knew what the group, who had emitted a sweet cannabis odor when they'd stood, was going to say before they said it.

"Aliens. Come to conquer us. Just like in *War of the Worlds*."

"Uplifting, Curtis," another in the group responded. "But it does look like them lights you see on the History Channel."

Billy stood and helped Cooper to her feet. "What do you think?"

"Meteor is my first choice."

"Safe bet, but I'm not so sure. It moves like a meteor but really doesn't look like one. Watch how it changes shape the closer it gets."

The moving light increased in speed and Cooper wondered about its twinkle. "Not a U.F.O., huh?"

Billy put his arm around Cooper's shoulders and tugged her closer. "If it is, I hope it lands right here. It's the only kind of evidence that will ever work."

"For you to believe in them?"

Billy nodded. "If it is a U.F.O., I'm thinking it wouldn't be taking such a meteor-like path. It's heading in one direction and that's the way it's stayed."

Cooper grabbed Billy's fingertips that were draped over her shoulder. "If it is a meteor, let's hope it doesn't land here."

"That would be a shitty way for it all to end."

Cooper faced his silhouette as Billy continued to stare at the light. "It's almost December twenty-first," she said.

"Yeah, but we still got another year."

The groups with fires burning had put them out. The entire population around the lagoon was now standing and gawking at the light. "Flying saucer," someone yelled. "Take me to your leader," another added and was quickly encored by a short burst of snickering.

As it traversed the sky, the light grew three times larger than any of the stars around it. It entered Orion's Belt, which was prominently displayed upside down, and disappeared behind the belt's center star. When the light exited the belt, its growth stopped. Horizontally, it had moved to the center of the sky but was no longer moving closer.

"What *does* that look like to you?" Billy asked.

Someone at a distance behind them answered his question. "Jesus is born," they yelled.

"Bethlehem Star?" Cooper said.

Billy nodded. "Doesn't it?"

The object did look a lot like many of the classic renderings, Cooper thought. It had a total of eight prominent points. The top and bottom points were long and the two center points stretched left and right at only half the length. Tinier points filled the spaces in between.

"You know what else it looks like?" Billy added. He reached into the cargo pocket of his shorts and pulled out a book that Cooper immediately thought was a well-used journal. Its tan, leather-looking cover was very flimsy, having been opened and closed for numerous entries, and it flopped as Billy brought the book up in front of her.

"I've been engaged in a little activity for the past two-and-a-half-plus years." When Billy flipped the book over, Cooper saw a Creation Dagger, drawn meticulously with a gold-tipped pen, on the back cover. It looked just like the inscription on the back of the Book of the Djed.

"From memory?" she said.

"Yes, for the most part." Billy opened the book to a page near the middle where he'd penciled in the four glyphs that had been revealed in the real Book. He'd even used color on some of them, particularly the bird of fire. Steady hand strokes of orange, red, yellow and pencil gray popped from the top of the page. The fourth drawing down looked nearly identical to the light in the sky, which had moved a little right of center. "I'm sure this is what I saw on Debbie's pill." He tapped the image with one finger.

"And so the conundrum is: what the hell is it doing in the Book of the Djed? A pill?"

"A symbol. A riddle."

"That some nutcase billionaire is selling some bad shit to people?"

"He doesn't sell it. He gives it away. Just like he's apparently done right here in Nexpa."

"For what purpose? To make everyone healthy, right? Very altruistic."

"You know that ain't right. Manson's some kind of cubit, a special kind, maybe a demon or Satan himself—and he can see through the eyes of other cubits. There's got to be something else."

"That idea creeps me out. That means he could see you but you wouldn't know he's watching."

"Until the video on YouTube started going viral, he would have never known where to find me. But now, I…we need to stay prepared."

Cooper stared at the six partygoers, thinking about how a stoned cubit would act. "You think that…Rio is one?"

Billy's eyes popped wide open. He set his Book clone, still open, on his lap. "Not until now. Is that wishful thinking? I mean, really. You think a chick like that could be a cubit?"

"You mean a beautiful bombshell like that couldn't possibly be dead. She made me so mad."

Billy looked hard into her eyes. "Jealousy," he whispered. "Now *that* is stranger than usual." He kissed her with one of his friendly but not so passionate pecks to the corner of her lips. "She's not my girl," his hushed voice continued. "You are. And besides, I've always been partial to strawberry blondes, orange pants, and women who aren't over six-feet tall."

They embraced for their first really passionate kiss since Tulum back in 2008. It was certainly her imagination, but Cooper swore the Bethlehem Star over the ocean brightened the more their lips squashed and tongues explored. When she pulled away, her left eye still peripherally focused on the light in the sky. "Are you going to see her again?"

"Not intentionally. She came by last night to change her surf time for this morning and tried, I think, to 'wiggle' her way inside. You know…the way women do."

"I do know." Cooper was happy that he'd confessed about Rio's visit and she was thrilled that nothing had happened. Her jealous twinge relaxed and she kissed him on the cheek.

"She also wigged out this morning. You should have seen it. Such ugly words coming from such a…"

"You can say it. I agree. She does have a beautiful body." Billy told her all about ugly Rio and her reaction to Buck's little white lie concerning the Jackass Gang's bail bond. When he finished, she grabbed the book from his lap and flipped through the first half of it. "This is fascinating. You know, we mortals aren't supposed to be able to see any of the other pages of the Book. This almost makes me feel like a Daykeeper."

Billy hugged her shoulders within one arm. "Trust me. You don't want any of that action."

"I don't know." She lolled her ear onto the back of Billy's knuckles. "I saw you survive three bullets at Tulum and another couple at Hondo."

"You want to know what invincibility is like?" Billy replied calmly, matter-of-factly, as if he really needed to tell someone what he was feeling. "That was Cower's big tease, wasn't it? I can tell you—it ain't all it's cracked up to be. I suppose if you were the Manson type, you could use your invincibility for all kinds of self-serving needs but…"

"Daykeepers aren't like that," Cooper finished. "You are Good and they are Evil. You save and they kill. You respect the power to give or take life and they abuse it."

"I am to save the world and they want to destroy it. You know how much that sucks, the idea of saving the world, especially when you have no idea how you are supposed to do so?"

Cooper released the front cover of the book and it flopped closed. "Maybe that's a part of it. If you knew how you were going to die, wouldn't that ruin the rest of your life?"

"You don't know how many times I thought of that very thing back on Sebastian's Island, back in the cliff caves. The entire process of reading the Book of the Djed each and every day, memorizing every tiny cursive stroke and every stroke's placement on every written page made me wonder if I was reading my own obituary. Fortunately, I didn't, and still don't, understand a lot of what was memorized beyond what Alixel and Lax explained. I guess that's what keeps me sane: not knowing how it's all going to end."

"An insane Daykeeper," Cooper said. "Now that's about as scary as it gets."

"I think we have another word for such a thing…a cubit."

Again, Cooper looked over at the nearby group of teens who were now passing around a joint. "An insane stoned Daykeeper," she said.

Billy giggled in a way that accepted her absurdity. "You know," he said. "You can come with me…to my mother's place in Tempe. Sedona is just a skip up the interstate from there. It's been a long time. If you lay low you could…"

The invitation opened something inside her, some hidden pocket of adoration that had been sealed so long ago. The slow drizzle of complete surrender escaped the mental confines built by men. It made her swoon. It filled her mind with possibilities. Perhaps, she really could love someone.

She could almost taste it.

But something else also drooled out, a darkness that had been love's keeper: hatred and revenge. And she knew at that very moment that Billy could never be completely hers until she erased the cause of her heart's burden. Danny Kerskker. "Thank you, Billy. I'll take you up on that invitation but…"

"But you have an invincible knight to take care of first," Billy finished and cupped her face within both of his palms. "You know how dangerous that's going to be?"

"You taught me all about danger, Billy." She searched his brown eyes for all of those things she wanted him to say. "And how to avoid it."

He kissed her as passionately as he had moments ago and pulled back a few inches from her face. "I think tomorrow evening is going to be one special night," he said.

Do you know that I love you? For a moment Cooper thought she'd actually said it. The words sat there, between teeth and tongue, like a wild, caged beast.

"You want to head in?" Billy continued.

Do you know that I love you? Cooper pressed her tongue to the roof of her mouth to try and make the words go away. "No," she said. "I'd rather stay here for a little while longer."

The light that looked like the symbol in Billy's hand-sketched book continued traveling across the sky until it disappeared beyond the northern horizon an hour later. Some thought it had been an aircraft or a satellite high in orbit. Others, like the stoners next to them, swore that it had been a flying saucer.

Cooper thought its appearance had been meant to validate their departure. It looked like the symbol stamped into the Popstar pill. It looked like the sparkle she'd seen in Billy's eyes as he'd massaged her cheeks and kissed her lips.

She thought it was a sign of love.

0-TIME: PREDICATE

DAYKEEPERS CAN

Tuesday, December 20, 2011

Caleta de Campos was a town built on cliffs that nature had carved into a bay made for fishing and diving and fun. The coastal sands shaded toward yellow and the locals had to constantly reassure visitors that the beaches were not polluted. Undersea minerals had made the Caleta beaches look as if a giant had peed on it.

Billy drove Jerry's SUV into the town just as most businesses were opening, which in the laid back culture of the area was close to nine-thirty. The sunny December day had drawn many people to the town's center and both locals and visitors meandered about, looking for that perfect Mexican-flavored Christmas gift.

"You want anything from the market?" Cooper asked Billy as they exited the vehicle.

"No, thanks," he said. "I'm going to get some breakfast at the coffee shop, though. You want to join me before shopping?"

"Had something at the restaurant before we left. I'll meet you back here in about two hours."

Cooper was wearing her new orange capris again and Billy knew she knew he was looking at them as she walked away. She turned and smiled and shook it once or twice before disappearing in the crowd.

Internet service was provided at several Caleta locations. Billy's favorite was a New England-style coffee shop just a couple of blocks away. He liked the place more for the décor's similarity to stateside coffee shops than for its digital connections. He'd mostly given up the Internet as a self-imposed restriction to laying low. Networks were smarter than most people knew and just about anyone could be tracked if the trackers were diligent enough. Billy had never wanted to take that chance, but it was irrelevant now that YouTube had pretty much geosynced his location with the Billy Boardies video.

He entered The Crosses just before ten o'clock and took a seat in front of a computer flat screen near the tall, storefront window. Sunshine hit him square in the face and he stood to pull the window blind.

"Let me get that for you," said Trisha Cross, the thirty-something daughter of the shop owners. "You want the usual?"

"Coffee and a cookie, yes," he replied.

"House blend and chocolate chip?"

Billy nodded. "Just like back home."

Trisha left and Billy grabbed his research notebook from one thigh pocket of his cargo shorts. The thing was beat all to hell, having survived Sedona and Tulum and the wilds of the Mexican jungle. Almost every one of the book's fifty pages was filled with some note or sketch or brainstormed mind map. The spiral binding had helped maintain its overall integrity but even *it* showed age, the wires bent at angles that he pried up so the pages would turn.

He flipped straight to the notes he'd made back in Sedona's public library that pertained to the wonder pill, Phoenix International, and Richard Manson. Trisha delivered his coffee and cookie as he began to cross-reference.

"Popstar" was the first search term he used but the results were limited to celebrity web pages, a new talent show in the U.K., and a couple of academic articles pertaining to marketing, branding and other boring higher education banter.

"Popstar health pill" returned more useful results. The very first usable link (under all the advertisement crap), referenced the exact *Sedona Red Rock News* article he'd read in the library, the one titled "Llama Lunatic Mountain Bike Race Begins Monday." He reread it:

> The City of Sedona and the Village of Oak Creek announce the first annual Llama Lunatic Mountain Bike Race to be held on Monday, Dec. 1.

> In cooperation with the National Parks Service and sponsorship by BETH Pharmaceuticals, the race will traverse a loop marked by the Llama Bike Trail. National race professionals will be challenged by sharp natural benches, slickrock, big drops and, perhaps, a cactus or two as they traverse the relatively new trail around Bell Rock and Courthouse Butte and up the challenging rise of Lee Mountain.
>
> "This is an event we've been working on for a couple of years," said Gin Arropo, mayor of Sedona. "The beauty of Sedona's autumn will bring in dozens of prominent athletes from all over the country which will be a holiday boon for local merchants."
>
> BETH Pharmaceuticals, manufacturer of the popular Popstar health pill, has guaranteed a purse of over $50,000 to participants.
>
> "BETH Pharma pledges to bring everyone total health," said the company's president, Richard Manson. "We can't think of a better cooperative effort to bring this mission to these superb athletes and to the people of Arizona."
>
> Stretches of the Llama Trail will be cordoned off for spectators along the entire route. The National Park Service reminds you that if you visit any of Sedona's beautiful natural parks to "Take what you bring and leave what you find." Please visit our local adventure merchants for further information.

What a difference three years had made. When he'd read the article just after Thanksgiving back in 2008, he hadn't even known Lax and his son Aaron beyond their chance meeting in a parking lot. Now Lax was dead. The "invincible" Daykeeper had sacrificed himself to help save Marcy under Lee Mountain, in the sacred Great Hall of the Anasazi, where a giant hawk named Osi had merged with Lax's mortal soul.

"Invincible," he said to the computer screen, thinking about Lax… thinking about himself. "No, not invincible. Immortal." He couldn't help but to shed a tear for his friend and felt oddly comfortable with the thought of joining Lax and his sister in immortality one day.

He continued reading the search results to find a strange anomaly. Everything that referenced "popstar" as it pertained to BETH Pharmaceuticals was dated before 2009. This curiosity led him back one web page to the search results referencing academic articles and branding. He clicked one and in the abstract, he immediately found an answer.

> **Rebranding a Mistake**
>
> Abstract: In a corporate culture where profit equals success, few multi-national companies can survive the combination of brand reconditioning and a complete sales remodeling. This article describes how one corporation, Phoenix International (PIIL), and its subsidiary BETH Pharmaceuticals (BETH), did just that. After successful trials in 2008 of the then branded "Popstar" pill, BETH sold the supplement as a FDA-approved prescription medication that met with dismal success. Early in 2009, PIIL decided to rebrand the drug, take it off the market as a prescription medication and started giving it away at no cost. BethStar, as the supplement became known, was the marketing genius of Taylor and Jones of New York, NY. Touting the perception of the Bethlehem Star which guided the wise men toward salvation, "BethStar" implies the same thing: salvation through a healthier body and mind. With partnerships that include Apple Inc. and the X-Games, coupled with the no-cost incentive, PIIL has successfully rebranded itself as cool, hip and trustworthy and has increased its net worth using the tried and true, "Give something for nothing" concept that has become the mantra of other successful corporations such as Google, Facebook and Amazon.

Billy copied the word "BethStar" and pasted it in a new search. The results were plentiful with link titles full of the words "miracle, panacea, and mystery." It was a miracle, one web site explained, because it had helped save many thousands from famine in Africa, Asia and several Latin American countries. For those who lived in rich societies like the United States, it was a panacea because it apparently cured just about every negative health-related issue including obesity, high cholesterol, and diabetes among dozens of others. It was a mystery because no one knew exactly how it worked. BETH Pharmaceuticals' "secret formula" was protected by patent and none at the drug giant was willing to give up any information. That it reacted with human DNA in a unique way was about all any scientist or reporter ever got. As long as it passed clinical trials, which it had, government agencies across the world had never questioned its processes.

One fascinating cross reference led him to a website that documented the remarkable rise and fall of a man named Ben Reely. A year ago almost to the very day, Reely had survived an attempted murder by a guest on his popular cable news show Fox News Morning. Billy stopped reading and clicked a link to the YouTube video that documented the event.

> *...with me today is my friend and award-winning documentarian, Michael Arden, who knows all about it. Michael has been working on what has been a—what would you call it—undercover assignment for Fox News...*

Michael Arden. Billy opened up a new browser window, typed in the name and clicked the first link that went to Fox's web site. He resized both windows so that he could watch and read at the same time. In the video, a man who looked to be twice Billy's age suddenly produced a handgun from under the anchor's desk, stood, pointed it directly at Reely's head and clicked through two empty cylinders. Reely flinched and…to Billy, it was more like a stumble than a leap. The way his body collided with the assailant's looked like "brave Ben Reely" (a term he was reading on Fox's web page as he watched the video) had almost passed out. Regardless of how it had appeared, Reely's hand had deflected Arden's third pull of the trigger which had fired a bullet that had almost killed a female stagehand. In the video, a mass of bodies assaulted the stage and the video ended.

Billy's full concentration went to the worded account on Fox's website which had hundreds of reader comments added at the end. Billy read through the first few.

> *What a piece of crap Reely is and always will be. The SOB passed out!*
> *How could anyone get into the Fox news studio with a loaded gun?*
> *He was so brave...that's why I love him so much :)*

There was no response to the first comment but the second had the following addition: *No one brought a gun into the studio. The gun is a requested requirement of Reely's. He's had that thing under his desk every day since taking the job five years ago.*

As far as bravery was concerned, Fox's response went much further than a one sentence response to a feedback comment. News anchors pushed their brave shining star for the next five months. Reely had become the face of Fox and the poster boy for Fox's definition of news reporting as "hard, gutty and, above all, fearless." Reely had used his overwhelming celebrity status to promote a new topic (which he'd been proficient at doing to an annoying, endless degree).

BethStar was no longer some scary corporate conspiracy bent on mind control. BethStar, according to Reely's incessant promotion, was a miracle, a panacea, and a mystery. The combination of Reely's push of the pill and an award-winning documentary that Billy found cross-referenced to Arden's name, had accelerated BethStar's acceptance, particularly in third world countries where human health conditions were catastrophic.

Billy clicked a couple of more links, found a picture of the BethStar pill, stared at it until he was positive that the star in the middle of it was the same one he'd seen in Debbie's kitchen, then leaned back to realize he'd not even touched his coffee and cookie. He took a bite and a sip as Trisha walked up to his table.

"Not good today, Billy?" she asked.

Billy took another bite and sip. "Fantastic, as usual. Just got caught up on the Web."

"I know what you mean. Sucks really…hey." She pointed at the computer screen. "My mom takes those. I really think they saved her life."

"BethStar?" Billy asked.

"I don't know what they're called but I'd recognize the logo anywhere."

"How does she get them?"

"Distribution point."

"Distribution point? You mean the pharmacy?"

"No. It's what you would call the local health department back in the States. They give them away absolutely free."

"How long has this been going on?"

"Oh…a month, maybe two. Mom started them about three weeks ago and you should have seen it—her—just like a kid again. She was so run down, but not anymore."

Billy drank more coffee. "Wow. That's great news for her…and for you."

"Yeah. I just hope she doesn't kill herself."

"What do you mean?"

"She's out parasailing today. She's never done that before." Trisha grinned and pointed at his cookie. "You want something else?"

"No. I'm good. Do you suppose your mom will be back in today?"

Trisha shrugged. "Beats me. And to tell you the truth, it's a bit annoying. I love her to the max, but she's acting so, I don't know, like a teenager. Can't rely on her for work, but…she deserves a break."

Billy grinned not because he wanted to but because he thought that's the reaction Trisha wanted. "Could you tell your mom that I might stop back in on the way out of town today?"

"Absolutely."

"One other thing…where's the 'health' department located?"

"A couple of blocks away from the police station, but I'd say it's pretty busy over that way today."

"How so?"

"You didn't hear? Someone broke out some prisoners this morning. They killed at least one of the officers and injured a couple more. This place hasn't seen that kind of action since Buck came to town."

"Do you know if the sheriff was one of the injured?"

"Not sure. You know how rumors go. Some said yes. Some said no. I haven't seen him."

Billy dropped cash on the table, took another bite of cookie, and washed it down with the remaining lukewarm coffee. As he exited the coffee shop, he didn't notice Duncan Swallow who stood near a lamppost just a few yards from The Crosses storefront window. Once Billy had turned the corner of the next block, Swallow took pursuit, stopping just for a moment to gaze through the coffee shop window at the computer screen on which Billy had been viewing the white oval pill and the unique star embossed into its surface.

Cooper hadn't said anything to Billy, but before they'd left the restaurant that morning, Debbie had asked her to pick up some medication for her stomach cramps. The location was on the other side of town, pretty close to where Ron Buck had jailed the assholes that had stolen Billy's motorcycle, and Cooper decided to make it her last stop.

Her short, athletic figure, sparkling strawberry blonde hair and next-to-brand-new, sunset orange capris and white top turned dozens of men's heads as she walked the cracked brick and dirt sidewalks of Caleta's town center toward the farmer's market. Much of the fresh ingredients for Hunters Restaurant (especially the native Mexican choices) came from the market and, over the years, she had gotten to know many of the producers, which ones were honest, which had trustworthy products, and which to avoid altogether.

She purchased a bagful of essentials that carried easily (mostly herbs and spices), asked lots of questions about crop health and which fruits and vegetables were at peak, and mentally noted how each could be served in existing or new recipes. One farmer, a very old Mexican man who always wore a sombrero, offered to deliver any of the produce she purchased from him so she wouldn't have to carry it around town. Cooper took him up on the offer and pointed out a couple of hundred pesos worth of items which the man quickly and efficiently plucked from the tables, wrapped in newspaper and placed into paper bags. For each bag he filled, he wrote "chica" on it, which literally translated to *hot babe*.

"Gracias," she said to him and smiled. "Usted está especie."

The old man had four teeth and all of them gleamed yellow when he grinned. "Un minuto por favor," he said, walked to a table topped with round, green produce, grabbed two of the hand-sized fuzzy balls, wrapped them in newspaper and placed them in a small paper bag with paper handles. "Dulces para los dulces." When Cooper offered him twenty pesos, the old man waved her hand away. "Para la navidad."

A Christmas present.

She sniffed the open bag and was overwhelmed by the pure sugary sweet aroma that mixed together oranges, pineapples, and, strangely, cinnamon. "Mmmm," she moaned. "Gracias." The old man glared hungrily at her which, suddenly, made her feel uncomfortable. She waved and said good-bye and tried not to look back as she walked off.

She visited half a dozen shops (some indoor and some roadside), found a few Christmas-themed decorative pieces for the restaurant, looked at many blouses but failed to find anything that matched her capris better than the white button-up shirt she was wearing, and started looking for the address that Debbie had given her. She became lost for a few minutes but readjusted her course when she got to the south end of Caleta's bay. One of the town's oldest stone buildings occupied an area near the address about a hundred yards away, but there were no other buildings within a block of it. It was an odd place for a pharmacy, Cooper thought. Weeds were everywhere, a few windows were cracked or busted out completely, and the tin roof was as rusty red as the brick pavers that still mostly resembled a sidewalk in front of it.

She walked to the building's heavy front door (which was also in need of repair), but could hear nothing inside. She knocked and her knuckles' force pushed the door open on squeaky hinges. She remained cautiously outside even though, through the open doorway, she saw that the interior was completely modern, well lit, well maintained, and there were at least ten people sitting silently in chairs, reading magazines or books or whatever was on their smartphone screens. When she stepped inside, she thought she'd been transported to a doctor's office, complete with a middle-aged receptionist who beckoned Cooper over to her long, metal desk.

"May I help you, señora?" the Mexican woman said.

Unlike a doctor's office, Cooper saw no doctors, no examination rooms, no medical equipment and not even one of those wall-suffocating file cabinets that housed patients' records. The only other door in the room was closed behind the receptionist but it looked more like a closet. "I'm here to pick up a prescription for Debbie Hunter," she said.

"A minute, por favor," the receptionist replied, then got up, went through the narrow door, and closed it.

Cooper turned around to study those that were waiting. They varied in age, sex and, even, nationality. She knew none of them and none of them cared enough about her presence to look up from their reading material.

"Here you go." The receptionist's sudden voice startled Cooper. "Something else? Maybe for you?"

Cooper turned back to face the woman and took the white bag which had been stapled closed. "What? For me? I don't have stomach cramps."

"You no need them. We just need your blood signature."

"We? Who is we? What? Blood?" Cooper looked at the bag. Nothing was written on it.

"The goormant. It is a free service."

It took a moment for Cooper to realize that the woman had just said *government*. "No thanks," Cooper said. "Just picking up these for a friend."

"If you change your mind, we are here."

The receptionist's smile was creepy and false and Cooper stepped quickly away from her. When she opened the front door to exit, Duncan Swallow was standing outside as if waiting for her. Cooper quickly slipped the pill bag in with the bag of sweet green fruits.

"Swallow, is it?" she asked him.

Except for a change in clothes, Swallow looked no different than he had at the restaurant or at Debbie's dinner party. "Your boyfriend needs you," his monotonic voice said.

"Excuse me?"

"At the police station. There has been a murder."

"What?" Cooper exclaimed but she didn't wait for an answer.

Five minutes later, she pushed through a crowd of people who stood outside the police station; yellow crime scene tape blocked entry into it. She saw Billy inside.

"Hey," she yelled, but Billy didn't hear her. "Billy!" she yelled again and ducked under the tape. A young deputy that she didn't know immediately grabbed her arm and screamed Spanish at her so fast she had no idea what he said.

Billy came out and confronted the deputy and he released her. "Some crazy shit," he told Cooper. "Someone busted out the guys who stole my bike, killed one of the deputies, injured another and one is still missing."

"Where's Ron? Is he okay?"

"He's fine but really shaken up as you can probably imagine. He's out looking for them right now. It happened this morning but there were only a few witnesses. Buck said he was going to Nexpa first since that's where they'd caused so much trouble."

"They wouldn't go back to the restaurant would they?"

Billy hesitated as if he'd not thought of that. "I, uh…maybe we should call them."

Billy used the phone inside the station and Cooper listened as Billy's replies of *Uh-huh*, *yes* and *okay* did little to ease her apprehension. The holding cells for criminals were in a larger room that was connected to the main office by a doublewide pass-through. Red splatters marked the floor beyond the pass-through but there was no body. Billy hung up the phone.

"That was Debbie. Buck has already been there but no one has seen any of them."

"We should go back," Cooper insisted.

"Debbie said you would say that and she said that if you did, to tell you not to worry, to go to the waterfalls, regardless. Buck told her the suspects probably fled into the jungle, but he stationed a few of his deputies around the area as a precaution. A couple of federales are also combing the area."

"How am I supposed to not worry?"

Billy shrugged. "I know. Me too. But she insisted."

Cooper grunted.

"And there's something else. One of the killers…a witness said that she was the prettiest gringo she'd ever seen."

"Rio?"

"She did get really bent when Buck teased her about the bail bond for her buddies and that could have provided a motive. Only thing is…the witness claimed that the woman's hair was red, not blonde."

The young deputy who had verbally assaulted Cooper came into the station. "They got one," he said. "Found her near the main road. They shot her three times."

"Her?" Cooper asked. "The one with the red hair?"

"The red hair was false." The deputy grabbed his own short hair as if trying to find the right word. "A wig. She is blonde."

"The others?" Billy asked.

"Not yet but they think by tonight."

"That's a relief," Billy said to Cooper. "You know, we can still go back if you want. The waterfalls can wait just a little longer."

Cooper thought about how harshly Debbie would scold her for months ahead. Her boss, and friend, had pulled some big strings to get them the best room with all of the amenities, and a private hiking tour of the falls. Besides, it sounded like Rio was dead and *that* strangely made things better. "Well… if they've been caught, what's to worry?"

"You sure?"

"Can we get out of here?" Cooper said, sniffing the air. "It smells like blood."

Cascada de Mariposas was the perfect name for it. Butterfly Waterfalls. Carved by nature into the east face of a one-hundred-foot tall ravine wall, three rock formations broke the cascade of frothy water halfway up. The larger butterfly-looking rock (Mama) jutted from the ravine wall above two smaller butterfly-looking rocks (Dos bebés), and pummeling water from above created a misty, rainbow halo around all three. During the winter jungle wet season, the water and rocks and angelic aura were breathtaking to behold from ground level. Though he'd seen them a couple of times before, Billy gasped the moment he stepped from Jerry's SUV.

"They're marvelous today," he said to Cooper who carried a shopping bag of Caleta market goodies and a small duffle bag full of overnight necessities. "They say there's a cave behind Mama butterfly."

"There is," Cooper replied. "That's what's on our agenda for the evening."

"I didn't know they did that."

"They don't…usually…unless you have a friend named Debbie Hunter. She really came through for us."

Billy stood there for a minute longer, staring at the water as it ripped into three pieces around the butterflies and wondered how the hell anyone could hike up there. The ravine face looked quite steep and no trails were visible. He shrugged and walked with Cooper to the first of the four Mariposa Cottages.

"We are in this one, number four," Cooper said. "Debbie got the key for me yesterday."

"After you," he said and she opened the door and entered.

There really wasn't much to the room beyond a small, four-drawer dresser and the rectangular mirror above it, a rattan loveseat, two matching rattan chairs, and three oil lamps: one on the dresser, and one on each of the two small tables that bookended a queen-sized bed. Billy suddenly blushed and turned away.

"Any bathrooms?" he asked.

"One community bathhouse outside."

He walked around the bed and looked out the single-pane window beside it to find only dense foliage. When he turned back around, Cooper was sitting on the bed and smiling at him, one orange capri-clad leg flopped lazily across the mattress, exposing one strong calf muscle. "What?" he asked.

"You haven't said anything about my new pants."

"You never asked."

"Billy Jo Presser! You know a girl shouldn't have to ask for a compliment."

Billy sat on the bed next to her. "You got some hot pants there," he said. "So what's in the sack?" He pointed at the brown paper with handles that she'd set on the bed between them.

"Food and…"

Someone knocked on the door and Cooper answered it. Mrs. Giovanni stood in the doorway with a basket of assorted fruits and cheeses. "Welcome," she said with an Italian accent so thick Billy thought he'd been transported to Europe. "An appetizer for the lovers."

Cooper cleared her throat. "It looks wonderful. That's very kind."

"Debbie Hunter said you two deserved the Mariposa package." She handed the basket to Cooper. "That's dinner for two and champagne at sunset."

"Did she ask about a tour of the falls by chance?"

Mrs. Giovanni smiled—big. "That's where your dinner is and, well, you'll see. The guide will be by in about an hour or so. If you didn't bring hiking boots, we have some extras."

"We didn't. I didn't even think…"

"Already taken care of. Debbie told us your sizes." Mrs. Giovanni backed away from the door and offered a cute little wave at Billy. "Enjoy the basket."

Cooper closed the door. "Debbie's something else," she said and set the basket on the top of the dresser.

"She's something all right. She wants us together in the best kind of way."

"Mariposa package," Cooper said and traveled three steps with a sexy hip shake. "For lovers." She leaned forward and kissed Billy gently, quickly. "But after what happened in town…let's have something to eat while we talk. What did you find out?"

Billy told her what his research had uncovered concerning BethStar, its popularity and its widespread use. He reminded her that the pills were created by a subsidiary of Richard Manson's mega-corporation and both agreed that something must be wrong with the drug even though it had saved so many thousands of lives and had made thousands more much healthier. "Trisha Cross said her mother started taking them a couple of weeks ago and the improvements have been phenomenal."

Cooper ate one of the last two wedges of an orange she'd peeled and offered Billy the final slice which he took and ate. "I think you're right about Debbie. She's taking it, too." Billy licked orange juice from his lips and his eyebrows rose with curiosity as Cooper reached into her shopping bag and produced a much smaller white bag. She thumbed the stapled flap and told Billy about Debbie's request that morning.

"You went to the distribution point?" Billy asked. "What was it like?"

"What's a distribution point?"

"That's what Trisha called it. Not pharmacy or doctor's office but distribution point. Doesn't sound very 'medical' does it?"

"It wasn't. It was more like some sterile crack house…out away from everything in an old, turn-of-the-century building with people inside just sitting and waiting and kind of out of it. As if they were Jonesing for a hit. I walked right in, got the stuff with no ID of any kind and left, and…" She pulled the flap of the bag free from the staple. "That Swallow character was there."

"Swallow? Why would he be there?"

"Do you think he was following me?" Cooper opened the white bag and dumped the single, red pill bottle onto the mattress where it rolled into a pile of large orange peels.

"Why would you say that?"

"He was in the restaurant yesterday. He talked to Debbie, then Debbie had another bout of stomach cramps, then she asked me this morning to get these pills, then Swallow showed up."

"Coincidence…" He said it but immediately dumped the idea. "No. I don't think it was a coincidence that I saw him with Rio and one of her asshole leather-jackets, so I doubt it's a coincidence that he keeps showing up wherever we are." Billy grabbed the pill bottle and twisted the cap. "You think Debbie will be pissed that we looked into her medicine?"

Cooper shifted closer to him. "It's not medicine, right? And if it's hurting her then she shouldn't have it anyway."

"Before we jump to conclusions…" He tilted the bottle and a dozen white, oval pills flopped into the palm of his hand. On one side of each of them was the symbol of the Bethlehem Star—the symbol of chaos—the fourth symbol in the Book of the Djed. "Well, there you have it. I'm not crazy." He sniffed one pill but was careful to keep it away from his lips, then scooped all of them back into the bottle and capped it.

"So what do we do about it?" Cooper asked while dropping the pill bottle back into its bag.

"We do what we can for those we care about. We go to this 'distribution point' with Sheriff Buck and a couple of deputies and demand a search. We confiscate and destroy."

"Without a warrant?"

"Remember. We're in Mexico. Sheriff Buck is all the warrant needed. If he cares about Debbie and his community, he'll trust us. Besides, one of his deputies may have been murdered because of these pills. Rio and her gang and Swallow—all in collusion."

"Drug dealers?" Cooper tossed the white bag back and forth between both hands and the pills rattled inside. "I don't know. You said that BethStar had been widely distributed so it must be legal." She dropped the white bag back into the larger shopping bag. "What if they're here for another reason?"

"Yeah…surfing lessons."

"Or…"

Billy remembered Cooper's suggestion the night before. *Could Rio be a cubit?* "Or me," he said, and his hand instinctively went to his chest and rested atop the sheathed dagger.

They waited another hour before the guide showed up, which gave them an opportunity to talk about the future, about leaving Nexpa, about the idea of not seeing each other after having been through so much for the past three years. Cooper almost cried and Billy had to pull her tight to his body for reassurance. In those last few moments before the guide knocked, Billy finally felt the spurt that runs from the heart, down through the toes, up across the spine and into the back of the head. This same spurt caused emotional wars and stitched together polar opposites. It made one swoon, shiver, hyperventilate and submit. Billy stroked the natural waves on the top of her head with his lips, sniffed her ocean breeze aroma, pressed his cheek into the softness. And when she finally titled her head up, her eyes' moisture told him the truth. It was the irreversible path they were both about to take, one less traveled because lust was so much easier. It wasn't convenient and it fulfilled nothing sentient. True love served no one. The vassalage was the onus of the bearer.

Billy continued floating in this serenity as they hiked up the ravine and, given Cooper's almost absolute silence, he knew she must be feeling the same way. It was more than anticipation—it was culmination. And this was the perfect moment.

They were still at least a fifty feet from the ribbon of falling water that crashed against the mother butterfly when the guide departed. He had been told to do so. They were to be left alone. He pointed out a path that could not be seen from anywhere except where they now stood, then turned around and quickly disappeared.

The higher they climbed, the wetter the air became, cleaner smelling, denser with oxygen and lighter to breathe. The waterfall splashes became more than teardrops. They hit Billy's cheeks like soft golf balls, dousing entire patches of skin until his face was drenched. Cooper suffered the same wondrous assault. Her hair matted to her head and she shook it to get the excess water out of her eyes. When she smiled, her lips parted liquid runners that continued around the corners and drooled off of her chin.

Mama Butterfly camouflaged the opening until Billy was just a few yards away. There was just a sliver, about as wide as his shoulders, but the light glowing from beyond the narrow space convinced him to move forward. At his feet, the jungle-trampled path they'd followed transitioned into a slippery, curly passage of rock that had been created over centuries of cascading water. He squeezed Cooper's hand and slowly shuffled across the slick path, a thin layer of water testing his footing and courage.

Few ever went to the cave, the guide had said on their journey up the ravine, and many who'd dared had lost their lives. But Billy had experience with caves on the sides of cliffs near water, and the closer he moved toward the flickering orange-yellow opening, the faster his heart raced and the more his mind quickened. Splashes now completely drenched his and Cooper's bodies. The thunder of the fall's might against the rocks overpowered any warning or encouragement that Billy might have had for Cooper but she didn't need any. She followed him lock step through the narrow passage behind the rock, ignorant, as he was, of how quickly the falls could rip them apart with one false step.

The cave behind the butterflies wasn't very wide but its depth was at least three times more than the one on Sebastian's Island. The height of its flat floor to domed ceiling was just enough for both of them to stand. It was illuminated by three fat candles and one gas lamp. Furnishings included an inflatable mattress (that had already been inflated), a couple of blankets, a picnic basket that looked like it had been taken from the set of *Little House on the Prairie*, a small Igloo cooler, and several incense sticks that stood unlit and erect from sand-filled clay cups.

Both of them moved into the chamber, scanned the perimeter and simultaneously turned. Billy gasped as did Cooper, but only Cooper fell onto the plastic air of the mattress beneath her. Billy grabbed her outstretched arm.

In front of them, the sun was still an hour from setting beyond the veil of rushing water a hundred feet above the earth's surface. Rays of light poked and peeked through the crystal wet layers. An enchantment. No wonder so many had lost their lives, Billy thought. The vision—you had to jump into it because it was so beautiful—a salvation.

Billy flopped down next to Cooper. His exclamation bounced against the wet wall and reflected back into his and Cooper's face. "Ahh," is all his mouth could manage and the echo of the butterflies, which had become much more than rock, redoubled his awestruck pleasure.

"Why?" Cooper exclaimed. "Why us? Why are we here? Why should we see such beauty when no one else can?"

Billy's gaze remained on the falling water, on its prisms of sun orange and sky blue. He answered without looking at her. "Because we were chosen." And then he did…

Turn to her…

Embrace her…

Pull her closer…

Skin, elastic wet…

Breaths, consuming…

Everything…

Their clothes came off as the sun twinkled, naked.

Their sweat drooled in tributary rivulets as the waterfall crashed, dissonant.

Combining and coalescing and coming to…

Billy's eyes fluttered and opened and he saw Cooper's head lying against his chest, against the amulet. The pure serenity of her exhausted naked body against his flesh, intertwined and united, tossed all doubts aside. Daykeepers could love, could make love, could accept it and desire it. The slurry of sweat on the plastic air mattress proved it physically, but it was the visions within the waterfall of Pacific dusk that confirmed such enigmatic ideals. Cascading slivers of water slowed to the beat of his heart, and his heart slowed to match this only moment that time would ever offer.

Alixel appeared in one of the crystal slices of suspended falling water, her face looking just as it did back in Port Aransas just before she'd departed within the arms of the hurricane. The orange streaks along each temple flowed down in loops behind the ears, twisted within night-black hair, her skin dark and ancient, her eyes soothing and wise.

You have to do it for all of us, she said. *The future is in your hands.*

Her beauty sparkled atop the prism of reflected sunset and if Cooper had not been cuddled against his chest, he would have stood and walked right through the waterfall, believing as he fell from the butterfly rocks that Alixel truly was there, really was talking, and had actually returned.

The slice of suspended water moved incredibly slow. Above Alixel, her brother appeared within a second, suspended water crystal moment. And because Billy had gotten to know Lax a lot more than Alixel, had been there when the immortal giant had taken his last breath, his appearance made Billy cry.

Remember what I told you about immortality? Lax said. *You too will serve like us, to protect from man what he should not know. But first you must fulfill your own fate…and…*

Billy started to rise because the sound of falling, crashing water got louder, because it seemed as though the frozen moment of time was about to end. "Yes," he said to the image and Cooper stirred beneath him.

Tell Aaron I do love him so, Lax finished, his broad, mighty chin pressing against the sparkling water, his lips pleading.

And just before time resumed as humans understood it, the Daykeepers, both Alixel and Lax, disappeared from their suspended watery vessels. In their place…

The cave suddenly became very dark though the sun remained above the horizon. In his dreamlike trance, Billy saw that the candles still flickered and the gas lamp still glowed, but the room somehow now swallowed whatever light they emitted. In the waterfall, the faces of his friends dissolved except for the eyes: two sets of them, red as blood with silver sparkles twisting chaotically within the pupils.

Help me, help me, the four eyeballs said. *Love, love, love, love, love—why don't you get a real fucking job?*

They were the eyes of the cubits. They were the eyes of Richard Manson. They grew larger, separating themselves from the flow of water and moved into the cave, suffocating its intimacy, suffocating Billy, the lunatic silver sparkles dancing frantically within bloody, spongy sockets.

*You are not a Daykeepe*r, the four eyes said. *They lied to you. You are just like us. You are just like me. You are a cubit.*

"NO!" Billy screamed.

The cave grew sunset bright again and he and Cooper rose together. The eyes were gone as was the moment.

"Billy?" Cooper moaned. "What?" She wrapped her body within his shirt, looked at his horrified expression, and turned toward the waterfall. He grabbed her hand and brought it to his lips, kissed the fingertips. He couldn't stop shaking. "Your hand…" She pointed. In his palm, the scar of the dagger star glowed soft red. Cooper stroked it with her fingers. "What happened?"

"I saw them. I saw Alixel. I saw Lax. I saw…" Billy looked at the scar and immediately grabbed for the dagger which he'd taken off to make love to Cooper.

"It's right here," Cooper said, reaching behind the Igloo cooler. "You gave it to me just before we…" Cooper blinked. "You don't remember?"

"I do remember…everything important…believe me. But there's something wrong." She handed him the sheathed dagger and he pulled it free, turned it in his hand, matched the star scar in his palm with the one in the dagger's haft, felt them lock together, watched as the spaces between his fingers emitted soft red rays of light that disappeared a second later. Both of them looked at the waterfall, at the sliver of space that allowed entrance into the cave; a rock skittered down the face of the ravine just beyond it.

Billy pulled his shorts on, strapped the sheath in place, and stood while Cooper dressed. He didn't take his eyes off the entrance. The dagger's warmth told him what must be outside. He placed a finger to his lips to silence anything Cooper might say then stepped cautiously to the cave opening, the dagger at his side. When he craned his head forward to look beyond the edge of falling water, he saw no one—at first. The sun had just touched the ocean and shadows dominated the landscape.

"Amigo!" a voice yelled and echoed from the jungle path at the point where the guide had left them about thirty yards away. "Are you good?" The bushes shook and the guide appeared from among the foliage. "I hear screaming and thought you fell."

Water mist massed on Billy's forehead and he blinked some of it away from his eyes. He didn't answer the guide but he did look down and had to grab the rock wall to prevent vertigo from taking him. A hundred feet below, the waterfall crashed into a wide stream that, a mile away, emptied into the Rio Nexpa. Broken rocks and trees were everywhere and lying among them at the stream's perimeter was a body. Billy blinked, shook his head, squinted. It was twisted like a pretzel, the legs and arms, shattered, the torso…

It was wearing a leather jacket.

That the body at the bottom of the ravine was that of the leader of the Jackass Gang was easier to believe than Billy's explanation that the leader was a cubit and that it had lost its footing while attempting to assault Billy and Cooper as they'd made love. Even though the leather clad body was busted all to hell, as a cubit, it would have reshaped itself somehow, it would have risen with mangled bone and flesh, it would have limped or crawled or rolled, but it would have regenerated, just like Albert Stine had, just like Stephanie Drake had, just like they all did without a Creation Dagger's blade jammed into the back of their skulls. But the body never moved. During their entire trek back down the ravine, each time Billy or Cooper or the guide looked in that direction, the clump of flesh and bone remained, moving only because the might of the water slammed against it. By the time they'd gotten back to the cottage, complete darkness consumed everything except for the oil-lit lamps glowing inside the rooms. The guide said that he would call the authorities and left them.

"If you're right," Cooper said, "then they do know where we are. Which means…"

"They're already here," Billy looked over his shoulder then entered the cottage. "Which means anyone could be one." Cooper followed him inside and he closed the door. "We'll wait here until Buck or one of his men arrives and go from there. In the meantime, do we have any of that fruit left? We didn't even get a chance to eat whatever Debbie put in the basket."

"One orange," she said. "But I picked up something else at the market. We could try that." Billy nodded and sat on the bed and Cooper joined him. She reached into her shopping bag.

"Cooper," Billy said. "I'm sorry. I'm sorry that, you know, it didn't work out the way a first time should."

Cooper pulled out a wad of crumpled newspaper and unraveled one of the fuzzy green fruits. She laid it on the bed and grabbed Billy's hand, the one with the star scar. "Are you kidding? You are wonderful. You are…it was… the best thing I could have ever imagined. I only wish your troubled mind could have enjoyed it."

Billy embraced her and stroked one of her ears. "It wasn't like that. I did enjoy it. It was spectacular. You stopped time."

Cooper shifted forward and looked him hard in the face. "I stopped it? Only Daykeepers can do that."

Billy inched closer, his lips a breath away. "Only love can do that."

The green ball of fruit rolled off the bed as Billy and Cooper made love again. Billy remembered every single touch this time because there were no visions of past friends or fiends interrupting the quiet solace within the cottage. There were, however, red eyes with chaotic silver specks, but Billy nor Cooper saw them. Above the bed and through the window, Rio stared in from the jungle outside, a curious twist of angst chiseled on her face as Richard Manson used his cubit to gawk at the sweaty sex of humanity.

Billy had said it first and that was fine with Cooper because if he hadn't, "love" may never have come out of her mouth. And she did love him. For every minute that passed as he lay there dozing with a sheen of sweat across his body, that absolute truth was inarguable. Whatever walls of denial that had been built, Billy had knocked over in the cave and had completely shattered in the cottage.

She laid beside him, tracing the concavity between his breasts with one finger, the Djed amulet cocked to one side, the dagger sheathed but, again, unstrapped and on the floor next to the fuzzy green fruit that had rolled off the bed. When she grabbed the amulet, Billy stirred but didn't wake. She rolled it in the palm of her hand and turned her arm over. The tattoo on her wrist that Chris Cower had convinced her to get so long ago almost looked exactly like it, except, of course, for the rattlesnake fang marks. But that had been another world in another time. Nothing would ever be the same again, she thought. She was now Cooper Reyes, a woman capable of loving a man and the man she loved was invincible. The amulet provided such power. The amulet when worn could…

A rush of temptation sped through her. She remembered how Cower had coaxed her into helping him steal the Cubit. She remembered how that lie had made her imagine being a God, of possessing such power just by having something so precious as the Djed amulet. What if she did try it on, just for a moment? Temptation.

But the lure of the past was immediately erased as she turned the amulet and on the back side of it saw a reflection of the window above and behind her. Red eyes. She jerked up and turned quickly around, peered at the black square of glass and wondered. Had she really seen them or was it her mind's warning against the temptation she'd just experienced? The jungle outside moved. The brush and the branches were mostly shadow, and they scraped the window glass.

Cooper dressed and opened the cottage door as Billy woke and propped himself up on one elbow. "Rest," she said. "I need to use the bathroom. Be back in a minute." Billy brushed his hand against the amulet and waved.

Outside, Cooper immediately walked to the back of the building, peered cautiously into the shadowy vacancy that separated the jungle from the window. There were no eyes but she did see two orbs of light that weren't red. The lamps inside cast yellow-orange, eyeball-looking reflections against the glass panes and she wondered if that is exactly what she'd seen.

She thought about the mangled body of the leather-clad gang leader, looked to her right in the direction where the body had fallen. If it had been a cubit, it probably would have attacked them already. If it had been a cubit, it wouldn't have cared to take time snooping behind windows.

Jerry's SUV was parked in her line of sight and she walked to it, thinking that, if she was wrong, what better place to hide than inside a vehicle they would soon be driving home. Circling the SUV, she peered into all of its tinted windows but there were no red eyes; there were no hidden cubits. And she tripped. At her feet was a broken tree branch that had been driven into the left front tire of the SUV, flattening it. The stick's upward angle into the rubber suggested that they'd driven over it on the way to the cottages. She reached down and tried, unsuccessfully, to pull it out.

Since they would be going nowhere with a flat tire, Cooper decided to change it. She opened the driver's door, hit the rear hatch button and went to the back of the SUV. She lifted the hatch and prodded the dark compartment with blind hands, found the floorboard latch, and pulled it up. But the spare tire was gone. In its place, all crumpled and crushed like a wad of garbage was one of Buck's deputies. She stumbled backward and fell flat on her ass, and heard the raspy breathing before she saw the cubit emerge from the jungle tree line behind her.

Ehhh-hee-ehhh-hee.

She rolled onto hands and knees.

Ehhh-hee-hee-hee.

The Jackass Gang leader stood askew, trying to balance on its horribly fractured accordion-legs. Most of its leather jacket remained intact but the damage to the body underneath leaked out in coagulated blood spots from the collar and from between the zippered front. A piece of collar bone stuck straight up and acted almost like a tripod against the cubit's lolling, mangled, head. It slid-walked one step closer. "Pooper," it said. "I want you Pooper."

Cooper stood and backpedaled from the approaching monster, tripped against the SUV's open hatch, and slung her hands backward for support; both landed on the squishy flesh of the ripe dead deputy.

"You like sex," the cubit said and wobbled forward "Yes. I like sex. We like sex, Pooper."

Cooper's hands roamed across flesh, found holes she didn't want to think about, and landed on the hard steel of a crowbar.

"Yes…unngghhhhh." The cubit's one functioning hand unzipped its wet and muddy pants but it couldn't lower them past the hips which also had bone fragments sticking through the flesh.

Cooper bolted forward, the flat, sharp end of the crowbar leading her assault, and she shoved it into the open mouth crevice of the cubit. She yanked it free, drew the crowbar up, and swung it against the head with all of her strength. The crack of metal on bone sent the cubit to the ground where it writhed and kicked and screamed grotesque gurgles.

Behind her, glass shattered inside the cottage and she saw the room's illumination dim through the cottage's back window. She ran. When she came to the front of the building, the door was wide open and inside was Rio. She had Billy's amulet in one hand and a fistful of Billy's long hair in the other. Behind her, on the floor, was the sheathed Creation Dagger and the star in its haft blazed red. Rio followed Cooper's gaze.

"Go ahead." Rio's lips moved but her voice was Manson's. "If you love him you'll do it." Rio's once blue eyes were now those of a possessed cubit. The red orbs matched the color of the dagger's aura. She lifted the arm that clutched Billy's hair and both of Billy's hands came up in an attempt to loosen the grip. "Is this what fucking does to a Daykeeper? He didn't even hear me coming though I'm sure he heard you coming."

Cooper stepped inside and gauged how quickly she could dive for the dagger.

"This is it. Your last chance. He's not invincible without the amulet." Rio waved it teasingly and laughed, which was quite creepy since it was Manson's harsh baritone that blew through Rio's lips.

Cooper stepped forward.

"Ah-ah-ah," Rio yanked on Billy's hair and Billy screamed. This shifted Rio's attention for the fraction of a second Cooper used to dive for the dagger.

Three things happened almost simultaneously. Rio's foot slammed down on the dagger's sheath just before Cooper could reach it, Billy flung one arm out and snatched the amulet away from the cubit's grasp, and Ron Buck and two of his deputies came through the door with weapons drawn.

"Shoot!" Billy yelled. "Shoot her now."

The Rio cubit kicked Cooper in the side of the head and pulled Billy closer. It stuck a pink tongue out and licked the entire side of Billy's face.

"Do it!" Cooper screamed. "Ron…please."

One of the deputies unloaded his pistol and the second deputy followed the lead. "Stop," Buck yelled. "You'll hit them both!" But it was too late. Both Billy and the Rio cubit flailed backward against the dresser, shattering the oil lamp on top. The surface of the dresser ignited and the fire snatched a hold of the cubit's blonde hair. Flames raced up the long locks and the cubit released Billy who slumped to the floor with bullet holes in his naked chest. With hair afire, the Rio cubit lunged at Buck who tried to stop it with his own blast of ammunition. Bullets knocked the cubit sideways and it fell against one of the deputies, igniting the man's uniform.

Rio's beauty became black and bubbly from the neck up but this didn't stop it from tearing off one of the flaming deputies arms at the elbow and using it to break the other deputy's face. Buck backpedaled away from what was too unreal for him to accept. He'd never seen a cubit before and, like most who experienced first encounters with cubits, his body froze in shock.

The fire raging atop the Rio cubit's head spread down its body and this made the cubit change its course of action. Instead of killing both deputies, it ran off, its hands beating at the raging flames, its direction toward the waterfall and stream.

Cooper immediately jumped up and tackled the fire-engulfed deputy, rolled with him on the ground outside the cottage until the flames were extinguished, then sat there, her breaths heaving.

Buck's shock left him the moment the cubit ran off and he quickly ran to his burnt deputy and used his belt to make a tourniquet for what remained of the man's arm.

"Billy?" Cooper said. "Billy?" She crawled up and scuttled forward, back through the cottage door to where Billy's body lay slumped against one wall. Three bullets had found his chest and one had entered his mid-section. The Djed amulet lay on the floor an inch from his right hand of outstretched fingers.

Cooper snatched the amulet and tossed the necklace around Billy's head, waited for the miracle to happen, waited for the bullets to magically rise from his chest, waited in vain. He'd stopped breathing. There was no pulse.

From behind her, the Creation Dagger now pulsed a blinding red light, and hummed…soothingly, invitingly. It seemed to talk to Cooper and Cooper swore she heard it say, "Save him." She remembered (and perhaps the amulet now initiated the memory) Billy using the blade of the dagger to save Hondo. She remembered how he'd shoved the blade into the dying man's belly.

Cooper unsheathed the dagger and brought the blade up against one of the red holes next to Billy's left nipple then stuck it in. Energy buzzed the length of her arm and she could actually feel the bullet as the blade grabbed it. The extraction was accompanied by a sharp sucking sound and after the first bullet was out, she worked on the other three. Her efforts did not restart his heart so she began CPR just as Buck screamed, "Look out!"

The Jackass Gang leader cubit stumbled through the door, the tire iron in one crooked hand, its mouth agape from where Cooper had skewered it earlier. Beyond the lurching monster, Cooper saw Buck lying motionless on his back next to both of his deputies. The cubit swung the tire iron haphazardly and whacked a big chunk out of the four-drawer dresser. Cooper kicked one of its crooked legs and the cubit fell right on top of her. Its mangled arms vised around Cooper's body and the cubit starting thrusting its hips against her groin. She tried to push off but the cubit's overwhelming strength squeezed her closer as if it was trying to penetrate her with its flaccid, dead penis.

And then, all at once, the leather-clad cubit's strength extinguished. The arms went limp and Cooper pushed. As it fell to the side, Billy was there, the dagger in his right hand, the blade pointing toward the damage it had just made in the back of the cubit's head. The cubit trembled on the cottage floor and became ashes and bone within seconds.

Buck slowly rolled onto his knees; his forehead was bleeding. He surveyed his suffering deputies and said, "What in God's name were they?"

"Not in God's name," Billy said. "And you don't want to know."

Buck stood and touched the sticky wetness drooling down one side of his face. "But I do," he said. "I do because they are all over the place. They fired the restaurant."

"Cubits did?" Cooper asked. "How many?"

"Half the town," Buck said. "What's a cubit?"

Cooper helped Billy and Buck get his men into the back of the cruiser then she sat in the front seat between them as Buck sped along the Pacific front road from Caleta toward Nexpa. Halfway there, Cooper saw the fire before Billy exclaimed, "The Hunters!"

Buck drove up to the blazing homestead to find Jerry lying in the driveway face-first. Buck drew his gun and exited the car, and Billy and Cooper followed him. Jerry was dead. A shotgun blast had blown a giant hole in his back.

"Debbie!" Cooper screamed. "Debbie!" But the only sound was that of the Hunters' home as it collapsed inward, the flames thrusting outward. The front of the blazing building tottered for a moment then tumbled toward them. Buck grabbed Billy and Billy grabbed Cooper and all three of them stumbled backward as the flaming wall dropped onto Jerry's body.

Cooper started crying and Billy had to force her back into the cruiser. "She's not in there," he said to her. "She can't be."

"We'll find her," Buck offered. "Then we're getting the hell out of here. If what you said about these cubit things is true, there's no future for any of us here."

When they arrived in Nexpa, several buildings were on fire, including Hunters Restaurant. Buck stopped the car and they all got out except for the deputy with the missing piece of arm. Buck leaned in to find that he was still breathing but unconscious. He offered Billy the deputy's gun. "Gather your belongings. I'm going to find Debbie," he said. "Get back to the car as soon as you can." Billy waved the gun away but Cooper grabbed it anyway. "If we're not back in twenty minutes, don't wait. You get my deputy back to Caleta."

Buck and his second deputy headed toward the flaming remains of Hunters Restaurant while Cooper followed Billy back to his bungalow. People she didn't know ran in all directions. Many more that she did know walked casually among the chaos as if Nexpa Burning was some holiday event they'd all come out to watch. The Hunter's waiter, Tad, was one of them. He stood in a tree line twenty yards away and as she approached, Cooper tightened her grip on the deputy's gun.

"Tad," she said to him.

"Beautiful," Tad said, staring straight ahead, his eyes red but, Cooper thought, not like a cubit's; they were bloodshot and glassy as if he'd been smoking dope. "I feel beautiful." He smiled at Cooper but when he turned to look at Billy, his expression changed. "You!" he growled. "It's all because of you. No more Nexpa because of you." And then he attacked. Billy pushed Cooper to the side as Tad jumped on top of him. "You, you, you…" They rolled twice before Cooper made the decision to fire. Bullets wouldn't kill a cubit but they could provide enough force to damage one long enough for Billy to unsheathe his dagger. She shot Tad directly in the center of his spine and Tad lurched forward, grabbed at the hole behind him, shuddered for two seconds then fell off of Billy.

"He's dead," Billy said. "He's not a cubit, but something's got control of him."

Cooper gasped and dropped the gun. "He was acting like…I thought…"

"Come on," Billy said. "We don't have time."

Billy raced up the steps to his bungalow with Cooper close behind. He threw open the door and immediately headed for the bathroom.

"This what you're looking for?" Duncan Swallow stepped into the bathroom doorway. Billy's research notebook and his journal facsimile of the Book of the Djed were both in his left hand. His eyes boiled red and the silver sparkles raced. "You're a shitty artist," Richard Manson's voice said to Billy. "Where's the real thing?"

"Cram it, Manson," Billy said to Swallow and pulled out his dagger.

"You'll need more than one of those to stop me," Manson's voice said. "And time's on my side. Perhaps your little slut, there, can help you find them."

"What?" Billy asked, puzzled.

"You bring me the Book of the Djed and you can have all the little daggers your heart desires."

"Like the one you gave Kerskker?" Cooper said.

Swallow managed a look of surprise. "Sharp cookie slut," Manson said. "But that's only the beginning. The world will know in just a few days. The world will know that it's all going to end. And both of you are going to help that happen." Swallow swiped one hand through its black, matted hair then threw Billy's books at him and charged.

Billy took him down much too easily, Cooper thought. He simply stepped aside, arched the dagger, and planted it without resistance from the cubit. Swallow howled a maniacal laughter that changed in volume and pitch as the face molted. Its red eyes burst from the sockets and the face morphed into a slurry that filled the mouth and gagged the laughter until all of its flesh turned to ash. Billy grabbed his books, ran to the bathroom and took his boardies from the shower rod, then, together, he and Cooper ran.

Back on the beach, Billy gave Cooper the books. "You hold onto these. You might need them."

"What? Don't you mean we will need them?"

"No. I mean *you* will need them. The time has come. The time we were both dreading. Stay here. I'll be right back."

"But we're getting out of here together, right?"

"Stay here. There's something I need from the shop."

Cooper stood between dirt wheel ruts as she watched Billy run to his surf shop fifty yards away. He disappeared for a moment and when he reappeared, he stopped and stood and looked at her. Instead of running back, he ran away in a straight line toward the shadowy froth of black ocean. Something was out there but Cooper couldn't quite tell what. Black shapes floated atop the water's surface, bobbing in unison with the waves.

"BILLY!" she screamed. "BILLY, NO!"

Suddenly, the thing that had been Rio came running at her from the jungle shadows to her right. Her blackened face had Manson's blood-red eyes. "Help me, help me," Manson taunted. "You fucking whore."

Because she'd dropped the deputy's gun during the encounter with Tad, she had no defense and she screamed even louder, "BILLY! HELP ME!"

Sheriff Buck rammed the burnt cubit with the police cruiser, sending it twenty feet through the air where it planted head first into the sand. He stopped the car and got out, then shoved Cooper inside. The burnt bald Rio popped its head up and ran at Buck, hopping on the one good leg that remained. It tried to talk but could only spit sand. Cooper locked the cruiser's doors and cowered against the seat as Buck put three bullets into the hopping leg of the cubit which took it down immediately.

From all directions, dozens of people or cubits or whatever the hell they were, attacked. Cooper gripped the steering wheel as Buck ran to the trunk of the car, grabbed a shotgun and screamed, "Get the hell outta here," while he reloaded. He emptied one shotgun blast into a woman to whom Cooper had served lunch for the last three years, blowing her almost in two. "Now!" he demanded.

When Cooper finally hit the accelerator, Debbie Hunter was behind the car and she attacked Buck. The trunk, still open, flapped like a metal mouth chewing air. In random intervals it blocked Cooper's vision through the rear view mirror.

Debbie Hunter was on top of Buck…

Buck was on top of her…

Buck shot her with his handgun…

The Rio torso grabbed his legs…

Buck went down…

Cooper started crying because she was too afraid to turn back. She did stop the car, though. Once she was out of immediate danger, she rolled down the window, wiped her face with the back of both hands, and leaned out to look for Billy.

She saw him in the ocean about a hundred yards out. She knew it was Billy because the amulet was glowing a soft green aura that encircled him, his dark outline set in the middle of the light.

She knew that it was him because he was swimming with dolphins.

0-TIME: PREDICATE
REUNION

John and Sebastian left the island for good on December 22 because of three specific events.

The first was Hurricane Ida. Less than a year after Billy and Cooper left, Ida belted the island with so much force that the hut-home (which they'd built into quite a nice living space) had blown out to sea. The tidewaters had gotten so high that even Sebastian's underground shelter had been water-ravaged. They'd had to wait out the storm inside a rocky crevice located on a hill near the island's highest point where Sebastian had stored a lot of dry goods over the past twenty years. Cleanup had been very depressing. The irrigation system and hybrid garden that they'd been so proud of—completely devastated. All of the handcrafted furniture and eating accessories—gone. They would not survive another year on the island without restocking vegetables seeds, collecting more construction materials, and replenishing fresh water. So, they'd had to travel to the mainland on several occasions after Ida's wrath. John's contact in Merida, a former sergeant named Roger Braun whom he'd served with in the Marine Corps back in the early 90s, had maintained John's dive shop and his low profile. Even in 2011, John and Sebastian were still regarded as part of the "Tulum Terroristas" who'd desecrated the sacred Mayan ruins with bullets and had murdered several of its guards. A stray wanted poster could still be found attached to some obscure city wall, their crudely drawn faces enough to possibly spark attention.

The second event that caused them to abandon the island had to do with an announcement that John had read in Merida's city paper just a week before they left. Richard Manson, the billionaire owner of much of the city's real estate, had discovered that the Mayan prediction surrounding the December 21, 2012 end date was actually true and he wanted to prepare the world a full year in advance. A press conference was to be held at the Phoenix Tower plaza on Christmas Eve. Rumors were that Manson had found proof that the sun would eject a coronal mass that would decimate much of the planet's resources and send mankind back a few centuries in evolution.

The third event, and the one that really sealed the decision, was the drawing of the fifth symbol at the bottom of the center page in the Book of the Djed. Of the many Mayan glyphs that John and Sebastian had come across over the years of living in the Yucatán, one was particularly universal: circles drawn as a spiral, designating the life-sustaining force of the sun that all cultures worshipped. Back on the island, the day after John had read about Manson's impending announcement, he'd been restocking the dry goods inside the crevice on the hill and the Book had beckoned him. He'd stashed it at the bottom of a cardboard box full of several bags of Uncle Ben's instant rice, and the Book had drawn his attention not because he'd heard or seen or smelled anything unusual but because of something more akin to ESP. When he'd plucked it from the box and had opened it, the symbol had drawn itself right before his eyes, the fine pencil-like strokes scratching oblong circles, spiraling one inside the other. He'd placed his finger over the image as it was being written and had felt the heavenly hand pressing down on his flesh, pressing down on the paper. It had been a wonderfully creepy perception, his finger experiencing something fingers never felt. But the sun symbol had not been what freaked him out to the point of slamming the Book shut and gasping like a little girl. It had been when the symbols, all five of them, either changed colors or moved into new positions on the page: the phoenix bird at the top "flew" backward an inch to the right; the five sixes and nines morphed together and created a circle of five numerals (sixes if you looked at them one way and nines if you looked at them the other) that repositioned itself, still below the firebird, a few inches to the left. Below the circle of six-nines, the Djed stayed in the same position on the page but green strokes suddenly appeared within its pencil gray outline. The chaos star that Billy had said was stamped on the wonder drug shifted down just a bit and its eight-points either caught some reflection from the sun's rays poking into the crevice or they somehow self-illuminated. When John had tried to turn the page to see if the illumination was coming from the back side of the page, the Book had slammed shut, on its own, and John had not been able to open it again.

Sebastian hadn't been particularly happy about leaving his island. He'd argued that if the world was going to end, the safest place to be was right where they were. Supplies were limited but, he'd said, at least there were no freaked-out, fundamentalist idiots to contend with. The thought of being left alone, however, was not a comforting alternative and so he'd reluctantly packed up what his Sea Ray could carry and had moved with John to Merida, back to the scuba shop that John had operated before escorting Billy and Cooper to Chichen Itza three years before.

"Manson's announcement is scheduled for five o'clock," Roger reminded John as they both helped Sebastian with his scuba tank. "You really think going over there is necessary? We could watch it on TV and avoid what is sure to be a madhouse of a crowd. Besides, why take a chance at all? You know there's still plenty of people looking for you two. I yanked down another wanted poster from inside the tackle shop just yesterday." Roger was half the size of John but very stocky, agile and cunning. He'd grown up in Boston and as a dedicated Red Sox fan, his ball cap was always on his head, except, of course, when he was diving. He now removed the cap and a folded piece of paper fell from the top of his head and into one hand. "Here."

John took the paper and Sebastian craned his head forward while unzipping his wetsuit. "This doesn't look anything like me," John said, staring at the wanted poster. "Looks like a little kid drew this. Sebastian, on other hand, hasn't changed a lick since Tulum."

"Are you crazy?" Sebastian said. "I looked a lot older back then. And you. You don't need much skill to draw a big round head and color it in with a black pencil." The poster noted an offer of 100,000 pesos for information leading to the capture of the Tulum Terroristas. "I wonder why Billy and Cooper aren't on it?"

"People around here knew you guys," Roger explained. "Apparently, no one got a good look at the other two."

John gave Roger the poster paper. "I'm thinking no one is going to be paying any attention to anything other than Richard Manson and his crazy talk," John said. "Besides, I've got this feeling that we need to be there." He'd never said anything to Roger about Manson's connection to cubits or daggers or prophecies, and even though the two Marines had seen some pretty heinous action in Gulf War I, and had saved each other's asses on numerous occasions, John thought Roger would have never helped them had he said anything about walking dead people or the man who seemed to control them.

"Feeling?" Roger crumpled the poster and threw it on the floor of the dive shop. "There was a time that when you got 'feelings,' people died."

"Day's still young. So you going with us or no?

"No. I can't stand crowds and I really can't stand Richard Manson. He's such a pompous ass. I don't see a need to add my presence to his own self love."

"You mind if we take the truck?"

Roger cocked his Red Sox cap sideways. "Don't fuck it up. You haven't driven anything on four wheels for years."

"Fuck it up? You're kidding." John pointed at Roger's beat up F-150 parked outside the shop's storefront window. "I'd offer to give it a wash but I'm afraid I'd blow all the rust away and there'd be nothing left to hold it together."

Roger tossed him the keys. "Whatever, Gordon. You could stop at Pepe's on the way back and get me dozen of those little fuckin' tacos. I'm starved."

"Hot or superfire?"

"Half and half."

John turned to Sebastian. "You ready to do this?"

Sebastian looked extremely complacent. "I don't think so, but do I have a choice?"

The media had made it an event before the event ever took place. It wasn't every day that the richest man in the world was about to tell the world that the world was going to end. Such sensationalistic drivel, whether true or not, wasn't good for business. People didn't invest in companies owned by nut jobs. But this was Richard Manson and when Richard Manson spoke, oil markets shifted, commodity stock prices moved, and people won or lost fortunes in an instant.

The Spanish tabloids, always a good source for the sensational, announced that the Christian apocalypse was finally upon the planet. Most articles went well beyond Manson's tease of impending sun flares and coronal mass ejections to include catastrophic volcanic eruptions, coastline decimating tsunamis, and a planet-wide rain of fire that would last five years.

Of course, the Mayan end date prediction served to occupy plenty of space in the papers and time on the air. Prognosticators and scientists and evangelical namesakes came out of the woodwork to posit their own evidence that could never be substantiated. No one could prove anything because no one could predict nature, particularly a year in advance of catastrophe.

But this was Richard Manson. He'd saved the lives of countless people across the globe by giving away his now infamous BethStar wonder drug. How could someone who was so altruistic purposely scare the crap out of all humanity unless he knew something that no one else did (which seemed plausible for the richest man in the world)? Not only might Manson know something catastrophic was going to happen, he might also know of a way to stop the End of Days prophecy.

Dozens of satellite trucks encircled the Phoenix Tower plaza. The representation was worldwide. Even the most popular news bloggers, video novices, and wannabe info stars had amassed in numbers. Every inch of the plaza was occupied by the curious, the critic, or the lurid.

John had to park the truck several blocks away and, by coincidence, found space in the same garage where Billy had parked Stephanie Drake's Cavalier back when they'd all first met. He and Sebastian pushed through a mass of people meandering on the sidewalk and when John passed the History Museum of Merida, he stopped and turned toward it as a memory rush took him back inside to the moment before he'd saved Cooper's life for the first time. He remembered looking into the Manuel cubit's eyes and the silver swirls that danced within them, not knowing then that Richard Manson was looking at him through one of his dead surrogates. If the world only knew who this man really was. If they only believed that the devil did exist.

"John? John Brown Gordon!"

John had to shake his head and blink several times to make sure the face was really Cooper's. She stood in the museum's doorway as if she'd been waiting for him.

"I knew it. I just knew it," she said, her smile widening, her open arms coming forward, invitingly. She ran down the short flight of steps and tripped into his thick arms. John gently grabbed the back of her head, stroked her short hair, pulled her back and kissed her forehead. His hands came around and cupped her cheeks and her entire face almost disappeared into his loving grasp. Sebastian cleared his throat and John released her so that she could hug him as well.

"What brings you here?" Sebastian asked her.

"Same thing that brings you two."

"John's got more insight to that answer than I do. I'm just along for the ride."

"Manson," John said. "And the Book." He looked around the mass of people. "Billy?"

Cooper shook her head.

"You mean he…?"

"No. He's alive." Cooper quickly told them of the last moment she saw Billy.

"Gone swimming with dolphins again," John said and smiled. "Well, I guess it's just the three of us."

Cooper grabbed each of their hands and started along the packed sidewalk. "For now," she said, "but not for long. I'm heading back home to Puerto Rico. A Creation Dagger has shown up there in the possession of my ex-husband."

John stopped in the middle of the walk, forcing the crowd to move around him. The screech of an intercom system resounded from the plaza square and someone said, "Testing. One, two, three. Testing."

Cooper continued, "I'll fill you in later but right now… Come on."

The streets surrounding the plaza were decorated for the holidays and as the sun continued its descent, multicolored lights flickered on around light poles, bench seats, palm trees and a giant pine tree that Manson had flown in from Vermont. The hundred-and-thirty-foot tree that eclipsed the first thirteen floors of the Phoenix Tower behind it had been hyped by Manson as being larger than the one at Rockefeller Center or Washington D.C. Supposedly, he'd paid upwards of twenty thousand dollars to acquire it, ship it and decorate it.

They couldn't get anywhere near the stage where Manson appeared. He was bookended by two bodyguards wearing dark sunglasses and dressed in three-piece suits though John knew the man-beast needed no such protection. He guessed that they were cubits and they were present more for media effect than anything else.

"The one on the right," Cooper said. "He looks like the same one that attacked us in Hondo." Both John and Sebastian looked at her as if she was crazy. "Another long story."

No one introduced Manson. He stepped right up to the podium microphone. A thousand shutter clicks snapped like digital crickets.

John had totally expected Manson to be wearing a three-piece black suit with red tie, his hair slicked back, every flaw in his face touched up by otherworldly cosmetics just like the devil in disguise was supposed to look—just like Al Pacino. But Richard Manson was much too casual for the likes of Al Pacino. He had an I'm-a-rad-dude-brand, to maintain. Men that made friends with Apple and sponsored the X-Games would not be caught dead in a suit, not in public, at least.

Manson looked more like he was dressed for a casual stroll on a Yucatán beach. His light colored button-up shirt and slacks were tailored to fit loosely, the pant cuffs lying across the leather straps of open-toed sandals. His hair was dark, but it was long and feathery with streaks of white at the temples.

When the wind blew, long bangs dropped across his forehead and he jerked his head backward to clear them from his eyes before he spoke.

"Feliz navidad," he said, lifting his arms high and waving with both hands. "First, let me wish all of you a very merry Christmas. Such an appropriate moment: the celebration of our savior, Jesus Christ."

John wasn't the most religious man in the world but even he had to cringe when Manson said Christ's name. Cooper scowled and Sebastian reacted by flipping Manson off which was ineffective at his distance to the stage. There was, however, a tall man with bleached hair standing in the crowd a few feet from the stage that also shot the finger, and the bodyguard, whom Cooper had pointed out, took one step closer in his direction.

Manson continued, "It's about saving that I brought you all here tonight."

"When's the world gonna end?" someone yelled. This caused a massive amount of chatter. A few people screamed. When the loudspeakers offered a screech of feedback, most everyone hushed except for the tall man with the bleached hair.

"You suck! Scaring everyone like this! Get out of here and go back to killing the poor with your money!" The bodyguard moved to the edge of the stage directly in front of the enraged man.

"Excuse me, sir," Manson said, his voice remaining mostly temperate though John picked up on the slight nuance of irritation. "I save the poor." He pointed at the camera crews that were assembled on the opposite side of the stage. "Haven't I?" he said to them. "How many tens of thousands? And now I'm trying to save all of you."

"Kiss my ass!" the bleached hair man said. "You're a big fucking liar!"

The bodyguard jumped off the stage, immediately grabbed the man, and forcefully escorted him toward the right side of the stage.

"Is this the way you…" the man started to yell. John wasn't sure if the bodyguard punched him or grabbed his mouth, but the man immediately shut up and disappeared from the crowd.

"There will be no toleration for swearing on national television, sir, especially on Christmas Eve," Manson said. "Now, if you will please bear with me. It isn't easy being the messenger of bad news, especially on a night like this." He cleared his throat. "To put it plainly, our world is coming to an end…"

John couldn't believe how many people screamed at that moment, most of them standing along the perimeter of the plaza. Is that all it took to cause widespread panic, he thought: a big Christmas tree, a microphone and a few billion dollars?

"Please, please." Manson tried to calm everyone. "My announcement has to do with saving life, not death."

A CNN reporter yelled out, "What proof do you have that a massive solar flare could destroy the earth?"

"Coronal mass ejection," Manson corrected him. "Much more powerful. And I didn't say 'destroy the earth.' In all of my press releases, I've been very careful so as not to create this kind of panic. I said the world is coming to an end as we know it."

Another reporter chimed in, "And what, exactly, does that mean?"

"It means that, just as was predicted in the Bible and by the ancient Maya and by just about every culture that has existed, in the end, Man will be tested." Manson grabbed the wireless mic from the podium and walked the stage, his tone changing to that of a preacher. "For anyone who speaks in a tongue does not speak to people but to God. Indeed, no one understands them; they utter mysteries by the Spirit. But the one who prophesies speaks to people for their strengthening, encouraging and comfort. Now, brothers and sisters, if I come to you and speak in tongues, what good will I be to you, unless I bring you some revelation or knowledge or prophecy or word of instruction?"

People started screaming again and the CNN reporter reminded Manson what he'd said about creating panic. He told Manson that he was, at that moment, receiving satellite reports of extreme unrest in several Mexican cities.

"We all knew this day would come sooner or later," Manson told the reporter, while speaking into the microphone. "I'm just trying to help save humanity by warning you a full year in advance. This will give everyone a chance to avoid the panic that will certainly destroy you. This will give everyone a chance to believe that I can, indeed, stop the sun from decimating power, transportation, communication and agriculture. I can stop the real horror that will ensue when towns run out of clean water, when city stores become barren because trucks can't run without fuel, when nations can no longer protect themselves with invisible weapons guided by invisible satellites using computer joysticks."

"And just how do you plan on doing that?!"

John turned toward Cooper, surprised that she had just yelled those words. Manson stopped pacing the stage and put a hand to his forehead as if looking across a vast sea and said, "With the Cubit, of course."

A Mexican woman with no teeth and ages of wrinkles stood beside Cooper. She now turned and stared straight at her. John couldn't believe that her eyes were that of a cubit, red and silver swirly. Up on the stage, Manson turned his back to the crowd and hunched forward. "But you know that already, don't you, Cooper?" the old woman said in Manson's voice. "You know all about the Cubit, little Johnny." The old woman shifted her gaze to Sebastian. "Aren't you fucking dead yet, old fuck?" The woman turned back around as did Manson. In his hand was a Creation Dagger and he lifted it above his head. Every reporter and paparazzi waved their hands and shouted and snapped photographs.

"Calm down everyone, please. I know you have a zillion questions and my staff has provided a brief for anyone interested, but what I can tell you, what I can guarantee you all, is that the Mayans were right. On December 21 of next year, the end date will arrive, the sun will blast the earth with too much energy, and all of us will kill each other for the tiny scraps of existence that will remain unless we find the rest of these and the Cubit. The mass of questions, screams and confusion made it impossible for Manson to control the information flow any longer. He walked off the back of the stage and, with a dozen men surrounding him, was escorted under the huge Christmas tree and into his glass tower. One bodyguard remained on stage and he told the reporters that each would receive further information upon request. He gave them an email address.

As the harried crowd began to disperse, the old woman turned back to face Cooper. The red eyes and silver swirls were, again, blazing. "What'd ya think of that?" Manson said.

"Coward," Cooper answered and grabbed the old woman's ratty shawl.

"You wouldn't harm an old lady, would you? If you want a piece of me, you know where I am." John, Cooper and Sebastian all looked up to the darkening outline of the fortieth floor.

Four men wearing sunglasses suddenly surrounded them. John placed his meaty arms around both of his friends and walked with them toward the towering Christmas tree. He looked up once more before entering Manson's skyscraper. The white light outline of the large cross at the top of the tree aligned directly in the center of the fortieth floor windows.

"Come in. Don't be bashful." Manson's voice came from deep within the incredibly dim and tremendously wide-open space of the fortieth floor. "Shit. What am I saying? Like any one of you would be that boring."

John stood protectively in front of Cooper; Sebastian stood beside him. As the elevator doors closed behind them, one of Manson's bodyguards appeared from the shadows. Manson still could not be seen.

"I'd like to introduce you to my acquaintance," Manson said. "You know him, Cooper, as Julio. Billy knows him as Chester, others simply call him Pitchfork Man. Now that's a name that sticks to a person, eh?"

Cooper squinted into the darkness beyond the bodyguard. "And assassin of billionaire competitors," she said.

"You know what they say," Manson's voice answered. "Those with the most planetary resources wins." He cackled, once.

"You could have chosen any day," Cooper said, "but you purposefully chose Christmas Eve, when people are the most happy and forgiving and loving."

"Yes," Manson replied. "It is the most effective." After a short pause he added, "Where's William?"

"Who?" Cooper asked.

"Billy Jo Presser, the Daykeeper, and that wonderful Book of his."

"Somewhere that you'll never find him."

"His mommy's house?"

"How would you…" Cooper began then immediately shut up.

"How do I know Billy went to see his mother? How in God's name could I know where he is when the amulet is supposed to hide his location from all that possess daggers?"

Cooper shrugged.

"I know because I'm a good guesser. Guessing has made me billions. And honesty has given you away more times than now. But that doesn't matter, really. I have better methods for taking care of Daykeepers, just like I did with his Injun friend and sister."

"They weren't Indian. They were Anasazi."

"Yeah, yeah. Whatever. Still the fact remains. I'll find him and I'll take the Book and he'll die, then all will be said and done. And the best part: you…all of you chummy buddies are going to help me."

John took a step toward the voice. "What in the hell are you up to, you freak?" he said.

"Back off, little man. You're lucky I've decided to keep you alive."

"You sure about that?" John took another step, this time directly toward the shadowy bodyguard who did not move beyond lifting his arm to readjust his sunglasses.

"Ah, ah, ah," Manson warned. "Men without daggers should be careful. Now, you wouldn't happen to have one of those daggers on you, would you?" A table lamp switched on and John saw Manson standing another ten yards away. "No. I didn't think so. And you know why that is? It's because I know where all of them are…well, except for Billy's. As I'm sure he's told you, those with daggers can see others with daggers." Manson presented the Creation of the Antichrist dagger grasped in his left hand. "Unfortunately, and this is the really funny, ironic part, I can't see Billy because he wears the amulet but, by wearing the amulet, he can't see where all the other daggers are. And he needs them, much more than I do." Cooper suddenly sprinted from behind John and halved the distance between herself and Manson before the bodyguard snatched her by the shirt and threw her backward. She landed sideways and slid across waxy wood floorboards all the way to John's feet. "Feisty as ever. You're going to need that."

John helped Cooper to her feet. "Why did you bring us here?" he said.

"Oh? I think you've got that all wrong. You came because…I don't know…perhaps your God told you to. Perhaps Billy told you to." Manson snapped on a second lamp and the area he stood in became clearer. To John, it looked like a large and lush living room. Two long, leather brown couches sat on either end of an oriental rug that was larger than the floor of his entire scuba shop. The two lamps sat atop cherry wood end tables next to the armrest of each couch. Manson stood in the middle of the carpet. Behind him was a lifeless, stone-faced fireplace. He pointed the dagger at Cooper. "I could use a girl like you, if you know what I mean. Cooper Reyes, cubited lover of a Daykeeper. Talk about infiltration. You could fuck him and kill him all at the same time."

"You can't kill a Daykeeper," Cooper snapped. "But a Daykeeper could kill the Devil."

"Is that what you think I am? Such abstraction. Do you see horns and a pitchfork and a red latex bodysuit with a long, pointed tail waving viciously across cauldrons of boiling fire? I appreciate the mythological comic strip entertainment value, but that's not me—though I admit, I've had a pitchfork or two in my days." Manson snapped his fingers and Chester, the bodyguard, walked over and stood beside the triumvirate. It was Sebastian's turn to take a forward stance and the bodyguard pushed him with such force, he backpedaled all the way to the giant rug, tripped on it, and fell. Manson stooped, snatched Sebastian's upper arm, and eased him onto one of the couches. "Old men should not be attempting young feats of courage but, you are Sebastian Bondager after all…the Tulum Terrorist, and the young child who could have stopped all of this before it ever happened." Manson laughed loudly and it echoed within whatever depth the room shadows hid.

"You son-of-a-bitch," Sebastian growled. "It was you. You killed my mother. You killed my village. You…dressed like a goddamned Nazi."

"Yes and no. I've taken many, many forms but, more so, I've been an influence, one that existed well before any Richard Manson was born. In fact, if it wasn't for me, Manson would have ended his life in shame a long time ago. You want to call me Devil and Lucifer and the Dark Man. Fine. Call me whatever your meager little mortal minds can fathom. Truth is…well it's simple, really. I'm the opposite of Good. I make Good a reality. Without me, where's the love in the world? Without me, where's the hope? If you just wouldn't have eaten that apple from the Tree of Knowledge." Manson shook his head.

"You mean if man had not created religion," Cooper said.

Manson waved Cooper and John forward, and Chester, though smaller in stature, moved behind John and pushed him. John turned to face the cubit, thought about a couple of death blows he'd learned long ago, then decided against fighting—at least for now. Chester grinned, his puffy cheeks rising up and under his dark sunglasses. John took Cooper's hand and led her to the rug. They stood within a foot of Manson.

"You sure you don't want to change sides?" Manson asked Cooper as he swiped one of his long, silver-streaked bangs from eyes that were darker red than any cubit's eyes and swirled with silver jagged spikes of lightning. "It's so much less painful to do so willingly. Getting eaten by something that looks exactly like you—oh, God—that tends to drive a person mad while feeling the pain of flesh ripped from the bones. I understand that burning flesh is the only thing that is more miserable." He reached out to touch Cooper's face and John quickly snatched his wrist. Manson raised the dagger from his side and planted it in the back of John's hand. The blade sank between the bones and continued all the way through both John's hand and Manson's wrist. When he pulled the dagger free, Cooper grabbed John's bleeding hand and applied pressure. Manson's wrist showed no more damage than a paper cut which stitched itself back together in less than a second. "You're bleeding all over my rug," Manson said. "Give me your hand."

"Kiss my ass," John replied.

"It doesn't have to be like this…painful…not yet. But if you grab me again…Now give me the fucking hand. That rug cost me four hundred Gs."

Cooper offered John's hand to Manson who swiped the dagger blade across the wound. Seconds later it stopped bleeding. A minute later, it healed completely. A tingly sensation remained that reminded John of the feeling he'd had right after Billy had removed the bullet from his chest after they'd been ambushed in the jungle on the way to save Cooper from the Zetas. He scratched it. "You weren't going to provide them with any answers," he said to Manson. "You wanted to see how panicked people would become with just the mention of the end of the world. You got off on it. You wanted to prove the power of lies."

Manson wiped the dagger's blade across his tan, baggy beachy slacks and a red streak remained. "But it's not a lie. The sun will do what the sun will do and nothing can stop it except for…"

"Wait. No," John said. "You already have it."

"Thanks to Daykeepers who can't follow their own destinies."

Manson turned his back to them, walked to one of the end tables, and grabbed what looked like a remote control. "Please. All of you sit. I insist." John led Cooper to the couch and both sat beside Sebastian.

"Unlike what you might think, I am not a cubit. You have to understand the fine details of the cubit collective to know that I am…well let's place it within a business context…I am the boss. I have executives who have groups that have designated tasks to perform which hopefully end up in profit."

"You profit from controlling people," John said as a statement of fact.

"Yes. Good ones and bad." He pointed the remote at the shadowy fireplace and it started to move. It sounded, to John, like an Egyptian crypt opening in any one of a hundred monster movies: squeaky wheels and the crushing scrape of rocks moving across rocks. The entire stone face of the fireplace slid to the left as one floor-to-ceiling piece and a red, vertical line appeared that brightened and broadened the wider the opening became. Behind the fireplace was the Cubit. It pulsed a gentle crimson as if it was asleep. It was hard to tell if the throne pedestal on which the Cubit sat was the real thing or a really great knock-off. It looked just like the one under the Caracol at Chichen Itza and inside the cenote at Tulum. "This is what's going to save the planet."

"That thing kills people," Cooper said.

"Yes."

"And then it takes their place as an evil incarnation."

"Yes."

"And you control them."

"Uh-huh."

"But you can't get everyone in the world to touch it."

"You are a sharp one, Cooper, but that has nothing to do with how it's going to save the planet. I only need to convert a few to convince everyone."

John said, "To convince them of what?"

"That on the twenty-first of December in the year 2012, the Cubit will create a shield against the sun's global threat."

"You've got to be kidding."

"Oh, no. I'm quite serious. It is a fact that the sun will pummel the earth with electromagnetic radiation, and it's also a fact that the Cubit has an energy all its own—an anti-electromagnetic radiation if you will."

All of them looked at the Cubit, at the red glow. John had seen it do some pretty spectacular things but a force field against the sun? "Assuming what you say is true," he said, "you get to save the planet, then what?"

"The world goes on."

"You mean Manson's world," Cooper added. "You want the next age to be filled with chaos and suffering and death."

Manson smiled and he clicked the remote. The stone fireplace slid back into place, the stone crunchy sound ending when the crimson light behind it disappeared. "So what's the difference in today's world?"

"There will be no love and no hope," Sebastian growled and started to rise, but John held him down.

"And no revenge," Manson added and pointed his remote at the darkness right in front of them. He clicked a button and a huge media screen flickered into life. It was anchored against some distant dark wall that the screen's immense glow only revealed as shadowy.

The screen showed Google Maps' image of a revolving Earth. It centered on the United States and zoomed into the eastern part of Kansas until a red marker appeared with the words "Pickett's Crossing" above it. The map faded and in its place came a newscast from a Kansas television station. A reporter was talking to a police official.

"You know who that policeman is, Sebastian?"

Sebastian didn't acknowledge the question.

"You mean he doesn't look at all familiar?"

Sebastian remained silent.

"Who was it that killed your mother, who plastered her with the black chechen negro sap right in front of her poor little son's eyes? Who was it that the poor little boy wanted to kill more than anything in the world? A Nazi? Take a good look."

Sebastian rose from the couch and John let him. He walked closer to the big screen just as the reporter was asking the policeman about an artifact he'd supposedly found in the ruins of a farm that had exploded some years ago. The policeman denied such possession but offered to show the reporter the ruins of the Bender Farm if desired. Sebastian gasped and craned his head closer, stumbled closer, tripped and fell against the wall under the big screen. John and Cooper both jumped to their feet but Manson told them to stop and wait. Sebastian slowly rose from his knees then stood in front of the screen. The policeman's face was right next to his, which gave the appearance that the policeman was looking at Sebastian.

"It is," Sebastian said. "But it can't be…"

Manson shook his head. "You know that isn't true. Of course it's him. The man who killed your mother. The Gestapo motherfucker that deep down inside, stored in places you just can't get to, you've always wanted for revenge. Cut his hair a bit and stick a little Hitler mustache on him and voila!"

"He has a Creation Dagger?" John asked.

Manson snapped his fingers and a second bodyguard appeared from the shadows beyond the media screen. He grabbed Sebastian's arm and led him back to the couch. "Not after Sebastian gets through with him," Manson said. "Not after Sebastian steals the dagger and slices his cubited head off with it. Right? Isn't that what you would do given the chance?"

Sebastian's breaths spewed almost uncontrollably. He nodded.

"And you, Cooper," Manson turned back toward the screen and clicked the remote.

"I already know what you are going to show me," she said.

"Yes. I know. But let's take a look anyway."

Again the screen started with Google Maps' Earth image, but this time it zoomed into the town of Ceiba, Puerto Rico. The screen cross-faded to a broadcast of a full contact jousting event, but the video was not professional and was shaky, having been captured with a smartphone not twenty feet from the action.

Two armored riders on armored horses sped toward each other, lances erect and ready for the collision. The knight in gold unseated the knight in black and it was only when the black knight removed his helmet that Cooper muttered, "Kerskker."

"Wait for it," Manson said.

"I thought that asshole's claim to fame was that he was the undefeated king of the sport."

"Undefeated, no. King of the sport in competition, yes. But his claim to fame is…" Manson gestured toward the screen.

"His invincible dagger," Cooper finished.

The male smartphone user's voice giggled a bit as Kerskker revealed the Creation Dagger. The knight in gold jumped off his horse but did not remove any armor. *Do it!* the smartphone user said as Kerskker stood and jammed the dagger into the golden knight's breastplate. It easily pierced metal that was thick enough to stop a lance moving at thirty miles an hour. Kerskker flipped the golden knight's helmet open and told the red-bearded man inside, *No one unseats Triple K and lives to tell about.* He then twisted the dagger and the knight fell, dead. The smartphone user clapped and whistled and the video shook in concert with the jubilation. Kerskker bowed for the camera, then the user flipped the smartphone around to reveal the face of a kid that no one in Manson's huge living room knew. Everyone did, however, recognize the red eyes and silver sparks of a cubit.

"Another of your surrogates?" Cooper said.

"Yes," Manson replied and clicked his remote. "Both of them. You are the only ones to ever see that video, but rumors of it spread throughout Puerto Rico. You know why your ex-husband is the king of full contact jousting? It's because other knights are afraid of dying in a similar fashion."

"So they all just let him win."

The media screen went dark for a moment before Google's Earth image rotated once more. "Sometimes. He does win a few on his own. But you know as well as I do that Danny Kerskker is a big fucking coward without enough common sense to keep the beautiful woman he married. He screwed you royal, Cooper. He made you who you are today: full of vinegar with a heart that will never open to any man. He took love from you. Now doesn't that piss you off?" Manson smiled as the Google Earth globe stopped above Australia and zoomed into Cairns and the Great Barrier Reef. He didn't wait for Cooper to answer. "Now then. What do we have here? One of the greatest scuba destinations on the planet. Scuba diving…hmmm. Who in here other than Sebastian Bondager is a professional scuba diver?"

John took a deep breath. He had no idea where Manson was going with this. John had never even been to Australia, let alone to the Great Barrier Reef. He'd always wanted to go but that had been wishful thinking, a dream really, one he'd shared with Sebastian and…

"That's right, Johnny," Manson said when he saw the realization spread into John's expression. "Tell 'em what he's won. An ex-spy lover turned militant."

This time the media screen faded from Google Earth to a FOX News report from Cairns, Australia.

Middle East terrorism moves to a new country, a reporter's voiceover explained, *and now the leader is backed by the promise of magic. Majjar Fodii, a former organizer and government double agent for al Qaeda during the first Gulf War has resurfaced in Australia as the ringleader for the militant group Jamaah Islamiah, also known as JI. Following, is exclusive FOX News video that was obtained by patriotic sources close to the leader. As you will see, Fodii has absolutely no compassion for anyone that does not follow her radical Islamic ideals. We warn you that the video you are about to see may be unfit for some viewers.*

FOX's exclusive showed the close-up of a person (whether male or female was uncertain because of the black hood that covered the face) being beheaded by a Creation Dagger. When the camera zoomed out, a female with dark skin, and dark hair rolled up into a bun, had the bloody dagger in one hand. *Follow me or follow death*, the woman said. The reporter's voiceover went on to talk about two recent terrorist attempts that had failed, one in Sydney and one in Melbourne. Fodii's group, the reporter explained, had taken responsibility for both.

Cooper and Sebastian stared curiously at John as Manson turned off the media screen.

"Oh. I see. John Brown Gordon hasn't told either of you about his past love affair. She pretty much duped the king of black ops. She pretty much ruined any chance for John and his fellow Marines to take out Saddam Hussein before the Gulf Wars ever started. She fucked him, didn't she Johnny? Literally and figuratively. An al Qaeda spy. A double-crossing piece of ass that totally fooled one of this country's best covert operators. And now look at her. A militant leader with an invincible blade. She'll be all the rage once other militants find out what she has and what it can do. And it won't take long for the media to put *all* of the pieces together now that I've thrown them a bone. These seemingly unrelated, unbelievable, fantastic accounts, as you can see, are all merging into one. It won't be long before reporters, paparazzi and other sensationalists will be making the words 'Creation Dagger' and 'Cubit' a household name. You'll be lucky to even get close enough to a dagger without being broadcast across the world."

"So, when do we go?" John asked and stood. Cooper and Sebastian followed his lead.

"Goddamned smart bunch of people huggers—all of you." Manson clapped his hands together.

John took two giant steps and stood nose-to-nose with Manson. Chester the bodyguard started forward but was halted when Manson raised the hand holding his Creation Dagger and waved it. "I'll be back for that," John said, his voice even and confident. "And the Cubit, too. We're going to stop whatever it is you're trying to do. Mine will be the last face you'll ever see, I shit you not."

Manson raised his free hand and dropped it onto John's thick shoulder. "You believe what you want, little man. Hope and faith are all you have left…but not for long. This world needs a new leader and you're looking at him. Deal with it." He released John and turned his back to him. "You get the daggers and I'll get the Book and you'll get the chance to meet your maker." Manson nodded toward the stone fireplace that hid the Cubit.

Media Release
Phoenix International
December 24, 2011

For Immediate Release

Friends:

Every moment of my life has been dedicated to the sanctity of man. It's not easy being the one who, by his own, skilled, cognizance can build upon a breadth of knowledge known only to a chosen few. My financial situation has aided me - has aided you. A person can only enter the back door's dark secrets when money is the player's ticket.

Government is crooked. It lies to you. And it knows better. Like I know better.

Scientists hired by the government have known that our sun will…and I say WILL…get very angry during the first half of December in 2012. The sun will, kind of, burp what is known as a coronal mass ejection. This is not an unusual celestial event. Scientists around the globe will tell you that CMEs often happen. A bunch of plasma is shot into the solar system and, for the most part, the planet Mercury eats it.

But on, or near, December 21 in the year 2012 of our Lord, the CME will be the largest ever known in recorded scientific history. The magnitude of the ejection is also complicated by its vector, meaning, it's going to be directed right at Mother Earth.

Most of you reading this will think that Richard Manson is full of shit, but I remind you. I know things because I can know them. I know what the scientists at the Dish in Australia are not telling the world. I'm giving you the resources to verify what others have, until now, hidden from the population (see Appendix A).

With great power comes great responsibility…I love that Spiderman quote. And it's true. My power leads to this responsibility: Tell the world what others are afraid to tell them and, then, figure out how to remedy such catastrophic implications so the world does not panic.

Phoenix International is, and has always been, a socially responsible citizen. I, WE, have helped the world become healthier and have done so altruistically. PIIL has never profited, and will never profit, from the distribution of BethStar. Statistics reveal the benefits of the supplement to entire communities—and, in fact, countries. My scientists have been given the green light to wash away all of the rigmarole that is attached to everyday commercial bullshit. Fast food sucks. BethStar cures this suck. It's proven (see Appendix B).

So the real answer that you have come to this document to realize is the continued salvation of mankind. Being healthy means nothing if you are dead. And on December 21, without my help, the world will spin toward death. There is nothing that can stop a massive CME from coating this planet with an amount of radiation such that all communication, all transportation, all electrification will abruptly stop.

I have in my possession, the element which can, for the lack of a better metaphor, create a force field around the earth. The device is known as a Cubit. Archeologists unearthed the device a few years ago but you wouldn't know that. Why would those that control want any possibility of that control being lost?

I showed the world, earlier tonight (December 24, 2011) what is known as a Creation Dagger. There are five of them known to be in existence. I have one and I know where most of the others are. The Cubit, which in a year will detour the sun's harmful radiation, can only work if all five daggers are together at that moment in time. But beware. These daggers in the hands of some will end this world as we all know it.

Now, I know what some of you are thinking. Richard Manson is a nutcase. In every other circumstance, I would think the same thing. But I have dedicated so much, so far, to this world. I knew how to stop the insanity of the health care crisis...of third-world disease...of everything that men in power will not reveal.

The Cubit can stop the CME ejection that will, absolutely, destroy our world. No fuel. No water. No electricity. No Internet. No nothing.

Phoenix International will save us all.

If you have any additional questions, I will be glad to answer them. Respond to this email with any inquiries.

Sincerely,

Richard Manson

It was everything you told no one but John no longer had that luxury. Pride. Honor. Brotherhood. When any one of them was broken all were in jeopardy. As a Marine, you sacrificed your soul to uphold such values no matter what. The sanctity of the Corps included the blood of ghosts, whether real, anticipated, or lost. When *you* fucked up, the *Corps* fucked up and that was not acceptable. On the drive back to the dive shop, John told his friends about how he'd fucked up.

Back in 1990, John, Strykor and Roger had all eagerly jumped at the chance to serve as pawns in an impossible mission to stop Saddam Hussein. The Corps had provided everything they'd needed: weapons, guts and subversive contacts. They'd gotten within minutes of stopping one war that would ultimately lead to others.

But Majjar Fodii had deceived them all, especially John Brown Gordon. The tease had been absolute. Strykor, by the Corps' own description of him, had been "one crazy mother that no one could fool." Roger had been the most intellectual of the bunch, having the advantage of logic that went far beyond most soldiers' capacities to reason. John had been the heavy, the leader, the only Marine who could have managed Strykor's insanity and Roger's intellect in an effort to stop the world's most hated dictator. Fodii had been a "U.S. Government spy," but she'd used that false moniker to steal John's flowering love, and that had almost killed them all.

"What does Fodii have to do with Cairns and the Great Barrier Reef?" Cooper asked as she squirmed uncomfortably on the truck's bench seat between John and Sebastian, watching nervously as John dodged nighttime Mexican traffic.

"It's the location of one of the greatest scuba adventures anywhere. It's the place where we'd promised to meet once the mission was over."

"A lie," Sebastian said.

John nodded. "One of many."

"You loved," Cooper said and patted John's knee. "And that's always a good thing."

"Your history and love are as brash as mine."

"Yes. And it was a mistake to use it as a crutch for as long as I did."

John turned his body as much toward Cooper as the truck's interior would allow. "You and Billy?" Cooper nodded and John smiled, big, his cheeks bulging happiness in a way that Cooper had not seen in a very long time. "Fantastic."

"But it still doesn't change the way I feel about Kerskker. Manson was right. Revenge is a very powerful thing—perhaps even more so than love. Regardless, we do have to get the daggers if we and Billy are going to stop Manson."

"Yes." John sat straight, his thick arms coddling the steering wheel. "I've been thinking that the daggers are not what he wants. I think he just wants the Book and he thinks Billy has it. I think that he knows Billy will eventually reunite with one or all of us and, through whatever connection the daggers make, will find him. I think, too, that he wants us to suffer along the way. He wants us to do like cubits do, to kill without remorse because of the extremity of the sin of revenge in each of us. We are his pawns."

"Well, I don't give a shit what Manson gets off on," Sebastian said, tapping his foot nervously. "I'm going to kill the fucker that killed my mother. It's really more about that, for me, than it is for anything else."

Neither Cooper nor John responded to Sebastian's anger but John felt that same thing. Revenge was a powerful motivator, particularly when coupled with the lies of love.

Pepe's Taco Bar was only a few blocks from John's dive shop and as they passed it, Cooper reminded him that Roger wanted some mini-tacos as the price for using his truck. John, however, wasn't paying any attention to Pepe's or to Cooper. Something ahead just wasn't right. His Marine-learned instincts were kicking in…or, perhaps, it was the Book, again. He started feeling that same extra sensory perception, as if the Book was asking for help. He hammered down on the truck's accelerator pad.

"What?" Sebastian asked.

"Something's wrong," John said while steering the truck around slower traffic. "The dive shop." He nodded ahead.

"Shit!" Sebastian yelled. "Where the fuck's my boat!"

When John screeched to a stop, he and Cooper ran from the truck to the busted front door of the dive shop while Sebastian took off in the direction of the short, wooden dock behind the shop to an array of glowing deck lamps where his boat had been tied.

John snapped on the lights but only two of the four illuminated. The interior was in shambles. Not one cabinet, corner or crevice had been left untouched. Scuba equipment was scattered everywhere. John's first thought was of the Book. Manson's men had been there while Manson had confronted them back in town. It was Cooper that reminded him of his friend.

"Roger," she said. "Do you think they…"

John started plowing through the broken room, saying Roger's name as he moved large pieces. "Any blood?" he asked Cooper. "Do you see any blood?"

"No. None."

Sebastian entered. His face looked as dismal as the scuba shop. "My boat. It's gone. I think they sunk it."

"You ask the fishermen next door?" John said.

"Not there. No one's around. Those bastards must have scared 'em all away." John had never seen Sebastian cry until now. "They took my mom, took my boat, took my life. Goddammit! Goddammit all to hell!"

"The Book," Cooper said. "Did they get the Book?"

"Fuck a goddamn book," Sebastian growled, wiping away a tear as if it was acid.

John stepped toward Sebastian over what once was the dive shop's front counter and the crushed cash box it contained. Pesos were strewn everywhere. "Remember our purpose. Remember our goal."

"Your goal, not mine! I'm gonna kill that bastard. I'm gonna kill him then I'm gonna sink him right next to my boat!" Sebastian backpedaled out the busted door, tripped and fell. When John moved to help him, he quickly shuffled up onto his feet and ran back to the dimly lit deck.

"Is this it?" Cooper asked, one hand propping up a scuba tank atop a pile of air hoses.

John nodded. "Check it."

Roger Braun was indeed a clever person. In the years he'd watched after John's dive shop, he'd occasionally dealt in some "questionable" bartering, mostly small stuff like marijuana. There'd been more than a few times that scuba enthusiasts had paid him in dope, and Roger (not a smoker himself) had traded the dope for scuba equipment and a collectible antique gun or two. He'd hid the dope he'd acquired in the shop, using quite a unique camouflage strategy: a scuba tank. He'd crafted the piece himself by cutting off the top, threading it and the body, and installing a pocket inside so the dope wouldn't fall all the way to the bottom of the tank. This is where John had stashed the Book.

Cooper tried to unscrew it but was unable. John stepped over to help. As he gave the tank top a hefty twist, Sebastian came running back into the shop.

"Not sunk. Holy shit, it's Roger!"

John, Cooper, Sebastian and Roger spent Christmas Eve floating five miles offshore on Sebastian's Sea Ray. Roger had just finished telling them how the two men in dark suits and sunglasses had pulled up in a black SUV while he had been tuning up Sebastian's boat. Roger had untied the Sea Ray and had used a long paddle to guide the boat away from the dock. He'd told them that he'd heard the destruction and that he was sorry for not having done anything about it.

"You saved the boat," Sebastian said.

"And your scuba tank saved the Book," John added. "Nothing to be sorry about."

Cooper walked up from the cabin onto the bow where she'd laid a blanket and a setting of four plates. Their Christmas Eve meal consisted of a couple of turkey sandwiches, two cans of mandarin oranges, some Uncle Ben's instant rice that Cooper had prepared in the cabin kitchen, and a jug of sangria that Roger had been sipping from when Manson's men had arrived. A Coleman Lantern provided light in the middle of the setting and Cooper sat, her face glow joining the others. "Dig in," she said and poured each a coffee cup full of wine.

"What is it with that Book, anyway?" Roger asked, adjusting his Red Sox ball cap as his lips smacked against a spoonful of rice. "You know, I'm not much of a metaphysical kind of guy, but I swear to you that thing warned me about them G-men before they ever got here."

"Not G-men," John said. "More like henchmen."

"Manson's?" Roger asked.

"Yeah. And they were looking for it. Would have killed you to get it."

Roger downed his cup of sangria and poured some more. "So, you gonna fill me in or what?"

John gave him an abstract of what had transpired that night. He explained that they would all be leaving in the morning. Manson had arranged forged papers and passes, and security logs had been expunged so that the Tulum Terrorists would not be recognized on the way to their individual destinations.

"Good. Okay," Roger said. "But the Book. What about the Book? I can't get that incessant buzzing noise out of my head."

John waited until everyone had cleaned their plates and only the half jug of sangria and four coffee cups remained on the blanket before he went to the cabin to retrieve it. He set the Book in the middle of the blanket. "Manson wants this more than anything in the world," he said. "It contains info that he needs himself or needs to prevent others from having."

"What info?" Roger asked, his eyes becoming as red as the wine and his Red Sox cap. "Let's see." He reached forward and tried to open it but couldn't. "Ain't gonna help much if you can't read it."

Cooper set her half-empty wine cup on the blanket. "It's not meant for just anyone to read except for one page in the middle." She grabbed the Book and held it flat against the palm of her right hand where the back cover touched the djed tattoo on the back of her wrist. "Funny that it didn't open for you," she said to Roger.

"Won't open for me anymore, either," John said.

But when Cooper yanked on it, the Book's first ten pages flipped forward as one stuck-together mass, to reveal the page of symbols. John shook his head, but wasn't surprised. Nothing about the Book surprised him anymore.

Cooper gasped at the colors and illumination that John had witnessed back on Sebastian's Island. "It's almost complete. The last symbol…it's…"

"The sun," Roger finished. "And there's a little man under the sun." John leaned forward. The *little man* outline had not been there when he'd last seen it. "And it looks like the little man is praying to it," Roger added.

Simultaneously, all four of them looked up into the densely star-packed sky. There was no moon and there was no sun but every one of them said a prayer.

0-TIME: PREDICATE

CREATION OF GOOD AND EVIL

All we have to decide is what to do with the time that is given to us. There are other forces at work in this world besides the will of evil.

-Gandalf

Saturday, December 24, 2011

It had been the hardest thing he'd ever had to do, even worse than killing his best friend, Bottlenose, back in Port Aransas. But Bottlenose had been a cubit—Cooper was his love. The decision had been instinctual, his Daykeeper's second heartbeat hammering out the alarm bell that the time had finally come for him to start getting busy.

After leaving Duncan Swallow's cubit dead on the bungalow floor, he'd seen them from the deck at the top of the steps: three dolphins, one pink, waiting for him in the swells. By the time they'd reached the beach and he'd given Cooper his notebook and journal, he'd known that love was important, but his Daykeeper's responsibility trumped everything, and *that* cost for invincibility really sucked. It had sucked even worse when he'd stood next to his looted surf shop to change into his boardies and had turned back to see Cooper being attacked by the Rio cubit. Thankfully, Buck had saved her by ramming Rio with his police car and Cooper had used the police car to escape. Billy had run to the surf then. He'd seen Cooper one last time when she'd stopped the police car to look for him, then she'd sped out of sight. What had happened to Buck and Debbie, he'd never known. The pink dolphin had pulled him under the water just as the two had been swarmed by another dozen Nexpa residents.

That's when Billy had entered the same "other world" that he'd experienced back in the cliff caves. The pink dolphin that had pulled him down into the Pacific was the very same one from Sebastian's Island, the one that had shown him life under the sea, that had communicated ideas meant only for immortals interested in saving the planet, that had proven to him how superheroes were not in comic books.

The three dolphins had helped him navigate the waters up the entire Mexican Pacific coast, into the Gulf of California and to the mouth of the Colorado River. In the day and a half excursion, he'd been able to stay under water just as long as the dolphins and he'd cruised with them on the surface by holding their fins just like a Sea World performer. In fact, Billy was sure that, on at least two occasions, humans on boats had seen the spectacle.

The first incident had been with a luxury cruise liner. It had passed them right outside of Cabo San Lucas and had blown its fog horn to signal to its passengers that something interesting was to be seen off the port side. The distance to the ship had been too great for anyone without optical magnification to verify that a human being was actually skirting along the top of the Pacific Ocean with a trio of dolphins, but he was sure they'd been close enough to spark memories in some. He was sure that those who did have binoculars would tell incredulous stories about a man and his dolphins and the shots of tequila that had caused their delusions.

The second incident had been hallway up the Gulf when a small Mexican fishing boat had not only seen them, but had come racing after them. The fishermen had nearly blown their engine to catch up with nets ready for the capture of something they couldn't possibly understand. But Billy had held tight as the dolphins had dove seconds before the nets had hit the water above them. The dolphins had only been having fun with the fishermen and Billy had shared in their playful joy both physically and spiritually.

It was this playfulness with life, the serenity and assurance of a live-by-the-moment mantra, that changed Billy the most during his days with the dolphins. It infused him with more than courage or bravery since those were purely human ideal concepts. He came to understand a *knowing* that life would work out as the universe had planned it and that he was instrumental in that future. Absolutely nothing could be done about it. Worry, no longer, would be a nemesis, but Concern would always direct his actions. After all, he was still human so love was possible: for dolphins, for fishermen and for Cooper.

By the time he crawled up onto the muddy banks along the Colorado

River, Billy knew exactly what it meant to be a Daykeeper. He was the pawn in the hand of the Great Spirit who would knock down knights and queens and kings by moving one step at a time.

He waved at his finned friends and they waved back with their bottle noses and Billy sat there in the tremendously dry December heat thinking about the trek across the Sonoran Desert that he was about to undertake. And a hand dropped onto his shoulder from behind.

"That was awesome, dude." The man looked nothing like someone who'd use the word "dude" but his wife certainly did. They both had some pretty expensive cameras hanging from their necks.

Billy stood and wiped the mud from his boardies. "What are you two doing way out here in the middle of nowhere?"

"Funny. I was just gonna ask you the same. This ain't no place for a man with no hat." The man looked to be in his fifties and this became more evident when he shifted the broad brim of his straw hat to reveal a few more wrinkles and a lot less hair. "Looks like you had some friends though."

Billy looked back at the water, thinking about the dolphins and the journey they'd made. "Yes. Very good friends."

The man's wife walked a few steps to stand beside her husband. "Never seen a pink dolphin before. Nat Geo is going to go bonkers."

"Nat Geo?" Billy asked.

"National Geographic," the man said. "We're photojournalists, here to document the damage that agricultural runoff has done to the lower Colorado. Not many come down to these parts but we were quick to accept, weren't we, hon?" His wife smiled a face full of freckles. "So what brings *you* out here?"

"Banditos took my boat," Billy said. "The dolphins rescued me."

"Hot damn," the woman said. "That's a much better story."

Billy nodded. "That ain't the most of it."

"Right on," the man said. "We're heading back to the states within the next day. Care to tag along, seeing's that the walk would definitely kill you? We got plenty of room in the Nat Geo RV. Maybe you'll tell us a little more about them banditos…"

"…and the pink dolphin that saved you," his giddy wife added.

Billy told them. He knew that his story would surface soon anyway and he really wasn't one for keeping any more secrets. Perhaps, he thought, the professional photography team known as the Jones' (the man's first name was Leo and his wife's name was Anna), could even provide some validity to what would certainly seem to most, lunacy. He'd have to continue laying as low as possible until the time was right, but stories…he had a few, which he told them all the way to Phoenix. He'd shown them his dagger and they'd taken a picture of it. He'd shown them the Djed amulet and they'd recorded that as well. He told them about the Cubit and about cubits and they had listened intently, never once questioning his sanity. His revelation was his Christmas gift to the world, he'd said, and he'd begged them to use the information wisely.

"Definitely," Anna told him as they dropped him off at the campus of Arizona State University in the early afternoon. "That's one quacky story and we love our jobs."

"Peace," Billy told them and offered the hand sign.

"And love," Leo added, then waved goodbye.

The Jones' had given him a printed T-shirt with the yellow square logo of National Geographic and he used one sleeve to wipe sweat from his brow. It was Saturday, the day before Christmas and the campus was mostly abandoned. A few college-aged skateboarders roamed the sidewalks and Billy asked one of them if he knew Elizabeth Presser, a professor of chemistry at the school.

"Nope," the skateboarder said. "But the chem building is over there." He pointed. "Good luck finding any working stiffs around here today, especially professors." He looked a Billy's boardies. "Nice, man. Where'd you get them?"

"Special order from Mexico," Billy said.

"Rad. I'll have to check 'em online."

Billy nodded. "You'll find them there for sure. Thanks for the info." The skateboarders rolled off in the opposite direction as he walked toward the chemistry building.

Phoenix in winter was much like Nexpa in winter except for the influence of the ocean. The sky was magnificently blue and cloudless and smelled less like salt and more like dust. A cool seventy-degree wind ruffled his long, blonde locks which got him wondering what his mom was going to think about his hair. Jo Presser had absolutely hated long hair and, being the compliant wife, his mom had always urged Billy to maintain it above shoulder length. This kind of psychologically-enforced compliance, Billy thought, was probably one of the reasons they'd divorced. It was certainly one reason why he'd left the college Jo had insisted he attend and why he'd moved to a beach town of the likes that Jo utterly hated. Billy had been spiteful in lieu of being thoughtful since it was his mother who had suffered the greatest casualty, but that had been long ago, before his knowledge of Daykeepers and their better understanding of the things that made the world good.

The main entry to the modern brick and concrete building that housed the chemistry department was locked. Billy pressed his head against one glass door, looking for some sign of activity or wall-mounted directory that would reveal further information about his mother. At the far side of the interior lobby, a guard saw him but remained seated. Billy tapped the glass with one hand and when the guard didn't move, smacked it with a closed fist. The guard left the television he was watching and strolled to the door.

"What?" the young, skinny kid said from behind the glass.

Billy yelled, "Can I ask you something?"

"You just did," the kid guard responded.

"Open the door."

"It's Christmas Eve for God's sake. Don't you have some better place to be?"

Billy thought that was exactly what the guard felt about himself. Having pulled the security shift today was this guy's pissing point. "I haven't seen my mother in five years," Billy pleaded. "Elizabeth Presser, please?"

The expression of indignation immediately left the guard's face. He opened the door. "You're Dr. Presser's son?"

Billy nodded. "Yes."

"She said you might be around but…"

Billy entered and the door automatically closed behind him. "But what?"

"She said that last Christmas, too." He stared at Billy as if he was a ghost. "Me and the boys have had a bet that you don't even exist."

"Well, I do. Don't you see the resemblance?"

The boy guard scratched his bald chin. "Truth be known…yeah. You look just like her, except for the long hair."

"Can you tell me where she lives? I've lost track of…of time, and…"

"She says the same thing. She says it a lot. I…we think she's lost her…" The guard shook his head as if the next few words were totally inappropriate to tell a ghost who was the son of someone whom he'd bet money was losing their mind. "Her house is just off campus but she really doesn't live there; she pretty much lives here. Hardly ever leaves anymore." The guard apparently saw the expressed stress on Billy's face. "I mean, she's one dedicated professor."

"She's here…now?" The guard nodded. "Can you show me?"

"I'll take you, even though it's gonna cost me twenty bucks."

"I guarantee you, you've won." Billy smiled but that didn't ease the odd tension that suddenly turned the guard's face red.

Dr. Presser was working on the second floor and the guard took Billy straight to her, knocked a tiny tap with one knuckle on a door labeled "Microbiology Lab," and waited for a response. He knocked again…then once more.

"Yes!" a voice from within impatiently grumbled.

"Your son, Dr. Presser. Just like you said."

Something rolled and shattered, then a soft and quick shuffling of footsteps approached the closed door. "Another game?" Dr. Presser asked.

"Of course not, doctor. You told us before…"

"I told you not to disturb me."

"But your son. You said that he was coming to see you."

The latch on the door turned, the door swung inward, and a woman with a full head of silver hair cut to the neckline showed part of her face through the opening. Her reaction was immediate. The door flung fast and furious against the inside wall and Elizabeth Presser consumed her son with open arms. The guard quickly walked away.

"Dear God," she whispered in his ear, her breath a bit pungent from drinking too much coffee. "I really didn't know if I'd ever see you again." She pulled back and kissed his forehead and her hands became wrapped in his hair. "Why Billy Jo Presser. What of all this?"

"It's the in thing, mom. Do you know how happy I am to see you?" This time Billy consumed his mother with another hug.

"Come in. Come in." Elizabeth offered him the door and once inside, she closed and locked it.

"What are you doing here on Christmas Eve? Working?"

"All in good time. I have some things that are really important to share with you but right now, I just want to look and listen. You got my note, I take it."

"Just last Monday. Pretty clever of you."

"No. Lucky. I don't use the Internet for anything except research, but thanks to one of my unruly students who likes to watch YouTube instead of take notes, I saw your beach shorts…" She looked down. "…that looked just like these."

"Crazy, huh? How something so simple can be such a hit. I never really intended for them to go viral. That's the Internet for you—always making something much larger than it really is." Elizabeth led Billy further into the bright lab where huge pieces of research equipment occupied walls of space. LEDs blinked and digital screens presented graphs and sine waves and molecular structures that reminded him of M.I.T., which reminded him of dropping out of college. "Is this where you always go for vacation?"

Elizabeth looked astonished by the observation. "This is my vacation, and my home, and my work. Ever since your father left…Here, sit down. Enough about me. Where have *you* been for the last five years?"

Within the sterility of the lab, Billy found it unusual that it contained a corner furnished with three cushy, fabric-covered chairs and a couch. The mini-living space also sported a wall-mounted flat screen which was dialed into Pandora on the Internet. The television displayed the bouncing icon of a Greed Day album cover but no sound was coming from it. Billy dropped into one of the chairs. "I've been…changed," he said.

Elizabeth sat on the couch beside him. "Haven't we all? You were a restaurant owner the last time I knew."

"Still am, in a way. I have a manager looking after things now."

"I see. So the hurricane that hit Port Aransas didn't destroy it after all."

Guilt flooded into Billy's heart. He'd never even thought about contacting his parents after Hurricane Antiago hit the island back in 2008. "I'm sorry. I should have called. I should have before that and after that and…"

"It's hard living with a man like Jo Presser. I'm sure it's just as hard being his son. I don't want to be judgmental. I didn't mean it that way. What's in the past, stays in the past."

"You said something about his leaving."

Elizabeth stopped looking at him for the first time since she'd opened the lab door and gazed across the room where the thick cylinder of an electron microscope seemingly sprouted from the floor. She nodded. "About a year ago. I got into some new research that took a big chunk of my time away from him…or should I say, took a big chunk of time away from my wiferly household duties."

"Wiferly?"

Elizabeth returned her attention to him. "His adjective for 'duties of a wife.' I think you know what I mean."

"He never called it that. He just got upset every time you had late classes or meetings or grant work."

"Yeah, well, he changed, too." She reached out and grabbed his hand. "So now that you have a manager, have you been looking to expand?"

Billy shook his head. "No. I guess you could say I've been traveling."

Her face lit up. "How exciting! I've always wanted to do that. Tell me more."

Why he was hesitant, he couldn't understand. He'd told two complete photojournalist strangers just about everything he *needed* to tell his mother. Perhaps it was the way she looked at him. Forlorn circles sagged under eyes that were as brown as his own. She didn't really smile the way he remembered; it seemed forced even though he was sure she was overwhelmed by his presence. She looked extremely overworked and stressed. Telling her that he was a Daykeeper, and explaining all the fine details that had evolved around him becoming one, he thought, would only add pressure. So he started slowly. "I have something to show you." He yanked the Velcro strap on his boardies' pocket and took out the Djed amulet. "In one of the places I traveled, I found this." He held it in the palm of his hand and when his mother tried to take it, he rolled his fingers around the four crosses but didn't pull his hand back. "It's very special. It...helps me connect."

She patted the hand and the amulet. "It looks very special. That's a Djed isn't it?" Billy nodded, only a little surprised that she knew. "So you've been to Egypt?"

"Not for this. Sedona."

His mother's eyebrows, which still contained flecks of youthful auburn hair, squashed inward. "Hmmm. Egyptian trinkets in Sedona, Arizona. How...unique."

"Not a trinket, mom—an artifact. I found it in a..." Billy searched quickly for a truth that wasn't complete, "...in an archeological dig."

The pause that ensued was relentless, a silence meant to teach understanding or measure ignorance. "Well, you must really enjoy it or else you wouldn't have kept it so close," she finally said. "But why in your pocket? It has such a beautiful chain. Are those dolphins?"

Billy nodded. "My Nahual."

"Your?..."

"Nahual. My animal spirit."

His mother gasped but it was almost inaudible. "Since when did you start believing in spirits?" She placed the necklace around Billy's neck.

"Since the island hurricane. Such exhibitions of Nature's force have a way of doing that to a person." His mother had a strange look in her eye that was quite pleasing, particularly since most of the strange-look-in-the-eyes he'd recently experienced had been filled with blood and lightning. "Mom. This artifact means that I'm invincible."

Dr. Elizabeth Presser did have a home away from the lab and she drove Billy there an hour after he reentered her life. It wasn't far; just a mile or so down University Drive. In the divorce settlement, she'd gotten the house and Jo had gotten the savings account. On the drive over, she told Billy that the financial split had been equitable and nothing except a few personal, shared belongings had been contested. Jo was living back in Connecticut where Billy had grown up much of his young life and he was still an architect with his own firm and making tons of money—which was something he loved.

Her house reminded Billy a lot of the Hunter's ranch style home before it burned down. There was no huge living room built for entertaining and the back yard did not meet the Mexican jungle, but the home's size and basic layout was pretty much the same. It, of course, reminded Billy of his lost friends: Jerry lying dead in his own fire-blackened driveway; Debbie and Sheriff Buck scrapping on the ground among the chaos that consumed the Nexpa beach just before he'd submerged with the dolphins.

His mother poured each of them a glass of iced sun tea and they went out on the back porch to watch the dusk's red streaks above the six-foot wooden fence that separated her house from her neighbors. It was much harder explaining everything to her than it had been to the Nat Geo Joneses. For every new revelation he uncovered, he felt another squirt of guilt race through him, guilt for not having called, guilt for not asking advice, guilt for leaving home, not because of her, but because of his father and then never telling her this, guilt for not having been there when Jo Presser left her. Of all of the responses he thought his mother would give, he didn't anticipate what she actually said.

"I know Richard Manson."

Billy's mouth dropped farther than his mother's had at any moment during his own admissions. "What? How?"

"And I think he named that health pill after me."

"Bringing Everyone Total Health?" It took Billy a second to realize her nickname was naturally *Beth*, but no one had ever called her that. "Oh, I see. But there are lots of Beths in the world."

"None that he had a crush on when he was a graduate student at the university." She thumbed in the direction of the ASU campus then turned the thumb toward herself. "It's one of the reasons I sent you that letter. The world works in mysterious ways, Billy—of that I'm sure you are now convinced. It always comes full circle. How much do you know of Richard?"

Hearing her talk of the Evil by his human first name unnerved him. "He's the beast that Revelation talks about."

His mother's eyebrows, again, showed surprise. "Now you're reading the Bible?"

"I do at times just to appreciate such an archive of thought."

"Said like a mother's scientist. I hope you'll forgive me for not taking you to church more often."

"It's not my place to forgive." Billy gently grabbed his mother's thumb and then her hand. "Mine is only to accept."

"You have changed. You seem much wiser than your age. A Daykeeper's quality, no doubt?"

He released her thumb and her hand found the glass of tea which was empty except for a few ice cubes. "And it's getting stronger. I think I'm supposed to kill Rich… Manson."

The statement didn't faze his mother one bit. "Let me refill your glass and then it will be my turn to tell you a story that I've never shared with another living soul."

In the fall semester of 1983, Elizabeth Delone met Jo Presser while attending Arizona State University and they immediately started dating. She was a senior undergraduate biochemistry major and he was a junior in the engineering program which he later changed to architecture. The following January, Richard Manson entered her life.

When Manson arrived in Arizona, he'd not yet been possessed by the Great Darkness, but he was, and had always been, a lambasting creep, self-loved, over confident, and sharp as a tack. He'd come to ASU for many reasons after getting his undergraduate degree at Pepperdine where he'd "majored" more in the Malibu surf culture than in their engineering program. He had, in fact, won a couple of surfing competitions and for a short time, had basked in stardom which had jacked up an overcharged ego even further.

Manson was an exceptionally smart person, the type that scored As on tests without really studying. He'd spend hours in the surf and pull a 3.95. This was envied (he knew it) and it helped shape an egotistic personality that really pissed off just about everyone…a smugness that evolved into a life with no true friends. His only acquaintances were those short-lived relationships that he accepted for the purpose of self-gratification: sex, business propositions, learning. To be with him was to share his success if not for just a short time, and there was a world of people whom he influenced this way.

He chose ASU because he wanted to separate himself from the west coast surfing culture that had become boring because he had grown fat, gaining almost thirty pounds since his competition days as a sophomore. He chose ASU because it offered research programs that intrigued him, particularly one involving the pioneering human genome efforts of the 1980s. He became obsessed with finding a way to manipulate the genome for the purpose of increasing everyone's chance for a healthier life, mostly his own. He thought he could do it without much effort. He thought his smarts could outwit the microscopic complexities of DNA. He fancied the idea of inventing the next big craze that could make him rich.

Elizabeth, a tall slender blonde at the time, sat in the front row of the advanced chemistry class that Manson taught as a graduate researcher. He took an immediate shine to her and decided that she would be his girl regardless of the fact that she already had a boyfriend. He thought she'd be easy. Even though he was still a bit overweight, he was confident in his beauty. He was the new star of the Bio-Engineering Research Department. He was unraveling the secrets of the human genome. He was every girl's big catch.

Elizabeth wanted nothing to do with him. Not only would she not destroy a good relationship with Jo, she'd heard from her close friend, Frederico Fernandez, about Manson's obsession with her. Because they shared lab space (Frederico worked with early advances in nanotech while Manson struggled with the human genome), Frederico had kept a suspicious eye on Manson the entire 1984 spring semester, even "befriending" the man just to get closer, to find out what he was up to.

One night, Manson came into the lab incredibly drunk and proceeded to tell Frederico all about this cute blonde named Elizabeth Delone, about how she'd continued to dodge his advances, about how "no girl in their right mind wouldn't want to hook up with a stud like me." Manson had rambled on and had become angry when Frederico had mentioned Elizabeth's boyfriend with whom she'd recently become engaged. Manson had then changed the subject, apparently wanting to manipulate Frederico into his own confederacy by asking him for help. Could the young nanotech scientist's microscopic work help him get past a stumbling block in his own DNA research? Frederico, of course, had immediately denied Manson and Manson had stormed and stumbled out of the lab, screaming something about Jack Daniels.

As Elizabeth was nearing graduation in May, she, like most new graduates, came upon some rough financial times. Neither she nor Jo had ever received family support to attend college and both had pretty much lived off of student loans, but that money had dried up. Elizabeth couldn't get credit because she had no credit and though she knew of several job prospects, all of them required a diploma. And so, that's how Elizabeth Delone was finally forced to connect with Manson. It seemed that the young DNA researcher had finally figured out a key for unlocking genes that controlled metabolic rate. Manson was offering upwards of two thousand dollars for five volunteers who would, over a month, help him test the effects of this new discovery. Unfortunately, it wouldn't be until after the experiments were completed near the end of the academic year that Frederico discovered how Manson had falsified research data, and how he'd stolen some of Frederico's work, though Frederico had never been able to prove it.

Hundreds of students signed up and both Elizabeth and Jo were among the five selected. She should have been concerned. She should have listened to Jo, how he'd tried to convince her that there were better ways to make money, but Elizabeth had argued that four thousand dollars would not only help them survive the last month of college, it would provide a great start to their future together. All they had to do was take a little pill, have a little blood drawn every now and then and, once a week, complete some exercise routines while being monitored for improvement. Basic stuff. Elizabeth had even talked with the director of the research board, had reviewed Manson's request for human subject experiments, and had been convinced that the proposed study was sound and, quite frankly, intriguing.

The first warning sign was with Jo. He and Elizabeth had a very healthy relationship which included casual, protected sex. Two weeks into the experiments, Jo lost his erection. Both of them considered it stress-related. Finals were on the horizon and Manson's money only trickled in at a hundred dollars a week with the promise of the balance after the research was completed (a little caveat they'd not discovered until after the experiments had started).

The second warning sign, which none of them had ever noticed, was the increase in the number of lab rats. Almost all of the females had quadrupled their litters, necessitating a temporary expansion of the "rat room."

The final warning came on the night that Manson changed. Elizabeth remembered this part particularly well. It was Monday, April 30, just a few days before the experiments were to end. All five volunteers were running on treadmills with monitors attached to their chests when Manson crept into the room. It was as if Manson had never been in the ASU lab, or any lab for that matter. He stooped more than he stood, his hair was disheveled, and he smelled quite offensive, almost rotten.

The other volunteers stopped their treadmills, yanked off their heart monitors and ran from the lab. They'd seen that Manson had changed. They'd seen that Manson was possessed. He was no longer the slimeball thief of other's research, or the obnoxious creep who'd taken jealousy to a new extreme by adding a little extra chemical soup to Jo's experimental doses to make him impotent. Now, he was much worse. Inhuman, really. Elizabeth saw it in his eyes when she'd finally turned to look at him. She heard the demonic insanity when he'd called her name.

"Bethhhh. Where is it?"

Jo immediately swiped the monitors from his body and took two steps before Manson broke his arm and threw him like a rag doll.

"Bethhhh. Where is the Cubit?"

Manson had become something right out of *The Exorcist*, but darker, more hellish, the pure opposite of God. When Elizabeth ran to Jo's side, the Manson thing started destroying the room, repeating *Where is it?* over and over again. Little was left of the lab by the time security showed up with their useless little batons and lack of courage. Seeing Manson scared all three of them away, then Manson stood for the longest time, just staring at Elizabeth, a creepy smile on his crazy face. It was a hungry look, one that would yank Elizabeth from sleep for months to come. He could have killed her, but he just stood there as if admiring her courage, as if conflict between hate and love was playing Russian roulette behind the boiling red eyes that sparkled with blue-white lightning.

"I must find it," he finally said, then stumbled through the scattered wrecks he'd made out of the lab room door and disappeared until the 1990s when his name became synonymous with Big Oil, pharmaceuticals and wealth as the CEO of Phoenix International.

Elizabeth found that she was pregnant a month after graduation. She kept that knowledge from Jo until Frederico finally convinced her that Jo had to be the father, impotence or not. If Jo had been the only man she'd ever slept with, Frederico helped her reason, then there was no other answer. She and Jo were married that summer and in 1985, a son was born. Jo wanted the baby to take his name, become Jo Presser II, but Elizabeth insisted that he be named after her grandfather, William Delone. "Jo" would make a good middle name, she said, and Jo begrudgingly agreed.

Jo's impotence remained and as Billy grew older, Jo started questioning why his son lacked any of his physical attributes, why his kid was always rebellious, why he was more a flower child than a stone-chiseled business suit. He started questioning who else Elizabeth might have slept with back in college. He started to wonder about Richard Manson. He started to believe that Billy was not his son.

"Please don't tell me, mom. Please." Billy had not taken a sip out of his full glass of tea from the moment his mother had started her story. All of the ice had melted and the glass had sweated a dense wet circle onto the patio's glass table.

"Don't tell you what?" His mother didn't look at him, only stared at the neighbor's house Christmas lights as they blinked in the darkness.

"Is Jo Presser my father?"

When she finally turned to face him, tears were all over her cheeks. She sniffed and tried to drink from the tea glass between gasps of sorrow. "I don't know," she said. "I really don't. We never had sex…oh God. But he was doing something with those experiments. He made Jo impotent. He made those rats have babies. There's one thing I am sure of—you are *my* son."

"Why have you waited so long to tell me this?"

"Why does any mother do the things she does for her children? To protect them. When you disappeared from Texas three years ago, I wondered if I'd done the wrong thing; I wondered that if I ever lost you without telling you the truth, I'd never be able to live with myself. I think my psychological paranoia was a determining factor for driving Jo away. It was by pure coincidence that you reappeared just at the right moment."

Right moment, Billy thought. There were no right moments anymore. Everything happened for a reason. "What do you mean?"

"My friend, Frederico Fernandez."

"The scientist who tried to warn you about Manson?"

"Yes."

"He has reconnected?"

"Not exactly."

Billy turned his chair completely in the direction of his mother. He reached forward and wiped the new tears from her face. "What?"

"A man came to see me a week and a half ago. He said he had proof that Manson was trying to control the world."

"BethStar," Billy said. His mother's wet eyes did not show surprise. "Who's the man?"

She opened her mouth to respond just as the patio door slid open. Lax's adopted son from Sedona, Aaron, stepped through and answered. "His name is Michael Arden."

Michael had returned to the United States because he couldn't let Richard Manson get away with it, and because there was only one person in the world that was going to believe him, given that the "incident" at *Fox News Morning* nearly a year ago had pretty much decimated his reputation. He'd finally come to grips with the fact that he *could* stop Manson, but he just didn't have the resources.

Shortly after he'd almost shot and killed Ben Reely, Michael had been convinced something was in the supplement that not only "adjusted" the human metabolism but the human mind as well. He'd had absolutely no control over his own actions until the studio staff had tackled him. Once subdued, the mind control had disappeared and had never resurfaced. He'd been hiding in Australia ever since, wondering if the nanobots that Manson had placed in his bloodstream were actually gone or were merely dormant and floating around, waiting for the command to kill again, which had made him one neurotic basket case.

Fox had dropped all charges on his felonious attempt. Michael knew something and the powers of the gigantic news organization needed that knowledge: just a simple, little web address. Fred Fernandez's documented proof. Michael believed that Fox had wanted it for the purpose of suppression not revelation and he'd used the assumption to avoid prosecution. Then he'd fled. He'd cowered outside of Sydney, hiding in his brother's Blue Mountain lodge, jerky and jumpy whenever anyone came near. Trust for anyone, except his brother, had become a foreign concept.

He'd met with as much scrutiny from Dr. Elizabeth Presser when he'd arrived in Phoenix two weeks ago. Apparently, as a biochemist herself, she'd heard about the incident on Fox. She'd told him that he was crazy. She'd told him to leave and never return or else she'd make sure that, this time, he'd go to prison.

Then he'd mentioned Fernandez and Manson and how he knew that Manson had murdered Fred for the information that Fox wanted, the information that he was going to reveal only to her. He'd told Dr. Presser that Fred had been a great friend and that he'd mentioned her name often as someone that could be trusted—and then he'd given her the Dark Web address.

It had been a tense moment for both of them: she, with a total stranger who seemed to know a bit too much about her and who suddenly turned and locked her lab room door, and he, with the final expunging of the string of numbers that had been locked inside his head for almost a year. He didn't even know if he'd remembered it correctly, but he'd never taken the chance to find out. Fred had told him that once access was made, an internal program on the Dark Web server would erase the information, permanently.

When she'd typed in the address and had hit the return key, it took the computer monitor an uncomfortably long five seconds to do anything. Then, Fred's recording of BethStar's octagonal nanobot reaction played out in front of them just as it had the last night Michael had seen Fred alive. All of the rest of the evidence had been zipped up into one file and a link labeled "Right Click" promoted it after the recording had finished. When Dr. Presser had rolled the cursor over the link and had clicked the right mouse button, a message had popped up. It was from Fred.

> Congratulations Mikey. The Runes are safe. We can now defeat the ghouls. Please take care with it. It is our only Excalibur and there are many that want to topple the castles. I fear this may be our last transaction so, dear friend, no good-byes…only good journeys.
>
> - FredRod

Below the message there'd been a button labeled "Download" and a timer which read :05. Michael and Dr. Presser had both cried a short set of tears as the download transpired and the entire web page went black. The web browser window had then crashed. Dr. Presser had relaunched the browser and had retyped the web address which had, again, immediately crashed the window. She'd tried a second computer and a third before finally giving up and racing back to the main computer to make absolutely certain the file had downloaded. When she'd extracted the file's contents and had opened the first Word document titled "A case for DNA manipulation by BETH," her entire demeanor had changed, becoming almost catatonic. All of her attention had locked onto the science she read and that's how Michael had left her. He'd not returned to the lab since. The ghouls were everywhere and he just couldn't take the chance that they'd find him…and then her…and then…game over.

Michael now sat in a white TV news van, watching Dr. Presser's house, wondering who it was that she'd brought home a few hours ago, wondering who the little Indian boy really was who'd been living with the doctor for weeks. He wondered if they were ghouls. He wondered if they were setting him up, using Dr. Presser, waiting for him to return, waiting to kill the man who'd uncovered their lies long ago and had finally found the proof. He wondered if anyone at the TV station was involved. Perhaps their willingness to give him a job was also a ruse. They'd too easily accepted his explanation about the Fox incident as having been caused by the unfortunate side effects of an anti-depressant drug. They'd too easily accepted his award-winning documentary as the only needed cross-reference for his reporting abilities. They'd too easily accepted his condition that he'd do no standups or anchor work or complete any assignments that required his face to be on camera. All they'd wanted was his propensity to gather information, particularly the investigative journalism skills that so few of their current employees possessed. Michael Arden wondered and worried about everything. He had to. Pitchfork Man was still out there, somewhere. The ghouls hid among the living and they were nearly impossible to detect anymore.

It was just before six-thirty and darkness had eclipsed Dr. Presser's house when the van's news radio crackled.

Michael, the dispatcher's voice said. *We need you back at the station, pronto. Some nutjob in Mexico is causing a panic. Please return immediately for a new assignment.*

"On my way," Michael said to the microphone, knowing that whatever they were about to ask him to do would be completed only if he had the time. Though she didn't know it, Dr. Presser needed him and he wasn't about to ignore the only person who could prove that Richard Manson was the Devil.

Billy almost fainted. It was because he was a Daykeeper that he did not drop right then and there. The history of Richard Manson and his mother, the connection to BethStar research, and the physical presence of Aaron all combined to make him swoon so badly that Aaron ran to his side to hold him steady.

"How…?" Billy gasped. "What…?" He choked on the word.

"Drink," Aaron said and lifted Billy's sweaty glass. "Forgive me." He patted Billy on the back and massaged one shoulder with a hearty grip.

"Aaron?" He turned in the chair while sipping from the glass. "Is it really you?" He looked at his mother.

"I was going to tell you," she said. "But there were more important things to say first."

Billy stood, grabbed both of Aaron's shoulders and held them at arm's length. The boy had grown much taller and his thin stature had filled into a stout thirteen-year-old. "What are you doing here?"

"The same as you," he said and initiated a hug which Billy overwhelmingly accepted. "Trying to save the world."

They separated and Billy asked, "How did you find me?"

"I found your mother. Sons always return to their mothers." There was something about him that was much older, Billy thought. A young wisdom. "My father asked me to bring something to you."

Billy blinked and shook his head. "But he is…"

"Nothing ever dies," Aaron reminded him and pointed at his head. "He still visits me, just like he still visits you."

Elizabeth walked to the patio door and opened it. "How about a little Christmas Eve cheer?" she said. "While you two reconnect."

Billy sat with Aaron at the kitchen table while his mother tuned her stereo to a radio station that played nonstop holiday music, then started a batch of Christmas tree cookies. She'd already made the dough and she rolled it out as Aaron began to recount his life over the past three years. Another Hopi elder, Will Crossbear, had taken him in and he'd started high school a year early. He told Billy that Sedona had been changing since he'd seen him last, that new leaders had taken over the city and the school systems seemed a little off, the studies directed away from science and math and more toward new history books that had been purchased just that year, history books that had omitted some important facts that Aaron had learned from Lax. Then he told Billy about the Great Hall of the Anasazi, about how Phoenix International and the new city leadership had finally defeated the Sedona electorate and had secured rights to the red rock area surrounding Lee Mountain. He told Billy and his mother (who joined them at the table after the Christmas cookies were done), how he'd gone into the underground sanctuary because the spirit of Lax had told him to, how that same spirit had guided him down the giant ceiba tree and into the Wayeb Chamber. He was to retrieve something before Richard Manson destroyed all evidence that the Great Hall ever existed and he'd escaped the sanctuary moments before the demolition crews had blown apart a thousand years of history.

"What did he ask you to get?" Billy said.

Aaron reached into his pocket and set two stone relics on the table next to the plate of green-sprinkled cookies. Billy knew immediately where they'd come from: the right side of the temple wall where Lax had said the glyphs of past Daykeepers had been enshrined forever. One of the hand-sized stone tablets was etched in the form of a jaguar. The other was etched with the bird glyph that Billy had seen just after Lax had died.

Billy pointed at the bird. "Lax," he whispered. "His nahual?"

Aaron nodded and pointed at the jaguar. "And his sister. She is of the land. He is of the sky." Aaron's attention quickly shifted to Billy's neck and he reached forward to grab the necklace that Cooper had given him. He gently pulled it forward and the Djed amulet popped from the neckline of Billy's National Geographic T-shirt. "And you," he continued. "The dolphin. The spirit of the water."

"Is that what Lax wanted you to tell me?"

Aaron nodded again. "That...and many more things. But we have to wait for the other who is going to help us."

Elizabeth quickly understood. "You mean Arden."

"Yes."

"What about Arden?" Billy interjected. "I thought he was a crazy man that tried to kill someone on TV."

"It wasn't his fault," his mother countered. "It was the BethStar. And I'm going to prove it."

"I knew it," Billy said and slapped the table. One cookie rumbled off its plate. "But that stuff is just about everywhere, now. How are we going to stop it…to stop HIM?"

"That's my next task," his mother said.

At that moment, a top-of-the-hour news break came on the radio station.

According to Richard Manson, billionaire owner of Phoenix International and creator of the popular health pill BethStar, the world is going to end in one year.

All three of them looked at each other, then Elizabeth stood and walked to her TV flat screen. When she turned it on, the same breaking news story was on CNN. A recording of Manson's announcement from the front of the Phoenix Tower played through commentary by the CNN news staff. Interspersed in the talk were clips of live feeds from several cities and towns across the world. Some video showed panic and mayhem while others promoted callous disregard for such apocalyptic banter. In one shot from the Phoenix Tower plaza, the CNN camera panned the suffocating audience as Manson revealed his truth, and stopped for a moment on a woman in the audience who was flipping off the speaker.

"Cooper," Billy said, pointing at the screen. "And Sebastian and John. Thank God they made it."

0-TIME: PREDICATE

CREATION OF MAN

Never fear words. Only fear the men who say them.

-Anonymous

Cooper's father had hated just about all of the American men from the naval base, but as far as Seaman Danny Kerskker was concerned, he'd absolutely despised that son-of-a-bitch. It was evident in the way her Papa's eyes immediately went bloodshot every time Kerskker came around. "Mango Bajito," he'd call him—a punkass, low-life liar whom he wanted nowhere near his only daughter. Though her Mama had never really confessed, Cooper had always suspected that she hated him just as much as did Papa but that her concern for Cooper's feelings always trumped any display of her own emotions. That all ended the day Kerskker proposed and took Cooper from her home to live with him in Texas.

"He's no good," Papa had warned. "He'll drop you and then you'll want to come home and there will be no home for you here."

Kerskker had been waiting outside the family's house, tapping an indifferent foot with his indifferent attitude that always leaned toward what was best for Kerskker before considering anything else. Too bad Cooper had not known that then. She'd been in love, not so much with the man as with his promises. She'd just turned eighteen and had graduated from high school the month before, and even with an education, she'd never thought her home in Ceiba would provide for the glamorous future that Kerskker had said awaited.

"You'll be in the great state of Texas where everything is possible," he'd promised. "And once I retire from the navy, we'll not have to work a day in our lives again."

Mango Bajito. Kerskker had proven that he was the poster boy for punkass liars.

Cooper never really understood why Kerskker had wanted to marry her, but she suspected that it was either because he thought that having a wife while serving in the military provided some kind of heightened self-status or, most likely, he'd done it out of pure spite for her father. Love had certainly not been the reason. He'd divorced her in Amarillo a month after they'd married, leaving Cooper alone in a foreign land and with a family that no longer wanted her home.

As a Puerto Rican, she was a legitimate U.S. citizen but the *Mango Bajito* had stolen her identification the morning he'd scurried out of town. She'd had to live as one of thousands of illegal immigrants, a beautiful, tan-skinned, eighteen-year-old girl whose only destiny was everything too unsavory to fathom.

Fortunately, Bonita Reyes had found her first.

The Reyes family had been an influential member of a dozen agricultural cooperatives in three southwestern states. Bonita was the wife of the family elder Carl Reyes who'd gained citizenship from Mexico because his father, ironically, had been a U.S. soldier in World War II. The family's controlling interests in cotton and corn and citrus had made them very rich but, because of their ancestry, had also made them the continual target of white farmers who'd kept them under scrutiny for hiring illegal immigrants, a practice that Carl had sworn against his entire life. Workers for all of the Reyes farming interests were hired by the book as far as Carl could control. Managers who'd been found to practice otherwise had been immediately fired (which was one point of argument that had consistently gotten claims against them thrown out of court).

The day after Kerskker had left her in an apartment with one month's rent past due, she'd started to look for a job, but the burger-flipping businesses and the janitorial businesses and the secretarial businesses had all turned her down for lack of proper ID. Within the following week, she'd learned how dirty and deceitful men other than Kerskker could be. With food gone and the sleazy landlord threatening eviction if she couldn't provide "other means of payment," Cooper had finally given into the temptation of becoming something called an exotic dancer. She could make a couple of hundred dollars a night if she really tried, the owner of the Amarillo Roadhouse had promised. He'd even given her front money to pay the rent and buy some food.

That first night in the Roadhouse had been, perhaps, the worst experience she'd ever had. Papa had always protected her from such things. Papa had always taught her right from wrong. Papa had told her about men like these, like Kerskker, who only wanted one thing.

Mango Bajitos, every one of them.

In an odd twist of fate, both for herself and for Carl Reyes, her performance that night would change both of their lives forever. Cooper would never again strip for any man that she did not love, and Carl would never again visit such establishments where women do.

As important as he was to the business of agriculture, the leader of the Reyes family had one great weakness: watching naked women dance. Bonita had expected this aberrant behavior for some time (as she would tell Cooper much later), but until she'd walked into the Roadhouse during Cooper's performance to find Carl folding a twenty dollar bill into her g-string, Bonita had always hoped she'd been wrong. When Bonita screamed his name, Carl had jumped with the folded twenty still gripped in his hand and had ripped the g-string right off of Cooper's body. Men had howled and the money had flown, but Cooper had fled the stage and had refused to return even though the Roadhouse's owner had threatened to withhold the advance he'd promised so that she could pay rent and eat.

"Get out there or get outta here," he'd said, trying to withhold a towel with which Cooper was trying to cover herself while gripping Cooper's thin wrist so hard she thought it might break.

"No! I don't think so," Bonita had countered. She'd come through the dressing room door with Carl in tow. "Hands off, pendejo. She is my daughter."

The owner had immediately released her, claiming no fault of his own and blaming the entire ordeal on "the little whore."

Bonita had walked over then, leaving Carl whose eyes had remained locked onto the grimy floor, and had wrapped Cooper in the towel. "Come on, honey. We're all outta here."

Bonita had saved her in many more ways than Bonita could have ever understood, and in a display of gratitude that also had the ancillary effect of preventing a life with a name like Cooper Kerskker, Cooper had asked to change her legal name to Reyes. The deed was a Band-Aid of sorts, one that could help heal the surface of her pain, but not its roots. The one thing that would never be soothed-over, thoroughly healed, or forgotten was Cooper's distrust in men. This scar would forever follow her into the Reyes' citrus groves where she'd earned enough money for college, onto Arizona State University where she'd acquired a degree in psychology, and into Sedona where her true love had become the cultures of so many American Indian tribes. Her sexual encounter with Christopher Cower had only served to magnify her distrust, even though her own willingness to give of herself had been for selfish reasons—to find the secrets of the Djed. To become invincible.

It was a cruel twist of irony, she thought. To have finally found invincibility in the only man she would ever love but who, by fate, was destined for a world much greater than one woman. She only hoped that the dolphins had saved him as much as he (and Bonita) had saved her.

Sunday, December 25, 2011

When Cooper exited the airport around noon with nothing except a backpack full of a couple of days clothing and Billy's two books, no one was there to meet her except panhandlers, and this was a relief. The flight had been quick, just a jump over the Caribbean, but it had given her enough time to reflect on the man she had to kill. As the plane had begun its final descent, however, she'd suddenly turned fearful that Manson had "told" Kerskker that she was coming and that Triple K would be waiting for her.

The airport had been converted from the Roosevelt Roads Naval Station where Kerskker had been stationed. The base had been closed since 2004 but its ghosts remained. As she walked the old barracks road, she passed the spot where Kerskker had lived. For a moment, she thought she saw his horse and black armor, but it was just a man pushing a tall cart inside the barracks that had been converted into a business warehouse storage facility. How long had it been? Fifteen years? Lots had changed and she wondered if anyone was left that she knew. She wondered if Papa would ignore her as he'd promised when she'd left. She wondered if her Mama would still take up for her. Fifteen years was plenty of time for healing and she needed them so much. She needed them to accept her. She needed them to know that she was going to erase the beast they loathed. She was going to make amends.

Ceiba was at the end of a mile-long stretch of highway and as she walked the asphalt, three cabs at different points in the journey pulled over on the shoulder. Rangy men with stained teeth asked her if she needed a ride. One even offered a free trip to town but Cooper was having none of it. With men like these mango bajitos, nothing was ever, truly free.

Her parents' house (if it, indeed, still existed) was located on the northeast side of the town near the water. She walked from the highway along an exit ramp that morphed into the town's main road, and acknowledged those people that acknowledged her, each one looking at her as if she was a stranger. Most of the buildings were just as she remembered—old world, turn of the nineteenth century, some with fresh paint, some looking like the flaking paint was all that held them together—but she recognized no one. Even the few elderly that sat on rickety wooden chairs outside their shops or their homes were unfamiliar. And that *was* creepy. It had only been fifteen years, not even one complete generation. She supposed that when the American naval base had dissolved, most of the prosperity of Ceiba had gone with it, including the people.

One landmark that had much improved was the baseball field where she'd gone as a kid to watch aspiring highschoolers play the sport that they believed would make them millions in the States. It's where she'd met Kerskker. He'd played for the Navy's team, right field, and he'd been half good at it. In fact, it was a long fly ball that he'd jumped the wall to snag that had initially brought them together. He'd pretty much fallen right in her lap.

A block wall that was painted grass green now surrounded the field. A sign mounted against the wall informed readers that jousting took place every Wednesday and Saturday night. She had to hoist herself up the sign's six-foot height to see inside, and was astonished to find that a baseball diamond wasn't the only thing landscaped into the playing surface. In the gap between second base and centerfield was a jousting run. Grass had been trampled into clumps of hard earth along the opposing horse tracks, and on each end of the jousting line were tall flag poles with the crests of opposing knights hanging from each. This was Kerskker's new world and his new field of play.

"'Scuse me."

The voice was plainly American and had an East Coast wang to it. Cooper dropped from the wall and turned around.

"You live in these parts?" The woman looked to be in her early twenties, a brunette with shoulder length hair who wore a black pantsuit in the humid Puerto Rican sun. Cooper remained silent and gave the woman a look as if she didn't understand English.

"Do you know anything about full contact jousting?"

Cooper continued staring at her.

"I'm with a news crew from New York…in the United States."

Cooper smiled.

"Yes. New York. We're looking for someone who can tell us about Triple K."

Cooper smiled even wider.

"You know Triple K? The king of the joust?"

Cooper nodded.

"Can you tell me where he is?"

Cooper kept smiling.

"Donde es Triple K?"

The reporter's attempted accent was horrible, sounding more like "donny is," but Cooper pointed toward the middle of town anyway. "Es en La Ceiba," she said.

The woman's expression turned into frustration. "I know that, but where in La Ceiba?"

"Es en La Ceiba," Cooper repeated.

The woman threw her hands in the air and walked away. "Jesus Christ," she said. "Doesn't anyone speak freakin English around here?" She joined a man who was about her same age that was standing near the entrance to the field. She pointed at Cooper and shrugged her shoulders, then the two got into a blue sedan and drove off.

Cooper thanked her instincts for not saying anything to the woman. The last thing she needed was the media. It was interesting that a New York news team had come to Puerto Rico just because of a local who was good at playing a local sport. She supposed that the real reason for the media interest was Kerskker's dagger. It was identical to the one Manson had shown the world during his news conference the night before.

Cooper left the ball field and continued along the outskirts of the city. After the encounter with the news woman, she suddenly felt fortunate that she'd not run into anyone she knew. It was best that only her Mama, her Papa and Kerskker (who, as a cubit, was connected to Manson) knew she was there.

She walked along dirt paths that were puddled in some spots through short, tropical greenery that inundated the east coast of Puerto Rico; there was no housing here since the sea level made living too risky when the tropical waves hit the island. The trampled byways reminded her of her youth, of traveling similar paths on her way to school and to the market and to work. Her Mama would accompany her on some of the journeys, particularly in the last year after she and Kerskker had started dating. Papa had always voiced his hatred for the Navy man but Mama, the devout Christian that she was, had never really said much. She'd "voiced" her opinions through her actions, by changing the subject at the dinner table, or handing Cooper a box of tissue when her father upset her, or walking to town with her on trampled wet paths meant more for frolicking children in search of imaginary adventures. Of course, as it had turned out, everything her Papa had ever said, every mean, hated word, had been absolutely true. Kerskker *had* killed her, though not in body but certainly in spirit. At least up until Billy Jo Presser had entered her life.

In the distance, Cooper saw the splashing crests of Puerto Medio Mundo, a popular spot for kayakers since the water was mostly flat and the regulations for boating in the port were quite lenient. Her parents' house was just a few thousand yards away from the water, sitting pretty much by itself in an area of tropical bush that had seen its share of floods over the decades. Papa had built the place in its location, purposely. Land was cheap, city regulations were absent, neighbors were negligible, and the water, which her father had always adored, was near. The home was built atop a five-foot foundation and it had rarely been the case that storm surges entered the living spaces. Papa had always been a smart man. Unfortunately, Cooper, like most children, never really understood her father's intelligence until she'd lived as an adult and had experienced life's hardships.

The dirt path led directly to a muddy front road that dead-ended at the house and as Cooper stood in front of the dirty, single-story, white clapboard house, she habitually opened the aluminum mailbox to retrieve its contents (something she always did as a kid). Only a single envelope was inside. The Christmas stamp on it was postmarked from the neighboring town of Fajardo and the return address was that of the Caribbean Medical Center. She took the letter and ascended the steps to her parents' home. She didn't knock, though she felt obligated to do so. It was Christmas and she was her parents' gift, a daughter who'd returned home to mend the ties of a life almost lost.

"Mama," she said as she entered. "Papa." The house was dead quiet. She roamed through the front living room, comforted by the familiar surroundings: Mama's wooden rocking chair and the red, knitted blanket draped over one arm; the rose pedal patterned couch with the same green and brown pillows she remembered throwing in temper tantrums as a child; the oil painting of Jesus Christ and his disciple, Peter. The evergreen striped wallpaper had peeled a bit more and the wooden floors had gathered a few more scratches, but for the most part, the living room was just as she'd left it almost fifteen years ago.

It wasn't odd that no one was home. What *was* odd was that there were no smells emanating from the kitchen. Mama had habitually prepared something every day: bread, jams, stews, roasts, cakes or cookies. Cooper couldn't remember a day when the house didn't smell good. But there was nothing except the gentle waft of sea salt and wetness. She walked into the kitchen which was rather small for the work that was done it. The range had been replaced with one that was less rustic and a microwave now sat on the small countertop, but, again, nothing else was much different. Even the old, laminated, metal table still suffocated one side of the kitchen and the same bowl of fake fruit sat in its center. She grabbed the banana because it looked so real, sniffed it, pinched it, replaced it, then dropped the envelope she'd taken from the mailbox beside it.

She opened the back door and it squeaked as she swung it wide and pushed through the screen door behind it. A rush of Caribbean air pressed her strawberry locks against her forehead and she stood there for a moment, breathing deeply, exhaling completely and thinking: where were her parents? It was Christmas and they were not home. There were only a few people she knew that they called friends and none of them lived in Ceiba. She assumed they must be with them and the thought made her sad. She'd missed so many Christmases all because of one man and one bad decision.

The yard had been kept, the tropical grass mowed, the brush trimmed back, the hip-high metal fence that locked in about forty yards of space in good repair. The old swing set was still back in the far right corner but its rusted surface made it look as if it had not been used in some time. One swing dangled at an angle and gently swayed with the wind, giving the impression that something invisible sat there. Cooper was immediately drawn to it. She descended the back steps and walked as if she was a child again, a half-skip in each step, her arms swinging freely, a tiny, happy grin scribbled on her cheeks. She grabbed the swing seat and sat, not caring about its rusty surface or that it might break the moment her weight settled into it. Her feet drug the grassy ground and she lifted them to start a gentle motion. Memories of childhood immediately assaulted her and she smiled. There'd been lots of good times, lots of simple times, lots of times that she wished she could return to, all the days before she'd grown up and obnoxiously believed she knew more than her parents. She stared at the moving ground, wondering where they were, and noticed something out of place on the other side of the yard: something sticking out of the trim grass.

She dropped from the swing and slowly walked toward it. It looked like a boulder at first but as she moved closer, she realized it was a tombstone. She shook her head, not wanting to know a truth that the tombstone seemed to scream at her. She didn't want to read the name chiseled into its surface. She prayed that it was not true. And then the tears fell like a storm.

Fellippe Juan Andaho
Born July 12, 1948
Into the arms of Jesus October 29, 2011

Her father had died just a couple of months ago and she'd never known. She dropped to her knees and lowered her forehead against the stone and the tears dropped from her cheeks and onto the single, lively red rose planted in front of the marker. She sobbed uncontrollably for five full minutes before she jumped and screamed because someone grabbed her from behind.

"Cooper?" the young female voice asked. "Is it really you?"

When she turned around, Cooper fell backward against the tombstone and her backpack crushed the rose. The wash of tears made it hard to see the woman's face and she squinted hard to flush them away. A hand was in front of her and she grabbed it.

"I am sorry," the woman said, helping Cooper to her feet. "You did not know. I wish I would have gotten here a little sooner."

Cooper wiped her face with the back of her hand. "What happened? And who are you?"

"I am watching the house for your Mama." The woman wasn't much out of her teens. "You don't remember me do you? I am Marianna. The daughter of your Papa's best friend."

It took Cooper a moment to find the face in her memory. "You were only five the last time I saw you."

"Sí. And you were going to Texas if I remember."

"What happened to Papa and where is Mama?"

"I really don't know how he died. Your Mama never said. She got sick shortly after and has been in the hospital since." Marianna grabbed both of Cooper's arms to hold her steady. "She has the leukemia." Cooper fell into Marianna's grasp. "I know. Shhhh." She patted the back of Cooper's head. "I will take you to see her."

Cooper pulled back and attempted a grateful smile but it faltered. "I shouldn't have left," she said, sniffing. "I should have come back."

Marianna walked Cooper away from the grave and gently caressed her shoulder. "She said your name last night. It was the only thing she has said in over a month."

"She doesn't talk?"

Marianna shook her head as they went back into the house and into the living room where they stopped for moment in front of the painting of Christ and Peter. "No. She has been in a coma." This brought a few more tears from both Cooper and Marianna. "But after last night, I really believed you would be here today. I really did. Miracles still happen. Maybe all she needs is you."

For three days, Cooper stayed by her Mama's bedside, staring at every last inch of her face, watching the tubes feed her and listening to the monitors beep. She never talked, but Cooper wasn't going to give up. If her mother had said her name once, she might do it again, and this time Mama would know that her daughter had returned to her and wake up.

Sitting alone gave her plenty of time to think about the power of the Creation Dagger to heal and if, somehow, it could take the leukemia away from Mama. Her blind faith grew the more she thought about it, but the question remained. How was she going to get the dagger from a powerful cubit who had almost certainly been pre-warned that Cooper Reyes Andaho had returned home to kill the thing that had taken so much from her? How could she do it? There was really only one way. Challenge Kerskker to a joust.

She'd remembered the sign on the wall of the converted baseball field that promoted tournament action every Wednesday and Saturday night, and just yesterday, when Marianna had stopped in for her daily visit, Cooper had asked her to take her to the match.

Now, they were on their way. The sun had already set and the lights from the field blazed a beckoning invitation. Parking was phenomenally horrible as thousands flocked. Cooper didn't have a plan, but she was certain that Manson would help lead the inevitable confrontation.

She and Marianna entered through one of the side gates where there were fewer people, and Cooper was immediately confronted by a man who said he was a private usher for the "Invincible Triple K." He told them that Triple K had been anxiously awaiting their arrival and he escorted them to a row of cushioned seats that were right behind the flagman's stand. Spectators along the row seemed exceptionally affluent, wearing expensive clothing and sporting pieces of jewelry that were worth more, collectively, than the incomes of all the thousands of people around them. A woman with a mink shawl tapped Cooper's forearm.

"So, you're his chosen for tonight," she said, her wrinkled eyes sparkling blue irises that were strangely intoxicating. "I wish he would choose me…just once." She turned to her just-as-old girlfriend. "Age equals a whole lot of knowledge in the sack." They cackled together and she licked the heavy red lipstick that looked really disgusting on her prunish lips. Her diamond necklace bounced a rainbow of stadium light into both Cooper and Marianna's faces and Cooper shifted in her seat so that her body language helped eliminate any further conversation.

From the area where the first base dugouts had been, a line of seven men marched in unison down the first base line and into centerfield. Each was dressed in Middle Ages red coats and pants with gold piping and tassels, and each carried a long-stemmed trumpet. The stadium lights dimmed and a spotlight encircled the trumpeters as each turned in a slightly different direction so that their seven instruments pointed toward every section of spectator seating. They began blaring some Gaelic tune to set the mood and a public announcer accompanied them, first in English and then in Spanish.

> Ladies and gentlemen. Welcome to Wednesday night, Full…Contact…Jousting.

The trumpeters' blasts became overpowered by the volume of cheers from the stands. Then, one by one, the announcer introduced the evening's five jousters. Each entered the stadium under a spotlight, trotted from left to right field with lances held upright by their sides, then came to a halt next to the flag stand. Triple K, of course, was last and was greeted with much greater fanfare. The whole ordeal reminded Cooper of entertainment wrestling in the United States. She could almost hear the words "are you ready to rumble" though the announcer never actually said them.

> And now, the undisputed champion of champions, with a record
> of 45 wins and no losses, the king of the knight and of the day,
> the awesome power of Triple K.

She couldn't see his face until Kerskker rode an incredibly large, black horse all the way across the outfield then back to center, stopped right in front of her, and lifted his black helmet face shield. The two old rich women swooned and giggled and Cooper inched farther away from them until her shoulder squashed against Marianna's.

"I have something for you, Cooper," Kerskker said, holding his steed steady. "My rod and my staff shall comfort you."

The old woman next to her grabbed Cooper's arm and shook it. "You are the maiden. You are the maiden."

"Get off!" she said, loosing eye contact with Kerskker as she pushed the woman away. When she turned back, Kerskker was right in front of her, the height of his mount bringing his head almost level with hers. His attention was on the old woman and though he said nothing to her, the woman cowered and her expression molted into one of pure fright. He turned back to acknowledge Cooper.

"Me lady," he said almost inaudibly. "I would hope that you will join me after I get rid of these cocksuckers. We have much to catch up on. But ditch the young bitch." His shiny black helmet nodded in Marianna's direction then he kicked his horse and sped away.

"He is the one, isn't he?" Marianna asked, the fear in her face almost as complete as that which still washed over the old woman. "He's the one that took you away."

Cooper didn't answer because her mind was much too busy calculating. The chair she sat in…it was some kind of sacrificial gift seating for the victor of the tournament. The knight that wins gets the "fair maiden." It was all a part of the show. It was all a part of the marketing. And Cooper saw the spotlight heading her way two seconds before it landed on her. She turned, grabbed Marianna's hand, and led her across the row, into the aisle, and toward the steps that led to the exit. Boos came from everywhere. Men shouted more than women, mostly in Spanish, and mostly in the connotation of "whores." They mingled in with the crowd that was still entering the field and pushed through the mass. Marianna was apparently frazzled and Cooper hugged her close as they hunkered low and half-jogged to Marianna's car.

"That pendejo. He is a real jerk," Marianna said. "I know now why you left him."

"Jerk is not the word for it." Cooper hugged her again. "I want you to go back. There's something I still have to do."

"Please," Marianna said. "He is not a good man. He has lots of stories around him. Now I understand. Now I know they are true. Did you see him? He…"

"Por favor. I will get a taxi ride back and I promise that I will be with Mama tonight."

Marianna, reluctantly, left Cooper standing in the overcrowded parking lot and drove away.

Puerto Rican jousting festivities were not unlike that which were enjoyed by football fans in the U.S. Many tailgaters offered Cooper a chance to mingle and she had no problem finding one that was, in fact, mostly American. She drank only one beer out of the dozens that the male partygoers offered. Some of the wives in the group took an immediate liking to Cooper and protectively gave her a seat away from their drunken husbands near the media screen that was broadcasting the event. One of the wives took particular interest.

"I saw you out there," the woman said. "The spectacle had not found your seat, but the lighting was good enough. Why did you leave? You pretty much ruined the plan."

The woman reminded Cooper of Bonita Reyes but much more Americanized. "I didn't know there was a plan," she said. "I just wanted to watch a joust."

"You didn't come here alone. Where is Marianna?"

Cooper blinked and looked at the second bottle of Bud she had just grabbed from a frosty cooler. "You know Marianna?"

"Of course. I am her mother, Sandra."

Cooper scratched a thin rut into the palm of her hand as she tried to open the bottle. "You know how ridiculous that sounds? How could I and you and…"

Sandra shrugged. "I am as surprised as you, but you have to know that I never let my daughter go anywhere without my knowledge, particularly after what that man did to your father." She pointed at the media screen just as Kerskker de-horsed the first of his competition.

"What do you mean?" Cooper asked.

Sandra hugged Cooper. "You don't know, do you? Mari told me as much." The woman whom she'd known for less than ten minutes jerked her forward at arm's length. "He killed your father and, as such, he killed your mother."

The news wasn't particularly surprising but it made Cooper so mad, tears came to her eyes. She took a sip from the beer bottle but couldn't taste it. She glared at the media screen—at Kerskker, as his lance splintered against a second opponent who fell from his horse. She glared at the black knight, listened to the crowd cheering him, but she thought of Manson, about how he must have known that her father was already dead when he'd confronted her back in Merida. He'd wanted it to be a surprise. He'd wanted her anger to overtake common sense so that death would come much more quickly when she tried to get the dagger. "Thank you," Cooper finally said. "To you and your daughter for taking care of her."

"You're welcome but, really, it was my husband who was responsible. He and your father made a pact long ago, shortly after you left home, a verbal will if you will. The pact was that should your father ever die before you returned home, my husband would look after your mother until you returned."

Cooper's heart sank a few fathoms farther. "Papa expected me to return?" she asked.

The crowd in the stadium screamed again and Cooper looked up at the tailgater's media screen. Kerskker was trotting around the perimeter of the stadium seating, waving his lance at the crowd, while two of his opponents squared off. The metal-clad prick couldn't even let the other contestants have any of the spotlight, she thought. His cavorting around the outfield attracted all attention directly on him.

"Of course he did, dear," Sandra said. "Parents say things they don't always mean, too. You should know family is family." She knelt in front of Cooper. "He always loved you. As the years passed, his guilt grew until that so-of-a-bitch returned first." She pointed at Kerskker's LCD image. "That really was the crushing blow. In the last months, his insides drove him so crazy that he tried to kill Kerskker. Blamed himself for everything.

"Is that how he died? Guilt because of me?"

"He died because he was a man bent on revenge." Sandra's eyes locked onto Cooper's and she snatched the hand that held the beer bottle, took the bottle from her, set it on the graveled lot, then massaged her knuckles. "He would have done it, I think, whether you ever returned or not. Kerskker goaded him into it. He told your father that he'd made you a whore and was living off the money you made for him. He told your father that you'd said you hated him and that you wished he was dead. He called your father just about every degrading word men use to instigate fights."

"And Papa believed him?"

"Why wouldn't he? What else did he know? The real tragedy, though, is your mother.

Cooper cried. She wasn't sure if Sandra's intent had been this all along, but thinking of her Mama—lying there unable to speak, or to hear Cooper tell her how much she loved her or how much she was missed—was just too much. She hated crying in front of total strangers and the discontent worsened when two more of the female tailgaters walked over and asked if everything was okay.

On the media screen, Kerskker rode his horse to the chairs that she and Mari had vacated and said into a microphone, "Where are you my fair maiden? Triple K will be waiting." He looked directly into the camera.

"You can't do it," Sandra whispered so the other wives couldn't hear. She wiped Cooper's cheeks with a napkin that smelled like barbeque sauce. "He'll kill you, too."

Cooper sniffed and concentrated on not crying. "Will you be here until the match is over?"

Sandra nodded.

"Do you mind if I stay until then?"

"Absolutely. I'm taking you back with me."

"You don't need to…"

"My promise to your Mama." Sandra patted her hand and noticed the djed tattoo with the snake fang scars. "Very strange. Que es?"

"A reminder of *my promise* to someone I care a whole lot about."

Most of the tailgating accessories had been put away and Sandra was just about ready to leave when Triple K appeared a hundred feet away. He exited through the field's side gates and into the parking lot, and was immediately smothered by a drove of fans, bodyguards and news people. Cooper recognized the woman reporter from New York who was closest to the undefeated knight. Kerskker's bodyguards pushed the screaming fans so that a circle of space opened for the New York camera crews to capture the interview.

"'Bout ready?" Sandra asked.

"Just a moment, please." Cooper said. The New York reporter finished her standup for the cameras then lowered her microphone as the camera crew turned off their equipment. Kerskker then leaned forward and whispered something to the reporter who drew back. Kerskker grabbed her arm and pulled her closer, his lips almost touching one ear. This time he pointed directly at Cooper. The reporter followed his finger and lifted a hand to her forehead as if shading some invisible light source. The reporter started walking in her direction and Cooper calmly said to Sandra, "Let's get out of here."

Sandra convinced Cooper to come to her home in Fajardo instead of returning to the hospital. She told Cooper that she looked as if she'd not slept in days, that she could hear Cooper's stomach growling for a good, home-cooked meal and, that the hospital had instruction to call her house if her Mama's condition changed. Still, it had been hard for Cooper to accept. She'd taken a big enough chance just going to the joust. What if her mother did wake up and no one was there? What if she did call out for her daughter and Cooper missed her only chance to tell her Mama all the things she not said in the last fifteen years? Again, she'd have to go on blind faith. Again, she'd have to trust the unknown future and truly believe that if her mother did come out of the coma, she'd be there when it happened. She told Sandra that she'd accept the offer, but that she would not burden them any longer once Thursday morning came.

As promised, Sandra Manana and her daughter provided wonderful food and a comfortable bed. Carlos Manana was absent from dinner and Sandra said that it was not unusual for her husband to stay the night on the water. Snapper and tuna was hard to catch since the industry had dried up in the last decade, and efforts to do so often required many days away from home to bring in a profitable catch. Cooper accepted the explanation, but she really believed that Carlos had not come home because of her. How could Carlos face the child who had put his best friend through so much hell?

Cooper never said as much to Sandra when she was dropped off at the hospital the next morning, but only offered thank yous and goodbyes. Sandra told her that Mari would continue checking on her parents' house and Cooper told Sandra that if anything changed with her Mama, she'd call immediately.

As soon as she entered the hospital, she heard the whispers and noticed the stares from some of the hospital staff, mostly the women. When she exited the elevator on the second floor, the morning nurse immediately came up to her. The nurse was about Mari's age and her eyes were wild with girlish excitement. She struggled with her English but Cooper understood just fine.

"Señorita. It is true? You are Triple K's…" she struggled for the right word. "You are his before wife?"

"Who told you that?" Cooper asked.

"It is on the TV. And she came here last night for you."

"Who came here?"

"The TV woman."

Now Cooper knew what Kerskker had whispered to the reporter after the match. He'd started a bunch of rumors. He'd started driving attention in Cooper's direction. "If she comes here again, tell her Nadie—No One! is allowed in that room, sí?"

The nurse nodded, but Cooper could tell that she had absolutely no idea what to say or do. She turned and walked toward the nurses' station farther down the hall as Cooper entered her mother's room, closed the door and locked it.

For the next two days, while Cooper stayed with her mother, her story (the one that Kerskker had cooked up about her) circulated throughout Puerto Rico and, with the influence of the New York news crew, much of the world. The hospital had been inundated with requests to interview Cooper, but the local police had denied them all because, one, the doctors had demanded it and, two, part of Kerskker's story had revealed that Cooper was one of the Tulum Terrorists who'd blasted her way out of the ruins three years ago. The police had no proof but until they did (or found Kerskker to be a liar), Cooper was in their custody. The police chief had placed guards outside her Mama's door, but that had not stopped one paparazzi miscreant who had disguised himself as an orderly and had gained access for two minutes before Cooper screamed to have him removed.

The police chief was another matter altogether. Cooper believed that he was either being manipulated with cash by Kerskker, or was, in fact, a cubit himself. This became more apparent late New Year's Eve when Kerskker was allowed into the hospital room after Cooper had explicitly told everyone that, of all the people who were absolutely forbidden inside, it was Triple K. She'd told the authorities that Triple K had abused her in their previous relationship and that he might do so again.

When the mango bajito entered, Cooper was leaning over her Mama because she thought she'd heard her speak.

"Cooper Reyes. Whatever happened to Kerskker? Remember…till death do us part?"

His voice immediately made the orange juice she'd drank just moments before rise into her throat. When she turned around, she hardly recognized him. His short hair had been bleached white in streaks that were layered against his natural auburn strands. His goatee was pure white and his cheeks were sunken, giving his chin a pronounced squareness. He wasn't bad looking to anyone who didn't know he was a cubit. The good thing was that his eyes were not currently occupied by Manson's influence. Their hazel brown translucence was exactly as she'd remembered the night before he had left her stranded in Amarillo. "You know why I returned home," she said as a matter of fact. "To part us permanently."

"Yes…how exciting," Kerskker said, walking closer. "How do you plan on doing such a thing?"

"I plan on ramming that dagger right up your dead asshole."

"Coop—you don't mind if I call you that do you?"

"You're going to do whatever you want to no matter what."

"True, true. But we can be civilized for tonight, can't we? I mean, it's almost twenty-twelve." He pointed at the television where Ryan Seacrest was introducing the next act in Times Square.

"You fucking suck," she said.

"No. I'm a cubit. Vampires are for adolescent nut jobs who have no real imagination."

Cooper stood up straight, her hand still clasped in her Mama's limp grip. "Why Papa? You didn't have to kill him. What purpose was there in that?"

"No purpose. I did it…well, because I just couldn't control myself."

Cooper suddenly felt something between her fingers—her Mama's hand—she thought she felt some surge of strength against her pinky. She looked down but the pressure quickly dissipated. When she looked back up, she gasped. Kerskker's eyes were now red as blood and the silver sparkles raged at their centers.

"I killed him because it was fun," Manson said through Kerskker's lips. "I killed him just to piss you off. How am I doing?"

"Go to hell."

"Funny you should mention that. It's where we're all headed unless you can take the dagger from me." From behind Kerskker's back, Manson produced the Creation of Man Dagger and waved it in front of her just as her Mama's grip, again, pressed against her fingers. She didn't look down this time but Manson saw the muscles flex. "You ever consider that one of these might cure cancer? They can do just about everything else."

"I don't know," Cooper lied, knowing that Manson was fucking with her again. "Why don't we try it and find out?" She offered her free hand to him. "We'll call it even for murdering my Papa."

Kerskker's mouth opened wide and Manson bellowed laughter. "Tell you what. I'll give you a chance, but you gotta earn it."

"I'm listening."

"A joust," Manson snickered. "Now, don't tell me the thought hasn't crossed your mind. Just think of it. Pissed off wife of abusive husband returns for revenge. The wife is one of the Tulum Terrorists and the husband is Triple K himself."

"Agreed…but only on my terms."

Manson giggled through Kerskker's lips. "You know, when I saw you at the joust, I never realized how much spunk you really do have. What's the terms?" And then he added under his breath, "This is getting good."

"Not on the jousting field and with no crowds or media or hoopla of any kind."

"Okay. So, you wanna do it right here in front of your comatose Mama?"

Cooper controlled her welling anger. "Better. Behind my parents' house so my father can watch me kill you."

"Touching. So goddamned ethereal of you. Tell you what. I'll agree if you'll let me bury you and your mother as far away from him as possible."

"I'm not going to have to worry about that. Monday evening good for you? You will be sporting and give me a day to practice."

"Of course. I'll even provide you with a trainer and gear. See, I *can* be reasonable."

"I highly doubt that." Cooper squeezed her Mama's hand. "Remember. Just the two of us. Monday at midnight."

Manson cackled once again and replaced the dagger behind Kerskker's back. "Perfect. Hope you get encouragement from your mommy." He turned around and for a fraction of a second, Cooper almost leaped for the white haft of the dagger that stuck out of his waistband. "I'll have an escort for you tomorrow to take you to my private training facility," he said. "No tricks. I promise." Then Kerskker left.

It was just minutes before the ball dropped when Mama woke from her coma. Cooper had been sitting right beside her, their hands clasped tightly from the moment Kerskker (and Manson) had left. She'd been contemplating how heavy the armor would be, how awkward the lance would be to hold in front of her, how she could control a mighty horse running at thirty miles an hour. Mama had jerked her hand hard which broke Cooper from thought. When Cooper looked down, Mama's dark brown eyes were staring straight at her and this made Cooper involuntarily yelp.

"The light," Mama said. "I saw the light."

Cooper patted her hand then touched her face. "Mama. I love you so much."

"The light," she repeated. "It is so beautiful. I will see you there one day."

Cooper's lips trembled. "Please, Mama. Be still."

"You have to do it. Here. I have been waiting many years to give this to you."

Behind Cooper, Ryan Seacrest counted down from ten. Cooper grabbed the remote and turned him off. When she turned back around, Mama had, in her lap, a wooden box that was about a foot long and a third as wide. It was her trinket box that had been hand-carved out of a native ceiba tree. She'd had it since before Cooper was born. In it, she'd stored all of her important memories including costume jewelry worn as a child and a couple of keepsakes from when she and Fellippe had met. "You carry it for luck," she said. "You put your memories inside."

Cooper wondered from where Mama had produced the box. In all of the days she'd been in the room, Cooper had never seen it. She suspected that Mama had kept it under the bed sheets, which made a lot of sense. In times of trouble, she'd always slept with it for good luck.

Mama tried to raise her head but could not. "You remember when you were a little girl and Papa took you fishing for the first time?"

"Mama, please," Cooper pleaded.

"You remember what happened?"

Cooper tried to conjure the memory but it had been so long ago."

"Remember," Mama repeated and placed the trinket box in Cooper's free hand.

The monitors stopped beeping and the tubes stopped feeding and the grip went limp as Mama died.

When Cooper was only five years old, her father took her out on the Caribbean for the first time. The boat was nothing more than a small fishing skiff, but it had been sufficient for the short distance he'd planned for them. He was going to show her how to string a line and bait a hook and cast without ripping her skin open or falling overboard. He'd not really expected to "catch" anything and, in fact, used bait that was more freshwater appropriate than Caribbean.

Once they were a mile offshore, he baited and cast and reeled in nothing, then repeated the process another dozen times, trying to maintain the young girl's attention longer than a few minutes. Young Cooper was fascinated more by the white caps, pointing at them and smiling and saying how beautiful they were. Then it came time for her to try. To her Papa's amazement, his little girl zipped out a line twenty feet on the first try. "Excelente, niña," proud Papa said as a fish took the bait.

A young, thirty-pound albacore jerked the line so hard, niña Cooper's hand got caught between the line, the reel, and the rod, and overboard she went. Her father had already taught her to swim but he dove in right after her. Fortunately, the fishing rod released her hand the moment she hit the pretty little white caps she'd been adoring all afternoon. Unfortunately, a passing tiger shark turned toward the sudden meal that splashed atop the water.

"Darse un baño, niña," Papa had yelled. "Swim!"

Cooper had turned to see what was upsetting Papa so much. The shark fin was ten yards from her, but she had not yet learned to be afraid of it. She bobbed without moving as Papa yanked her arm. When the shark was within striking distance, the fin suddenly disappeared. It had been gaining speed, slicing through the water like a razor blade, and then it was just gone.

Once Papa and niña Cooper was aboard the boat, they looked back into the water. The shark wasn't there but the dolphin that had saved their lives was.

Cooper had never understood the magnitude of what had happened, and no one had ever explained it to her. She'd fallen in the water and had watched a beautiful dolphin jump across pretty white waves. Once Mama had found out, she'd never let on how horrified she'd been and the whole incident had been forgotten.

Until the moment before she died.

It was Monday night. They'd buried Mama next to her husband in the backyard, yesterday morning, New Year's Day. It had been quick and without anyone but the doctors knowing that she'd died. When Kerskker's police chief bodyguards had escorted Cooper to his private training facility, Sandra and Mari had snuck the body out along with Cooper's backpack that still contained Billy's books. Cooper was going to miss the burial, but that was better than having the entire world present. Besides, now both of her parents would watch, together, as Cooper killed their greatest nemesis, permanently.

In a way, it was fitting. The Black Knight against the Bolt of Lightning. That's what she'd called herself because the trainers had told her that no knight fights nameless. The armor had been easier to manage than she'd imagined. She'd even been as one with the horse, though it was twice as large and three times more powerful than anything she'd ridden while living with Bonita Reyes. The problem point was the lance. It felt much too awkward just holding it upright, let alone at the horizontal striking position needed to unhorse Triple K. In practice, she'd only been able to lift it against the dummy target once and for only a second.

But the time had come, ready or not. She'd have to whack the hell out of him, drop him to the ground, and go for the dagger she hoped he still kept just above the waistline in the back of his suit of armor. She'd need a miracle, a heavy dose of blind faith, and the luck of her Mama's trinket box which she'd strapped to the saddle of her horse.

The jousting crew had arrived around ten o'clock to set up the torches and the fence that would mark the jousting line a couple of dozen yards from the sea port. A storm was expected and if it hit before they started, the torches would get doused, so the crew had a backup lot of charged solar-powered lanterns. These weren't as "Middle Aged" as big, flaming torches, but there were no rainouts in jousting. Besides, how were the dozen reporters who showed up ten minutes before midnight going to get their story? Yes, Manson had lied—imagine that. The world was going to watch Triple K lose his first match and his cubited life and, quite frankly, that was fine with Cooper. Perhaps heaven had a rewind button that her Mama and Papa could play over and over again.

There was no grandiose stadium presentation, no overbearing announcer, no box seating with fair maidens waiting for their Triple K hero—just Cooper on a tan horse gilded with ivory cloth and metal, and Kerskker on his black horse with red crests. Triple K's eyes boiled blood red—Manson wasn't going to miss this front seat chance for the world.

The news crews lined up just beyond the graves. The reporter from New York was there, as was the orderly paparazzi that had snuck into Mama's room. Cooper noticed a third familiar face as well: the cubited kid with the smartphone that had recorded Kerskker killing the Golden Knight with the Creation Dagger, the same recording that Manson had shown her Christmas Eve on the fortieth floor of the Phoenix Tower. Cooper guessed that he was there for more than smartphone archiving and she immediately trotted up to him, lowered her lance at his eyeball, and warned him that if he got involved, he'd lose more than an eye. The cubit only laughed and the New York news crew caught it all on camera. Cooper played it up. "That goes for all of you. Stay back and stay out of it or none of you will leave here alive." As if understanding her intent, her horse reared up and kicked both legs toward the smartphone cubit in unison with the first bolt of lightning that jagged behind them. Cameras flashed as the thunder roared.

A light rain began as the two horses took their marks on either end of the jousting fence. Winds blew the torch flames diagonally. Manson lifted Kerskker's lance to signal that he was ready; his red eyes glowed through the slits in the knight's helmet. Cooper lifted her lance assuredly, but could already feel its weighted strain on her right forearm. She rubbed Mama's trinket box with her left fist as the fingers strangled the reins, and looked over her shoulder at her parents' shadowy graves. The smartphone cubit yelled, "Let's get on with it," then Manson kicked Kerskker's horse and raced toward her.

Cooper kicked and her horse accelerated so fast, she almost fell. Manson's eyes closed in and constantly blinked because of the rain. On the first pass, both of them missed. Kerskker's lance glanced off Cooper's shoulder. Cooper had been unable to even lift her weapon to the appropriate angle.

The rain fell harder. The torch near the center of the joust line died almost completely, leaving a dark patch on Cooper's side. Perhaps she could use it as an advantage, she thought. Manson wasn't the real jouster, Kerskker was. With his control over Triple K's body, the true, undefeated knight was not a hundred percent. Additionally, the back of Cooper's right wrist began to itch incredibly bad, and when she looked down, from out of the metal sleeve that encapsulated her hand, was a greenish glow—the djed tattoo; it had come alive. Cooper kicked her horse to time its run so that they would intersect with the torch that now died.

Manson guided Kerskker's horse to full speed and entered the dark patch. This time, her forearm did not deny her. This time the lance lowered perfectly horizontal. She disappeared into shadow for the fraction of a second it took to land her point in Kerskker's chest. In that same fraction of time, every ounce of oxygen blew out of Cooper's lungs as if she'd hit a wall. Her body flipped into the rainy air and crumpled in a metal heap onto wet earth. Blood ran into her eyes and mouth. She gasped for breath and blew red bubbles. For a moment, she thought her back was broken, but then one leg moved. Raindrops drizzled into the eye slits of her helmet and she tried to turn her head but couldn't. Someone had a hold of it. Her faceplate was lifted, and Kerskker's head blocked the rain. Manson was no longer in him but that meant nothing. He was going to kill her and he said as much at that moment. "You wanted the dagger. Well, here it…" When Kerskker reached behind his back, his hand came up empty. He threw his helmet off and turned away to scuttle across wet grass, his hands searching for the one thing that had made him invincible.

Cooper turned on her side just in time to see the smartphone cubit's eyes turn red. In his hand was the dagger and he snuck up behind Kerskker and stabbed him in the back of the head. "You couldn't even kill one stupid little whore," he said to the withering pile of ash and bone. "And you almost let her have the dagger." Manson turned the smartphone kid to face the cameras. "If Triple K can't have it then nobody will." He then pivoted toward the sea, reared back, and launched the dagger just as Cooper stabbed him in the small of his back with her lance. The dagger lost its intended altitude and landed somewhere in the dark, bushy jungle between the torches and the water. She tried to run but could only kneel. The New York news woman, however, sprinted wildly through the wet vegetation in the direction that the dagger had flown. Cooper's horse stood beside her and she pulled herself up, her body not centered on the saddle, as the horse took off and easily outdistanced the news woman. Cooper nearly fell, but caught the strap that she'd used to tie Mama's trinket box to the saddle, and this kept her atop the saddle for an additional fifty feet before the strap snapped and she fell with the trinket box in hand.

Blind faith was all that she'd needed and blind faith came through again. The dagger rested just a foot away. She wrested the body armor from her torso, opened the trinket box, and maneuvered the dagger into it. She then ran as far as her aching back would allow, spitting away rain-mixed blood that drooled down from the cut in her forehead. She had just one option and she took it.

The storm now opened up in sheets and it provided camouflage as Cooper dove into the sea. Rain pelted the water's surface so hard she could hardly breathe. All she had to do, she thought, was to follow the shoreline until she was out of sight, but the wading, while holding onto the trinket box as the rain came straight up into her nose, was nearly impossible.

That's when Billy's nahual showed up. It was as if he'd sent it himself. The dolphin's fin caught Cooper's free hand and it moved her slowly around the perimeter of land, taking its time, randomly cackling with its unique laugh until almost thirty minutes later, when the storm had finally cleared and Cooper heard a familiar voice. She looked up from the water to see Marianna's face staring down at her. Mother Sandra and father Carlos stood in the boat beside her.

The Mananas had been watching the entire event from the safety of Puerto Medio Mundo, and when Carlos' hand swung down and grabbed Cooper's, they were both saved. He hoisted her into the boat and a group hug ensued. Behind them, the dolphin joined in and though she would never tell a living soul, Cooper swore she heard it say, "Remember."

The dolphin and her father's best friend had, once again, saved her from the shark.

0-TIME: PREDICATE

CREATION OF RELIGION

Beloved, do not be surprised at the fiery ordeal among you, which comes upon you for your testing, as though some strange thing were happening to you.

- Peter 4:12

Pickett's Crossing, Kansas
Friday, January 6, 2012

Sebastian just wanted a drink. Hard. A double. Forget the Cuervo—even a watered down, crappy rail tequila would have worked. Anything to quiet the adrenaline rush. Just one big swallow to help an old man forget that he'd just robbed the Pickett's Crossing sheriff's house.

Before entering the bar, he straightened his appearance, pulling the waistline of his blue jeans up while dusting off both knees. He scratched what peanut butter remained from one long sleeve of his forest green plaid shirt and looked once more behind and around, peering for those he thought were following him (seemed like someone was always following him) just as dusk fell beyond Kansas Route 22 and acres of winter-dead farmland. He'd ran into the sheriff's kitchen table while groping in the darkness and had not known that he'd swiped the sandwich with his elbow until just a few minutes ago. Now he worried that a forgotten snack might be his undoing. A crazy thought perhaps, but this was a small town bar in a small town community that he'd found to be so tightly knit even peanut butter might be recognized, particularly if it came from the sheriff's house.

Static music from within the bar greeted Sebastian through an intercom near the front door. When he pressed the intercom's button, no one said anything; there was only the crackled filter of live music. A buzzer sounded and the door unlocked with a click.

The band at the back of the wide open room was in the second chorus of *Proud Mary.*

Big wheel a keep on turnin'
Proud Mary keep on burnin'

"Five bucks," the doorman said, a bit of frosty smoke rolling from his lips as the outside chill invaded the bar. Sebastian had been in town for nearly two weeks and had yet to meet everyone at Big T's Bar. He didn't know the doorman.

"Must be a good band," Sebastian offered.

"All the way from Kansas City," the doorman said, studying Sebastian's posture. "Do I know you?"

"Probably." Sebastian pulled a five dollar bill from one pants pocket. "Been doing some research over at the Bender Farm."

The doorman's chaffed hand snatched the bill and placed it in a metal money box. "Yeah. I heard about that. Lookin' for something buried out there by that crazy Bender woman. Havin' much luck?"

Sebastian thought about the sheriff's house where the treasure had actually been found. The investigation at the Bender Farm was only a diversion. He absently scratched his elbow and another crumb of peanut butter dropped from the fabric. "No," he said and smiled. "Not sure that I'm going to. Thinkin' of heading out, actually."

"But decided you'd stop in for one more drink." The doorman returned his smile though Sebastian believed it was forced.

"Yes." Sebastian took a step past the doorman. "Best drinking hole this side of Pickett's Crossing."

The doorman grabbed his hand and Sebastian jumped with surprise. "Stamp for reentry," he said and pressed the rubber stamp of a red star onto the back of Sebastian's hand.

"Don't think I'll need it but thanks anyway."

"Enjoy." The doorman thumbed the buzzer to unlock the front door for a new guest.

Sebastian approached the bar on the left while the band took a break and the slow groove of *rolling on the river* was replaced by several dozen chattering voices. Someone laughed loudly and slapped a table.

"You know I'm not gonna serve ya," Big T said.

Sebastian stood between two empty stools. On the wall behind the bar was a flat screen television. A trivia game was in play. Babe Ruth was revealed as the answer and someone else slapped a table. Big T was the owner and bartender. He'd not served Sebastian a drop since finding out three days ago that the out-of-towner had gotten serious with the sheriff's housekeeper.

"Just one rail shot?" Sebastian asked, trying not to sound as if he was groveling. "It's my last night in town."

"So you'll be leaving Beaty then, and you'll not be coming back?" Big T leaned forward, halving the distance across the top of the bar. His T-shirt was at least two sizes too small which made his torso look so much bigger than it really was. He lifted one hairy arm and pointed toward two men and a woman that were playing darts on the far side of the room.

Sebastian quickly weighed the situation. If he responded with what he really wanted to say—*Beaty is her own woman and can decide for herself*—he might not get that drink. Worse, he knew that Big T had been hot on the sheriff's housekeeper long before Sebastian Bondager ever pulled into town, and such an aggressive reply might bring Big T right over the bar. Sebastian was tougher than most men in their seventies, but certainly no match for a jealous behemoth of any age. He turned to look at the dart players. "Just want to say good-bye. Perhaps buy her a drink, too."

Big T hesitated. "Cuervo, isn't it?"

"And a scotch for Beaty."

Big T poured both drinks and set them on the bar. "Hope you had a wonderful time in our little town of sliced heaven."

Sebastian knew that Big T had meant to say *our little slice of heaven*, but he went with it. "Sliced heaven. You nailed it." He took the drinks and walked around the center of the room where most people sat at square tables playing trivia in groups of four. Someone yelled, "In your face," as Sebastian approached the dart players. To the right of the dartboard, two men were setting up the bar's only pool table for a new game.

"Scotch on the rocks," he said to Beaty who looked much younger than her fifty-five years. She held three steel-pointed darts and smiled when she turned to him. The corner of her lip quivered. She grabbed the drink.

"I've got mine," she said. "Did you get yours?" She took a sip and peered above the glass rim at the crowd.

Sebastian knew she wasn't talking about the double-shot of tequila that his lips had not yet touched. She was referring, of course, to his theft. He nodded then hesitantly raised his glass for a toast, thinking about Big T's eyes and how they were probably burning a hole right through his skull at that very moment. Beaty touched his glass with her own and they finished off the drinks in unison. He stepped forward and lowered his voice. "We gotta go now."

"You gotta go," one of the pool players said as he chalked his stick for the break.

Sebastian gently grabbed Beaty's arm and both of them took three steps away from the table. "After the game," Beaty insisted, her voice not as hushed. "Can't just leave in the middle of a game of 501, especially one that I'm winning."

"But what if he shows up?" Sebastian looked at the two other dart players. He knew neither.

"What if he does? He hasn't found out yet. I know that son-of-bitch well enough…"

"Your turn," said the tall man leaning against a wall near the dartboard. "One-eighty wins the game. You could do it in three darts but that means three trip-twenties."

"One hundred and eighty," the other male dart player said, doing a very good impression of an announcer from the professional English games he'd no doubt watched on television. "Better than my two hundred and fifty." Again, he added the accent.

"Five minutes," Beaty said and turned without waiting for Sebastian to reply.

Strangely, his elbow began to itch around the area where the peanut butter leftovers remained embedded in his shirt sleeve. He scratched it while watching the band get ready for the next set. Over at the bar, Big T was serving a young couple, but Sebastian could only see the stretched T-shirt of one thick shoulder from beyond the carpet-padded column in the center of the room.

"Triple one," the tall dart player said. "That plus two twenties and…"

"One hundred and thirty-seven," the English-accented dart player added.

Five minutes was too long, Sebastian thought. One minute was too long. He just had that feeling.

The lights in the bar dimmed as the band began their set with *Desperado*. Several couples got up to dance. Those that remained seated tapped at handheld trivia controllers that cast white, glowing circles from illuminated touchpads onto each contestant's face. When a new question popped up, the background behind all of the touchpads' lettering turned dark red and across the center of the room, dozens of faces suddenly became crimson.

That's when Sheriff Greely, alias the Nazi cubit bastard that had killed Sebastian's mother, walked in.

"I have to use the bathroom," Sebastian said to Beaty who was awaiting her dart-throwing turn. He nodded in the direction of the sheriff. "Meet you outside in five minutes."

"I'm tellin' ya." Beaty rubbed one of his shoulders. "He couldn't know anything yet. But if it makes you feel better, you go on and use the bathroom for five whole minutes, not that that would be suspicious or anything."

Sebastian tilted his head onto Beaty's soothing, strong fingers, then raised it quickly when he saw Big T's big T-shirt on the other side of the room. "You're right, of course. But I'd still rather not deal with him right now. I think I'd give everything away."

"Go on then. Circle around the back. I'll keep him busy as I finish off these two fellas then I'll meet you outside."

Not caring where Big T was or what he was looking at, Sebastian grabbed her cheeks, placing one gently into the palm of each of his wrinkled but strong hands. "Are you sure you're okay with all of this? You were never supposed to be included."

"Yes. You've said that before. And I've answered you." Beaty grabbed his hands and lowered them. "Outside. Just a few minutes longer."

Sebastian turned away and from the corner of his eye he saw the sheriff coming around the center tables. Sebastian quickly walked in the opposite direction, moving toward the band and dancing couples, then crossed in front of the short stage. Halfway across the dance floor, *Desperado* ended and the lights came up.

Before it's too-oo-ooo laaaa-te...

People clapped and turned toward the band. Had he not stopped walking, it wouldn't have been so awkward. Instinctively, he turned to one band member and said, "Sweet home," then walked from the stage to the opposite side of the room and straight through a crowd standing around the long bar. He didn't look at Big T nor did he acknowledge the doorman as he exited, and the door closed on the first notes of *Sweet Home Alabama*.

Outside, dozens of cars were parked nose first in one long line and Sebastian stepped from Big T Bar's wooden porch onto the icy gravel-packed lot. He'd parked his Ford Taurus, a rental, at the south end, to his right, and he walked briskly in that direction, his leather loafers kicking chunks of frozen rocks, his quick breaths swirling briefly under the parking lot lamp lights.

He passed a staggering couple that looked too young to be drinking, and removed the car keys from his pants pocket. The Taurus was twenty feet away when he pressed the key fob to unlock the door. The interior lights did not come on. He pressed it again. Nothing. He stepped to the driver's side door and pointed the fob directly at the lock and tried it without success. He turned the key in his hand and pointed it at the lock, but as he slid the key in, the interior lights came on and the door clicked open. "Cheap rentals," he said to the door, removed the car key and got in.

The first thing Sebastian did when he was settled behind the wheel was to look at the glove box where he'd stashed the dagger. Every minute counted. Kansas roads were long and flat and occupied only sparsely. There would be no place to hide. They needed to get far and fast.

Sebastian reached for the glove box. He just wanted to hold it. There was a wonderful energy that flowed from it into one's grasp and Sebastian felt an overwhelming need for that extra lift, that confidence-inspiring vibration that had raced all the way to his very soul when he'd grabbed it from the sheriff's bed side table (just where Beaty had told him it would be) less than thirty minutes ago.

He touched the glove box latch just as the passenger door opened and Beaty slid in. "That was fast," Sebastian said, sitting up.

"You said we're in a hurry."

"What did he say? What did you tell him?"

"I told him that I was going home to cook up some pies for tomorrow's pot luck dinner at church. He just smiled. Didn't say much of anything."

"Greely goes to church?" The very thought of a cubit in church made Sebastian's stomach turn.

"He absolutely loves it there."

Sebastian shook the thought away and buried it for later consideration. "Did he see me?"

"If he did, he wasn't letting on." She placed her hand on the glove box. "The dagger. It's in here isn't it? Can I see it?"

Sebastian moved his hand next to Beaty's fingers. "Once we get far away from here."

Beaty frowned which was something Sebastian had rarely seen her do in the short time he'd been with her. She dropped back into the seat and stared at the glove box as Sebastian started the car.

When Sebastian had arrived in Pickett's Crossing shortly after Christmas, he'd faced a whole lot of curious, gossipy people. He was an aging out-of-towner, showed up without advanced notice, checked into The Crossing Motel, said he was a government official from the NOAA (an acronym he'd had to explain to the mayor) who was on official business, said he was here to look for something supposedly buried in that old blowed-up Bender place, said he'd not be here but for a couple of weeks and then he'd be on his way.

Why he was in the Crossing and what he was supposed to be doing created immense suspicion: an old man from a government agency that deals with oceans…here? It didn't make sense to the mayor but it didn't need to. Any background check would show that Sebastian was a NOAA employee if not only part-time; his immense diving experience still had some value, particularly in Mexican waters. Sebastian also hoped that any background check to uncover the reason why he was in the Crossing would begin enough red tape that by the time the agency determined the truth and told the mayor, Sebastian would be long gone.

At least that had been the plan. What he had not anticipated was the Crossing's overreaction to the color of his skin. Not quite black. Not quite white. More Latino than anything else but to watch these locals' stares, you'd think they'd never seen anyone south of Kansas. When he'd first arrived, the eyes in town followed him wherever he went. It had taken an entire week before the guests at Big T's Bar had gotten used to his presence—all guests except, of course, for Beaty.

The sheriff's housekeeper had taken a shine to Sebastian that first night he'd been in town. To her, he was a mysterious, dark-skinned G-man looking for buried treasure. If he had been more the age of Harrison Ford in the first *Indiana Jones* movie, he'd had Crossing women buying him drinks just to listen to him talk, just to listen to the mystery man's adventure stories and wish they, too, were a part of them.

But only Beaty had bought him one—in fact, she'd bought him three. She'd been talking to Big T when Sebastian had entered, and the stares of just about everyone in the place turned toward him. He'd only ordered coffee, thinking that there'd be enough about him for these people to talk about, thinking that he didn't need "lush" added to the list. For almost thirty minutes, Big T had not paid him much attention. He'd been locked in conversation with Beaty while Sebastian had been watching Sports Center highlights on the flat screen television, his thoughts on trying to break the ice with these strangers, how he could ask them questions without giving up the real reason why he was here: to get the dagger from a long dead nemesis now living as a man known as Sheriff Greely.

"You interested in liquor?" Big T asked, shaking Sebastian from his thoughts.

Big T's too-small-of-a-T-shirt stretched the logo of Red Bull across his chest. Sebastian looked at his empty cup then at Big T. "How about a shot of

Bailey's in a second cup of joe?" he said, politely.

"Don't have it." Big T's big hands rested on the bar top. His eyes were moist and red and had a little bit of impatience in them.

And then, suddenly, Beaty was there. She'd moved to the stool beside him without making a sound. "Let me get you something," she interjected. "A welcome to the Crossing drink."

A strange woman had not bought Sebastian a drink in quite a long time. It would have been rude and without pride to refuse. "Tequila," he said, not really hearing his own words. "Cuervo if you have it—straight up."

"Top me off, too," Beaty said to Big T.

It wasn't quite anger, but some kind of hateful expression fell of Big T's face as he turned away, walked to the sweaty glass that Beaty had been drinking from and snatched it.

"So, you're the G-man everyone has been talking about?" Beaty said, a strange little smile jerking one corner of her mouth. Her lips were painted a soft violet.

"Sebastian. G-man sounds too formal." He held his hand for a shake and she firmly gripped it and pumped it twice.

"Beaty, they call me."

"Betty?"

"No. Beaty. Short for Beatrice."

Sebastian blinked then looked her over from head to waist.

"Yeah. I know," Beaty said. "Doesn't look like a Beatrice does it?"

Sebastian shook his head. "It looks…" Big T set both drinks down with a hardwood thud and Sebastian's gaze shifted. He grabbed his Cuervo shot and raised it. "To Beaty, and how she doesn't look like Beatrice."

Beaty toasted and together they drank while Big T's expression slowly dissolved more into bewilderment and depression.

And that's how Sebastian had broken the ice. What he hadn't known at the time was that Beaty was the sheriff's housekeeper. Billy Jo Presser had told him how such moments were fated. *"Coincidence and Fate are cooperatively disguised,"* he'd often say. *"Never take one over the other for granted."*

And Sebastian hadn't. That first night in Pickett's Crossing had been pure fate, he was sure of it. He'd come to get the cubit's dagger and the cubit's housekeeper had showed up with an overzealous attraction for the new man in town.

As the days had elapsed, fate had continued to aid his search. Beaty had revealed several curious snippets of info, one snip at a time, one night at Big T's at a time, for nearly a week. She'd told him how ruthless Greely was and how everyone in town kept out of his way. She'd said that there had been more than one person who'd tried "wrangling" with the sheriff, only to disappear a day later.

Sebastian never told Beaty what Greely really was. Even after their romance had started, after that first week he was in town, Sebastian had kept that part a secret. Believing in cubits was something few could reason with.

It had crossed Sebastian's mind that, just perhaps, Beaty was a cubit, too. The abominations had gotten very good at faking life. Even for Sebastian, it was hard to tell anymore. Really, there were only a couple of ways a person might know if someone was a cubit. The easiest method, Sebastian believed, would be to attempt sex with one you thought was a cubit, but the thought of taking such a chance and getting it wrong made him hesitant to try. How would sex with a cubit turn out? Just the naked thought of it was always enough to jerk a little bile into his throat.

Beaty had finally come to his motel room three days ago. She'd found the dagger for the first time while cleaning Greely's bedroom. Though Sebastian had never told her what he'd supposedly been looking for at the Bender Farm, Beaty had reasoned that the sheriff had already found it.

"Yes," Sebastian had said. "That's what I've been looking for. Don't tell him. Between you and me, mums the word." He'd turned off the motel television and had asked Beaty to sit. The bed had been her only option and she'd happily accepted its firm invitation. "The dagger is the reason why those that wrangle with Greely turn up missing. It's very special. The story goes, it can make you invincible."

Perhaps she'd seen some confirmation of such invincibility, Sebastian had thought, or perhaps she was so lonely and desirous of change that she'd accept even the most fanciful of ideas if it meant a break from hick-town boredom. Either way, Beaty had accepted the idea rather easily.

Sebastian had found that Beaty was not a cubit, and in the hour after they'd made love (a feat in which Sebastian still proudly felt competent even at his age), he'd told her of his many adventures diving in the Yucatán, about sunken treasure and underground water caves and the massive variety of sea life he'd come across, including the tiger shark that had chomped off a piece of his calf muscle and had left the scar that Beaty had commented on during their lovemaking.

"I want to go there," she'd said, stroking his thin chest. "I want to go to Mexico."

Sebastian's story had sealed a pact in which she had agreed to help him steal the dagger, but only if he agreed to take her with him when he left the Crossing. She'd said that she'd had enough of the town. She'd said that she wanted to quit it. She'd said that her dear friend Janine Bender, before blowing up her own farm, had always talked about paradise and that it was now time for her, Beaty, to find her own.

The dagger for a promise.

If that's what it took, then so be it. He'd take her with him, but a return to the Yucatán anytime soon was improbable. Presser needed the dagger and finding him without first getting killed was to be Sebastian's next labor.

"Now?" Beaty urged. They'd been on the road for less than five minutes.

"Patience," Sebastian said, maintaining an attention to the rear view mirrors as he'd been doing since leaving Big T's. A new set of headlights appeared in the early evening darkness behind them. "It's not going anywhere."

"What is it?" Beaty said. "I mean…really? Does it have the power you said it has?"

"Absolutely."

"Invincibility?"

"And the only way to kill a cubit."

"What's that? What's a cubit?"

"Sheriff Greely is a cubit."

Beaty shook her head. "Not following."

The headlights behind now switched to high beams but remained a few hundred yards away. It was then that both of them noticed the dull red glow emitting from the edges of the glove box door. Beaty immediately opened it and the dagger, wrapped inside a soft cloth, almost sprang from the tight enclosure. It rolled onto the back side of the open glove box door and partially unraveled from the cloth, exposing a very sharp and very thin tip that twinkled in the dashboard lights. Still hidden, the dagger's haft seemingly pulsed and jittered, acting as if it were alive, its dull red glow growing brighter as Beaty unrolled it with the tip of one finger. She picked it up to search for the source of light.

"The star," Sebastian said. "It's in the star."

Beaty turned the dagger over to find a five-pointed star made of gold. The red jewel in one of its points began to pulse.

"Grip it tightly," Sebastian said. "You'll really feel it then."

Beaty did so and a most serene expression swept across her face. Her head bobbed to the beat of her heart. Her closed eyes fluttered. Her hand and the dagger matched the life beat, raising and lowering in unison with her head as if she was listening to a song only she could hear. And then she started humming words that caught Sebastian by surprise.

"He's gonna get you," she said as if they were lyrics to a song. "He's gonna get you, boy."

"What?" Sebastian looked over at Beaty's closed eyes and gritting teeth grin.

"Sheriff Greely's gonna get the little Yucatán boy," she hummed. "Sheriff Greely's gonna make it all right."

Sebastian reached for the dagger but Beaty yanked it away. The red glow from the star point intensified as the blazing headlights from behind suddenly raced up to within thirty feet of the Taurus's bumper. Sebastian heard the angry growl of the truck's engine. The truck's height had been modified so that the high beams shot squarely into the rear view mirror.

Beaty stopped humming. "He's gonna get you," she said, suddenly smiling. "This car ain't no match for that truck."

"Give me the dagger," Sebastian demanded, trying to remain calm though he knew he'd been set up. He held his right hand out while the left remained on the steering wheel. "I know what to do with it. You don't."

"Oh, don't I?" Beaty said and drove the dagger's blade through the palm of Sebastian's open hand. The blade sank through the meat and three inches of it protruded from between the veins on the back on his hand right where Big T's doorman had hand-stamped a red star.

Sebastian screamed and pulled away, taking the dagger from Beaty's grip because it was implanted in his hand. She leapt at him then, grabbed for the dagger, scratched at his face, screamed obscenities.

"You can't have my sheriff," she raged. "And you can't have the fucking dagger. What would poor Tommy Greely do without it?"

At that moment, the Taurus raced forward even though Sebastian had not touched the accelerator. Beaty beat his shoulder with both hands and he instinctively backslapped her, not thinking about the dagger's blade and how it still protruded from the back of his hand. The dagger's point missed her left eye by the smallest fraction and carved a thin slice of meat from her upper cheek bone. The force of his backhand knocked Beaty out and she slumped over against the passenger door window as blood rolled from the face slice onto the collar of her jacket.

Sebastian set the bloody fingers of his daggered hand on the top of the steering wheel, the blade sticking straight up, his vision of the road ahead divided by its sharp metal. Below the blade, the Taurus's digital speedometer read 85 and the car continued to accelerate. He mashed the brake pedal and it sank to the floor. He remembered how the car had acted strangely when he'd tried to unlock it back at Big T's. Now he wondered if Sheriff Greely had tampered with it before entering the bar. He wondered if the sheriff was following just to watch the climactic end to his, and Beaty's, deception. But, as the Taurus hit…

…89…

The sheriff's truck backed off several hundred yards.

…93…

The trailing truck's headlights switched from high to low and the distance between them increased.

…96…

The headlights turned off. Apparently, the truck had stopped.

…100…

Sebastian thought of the emergency brake but the handle to engage it was down by his left knee which meant that he'd have to take his one good hand off the steering wheel. He used his knee to drive while he yanked the handle. It broke in his grasp.

…105…

He tried to pull the dagger out of his right hand but instead of releasing, the blade seemingly gripped his serrated flesh with even more tenacity and its starry red point glowed brighter.

Sebastian stared helplessly at the speedometer as it reached 110. He tried the brake again and the pedal sank only halfway to the floor this time, slowing the car's momentum below a hundred miles per hour. He sighed.

And then Beaty was on him again, punching, grappling, trying to yank the dagger out of his hand, twisting it back and forth and slicing through tendon and vein and blood. The car swerved to the right and slid across the dusty shoulder and Sebastian caught it just before losing control.

"Give me the fucking dagger!" Beaty screamed. "Give—me—the—fucking—dagger!"

Sebastian knew that in less than a mile, Kansas Route 22 would take a sharp turn to the left as the two-lane road ascended a short hill. If the Taurus hit that turn at their current speed there would be no saving them.

"You're gonna kill us both!" Sebastian yelled.

"No," Beaty growled. "I'm gonna kill you."

She acted just like a cubit but Sebastian had made love to her. Cubits couldn't do that. *Right?*

Right!

Sebastian's stomach churned as a road sign zipped past, warning of the thirty mile-per-hour turn just ahead. He tried the brake pedal again and, this time, it caught immediately. The car slowed from seventy-five to seventy to sixty as he applied even pressure to avoid a spinout.

Beaty's two-handed grip was stronger than Sebastian's one arm. She pounded his daggered hand against the car's dashboard, each thrust opening a new hole in the rental's vinyl and plastic, until they entered the turn. Sebastian had braked to fifty miles-per-hour, a speed he thought he'd be able to manage even with one arm, but Beaty had a different ending in mind. She slammed his hand once more into the dashboard with enough force that the dagger's blade anchored it in place, then grabbed the steering wheel with both free hands and yanked—hard.

Before the car tumbled over the embankment, Sebastian's only thought was of failure.

"I'm sorry," he whispered as the bottom of the car became its top and seventy-seven years of guilt, frustration, and unfulfilled vengeance swarmed into the minute remainder of his memory…

A vision of himself…five-years-old.

A vision of his mother…tied to a chechen negro tree…its black poison drooling down her body.

Suffering.

Her bubbling, tarred skin.

Laughter.

The Nazi who had taken everything away.

His father's Creation Dagger cupped in his own hand.

His inability to use it.

His inability to save his mother's life.

His inability to stop the war before it ever started.

Inability.

Irrelevant.

Failure.

Richard Manson watched with Greely's cubited eyes as the Taurus remained on the road less than a second longer. When it hit the hard, cold shoulder with the car's nose pointed in the opposite direction of the turn, all it took was one heaping patch of solid ground to send it spinning, flipping and rolling off the embankment and into a landscaped tree line. There were only three oaks in the tree line but the Taurus hit every one of them. The first two tore off just about every door the car had and ejected Beaty along with an array of metal splinters, sparks, and glass. The impact with the third oak made the car explode. The Taurus slid down the charring bark of the tree and, for a full minute, stood like a ladder on fire before toppling over onto what remained of its roof.

The explosion could have been seen for miles in the early evening darkness but no one came to the rescue, even though rescue was no longer possible. The Greely cubit had blockaded and detoured Route 22 traffic another dozen miles ahead and had, with the help of Manson, chosen this turn because of its isolation from nearby farmhouses. It had been a great plan: to close the book on the life of Sebastian Bondager; to show the other "apostles" that none of them were invincible and that the meek would not inherit this earth. Bondager's death and the fact that the Creation of Religion dagger would remain in the possession of a cubit, would undoubtedly bring the others. And one by one…

Beyond the tree-raptured perimeter, a tire suddenly popped and the Greely cubit jerked in the direction of the source to find Beaty's body. It lay a good twenty yards beyond the broken trees. She'd not been cooked but she was definitely dead. Both arms and legs were broken and curled completely behind her which made the torso look stumpy.

The Greely cubit skittered down the embankment and walked to within a dozen feet of the wreckage. A few flickering, foot-high flames provided the light that helped it locate the dagger still implanted in what remained of the car's dashboard. Bondager's blackened hand was still attached. The rest of his arm and body were rolled up in a mess of curled steel and melted plastic a few feet further to the left. A windshield wiper blade stuck straight up from one burnt thigh and a small, lighter-sized flame ate away at the gooey rubber that remained at the tip of the wiper.

Manson, with the Greely cubit's hand, grasped the dagger, thinking that it would be hot, but it wasn't. The blade came out of the dashboard rather easily and Manson raised it toward the Greely cubit's eyes. Bondager's hand looked like a deformed, overcooked spider.

"No, Sebastian," Manson said through the cubit's lips. "I don't think this dagger is gonna be bringing your old ass back to life." He flicked Bondager's hand from the blade of the dagger then marveled at its indestructibility, thought about the future, relished in the belief that he controlled every…

Manson felt it in the back of his own skull and this made him immediately sever his connection with the Greely cubit. He knew that it was death, the long blade of a Creation Dagger entering the kill spot, the eradication of another of his cubited minions. What he didn't understand was how.

Cooper Reyes yanked her dagger from the cubit's skull and watched it dissolve to bones before wiping away her tears. If only she'd arrived a few minutes sooner Sebastian would still be alive. Having both daggers was important, maybe even more so than losing a good friend, but convincing herself of this, right now, was impossible. She could have saved them both. She should have saved them both.

She reached down and took Sebastian's dagger from the pile of cubit ash then placed it and her own dagger inside her Mama's trinket box, closed it, and flipped two gold latches to lock it. She walked to Sebastian's remains, yanked the wiper blade from his blackened thigh and threw it as far as she could.

"Forgive me, dear friend," she said as if consoling a spirit she knew floated invisibly nearby. "It wasn't supposed to happen this way."

0-Time: Predicate

Creation of the Antichrist

If you dance with the devil, the devil don't change, the devil changes you.

-8mm

The worst thing about being the Antichrist was that you just couldn't be everywhere at the same time. Manson had to choose which cubit he'd jump into. He could only manipulate one situation at a time, using his cubits as a kind of periscope in a sea of humanity. It was true that whatever cubits did was always terribly bad, but without his direction, a cubit's conduct was not always to Manson's best interest. Albert Stine, Lafitte and Kerskker had been good extreme examples. All cubits were dead, nasty, evil creatures that were selfishly inspired to act for the satisfaction of their own cruel intent, some to the point of actually believing they could become what Manson was destined to be: ruler of the new Age of Chaos. But he couldn't manipulate a thousand decisions all at once, at least not yet. BethStar would enable that power.

The old S.S. Nazi murderer, a.k.a. Sheriff Thomas Greely, had been doing splendidly up until 2007, but being the pure evil he was, both in life and in death, he'd had those same Stine-like aspirations. He'd gone off-script much too often, particularly back when Chris Cower had blown through town. Still, Greely had always served a purpose, if not only for the fear he instilled in others, but Manson had finally given up on him after nearly blowing his plans to kill Bondager. If Cooper had not gotten to Greely first, Manson certainly would have.

Manipulating Beatrice had been much easier, as was the case for most coercible, Faustian mortals. Using his cubit surrogate Big T, Manson had guaranteed Beaty a life of luxury. The dagger was worth millions, Big T had told her. All she had to do was play the game: become the sheriff's housekeeper, convince the town of this, convince Bondager that she was sick of the town, pretend to fall in love, trick the old fuck into thinking he was saving her life, act as though she would conspire to steal the dagger, then once she had it, millions would be hers.

Lies and liars—all of them—and all for one purpose.

Manson had accepted the Great Darkness into his soul back in 1984, but now it was more a pain in the ass than anything else. Being the Lord of all things Bad was a chore. Evil had as many idiots working for it as did Good. He just couldn't trust any of them. But the end was coming and, thankfully, it wouldn't be long. He knew what he had to do—mostly. He had to take his Creation of the Antichrist dagger and shove it into the Cubit on December 21, 2012. This would not only save humanity from the sun, it would turn them into slaves that he could control. The Cubit would remain alive and pertinent, spewing occasional dark leaders that would take their proper positions across the globe. The problem was: he didn't know at what time the ceremonial dagger stabbing was supposed to occur, and he had absolutely no clue where it was destined to happen. That's what the Book of the Djed was going to tell him. That's why he needed it so badly, and the three daggers that were of no use to him, were supposed to help him get it.

He'd recovered all four daggers shortly after the Port Aransas hurricane. They'd somehow returned to the pedestals under the Caracol in Chichen Itza and in the cenote outside of Tulum. Manson had found the first two when he'd gone back to get the Cubit. The other two, he'd sent Chester to retrieve from two Mexican stoners who had tried to sell their "totally cool" discoveries to a local pawn shop in Merida—a business franchise that Phoenix International just happened to own.

Manson had kept the Creation of the Antichrist dagger—knowing that he would need it because the Great Darkness had told him as much—and had spread the others out in hopes of luring the Daykeeper or his friends. One of them had the Book. To maximize suffering, he'd given one to the cubit Cooper most despised, one to the cubit that most haunted Bondager, and one to the cubit that John Brown Gordon most wanted for revenge.

Manson had erased Sebastian, but Cooper—somehow, she'd tricked him. Somehow, she'd beaten Triple K. Somehow, she'd kept Manson from finding her through the connection he had with daggers. Somehow, she'd snuck up on him, had surprised him, had taken out the second of his cubit surrogates.

And that's exactly why Manson was now concentrating on Phoenix. Elizabeth was here. Billy was here. Sooner or later, Cooper would be, too.

Manson jumped back into Chester Kalimaris who was sitting in a black SUV outside Presser's house. They were all in there, including that little Indian boy from Sedona. Since Christmas, he'd carefully gone through the house when no one was home, had followed Billy and the boy all around the valley—watching them go to the movies together, to the park together, fishing together, even playing with little monster trucks together—trying to determine where the Book might be. He'd been unsuccessful with getting into the lab where Elizabeth worked since the place was well-guarded and murdering any of the young pseudo-cops would have only created unnecessary attention. But he wasn't going to give up. Either Billy had it, Cooper did, or the big black Marine did. All he had to do was wait. Nearly a year remained and he'd already proven that he could outlast the ages.

What Manson didn't anticipate was what happened next. Through Chester's eyes, he saw that bothersome twerp whom he'd used to augment the popularity of BethStar and to scare the living shit out of Fox's Ben Reely. Michael Arden was his name and Manson thought he'd sufficiently scared him off, but there he was, sitting in a white van directly across the street, staring at him, pointing his middle finger at him, rolling down his window and yelling out that he'd found proof and that nothing was going to stop him this time.

When Arden's van peeled out, Manson, as Chester, took off in pursuit.

A video created by a news station from New York had started all the fuss that led Michael's decision to finally confront Pitchfork Man. Up until now, he'd kept an incredibly safe distance. Pitchfork Man scared him more than fear was defined. But Michael had uncovered important information about the boy from Sedona just a day ago and he had to tell Elizabeth Presser. She was living with a lie.

When Pitchfork Man looked at him, Michael almost shit himself. The ghoul's eyes were blazing red and it actually looked surprised to see him which, even with his intestines tied in a knot, made Michael smile; he revved the news van's engine a little louder, then peeled out.

Pitchfork Man had been following Elizabeth and, as Michael had also discovered, her son since Christmas. Whenever the son had left the house (and this was usually with the boy), the ghoul had followed. When the doctor had gone to the lab, the ghoul had followed. When they were all at home together, the ghoul had stayed in his black SUV just a block away, remaining there until one of them, once again, left. If both left at the same time, the ghoul had always followed the son.

Michael had been staking the place out since Christmas as well, but it was only since last Tuesday that he was "officially" doing so. The television news station manager had asked him to find out if the video from Puerto Rico was real; someone connected to it, an anonymous source had said, was supposedly living in Phoenix. This had given Michael cart blanche to use any resources the station could offer, including the help of an intern which Michael had quickly accepted. Theodore was his name, and he was now a part of the plan to lure Pitchfork Man away from the doctor's house.

As expected, the black SUV took up the chase. Theodore was in a second, identical, unmarked news van that was parked under the I-10 cloverleaf interchange just a few miles away. The plan was for Michael to gain enough distance from the ghoul so that when he sped below the underpass, Theodore would take off, continuing straight down Broadway Road while Michael took the cloverleaf onto I-10. Hopefully, the ghoul would take the bait and follow Theodore all the way to the television station where (Michael also hoped) Theodore could find safety and, if the ghoul followed him inside, one hell of a story. He'd not told Theodore who the driver really was, just that he was a witness to the Puerto Rico murders revealed in the video. The diversion would give Michael fifteen, maybe twenty minutes tops to get back to the doctor's house and warn her about the boy who called himself Aaron.

In the first mile, all was going to plan. He'd been fortunate to make every traffic light and, at one intersection, had gained a considerable distance on the SUV when Pitchfork Man was forced to slow for turning traffic. Michael had gambled that the ghoul would not want to cause attention, so crashing through traffic (he'd hoped) would not be an option. The gamble played out until he was within eyesight of the interstate underpass. That's when the SUV rammed the first vehicle, sending it careening into a line of parked cars. As for the second vehicle that got in the way, the ghoul simply T-boned the car's rear bumper which spun it in two complete circles. It was going to be close. Michael saw Theodore pull off the shoulder and into traffic just as he rounded the final corner before the underpass. Michael sped up the on-ramp so fast, he almost flipped the van. In his mirrors, he watched for the busted front end of the SUV until he crossed over Broadway and looked down. Pitchfork Man had taken the bait and Theodore was doing an excellent job at speeding without crashing. Michael took the next exit, circled back, and headed for Dr. Presser's house.

Billy had known for some time that Manson's bodyguard, a.k.a. Chester Kalimaris, had been following him during the day and watching the house at night. Why he hadn't tried anything yet made Billy curious, but not particularly worried. Perhaps it was as simple as Manson's realization that a Daykeeper could easily dispatch one, measly cubit. Perhaps Manson was amassing dozens of cubits and, at some point, he'd planned to unleash all of them at once. But he hadn't.

A more believable scenario was that he was going to kidnap his mother. Manson, through Chester, could have held her hostage to bargain for Billy's dagger and the Djed amulet. But he hadn't.

Manson must have known that Aaron was connected to the story of Daykeepers. He could have had Chester kill the boy just out of spite, just to show Billy he could get to all that he cared about. Daykeepers loved—murdering Aaron would have, at least, demolished some part of Billy's soul. But he hadn't.

Manson (through Chester) was waiting for something: a person, an event, a moment in time—whatever it was, Billy continued forward. He, too, would wait.

In the meantime, Billy had gotten to know Aaron much better. While his mother labored away at uncovering the truth about BethStar, he and Aaron had become quite close. Conversations with the youngster had been full of daily surprises—a kind of surprise-du-jour.

The day after Christmas, when Billy had first noticed Chester's SUV, he and Aaron had visited the local park for no other reason than to swing. Aaron had never done such a simple kid thing and Billy had been happy to teach the simple kid task. They'd sat for an entire hour, talking about flying without wings, wondering what it would be like to do a complete three-sixty around the swing set's top cross post, how chains connected to narrow bendy seats could promote so much joy.

A couple of days later, Billy had taken Aaron to the backend of a Walmart parking lot where he'd surprised Lax's adopted son with a pair of remote-controlled four wheelers. Neither was painted Grave Digger green, but they'd had a blast nonetheless. Aaron had asked him about Lax, about how he'd died, about the worth of life—all life. The discussion had wavered on academic at times, Aaron asking questions as if repeating some Discovery

Channel special he'd recently seen. He'd asked Billy what it was like to be a Daykeeper, to be invincible, to not worry about all of those things the cable stations suggested happened when a person died.

All that Billy could say was something about superheroes, how none were really invincible because all had been created by mortals. He'd told him that if he knew what happened after life, he'd probably be dead. No one, he'd said, was supposed to know the answer to that.

Then Aaron had surprised him with a suggestion: "What if we are dead right now and what we call death is really life?" He'd suggested that everybody already lived in hell and death was the transition. If you learn on earth, he'd said, then you can escape.

Billy had understood that day what the term "heavy heart" really meant. He'd had no answers for the boy, only consolation. "If you're right," Billy had said, "then your father is alive today."

Just yesterday, Billy had taken Aaron to see a movie at the Dollar Matinee Theater where previously released movies could be seen for a buck. Aaron had suggested it. He'd wanted to watch *2012.* When the movie had ended, Aaron had been extremely upset. "That's not how it's going to happen," he'd said. "People will figure out how to survive. The last five days will be key. The *Wayeb* is waiting to test us all." Billy hadn't heard that word in so long, he'd almost forgotten its meaning: the Mayan's final month of the year, the last five days when Evil tried to cross into the world of life, the days of temptation, of redemption, of conciliation, of real honest to goodness truth. Succumb to Wayeb, Billy remembered, and you could write your ass off to eternal damnation which really meant, if you followed young Aaron's logic, you'd be reincarnated to live Hell on earth all over again.

Yes. Aaron had learned well from a Daykeeper teacher and when Friday rolled around, Aaron had one more surprise up his sleeve for both Billy and his mother. It was just before nightfall when he brought them together around Elizabeth's kitchen table and set the stone, glyph-faced tablets he'd taken from the Great Hall on its glass surface. He told them that it was time. The "other" would be joining them shortly. It was time for the revealing. It's what his father, Alaxel, Daykeeper of all that was and all that would ever be, had told him to do.

It started with so much stereotypical evocation Billy thought, at first, it was all just a ruse. The house lights dimmed though none of them had moved from the table. Aaron asked that they all hold hands and close their eyes.

There were no candles, just wall socket night lights, but the glass tabletop glowed nonetheless. The two stones provided the necessary energy and they provided the sudden otherworldly voices.

The first was that of an old man who began by speaking in a language that Billy not only didn't understand, but had never heard before. There was a lot of tongue to the roof of the mouth clicking that morphed into easily understood English, a kind of ethereal translation. It was a story, Billy realized. The old man was talking about boats and fish and angry seas. He was talking about famine and survival and hope. Billy opened his eyes at the same time as did his mother, but neither she, nor Aaron (whose eyelids remained clenched), was saying anything.

The next voice was also male but it sounded very young and it also began in a strange language that was translated into English. The tone of the voice was fear as it spoke of hangings and beheadings and wanton acts of human suffering.

A woman's voice evolved next; it was Latin, Billy thought. The English translation made references to great victories, plentitude and a feeling of protection, then quickly gradated to dismal reckonings.

All of a sudden, Billy understood. He blurted out, "Daykeepers! They are Daykeepers!"

Aaron squeezed his hand to hush him and the next very familiar Daykeepers entered the vision. In the Book, they were represented by sixes and nines, 623 B.C. and 622 A.D., and the birthdate that came right in the middle. Buddha, Mohammed, and Christ. Daykeepers kept revealing themselves, talking of the times when their invincibility had ended because of the first three Creations. The Mayan Eka and the Anasazi Samaal talked about the decimation of their civilizations, then they were followed by…

…the Twins.

Alixel's face entered the vision. She was just as Billy remembered from the vision in the waterfall and she repeated what she'd told him back then: *The future is in your hands. You have to do it—for all of us.* Then her ethereal expression became one of surprise as her ghostly figure turned and glared at something that was just beyond the aura of the séance.

At that moment, Michael Arden entered the house from the back porch, yelling, "He's not him! He's not him!"

Billy stood. "Quiet!" he snapped. "I don't know why you've taken so long, but Aaron says you are supposed to be here, so take a seat."

"But..."

"Sit!"

Michael took the seat opposite Aaron and his eyes never left the boy's face. He was afraid of him; that much was evident. "I have to tell you something," he insisted. "We don't have time for this bullshit. Pitchfork Man is coming. He'll be here in minutes. We have to get out of here. We have to get to the lab and collect the evidence and run. I have a van."

Aaron grabbed Elizabeth's hand then Billy's and closed his eyes. Elizabeth and Billy presented their free hands to Michael who looked at the offering as if to touch them meant instant death.

"Take them," Billy urged. "Now! You said we don't have time for this so do it!"

When Michael completed the circle of hands, the stone tablets from the Great Hall began trembling and spun atop the table. The vision of Alixel returned and she held her hands out toward each of them as the stone-etched jaguar glyph leapt up and into her. The morph was miraculous, the jaguar spots integrating into the red streaks in her hair, her eyes and ears evolving into the certain cunning of the animal that symbolized the spirit of Land.

A tremendous clinking of rock on glass caused all of them to open their eyes in time to see the stone tablet that had contained the jaguar glyph, bounce up on its edge, spin like a top, and vanish in a flash of white light. The stone with the bird glyph remained and Billy expected that the next vision would be Alixel's twin brother, but that's not what he saw.

The glass tabletop became a translucent map of the world. The stone tablet now rested atop the Australian continent while, to the right of it, a smudge of darkness developed just off the South American Pacific coast. It wasn't real, of course, but every sense in Billy's Daykeeper body told him that the smudge symbolized something darker than black, more putrid than rot and more ghastly than any imaginable horror. The smudge turned black as it moved up the Chilean coast, into Central America, then to Mexico, and finally up the Gulf of California. It traced the exact route that Billy had taken to Arizona where it stopped and hovered over Phoenix. An image of Richard Manson suddenly appeared right next to the dark rift and the two coalesced into what Billy perceived as the moment of possession that had taken over Manson back when he and his mother were in college.

Michael suddenly pointed at Aaron. "See," he yelled. "He's not Aaron Crossbear. He is the darkness. Aaron Crossbear died in an explosion under Lee Mountain in Sedona, Arizona." Michael reached into his pocket and tossed a folded newspaper onto the table next to the stone. His mother grabbed it before Billy had the chance. She unfolded it and read from the headline story of a November edition of the *Sedona Red Rock News*. "City outraged over death of young boy," she said. "City officials said that Aaron Crossbear, the adopted son of Will Crossbear, died in a planned explosion as part of Phoenix International's new resort project on the west side of Lee Mountain." She turned the paper around and there, on the front page, was a head shot of the boy who sat at their table.

Billy stood so quickly his chair slid into the wall behind him and toppled. "Aaron!" he said. Aaron stood, then Michael and Elizabeth joined Billy on the opposite side of the table.

"I am Aaron," the boy said. "And I am also your friend. Remember what I told you the night before we left for the Great Hall?"

Billy's jaw dropped. "You said that we shouldn't let the definition of death become the definition of life."

"And?"

"You said that even if we think we have a choice, we do not."

Elizabeth and Michael looked totally perplexed and the confusion intensified when the remaining stone started spinning on the table. Billy knew what was going to happen before the bird glyph sprang from it. It looked just like Osi, only a smaller version of the giant hawk. It hovered over the table as if some invisible gust of wind gave its wings lift. Its beak moved in unison with Aaron's lips.

"The final destination," both said. "Seal the Evil forever. Don't let men stop you. Suffer the five days of reckoning and renew the earth."

The bird looked so real, Billy reached out to touch its wing, but it dove at the kitchen table before he could make contact. It swept away the dark-spotted Evil hovering over Phoenix and the world map vanished, then it turned toward Aaron and flew right into the boy's chest. Aaron smiled, his grin as wide as Lax's had ever been, then he and the stone tablet vanished.

"No!" Billy screamed. "Don't leave me!"

"Look," Elizabeth said, pointing at the tabletop.

Lax's wispy-white afterglow still blotted Billy's vision and he rubbed his eyes. The bird—Lax—had scratched something into its surface. All three of them leaned forward. "What is it?" Elizabeth said. Billy shook his head but Michael stared, emotionless.

"Arden. Do you know?" Billy asked.

"Michael," he responded. "It's Michael. And…and…I'm sorry. Oh, dear God. I heard him, too. The final destination. The renewal of the earth." He pointed at the etching and turned his head.

"It's familiar," Michael continued. "I've seen this somewhere before."

Now we all know.

The voice came from Elizabeth's dark living room.

The final destination. The pedestal. The key. The beginning of the end.

Michael screamed like a little girl but jumped in front of Elizabeth as did Billy.

The assassin Chester Kalimaris, alias Pitchfork Man, stepped into the dim kitchen light. Its eyes boiled red; the pupils cracked electric blue. "I do so love Daykeepers," the cubit grunted, excited.

Billy's glowing red dagger was out of its sheath in an instant as Chester's hand crashed through the glass tabletop. Michael grabbed Elizabeth and backpedaled with her into the kitchen counter cul-de-sac, trapped except for a small window above the kitchen sink.

"Son," Manson said, his voice a creepy bass that sounded hungry. "Pretty fucked up, eh? If it's any consolation, I never intended to create a Daykeeper. Getting her pregnant was an experiment gone awry."

"An experiment gone awry?" Elizabeth calmly said. "I think it went just as the good Lord planned. Now you have your equal to contend with and I'm glad I could be of service."

"Equal?" Chester's lips said, grimacing. "Noooo. Just ask all those other Daykeepers. Not equal. Not invincible. Dead."

Billy slashed out with the dagger and Chester dodged it and punched his arm, but Billy held tight. "I don't accept that I'm your son," he growled and jabbed at Chester's red eyes.

"In all of the lies I take honor in distributing, this is not one of them. A bit of my sperm, a few nanobots, my beloved Beth, and Voila! Baby stew time." He looked directly at Michael. "Freddie's nanobots are really a miracle of science. Too bad the greasy wetback ain't around to see what a real scientist can do with them."

"I know what you have planned," Elizabeth said. "I figured it all out and stored the evidence in a place you'll never find. Once I release it to the media, your dream of a new world order will be no more."

Chester hesitated for just a moment which gave Billy the opening to drive the dagger into its stomach. Blood squirted everywhere but the cubit didn't go down. Chester actually turned the spewing wound at Elizabeth and

Michael, spraying them like a garden spigot. Then, it spun in a complete circle with feet easily moving atop the blood-splattered, glass shard-covered floor, and caught Billy by surprise, backhanding the dagger from his grip. The dagger flipped once and stuck in the wall out of reach behind him.

"You can't kill me," Billy said.

"Perhaps. But I can make you wish you were dead." The cubit took one step but went no further. Almost all blood was gone from its body, but that's not the reason it froze. It lifted its head like a bloodhound on the scent.

Beams of light suddenly flashed in several directions, entering the dark house through the windows. Pitchfork Man regained its composure and growled. It grabbed Billy's arm and broke it, then pulled Billy closer, grabbed the necklace that held the Djed amulet and…

"Triple K!" a voice screamed from the darkness.

Manson turned his cubit toward the declaration.

"Whatever it is you're calling yourself today, it's time to die."

More lights flashed into the house and Cooper stepped into the midst of the melee. Through the windows behind her, men ran with cameras and reporters ran with microphones. At Cooper's feet lay her Mama's trinket box. In her hands were two daggers.

"It thought I smelled shit," Manson said. "You sure you know how to use those?"

"Took out your Marcy cubit didn't I? Now, it's your turn."

But Cooper never had the chance. Elizabeth had found Billy's dagger, had yanked it from the wall, and had rammed it into the cubit's skull, twisting it back and forth and back again.

Michael slipped and slid past the molting cubit and kicked it as it disintegrated, then yelled out to all of them, "Let's get out of here. Go to the backyard and wait for a moment."

As the triumvirate crept out to the back porch, Michael went to the front door and opened it. Theodore was standing there with a microphone. "I followed him back here and brought the forces," he said.

"Great job, kid," Michael said. He opened the door wide and a half a dozen people entered. "The kitchen. It's a blood bath."

As their attention was drawn to the kitchen, Michael joined his compatriots on the porch, slowly lifted the fence gate latch, and led everyone to his van which he'd parked several yards away. Once they were all inside, he stealthily drove away. "It's time to go," he said.

"Where?" Billy asked.

"To the final destination. To the land of the Down Under."

0-Time
Presage

Cairns, Australia

The Cairns Post, Monday, November 12, 2012

U.S. President to Visit Cairns for Talks on JI

Australian Prime Minister Julia Gillard, will welcome the United States' newly elected president on Wednesday for talks concerning rising security issues sparked by recent terrorists threats from the Islamic extremists group Jamaah Islamiah, also known as JI.

The public display of beheadings and several bomb threats in Perth and Sydney have necessitated that the Australian government take action after months of laissez-faire leadership.

"The United States has a history with JI's leader, Majjar Fodii," Gillard said. "We hope to forge a security alliance with the U.S. so that our combined knowledge will root out all of these radicals."

Sources say that Fodii was a former organizer and double agent for al Qaeda during the first Gulf War who thwarted U.S.-backed efforts to assassinate Saddam Hussein.

Fodii can be seen in many of the beheading videos. She uses a weapon very similar to the one displayed by billionaire Richard Manson last December, but no verification is available as to its authenticity. Manson nor any of his spokespersons would comment.

The president's visit to Cairns coincides with the 2012 total solar eclipse. The city is one of the few populated places that will witness the event. Thousands of star-gazing tourists are expected that will challenge the prime minister's security measures, but her staff has reassured the public that safety is her number one concern.

Gillard said, "We will be talking security and partaking in security while enjoying two of this country's greatest wonders: the Great Barrier Reef and a total eclipse."

The location of the meeting is top secret but sources suggest that a barrier reef island is the obvious choice.

Sun Shows Signs of Manson Mania

If you've stocked up on barrels of fresh water, shelves of canned and dehydrated foods and tanks of fuel, you've probably caught a little bit of what has become known as Manson Mania—and now there's scientific evidence that the "mania" might be justified.

The term was first coined to describe the hoarding of commodities shortly after Richard Manson, CEO of Phoenix International and billionaire responsible for the supplement BethStar, announced that the sun would eject an earth-altering blast of radiation on December 21.

Dr. Chi Yurilo of the Australian Astronomical Observatory in New South Wales released observational data that, he says, shows that the sun has turned a bit angrier since the first of the year.

"To pinpoint the exact moment that a coronal mass ejection might take place, even without regard for the direction of its ejection, is quite difficult," Yurilo said. "But recent measurements suggest that a few erupting solar flares have the potential for a trajectory toward the earth near the end of this year or early next year."

Scientific peers have suggested that it is highly irresponsible of Yurilo to make statements that cannot be verified, especially given the global unrest that Manson Mania has created.

"I'm not guaranteeing anything," Yurilo responded to these critics. "To imply that I am anywhere close to as crazy as Manson borders on libel. Look at the data. Decide for yourself."

Independent researchers interviewed by the *Post* have confirmed that Yurilo's data is authentic but not conclusive as to when or even if Manson's predicted solar eruption would happen.

Australian Scientist Delivers Proof BethStar No Miracle

A scientific report from a source known only as Frederico has delivered convincing evidence that the popular supplement known as BethStar is a danger, not miracle, to public health.

The report, which has been vetted by a number of scientists, reveals that BethStar is composed of minute quantities of nanobots which are, basically, imperceptible small machines that do work at the atomic level. The report shows that the nanobots are active and are responsible for the manipulation of human genes which causes changes in the metabolism, thus making the host healthy.

Accompanying the report was an accusation that health was not the sole purpose of BethStar's distribution.

"If nanobots can control the internal pieces of the human body and make it healthy," the author said, "then they can control just about anything else for which they've been programmed, including the human brain."

The author includes a log of dozens of cities around the world where sudden, random violence in the last two years is purported to have been caused by BethStar's manipulation of the brains of citizen populations.

Richard Manson, CEO of the company responsible for BethStar development and distribution, denies these claims.

"While it is true that nanobot technology has provided a miracle cure for the well-being of millions of people, to suggest that I or my company has any vicious intent is dogmatic balderdash."

Manson also said that the author of the report is an individual who has tried to blackmail him in the past and should be arrested.

"Frederico is a joke. The real author is a scientist from Arizona who fled the country and is supposedly living somewhere in Australia. Find Elizabeth Presser and you'll find the liar."

Manson referred the *Post* to a video on YouTube captured by a news crew in Phoenix, Arizona, that shows what looks like the aftermath of a massacre in the home of Dr. Elizabeth Presser, a former employee of Arizona

State University (ASU). Spokespersons at ASU would not comment.

Whether Frederico or Elizabeth Presser, the author of the report and accusation warns of a premeditated actuation of the nanobots on the date of Manson's so-called solar event. The author says that on December 21, the nanobots will be activated for whatever purposes the maker has chosen. The author also says that heavy doses of thermal radiation can make the nanobots impotent which puts a new spin on Manson's guarantee that he can stop the coronal mass ejection (CME) from taking the earth back to the dark ages.

"Presser would rather the entire planet's population die than admit her research is a lie meant for revenge," Manson said. "She is a very dangerous woman and should be stopped at all costs."

The report suggests that the supposed world-altering CME can stop a devious plot by Manson to control the minds of those who've ingested BethStar and that his "force field," which he has referred to as a Cubit, is for the purpose of guaranteeing that extreme thermal radiation does not stop his nanobots from taking over the planet.

Invasion of the Bodysnatchers it isn't, but the story does seem a bit too sci-fi for this news journalist.

John set the newspaper on the table. Instead of naming it *The Cairns Post*, today's edition, he thought, seemed more appropriately titled, *The Manson Report.* Not only were the majority of the headline articles in some way connected to Manson Mania, there were plenty of advertisements touting specials for all kinds of survival equipment, food supplies, weapons and underground shelters. He'd never lived during the height of the 1950s cold war propaganda, but he imagined the fever to have been very similar: profiteering based on unseen fears that had been emboldened by the popular media.

Of course, John knew better. That's why he'd been in Australia for more than ten months. That's why he'd slowly infiltrated the JI. That's why he was waiting in a seedy apartment in a section of Cairns that no tourists ever visited. The contact would arrive at any moment, a front man for the Fodii leadership, a defector who was, to the best of John's knowledge, not a cubit and was not on BethStar, who was not a double agent, who was legitimately interested in John's help to acquire the dagger of death and, thus, overthrow Fodii. The promise of power did that to people and John had cleverly built the promise over months of belabored covert cunning.

Shortly after he'd arrived in the Land Down Under, he'd been immediately picked up by local military Intelligence. John had assumed that Manson had set him up, had pretended to provide papers for passage into the country, and had informed the authorities that a Tulum Terrorist was theirs for the taking. But that's not what had happened. Intelligence had nabbed him not because of false accusations that he was a terrorist, but because John Brown Gordon had been a black ops Marine responsible for nearly stopping a terrorist regime in 1990. They'd offered John a choice: go undercover again to "get that bitch who double-crossed you" or land in prison for the false Tulum terrorist's acts of which he'd been accused.

Billy had often touted blind faith as a central force in moving the world toward its planned destination. Getting government authorities to help him complete the assignment to retrieve the Creation Dagger from Majjar Fodii seemed to vindicate, once again, that belief.

The JI front man's name was Jupe…just Jupe and nothing more. According to John's government sources, Jupe had been responsible for the planting of a bomb at a popular Perth restaurant a few months back. They'd pinpointed his hideout in a tent city built in the Northern Territory shortly after they'd thwarted the attempt, and had sent John to do his thing, all alone this time, without Roger and without Strykor. Getting accepted into Jupe's cell of the JI had been tough, but not much different than it had been with Hussein's Ba'athists. He'd made up the common story that he hated the pigs in America and all countries like America, and had touted himself as a pretty damn good tracker, the proof being that he'd tracked Jupe from Perth into the Territory and had found him. He'd had to prove his hatred for all things "western" by assassinating a random western target in the city of his choosing. Fodii, according to John's resources, was last known to have been living somewhere in or near Cairns so, to get himself closer to the real target, he'd chosen that city for his induction "where all the infidels of western culture come to rape the reefs of the Great Barrier."

Just a month ago, he'd "assassinated" a young boy and his mother. Local Intelligence had set the marks, had provided the false reality with standard splatter packs and kevlar, had made sure that Jupe and the three other JI terrorists who'd been watching from buildings surrounding the popular Cairns Pier had been convinced that John's sniper rifle shots had killed the tourists.

With a bit of trust now built and a growing knowledge that Jupe and his men were planning to overthrow Fodii, John had set the hook. He'd told them that he could help. He'd told them that he knew a whole lot about the dagger of death that gave Fodii so much power. He'd told them that he'd actually held one in his hand and had gone into great detail about how it felt, the energy it provided, the power it, indeed, promoted. He'd told Jupe and his men that it was the true Sword of Islam. And they had believed him.

John, for the dozenth time, looked out the grimy window of the second-story apartment. Bad streets in bad parts of towns were the same all over the world and Cairns was no different. Blinking, dying, incandescent street lamps provided little comfort and a lot of camouflage for the discrepancies he watched being bartered on the street corner below. Inside, wall paint curled like fresh wood shavings with edges tinged brown from unkept age. The refrigerator worked, but only some of the time, and never to its full, chilly potential. The mattress sucked, the couch sagged, one of the two wooden chairs was broken, and the television received a signal only when it wanted to. But he did have running water which he never drank, and a working gas stove which he never used. He was living there for only one reason.

Jupe knocked the way he said he would: three quick raps, three short raps, and three quick raps. John had told him to come alone and when he opened the door and looked past Jupe down the dark hallway, he saw no one else. John closed the door and Jupe looked cautiously around, even though there was no place to hide an accomplice.

"How?" Jupe immediately said, jumping right to the point of their meeting. "How are we going to get the glorious sword?"

John asked Jupe to sit and the terrorist sank into the flat couch cushions while John pulled up the one good wooden chair. "I have something she wants."

"You mean other than you?"

John tried not to look surprised. "What do you mean?"

"She knows who you are. I know who you are, Marine. Bad-ass black ops Marine. Tried to kill Saddam not so long ago. At least that's what Fodii told me. Is this true?"

John had expected that his cover would be blown sooner or later. "That was then," he said. "She fucked me. She almost killed all of us."

"Umm-hmm." Jupe did not take his eyes off of any part of John's face. "She verified that you did have a dagger back then. She said that she knew of its power a long time ago. And she laughed when she told me she'd fucked you and then had fucked you and your boys by telling Saddam of your intents." Neither of them said a word for almost a minute, just intensely stared. "Revenge, isn't it? You'll kill her for the purpose of revenge."

"I'll kill her because she's a terrorist just like you."

Jupe laughed quite loudly. "It's a wicked game we play, eh Little John?" He shifted on the couch to find a more comfortable flat spot. "So, you have the Book, don't you?"

"I do."

"You're right about one thing. That bitch sure does want whatever the Book is. It'll play right into our hands. I don't suppose you have it with you?"

John purposely scooted his chair quickly forward and it squealed loud enough to make Jupe jump. "What do you think?" John grinned. "Are we gonna continue playing Who Knows What or are we gonna plan my revenge and your ascent to the throne?"

"Isn't it a wonder," Jupe said, sitting up straight so that his head was almost level with John's massive chest, "how two enemies who wish both were dead can come together for mutual benefit?"

"Where and when?" John asked.

"The when, of course, is the eclipse. In two days, you will go to Hamilton Island along the Great Barrier Reef with the Book."

"Where on the island?" John asked.

Jupe stood as did John. "You'll know. Just be there Wednesday morning when the sun goes dark. Your Intelligence buddies, I'm sure, will help you. Fodii will make contact at her leisure."

"And you, Jupe?"

"I have my own buddies. Fodii can't know everything. We'll be waiting in the wings."

"And once I kill her, how do you know I'll give you the dagger?"

Jupe walked to the door and opened it. "Because you won't have a choice," he said, grinned and disappeared into the shadows.

The last time John had no faith was every day of his life before 1990. That's the year he met Alaxel, alias Lax, alias the Daykeeper. It's also the year in which he'd tried to assassinate Saddam Hussein.

Confidence to take on the dictator had come in the form of the Creation of Good and Evil Dagger which, ironically (or fatefully), Fodii now possessed. John had been on extended leave for belting a fellow officer who had gone much too far with his country southern racial remarks. The Corps had not wanted to discharge John—he was much too valuable an asset—but the Corps couldn't have its soldiers randomly beating the shit out of each other either and had to maintain the Code. So they'd sent him home for a month, back to Merida, back to the sea and scuba diving and the distance both offered from the racism that had caused him to lose all faith in humanity for the first two decades of his life.

It was in his dive shop that he'd first encountered Alaxel. John often thought of that day as one of salvation. Alax had made him realize that changing men's attitudes such as those engrained in racism was nearly impossible. Dark hearts would forever remain dark-hearted unless the world changed, he'd said. Evil could be eradicated. Good could exist without it. Opposites were not always necessary. In a world without the dark-hearted, hope would be unnecessary.

During the month of his military leave, John had learned all about cubits and daggers and the power of Daykeepers, and when Alax had told him what he must do because the world was about to take a horrible turn for the worst, John had accepted the labor, knowing that the whole of his life had led up to this singular, important moment.

Alax had given John his Creation Dagger to kill Saddam Hussein. What Alax had never told him, though, was the entire truth. No mortal could ever be told entire truths. Knowing the future was dangerous to such fragile creatures such as human beings. The attempt on Saddam's life had never been about ousting a dictator. It had been about meeting the woman who, twenty-two years later, he would confront again with the Creation Dagger as the central focus.

John was a pawn for Good. Perhaps he really was some kind of disciple. Perhaps a big, black man whose given name was John Brown, was supposed to help in the abolishment of the dark-hearted from this world forever.

And as the day of the total solar eclipse arrived, forty-two years from the date of his birth, John's faith had become, finally, irrevocable.

Seven Spirit Bay on the Cobourg Peninsula, Australia
Tuesday, November 13

Cooper sat alone on a patch of green grass by the crystal blue water of the Timor Sea, her right arm propping her up sideways as she stared at her Mama's trinket box for the hundredth time, knowing that it could not be opened and the contents handled until Billy said so. The two daggers inside could save them from anything, particularly cubits, but to hold one would tell Manson where they were.

Seven Spirit Bay was better than even Nexpa had been. There wasn't any surfing but the Indonesian seas provided an ocean-like atmosphere. The location was so remote, a person could go an entire day without running into another human being. Michael had set everything up. He had been, quite frankly, their savior. From the escape out of Phoenix, to the stealthy drive from the Darwin Airport to Seven Bay, Michael, it seemed, had known exactly what to do at exactly the right time. He had a lot of contacts in his Australian homeland, people who would not talk, many of which were of Arnhem aboriginal descent who hated everything western culture had done to them. If taking down a corporation such as Phoenix International was something they could help perpetuate, most of the Arnhem were more than happy to lend whatever services Michael requested, including lab space at Charles Darwin University where Elizabeth Presser had been able to continue her research, had finally found a way to stop the nanobots in Manson's BethStar, and had reported as much to the Australian media under the pseudonym of her and Michael's good friend, Frederico.

"Thinking about opening it?" Billy said, strolling up from behind.

"I think about it every day," Cooper replied, turning over on her back so that she could kiss Billy as he knelt beside her and lowered his head. "I think about the moment in time when we *will* open it and what that moment will mean."

"You shouldn't worry your precious thoughts with such things you cannot control. There's so much more to think about."

"Like you," Cooper said and smiled as she wrapped her arms around Billy's neck.

"Like us." Billy kissed her again.

"We're not gonna make it, are we?"

"Precious thoughts," Billy repeated. "Take deep breaths. Out with the Bad…"

"…and in with the Good," Cooper finished. She sat up and Billy sat next to her. The sea was invitingly calm and reminded her a lot of the day when her father had taken her fishing for the first time. The gentle white caps lured her senses.

"What do you see?" Billy asked.

"Memories." Cooper dropped her head onto Billy's shoulder. "We've got a few, don't we?"

"That's what makes us human."

When Cooper shifted her gaze to Billy's face, his smiling lips were just inches away. He was a Daykeeper but he was human. He was invincible, but his bones could still break. He would live for hundreds of years, but right now he was still in his twenties, young and wise and knowing without really knowing how he knew so many things. He protected her as much with his kindness as he did with the spiritual power that had been bestowed upon him. Cooper had, at one time, fantasized about invincibility, but that had been back in the Chris Cower days of lies and mistrust, a part of her memories that she wished were vanquished. She, of course, knew better now. She wouldn't want Billy's job for all the riches in the world. She did, however, accept the role of close friend and love. She was his second set of eyes and ears and she provided him with another way of looking at the world around them. She could tell him "no" or that his reasoning made little sense, and he would, most of the time, accept it in the sum of his logic. Billy was a Daykeeper, a prophet to the earth in the same capacity as those that came before him, but he was also, in so many more ways, just a man in love with not only Cooper, but with all of the wonders that most humans took for granted.

"So, tomorrow is the big day," Cooper said and lifted her head from his shoulder.

"Yes. Once the eclipse passes, the sun will begin showing evidence of what many will believe is the coming of Doomsday, of Revelation. My father has already planted the seed in their heads. All we can do is hope that mankind can survive the five days following December twenty-first, the five days of the Wayeb.

Cooper grabbed his shoulder and turned him sideways. "He's not your father. Stop saying that." This was one of those subjects for which his reasoning made no sense to her and, no matter what she said, his logic would not accept it.

His smile faltered. "But what if he is? My mother thinks it's possible."

"Billy Jo Presser! We've been over this a million times. Even if Manson was able to manipulate some genetic structure within your mother that caused her pregnancy, that doesn't automatically mean it was his…"

Billy blinked and frowned. "His fertilizer?"

Cooper shivered and leaned away from him. "He must have found another way. He must have discovered how to initiate conception without… fertilizer."

"That *would be* a miracle of science." Billy grabbed her by the shoulders and pulled her close. "Perhaps you're right. I was conceived by the immortals, the Gods, the Great Spirit."

Cooper accepted his warm embrace and new smile. "It's happened before," she said, softly.

"I know. I know." He massaged her shoulder and kissed the top of her head. "But I'm no superhero."

Fallen tree branches and brush crackled from behind. "What are you two lovebirds up to?" Elizabeth Presser asked and walked up to stand in front of them.

"Just talking," Billy replied.

"You guys do a lot of that." Billy's Mama seemed much happier now than when Cooper had first met her. Her research in Darwin and her recent discoveries concerning BethStar had magnified Elizabeth's enlightenment. "I wanted to tell you that I might know something about the whereabouts of your friend, John."

Both Billy and Cooper quickly stood.

"You told me that he was on a mission to acquire another dagger. You said that the dagger was in the possession of one of the JI terrorists. At the university, yesterday, I read in the local paper that the President of the United States is coming to Cairns for the purpose of helping delegate the JI terrorist threat with the Australian prime minister…and to observe the solar eclipse."

"How does that help us locate John?" Billy asked.

"Think about it, son. Logic. We are scientists after all."

Billy took a moment but said nothing.

"The president is coming to Cairns," his mother explained. "He's going to be in talks with factions of the JI. The leader of the JI has a Creation Dagger. The leader of the JI is a cubit. John's mission is to retrieve the Creation Dagger."

Cooper realized what Billy's mother was inferring at the same moment that Billy said, "Assassination."

"This is Richard Manson we're talking about. He likes to use people for his own twisted purposes."

"Fodii is going to try and kill the president?" Billy repeated.

"Not Fodii—Manson. He'll use her just like he tried to use Triple K to kill you, Cooper."

"And John will find a way to be there," Billy concluded. "Do you think he knows about an assassination attempt?"

"Impossible to know for sure, but you've said he's a pretty sharp Marine."

"Well, we've got to go find him…to warn him." Billy turned as if he was about to run off in the direction of Cairns a thousand miles away, but Cooper grabbed his arm.

"You can't go anywhere," Cooper said. "You have more important things to do like staying put until the time is right…Your words, remember?"

"But it's John…and the president."

"We don't even know for sure that an attempt will be made."

"No worries," Elizabeth said, the Australian culture already rooted in her own language. "Michael left for Cairns this morning after he brought me over from the university. When I told him what I've just told you, he was convinced that Richard Manson was going to kill the president."

"Mother," Billy grunted. "Might that be a bit irrational? You may have unnecessarily put his life in jeopardy. John is there. His purpose is to retrieve the dagger and bring the Book back to us."

Elizabeth turned away and let the sea breeze ruffle gray hair that had grown to the middle of her back. "There is such a thing as having too much faith," she said. "After what I've seen in the past year, I'll give in to the fact that fate does exist, but it can only exist in the presence of logic. Manson wants to rule the world, there's no doubt about that, but we have to remember that he, too, was a scientist turned rotten. Evil took him on a path of fate built on suffering and gave him the Cubit with which to accomplish such supernal pursuits. But he also created a backup plan based purely on science. If the Cubit couldn't guarantee him the world, his nanobots would." She turned and her hair blew across her face. "Your spiritual power comes from the Creation Daggers, the Book and the amulet you wear. There's no logic in them as there is no logic in the Cubit. But you, son, have something that Manson does not. People willing to give their lives for you. People who do logical things like creating a backup plan just in case blind faith doesn't work out. People who know that instinct with better light let in by death serves a purpose that is reasonable. Michael understands the possibility of death. But he also knows that sacrifice is, many times, a means to an end. If he should die so that John can get to us the fourth Creation Dagger, we can consider that both logical and fateful, but it certainly cannot be said that such a decision is irrational."

She was right, Cooper thought, and she could see the same understanding in Billy's expression. A world that divided logic and consequence and fate and belief into individualized pieces to be argued over as righteous was the world they now lived in. Transcendence would come only with an acceptance that faith and science existed simultaneously. Once December twenty-first passed, black and white would have only one shade and the five days that followed would either turn the world gray or wipe it out in a blaze of irrationality.

It was close to midnight on the night before the total eclipse, and John sat on a bed in a plush Hamilton Island, Reef View Hotel room with the Book resting next to his thigh, waiting to be called for bodyguard duty, which gave him ample time to miss his friends—a lot—particularly, Sebastian. He would never forget holding the man by his shirt, lifting him from his own boat and almost tossing him to the merciless depths of the Caribbean. Panic, was the word for it: an unreasonable response to an unreasonable determination that the immediate future held nothing but grim details. He wished that he could tell his friend that he was sorry. He wished that Cooper was so close that he could save her all over again. He wished Billy could guide him in all of the ways that Alax had. A Marine's decisions were determined by the Code and the Code had very little patience with true friendships.

In their debriefing after his meeting with Jupe in the gloomy arena of darkside Cairns, John had told Intelligence just enough for them to agree that he should be one of the two Secret Service bodyguards that confronted the public during presidential appearances: one of those well-dressed, expressionless men who looked at every nuance of every person who came within a breath of the leader of the free world. But the simple truth was that John had planned to use the president to acquire what, he was convinced, could save freedom. He was going to use the president for the purpose of revenge. Whatever happened to him after that was up to blind faith, and it was this very thought that kept him awake, reminiscing.

When he closed his eyes, he could see his friends' faces though he hadn't a clue where any of them were. His massive chest rose and fell with uneven breaths. He smiled awkwardly. When he opened his eyes, he looked at the Book once again, tried to open it once again, hoped once again that something inside would reveal some necessary truth that could ease his apprehension.

The island's Master of the Guard had, about an hour ago, informed him that talks between Majjar Fodii, the president, and the Australian prime minister had broken down. Instead of appearing in person, the terrorist had sent them a live video feed showing Fodii with the Creation Dagger planted firmly against the throat of the U.S. Ambassador to Australia. Fodii had demanded global media airtime. Fodii wanted the president to organize a news conference in which Fodii's aberrations could be broadcast via a live video feed from an undisclosed location or the ambassador would die.

What John suspected and told no one was that Fodii's hostage threats were a ruse. Jupe had told him that the meeting place and time in which Fodii would make her appearance would be, to John, evident, and John realized the president's news conference was it. John suspected and told no one that Fodii's video feed demand was also a ruse. Fodii would either tape the whole thing or have someone else wear her black hood and mimic her Islamic banter while Fodii waited in the conference room shadows with her Jupe accomplice. It would be John's one and only chance to lure her out, to lure Manson out. He'd have the Book with him, of course. That had been the deal. A trade.

Right there in front of the President of the United States. There would be that perfect moment when the attack came, an ambush, when the president's life would be in jeopardy and the Creation of Good and Evil Dagger would come out of hiding, its invincible blade bearing down.

He looked at the Book again, prayed that it would talk to him, wished for one more sign, one that could comfort him, one of guarantees. Instead, knuckles against his hotel room door made him look up.

"John."

It was the voice of the Intelligence officer that had debriefed him nearly twenty-four hours ago, and he suddenly worried that he'd unintentionally spoken aloud. His room was, by procedure, bugged. *Had they heard what he'd not told them?*

The door opened and the too-tall-to-be-so-skinny man entered. John, again, sarcastically wondered if the officer's gene pool had come straight from a stack of two-by-fours. "Still no green light. You look as if you're pondering something important."

John looked up at the ceiling smoke detector, wondering if two-by-four had placed a camera inside. "Nothing. Just prepping the mind."

The Intelligence officer strolled toward the bed. "That's good. We wouldn't want our forward guard thinking of anything more than our president's life."

John stood, and though he was a few inches shorter than the officer, his width was more than quadruple. Two-by-four didn't move an inch. "Of course," John said. "But we both know you guys are using me as bait. Fodii may not be around, but you are quite certain that Jupe is going to make an attempt."

"Based on what you told us, yes. That is, if what you told us is everything."

"And why wouldn't it be? I'm a Marine and I serve the Code."

The officer looked at the bed, at the Book. "Man of faith?"

"Aren't we all." John stepped between the officer and the Book.

"Don't think I've ever seen such a unique Bible."

"Who says it's a Bible?"

The officer craned his neck to look around John's massive shoulder. "Mind if I take a look?"

"I do. Some things are sacred, are they not?"

"Not when the president's security is in question."

"The Master of Arms has already verified my spiritual tome. Ask him." John took one giant step forward and his shadow consumed every part of two-by-four's body except for the lamp lit illumination of his forehead, eyes and half a nose.

"We all need a little faith, don't we John Brown Gordon?"

"Anything else?" John grinned but his lips felt pressured to do so.

"You might want to try a little shut eye. I suspect the president will wait until U.S. primetime to go live; that's what Fodii wants, anyway—some nut job idealistic connection with the eclipse."

"Thank you," John said. "I'll take it under advisement. Would you like me to show you the door?"

"Remember the purpose of this meeting," two-by-four said. "It is to save lives."

John nodded, knowing that Intelligence hadn't a clue of the real ramifications for what would transpire in the next few hours.

Shortly after they'd escaped Phoenix, Cooper had returned Billy's research notebook and the journal in which he'd tried to duplicate the content of the Book of the Djed. Since then, he'd stashed them away, which was not difficult in a place like Seven Spirit Bay where many of the hundred or so guests already kept to themselves. On occasion (like right now), he'd look through them for inspiration and reflection: of what had brought them to this moment and of what future still awaited. Back in February, Cooper had described what she and John and Sebastian and Roger had seen the night before they'd left Mexico for the final time, and Billy had replicated that final drawing at the bottom of the page of symbols in his own "Book," a glyph that looked just like Man standing under the Sun.

Night had fallen across the sea and the full dark side of the new moon thickened the sparkling layer of Milky Way stars that sandwiched the dark rift. He sat on a tropical wood porch outside the one-room cottage he and Cooper had been living in since arriving in Australia. His journal sat on the porch decking next to him while in his lap rested his research notebook. He opened it to where, on the left page, he'd written what Lax had divined through Aaron's spiritual ghost back in his mother's Arizona house:

> *The final destination. Seal the Evil forever. Don't let men stop you. Suffer the five days of reckoning and renew the earth.*

Man had to suffer for five days, Billy thought, and the only way that was going to happen was if Billy stopped Manson and his men and sealed the Cubit at the final destination.

On the right page, he'd retraced, to the best of his recollection, the strange letters that had been scratched into the glass surface of his mother's kitchen table.

Michael had already told him what the scratching meant. The letters had not looked like any language Billy had ever seen until Michael had told him to flip his notebook upside down.

Uluru: the aboriginal name for the infamous red rock monolith located in the southern part of the Northern Territory, better known as Ayer's Rock. *That's the final destination,* Michael had suggested. *The word means "to wail at the meeting place." That's where we'll know.*

"Figure it out?" Cooper was suddenly beside him. Billy only shook his head. "You gonna stare at it all night? Those words? Waiting for an answer from the Milky Way?"

Billy didn't mean to frown when he finally looked at her, but what she'd said suddenly reminded him of Joel Canton, the old fisherman who'd cleverly used candy as bait. What she said reminded him of Stephanie Drake and her dolphin-clad outfit she'd worn the night they'd gone to the luau. He thought of Janine Bender and how, back in Boynton Canyon, he'd spiritually connected to her son, Lenny, while standing within the medicine wheel of Yavapai Indians. He thought about what his mother had said earlier in the day, how there were *people willing to give their lives for you,* which made him think about all of his friends' deaths.

And he cried. Big fat tears dressed the open notebook pages with fresh personality. A few of the pen strokes smeared before he closed it.

"I'm sorry," Cooper said. "I didn't mean to…"

"You didn't. It's just that so many have suffered so much and it's taken so long. I don't know how *you've* managed."

"I love you Billy Jo Presser. No other explanation is necessary." Cooper knelt and cuddled him from behind. "A wee bit of sleep might help…well, you know—out with the Bad, in with the Good."

Billy leaned back into her comforting caress and his notebook toppled from his lap to the green grass at his feet. Her heart beat delicately against the back of his head, lifted a few of his shoulder-length blonde strands like a gentle breeze. The harmonic rhythm made his eyes flutter, and when she started humming and rocking gently, he knew sleep was not far off. She'd done this before to cleanse his troubled mind. She'd hugged and hummed and had sang the same song that she now repeated—a lullaby from her Mama.

Lullaby baby. Lullaby now.
Sleep my baby. Sleep my love.
This pretty baby who was born in the morning,
Wants to be taken for a jalopy ride.

This sweet baby who was born during the day,
Wants to be taken to the candy shop.

This pretty baby who was born at night,
Wants to be taken for a stroller ride.

This pretty baby wants to sleep
But the naughty sleep doesn't want to come.

This pretty baby who was born at night,
Wants to be taken for a stroller ride.

Reef View Hotel Conference Room
Wednesday Morning, November 14

Among the suffocating local Fox network and international news crews was Maggie Liester, anchor extraordinaire for the historically popular New York broadcast station, WNBC. Liester had risen in the past year to become one of the most sought after on-air talents. Her middle-market news crew had captured Triple K's death, which had gone viral on the Internet almost immediately. The video had made her famous because it had sparked so much controversy. Some had said it contained mere studio effect, something thrown together during a late night, Long Island storm; crafty, yes…clever, certainly…but legit? The video had some major flaws in it, the critics had said, and they came right at the moment of most interest: when the scrawny kid holding a smartphone in one hand and a Creation Dagger in the other, stabbed Triple K. At that moment, Liester's cameraman had decided that the raindrops on his camera lens needed a quick wipe down. In the video capture, the kid's arm swung in a large arc toward the back of Triple K's neck then—Wipe—the haft of the weapon (all blurry and smearing from the streaks on the camera lens) was sticking out of the knight's neck and the invincible knight's body was molting into nothingness. How convenient, the critics had said. Classic cinematic jump cut.

Many others, though, had determined that the video *was* legit. They had made the connection. The evidence had been clear to them. What Manson had said on Christmas Eve, and had later released in a written statement, was absolutely correct. The Creation Daggers were not of this earth. The Creation Daggers, in the hands of the wrong people, could end this world. Their power was evident, if you believed what you saw in Maggie Liester's infamous footage.

John stood in front of the door to the backroom where the president was preparing his entrance. The conference room had way too many windows for the likes of the Service, but it was the most securable space of its size on the island. The agenda for the conference was a bit complex, having been determined by the president and Intelligence. Since early morning in Cairns coincided with the evening newscasts fourteen hours earlier in the U.S., the president first wanted his country to "share with him" the total eclipse of the sun, which had begun when John arrived an hour ago. Numerous wireless cameras had been set up outside, and all were feeding the celestial spectacle right into the six o'clock homes of millions of Americans.

Next on the agenda was a deception. Fodii, with the ambassador hostage in hand, had demanded live airtime to endorse her terrorist extremism. The president had agreed but had never even considered doing such a thing. He and Intelligence would let the live feed run, would blame the eclipse for magnetic interference and satellite malfunction, would use Fodii's live signal to trace its source, and would send in the Seals to take care of business. Intelligence already knew that Fodii's hideout was somewhere close by, perhaps on one of the neighboring barrier islands, but they'd been unable to trace communications from the terrorist so far.

While this all played out—the tracing of Fodii's signal and the Seals' deployment—the president's news conference would not be live as had been promised; it would be recorded without the knowledge of anyone, including the media attendees who'd been allowed to bring their cameras but had been forbidden to broadcast anything until the conference was over. The president would stand at the podium at the moment of full eclipse and give a speech that condemned Fodii, that would reveal Fodii's capture (which at the moment of the speech would not yet have happened), that would crucify terrorism—then he'd take questions, take credit, and take off just as the sun reemerged from behind the moon. If everything went according to plan, the U.S. ambassador would be saved and Fodii would join Bin Laden at the bottom of the sea. Case closed.

But there would be no broadcast signals from Fodii. There would be no tracing of anything that the Seals could use. John knew that the terrorist, herself, which in this case was actually Richard Manson, would be in the audience.

Two-by-four stood at the back of the fifty-foot-square conference room and stared straight at John who shrugged in the most inconspicuous way he could. Both men scanned the faces of the crowd that sat in rows of folding metal chairs and stood in numbers behind the rows and along the walls to either side. Intelligence was looking for Jupe. John was looking for Fodii. John centered his attention on Maggie Liester who stood near the front of the room along the wall of windows to his right, and this drew two-by-four in the news anchor's direction.

A knock on the backroom door alerted John that the president would emerge in ten minutes. He looked through the conference room windows above Liester where, nestled within the forefront of Hamilton Island's short mountain peaks, the rising sun sat like a sliced orange in a bowl, its majesty chomped by the moon like a disease that had nearly consumed its magnificent host.

John unbuttoned his suit jacket and removed it, released the strap on his shoulder-holstered Baretta, reached around and stroked the leathery cloth face of the Book which he'd stashed in his pants waistband, turned around to open the backroom door, and inhaled one final, deep good breath.

Like a pigeon from hell, sleep delivered the images. The death of Billy's friends. Steph's head cracked against the roof of her Cavalier and he did nothing. Janine and Joel perished atop Port A sand piles and he did nothing. He even stabbed his best friend, Bottlenose. Then there was Alixel and Lax and Sebastian and…

How many more? He thought as he woke with a start. John…Michael… the president? What good would there be in killing the President of the United States? Turmoil, of course. Chaos. Leadership was going to be paramount very soon. It was the one last character attribute that would have any chance at steering the paranoid once everything started coming apart. The power of love and hope, for many, would be lost and this seemed to be right up Manson's sick alley.

Cooper had left him on the porch hours ago and when he jerked from sleep, the stars were gone. A thin, blue-black band of clouds hovered in an arc above the eastern horizon and above them, the sun was two-thirds gone.

He slowly pushed his stiff spine into a sitting position and looked for Cooper. The cottage door, which was nothing more than a vine-strapped collation of bamboo, stood open. He couldn't see her, but a small gas lamp revealed the shadow of her bed and resting body.

He stood, scratched his head, and collected his research notebook and journal which Cooper had stacked next to him. He went inside the cottage, set the books on a small bamboo end table, and just stood and stared at her, at the fetal scrunch of her body that brought her bare knees up toward her elbows, at the strawberry-blonde curls of hair drooping across her cheeks and looping through the fingers of one hand. Her calm breaths made the curls dance and then she said something, an indecipherable mumble. He stepped forward and leaned over.

Mmmm...mmmm...mmmm...

Billy jerked up and looked around the room.

Mmmm...mmmm...mmmm...

The remaining sliver of sun shot a stream of waking amber light straight across the Timor Sea and through the cottage's open doorway. Inside the sunbeam, Billy saw…he blinked.

Mmmm...mmmm...mmmm...

The Cubit! He blinked again and shuffled backward, almost falling onto Cooper's sleeping body. It wasn't real, of course, but he could see it and hear it nonetheless. Against his chest, the Creation of the End Dagger glowed red with warmth. He unbuttoned his shirt, unsheathed it, carried it in his right hand, approached the apparition; the edges of the Cubit's sealed lid pulsed with the same rhythm as the dagger.

Mmmm...mmmm...mmmm...

The Cubit's translucence allowed him to see the wooden floor underneath and when he poked at the box with the dagger, he thought the blade would pass right through…but it didn't. The dagger's thin point touched the lid and Billy felt the pressure of resistance against his wrist. The Cubit apparition reacted angrily, shaking its ghostly self as if a lethal dose of death was about to be injected into it.

MMMM...MMMM...MMMM...

The lid started to rise and Billy reacted by pushing the dagger downward; its glow became a blaze. The blade disappeared an inch into the apparition and the Cubit's lid shook as if something inside wanted out.

"MMM…MMM…MAMA!"

Billy jumped and turned at the same time. The dagger fell from his hand and thumped against the wood floor. If the Cubit had not been an apparition, he would have tripped over it.

"Mama," Cooper said again, her volume a few decibels softer, and started crying.

The remaining sunlight warmed Billy's spine and when he looked down, the Cubit was gone. His dagger sat idle on the floor at his feet and he picked it up, considered it and the ghostly experience for a moment, then walked quickly to Cooper's bedside. He mopped the sweat from her brow and one finger tangled in one strawberry curl.

"She came out of the grave!" Cooper said, panting. She rolled on her back and her eyes pierced Billy's. "She came out of the grave and the grave was the Cubit!"

"Shhh," Billy softly said. "It was all a dream." He glanced at the doorway then back again.

"A nightmare," Cooper said and whimpered.

Billy leaned closer and touched her cheeks with both hands. "It's all right. I'm here." Cooper grabbed his hands and her fingernails dove into his skin but he didn't flinch. She lolled her head against his chest, against the Djed amulet that dangled in the open V made by his unbuttoned shirt. He tried to console her but the eclipse only magnified the dark thought of the Cubit that both of them had simultaneously experienced. Though the air swirled an Australian summer breeze through the open cottage windows, Billy suddenly felt very cold. The sun had, after so many millions of years, begun to change. And Man stood in its way.

Unbeknownst to John, the Secret Service had killed Jupe and two accomplices as they'd attempted to sabotage the hotel's electrical systems moments before the president emerged from the backroom. Also unbeknownst to John was Fodii's disguise as Maggie Liester's news camera operator. She looked just like a man, had full facial hair, and wore dark sunglasses to hide the red-eyed evidence that she was really a Manson-controlled cubit. For those who were the true players of destiny, the cards were stacked perfectly. The Intelligent two-by-four stood significantly insignificant. He looked for a perpetrator that crouched, incognito, right in front of him.

When the president emerged, John led him forward, toward the podium, his eyes roaming for the imminent attack. Beyond the breadth of the conference room windows, the moon slowly consumed nearly all of the sun's orange face and the room dimmed in concert with the celestial shadow.

The Aboriginals called it dreamtime. Billy had experienced it on many occasions both before he'd become a Daykeeper and since. Visions. Alternate realities. A sixth sense. Knowing without really knowing how you knew. It was his destiny to know. A lonely burden. All because he was meant to. The world's selfish demand on a poor unsuspecting soul. All of the Daykeepers before him had knelt to the expectation, accepting such inexplicable self-sacrifice in exchange for a life neverending.

But for Billy, right now, it was different—because of Cooper. It was unlike it had ever been for any Daykeeper before him. Such supreme knowledge had never been available to mere mortals, but everything that was going to happen from now until whatever awaited at Uluru would include a bond between prayer and savior.

Billy and Cooper held each other tightly, not only with arms and skin but with soul, and they sat on the shores of the Timor Sea, staring at the dark orb of the shadowed sun, seeing together, feeling together, experiencing the hardship of a friend who was determined to satisfy his deed. John Brown Gordon.

The Secret Service bodyguard closest to the light switch flicked it up just as Fodii dropped her video camera and ran forward. The switch didn't work and the entire conference room went dark as the eclipsing moon shadow swallowed the sun. Lights mounted atop six other news cameras provided the only illumination in the room. Metal glistened in the palm of Fodii's hand: the blade of the Creation of Good and Evil.

At the moment that the total eclipse transformed the morning, Cooper's heart beat feverishly against his chest. She stared with him straight into the moon shadow. He believed that she saw what he was seeing: John and the president and the bearded attacker. When she hunched forward at the same moment he did, Billy knew that she was also dodging the blade that almost killed the president. When she gasped at the same moment he did, he knew that she also saw the blade sweep around for a second attempt. When she screamed, he knew that she did so because John jumped.

The president was quite agile and wily and had been trained to always be prepared. When Manson (as Fodii) leapt at him, the president knelt and the dagger's blade chopped off two strands of hair from the top of his head. When Manson pivoted around and a swarm of bodyguards dove at her, John dropped atop the president's back, exposing the Book stashed in his waistband. This had been John's plan all along. Bait. The president. The Book. He'd known that the only way he might get the dagger from his nemesis was to be impaled by it. And that's exactly what Manson did—right into the kidney just inches above the top of the Book. What John had not expected, was an angel whose name was Michael.

Billy's perspective now floated above the melee. Light was provided only in concentrated spotlight beams from each of the news cameras. When Fodii stabbed John, she took the Book and then kicked three bodyguards with such force that each instantly became incapacitated balls of throbbing flesh. She pivoted and crouched and grabbed the Book's cover just as a beam of bright white light streamed in a thin plane, no thicker than piece of paper, from the center of it. Fodii pulled the Book open and its light engulfed the room.

From the right side of his vision, Billy saw Michael who had been standing with the Fox news crew, a camera on his shoulder, waiting. He now dove at Fodii and knocked the Book from her grip. Fodii's snarl shook the room and as she stood, panting with anger, she punched two more bodyguards in the head, killing them instantly. Michael dropped to his knees near the Book but was still a foot away when Fodii stepped in front of him.

"Give it to me," Manson said through Fodii's lips. "The game is over. You have lost."

"Nothing is over until the Lord says so," Michael countered.

From behind both of them, John squirmed. The president had already rolled from under John's body and was now looking down at him, at the dagger's haft which protruded from his bodyguard's back.

"What is your name?" the president said.

"John Brown Gordon…sir." He grimaced.

"John Brown?" The president's eyes rolled with intrepid understanding. "Freedom."

John's body jerked involuntarily. He tried to grab the dagger from its secure place inside his kidney. "More than that," John said. "It's time."

"Time? What time?"

John pushed his huge chest away from the floor. The muscles of his upper arms rippled, bulged. He craned his mighty head upward. "Time for the beginning." John tried once more to grab the dagger, falling back to the floor as he did so, and the president's hand led the wandering appendage to its target. Together, they pulled it free. "Michael," John gasped. "It belongs to the angels."

Five feet away, the Book warbled because Manson, as Fodii, touched it.

When the Book opened, Cooper shielded her eyes. Its light was too intense. In that instant, she looked at Billy who was crying. She reached up and grabbed one of his tears, let it roll on the pad of her index finger. She studied its salty smear, questioned it, then looked back at the black sun and saw…

John Brown Gordon died in the service of his country at the moment of full eclipse. He'd lived a life of separation because of his race, because of his size, because of his aggressive choices. He'd tried to change the world more than once and, in death, had finally succeeded. His true friends experienced his passing even though they didn't hold his hand. He left the world with a wide-eyed glare and a smile of knowing.

The president rolled the big man onto his back and swiped his open eyelids closed. In the president's hand was the Creation of Good and Evil and he looked up because the Book beckoned him.

One of the Fox News anchors had taken Michael's camera and now started recording as Michael and Fodii Manson each grabbed a cover of the Book and pulled in opposite directions, opening it to reveal the key page that was smothered in a light so bright, both of them covered their eyes with their free forearms. Neither would release the tome even though their combined grips tempted a tear that would nullify any advantage the Book had for Good or Evil. Fodii Manson reached out, squinting to avoid the light's intensity, grabbed Michael's wrist, squashed it so that he released the Book. The absence of Fodii's counterforce sent Michael sprawling backward into the first row of unfolded metal chairs. Fodii Manson now proudly held the open Book with both hands, and stared straight into the light, looking for the final clue that he thought the key page was about present. It was at that moment that two things happened simultaneously. The sun poked out from behind the moon, casting a sliver of red-orange light through the conference room windows, and the president rammed the Creation Dagger into the back of Fodii Manson's neck. A dozen Secret Service men, including the scrawny two-by-four Intelligence officer, ran and dove at the center of the confrontation. Michael was tackled from behind and fell face-forward into the presidential pile. Slowly, like a football scrum after the scramble for a loose ball, the human pile peeled away. When Michael was yanked out, he grabbed his stomach as if in horrible pain and dropped to his knees, bowed forward and glared at the floor. His Fox News cohort momentarily moved the camera from his shoulder and yelled, "Michael. Are you all right?"

When the pile cleared, all that remained was the president and a scattered mound of ash and bones. The Creation Dagger was gone as was the Book. "The weapon, sir," one of the bodyguards said. "Where's the weapon?"

The president brushed ash from his pants and looked over at John's body then at Michael. "Your name is Michael," he said.

Michael looked up but still held his stomach in pain. A blood spatter larger than his hand stained the shirt. "Yes, Mr. President."

"Like the angel," the president said, "from the Bible."

"I…"

The president walked over and knelt beside him, gazed at the bulge under Michael's bloody shirt that had the shape of a book, but didn't question it. Instead, he said, "He was your friend," and nodded toward John.

"No, sir. I didn't even know him."

"But you tried to save him. Why?"

"Because I was told to. I was told to get…" He looked at his stomach and the blood on his shirt.

"Can you tell me, Michael, what time it is?" The president reached out and grabbed one of Michael's shoulders.

"Time?" Michael said. "It's time for the Wayeb. It's time for penance. It's time for the new beginning. It's time for the sun." He nodded toward the windows where the red-orange solar slivers grew wider.

The president stood and beckoned the Fox News anchor forward. "You have an injured man here," he said, "Tend to him."

As the anchor gave his camera to another of the crew and moved forward, Michael slowly stood, both hands remaining firmly against what was under his shirt. "Mr. President," he said, pleading. "Beware of Richard Manson."

Billy saw the key page as clearly as if he'd been sitting on the shoulders of the cubit that called herself Fodii. It was flipped to the left of the opened Book, resting atop the page of symbols. The light blazing from it was unbelievably white—a color he'd never seen before, but he couldn't take his eyes off of it, off of what he saw. Way back when he'd first seen the key page, it had been sticking out of the satchel of another cubit named Albert Stine. At the top of the page had been the symbols of the Creation Dagger and the Wayeb. He remembered thinking that the page was some kind of treasure map or priceless ancient artifact. He'd been right on both accounts. Not only had the key page led him toward the place where he'd become a Daykeeper, it now told him how the Wayeb would begin.

Just as it had become when he'd gazed upon it in the Great Hall of the Anasazi, the key page was, again, translucent. He saw what was above it, on it and through it all at the same time. Above it, floated a holographic rendering of the Cubit. It glowed a faint wooden red color that made it stand out in the blinding whiteness. On the key page, the dagger symbol drawn at the top of it now moved downward and split into four additional duplicate glyphs. The four new daggers crept into four different positions under the floating Cubit, each stopping at a point that intersected with the Cubit's lid. The fifth dagger squirmed toward the bottom of the page and its point found a place directly under the star in the front face of the floating Cubit. Through the key page, Billy saw each of the five drawings on the page of symbols in reverse, as if the heavy heavenly hand that had drawn them there had pressed so firmly that each—the phoenix, the 6s and 9s, the Djed, the chaos star, and the Sun over Man—had been embossed into the paper. These symbols, too, moved across their page and each now rested under a different dagger, under a different part of the holographic Cubit, vertically lining up.

The three-dimensional experience brightened even whiter and Billy tried to close his eyes but couldn't. He wouldn't. His brain was searching for meaning. He was remembering—the image of the Cubit he'd seen floating in the doorway less than an hour ago. He'd pulled out his dagger and had tried to…

And then he knew beyond a shadow of a doubt: the five daggers could seal the Cubit! They could seal it if placed in the exact locations that the key page was now revealing. Billy stared harder so that the image burned into him, so that the image would never be forgotten.

"Billy!"

Someone was shaking him.

"Billy! Stop! Stop it, now!"

He blinked and looked away from the Book, floated away from the alternate reality, saw the president and Michael and John all fading. Then he saw nothing but the sun.

"Billy, please."

Cooper turned his shoulders to face her. Billy's irises and pupils were as white as the center of the Book of the Djed had been. And he was blind.

CBSNews.com
Wednesday, November 21, 2012

Video Sparks Petition for Presidential Election Recall

A video released yesterday has ignited a cry for a petition to recall the presidential election because, the distributors of the video say, the recording provides evidence that the President of the United States is a terrorist.

The video [see CBSNews video link] is the only known recorded evidence of the mayhem during the attempted assassination of the president during the total solar eclipse outside of Cairns, Australia a week ago. The choppy recording appears to show the president stabbing one of his own bodyguards in the back before attacking a second man who was confronting the terrorist known as Majjar Fodii. Darkness from the eclipse combined with flashes from camera lights make the video hard to comprehend.

An anonymous group sent the recording to most major news outlets Tuesday morning. WNBC in New York has denied responsibility and said that their popular news anchor Maggie Liester, infamous for another video similar to that sent yesterday, was at the news conference but that she had been tackled by intelligence officers when the assassination attempt was made.

"Before the terrorist attacked the president's bodyguard, I was knocked over by men who were trying to grab Fodii," Liester said. "That's when the shit really hit the fan, but all I could see from the floor was asses and elbows." Liester added that the anonymous video was the only way she'd seen what she had missed.

Billionaire Richard Manson, contributor of more than $10 million dollars toward a new super PAC entitled "Recall," said today that the video is proof enough.

"I told everyone back on Christmas Eve in 2011 that those Creation Daggers, when in the hands of the wrong people, could end the world as we know it. The video plainly shows the president stabbing his own bodyguard with one. He was plainly trying to save the terrorist. The president must be one of them, or worse. He apparently has had a Creation Dagger for quite some time and has used it to amass too much power."

The White House denied all accusations, saying that they were "unacceptable nonsense" and calling out Manson's own possession of what he has called a Creation Dagger.

Manson is famously remembered for a worldwide news conference last year in which he promised to save the planet from a climate-altering coronal mass ejection which he claimed would hit the earth around December 21.

Popular Science News App
Sunday, November 25, 2012

Solar Activity Increases

Coronal Mass Ejections (CME) have been growing in number, intensity and speed since the solar eclipse more than ten days ago, said scientists at NASA's Goddard Space Flight Center in Greenbelt, Md. Using the Solar and Heliospheric Observatory (SOHO), a spacecraft mission launched in 1995 designed to study the sun, the CME events have been recorded as expected but not worrisome.

"The solar system goes through these 11-12 year cycles. It's expected," said NASA scientist Dr. Samuel Eaks, a SOHO project leader.

None of the CMEs have been directed at earth, NASA said, and none have been anywhere the intensity of one of the greatest space weather events ever recorded known as the 1859 Carrington Event when telegraph systems all over the world failed and telegraph operators were shocked by the sun's massive CME.

"CMEs are usually nothing more than spectacular light shows when viewed from terrestrial viewpoints," Eaks said. "Enjoy the spectacle as it will be coming to an end in just a few months."

CBSNews.com
Wednesday, November 28, 2012

New Science Advisor Has Evidence Against BethStar

One week after the creation of a post-election super PAC by billionaire Richard Manson [link to Article from Nov. 21], the U.S. President is striking back.

The president's new science advisor, Dr. Elizabeth Presser has provided evidence that Manson's corporate giant Phoenix International was responsible for the manufacture and distribution of the designer drug known as PUSH*, which became quickly popular then quickly disappeared back at the end of 2010. Presser has also provided evidence that PUSH* and the miracle health pill, BethStar, are nearly identical in their molecular design. According to the president, Dr. Presser has determined that Manson knowingly and willingly distributed this potentially harmful drug to millions of people across the globe.

"Richard Manson is not to be trusted," the president said in a news conference earlier today. "He won't save the world on December 21 or on any other day. If you are taking the BethStar supplement, stop now."

The president declined reporter's questions to further explain his position, but sources say what the president didn't mention was his suspicion that the BethStar pills contain what are known as nanobots. Sources say that there is a connection between this suspicion and one that was made by an award-winning documentarian, Michael Arden, back in 2010, during the height of the PUSH* drug influence.

The president's announcement today has fueled anger across the political aisle. Both House and Senate members have called the president's science advisor "a kook" and that her "accusations against a man who has saved the world from suffering are skeptical at best."

Tens of thousands have already signed the post-election recall petition and there is little evidence to show that the effort will slow. Most political pundits believe that the super PAC "Recall" will collect the necessary signatures for a recall election before the president takes the oath in January.

National Geographic Magazine
Wednesday, December 5, 2012

Man From the Sea Talks to Dolphins

National Geographic photojournalists Leo and Anna Jones have released an astonishing collection of photographs taken while documenting river run off into the Baja gulf earlier in the year. The photographs (see opposite page) show a man emerging from the Gulf of California with a group of dolphins, one of them pink. The Jones' claim that the man, later identified as Billy Jo Presser, was talking to the dolphins when they captured him on film. The photographs appear to justify the claim.

"He had an amazing story to tell," Anna Jones said. "He claimed to have swum with the dolphins all the way from Nexpa, a small surfing and fishing village in Mexico some thirteen hundred miles to the south. Of course, anyone who might have been stranded in the Sonoran Desert would succumb to dehydration-induced aberrations, but Billy showed no signs of any need for medical treatment. He was quite convincing."

The Jones' said that they drove the man to Tempe, Arizona, and dropped him off outside of the campus at Arizona State University (ASU) where he was supposed to meet his mother. Coincidentally, the United States president's new science advisor has the same last name and worked at ASU up until a time that closely coincides with the Jones' story.

The whereabouts of the Man From the Sea are unknown and the president's media relations team has denied any knowledge of him, but it is certain that National Geographic's team of award-winning photojournalists has once again captured amazing and controversial moments in time.

CBSNews.com, FLASHFILE
Friday, December 14, 2012

A Week Before the End; Manson Gone

Following news on December 12 that scientists now agree with recent claims of an earth-altering coronal mass ejection (CME) hitting the planet, tens of thousands of people have been massing at ancient worship sites and geographic locations known for their intense ley line energies. Dozens of ancient Mayan ruins in Mexico and Guatemala have seen a dramatic influx of people who believe that these sites will save them when the CME hits. Other locations of mass migration include the monoliths on Easter Island, the Great Pyramids of Egypt, Stonehenge and the red rock country of central Arizona among dozens of others across the world. Some of the holy migrators believe that the site they have fled to is the same one that their savior, Richard Manson, will choose to release what he said would stop the CME back on Christmas Eve in 2011. Manson has not been seen since the release of evidence that his BethStar pill has been linked to the designer drug PUSH* and that BethStar contains potentially harmful ingredients.

Ayers Rock Resort, Northern Territory, Australia
December 20, 2012

For the fourth time since Michael had been sitting in the lobby, the President of the United States was urging all people to take necessary precautions as the CME was now imminent. When Michael changed the TV station, there he was again, saying the same recorded thing. Not one of the other resort guests stopped to watch with him. He thought they were either too numb from the numerous media messages they'd already encountered, didn't believe in the U.S. president's warning, were completely deaf and dumb or, most likely, were walking products of Richard Manson's manipulations. After all, this was Manson's property. Phoenix International had purchased it the day after Pitchfork Man had infiltrated Elizabeth Presser's home and had seen the prophetic writing on the kitchen's table top.

Uluru, scratched in glass upside down, was within a few minutes' drive.

Manson had turned the resort into some kind of health haven where guests were fed BethStar pills like candy. It didn't matter that scientists in the United States had offered a warning. Ayers Rock Resort had been marked as the Fountain of Youth where age was put on hold and anyone who could front the bill was guaranteed life forevermore. Given the fact that the sun was about to test mankind, the resort was now home to the richest, most self-absorbing people the planet had to offer.

"...an immense solar flare will hit the earth tomorrow," the president said again and Michael turned the station to an Australian Rules football recap. A news ticker rolled along the bottom of the screen.

Tens of thousands amass at the Vatican today after U.S. President warns of impending solar calamity.

Considering the severity of what was about to happen, the world seemed to be taking the news fairly well, Michael thought. There had not been many cases of rioting panic except for the places where rioting panic had always been a norm. Part of the reason was because billionaire Richard Manson had promised salvation, had guaranteed that he could stop the sun, and an incredible number of people across the globe were now counting on it, regardless of the accusations that BethStar was a form of mind control. These people had carelessly massed in places where they'd prayed on knees and worshipped stones instead of finding food and water and shelter underground. It was happening in the U.S. It was happening in Australia. It was happening everywhere. It was this complacency that the president kept warning everyone to avoid. The president knew that Manson wasn't going to stop the sun because he knew that Billy Jo Presser and Cooper Reyes and Michael Arden were going to stop him. The president knew that the sun's rays *had to* pummel the earth because only such an extreme radiation blast could deactivate the BethStar nanobots. The president knew these things because Elizabeth Presser had shown him the evidence and the president knew of Dr. Presser because Michael had told him about her shortly after he'd saved the leader of the free world from assassination.

An hour after Fodii's remains had been swept from the floor of the Reef View Hotel conference room, a tall, thin man had visited Michael just minutes before his scheduled flight back to Cairns. Michael had wrapped the dagger in a hotel hand towel and both it and the Book were stashed in his brown, canvas carry-on.

He scratched his belly where the dagger had sliced through skin, lifted his shirt, and examined the wound. Billy had told him of the healing powers of the Creation Daggers and the hard scab, which had already started to peel, was evidence.

"The president would like to see you," said the thin man, who'd taken it upon himself to open Michael's hotel room door. He pointed at Michael's carry-on. "And bring that with you. We'll escort you back to the mainland."

The thin man who said he was with Intelligence escorted Michael into the elevator and up to the penthouse suite where two bodyguards greeted them. The door to the penthouse suite was open and Michael saw the president sitting behind a desk beyond the doorway. The president waved, invitingly. The Intelligence officer walked him into the room and the bodyguards closed the door behind them but remained outside.

"Who is Richard Manson?" the president said and tapped the point of a pen against a stack of paper sitting on the desk.

"Sir?" Michael said, stepping away from the Intelligence officer who'd found it necessary to crowd him since leaving his hotel room fifteen floors below. "He's the billionaire that..."

The president raised his left hand and spun the pen between two fingers. "Would you please leave us," he said to the Intelligence officer.

"But," the skinny man said. "Is that wise, sir?"

"Angels will look after me. And I don't want any monitoring going on either. It's just me and Michael, understand?"

The Intelligence office nodded and left the room and the president came from behind the desk, flipped the pen onto the desk top, the offered Michael one of two cloth armchairs sitting next to each other on the left side of the room. He pointed at Michael's carry-on.

"Are they in there?"

"What, sir?"

"The weapon that looks like the one Manson waved at the world last Christmas Eve. The one I used to kill that thing. And the book with the bright light."

Michael didn't say anything and looked over his shoulder at the door.

"You can tell me," the president said, "and I'll believe you. I haven't seen anything like what happened this morning except, of course, in the movie theater."

"Richard Manson is the Antichrist," Michael whispered. "The Book says so." He thought the president would throw him out of the room but, instead, he leaned forward and placed his hands on his knees.

"Tell me more."

And Michael did. With a hushed voice that made the president move his chair closer, Michael told him everything he knew. He told him about Phoenix International and the BethStar nanobots. He told him about Elizabeth Presser and the evidence he'd help her uncover. He told him that the sun was going to place the world in grave jeopardy and that there really was a device called the Cubit that could protect the planet. He told him that Dr. Presser had found that the sun's coming intense ejection could deactivate Manson's nanobots and that Presser's son was going to make sure that happened.

Michael then explained what Billy had told him about the Djed, and Daykeepers, and cubits, and the Book, and the five Creation Daggers that Billy needed to stop Manson from taking further control of earth's future. Michael told the president that acquiring Fodii's dagger and the Book was the reason why he'd come to the Great Barrier Reef.

When Michael had finished, the president asked, "And John Brown Gordon? The man who saved my life?"

"Like I said, I didn't know him. Billy always called him his friend. He helped Billy find his fate."

"An honorable soldier," the president said. "Self-sacrifice for freedom."

"Not if Manson gets his way."

"Well, we'll just have to make sure that doesn't happen, but I need your help. I need some evidence."

Michael looked down at his carry-on.

"No. Not them. You need them. What I need is to talk with Dr. Presser. Can you arrange that?"

"Can you get me some transportation?"

The president smiled. "You're kidding, right?" he said and stood. "But first we have to take care of something very important."

John Brown Gordon was laid to rest along the Outer Barrier Reef.

The president and Michael saluted the casket as it slid off the back end of a U.S. naval destroyer. Seven guns fired three times and with each resounding percussion, Michael's nerves jumped. "Taps" played in the background as John finally found peace in the one place he'd always dreamed of as paradise.

Michael was then escorted to a helicopter and two Secret Service men jumped on board with him.

"You need to convince her that she can help me help her son," the president shouted as the blades chopped air overhead. "I'll be here waiting."

Elizabeth Presser became the president's senior science advisor the day after Michael had returned to Seven Spirit Bay. Her departure in the military aircraft had been a tough moment for Billy. He'd reconnected with his mother and they had worked through the complexity of their difficult past. Predominately, they'd finally reasoned that there was no solid evidence indicating that Billy was Richard Manson's biological son. Together, they'd reasoned that Billy was the product of genetic irregularity catalyzed by science and fulfilled by faith.

After Dr. Presser had left, Michael had given Billy the Book and had rolled the Creation of Good and Evil dagger from the hotel hand towel (taking care not to touch it) into Cooper's trinket box where it had settled snuggly against the two other daggers.

And then they'd waited. They'd waited until Billy had said it was time to go. They'd waited until the sun had turned blood red on the day before the end of the world.

Michael jerked from trance when he realized that someone was standing beside him in the resort lobby. The man's head was glistening bald and he looked just like Yule Brenner. The guy stared straight at the television, expressionless, seemingly oblivious of Michael's presence. If he had been wearing a black hat and belt with pistols, Michael would have sworn the killer from one of his favorite movies *Westworld* was standing right next to him. Silver sparkles lit up the center of both of Yule's eyes and Michael's nerves caused a hiccup. On the TV, an Australian Rules football game recap had turned the screen bright white and Michael realized Yule's eyes had caught the reflection. The man looked down at Michael whose mouth was agape in preparation for another hiccup.

"Flies," the Yule impersonator said.

Michael shook his head, hiccupped, but did not take his eyes off of the man's silver pupil stare.

"Flies," the man repeated. "Keep that mouth open like that and flies are gonna fly right down your goozlepipe."

"Goozle…?" Michael closed his mouth.

"Pipe," the man added and laughed. "You look like crap. First day here?"

Michael nodded, once.

"Give it a few days. You'll get better." Yule then reached into his pocket and pulled out a fist. When his hand opened, three BethStar pills rolled into his lifeline. "Need one?"

Michael shook his head. "I'm good."

"Yes. Well that is a matter of opinion."

The double glass doors that led to the courtyard where the pool and rooms were located slid open. Cooper led Billy by the hand into the lobby. "A new friend?" she said to Michael while scowling at the man who had not yet closed his hand. "We have plenty," she told him. "Beat it."

The bald man huffed, shrugged, and stuck his nose in the air as he slammed all three pills down his goozlepipe. He left the lobby through a second set of sliding glass doors that led outside to the front of the resort.

"I hate these people," Cooper said. "You can't get anything from them that doesn't lead to some self-loving diatribe of selfishness."

Billy shifted his dark sunglasses up the bridge of his nose with the same hand that carried his walking stick. "Manson has less than twenty-four hours and he's got to bring the Cubit with him. He bought this place for more than just creating a mecca of nanobot-infused humans. This is a staging ground, the only one within three hundred miles of Uluru. He'll use its satellite resources to show the world how he is their savior."

"And then he'll hit the switch," Michael said as he stood from the lobby couch. "Everyone with those nanobots streaming through their system will instantly become his servants." He looked back at the TV, saw that the football recap had ended and the U.S. President was again pleading with the world to take the sun seriously, and was reminded of the president's pledge to him, of Manson's manipulation of him, of Frederico's death, of the brave Marine he'd never known, of Billy and Cooper and their sacrifices. "But we're going to stop him," he added and walked to the hotel's entrance. "We don't have a choice."

There was an old adage that Billy's mother had told him right before she'd taken off in the helicopter with the Secret Service men.

The blind can see forever.

She, of course, had been trying to comfort Billy with his unexpected disability. But she'd been right. The bright white light he'd seen streaming from the center of the Book of the Djed while he'd been locked in the transference that had him floating above Majjar Fodii *was* forever. And now, that's all he saw: bright whiteness that held within it something immaterial, unimaginable and beyond human understanding. He thought that the whiteness was what some said they had experienced while on the brink of death, at the moment before they had crossed over into whatever they believed awaited once their time on earth had passed. To Billy, it was an abyss where all things really existed, hidden from the conscious lives of mortals. It was the beginning and it was forever. Not death. Not heaven. It was a realm where life was measured by the cooperation and the coalescence of its membership, without judgment, without disdain, without hardship. It was where mankind could find itself if only the next Great Cycle was not dictated by Richard Manson and the millions of surrogates he'd indoctrinated either through cubiting them or fooling them into an addiction full of BethStar.

Though Billy's blindness was manifest as a sense of white purity, his human memories applied pictures of sight. His intellect and experience helped shape these mental snapshots and guided him forward. Occasionally, new information that was attached to neither intellect nor experience had integrated in ways which provided presage of warning that guided him and provided a certain peace of mind. Daykeepers often appeared—some he knew, some he did not, but all were influential. Their experiences became Billy's and from the moment he'd been blinded by the solar eclipse to the moment he'd arrived at Uluru, he'd felt he'd aged a few thousand years.

"So where are we supposed to go now?" Cooper asked from the passenger's seat of a rented Prius.

Billy sat in the backseat, by himself, the Book opened across his lap. He flipped forward to the key page where the five little daggers had formed the points of a symmetrical star, flipped back to the page of symbols where each of the five glyphs had moved into mirrored positions under the key page daggers, and stared. No Daykeepers helped him. No presage. Nothing except the whiteness. "I don't know," he said, trying to block out the dimension of mortals, trying to find the mental pictures that would tell him where, at Uluru, they were supposed to find Manson and his dagger, find the Cubit, and seal it forever.

"How about the second half of it?" Cooper asked. "Has anything been written there?"

"Not until the Wayeb," Billy said. "It is for us to document what happens next."

Michael, who was driving, parked in an empty spot along the road encircling the massive red rock and turned in his seat. "Are you sure? You want us to take a look?" He reached over the backrest and Billy coddled the Book closer.

"It won't open for you." Billy tried to remain calm but his frail human heart and mind sparked emotion. Cooper smiled at him and for a moment, Billy thought he could see her gleaming face.

"You want to be sure, right?" Cooper said to him. "We're here to help." Billy eased his grip on the Book and nodded. "You turn the pages and we'll tell you if anything has been written."

Billy did so, thumbing through each of the remaining nine pages, pausing with each flip so that Michael and Cooper could assure themselves that Billy's intuition was correct. He started to close the Book when Cooper exclaimed, "Wait! Turn back."

"I don't see anything," Michael said.

"Not the pages. Inside the back cover."

Billy flipped the Book over and opened the back cover.

"There." Cooper pointed. "What is that?"

Michael leaned forward as Billy lifted the open Book closer to both of their craning necks. "Water stains?" he suggested.

Cooper huffed, turned back in her seat, and exited the car. She opened the back door and slid in beside Billy, then lowered her head closer. Her pinky traced the marks. She took Billy's right hand and extended the index finger, then traced the marks with it. "What do you think?"

Billy couldn't feel anything other than the leathery-cloth texture of the cover, but as Cooper moved his finger, lifted it, moved it again, and lifted it repeatedly, he said, "One. One. Dot. Dot. One. One."

Cooper released his hand. "The two dots are actually on top of each other, like a colon," she explained.

"Eleven-colon-eleven." Both Billy and Michael said it simultaneously.

"I don't know," Cooper said. "Maybe you're right, Michael. Maybe they are just coincidental stains and I'm trying too hard to find an answer."

Billy grabbed her hand and caressed its silky softness. He stared at her through the tint of his sunglasses, wishing, again, that he could see her beautiful face. "Since when has the Book been coincidental?"

"Do you know what it means?" she asked.

"Not yet."

A tour bus pulled in behind them and parked, and a rush of tourists sprang from its door. Billy snapped the Book closed. "Looks like it's time for a walkabout. Aaron and Lax led us here. Let's find out why."

Cooper dropped the Book of the Djed into her backpack where her mother's trinket box already rested, then all three of them mixed in with the bus tour group and entered, unquestioned, into the aboriginal reservation that surrounded the red rock monolith. Many of the tourists wore head nets that protected their faces from the intrusive swarms of flies that were drawn to the moisture of eyes, noses and mouths. Those that were unprotected performed what the locals called the "Aussie wave" as their hands constantly swatted at the flying nuisances. Michael had warned Cooper and Billy about the insects and had sprayed all of them with repellent before the sun had risen.

To Cooper, it was almost like being home, back in Sedona. She was used to majestic red rocks that had been sculpted by Mother Earth and rusty crystal rivulets etched into the arid ground. It reminded her of her kitchen counters, of her house she'd left abandoned so many years ago; it reminded her that if she'd only avoided one pothole on the day that she'd met Marcy Ruminski, none of everything after that would have happened. She wouldn't be here, she wouldn't be in love and, certainly, she would never have learned to believe in fate.

Cooper led Billy by the hand as she guided the three of them in the opposite direction from that of the tour group. Michael lagged behind as he constantly stared at the massive sandstone wonder. He stopped to study some of the aboriginal glyphs that were drawn on the side of Uluru and waved his hand at Cooper. "You go on," he yelled. "I'll look for clues on this side; you two look for them on the other. We'll meet up at the entrance."

Cooper nodded and continued walking a trampled pedestrian path, bypassing several pockets within the great rock where more glyphs were scrawled, knowing that Michael would soon inspect them. For some reason, she felt that the answer would not be in the aboriginal rock art. That seemed too obvious. The answer, she suspected, would come when they least expected it. That's how it had been up to this point. Why would Fate change its strategy now?

"Cooper," Billy said. "What do you see?"

She squeezed his hand and led him around a clump of broken rocks and spiky spinifex grass. "Red," she said. "Just about everything. Even the sun is red."

"Like walking through hell?"

Cooper hadn't thought of that analogy. "Perhaps from a biblical perspective. But I'm not sure if hell has such beautiful wildlife and green bushes and grasses. There's no fire and brimstone…I can tell you that much."

"But as far as places on earth. Would this be where one might find the devil?"

Cooper stopped and stared at Billy's sunglasses, briefly looked up at Uluru, then around and across toward the horizon. "What are you…" but she knew what he meant before she could finish the question. "Manson."

"I don't know why, but I keep hearing Clint Eastwood in my head, like some kind of weird warning, just like what happened back in Boynton Canyon."

Cooper should have been surprised that Billy was now reliving experiences from Sedona just as she had been moments before, but she wasn't. She felt that they'd become so connected, particularly since Billy had been blinded, even their thoughts merged. "What's he saying?"

"Get ready little lady. Hell is coming to breakfast."

"But it's past noon."

"I guess you can eat breakfast anytime." He took a step forward, initiating their continued journey around the great monolith.

Ten minutes later, they came across an area where lots of tourists and lots of tents merged a few dozen yards from the rock face. Cooper read from a sign nailed to a four-foot post:

> Aboriginal Artist Cooperative. All purchases of artwork directly benefits the artists and their families. No cameras permitted.

The small tent city was surrounded by a split rail fence that could have easily been ducked through, but everyone, except a few playful children, respected the boundary. They entered an opening in the fence that had a banner stretched between two posts above it. It was emblazoned with the word "Welcome" in ten different languages.

Just three steps inside the first tent, Billy was immediately drawn to a woman whose half a dozen tapestries hung from ropes strung around her twenty-foot corner space. No one else seemed interested in her multicolored pieces that were more art than practical. Billy asked Cooper to lead him over and Billy grabbed one of the pieces lying folded on a narrow table in front of the woman. He ran his fingers over the concentric circular rills in the patterns as the tapestry woman leaned forward. She was plump and middle-aged and knew that Billy was blind.

"I have more to show you," she said to Billy, then turned toward Cooper. "He'll be fine." She patted the knuckles of his hand as it stroked her creative work.

The tapestry woman emoted immense trust and Cooper had the feeling that she wanted to be alone with Billy. Cooper thought that this might be one of those unsuspecting moments when answers were delivered by Fate. "Okay," she said. "Be back in a few minutes."

Cooper wrapped her fingers around the straps of her backpack and wandered through the artists stations, each one twenty to forty feet in size, each one displaying similar geometric shapes, animal outlines and patterns of waves and lines all on differing artistic media such as canvas or cloth or pottery or wood or rock or, in one space, the human body. When Cooper passed this artist's rickety table, the young boy who could not have been older than twelve, asked if she wanted her body to be made sacred again. The boy had painted his own bald head with a white spiral that started at the crown of his skull and ended an inch above his eyebrows. He pointed at Cooper's right arm and she looked down to see that her hand, which still clung to one backpack strap, was turned so that her wrist revealed the djed tattoo and the rattlesnake fang scars.

"The snake and the cross. Those are conflicting—on your arm—in your soul. I can make it right again," he said and blinked several times, which drew Cooper's attention to his eyes of different color. One was dark brown and the other was a soft shade of hazel. A hefty wind blew through the space and a flap of the canvas tent wall flew off beside them, revealing the perimeter spilt rail fence outside, thirty yards away. "Even the wind says so," the boy added.

"Do you know this symbol?" Cooper asked, nodding at the tattoo.

"Four lines. Four crosses. A new beginning."

"And how could you know that those were made by a snake?" She released her backpack straps and touched each of the four scars with her left hand.

"Because you told me."

Cooper thought about that. Had she? Through the tent flap opening, the wind swirled dusty clouds and the fence disappeared for a moment. She looked back at the boy. "I don't think so," she said.

"They are scars from a snake, yes?"

Cooper nodded.

"So let me make it right."

The boy's smiling, multicolored eyes made it easy for Cooper to stick out her arm. The boy gently grabbed it with one hand, and with the other, snatched a very thin bristled paint brush with a pearly, white handle from a large canister full of brushes, and dipped it into a smear of red paint from a palette next to the canister. Very methodically, the boy traced the outline of each of the four crosses. He didn't bother with the djed tattoo's vertical post, but he did add a pair of additional marks. These additions took him twice as long to apply as did the tracing of the crosses and when he was finished,

Cooper lifted her hand, fingertips up, to her face. The boy had added two dots between the top two crosses and the bottom two. She immediately wondered why it had taken the boy so long to draw two simple dots until she moved her wrist to within an inch of her eyes. They weren't dots. They were spirals that looked exactly like the fifth symbol on the page of symbols in the Book. If fact, they looked just like the self-painting the boy had done to his bald head. The two dots were glyphs representing the sun.

Fingers suddenly curled around her forearm and, with gentle pressure, twisted it sideways. Cooper looked above her arm and straight into the boy's odd eyes. His stare shifted from her own and down to her wrist which was now horizontal to her eyesight. Her wrist read eleven-colon-eleven—the same marks that had been revealed inside the back cover of the Book of the Djed.

Cooper suddenly felt faint and she swooned and closed her eyes. Had the boy not been holding her, she would have fallen straight back. Another gust of wind swept across her moist cheeks and she heard the tent flap flapping. When she opened her eyes, the boy's hand was gone. In fact, the boy wasn't even there and neither were his brushes or paint palette or the makeshift table he'd used to display them. Her arm, still held horizontally forward, now rested against one of the thick poles that held up the tent roof. She leaned back and looked at her wrist to find that the boy's artwork was still there.

Through the open tent flap, about ten yards away and next to the split rail fence, was another aboriginal artist who was displaying framed paintings. A couple of people stopped for a moment to look at his pieces, then continued on and out of Cooper's sight. The painter turned and looked at her, then smiled.

Cooper blinked at the space where the boy had been then blinked at the painter. It didn't make sense. The man outside had not been there. The boy inside, had—the proof was sketched on her wrist.

She ducked through the tent opening and slowly, almost cautiously, walked over. She pretended to look at the dozen or so framed pieces, all of which showcased Uluru from different angles and from different distances.

"May I help you find something?" the painter asked.

Cooper looked up. Sunglasses covered his eyes and white streaks of paint occupied both bulbous cheeks. When he smiled, a hundred wrinkles divided the surface of his lips into a hundred sections. Whiskers from his gray beard and mustache also had streaks of white paint smeared through them. He stroked the beard and moved his hand to his head to adjust a knit cap that hid most of his hefty strands of equally gray hair. The pattern sewn into the cap matched the twirling symbols of the sun that the boy had added to the djed tattoo. "Not sure," Cooper said. "What do you have?"

"Seeing is knowing." The painter turned in his chair and flipped through a collection of more paintings stored in a cardboard box. He pulled one out and set it on his lap. "What do you think of this one?"

All Cooper could do was gasp. No other reaction would have been appropriate.

"Is this what you've been looking for?" The painter smiled, revealing a set of unusually white teeth.

The painting was not of Uluru. It looked, in many ways, just like the numerous red rock gorges that inundated the vicinity in and around Sedona. Two red rock walls stood on either side of the painting and as they came together in the distance, a V-shape full of blue sky was formed. In the middle of the V of blue was the sun, red as the rocks beside it, and sending rays of solar light down onto the floor of the gorge where an outcropping of indigenous plants surrounded a calm pool of water. The reflections of the two rock walls, the sun rays and the sun itself were revealed in the small pool as a symbol that Cooper was now very familiar with: one-one-colon-one-one.

"This is the third time I've seen this sequence of numbers in the last hour," she said. "Do you know where this is?"

"Of course. Seeing is knowing."

"Can you tell me where?"

"It is here." The painter tapped the painting on his lap.

"It's here at Uluru?"

The painter shook his head.

"Then why the heck did we come here?" She said to herself much more loudly than she had intended.

"You came here because you are looking for something and I can help you find it."

"So, you can take me to this place?"

"That's why you are here."

At that moment, Michael led Billy through the opening in the tent and both walked over.

"This man knows where we are supposed to go," Cooper said to them.

Michael looked at the aboriginal then down at the painting. "Eleven-colon-eleven. Just like in the Book."

"And a boy painted this on my arm just a few minutes ago." Cooper showed Michael.

"Eleven-colon-eleven," Michael repeated.

"What is your name?" Billy suddenly asked the painter.

"Today, I am alpha. Tomorrow, omega."

"The beginning and the end," Billy said.

"The phoenix and the sun," the painter added.

This was the first time that Cooper wondered if the painter was actually blind. She watched the two sunglass-clad men stare directly into each other's shaded eyes then stuck her arm with the newly stenciled tattoo between the stare and waved it.

"No. I'm not blind," the painter said. "But Billy is."

Cooper gasped. "How do you know his name?"

The painter grinned and looked at her tattoo. "Because you told me."

Cooper looked over at the tent flap opening then back at the painter whose grin had widened.

Billy asked, "How much?"

"No money," the painter said. "A trade. I need something to keep my paintbrushes safe." He stared at Cooper's backpack.

"This?" Cooper asked, thumbing the straps of the pack.

"No. I have many packs. They are too flimsy. My brushes could break."

Billy stepped behind Cooper. "He wants your trinket box," he said, unzipping the pack.

Cooper jerked away. "No," she demanded. "Es mi Mamas."

"Your Mama," Billy said, "is going to help save our world."

"But the daggers?" Cooper looked at the painter whose wide grin had not faltered a bit.

"The trinket box," the painter said, "and I'll show you where the devil is headed."

For a moment, Cooper felt as though she was standing alone. All three men looked at her as if she held the key to salvation but was too selfish to give it up. The painter's head slowly bobbed up and down. Michael stood motionless but his heavy breathing belied his anxiety. She turned around to allow Billy access to the backpack, and he reached inside and pulled out Cooper's Mama's trinket box. He opened it and all four of them craned their necks forward to look at the three daggers inside, all identical except for the stars in their hafts. Billy scooped all three of them up then handed the box to the painter. He started to place the daggers back in the backpack when the painter's voice stopped him.

"May I see one of those?"

Billy plucked the Creation of Religion dagger from the bunch and held it out.

"Wait," Cooper said. "If he touches it, Manson will know where we are."

Billy turned to look at Cooper as the painter grabbed the dagger. "I know."

"Beautiful," the painter said, twirling the dagger between both hands. "I have only seen them in my dreams." He tried to return the dagger but Billy held his hands palms up.

"You hold onto it…" Billy hesitated. "What is your name?"

"I am Jerara," the painter said.

"You hold onto it, Jerara. I have a feeling you might need it."

"No. Keep them all close to you. Don't let them out of your sight, particularly now." He returned the dagger and Billy dropped all three in the backpack. Jerara looked toward the horizon where the red sun blazed atop the red rock outcropping known as The Olgas a few miles away and pointed. "In the Walpa Gorge. We should be there before the sun goes down. I'll get what we'll need to stay the night. Tomorrow morning, hell is coming for breakfast."

Cooper gasped. Those words were what Billy had said he'd heard coming from the voices in his head. She gasped again when Jerara took off his sunglasses. One of his eyes was dark brown—the other, a gentle shade of hazel.

0-TIME: PRESAGE

CREATION OF THE END

THE WAYEB

December 21, 2012

It was almost like it had been in Jerara's painting, minus the reflection on the small pool of water, since, when they'd arrived the night before, the sun had already fallen well below the V-shape made by the red walls of the Walpa Gorge.

Jerara had arranged their overnight stay with the park rangers, and the rangers had graciously accepted all of them, had even supplied sleeping bags, water, and some dehydrated foodstuffs. Soon after they'd arrived, Jerara had made a small campfire and had led them through numerous ceremonial songs that, he'd said, were meant to appease the sun and give hope to all things for which the sun had provided life.

It had crossed Billy's mind that Jerara might be a Daykeeper or, at least, some kind of aboriginal shaman closely related to Daykeepers. From what Cooper had told him, Jerara had transformed from a small boy to an old man within minutes. He'd not questioned her assumptions. They'd seen so many transformations of human and animal minds, bodies and souls there really was no reason to question such things anymore. All of it had been purposeful.

All of it had led them here.

Billy had slept more soundly than he had since becoming blind, but when he woke three hours after daybreak, nothing calm greeted him. Michael was screaming, his voice far off but bouncing against the gorge walls, which confused Billy. He looked blindly around, unsure of his bearing.

"Billy," Cooper suddenly said as her hand grabbed his arm.

Billy turned in the direction of her voice. "What?" he asked. "Where's Michael?"

"He's running toward us from the gorge entry." She helped him to his feet. "My God. It is hell. You were right."

"What do you mean?"

"The sun. Everything is red and hell-looking. Can't you feel it?"

He'd been jerked from sleep so abruptly, he'd not really felt the heat that now slapped him right in the face. It was at least ten degrees hotter than it had been the day before and seemed to be getting warmer in the few minutes he was thinking about it. "It's happening," he said. "Don't look at it."

"I can't see it," she said. "Not yet. It's still behind the gorge wall. But everything looks like a red filter has been placed on it. Even the little pool of water, and…I swear it looks like it's boiling. There's little bubbles coming out of it."

Michael's voice was getting closer and he was yelling something about Jerara, but his rushed breaths made the words hard to understand.

"The daggers," Billy said. "And the Book."

"Yes," Cooper assured him. "I have the backpack right here." She lifted it so Billy could touch it. "What now?"

"He's coming," Billy said. "Can't you hear it?"

"Who? Michael?"

"No—Him."

Cooper could almost hear the earth tremble moments before Manson and his small army of followers came around the last bend in the gorge. Michael nearly collapsed from the heat.

"He took out a couple with one of those big boulders on top of the rock wall," Michael panted. "Rolled it right down on top of them just like something out of a roadrunner cartoon. Then one of them shot him."

"Jerara." Billy said.

"Yeah. They shot him then stuck him in a goddamned box."

"The Cubit."

"That thing sucked him inside like it was hungry."

"A good description," Cooper said. "It's always hungry."

Cooper, Billy and Michael still remained within the shadows of the higher, easterly gorge walls but the bend in the path where Manson appeared was bathed in bright, red sunshine. At least a hundred people walked behind him. On the shoulders of four of them, three men and one woman, were the ends of two long poles which supported a platform that carried the Cubit. Walking near Manson but just a pace behind, was the bald-headed man from the resort that Michael had referred to as Yule Brenner. He clenched a rifle between both hands, the barrel pointed up at the sun, and chambered a round, the bolt-action slide echoing metallic across the faces of the rock walls.

"Isn't this fancy," Manson shouted, still fifty yards away. "I would have expected my son, but you two? You should be dead already."

"I'm not your son," Billy loudly grumbled. Cooper's attention was drawn to Billy's chest. The Creation of the End Dagger had started to glow. She could see the star in its haft through his unbuttoned, sweaty shirt.

"No time for argument. Just take it on fact that my juice created you. It makes sense; you gotta admit that. Here we are…together for the finale of the world…father and son, united at last."

Manson, Yule, and the four Cubit bearers continued forward just as the sun's right hemisphere slowly moved into the V-shape created by the merge of the gorge walls. Bright red light quickly eliminated all shadows and Cooper felt the sudden increased heat. The earth trembled again. Directly behind her, the pool of water bubbled more anxiously, spitting tiny burps of steam.

"I see that you are just as much a coward as mom said you were," Billy shouted. "Can't take on the three of us by yourself? Gotta bring your cubit drones with you."

Manson laughed. "Not cubits, dear boy. Well, at least, not all of them. They represent the future of the world. Healthy, long-living, proper-minded humans. I offered them the Fountain of Youth and they happily drank from it."

"You're a fucking disease," Michael shouted and suddenly ran at Manson until Yule shot a hole in the ground at his feet ten yards away.

"You'll much better serve me than be dead, Mikey," Manson said. "A long life of suffering in exchange for the crap you've put me through."

"Is that what your Fountain of Youth is all about?" Michael demanded. "Human suffering?"

Cooper felt it again, but this time the earth's tremble was much more pronounced. Behind her, the sun's circle was almost fully exposed. Tendrils of bloody fire veins snaked slithery patterns across its red surface.

"The sun is about to cause as much suffering as your race can handle," Manson said. "That is, unless I stop it. So, do your fellow humans a favor and back off. Let me save the world."

"You're a liar," Michael grumbled. "Frederico proved it. Dr. Presser proved it. The sun's rays are the only thing that can stop your…your robots."

"Yeah. Well who's going to stop me?"

"I am." Billy said and stood beside Michael. His dagger was out and the hand that held it was encased in a bright red glow. Billy adjusted his sunglasses and looked straight ahead. "If I don't get this one in the back of your head, I've got three more chances."

"You've done well up to this point…all of you," Manson said. "You bested some of my worst cubits. Albert, Lafitte, Triple K, Greely, Fodii, even Michael's beloved Pitchfork Man. But for what? Daggers and Books that will do you no good without this." He presented the Creation of the Antichrist dagger from behind his back. "It was fun sending you all on wild goose chases. Even in your journey for the daggers, you should have known you were never going to get this from me. Fate is a ridiculous character on a ridiculous stage built on the concept of imperfection. You have been pawns…my pawns. You discovered all of the clues, sacrificed all of your friends, determined where and when and how, and helped Fate relish in this final scene: the transition of an age of suffering to one that is more properly plotted."

"With you as the director," Billy said, stepping a foot in front of Michael and two feet closer to Manson, his dagger thrust forward and ready.

"You know what the real irony is?" Manson continued. "All I need is this one dagger to stop the sun. I stick it into the star in the Cubit, twist it around a few times and the Cubit does its thing so the sun doesn't destroy the power grid. No depletion of life-sustaining resources. No looting or pillaging or murder of one's own neighbors just to acquire their food and water. No gangs of indigent humans that are so panic-stricken, so fearful that their mighty Gods have finally put the hammer down, so impatient to wait for ingenuity to conquer fear, that they would end the world in a matter of days. The irony is, I'm here to save humanity by controlling its freewill. Just like it was before Adam ate the apple. Just like it should have been from that day forward. I am not the snake—I am the savior."

"You're wrong," Cooper yelled, and started to walk forward with the backpack clenched in one fist. "Billy is the savior. He is a Daykeeper."

"Stay back," Billy ordered Cooper. "He's baiting us. Keep what we have safe."

Manson snickered. "If I would have thought that those daggers and the Book would have been any real threat, don't you think I'd have them already?"

"You tried," Billy said. "You failed."

Manson laughed so loudly that the red rock walls around them shook. "Baldy," he said to the Yule Brenner-looking man with the rifle. "That woman over there is a blasphemous whore who has soiled my perfect son with love that no Daykeeper should ever endure. Shoot her."

Baldy lowered the rifle, set the sights, and fired just as Billy leapt in front of the bullet. Cooper knew that bullets couldn't harm him but she screamed anyway. The rifle's recoil sent a shockwave through the gorge that made everything shake. Billy fell to the ground, rolled up on one knee as Baldy chambered another round, then turned abruptly toward Cooper. He didn't look at her and neither did Michael when he turned in unison with Billy, nor did any of Manson's surrogates who were already facing her. They all stared above her. They all stared at the sun.

At that moment, the earthquake started. Red dust rained down the gorge walls. Tiny pebbles skittered across Cooper's feet and sank into the pool of bubbling water behind her. Some of the BethStar recipients stood comatose as if all of their natural survival mechanisms had been totally erased, while others jockeyed for things to hold onto. The four surrogates that had been holding up the Cubit platform remained as they were until a rock, about the size of a human head, fell from overhead, bounced against a larger boulder on the ground, and tore through the kneecap of one of the rear throne-bearers. The Cubit remained aloft for another second before crashing into and rolling across the ground where it settled upright. The red star directly under the front side of its lid blazed as brightly as the sun above it.

Manson, Baldy, and the three remaining throne-bearers stumbled forward just as a flurry of rocks and boulders rumbled down both sides of the gorge, burying many of the reticent surrogates and creating an impasse for those that had survived behind it. The water at Cooper's feet bubbled much more viciously until, suddenly, the entire pool disappeared as the ground cracked open. The top layer of earth followed the water into the sinking hole and as the hole spread out, it grabbed Cooper's heels. She flailed for an instant, trying to use the backpack for balance, then toppled backward and disappeared.

When the earthquake stopped, Billy stood staring at the spot where Cooper had been. He couldn't see but he did. Inside the whiteness of his blindness, the moment before the ground opened up, he'd seen Jerara's painting, except that it hadn't been a painting; it had been real. The sun and the gorge walls had reflected off the small pool of water, marking the symbol eleven-colon-eleven. And then Cooper had disappeared. A scream boiled inside, rising up acidic into the back of his throat. He clenched the Creation of the End Dagger so hard, the star in the haft buried into the scar it had made in the palm of his hand like a key in a lock. And then it came. A rabid lion could not have bellowed as loud.

"NOOOO!"

He started to run toward the hole but a hand grabbed him and held him back.

"Where you think your goin', asshole?"

Billy didn't have to think about it. He spun around and thrust the dagger out at the same time. The seven-inch blade decapitated the Yule Brenner bald man. The head jumped off his bloody shoulders and rolled ten yards past Manson's feet where it settled near boulders that were similar in size. The rifle fell from limp hands then the body jerked forward and Billy pushed it aside.

Michael took advantage of the moment and scooped the rifle up from the blood-dusty ground. He chambered a shot and pointed the barrel at Manson's face.

"Back off you useless piece of shit," he growled.

"Shoot, pussy," Manson countered. "Come on, you scared little shit. You're the biggest mistake I ever made. I should have had Chester pitchfork you right in the face back in New York. There's no place in the new world for cowards like you. Come on. Do it! Set your soul free."

Michael shot Manson right in the chest. The bullet blew through his body and drilled the female throne-bearer who was standing right behind him. Manson didn't flinch but his surrogate, clenched her face, vaulted backward and bounced off of one corner of the Cubit, rolled and writhed on the ground, kicked bloody dirt from where Baldy had been decapitated, then stiffened.

Manson stuck the blade of the Creation of the Antichrist Dagger into the bullet hole, twisted it a few times, then pulled it out. "Ahh. Good as new." He grinned. "Anything else you got for me, pussy coward?"

Billy slashed out with his dagger but missed Manson by a full five feet.

"Blind as bat. You can't see me. You can't see the Cubit. You can't even see your sweet lover's body all broken and dead at the bottom of the sinkhole. You lost your daggers. You have no Book. Watcha' gonna do, my son? What in the fuck are you going to do now?"

"I'M NOT YOUR SON!" Billy screamed, threw off his sunglasses and thrashed out in the direction of Manson's voice. Manson stepped gingerly aside and easily punched the dagger from Billy's hand. It twirled in the air, its blade reflecting the boiling heat of the red sun, and stuck straight-up in the ground between Michael's boots. Michael dropped the gun and grabbed the dagger.

"Come on, Billy," Michael said, and grabbed Billy's arm. "Let's go help Cooper. I heard her. She's not dead." Michael led Billy toward the hole, shuffling backward as he held the dagger out in front of them.

"You're gonna look awful funny with that dagger sticking out of your asshole," Mason said, leading his two remaining surrogates forward. "Get him."

While Michael's attention was on Manson, Billy's feet prodded the ground for the hole. When he found it, he halted Michael's backpedal. "Can you see her?" he asked.

Michael turned and looked down. "My God," he exclaimed.

"What is it?" Billy asked and also looked down. "Is she okay?"

"A staircase. A spiral rock staircase. And there's a light, glowing red, pulsing."

"Can you see her?"

"No…wait. There's she is. At the bottom of the last step. She's moving."

"…Billy…" Cooper moaned. "It's down here, Billy."

"You go on," Michael said. "I'll join you after I cut off Manson's head and bring you his dagger."

Billy stepped into the hole, more concerned for Cooper than for the plausibility of Michael's courage. He used his hands to slowly guide him, his feet slipping on the wet dirty steps, his hands grasping for walls that weren't there. He heard the scuffle above, heard the agonized screech of dying cubits and knew that Michael was handling himself well. But as he neared the middle of the staircase, he turned and looked up. Michael screamed.

When Michael turned around, both of Manson's men were already on top of him. These two were unlike Baldy. When he sliced off one of their arms with the dagger and the thing used it to beat Michael in the head, he realized that these were cubits and that, as Billy had told him back at Seven Bay, the only way to kill a cubit was to plant the blade into the back of the head.

Michael had held a dagger before (he'd carried one back from Cairns) but he'd never used it. The fear of death, a sudden adrenal squirt, or the convenient assistance from some greater power—whatever the reason, Michael suddenly found the prowess. He stabbed the cubit, who was beating him with its own arm, right in the eye, which made it stumble backward. He spun around and lashed out at the second cubit, chopped of its ear, then counter spun, and planted the dagger into the base of its skull. It screeched and writhed and withered into ash as the remaining cubit charged again. Michael kicked it in the chest then crouched and busted its kneecap with the heel of his boot. As the cubit tried to rise on one leg, Michael finished it off and stepped back to watch it deteriorate into the red dust gorge floor.

"Impressive," Manson said, his own dagger out and ready for an assault. "But I have something you don't." Manson moved his dagger behind his back, sheathing it into some hidden recess, then drew the empty hand forward, stuck it into his pants pocket, and pulled out an iPhone. He thumbed the screen then looked up at Michael. "Do you remember your experience in the Fox News studio? You ever wonder what the hell happened to you? Slip sliding away, my man. Slip sliding away." Manson raised his arm and pointed it at Michael as he slid his thumb up the length of the phone.

The nanobots in Michael's body immediately went to work, shutting down his nervous system, constricting his aorta, collapsing his lungs. In the last moment of consciousness, he threw both arms in the air, and the dagger skittered across the red dirt and into the hole.

Cooper had finally risen to her feet, favoring her left leg which was horribly bruised, when she heard the clank of metal on rock. She looked up the spiral staircase to see Billy retrieve his dagger.

"Michael?" she said.

Billy shook his head. "Manson will be coming."

Cooper hobbled up the staircase to help Billy descend the remaining steps. "There's another one of those pedestals down here. It's almost like the others except that there's only one mark on the front of it: a single Creation Dagger." She grabbed the backpack and led Billy into the chamber.

Behind them, pebbles rolled down the steps. Footfalls crunched and squished and Manson's rushed breaths filled the chamber. "T-i-i-i-i-me, is on my side. Yes it is," he sang. When he appeared beyond the arched walls of the chamber's entrance, the Cubit was in his arms. He smiled, his grin wide and confident. "Time to save the world."

Cooper knew that Billy had to seal the Cubit. She understood that the

Cubit had to be on the pedestal if he was to accomplish this singular mission. She knew that there were only minutes left before the next epoch would begin. "Would you like some help?" she asked Manson.

This seemed to throw Manson off his game. "What, whore-slut?"

"We've got to seal that damned thing. The least I can do is help you get it into the proper position."

"Kind of you, but just back the fuck off."

Manson looked directly at Billy who offered no retreat. Cooper assumed that Billy was also waiting for Manson to put the Cubit on the pedestal. She knelt, unzipped the backpack, and pulled out its contents.

Manson gingerly stepped forward, set the Cubit on the pedestal's waist-high surface, tapped his toe for a few more seconds, looked at his arm as if looking at a wristwatch that was not there, and said, "Time's up." He moved his hand to the dagger sheathed at the base of his spine, drew it forward and shoved it into the star in the front of the Cubit. At that moment, both Cooper and Billy turned toward the arched entry. Michael flailed forward, waving his arms, stumbling, uncontrolled. He flopped against Manson like a rag doll and Manson turned, surprised.

With Manson's attention diverted, Cooper sprang into action. She pulled Billy forward and set the Book atop the Cubit. The lid of the Cubit rumbled and trembled as if it was about to blow apart. Billy turned to the page of symbols, flipped forward to the key page, flipped back again. "I can't see it!" he said. "I don't know where they go!"

The lid of the Cubit suddenly blew open, sending Billy and the Book through the air and against the chamber's rocky surface. Cooper leapt on top of the Cubit, disregarding the consequences of touching it, and used her body weight to push the lid back down until Manson swatted her aside. The lid, again, stood straight up and the Cubit's contents pressed against the four wooden walls.

Manson looked into the Cubit, his grin as wide as any devil's. He then turned and looked right at Cooper. His pupils roiled in a moiré of silver and crimson red. "Welcome to the new…"

From inside the Cubit, a hand emerged. It snatched Manson's neck and pulled him forward. Manson struggled against the grip. His hands gripped both edges of the Cubit and pushed back, but the force from within was too much and the hand yanked Manson into the Cubit head first. The Cubit sucked his body down…down…until only his feet, now bare because the aggressive Cubit had shaken the shoes off, remained. As soon as the feet disappeared, Cooper jumped up, yanked the Creation of the Antichrist dagger from the Cubit, and grabbed the lid. As she was forcing it down, she looked inside. The bottoms of both of Manson's feet were surrounded by fire and they descended into pinpoints. The pinpoints twisted and transformed into two eyeballs. She heard a voice say "Now!" and the two eyeballs filled with color: one was dark brown and the other was a gentle shade of hazel.

Billy heard the struggle and saw a stream of red fire split the whiteness of his blindness. The fire stream narrowed into a point that looked just like the blade of a Creation Dagger.

"There's four red circles on top of the Cubit," Cooper yelled.

The Book was in his lap and Billy "saw" every page from memory. He flipped from the very front, to the page of symbols, to the key, and forward through all of the blank pages to the back cover where the eleven-colon-eleven was embossed.

He stood, collected the four daggers together and stepped to the Cubit. He gave the daggers to Cooper. "Stick them into the circles. That must be how we seal it."

The Cubit rumbled. Billy could feel its energy. It was about to blow. It was about to stop the sun's rays. It was about to save humanity from the suffering of the next five days. It was about ensure that Manson's nanobots would take control even though Fate had taken Manson to hell.

"Wait!" Billy suddenly bellowed. His hand was atop the page of symbols. His fingers scanned the pages. There were rills in the page that reminded him of the textile artist from the aboriginal artist cooperative. The rills formed a pattern. The rills were a language. The rills were braille. The rills told him which dagger was supposed to go in which location and in what specific order.

Billy shouted out the directions and Cooper planted each of four Creation Daggers into the lid of the Cubit, saving Billy's Creation of the End Dagger for last. She pushed it into the star on the face of the Cubit and the box trembled once more before dying. Cooper, whose full weight was on top of the wooden cube, crushed it. All of the power of the Cubit splintered into a pile of kindling.

The power of the sun's coronal mass ejection saved Michael's life. It destroyed the nanobots that Manson had injected into him back in 2010.

The effects of the rays were also evident at Ayer's Rock Resort. All of the guests, at least those that had not followed Manson into the gorge to be crushed by the earthquake, were "human" again, the nanobots in them now dormant. Across the globe, however, the challenges were much greater. The sun had wiped out all electricity, all satellite communication, all of the things that humans had become reliant on as a part of what they believed life was predicated upon.

Billy knew of the struggles that men made for themselves. He was a Daykeeper. His responsibility was survival. And as he sat on a couch, cuddling Cooper and grasping Michael's hand in the lobby of the Ayer's Rock Resort, he told a confused, fearful mass of people, the wisdom of ages.

"The Mayan's warnings…" he said. "In fact, all ancient civilizations' warnings demand that we don't repeat history. We all have our Wayeb. We all have our days of reckoning. The key to survival is how we come together in times of great challenge. Survival is not a right. Survival is a privilege."

The Book was in his lap. He turned to the first blank page past the key and began writing.

Chapter 1

1 In the beginning God created the heaven and the
earth.

2 And the earth was without form, and void; and
darkness was upon the face of the deep. And the Spirit
of God moved upon the face of the waters.

3 And God said, Let there be light: and there was
light.

www.ingramcontent.com/pod-product-compliance
Lightning Source LLC
Chambersburg PA
CBHW060603310726
48982CB00008B/1225/J

* 9 7 8 0 9 8 2 5 1 2 9 7 5 *